How We Live

AN

ANTHOLOGY

EDITED BY

Penney Chapin Hills

AND

L. Rust Hills

HOW WE LIVE

Contemporary Life in
Contemporary
Fiction

THE MACMILLAN COMPANY

NEW YORK

Library of Congress Catalog Card Number: 68-11266

Second Printing 1968

The Macmillan Company, New York
Collier-Macmillan Canada Ltd., Toronto, Ontario

Printed in the United States of America

FOR

Paula and Henry

AND

Piera and Stefan

Contents

Part One. The Way We Live Now

IN COMMUNITIES

AT WORK

Part Two. Differentiations and Confusions

IN RELIGION—JEWISH CONFLICTS IN CULTURAL ASSIMILATION

IN RACE—THE VISIBLE NEGRO

CONTENTS

IN CLASS—MINUTE DISTINCTIONS IN THE MIDDLE

Part Three. The Eye of Fiction

IN SOME OVERVIEWS

IN SOME STRATAGEMS

APPENDIX. IN DEFENSE OF CONTEMPORARY FICTION

An Introductory Note

This anthology is intended to demonstrate two things, both of them contrary to current general opinion. First, we believe that contemporary fiction is flourishing—even though nobody much reads it. Second, we're convinced that contemporary fiction is relevant, has much to tell us about how we live, presents a kind of complex truth about ourselves and our society that can be found neither in the analyses and statistics of the psychologists and sociologists nor in the recently popular "new" reportage, which attempts to bring fact somehow "alive" by borrowing superficial methods of fiction. A central premise of this book is that just as when we try to understand any past civilization we turn first to its Art, so for an understanding of how we live now we should turn first to the literary art that expresses and describes our own era. Also: however valid for the training of future literary critics may be the way fiction is now taught in most of our colleges and universities —that is, according to the tenets of the still so-called "New Criticism," which emphasizes the separateness of the art "object" from both author and reader—these methods have produced a generation of ordinary readers apparently unable to see the very great deal that contemporary fiction has to tell us about ourselves and our troubled times. Fiction has a special way of seeing and showing, that cultural historians, analytic psychologists, and the more literate sociologists have always appreciated as significant and useful. Our thesis will be that as well as vividly and accurately depicting manners and mores, modern fiction even more importantly expresses the morality, the emotional essence, of the way we live now. Further argument about these matters is relegated to Part Three of this book, "The Eye of Fiction," and to the Appendix, "In Defense of Contemporary Fiction," for we believe that the fiction itself provides the best proof of our claims for it.

But even though this is an anthology, we hope we have been really editors, not simply compilers. We have intended the book to be read through from beginning to end, not to be dipped into, and we've arranged the fiction so as to make certain points in sequence. But no particular school or scheme of psychology or sociology is used to order the selections; in fact, the sociological theory used may be so broad as to seem like shallow common sense. What contemporary fiction seems to us to say about contemporary life is throughout the book, implicit in the selection and arrangement of the stories and novel excerpts, and explicit in the italicized afternotes, section prefaces, and other apparatus. Our interpretations are not offered as either necessary to the understanding of these stories or as definitive interpretations of their relationship to the way we live now. We have placed them after the stories, so as not to disturb the reader's own initial reading. It seems to us that anyone who doesn't like them can simply skip them. They are neither literary criticism nor sociological analysis; perhaps they are no more than evidence of our belief that reading fiction with intent to understand should not be confined to those with specialized professional competence. If sometimes the introductions and explications seem obtrusive or overobvious, like a too-anxious host who wants his antagonistic guests to like one another, then we say in defense that one of the chief troubles of our troubled times has been that contemporary readers and contemporary writers haven't got along all that well in the past, and although there may be reasons that they may never be friends, they'll never know until they have met and have tried to understand one another. We hope for the reader what we feel we ourselves have experienced: that the attempt to read fiction with understanding invariably yields a rewarding complexity of meaning that provides a continuing source of insight into the complexity of the way we live now.

Our purpose has been not to apologize for contemporary fiction, but to celebrate it.

PENNEY CHAPIN HILLS

L. RUST HILLS

". . . to celebrate a world that lies spread out around us like a bewildering and stupendous dream . . ."

—JOHN CHEEVER

The Way We Live Now

ALONE

·

IN FAMILIES

·

IN COMMUNITIES

·

AT WORK

Part One

THE WAY WE LIVE NOW

IT HAS BECOME A CLICHÉ *to say that nowadays the only constant seems to be change, and even change seems to be changing, growing constantly faster. While open revolution and war are confined to the "underdeveloped" countries, there seems to be a process of social disorganization at work even in our safe and affluent nation. The way things were before World War II seems entirely different from the way things are now. While on the technological level these changes represent incredible "progress," with all its connotations of a richer, better world, on the social level the effect on the individual is of disintegration of the traditional structures and strictures that in the past served to support and guide him in his thinking, feeling, and behavior. The central forces at work in contemporary American society— industrialization, urbanization, and bureaucratization—all tend toward standardization and depersonalization of our lives. The agents of these forces—mass production, mass marketing, mass communication, mass education, and so on—all lead us rapidly toward the evolving mass society. But while the nation as a whole may be becoming less diverse, each individual's experience is of a greater variety of worlds and ways, confronting him with many more choices but many fewer reasons, codes, and norms to guide him to any particular choice. Against the tendencies toward standardization stand such forces of discrimination and differentiation as religion, race, and class—all aspects of a social order that is in the process of disintegration. The effect on the individual of the breaking-down of these bastions of the old ordering of things is shown in the stories in Part II, "Differentiations and Confusions." In Part I the selections are concerned with the individual alone and with the effects on him of changing patterns in the most basic social institutions—first the family, then the community— and then changes in the nature of work in this country. No suggestion is made that this survey is comprehensive of life in America today, much less historical. Our intention is less to show how things have changed, than to show how things are now. All these matters of family and community and work and religion and race and class are of course interrelated; and although we have separated them by our categorizing, the stories themselves show these interrelations clearly.*

As fiction is always by its nature concerned primarily with the individual in his interaction with his family, friends, neighbors, colleagues, and his culture as a whole, so we will begin with the individual . . .

The Way We Live Now

ALONE

Few choose or are able to live alone, in fiction or in life, yet contemporary fiction often portrays an individual in a kind of isolation that is psychological rather than physical. It is part of the individual's emotional reaction to the chaos and confusion of a time of social disorganization and cultural change. The classic psychological and sociological theoretical concepts for this effect—"alienation" and "anomie"—have become very familiar to us as more and more experts of various sorts speak out against what our society is doing to the individual. The effects of all this seem to be hastened because many American men and women, released by the new technology from many of the obligations and preoccupations of work, now have the opportunity—formerly available only to the leisured rich— to engage in what sometimes seems to be a nationwide, coast-to-coast, collective-individual search for "self." Many others find it difficult to take this "crisis of the individual" seriously: there is something comical about Life *magazine running a four-part series called "The Struggle to Be an Individual." As the final story in this section shows, so much talk about the absurdity and meaninglessness of modern existence is getting to be absurd and meaningless. Yet a constantly increasing number of individuals do in fact experience deep emotional crises, and to such a significant extent and in such a way that the experience is clearly attributable to the chaos and disorder and insecurity of modern life. The individual may feel he is without goals, without guidance from within or without; his life seems not to have purpose or meaning or direction; he lacks identity; he suffers feelings of restlessness and longing; he feels empty and "hollow"; his way of life seems futile and impermanent; he feels "atomized," "adrift," "dead center," "immobile," "hung up." All these direct statements are admittedly the standard, fashionable clichés about the "normlessness of modern life"; but while one may feel impatience with so much talk about these symptoms, it is still necessary to confront the fact that they are very much, and increasingly, an aspect of how we live now.*

In the fiction that follows, these matters are dramatized to show their effects on an individual who is somehow isolated from others. But they are always treated with a good deal more complexity of meaning, and never, thankfully, without humor.

19

JOHN BARTH

The Remobilization of
Jacob Horner

◇◇◇◇◇◇◇

IN SEPTEMBER it was time to see the Doctor again: I drove out to the Remobilization Farm one morning during the first week of the month. Because the weather was fine, a number of the Doctor's other patients, quite old men and women, were taking the air, seated in their wheel chairs or in the ancient cane chairs along the porch. As usual, they greeted me a little suspiciously with their eyes; visitors of any sort, but particularly of my age, were rare at the farm, and were not welcomed. Ignoring their stony glances, I went inside to pay my respects to Mrs. Dockey, the receptionist-nurse. I found her in consultation with the Doctor himself.

"Good day, Horner," the Doctor beamed.

"Good morning, sir. Good morning, Mrs. Dockey."

That large, masculine woman nodded shortly without speaking—her custom—and the Doctor told me to wait for him in the Progress and Advice Room, which, along with the dining room, the kitchen, the reception room, the bathroom, and the Treatment Room, constituted the first floor of the old frame house. Upstairs the partitions between the original bedrooms had been removed to form two dormitories, one for the men and one for the women. The Doctor had his own small bedroom upstairs, too, and there were two bathrooms. I did not know at that time where Mrs. Dockey slept, or whether she slept at the farm at all. She was a most uncommunicative woman.

I had first met the Doctor quite by chance on the morning of March 17, 1951, in what passes for the grand concourse of the Pennsylvania Railroad Station in Baltimore. It happened to be the day after my twenty-eighth birthday, and I was sitting on one of the benches in the station with my suitcase beside me. I was in an unusual condition: I couldn't move. On the previous day I had checked out of my room in an establishment on St. Paul and 33rd Streets owned by the university. I had roomed there since September of the year before, when, halfheartedly, I matriculated as a graduate student and began work on the degree that I was scheduled to complete the following June.

But on March 16, my birthday, with my oral examination passed but my master's thesis not even begun, I packed my suitcase and left the room to take a trip somewhere. Because I have learned not to be much interested in causes and biographies, I shall ascribe this romantic move to simple birthday despondency, a phenomenon sufficiently familiar to enough people so that I need not explain it further. Birthday despondency, let us say, had reminded me that I had no self-convincing reason for continuing for a moment longer to do any of the things that I happened to be doing with myself as of seven o'clock on the evening of March 16, 1951. I had thirty dollars and some change in my pocket: when my suitcase was filled I hailed a taxi, went to Pennsylvania Station, and stood in the ticket line.

"Yes?" said the ticket agent when my turn came.

"Ah—this will sound theatrical to you," I said, with some embarrassment, "but I have thirty dollars or so to take a trip on. Would you mind telling me some of the places I could ride to from here, for, say, twenty dollars?"

The man showed no surprise at my request. He gave me an understanding if unsympathetic look and consulted some sort of rate scales.

"You can go to Cincinnati, Ohio," he declared. "You can go to Crestline, Ohio. And let's see, now—you can go to Dayton, Ohio. Or Lima, Ohio. That's a nice town. I have some of my wife's people up around Lima, Ohio. Want to go there?"

"Cincinnati, Ohio," I repeated, unconvinced. "Crestline, Ohio; Dayton, Ohio; and Lima, Ohio. Thank you very much. I'll make up my mind and come back."

So I left the ticket window and took a seat on one of the benches in the middle of the concourse to make up my mind. And it was there that I simply ran out of motives, as a car runs out of gas. There was no reason to go to Cincinnati, Ohio. There was no reason to go to Crestline, Ohio. Or Dayton, Ohio; or Lima, Ohio. There was no reason, either, to go back to the apartment hotel, or for that matter to go anywhere. There was no reason to do anything. My eyes, as the German classicist Winckelmann said inaccurately of the eyes of Greek statues, were sightless, gazing on eternity, fixed on ultimacy, and when that is the case there is no reason to do anything—even to change the focus of one's eyes. Which is perhaps why the statues stand still. It is the malady *cosmopsis*, the cosmic view, that afflicted me. When one has it, one is frozen like the bullfrog when the hunter's light strikes him full in the eyes, only with *cosmopsis* there is no hunter, and no quick hand to terminate the moment—there's only the light.

Shortsighted animals all around me hurried in and out of doors leading down to the tracks; trains arrived and departed. Women, children, salesmen, soldiers, and redcaps hurried across the concourse toward immediate destinations, but I sat immobile on the bench. After a while Cincinnati, Crestline, Dayton, and Lima dropped from my mind, and their place was taken by that test-pattern of my consciousness, *Pepsi-Cola hits the spot,* intoned with silent oracularity. But it, too, petered away into the void, and nothing appeared in its stead.

If you look like a vagrant it is difficult to occupy a train-station bench all night, even in a busy terminal, but if you are reasonably well-dressed, have a suitcase at your side, and sit erect, policemen and railroad employees will not disturb you. I was sitting in the same place, in the same position, when the sun struck the grimy station windows next morning, and in the nature of the case I suppose I would have remained thus indefinitely, but about nine o'clock a small, dapper fellow in his fifties stepped in front of me and stared directly into my eyes. He was bald, dark-eyed, and dignified, a Negro, and wore a graying mustache and a trim tweed suit to match. The fact that I did not stir even the pupils of my eyes under his gaze is an index to my condition, for ordinarily I find it next to impossible to return the stare of a stranger.

"Weren't you sitting here like this last night?" he asked me sharply. I did not reply. He came close, bent his face down toward mine, and moved an upthrust finger back and forth about two inches from my eyes. But my eyes did not follow his finger. He stepped back and regarded me critically, then snapped his fingers almost on the point of my nose. I blinked involuntarily, although my head did not jerk back.

"Ah," he said, satisfied, and regarded me again. "Does this happen to you often, young man?"

Perhaps because of the brisk assuredness of his voice, the *no* welled up in me like a belch. And I realized as soon as I deliberately held my tongue (there being in the last analysis no reason to answer his question at all) that as of that moment I was artificially prolonging what had been a genuine physical immobility. Not to choose at all is unthinkable: what I had done before was simply choose not to act, since I had been at rest when the situation arose. Now, however, it was harder—"more of a choice," so to speak—to hold my tongue than to croak out something that filled my mouth, and so after a moment I said, "No."

Then, of course, the trance was broken. I was embarrassed, and rose stiffly from the bench to leave.

"Where will you go?" my examiner asked with a smile.

"What?" I frowned at him. "Oh—get a bus home, I guess. See you around."

"Wait." His voice was mild, but entirely commanding. "Won't you have coffee with me? I'm a physician, and I'd be interested in discussing your case."

"I don't have any case," I said awkwardly. "I was just—sitting there for a minute or so."

"No. I saw you there last night at ten o'clock when I came in from New York," the Doctor said. "You were sitting in the same position. You *were* paralyzed, weren't you?"

I laughed. "Well, if you want to call it that, but there's nothing wrong with me. I don't know what came over me."

"Of course you don't, but I do. My specialty is various sorts of physical immobility. You're lucky I came by this morning."

"Oh, you don't understand—"

"I brought you out of it, didn't I?" he said cheerfully. "Here." He took a fifty-cent piece from his pocket and handed it to me and I accepted it before I realized what he'd done. "I can't go into that lounge over there. Go get two cups of coffee for us and we'll sit here a minute and decide what to do."

"No, listen, I—"

"Why not?" He laughed. "Go on, now. I'll wait here."

Why not, indeed?

"I have my own money," I protested lamely, offering him his fifty-cent piece back, but he waved me away and lit a cigar.

"Now, hurry up," he ordered around the cigar. "Move fast, or you might get stuck again. Don't think of anything but the coffee I've asked you to get."

"All right." I turned and walked with dignity toward the lounge, just off the concourse.

"Fast!" The Doctor laughed behind me. I flushed, and quickened my step.

While I waited for the coffee I tried to feel the curiosity about my invalidity and my rescuer that it seemed appropriate I should feel, but I was too weary in mind and body to wonder at anything. I do not mean to suggest that my condition had been unpleasant—it was entirely anesthetic in its advanced stage, and even a little bit pleasant in its inception—but it was fatiguing, as an overlong sleep is fatiguing, and one had the same reluctance to throw it off that he has to get out of bed when he has slept around the clock. Indeed, as the Doctor had warned (it was at this time, not knowing my benefactor's name, that I began to think of him with a capital D), to slip back into immobility at the coffee counter would have been extremely easy: I felt my mind begin to settle into rigidity, and only the clerk's peremptory, "Thirty cents, please," brought me back to action— luckily, because the Doctor could not have entered the white lounge to help me. I paid the clerk and took the paper cups of coffee back to the bench.

"Good," the Doctor said. "Sit down."

I hesitated. I was standing directly in front of him.

"Here!" he laughed. "On this side!"

I sat where ordered and we sipped our coffee. I rather expected to be asked questions about myself, but the Doctor ignored me.

"Thanks for the coffee," I said. He glanced at me impassibly for a moment, as though I were a hitherto silent parrot who had suddenly blurted a brief piece of nonsense, and then he returned his attention to the crowd in the station.

"I have one or two calls to make before we catch the bus," he announced without looking at me. "Won't take long. I wanted to see if you were still here before I left town."

"What do you mean, catch the bus?"

"You'll have to come over to the farm—my Remobilization Farm near Wicomico—for a day or so, for observation," he explained coldly. "You don't have anything else to do, do you?"

"Well, I should get back to the university, I guess. I'm a student."

"Oh!" He chuckled. "Might as well forget about that for a while. You can come back in a few days if you want to."

"Say, you know, really, I think you must have a misconception about what was wrong with me a while ago. I'm not a paralytic. It's all just silly. I'll explain it to you if you want to hear it."

"No, you needn't bother. No offense intended, but the things you think are important probably aren't even relevant. I'm never very curious about my patients' histories. Rather not hear them, in fact—just clutters things up. It doesn't much matter what caused it anyhow, does it?" He grinned. "My farm's like a nunnery in that respect—I never bother about why my patients come there. Forget about causes; I'm no psychoanalyst."

"But that's what I mean, sir." I explained, laughing uncomfortably. "There's nothing physically wrong with me."

"Except that you couldn't move," the Doctor said. "What's your name?"

"Jacob Horner. I'm a graduate student up at Johns Hopkins—"

"Ah, ah," he warned. "No biography, Jacob Horner." He finished his coffee and stood up. "Come on, now, we'll get a cab. Bring your suitcase along."

"Oh, wait, now!"

"Yes?"

I fumbled for protests: the thing was absurd. "Well—this is absurd."

"Yes. So?"

I hesitated, blinking, wetting my lips.

"Think, think!" the Doctor said brusquely.

My mind raced like a car engine when the clutch is disengaged. There was no answer.

"Well, I—are you sure it's all right?" I asked, not knowing what my question signified.

The Doctor made a short, derisive sound (a sort of "Huf!") and turned away. I shook my head—at the same moment aware that I was watching myself act bewildered—and then fetched up my suitcase and followed after him, out to the line of taxicabs at the curb.

Thus began my *alliance* with the Doctor. He stopped first at an establishment on North Howard Street, to order two wheel chairs, three pairs of crutches, and certain other apparatus for the farm, and then at a pharmaceutical supply house on South Paca Street, where he also gave some sort of order. Then we went to the bus terminal and took the bus to the Eastern Shore. The Doctor's Mercury station wagon was parked at the Wicomico bus depot; he drove to the little settlement of Vineland, about three miles south of Wicomico, turned off into a secondary road, and finally drove up a long, winding dirt lane to the Remobilization Farm, an aged but white-painted clapboard house in a clump of oaks on a knoll overlooking a creek. The patients on the porch, senile men and women, welcomed the Doctor with querulous enthusiasm, and he returned their greeting. Me they regarded with open suspicion, if not hostility, but the Doctor made no explanation of my presence; for that matter, I should have been hard put to explain it myself.

Inside, I was introduced to the muscular Mrs. Dockey and taken to the Progress and Advice Room for my first interview. I waited alone in that clean room—which, though bare, was not really clinical-looking—for some ten minutes, and then the Doctor entered and took his seat very much in front of me. He had donned a white medical-looking jacket and appeared entirely official and competent.

"I'll make a few things clear very quickly, Jacob," he said, leaning forward with his hands on his knees and rolling his cigar around in his mouth between sentences. "The farm, as you can see, is designed for the treatment of paralytics. Most of my patients are old people, but you mustn't infer from that that this is a nursing home for the aged. Perhaps you noticed when we drove up that my patients like me. They do. It has happened several times in the past that for one reason or another I have seen fit to change the location of the farm. Once it was outside of Troy, New York; another time near Fond du Lac, Wisconsin; another time near Biloxi, Mississippi. And we've been other places, too. Nearly all the patients I have on the farm now have been with me at least since Fond du Lac, and if I should have to move tomorrow to Helena, Montana, or The Rockaways, most of them would go with me, and not because they haven't anywhere else to go. But don't think I have an equal love for them. They're just more or less interesting problems in immobility, for which I find it satisfying to work out therapies. I tell this to you, but not to them, because your problem is such that this information is harmless. And for that matter, you've no way of knowing whether anything I've said or will say is the truth, or just a part of my general therapy for you. You can't even tell whether your doubt in this matter is an honestly founded doubt or just a part of your treatment: access to the truth, Jacob, even belief that there is such a thing, is itself therapeutic or antitherapeutic, depending on the problem. The reality of your problem is all that you can be sure of."

"Yes, sir."

"Why do you say that?" the Doctor asked.

"Say what?"

" 'Yes, sir.' Why do you say 'Yes, sir'?"

"Oh—I was just acknowledging what you said before."

"Acknowledging the truth of what I said or merely the fact that I said it?"

"Well," I hesitated, flustered. "I don't know, sir."

"You don't know whether to say you were acknowledging the truth of my statements, when actually you weren't, or to say you were simply acknowledging that I said something, at the risk of offending me by the implication that you don't agree with any of it. Eh?"

"Oh, I agree with *some* of it," I assured him.

"What parts of it do you agree with? Which statements?" the Doctor asked.

"I don't know: I guess—" I searched my mind hastily to remember even one thing that he'd said. He regarded my floundering for a minute and then went on as if the interruption hadn't occurred.

"Agapotherapy—devotion-therapy—is often useful with older patients," he said. "One of the things that work toward restoring their mobility is devotion to some figure, a doctor or other kind of administrator. It keeps their allegiances from becoming divided. For that reason I'd move the farm occasionally even if other circumstances didn't make it desirable. It does them good to decide to follow me. Agapotherapy is one small therapy in a great number, some consecutive, some simultaneous, which are exercised on the patients. No two patients have the same schedule of therapies, because no two people are ever paralyzed in the same way. The authors of medical textbooks," he added with some contempt, "like everyone else, can reach generality only by ignoring enough particularity. They speak of paralysis, and the treatment of paralytics, as though one read the textbook and then followed the rules for getting paralyzed properly. There is no such thing as *paralysis,* Jacob. There is only paralyzed Jacob Horner. And I don't treat paralysis: I schedule therapies to mobilize John Doe or Jacob

Horner, as the case may be. That's why I ignore you when you say you aren't paralyzed like the people out on the porch are paralyzed. I don't treat your paralysis; I treat paralyzed you. Please don't say 'Yes, sir.' "

The urge to acknowledge is an almost irresistible habit, but I managed to sit silent and not even nod.

"There are several things wrong with you, I think. I daresay you don't know the seating capacity of the Cleveland Municipal Stadium, do you?"

"What?"

The Doctor did not smile. "You suggest that my question is absurd, when you have no grounds for knowing whether it is or not—you obviously heard me and understood me. Probably you want to delay my learning that you *don't* know the seating capacity of Cleveland Municipal Stadium, since your vanity would be ruffled if the question *weren't* absurd, and even if it were. It makes no difference whether it is or not, Jacob Horner: it's a question asked you by your Doctor. Now, is there any ultimate reason why the Cleveland Stadium shouldn't seat fifty-seven thousand, four hundred, eighty-eight people?"

"None that I can think of." I grinned.

"Don't pretend to be amused. Of course there's not. Is there any reason why it shouldn't seat eighty-eight thousand, four hundred, seventy-five people?"

"No, sir."

"Indeed not. Then as far as Reason is concerned, its seating capacity could be almost anything. Logic will never give you the answer to my question. Only Knowledge of the World will answer it. There's no ultimate reason at all why the Cleveland Stadium should seat exactly seventy-three thousand, eight hundred and eleven people, but it happens that it does. There's no reason in the long run why Italy shouldn't be shaped like a sausage instead of a boot, but that doesn't happen to be the case. *The world is everything that is the case*, and what the case is, is not a matter of logic. If you don't simply *know* how many people can sit in the Cleveland Municipal Stadium, you have no real reason for choosing one number over another, assuming you can make a choice at all—do you understand? But if you have some Knowledge of the World you may be able to say 'Seventy-three thousand, eight hundred and eleven,' just like that. No choice is involved."

"Well," I said, "you'd still have to choose whether to answer the question or not, or whether to answer it correctly, even if you knew the right answer, wouldn't you?"

The Doctor's tranquil stare told me my question was somewhat silly, though it seemed reasonable enough to me.

"One of the things you'll have to do," he said dryly, "is buy a copy of the *World Almanac* for 1951 and begin to study it scrupulously. This is intended as a discipline, and you'll have to pursue it diligently, perhaps for a number of years. Informational Therapy is one of a number of therapies we'll have to initiate at once."

I shook my head and chuckled genially. "Do all your patients memorize the *World Almanac,* Doctor?"

I might as well not have spoken.

"Mrs. Dockey will show you to your bed," the Doctor said, rising to go. "I'll speak to you again presently." At the door he stopped and added, "One, perhaps two of the older men may attempt familiarities with you at night up in the dormitory. They're on Sexual Therapy. But unless you're accustomed to that sort of thing I don't think you should accept their advances. You should keep your life as uncomplicated as possible, at least for a while. Reject them gently, and they'll go back to each other."

There was little I could say. After a while Mrs. Dockey showed me my bed in the men's dormitory. I was not introduced to my roommates, nor did I introduce myself. In fact, during the three days that I remained at the farm not a dozen words were exchanged between us. When I left they were uniformly glad to see me go.

The Doctor spent two or three one-hour sessions with me each day. He asked me virtually nothing about myself; the conversations consisted mostly of harangues against the medical profession for its stupidity in matters of paralysis, and imputations that my condition was the result of defective character and intelligence.

"You claim to be unable to choose in many situations," he said once. "Well, I claim that that inability is only theoretically inherent in situations when there's no chooser. Given a particular chooser, it's unthinkable. So, since the inability *was* displayed in your case, the fault lies not in the situation but in the fact that there was no chooser. Choosing is existence: to the extent that you don't choose, you don't exist. Now, everything we do must be oriented toward choice and action. It doesn't matter whether this action is more or less reasonable than inaction; the point is that it is its opposite."

"But why should anyone prefer it?" I asked.

"There's no reason why you should prefer it, and no reason why you shouldn't. One is a patient simply because he chooses a condition that only therapy can bring him to, not because one condition is inherently better than another. My therapies for a while will be directed toward making you conscious of your existence. It doesn't matter whether you act constructively or even consistently, so long as you act. It doesn't matter to the case whether your character is admirable or not, so long as you think you have one."

"I don't understand why you should choose to treat anyone, Doctor," I said.

"That's my business, not yours."

And so it went. I was charged, directly or indirectly, with everything from intellectual dishonesty and vanity to nonexistence. If I protested, the Doctor observed that my protests indicated my belief in the truth of his statements. If I only listened glumly, he observed that my glumness indicated my belief in the truth of his statements.

"All right, then," I said at last, giving up. "Everything you say is true, all of it is the truth."

The Doctor listened calmly. "You don't know what you're talking about," he said. "There's no such thing as truth as you conceive it."

These apparently pointless interviews did not constitute my only activity at the farm. Before every meal all the patients were made to perform various calisthenics under the direction of Mrs. Dockey. For the older patients these were usually very simple—perhaps a mere nodding of the head or flexing of the arms—although some of the old folks could execute really surprising feats: one gentleman in his seventies was an excellent rope climber, and two old ladies turned agile somersaults. For each patient Mrs. Dockey prescribed different activities; my own special prescription was to keep some sort of visible motion going all the time. If nothing else, I was constrained to keep a finger wiggling or a foot tapping, say, during mealtimes, when more involved movements would have made eating difficult. And I was told to rock from side to side in my bed all night long: not an unreasonable request, as it happened, for I did this habitually anyhow, even in my sleep—a habit carried over from childhood.

"Motion! Motion!" the Doctor would say, almost exalted. "You must be always *conscious* of motion!"

There were special diets and, for many patients, special drugs. I learned of Nutritional Therapy, Medicinal Therapy, Surgical Therapy, Dynamic Therapy, Informational Therapy, Conversational Therapy, Sexual Therapy, Devotional Therapy, Occupational and Preoccupational Therapy, Virtue and Vice Therapy, Theotherapy and Atheotherapy—and, later, Mythotherapy, Philosophical Therapy, Scriptotherapy, and many, many other therapies practiced in various combinations and sequences by the patients. Everything, to the Doctor, was either therapeutic, antitherapeutic, or irrelevant. He was a kind of superpragmatist.

At the end of my last session—it had been decided that I was to return to Baltimore experimentally, to see whether and how soon my immobility might recur—the Doctor gave me some parting instructions.

"It would not be well in your particular case to believe in God," he said. "Religion will only make you despondent. But until we work out something for you it will be useful to subscribe to some philosophy. Why don't you read Sartre and become an existentialist? It will keep you moving until we find something more suitable for you. Study the *World Almanac:* it is to be your breviary for a while. Take a day job, preferably factory work, but not so simple that you are able to think coherently while working. Something involving sequential operations would be nice. Go out in the evenings; play cards with people. I don't recommend buying a television set just yet. Exercise frequently. Take long walks, but always to a previously determined destination; and when you get there, walk right home again, briskly. And move out of your present quarters; the association is unhealthy for you. Don't get married or have love affairs yet, even if you aren't courageous enough to hire prostitutes. Above all, act impulsively; don't let yourself get stuck between alternatives, or you're lost. You're not that strong. If the alternatives are side by side, choose the one on the left; if they're consecutive in time, choose the earlier. If neither of these applies, choose the alternative whose name begins with the earlier letter of the alphabet. These are the principles of Sinistrality, Antecedence, and Alphabetical Priority—there are others, and they're arbitrary, but useful. Good-by."

"Good-by, Doctor," I said, and prepared to leave.

"If you have another attack and manage to recover from it, contact me as soon as you can. If nothing happens, come back in three months. My services will cost you ten dollars a visit—no charge for this one. I have a limited interest in your case, Jacob, and in the vacuum you have for a self. That *is* your case. Remember, keep moving all the time. Be *engagé*. Join things."

I left, somewhat dazed, and took the bus back to Baltimore. There, out of it all, I had a chance to attempt to decide what I thought of the Doctor, the Remobilization Farm, the endless list of therapies, and my own position. One thing seemed fairly clear: the Doctor was operating either outside the law or on its fringes. Sexual Therapy, to name only one thing, could scarcely be sanctioned by the American Medical Association. This doubtless was the reason for the farm's frequent relocation. It was also apparent that he was a crank—though perhaps not an ineffective one—and one wondered whether he had any sort of license to practice medicine at all. Because—his rationalizations aside—I was so clearly different from his other patients, I could only assume that he had some sort of special interest in my case: perhaps he was a frustrated psychoanalyst. At worst he was some combination of quack and prophet running a semilegitimate rest home for senile eccentrics; and yet one couldn't easily laugh off his forcefulness, and his insights frequently struck home. As a matter of fact, I was unable to make any judgment one way or the other about him or the farm or the therapies.

A most extraordinary doctor. Although I kept telling myself that I was just going along with the joke, I actually did move to East Chase Street; I took a job as an assembler on the line of the Chevrolet factory out on Broening Highway, where I operated an air wrench that belted leaf springs on the left side of Chevrolet chasses, and I joined the UAW. I read Sartre, but had difficulty deciding how to apply him to specific situations. (How did existentialism help one decide whether to carry one's lunch to work or buy it in the factory cafeteria? I had no head for philosophy.) I played poker with my fellow assemblers, took walks from Chase Street down to the waterfront and back, and attended B movies. Temperamentally I was already pretty much of an atheist most of the time, and the proscription of women was a small burden, for I was not, as a rule, heavily sexed. I applied Sinistrality, Antecedence, and Alphabetical Priority religiously (though in some instances I found it hard to decide which of those devices best fitted the situation). And every quarter for the next two years I drove over to the Remobilization Farm for advice. It would be idle for me to speculate further on why I assented to this curious alliance, which more often than not was insulting to me—I presume that anyone interested in causes will have found plenty to pick from by now in this account.

I left myself sitting in the Progress and Advice Room, I believe, in September of 1953, waiting for the Doctor. My mood on this morning was an unusual one; as a rule I was almost "weatherless" the moment I entered the farmhouse, and I suppose that weatherlessness is the ideal condition for receiving advice, but on this morning, although I felt unemotional, I was not without weather. I felt dry, clear, and competent, for some reason or other—quite sharp and not a bit humble. In meteorological terms, my weather was *sec supérieur*.

"How are you these days, Horner?" the Doctor asked as he entered the room.

"Just fine, Doctor," I replied breezily. "How's yourself?"

The Doctor took his seat, spread his knees, and regarded me critically, not answering my question.

"Have you begun teaching yet?"

"Nope. Start next week. Two sections of grammar and two of composition."

"Ah." He rolled his cigar around in his mouth. He was studying me, not what I said. "You shouldn't be teaching composition."

"Can't have everything," I said cheerfully, stretching my legs out under his chair and clasping my hands behind my head. "It was that or nothing, so I took it."

The Doctor observed the position of my legs and arms.

"Who is this confident fellow you've befriended?" he asked. "One of the other teachers? He's terribly sure of himself!"

I blushed: it occurred to me that I was imitating one of my office mates, an exuberant teacher of history. "Why do you say I'm imitating somebody?"

"I didn't," the Doctor smiled. "I only asked who was the forceful fellow you've obviously met."

"None of your business, sir."

"Oh, my. Very good. It's a pity you can't take over that manner consistently—you'd never need my services again! But you're not stable enough for that yet, Jacob. Besides, you couldn't act like him when you're in his company, could you? Anyway I'm pleased to see you assuming a role. You do it, evidently, in order to face up to me: a character like your friend's would never allow itself to be insulted by some crank with his string of implausible therapies, eh?"

"That's right, Doctor," I said, but much of the fire had gone out of me under his analysis.

"This indicates to me that you're ready for Mythotherapy, since you seem to be already practicing it without knowing it, and therapeutically, too. But it's best you be aware of what you're doing, so that you won't break down through ignorance. Some time ago I told you to become an existentialist. Did you read Sartre?"

"Some things. Frankly I really didn't get to be an existentialist."

"No? Well, no matter now. Mythotherapy is based on two assumptions: that human existence precedes human essence, if either of the two terms really signifies anything; and that a man is free not only to choose his own essence but to change it at will. Those are both good existentialist premises, and whether they're true or false is of no concern to us—they're *useful* in your case."

He went on to explain Mythotherapy.

"In life," he said, "there are no essentially major or minor characters. To that extent, all fiction and biography, and most historiography, is a lie. Everyone is necessarily the hero of his own life story. Suppose you're an usher in a wedding. From the groom's viewpoint he's the major character; the others play supporting parts, even the bride. From your viewpoint, though, the wedding is a minor episode in the very interesting history of *your* life, and the bride and groom both are minor figures. What you've done is choose to *play the part* of a minor character: it can be pleasant for you to *pretend to be* less important than you know you are, as Odysseus does when he disguises as a swineherd. And every member of the congregation at the wedding sees himself as the major character, condescending to witness the spectacle. So in this sense fiction isn't a lie at all, but a true representation of the distortion that everyone makes of life.

"Now, not only are we the heroes of our own life stories—we're the ones who conceive the story, and give other people the essences of minor characters. But since no man's life story as a rule is ever one story with a coherent plot, we're always reconceiving just the sort of hero we are, and consequently just the sort of minor roles the other people are supposed to play. This is generally true. If any man displays almost the same character day in and day out, all day long, it's either because he has no imagination, like an actor who can play only one role, or because he has an imagination so comprehensive that he sees each particular situation of his life as an episode in some grand over-all plot, and can so distort the situations that the same type of hero can deal with them all. But this is most unusual.

"This kind of role-assigning is mythmaking, and when it's done consciously or unconsciously for the purpose of aggrandizing or protecting your ego—and it's probably done for this purpose all the time—it becomes Mythotherapy. Here's the point: an immobility such as you experienced that time in Penn Station is possible only to a person who for some reason or other has ceased to participate in Mythotherapy. At that time on the bench you were neither a major nor a minor character: you were no character at all. It's because this has happened once that it's necessary for me to explain to you something that comes quite naturally to everyone else. It's like teaching a paralytic how to walk again.

"I've said you're too unstable to play any one part all the time—you're also too unimaginative—so for you these crises had better be met by changing scripts as often as necessary. This should come naturally to you; the important thing for you is to realize what you're doing so you won't get caught without a script, or with the wrong script in a given situation. You did quite well, for example, for a beginner, to walk in here so confidently and almost arrogantly a while ago, and assign me the role of a quack. But you must be able to change masks at once if by some means or other I'm able to make the one you walked in with untenable. Perhaps—I'm just suggesting an offhand possibility—you could change to thinking of me as The Sagacious Old Mentor, a kind of Machiavellian Nestor, say, and yourself as The Ingenuous But Promising Young Protégé, a young Alexander, who someday will put all these teachings into practice and far outshine the master. Do you get the idea? Or—this is repugnant, but it could be used as a last resort—The Silently Indignant Young Man, who tolerates the ravings of a Senile Crank but who will leave this house unsullied by them. I call this repugnant because if you ever used it you'd cut yourself off from much that you haven't learned yet.

"It's extremely important that you learn to assume these masks wholeheartedly. Don't think there's anything behind them: *ego* means *I*, and *I* means *ego,* and the ego by definition is a mask. Where there's no ego—this is you on the bench—there's no *I*. If you sometimes have the feeling that your mask is *insincere*—impossible word!—it's only because one of your masks is incompatible with another. You mustn't put on two at a time. There's a source of conflict; and conflict between masks, like absence of masks, is a source of immobility. The more sharply you can dramatize your situation and define your own role and everybody else's role, the safer you'll be. It doesn't matter in Mythotherapy for paralytics whether your role is major or minor, as long as it's clearly conceived, but in the nature of things it'll normally always be major. Now say something."

I could not.

"Say something!" the Doctor ordered. "Move! Take a role!"

I tried hard to think of one, but I could not.

"Damn you!" the Doctor cried. He kicked back his chair and leaped upon me, throwing me to the floor and pounding me roughly.

"Hey!" I hollered, entirely startled by his attack. "Cut it out! What the hell!" I struggled with him, and being both larger and stronger than he, soon had him off me. We stood facing each other warily, panting from the exertion.

"You watch that stuff!" I said belligerently. "I could make plenty of trouble for you if I wanted to, I'll bet!"

"Anything wrong?" asked Mrs. Dockey, sticking her head into the room. I would not want to tangle with her.

"No, not now." The Doctor smiled, brushing the knees of his white trousers. "A little Pugilistic Therapy for Jacob Horner. No trouble." She closed the door.

"Now, shall we continue our talk?" he asked me, his eyes twinkling. "You were speaking in a manly way about making trouble."

But I was no longer in a mood to go along with the whole ridiculous business. I'd had enough of the old lunatic for this quarter.

"Or perhaps you've had enough of The Old Crank for today, eh?"

"What would the sheriff in Wicomico think of this farm?" I grumbled. "Suppose the police were sent out to investigate Sexual Therapy?"

The Doctor was unruffled by my threats.

"Do you intend to send them?" he asked pleasantly.

"Do you think I wouldn't?"

"I've no idea," he said, still undisturbed.

"Do you dare me to?"

This question, for some reason or other, visibly upset him: he looked at me sharply.

"Indeed I do not," he said at once. "I'm sure you're quite able to do it. I'm sorry if my tactic for mobilizing you just then made you angry. I did it with all good intent. You *were* paralyzed again, you know."

"You and your paralysis!" I sneered.

"You *have* had enough for today, Horner!" the Doctor said. He too was angry now. "Get out! I hope you get paralyzed driving sixty miles an hour on your way home!" He raised his voice. "Get out of here, you damned moron!"

His obviously genuine anger immediately removed mine, which after the first instant had of course been only a novel mask.

"I'm sorry, Doctor," I said. "I won't lose my temper again."

We exchanged smiles.

"Why not?" He laughed. "It's both therapeutic and pleasant to lose your temper in certain situations." He relit his cigar, which had been dropped during our scuffle. "Two interesting things were demonstrated in the past few minutes, Jacob Horner. I can't tell you about them until your next visit. Good-by, now. Don't forget to pay Mrs. Dockey."

Out he strode, cool as could be, and a few moments later out strode I: A Trifle Shaken. But Sure Of My Strength.

❖

Although John Barth's reputation as one of our major American writers has grown with the publication of each of his four novels, it has never caught up with his achievement. There is in his work more intellectuality than is usual in the main tradition in American fiction; that, and the almost chilling wit, the mockery implicit in both his vision and his manner, which lead him to portray as comic, situations other writers might treat as pathetic or tragic—these qualities have perhaps cut him off from the large popular readership the excellence of his work should command. His first novel, The Floating Opera, *published in 1956, sold few copies, although it was a candidate for the National Book Award. His second novel,* The End of the Road *(1958), brought him the enthusiastic attention of some few discerning critics but was not read widely. With the publication in 1960 of a huge (eight hundred and six pages) parody or travesty of a historical novel,* The Sot-Weed Factor, *set for the most part in some wildly imagined version of Maryland's Eastern Shore in the days of the first settlers, his audience grew, for the book was recognized as obviously a work of genius— perverse and self-indulgent and stretching the novel form to its limits, it was said, but still genius. Yet the ironies in his career and reputation continued. Very near to becoming a "cult" writer, Barth published in 1966 what most reviewers considered his most difficult and "unreadable" book yet,* Giles Goat-Boy, *or* The Revised New Syllabus, *seven hundred pages of outlandish, futuristic goings-on in an age when goats and computers copulate, projected by metaphors from the New Testament and academia. Although it was found to be actually quite readable by enough of the public to put the book on best-seller lists for weeks, it was then, scandalously, not even nominated for the 1966 National Book Award. The author was born in Cambridge, Maryland, in 1930, studied for a Ph.D. in aesthetics at Johns Hopkins, taught for many years at Penn State, and is Professor of English at the State University of New York at Buffalo. It is to be hoped that when he publishes his next book, both the critics and public will catch up with him at the same time.*

Jacob Horner, immobilized on his bench, with no reason to go anywhere, can be considered the archetypal, the ad absurdum *ultimate of a kind of directionless, adrift "hero" one finds increasingly in contemporary fiction. The situation occurs in too many books for a listing to be attempted* here, but *Saul Bellow's* Dangling Man *(1944) and Alan Harrington's* The Revelations of Dr. Modesto *(1955) should be noted as early examples. Many such novels also present, counterpoised against the hung-up hero, an active adviser, often and oddly enough a charlatan doctor of some sort: as, for instance, Dr. Lorenz T. Goodykuntz in Thomas Berger's* Reinhart in Love, *with his nonsensical "Comprehensive Nonchemical Medicine"; or Dr. Modesto, with his mail-order courses in "Centralism," a method of achieving success and making people love one by adopting a role of superconformity. Variations on this central situation, then, are far from uncommon, and the doctors—although invariably eloquent and always plausibly consistent—are shown to be offering false counsel. Sometimes these authors are of course commenting more or less directly on the methods of psychoanalysts anxious to reactivate their patients no-matter-what. But what more often seems to be involved is an attack on science in general, an expression of distrust for the experts and technologists who seem to know what we all ought to do, but whose glib plausibilities scarcely conceal a value-free, meaningless pragmatism. In what the Doctor says to Jacob there are of course elements of existential thought, but he is really, as Jacob says, "a kind of superpragmatist." The Doctor speaks clearly, and there is little need for explication. He admits the irrelevance of truth or reason or logic, and his marvelously absurd principles of Sinistrality, Antecedence, and Alphabetical Priority as ways of determining choice of action show how arbitrary and meaningless any action is. The story as printed above is actually an excerpt from the novel* The End of the Road, *and the novel shows what may be obscured in the story: that although the Doctor's therapies do remobilize Jacob Horner, the purposeless and arbitrary action he subsequently takes leads to a gruesome catastrophe. Thus* The End of the Road *clearly develops the following dilemma: to choose to act without reason is wrong, but there is no reason to take any one action instead of any other action; acting, however, is existence, and to fail to act is to fail to exist. And in his first novel,* The Floating Opera, *Barth showed that to choose to cease to exist (to commit suicide) is to choose an action without reason. The predicament is presented as permanent (Barth sometimes seems to be using our own times only as an example), but we will see in what follows that both for multiplicity of choice and for absurdity of alternative, there seems never to have been an age that offered anything like what is being offered now.*

STANLEY ELKIN

I Look Out For Ed Wolfe

◇◇◇◇◇◇◇

HE WAS AN ORPHAN, and, to himself, he seemed like one, looked like one. His orphan's features were as true of himself as are their pale, pinched faces to the blind. At twenty-seven he was a neat, thin young man in white shirts and light suits with lintless pockets. Something about him suggested the ruthless isolation, the hard self-sufficiency of the orphaned, the peculiar dignity of men seen eating alone in restaurants on national holidays. Yet it was this perhaps which shamed him chiefly, for there was a suggestion, too, that his impregnability was a myth, a smell not of the furnished room which he did not inhabit, but of the three-room apartment on a good street which he did. The very excellence of his taste, conditioned by need and lack, lent to him the odd, maidenly primness of the lonely.

He saved the photographs of strangers and imprisoned them behind clear plastic windows in his wallet. In the sound of his own voice he detected the accent of the night school and the correspondence course, and nothing of the fat, sunny ring of the word's casually afternooned. He strove against himself, a supererogatory enemy, and sought by a kind of helpless abrasion, as one rubs wood, the gleaming self beneath. An orphan's thinness, he thought, was no accident.

Returning from lunch, he entered the office building where he worked. It was an old building, squat and gargoyled, brightly patched where sandblasters had once worked and then, for some reason, quit before they had finished. He entered the lobby, which smelled always of disinfectant, and walked past the wide, dirty glass of the cigarette-and-candy counter to the single elevator, as thickly barred as a cell.

The building was an outlaw. Low rents and a downtown address and the landlord's indifference had brought together from the peripheries of business and professionalism a strange band of entrepreneurs and visionaries, men desperately but imaginatively failing: an eye doctor who corrected vision by massage; a radio evangelist; a black-belt judo champion; a self-help organization for crippled veterans; dealers in pornographic books, in paper flowers, in fireworks, in plastic jewelry, in the artificial, in the artfully made, in the imitated, in the copied, in the stolen, the unreal, the perversion, the plastic, the *schlak*.

On the third floor the elevator opened and the young man, Ed Wolfe, stepped out.

He passed the Association for the Indians, passed Plasti-Pens, passed *Coffin & Tombstone,* passed Soldier Toys, passed Prayer-a-Day. He walked by the open door of C. Morris Brut, Chiropractor, and saw him, alone, standing at a mad attention, framed in the arching golden nimbus of his inverted name on the window, squeezing handballs.

He looked quickly away, but Dr. Brut saw him and came toward him, putting the handballs in his shirt pocket, where they bulged awkwardly. He held him by the elbow. Ed Wolfe looked down at the yellowing tile, infinitely diamonded, chipped, the floor of a public toilet, and saw Dr. Brut's dusty shoes. He stared sadly at the jagged, broken glass of the mail chute.

"Ed Wolfe, take care of yourself," Dr. Brut said.

"Right."

"Regard your position in life. A tall man like yourself looks terrible when he slumps. Don't be a *schlump*. It's not good for the organs."

"I'll watch it."

"When the organs get out of line the man begins to die."

"I know."

"You say so. How many guys make promises. Brains in the brainpan. Balls in the strap. The bastards downtown." Dr. Brut meant doctors in hospitals, in clinics, on boards, non-orphans with M.D. degrees and special license plates and respectable patients who had Blue Cross, charts, died in clean hospital rooms. They were the bastards downtown, his personal New Deal, his neighborhood Wall Street banker. A disease cartel. "They won't tell you. The white bread kills you. The cigarettes. The whiskey. The sneakers. The high heels. They won't tell you. Me, *I'll* tell you."

"I appreciate it."

"Wise guy. Punk. I'm a friend. I give a father's advice."

"I'm an orphan."

"I'll adopt you."

"I'm late to work."

"We'll open a clinic. 'C. Morris Brut and Adopted Son.' "

"It's something to think about."

"Poetry," Dr. Brut said and walked back to his office, his posture stiff, awkward, a man in a million who knew how to hold himself.

Ed Wolfe went on to his own office. The sad-faced telephone girl was saying, "Cornucopia Finance Corporation." She pulled the wire out of the board and slipped her headset around her neck, where it hung like a delicate horse collar. "Mr. La Meck wants to see you. But don't go in yet. He's talking to somebody."

He went toward his desk at one end of the big main office. Standing, fists on the desk, he turned to the girl. "What happened to my call cards?"

"Mr. La Meck took them," she said.

"Give me the carbons," Ed Wolfe said. "I've got to make some calls."

The girl looked embarrassed. Her face went through a weird change, the sadness taking on an impossible burden of shame, so that she seemed massively tragic, like a hit-and-run driver. "I'll get them," she said, moving out of the chair heavily. Ed Wolfe thought of Dr. Brut.

He took the carbons and fanned them out on the desk, then picked one in an intense, random gesture like someone drawing a number on a public stage. He dialed rapidly.

As the phone buzzed brokenly in his ear he felt the old excitement. Someone at the other end greeted him sleepily.

"Mr. Flay? This is Ed Wolfe at Cornucopia Finance." (Can you cope, can you cope? he hummed to himself.)

"Who?"

"Ed Wolfe. I've got an unpleasant duty," he began pleasantly. "You've skipped two payments."

"I didn't skip nothing. I called the girl. She said it was okay."

"That was three months ago. She meant it was all right to miss a few days. Listen, Mr. Flay, we've got that call recorded, too. Nothing gets by."

"I'm a little short."

"Grow."

"I couldn't help it," the man said. Ed Wolfe didn't like the cringing tone. Petulance and anger he could meet with his own petulance, his own anger. But guilt would have to be met with his own guilt, and that, here, was irrelevant.

"Don't con me, Flay. You're a troublemaker. What are you, Flay, a Polish person? Flay isn't a Polish name, but your address . . ."

"What's that?"

"What are you? Are you Polish?"

"What's that to you? What difference does it make?" That's more like it, Ed Wolfe thought warmly.

"That's what you are, Flay. You're a Pole. It's guys like you who give your race a bad name. Half our bugouts are Polish persons."

"Listen. You can't . . ."

He began to shout. "*You* listen. You wanted the car. The refrigerator. The chintzy furniture. The sectional you saw in the funny papers. And we paid for it, right?"

"Listen. The money I owe is one thing, the way . . ."

"We paid for it, right?"

"That doesn't . . ."

"Right? *Right?*"

"Yes, you . . ."

"Okay. You're in trouble, Warsaw. You're in terrible trouble. It means a lien. A judgment. We've got lawyers. You've got nothing. We'll pull the furniture the hell out of there. The car. Everything."

"Wait," he said. "Listen, my brother-in-law . . ."

Ed Wolfe broke in sharply. "He's got money?"

"I don't know. A little. I don't know."

"Get it. If you're short, grow. This is America."

"I don't know if he'll let me have it."

"Steal it. This is America. Good-by."

"Wait a minute. Please."

"That's it. There are other Polish persons on my list. This time it was just a friendly warning. Cornucopia wants its money. Cornucopia. Can you cope? Can you cope? Just a friendly warning, Polish-American. Next time we come with the lawyers and the machine guns. Am I making myself clear?"

"I'll try to get it to you."

Ed Wolfe hung up. He pulled a handkerchief from his drawer and wiped his face. His chest was heaving. He took another call card. The girl came by and stood beside his desk. "Mr. La Meck can see you now," she mourned.

"Later. I'm calling." The number was already ringing.

"Please, Mr. Wolfe."

"Later, I said. In a minute." The girl went away. "Hello. Let me speak with your husband, madam. I am Ed Wolfe of Cornucopia Finance. He can't cope. Your husband can't cope."

The woman made an excuse. "Put him on, goddamn it. We know he's out of work. Nothing gets by. Nothing."

There was a hand on the receiver beside his own, the wide male fingers pink and vaguely perfumed, the nails manicured. For a moment he struggled with it fitfully, as though the hand itself were all he had to contend with. Then he recognized La Meck and let go. La Meck pulled the phone quickly toward his mouth and spoke softly into it, words of apology, some ingenious excuse Ed Wolfe couldn't hear. He put the receiver down beside the phone itself and Ed Wolfe picked it up and returned it to its cradle.

"Ed," La Meck said, "come into the office with me."

Ed Wolfe followed La Meck, his eyes on La Meck's behind.

La Meck stopped at his office door. Looking around, he shook his head sadly, and Ed Wolfe nodded in agreement. La Meck let him enter first. While La Meck stood, Ed Wolfe could discern a kind of sadness in his slouch, but once the man was seated behind his desk he seemed restored, once again certain of the world's soundness. "All right," La Meck began, "I won't lie to you."

Lie to me. Lie to me, Ed Wolfe prayed silently.

"You're in here for me to fire you. You're not being laid off. I'm not going to tell you that I think you'd be happier some place else, that the collection business isn't your game, that profits don't justify our keeping you around. Profits are terrific, and if collection isn't your game it's because you haven't got a game. As far as your being happier some place else, that's bullshit. You're not supposed to be happy. It isn't in the cards for you. You're a fall-guy type, God bless you, and though I like you personally I've got no use for you in my office."

I'd like to get you on the other end of a telephone some day, Ed Wolfe thought miserably.

"Don't ask me for a reference," La Meck said. "I couldn't give you one."

"No, no," Ed Wolfe said. "I wouldn't ask you for a reference." A helpless civility was all he was capable of. If you're going to suffer, *suffer,* he told himself.

"Look," La Meck said, his tone changing, shifting from brutality to compassion as though there were no difference between the two, "you've got a kind of quality, a real feeling for collection. I'm frank to tell you, when you first came to work for us I figured you wouldn't last. I put you on the phones because I wanted you to see the toughest part first. A lot of people can't do it. You take a guy who's already down and bury him deeper. It's heart-wringing work. But you, you were amazing. An artist. You had a real thing for the deadbeat soul, I thought. But we started to get complaints, and I had to warn you. Didn't I warn you? I should have suspected something when the delinquent accounts started to turn over again. It was like rancid butter turning sweet. So I don't say this to knock your technique. Your technique's terrific. With you around we could have laid off the lawyers. But Ed, you're a gangster. A gangster."

That's it, Ed Wolfe thought. I'm a gangster. Babyface Wolfe at nobody's door.

"Well," La Meck said, "I guess we owe you some money."

"Two weeks' pay," Ed Wolfe said.

"And two weeks in lieu of notice," La Meck said grandly.

"And a week's pay for my vacation."

"You haven't been here a year," La Meck said.

"It would have been a year in another month. I've earned the vacation."

"What the hell," La Meck said. "A week's pay for vacation."

La Meck figured on a pad, and, tearing off a sheet, handed it to Ed Wolfe. "Does that check with your figures?" he asked.

Ed Wolfe, who had no figures, was amazed to see that his check was so large. After the deductions he made $92.73 a week. Five $92.73's was evidently $463.65. It was a lot of money. "That seems to be right," he told La Meck.

La Meck gave him a check and Ed Wolfe got up. Already it was as though he had never worked there. When La Meck handed him the check he almost couldn't think what it was for. There should have been a photographer there to record the ceremony: ORPHAN AWARDED CHECK BY BUSINESSMAN.

"Good-by, Mr. La Meck," he said. "It has been an interesting association," he added foolishly.

"Good-by, Ed," La Meck answered, putting his arm around Ed Wolfe's shoulders and leading him to the door. "I'm sorry it had to end this way." He shook Ed Wolfe's hand seriously and looked into his eyes. He had a hard grip.

Quantity and quality, Ed Wolfe thought.

"One thing, Ed. Watch yourself. Your mistake here was that you took the job too seriously. You hated the chiselers."

No, no, I loved them, he thought.

"You've got to watch it. Don't love. Don't hate. That's the secret. Detachment and caution. Look out for Ed Wolfe."

"I'll watch out for him," he said giddily, and in a moment he was out of La Meck's office, and the main office, and the elevator, and the building itself, loose in the world, as cautious and as detached as La Meck could want him.

He took the car from the parking lot, handing the attendant the two dollars. The man gave him back fifty cents. "That's right," Ed Wolfe said, "it's only two o'clock." He put the half-dollar in his pocket, and, on an impulse, took out his wallet. He had twelve dollars. He counted his change. Eighty-two cents. With his finger, on the dusty dashboard, he added $12.82 to $463.65. He had $476.47. Does that check with your figures? he asked himself and drove into the crowded traffic.

Proceeding slowly, past his old building, past garages, past bar-and-grills, past second-rate hotels, he followed the traffic further downtown. He drove into the deepest part of the city, down and downtown to the bottom, the foundation, the city's navel. He watched the shoppers and tourists and messengers and men with appointments. He was tranquil, serene. It was something he could be content to do forever. He could use his check to buy gas, to take his meals at drive-in restaurants, to pay tolls. It would be a pleasant life, a great life, and he contemplated it thoughtfully. To drive at fifteen or twenty miles an hour through eternity, stopping at stoplights and signs, pulling over to the curb at the sound of sirens and the sight of funerals, obeying all traffic laws, making obedience to them his very code.

Ed Wolfe, the Flying Dutchman, the Wandering Jew, the Off and Running Orphan, "Look Out for Ed Wolfe," a ghostly wailing down the city's corridors. What would be bad? he thought.

In the morning, out of habit, he dressed himself in a white shirt and light suit. Before he went downstairs he saw that his check and his twelve dollars were still in his wallet. Carefully he counted the eighty-two cents that he had placed on the dresser the night before, put the coins in his pocket, and went downstairs to his car.

Something green had been shoved under the wiper blade on the driver's side.

YOUR CAR WILL NEVER BE WORTH MORE THAN IT IS WORTH RIGHT NOW! WHY WAIT FOR DEPRECIATION TO MAKE YOU AUTOMOTIVELY BANKRUPT? I WILL BUY THIS CAR AND PAY YOU CASH! I WILL NOT CHEAT YOU!

Ed Wolfe considered his car thoughtfully a moment and then got in. That day he drove through the city, playing the car radio softly. He heard the news on the hour and half-hour. He listened to Art Linkletter, far away and in another world. He heard Bing Crosby's ancient voice, and thought sadly, Depreciation. When his tank was almost empty he thought wearily of having to have it filled and could see himself, bored and discontented behind the bug-stained glass, forced into a patience he did not feel, having to decide whether to take the Green Stamps the attendant tried to extend. Put money in your purse, Ed Wolfe, he thought. Cash! he thought with passion.

He went to the address on the circular.

He drove up onto the gravel lot but remained in his car. In a moment a man came out of a small wooden shack and walked toward Ed Wolfe's car. If he was appraising it he gave no sign. He stood at the side of the automobile and waited while Ed Wolfe got out.

"Look around," the man said. "No pennants, no strings of electric lights." He saw the advertisement in Ed Wolfe's hand. "I ran the ad off on my brother-in-law's mimeograph. My kid stole the paper from his school."

Ed Wolfe looked at him.

"The place looks like a goddamn parking lot. When the snow starts falling I get rid of the cars and move the Christmas trees in. No overhead. That's the beauty of a volume business."

Ed Wolfe looked pointedly at the nearly empty lot.

"That's right," the man said. "It's slow. I'm giving the policy one more chance. Then I cheat the public just like everybody else. You're just in time. Come on, I'll show you a beautiful car."

"I want to sell my car," Ed Wolfe said.

"Sure, sure," the man said. "You want to trade with me. I give top allowances. I play fair."

"I want you to buy my car."

The man looked at him closely. "What do you want? You want me to go into the office and put on the ten-gallon hat? It's my only overhead, so I guess you're entitled to see it. You're paying for it. I put on this big frigging hat, see, and I become Texas Willie Waxelman, the Mad Cowboy. If that's what you want, I can get it in a minute."

It's incredible, Ed Wolfe thought. There are bastards everywhere who hate other bastards downtown everywhere. "I don't want to trade my car in," he said. "I want to sell it. I, too, want to reduce my inventory."

The man smiled sadly. "You want me to buy *your* car. You run in and put on the hat. I'm an automobile *salesman,* kid."

"No, you're not," Ed Wolfe said. "I was with Cornucopia Finance. We handled your paper. You're an automobile *buyer.* Your business is in buying up four- and five-year-old cars like mine from people who need dough fast and then auctioning them off to the trade."

The man turned away and Ed Wolfe followed him. Inside the shack the man said, "I'll give you two hundred."

"I need six hundred," Ed Wolfe said.

"I'll lend you the hat. Hold up a goddamn stagecoach."

"Give me five."

"I'll give you two-fifty and we'll part friends."

"Four hundred and fifty."

"Three hundred. Here," the man said, reaching his hand into an opened safe and taking out three sheaves of thick, banded bills. He held the money out to Ed Wolfe. "Go ahead, count it."

Absently Ed Wolfe took the money. The bills were stiff like money in a teller's drawer, their value as decorous and untapped as a sheet of postage stamps. He held the money, pleased by its weight. "Tens and fives," he said, grinning.

"You bet," the man said, taking the money back. "You want to sell your car?"

"Yes," Ed Wolfe said. "Give me the money," he said hoarsely.

He had been to the bank, had stood in the patient, slow, money-conscious line, had presented his formidable check to the impassive teller, hoping the four hundred and sixty-three dollars and sixty-five cents she counted out would seem his week's salary to the man who waited behind him. Fool, he thought, it will seem two weeks' pay and two weeks in lieu of notice and a week for vacation for the hell of it, the three-week margin of an orphan.

"Thank you," the teller said, already looking beyond Ed Wolfe to the man behind him.

"Wait," Ed Wolfe said. "Here." He handed her a white withdrawal slip.

She took it impatiently and walked to a file. "You're closing your savings account?" she asked loudly.

"Yes," Ed Wolfe answered, embarrassed.

"I'll have a cashier's check made out for this."

"No, no," Ed Wolfe said desperately. "Give me cash."

"Sir, we make out a cashier's check and cash it for you," the teller explained.

"Oh," Ed Wolfe said. "I see."

When the teller had given him the two hundred fourteen dollars and twenty-three cents, he went to the next window, where he made out a check for $38.91. It was what he had in his checking account.

On Ed Wolfe's kitchen table was a thousand dollars. That day he had spent one dollar and ninety cents. He had twenty-seven dollars and seventy-one cents in his pocket. For expenses. "For attrition," he said aloud. "The cost of living. For streetcars and newspapers and half-gallons of milk and loaves of white bread. For the movies. For a cup of coffee." He went to his pantry. He counted the cans and packages, the boxes and bottles. "The three weeks again," he said. "The orphan's nutritional margin." He looked in his icebox. In the freezer he poked around among white packages of frozen meat. He looked brightly into the vegetable tray. A whole lettuce. Five tomatoes. Several slices of cucumber. Browning celery. On another shelf four bananas. Three and a half apples. A cut pineapple. Some grapes, loose and collapsing darkly in a white bowl. A quarter-pound of butter. A few eggs. Another egg, broken last week, congealing in a blue dish. Things in plastic bowls, in jars, forgotten, faintly mysterious leftovers, faintly rotten, vaguely futured, equivocal garbage. He closed the door, feeling a draft. "Really," he said, "it's quite cozy." He looked at the thousand dollars on the kitchen table. "It's not enough," he said. "It's not enough," he shouted. "It's not enough to be cautious on. La Meck, you bastard, detachment comes higher, what do you think? You think it's cheap?" He raged against himself. It was the way he used to speak to people on the telephone. "Wake up. Orphan! Jerk! Wake up. It costs to be detached."

He moved solidly through the small apartment and lay down on his bed with his shoes still on, putting his hands behind his head luxuriously. It's marvelous, he thought. Tomorrow I'll buy a trench coat. I'll take my meals in piano bars. He lit a cigarette. *"I'll never smile again,"* he sang, smiling. "All right, Eddie, play it again," he said. "Mistuh Wuf, you don' wan' ta heah dat ol' song no maw. You know whut it do to you. She ain' wuth it, Mistuh Wuf." He nodded. "Again, Eddie." Eddie played his black ass off. "The way I see it, Eddie," he said, taking a long, sad drink of warm Scotch, "there are orphans and there are orphans." The overhead fan chuffed slowly, stirring the potted palmetto leaves.

He sat up in the bed, grinding his heels across the sheets. "There are orphans and there are orphans," he said. "I'll move. I'll liquidate. I'll sell out."

He went to the phone, called his landlady and made an appointment to see her.

It was a time of ruthless parting from his things, but there was no bitterness in it. He was a born salesman, he told himself. A disposer, a natural dumper. He administered severance. As detached as a funeral director, what he had learned was to say good-by. It was a talent of a sort. And he had never felt quite so interested. He supposed he was doing what he had been meant for—what, perhaps, everyone was meant for. He sold and he sold, each day spinning off little pieces of himself, like controlled explosions of the sun. Now his life was a series of speeches, of nearly earnest pitches. What he remembered of the day was what he had said. What others said to him, or even whether they spoke at all, he was unsure of.

Tuesday he told his landlady, "Buy my furniture. It's new. It's good stuff. It's expensive. You can forget about that. Put it out of your mind. I want to sell it. I'll show you bills for over seven hundred dollars. Forget the bills. Consider my character. Consider the man. Only the man. That's how to get your bargains. Examine. Examine. I could tell you about inner springs; I could talk to you of leather. But I won't. I don't. I smoke, but I'm careful. I can show you the ashtrays. You won't find cigarette holes in *my* tables. Examine. I drink. I'm a drinker. I drink. But I hold it. You won't find alcohol stains. May I be frank? I make love. Again, I could show you the bills. But I'm cautious. My sheets are virginal, white.

"Two hundred fifty dollars, landlady. Sit on that sofa. That chair. Buy my furniture. Rent the apartment furnished. Deduct what you pay from your taxes. Collect additional rents. Realize enormous profits. Wallow in gravy. Get it, landlady? Get it, landlady! Two hundred fifty dollars. Don't disclose the figure or my name. I want to remain anonymous."

He took her into his bedroom. "The piece of resistance, landlady. What you're really buying is the bedroom stuff. This is where I do all my dreaming. What do you think? Elegance. *Elegance!* I throw in the living-room rug. That I throw in. You have to take that or it's no deal. Give me cash and I move tomorrow."

Wednesday he said, "I heard you buy books. That must be interesting. And sad. It must be very sad. A man who loves books doesn't like to sell them. It would be the last thing. Excuse me. I've got no right to talk to you this way. You buy books and I've got books to sell. There. It's business now. As it should be. My library—" He smiled helplessly. "Excuse me. Such a grand name. Library." He began again slowly. "My books, my books are in there. Look them over. I'm afraid my taste has been rather eclectic. You see, my education has not been formal. There are over eleven hundred. Of course, many are paperbacks. Well, you can see that. I feel as if I'm selling my mind."

The book buyer gave Ed Wolfe one hundred twenty dollars for his mind.

On Thursday he wrote a letter:

American Annuity & Life Insurance Company,
Suite 410,
Lipton-Hill Building,
2007 Beverly Street, S.W.,
Boston 19, Massachusetts

Dear Sirs,

I am writing in regard to Policy Number 593-000-34-78, a $5,000, twenty-year annuity held by Edward Wolfe of the address below.

Although only four payments have been made, and sixteen years remain before the policy matures, I find I must make application for the immediate return of my payments and cancel the policy.

I have read the "In event of cancellation" clause in my policy, and realize that I am entitled to only a flat three percent interest on the "total paid-in amount of the partial amortizement." Your records will show that I have made four payments of $198.45 each. If your figures check with mine this would come to $793.80. Adding three percent interest to this amount ($23.81), your company owes me $817.61.

Your prompt attention to my request would be gratefully appreciated, although I feel, frankly, as though I were selling my future.

On Monday someone came to buy his record collection. "What do you want to hear? I'll put something comfortable on while we talk. What do you like? Here, try this. Go ahead, put it on the machine. By the edges, man. By the edges! I feel as if I'm selling my throat. Never mind about that. Dig the sounds. Orphans up from Orleans singing the news of chain gangs to café society. You can smell the freight trains, man. Recorded during actual performance. You can hear the ice cubes clinkin' in the glasses, the waiters picking up their tips. I have jazz. Folk. Classical. Broadway. Spoken word. Spoken word, man! I feel as though I'm selling my ears. The stuff lives in my heart or I wouldn't sell. I have a one-price throat, one-price ears. Sixty dollars for the noise the world makes, man. But remember, I'll be watching. By the edges. *Only by the edges!*"

On Friday he went to a pawnshop in a Checker cab.

"*You?* You buy gold? You buy clothes? You buy Hawaiian guitars? You buy pistols for resale to suicides? I wouldn't have recognized you. Where's the skullcap, the garters around the sleeves? The cigar I wouldn't ask you about. You look like anybody. You look like everybody. I don't know what to say. I'm stuck. I don't know how to deal with you. I was going to tell you something sordid, you know? You know what I mean? Okay, I'll give you facts.

"The fact is, I'm the average man. That's what the fact is. Eleven shirts, 15 neck, 34 sleeve. Six slacks, 32 waist. Five suits at 38 long. Shoes 10-C. A 7½ hat. You know something? Those marginal restaurants where you can never remember whether they'll let you in without a jacket? Well, the jackets they lend you in those places always fit me. That's the kind of guy you're dealing with. You can have confidence. Look at the clothes. Feel the material. And there's one thing about me. I'm fastidious. Fastidious. Immaculate. You think I'd be clumsy. A fall guy falls down, right? There's not a mark on the clothes. Inside? Inside it's another story. I don't speak of inside. Inside it's all Band-Aids, plaster, iodine, sticky stuff for burns. But outside—fastidiousness, immaculation, reality! My clothes will fly off your racks. I promise. I feel as if I'm selling my skin. Does that check with your figures?

"So now you know. It's me, Ed Wolfe. Ed Wolfe, the orphan? I lived in the orphanage for sixteen years. They gave me a name. It was a Jewish orphanage, so they gave me a Jewish name. Almost. That is, they couldn't know for sure themselves, so they kept it deliberately vague. I'm a foundling. A lostling. Who needs it, right? Who the hell needs it? I'm at loose ends, pawnbroker. I'm at loose ends out of looser beginnings. I need the money to stay alive. All you can give me.

"Here's a good watch. Here's a bad one. For good times and bad. That's life, right? You can sell them as a package deal. Here are radios. You like Art Linkletter? A phonograph. Automatic. Three speeds. Two speakers. One thing and another thing, see? And a pressure cooker. It's valueless to me, frankly. No pressure. I can live only on cold meals. Spartan. Spartan.

"I feel as if I'm selling—this is the last of it, I have no more things—I feel as if I'm selling my things."

On Saturday he called the phone company: "Operator? Let me speak to your supervisor, please.

"Supervisor? Supervisor, I am Ed Wolfe, your subscriber at TErrace 7-3572. There is nothing wrong with the service. The service has been excellent. No one calls, but you have nothing to do with that. However, I must cancel. I find that I no longer have any need of a telephone. Please connect me with the business office.

"Business office? Business office, this is Ed Wolfe. My telephone number is TErrace 7-3572. I am closing my account with you. When the service was first installed I had to surrender a twenty-five-dollar deposit to your company. It was understood that the deposit was to be refunded when our connection with each other had been terminated. Disconnect me. Deduct what I owe on my current account from my deposit and refund the rest immediately. Business office, I feel as if I'm selling my mouth."

When he had nothing left to sell, when that was finally that, he stayed until he had finished all the food and then moved from his old apartment into a small, thinly furnished room. He took with him a single carton of clothing —the suit, the few shirts, the socks, the pajamas, the underwear and overcoat he did not sell. It was in preparing this carton that he discovered the hangers. There were hundreds of them. His own, previous tenants'. Hundreds. In each closet, on rods, in dark, dark corners, was this anonymous residue of all their lives. He unpacked his carton and put the hangers inside. They made a weight. He took them to the pawnshop and demanded a dollar for them. They were worth more, he argued. In an A&P he got another carton for nothing and went back to repack his clothes.

At the new place the landlord gave him his key.

"You got anything else?" the landlord asked. "I could give you a hand."

"No," he said. "Nothing."

Following the landlord up the deep stairs he was conscious of the $2,479.03 he had packed into the pockets of the suit and shirts and pajamas and overcoat inside the carton. It was like carrying a community of economically viable dolls.

When the landlord left him he opened the carton and gathered all his money together. In fading light he reviewed the figures he had entered in the pages of an old spiral notebook:

Pay	$463.65
Cash	12.82
Car	300.00
Savings	214.23
Checking	38.91
Furniture (& bedding)	250.00
Books	120.00
Insurance	817.61
Records	60.00
Pawned:	
Clothes	110.00
2 watches	18.00
2 radios	12.00
Phonograph	35.00
Pressure cooker	6.00
Phone deposit (less bill)	19.81
Hangers	1.00
Total	$2,479.03

So, he thought, that was what he was worth. That was the going rate for orphans in a wicked world. Something under $2,500. He took his pencil and crossed out all the nouns on his list. He tore the list carefully from top to bottom and crumpled the half which inventoried his ex-possessions. Then he crumpled the other half.

He went to the window and pushed aside the loose, broken shade. He opened the window and set both lists on the ledge. He made a ring of his forefinger and thumb and flicked the paper balls into the street. "Look out for Ed Wolfe," he said softly.

In six weeks the season changed. The afternoons failed. The steam failed. He was as unafraid of the dark as he had been of the sunlight. He longed for a special grief, to be touched by anguish or terror, but when he saw the others in the street, in the cafeteria, in the theater, in the hallway, on the stairs, at the newsstand, in the basement rushing their fouled linen from basket to machine, he stood, as indifferent to their errand, their appetite, their joy, their greeting, their effort, their curiosity, their grime, as he was to his own. No envy wrenched him, no despair unhoped him, but, gradually, he became restless.

He began to spend, not recklessly so much as indifferently. At first he was able to recall for weeks what he spent on a given day. It was his way of telling time. Now he had difficulty remembering, and could tell how much his life was costing only by subtracting what he had left from his original two thousand four hundred seventy-nine dollars and three cents. In eleven weeks he had spent six hundred and seventy-seven dollars and thirty-four cents. It was almost three times more than he had planned. He became panicky. He had come to think of his money as his life. Spending it was the abrasion again, the old habit of self-buffing to come to the thing beneath. He could not draw infinitely on his credit. It was limited. Limited. He checked his figures. He had eighteen hundred and one dollars, sixty-nine cents. He warned himself, "Rothschild, child. Rockefeller, feller. Look out, Ed Wolfe. Look out."

He argued with his landlord and won a five-dollar reduction in his rent. He was constantly hungry, wore clothes stingily, realized an old reassurance in his thin pain, his vague fetidness. He surrendered his dimes, his quarters, his half-dollars in a kind of sober anger. In seven more weeks he spent only one hundred and thirty dollars and fifty-one cents. He checked his figures. He had sixteen hundred seventy-one dollars, eighteen cents. He had spent almost twice what he had anticipated. "It's all right," he said. "I've reversed the trend. I can catch up." He held the money in his hand. He could smell his soiled underwear. "Nah, nah," he said. "It's not enough."

It was not enough, it was not enough, it was not enough. He had painted himself into a corner. Death by *cul-de-sac*. He had nothing left to sell, the born salesman. The born champion, long-distance, Ed Wolfe of a salesman lay in his room, winded, wounded, wondering where his next pitch was coming from, at one with the ages.

He put on his suit, took his sixteen hundred seventy-one dollars and eighteen cents and went down into the street. It was a warm night. He would walk downtown. The ice which just days before had covered the sidewalk was dissolved to slush. In darkness he walked through a thawing, melting world. There was something on the edge of the air, the warm, moist odor of the change of the season. He was touched despite himself. "I'll take a bus," he threatened. "I'll take a bus and close the windows and ride over the wheel."

He had dinner and some drinks in a hotel. When he finished he was feeling pretty good. He didn't want to go back. He looked at the bills thick in his wallet and went over to the desk clerk. "Where's the action?" he whispered. The clerk looked at him, startled. He went over to the bell captain. "Where's the action?" he asked and gave the man a dollar. He winked. The man stared at him helplessly.

"Sir?" the bell captain said, looking at the dollar.

Ed Wolfe nudged him in his gold buttons. He winked again. "Nice town you got here," he said expansively. "I'm a salesman, you understand, and this is a new territory for me. Now if I were in Beantown or Philly or L.A. or Vegas or Big D or Frisco or Cincy—why, I'd know what was what. I'd be okay, know what I mean?" He winked once more. "Keep the buck, kid," he said. "Keep it, keep it," he said, walking off.

In the lobby a man sat in a deep chair, *The Wall Street Journal* opened wide across his face. "Where's the action?" Ed Wolfe said, peering over the top of the paper into the crown of the man's hat.

"What's that?" the man asked.

Ed Wolfe, surprised, saw that the man was a Negro.

"What's that?" the man repeated, vaguely nervous. Embarrassed, Ed Wolfe watched him guiltily, as though he had been caught in an act of bigotry.

"I thought you were someone else," he said lamely. The man smiled and lifted the paper to his face. Ed Wolfe stood before the opened paper, conscious of mildly teetering. He felt lousy, awkward, complicatedly irritated and ashamed, the mere act of hurting someone's feelings suddenly the most that could be held against him. It came to him how completely he had failed to make himself felt. "Look out for Ed Wolfe, indeed," he said aloud. The man lowered his paper. "Some of my best friends are Co-manches," Ed Wolfe said. "Can I buy you a drink?"

"No," the man said.

"Resistance, eh?" Ed Wolfe said. "That's good. Resistance is good. A deal closed without resistance is no deal. Let me introduce myself. I'm Ed Wolfe. What's your name?"

"Please, I'm not bothering anybody. Leave me alone."

"Why?" Ed Wolfe asked.

The man stared at him and Ed Wolfe sat suddenly down beside him. "I won't press it," he said generously. "Where's the action? Where *is* it? Fold the paper, man. You're playing somebody else's gig." He leaned across the space between them and took the man by the arm. He pulled at him gently, awed by his own boldness. It was the first time since he had shaken hands with La Meck that he had touched anyone physically. What he was risking surprised and puzzled him. In all those months to have touched only two people, to have touched *even* two people! To feel their life, even, as now, through the unyielding wool of clothing, was disturbing. He was unused to it, frightened and oddly moved. Bewildered, the man looked at Ed Wolfe timidly and allowed himself to be taken toward the cocktail lounge.

They took a table near the bar. There, in the alcoholic dark, within earshot of the easy banter of the regulars, Ed Wolfe seated the Negro and then himself. He looked around the room and listened for a moment, then turned back to the Negro. Smoothly boozy, he pledged the man's health when the girl brought their drinks. He drank stolidly, abstractedly. Coming to life briefly, he indicated the men and women around them, their suntans apparent even in the dark. "Pilots," he said. "All of them. Airline pilots. The girls are all stewardesses and the pilots lay them." He ordered more drinks. He did not like liquor, and liberally poured ginger ale into his bourbon. He ordered more drinks and forgot the ginger ale. *"Goyim,"* he said. "White *goyim*. American *goyim*." He stared at the Negro. He leaned across the table. "Little Orphan Annie, what the hell kind of an orphan is that with all her millions and her white American *goyim* friends to bail her out?"

He watched them narrowly, drunkenly. He had seen them before—in good motels, in airports, in bars—and he wondered about them, seeing them, he supposed, as Negroes or children of the poor must have seen him when he had sometimes driven his car through slums. They were re-moved, aloof—he meant it—a different breed. He turned and saw the Negro, and could not think for a moment what the man was doing there. The Negro slouched in his chair, his great white eyes hooded. "You want to hang around here?" Ed Wolfe asked him.

"It's your party," the man said.

"Then let's go some place else," Ed Wolfe said. "I get nervous here."

"I know a place," the Negro said.

"You know a place. You're a stranger here."

"No, man," the Negro said. "This is my home town. I come down here sometimes just to sit in the lobby and read the newspapers. It looks good, you know what I mean? It looks good for the race."

"The Wall Street Journal? You're kidding Ed Wolfe. Watch that."

"No," the Negro said. "Honest."

"I'll be damned," Ed Wolfe said. "I come for the same reasons."

"Yeah," the Negro said. "No shit?"

"Sure, the same reasons." He laughed. "Let's get out of here." He tried to stand, but fell back in his chair. "Hey, help me up," he said loudly. The Negro got up and came around to Ed Wolfe's side of the table. Leaning over, he raised him to his feet. Some of the others in the room looked at them curiously. "It's all right," Ed Wolfe said. "He's my man. I take him with me everywhere. It looks good for the race." With their arms around each other's shoulders they stumbled out of the bar and through the lobby.

In the street Ed Wolfe leaned against the building, and the Negro hailed a cab, the dark left hand shooting up boldly, the long black body stretching forward, raised on tiptoes, the head turned sharply along the left shoulder. Ed Wolfe knew that he had never done it before. The Negro came up beside him and guided Ed Wolfe toward the curb. Holding the door open, he shoved him into the cab with his left hand. Ed Wolfe lurched against the cushioned seat awkwardly. The Negro gave the driver an address and the car moved off. Ed Wolfe reached for the window handle and rolled it down rapidly. He shoved his head out the window of the taxi and smiled and waved at the people along the curb.

"Hey man, close the window," the Negro said after a moment. "Close the window. The cops, the cops."

Ed Wolfe laid his head on the edge of the taxi window and looked up at the Negro, who was leaning over him, smiling; he seemed to be trying to tell him something.

"Where we going, man?" Ed Wolfe asked.

"We're there," the Negro said, sliding along the seat toward the door.

"One ninety-five," the driver said.

"It's your party," Ed Wolfe told the Negro, waving away responsibility. The Negro looked disappointed, but reached into his pocket.

Did he see what I had on me? Ed Wolfe wondered anxiously. Jerk, drunk, you'll be rolled. They'll cut your throat and leave your skin in an alley. Be careful.

"Come on, Ed," the Negro said. He took Ed Wolfe by the arm and got him out of the taxi.

Fake. Fake, Ed Wolfe thought. Murderer. Nigger. Razor man.

The Negro pulled him toward a doorway. "You'll meet my friends," he said.

"Yeah, yeah," Ed Wolfe said. "I've heard so much about them."

"Hold it a second," the Negro said. He went up to the window and pressed his ear against the opaque glass.

Ed Wolfe watched him without making a move.

"Here's the place," the Negro said proudly.

"Sure," Ed Wolfe said. "Sure it is."

"Come on, man," the Negro urged him.

"I'm coming, I'm coming," Ed Wolfe said. "But my head is bending low," he mumbled.

The Negro took out a ring of keys, selected one and put it in the door. Ed Wolfe followed him through.

"Hey, Oliver," somebody called. "Hey, baby, it's Oliver. Oliver looks good. He looks *good.*"

"Hello, Mopiani," the Negro said to a short blackman.

"How is stuff, Oliver?" Mopiani said to him.

"How's the market?" a man next to Mopiani asked, with a laugh.

"Ain't no mahket, baby. It's a *sto',*" somebody else said.

A woman stopped, looked at Ed Wolfe for a moment, and asked, "Who's the ofay, Oliver?"

"That's Oliver's broker, baby."

"Oliver's broker looks good," Mopiani said. "He looks *good.*"

"This is my friend, Mr. Ed Wolfe," Oliver told them.

"Hey there," Mopiani said.

"Charmed," Ed Wolfe said.

"How's it going, man," a Negro said indifferently.

"Delighted," Ed Wolfe said.

He let Oliver lead him to a table.

"I'll get the drinks, Ed," Oliver said, leaving him.

Ed Wolfe looked at the room glumly. People were drinking steadily, gaily. They kept their bottles under their chairs in paper bags. He watched a man take a bag from beneath his chair, raise it and twist the open end of the bag carefully around the neck of the bottle so that it resembled a bottle of champagne swaddled in its toweling. The man poured liquor into his glass grandly. At the dark far end of the room some musicians were playing and three or four couples danced dreamily in front of them. He watched the musicians closely and was vaguely reminded of the airline pilots.

In a few minutes Oliver returned with a paper bag and some glasses. A girl was with him. "Mary Roberta, Ed Wolfe," he said, very pleased. Ed Wolfe stood up clumsily and the girl nodded.

"No more ice," Oliver explained.

"What the hell," Ed Wolfe said.

Mary Roberta sat down and Oliver pushed her chair up to the table. She sat with her hands in her lap and Oliver pushed her as though she were a cripple.

"Real nice little place here, Ollie," Ed Wolfe said.

"Oh, it's just the club," Oliver said.

"Real nice," Ed Wolfe said.

Oliver opened the bottle, then poured liquor into their glasses and put the paper bag under his chair. Oliver raised his glass. Ed Wolfe touched it lamely with his own and leaned back, drinking. When he put it down empty, Oliver filled it again from the paper bag. Ed Wolfe drank sluggishly, like one falling asleep, and listened, numbed, to Oliver and the girl. His glass never seemed to be empty any more. He drank steadily, but the liquor seemed to remain at the same level in the glass. He was conscious that someone else had joined them at the table. "Oliver's broker looks good," he heard somebody say. Mopiani. Warm and drowsy and gently detached, he listened, feeling as he had in barbershops, having his hair cut, conscious of the barber, unseen behind him, touching his hair and scalp with his warm fingers. "You see, Bert? He looks good," Mopiani was saying.

With great effort Ed Wolfe shifted in his chair, turning to the girl.

"Thought you were giving out on us, Ed," Oliver said. "That's it. That's it."

The girl sat with her hands folded in her lap.

"Mary Roberta," Ed Wolfe said.

"Uh huh," the girl said.

"Mary Roberta."

"Yes," the girl said. "That's right."

"You want to dance?" Ed Wolfe asked.

"All right," she said. "I guess so."

"That's it, that's it," Oliver said. "Stir yourself."

Ed Wolfe rose clumsily, cautiously, like one standing in a stalled Ferris wheel, and went around behind her chair, pulling it far back from the table with the girl in it. He took her warm, bare arm and moved toward the dancers. Mopiani passed them with a bottle. "Looks good, looks good," Mopiani said approvingly. He pulled her against him to let Mopiani pass, tightening the grip of his pale hand on her brown arm. A muscle leaped beneath the girl's smooth skin, filling his palm. At the edge of the dance floor he leaned forward into the girl's arms and they moved slowly, thickly across the floor. He held the girl close, conscious of her weight, the life beneath her body, just under her skin. Sick, he remembered a jumping bean he had held once in his palm, awed and frightened by the invisible life, jerking and hysterical, inside the stony shell. The girl moved with him in the music, Ed Wolfe astonished by the burden of her life. He stumbled away from her deliberately. Grinning, he moved ungently back against her. "Look out for Ed Wolfe," he crooned.

The girl stiffened and held him away from her, dancing self-consciously. Brooding, Ed Wolfe tried to concentrate on the lost rhythm. They danced in silence for a while.

"What do you do?" she asked him finally.

"I'm a salesman," he told her gloomily.

"Door to door?"

"Floor to ceiling. Wall to wall."

"Too much," she said.

"I'm a pusher," he said, suddenly angry. She looked frightened. "But

I'm not hooked myself. It's a weakness in my character. I can't get hooked. Ach, what would you *goyim* know about it?"

"Take it easy," she said. "What's the matter with you? Do you want to sit down?"

"I can't push sitting down," he said.

"Hey," she said, "don't talk so loud."

"Boy," he said, "you black Protestants. What's that song you people sing?"

"Come on," she said.

"Sometimes I feel like a motherless child," he sang roughly. The other dancers watched him nervously. "That's our national anthem, man," he said to a couple that had stopped dancing to look at him. "That's our song, sweethearts," he said, looking around him. "All right, *mine* then. I'm an orphan."

"Oh, come on," the girl said, exasperated, "an orphan. A grown man."

He pulled away from her. The band stopped playing. "Hell," he said loudly, "from the beginning. Orphan. Bachelor. Widower. Only child. All my names scorn me. I'm a survivor. I'm a goddamned survivor, that's what." The other couples crowded around him now. People got up from their tables. He could see them, on tiptoes, stretching their necks over the heads of the dancers. No, he thought. No, no. Detachment and caution. The La Meck Plan. They'll kill you. They'll kill you and kill you. He edged away from them, moving carefully backward against the bandstand. People pushed forward onto the dance floor to watch him. He could hear their questions, could see heads darting from behind backs and suddenly appearing over shoulders as they strained to get a look at him.

He grabbed Mary Roberta's hand, pulling her to him fiercely. He pulled and pushed her up onto the bandstand and then climbed up beside her. The trumpet player, bewildered, made room for him. "Tell you what I'm going to do," he shouted over their heads. "Tell you what I'm going to do."

Everyone was listening to him now.

"Tell you what I'm going to do," he began again.

Quietly they waited for him to go on.

"I don't *know* what I'm going to do," he shouted. "I don't *know* what I'm going to do. Isn't that a hell of a note?

"Isn't it?" he demanded.

"Brothers and sisters," he shouted, "and as an only child bachelor orphan I use the term playfully, you understand. Brothers and sisters, I tell you what I'm *not* going to do. I'm no consumer. Nobody's death can make me that. I won't consume. I mean, it's a question of identity, right? Closer, come up closer, buddies. You don't want to miss any of this."

"Oliver's broker looks good up there. Mary Roberta looks good. She looks good," Mopiani said below him.

"Right, Mopiani. She looks good, she looks *good,"* Ed Wolfe called loudly. "So I tell you what I'm going to do. What am I bid? What am I bid for this fine strong wench? Daughter of a chief, masters, Dear dark daughter of a dead dinge chief. Look at those arms. Those arms, those arms. What am I bid?"

They looked at him, astonished.

"What am I bid?" he demanded. "Reluctant, masters? Reluctant masters, masters? Say, what's the matter with you darkies? Come on, what am I bid?" He turned to the girl. "No one wants you, honey," he said. "Folks, folks, I'd buy her myself, but I've already told you. I'm not a consumer. Please forgive me, miss."

He heard them shifting uncomfortably.

"Look," he said patiently, "the management has asked me to remind you that this is a living human being. This is the real thing, the genuine article, the goods. Oh, I told them I wasn't the right man for this job. As an orphan I have no conviction about the product. Now, you should have seen me in my old job. I could be rough. *Rough!* I hurt people. Can you imagine? I actually caused them pain. I mean, what the hell, I was an orphan. I *could* hurt people. An orphan doesn't have to bother with love. An orphan's like a nigger in that respect. Emancipated. But you people are another problem entirely. That's why I came here tonight. There are parents among you. I can feel it. There's even a sense of parents behind those parents. My God, don't any of you folks ever die? So what's holding us up? We're not making any money. Come on, what am I bid?"

"Shut up, mister." The voice was raised hollowly some place in the back of the crowd.

Ed Wolfe could not see the owner of the voice.

"He's not in," Ed Wolfe said.

"Shut up. What right you got to come down here and speak to us like that?"

"He's not in, I tell you. I'm his brother."

"You're a guest. A guest got no call to talk like that."

"He's out. I'm his father. He didn't tell me and I don't know when he'll be back."

"You can't make fun of us," the voice said.

"He isn't here. I'm his son."

"Bring that girl down off that stage!"

"Speaking," Ed Wolfe said brightly.

"Let go of that girl!" someone called angrily.

The girl moved closer to him.

"She's mine," Ed Wolfe said. "I danced with her."

"Get her down from there!"

"Okay," he said giddily. "Okay. All right." He let go of the girl's hand and pulled out his wallet. The girl did not move. He took out the bills and dropped the wallet to the floor.

"Damned drunk!" someone shouted.

"That whitey's crazy," someone else said.

"Here," Ed Wolfe said. "There's over sixteen hundred dollars here," he yelled, waving the money. It was, for him, like holding so much paper. "I'll start the bidding. I hear over sixteen hundred dollars once. I hear over sixteen hundred dollars twice. I hear it three times. Sold! A deal's a deal," he cried, flinging the money high over their heads. He saw them reach helplessly, noiselessly toward the bills, heard distinctly the sound of paper tearing.

He faced the girl. "Good-by," he said.

She reached forward, taking his hand.

"Good-by," he said again, "I'm leaving."

She held his hand, squeezing it. He looked down at the luxuriant brown hand, seeing beneath it the fine articulation of bones, the rich sudden rush of muscle. Inside her own he saw, indifferently, his own pale hand, lifeless and serene, still and infinitely free.

❖

Stanley Elkin is another fine American writer whose work has not yet achieved the attention or audience it deserves. He was born in New York City in 1930, took his Ph.D. in English at the University of Illinois, and has been teaching for several years at Washington University in St. Louis, Missouri. His short stories were much admired when they first appeared, at the beginning in such "little" literary magazines as Accent *and* Paris Review *and then later in* Esquire *and* The Saturday Evening Post, *and they were much reprinted in the two best-of-the-year anthologies; but when they were collected in 1966, under the title* Criers and Kibitzers, Kibitzers and Criers, *they were neither widely reviewed nor widely read. The same indifferent reception had been given a novel Elkin had published two years earlier. Called* Boswell, *it recounted the adventures, in high places and low, all over America and Europe, of a modern James Boswell, by original profession a strong man and wrestler, who wanders to fulfill his destiny: to be friend and companion to all the great and famous men and women of the world. The book fully realized the many opportunities for satire and situation inherent in such a contemporary picaresque form. A second novel,* A Bad Man, *published in 1967, has been well and widely reviewed, perhaps marking the end of Elkin's neglect. Elkin's work, more than that of most contemporary American writers, has an especially distinct and original "voice." The language and dialogue in his novels and stories are to some extent derived from the cadences and reiterations of Jewish speech patterns, but he has modified them and heightened them to create a vivid style that is characteristically and effectively and recognizably his own.*

One of the central themes in Elkin's work is the quest for identity. Boswell, of course, is full of it, for the hero's destined role requires constant shifts of personality and identity. A fine flashback section of A Bad Man *is involved with a Jewish boy's conflicts in cultural identity in a diaspora extended to the American frontier. One remarkable long story, "On a Field, Rampant," is really a fable of identity: from birth the hero has had a beautiful medallion that promises to make him different from others, that seems to single him out for some marvelous purpose; but as the years go by and nothing happens, he travels the world seeking the meaning of this special life that's been hung round his neck, only to find of course that it never has any special meaning at all. "I Look Out For Ed Wolfe" presents the opposite side of the matter. Here the hero is born as an orphan—that is, without a tradition or a family, alone from the beginning, without any given identity at all really. In the beginning of the story he is shown striving against himself, using and bullying others as he "sought by a kind of helpless abrasion, as one rubs wood, the gleaming self beneath." The story then describes the removal, one by one, of the identities he has accumulated. Fired from his job for identifying too closely with it, he sheds all the "things" of his life that had comprised his attributes: his car, his books and records, his clothes, his apartment. "Disconnect me," he says to the telephone company. It is made clear that the $2,479.03 that he is "worth" is apparently what he is, as men are known and valued in a commercial society. At the end, before he throws even this away, he tries to sell even the possibilities for love or sex. "I'm no consumer," he says. "I won't consume. I mean, it's a question of identity, right?" Conceivably the story could be read as an analogy to psychoanalysis: the peeling off of the layers of consciousness to reveal the self within. But Elkin makes the point in the last lines that Ed Wolfe now considers himself "indifferently"; he is "lifeless and serene, still and infinitely free"—perhaps only now having come to the realization of the pointlessness of any action, the dilemma that immobilized Jacob Horner. Although both heroes may seem extravagant and unlikely representatives of modern man, exaggeration of the characters and situation is functional, demonstrating the unworkability and ultimate absurdity of the "solutions" they find to their problems.*

MAUREEN HOWARD

Bridgeport Bus

◇◇◇◇◇◇◇◇

FIRST I WILL WRITE:

When I go home, I walk through all the dim two-family-house streets where the colors are brown and grey with what they call cream trim. On the route I take—eight thirty in the morning, five at night—there are four houses which are repainted in pastels, pink and pale green, with aluminum around the doors; the windows and their front stoops are faced with quarter-inch fake stone. When my nerves are raw from the meaningless day at work I see nothing more than four ugly houses, their vulgar shapes, their sameness, defined by the light colors and bright metal. On better days I think these houses have beauty, reflect some hope shared by the Italians who own them: I suppose their blank painted faces would look fine in the Mediterranean sun or in a summer town on the Long Island Shore.

I turn to walk up the hill where I live—here the dark houses are equally bad, though they are presumed to be better, with an extra bedroom in each flat and the upstairs flat bulged out over the downstairs porch. When I look up the hill there are dirty window eyes and huge indolent growths on each idiot brow, a row of monster heads to greet me. I turn back and see the city stretched out dead at my feet. I think about New York or San Francisco or Paris, the scene in which young Gide (it's the first entry in his journals) looks down on beautiful and mist-grey Paris across the imaginary writing desk of an artist. I started that book but something happened, my brother's children, my mother's gall bladder, something happened so I never finished. The actor says, "You see all that down there" (panorama of city at night), "all that," he says to Rita Hayworth, "will be yours." When I look down I see my city on the banks of the exhausted Naugatuck. There is a line of rust along the shore that smells of rubber—the gardens, if I may be allowed, of factories, and then the hills with all the streets of brown houses coming up towards me and towards my street of superior brown houses.

When I go home my mother and I play a cannibal game; we eat each other over the years, tender morsel by morsel, until there is nothing left but dry bone and wig. She is winning—needless to say has had so much more experience—she meets me in the front room, hiding behind the evening paper, a fat self-indulgent body, her starved mind hungry for me. I am on guard when I first come from work—what means had she devised during the day for devouring me? I stand under the dark-stained arch, an anxious thrill rising in me, and just wait, watching but not seeing the elephant chairs and my bloated old mother behind her paper. This room, stuffed with darkness, day or night, any season, is a monochrome of immobility; heavy chairs, lame tables, parchment shades and curtains of ecru lace, all colorless as time—all under a layer of antediluvian silt. Arrangement in grey and black, portrait of my mother profiled, soft and bulky in her sagging chair: a big Irishwoman full of life with eyes ready to cry. For contrast, her white hair crimped in a prim and Protestant roll, seen against the walls (a deeper tone) papered in potato skins. A coat of yellow varnish, the years of our aboriginal love, over the entire picture. I have not long to wait, contemplating the classic scene of home, for she speaks up right away.

"Ag?" she says, not looking at me, and I don't answer, but I entertain myself with the notion that one day it will be someone else come in the front door, a rapist or a mad killer and she'll be caught there reading the obituaries or the society page or looking up her TV programs for the night. "Ag, I bought snowsuits today for the children downtown."

"In April? That's fine."

"On sale, Ag. Sometimes I don't think you use your head. There's been sales advertised downtown all week. I bought them big for next year." She smiles at me, puffy and red in the face, self-satisfied, imitating all the well-to-do Irish.

"I don't read that paper. How much?" I ask.

"Well, that's it—only twenty dollars," mother says.

"Sixty dollars?"

"Yes, for *three* children. I guess I can multiply as well as you, Mary Agnes." Then she's had enough and pushes herself out of the chair to waddle off and get supper.

"Sixty dollars," I say after her, "and what's wrong with the ones you bought last year, not on sale? Can't they pass the clothes on? Can't Catherine wear Patrick's snowsuit? I didn't know a goddamn girl's coat buttoned from right to left when I was their age."

"I don't like to hear you talk that way, Mary Agnes." And then she will say, hurt to wrench my heart—and it works every time—my heart *is* wrenched looking at her raw face, tears swelling. Her blood pressure is up. "Your father, rest his soul, was poor. It's a sad thing, Ag, when you've no more feeling left for your brother and his family way up there in Buffalo. It doesn't matter about me, but it's sad."

We never get more violent than that. I am cursed with gentility and can hardly do better than an occasional name of the Lord in vain, but after each argument I like to look at myself in my own room or in the blue glass mirror in the dining room. There I can see what part of me she has pricked at—her favorite soft flesh around the eyes or my shamefully concave chest. I am gaunt, you might guess it, five-foot eleven, one hundred and eighteen pounds. But why do I start with such heightened drama when there are the usual tidbits: my mail is opened, my bureau drawers rearranged, Clorox put in the machine with a new dress, or: "Ag?" (Once again it is only me, not the sex maniac I dream of, and she goes on at me behind the paper.) "Christine Doyle called about the Sodality Tea and she said wouldn't you pour. Isn't that nice?"

"And you said yes?"

"Yes, isn't that nice." Then she is wise enough to hurry right on and read me something out of the paper: "Well, poor Tom Heffernan died, that's a blessing. They say his body was full of it."

You will think now that I am stupid and incompetent, but you would be surprised how I can gnaw at my mother just by reading for hours, or not speaking, or muttering "Christ" in the direction of the television set as I pass through the front room. And, my choicest bone of contention, I take night courses every year instead of making myself one bit attractive to the gelded, balding boys that my mother is able to find in limitless supply. "Tess Mueller is coming over with that nice son who works in the bank," she announces from behind her paper. I get a quick flash of Fred Mueller, a harmless pudding-beast caged at the People's Trust, counting out my money and saying, "Cold enough for you?" or "Long time no see."

"That's a shame," I tell my mother, "because I'm going to the library in New Haven tonight."

"The library, the *library*—" shrieks of coronary outrage.

"The University, mother. Hundreds of men."

But she is gasping now and slaps her beloved *Evening American* against the brown velour chair. "That's what I'm to tell Tess when she brings that nice boy, that you've gone to the *library?*"

"Oh, you'd be surprised—hundreds of men . . ." But never use even the simplest sarcasm on children because they don't get it, and I wonder if I should illustrate my point for mother: maybe a story about a nun, a Sister of Mercy, working on Cardinal Newman in the stack; she meets up with an emeritus professor, a medievalist who has just been writing a piece on the clerical orgies at Cluny. Scene: the Sterling Memorial Library in the $9860.2n$'s. Time: four o'clock in the week of Septuagesima. It is a moment of transition and the lights have not yet been turned on. . . .

Mother smooths out the newspaper, folds it, tucks it under her arm with finality: she is finished, through with me. "Ag," she says, "you are thirty-five years old."

This is her master stroke. What I should have written to begin with is that I am Mary Agnes Keely, a thirty-five-year-old virgin. All narrative should begin with essentials, instead of the oblique device—picture of a city, a house—that flirts with the truth in a maidenly way. I am called Ag, named Mary after guess who and Agnes after the child martyr. She defended her virginity before it had even a literary value, so I have never had much sympathy with her. At the age of thirteen can you honestly say there is a choice—I mean between a lion and a dirty, nasty man? I cannot believe in a world which honors that prissy little girl, and dishonors me as no more than one of a million social misfits, and lets me be fed daily to my ravenous old mother. "Ag," she will say, her mouth watering, "you are thirty-five years old."

As I write this, I am calm for the first time in years, sitting at my dressing table where I can look at myself often, and I admire the freshness that has come to my cheeks this evening and what seems to be a new firm quality to my throat. I had laid out a thick pad of yellow theme paper and with a smooth, satisfying ball point pen I have begun to write. I can hear my mother at the telephone out in the kitchen. She is whining, aggrieved, to the long distance operator and is asking again, the fifth time in the hour, if the girl will dial her son in Buffalo. My brother and his family don't seem to be at home; that's the straw, she tells my Aunt Mae in a lengthy call, that broke the camel's back in her already broken heart. She has told her sad story to Aunt Mae and to her younger sister Aunt Lil. From what I can overhear, Aunt Lil will be over after supper, done up in her ranch mink stole, to talk to me and try to straighten things out, though nothing is tangled as far as I'm concerned—things are straighter than they have ever been, and I intend to set the whole scene down on my pleasant yellow pad.

It is spring now, but nine weeks ago tonight it was winter, the beginning of February. I came in from the wet gloom of the brown streets to the shriveled gloom of our house—there was mother with the *Evening American,* but she didn't ask who it was standing under the arch, so immediately I knew there was to be an announcement on a grand scale.

"Is it still raining, Ag?" she asked, sweetness itself.

"Yes," I said.

Then she put down the paper so I could see that she had been to the Edna-Lou Beauty Shop. Her hair had a fresh rinse of purple and was kinked in to the head. She was wearing her best stylish-stout wine crepe with a surplice top, and her new Enna Jettick shoes. "Well, wouldn't you just know," my mother said with false petulance, "wouldn't you just know it would rain tonight." She waited, preening out her fat bosom, but I wouldn't ask, so she heaved out of the chair. "Dinner is almost on the table. We have to eat early tonight, Ag, because of the novena."

"The novena!" I said. Her backside looked broader than ever as she hustled out to the kitchen. Ever since I was a girl, for over twenty years that would be, I had to drag my mother to that novena in the winter, tugging her up the church steps like an impossible rolled mattress and stuffing her into a pew. Then the Rosary, the Aspirations, the Benediction, the Prayer for Peace . . . the whole thing started just before the war and was addressed to Our Lady of Fatima who, as I recall, appeared to some prepubescent Portuguese and said the world was coming to an end—as though that were news. So off to the novena and afterwards from St. Augustine's to Friedman's Dairy with the Scanlan sisters, Aunt Mae, and a toothy schoolteacher named Louise Conroy, there to reap the reward: heavenly hot fudge sundaes, topped with whipped cream, and a symposium on every hysterectomy in town. Unfortunately, when the novena was four-ninths or five-ninths over it coincided with Lent, so that my mother and her friends would stand in the back of the church and debate about going to Friedman's, but they always went, denying themselves nuts and whipped cream to commemorate the forty days and forty nights in the desert. Nine weeks ago tonight the novena began.

"I've put your dinner out," my mother called and I walked slowly out to the kitchen. She had already settled herself behind a dish of glutinous brown stew.

"I have my course tonight, mother." *En route* I had switched from the Spenser-Milton seminar which was to be given on Friday evenings to Modern French Poetry.

"You have what?" Poor mother, she saw I was serious.

I sat down opposite her, just as loose and easy, and said, "My French course. It comes on Thursdays."

"God knows," she started her harangue right away, "you were brought up a good Catholic girl that you should choose a lot of dirty French books over your religion. And thank the good Lord," (with a tremolo) "your father is not here to see you an ingrate to your mother . . . a woman the age of you, Mary Agnes, thirty-five years old . . ." and on and on with a sad scum forming on her stew. She looked hateful with all the veins jumping in her face, yet I almost cried, out of a perverse love for her ravings, I was consumed, ready to say yes I would go with her and try to stop the end of the world, but she said, "I will pray for you, Mary Agnes," with her lips all pursed up. That was new, as though she were sucking the marrow out of my bones, and for eight weeks I have heard it—how she is praying for me, for a woman who would let her old mother go down the slippery hills and up the church steps alone at night.

It must have been her praying for me that started me on the pastel houses. I had to have something to come back with after all. Three or four times a week when I came in from work, I told my mother about the Italian houses, the houses that are painted pink and pale green. I would mention how gay they look on a rainy day or remark what a lovely aluminum curlycued C the Capizzolis had put on their front door, or how I admired the Riccios' empty urn, a cemetery urn painted red, standing in front of their peachy pink house. And all the while I had no knowledge, I will swear to it, that I was provoking her more than usual. Yes, I was nibbling! And there were the expected retorts about foreigners: "They weren't stupid. They knew how to improve their property." But when I told her I liked the Italian houses it was only partially true. I had come to love them. I left the house early to hurry down my street and around the corner to the first one, the Marcuccis', who had left corrugated metal awnings up all winter long waiting for sun, and then on to the Riccios' splendid red urn that promised to have flowers and to the Capizzolis' with all the twisted aluminum and the pressed stone that had no geological limitations. A few grey blocks on, near my office, was the last house—I don't know the people—a three-family aqua wonder with glass bricks set around each window to modernize it and the front yard cemented up except for a small patch of dirt the shape of an irrigation pan. There some hardy ivy grew all winter, green. It was an oasis that I rushed to, and one day I walked into the cement yard and picked an ivy leaf. The urn, the awnings, the ivy remembered another season, though I suppose it was the future that I really admired in them, because I had none.

One night I said to my mother, "That's how I get to work and back, from one bright house to the next. I think lots of people go on that way, from one bowling night to the next, or even from meal to meal."

I thought she hadn't heard—she hardly ever did when I explained things—but later by the blue light of the television set she said, "You used to be a good, plain girl, Ag. I can't see what's changed you."

I bought a red silk dress at this time and let my hair grow. At the office they all said how snappy Miss Ag was looking—there I command respect for seventeen years as a cheerful drudge. I am secretary to the president of the Standard Zipper Company. Everyone knows the type, a pinch-faced lady, supports an old mother, can locate every paper clip and advise her boss not to merge with Reddi-Zip, Inc. It makes the salesmen laugh to say I know all the ups and downs. It is pathetic . . . I think of a million flies over America, zip, zip, zip down the trolley—miners, truck drivers, farmers, junior executives, Hollywood stars—never an embarrassing moment, due to the efficiency and diligence of Mary Agnes Keely. I think of the harassed women catching their flesh . . . you must never hurry, I know that . . . and the tossing babies kept warm for the night and the suitcases and tents and silver bags, everything is closing and opening like breath going in and out, while I am sealed—as though our 72-inch model were stitched into me from the toes up and the zipper stuck forever on a broken track under my hawk-Irish nose. It's pathetic, but funny.

I mentioned the dress, the novena naturally, and I shall want to write about my course. My brother went to college, but after my father died my mother took the money that was meant for me and bought our wen-browed dark house so that we would always have a roof over our empty heads. I started filing at Standard Zipper and taking courses at night, and I discovered that being a homely gawk, I was smart. Well, I was smarter than anyone at the Teachers College and as smart as the Saturday morning crowd at Columbia. I have a world now, about the size of a circle of light thrown by a desk lamp, that is mine and safe from my mother and the zipper company and my brother's children. It is the one space in which I am free of self-pity and I hold it sacred like some impossible belief in guardian angels, because when I am outside of the circle of light I can see that it is dim and small. Someone is always saying how fine it is and what a mark of maturity to be able to think, to read; but I'm sure it is a cowardice for most people. I mean that we should want to stand in an amphitheater with spotlights on us, like F.D.R. in a black cape, and say something significant: "At last, my friends, we know the world can come to an end."

Well, my small circle of light, the reading lamp, had been shining with special brightness since the beginning of February because of my course in the modern French poets—they spoke to me. That happens now and again, even when you become a sophisticated reader with all kinds of critical impedimenta: you read something that is so direct, so pertinent to exactly where you are—the way you feel and your precise frame of mind. That is the rapport I had—I still do have—with Nerval, with Baudelaire, with Rimbaud. Not only what they say in brilliant, disparate images but with their diseased, eccentric lives. I feel pain where I have never been touched, dissipation in my early-to-bed soul. (Have I written an Illumination?)

(My mother has got through to my brother in Buffalo. She has only to hear his voice to cry, so what must it be tonight, an ancient keening racially remembered that cannot stop. I wonder if she will ask me to talk to him, way up there in Buffalo. "Hello," I will say, "how are you? How are the kids? Yes," I will say, "everything is fine here. The weather is fine. I am going away." She is wailing. She will not ask me to speak to him on the phone, but no matter where I may go I will get the bill . . . I always pay. If I were to leave my room and see my mother leaning heavily on the refrigerator, daubing at her wet eyes and nose with a disintegrated Kleenex, weeping and weeping to the child she loves, my brother . . . then I could not go. I would offer myself to her, the last sweet bite, a soupçon airy and delicious to restore her, humanity fudge. Warriors did that—not so long ago as we like to think—ate the heart of the enemy . . . I will stay in my room.)

Now let me tell you what has happened. I have told you about the red dress, the novena, the pastel houses and the French poets. Tonight I came home, a Thursday, and turned up the hill to my house. The scene was wrong: the weather had been fine all day, from the window of the zipper factory, and the sun still glowed, low and late on my dirty brown street, but there was a flash of electric blue—intense Immigrant Blue. Then I ran up the hill to my house, because it was *my* house with that cheap blue all over the front and half way down the side, and I ran up the steps, my feet sticking to the gluey wet paint. Inside there she was with the newspaper held up higher than usual, waiting for me. "Ag," she said, "is that you?"

"You know it's me," I shouted. "You know that." I tore the *Evening American* from her face. The smile she had prepared to greet me with was plastered on her speechless mouth. "You have gone out of your mind," I said evenly, *"out of your mind."*

"Now, Mary Agnes, the painters came today . . ."

"The house is blue."

". . . the painters came today, Mary Agnes, and I had it in mind for a while with the house so run down, and I wanted to do something for you, something to please you, Ag."

"The house is blue."

"Well that's it." Her voice rose an octave—her face was flushed. "You've been talking up those houses the Italians own for weeks now, every day it seems you're at me about the colors and the decoration." Now she got up and began to gather the torn newspaper, stooping as best she could with the blood rushing to her head and those veins jumping faster than I have ever seen. "You've been plaguing me with those colored houses, but there is no pleasing you, Mary Agnes."

"In the first place we are not Italians," I said.

"Well you don't have to tell me," she screamed, "you're the big mixer, aren't you, with all your talk about those wops. . . . It wasn't me wanted the house blue."

"We are not Italians," I said again—and in a whisper: "We are withered brown people. Can't you see that? Can't you see one rotten thing?"

"No, I don't like the way you speak to your mother—out of dirty French books I've seen in your room. I bless the day your father died, not to see you like this, a heretic and a spiteful woman."

I grabbed her fat arm when she turned from me and held her. "Now tell me," I said, "how much does it cost to paint a house?"

But she only started to cry, so that I had to answer. "It's my bank account, isn't it?—spread all over the front of this house."

"You'd go off and leave your mother to die, Mary Agnes." Then I saw the working of her voracious mind. Her words grated through the sobs: "You've no more feeling than stone; you'd go off to Europe with the money, and let me walk up to church in the winter and go off in the summer and leave me alone, all alone when I chose that color for you."

Then I began to cry and threw myself into an elephant chair. "For me. For me. That is the color of your Holy Mary. Must the whole street know, the whole city that I am a virgin and thirty-five." I pounded the bulky chair thinking it was my mother's body. She must have felt I was wild—staring up at her with my ravaged face. I was suddenly smiling and sure. "All this," I said pleasantly looking around the front room, "has no importance." My mother thought I meant only our house. "Now I am going to play Bridgeport Bus, once and for all I am going to play Bridgeport Bus and I will go away." (It is a wonderful game, Bridgeport Bus: you line up the dining room chairs in two aisles and you collect fares and joggle along through the Naugatuck valley talking to all the passengers and then get off at Bridgeport.) Mother went out weeping into the kitchen, but I stayed there hugging the large bosom back of the chair.

Aunt Lil has come and gone. She stuck her head into my room and seeing that I was calm, writing on my yellow pad, she went to comfort my mother, saying, I imagine, that it was one of our arguments like any other. Then I could hear mother, loud and choking to Aunt Lil that she would not finish her novena tonight. She is too ill from the exertion and all the shouting. Oh, M. Rimbaud—"This can only be the end of the world, kept going." It is obvious that I will not finish my course . . . no matter.

I intend to travel light, only the red silk dress, some books, my cosmetics, though my face has a surprising fullness and the skin on my neck seems tight, like the skin of an out-of-season, hothouse fruit. I am like that, maturing too late, therefore I may be more valuable . . . that is one of the questions to be asked, still unplucked. My girlish head luxuriates in absurd decisions: I will take the Bridgeport Bus and joggle to the railroad station and then choose between Boston and New York. I may take my rhinestone earrings or I may leave them behind. Shall I call a taxi to take me to the bus depot or shall I walk so that I can see for the last time my obscure, night-dark city with its hills rising—unlit funeral pyres, grey and brown, rising from the beach of industrial rubble . . . and the river used up, ashamed like a deserted woman. "So long!" I will say. "You have loved me like a mother. I take nothing from you but the bare necessities; one suitcase, the beginning of this story. So long, sweet Mother, good night, good night."

The wise boy Rimbaud writes: "The hour of flight will be the hour of death for me." Let me establish that I *know* this as concretely as I comprehend a world of zippers. So having cleared myself of some naïveté, I have only to put on my coat and go—through the living room where my mother is soothed at last by her television, watching lives much more professional than ours. "Let's not say good-bye, only *Adieu, bon appétit. . . .*"

⬦

Maureen Howard was born in Bridgeport, Connecticut, in 1930, educated at Smith College, and worked in publishing and advertising in New York City. She has lived in Rome and London and now lives in New Jersey, where her husband teaches literature at Rutgers University. Her short stories, most of which have appeared in The Hudson Review, *have been anthologized in the best-of-the-year collections, and she has published two novels:* Not a Word About Nightingales *(1962) and* Bridgeport Bus *(1965).*

"Bridgeport Bus" reads very satisfactorily as a short story, but it appears in the novel as a first chapter. The subsequent career of the heroine, Ag, reveals much about the disintegrating forces of life in New York City on a single woman and makes very clear that Ag's final action in this story is a flight rather than an escape: guilt about deserting her mother follows with her. In the story her plight is that of the "emancipated" but nonetheless trapped single woman. A spinster and a virgin at thirty-five, she has no feminine place in her mother's home. Emancipation through education and efficiency—the old feminist dream for the ugly and unchosen woman —has provided her with little comfort. Her efficiency as secretary to the president of a zipper company seems to her only "pathetic, but funny." Her new-found education has served only to bring her into community with the "diseased, eccentric" modern French poets, who echo her feelings of alienation and despair. The urban ugliness in which she lives is relieved only by the pastel houses of her Italian neighbors, which represent her longing for another life—a more romantic and passionate, more "Mediterranean" life. When the money she might have used to go to Europe is spent by her mother to have their brown house painted blue, it seems to Ag not only unsuitable ("We are not Italians") but also to make her romantic longings ridiculous and obvious ("Must the whole street know"). And although she realizes, with Rimbaud, that "the hour of flight will be the hour of death," she resolves to flee the trap that her life has become.

For women, past or potential childbearers all, isolation is not conceivable to the same drastic extent that it is for men: to be alone in a fruitful way is an educated female conceit, a way out of the bleak sterility of unfulfilled femininity, and thus both a death and a hope. It takes a different form, still a concrete reality and an ideal, within the feminine context of family—as is shown, for example, in "Two Short Sad Stories from a Long and Happy Life," by Grace Paley (pages 349 ff).

EVAN S. CONNELL, JR.

The Suicide

◇◇◇◇◇◇◇

SINCE NOON a cold rain had been falling, and the ducks floated as silently and stiffly as decoys among the reeds at the edge of the lake. The sailboats were moored; the village shops were closing for the night.

Leon, having ordered supper, was warming his hands over a candle. He felt chilled and exhausted. He had been playing cards most of the day at the Po-Po Club. As soon as I've eaten, he said to himself, I'll go straight home, take a warm bath and get a long night's sleep. He rubbed his hands and shut his eyes, shivering as a gust of rain swept across the colored glass windows. The more he thought of going home to bed, the more agreeable it seemed. When he opened his eyes, there stood Bébert, dripping wet.

"I've been looking everywhere for you!" Bébert exclaimed. "They told me at the club that you'd been there and left saying you were going to eat, but nobody knew where."

Leon gazed at him in surprise. "Is anything wrong? You look anxious about something."

"Well, yes, I'd say so," Bébert remarked, sitting down at the table. He pulled out a handkerchief and wiped the rain from his face and then mopped his hands. "Yes, indeed, I'd say there's something wrong," he continued. "And if you want to know the truth, there's plenty of reason for me to look anxious. There's plenty of reason for you to look anxious too, as far as that goes. The fact is, just a few minutes ago I received a call from Maggie, who says that Andrea is extremely distraught and is threatening to kill herself."

"Is that right!" said Leon, looking at him with interest. "I had no idea Andrea was feeling depressed."

"Nor did I," said Bébert. "You can imagine how the news astonished me."

"I'm not altogether surprised," Leon said. "I admit that you startled me, but of course we both know that Andrea isn't the most stable person on earth. In fact, the more I think about it, the more it seems to me I've halfway suspected she'd do something like this sooner or later."

"Really?" Bébert asked. "Well, there are various ways of looking at it.

But suicide's a nasty business in any case." All at once he sneezed. "Excuse me! You wouldn't believe how cold it is outside. I'm stiff as a board. It's nice enough in here, though."

"Did you walk all the way from the club?"

"Yes. As a matter of fact, I ran part of the way. I'm supposed to get you to go and see Andrea. Apparently it's a matter of life and death."

"But what am I supposed to do?" Leon asked. "Incidentally, who told you to come and get me?"

"Maggie said that you were a close friend of Andrea, and naturally you should be notified. She assumed you'd know what to do. I don't remember her exact words. The whole affair is confusing. I haven't had much experience in this sort of thing."

"But I really don't have the vaguest idea what to do," Leon said, pinching his lip and frowning. "Why didn't Maggie take care of the situation?"

Bébert shrugged. "She was terribly upset. She asked for you; it's as simple as that. Everybody knows you and Andrea are good friends."

Leon smiled. "Not in the way you seem to be suggesting. We're friends, true enough. We've gone out together occasionally. She's very attractive and I'd be the first to admit I've had ideas, but that's as far as things went, believe me."

"I'll take your word for it. Of course, people do assume that you and she are closer than you pretend. But that's neither here nor there."

"It's the truth. I'm not just saying so."

"All right, I'm only repeating what I've heard."

"I can't understand why Maggie sent for me," said Leon after a pause.

"Possibly Andrea asked her to locate you."

"That doesn't make sense. It isn't like Andrea. And if you want my opinion, I'd say she's despondent because of Schumann getting married."

"Schumann?" cried Bébert. "You mean to say that Andrea has been seeing Schumann!"

"That's what I hear."

"I don't believe a word of it. Not one word."

"Well, I don't know," said Leon. "Stranger things have happened. I once knew a girl who seemed like a perfectly ordinary sort of girl, but later I heard that she had fallen in love with an acrobat. You just can't tell."

"That reminds me—did you know there's to be a carnival in town next week?"

"Yes, I noticed the poster at the club."

"Are you planning to go?"

"If there's nothing better to do. Frankly, I don't care much for spectacles of that sort." Leon stretched out his hands again to the candle. "You know, I really don't understand why Maggie was asking for me. It's as though I had something to do with all this, but I assure you I haven't. This morning I was working on the boat and this afternoon I was at the club. I haven't seen Andrea for at least a week, come to think of it. And as soon as I finish dinner I'm going home. I don't want to catch cold. It's a bad night."

"I'm only doing as I was asked," said Bébert.

"H'm'm. Well, to be honest about it, I feel more or less inadequate. Ever since I was a child I've had a feeling of being somehow not too effective when it comes to emergencies, I don't know why. Of course, nobody's perfect; we all have our weaknesses."

"I'm the same," Bébert replied. "I have the best of intentions, but I never know quite how to proceed. A fire, let's say, well! That's enough to throw me in a panic. I gallop back and forth explaining to everybody that there's a fire, but of course that's hardly the way to put it out. Now in this particular case—Andrea, I mean—I came dashing up the street with a message, but beyond that I didn't have an idea in my head! So you see I know exactly what you mean. But I don't really think of you as ineffectual. You've always struck me as being very calm and collected. That's a good thing. I envy you, in fact."

"Well," said Leon, "in any event, it's disturbing to know about Andrea. On the other hand, I find myself wondering if she's really as depressed as Maggie says."

"Oh, there's no doubt of it! Not a doubt in the world. Maggie told me that Andrea was completely hysterical. Threatening to slash her wrists! Just the thought of something like that is enough to terrify me."

"Did it come on suddenly?"

"I'm so upset I can hardly think. Did *what* come on suddenly?"

"Has Andrea been in this state for some time, or did she collapse without warning?"

"I don't know. If Maggie told me I've forgotten. If a thing's important you can trust me to forget it."

"She's planning to slash her wrists, you say. That's unusual."

"How so?"

"Andrea's fastidious. She seems to me the type that would take poison."

"Really? How awful! You could be right. But then I don't know her too well."

"Women rarely shoot themselves, either. Did you know that? They jump off buildings or take too many sleeping pills, but they don't care much for guns or knives. I don't know why it is, except that there's something basically different about them. And they often go in for gas. They shut the windows and put on a transparent negligee and arrange themselves on the sofa. You read about it in the papers every day."

"I can't bear to think about such things," said Bébert. "It gives me cold chills."

"Getting back to Andrea, didn't Maggie give you any clues as to just why she happens to be in this condition?"

Bébert was silent for a while. "No," he said at last, frowning. "All I know is that she was weeping and creating a scene, so Maggie telephoned the club, and it was just my luck to be there. I shouldn't say that, but it's true. There I was playing chess with some fellow from New York, when they came around asking if anybody knew where you were. Well, I made the mistake of being curious, so they assumed I must know. That's how I got involved. I shouldn't have said a word. At any rate, before I knew what was happening I found myself on the telephone talking to Maggie, and as she seemed so desperate and kept asking for you I thought to myself, the simplest way to get out of this mess is to try and find you. That's the story in a nutshell. So here I am, wet as a dog! And I had a good game going for me, if I do say so. I'd pinned his rook; he didn't have any idea what to do—you should have seen him twisting his hands together and studying the board." Bébert laughed.

"Who did you say you were playing?"

"You don't know him. He's visiting that tennis player with the red moustache. They came into the club just after you left, evidently. Then I happened to come in, and this New Yorker for some reason challenged me to a game; I don't know why. You'd think he'd rather play with his friend, but he took one look at me and said, 'What about you? You look like a chess player.' I had to admit that I was, although not a very good one, and I told him so. Well, he gave me a superior little smile and I must admit that annoyed me. I wasn't pretending to be modest. The fact is, I scarcely ever win a game. Practically everybody beats me."

"Is that so? I had the impression you played very well. I wouldn't take you for an aggressive player, but I should think you'd win your share."

"No, I almost always lose. But tonight I got off to a good start, and that makes all the difference. I offered a bishop pawn, and to my surprise he took it, which is exactly what I was hoping he'd do. Then I moved out with the queen and threw him in check right away. He was completely startled —you should have seen his face! It knocked him off his game, I suppose. One isn't expected to open with the queen attack, you know; the textbooks advise against it. But it worked. Whatever he had in mind, he didn't have a chance to get started. There he was with his back to the wall. And things moved along from there quite nicely. It's the beginning that's important."

"Ah! Excuse me, here's my soup," Leon said, and placing both hands on the table he leaned forward to smell the soup.

Bébert watched attentively. Leon stirred the soup, lifted a spoonful and blew on it.

"Looks very hot," said Bébert.

Leon nodded and then tasted it. "But it's good."

"There's nothing better than hot soup on a bad night," said Bébert.

"Not many things, at any rate."

"Aren't you coming to see what you can do about Andrea? I thought you were planning to cancel your order."

"I've been thinking about it," said Leon. "But of course if she's firmly made up her mind to kill herself, why, chances are that she'll do it. Look at the case this way. Suppose we go to see her and tell her things aren't really half as bad as she thinks, and so on and so forth. Now, if she's determined to kill herself she won't believe a word we say, will she? Women are like that."

"I wasn't planning to go," said Bébert immediately.

Leon took another spoonful of soup.

"I'm just running an errand, so to speak," Bébert continued. "That's the extent of it. You could think of me as a messenger."

"I thought you wanted the two of us to go and see her."

"Oh, no!" exclaimed Bébert. "You misunderstand!"

Leon was annoyed. "But why did they send for me? That's what I can't understand. You'd think I was her lover."

"I believe you," Bébert said, who had placed both elbows on the table and now sat with his chin cupped in his hands watching Leon eat the soup. "Don't you think we ought to go see her?" he asked after a little while. "It sounds like a crucial situation. Not that it's any of my business, of course. They asked if I could find you, and I thought perhaps I could. I remembered that you liked this place."

"Yes, the food's good here," Leon said. He began grinding pepper into his bowl.

"I shouldn't think you could taste anything, not with all that. I take very little seasoning. I read somewhere or other that pepper weakens the senses and leads to any number of complications, some of them quite serious. There was one fellow who sprinkled paprika on everything until finally he developed pleurisy, and the doctors say it was the paprika that caused it. That doesn't sound reasonable, but you never know. As for myself, I'm not afraid of pleurisy, but I do get cramps if I eat certain things. Well!" he exclaimed, straightening up. "There was a flash of lightning if ever I saw one! What a storm! And it's odd for this time of year. Usually the weather isn't too bad, nothing like this, anyhow."

Leon wiped his lips with the napkin. "Hand me the bread, will you?"

Bébert silently gave him the basket.

"You're worried about Andrea, aren't you?" Leon asked, as he twisted off a piece of bread.

"I certainly am. You should be too. I don't know how you can sit there placidly eating your dinner as though nothing in the world was wrong when she could be slashing her wrists at this very instant, for all we know."

"But you've forgotten one thing."

"What's that?"

"Maggie is there. Maggie wouldn't let her do anything foolish, so as I see it there isn't much to worry about."

"How can you be so sure? There was simply this telephone call, you understand, and Maggie was excited—I could tell!"

"That's bad, I admit. It isn't like Maggie to be excited."

"Furthermore, I can't positively state that Maggie was with Andrea. It's conceivable, you know, she simply received word that Andrea was planning to do something drastic. I should have asked; that's my fault. I didn't think of it. You see what I mean when I say I'm no good at emergencies? I just came flying down here to try to locate you. I'm so impulsive. It seems as though I'm always rushing off in one direction or another, and then people such as yourself who have a naturally phlegmatic nature are able to calmly butter their bread and ask about specific items, and then I'm forced to confess that I don't know. It's embarrassing. Whenever something like this happens, I promptly say to myself that I've got to take action when, of course, the intelligent thing is not to go running around helter-skelter."

"I don't regard myself as phlegmatic."

"You're always perfectly in control of yourself."

"Well," said Leon, "that's different. Anyway, you know how it is. We each have a varying tempo, different ways of doing things, so to speak. It's true that you're more or less impulsive—at least that's been my observation—but there's nothing wrong with that. In fact, I wish I could be more like you. I'm perhaps inclined to be a trifle sluggish. Right now, for instance, you could be right and I might be absolutely wrong. Here I am, as you point out, buttering a piece of bread when at this very moment Andrea might be lying in a pool of blood. Suppose, for example, this really turns out to be the case and we find out that a tragedy occurred while I was here eating supper. How would I feel? You can imagine. I'd feel a sense of guilt for the rest of my life."

Bébert nodded enthusiastically. "And you wouldn't be alone! Even though I really haven't anything to do with all this, I'd feel a sense of guilt right along with you. I know exactly what you're trying to express. When these things occur, it's simply no use telling yourself after it's all over that you weren't to blame. You know in your heart that you should have done something about it. You should have been able to avert the tragedy. People are pretty much alike in that respect, at least this is my own opinion. Their hearts are in the right place, but somehow they don't behave the way they know they ought. It's queer. I've often thought about it. You're right. You're absolutely right."

"Shh!" Leon whispered, holding up a finger.

"What's the matter?"

"Can't you hear the ducks?"

"Ducks?"

"It sounds as though they're taking off. I thought they'd stay where they were, considering it's such a bad night."

"Well, I don't suppose they mind the weather," said Bébert.

"Ah! This looks worth waiting for," Leon remarked as the waitress placed a large salad in front of him.

"What do you have there?" Bébert asked, looking at it closely. "Is that a Roquefort dressing?"

"Yes. My favorite. I never get tired of it."

"Salads are good for you. When I was a child my mother told me they were, and naturally just like a child that was enough to put me off salad for years. I refused to eat one for no reason except that they were supposed to be good for me. But now I must admit I love them."

Leon was grinding pepper on the salad. Bébert watched with a look of disapproval.

"What do you think ought to be done?" Leon asked.

"As far as Andrea is concerned?"

Leon paused and looked at him curiously. "Well, what else did you think I was talking about?"

"You needn't be snappish."

"I apologize," Leon said. "You've got me on edge."

"As I've previously explained with utter clarity, this entire affair has nothing to do with me personally. Strictly speaking, my job is finished. I've notified you, that's all I set out to do. From here on it's up to you for better or worse. But frankly, I don't see how you can go right on eating at a time like this."

"Don't be ridiculous," Leon said with his eyes fixed on the salad.

"Well! If that's how you're going to act," said Bébert, "I'll just be leaving. I can't honestly say I enjoy being spoken to in that tone of voice. Furthermore, I certainly don't feel that I was being ridiculous."

"Let's not argue. Perhaps you misunderstood what I meant. Now look here—the important point is whether or not Andrea actually plans to end it all. What do you think? Is she, or not?"

"I'd say there's not much question about it."

"By the way, you know she's divorced, don't you?"

"One hears rumors. I don't believe everything. Repeating rumors can be malicious."

"I know for a fact that she is a divorcée. I don't know what the husband was like, but if he was anything like Andrea, they must have made a pair. You were at the beach that time she started kicking sand at everybody, weren't you? No reason for it, she just decided she disliked everybody. She flies off the handle every once in a while."

"I wasn't at the beach, though I did hear about that episode. I remember being surprised, because I'd always thought of Andrea as not being the type to raise a fuss. She seems so mature."

"She's not as old as she looks. She's twenty-three."

"No! Are you sure?"

"Positive." Leon took a sip of wine and inspected the bottle. "Here, this is very good. Have a glass."

"No, no. Thank you. I never can guess how wine will affect me. At times it disagrees with my stomach. I believe I'll just have a cigarette, though, if the smoke won't disturb you while you're eating."

"Go ahead; one gets used to it nowadays. You'd think we were all living inside a furnace. I'm as guilty as the rest. Puff-puff-puff, morning, noon and night. The first of the year I'm going to quit."

"I've tried to quit several times," Bébert said as he struck a match. "I simply don't have the willpower. But you say Andrea is only twenty-three? That's amazing!"

"She's been around. Probably that's why people tend to associate her with me. Since I have a poor reputation they probably assume the two of us have something going."

"What makes you say you have a poor reputation?"

"It's true, isn't it? Be honest."

Bébert looked thoughtful. "No worse than anyone else who spends a lot of time at the club. I'm there half my life, you know, so I'm hardly in a position to be criticizing. On the other hand, it's probably true that certain persons who don't go there very often think that some of us are wasting a lot of time, if that's what you mean. Otherwise, though, I don't feel that you have a bad reputation. We're all in the same boat. Practically every night the club's full of the same old faces."

"What else is there to do? That's what I answer when anybody asks why I'm always around."

"And it's true!" Bébert exclaimed. "You can only go to the movies every so often, and what else is there? The club's a nice place to spend your time. It isn't too expensive and there aren't many fights."

"Even so, the first of the year I'm going to stop spending so much time there," said Leon. "It repels me. Here, try a bite of this salad."

"All right," said Bébert, laughing. "How often do you eat at this place, by the way?"

"Oh, twice a week, more or less. It depends on the chef's special. I almost always have the special, although you have to get here early; otherwise it's gone. I've been here as early as six o'clock some nights and the special was gone."

"I've never tried it. I don't come here often, maybe once a month. I do enjoy the lobster tail. I suppose you've tried that, haven't you?"

"Yes, it's delicious. But it costs too much."

"It certainly does! What's on special tonight?"

"Baked sugar-cured ham with bread crumbs and cranberry sauce."

"What an odd combination!"

"You get to trust the chef. He improvises, and sometimes it's a little strange. For instance, last week he cooked a chicken risotto that had an unusual taste. I've been wondering what he put in it. But ordinarily the special is a good bet. The baked ham is fair, although he does better with the pocket of veal."

"I don't know why they don't serve dinners at the club," said Bébert reflectively.

"I've wondered. It must be the cost of outfitting a kitchen."

"You know how much plumbers and electricians are making these days, I suppose?"

Leon held up both hands. "Don't say a word! They earn six times what I do."

"You wouldn't believe it. Just last week an electrician's helper came into the bank to deposit his weekly check, and I was absolutely dumbfounded. I thought he'd stolen it."

Leon shook his head and continued eating the salad. Rain swept across the windows. Bébert sat watching a drop of wax roll down the candle; every little while he shivered as though remembering the cold outside. Presently the waitress brought Leon's baked ham, and with it the cranberry sauce, some parsley and Mexican beans and a dish of corn pudding. A little cloud of steam rose above the plate.

"I don't have much appetite," Leon said. "I don't know why."

"It looks delicious," Bébert said. "In fact, if you don't mind my saying so, I could almost eat it myself."

Leon picked up his knife and fork and said, as he prepared to attack the dish, "I was thinking about Andrea. There wasn't a thing on my mind, but then you came in here and told me about her being so despondent, and since then I haven't felt particularly hungry." He cut a slice of ham, which he put into his mouth and began to chew with an expression of pleasure.

Bébert looked at him and then at the ham on the plate.

"Why don't you have some of that corn pudding?" Leon asked. "I'm not really very hungry."

"I'm not either, in fact," said Bébert. "It's just that suddenly the ham looked very good, as you say. How is it?"

"Excellent!" said Leon. "Excellent." He began to cut himself another piece, but then lowered the knife and said, "Look here, I've got an idea. While I'm having dinner you could run up to see Andrea. You could find out how she is and come back and let me know. How does that sound? I should have thought of it before."

"I don't think that's a good idea," said Bébert.

"No? Why not?"

"Well, first of all, you've got to consider her feelings. You're the one she's expecting. How does it look when you're expecting a certain person and all of a sudden there's somebody else at the door? That can be quite a shock, particularly so when you're in a bad state. It might even be fatal. You yourself told me just a little while ago that she's unstable. There'd be no way of guessing what she might do. There's a knock at the door, she thinks it's you and she flings open the door, and there I am! What happens next? It could be extremely awkward; you can see that."

"You're forgetting she's desperate," said Leon, who was cutting another piece of ham. "There's nothing worse than feeling desperate. I ought to know; I've had that feeling myself once or twice. It's terrible. You don't know which way to turn."

"Those are the truest words ever spoken," said Bébert.

Leon helped himself to the corn pudding. "Just let us suppose," he went on after a little while, "that Andrea is by herself. You say you forgot to ask Maggie whether she was with Andrea or not. All right, suppose there's nobody with her; what about that? Wouldn't you be glad to see anybody, no matter who it was, even though it didn't happen to be exactly the person you were expecting?"

"You're right," Bébert admitted, nodding. "I hadn't thought of it like that. I agree with you one hundred percent. But still, the main thing is that she's expecting you. That's the important point."

Leon stopped chewing and gazed at Bébert curiously. "But you said it was Maggie who asked where I was. Did Andrea herself ask for me? There's all the difference in the world."

"You're right again; I should have asked specific questions. I never think about things until it's too late. It's just the way I am. I forgot, that's all. The first thing I thought was that here was an emergency and something had to be done immediately."

"Well, it's nothing to be embarrassed about," Leon said and resumed eating.

Bébert frowned. "As a matter of fact, I remember one time six or eight years ago I was witness to an accident, and virtually the same thing occurred. It must have been at least six years ago, because I was going around at that time with a blond girl by the name of Claudine, but I don't think you knew her. She was a very good swimmer." He paused and then shrugged. "There. You see? Already I've forgotten what I was going to tell you."

"An accident. Something about an accident."

"Oh! Yes. A taxicab ran over this fellow who was selling newspapers. Papers flew all over the street. I never saw anything like it. It was a windy day too. The confusion was unbelievable. Everybody honking and traffic tied up for blocks. You can imagine the scene. At any rate, I just happened to be standing on the corner waiting to go across when the taxi hit this fellow. I've never seen anything so horrible. He turned a somersault in midair and came down sitting. Well, he just sat there in front of the taxi and leaned back slowly on his elbows with the oddest expression on his face. I was petrified. I simply stood there and gawked at him like an imbecile. The only consolation was that everybody did the same. It was just as though nobody wanted to get mixed up in it. Of course everybody felt sorry for him, but at the same time they didn't quite want to get involved, seeing it was none of their business. They were pretty thankful they weren't the one who'd got hit. In fact, I remember thinking at the time that this was the reason I didn't make a move to help him. I was afraid I'd get some blood on my hands, in case he was bleeding. Then too, you could be called into court and involved in lawsuits and so on. One thing leads to another, particularly in cases like this. There's just no telling."

"What happened?" Leon asked without looking up from his plate.

"Oh, the spell was finally broken, so to speak. Everybody gathered around and started offering advice, but naturally one person said to wrap him in a blanket and somebody else said not to move him and somebody else thought he needed a drink. I must say, I certainly could have used a drink right at that moment. At any event, an ambulance finally arrived with the siren on and the lights flashing, and there was a great deal of commotion before they managed to get the poor fellow loaded on a stretcher and carried away. I never did find out what became of him. Some woman fainted, and at first the ambulance stewards supposed she was the victim. Oh, it was a pretty mess!"

"I can imagine," said Leon.

"Frankly, I'm terrified of accidents. Except for that one time, I've never gotten involved; I always seem to be somewhere else when anything happens. It's almost mysterious. It isn't that I go out of my way to avoid incidents; it's just that I'm almost always getting there after it's over, or else I leave not five minutes before something occurs. It's amazing, when I think of it."

"That's so. There are certain people who do seem to miss everything, just as other people are always breaking a leg or having their house burn down, or getting robbed. Nobody knows why it is, but it does make you wonder."

Bébert nodded.

"Now, take Andrea, for instance," Leon continued, filling up his wineglass. "Wouldn't you say she's a perfect instance of what we're discussing?"

"I don't know," said Bébert promptly. "I'm not well acquainted with her, as I've already pointed out. We've run into each other a number of times, yes, and we're on friendly terms, but aside from that I can't truthfully say I know much about her. This thing tonight was a great shock."

"Yes, it was for me too," said Leon thoughtfully.

"There I was playing chess at the club, when all of a sudden I find myself mixed up in a business that's completely foreign to me and have to come flying down the street getting soaked to the bone trying to find out where you are. It was no picnic. I don't care for things of this sort. I don't have the temperament for it. But as to what you were saying, you could be right. Divorced, and then that scene at the beach, and now this! It makes you wonder what will happen next."

"She's not realistic, that's her trouble."

"Well, who is? Take my uncle on my mother's side, for example. An absolute mystic! I remember him quite well, although he died when I was little. He used to interpret dreams and read tea leaves, and he could read your history on the palm of your hand so that you'd swear he'd been following you around. It was absolutely incredible! Even my father was impressed, and there were very few things on this earth that could impress my father. Why, when the *Hindenburg* crashed at that airport in New York—or New Jersey, I think it was—anyway my father when he heard the news didn't so much as bat an eye. 'That's quite a tragedy,' he said. Those were his exact words. 'That's quite a tragedy.' Everybody else was simply horrified and went around telling people, but not my father. That's the way he was about everything."

"I remember the *Hindenburg* disaster," Leon said.

"People discussed it for weeks! The thing caught fire and exploded. There were photos in all the newspapers and magazines. They were using helium instead of hydrogen."

"No, it was hydrogen instead of helium."

"Are you sure? Well, it doesn't matter. I just recall that the whole thing caught fire and blew up. People trying to escape twisting red-hot metal bars with their bare hands! It's remarkable what people can do when they have to. I remember reading somewhere about a man who picked up a three-thousand-pound safe and threw it out a window because the building caught fire and there were some valuable papers in the safe. The funny thing is, if he'd simply stopped a minute to think, he'd have realized the papers would be all right where they were because the safe was fireproof. But he got excited and just picked up this enormous object and flung it out the window as though it was a cigar box. Later on, of course, he couldn't begin to budge it."

"That's the adrenaline in the bloodstream. When you get excited about anything, the body secretes adrenaline. It's some sort of a survival response. It goes back to the time of the cave man. It gives you additional strength for emergencies."

"Yes, that's what I've heard. It's a good thing, I guess."

"Here, why don't you have some of this wine? Really, I should have ordered a small bottle. Ordinarily I do, but tonight I felt extravagant for some reason. Maybe it was the bad weather. The weather affects me that way. I'm subject to moods."

Bébert shook his head, but then after a moment he said, "All right, I will. Usually I don't drink wine on account of my stomach, but I'll make an exception." He plucked a glass from the next table and neatly wiped the rim with a napkin. Leon filled the glass and Bébert held it to the light.

"I never can tell a thing by doing that," said Leon.

"Neither can I," said Bébert, "but I do it just to be on the safe side. You never know. It could be full of sediment."

"There's a great deal to be learned about wines," Leon said. "I keep telling myself that I ought to take time and brush up on a few things. It gives you a better status with women. They appreciate a man who knows all about wines and fabrics."

"You're right, particularly about fabrics. I've noticed that a woman will be impressed if a man can glance at a dress or a suit and make some intelligent remark about it. That's because they don't expect men to know about such things."

"Women have a great many misconceptions. I could give you a list as long as my arm; it wouldn't be any trouble. You can't be too careful about dealing with them, because you can't predict what will happen. They do things without a reason. Then, if you make the mistake of asking why they've done this or that, they attack you. It's just the way they are."

"Like birds in flight," said Bébert.

"Exactly," said Leon, although he did not see the resemblance. "You've nailed it down. That's how they are. Andrea's the perfect example. But she might be feeling somewhat better by this time. What do you think?"

"I should think so," Bébert agreed, "after all this time."

"That's right. She's had a chance to think it over and realize how foolishly she was behaving. I'd even go so far as to make a guess that she's laughing over it by now. They're very changeable, you know."

"They're just like chameleons. They get over these things. Take my sister. Why, you wouldn't believe it, but when we were children it seemed to me that five times a day, at least, my sister was screaming about something or other, but then the next thing I knew she was playing with her dolls as though nothing had happened. They have extraordinary powers of recuperation. They're much stronger than men, as a matter of fact."

Leon smiled. "You don't know how right you are."

"What do you mean?"

"Never mind. At times they're feeble enough."

"Feeble, did you say? That's not a word I'd use in connection with them. Of course, your experiences may have been different."

"I imagine we all have the same experience."

At this Bébert burst out laughing. "Well, you were talking about having a reputation, and in that respect I must admit you certainly do. Everybody knows your favorite dish isn't printed on the menu, if you don't mind my saying so."

"Oh, I'm no worse than the rest. We're all alike. It's just that I'm not as discreet."

"It pays to be cautious, I've found. It's easy to get yourself in a jam." Bébert snapped his fingers. "It can happen just like that! One minute you're all right and the next minute you hardly know what hit you. You've got about as much chance as a pig in a butcher shop."

"It's not all that bad," said Leon thoughtfully, "not if you keep on your toes. Anyway, you can't do without them, so you've got to run a few risks. That's how I feel about it. You can criticize me if you like; I'm only being truthful. It's no fun being left out in the cold."

"There's something to what you say," Bébert remarked. "I should be more like you. You always know what you're up to. I can't help admiring you for that."

Leon, who had eaten everything in sight, swallowed the rest of the wine and patted his lips with the napkin.

"It's foolish to get excited about things," Bébert continued. "I should have learned by now that if you let well enough alone, why sooner or later the matter will straighten itself out, chances are. But women in particular don't realize this. If you simply let nature take its course, though, there's no reason to get upset. What do you think?"

Leon belched. "I don't know," he admitted. "It seems as though every time I eat too much I have trouble concentrating. My head feels strange."

"It could be your pancreas. They say that if you develop a bad pancreas you have any number of symptoms."

"Maybe," Leon said doubtfully. "I think, though, that I just ate too much."

"Well, you ate quickly too. I noticed that. It's bad for you. I have a cousin who eats as if the world was coming to an end, and there's always something wrong with him. Backaches, hangnail, pinkeye, warts—if it isn't one thing it's another! He's always running off to the doctor. I've told him what the trouble is, but he doesn't listen. 'Mind your own business,' he says. So I don't even speak to him anymore. It's not my affair if he wants to kill himself by gobbling. Furthermore, it shows. He's terribly overweight. He used to be thin as a rail. That's what happens when you're too proud to accept advice."

"How many people can you name who do take advice? They all think they know what they're doing."

"Right!" said Bébert. "I've observed the same thing, and it never ceases to amaze me."

"You take this case we've been discussing. What about that?"

"Andrea?"

"Yes."

"I'm afraid I don't follow you."

"Simply this: What sort of advice could you give her?"

Bébert sank back in his chair. "That's quite a question. You asked a hard one that time."

"Let's assume she's right here at the table and it's as plain as the nose on your face what she's up to. She's on the point of doing something drastic. Now then, how are you going to approach this hypothetical problem?"

"To tell the truth," Bébert replied after some moments of thought, "I wouldn't know how to begin."

"So you'd leave it all up to her, is that right? You'd simply let nature take its course?"

"I see what you're getting at. What would you do? How would you handle it?"

"Oh," Leon said, "I'm not trying to give the impression that there's an easy way out. If one thing didn't work, you'd have to try something else. In a sense, you'd find yourself caught between two fires. You might do the wrong thing very easily. It would be touchy, to say the least."

"Judging from what little I've seen of her," Bébert remarked, "I'd say she's very strong-willed, and in a situation such as you were describing she might even grow dangerous. She's capable of anything. In fact, although I don't know whether you agree with this or not, it might not be a bad idea to leave her utterly alone, because she might not want to be disturbed. The more I think of it, in fact, the more I think that's the proper course to follow. People frequently wish to be left alone, especially if they don't happen to be feeling up to par. My cousin used to complain about his intestines, but then he'd get furious when I tried to help. It makes you wonder. You want to help people, but the first thing they do is turn right around and virtually bite your head off for trying to be of some assistance. It's happened to me more than once. On the whole, if a person isn't quite up to snuff, the best thing for them is to be left alone. No telephone calls or visitors. I sometimes lie down with a damp cloth over my forehead and rest for several hours without thinking about anything in the world. It restores your confidence."

"Well, anyhow," said Leon absently, "I don't think we ought to go up there. Besides, she's probably had enough excitement for one day."

"I agree one hundred percent! After all, we wouldn't want to be held responsible for complicating matters."

"That's rather a droll thought," Leon said, and began picking his teeth with a match.

"I see nothing droll about it," said Bébert crisply. "My father once told me about some man who met an old friend unexpectedly while he was out swimming, and suffered a heart attack then and there. He drowned right in the water! It goes to show, you can't tell how people are going to react."

Leon had been examining the check while Bébert was talking. He opened his wallet and said, "As soon as I pay this, I think perhaps we ought to go back to the club and find out if there's any news. I can't get over a feeling that this whole business ought to be looked into."

"I agree with that wholeheartedly," said Bébert. "We'll gather some firsthand reports and see what's up. Incidentally, I notice it's stopped raining."

"I noticed," said Leon, unwrapping a cigar. "Well, then. So the matter's settled."

"Yes," Bébert said, "and to put it mildly, I feel relieved. I couldn't begin to tell you how much. Let's rush back to the club and find out what's what."

"That strikes me as a good idea," said Leon.

◇

Evan S. Connell, Jr., was born in Kansas City in 1924, attended Dartmouth College, lived in Paris and Barcelona, then settled in San Francisco, where he has studied and taught writing and been an editor of Contact *magazine. His first published work was a collection of short stories,* The Anatomy Lesson *(1957), and he has since published another,* At the Crossroads *(1965). His first published novel was* Mrs. Bridge *(1959), which appears in a shortened form beginning on page 210. But he had earlier written and later rewritten a novel projecting his experiences in the Naval Air Force,* The Patriot, *published in 1960. There is as well a book-length poem,* Notes from a Bottle Found on the Beach at Carmel *(1963), and his most recent novel,* The Diary of a Rapist *(1966), an extraordinarily relevant book, documenting the fatal relationship between powerlessness and violence— two of the most characteristic symptoms of our times. The book was not much read, however, and Connell is another example of an American writer whose achievement is well in advance of his reputation.*

"The Suicide" is the first in a series Connell has written about Leon & Bébert (their names are supposed to be joined by the ampersand). Many have felt them to be delightful comic characters appallingly representative of our times; other readers must realize that the exasperation they feel with the two young men is functional, an entirely intended reaction. "The Suicide" shows the intricate ways in which people who have become incapable of involvement with others justify and rationalize their apartness. Leon & Bébert use all the clichés of ritualized, routine, meaningless conversation (how hard it is to stop smoking, the high wages of electricians and plumbers, their own little faults of character, the food, the wine, the weather) in order to avoid the crisis they are faced with. That they are not alone in their unwillingness to accept responsibility for others is indicated by the virtually proverbial nature of their justifications for inaction: "It pays to be cautious . . . it's easy to get yourself in a jam . . . it's foolish to get excited about things . . . if you let well enough alone . . . sooner or later the matter will straighten itself out . . . simply let nature take its course . . . there's no reason to get upset. . . ." They rationalize that they are powerless anyway: as Leon reasons, nothing they could do would have any effect on the strong-willed Andrea. Bébert excuses his failure to act when the taxicab hit the paper boy: "The only consolation was that everybody did the same . . . nobody wanted to get mixed up in it . . . they didn't

quite want to get involved, seeing it was none of their business." People are afraid they'll get blood on their hands or "be called into court and involved in lawsuits and so on." Each of them thinks the other should go do something about Andrea. But "if a person isn't quite up to snuff, the best thing for them is to be left alone." People sometimes "virtually bite your head off for trying to be of some assistance." Neither wants "to be held responsible for complicating matters." The story, then, is a veritable catalogue of the "reasons" we offer for not accepting responsibility for or involvement with others—although the author has of course extended and exaggerated this inactivity to absurd lengths. As a result of cutting themselves off so entirely from any real involvement with others, Leon & Bébert live lives of no purpose whatsoever: they spend their time playing games at the Po-Po Club because "you can only go to the movies every so often, and what else is there?" It is a world of cozy, shared aloneness, solaced by gossip, good food in warm restaurants, and the constant reassuring of one another that nothing is required of them beyond the satisfaction of their curiosity. They experience and "know" only what they have heard, only what they can resolve into homily. Like the ducks in the opening paragraph, they are "as decoys among the reeds at the edge of the lake"; they only resemble life.

NORMAN MAILER

Prologue: The Man Who Studied Yoga

◇◇◇◇◇◇◇

I WOULD INTRODUCE MYSELF if it were not useless. The name I had last night will not be the same as the name I have tonight. For the moment, then, let me say that I am thinking of Sam Slovoda. Obligatorily, I study him, Sam Slovoda who is neither ordinary nor extraordinary, who is not young nor yet old, nor tall nor short. He is sleeping, and it is fit to describe him now, for like most humans he prefers sleeping to not sleeping. He is a mild pleasant-looking man who has just turned forty. If the crown of his head reveals a little bald spot, he has nourished in compensation the vanity of a mustache. He has generally when he is awake an agreeable manner, at least with strangers; he appears friendly, tolerant, and genial. The fact is that like most of us, he is full of envy, full of spite, a gossip, a man who is pleased to find others are unhappy as he, and yet—this is the worst to be said—he is a decent man. He is better than most. He would prefer to see a more equitable world, he scorns prejudice and privilege, he tries to hurt no one, he wishes to be liked. I will go even further. He has one serious virtue —he is not fond of himself, he wishes he were better. He would like to free himself of envy, of the annoying necessity to talk about his friends, he would like to love people more; specifically, he would like to love his wife more, and to love his two daughters without the tormenting if nonetheless irremediable vexation that they closet his life in the dusty web of domestic responsibilities and drudging for money.

How often he tells himself with contempt that he has the cruelty of a kind weak man.

May I state that I do not dislike Sam Slovoda; it is just that I am disappointed in him. He has tried too many things and never with a whole heart. He has wanted to be a serious novelist and now merely indulges the ambition; he wished to be of consequence in the world, and has ended, temporarily perhaps, as an overworked writer of continuity for comic

88

magazines; when he was young he tried to be a bohemian and instead acquired a wife and family. Of his appetite for a variety of new experience I may say that it is matched only by his fear of new people and novel situations.

I will give an instance. Yesterday, Sam was walking along the street and a bum approached him for money. Sam did not see the man until too late; lost in some inconsequential thought, he looked up only in time to see a huge wretch of a fellow with a red twisted face and an outstretched hand. Sam is like so many; each time a derelict asks for a dime, he feels a coward if he pays the money, and is ashamed of himself if he doesn't. This once, Sam happened to think, "I will not be bullied," and hurried past. But the bum was not to be lost so easily. "Have a heart, Jack," he called after Sam in a whiskey voice, "I need a drink bad." Sam stopped. He began to laugh. "Just so it isn't for coffee, here's a quarter," he said, and he laughed, and the bum laughed. "You're a man's man," the bum said. Sam went away pleased with himself, thinking about such things as the community which existed between all people. It was cheap of Sam. He should know better. He should know he was merely relieved the situation had turned out so well. Although he thinks he is sorry for bums, Sam really hates them. Who knows what violence they can offer?

At this time, there is a powerful interest in Sam's life, but many would ridicule it. He is in the process of being psychoanalyzed. Myself, I do not jeer. It has created the most unusual situation between Sam and me. I could go into details but they are perhaps premature. It would be better to watch Sam awaken.

His wife, Eleanor, has been up for an hour, and she has shut the window and neglected to turn off the radiator. The room is stifling. Sam groans in a stupor which is neither sleep nor refreshment, opens one eye, yawns, groans again, and lies twisted, strangled and trussed in pajamas which are too large for him. How painful it is for him to rise. Last night there was a party, and this morning, Sunday morning, he is awakening with a hangover. Invariably, he is depressed in the morning, and it is no different today. He finds himself in the flat and familiar dispirit of nearly all days.

It is snowing outside. Sam finally lurches to the window, and opens it for air. With the oxygen of a winter morning clearing his brain, he looks down six stories into the giant quadrangle of the Queens housing development in which he lives, staring morosely at the inch of slush which covers the monotonous artificial park that separates his apartment building from an identical structure not two hundred feet away. The walks are black where the snow has melted, and in the children's playground, all but deserted, one swing oscillates back and forth, pushed by an irritable little boy who plays by himself among the empty benches, swaddled in galoshes, muffler, and overcoat. The snow falls sluggishly, a wet snow which probably will turn to rain. The little boy in the playground gives one last disgusted shove to the swing and trudges away gloomily, his overshoes leaving a small animal track behind him. Back of Sam, in the four-room apartment he knows like a blind man, there is only the sound of Eleanor making breakfast.

Well, thinks Sam, the depression in the morning is a stage of his analysis, Dr. Sergius has said.

This is the way Sam often phrases his thoughts. It is not altogether his fault. Most of the people he knows think that way and talk that way, and Sam is not the strongest of men. His language is doomed to the fashion of the moment. I have heard him remark mildly, almost apologetically, about his daughters: "My relation with them still suffers because I haven't worked through all my feminine identifications." The saddest thing is that the sentence has meaning to Sam even if it will not have meaning to you. A great many ruminations, discoveries, and memories contribute their connotation to Sam. It has the significance of a cherished line of poetry to him.

Although Eleanor is not being analyzed, she talks in a similar way. I have heard her remark in company, "Oh, you know Sam, he not only thinks I'm his mother, he blames me for being born." Like most women, Eleanor can be depended upon to employ the idiom of her husband.

What amuses me is that Sam is critical of the way others speak. At the party last night he was talking to a Hollywood writer, a young man with a great deal of energy and enthusiasm. The young man spoke something like this: "You see, boychick, I can spike any script with yaks, but the thing I can't do is heartbreak. My wife says she's gonna give me heartbreak. The trouble is I've had a real solid-type life. I mean I've had my ups and downs like all of humanity, but there's never been a shriek in my life. I don't know how to write shrieks."

On the trip home, Sam had said to Eleanor, "It was disgraceful. A writer should have some respect for language."

Eleanor answered with a burlesque of Sam's indignation. "Listen, I'm a real artist-type. Culture is for comic-strip writers."

Generally, I find Eleanor attractive. In the ten years they have been married she has grown plump, and her dark hair which once was long is now cropped in a mannish cut of the prevailing mode. But, this is quibbling. She still possesses her best quality, a healthy exuberance which glows in her dark eyes and beams in her smile. She has beautiful teeth. She seems aware of her body and pleased with it. Sam tells himself he would do well to realize how much he needs her. Since he has been in analysis he has come to discover that he remains with Eleanor for more essential reasons than mere responsibility. Even if there were no children, he would probably cleave to her.

Unhappily, it is more complicated than that. She is always—to use their phrase—competing with him. At those times I do not like Eleanor, I am irritated by her lack of honesty. She is too sharp-tongued, and she does not often give Sam what he needs most, a steady flow of uncritical encouragement to counteract the harshness with which he views himself. Like so many who are articulate on the subject, Eleanor will tell you that she resents being a woman. As Sam is disappointed in life, so is Eleanor. She feels Sam has cheated her from a proper development of her potentialities and talent, even as Sam feels cheated. I call her dishonest because she is not so ready as Sam to put the blame on herself.

Sam, of course, can say all this himself. It is just that he experiences it in a somewhat different way. Like most men who have been married for ten years, he finds that his wife is not quite real to him. Last night at the party, there were perhaps half a dozen people whom he met for the first time, and he talked animatedly with them, sensing their reactions, feeling their responses, aware of the life in them, as they were aware of the life in him. Eleanor, however, exists in his nerves. She is a rather vague embodiment, he thinks of her as "she" most of the time, someone to conceal things from. Invariably, he feels uneasy with her. It is too bad. No matter how inevitable, I am always sorry when love melts into that pomade of affection, resentment, boredom and occasional compassion which is the best we may expect of a man and woman who have lived together a long time. So often, it is worse, so often no more than hatred.

They are eating breakfast now, and Eleanor is chatting about the party. She is pretending to be jealous about a young girl in a strapless evening gown, and indeed, she does not have to pretend altogether. Sam, with liquor inside him, had been leaning over the girl; obviously he had coveted her. Yet, this morning, when Eleanor begins to talk about her, Sam tries to be puzzled.

"Which girl was it now?" he asks a second time.

"Oh, you know, the hysteric," Eleanor says, "the one who was parading her bazooms in your face." Eleanor has ways of impressing certain notions upon Sam. "She's Charlie's new girl."

"I didn't know that," Sam mutters. "He didn't seem to be near her all evening."

Eleanor spreads marmalade over her toast and takes a bite with evident enjoyment. "Apparently, they're all involved. Charles was funny about it. He said he's come to the conclusion that the great affairs of history are between hysterical women and detached men."

"Charles hates women," Sam says smugly. "If you notice, almost everything he says about them is a discharge of aggression." Sam has the best of reasons for not liking Charles. It takes more than ordinary character for a middle-aged husband to approve of a friend who moves easily from woman to woman.

"At least Charles discharges his aggression," Eleanor remarks.

"He's almost a classic example of the Don Juan complex. You notice how masochistic his women are?"

"I know a man or two who's just as masochistic."

Sam sips his coffee. "What made you say the girl was an hysteric?"

Eleanor shrugs. "She's an actress. And I could see she was a tease."

"You can't jump to conclusions," Sam lectures. "I had the impression she was a compulsive. Don't forget you've got to distinguish between the outer defenses, and the more deeply rooted conflicts."

I must confess that this conversation bores me. As a sample it is representative of the way Sam and Eleanor talk to each other. In Sam's defense I can say nothing; he has always been too partial to jargon.

I am often struck by how eager we are to reveal all sorts of supposedly ugly secrets about ourselves. We can explain the hatred we feel for our parents, we are rather pleased with the perversions to which we are prone. We seem determinedly proud to be superior to ourselves. No motive is too terrible for our inspection. Let someone hint, however, that we have bad table manners and we fly into a rage. Sam will agree to anything you may say about him, provided it is sufficiently serious—he will be the first to agree he has fantasies of murdering his wife. But tell him that he is afraid of waiters, or imply to Eleanor that she is a nag, and they will be quite annoyed.

Sam has noticed this himself. There are times when he can hear the jargon in his voice, and it offends him. Yet, he seems powerless to change his habits.

An example: He is sitting in an armchair now, brooding upon his breakfast, while Eleanor does the dishes. The two daughters are not home; they have gone to visit their grandmother for the weekend. Sam has encouraged the visit. He had looked forward to the liberty Eleanor and he would enjoy. For the past few weeks the children had seemed to make the most impossible demands upon his attention. Yet now they are gone and he misses them, he even misses their noise. Sam, however, cannot accept the notion that many people are dissatisfied with the present, and either dream of the past or anticipate the future. Sam must call this ambivalence over possessions. Once he even felt obliged to ask his analyst, Dr. Sergius, if ambivalence over possessions did not characterize him almost perfectly, and Sergius, whom I always picture with the flat precision of a coin's head— bald skull and horn-rimmed glasses—answered in his German accent, "But, my dear Mr. Slovoda, as I have told you, it would make me happiest if you did not include in your reading these psychoanalytical text-works."

At such rebukes, Sam can only wince. It is so right, he tells himself, he is exactly the sort of ambitious fool who uses big words when small ones would do.

2

While Sam sits in the armchair, gray winter light is entering the windows, snow falls outside. He sits alone in a modern seat, staring at the gray, green, and beige decor of their living room. Eleanor was a painter before they were married, and she has arranged this room. It is very pleasant, but like many husbands, Sam resents it, resents the reproductions of modern painters upon the wall, the slender coffee table, a free-form poised like a spider on wire legs, its feet set onto a straw rug. In the corner, most odious of all, is the playmate of his children, a hippopotamus of a television-radio-and-phonograph cabinet with the blind monstrous snout of the video tube.

Eleanor had set the Sunday paper near his hand. Soon, Sam intends to go to work. For a year, he has been giving a day once a month or twice a month to a bit of thought and a little writing on a novel he hopes to begin some time. Last night he told himself he would work today. But he has little enthusiasm now. He is tired, he is too depressed. Writing for the comic strips seems to exhaust his imagination.

Sam reads the paper as if he were peeling an enormous banana. Flap after flap of newsprint is stripped away and cast upon the straw rug until only the magazine section is left. Sam glances through it with restless irritability. A biography of a political figure runs its flatulent prose into the giant crossword puzzle at the back. An account of a picturesque corner of the city becomes lost in statistics and exhortations on juvenile delinquency, finally to emerge with photographs about the new style of living which desert architecture provides. Sam looks at a wall of windows in rotogravure with a yucca tree framing the pool.

There is an article about a workingman. His wife and his family are described, his apartment, his salary and his budget. Sam reads a description of what the worker has every evening for dinner, and how he spends each night of the week. The essay makes its point; the typical American workingman must watch his pennies, but he is nonetheless secure and serene. He would not exchange his life for another.

Sam is indignant. A year ago he had written a similar article in an attempt to earn some extra money. Subtly, or so he thought, he had suggested that the average workingman was raddled with insecurity. Naturally, the article had been rejected.

Sam throws the magazine section away. Moments of such anger torment him frequently. Despite himself, Sam is enraged at editorial dishonesty, at the smooth strifeless world which such articles present. How angry he is—how angry and how helpless. "It is the actions of men and not their sentiments which make history," he thinks to himself, and smiles wryly. In his living room he would go out to tilt the windmills of a vast, powerful, and hypocritical society; in his week of work he labors in an editorial cubicle to create space-ships, violent death, women with golden tresses and wanton breasts, men who act with their fists and speak with patriotic slogans.

I know what Sam feels. As he sits in the armchair, the Sunday papers are strewn around him, carrying their war news, their murders, their parleys, their entertainments, mummery of a real world which no one can grasp. It is terribly frustrating. One does not know where to begin.

Today, Sam considers himself half a fool for having been a radical. There is no longer much consolation in the thought that the majority of men who succeed in a corrupt and acquisitive society are themselves obligatorily corrupt, and one's failure is therefore the price of one's idealism. Sam cannot recapture the pleasurable bitterness which resides in the notion that one has suffered for one's principles. Sergius is too hard on him for that.

They have done a lot of work on the subject. Sergius feels that Sam's concern with world affairs has always been spurious. For example, they have uncovered in analysis that Sam wrote his article about the worker in such a way as to make certain it would be refused. Sam, after all, hates editors; to have such a piece accepted would mean he is no better than they, that he is a mediocrity. So long as he fails he is not obliged to measure himself. Sam, therefore, is being unrealistic. He rejects the world with his intellect, and this enables him not to face the more direct realities of his present life.

Sam will argue with Sergius but it is very difficult. He will say, "Perhaps you sneer at radicals because it is more comfortable to ignore such ideas. Once you became interested it might introduce certain unpleasant changes in your life."

"Why," says Sergius, "do you feel it so necessary to assume that I am a bourgeois interested only in my comfort?"

"How can I discuss these things," says Sam, "if you insist that my opinions are the expression of neurotic needs, and your opinions are merely dispassionate medical advice?"

"You are so anxious to defeat me in an argument," Sergius will reply. "Would you admit it is painful to relinquish the sense of importance which intellectual discussion provides you?"

I believe Sergius has his effect. Sam often has thoughts these days which would have been repellent to him years ago. For instance, at the moment, Sam is thinking it might be better to live the life of a worker, a simple life, to be completely absorbed with such necessities as food and money. Then one could believe that to be happy it was necessary only to have more money, more goods, less worries. It would be nice, Sam thinks wistfully, to believe that the source of one's unhappiness comes not from oneself, but from the fault of the boss, or the world, or bad luck.

Sam has these casual daydreams frequently. He likes to think about other lives he might have led, and he envies the most astonishing variety of occupations. It is easy enough to see why he should wish for the life of an executive with the power and sense of command it may offer, but virtually from the same impulse Sam will wish himself a bohemian living in an unheated loft, his life a catch-as-catch-can from day to day. Once, after reading an article, Sam even wished himself a priest. For about ten minutes it seemed beautiful to him to surrender his life to God. Such fancies are common, I know. It is just that I, far better than Sam, know how serious he really is, how fanciful, how elaborate, his imagination can be.

The phone is ringing. Sam can hear Eleanor shouting at him to answer. He picks up the receiver with a start. It is Marvin Rossman, who is an old friend, and Marvin has an unusual request. They talk for several minutes, and Sam squirms a little in his seat. As he is about to hang up, he laughs. "Why, no, Marvin, it gives me a sense of adventure," he says.

Eleanor has come into the room toward the end of this conversation. "What is it all about?" she asks.

Sam is obviously a bit agitated. Whenever he attempts to be most casual, Eleanor can well suspect him. "It seems," he says slowly, "that Marvin has acquired a pornographic movie."

"From whom?" Eleanor asks.

"He said something about an old boy friend of Louise's."

Eleanor laughs. "I can't imagine Louise having an old boy friend with a dirty movie."

"Well, people are full of surprises," Sam says mildly.

"Look here," says Eleanor suddenly. "Why did he call us?"

"It was about our projector."

"They want to use it?" Eleanor asks.

"That's right." Sam hesitates. "I invited them over."

"Did it ever occur to you I might want to spend my Sunday some other way?" Eleanor asks crossly.

"We're not doing anything," Sam mumbles. Like most men, he feels obliged to act quite nonchalant about pornography. "I'll tell you, I am sort of curious about the film. I've never seen one, you know."

"Try anything once, is that it?"

"Something of the sort." Sam is trying to conceal his excitement. The truth is that in common with most of us, he is fascinated by pornography. It is a minor preoccupation, but more from lack of opportunity than anything else. Once or twice, Sam has bought the sets of nude photographs which are sold in marginal bookstores, and with guilty excitement has hidden them in the apartment.

"Oh, this is silly," Eleanor says. "You were going to work today."

"I'm just not in the mood."

"I'll have to feed them," Eleanor complains. "Do we have enough liquor?"

"We can get beer." Sam pauses. "Alan Sperber and his wife are coming too."

"Sam, you're a child."

"Look, Eleanor," says Sam, controlling his voice, "if it's too much trouble, I can take the projector over there."

"I ought to make you do that."

"Am I such an idiot that I must consult you before I invite friends to the house?"

Eleanor has the intuition that Sam, if he allowed himself, could well drown in pornography. She is quite annoyed at him, but she would never dream of allowing Sam to take the projector over to Marvin Rossman's where he could view the movie without her—that seems indefinably dangerous. Besides she would like to see it, too. The mother in Eleanor is certain it cannot hurt her.

"All right, Sam," she says, "but you are a child."

More exactly, an adolescent, Sam decides. Ever since Marvin phoned, Sam has felt the nervous glee of an adolescent locking himself in the bathroom. "Anal fixation," Sam thinks automatically.

While Eleanor goes down to buy beer and cold cuts in a delicatessen, Sam gets out the projector and begins to clean it. He is far from methodical in this. He knows the machine is all right, he has shown movies of Eleanor and his daughters only a few weeks ago, but from the moment Eleanor left the apartment, Sam has been consumed by an anxiety that the projection bulb is burned out. Once he has examined it, he begins to fret about the motor. He wonders if it needs oiling, he blunders through a drawer of household tools looking for an oil can. It is ridiculous. Sam knows that what he is trying to keep out of his mind are the reactions Sergius will have. Sergius will want to "work through" all of Sam's reasons for seeing the movie. Well, Sam tells himself, he knows in advance what will be discovered: detachment, not wanting to accept Eleanor as a sexual partner, evasion of responsibility, etc. etc. The devil with Sergius. Sam has never seen a dirty movie, and he certainly wants to.

He feels obliged to laugh at himself. He could not be more nervous, he knows, if he were about to make love to a woman he had never touched before. It is really disgraceful.

When Eleanor comes back, Sam hovers about her. He is uncomfortable with her silence. "I suppose they'll be here soon," Sam says.

"Probably."

Sam does not know if he is angry at Eleanor or apprehensive that she is angry at him. Much to his surprise he catches her by the waist and hears himself saying, "You know, maybe tonight when they're gone . . . I mean, we do have the apartment to ourselves." Eleanor moves neither toward him nor away from him. "Darling, it's not because of the movie," Sam goes on, "I swear. Don't you think maybe we could . . ."

"Maybe," says Eleanor.

3

The company has arrived, and it may be well to say a word or two about them. Marvin Rossman who has brought the film is a dentist, although it might be more accurate to describe him as a frustrated doctor. Rossman is full of statistics and items of odd information about the malpractice of physicians, and he will tell these things in his habitually gloomy voice, a voice so slow, so sad, that it almost conceals the humor of his remarks. Or, perhaps, that is what creates his humor. In his spare time, he is a sculptor, and if Eleanor may be trusted, he is not without talent. I often picture him working in the studio loft he has rented, his tall bony frame the image of dejection. He will pat a piece of clay to the armature, he will rub it sadly with his thumb, he will shrug, he does not believe that anything of merit could come from him. When he talked to Sam over the phone, he was pessimistic about the film they were to see. "It can't be any good," he said in his melancholy voice. "I know it'll be a disappointment." Like Sam, he has a mustache, but Rossman's will droop at the corners.

Alan Sperber who has come with Rossman is the subject of some curiosity for the Slovodas. He is not precisely womanish; in fact, he is a large plump man, but his voice is too soft, his manners too precise. He is genial, yet he is finicky; waspish, yet bland; he is fond of telling long, rather affected stories, he is always prepared with a new one, but to general conversation he contributes little. As a lawyer, he seems mis-cast. One cannot imagine him inspiring a client to confidence. He is the sort of heavy florid man who seems boyish at forty, and the bow ties and gray flannel suits he wears do not make him appear more mature.

Roslyn Sperber, his wife, used to be a school teacher, and she is a quiet nervous woman who talks a great deal when she is drunk. She is normally quite pleasant, and has only one habit which is annoying to any degree. It is a little flaw, but social life is not unlike marriage in that habit determines far more than vice or virtue. This mannerism which has become so offensive to the friends of the Sperbers is Roslyn's social pretension. Perhaps I should say intellectual pretension. She entertains people as if she were conducting a salon, and in her birdlike voice is forever forcing her guests to accept still another intellectual canapé. "You must hear Sam's view of the world market," she will say, or "Has Louise told you her statistics on divorce?" It is quite pathetic, for she is so eager to please. I have seen her eyes fill with tears at a sharp word from Alan.

Marvin Rossman's wife, Louise, is a touch grim and definite in her opinions. She is a social welfare worker, and will declare herself with force whenever conversation impinges on those matters where she is expert. She is quite opposed to psychoanalysis, and will say without quarter, "It's all very well for people in the upper-middle area—" She is referring to the upper middle class—"but it takes more than a couch to solve the problems of . . ." and she will list narcotics, juvenile delinquency, psychosis, relief distribution, slum housing, and other descriptions of our period. She recites these categories with an odd anticipation. One would guess she was ordering a meal.

Sam is fond of Marvin but he cannot abide Louise. "You'd think she discovered poverty," he will complain to Eleanor.

The Slovodas do feel superior to the Rossmans and the Sperbers. If pressed, they could not offer the most convincing explanation why. I suppose what it comes down to is that Sam and Eleanor do not think of themselves as really belonging to a class, and they feel that the Sperbers and Rossmans are petit bourgeois. I find it hard to explain their attitude. Their company feels as much discomfort and will apologize as often as the Slovodas for the money they have, and the money they hope to earn. They are all of them equally concerned with progressive education and the methods of raising children to be well-adjusted—indeed, they are discussing that now—consider themselves relatively free of sexual taboo, or put more properly, Sam and Eleanor are no less possessive than the others. The Slovodas' culture is not more profound; I should be hard-put to say that Sam is more widely read, more seriously informed, than Marvin or Alan, or for that matter, Louise. Probably, it comes to this: Sam, in his heart, thinks himself a rebel, and there are few rebels who do not claim an original mind. Eleanor has been a bohemian and considers herself more sophisticated than her friends who merely went to college and got married. Louise Rossman could express it more soundly. "Artists, writers, and people of the creative layer have in their occupational ideology the belief that they are classless."

One thing I might remark about the company. They are all being the most unconscionable hypocrites. They have rushed across half the city of New York to see a pornographic film, and they are not at all interested in each other at the moment. The women are giggling like tickled children at remarks which cannot possibly be so funny. Yet they are all determined to talk for a respectable period of time. No less, it must be serious talk. Roslyn has said once, "I feel so funny at the thought of seeing such a movie," and the others passed her statement by.

At the moment, Sam is talking about value. I might note that Sam loves conversation and thrives when he can expound an idea. "What are our values today?" he asks. "It's really fantastic when you stop to think of it. Take any bright, talented kid who's getting out of college now."

"My kid brother, for example," Marvin interposes morosely. He passes his bony hand over his sad mustache, and somehow the remark has become amusing, much as if Marvin had said, "Oh, yes, you have reminded me of the trials, the worries, and the cares which my fabulous younger brother heaps upon me."

"All right, take him," Sam says. "What does he want to be?"

"He doesn't want to be anything," says Marvin.

"That's my point," Sam says excitedly. "Rather than work at certain occupations, the best of these kids would rather do nothing at all."

"Alan has a cousin," Roslyn says, "who swears he'll wash dishes before he becomes a businessman."

"I wish that were true," Eleanor interrupts. "It seems to me everybody is conforming more and more these days."

They argue about this. Sam and Eleanor claim the country is suffering from hysteria; Alan Sperber disagrees and says it's merely a reflection of the headlines; Louise says no adequate criteria exist to measure hysteria; Marvin says he doesn't know anything at all.

"More solid liberal gains are being made in this period," says Alan, "than you would believe. Consider the Negro . . ."

"Is the Negro any less maladjusted?" Eleanor shouts with passion.

Sam maneuvers the conversation back to his thesis. "The values of the young today, and by the young I mean the cream of the kids, the ones with ideas, are a reaction of indifference to the culture crisis. It really is despair. All they know is what they don't want to do."

"That is easier," Alan says genially.

"It's not altogether unhealthy," Sam says. "It's a corrective for smugness and the false value of the past, but it has created new false value." He thinks it worth emphasizing. "False value seems always to beget further false value."

"Define your terms," says Louise, the scientist.

"No, look," Sam says, "there's no revolt, there's no acceptance. Kids today don't want to get married, and . . ."

Eleanor interrupts. "Why should a girl rush to get married? She loses all chance for developing herself."

Sam shrugs. They are all talking at once. "Kids don't want to get married," he repeats, "and they don't want not to get married. They merely drift."

"It's a problem we'll all have to face with our own kids in ten years," Alan says, "although I think you make too much of it, Sam."

"My daughter," Marvin states. "She's embarrassed I'm a dentist. Even more embarrassed than I am." They laugh.

Sam tells a story about his youngest, Carol Ann. It seems he had a fight with her, and she went to her room. Sam followed, he called through the door.

"No answer," Sam says. "I called her again, 'Carol Ann.' I was a little worried you understand, because she seemed so upset, so I said to her, 'Carol Ann, you know I love you.' What do you think she answered?"

"What?" asks Roslyn.

"She said, 'Daddie, why are you so anxious?' "

They all laugh again. There are murmurs about what a clever thing it was to say. In the silence which follows, Roslyn leans forward and says quickly in her high voice, "You must get Alan to tell you his wonderful story about the man who studied yogi."

"Yoga," Alan corrects. "It's too long to tell."

The company prevails on him.

"Well," says Alan, in his genial courtroom voice, "it concerns a friend of mine named Cassius O'Shaughnessy."

"You don't mean Jerry O'Shaughnessy, do you?" asks Sam.

Alan does not know Jerry O'Shaughnessy. "No, no, this is Cassius O'Shaughnessy," he says. "He's really quite an extraordinary fellow." Alan sits plumply in his chair, fingering his bow-tie. They are all used to his stories, which are told in a formal style and exhibit the attempt to recapture a certain note of urbanity, wit, and élan which Alan has probably copied from someone else. Sam and Eleanor respect his ability to tell these stories, but they resent the fact that he talks *at* them.

"You'd think we were a jury of his inferiors," Eleanor has said. "I hate being talked down to." What she resents is Alan's quiet implication that his antecedents, his social position, in total his life outside the room is superior to the life within. Eleanor now takes the promise from Alan's story by remarking, "Yes, and let's see the movie when Alan has finished."

"Sssh," Roslyn says.

"Cassius was at college a good while before me," says Alan, "but I knew him while I was an undergraduate. He would drop in and visit from time to time. An absolutely extraordinary fellow. The most amazing career. You see, he's done about everything."

"I love the way Alan tells it," Roslyn pipes nervously.

"Cassius was in France with Dos Passos and Cummings, he was even arrested with e.e. After the war, he was one of the founders of the dadaist school, and for awhile I understand he was Fitzgerald's guide to the gold of the Côte d'Azur. He knew everybody, he did everything. Do you realize that before the twenties had ended, Cassius had managed his father's business and then entered a monastery? It is said he influenced T. S. Eliot."

"Today, we'd call Cassius a psychopath," Marvin observes.

"Cassius called himself a great dilettante," Alan answers, "although perhaps the nineteenth-century Russian conception of the great sinner would be more appropriate. What do you say if I tell you this was only the beginning of his career?"

"What's the point?" Louise asks.

"Not yet," says Alan, holding up a hand. His manner seems to say that if his audience cannot appreciate the story, he does not feel obliged to continue. "Cassius studied Marx in the monastery. He broke his vows, quit the Church, and became a Communist. All through the thirties he was a figure in the party, going to Moscow, involved in all the Party struggles. He left only during the Moscow trials."

Alan's manner while he relates such stories is somewhat effeminate. He talks with little caresses of his hand, he mentions names and places with a lingering ease as if to suggest that his audience and he are aware, above all, of nuance. The story as Alan tells it is drawn over-long. Suffice it, that the man about whom he is talking, Cassius O'Shaughnessy, becomes a Trotskyist, becomes an anarchist, is a pacifist during the Second World War, and suffers it from a prison cell.

"I may say," Alan goes on, "that I worked for his defense, and was successful in getting him acquitted. Imagine my dolor when I learned that he had turned his back on his anarchist friends and was living with gangsters."

"This is weird," Eleanor says.

"Weird, it is," Alan agrees. "Cassius got into some scrape, and disappeared. What could you do with him? I learned only recently that he had gone to India and was studying yoga. In fact, I learned it from Cassius himself. I asked him of his experiences at Brahna-puth-thar, and he told me the following story."

Now, Alan's voice alters, he assumes the part of Cassius, and speaks in a tone weary of experience, wise and sad in its knowledge. " 'I was sitting on my haunches contemplating my navel,' Cassius said to me, 'when of a sudden I discovered my navel under a different aspect. It seemed to me that if I were to give a counter-clockwise twist, my navel would unscrew.' "

Alan looks up, he surveys his audience, which is now rapt and uneasy, not certain as yet whether a joke is to come. Alan's thumb and forefinger pluck at the middle of his ample belly, his feet are crossed upon the carpet in symbolic suggestion of Cassius upon his haunches.

" 'Taking a deep breath, I turned, and the abysses of Vishtarni loomed beneath. My navel had begun to unscrew. I knew I was about to accept the reward of three years of contemplation. So,' said Cassius, 'I turned again, and my navel unscrewed a little more. I turned and I turned,' " Alan's fingers now revolving upon his belly, " 'and after a period I knew that with one more turn my navel would unscrew itself forever. At the edge of revelation I took one sweet breath, and turned my navel free.' "

Alan looks up at his audience.

" 'Damn,' said Cassius, 'if my ass didn't fall off.' "

4

The story has left the audience in an exasperated mood. It has been a most untypical story for Alan to tell, a little out of place, not offensive exactly, but irritating and inconsequential. Sam is the only one to laugh with more than bewildered courtesy, and his mirth seems excessive to everyone but Alan, and of course, Roslyn, who feels as if she has been the producer. I suppose what it reduces to is a lack of taste. Perhaps that is why Alan is not the lawyer one would expect. He does not have that appreciation—as necessary in his trade as for an actor—of what is desired at any moment, of that which will encourage, as opposed to that which does not encourage, a stimulating but smooth progression of logic and sentiment. Only a fool would tell so long a story when everyone is awaiting the movie.

Now, they are preparing. The men shift armchairs to correspond with the couch, the projector is set up, the screen is unfolded. Sam attempts to talk while he is threading the film, but no one listens. They seem to realize suddenly that a frightful demand has been placed upon them. One does not study pornography in a living room with a beer glass in one's hand, and friends at the elbow. It is the most unsatisfactory of compromises; one can draw neither the benefit of solitary contemplation nor of social exchange. There is, at bottom, the same exasperated fright which one experiences in turning the shower tap and receiving cold water when the flesh has been prepared for heat. Perhaps that is why they are laughing so much now that the movie is begun.

A title, *The Evil Act,* twitches on the screen, shot with scars, holes, and the dust-lines of age. A man and woman are sitting on a couch, they are having coffee. They chat. What they say is conveyed by printed words upon an ornately flowered card, interjected between glimpses of their casual gestures, a cup to the mouth, a smile, a cigarette being lit. The man's name, it seems, is Frankie Idell; he is talking to his wife Magnolia. Frankie is dark, he is sinister, he confides in Magnolia, his dark counterpart, with a grimace of his brows, black from make-up pencil.

FRANKIE: She will be here soon.

MAGNOLIA: This time the little vixen will not escape.

FRANKIE: No, my dear, this time we are prepared.

He looks at his watch.

FRANKIE: Listen, she knocks!

There is a shot of a tall blond woman knocking on the door. She is probably over thirty, but by her short dress and ribboned hat, it is suggested that she is a girl of fifteen.

FRANKIE: Come in, Eleanor.

As may be expected, the audience laughs hysterically at this. It is so wonderful a coincidence. "How I remember Frankie," says Eleanor Slovoda, and Roslyn Sperber is the only one not amused. In the midst of the others' laughter, she says in a worried tone, obviously adrift upon her own concerns, "Do you think we'll have to stop the film in the middle to let the bulb cool off?" The others hoot, they giggle, they are weak from the combination of their own remarks and the action of the plot.

Frankie and Magnolia have sat down on either side of the heroine, Eleanor. A moment passes. Suddenly, stiffly, they attack. Magnolia from her side kisses Eleanor, and Frankie commits an indecent caress.

ELEANOR: How dare you? Stop!

MAGNOLIA: Scream, my little one. It will do you no good. The walls are soundproofed.

FRANKIE: We've fixed a way to make you come across.

ELEANOR: This is hideous. I am hitherto undefiled. Do not touch me!

The captions fade away. A new title takes their place. It says, "But

There Is No Escape From the Determined Pair." On the fade-in, we discover Eleanor in the most distressing situation. Her hands are tied to loops running from the ceiling, and she can only writhe in helpless perturbation before the deliberate and progressive advances of Frankie and Magnolia. Slowly they humiliate her, with relish they probe her.

The audience laughs no longer. A hush has come upon them. Eyes unblinking, they devour the images upon Sam Slovoda's screen.

Eleanor is without clothing. As the last piece is pulled away, Frankie and Magnolia circle about her in a grotesque of pantomime, a leering of lips, limbs in a distortion of desire. Eleanor faints. Adroitly, Magnolia cuts her bonds. We see Frankie carrying her inert body.

Now, Eleanor is trussed to a bed, and the husband and wife are tormenting her with feathers. Bodies curl upon the bed in postures so complicated, in combinations so advanced, that the audience leans forward, Sperbers, Rossmans, and Slovodas, as if tempted to embrace the moving images. The hands trace abstract circles upon the screen, passes and recoveries upon a white background so illumined that hollows and swells, limb to belly and mouth to undescribables, tip of a nipple, orb of a navel swim in giant magnification, flow and slide in a lurching yawing fall, blotting out the camera eye.

A little murmur, all unconscious, passes from their lips. The audience sways, each now finally lost in himself, communing hungrily with shadows, a violated, or violating, fantasy triumphant.

At picture's end, Eleanor the virgin whore is released from the bed. She kisses Frankie, she kisses Magnolia. "You dears," she says. "Let's do it again." The projector lamp burns empty light, the machine keeps turning, the tag of film goes slap-tap, slap-tap, slap-tap, slap-tap, slap-tap, slap-tap.

"Sam, turn it off," says Eleanor.

But when the room lights are on, they cannot look at one another. "Can we see it again?" someone mutters. So, again, Eleanor knocks on the door, is tied, defiled, ravished, and made rapturous. They watch it soberly now, the room hot with the heat of their bodies, the darkness a balm for orgiastic vision. To the Deer Park, Sam is thinking, to the Deer Park of Louis XV, were brought the most beautiful maidens of France, and there they stayed, dressed in fabulous silks, perfumed and wigged, the mole drawn upon their cheek, ladies of pleasure awaiting the pleasure of the king. So Louis had stripped an empire, bankrupt a treasury, prepared a deluge, while in his garden on summer evenings the maidens performed their pageants, eighteenth-century tableaux of the evil act, beauteous instruments of one man's desire, lewd translation of a king's power. That century men sought wealth so they might use its fruits; this epoch men lusted for power in order to amass more power, a compounding of power into pyramids of abstraction whose yield are cannon and wire enclosure, pillars of statistics to the men who are the kings of this century and do no more in power's leisure time than go to church, claim to love their wives, and eat vegetables.

Is it possible, Sam wonders, that each of them here, two Rossmans, two Sperbers, two Slovodas, will cast off their clothes when the movie is done, and perform the orgy which tickles at the heart of their desire? They will not, he knows, they will make jokes when the projector is put away, they will gorge the plate of delicatessen Eleanor provides, and swallow more beer, he among them. He will be the first to make jokes.

Sam is right. The movie has made him extraordinarily alive to the limits of them all. While they sit with red faces, eyes bugged, glutting sandwiches of ham, salami, and tongue, he begins the teasing.

"Roslyn," he calls out, "is the bulb cooled off yet?"

She cannot answer him. She chokes on beer, her face glazes, she is helpless with self-protecting laughter.

"Why are you so anxious, daddie?" Eleanor says quickly.

They begin to discuss the film. As intelligent people they must dominate it. Someone wonders about the actors in the piece, and discussion begins afresh. "I fail to see," says Louise, "why they should be hard to classify. Pornography is a job to the criminal and prostitute element."

"No, you won't find an ordinary prostitute doing this," Sam insists. "It requires a particular kind of personality."

"They have to be exhibitionists," says Eleanor.

"It's all economic," Louise maintains.

"I wonder what those girls felt," Roslyn asks. "I feel sorry for them."

"I'd like to be the camera man," says Alan.

"I'd like to be Frankie," says Marvin sadly.

There is a limit to how long such a conversation may continue. The jokes lapse into silence. They are all busy eating. When they begin to talk again, it is of other things. Each dollop of food sops the agitation which the movie has spilled. They gossip about the party the night before, they discuss which single men are interested in which women, who got drunk, who got sick, who said the wrong thing, who went home with someone else's date. When this is exhausted, one of them mentions a play the others have not seen. Soon they are talking about books, a concert, a one-man show by an artist who is a friend. Dependably, conversation will voyage its orbit. While the men talk of politics, the women are discussing fashions, progressive schools, and recipes they have attempted. Sam is uncomfortable with the division; he knows Eleanor will resent it, he knows she will complain later of the insularity of men and the basic contempt they feel for women's intelligence.

"But you collaborated," Sam will argue. "No one forced you to be with the women."

"Was I to leave them alone?" Eleanor will answer.

"Well, why do the women always have to go off by themselves?"

"Because the men aren't interested in what we have to say."

Sam sighs. He has been talking with interest, but really he is bored. These are nice pleasant people, he thinks, but they are ordinary people, exactly the sort he has spent so many years with, making little jokes, little gossip, living little everyday events, a close circle where everyone mothers the others by his presence. The womb of middle-class life, Sam decides heavily. He is in a bad mood indeed. Everything is laden with dissatisfaction.

Alan has joined the women. He delights in preparing odd dishes when friends visit the Sperbers, and he is describing to Eleanor how he makes blueberry pancakes. Marvin draws closer to Sam.

"I wanted to tell you," he says, "Alan's story reminded me. I saw Jerry O'Shaughnessy the other day."

"Where was he?"

Marvin is hesitant. "It was a shock, Sam. He's on the Bowery. I guess he's become a wino."

"He always drank a lot," says Sam.

"Yeah." Marvin cracks his bony knuckles. "What a stinking time this is, Sam."

"It's probably like the years after 1905 in Russia," Sam says.

"No revolutionary party will come out of this."

"No," Sam says, "nothing will come."

He is thinking of Jerry O'Shaughnessy. What did he look like? what did he say? Sam asks Marvin, and clucks his tongue at the dispiriting answer. It is a shock to him. He draws closer to Marvin, he feels a bond. They have, after all, been through some years together. In the thirties they have been in the Communist Party, they have quit together, they are both weary of politics today, still radicals out of habit, but without enthusiasm and without a cause. "Jerry was a hero to me," Sam says.

"To all of us," says Marvin.

The fabulous Jerry O'Shaughnessy, thinks Sam. In the old days, in the Party, they had made a legend of him. All of them with their middle-class origins and their desire to know a worker-hero.

I may say that I was never so fond of Jerry O'Shaughnessy as was Sam. I thought him a showman and too pleased with himself. Sam, however, with his timidity, his desire to travel, to have adventure and know many women, was obliged to adore O'Shaughnessy. At least he was enraptured with his career.

Poor Jerry who ends as a bum. He has been everything else. He has been a trapper in Alaska, a chauffeur for gangsters, an officer in the Foreign Legion, a labor organizer. His nose was broken, there were scars on his chin. When he talked about his years at sea or his experiences in Spain, the stenographers and garment workers, the radio writers and unemployed actors would listen to his speeches as if he were the prophet of new romance, and their blood would be charged with the magic of revolutionary vision. A man with tremendous charm. In those days it had been easy to confuse his love for himself with his love for all underprivileged workingmen.

"I thought he was still in the Party," Sam says.

"No," says Marvin, "I remember they kicked him out a couple of years ago. He was supposed to have piddled some funds, that's what they say."

"I wish he'd taken the treasury," Sam remarks bitterly. "The Party used him for years."

Marvin shrugs. "They used each other." His mustache droops. "Let me tell you about Sonderson. You know he's still in the Party. The most progressive dentist in New York." They laugh.

While Marvin tells the story, Sam is thinking of other things. Since he has quit Party work, he has studied a great deal. He can tell you about prison camps and the secret police, political murders, the Moscow trials, the exploitation of Soviet labor, the privileges of the bureaucracy; it is all painful to him. He is straddled between the loss of a country he has never seen, and his repudiation of the country in which he lives. "Doesn't the Party seem a horror now?" he bursts out.

Marvin nods. They are trying to comprehend the distance between Party members they have known, people by turns pathetic, likable, or annoying —people not unlike themselves—and in contrast the immensity of historic logic which deploys along statistics of the dead.

"It's all schizoid," Sam says. "Modern life is schizoid."

Marvin agrees. They have agreed on this many times, bored with the petulance of their small voices, yet needing the comfort of such complaints. Marvin asks Sam if he has given up his novel, and Sam says, "Temporarily." He cannot find a form, he explains. He does not want to write a realistic novel, because reality is no longer realistic. "I don't know what it is," says Sam. "To tell you the truth I think I'm kidding myself. I'll never finish this book. I just like to entertain the idea I'll do something good some day." They sit there in friendly depression. Conversation has cooled. Alan and the women are no longer talking.

"Marvin," asks Louise, "what time is it?"

They are ready to go. Sam must say directly what he had hoped to approach by suggestion. "I was wondering," he whispers to Rossman, "would you mind if I held onto the film for a day or two?"

Marvin looks at him. "Oh, why of course, Sam," he says in his morose voice. "I know how it is." He pats Sam on the shoulder as if, symbolically, to convey the exchange of ownership. They are fellow conspirators.

"If you ever want to borrow the projector," Sam suggests.

"Nah," says Marvin, "I don't know that it would make much difference."

5

It has been, when all is said, a most annoying day. As Sam and Eleanor tidy the apartment, emptying ash trays and washing the few dishes, they are fond neither of themselves nor each other. "What a waste today has been," Eleanor remarks, and Sam can only agree. He has done no writing, he has not been outdoors, and still it is late in the evening, and he has talked too much, eaten too much, is nervous from the movie they have seen. He knows that he will watch it again with Eleanor before they go to sleep; she has given her assent to that. But as is so often the case with Sam these days, he cannot await their embrace with any sure anticipation. Eleanor may be in the mood or Eleanor may not; there is no way he can control the issue. It is depressing; Sam knows that he circles about Eleanor at such times with the guilty maneuvers of a sad hound. Resent her as he must, be furious with himself as he will, there is not very much he can do about it. Often, after they have made love, they will lie beside each other in silence, each offended, each certain the other is to blame. At such times, memory tickles them with a cruel feather. Not always has it been like this. When they were first married, and indeed for the six months they lived together before marriage, everything was quite different. Their affair was very exciting to them; each told the other with some hyperbole but no real mistruth that no one in the past had ever been comparable as lover.

I suppose I am a romantic. I always feel that this is the best time in people's lives. There is, after all, so little we accomplish, and that short period when we are beloved and triumph as lovers is sweet with power. Rarely are we concerned then with our lack of importance; we are too important. In Sam's case, disillusion means even more. Like so many young men, he entertained the secret conceit that he was an extraordinary lover. One cannot really believe this without supporting at the same time the equally secret conviction that one is fundamentally inept. It is—no matter what Sergius would say—a more dramatic and therefore more attractive view of oneself than the sober notion which Sam now accepts with grudging wisdom, that the man as lover is dependent upon the bounty of the woman. As I say, he accepts the notion, it is one of the lineaments of maturity, but there is a part of him which, no matter how harried by analysis, cannot relinquish the antagonism he feels that Eleanor has respected his private talent so poorly, and has not allowed him to confer its benefits upon more women. I mock Sam, but he would mock himself on this. It hardly matters; mockery cannot accomplish everything, and Sam seethes with that most private and tender pain: even worse than being unattractive to the world is to be unattractive to one's mate; or, what is the same and describes Sam's case more accurately, never to know in advance when he shall be undesirable to Eleanor.

I make perhaps too much of the subject, but that is only because it is so important to Sam. Relations between Eleanor and him are not really that bad—I know other couples who have much less or nothing at all. But comparisons are poor comfort to Sam; his standards are so high. So are Eleanor's. I am convinced the most unfortunate people are those who would make an art of love. It sours other effort. Of all artists, they are certainly the most wretched.

Shall I furnish a model? Sam and Eleanor are on the couch, and the projector adjusted to its slowest speed, is retracing the elaborate panto-mime of the three principals. If one could allow these shadows a life . . . but indeed such life has been given them. Sam and Eleanor are no more than an itch, a smart, a threshold of satisfaction; the important share of themselves has steeped itself in Frankie, Magnolia, and Eleanor-of-the-film. Indeed the variations are beyond telling. It is the most outrageous orgy performed by five ghosts.

Self-critical Sam! He makes love in front of a movie, and one cannot say that it is unsatisfactory any more than one can say it is pleasant. It is dirty, downright porno-dirty, it is a lewd slop-brush slapped through the middle of domestic exasperations and breakfast eggs. It is so dirty that only half of Sam—he is quite divisible into fractions—can be exercised at all. The part that is his brain worries along like a cuckolded burgher. He is taking the pulse of his anxiety. Will he last long enough to satisfy Eleanor? Will the children come back tonight? He cannot help it. In the midst of the circus, he is suddenly convinced the children will walk through the door. "Why are you so anxious, daddie?"

So it goes. Sam the lover is conscious of exertion. One moment he is Frankie Idell, destroyer of virgins—take that! you whore!—at the next, body moving, hands caressing, he is no more than some lines from a psychoanalytical text. He is thinking about the sensitivity of his scrotum. He has read that this is a portent of femininity in a male. How strong is his latent homosexuality, worries Sam, thrusting stiffly, warm sweat running cold. Does he identify with Eleanor-of-the-film?

Technically, the climax is satisfactory. They lie together in the dark, the film ended, the projector humming its lonely revolutions in the quiet room. Sam gets up to turn it off; he comes back and kisses Eleanor upon the mouth. Apparently, she has enjoyed herself more than he; she is tender and fondles the tip of his nose.

"You know, Sam," she says from her space beside him, "I think I saw this picture before?"

"When?"

"Oh, you know when. That time."

Sam thinks dully that women are always most loving when they can reminisce about infidelity.

"That time!" he repeats.

"I think so."

Racing forward from memory like the approaching star which begins as a point on the mind and swells to explode the eyeball with its odious image, Sam remembers, and is weak in the dark. It is ten years, eleven perhaps, before they were married, yet after they were lovers. Eleanor has told him, but she has always been vague about details. There had been two men, it seemed, and another girl, and all had been drunk. They had seen movie after movie. With reluctant fascination, Sam can conceive the rest. How it had pained him, how excited him. It is years now since he has remembered, but he remembers. In the darkness he wonders at the unreasonableness of jealous pain. That night was impossible to imagine any longer—therefore it is more real; Eleanor his plump wife who presses a pigeon's shape against her housecoat, forgotten heroine of black orgies. It had been meaningless, Eleanor claimed; it was Sam she loved, and the other had been no more than a fancy of which she wished to rid herself. Would it be the same today, thinks Sam, or had Eleanor been loved by Frankie, by Frankie of the other movies, by Frankie of the two men she never saw again on that night so long ago?

The pleasure he gets from this pain, Sam thinks furiously.

It is not altogether perverse. If Eleanor causes him pain, it means after all that she is alive for him. I have often observed that the reality of a person depends upon their ability to hurt us; Eleanor as the vague accusing embodiment of the wife is different, altogether different, from Eleanor who lies warmly in Sam's bed, an attractive Eleanor who may wound his flesh. Thus, brother to the pleasure of pain, is the sweeter pleasure which follows pain. Sam, tired, lies in Eleanor's arms, and they talk with the cozy trade words of old professionals, agreeing that they will not make love again before a movie, that it was exciting, but also not without detachment, that all in all it has been good but not quite right, that she had loved this action he had done, and was uncertain about another. It is their old familiar critique, a sign that they are intimate and well-disposed. They do not talk about the act when it has failed to fire; then they go silently to sleep. But, now, Eleanor's enjoyment having mollified Sam's sense of no enjoyment, they talk with the apologetics and encomiums of familiar mates. Eleanor falls asleep, and Sam falls almost asleep, curling next to her warm body, his hand over her round belly with the satisfaction of a sculptor. He is drowsy, and he thinks drowsily that these few moments of creature-pleasure, this brief compassion he can feel for the body that trusts itself to sleep beside him, his comfort in its warmth, is perhaps all the meaning he may ask for his life. That out of disappointment, frustration, and the passage of dreary years come these few moments when he is close to her, and their years

together possess a connotation more rewarding than the sum of all which
has gone into them.

But then he thinks of the novel he wants to write, and he is wide-awake
again. Like the sleeping pill which fails to work and leaves one warped in
an exaggeration of the ills which sought the drug, Sam passes through the
promise of sex-emptied sleep, and is left with nervous loins, swollen jealousy
of an act ten years dead, and sweating irritable resentment of the woman's
body which hinders his limbs. He has wasted the day, he tells himself, he
has wasted the day as he has wasted so many days of his life, and tomorrow in the office he will be no more than his ten-fingers typing plot and
words for Bramba the Venusian and Lee-Lee Deeds, Hollywood Star,
while that huge work with which he has cheated himself, holding it before
him as a covenant of his worth, that enormous novel which would lift him
at a bound from the impasse in which he stifles, whose dozens of characters
would develop a vision of life in bountiful complexity, lies foundered,
rotting on a beach of purposeless effort. Notes here, pages there, it sprawls
through a formless wreck of incidental ideas and half-episodes, utterly
without shape. He has not even a hero for it.

One could not have a hero today, Sam thinks, a man of action and
contemplation, capable of sin, large enough for good, a man immense.
There is only a modern hero damned by no more than the ugliness of
wishes whose satisfaction he will never know. One needs a man who could
walk the stage, someone who—no matter who, not himself. Someone, Sam
thinks, who reasonably could not exist.

The novelist, thinks Sam, perspiring beneath blankets, must live in
paranoia and seek to be one with the world; he must be terrified of experience and hungry for it; he must think himself nothing and believe he is
superior to all. The feminine in his nature cries for proof he is a man; he
dreams of power and is without capacity to gain it; he loves himself above
all and therefore despises all that he is.

He is, thinks Sam, he is part of the perfect prescription, and yet he is not
a novelist. He lacks energy and belief. It is left for him to write an article
some day about the temperament of the ideal novelist.

In the darkness, memories rise, yeast-swells of apprehension. Out of
bohemian days so long ago, comes the friend of Eleanor, a girl who had
been sick and was committed to an institution. They visited her, Sam and
Eleanor, they took the suburban train and sat on the lawn of the asylum
grounds while patients circled about intoning a private litany, or shuddering in boob-blundering fright from an insect that crossed their skin. The
friend had been silent. She had smiled, she had answered their questions
with the fewest words, and had returned again to her study of sunlight and
blue sky. As they were about to leave, the girl had taken Sam aside. "They
violate me," she said in a whisper. "Every night when the doors are locked,
they come to my room and they make the movie. I am the heroine and am

subjected to all variety of sexual viciousness. Tell them to leave me alone so I may enter the convent." And while she talked, in a horror of her body, one arm scrubbed the other. Poor tortured friend. They had seen her again, and she babbled, her face had coarsened into an idiot leer.

Sam sweats. There is so little he knows, and so much to know. Youth of the depression with its economic terms, what can he know of madness or religion? They are both so alien to him. He is the mongrel, Sam thinks, brought up without religion from a mother half-Protestant and half-Catholic, and a father half-Catholic and half-Jew. He is the quarter-Jew, and yet he is a Jew, or so he feels himself, knowing nothing of Gospel, tabernacle, or Mass, the Jew through accident, through state of mind. What, whatever did he know of penance? self-sacrifice? mortification of the flesh? the love of his fellow man? Am I concerned with my relation to God? ponders Sam, and smiles sourly in the darkness. No, that has never concerned him, he thinks, not for better nor for worse. "They are making the movie," says the girl into the ear of memory, "and so I cannot enter the convent."

How hideous was the mental hospital. A concentration camp, decides Sam. Perhaps it would be the world some day, or was that only his projection of feelings of hopelessness? "Do not try to solve the problems of the world," he hears from Sergius, and pounds a lumpy pillow.

However could he organize his novel? What form to give it? It is so complex. Too loose, thinks Sam, too scattered. Will he ever fall asleep? Wearily, limbs tense, his stomach too keen, he plays again the game of putting himself to sleep. "I do not feel my toes," Sam says to himself. "My toes are dead, my calves are asleep, my calves are sleeping . . ."

In the middle from wakefulness to slumber, in the torpor which floats beneath blankets, I give an idea to Sam. "Destroy time, and chaos may be ordered," I say to him.

"Destroy time, and chaos may be ordered," he repeats after me, and in desperation to seek his coma, mutters back, "I do not feel my nose, my nose is numb, my eyes are heavy, my eyes are heavy."

So Sam enters the universe of sleep, a man who seeks to live in such a way as to avoid pain, and succeeds merely in avoiding pleasure. What a dreary compromise is life!

⟡

Norman Mailer was born in New Jersey, grew up in Brooklyn, where he now lives, and was educated at Harvard. His best-selling war novel, The Naked and the Dead *(1945), is related to his experience as a rifleman on Leyte in World War II. His second novel was* Barbary Shore *(1951), a heavily symboled story of politics, set in a Brooklyn rooming house. His third novel was* The Deer Park *(1955), set in a desert resort near Holly-wood, where Mailer had worked as a screenwriter; it is the novel consid-ered most central to his work; he has reworked it into a play produced off-Broadway in 1967. A fourth novel,* An American Dream *(1965), was originally written under conditions of serial deadline for* Esquire *magazine. There is a fifth novel, a short one called* Why Are We in Vietnam? *(1967), that may or may not be attempting to answer the title question in terms of the actions and reactions of some rich Texans on a bear hunt in Alaska. There is a collection of poems,* Death to the Ladies, and Other Disasters *(1962), and he has published three other books:* Advertisements for Myself *(1959),* The Presidential Papers *(1963), and* Cannibals and Christians *(1966). These three collections indicate that Mailer has done interesting work in virtually every form: short poems and long poems, plays and play-lets, short stories, essays, reviews, criticism, dialogues, interviews, self-interviews, conversations, reportage, movie treatments, as well as the strange new form that he invented to string all these pieces together, the self-advertisement, in which he describes the circumstances under which they were written and how they relate to one another and to the rest of his work. He seems to have original ideas and perceptions in every area— local politics and foreign policy, architecture, literature, philosophy, sports, medicine—and although sometimes the ideas themselves are so original as to seem outlandish, his pieces are nevertheless always brilliantly written, carefully argued, and informed by wide reading and direct experience. In-evitably, having written so much else—and having spent an amount of time becoming a public figure—he has fallen behind in the ambitious program of novel writing which he set himself.*

"The Man Who Studied Yoga" was written in 1952 and is the gateway to this later fiction, at least as it was originally projected. A novella, it can be read very satisfactorily as an independent work, but an understanding of the point of view used, and some other matters, may help illuminate its meanings. The "I" narrator, who declines to introduce himself at the be-ginning and who comments on the story intermittently, is Sergius O'Shaugh-nessy, a figure from Sam Slovoda's dream life, compounded of his psycho-analyst, Dr. Sergius, and the two adventurous O'Shaughnessys mentioned in the story, Jerry and Cassius. It should be understood that "The Man Who Studied Yoga" was originally intended as the prologue to a projected sequence of eight novels, only the first of which, The Deer Park, *has yet been written, although sections of a second appear at the end of* Advertise-ments for Myself. *Mailer is ambiguous in his statements about whether the project has been abandoned. Sergius O'Shaughnessy, the narrator of* The Deer Park, *was to be the mythical hero of all eight books, encountering fabulous adventures as he traveled through various worlds—pleasure, busi-ness, crime, and so on—each book comprising a separate dream of Sam Slovoda during the night following the incidents described in "The Man*

Who Studied Yoga." The many interrelationships and correspondences between The Deer Park *and "The Man Who Studied Yoga" are subtle and revealing of both works; but what need concern us now is only the extraordinary validity of the point of view used in the novella. Sergius O'Shaughnessy knows Sam Slovoda as both man and dreamer, as no man ever knew any other. As he says, "It is just that I, far better than Sam, know how serious he really is, how fanciful, how elaborate, his imagination can be." Sergius and Sam are the very antithesis of each other, yet they are one and the same, for Sergius is the thwarted potential of Sam. Sam goes to sleep thinking: "One could not have a hero today . . . a man of action and contemplation, capable of sin, large enough for good, a man immense . . . someone who—no matter who, not himself." Yet Sergius is himself; not only Sergius and all his heroics but also all the other vigorous characters and situations are products of Sam's elaborately fanciful mind, an imagination that in real life is sapped by Sam's profession—writing continuity for comic books. "How angry he is," says Sergius, the liberated and compassionate projection of Sam's trapped and envious self, "how angry and how helpless." All the excellence and passion of his dreams unavailable to him, "damned by no more than the ugliness of wishes whose satisfaction he will never know," Sam Slovoda is powerless to express himself; as such, as he himself realizes, he is "only a modern hero."*

A Shower of Gold

◈◈◈◈◈◈◈

BECAUSE HE NEEDED THE MONEY Peterson answered an ad that said *"We'll pay you* to be on TV if your opinions are strong enough or your personal experiences have a flavor of the unusual." He called the number and was told to come to Room 1551 in the Graybar Building on Lexington. This he did and after spending twenty minutes with a Miss Arbor who asked him if he had ever been in analysis was okayed for a program called *Who Am I?* "What do you have strong opinions about?" Miss Arbor asked. "Art," Peterson said, "life, money." "For instance?" "I believe," Peterson said, "that the learning ability of mice can be lowered or increased by regulating the amount of serotonin in the brain. I believe that schizophrenics have a high incidence of unusual fingerprints, including lines that make almost complete circles. I believe that the dreamer watches his dream in sleep, by moving his eyes." *"That's very interesting!"* Miss Arbor cried. "It's all in the *World Almanac,"* Peterson replied.

"I see you're a sculptor," Miss Arbor said, "that's wonderful." "What is the nature of the program?" Peterson asked. "I've never seen it." "Let me answer your question with another question," Miss Arbor said. "Mr. Peterson, are you absurd?" Her enormous lips were smeared with a glowing white cream. "I beg your pardon?" "I mean," Miss Arbor said earnestly, "do you encounter your own existence as gratuitous? Do you feel *de trop?* Is there nausea?" "I have an enlarged liver," Peterson offered. "That's *excellent!"* Miss Arbor exclaimed. "That's a *very* good beginning! *Who Am I?* tries, Mr. Peterson, to discover what people *really are.* People today, we feel, are hidden away inside themselves, alienated, desperate, living in anguish, despair and bad faith. Why have we been thrown here, and abandoned? That's the question we try to answer, Mr. Peterson. Man stands alone in a featureless, anonymous landscape, in fear and trembling and sickness unto death. God is dead. Nothingness everywhere. Dread. Estrangement. Finitude. *Who Am I?* approaches these problems in a root radical way." "On television?" "We're interested in basics, Mr. Peterson. We don't play around." "I see," Peterson said, wondering about the amount of the fee. "What I want to know now, Mr. Peterson, is this: are you *interested* in absurdity?" "Miss Arbor," he said, "to tell you the truth, I don't know. I'm not sure I believe in it." "Oh, Mr. Peterson!" Miss Arbor said, shocked. "Don't *say* that! You'll be . . ." "Punished?" Peterson suggested. *"You* may not be interested in absurdity," she said firmly, "but absurdity is interested in *you."* "I have a lot of problems, if that helps," Peterson said. "Existence is problematic for you," Miss Arbor said, relieved. "The fee is two hundred dollars."

"I'm going to be on television," Peterson said to his dealer. "A terrible shame," Jean-Claude responded. "Is it unavoidable?" "It's unavoidable," Peterson said, "if I want to eat." "How much?" Jean-Claude asked and Peterson said: "Two hundred." He looked around the gallery to see if any of his works were on display. "A ridiculous compensation considering the infamy. Are you using your own name?" "You haven't by any chance . . ." "No one is buying," Jean-Claude said. "Undoubtedly it is the weather. People are thinking in terms of—what do you call those things?—Chris-Crafts. To boat with. You would not consider again what I spoke to you about before?" "No," Peterson said, "I wouldn't consider it." "Two little ones would move much, much faster than a single huge big one," Jean-Claude said, looking away. "To saw it across the middle would be a very simple matter." "It's supposed to be a work of art," Peterson said, as calmly as possible. "You don't go around sawing works of art across the middle, remember?" "That place where it saws," Jean-Claude said, "is not very difficult. I can put my two hands around it." He made a circle with his two hands to demonstrate. "Invariably when I look at that piece I see two pieces. Are you absolutely sure you didn't conceive it wrongly in the first instance?" "Absolutely," Peterson said. Not a single piece of his was on view, and his liver expanded in rage and hatred. "You have a very roman-tic impulse," Jean-Claude said. "I admire, dimly, the posture. You read too much in the history of art. It estranges you from those possibilities for authentic selfhood that inhere in the present century." "I know," Peterson said, "could you let me have twenty until the first?"

Peterson sat in his loft on lower Broadway drinking Rheingold and thinking about the President. He had always felt close to the President but felt now that he had, in agreeing to appear on the television program, done something slightly disgraceful, of which the President would not approve. But I needed the money, he told himself, the telephone is turned off and the kitten is crying for milk. And I'm running out of beer. The President feels that the arts should be encouraged, Peterson reflected, surely he doesn't want me to go without beer? He wondered if what he was feeling was

simple guilt at having sold himself to television or something more elegant:
nausea? His liver groaned within him and he considered a situation in
which his new relationship with the President was announced. He was
working in the loft. The piece in hand was to be called *Season's Greetings*
and combined three auto radiators, one from a Chevrolet Tudor, one from
a Ford pickup, one from a 1932 Essex, with part of a former telephone
switchboard and other items. The arrangement seemed right and he began
welding. After a time the mass was freestanding. A couple of hours had
passed. He put down the torch, lifted off the mask. He walked over to the
refrigerator and found a sandwich left by a friendly junk dealer. It was a
sandwich made hastily and without inspiration: a thin slice of ham between
two pieces of bread. He ate it gratefully nevertheless. He stood looking at
the work, moving from time to time so as to view it from a new angle.
Then the door to the loft burst open and the President ran in, trailing a
sixteen-pound sledge. His first blow cracked the principal weld in *Season's
Greetings,* the two halves parting like lovers, clinging for a moment and
then rushing off in opposite directions. Twelve Secret Service men held
Peterson in a paralyzing combination of secret grips. He's looking good,
Peterson thought, very good, healthy, mature, fit, trustworthy. I like his
suit. The President's second and third blows smashed the Essex radiator
and the Chevrolet radiator. Then he attacked the welding torch, the plaster
sketches on the workbench, the Rodin cast and the Giacometti stickman
Peterson had bought in Paris. *"But Mr. President!"* Peterson shouted. *"I
thought we were friends!"* A Secret Service man bit him in the back of the
neck. Then the President lifted the sledge high in the air, turned toward
Peterson, and said: "Your liver is diseased? That's a good sign. You're
making progress. You're thinking."

   "I happen to think that guy in the White House is doing a pretty darn
good job." Peterson's barber, a man named Kitchen who was also a lay
analyst and the author of four books titled *The Decision To Be,* was the
only person in the world to whom he had confided his former sense of
community with the President. "As far as his relationship with you personally goes," the barber continued, "it's essentially a kind of I-Thou relationship, if you know what I mean. You got to handle it with full awareness of
the implications. In the end one experiences only oneself, Nietzsche said.
When you're angry with the President, what you experience is self-as-angry-
with-the-President. When things are okay between you and him, what you
experience is self-as-swinging-with-the-President. Well and good. *But,"*
Kitchen said, lathering up, "you want the relationship to be such that what
you experience is the President-as-swinging-with-you. You want *his* reality,
get it? So that you can break out of the hell of solipsism. How about a little
more off the sides?" "Everybody knows the language but me," Peterson
said irritably. "Look," Kitchen said, "when you talk about me to some-

body else, you say 'my barber,' don't you? Sure you do. In the same way, I look at you as being 'my customer,' get it? But you don't regard yourself as being 'my' customer and I don't regard myself as 'your' barber. Oh, it's hell all right." The razor moved like a switchblade across the back of Peterson's neck. "Like Pascal said: 'The natural misfortune of our mortal and feeble condition is so wretched that when we consider it closely, nothing can console us.' " The razor rocketed around an ear. "Listen," Peterson said, "what do you think of this television program called *Who Am I?* Ever seen it?" "Frankly," the barber said, "it smells of the library. But they do a job on those people, I'll tell you that." "What do you mean?" Peterson said excitedly. "What kind of a job?" The cloth was whisked away and shaken with a sharp popping sound. "It's too horrible even to talk about," Kitchen said. "But it's what they deserve, those crumbs." "Which crumbs?" Peterson asked.

That night a tall foreign-looking man with a switchblade big as a butcherknife open in his hand walked into the loft without knocking and said "Good evening, Mr. Peterson, I am the cat-piano player, is there anything you'd particularly like to hear?" "Cat-piano?" Peterson said, gasping, shrinking from the knife. "What are you talking about? What do you want?" A biography of Nolde slid from his lap to the floor. "The cat-piano," said the visitor, "is an instrument of the devil, a diabolical instrument. You needn't sweat quite so much," he added, sounding aggrieved. Peterson tried to be brave. "I don't understand," he said. "Let me explain," the tall foreign-looking man said graciously. "The keyboard consists of eight cats—the octave—encased in the body of the instrument in such a way that only their heads and forepaws protrude. The player presses upon the appropriate paws, and the appropriate cats respond with a kind of shriek. There is also provision made for pulling their tails. A tail-puller, or perhaps I should say tail *player"* (he smiled a disingenuous smile) "is stationed at the rear of the instrument, where the tails are. At the correct moment the tail-puller pulls the correct tail. The tail-note is of course quite different from the paw-note and produces sounds in the upper registers. Have you ever seen such an instrument, Mr. Peterson?" "No, and I don't believe it exists," Peterson said heroically. "There is an excellent early seventeenth-century engraving by Franz van der Wyngaert, Mr. Peterson, in which a cat-piano appears. Played, as it happens, by a man with a wooden leg. You will observe my own leg." The cat-piano player hoisted his trousers and a leglike contraption of wood, metal and plastic appeared. "And now, would you like to make a request? 'The Martyrdom of St. Sebastian'? The 'Romeo and Juliet' overture? 'Holiday for Strings'?" "But why—" Peterson began. "The kitten is crying for milk, Mr. Peterson. And whenever a kitten cries, the cat-piano plays." "But it's not my kitten," Peterson said reasonably. "It's just a kitten that wished itself on me. I've been trying to give it away. I'm not sure it's still around. I haven't seen it since the day before yesterday." The kitten appeared, looked at Peterson reproachfully, and then rubbed itself against the cat-piano player's mechanical leg. "Wait a minute!" Peterson exclaimed. "This thing is rigged! That cat hasn't been here in two days. What do you want from me? What am I supposed to do?" "Choices, Mr. Peterson, choices. You *chose* that kitten as a way of encountering that which you are not, that is to say, kitten. An effort on the part of the *pour-soi* to—" "But it chose me!" Peterson cried, "the door was open and the first thing I knew it was lying in my bed, under the Army blanket. I didn't have anything to do with it!" The cat-piano player repeated his disingenuous smile. "Yes, Mr. Peterson, I know, I know. Things are done to you, it is all a gigantic conspiracy. I've heard the story a hundred times. But the kitten is here, is it not? The kitten is weeping, is it not?" Peterson looked at the kitten, which was crying huge tigerish tears into its empty dish. *"Listen,* Mr. Peterson," the cat-piano player said, *"listen!"* The blade of his immense knife jumped back into the handle with a thwack! and the hideous music began.

The day after the hideous music began the three girls from California arrived. Peterson opened his door, hesitantly, in response to an insistent ringing, and found himself being stared at by the three girls in blue jeans and heavy sweaters, carrying suitcases. "I'm Sherry," the first girl said, "and this is Ann and this is Louise. We're from California and we need a place to stay." They were homely and extremely purposeful. "I'm sorry," Peterson said, "I can't—" "We sleep anywhere," Sherry said, looking past him into the vastness of his loft, "on the floor if we have to. We've done it before." Ann and Louise stood on their toes to get a good look. "What's that funny music?" Sherry asked, "it sounds pretty far-out. We really won't be any trouble at all and it'll just be a little while until we make a connection." "Yes," Peterson said, "but why me?" "You're an artist," Sherry said sternly, "we saw the A.I.R. sign downstairs." Peterson cursed the fire laws which made posting of the signs obligatory. "Listen," he said, "I can't even feed the cat. I can't even keep myself in beer. This is not the place. You won't be happy here. My work isn't authentic. I'm a minor artist." "The natural misfortune of our mortal and feeble condition is so wretched that when we consider it closely, nothing can console us," Sherry said. "That's Pascal." "I know," Peterson said, weakly. "Where is the john?" Louise asked. Ann marched into the kitchen and began to prepare, from supplies removed from her rucksack, something called *veal engagé.* "Kiss me," Sherry said, "I need love." Peterson flew to his friendly neighborhood bar, ordered a double brandy, and wedged himself into a telephone booth. "Miss Arbor? This is Hank Peterson. Listen, Miss Arbor, I can't do it. No, I mean really. I'm being punished horribly for even thinking about it. No, I

mean it. You can't imagine what's going on around here. Please, get somebody else? I'd regard it as a great personal favor. Miss Arbor? Please?"

The other contestants were a young man in white pajamas named Arthur
Pick, a karate expert, and an airline pilot in full uniform, Wallace E. Rice.
"Just be natural," Miss Arbor said, "and of course be frank. We score on
the basis of the validity of your answers, and of course that's measured by
the polygraph." "What's this about a polygraph?" the airline pilot said.
"The polygraph measures the validity of your answers," Miss Arbor said,
her lips glowing whitely. "How else are we going to know if you're . . ."
"Lying?" Wallace E. Rice supplied. The contestants were connected to the
machine and the machine to a large illuminated tote board hanging over
their heads. The master of ceremonies, Peterson noted without pleasure,
resembled the President and did not look at all friendly.

The program began with Arthur Pick. Arthur Pick got up in his white
pajamas and gave a karate demonstration in which he broke three half-inch
pine boards with a single kick of his naked left foot. Then he told how he
had disarmed a bandit, late at night at the A&P where he was an assistant
manager, with a maneuver called a "rip-choong" which he demonstrated
on the announcer. "How about that?" the announcer caroled. "Isn't that
something? Audience?" The audience responded enthusiastically and Arthur Pick stood modestly with his hands behind his back. "Now," the
announcer said, "let's play *Who Am I?* And here's your host, *Bill Lemmon!*" No, he doesn't look like the President, Peterson decided. "Arthur,"
Bill Lemmon said, "for twenty dollars—do you love your mother?" "Yes,"
Arthur Pick said. "Yes, of course." A bell rang, the tote board flashed, and
the audience screamed. "He's lying!" the announcer shouted, "lying! lying!
lying!" "Arthur," Bill Lemmon said, looking at his index cards, "the polygraph shows that the validity of your answer is . . . questionable. Would
you like to try it again? Take another crack at it?" "You're crazy," Arthur
Pick said. "Of course I love my mother." He was fishing around inside his
pajamas for a handkerchief. "Is your mother watching the show tonight,
Arthur?" "Yes, Bill, she is." "How long have you been studying karate?"
"Two years, Bill." "And who paid for the lessons?" Arthur Pick hesitated.
Then he said: "My mother, Bill." "They were pretty expensive, weren't
they, Arthur?" "Yes, Bill, they were." "How expensive?" "Five dollars an
hour." "Your mother doesn't make very much money, does she, Arthur?"
"No, Bill, she doesn't." "Arthur, what does your mother do for a living?"
"She's a garment worker, Bill. In the garment district." "And how long has
she worked down there?" "All her life, I guess. Since my old man died."
"And she doesn't make very much money, you said." "No. But she *wanted*
to pay for the lessons. She *insisted* on it." Bill Lemmon said: "She wanted
a son who could break boards with his feet?" Peterson's liver leaped and

the tote board spelled out, in huge, glowing white letters, the words BAD FAITH. The airline pilot, Wallace E. Rice, was led to reveal that he had been caught, on a flight from Omaha to Miami, with a stewardess sitting on his lap and wearing his captain's cap, that the flight engineer had taken a Polaroid picture, and that he had been given involuntary retirement after nineteen years of faithful service. "It was perfectly safe," Wallace E. Rice said. "You don't understand, the automatic pilot can fly that plane better than I can." He further confessed to a lifelong and intolerable itch after stewardesses which had much to do, he said, with the way their jackets fell just on top of their hips, and his own jacket with the three gold stripes on the sleeve darkened with sweat until it was black.

I was wrong, Peterson thought, the world is absurd. The absurdity is punishing me for not believing in it. I affirm the absurdity. On the other hand, absurdity is itself absurd. Before the emcee could ask the first question, Peterson began to talk. "Yesterday," Peterson said to the television audience, "in the typewriter in front of the Olivetti showroom on Fifth Avenue, I found a recipe for Ten Ingredient Soup that included a stone from a toad's head. And while I stood there marveling a nice old lady pasted on the elbow of my best Haspel suit a little blue sticker reading THIS INDIVIDUAL IS A PART OF THE COMMUNIST CONSPIRACY FOR GLOBAL DOMINATION OF THE ENTIRE GLOBE. Coming home I passed a sign that said in ten-foot letters COWARD SHOES and heard a man singing 'Golden Earrings' in a horrible voice, and last night I dreamed there was a shoot-out at our house on Meat Street and my mother shoved me in a closet to get me out of the line of fire." The emcee waved at the floor manager to turn Peterson off, but Peterson kept talking. "In this kind of a world," Peterson said, "absurd if you will, possibilities nevertheless proliferate and escalate all around us and there are opportunities for beginning again. I am a minor artist and my dealer won't even display my work if he can help it but minor is as minor does and lightning may strike even yet. Don't be reconciled. Turn off your television sets," Peterson said, "cash in your life insurance, indulge in a mindless optimism. Visit girls at dusk. Play the guitar. How can you be alienated without first having been connected? Think back and remember how it was." A man on the floor in front of Peterson was waving a piece of cardboard on which something threatening was written but Peterson ignored him and concentrated on the camera with the little red light. The little red light jumped from camera to camera in an attempt to throw him off balance but Peterson was too smart for it and followed wherever it went. "My mother was a royal virgin," Peterson said, "and my father a shower of gold. My childhood was pastoral and energetic and rich in experiences which developed my character. As a young man I was noble in reason, infinite in faculty, in form express and admirable, and in apprehension . . ." Peterson went on and on and although he was, in a sense, lying, in a sense he was not.

⟡

Donald Barthelme is a young Texan living in New York City who in 1964 published a collection of fourteen crazy stories, called for no known reason Come Back, Dr. Caligari. *Several of them appeared first in* The New Yorker *magazine, which has since enthusiastically taken over his work more or less entirely, publishing not only his subsequent stories but also the bizarre novella-length* Snow White *(1967). This peculiar fable of our times has seven dwarves that may or may not be seven identities of one man. In Barthelme stories it is never easy to tell exactly what is happening. At any rate, in what seems almost a symbolic working-out of the anomic society's vulnerability to totalitarianism, the gentle dwarves hang the one of their number called Bill, their leader who refuses to lead, and take in Hogo, "a brute perhaps but an efficient brute." Barthelme refuses to use traditional character-and-plot fiction methods in his stories, and he writes in a swift-moving style that brilliantly parodies not only the commercial cant of our time but also the intellectual jargon in which it is always being deplored.*

In "A Shower of Gold" Barthelme is at once satirizing current preoccupations with alienation and identity and absurdity, and using these themes for his own purposes. The ultimate in sadistic television shows is called Who Am I?, *a program deliberately designed to destroy the man whose "opinions are strong" and whose "personal experiences have a flavor of the unusual." The program represents an example of how co-optation by the mass media quickly neutralizes even the most radical ideas, simply by making them fashionable. ("On television?" Peterson asks Miss Arbor. "We're interested in basics, Mr. Peterson," she replies. "We don't play around.") Even Peterson's barber has written four books titled* The Decision To Be *and quotes Nietzsche and Pascal on the subject. So much talk about absurdity is obviously getting to be absurd. But Peterson is presented as an artist of integrity (at least, he refuses to saw one of his junk-sculptures in half, in order to sell it) in a time when the artist is at bay (the President himself invades Peterson's studio to destroy his work). Asked to expose himself as a fraud for the mass entertainment, he refuses. "In a sense, lying, in a sense . . . not," he persists—as the artist must—in holding his own strong beliefs and in telling his own personal story.*

⟡⟡

Each of the stories in this section dramatizes a different aspect of the modern condition of the non-hero: trapped in immobility; questing identity; longing for love and meaning; preoccupied with self and unable to accept responsibility for others; powerless to express his own uniqueness; alone in an absurd and meaningless world. While none of these people represent "social problems," the tensions of their lives, above all the inability to extract a sense of unique meaning from their existence, suggest a lack of social definition and reflect the impact of accelerating change in the basic social institutions. We turn next to how things are changing in the way we live in the most primary social group of all . . .

The Way We Live Now

IN FAMILIES

The family—primary social group, cradle of socialization, its origins lost in the mists of antiquity, and so forth—is obviously to some extent a given, an unchanging item in even the most changeable times: father, mother, and child seem to be what it takes to make a family no matter what. Yet patterns of family life in any larger sense of the word differ wildly from culture to culture around the world and from century to century through history. And today in America "the family" takes a variety of forms whose simultaneous existence makes them seem almost as bewildering. The rate of change in our times and in our country is now so fast that it is difficult to speak coherently of "trends" or of histories of change simply because an "old" order (common as recently as twenty years ago) still exists side by side with what is thought of as "new"; and what is common and "new" now exists side by side with patterns of living that suggest what may be common in the future—that is, virtually, tomorrow. With this disclaimer, then, and many others implied, we can describe the "history" of the American family "in our own time" simply by pointing to what everybody knows: that in the more-or-less all-inclusive middle class, families have grown smaller. This does not mean that there have been fewer children: as everyone also knows, there has been (or is) a "population explosion." It is simply that the number of people per family household has decreased. This is the well-known change from the so-called "extended" family structure, which included in the household nice maiden aunts, idiot children, lame old grandparents, and so forth, over to the so-called "nuclear" family structure, which includes only Dad, Mom, and the kids—the "family of procreation." Vast economic changes and consequent social changes purportedly brought this about: it is commonly shown by citing a hypothetical farm family with lots of room for all those relatives and lots of chores for them to do, as against an urban or suburban family in their cramped quarters with "modern conveniences" that do the little work there is to do. The geographical and social mobility required by changing occupational patterns also has contributed to diminishing of the sphere of influence of the family. Now the sick, the retarded, the aged, are for the most part segregated in specialized institutions or settings. Schools have taken over the children earlier and to a greater extent. *Work, play, and school send each individual out on his own; and if the family gets together at all, it is more likely to be for TV than for Sunday dinner. Years of "empty nest" sometimes precede and certainly follow the housebound years of small children. In one way or another, the family has been whittled down to fit. Isolated but mobile, flexible, tolerant, adjustable, anxious to conform to modern ways, the nuclear family seems ideally suited to the way we live now. Yet it seems not to be the whole solution. As everyone again knows: "One marriage in four . . ." Divorce is having such an effect on family structure that virtually as common nowadays as the model mother-father-child nuclear family is some lopsided mutation of it: either one parent too many, or one parent too few. And through divorce and remarriage and re-remarriage and such arrangements as "summer with Daddy's family" and "winter with Mommy and her new husband" and a bewildering variety of other accommodations and adjustments, the basic nuclear family may be growing again into quasi-kinship systems of half-brothers and stepparents and "divorce cousins" that greatly resemble the old extended family structure. This is especially true, of course, when money is not regarded as a problem in keeping such agglomerations going; among the working-class poor and the very rich who are either place-bound or place-based, large families and extensive family interrelationships are common anyway. As we will repeatedly specify, most of what this book has to say about how we live applies to those of us who are neither very rich nor very poor.*

The stories that follow have been arranged in an order that reflects this "history" of simultaneous contemporary American family forms. But it must be remembered that their intention, before they landed in this anthology, may have had nothing to do with family at all. They are stories, not treatises on family life. What they seem to us to offer, arranged in this way, is not so much a history as a spectrum of some of the ways we live in families now.

JOHN UPDIKE

The Family Meadow

◇◇◇◇◇◇◇

THE FAMILY always reconvenes in the meadow. For generations it has been traditional, this particular New Jersey meadow, with its great walnut tree making shade for the tables and its slow little creek where the children can push themselves about in a rowboat and nibble watercress and pretend to fish. Early this morning, Uncle Jesse came down from the stone house that his father's father's brother had built and drove the stakes, with their carefully tied rag flags, that would tell the cars where to park. The air was still, inert with the postdawn laziness that foretells the effort of a hot day, and between blows of his hammer Jesse heard the breakfast dishes clinking beneath the kitchen window and the younger collie barking behind the house. A mild man, Jesse moved scrupulously, mildly through the wet grass that he had scythed yesterday. The legs of his gray workman's pants slowly grew soaked with dew and milkweed spittle. When the stakes were planted, he walked out the lane with the REUNION signs, past the houses. He avoided looking at the houses, as if glancing into their wide dead windows would wake them.

By nine o'clock Henry has come up from Camden with a carful—Eva, Mary, Fritz, Fred, the twins, and, incredibly, Aunt Eula. It is incredible she is still alive, after seven strokes. Her shrivelled head munches irritably and her arms twitch, trying to shake off assistance, as if she intends to dance. They settle her in an aluminum chair beneath the walnut tree. She faces the creek, and the helpless waggle of her old skull seems to establish itself in sympathy with the oscillating shimmer of the sunlight on the slow water. The men, working in silent pairs whose unison is as profound as blood, carry down the tables from the barn, where they are stacked from one year to the next. In truth, it has been three summers since the last reunion, and it was feared that there might never be another. Aunt Jocelyn, her gray hair done up in braids, comes out of her kitchen to say hello on the dirt drive. Behind her lingers her granddaughter, Karen, in white Levis and bare feet, with something shadowy and doubtful about her dark eyes, as if she had been intensely watching television. The girl's father—not here; he is working in Philadelphia—is Italian, and as she matures an alien beauty estranges her, so that during her annual visits to her grandparents' place, which when she was a child had seemed to her a green island, it is now she herself, at thirteen, who seems the island. She feels surrounded by the past, cut off from the images—a luncheonette, a civic swimming pool, an auditorium festooned with crêpe paper—that represent life to her, the present, her youth. The air around her feels brown, as in old photographs. These men greeting her seem to have stepped from an album. The men, remembering their original prejudice against her mother's marrying a Catholic, are especially cordial to her, so jovially attentive that Jocelyn suddenly puts her arm around the girl, expressing a strange multitude of things; that she loves her, that she is one of them, that she needs to be shielded, suddenly, from the pronged kidding of men.

By ten-thirty Horace's crowd has come down from Trenton, and the Oranges clan is arriving, in several cars. The first car says it dropped Cousin Claude in downtown Burlington because he was sure that the second car, which had faded out of sight behind them, needed to be told the way. The second car, with a whoop of hilarity, says it took the bypass and never saw him. He arrives in a third car, driven by Jimmy and Ethel Thompson from Morristown, who say they saw this forlorn figure standing along Route 130 trying to thumb a ride and as they were passing him Ethel cried, "Why, I think that's Claude." Zealous and reckless, a true believer in good deeds, Claude is always getting into scrapes like this, and enjoying it. He stands surrounded by laughing women, a typical man of this family, tall, with a tribal boyishness, a stubborn refusal to look his age, to lose his hair. Though his face is pitted and gouged by melancholy, Claude looks closer to forty than the sixty he is, and, though he works in Newark, he still speaks with the rural softness and slide of middle New Jersey. He has the gift—the privilege—of making these women laugh; the women uniformly run to fat and their laughter has a sameness, a quality both naïve and merciless, as if laughter meant too much to them. Jimmy and Ethel Thompson, whose name is not the family name, stand off to one side, in the unscythed grass, a fragile elderly couple whose links to family have all died away but who come because they received a mimeographed postcard inviting them. They are like those isolated corners of interjections and foreign syllables in a poorly planned crossword puzzle.

The twins bring down from the barn the horseshoes and the quoits. Uncle Jesse drives the stakes and pegs in the places that, after three summers, still show as spots of depressed sparseness in the grass. The sun, reaching toward noon, domineers over the meadow; the shade of the walnut tree grows smaller and more noticeably cool. By noon, all have arrived, including the Dodge station wagon from central Pennsylvania, the young pregnant Wilmington cousin who married an airline pilot, and the White Plains people, who climb from their car looking like clowns, wearing red-striped shorts and rhinestone-studded sunglasses. Handshakes are exchanged that feel to one man like a knobbed wood carving and to the other like a cow's slippery, unresisting teat. Women kiss, kiss stickily, with little overlapping patches of adhesive cheek and clicking conflicts of spectacle rims, under the white unslanting sun. The very insects shrink toward the shade. The eating begins. Clams steam, corn steams, salad wilts, butter runs, hot dogs turn, torn chicken shines in the savage light. Iced tea, brewed in forty-quart milk cans, chuckles when sloshed. Paper plates buckle on broad laps. Plastic butter knives, asked to cut cold ham, refuse. Children underfoot in the pleased frenzy eat only potato chips. Somehow, as the first wave of appetite subsides, the long tables turn musical, and a murmur rises to the blank sky, a cackle rendered harmonious by a remote singleness of ancestor; a kind of fabric is woven and hung, a tapestry of the family fortunes, the threads of which include milkmen, ministers, mailmen, bankruptcy, death by war, death by automobile, insanity—a strangely prevalent thread, the thread of insanity. Never far from a farm or the memory of a farm, the family has hovered in honorable obscurity, between poverty and wealth, between jail and high office. Real-estate dealers, schoolteachers, veterinarians are its noblemen; butchers, electricians, door-to-door salesmen its yeomen. Protestant, teetotalling, and undaring, ironically virtuous and mildly proud, it has added to America's statistics without altering their meaning. Whence, then, this strange joy?

Watermelons smelling of childhood cellars are produced and massively sliced. The sun passes noon and the shadows relax in the intimate grass of this antique meadow. To the music of reminiscence is added the rhythmic chunking of thrown quoits. They are held curiously, between a straight thumb and four fingers curled as a unit, close to the chest, and thrown with a soft constrained motion that implies realms of unused strength. The twins and the children, as if superstitiously, have yielded the game to the older men, Fritz and Ed, Fred and Jesse, who, in pairs, after due estimation and measurement of the fall, pick up their four quoits, clink them together to clean them, and alternately send them back through the air on a high arc, floating with a spin-held slant like that of gyroscopes. The other pair measures, decides, and stoops. When they tap their quoits together, decades fall away. Even their competitive crowing has something measured about it, something patient, like the studied way their shirtsleeves are rolled up above their elbows. The backs of their shirts are ageless. Generations have sweated in just this style, under the arms, across the shoulder blades, and wherever the suspenders rub. The younger men and the teen-age girls play a softball game along the base paths that Jesse has scythed. The children discover the rowboat and, using the oars as poles, bump from bank to bank. When they dip their hands into the calm brown water, where no fish lives, a mother watching from beneath the walnut tree shrieks, "Keep your hands inside the boat! Uncle Jesse says the creek's polluted!"

And there is a stagnant fragrance the lengthening afternoon strains from the happy meadow. Aunt Eula nods herself asleep, and her false teeth slip down, so her face seems mummified and the children giggle in terror. Flies, an exploding population, discover the remains of the picnic and skate giddily on its odors. The softball game grows boring, except to the airline pilot, a rather fancy gloveman excited by the admiration of Cousin Karen in her tight white Levis. The Pennsylvania and New York people begin to pack their cars. The time has come for the photograph. Their history is kept by these photographs of timeless people in changing costumes standing linked and flushed in a moment of midsummer heat. All line up, from resurrected Aunt Eula, twitching and snapping like a mud turtle, to the unborn baby in the belly of the Delaware cousin. To get them all in, Jesse has to squat, but in doing so he brings the houses into his viewfinder. He does not want them in the picture, he does not want them there at all. They surround his meadow on three sides, raw ranch shacks built from one bastard design but painted in a patchwork of pastel shades. Their back yards, each nurturing an aluminum clothes tree, come right to the far bank of the creek, polluting it, and though a tall link fence holds back the children who have gathered in these yards to watch the picnic as if it were a circus or a zoo, the stare of the houses—mismatched kitchen windows squinting above the gaping cement mouth of a garage—cannot be held back. Not only do they stare, they speak, so that Jesse can hear them even at night. *Sell*, they say. *Sell*.

❖

John Updike was born in 1932 in Shillington, Pennsylvania, graduated from Harvard, and now lives in Ipswich, Massachusetts. He has published four novels, The Poorhouse Fair *(1959),* Rabbit, Run *(1960),* The Centaur *(1963), and* Of the Farm *(1965); two books of poetry,* The Carpentered Hen *(1958) and* Telephone Poles *(1963); a book of essays,* Assorted Prose *(1965); and three collections of short stories,* The Same Door *(1959),* Pigeon Feathers *(1962), and* The Music School *(1966). That is ten books in eight years, a considerable amount for a young man to have written. Yet none of his work is careless: it is in fact a criticism often, and of course unfairly, made of his work that it is somehow too polished, too "smooth." Because a great proportion of his work first appeared in* The New Yorker, *he is sometimes associated too with that magazine's reputed emphasis on style as being somehow more important than content in fiction. Again this is unfair, for Updike's stories, especially when read in collection, prove to have a great deal—cumulatively and individually—to tell us about how we live now. More than any other American writer he has exploited the methods James Joyce used in* Dubliners *and in his "epiphanies"; often in sketches and stories that may seem slight at first, Updike employs his brilliant style to make ordinary moments luminous and meaningful—moments of the sort that are experienced by us all, but rarely so fully realized or understood.*

In "The Family Meadow" Updike shows how anachronistic the extended family is and how frail its meaning has come to be. Most writers would develop such a theme in the form of a long family chronicle set in the West or Midwest, but Updike characteristically does it as a five-page sketch, describing only the events of one day in a meadow on the edge of megalopolis. This large family is no longer rural, no longer homogenous, no longer made feasible and useful by large areas of commonly held, communally farmed land. The family is scattered, now living mostly in cities and suburbs. As a consequence it is variegated: one member has married an airline pilot, another an Italian Roman Catholic who works in Philadelphia. They are estranged from one another: to the farmers the White Plains crowd seem like clowns in their suburban leisure wear; even handshakes feel strange. Thus, even in the midst of her family, a member of the youngest generation feels isolated from the images that compose her own life—a luncheonette, a civic swimming pool, and so on—as if she had made a leap backward in time: "The air around her feels brown, as in old photographs. These men greeting her seem to have stepped from an album." What has happened to this family is typical of what has happened in America, for the family "has added to America's statistics without altering their meaning." And Updike makes it clear that it is the continuing urbanization of America that has destroyed the viability of the land-based extended family. Jesse does not want the encroaching houses in his group photograph of the family; but they represent, as is said of the flies at the picnic, "an exploding population," and "the stare of the houses . . . cannot be held back."

GEORGE P. ELLIOTT

A Family Matter

◇◇◇◇◇◇◇

IN THE SUMMER of his thirty-fifth year Bryan Mott, second son of the inventor Gordon Mott, received the following letter from his father.

My dear Bryan,

Ever since Thelma's unhappy death this spring, I have had the growing feeling that her daughter Jessica (I believe I sent you a picture of her, a charming thing) not only does not need me but what is worse does not want me hanging around. In my day, and it is obviously my day no longer, a girl of twenty would have sought the wise counsel of a man like myself in a thousand concerns. There is no reason for her to think I lack wisdom, and I haven't bothered her much; yet everything I say bores her to death (the expression is hers). Now that she's home for the summer vacation I have been feeling superannuated, and besides I abominate the New York heat.

Therefore I have decided to renew my acquaintance with my sons, beginning with you.

According to the ticket I have before me, I shall arrive at the SP station in Oakland at 8:03 P.M. July 11. If I don't see you at the station I'll take a cab on out.

There's a lot more to say, but since I'll be seeing you so soon I won't bother to write it down.

The check enclosed is to cover any extra expenses you may run on my account. I don't eat much but I do cause a lot of trouble. Which Martha will bear the brunt of, so I've made it out to her.

Give my best to her and the children. I hope she is a little mellowed by having had children. A psychoanalyst told me once —I've tried everything, mineral water, body-building, psycho-analysis—that the reason I've had so many wives was that I was seeking a mother-substitute. Which may be so, and if it is then Martha as she was when you first married her is not the one for me. Charming, intelligent, companionable, but how unmaternal.

I look forward to getting to know your children—and you too.

Gordon

That flippancy about the psychoanalyst sounds worse than I meant it to sound. I never really went to one; he was just a friend of Diana's. There's nothing more the matter with me than there is with anyone else. It's New York. A dreadful atmosphere.

The letter arrived on a Monday morning, ten days before the eleventh. Aylmer fetched the mail to his mother, who was in the midst of washing clothes. At her prolonged wail Bryan came running out of his writing room to see what had happened, and Roxana sang out from her sand pile, "What's the matter, Mommy?"

"I won't be able to write a word while he's here," Bryan groaned.

"He's your father," said Martha darkly.

"Grampa Gordon?" asked Aylmer.

"Yes dear," his mother answered, "Grampa Gordon. Go out and play with Zan."

"And stay out," said Bryan.

"Oh why couldn't this letter have come at any other time?" said Martha belligerently, but not exactly to Bryan.

"Because there was no other time."

"I suppose so."

"Of course," Bryan continued, "it might have arrived the afternoon of the eleventh. Then I could at least have written for the next ten days."

"Oh come on, you sensitive plant. You haven't lived in the same city with your father since you were ten."

"Twelve. But it's the childhood experiences that leave their deepest impress on the soul."

"Carry out this basket of wet clothes, and then go back to your room and do something about it. He's *your* father."

"Laundering seems to dull your razorlike wit, my love."

"Daddy," said Roxana at the back door, "is Grampa going to sleep in the cellar?"

At which there was another wail from Martha. "Where is he going to sleep?"

And Bryan ducked back to his room, where he tried to pick up the thread of his thought—he was translating Racine—but failed. He sighed, but to maintain his honor he stayed in his room till lunchtime reading a novel.

For lunch there were peanut butter sandwiches and raw carrots. Bryan did not object in words but he created a ruckus by putting jam on his peanut butter. The children were not allowed jam except on state occasions —their teeth.

"I suppose," said Martha, "your father will wreck what little discipline you let me keep over the children. The old goat. He probably wouldn't give them a second glance if he didn't think I'd mind."

"The size of the pitcher, my love, has nothing to do with the size of the ear. Caution."

"Do you have to be so coy, Bryan? After all . . ."

"My maternal little wife," said Bryan patting her behind as she poured the milk, "I think Gordon will find you as maternal as he could wish."

"And that's another thing," said Martha whirling so vigorously that she kicked the table and knocked Roxana's milk over. "I never read such an insulting letter in my life. If you suppose," she continued, while mopping up Roxana and the floor, "that I'm going to coddle a white-haired, broken-down old roué, you're thicker than even I thought."

"Well," said Bryan, "where is he going to sleep?"

"He paid *me* to worry about it, darling. So go back to *Phèdre* and don't fret your poetic soul about such mundane matters."

"You're pretty snippy for a person who opens other people's letters."

"Bryan, really, it was from your father."

"All I have to say is—he does not sleep in my writing room."

He marched out, his pennon ragged but flying.

Racine could not hold his attention, and by two he had finished the novel. He was working on the composition of a literary crossword puzzle— he had had a number published under another name—when the door opened to Martha.

"I know you can't be working, darling," she began, but hesitated when she saw him hunched over his desk. "You could help me, couldn't you?"

He leaned back in his chair but did not turn to face her.

" '*Un dieu vengeur te suit, tu ne peux l'éviter.*
Je t'aimais; et je sens que malgré ton offense
Mes entrailles pour toi se troublent par avance.' "

"I'm sorry," she said. "I'll take the children down shopping."

His problem was to find a nine-letter name whose first two letters were SH and whose seventh was W. There was none so he made a name up, Shaddower in this case: "That the sun may not shine in broad day" or "Shamus."

When Justin Mott, the third son, returned from work his wife handed him the following letter and told him the peas were nearly cooked. He read it fast.

My dear Justin,

I have before me a ticket which says I am to arrive in Oak-land on July 11 at 8:03 P.M. I bought this ticket because I am getting old and want to see my sons. The truth is no one needs me in New York. Oakland is home.

I know from Charlene's most daughterly letters that you have an extra room for me. I shan't be more trouble than Charlene can bear, I hope, and I can't tell you how much I want to make the acquaintance of all three of you. Imagine, I have never seen my most beautiful grandson! How fortunate you are in your wife, Justin. Do with her better than I did with your mother. I hope Diana's well. Give Charlene a kiss for me. I haven't seen her since your wedding. Or you either, my dear son.

Your father

"What did he have to say, honey?" asked Charlene as she was taking off her apron.

"Here, baby, get into your high chair," said Justin picking up Michael.

Michael was well into his second year and not nearly so helpless as his parents supposed. As it was, picked up and stuffed into his high chair, he found it engaging to kick up the tray and poke one foot out through the side. There was more to put down in Michael than there was zeal in his parents for putting it down; they were young too.

"My, smoked pork chops and peas. What could be better? What do you get, baby? Scraped liver and spinach as usual?"

"And he loves it. What did your father say in his letter?"

"Let's not talk about disagreeable subjects while we eat."

"He said he was coming out here to visit."

"Yes."

"Glube blg wawa ffrts cheese," said Michael.

"You see, he wants cheese," said Justin.

"It just means he's feeling good."

"You won't even give my son cheese when he wants it."

"Yackety yackety. Get the cheese yourself if you want to."

He went to the icebox and got a piece of cheddar. Michael dunked the cheddar in his spinach and threw it onto the floor. Justin ungraciously mopped up.

"He's getting old and wants to see his sons," said Charlene as she picked a bone.

"So he says," answered Justin with a malevolent glance.

"Oakland is his real home now. No one needs him in New York."

"Look, you've read the letter. Let's not talk about it."

"I did not. When did I have a chance?"

"How do I know? While I was fussing with Mickey."

"But the letter's in your pocket."

"Well, maybe you steamed it open and resealed it."

But Charlene had burst into tears, and Michael was starting up slowly but ominously, like a fire siren.

Charlene was thought by some of her friends to be psychic; how else could she win at bridge so often? But Justin was a businessman.

"You don't believe me," she sobbed.

"I'm sorry, honey," he said with irritation as he bent over her, hugging her shoulders with one hand and tickling Michael's stomach with the other. "So you didn't read the letter. I still don't see . . ."

"I wouldn't dream of steaming open a letter."

"Well, I guess it's just a woman's intuition," he said.

"Thassawrai, thassawrai. Mama, mama."

His parents turned on him like heliotropes.

"Did you hear that?"

"He said 'That's all right.' "

"Cheese, cheese, cheese, cheese."

Michael crowed. His parents embraced.

"I'm sorry, baby," said Justin to his wife. "Here, read it, I'm sorry."

"It's just that you were so rough," she said. She disclaimed any pride in being psychic, but only did what she was prompted to do in these matters. "Well, I think it's sweet of your father to just come like this. Real family-like. Do you suppose he'll mind if I call him Gordon?"

"I don't suppose he'll mind if you call him Gordon."

"Are you being sarcastic, Justin?"

"Only irritated. Why should he mind?"

"I don't know. I just remember him as a very courtly old man. Sort of like a nobleman. An earl say."

Justin did not respond; he was mustering his miscellaneous knowledge of his father so that he might demolish in an orderly and accurate fashion this picture of him as an earl.

"We ought to get an innerspring mattress for the guest bed and a new rug for the guest room. I saw a bargain in rugs just yesterday."

"We ought not. It's a good bed and a good enough rug. Your mother didn't complain of them when she stayed with us when Michael was born."

"Oh, mother. But we don't know how long your father is going to be with us. He didn't say. Maybe he even wants to settle down with us for the rest of his life."

"Oh no, oh no," said Justin, at first with the inflection of determination and then with that of horror. "Oh no, oh no, no, no."

"Why not? He has no one to take care of him."

"I don't know why not. Just not. He has three sons and two living wives. Why should he stay with us?"

"I like him."

"I don't."

"Justin!"

"He may stay here a couple of weeks, a month even. Then he goes to visit Roscoe or Bryan."

"I don't think Mickey will like firecrackers."

"And why not? He's a boy isn't he?"

"A baby boy. I was thinking, we ought to get Nancy to stay with him Thursday evening."

"Why Nancy? Is she sound absorbent?"

"We're going to Roscoe's on Thursday, to watch the fireworks over Lake Merritt. Can't you even remember your own family?"

"Oh yes . . . Mickey is my son. He can stand a little noise."

"I don't think so," she said lightly. Scowl darkened Justin's face. Seeing this little victory she added, "You frightened him, honey."

With the slightest readjustment of muscles his scowl became an anxious frown.

"I don't know how it is, but I manage a factory with a hundred and fifty men in it with less trouble than I manage you. In fact, I don't manage you at all. You always make me feel in the wrong."

She suppressed a very quiet smile and patted him on the arm.

"Tell me what happened today, dear," she said. "It's harder to manage a hundred and fifty than one."

Justin, not perceiving the fallacy in this proposition, brightened and gave her an account of his day as he always did. He did not yet know that she was not interested in his factory life; indeed she did not yet know it herself. She would respond to his statements with an occasional polite yes and is that so and really, but her eyes were not in harmony with her voice. He thought it was her way, and talked on.

Roscoe Mott, the eldest son, received no such letter from his father. Roscoe was forty, spare, and slightly dandyish. He was in the habit of watching an interlocutor with the air of one who seeks confirmation of his opinion of himself. This opinion fluctuated on the scale of pride rather extremely, and did not always receive confirmation. His wife, for example, did not give it him promiscuously.

"Roscoe," she said somewhat thickly for she had toothpicks between her lips, "do we have enough seltzer?"

"Hrmph," he answered from the dining room. He was ranging through the house with hostly eye alert that he might rectify error.

"You know you should see to it," she said as she rolled another delicacy in a strip of bacon.

"I am sure we have enough, Edwa."

"The last three Fourths we ran out of seltzer," she said as she speared the bacon. "And we ran out when the Tollertons dropped by. You always say you'll take care of the drinks but just look . . ."

"All right, I'll get it, all right."

"You might as well get John to go."

"All right. John!" There was no response. "I suppose he's around, Edwa? John!"

"There's no use shouting. He went down to the lake to watch them set up the stage for the fireworks."

"You might have told me. I suppose Henry has a date as usual?"

"Oh Roscoe, how can you talk so harshly about him? This may be the last summer he'll be with us. Who knows when he will love us so much again?"

"Hrmph."

"Well as long as you're going, dear, you might just as well get another package of cocktail napkins. There are so many of us."

"Yes, yes, yes. That's all?" He put on his hat, an exact, gray homburg.

"Don't forget, everybody takes seltzer but Martha."

Yet it had been the napkins she had wanted, and that had suggested sending him out in the first place.

As he left, he met Bryan and his family arriving, and by the time he had returned, Justin and Charlene had installed Michael in the baby bed upstairs. There was scarcely time for a highball before dinner was ready.

"We must hurry with dinner," he said serving. "It'll soon be time for the fireworks."

"The children won't want to miss them," said Edwa.

"If the children are the ones who won't want to miss them," said Martha, "then why must we bolt our food?"

"Honey," said Charlene to Justin before Edwa could have responded had she wished to, "do you suppose we ought to go home and get baby's cod liver oil?"

"Can't you give it to him tomorrow morning?"

"Yes."

"Then don't worry."

"And powder his bottom and button his sleepers," said Bryan in a crooning voice to Charlene beside him, "tuck him in tight and kiss him and tell him you love him, leave the door open just a crack and sing him good night."

She looked at him sentimentally, put her hand on his arm, and said, "You and Martha ought to have another baby."

"Ah, but it's not as simple as all that."

"It should be, for you. Really."

Bryan watched her a moment.

And Martha and Edwa were both watching him watch her, though he didn't notice it. Bryan had so many internal eyes, some like Edwa's and more like Martha's, scrutinizing him day and night that he paid very little attention to watchful eyes outside himself. Which accounted, among other things, for his attire as of a workingman at a ball game, in contrast to Roscoe's gray flannels and Justin's soft, expensive, sporty clothes.

"You know," said Bryan remembering Roscoe's injunction to hurry, "here we are, the assembled sons of Gordon." He held forth his glass of wine and drained it as though drinking a toast. "Sons of the famous Mott. True, Roscoe is known in the best real estate circles of the Bay Area, and I am known to critics and editors of literary magazines, and Justin is making his mark in the realm of tubes and condensers and frequency modulation. But essentially we are the three who are identified at a party, should someone want to know, as the sons of Gordon Mott. That at least we have in common, the shuddering loin."

He paused to pour himself another glass of wine and drink it. During the interval Martha said, "Pass the beets please," and Edwa urged Justin to have some more cold tongue. Bryan went on.

"He has set us an example which we have not followed, encumbered as we are by charming and devoted wives." He saluted each; only Charlene liked it. "Yet I propose that each of us, since we are not apt to act on our impulses as splendidly as he has done, tell a love story on occasions of our forgathering like this."

"Really Bryan," said his wife.

"I hardly think we have time now," said Roscoe.

"You are the senior brother," said Bryan. "Why don't you start off?"

"No," said Charlene before Roscoe could object, "you must start. You thought of it and anyway you have one to tell or you wouldn't have brought the subject up."

"That's true," Bryan said, "that's perfectly true. I am seen through." Martha snorted and Edwa stirred in her chair. "Very well, my story. I was down in the book section of the Good Will store one day. You know, down on Broadway and 5th or 6th."

"We know," said Martha.

"I was just looking around rather aimlessly, at Winston Churchill and F. Marion Crawford and Somebody Canfield. I noticed, only because she was in my way, a young woman also looking at books. She was perfectly unnoteworthy, perfectly. Hair-colored hair and eye-colored eyes and clothes that were a perfection of the ordinary. I doubt if I would recognize her again. She had good wrists though, very delicate and supple, only with listless, chapped hands."

"It takes a queen," said Charlene, "to look like anything in the Good Will."

"Yes, yes, that's it. That's what I was trying to get at," he said turning to her and addressing the rest of his story to her. "Nothing was happening when presently a young man, her gray counterpart, walked in and came up to her. She started a little when he touched her shoulder. 'Peter!' she said. 'How did you know I was here?' He smiled at her with a tenderness I cannot describe. His ordinary face suddenly shone with a love so little ordinary, so pure and true, that I held my breath to hear what he would reply. Her face reflected some of his radiance, very quietly. They had halos. You understand, they were not touching each other at all. He stooped a little, and she still held a copy of some novel or other. They just looked into each other's eyes, smiling a little, aware of me and indifferent to my presence as though I had been another book. There was only a moment of this before he replied: 'How do I know my foot is in my shoe?' That was all the answer she needed. They walked out with little fingers linked, not talking, as ordinary as ever, and I have never forgotten them."

Bryan looked about the table commandingly; there was to be a moment of respectful, not to say reverent, contemplation following this apologue.

Charlene seemed sunk deepest of all, chin in hand, eyes in nether space, when dreamily she said, "How did you remember his name was Peter?"

"What difference does it make?" he snapped.

The sound of jaws in motion returned to the room.

"Well how?"

"Who cares what his real name was?"

"If you don't even know his real name how do we know it was a real story?"

"Reality is of the essence, not the detail," he said intending to silence her and nearly succeeding.

"I don't see," Martha put in, "anything so wonderful about what he said. Anybody knows where his foot is."

"How stupid can you get?" said Bryan wrathfully to Martha.

"It was really a very sweet story," said Charlene to him sweetly, making amends.

"Thank you, my dear, for those few kind words.—Come on, Justin, you must have one to tell."

"I don't want to."

"Honey," said Charlene.

"Well, all right. I'm no good at it, but the PBX operator down at the plant fell in love with the stationary engineer. He used to flirt with her, and he flirted too much. Well, he took her out a couple of times and when she found out he was married she ran off to Reno with the truck driver in the company pickup. He'd been in love with her for months but he had a birthmark on his neck."

"Not a bad situation," said Bryan.

"I think it's too bad for the truck driver," said Edwa.

"Justin," said Charlene gazing at him intently, "you never told me this story. When did it happen?"

"Last month, and I told you." His eyes opened wider. "At dinner once."

"There should be at least one more complication," said Bryan. "Pregnancy, relationship, threat, misunderstanding, something."

"I like it," said Martha, "just as it is."

"I forgot to say," said Justin wrenching his eyes from Charlene, "the truck driver is the brother of the engineer's wife."

"Ah, now we're getting some place," said Bryan.

"Really, honey," said Charlene, her eyes on the table, "I don't remember."

"You said at the time what a terrible way to get married it was."

"I must have been thinking of baby at the time you told it."

But she didn't believe herself, and no one else, who was paying any real attention, believed her either. Martha perceived that Justin and Charlene were making some unhappy discovery about themselves; therefore, having a profound trust in decorum as the lubricant of life, she began clearing table, to create stir and bustle that would restore the young couple to their social selves.

"No story, Roscoe?" said Bryan.

"Well, you know," said Roscoe with a condescending smile, "there's hardly time."

"Roscoe," said Bryan not without malice, "you looked remarkably like Gordon just then—the way you took out your watch and peered down your nose at it."

"Hrmph," said Roscoe, who viewed his character as being essentially an inversion of his father's.

"Gordon, Gordon, Gordon," said Edwa as she poured cream over her pudding. "Why all this talk about Gordon, Bryan? If you've mentioned him once you've mentioned him a dozen times."

"Bryan wants to see him," said Charlene in her automatic way.

"Come, my little oracle," he said as though she were dear to him but weak in the head, "wants to or expects to?"

"Wants to," she said defiantly.

"Maybe she's right," said Bryan to himself, only aloud, "maybe that's what I really want. She's an odd one.—My sweet, my pure, my apple-cheeked Cassandra, can you tell me why . . ."

"Justin!" she cried out. "You can't just sit there and let him insult me, even if he is your brother."

"Oh Charlene," said Justin.

"What in the world!" said Bryan.

Martha was gagging her laughter with her napkin.

"I won't sit by him another minute." Charlene got up, pudding in hand, and made a place for herself beside Justin. Once there she pressed his foot with hers, and whispered to him how horrible Bryan was, and paid no attention to Bryan's rather stiff-necked explanation of himself.

So love filled up the gap that Justin had found, and after that Charlene would not ask him much about his day at the plant and he would volunteer her very little; and there would be less to talk about when he came home from work, so they would talk even more about Michael.

Roscoe, who had gathered from Charlene's shift that some sort of re-alignment was going on, turned to Bryan with a rather stately motion and said, "What have you heard from father recently?"

"He's coming to visit us next week."

"What!" said Charlene, Edwa, Roscoe, Justin.

"I got a letter a few days ago saying he was coming for a visit the eleventh. Is there anything so remarkable about that?"

"Who was he going to stay with?" asked Justin.

"I said I got the letter."

"He's going to stay with you?"

"For pity's sake, yes. What is there . . ."

"I got the same letter," said Justin, "only he said he was going to stay with us."

"What!" said Martha, Edwa, Roscoe, Bryan.

"Why," said Edwa in slow astonishment, "he did not write us a letter."

"It's a doubtful honor either way," said Bryan.

"But I write to him at least twice a year," said Edwa, who was not much interested in honor.

Two letters a year were as many as were written to Gordon by all the others in the room combined; they were silent.

"How very thoughtless of him," she said, and meant at least that.

There was a great *crack* outdoors, and the dark sky flashed bluish-white.

"The fireworks!" said Edwa.

"The children won't want to miss them," said Roscoe.

But the kitchen was empty.

"They must be up on the roof of the apartment house down the street," said Edwa. "Let's go down."

"I'd better stay with baby, hadn't I, honey?" said Charlene to Justin, her hands on his shoulders.

It rose to his lips to say he was going with the others, but he hugged her instead and said, "Sure, honey, I'll wait with you. We can watch from here."

The fireworks were a great success with the children. It was eleven before the families had reassembled themselves at Roscoe's. Bryan had been unable to interest anyone in talking about Gordon's letters; he felt even a little snubbed. He had decided to go over to see Charlene the next afternoon, ostensibly to talk about the letters, really to make friends with her again. But he changed his mind; as everyone was saying their good nights she ducked into her car before he could kiss her on both cheeks as he always had done before. He kissed Edwa, instead, as he seldom did; she patted him as if he were a child, and sent him home.

The children were all in bed, and Roscoe was lying in bed watching Edwa work on her hair.

"On days like this," he said, "I'm thankful that all our family live in Oakland."

"Your head doesn't ache?" she said through her hairpins. It usually ached after family gatherings.

"No, not a bit. Fine young woman, Charlene."

"Mommy!" Mary called out.

"Not asleep!" said Edwa to Roscoe. "What, dear?" she said to Mary at the door of the girls' room; she was still fixing her hair.

"Roxana said that's how it would be at the end of the world, Mommy."

"Well, we'll never see it, honey. Go to sleep."

"She said it might happen any old day now."

"Oh no, it won't. She's wrong."

"She said so. She said she read it in a book."

"She was teasing, honey. Go to sleep."

"How do you know it won't?"

"God wouldn't let it happen."

"Oh."

"Sometimes," said Roscoe when she had returned, "I wish we didn't have to tell the children so many lies."

"What lies? I never tell them lies."

"Oh well, whatever you want to call it. The world may end any day you know. Stars do explode."

"Nonsense," said Edwa turning out the light, "that's a Mottish idea."

She got into bed and told him good-night, and she was sound asleep before he had finally adjusted his pillow.

2

"Well my boy," said Gordon, "you seem to lead a very agreeable life."

Martha was just joining them, having put the children to bed. They were sitting about the fireplace, in which there was a small fire that was warming the darkness more than any chill in the air. Bryan disliked the thought of building a fire, but when it was actually burning he could stupefy himself gazing into the flames and afterward the embers dying down.

"We like it," he answered noncommittally.

"The children like it," said Martha positively.

"Indeed, indeed. Well they should. Tell me, Bryan, what are you working on these days? I've only seen that one book of poems you published some years back."

"Four years ago. Only individual verses since then, in magazines, a few in anthologies. I'm working on a translation of Racine at the moment."

"Racine!"

"I've done most of *Phèdre* and half of *Andromaque*. It goes rather slowly."

"I've always gathered somehow that Racine was untranslatable."

"Have you? That's a rather old-fashioned notion, like the one that *Lear* won't go on stage."

"It's a very strong impression all the same."

"Have you ever read Racine in French?"

"Yes."

"Oh. Well, do you see any reason why he can't be translated like any other great poet?"

"Yes. It sounds like prose in English."

"You're a scientist," said Bryan with a levity that was yet not far from surliness.

"The thing is," said Martha, who was darning socks, "that Bryan likes challenges. Racine is supposed to be untranslatable; Bryan sets about translating him. He tries his hand at a novel; it turns out to be too short for a book and too long for a magazine. He starts a poetic play full of fine speeches, but he's never been backstage and he won't go because he can't stand little-theater characters; the play is unactable. His stories almost always have some shocking passage or idea in them; therefore they're published, if at all, only in magazines no one ever heard of, with names like *Stormy Petrel* or *K* or *Tangent* or *South Dakota Quarterly Review*."

"It sounds," said Gordon, "as though he were ducking out from under."

"That's our Bryan," said Martha. She got up and kissed him on the back of the neck, but he was staring into the fire.

"Yet his poetry suffers from none of these complaints that I can see."

"Yes, but being a poet is rather like being a bird watcher; what competition there is comes from other bird watchers, and they are really doing it for its own sake, and no one else takes it seriously at all. Still it's respectable and everyone knows about it, and most people have even looked at poems a few times."

"Usually in zoos."

"He can be more serious about writing poetry since it's a less serious occupation."

"I understand that perfectly," said Gordon. "I work much better on something that has no apparent utility than on, say, a problem in electronics."

"You do," said Bryan heavily, "you do, eh?—You," he said at Martha, "have said too much too soon and too fast. Even if what you said were true, as it is not, even so you should not have said it. At least, not like that."

"Why, darling . . ." she began.

"What was wrong with what she said?" said Gordon.

"What she left out."

"Which was?"

"The world. Would you rather have sherry or port, Gordon? The sherry is better."

"Sherry."

"Sherry for you," he said to her. He stood up with a bitter expression on his mouth, glanced at each of them a moment, and went for the sherry.

"Well," said Gordon, "I hope he doesn't put poison in the wine."

"Come."

"Come what?"

"We don't keep poison in the kitchen."

"Good. Perhaps we oughtn't to be so harsh on him."

"It was very wrong of me to have said all that."

There was a little stillness between them.

"I must make it up to him," said Martha.

"How?"

"How? What a question. I haven't thought about it."

"I ask because my wives were always threatening to make it up to me for something atrocious they'd done."

"Didn't they ever do it?"

"Sometimes they would get me all involved in a project I had no interest in, such as a family picnic with some brothers and sisters of theirs. That's as close as they ever got to it, as I remember."

"You were poor at picking wives I should say."

"I must exempt Thelma from this condemnation." Bryan entered. "You remember Thelma, Bryan?"

"We met her only once. What about her?"

"I was just extolling one of her many virtues to Martha. She could choose with consummate tact precisely what would please me."

"It's a pity she died. No one else can."

The conversation came to a brief pause, which was filled with the whicker of blades.

"That was unnecessary of me," said Bryan.

"Worse than that," said Martha.

"Well, well," said Gordon. "Perhaps the air is clearer now."

"Tell me," said Bryan, "what sort of a person was Thelma? I'd the impression she flowed with kindness rather than love."

"True. If we bore each other any love it was of a very pacific variety. She combined all the virtues of a nurse and a mistress, and I, I flatter myself, the best qualities of a patient and lover."

"But you are never sick," Martha exclaimed.

"Exactly. I was never sick. What better attribute can a patient have? And I was usually not around, which is a primary virtue in any lover."

"You talk of her so coolly," she said, "and here she's been dead only a few months. You really didn't love her, did you?"

"Pacifically. But the dead are so dead."

"I'm sleepy," said Bryan.

"Perhaps," said Martha, "we ought to clear up this misunderstanding about Justin and Charlene before Gordon goes to bed."

"There is no misunderstanding," said Bryan to her. "He knew what he was doing."

"I envy you two the openness of your warfare," said Gordon.

"Surely, Father, we could learn from you some of the subtleties of marital discord."

"Not at all, not at all. I was always, nearly always, courteous to my wives, but I used to murder them on an average of three times a month. That is not subtle."

"No," said Bryan.

"You mean," said Martha sharply, "in fancy."

"Well, there is a distinction," said Gordon, "though not, I am told, in the eyes of God."

"Bryan, you never had such an impulse, did you?" his wife asked.

"My dear, only the laws of the land have kept you from being an angel lo these many years."

"Motts," she said to her darning.

"You make it sound like an ugly little epithet," said Bryan.

"It was so intended."

"Your mother, Bryan, used to say Motts somewhat like that, only with heavier scorn. Maureen was cruder than you," he said addressing himself to Martha, "but a fine, high-spirited creature of the purest blood."

"I am not unacquainted with her," said Martha coolly.

"Ah, so you are, so you are. I find it difficult to remember that what is so totally past to me may have a living present of its own."

"Try it all the same."

"I will, I will indeed. And how is she now?"

"Mother seems contented enough with the man she lives with. Her second husband died a few years ago, you know."

"No, I didn't. Where is she living, Bryan?"

"Up in the Mother Lode country, in a little town named Poulterville."

"Tell me, does she still have, well, a physical life?"

"It was not ectoplasm that threw its arms about me last fall and called me her sweetest mistake."

"That last," said Martha, "was gratuitous of you."

"Oh," said Gordon, "that is exactly what he is. But what I meant by physical was, sexual."

"I am sure, Father . . ."

"No," said Martha, "she does not."

"It was perhaps indelicate of me to ask," said Gordon with a sigh.

"To ask me, yes," said Bryan.

"Well, well, no harm done."

"What's the matter?" asked Martha. "Past not past enough?"

"Oh it's dead now, but it kicked so when it was alive. She's not poor?"

"Not particularly. Tell me, what did she mean, I am a mistake?"

"Not what your low leer implies, son."

"Crude for a Mott," said Martha to Bryan, who was chagrined.

"Well, what did she mean and what do you mean?"

"I meant Maureen is, or was then, one of those who believe that the beautiful sentiment precedes the beautiful itch. With me her passion was handsome indeed, and by reverse logic she deduced that she must have loved me too. You were born before she discovered she didn't. The troubles we had while she was finding it out."

"So. I am the fruit of lust and hate."

"No!" cried Martha.

"Indeed not," said Gordon lightly. "Our desire was very great and very satisfied, and we were fond of each other. But the fondness she felt for me, when she came actually to look at it, seemed a pea beside the melon she had expected. A rather dry, yellowish pea at that."

"She does not speak of you bitterly," said Martha.

"I'm glad of that. A little regret perhaps?"

"Perhaps."

"I wish, Gordon, that you had not told me this in front of Martha."

"Husband and wife should have no secret one from the other," said his father.

"Huh," said Bryan, and left the room without saying good-night.

"You must promise me, Martha, not to use this against him."

"I will not."

"Use it?"

"Promise. I view Bryan in the only way a wife can view a husband tainted with genius—simple and dangerous and not quite explainable. A slightly divine fool."

"That's a very inaccurate description of him. He may be foolish sometimes, but a fool he is not."

"No, no, I mean fool in the old sense."

"A fool in the old sense he is not. From the way you said that I would guess that you read that about a slightly divine fool in some essay. Somebody like Chesterton, flashy and wrong most of the time."

"I did not!" she cried with great vigor because what he had said was true.

"If I were to use any such word for Bryan, I would say he was artless. And I wouldn't trust his artlessness very far either."

"Artless." She was still rallying.

"Yes. He assumes that everyone is going to like him, which is artless enough. Of course you know him better than I."

"Well, whatever you call it I don't know what I would do if I couldn't laugh at him once in a while."

"Yet you seem fond of him."

"Yet!" She stopped putting her darning away to glare at him a moment.

"Well, well, my dear. It seems you will stay married a while yet."

"Of which I am thankful and proud."

"But the time will come, my dear—I hope unfaithfulness is not one of your bugbears."

"We move faster nowadays," she said. "But then, I am not so indiscreet as you." And she left him these shards of meaning to piece together if he would. At most, he discovered, they would not construct a whole sense.

By the time Martha had seen that the children were tucked in and had turned out the hall light Bryan was in bed with his face to the wall.

"Darling," she said affectionately as she took off her stockings.

He rolled over and looked at her.

"I'm terribly sorry I hurt your feelings."

"Echch," he said, like a cat whose tail has been stepped on, and rolled back.

"Oh dear, now I've done it again."

She undressed in silence. As she began her nightly toilet she said in a musing tone, "Gordon seems to have an effect on both of us."

At which Bryan began a grunt that became a roar, and she said no more.

She got into bed and patted his arm and kissed the back of his neck; he did not respond. When she turned over to sleep she pressed her bottom to his; she wriggled it once in a friendly way and then again. The third time she did it he rolled over and hugged her and bit her ear rather hard; she said nothing, but turned her face to him. He kissed her, and very soon went to sleep, with his arm over her body and her scent in his nostrils most comfortably.

"My dear," said Gordon as Charlene brought tea in to the three men, "marriage and maternity are turning you into a beautiful woman."

"Thank you," she said not blushing. "How do you take your tea, Father?"

"Medium strong and, I hope, straight. What kind is it?"

"Oolong with a little Darjeeling."

"Perfect. You could not have pleased me more."

This time she did blush a little.

"Why do you wear that frock?" Gordon continued. "It's false-naïve for you, my dear."

"Why, it's sort of gay and young. Justin thought it set my figure off well. Didn't you, honey?"

"I like it," Justin said.

Charlene, without asking him, put two spoonfuls of sugar in Bryan's cup of tea and passed it to him with a knowing smile. He did not reach out for it.

"Charlene," he said mournfully, "it's Roscoe that likes sugar. I take lemon."

"Oh!" she said with dismay, but not much of it. "Really, Bryan, it's the only way I ever get you mixed up with Roscoe."

"It means something," said Bryan shaking his head. "I don't know what, but it must mean something. A dove was seen to fall lifeless before the Statue of Mars yesterday. Signs of an evil age."

"Oh Bryan baby," she said hugging his head and winking at Gordon over it, "I'll never do it again, I promise. Forgive me?"

"This once," he said with more lightness in his voice than in his eyes.

"You are too beautiful," said Gordon, "to hug your male relative."

"That for you," she said snapping her fingers under his nose. "Cream and sugar, honey?"

"Please," said Justin. "I'm going to bring Michael in."

"Oh, honey, not while we're having tea—please not."

"In his playpen, Sharly?"

"Oh that's all right." She turned to Gordon. "The other day he looked so wise and solemn for a minute, Father, just like you. I'm so glad you're getting to know him now when he's still nothing but pure candy."

"Wise," said Gordon reflectively. "Wise. That's it, Charlene. In another five or six years your figure will be mature and your face will be wiser. What a pity that all the bloom will be rubbed off by then. It's impossible to be pretty and wise at once, and wise is better."

"I would say," said Bryan, "that your present loveliness, Charlene, is its own reward. I do not need to wait five years to love you dearly."

"I would say," said Justin bearing Michael—he was cut off by a biff on the nose with a pan. "I would say," he recommenced a little truculently, "that she's mine to love now and she'll be mine to love five years from now and I hope she'll be mine to love fifty years from now when she's wrinkled and cranky."

Charlene beamed at his sentiment and smiled at the crudeness of its expression and ran over to hug Michael, who biffed her too. It was a good noisy pan.

"Pure candy, eh, Charlene?" said Bryan as diversionary. Being a poet he could not easily separate a sentiment from its expression, indeed it went against his grain even to try; besides, this particular sentiment at this particular time annoyed him.

"Well," she said nursing her bruise, "after all you expect little boys to be rough."

"Certainly," said Justin as he swung Michael by the feet in a great arc. "If they're not rough enough you make them rough. Rough and tough."

He hurled Michael through the air onto the davenport; for a moment the baby's eyes were huge and scared, but then they crinkled and he squealed with pleasure, demanding more.

"Very well, Justin," said Gordon, "you have now displayed yourself as a he-man with mate and male young. That, however . . ."

"And," said Justin loudly—he was irked at the ringing din of these pellets on his armor—"more coming."

"Really, my dear?" said Gordon to Charlene.

"Oh Justin," she said reddening.

"How soon, Sharly?" said Bryan, though that name for her was Justin's special right.

"It may just be a false alarm," she said. "Seven months."

"No false alarm," said Justin. "Three boys and a girl, that's what we're going to have."

He was putting Michael through some more calisthenics of an inuring sort. His face was stern, his motions were bold, and his hands on the baby were firm and gentle as any healer's—though he would not have agreed to this had he been asked.

"All that," said Gordon, "has nothing to do with Charlene's beauty. Which, as I said, is the sort that improves with age, acquaintance, and experience."

"Is that so?" said Justin where "Oh?" would have been enough.

"I think it is."

"I mean, you're only talking about the sort of beauty that hasn't got anything to do with love, just admiration. What really counts is the beauty seen with loving eyes. That hasn't got anything to do with wrinkles and bloom and all that."

"But I see her," said Bryan, "with the eyes of love. And though I love her dearly, I love her none the less for being young and beautiful."

"As long as you put that 'dearly' on," said Justin as he turned to Michael, finished with the conversation.

"I am fortunate in my daughter-in-law. I wonder if my son deserves her."

"Of course he does," said Charlene, who was pouring tea where none was wanted.

"Do you not find this conversation flattering?" asked Gordon.

"Yes. Flattering."

"Touché," said Bryan to his father.

"Touché."

"You are going to stay a week apiece with all three of us?" said Charlene.

"Why," said Gordon taken aback a little, "that was my intention."

"You're going to settle down for the rest of your life among your sons."

"Yes," he said, "I had planned to."

"Do you know where you're going to stay?" she asked, and everyone was silent in the pause before Gordon answered.

"No, not yet," he said, and went over to Michael, showing for the first time his age in his gait and posture. "I have not decided yet, nor have any of you." He advanced a great tickling finger at Michael, who bit it. He settled down to winning Michael over. "My dear," he said to Charlene, though in a soft voice for Michael's benefit, "you have done what I had not intended to have done. How could you state so surely what my intentions were?"

"It's just a knack," she said. "It hasn't got anything to do with anything. I knew it when you wrote those letters to Bryan and us."

"Really. I had not expected that result."

"Yes. I knew that was what you were saying. You're really very shy."

At which there was braying laughter from his two sons.

"He is too," said Charlene sharply to Bryan, in whom she combatted, as she often did, the Mottishness that she could least abide.

"He's usually thought of as something of a wolf with women, you know," said Bryan.

"Oh that," she said. "Anybody can be a wolf that wants to be."

"A shy wolf," said Bryan.

"If you don't know what that means you're not much of a poet."

"Oh I know what it means," said Bryan, who wanted her to think of him as indeed much of a poet. "I'm just wondering if it applies."

"Certainly it does. Take my word for it."

At eight o'clock Michael fell over the side of his crib onto the floor and howled about it. All three adults came flapping and clucking in, and the day was begun.

By the time Justin had shaved, breakfasted, and left for work Michael had forgotten about his mishap, and Charlene was beginning to agree that he was probably not maimed for life.

As they were sitting over coffee she said to Gordon, "But he never did it before."

"I gather as much, my dear," said Gordon. "He begins to cease to be a baby, to become a kid. But then, it's a gradual process and he's been a baby long enough."

"Not for me, he hasn't."

"He thinks so."

"How do you know what he thinks?"

"Cuddle him and find out for yourself."

She tried to cuddle him, but he stiffened and yelled. Finally she released him onto the floor. He immediately ran to the sinkboard and grabbed a paring knife, which Charlene took from him, and then into the front room where he began banging on the piano.

"Well," she said to Gordon, "even if you're right you oughtn't to be so happy about it."

"Don't you want him to grow up?"

"Of course!"

"How?"

"Oh heavens Father, you push me so."

"How?"

"Just the way everybody does I guess. Not really." She glared at him.

"As he needs you less you love him less."

"No!"

He paid no attention to her cry. "That's the ideal form of a nasty necessity."

"Oh Father, nasty?"

"Its nastiness is clear enough when the roles are inverted, as they are with me."

"How could you say such a thing?" she said. On her way around the table to him it occurred to her how he might say such a thing, and she added, "to me."

"Well," he said into her right clavicle, "I do not deny that there are saints. Let St. Charlene increase the mundane calendar."

"Don't say such things," she said as she returned to her place. "It isn't safe. You don't know what might be listening."

"No, you don't," he replied, repressing a rejoinder concerning hubris on Redwood Road.

There was a demolishing interruption from Michael; then dishes to wash and beds to make and lunch to prepare; and after lunch while Michael napped, conversation in the patio sun-bathing.

"Would you mind, Father," Charlene said in that tone with which one customarily approaches a tender subject, "telling me something that I have never been able to make out from what Justin has said?"

"I would not, though I do not know what it is."

"It's about Justin's mother," she said looking at his sunglasses through her sunglasses.

"Ah, Diana," he said smiling. "You know her?"

"Hardly at all. She's lived in Omaha ever since I knew Justin. I just went back to visit her with him one summer."

"What did you think of her?"

"Oh, she's a splendid person. So handsome and dignified and very intelligent. I think she thought I was too flighty for Justin."

"Very likely she did."

"I can't say how much I admire her. Still, I'm just as glad it's you that's here and not her. She is, maybe, just a little cool."

"Oh, just a little."

"I don't want to be unfair to her, and I'm sure she is splendid in her position—it's a fine orphanage you know, one of the very best in the country, they say, it's all her doing—still . . . you know."

"Oh, I know indeed."

"I don't mean it that way."

He did not respond.

"What I wondered is . . . You see, Justin sort of resents you, what you and his mother did. He blames you sort of, though he won't say why and she never mentioned it, and I wondered if you'd tell me what went wrong."

"She didn't die soon enough."

"Father!"

She sat up and took off her glasses.

"That is not true and it is not funny. Never say such a thing again."

"You asked me. I told you."

"Why do you make it so hard for people to love you? What do you mean by such a thing?"

The expression of hurt appeared on his face, but she ignored it.

"Explain yourself."

"I meant that she did not die in my heart soon enough."

"Go on."

"She was the only woman whom I ever both loved and hated at the same time. If I had just hated her I could have left her decently, as I did for another reason Bryan's mother. But I could not leave her. Her coldness and air of superiority infuriated me. She seemed to condescend to me. She made love as a favor. So I hurt her as badly as I could, though I thought at the time I was moved by passion; I was unfaithful to her with her sister. I believe I have never done anything more reprehensible. Does that satisfy you?"

"Oh, that last was not kind. But why did you ever love her?"

"She was handsome and very intelligent and not always so cold. The coldness grew with time. And I had just been having more sensuality than was good for me in Bryan's mother."

"How you must have hurt her."

"We need not talk about it," he said lightly.

"Oh, but we must. Why did you have to do it?"

"We really need not," he repeated, so that she lay back down again.

Presently she said, "Then you married Thelma?"

"Then I married Thelma. She was a saint of sorts too. I had hoped we might reside in Oakland as we were dying. You would have liked her."

"I am sure I would."

"And it is not nothing to administer an orphanage well."

"Of course not. It's a wonderful thing to do."

"Well," he said arising, "a not entirely unhappy ending. I am too hot."

He looked down at her smooth, round, golden body for a moment. Partly he was sorry that his own was so pale and gnarled, for in earlier years he would not have restrained his desire for her because she was

Justin's wife; but partly at this moment he was glad that it was so old, for he was kept by its age from making her unhappy, as he was sure he would once have done. He took himself into the house and set himself to thinking about electrons and their ways.

"Henry!" Edwa called up the stairs. "Come on down, Henry. Father Mott is here."

Gordon, in the living room, winced.

"Must she refer to me so? I am neither a priest nor a jolly old fellow with goodies in my bulging pockets."

"It's a custom," said Bryan, "like many another brought to us from the teeming middle plains of the nation."

"Let it teem in Nebrasky," said Gordon. "Here English is spoken. Roscoe, this is within your jurisdiction. See to it."

Roscoe, who was of the same height as his father, looked at him as though he were a good half-head taller; he managed this by holding himself very erect, tilting his face back a little, and looking down his bill like an ostrich.

"What would you prefer she call you to the children? Their other grandfather, you know, is often here."

"I don't know. Gordon, Grampa Gordon. Mott is not a name to be rolled on the tongue."

"Henry!" she called again. There was a trampling upstairs. "Come down now."

She joined the men.

"He's always going out in the evenings," she said apologetically. "There doesn't seem to be enough to hold the young people at home these days. But I made him promise," she said patting Gordon on the arm, "to spend a lot of time with his Father Mott before he leaves. He'll be with you all this evening, I know."

Gordon gave her a look (which was the only point of appearance that Justin shared with him) of pure, direct, calculating distaste. This he achieved by making his face blank as a sheep's and looking square-on at the object of his distaste.

"I'm sure we will both benefit by it," he said.

She saw that he was displeased with something but being conscious of no malice or error in her behavior she thought he was bilious and was sorry for him.

Henry entered, being large and dark of mane, and marked by acne. He was eighteen. He had had a date.

"Hello," he said to no one in particular.

"Well Henry," said Gordon, "it is planned that you sit at my feet in a sort of diffused discipleship and become wiser by a week."

Henry looked up from under his eyebrows at his grandfather, suspicious and buffalolike. An extraordinary distance separated his eyes, and they glowed with hostility.

"Huh," he said. "It is, is it?"

"He plans to be in law," said Edwa putting her arm about him. "Harvard Law School."

"What sort of law, Henry?" asked Gordon.

"I don't know," said Henry. "Any kind, I guess."

"Patent attorneys make a lot of money."

"I guess so."

"Oh I know it."

Henry had nothing more to say.

"Edwa," said Bryan, "may I get the stuff that Martha phoned about? She wanted to give it to the kids before suppertime."

"Are they sick?" asked Roscoe down to Bryan.

"Same thing that Clyde and Mary had." He turned to Henry. "And don't forget, nephew, there's always real estate."

"Well, well," said Roscoe. "Let the boy make up his own mind."

"Yes, let him," said Gordon as though agreeing to some other proposition.

Bryan and Edwa left for the medicine chest. When he presently returned to the room where Roscoe, Gordon, and Henry were still stiffly standing, Bryan heard a phrase that stopped him for a moment: "Law's at the very bottom of what we have, of course." A sort of film, like a chicken's second eyelid, only not physical, covered his eyes. This happened when he was thinking in a special way or when he was hurt or when he was very despondent; it let him know what was happening in the world without having to feel about it.

"Well," said Roscoe to him, "we'll see you a week from Saturday at the latest."

And for a considerable moment (the sheep, the ostrich, and the buffalo staring at the chicken eyes) Bryan considered what it was that law could be at the bottom of. But then they all four shook themselves, and he said, "A week from Saturday?"

"Yes, Henry's farewell dinner."

"You're leaving so soon?" asked Bryan.

"August tenth," said Henry, to whom it seemed none too soon. "I'm going to spend two or three weeks with some aunts in New York before I go on to Harvard."

"Two of Edwa's sisters. They are in import," said Roscoe.

"Well," said Bryan, "fine."

"Fine," said Gordon.

"Hrmph," said Roscoe down his beak.

"Yeh," said Henry.

"Well, good-bye," said Bryan. "I'll see you before long."

Gordon followed him, to get a briefcase he had left in Bryan's car. Bryan had transported him over from Justin's this afternoon for his week with Roscoe.

"My God," he said to Bryan, "a whole evening unarmed amongst them."

"A whole week," said Bryan. "There's always *Time*. They take it."

"You abandon me, then?"

"Ah, my dear father, hope is deciduous."

"I see you for the first time."

"And me without a tie on. Farewell, Father Henry-at-the-feet Mott. May quiring angels guard thee."

"Unnatural child."

When Gordon went back into the house he was greeted by Edwa and the four smaller children. They were all scrubbed and lined up and awkward for the occasion. Everyone, including Gordon, knew what to say and said it.

"Grampa Gordon," said Clyde sturdily after this midwestern ceremony was over. "I know how to tie a bowline."

"Oh Clyde," said Ann, who was impressed less by Gordon than the other children were, "don't bother him with the little-kid stuff."

"Well," said Clyde, who was the most impressed, "I can."

Gordon, who shared Ann's views on bowlines but after all was a grandfather, said in a kindly voice that he would like to see Clyde tie one; as he walked out with Clyde and John he winked and shrugged at Ann in a knowing way, as though she were an adult.

"Ann," said Mary when they were alone, "why did he wink at you?"

"Well," said Ann, who was not quite sure, "that's something you'll understand when you grow up."

"You're so grown up."

"Pretty much," said Ann. "Sometimes I feel a lot more grown up than you'd even understand."

"Huh," said Mary. "I suppose that's why you played seesaw with us today?"

Ann thumbed her nose at Mary and ran out of the room. Nosethumbing was something for which Mary could tattle on Ann, but seeing nothing to be gained by it she decided to go watch the bowline-tying instead.

Dinner was roast beef, broccoli, and mashed potatoes, cole slaw, bread and jam, and a choice of berry or custard pie. It was all very good, and Gordon ate far beyond his capacity; indeed, he was not allowed not to.

"Now, Father Mott," said Edwa as she served the pie, "we have a plan for every day this week. Sunday we're going to take a ride over to Marin County to the redwood grove."

"Can we all go?" said Clyde, who knew they all could not.

"Count me out," said Henry. "I've got a date."

"Perhaps," said Edwa to Clyde. "Don't worry, dear. Drink your milk. Monday we're going to have a picnic in Tilden Park. A real picnic."

"Can we ride the merry-go-round?" said Ann.

"Of course. We hope Daddy will be able to go with us."

"Grampa Gordon," said John, who was already bored by the calendar of coming events, "are you going to live with us?"

Gordon expected a dead silence after this question or a sharp reprimand. Instead Edwa spoke in her usual tone.

"I don't think Father Mott knows yet where he's going to settle down, John. He knows that he's welcome to stay with us as long as he wishes, but I think we should let him make up his own mind before we ask him."

She was the first one in Oakland, indeed the first one anywhere, to say these words to Gordon; he found he could tolerate even "Father Mott" from her in such a speech.

She finished the seven days.

"And there's one thing more important than all the rest: Henry's good-bye dinner. You can't disappoint us, Father. You will be here for it won't you?"

"If it is at all possible," said Gordon. He knew, he resolved that it would be quite impossible, but he could not find it in his heart to tell her so now.

Roscoe asked him if he wanted some more coffee, and Gordon looked at him in amazement. He had been more conscious of silent, watching Mary than of Roscoe. He was going to say something elaborate to Roscoe about being an absentee host, but the thought of translating it into Roscoe's language oppressed him. Instead he went into the living room and sat in a very comfortable chair which Edwa said was now sacred to him.

To him there the smaller children came for jokes and advice and to say good night. Roscoe had a headache and went to his room early. Edwa stayed with Gordon and Henry for a while listening to their logy conversation. She was spurred by it to relate much more entertaining experiences of her own; by ten she too went off to bed. The moment she was gone Henry excused himself and went rushing off into the adolescent night somewhere. Gordon found a copy of *Time* he hadn't read before and looked at it, but it wasn't annoying enough to keep him awake. By eleven o'clock, against the habit of years, he was in bed and asleep.

3

"Henry," said Bryan, "this is the last time you will think of us as your uncles and aunts, your dad and mom. When the Harvard tenants have moved into your head we will have acquired first names in your mind and we will seem annoying heirlooms you can't decently chuck out. Is it not sad, Rosalee?"

The pink and blue at Henry's side giggled.

"Bryan," said Roscoe, who liked Rosalee, "will you pass the yams? . . . My dear, this is the best ham I have ever eaten."

"Thank you," said Edwa. "Henry went clear to the city to get the ham and up to Berkeley to get the cake. My little boy," she said squeezing his forearm beside her to his annoyance.

"Henry," said Justin, who was feeling more than seven years older than his nephew, "I never went to college."

"My goodness," said Charlene, "he knows you never went to college. Why say it?"

"What I meant was, Henry, I envy you this opportunity I never took."

"Why?" said Martha, who was suddenly seized with the urge to bring him down.

"Why?" said Justin. "Everybody should have a college education."

"Can't you manage your factory without one?" she asked.

"Yes, but think of everything I'm missing."

"I doubt," she said, "whether a Ph.D. itself would enable you to see what you don't already see, Justin."

He did not know what she had done to him, but he knew that she had done something.

"It's just an advantage," he said, "and I'm glad you're getting it, Henry. Michael is going to Harvard if I have to do his homework myself to get him good grades in high school."

"Justin," said Charlene, "reads great books, like Aristotle."

"Is there anything wrong with that?" he demanded in a belligerent if cracked voice.

No one answered; he shrank into silence, so sitting a bird that not even Martha had the heart to shoot again.

"I did hope Father Mott could be here tonight," said Edwa. "Henry had so little chance to benefit from being with him. Such a rare opportunity," she said, beaming at Henry.

"Oh Mother," he said in a sort of pastel agony.

"Henry," whispered Rosalee leaning against him, "be nice to her. She loves you so much."

He growled.

"You were able to be with Father Mott a good deal these past days weren't you, dear?"

"Yes Mother," said Henry, who viewed it as being hobbled in barren pastures.

"I'm sure you benefited greatly from knowing him."

"Yes Mother," said Henry for Rosalee's sake, for he had not.

"We should all be thankful to have known him," said Charlene.

"Oh we are still going to know him," said Martha. "For years and years, I have no doubt."

"Father Mott does have the best of health."

"Well, I know," said Justin in a voice so loud that everyone looked at him, "where he's *not* going to live from now on."

There was a short silence, which each of the three women felt she must smooth over for Rosalee's sake.

"Honey," said Charlene, "you mustn't be so aggressive about it. We don't know."

"That's something for another time," said Edwa.

"Sometimes," said Justin, "I don't even feel like he was my father."

This was Roscoe's province.

"Justin," he said, "we will not talk about that at the table."

"How could *he* be my father?"

"That will be enough, Justin," said Roscoe in a very loud voice.

Henry held his breath. It seemed to Henry that he could not possibly be a true member of this family but that God had put him among these exquisite clowns to test him. The day was coming when his true rank should be revealed.

As soon as the silence had relaxed a little he spoke.

"Mom, when are we going to have dessert? Rosalee and I have to get going."

"Time to clear the table for dessert," said Edwa. "Everybody's ready?"

"I'll go lie down in the living room," said Bryan, "while you all gorge."

It was lonesome in the living room, but he stayed till they were through.

As Rosalee and Henry were in the hallway preparing to go she said to him in one of those whispers that are like the sound of a bugle at dawn, "You sure have the craziest family. How do you *stand* them?"

Edwa, who heard it, was cut to the quick; but Roscoe, to whose ears also the sound reached, heard it not. The others thought less of Rosalee than they had, and all the adults went into the living room logily.

"The children will be all right, dear?" said Roscoe.

"Ann and John are very good with them today," said Edwa.

"Can we hear Michael if he wakes up?" said Justin.

"I just took a peek at him, honey. He's sound asleep."

"Well," said Bryan, who was sprawled on the couch, "here we are. The last time we were assembled we had Gordon hanging over our heads."

"And now," said Martha, "we have him hanging around our necks."

"Martha!" said Charlene, "that's no way to talk."

"Why Martha," said Edwa, "you told me you didn't find him such a terrible burden."

"Not for a week, maybe, but what about for the rest of his life?"

"He's mighty damned healthy," said Justin.

"Honey!" said Charlene. "He's your father."

"How do I know? Only my mother knows whether that's true and she never said."

"Justin! That's unforgivable of you."

"He'll never live in my house," said Justin.

"Oh no?"

"No."

"The point is," said Bryan languidly, "he'll live with whomever he wants to live with. We have nothing to say about it."

And for putting that unpleasant doubt into words he was rewarded by having everyone turn against him.

"That," said Roscoe, "is scarcely true."

"He certainly can't live with us if we don't want him to," said Charlene.

"Say," said Justin, "whose side are you on anyway?"

"I'm not on your side," she said furiously. "I'm just against Bryan. And furthermore . . ."

"And furthermore," said Bryan, "your slip shows. Quit talking so much."

"You can't insult me!" she cried. "Justin!"

"Bah," said Justin.

"Are you trying to see," said Martha to Bryan, "just how mad you can get everybody?"

"I am sure," said Edwa, "that Father Mott will decide for himself where he is going to live. I know that he's welcome to live with any of us ('Oh yeh,' said Justin), but perhaps he might be encouraged to go live with Bryan as he ought."

"What!" cried Martha.

"Oh I see," said Bryan sitting up.

"Great," said Justin. "He lives off the old man anyhow."

"I see, I see," said Bryan.

"You do have plenty of room," said Edwa. "Bryan doesn't work. He could help Martha."

"If you think writing isn't work . . ."

"Shut up," said Martha. "Now, look here, Edwa, we're not taking him in just like that. I can't stand the old goat any more than anyone else can."

"Whose side are you on?" said Bryan.

"I'm on my own side," she said, "don't bother me."

Justin roared with laughter and Charlene scowled at him.

"I'm the only one who loves him," she said.

"That's all right," shouted Justin. "I hate him enough for two. Bryan gets Gordon."

Bryan strode over to him. "For two bits I'd knock your block off."

Justin fished a quarter out of his pocket. "Here you are, Blowhard. Let's see whose block gets knocked off."

Edwa and Roscoe separated them.

"Come now," said Roscoe. "When Gordon comes back from his vacation we'll talk to him about it. We won't make any decisions now."

"Oh the decision is made," said Justin. "Bryan gets him."

"Oh I do, do I? That for you, brother."

"You live off the old man. You can earn your keep for a change."

"Damn you. Who gave you a factory to manage? Who gave Roscoe a house and a fistful of shares in American Lite? What do you fatheads do with it?"

"Come on," said Martha, "Gordon will make up his own mind. You know that. Calm down."

"Justin," said Charlene, "if you don't quit insulting everybody I'll take Michael and go off to Mother's."

"Edwa," said Roscoe, "it was very ill-chosen of you to say that just then."

"Well, please, let's not disturb the children," said Edwa, who fancied she had heard scufflings on the stairs. She had.

"What did I ever do to get mixed up with a family like this?" said Justin. "Why don't you go to Greenwich Village with the other longhairs?" he said to Bryan.

"By God," said Bryan, "come outside and I'll show you who's the man around here. If you're not chicken that is."

"Chicken!" said Justin. "Against you? I'd be afraid of hurting you."

Charlene ran out in tears, and presently Michael began wailing. Justin left to follow her.

Martha walked, stiff-legged with fury, up to get Roxana and Aylmer. She found all six children sitting in the girls' room completely silent.

"Come on," she said with as much naturalness as she could summon. "We're going home now."

"Is anything the matter, Mommy?" said Roxana.

"You know there is," said Martha. "Don't ask foolish questions."

Edwa came in and quietly told her children to get ready for bed. With no objections, even ritualistic ones, they did as she bade.

"Aunt Edwa," said Aylmer, "we had a very good time."

"The ham was delicious," said Roxana.

"I'm glad you liked it," said Edwa.

"Come on," said Martha crossly and dragged them out.

"What's the matter?" said Roxana. "Don't you want us to be polite?"

"It's the wrong time," said Martha.

Justin and Charlene, with Michael in her arms, came out of the guest room and went straight out to their car without a word for anyone, even to Aylmer who said good night.

"They weren't kind," said Aylmer.

"It's never the right time to be unkind," said Roxana. "Is it Mommy?"

"No, no," said Martha, her voice full of both remorse and vexation. "Never."

The children bade Roscoe a long and very polite good night, with Bryan snapping at them to hurry up, and they went home.

Roscoe found Edwa preparing for bed.

"Edwa," he called from the bathroom, "where are the aspirin?"

"They might be on your night-stand."

"Yes. There are only two left."

"Isn't that enough?"

"I doubt it tonight."

"Well, they'll have to be."

"Are the children in bed?"

"Yes," she replied.

"I hope they didn't hear any of that disgraceful ruckus."

"I'm sure they did not. I don't think I'll bring the subject up with them. What do you think?"

"Of course not," he said. "Bryan was unforgivable."

"Well, you can hardly blame him." She was in bed settling herself.

"Well, he had to know sooner or later," he said.

"Roscoe," she said with a last flurry of feeling, "we're losing our first baby. Do you realize that?"

"Hrmph," he said; he did not think of Henry as his first baby and felt vaguely deficient as a father that he did not.

Bryan dropped his book and looked attentively at Martha.

"That's Gordon coming up the front steps," he said.

She dropped her darning. "Are you sure?"

"I can tell by his tread."

"Now darling," she said with alarm in her voice, "you must be firm. But do be polite."

"Oh yes," said Gordon, who had opened the door without having knocked, "oh gracious yes, do be polite."

"Gordon!" exclaimed Martha, standing up.

"Who else?"

"Why I thought it might have been Justin."

"Justin? Come, my dear Martha, since when has Justin taken to dropping in on you in the evenings?"

"I hoped he had come to apologize for something he said to Bryan."

"Well, Gordon," said Bryan, taking his coat.

"Mommy," came Roxana's voice from upstairs. "Who is it, Mommy?"

"Not asleep yet," said Martha.

"I have a couple of bags that the taxi driver left down at the foot of the stairs, Bryan." Bryan went for them. "Let me go kiss the children good night, Martha."

"Very well. I did not realize you liked them that well."

"Nor did I, my dear, until I spent a week at Tahoe in a guest hotel with none but elderly, respectable people."

"Can we come see him, Mommy?" called Aylmer.

"I'm coming right up, children," he said. "I have discovered that I am more attached to my grandchildren than I thought possible. One is so conscious of the irritations at the time one is with them, but afterwards that heaven of grandfathers, love without responsibility, is all that is left."

He bade them good night. Bryan put the suitcases in the guest room, Martha discovered that he had had his dinner at a restaurant, and they settled down in front of the empty fireplace.

"And what," said Gordon, bending forward and rubbing his hands as though there had been a blazing fire to warm them before, "what did Justin do that you should imagine he would come to apologize for it?"

"Well," said Bryan, "at Henry's farewell dinner we had a pretty terrific argument. He insulted me."

"Why?"

Martha looked distressed. Bryan gazed at her without expression for a moment before he answered.

"Well," said Bryan, "jealousy, I think. I had made rather a pass at Charlene before dinner."

"Oh," said Martha, looking greatly relieved, "he never knew about it."

"Maybe not with the top of his head," said Bryan, "but I think he knew it some place else."

"I hope that will teach you to lay off Charlene after this."

"Oh Martha," he said, "what's the good of a family dinner if I can't even kiss my pretty sister-in-law? Do you want me to read *Time* till dinner is served?"

"What frivolity," said Gordon. "Indeed, I might go so far as to say how jejune."

"He sounds worse than he is," said Martha. "At least worse than he is most of the time."

"The scoundrel's fallacy, that charm forgives all."

"Tell me, Gordon," said Bryan, "did you have a pleasant time at Tahoe?"

"What a paltry hypocrite. If you want me to believe such a question you've got to put a little conviction in it."

"Did you?"

"The weather and the scenery are, as you know, superb. This dispute with Justin the night of the dinner—was my name not brought up during the argument?"

"Yes."

"And with no excess of love, I dare say."

"No excess."

"Did you come to blows or stop at words?"

"Everyone conspired to keep us from actually fighting. I wish we had though, even if he'd beat me up a little. The satisfaction of landing one in the middle of that soul-less face is something I cannot forgo forever."

"And Roscoe, what role did he play?"

"Oh my heavens," said Martha, "quit beating about the bush. They were arguing about where you are going to live."

Her face was very strained as she said this.

"Well," said Gordon, "you did prick my little balloon of circumlocution very neatly."

"No circumlocution," she said, "but an elaborate system for making us uneasy."

"That was not my intention."

"Perhaps. It was your accomplishment."

"I don't think," said Gordon, "that I'll go to live with Justin."

"No," said Bryan, "neither does he. He, in fact, sometimes doubts that you are his father."

"A convenient doubt for one in his frame of mind, but not a probable one."

"He does seem to have more mother than father in him," said Bryan.

"Yes, to his hurt. Well, but Charlene is a most attractive woman. You, I take it, agree."

"I do. The spontaneity of her emotions is rare and winning."

"I had not thought of her that way," said Gordon. "How do you mean it?"

"I'm afraid," said Bryan, "that this is not a propitious time for me to elaborate upon that theme."

"Martha," said Gordon, "what do you think of her charms?"

"Not being the woman under discussion, but being a woman, I do not think my opinion would be unbiased."

"The power of her charm," said Gordon, "does not lessen your much subtler attraction, my dear."

"I have often been told that. I have never believed it."

"Martha," said Bryan, "believes that there is just so much admiration to go around. The more someone else gets, the less for her."

"Well," said Martha, "if there weren't so many Charlenes around maybe more men would make passes at my subtle attractions."

"Yours," said Gordon, "are not the charms that ripen and then fade, but rather the intellectual powers that only mature with time and endure into the impotence of old age. They partake of eternity."

"Lovely," she said. "But who kisses my enduring intellect?"

"I," said Bryan.

"When I'm old and withered," she said as though he had not spoken, "I suppose I'm to sit around hoarding my few drops of eternity and look down on other women, since all they have is a thousand pleasant memories?"

"Memories," said Gordon, "are the easiest substitute for satisfaction, but they are no satisfaction. I think I can speak with more authority than you about this."

"Well, use it on someone who's more impressed with it than I am. Let's drop me as a subject."

"Sorry," said Gordon. "When I said, Bryan, that I was not going to live with Justin, I was thinking of another reason than his distaste for the idea. I fancy I could have dealt with that."

"The boredom then?"

"Oh no, boredom can be dealt with too. I am going to continue my work wherever I settle down. There are books and concerts and pictures. No, I was thinking that wherever I settle I want to settle for good, and I distrust the permanence of Justin's household."

"Oh come, Gordon," said Martha, "not everyone divorces as readily as you."

"So it would appear," he replied. "However, it seems to me that if the time ever comes when Justin opposes or escapes from Charlene's rule, she will leave him."

Neither of the others said anything—Bryan because he agreed and Martha because she did not want another argument.

"And I do not want to be left high and dry."

"That leaves you three choices," said Bryan.

"Three?"

"Yes. Roscoe, myself, or living alone."

"Ah, living alone. I thought of that once or twice, but I rapidly put it out of my mind. I even thought of marrying again, but no. I have decided to be old."

"Do you mean that?" asked Martha. "Or are you being ironical as usual?"

"I mean it. The irony is a protection from the pain of admitting it. It is not pleasant to run down, but it is even less pleasant to have to watch yourself doing it."

"Well, even wives get old," she said.

"Yes, but a grandfather is a great deal closer to heaven than a husband. I exist only in relation to others, so that in solitude I would blow up like a balloon and pop. I am what the resistance of others makes me. And grandchildren are like the arms of the acclaiming populace bearing the victor home."

"Stirring," said Bryan. "Well, Roscoe has four acclaimers around the house to our two."

"True, but yours are so superior in quality."

And just before Martha could say what she was going to say he fore-stalled her.

"I believe you know very little about Roscoe's mother."

"Very little," said Bryan. "My mother said once she thought you still loved Roscoe's mother when you married her. That was three or four years after she'd died, wasn't it?"

"Over three years. Her name was Hannah. I have never loved anyone else so much as I loved her. I often wonder whether her memory did not influence my later relations with women. She remained perfect in my mind —she was yielding yet firm, like healthy young flesh, beautiful, not quite predictable, and she thought I was a god."

"She died just in time," said Martha, but when she saw the blind pain in his eyes she apologized almost tearfully for her cruelty, and left the room to make tea.

"She is very good at deflating the male ego," said Bryan.

"At least that," said Gordon, and seemed to be going to relapse into silence. ,

"What were you going to say about Roscoe's mother?"

"Just that the memory of her somehow is made stronger by Roscoe. Something of her lives in him; what, I could not say, nor how."

They were silent until Martha had brought the tea in.

"And furthermore," said Gordon looking steadily at Martha, "Edwa is a great deal pleasanter to live with than you are."

The confusion of wounded feelings, and gratitude that it was not they whom he was going to live with, and shame which kept her from respond-ing to this thrust reduced Martha to tears. Bryan looked very uncom-fortable.

"Well, we're quits," said Gordon. "I shall go to bed if you don't mind. You may take me to Roscoe's tomorrow."

"I'll make up the bed," said Martha going out again.

"You are very unkind to those you love," said Bryan to Gordon.

"Always, when I have trouble dominating them. That's the great thing about Roscoe—I have so little trouble keeping him under. Besides he has respect for me, and respect is fear and love combined in proportions that suit my taste excellently."

"Why do you always make the better cause appear the worse?"

"It is usually the correct explanation of motive, I have found, and when it is incorrect it is incorrect in such a gratifying way."

"Well," said Bryan standing up, "whenever you want a good conversa-tion you must call on us."

"That's why I came to you this evening," said Gordon. "One of the reasons. And when I want to recall my prime I will call on Charlene. You may tell Martha that she is not the least of the reasons I decided against settling down with you, nor the least of the reasons I almost did."

They went to the spare bedroom, where Martha was putting the finishing touches on the bed.

"May you both sleep well," said Gordon, meaning you ought to sleep badly.

"Of course," said Bryan, meaning I doubt if we will.

"It takes a lot to keep Bryan awake," said Martha, trying to mean by a brittle double-irony that a lot had happened.

"Oh?" said Gordon, and suddenly nobody knew what anybody meant any more.

Nobody knew what Martha meant by squeezing Gordon's hand hard and running from the room, or Gordon by turning his back to Bryan, or Bryan by approaching his father, flapping his right arm twice like a broken wing, and then going after Martha.

In bed Martha said to Bryan, "Oh darling, why was I so mean to him?"

"Well, don't worry about it. Now I can get back to work. I've lost the better part of six weeks."

"He made me be mean to him."

"No one is harder to forgive than the one who makes you behave badly."

"Is Edwa really easier to live with than I am?"

"No, of course not, my dear."

"Why does he try to be so sentimental with us? I didn't believe a word of that about Roscoe's mother, did you?"

"No, no, of course not."

"The old goat. He's so mean."

"Come, come. I love you dearly."

"You must forgive me for behaving like that," said Martha. "I'm sure he won't."

"I forgive you."

"I forgive you too. Well, I'll try to make it up to him."

Turning over, Bryan said, "Let's go to sleep now."

"I've got to do the wash in the morning," she said, and bottom to bottom they pretended to go to sleep.

❖

George P. Elliott was born in Knightstown, Indiana, in 1918, earned an M.A. from the University of California, and now teaches at Syracuse University. He has published three novels, Parktilden Village *(1958),* David Knudsen *(1962), and* In the World *(1965); a book of essays,* A Piece of Lettuce *(1964); and a narrative poem,* Fever and Chills *(1961). But he is perhaps best known for his many short stories—only ten of them were collected in* Among the Dangs *(1961)—which appeared mostly in the "little" literary magazines, and mostly in the 1950s, but which were invariably reprinted in one or the other of the best-of-the-year anthologies. His work can now be read in most every anthology of contemporary fiction. His stories are original and distinct not only from one another but from the work of anyone else: sometimes they are so fanciful as to seem rather like what science fiction ought to be; sometimes they are realistic and descriptive; often they are mystical and have religious themes or situations; and always they are very meaningful and relevant.*

"A Family Matter," though long, is precise and almost mathematical in the way it shows how the essence and style of three very different marriages relate back to three very different women who bore three very different sons. Gordon, "the inventor," fully aware of his own loves, errors, and present needs, finds his place in the family he likes least, because only it provides the respect ("respect is fear and love combined") and custom ("a very comfortable chair which Edwa said was now sacred to him") appropriate for a grandfather. Only the son of a mother who thought Gordon "was a god" can support him in his old age. In fact, there is an analogy here to Gordon as God and the death of God, which is in itself an analogy to the death of the patriarchal family. Neither Charlene's youth and beauty nor Martha's wit can propitiate Gordon in the way that Edwa's ritualistic ordering of her household and attentive reverence do. Bryan's is the family he is closest to (the artist, another inventor), but for them his presence is a disruption, a threat to the future, rather than the continuity with the past that only Roscoe and Edwa can provide.

PETER TAYLOR

Heads of Houses

◇◇◇◇◇◇◇

1. *The Foreign Parts and the Forget-Me-Nots*

KITTY'S OLD BACHELOR BROTHER gave Dwight a hand with the baggage
as far as the car, but Dwight would accept no more help than that. He had his
own method of fitting everything into the trunk. His Olivetti and his portable record-player went on the inside, where they would be most protected.
The overnight bag and the children's box of playthings went on the outside,
where they would be handy in case of an overnight stop. It was very neat
the way he did it. And he had long since learned how to hoist the two
heaviest pieces into the rack on top of the car with almost no effort, and
knew how to wedge them in up there so that they hardly needed the elastic
straps he had bought in Italy last summer. He was a big, lanky man, with a
lean jaw that listed to one side, and normally his movements were so
deliberate, and yet so faltering, that anyone who did not mistake him for a
sleepwalker recognized him at once for a college professor. But he never
appeared less professorial, and never felt less so, than when he was loading
the baggage on top of his little car. As he worked at it now, he was proud
of his speed and efficiency, and was not at all unhappy to have his father-in-
law watching from the porch of the big summer cottage.

From the porch, Kitty's father watched Dwight's packing activities with
a cold and critical eye. Only gypsies, Judge Parker felt, rode about the
country with their possessions tied all over the outside of their cars. Such
baggage this was, too! His son-in-law seemed purposely to have chosen the
two most disreputable-looking pieces to exhibit to the public eye. Perhaps
he had selected these two because they had more of the European stickers
on them than any of the other bags—not to mention the number of steam-
ship stickers proclaiming that the Dwight Clarks always travelled Tourist
Class!

Yet the exposed baggage was not half so irritating to Judge Parker as the
little foreign car itself. The car would have been bad enough if it had been

one of the showy, sporty models, but Dwight's car had a practical-foreign look to it that told the mountain people, over in the village, as well as the summer people from Nashville and Memphis, over in the resort grounds and at the Hotel, how committed Dwight was to whatever it was he thought he was committed to. The trouble was, it was a *big* little car. At first glance, you couldn't quite tell what was wrong with it. Yet it was little enough to have to have a baggage rack on top; and inside it there was too little room for Dwight and Kitty to take along even the one basket of fruit that Kitty's mother had bought for them yesterday. Judge Parker pushed himself as far back in his rocker as he safely could. For a moment he managed to put the banister railing between his eyes and the car. He meant *not* to be irritated. He had been warned by his wife to be careful about what he said to his son-in-law this morning. After all, the long summer visit from the children was nearly over now.

Busy at work, Dwight was conscious of having more audience than just Dad Parker—an unseen, and unseeing, audience inside the cottage. Certain noises he made, he knew, telegraphed his progress to Kitty. She was upstairs—in the half story, that is, where everybody but Dad and Mother Parker slept—making sure both children had used the bathroom before breakfast. (She knew he would not allow them time for the bathroom after breakfast.) And the same noises—the slamming down of the trunk lid, for instance, and even the scraping of the heavy bags over the little railing to the rack (the *galerie,* Dwight called it fondly)—would reach the ears of brother Henry, now stationed inside the screen door, considerately keeping hands off another man's work. The ears of Mother Parker would be reached, too, all the way back in the kitchen. Or, since breakfast must be about ready now, Mother Parker might be on the back porch, where the table was laid, waiting ever so patiently. Perhaps she was rearranging the fruit in the handmade basket, which she had bought at the arts-crafts shop, and which she was sure she could find space for in the car after everything else was in. . . . Everybody, in short, was keeping out of the way and being very patient and considerate. It really seemed to Dwight Clark that he and his little family might make their getaway, on this September morning, without harsh words from any quarter. He counted it almost a miracle that such a summer could be concluded without an open quarrel of any kind. Along toward the end of July, midway in the visit, he had thought it certain Kitty would not last. But now it was nearly over.

When the last strap over the bags was in place, Dwight stepped away from the car and admired his work. He even paused long enough to give a loving glance to the little black car itself, his English Ford, bought in France two summers ago. Such a sensible car it was, for a man who wanted other things out of life than just a car. No fins, no chromium, no high-test gasoline for him! And soon now he and Kitty would be settled inside it, and they would be on their way again, with just their own children, and headed back toward their own life: to the life at the University, to life in their sensible little prefab, with their own pictures and their own make-shift furniture (he could hardly wait for the sight of his books on the brick-and-board shelves!), to their plans for scrimping through another winter in order to go abroad again next summer—their life. Suddenly, he had a vision of them in Spain next summer, speeding along through Castile in the little black automobile, with the baggage piled high and casting its shadow on the hot roadside. He stepped toward the car again, with one long arm extended as if he were going to caress it. Instead, he gave the elastic straps—his Italian straps, he liked to call them—their final testing, snapping them against the bags with satisfaction, knowing that Kitty would hear, knowing that, for once, she would welcome this signal that he was all set.

He turned away from the car, half expecting to see Kitty and the children already on the porch. But they were still upstairs, of course; and breakfast had to be eaten yet. Even Dad Parker seemed to have disappeared from the porch. But, no, there he was, hiding behind the banisters. What was he up to? Usually the old gentleman kept his dignity, no matter what. It didn't matter, though. Dwight would pretend not to notice. He dropped his eyes to the ground. . . . As he advanced toward the house, he resolved that this one time he was not going to be impatient with Kitty about setting out. He would keep quiet at the breakfast table. One impatient word from anybody, at this point, might set off fireworks between Kitty and her mother, between Kitty and her father. (He glanced up, and, lo, Dad Parker had popped up in a normal position again.) Between Kitty and her ineffectual old bachelor brother, even. (He wished Henry would either get away from that door or come on outside where he could be seen.) And if she got into it with them, Dwight knew he could not resist joining her. It would be too bad, here at the last, but their impositions upon Kitty this summer had been quite beyond the pale—not to mention their general lack of appreciation of all she and he had undertaken to do for them, which, of course, he didn't mind for *himself;* and not to mention their show of resentment against *him,* toward the last, merely because he was taking Kitty away from them ten days earlier than the plans had originally called for. The truth was that they had no respect for his profession; they resented the fact that his department chairman could summon him back two weeks before classes would begin. . . . For a moment, he forgot that, in fact, the chairman had not summoned him back.

As Dwight approached the porch, in his slow, lumbering gait, Judge Parker suddenly rocked forward in his chair. Stretching his long torso still farther forward, he rested the elbows of his white shirtsleeves on the banister railing. Dwight, out there in the morning sun, seemed actually to be walking with his eyes closed. Perhaps he was only looking down, but, anyway, he came shambling across the lawn as though he didn't know where he was going. Judge Parker had noticed, before this, that when his son-in-law was let loose in a big open space, or even in a big room, he seemed to wander without any direction. The fellow was incapable of moving in a straight line from one point to another. He was the same way in an argument. Right now, no doubt, he had a theory about where the porch steps were, and he would blunder along till he arrived at the foot of them. But what a way of doing things, especially for a man who was always talking about the scientific approach. It had been, this summer, like having a great clumsy farm animal as a house guest. It had been hardest, the Judge reflected, on his wife, Jane. Poor old girl. Why, between the fellow's type-writer and record-player, she had hardly had one good afternoon nap out. And, oh, the ashtrays and the glasses that had been broken, and even the furniture. For a son-in-law they had the kind of man who couldn't sit in a straight chair without trying to balance himself on its back legs. . . . Out-of-doors he was worse, if anything. He had rented a power mower and cut the grass himself, instead of letting them hire some mountain white to do it, as they had in recent years. He had insisted, too, on helping the Judge weed and work his flower beds. As a result, Judge Parker's flowers had been trampled until he could hardly bear to look at some of the beds. A stray horse or cow couldn't have done more damage. All at once, he realized that there was an immediate danger of Dwight's stumbling into his rock garden, beside the porch steps, and crushing one of his ferns—his *Dryopteris spinulosa*. Somehow, he must wake the boy up. He must *say* something to him. He cleared his throat and began to speak. As he spoke, he allowed his big, well-manicured hands to drape themselves elegantly over the porch banisters.

"Professor Clark," he began, not knowing what he was going to say, but using his most affectionate form of address for Dwight. "Is it," he said, casting about for something amiable, "is it thirty-eight miles to the gallon you get?"

Dwight stopped, and looked up with a startled expression. He might really have been a man waked from sleepwalking. But gradually a suspicious, crooked smile appeared, twisting his chin still farther out of any normal alignment. "*Twenty*-eight to the gallon, Dad Parker," he said.

"Oh, yes, that's what I meant to say!"

What could have made him say *thirty,* he wondered. Not that he knew or cared anything about car mileage. It always annoyed him that people found it such an absorbing topic. Even Jane knew more about his Buick than he did, and whenever anyone asked him, he had to ask her what mileage they got.

But he couldn't let the exchange stop there. Dwight would think his slip was intentional. Worse still, his son Henry, behind the screen door, would be making *his* mental notes on how ill the summer had gone. The Judge had to make his interest seem genuine. "That does make it cheap to operate," he ventured. "And it has a four-cylinder motor. Think of that!"

"Six cylinders," said Dwight, no longer smiling.

The Judge made one more try. "Of course, of course. Yours is an Ambassador. It's the Consul that has four."

"Mine is called a Zephyr," Dwight said.

There was nothing left for Judge Parker to do but throw back his head and try to laugh it off. At any rate, he had saved his fern.

At the steps to the porch, a porch that encompassed the cottage on three sides and that was set very high, with dark green lattice-work underneath, and with the one steep flight of steps under the cupola, at the southwest corner—at the foot of the steps Dwight stopped and turned to look along the west side of the house. Dad Parker's lilac bushes grew there. Wood ashes were heaped about their roots. Beyond the lilacs was the rock pump house, and just beyond that Dwight had a view of Dad Parker's bed of forget-me-nots mixed with delphiniums. Or was it bachelor's-buttons mixed with ageratum? He was trying to get hold of himself after the Judge's sarcasm about the car. In effect, he was counting to a hundred, as Kitty had told him he must do this morning.

For the peace must be kept this morning, at any price—for Kitty's sake. For her and the children's sake he had to control himself through one more meal. And the only way he could was to convince himself that Dad Parker's mistakes about the car were real ones. With anybody but Judge Nathan Parker it would have been impossible. But in the case of the Judge it *was* possible. The man knew less than any Zulu about the workings of cars, to say nothing of models of foreign makes. This father-in-law of his most assuredly had some deep neurosis about anything vaguely mechanical. Even the innocent little Italian typewriter had offended him. And instead of coming right out and saying that Dwight's typing got on his nerves, he had had to ask his rhetorical questions, before the whole family, about whether Dwight thought good prose could be composed on "a machine." "I always found it necessary to write by briefs and decisions in longhand," he said, "if they were to sound like much." And the record-player, too. The Judge *despised* canned music; he preferred the music he made himself, on his violoncello, which instrument he frequently brought out of the closet after dinner at night, strumming it along with whatever popular stuff came over the radio. . . . There was not even a telephone in the cottage. That seemed to Dwight the *purest* affectation. Dad and Mother Parker were forever penning little notes to people over in the resort grounds, or at the Hotel. They carried on a voluminous correspondence with their friends back in Nashville. During the week, they wrote notes to brother Henry, who had to keep at his job at the courthouse in Nashville all summer long, and only came up to the Mountain for weekends. In fact, three weeks ago, when the generator on Dwight's car went dead, Dad Parker had insisted upon writing brother Henry about it. The garage in the mountain village could not furnish brushes and armatures for an English Ford, of course, but from the telephone office Dwight might have called some garage in Nashville, or

even in Chattanooga, which was nearer. Instead, he had had to tell Dad
Parker what was needed and let Henry attend to it. Henry did attend to it,
and very promptly. The parts arrived in the mail just two days later. When
the Judge returned from the village post office that morning, he handed
Dwight the two little packages, saying, "Well, Herr Professor, here are
your 'foreign parts.' " Everybody had laughed—even Kitty, for a moment.
But Dwight hadn't laughed. He had only stood examining the two little
brown packages, which were neatly and securely wrapped, as only an old
bachelor could have wrapped them, and addressed to him in Henry's old-
fashioned, clerkish-looking longhand.

At the foot of the porch steps, Dwight was listening hopefully for the
sound of Kitty's footsteps on the stairs inside. He remained there for
perhaps two or three minutes, with his eyes fixed in a trancelike gaze upon
the mass of broad-leaved forget-me-nots. (They *were* forget-me-nots, he
had decided.) Presently he saw out of the corner of his eye, without really
looking, that Dad Parker had produced the morning paper from somewhere and was offering him half of it, holding it out toward him without
saying a word. At the same moment, out in the rock pump house, the
pump's electric motor came on with a wheeze and a whine. Someone had
flushed the toilet upstairs. It was the first flush since Dwight came downstairs, and so he knew that Kitty and the children would not be along for
some minutes yet. There would have to be more flush.

As he went up to the porch to receive a section of the paper, the pump
continued to run, making a noise like a muffled siren. That was its *good*
sound. It *wasn't* thumping, which was its bad sound and meant trouble.
Probably the low ebb in understanding between Kitty and her mother this
summer had been during the second dry spell in July. Kitty had come to
the Mountain with the intention of relieving her mother of the laundry, as
well as of all cooking and dishwashing. Those were the things that Mother
Parker had hated about the Mountain when Kitty was growing up. She had
missed her good colored servants in Nashville and couldn't stand the
mountain "help" that was available. But it seemed that Kitty didn't understand how to operate her mother's new washing machine economically—
with reference to water, that is. During that dry spell, Mother Parker took
to hiding the table linen and bedsheets, and the old lady would rise in the
morning before Kitty did, and run them through the washer herself. No real
water crisis ever developed, but, realizing that Dad Parker would be helpless to deal with it if it did, Dwight got hold of the old manual that had
come with the pump, when it was installed a dozen years before, and
believed that he understood how to prime it, or even to "pull the pipe" in
an emergency. Having learned from the manual that every flush of the
toilet used five gallons of water, he estimated that during a dry spell it
wasn't safe to flush it more than three times in one day. And as a result of
this knowledge it became necessary for him to put a padlock on the bath-

room door so as to prevent Dwight, Jr., aged four, from sneaking upstairs and flushing the toilet just for kicks.

It seemed that the pump, like everybody else, was trying to make only its polite noises this morning. But just as Dwight was accepting his half of the newspaper, the pump gave one ominous, threatening thump. Dwight went tense all over. There had been no rain for nearly three weeks. There might yet be a crisis with the pump. In such case, brother Henry would be no more help than Dad Parker. It could, conceivably, delay Dwight's departure a whole day. If that happened, it might entail his pretending to get off a telegram to the chairman of his department. Moreover, he would have to do this before the eyes of brother Henry, in whom Kitty, in a weak moment, had confided the desperate measure they had taken to bring the summer visit to an end. It was Henry, lurking there in the shadows, that really depressed him. It seemed to him that Henry had come up for weekends this summer just to lurk in the shadows. Had he joined in one single game of croquet? He had not. And each time Dwight produced his miniature chess set, Henry had made excuses and put him off.

Dwight looked into Dad Parker's eyes to see if the thump had registered with him. But of course it *hadn't* registered. And when the motor went off peacefully, and when everything was all right again, that of course didn't register, either. To Dwight's searching look Dad Parker responded merely by knitting his shaggy brows and putting one hand up to his polka-dot bow tie to make out if anything was wrong there. Everything was fine with the Judge's tie, as it always was. He gave Dwight a baffled, pitying glance and then disappeared behind his half of the morning paper.

2. *The Garden House*

Dwight sat down on a little cane-bottomed chair and tilted it on its back legs. He opened his half of the paper. His was the second section, with the sports and the funnies. He had learned early in the summer to pretend he preferred to read that section first. Dad Parker had been delighted with this, naturally, but even so he hadn't been able to conceal his astonishment —to put it mildly—that a grown man could have such a preference. To the Judge it seemed the duty of all educated, responsible gentlemen to read the national and international news before breakfast every morning. He liked to have something important—and controversial, if possible—for the talk at the breakfast table.

Dwight, tilting back in his chair and hiding behind his paper, was listening for the pump to come on again. He felt positively panicky at the prospect of staying another day, or half day. One more flush of the toilet and he would be free. To think that five gallons of water *might* stand between him and his return to his own way of life! He found that he could not concentrate on the baseball scores, and he didn't even try to read "Pogo." Then, at last, the pump did come on, and it was all right. And again it went off with a single thump, which, as a matter of fact, it nearly always went off with.

Dwight sat wondering at his own keyed-up foolishness, but still he found it irksome that Dad Parker could sit over there calmly reading the paper, unaware even that there was such a thing as an electric pump on the place. It seemed that once the pump had been installed, the Judge had deafened his ears to it and put it forever out of his mind. This was just the way he had behaved during the worst dry spell. But Dwight understood fully why no water shortage could ever be a problem for Dad Parker. To begin with, he watered his flowers only with rain water that he brought in a bucket from the old cistern—water that was no longer considered safe for drinking. And Dad Parker, personally, still used the garden house.

The garden house! Dwight was alarmed again. The garden house? Was there any reason for the thought of it to disturb him? There must be. His subconscious mind had sent up a warning. The garden house was connected with some imminent threat to his well-being, possibly even to his departure this morning. Quickly, he began trying to trace it down, forming a mental image of the edifice itself, which was located a hundred yards to the east of the cottage, along the ridge of the Mountain. This structure was, without question, the sturdiest and most imposing on the Parkers' summer property. "Large, light and airy, it is most commodious"—that was how Dad Parker had described the building to Dwight when he and Kitty were first married and before Dwight had yet seen the family's summer place. And Dwight had never since heard him speak of the building except in similar lyrical terms. Like the pump house, it was built of native rock, quarried on the mountain-side just three or four miles away; but it had been built a half century back, when masonry work done on the Mountain was of a good deal higher order than it was nowadays. Family tradition had it that one spring soon after Kitty's grandfather had had their cottage built, the men of a local mountain family had constructed the garden house for the grandfather free of charge and entirely on their own initiative. It was standing there to surprise "the Old Judge," as the grandfather was still remembered and spoken of locally, when he and the family came up to the Mountain that July. The Old Judge had not actually been a judge at all, but an unusually influential and a tolerably rich lawyer, at Nashville, and he had befriended this mountain family sometime previous by representing them in a court action brought against one of their number for disturbing the peace. They had repaid him by constructing a garden house that was unique in the whole region. Its spacious interior was lighted by rows of transom windows, set high in three of the four walls. Below these windows, at comfortable intervals, were accommodations for eight persons, and underneath was a seemingly bottomless pit. Best of all, the building was so situated that when the door was not closed, its open doorway commanded a view of the valley that was unmatched anywhere on the Mountain. . . . It was there that Dad Parker usually went to read the first section of the paper, before breakfast every morning. And frequently he read the second section there, after breakfast. Suddenly a bell rang in Dwight's conscious mind, and the message came through. Dad Parker had, this morning, already read the first section of the paper once! From the east dormer window, half an hour before, Dwight had seen him returning from the garden house, paper in hand. It was extremely odd, to say the least, for him to sit there poring over the news a second time. Usually, when he had read the paper once, he knew it by heart and never needed to glance at it again— not even to prove a point in an argument. What was he up to? First he had hidden behind the banisters, now behind the paper.

Involuntarily, almost, Dwight tilted his chair still farther back, to get a look at Dad Parker's face. The chair creaked under his weight. Remembering he had already broken one of these chairs this summer, he quickly brought it back to all fours. Another broken chair might somehow delay their getting off! The chair wasn't damaged this time, but the glimpse Dwight had had of Dad Parker left him stunned. The old gentleman's face was as red as a beet, and he was reading something in the paper, something that made his eyes, normally set deep in their sockets, seem about to pop out of his head.

By the time the front legs of Dwight's chair hit the floor, the Judge had already closed the paper and begun folding it. As he tucked it safely under his arm, he looked at Dwight and gave him a grin that was clearly sheepish —guilty, even.

But deep in the old man's eyes was a look of firm resolve. A resolve, Dwight felt certain, that *he,* Dwight, should not under any circumstances see the front section of the paper before setting off this morning. Dwight couldn't imagine what the article might be. He had but one clue. He had observed, without thinking about it, that the Judge had had the paper open to the inside of the last page. That was where society news was printed, and it was one page that the Judge seldom read. Dwight realized now that Dad Parker had given him the second section as a kind of peace offering. And while going through the first section again he had stumbled on something awful.

From inside the cottage there came the sound of Kitty's and the children's footsteps on the stairs.

3. *An Old Bachelor Brother*

Henry Parker, just inside the screen door, heard Kitty and her children start downstairs. He pushed the door open and went out on the porch.

Through the screen he had been watching his father and his brother-in-law, hiding from each other behind their papers. He believed he knew precisely what thoughts were troubling the two men. He had refrained from joining them because ever since he arrived from Nashville last night he had sensed that his own presence only aggravated their present suffering. Each of them was suffering from an acute awareness that he was practicing a stupid deception upon the other, as well as from a fear that he might be discovered. His brother-in-law was leaving the Mountain under the pretense that he had been called back to his university. The Judge was concealing the fact that there was a party of house guests expected to arrive from Nashville this very day—almost as soon as the Clarks were out of the house— and that an elaborate garden party was planned for Monday, which would be Labor Day. Each man knew that Henry knew about his deception, and each wished, with Henry, that Henry could have stayed on in Nashville this one weekend. Henry couldn't stay in Nashville, however—for good and sufficient reasons—and just now he couldn't remain inside the screen door any longer. Kitty was on the stairs, and his mother was coming up the hall from the kitchen. His lingering there would be interpreted by them as peculiar.

Just as Henry made his appearance on the porch, Dwight and the Judge came to their feet. They, too, had heard the footsteps of the women and children. It was time for breakfast. Henry walked over to his father and said casually, "Wonder if I could have a glance at the paper?" The Judge glared at him as though his simple request were a personal insult.

"The paper," Henry repeated, reaching out a hand toward the newspaper, which the Judge now clutched under his upper arm. The Judge continued to glare, and Henry continued to hold out his hand. Henry's hands were of the same graceful and manly proportions as his father's, but, unlike the Judge, he didn't "use" his hands and make them "speak." He also had his father's same deep-set eyes, and the same high forehead—even higher, since his hair, unlike his father's, was beginning to recede. He glared back at his father, half in fun, supposing the refusal to be some kind of joke. Finally, he took hold of the paper and tried to pull it free. But the Judge held on.

"May I just glance at the headlines?" Henry said sharply, dropping his hand.

"No, you may not," said the Judge. "We are all going in to breakfast now."

Dwight stepped forward, smiling, and silently offered his section of the paper to Henry. Henry accepted it, but his heart sank when he looked into Dwight's face. Dwight's face, this morning, was the face of an appeaser. Only now did Henry realize that both men imagined he might, out of malice or stupidity, spill their beans at the breakfast table. The Judge, it seemed, meant to bluff and badger him into silence; Dwight intended to appease him.

Henry took the paper over to the edge of the porch, leaned against the banister, and lit a cigarette. His mother and sister were standing together in the doorway now, and his father had set out in their direction.

"Breakfast, everybody," said his mother. By "everybody," he knew, she meant him, because he was the only one who had ignored her appearance there. He glanced up from the paper, smiled at her and nodded, then returned his eyes to the paper, which he held carelessly on his knee.

"Henry has taken a notion to read the newspaper at this point," he heard his father say just before he marched inside the cottage.

His brother-in-law lingered a moment. There seemed to be something Dwight wanted to say to Henry. But Henry didn't look up; he couldn't bear to. Dwight moved off toward the doorway without speaking.

"Don't be difficult, Henry," his sister Kitty said cheerfully. Then she and her mother went inside, with Dwight following them.

Henry heard them go back through the cottage to the screened porch in the rear. He knew he would have to join them there presently. He supposed that, whether they knew it or not, they needed him. They were so weary of their own differences that any addition to their company would be welcome, even someone who knew too much.

And how much too much *he* knew!—about them, about himself, about everybody. That was the trouble with him, of course. *He* could have told them beforehand how this summer would turn out. But they had known, really, how it would turn out, and had gone ahead with it anyway; and that was the difference between him and them, and that was the story of his bachelorhood, the story of his life. He flicked his cigarette out onto the lawn and folded the paper neatly over the banister. No, it wasn't quite so simple as that, he thought—the real difference, the real story wasn't. But he had learned to think of himself sometimes as others thought of him, and to play the role he was assigned. It was an easy way to avoid thinking of how things really were with him. Here he was, so it appeared, an old-fashioned old bachelor son, without any other life of his own, pouting because his father had been rude to him on the veranda of their summer cottage on a bright September morning. Henry Parker was a man capable even of thinking inside this role assigned him, and not, for the time being, as a man whose other life was so much more real and so much more compli-cated that there were certain moments in his summer weekends at this familiar cottage when he had to remind himself who these people about him were. For thirteen years, "Life" to him had meant his life with Nora McLarnen, his love affair with a woman tied to another man through her children, tied to a husband who, like her, was a Roman Catholic and who, though they had been separated all those years, would not give her a divorce except on the most humiliating terms. Henry had learned how to think, on certain occasions with the family, as the fond old bachelor son. And he knew that presently he, the old bachelor, must get over his peeve and begin to have generous thoughts again about his father, and about the others, too.

It *had* been a wretched summer for all four of them, and they had got into the mess merely because they wanted to keep up the family ties. His mother was to be pitied most. His mother had finally arranged her summers at the cottage so that they were not all drudgery for her, the way they used to be when she had two small children, or even two big children, in the days when their cottage was not even wired for electricity and when, of course, she had no electric stove or refrigerator or washing machine and dryer. But in making their plans for this visit Dwight and Kitty had completely failed to understand this. Kitty had moved in and taken over where no taking over was needed. Not only that. Because Dwight had to do his writing—for ten years now they had been hearing about that book of his—and because Dwight and Kitty so disdained the social life that Mother and Dad had with the other summer residents, she had forgone almost all summer social life. Henry had it from his mother that the party on Monday was supposed to make it up to Dad's and her friends for their peculiar behavior this summer, and was not really intended as a celebration of their daughter's departure. To have concealed their plans was silly of them, but Mother had been afraid of how it might sound to Dwight and Kitty.

Kitty had to be a sympathetic figure, too, in the old bachelor's eyes. Kitty had written her mother beforehand that they would come to the Mountain only if she could be allowed to take over the housekeeping. Yet her mother had "frustrated" her at every turn. She wouldn't keep out of the kitchen, she wouldn't let Kitty do the washing. Further, Henry agreed with his sister that the cottage had suffered at their mother's hands, that it had none of the charm it had had when they were growing up. It was no longer a summer place, properly speaking. It was Nashville moved to the Mountain. There was no longer the lighting of kerosene lamps at twilight, no more chopping of wood for the stove, no more fetching of water from the cistern. The interior of the house had been utterly transformed. Rugs covered the floors everywhere—the splintery pine floors that Mother so deplored. The iron bedsteads had disappeared from the bedrooms; the living-room rockers were now used on the porch. Nowadays, cherry and maple antiques set the tone of the house. The dining room even ran to mahogany. And, for the living room, an oil portrait of the Old Judge had been brought up from the house in Nashville to hang above the new mantelpiece, with its broken ogee and fluted side columns. With such furnishings, Kitty complained, children had to be watched every minute, and could not have the run of the house the way they did when she and Henry and their visiting cousins were growing up. It was all changed.

As for the lot of the two men this summer—well, he should worry about them. When thinking of *them,* he couldn't quite keep it up as the sympathetic old bachelor who took other people's problems to heart. What was one summer, more or less, of not having things just as you wanted them? Next summer, or even tomorrow, or an hour from now, each of them would have it all his way again. And by any reasonable view of things that was what a man must do. A man couldn't afford to get lost in a labyrinth of self-doubts. And a man must be the head of his house. They were the heads of their houses, certainly, and they knew what they wanted, and they had their "values." Both of them knew, for instance, that they hated lying about small domestic matters, and tomorrow, or the next hour, would likely find them both berating their wives for having involved them in something that was "against their principles." Henry sighed audibly, took out another cigarette, then put it back in the package. If they but knew how practiced *he* was—without a wife—at lying about small domestic matters! If they knew his skill in that art, they wouldn't be worrying lest he make some faux pas at the breakfast table.

Finally, Henry bestirred himself. He crossed the porch and opened the screen door. Passing from the light of out-of-doors into the long, dark hall, which ran straight through the cottage to the back porch, he was reminded of something that had caught his attention when he was leaving Nashville, yesterday afternoon. As he was entering a railroad underpass, he glanced up and saw that there was something scrawled in large black letters high above the entrance. He had driven through this same tunnel countless times in the past, but the writing had never caught his attention before. It was the simple question *Have you had yours*—with the question mark left off. Perhaps it had been put there recently, or it might have been there for years. Some sort of black paint, or perhaps tar, had been used. And it was placed so high on the cement casement and was so crudely lettered that the author must have leaned over from above to do his work. Somehow, as he drove on through the tunnel, Henry had felt tempted to turn around at the other end and go back and read the inscription again, to make sure he had read it correctly. He hadn't turned around, of course, but during the eighty-mile drive to the Mountain the words had kept coming back to him. He thought of the trouble and time the author had taken to place his question there. He supposed the author's intention was obscene, that the question referred to fornication. And he had the vague feeling now that the question had turned up in his dreams last night; but he was seldom able to remember his dreams very distinctly. At any rate, the meaning of the question for him seemed very clear when it came back to him now, and it did not refer to fornication. The answer seemed clear, too: *He* had not had *his.* He had not had his what? Why, he had not had his Certainty. That was what the two men had. Neither of the two seemed ideally suited to the variety of it he had got; each of them, early in life, had merely begun acquiring whatever brand of Certainty was most available; and, apparently, if you didn't take that, you took none at all. Professor Dwight Clark was forever depending upon manuals and instruction books. (He even had an instruction book for his little Ford, and with the aid of it could install a new generator.) And Professor Clark had to keep going back to Europe, had literally to see every inch of it in order to believe in it enough to teach his history classes and do his writing. And the Judge's garden, while it contained only flowers and combinations of flowers that might have been found in any antebellum garden, was so symmetrically, so regularly laid out and so precisely and meticulously cared for that you felt the gardener must surely be some sweet-natured Frankenstein monster. And the decisions that the Judge handed down from the Bench were famous for their regard for the letter of the law. Lawyers seldom referred to him as "Judge Parker." By his friends he was spoken of as "Mr. Law." Amongst his enemies he was known as "Solomon's Baby." . . . But what was Henry Parker known as? Well, he wasn't much known. He was assistant to the registrar of deeds. He was Judge Parker's son; he was a Democrat, more or less. At the courthouse he was thought awfully well informed—about county government, for one thing. People came to him for information, and took it away with them, thinking it was something Henry Parker would never find any use for. He had passed a variety of civil-service examinations with the highest rating on record, but he had taken the examinations only to see what they were like and what was in them. He did his quiet, pleasant work in his comfortable office on the second floor of the courthouse. The building was well heated in the winter and cool in the summer. Two doors down the corridor from him, Nora McLarnen was usually at her typewriter in the license bureau. Their summers, his and Nora's, were all that made life tolerable. With *his* parents at the Mountain, and *her* two sons away at camp, they could go around together with no worry about embarrassing anyone that mattered to them. Their future was a question, a problem they had always vaguely hoped would somehow solve itself. That is, until this summer.

During past summers, Henry had come to the Mountain on weekends for the sake of his parents, or for the sake of making sure his mother had no reason to come down to Nashville on an errand or to see about him. But this summer he had come mostly for Nora's sake. Her older boy was now sixteen and had not wanted to go to camp. He had been at home, with a job as life-guard at one of the public swimming pools. Nora had wanted to devote her weekends to Jimmy. And by now, of course, the younger boy had returned from camp. For Labor Day, Nora had agreed to attend a picnic with the boys and their father—a picnic given by the insurance company for which John McLarnen was a salesman. All summer it had been on Nora's mind that the boys' growing up was going to change things. In the years just ahead they would need her perhaps more than before, and they would become sensitive to her relationship with Henry. She was thinking of quitting her job, she was thinking of letting her husband support her again, she was wondering if she mightn't yet manage to forgive John Mc-Larnen's unfaithfulness to her when she was the mother of two small children, if she hadn't as a younger woman been too intolerant of his coarse nature. She would not, of course, go back to her husband without Henry's consent. But with his consent Henry felt now pretty certain that she would go back to him. They had discussed the possibility several times, very rationally and objectively. They had not quarrelled about it, but they seemed to have quarrelled about almost everything else this summer. He thought he saw what was ahead.

He was so absorbed in his thoughts as he went down the hall that when he passed the open door to his parents' bedroom he at first gave no thought to the glimpse he had of his father in there. It was only when he was well past the door that he stopped dead still, realizing that his father was on his knees beside the bed. He was not praying, either. He was stuffing something under the mattress. And Henry did not have to look again to know that it was the newspaper he was hiding. He hurried on back to the screened porch, and, somehow, the sight of Dwight, bent over his grapefruit, wearing his travelling clothes—his dacron suit, his nylon tie, his wash-and-wear shirt—told Henry what it was the Judge had to conceal. There would be an article on the society page—something chatty in a column, probably—about those two couples who were driving up to visit the Nathan Parkers, and even a mention of the garden party on Monday.

4. *The Apples of Accord*

Kitty was determined that the two children should eat a good breakfast this morning, and she saw to it that they did. Mrs. Parker, who had insisted upon preparing and serving breakfast unassisted, was "up and down" all through the meal. The two women were kept so busy—or kept themselves so busy—that they seemed for the most part unmindful of the men. They took no notice of how long the Judge delayed coming to the table, or even that Henry actually appeared before his father did. When everybody had finished his grapefruit, and the men began making conversation amongst themselves, the two wives seemed even not to notice the extraordinarily amiable tone of their husbands' voices or the agreeable nature of their every remark. The only sign Kitty gave of following the conversation was to give a bemused smile or to nod her dark head sometimes when Dwight expressed agreement with her father. And sometimes when the Judge responded favorably to an opinion of Dwight's, Mrs. Parker would lift her eyebrows and tilt her head gracefully, as though listening to distant music.

Henry's first impression was that there had not, after all, been a crying need for his presence. His father and his brother-in-law, who a few minutes before had been hiding behind their papers to avoid talking to each other, were now bent upon keeping up a lively and friendly exchange. The Judge was seated at his end of the table, with Henry at his left and with Dwight on the other side of Henry at Mrs. Parker's right. Across the table from Henry and Dwight, Kitty sat between the two children.

The first topic, introduced by Dwight, was that of the routing to be followed on his trip. Dwight thought it best to go over to Nashville and then up through Louisville.

"You're absolutely right, Professor," the Judge agreed. "When heading for the Midwest, there is no avoiding Kentucky. But keep *off* Kentucky's back roads!"

Henry joined in, suggesting that the Knoxville-Middleboro-Lexington route was "not too bad" nowadays.

"I find the mountain driving more tiring," Dwight said politely, thus disposing of Henry's suggestion.

"And, incidentally, it is exactly a hundred and fifty miles out of your way to go by Knoxville and Middleboro," the Judge added, addressing Dwight.

Then, rather quickly, Dwight launched into a description of a rainstorm he had been caught in near Middleboro once. When he had finished, the Judge said he supposed there was nothing like being caught in a downpour in the mountains.

But the mention of Knoxville reminded the Judge of something he had come across in the morning paper, and his amnesia with regard to his hogging and hiding the first section was so thoroughgoing that he didn't hesitate to speak of what he had read. "There's an editorial today on that agitator up in East Tennessee," he said. "Looks as though they've finally settled his hash, thank God."

"I'm certainly glad," said Dwight. It was the case of the Yankee segregationist who had stirred up so much trouble. Dwight and the Judge by no means saw eye to eye on segregation, but here was one development in that controversy that they could agree on. "That judge at Knoxville had shown considerable courage," Dwight said.

"I suppose so. Yes, it's taken courage," said Judge Parker, grudgingly, yet pleased, as always, to hear any favorable comment on the judiciary. "But it is the law of the land. I don't see he had any alternative."

Henry opened his mouth, intending to say that the judge in question was known to be a man of principle, and if it had gone against his principle, Henry was sure that he would have . . . But he wasn't allowed to finish his thought, even, much less put it into words and speak it.

"Still and all, still and all," his father began again, in the way he had of beginning a sentence before he knew what he was going to say. "Still and all, he's a good man and knows the law. He was a Democrat, you know."

His use of "was" indicated only that it was a federal judge they were referring to, and that he was therefore as good as dead—politically, of course.

"No, I didn't know he was a Democrat," Dwight said, hugely gratified.

Here was another topic, indeed. Dwight and the Judge were both Democrats, and it didn't matter at the moment that they belonged to different wings of the party. But Dwight postponed for a little the felicity they would enjoy in that area. He had thought of something else that mustn't be passed up. "I understand," he said, pushing the last of his bacon into his mouth and chewing on it rather playfully, "I understand, Judge, that the Catholics have gotten the jump on everybody in Nashville."

The Judge closed his eyes, then opened them wide, suppressing a smile —or pretending to. "They've integrated, you mean?"

The machinations of the Catholic Church was a subject they never failed to agree on. "Not only in Nashville," Dwight said. "Everywhere."

"Very altruistic," said the Judge.

"Ah, yes. Very."

"If the *other* political parties were as much on their toes as that one, politics in this country would still be interesting."

Henry felt annoyed by this line they always took about the Catholic Church. Perhaps *he* should become a Catholic. That would give him his Certainty, all right. He grimaced inwardly, thinking of the suffering Nora's being a Catholic had brought the two of them. He realized that he resented the slur on the Church merely because the Church was something he associated with Nora. Silly as it seemed, Nora still came in the category of "Nashville Catholics." She was still a communicant, he supposed, and yet this proved that you could be a Catholic without developing the Certainty he had in mind. . . . But he didn't try to contribute anything on this subject. He had already seen that contributions from him were not necessary. Perhaps his father and his brother-in-law were no longer consciously trying to keep him silent, but they were in such high spirits over their forthcoming release from each other's company that each now had ears only for the other's voice. And, without knowing it, they seemed to be competing to see who could introduce the most felicitous subject.

From the subject of Nashville Catholics it was such an easy and natural step to Senator Kennedy, and so to national politics, that Henry was hardly aware when the shift came. Everybody had finished eating now. The men had pushed their chairs back a little way from the table. Dwight, in his exuberance, was happily tilting his, though presently Kitty gave him a sign and he stopped. Neither the Judge nor Dwight was sure of how good a candidate Kennedy would make. They both really wished that Truman— good old Truman—could head the ticket again. They both admired that man—not for the same reasons, but no matter.

Meanwhile, Kitty and her mother, having finished their own breakfasts and feeling quite comfortable about the way things were going with the men, began a private conversation at their corner of the table. It was about the basket of fruit, which Mrs. Parker still hoped they would find room for in the car. In order to make themselves heard above the men's talk and above the children, who were picking at each other across their mother's plate, it was necessary for them to raise their voices somewhat. Presently, this mere female chatter interfered with the conversation of the men. Judge Parker had just embarked on an account of the Democratic convention of 1926, which he had attended. He meant to draw a parallel between it and the 1960 convention-to-be. But the women's voices distracted him. He stopped his story, leaned forward and took a last sip of his coffee, and said very quietly, "Mother, Dwight and I are having some difficulty understanding each other."

Mrs. Parker blushed. She had thought things were going so well between the two men! How could *she* help them understand each other?

"Is the question of the basket of fruit really so important?" the Judge clarified.

Mrs. Parker tried to laugh. Kitty rallied to her support. "It's pretty important," she said good-naturedly.

Henry hated seeing his mother embarrassed. "I imagine it's as important as any other subject," he said.

The Judge's eyes blazed. He let his mouth fall open. "Can you please tell me in what sense it is as important as any *other* subject?"

Dwight Clark laughed aloud. Then he looked at Henry and said, unsmiling, "Politics is mere child's play, eh, Henry?" And, tossing his rumpled napkin beside his plate, he said, "Oh, well, we must get going."

"No," said the Judge. "Wait. I want to hear Henry's answer to my question."

"I do, too," said Dwight, and he snatched his napkin from the table again as if to prove it.

"We're waiting," said the Judge.

"At least theirs is a question that *can* be settled," Henry said, lamely.

"Oh," Dwight rejoined in his most ringing professorial voice, "since we can't, as individuals, settle the problems of the world, we'd best turn ostrich and bury our heads in the sand."

"That won't do, Henry," said Judge Parker. "We're still waiting."

So they *had* needed him, after all, Henry reflected. A common enemy was better than a peacemaker. He understood now that his own meek and mild behavior on the front porch had assured both men that he was not going to spill their beans. And in their eyes, now, he saw that they somehow hated him for it. But, he wondered, why had they thought he might do it, to begin with? Why in the world *should* he? Because he was an old bachelor with no life of his own? He knew that both the men, and the women, too, were bound to have known for years about his love affair with Nora McLarnen. But to themselves, of course, they lied willingly about such a large and unpleasant domestic matter. . . . He was an old bachelor without any life of his own! Oh, God, he thought, the realization sweeping over him suddenly that that's how it really would be soon, when he told Nora that she had his consent to go back to John McLarnen. He thought of his office in the courthouse and how it would seem when Nora was no longer behind her typewriter down the corridor. And he realized that the rest of his life with her, the part that had been supposed to mean the most, didn't matter to him at all. He couldn't remember that it *once* had mattered, that *once* the summer nights, when his parents and her children didn't have to be considered, had been all that mattered to him. He couldn't, because the time had come when he couldn't afford to remember it. All along, then, they had been right about him. All his hesitations and discriminations about what one could and could not do with one's life had been mere weakness. What else could it be? He was a bloodless old bachelor. It seemed that all his adult life the blood had been slowly draining out of him, and now the last drop was drained. John McLarnen, who could sell a quarter of a million dollars' worth of life insurance in one year, and whose wife could damned well take him or leave him as he was, was the better man.

While Dwight and the Judge waited for him to speak up, Henry sat with a vague smile on his lips, staring at the basket of fruit, which was placed on a little cherry washstand at the far end of the porch. He saw the two children, Susie and her little brother, slip out of their chairs and go over to the washstand. He heard his sister tell them not to finger the fruit. Suddenly he imagined he was seeing the fruit, the peaches and apples and pears, through little Dwight's eyes. How very real it looked.

"The basket of fruit," he said at last, "is a petty, ignoble, womanish consideration. And we men must not waste our minds on such." Intuitively, he had chosen the thing to say that would give them their golden opportunity. But before either of the men could speak, he heard his mother say, "Now, Henry," in an exasperated tone, and under her breath.

5. *The Juggler*

Judge Parker rested his two great white hands limply, incredulously on the table. "Henry," he said, "are you attempting to instruct your brother-in-law and me in our domestic relations?" He gazed a moment through the wire screening out into his flower garden. He was thinking that Henry always left himself wide open in an argument. Even Dwight could handle him.

"If that isn't an old bachelor for you," Dwight said, rising from his

chair. He wished Henry would wipe the foolish grin off his face. He supposed it was there to hide his disappointment. He had observed Henry, all
during the meal, trying to work up some antagonism between his father-in-
law and himself—about the roads, about religion, about politics.

The Judge was getting up from the table now, too, but he had more to
say. "While we discussed all manner of things that you might be expected
to know something about, you maintained a profound silence. And then you
felt compelled to speak on a subject of which you are profoundly ignorant."

" 'Our universities are riddled with them,' " Dwight said, savoring his
joke, feeling that nobody else but Kitty would get it. "Old bachelors who
will tell you how you can live on university pay and how to raise your
children. I know one, even, who teaches a marriage course."

"*You* might try that, Henry," said the Judge. And then he said, "We're
only joking, you know. No hard feelings?" He had thought, suddenly, of
the extra liquor that Henry was supposed to have brought up from Nashville for the party. Then he remembered that Jane had already asked
Henry. It was locked in the trunk of his old coupé.

"Henry knows we're kidding," Dwight said.

Kitty was helping her mother clear the table. Mrs. Parker was protesting,
saying that she had nothing else to do all day. Presently, she said to Henry,
"Henry, would you take the famous basket of fruit out front? I haven't
given up." She *hadn't* given up. How really wonderful it was, Henry
thought. And Kitty, too. She could so easily have agreed to take the whole
basketful along, could so easily have thrown the whole thing out once they
got down the Mountain. But it wouldn't have occurred to her.

"Will you gentlemen excuse me?" he said to the two men, smiling at
them. And the two men smiled back at him. They felt very good.

When they were all gathered out on the lawn, beside Dwight's car, Kitty
looked at her mother and father and said, "It's been a grand summer for
us. Just what we needed."

"It's been grand for *us,*" Mother Parker said, "though I'm afraid it's
spoilt us a good deal. We shouldn't have let you do so much."

"But we hope you'll do it again," Dad Parker said, "whenever you feel
up to it."

"I never dreamed I'd get so much done on my book in one summer,"
said Dwight, really meaning it, but thinking that nobody believed him. He
saw that brother Henry was pulling various little trinkets out of his pockets
for the children. He had bought them in Nashville, no doubt, and they
would be godsends on the trip. Henry knew so well how to please people
when he would. He was squatting down between the two children, and he
looked up at Dwight to say, "You're lucky to have work you can take all
over the world with you."

"Well, I'm sure it requires great powers of concentration," Mother Parker said. She went on to say that she marvelled at the way Dwight kept at it and that they were all proud of how high he stood in his field. As she spoke, she held herself very straight, and she seemed almost as tall as her husband. She had had Henry set the basket of fruit on an ivy-covered stump nearby. It was there to plead its own cause. She would not mention it again.

At breakfast, the children had been so excited about setting out for home that Kitty had had to force them to eat. In fact, even the night before, their eagerness to be on the way had been so apparent that Dwight had had to take them aside and warn them against hurting their grandparents' feelings. Yet now, at the last minute, they seemed genuinely reluctant to go. They clung to their uncle, saying they didn't see why they couldn't stay on a few days longer and let him enjoy the tiny tractor, the bag of marbles, and the sewing kit with them. It seemed to Dwight that their Uncle Henry had done his best to ignore the children during all his weekends at the Mountain, but now at the last minute he had filled their hands with treasure. And now it was Uncle Henry who was to have their last hugs and to lift little Dwight bodily into the car. When he turned away from the car, with the two children inside it, Henry took Dwight's hand and said, "I'm sorry we never had that chess game. I guess I was afraid you would beat me." It was as if he had seized Dwight and given him the same kind of hug he had given the children. Probably Henry had really wanted to play chess this summer, and probably he had wanted to be affectionate and attentive with the children. But the old bachelor in him had made him hold back. He could not give himself to people, or to anything—not for a whole season.

When finally they had all made their farewell speeches, had kissed and shaken hands and said again what a fine summer it had been, Dwight and Kitty hopped into the little car, and they drove away as quickly as if they had been running into the village on an errand. As they followed the winding driveway down to the public road, Dwight kept glancing at Kitty. He said, "Let's stop in the village and buy a copy of the morning paper."

"Let's not," she said, keeping her eyes straight ahead.

"All right," he said, "let's not." He thought she looked very sad, and he felt almost as though he were taking her away from home for the first time. But the next time he glanced at her, she smiled at him in a way that it seemed she hadn't smiled at him in more than two months. He realized that this summer he had come to think of her again as "having" her father's forehead, as "having" her mother's handsome head of hair and high cheekbones, and as "sharing" her brother's almost perfect teeth, which they were said to have inherited from their maternal grandmother's people. But now suddenly her features seemed entirely her own, borrowed from no one, the features of Dwight Clark's wife. He found himself pressing down on the accelerator, though he knew he would have to stop at the entrance to the road.

In the mirror he saw his two children, in the back seat, still waving to their grandparents through the rear window. Presently, Susie said, "Mama, look at Uncle Henry! Do you see what he's *doing?*" They had reached the entrance to the road now, and Dwight brought the car to a complete halt. Both he and Kitty looked back. Mother and Dad Parker had already started back into the cottage, but they had stopped on the porch steps and were still waving. Henry was still standing beside the ivy-covered stump where the basket of fruit rested. He had picked up two of the apples and was listlessly juggling them in the air. Dwight asked the children to get out of the way for a moment, and both of them ducked their heads. He wanted to have a good look, to see if Henry was doing it for the children's benefit. . . . Clearly he wasn't. He was staring off into space, in the opposite direction, lost in whatever thoughts such a man lost himself in.

Dwight put the car into motion again and turned out of the gravel driveway onto the macadam road, with Kitty and the children still looking back until they reached the point where the thick growth of sumac at the roadside cut off all view of the cottage, and the sweep of the green lawn, and the three relatives they had just said good-bye to for a while.

⬥

Peter Taylor was born in Trenton, Tennessee, in 1917, took his B.A. at Kenyon College in 1940, has taught at Kenyon, Ohio State, the University of North Carolina, and now teaches at the University of Virginia. He has published a novel, A Woman of Means *(1950), and a long play,* Tennessee Day in St. Louis *(1957), but he is best known for his short stories. He has written some fifty stories, and there are four collections of them:* A Long Fourth and Other Stories *(1948),* The Widows of Thornton *(1954),* Happy Families Are All Alike *(1959), and* Miss Leonora When Last Seen *(1963).*

In "Heads of Houses" we are given a good picture of the friendly conflict of the generations where nothing much is at stake except the continuity of "family ties." This continuity is maintained, in a mountain stronghold, based on wealth and community and a command of the past, despite irrevocably opposed notions of how one should act and talk and run a household now. The conflict is made beautifully explicit in details of the two generations' differing ways of life, and in the secret interpretations, or misinterpretations, each generation makes of the other's actions. It is the adroit way in which each generation manages to recognize this sequence of disagreements and "impositions" and "resentments" and yet determinedly keep them "hidden" and "secret" that has made it possible for the two families resolutely to go through with the carefully planned summer, wretched as it has been for both of them. This awareness of differences and the determination to ignore them, strengthened by being able to see through to a return to their own lives, when "each of them would have it all his way again," permit Dwight and the Judge to maneuver themselves through an "amiable" and "agreeable" but very hazardous last breakfast together. Each of the two heads of houses has his own "brand of Certainty" which each manages to keep at the last breakfast by excluding and victimizing poor Henry, bouncing their certainties off him, treating him, as he realizes, as "only a poor bachelor with no life of his own." Henry, privy to the secrets of both parties, has juggled the apples of accord for them all summer, as he is seen juggling the apples from the discordant basket of fruit in Dwight's last glimpse of him. He is the one on whom the events of the story have most consequence. He realizes that what he had thought were "stupid deceptions" on the part of both families had been necessary and useful to keep the larger family and its traditions intact by avoiding "an open quarrel of any kind." But he realizes too that in juggling the roles of his own life—as old-fashioned bachelor and as new-fangled, self-doubting, rational, adulterous man—his own deceptions had been harmful and useless self-deceptions. "All his hesitations and discriminations about what one could do and could not do with one's life had been mere weakness." Deception is useful only when it occurs as a result of Certainty. Then even deliberate self-deception can be useful, as is shown when Dwight and Kitty decide not to stop in town to get a copy of the local paper.

ROGER ANGELL

Summer in the Mountains

❖❖❖❖❖❖❖

MEG PORTER had a look of determination on her face as she listened to her mother. Her eyes were fixed on her mother, and occasionally she raised her eyebrows or nodded slightly at a pause in the conversation, but her lips were clamped firmly together, as if to hold back any words she might later regret, as if no one could wring from her the mildest complaint or even a sigh of boredom or resignation. It was, nevertheless, a look of remarkable hostility, particularly from a woman of thirty whose face was normally pretty and animated. Both her husband and her mother had seen this look before; her mother, Mrs. Brockway, had, in fact, come to think it was her daughter's normal expression, and it worried her, but somehow she had never brought herself to speak of it. Larry Porter had once mentioned it to his wife. She ought to try, he had said, to appear happier and more interested when her mother was with them. She had no idea how bad it looked, he said, and Mrs. Brockway would think that that was the way her only daughter *felt* about her, which, of course, wasn't true. And besides, it made her look old. But Meg Porter somehow couldn't shake the habit. Now Larry, sitting across the room, tried to get her attention, to remind her again, but Meg wouldn't take her rigid stare away from her mother.

"And since Dr. Stout couldn't see me at any other time," Mrs. Brockway was saying, "naturally I had to call Mrs. Lincoln and tell her I wouldn't be able to come to the symphony after all. It was really a shame, because I do get out so little, you know. But the doctor had said to come back for a little checkup when I noticed that shortness of breath again, and Tuesday morning I just felt as if I couldn't take any air into my lungs. Of course, it wouldn't worry me if there were someone living with me in the hotel, but even with the elevator boys right outside that you told me I could call any time, it just isn't the same. I sometimes wonder what would happen if anything *did* happen to me and nobody there with me." Meg Porter opened her mouth suddenly and took a breath, but her mother held her hand up and smiled. "No," she said. "I know what both Dr. Stout and that other one said. I'm fine, perfectly fine, and there's really nothing to worry about. For my age. I'm not trying to scare you, Meg. I know you call up, and you know I love that. Nearly every day. And there's always the phone, in case anything . . . I really don't worry at all." She smiled bravely and shook her head. "It's just being alone, that's all. I'm afraid I'll never really be used to it. Of course, I don't have to tell you how much I appreciate—No, you told me not to use that word, didn't you?" She looked slyly at her daughter. "Well, how much I *love* that apartment and how glad I am knowing that it's mine, or almost mine. I always want you and Larry to know that I don't forget that or take it for granted. Ever. Well!" She smoothed her skirt carefully and then looked at Larry. "Where are you two going tonight?"

Larry Porter took his eyes off his wife. "It's just to cocktails with the Bradleys. You know—you met them here Christmas Eve. And then we thought we'd go to dinner at Luchow's. But we won't be late. Shouldn't be later than ten or so. Of course, we can always come back before then if you want to get home earlier. We could just pick up a hamburger."

"Don't be silly, Larry," Mrs. Brockway said. "I wouldn't dream of it. Jane and I always have a wonderful time together. You know I love looking after her. It's so much like the old days, with Meg. After her father died and before she went away to college. I'll bet she doesn't even remember how close we used to be."

"Of course I remember, Mother," Meg Porter said. She leaned forward and took a cigarette out of a box on the table beside her chair. "We used to play games. And we went to the theater. And—"

"And every summer to Chocorua," Mrs. Brockway said. "Larry, you have no idea how she used to adore it there. Sometimes I wonder how you all ever started going to the beach."

"Jane is crazy about the beach, Mother," Meg said. "She wouldn't go any place else. And neither would I."

"Of course, dear," Mrs. Brockway said gently. "It isn't the place that counts. It's just being with people that counts. People you love. I just hope, Meg, that you're *with* Jane enough. She's such a responsive little girl, and you have no idea how suddenly it all ends. Before you know it, she'll be grown up and off married to somebody, with a busy life of her own and lots of friends and parties. And then you'll start thinking back about your life and you'll remember every hour you had together."

"Mother, for heaven's sake! You don't honestly think that I neglect—"

"Oh, no, Meg," Mrs. Brockway said, smiling again. "I just mean that Jane responds so. I hope you appreciate it. Why, I always look forward to these evenings we have together. Jane and I have such fine times it makes me feel like a real member of the family, just for a few hours, while you and Larry have a good time by yourselves. What I mean is, really, that at my age you know enough to appreciate a little child. They just *give* themselves, the way grownups can't. Nobody really understands that until they're as old as I am and their own children have gone."

"Oh, *Moth*-er," Meg said, helplessly dropping her hands.

Larry Porter stood up quickly, looking at his watch. "We'd better go, darling. It's past five-thirty. I'll tell Jane we're leaving. I think she's in her room watching that damned kid show again."

In the cab, a few minutes later, Meg was almost crying. "Oh, God, darling," she said to her husband, "why is she so awful, and why am I so awful to her? I've just got so that I think that every word is a hint or a slam or something, and I just can't stand it any more. There ought to be a compatibility test for parents and grown-up children to take together, and if they fail, there would be a law that said they couldn't see each other or couldn't live in the same city together. No, I don't mean that, either. I don't *really* feel that way—it's too hateful. It's just that Mother gets me all mixed up."

"I know," Larry Porter said. He lit a cigarette and handed it to her. "You had that look again. You never look that way except when she's there."

"I know I did. I can feel it coming over me and I can't stop it. Every time before she comes, I say to myself, This time will be different, this time we'll really get along, and she won't talk about herself and how lonely she is and how dreadful I am. But then the minute I see her I know it's going to be just the same."

"It's not your fault, Meg," Larry said gently. "It's just that she's old. That and the money."

"I know it. But we can't help the money. She needs it, and we want to give it to her. But why does she have to be so damned *grateful?* I've told her not to do that. It just ruins everything, and somehow it makes me feel as if we weren't doing enough for her, either. We all know she couldn't live with us, even if we had room. She doesn't really want that—she'd loathe it. And I'd go absolutely crazy and so would you."

"I wouldn't allow it," Larry said. "I'll never get us trapped with that."

"But what *does* she want?" Meg almost shouted. "I call her up. I have lunch with her. I go to the movies with her. We have her for dinner. We have her in to sit with Jane, because I honestly think she likes it. We get the best doctors for her and try to persuade her that she really is as well as she can expect. Why does she keep talking at me, then? Why does she make me feel so damned ungrateful and mean?"

Larry stared out at the passing lights for a moment before he answered. "I think," he said finally, "it's just that she's old and afraid, and she wants somebody to share that with her. And nobody can do it. You can't share being old with anybody."

Meg turned in the seat and quickly took hold of her husband's arm.

"Don't let me get that way, Larry," she said urgently. She squeezed his arm hard. "Promise me you'll do that, Larry. Don't ever let me get like that. Don't let me do that to Jane, ever."

In the apartment, after she and the little girl had eaten the supper she had cooked, Mrs. Brockway went to the living-room windows to draw the curtains. She felt tired, and there was a vague pain in her side. Before dinner, she and her granddaughter had played a game on the floor, throwing dice that sent little racing cars around a numbered course. She hadn't understood the game well and the floor had made her knees ache, but Jane had seemed excited and happy, and they had played it twice. Now she stood for a moment by the window and looked out at the darkness that meant that soon the little girl would have to go to bed. After that, after an hour or two, the Porters would be back. She would hear them laughing and talking as they came out of the elevator, and they would come in looking excited and happy, and Larry would offer her a drink, which she would refuse, and then it would be time for her to leave and go back to the barren hotel apartment, with the uncomfortable bed, and the furniture that was not hers, and the steam heat that killed every plant she bought, and the silent telephone, and the strange voices in the hall late at night—all the ugly and frightening familiarities that had somehow become the place where she lived. There were a few of her possessions left there—the set of Thackeray of her husband's, and the Spode teacups, which she had to keep on the mantelpiece—but they no longer seemed like her own. Sitting there by herself in the evenings after she had turned off the loud, confusing television, she often studied these treasures of hers and tried to remember how they had looked back in her own apartment, the one she had shared with Meg—where in the bookcase the set of Thackeray had stood and how the cups had looked among the other familiar china on the shelves in the dining room. But she could no longer remember. When her furniture had gone (Meg had pointed out that it would be foolish and expensive to keep up her old place or to store all her books and pictures and furniture), her remaining treasures had somehow lost their identity. Out of place and without companions, they had become exactly the same as everything else in her bare rooms—somebody else's belongings, which she was now expected to live with for a time.

It was this she tried to explain to her daughter when she came to Meg's house and saw it full of the warmth of lived-with and familiar objects: an album of records that Jane had left open on the floor, the dachshund's worn cushion beside the fireplace, the clamshell ashtrays, which the three of them had collected on the beach the summer before—all the evidence of plans made long ago and happily accomplished. Seeing this after the cold emptiness of her own long afternoons, after the terrors of a sudden pain in the night with no one to call out to, Mrs. Brockway always wanted to tell her daughter what she had here in her home, to cry desperately to her, "You don't know! You're so lucky here and you don't know it. You can't know what it's like to be without it, when it's all forgotten, when your own belongings are gone, and your house empty, and there are no more plans." But somehow it never came out that way. When she tried (without complaining) to explain all this to Meg, it ended in a recital of her days, of what she had eaten and what the doctor had said. Meg always became impatient and angry, and Mrs. Brockway went away feeling ashamed, because she had said it all wrong.

"Grandma, look!"

The little girl had made a small tower out of the piled-up dice from the game, and now she sent one of the tiny racing cars crashing into it, knocking the dice onto the rug. "Bang!" she cried. "He hit the pylon on that turn and now he's out of the race. Dang! Dang! Dang! Here comes the ambulance!"

Mrs. Brockway sighed and closed the curtains. She would have to hurry. The little girl would have to be put to bed soon. There was less than an hour for the two of them to be together.

"Let's read now, Jane, shall we?" Mrs. Brockway said. "I'll sit on the couch and you can lie beside me, and we'll read anything you want. We'll have a nice, quiet time together, won't we, darling?"

"O.K.," Jane said. She dropped the racing car and ran over to the bookcase. "Here," she said, pulling out a book. "This one. Read me *The Tinder Box,* Grandma."

Smiling, Mrs. Brockway sat down on the sofa. Sometimes Jane was exactly the way her mother had been as a little girl. Like Meg, she was suggestible; at one moment she could appear frighteningly violent, but she could change her mood and her interest in a second. The similarity made the grandmother feel warm and happy. Now she took the book from the eight-year-old. "All right," she said comfortably, turning the pages. *"The Tinder Box* it is. I know that story. It has those wonderful dogs with the big eyes. Now you sit down beside me, and I'll start." The little girl quickly curled her legs on the sofa, and Mrs. Brockway put her arm around her, pulled her close, and began to read: "A soldier came marching along the highroad. One, two! One, two!"

As she read the familiar story, Mrs. Brockway kept glancing at the little girl's face, intent on the page. Looking at her, the grandmother felt calm. At these moments, she knew that the fears and pains of her hotel bedroom were not really part of her at all. She was the same as she had always been, capable of anything as long as there was someone near her whom she loved and could make happy. Meg could no longer accept that from her, but this little girl, her granddaughter, did. She knew Jane depended on her. All that was needed was for them to be together more often, not just for a few hours on an occasional evening.

When Mrs. Brockway finished the story, Jane didn't move but kept staring at the page with an intent and abstracted expression. Suddenly, before the child sat up, before it was time for her to go to bed, Mrs. Brockway wanted to do something to preserve the moment, plan something that she could take back with her to her room, like a possession of her own—a guarantee of love and happiness to come.

She tightened her arm about her granddaughter. "Jane," she said softly, "how would you like to come and live with me for a little while? Just we two together. Wouldn't that be fun? We do have such nice, happy times together it would be fun to do it for a longer time. I know a lovely place we could go, perhaps in the summer, when your school is over and Mum and your father might like to take a little trip by themselves. Would you like that, Jane?"

"Where would Mum and Dad go?" Jane asked quietly.

"Oh, I don't know. Perhaps to Europe for a few weeks or on a motor trip somewhere in the summer. I haven't asked them, but perhaps, if you would like it, I could suggest it and they might think it was a good idea. They haven't been off by themselves for so long that they might say yes. And then you and I could go to the mountains together, to a place I know. I used to go there every single summer with your mother. We could get a lovely cottage, and there are mountains all around, all with long Indian names. And there's a lake, where you could learn to swim, right where your mother did. And you can climb mountains, and we could take little trips. Would you like that, Jane?"

"Could I have a bulldog?" Jane asked. "Jennifer French, at the beach, has a bulldog, and Dad said maybe I could have one sometime—a dog of my very own. Could I have one in the mountains?"

"Well, maybe, Jane. It all depends." Mrs. Brockway gave her another little hug. "We'd have to see, but we certainly could try. Wouldn't it be fun?"

"Yes, Grandma," Jane said. She sat up and looked at Mrs. Brockway. "And we can take the bulldog to climb the mountains and take him to the lake, and he'll learn to swim with me, won't he?"

Mrs. Brockway laughed aloud; actually, the plan didn't seem impossible at all. They might do it this very summer. It wasn't too late. She would be very practical and write and ask about cottages first and then speak to Meg after she had heard, so that there could be no difficulties or arguments. It was the simplest thing in the world. A whole summer with Jane, every moment of the long months with someone she loved. She pulled the child close. "We'll make a little secret of this, Jane, won't we? You won't tell Mum tomorrow, and then we'll talk to her about it together some day soon and surprise her, and she'll be so glad you can go to the mountains just the way she did."

"Not tell Mum?" Jane said doubtfully.

"Not right away, darling. It'll be a surprise, see? And then when we do tell her, you can explain how very much you want to go and spend the whole summer with Grandma. And after that, who knows? Perhaps we can do it again and we can stay even longer together. And we could go for a little trip next Christmas, just the two of us, on the train. Oh, you'll see! We'll have fine times together, and we'll have a lot of them!"

Mrs. Brockway had been hugging the child close to her for a long time, and now Jane began to struggle under her arm. She pulled herself away and stood up, and Mrs. Brockway was astonished to see that there were tears in her eyes.

"Go away for *Christmas?*" Jane said in a frightened voice. "Where will Mum and Dad be? Won't they be here for Christmas?"

Mrs. Brockway was frightened now, too. "Of course, darling," she said quickly, putting her hands out toward the child. "Of course they will. You don't have to go away for Christmas if you don't want to." She hadn't meant to go so far with her talk and plans. All that could come later. She caught Jane's hand and pulled her back to the couch. "You don't have to go anywhere, Jane," she said, trying to make her voice warm and soothing again. "Just to the mountains. Just this summer in the mountains, darling. You and I together."

But Jane roughly jerked her arm free and took three quick and defiant backward steps away from her. Mrs. Brockway again reached her hands out toward her granddaughter, and as she searched hopelessly for the words to recapture what she had lost, she suddenly thought she saw on the red, tear-streaked face of the little girl a flicker of expression she had noticed before in the eyes of the young and the strong—a bright, animal look of rejection and fear.

◈

Roger Angell was born in New York City, where he now lives with his wife and daughters, educated at Harvard, worked at Holiday, *and is now an editor of* The New Yorker, *where all of the stories in his only book,* The Stone Arbor *(1960), originally appeared.*

In "Summer in the Mountains," we see an increasingly common situation, that of the dispossessed mother who has outlived her husband. The grandmother, Mrs. Brockway, hasn't the equal footing necessary to maintain the battle of the generations on a friendly basis as the two families did during their summer in the mountains in "Heads of Houses." She has no house to be head of, no life of her own; she is like her few remaining possessions in her hotel apartment, which "had somehow lost their identity" and are "out of place and without companions." Older women alone, if

there is money enough, can be comfortably provided for, as Mrs. Brock-
way is; but it is certainly not comfort and not really even loneliness that is
her problem. Her trouble is her sense of uselessness, of not having someone
to care for. As she wants to tell her daughter, a busy and useful member
of the responsible generation: "You can't know what it's like to be without
it, when it's all forgotten, when your belongings are gone, and your house
empty, and there are no more plans." Plans are important to her because
they represent both some possible future to look forward to and also the
purposeful days of the past. She needs more than luncheons and occasional
baby-sitting; she needs a place and a function. Since the only function she
ever had was that of caring for her daughter, the only plan she is capable
of making is to recapture that way of life by taking over her granddaughter.
But her plans are met with "a bright, animal look of rejection and fear" from
the young, who guess, correctly, that her plans are not for their pleasure
but her sustenance. For she feels that she could recover herself, could be
"the same as she had always been, capable of anything as long as there was
someone near her whom she loved and could make happy." The need to
be needed can become more than merely oppressive to others. Like many
a widowed grandmother living out the remnant of a life whose only purpose
and pleasure have been caring for her family, Mrs. Brockway is more than
just a depressing dependent to the nuclear family, she is a threat to their
cohesive world.

ANATOLE BROYARD

Sunday Dinner in Brooklyn

❖❖❖❖❖❖❖

I TOOK A ROUNDABOUT ROUTE to the subway, and because I was going to Brooklyn the Village seemed to have at that moment all the charm of a Utrillo. It was only at times like this, in contrast to something else, that this neighborhood became attractive. Ugly in itself, it was a relief from certain kinds of beauty. To most of those like me who lived there, it was as inviting as a view of a squalid village would seem to a princess imprisoned in an ivory tower.

Since it was summer, the Italians were all outside on stoops and chairs or standing along the curb in their Sunday clothes, the old men in navy blue and the young men in powder blue suits, as though their generation was more washed out than the last. The mothers with their hair pulled back and their hands folded in their laps looked like Neanderthal madonnas, and they were dressed, of course, in black, since it was a miracle if someone in their families had not died within the year. The girls wore long pegged skirts which made their feet move incredibly fast. All of their movements seemed to be geared to this same tempo, and their faces were alert with the necessity of defending the one prize they had against mother and brother alike.

On the corner squatted their church—a huge casserole, fat, heavy, and plain as the women who prayed in it. Looking through the open doors as I passed, I saw the arches bending downward like a laborer under a heavy load. Even the bells of this church—presumably the voice of their god— were sour, and every Sunday morning I cursed them together with the priest who played some sort of chopsticks tune over and over on them.

On Thompson Street, a block and a half from where I lived, there was a stable, and here a horse's head poked through the window on the second floor. Above him, on the windowsill of the top floor, a geranium grew out of a rusty one-gallon can. Near the corner, a drunk slept in the sun against the wall of the Mills Hotel, and another drunk stood over him, holding out his hand, saying, "Shake, pal. Shake."

The waterless wading pond in the center of Washington Square, the bull's eye of the Village, was overflowing with guitar players, folk singers, folk dancers, conga drummers, communists, anarchists, voyeurs, frotteurs, fairies, dogs, children, Negroes, sightseers, psychotics, anthropology professors, heroin pushers, tea pushers, carriage pushers, lesbians, *New York Times* readers, people with portable radios, adenoidal girls looking for interesting boys, the uninteresting boys they would eventually wind up with, older girls between affairs, older boys on the lookout for younger girls, and so on. Where they stood, Fifth Avenue dribbled to its conclusion after penetrating Washington Arch.

Looking around, I didn't see any of my crew, so there was nothing else to do but head for the subway. At the entrance on Sixth Avenue and Waverly Place, I took a long breath like a deep-sea diver and went reluctantly underground.

The subway's roaring and screaming in the darkness, the passing under the river with the pressure in my ears—these were such a classical overture to going back home that I was weary of the joke. Riding the wrong way like that, I felt I had left Brooklyn for Manhattan only to discover on arriving that I had forgotten something I needed. Now, retracing my steps, I found the ride an endless torture, as it always inexplicably is under these circumstances, although when I was going in the other direction the distance passed unnoticed.

Of course it was my mother and father I'd forgotten, and I'd do it all over again next time too, but by now I accepted this as in the nature of things. They could hardly forget me though, because they had my picture on the mantel next to the clock. It was ten years old, that picture, but they never asked for a new one, and I was convinced that this was the way they still saw me. Like a criminal, I might alter my appearance, but they were not to be fooled. Each time I arrived, I could see their moist eyes washing away my disguise.

I was holding a book open on my lap—I always carried a book to Brooklyn, as an amulet or charm, a definition of my delicate ego—but for all the reading I did I might just as well have put it into the seat of my pants. My mind kept dropping down the page like a marble in a pinball machine until I finally gave it up, conceding that no book could successfully compete with my favorite fiction, my mother and father.

The train stopped, and a man who had been sitting across from me got out. He had been occupying the seat next to the window, at a right angle to the wall. Now a woman placed alone on the seat parallel to the wall and in front of the one he had vacated, quickly changed to his empty seat. Whereupon a man sitting on the outside of the seat corresponding to the one she now occupied but on my side of the train, jumped up to take her former seat, and the man next to me on the seat parallel to the wall shifted to the seat at his left knee just vacated. All of this was done dead-pan, but when I looked again at the woman to see how she was enjoying her new seat, I found her staring at me. She was sour and middle-aged, and her eyes, which were very small, were brooding deeply on me, full of a very personal distaste, as if she were imagining me as her own son. Something about me displeased the hell out of her—the way I was dressed, my haircut, or the expression on my face, which wasn't businesslike enough to spell security for her in her old age.

I didn't feel like answering this look, so I avoided her by staring myself at a man standing a few feet away from me. This man was very visibly chewing gum, and the movements of his bony jaws were so elaborate and so regular that they reminded me of printing presses. I noticed that he was studying himself in the window glass. Arresting his jaws in a position in which all the complications of structure were particularly conspicuous, he observed himself with the close and scientific attention of a Leonardo. Then the machine resumed its hypnotic movements. Now, shifting the gum this way and that, he worked out a wonderful variety of effects. Anyone watching him would have thought he was chewing over a problem. He began by taking it up languidly, indifferently, disarmingly, chewing with his front teeth, his mouth relaxed to the point where it was half open, when suddenly, without warning, he shifted the wad to the left side and began to work it over systematically between his molars. Very businesslike, he gave it an evenly paced pulverizing, and then, just before all the life ebbed out of it, he shifted it again to the center, where his teeth barely dented it, and his tongue turned it over and over in a revivifying massage.

As the train entered another station, without interrupting this ruminating, he stuck his hand through the rubber lip of the door in a Napoleonic attitude, and when the door drew back he flung his hand after it.

I could never chew gum like that, I was thinking, and then I saw the name of my own station through the open door and I jumped up and ran through it barely in time, absolutely confirming the lousy impression I had made on the sour-faced woman.

At the top of the stairs the sun hit me in the eye. It seemed to me that the sun was always shining in Brooklyn, drying clothes, curing rickets, evaporating puddles, inviting children out to play, and encouraging artificial-looking flowers in front yards. Against my will, it warmed over an ineffable melancholy in me. I felt that it was a great democratic source of central heating for this big house in which everyone lived together.

The streets were almost deserted, since everyone ate dinner at the same time in Brooklyn. I knew these streets so well I could have walked them with my eyes shut. There wasn't a tree I passed into which I hadn't thrown my knife, a wall against which I hadn't bounced my ball, a crack I hadn't avoided lest I break my mother's back. Now I saw them in slow motion; everything stood out in a kind of heavy-handed symbolism, as though I were the camera eye in an arty documentary film. When I was a boy, these streets had quickness and life for me, each detail daring me to do something, to match my wits, my strength, my speed, against them. Then I was always running. I saw things on the run and made my running commentary on them without breaking my stride, hurdling, skipping, dodging, but still racing forward . . . until one day I ran full tilt into myself and blocked my own path.

The scene was made even more sententious by the fact that it was Sunday. There was a tremendous vacuum left behind by God. In contrast to the kitchenlike intimacy of the church on Thompson Street—which in its ugliness succeeded in projecting its flock's image on the universe—the spiky shells on these blocks had a cold, punitive look, and seemed empty except for those few hours in the morning when people came with neutralized faces to pay their respects to a dead and departed deity.

From the corner, I could see my mother in the front yard. Her face was turned toward me, although I knew she couldn't see me at that distance. I had the feeling that wherever I was, her face was always turned toward me. Now she saw me, she was waving and talking. In a moment she would begin to shout. I was already smiling and gesticulating too. I modified my walk, making it playful. "Hello, Paul!" she was shouting. "How are you?" I was still too far to talk. I wanted to run, I always wanted to run those last few yards. I hated the last few steps, the final enormous gap, between us. Once we were close enough, like lovers in an embrace, we wouldn't be able to see each other so clearly.

I seized her by the shoulders and bent to kiss her. As usual, each of us offered a cheek. Quickly we turned our heads, and somehow miraculously avoided kissing each other on the lips, our heads turning just far enough so that each kissed the other with half a mouth in the middle of the cheek, making three or four smacks for good measure. My father was inside. He would have liked to come out too, but he felt he would be a spectacle, and besides he seemed to think that she ought to greet me alone, as though she were giving birth to me again.

He met me at the doorway, and we clogged up there, gesticulating and embracing. We always gesticulated too much, we distrusted language and thoughts. And all the while we were shouting, as if we were singing an opera. "Take off your coat!" they were shouting. "Take off your tie!" Sometimes I almost expected them to ask for my belt and shoelaces, but I suppose they knew that, after all, there was no way of disarming the dagger of the mind.

"Wait, I'll make you a martini!" my father shouted, and he ran off into the kitchen. "Sit down!" my mother shouted. "Make yourself comfortable!" Shoving me into my father's chair, she pressed the button on the arm and I was suddenly in a horizontal position. She switched the radio to WQXR, and one of the more familiar symphonies poured out like coal out of a chute.

This chair had been a gift to my father on one of his birthdays. My mother was delighted by the idea of the button. I never liked it. It always struck me as uncanny. I felt myself straining in it, trying to keep my head up a little. My father came in with the martini. I saw that it was amber. He never thought to make himself one. Like a servant.

The martini was sweet. Suddenly I realized that I loved them very much. But what was I going to do with them?

"Here's the Book Review," my mother said, handing me the paper. They both sat down, waiting for me to read it. How could I read it with them sitting there watching me as if I were performing a great feat? I was a spectacle, they assumed I didn't want to talk to them. I understood too that, in a way, they liked to believe I wasn't there just for a visit, and it was perfectly natural for me to be reading the Book Review of a Sunday afternoon.

I put the paper down, reassuring them that I'd read it later. We looked at each other for a moment, smiling. I felt that I was stretched out on a bier. Pressing the button, I allowed the back of the chair to come up. I smiled at my mother to show her I didn't mind the chair. I liked it, but I just felt like sitting up, I was such a bundle of energy.

"Well, how's everything, Paul?" she said. From the time I had been two years old, they had called me Bud, but somewhere in the last few years they began calling me Paul the way the outside world did. "Everything's fine," I said, realizing of course that they had no idea what that everything embodied. This vagueness was our tenderness. They'd have loved to know, but they were afraid of finding out something which might have offended not them, but me.

The dinner was ready. It was always ready when I arrived. Sometimes I had the fantasy of just walking by the house: my mother would be in the front yard, holding a box lunch in her hands. I would take the box without stopping. My face would be expressionless, hers grieving but controlled. My father would stand just inside the doorway. . . .

My mother brought in the roast and my father carved it with great concentration, as if he were carving out our destiny. He placed on my plate the portion he had always desired for me. My mother heaped potatoes, gravy, vegetables on my plate. "I know you like to eat," she said, smiling and heaping my plate still more. This was a fiction. I never ate heartily, but nevertheless I exclaimed, "You know me, Mom!"

Pretending I could scarcely wait, I attacked the roast with knife and fork, while my mother held back to observe this. "Home cooking," I mumbled around a mouthful, these two words speaking volumes to her. I wondered what she thought I ate every day, whether she ever speculated for a moment that I might have liked it better. As a matter of history, the first time I ate in the Automat, when I was about twelve, I discovered that my mother was not an especially good cook, and this had hurt me as much as anything in my childhood. I could hardly swallow the food for years after that, but practice makes perfect, and I had learned to chomp with the histrionic absorption of a movie hero on a picnic.

As we ate, we regressed in time, reingesting all the events that had separated us. We retraced our steps to the very beginning, and there, joining hands, we advanced again from the birth of the soft-eyed boy to my embarrassing and unassimilable prodigality there at the table. To their great surprise, it always came out the same. We always bumped up against the present. Each time we raised our eyes from the plate, we were startled to discover each other, so camouflaged by time. As soon as our eyes met, we jumped back, as from an abyss. In these encounters, we resembled two forever inhibited people who press against each other in the subway: both want the contact, but neither dares admit it.

It was like my friend Andrew's description of the first analyst he went to. This one was not a Freudian, he belonged to a group which held our difficulties to be "inter-personal," and so instead of having Andrew lie on a couch while he sat behind him, they faced each other across a table. There Andrew would lay out all the disgusting things he had done, avoiding the analyst's eye for fear of showing shame or triumph, but sneaking furtive glances now and then, while the analyst, on his side, had his hands full dissembling disapproval or any other sign which might conceivably have disturbed Andrew's flow. Occasionally, however, in darting about the room and briefly lighting on the table like flies, their eyes would collide, and in that split second shockingly copulate in a deep obscene surmise.

Our conversation consisted of answerable questions and unquestionable answers. As usual, my mother found that I looked thin. All my life, I had managed to stay thin as a reproach to her, and on her side, as if a mother's role were that of a fanatic taxidermist, she had done her best to stuff me. She asked me where I took my laundry. "Aren't the prices outrageous? And the way they boil your clothes in all that acid, a shirt doesn't last six months." She was working around to suggesting that I bring my laundry to her. Maybe those dirty shirts would tell her what she was so anxious, and so ashamed, to know. A smear of lipstick, a smell, a stain, might paint a Japanese picture.

My father discussed the last month's boxing matches. Since I occasionally watched televised bouts in a bar, this had become a regular gambit. With an old man's memory, which clings to things as a child clings to its mother, for fear of being abandoned, he recalled every blow. If I happened to disagree with him—by mistake, or because I wasn't following him—he revised his version accordingly. We fought those fights side by side.

When he wasn't talking about boxing, his remarks were designed to show me that he was a liberal, a man who understands. Yesterday he gave up his seat in the subway to a Negress. Jews are smart. Everybody does things without knowing why. Nobody can say who's right and who's wrong. There are two sides to every question.

I remembered him when he was ten feet tall and his every statement was a revelation of the absolute order of things. I tried to steer him around to himself, to push him gently back into his own indistinctly remembered convictions, but this only succeeded in panicking him. He tried to believe that the only difference between us was that I was "modern." He was going to be "modern" too, by denying everything he felt, and forgetting the few lessons life had taught him. He thought of my modernity as relentless and inescapable, a march of history which would let nothing—parents least of all—stand in its way.

My mother was smiling, and as I watched her over a forkful of mashed potatoes I realized that she was still pretty. I knew that smile from way back, I remembered how it had once outshone the sun in heaven. Only, it had had more of a Mona Lisa character then, an ambiguity that gave it a special quality of romance. Where was that romance now? I wondered. Which of us was unfaithful, and why? Each was caricatured by a love we didn't know how to express. Afraid to feel, we were condemned to think, and at the same time not to think. When—and how—had our oneness become three? What ingredient was added to my mixture to turn it to poison? What alchemy isolated my substance beyond their—and my—understanding? There we were, playing a painful game of blindman's buff. We began by bandaging our eyes; then the bandages had fallen away and we had realized that we were blind.

At last I judged that I had eaten enough, an exemplary amount. With all my blood and nerves busy in my stomach, I relaxed, I became flatulent with affection. My mother saw my face go blank and she beamed. Belly to belly, that was the only true way to talk.

My father was describing how, on the job, he had solved a problem that had stumped even the architect. He had just 'scribed a plumb line on the floor. "Well I'll be god-damned," the architect had said, "if old Pete hasn't gone and done it again!" As I listened to this story, I never doubted it for a moment, and I was proud of him. That was his reality, and in it he was still magnificent, just as my mother could calculate better than the Secretary of the Treasury, how much it would cost a newlywed couple to set up housekeeping. It was in these attitudes, like an old-fashioned photograph, that I thought of them most fondly, and although I had long since exiled myself from that Garden of Eden, it was something I could not root out of my feelings. This homely love was my history. Like a navel, it was a reminder that I hadn't been struck fully formed from my own brow. I remember a story an Army doctor told me, about a Negro soldier whose belly was ripped open in a fight. They sewed him up in time and saved his life, but when they pulled off the adhesive tape, his belly button—he had the old-fashioned protruding kind—came away with it. When he saw what had happened, the soldier was beside himself, in the full sense of that expression, and they couldn't calm him down until the doctor sewed his belly button back on.

I knew how he felt. Although I liked to imagine myself unfettered by human history, faced only by free choices, exquisitely irresponsible, it was still comforting to know that I hadn't been born in a bad novel like most of the people who spent their evenings in Village bars. Although they too probably came from Brooklyn or the Bronx, I couldn't imagine them with families. They seemed to have risen spontaneously from rotting social tissues, the way flies were thought to generate in filth, or in a wound.

I admit that whenever I considered my parents for any length of time, I generally arrived at a feeling of incredulity there too, but at least this is some kind of an emotion, and after all, how else can you look at a mother and father who hatched you like a plot and then couldn't read their own writing? They, too, were inevitably incredulous, always wondering. I could see them right there in that moment struggling with this puzzle which was hidden in the back of their minds the way people you read about now and then in the newspapers hide their children in a closet or a windowless room for twenty years. Always, without realizing it, they were wondering what I was, whether to be proud of me or ashamed, whether my strangeness was genius, sickness, or simply evil, whether I had sold my soul like Faust or was still learning to walk, whether I was a hero or an abortion. In the familiar terms, I was a failure. I had neither money, fame, nor any immediate prospect of either. At least if I had been an idiot, lurching up and down the sidewalk in front of the house, they could have lavished all their pent-up love on my helpless heart, but as it was they were never sure.

My father was still talking about the job. He seemed very proud to have a hand in this particular building, which had been given a lot of publicity and which was apparently expected to become a world-famous monument on Broadway. As superintendent, he had a set of plans, and he brought them out for me to see. I recognized the name of a large low-priced clothing chain which sold standard stuff on installments. Feigning a show of interest, I studied the plans. Besides some very ill-adapted functionalist architecture, the building boasted two tremendous figures—a male and a female nude—above its façade, on either side of the store name like parentheses. They were over fifty feet high, my father assured me, and would be draped in neon lights. "They're like the Statue of Liberty on Broadway," he said, and I knew by the tone of his voice that he was quoting somebody. "What are they supposed to stand for?" I asked, in spite of the feeling I had that this question was all wrong. He looked at me, surprised and a little embarrassed. He was searching his mind for an answer, and although by now I didn't want an answer, I didn't know how to stop what I had started. I looked at the plans again. The figures were sexless, without even the pretense of drapery or a fig leaf. I knew what they stood for. The Statue of Liberty, since it was a French gift, may be presumed to have something under her robes, but these were American-made, this was the naked truth.

My father moved his lips as if to speak, but said nothing. In spite of myself again, I turned on him inquiringly, and he dropped his eyes. "It seems like a mighty big job, Pop," I said. "They must have a lot of confidence in you." "You said a mouthful," he said quickly, plainly relieved. "The architect himself asked for me."

Primitive tools—a saw, a hammer, nails, a square rule, a leveler—these were not enough. I looked at my father, at his innocent face which had been chiseled into homely, heart-rending lines by the simplest kind of considerations, at his jaw made square by practical decisions, his mouth made thin by everyday resolutions, his eyes kept clear and alert with estimations of length, breadth, and height . . . and it struck me then that his head might have been done by a sculptor with a warm feeling for texture and no talent for portraiture, a craftsman with no idea of art.

Suddenly I felt a mushrooming urge to blurt out something—I don't know what—"I think you're great, Pop," or "I'm with you," or "To hell with them all," and this made me very nervous, so nervous I could hardly sit still. In desperation, I abruptly decided to leave. With my mouth still full of lemon meringue pie, I announced apologetically that I had an unbreakable appointment for which I was already late. I had been on the point of calling them up, I improvised, for that very reason, but I felt that even a short visit was better than none. I would come again soon and we would have a nice long talk.

They immediately fell into a frenzy of reassurances. Talking both at once, drowning each other out, they assured me that I didn't have to give explanations to them, they certainly understood how busy I was, and they had not the most infinitesimal wish to interfere with these quintessential commitments. Perish the thought—perish, in fact, the mother and father who would interrupt for a thousandth of a second their son's glorious onrush toward his entelechy. . . .

Caught up in their extravagance, I reiterated my determination to come again soon with all the fervor of MacArthur vowing to return to the Philippines. I again congratulated my mother for having served up a truly historic feast and made ready to leave, avoiding my own eyes in the mirror as I knotted my tie.

My father left the room for a moment and reappeared in his coat. He would walk me to the subway, he said. I was on the point of protesting, but I knew I shouldn't, so I said "O.K., Pop, let's go." I kissed my mother, and she walked out to the gate with us.

Closing the gate behind me, I said, "So long, Mom," and she answered, "So long, Bud," slipping unconsciously into my old nickname again. The sound of it moved me more than I would have thought possible, and I impulsively kissed her again before my father and I faded from her sight.

At the corner I looked back to see her still standing there, her features erased by distance, and I waved, although I knew she couldn't see me. To my astonishment, she waved back. I caught the movement of her arm in the corner of my eye just as I was turning my head. I couldn't believe I had actually seen it—I knew she couldn't see across the street without her glasses. I stopped and took a step back—she was gone. Had I imagined it? It seemed very important to me to find out, and then I realized that I believed she *knew* when I turned the corner, she *sensed* it. No, no, I expostulated with myself, she only knew how long it took us to reach the corner, and then she waved. . . .

"What's the matter?" It was my father, asking why I had stopped. "I was wondering how Mom could see this far," I said. "She just waved at us." "Yeah, she waves three, four times," he said indifferently, and we started off toward the subway again.

I was trying to dismiss a vague fear that he wouldn't stop at the subway entrance, that he would go all the way with me, then I reflected that he rarely came to visit me. My mother had never been to my place. "I can't climb all those steps," she would say, as if I lived on top of Parnassus. Once my father and I had walked, just as we were walking now, through the Village. He didn't remember the neighborhood very clearly—he said the last time he'd been there was before I was born—and he had looked around him like the sightseers who go through the streets in plastic-topped buses. On Fourth Street, we had passed a big fat lesbian dressed in men's clothes and with her hair cut like a man. My father favored her with a disapproving glance as she went by. "Put a dress on that bastard and he'd be a woman," he said, wholly unaware that it was.

A few minutes later, as we were walking through Waverly Place, he swept his arm over half a century's changes and said, "You know, this used to be all sportin' houses around here. . . ." and I could see that he was wondering how the simple, old-fashioned sportin' house—where you knew what you wanted and got what you paid for—had given way to this, had borne a brood of Hamlets and hermaphrodites whose sport was an ambiguous affair in which you never knew who was getting the f———ing or what unheard-of infections you risked in the bargain, and where you paid with your life. . . .

We had reached the subway entrance and I stopped, but he began to descend the steps. I seized him by the arm. "You don't have to walk me down, Pop," I said.

He was surprised. "That's all right," he said. "I haven't got anything else to do."

"Yeah, but what's the use of your breathing all those fumes and then having to come all the way up again?" I said, still holding his arm.

He was disappointed, I could see that he wanted to walk me down.

"O.K., Pop," I said, letting go of his arm and starting down, "I guess a few steps don't faze you, do they?"

"No," he said, "I'm used to them," and we went down together and he came back up alone.

❖

Anatole Broyard was born in New Orleans in 1926, spent most of his life in New York City, and now lives in Connecticut; he attended The New School in New York, where he now teaches short-story writing. "Sunday Dinner in Brooklyn" is part of a novel he's finishing; other parts have appeared in Hudson Review, discovery, *and* Fiction of the Fifties. *He writes very little, but whatever he does is much reprinted, translated, anthologized, admired.*

In "Sunday Dinner in Brooklyn" we see a different kind of conflict from that in the previous two stories, but one that's equally recognizable and prevalent. Like many young Americans—it sometimes seems most *young Americans—this son has chosen a way of life so different from his parents' that he is virtually cut off from them. Unlike Mrs. Brockway, he is dispossessed by his own choice. He has left "this big house in which everyone lived together," the "oneness" of his Brooklyn family childhood, for the cold, foreign, endlessly differentiated bohemian life in Greenwich Village. The parents' secure middle-class way of life, their house, eating habits, and furniture have remained unchanged. American life is nowadays so fluid that a young person may leap from one way of life to another while his parents remain firmly planted. Although the narrator now lives only a subway ride away, there is no sharing of his present self or life with his parents. The still considerable affection between parents and son is not enough to bridge the gap between their ways of life and ways of thought. Their affection has been arrested at the level of childhood, and they find no common ground for communication adult to adult. The son has opted for a "hellish" world which though "ugly in itself . . . was a relief from certain kinds of beauty." His "delicate ego" is at home in the bohemian life of the Village, and his mother and father have become "a fiction" for him, just as he appears to them to be in a "disguise." Neither geographical distance nor lack of love nor success has destroyed the former unity of this family. He realizes they are not "a rotting social tissue," nor is he simply "modern." They are a puzzle to one another, and as there is no answer to the puzzle there may be no answer to what the puzzle is caused by. There is no way of adjusting their shared past to a sharable present. What they have in common is "a feeling of incredulity." "How else can you look at a mother and father who hatched you like a plot and then couldn't read their own writing?" Each generation overinterprets the other, and overcompensates for possible misunderstandings, trying to arrive at the closeness they felt and remember and long for. The argumentative, self-pitying narrator is a typical product of the child-centered middle-class home where belief in the ultimate success of the child is based on his being part of the "relentless and inescapable march of history which would let nothing —parents least of all—stand in its way." The parents, instead of standing on their own convictions, surrender themselves to the ego of the offspring, who then finds he has no way of dealing with them except as part of his own invention. But his own ego, and his affection for them, requires that, as such, they remain the perfect idols of his childhood—his mother with a smile that "outshone the sun in heaven," his father, "ten feet tall."*

EVAN S. CONNELL, JR.

Notes from the File on

Mrs. Bridge

◇◇◇◇◇◇◇

Love and Marriage

HER FIRST NAME was India—she was never able to get used to it. It seemed to her that her parents must have been thinking of someone else when they named her. Or were they hoping for another sort of daughter? As a child she was often on the point of inquiring, but time passed, and she never did.

Now and then while she was growing up the idea came to her that she could get along very nicely without a husband, and, to the distress of her mother and father, this idea prevailed for a number of years after her education had been completed. But there came a summer evening and a young lawyer named Walter Bridge: very tall and dignified, red-haired, with a grimly determined, intelligent face, and rather stoop-shouldered so that even when he stood erect his coat hung lower in the front than in the back. She had known him for several years without finding him remarkable in any way, but on this summer evening, on the front porch of her parents' home, she toyed with a sprig of mint and looked at him attentively while pretending to listen to what he said. He was telling her that he intended to become rich and successful, and that one day he would take his wife—"whenever I finally decide to marry" he said, for he was not yet ready to commit himself—one day he would take his wife on a tour of Europe. He spoke of Ruskin and of Robert Ingersoll, and he read to her that evening on the porch, later, some verses from *The Rubáuját* while her parents were preparing for bed, and the locusts sang in the elm trees all around.

A few months after his father died she married Walter Bridge and moved with him to Kansas City, where he had decided to establish a practice.

All seemed well. The days passed, and the weeks, and the months, more swiftly than in childhood, and she felt no trepidation, except for certain moments in the depth of the night when, as she and her new husband lay drowsily clutching each other for reassurance, anticipating the dawn, the day, and another night which might prove them both immortal, Mrs. Bridge found herself wide awake. During these moments, resting in her husband's arms, she would stare at the ceiling, or at his face, which sleep robbed of strength, with an uneasy expression, as though she saw or heard some intimation of the great years ahead.

She was not certain what she wanted from life, or what to expect from it, for she had seen so little of it, but she was sure that in some way—because she willed it to be so—her wants and her expectations were the same.

For a while after their marriage she was in such demand that it was not unpleasant when he fell asleep. Presently, however, he began sleeping all night, and it was then she awoke more frequently, and looked into the darkness, wondering about the nature of men, doubtful of the future, until at last there came a night when she shook her husband awake and spoke of her own desire. Affably he placed one of his long white arms around her waist; she turned to him then, contentedly, expectantly, and secure. However nothing else occurred, and in a few minutes he had gone back to sleep.

This was the night Mrs. Bridge concluded that while marriage might be an equitable affair, love itself was not.

Children

Their first child, a girl, curiously dark, who seldom cried and who often seemed to want nothing more than to be left alone, was born when they had been married a little more than three years. They named her Ruth. After the delivery Mrs. Bridge's first coherent words were, "Is she normal?"

Two years later—Mrs. Bridge was then thirty-one—Carolyn appeared, about a month ahead of time, as though she were quite able to take care of herself, and was nicknamed "Corky." She was a chubby blonde, blue-eyed like her mother, more ebullient than Ruth, and more demanding.

Then, two years after Carolyn, a stern little boy was born, thin and red-haired like his father, and they named him Douglas. They had not wanted more than two children, but because the first two had been girls they had decided to try once more. Even if the third had also been a girl they would have let it go at that; there would have been no sense in continuing what would soon become amusing to other people.

Preliminary Training

She brought up her children very much as she herself had been brought up, and she hoped that when they were spoken of it would be in connection with their nice manners, their pleasant dispositions, and their cleanliness, for these were qualities she valued above all others.

With Ruth and later with Carolyn, because they were girls, she felt sure of her guidance; but with the boy she was at times obliged to guess and to hope, and as it turned out—not only with Douglas but with his two sisters—what she stressed was not at all what they remembered as they grew older.

What Ruth was to recall most vividly about childhood was an incident which Mrs. Bridge had virtually forgotten an hour after it occurred. One summer afternoon the entire family, with the exception of Mr. Bridge who was working, had gone to the neighborhood swimming pool; Douglas lay on a rubber sheet in the shade of an umbrella, kicking his thin bowed legs and gurgling, and Carolyn was splashing around in the wading pool. The day was exceptionally hot. Ruth took off her bathing suit and began walking across the terrace. This much she could hardly remember, but she was never to forget what happened next. Mrs. Bridge, having suddenly discovered Ruth was naked, snatched up the bathing suit and hurried after her. Ruth began to run, and being wet and slippery she squirmed out of the arms that reached for her from every direction. She thought it was a new game. Then she noticed the expression on her mother's face. Ruth became bewildered and then alarmed, and when she was finally caught she was screaming hysterically.

Marmalade

Her husband was as astute as he was energetic, and because he wanted so much for his family he went to his office quite early in the morning while most men were still asleep and he often stayed there working until late at night. He worked all day Saturday and part of Sunday, and holidays were nothing but a nuisance. Before very long the word had gone around that Walter Bridge was the man to handle the case.

The family saw very little of him. It was not unusual for an entire week to pass without any of the children seeing him. On Sunday morning they would come downstairs and he might be at the breakfast table; he greeted them pleasantly and they responded deferentially, and a little wistfully because they missed him. Sensing this, he would redouble his efforts at the office in order to give them everything they wanted.

Consequently they were able to move to a large home just off Ward Parkway several years sooner than they had expected, and because the house was so large they employed a young colored girl named Harriet to do the cooking and cleaning.

One morning at the breakfast table Carolyn said petulantly, "I'm sick and tired of orange marmalade!"

Mrs. Bridge, who was mashing an egg for her, replied patiently, "Now, Corky, just remember there are lots and lots of little girls in the world who don't have any marmalade at all."

Alice Jones

That summer Carolyn began playing with Alice Jones, the daughter of the colored gardener who worked next door. Every Saturday morning he would appear from the direction of the streetcar line, his daughter Alice capering wildly around him. As soon as they came in sight of the Bridges' house she would rush ahead, pigtails flying. In a minute she would be at the back door, pressing the bell with both hands. Often Mrs. Bridge would be in the kitchen polishing silver or planning the week-end menu while Harriet did the heavy cleaning somewhere else in the house, so Mrs. Bridge would answer the door.

Alice Jones was always out of breath from the run and her eyes were shining with expectation as she inquired if Corky could come out and play.

"Why, I think she can," Mrs. Bridge would say, and smile. "Providing you two behave yourselves." About this time the gardener would come walking up the neighbor's driveway and she would say through the screen door, "Good morning, Jones."

"Mornin', Mrs. Bridge," he always answered. "That child bothering you all?"

"Not a bit! We love having her."

By this time Carolyn would appear and the two children would begin their day. In spite of Carolyn's excellence at school she was not very imaginative, and no matter what she suggested they do that day Alice Jones had a better idea. Carolyn was a little stunned by some of the suggestions, and for a few minutes would grow petulant and arrogant, but when she found that Alice could not be intimidated she gave way and enjoyed herself.

One morning they decided to take apart the radio-phonograph and talk to the little people inside the cabinet; another morning they made sandwiches and filled a Thermos jug with milk because they planned to leave on a trip to Cedar Rabbits, Iowa. Again, they composed a long cheerful letter to Sears, Roebuck & Co. in which Alice told how she murdered people.

Some Saturdays they would stage extremely dramatic plays—the leading part always being taken by Alice Jones because, at her grade school in the north end of the city, she was invariably the Snow Queen or the Good Fairy or some other personage of equal distinction. Carolyn, whose stage experience had been limited to a Thanksgiving skit in which she had been an onion, seldom objected and in fact had some difficulty keeping up with the plot.

Long before noon they were at the back door, wanting to know if it was not yet lunchtime, and when at last Harriet, or perhaps Mrs. Bridge, set up the breakfast-room table for them they would turn on the radio so that during lunch they might listen to the livestock reports, which Alice Jones found hilarious.

One day a fire truck went by the house and Alice, wagging her head in amazement, exclaimed, "There they go again! Who they going to burn down this time?" Dismayed by the wickedness of the firemen, she rolled her eyes and sighed and helped herself to more caramel pudding.

Mrs. Bridge, who was making up a grocery list, paused and smiled affectionately at both children, pleased that Carolyn was not conscious of the difference between them.

Alice and her father appeared every Saturday, and the two children, occasionally joined by Ruth—who more often spent the day lying on the porch swing—would play together as comfortably as on the first Saturday they met. The gardener never failed to ask Mrs. Bridge if Alice was a nuisance; Mrs. Bridge always smiled and assured him she was not.

For a month each summer the Bridges went to Colorado; they hired Jones for this month to water the grass after he had finished working for the neighbors, and so Alice amused herself on the familiar grounds and frequently asked her father how soon Corky would be back.

"Soon enough," was his usual reply, but one day he paused, and as if considering the future, he told her, cryptically and a little sadly, "She liable not to come back, child."

But at last the vacation ended and Carolyn returned, full of sunshine and sophistication.

"The mountains are awfully big," she said primly, and, echoing her mother, "It was just grand."

Then Alice Jones said, "You know what I got in this here pocket?"

Carolyn, reluctant to become once more the planet instead of the star, affected disdain.

"Who cares?" she announced, coolly turning away.

"A human gizzard," murmured Alice with a mysterious expression, and before much longer Carolyn was convinced a summer in Kansas City would have been much more exciting than the mountains. She said as much to her mother, who replied a trifle brusquely, being harried at the moment, "Don't be silly, dear." And Mrs. Bridge was about to add that there must be other girls besides Alice to play with, but she did not say this; she hesitated, and said, "Corky, you know perfectly well you enjoyed Colorado." Soon, she knew, the girls would drift apart. Time would take care of the situation.

Of Ladies and Women

For semi-annual housecleaning Mrs. Bridge hired additional help. Carolyn answered the back door and reported to her mother, "The cleaning lady is here."

"Oh, fine," Mrs. Bridge said, and put away her sewing basket and went to the back door, smiling and saying genially, "How do you do? Come right in, won't you?"

That evening she instructed Carolyn. "You should say the cleaning 'woman.' A lady is someone like Mrs. Arlen or Mrs. Montgomery."

Table Manners

Mrs. Bridge said that she judged people by their shoes and by their manners at the table. If someone wore shoes with runover heels, or shoes that had not been shined for a long time, or shoes with broken laces, you could be pretty sure this person would be slovenly in other things as well. And there was no better way to judge a person's background than by watching him or her at the table.

The children learned it was impolite to talk while eating, or to chew with the mouth open, and as they grew older they learned the more subtle manners—not to butter an entire slice of bread, not to take more than one biscuit at a time, unless, of course, the hostess should insist. They were taught to keep their elbows close to their sides while cutting meat, and to hold the utensils in the tips of their fingers. They resisted the temptation to sop up the gravy with a piece of bread, and they made sure to leave a little of everything—not enough to be called wasteful, but just a little to indicate the meal had been sufficient. And, naturally, they learned that a lady or a gentleman does not fold up a napkin after having eaten in a public place.

The girls absorbed these matters with greater facility than Douglas, who tended to ask the reason for everything, sometimes observing that he thought it was all pretty silly. He seemed particularly unable to eat with his left hand lying in his lap; he wanted to leave it on the table, to prop himself up, as it were, and claimed he got a backache with one arm in his lap. Mrs. Bridge told him this was absurd, and when he wanted to know why he could not put his elbow on the table she replied, "Do you want to be different from everyone else?"

Douglas was doubtful, but after a long silence, and under the weight of his mother's tranquil gaze, he at last concluded he didn't.

The American habit of switching implements, however, continued to give him trouble and to make him rebellious. With elaborate care he would put down the knife, reach high across his plate and descend on the left side to pick up the fork, raising it high over the plate again as he returned to the starting position.

"Now stop acting ridiculous," she told him one day at lunch.

"Well, I sure bet the Egyptians don't have to eat this way," he muttered, giving "Egyptians" a vengeful emphasis.

"I doubt if they do," she replied calmly, expertly cutting a triangle of pineapple from her salad, "but you're not an Egyptian. So you eat the way Americans eat, and that's final."

Alice Jones Again

It seemed to Mrs. Bridge that Saturday came around quite often. She was selecting some sugar buns from the bakery man when Alice dashed up the driveway with a long piece of clothesline in her hand, and the first thing that came to Mrs. Bridge's mind was that the girl had stolen it.

"Good morning, Alice," she said. Alice dropped the clothesline on the back steps and ran directly into the house to find Carolyn. A few minutes later the gardener appeared and asked, as he always did, whether she was being a nuisance. Mrs. Bridge smiled briefly and shook her head, not knowing how to be truthful without hurting his feelings.

The children were in Carolyn's room playing jacks. Mrs. Bridge looked in on them after a while and asked why they didn't play out of doors, the day being so nice, and she thought—but could not be sure—that as she suggested this the little Negro girl gave her a rather strange look. In any event the suggestion appeared to take hold, because a few minutes later she heard them outside shouting with laughter about something.

Shortly before noon, while rearranging the handkerchiefs in her husband's bureau, Mrs. Bridge heard Carolyn singing at the top of her voice: "My mother, your mother, live across the way, eighteen-sixteen East Broadway! Every night they have a fight, and this is what they say—" Here Alice Jones took over the song: "Goddamn you, goddamn you, goddamn you, goddamn you—"

Mrs. Bridge rushed to the nearest window and looked down. One end of the clothesline was tied to the rose trellis. At the other end was Carolyn, churning the rope with both arms, and in the center was Alice leaping up and down.

Next week, when Alice came racing up the driveway and tried to open the screen door to the kitchen, she found it locked. Mrs. Bridge was in the kitchen and said, "Who is it, please?"

"It's me," replied Alice, rattling the door.

"Just a minute, Alice. I'll see if Carolyn is at home." She went into the living room and found her daughter looking at one of the movie magazines that Ruth had begun buying.

"Alice is here again. I'll tell her you're busy."

But at the first word Carolyn had jumped up and started for the back door.

About ten o'clock both of them came into the kitchen for a bottle of soda pop and wanted to know what there would be for lunch.

"Corky is having creamed tuna on toast and spinach," said Mrs. Bridge pleasantly.

Alice observed that she herself didn't care for spinach because it was made of old tea bags.

"I believe you're supposed to have lunch with your Daddy, aren't you?"

Alice heard a note in her voice which Carolyn did not; she glanced up at Mrs. Bridge with another of those queer, bright looks and after a moment of thought she said, "Yes'm."

Guest Towels

Boys, as everyone knew, were more trouble than girls, but to Mrs. Bridge it began to seem that Douglas was more trouble than both the girls together. Ruth, silent Ruth, was no trouble at all; Mrs. Bridge sometimes grew uneasy over this very fact, because it was slightly unnatural. Carolyn made up for Ruth, what with temper tantrums and fits of selfishness, but she was nothing compared to Douglas, who, strangely enough, never actually appeared to be attempting to make trouble; it was just that somehow he *was* trouble. Invariably there was something about him that needed to be corrected or attended to, though he himself was totally oblivious to this fact, or, if he was aware of it, was unconcerned. Whenever she encountered him he was either hungry, or dirty, or late, or needed a haircut, or had outgrown something, or had a nosebleed, or had just cut himself, or had lost something, or was just generally ragged and grimy looking. Mrs. Bridge could not understand it. She could take him down to the Plaza for a new pair of corduroy knickers and a week later he had worn a hole through the knee. He was invariably surprised and a little pained by her dismay; he felt fine—what else mattered?

He was hostile to guest towels. She knew this, but, because guest towels were no concern of his, there had never been any direct conflict over them. She had a supply of Margab, which were the best, at least in the opinion of everyone she knew, and whenever guests were coming to the house she would put the ordinary towels in the laundry and place several of these little pastel towels in each of the bathrooms. They were quite small, not much larger than a handkerchief, and no one ever touched them. After the visitors had gone home she would carefully lift them from the rack and replace them in the box till next time. Nobody touched them because they looked too nice; guests always did as she herself did in their homes—she would dry her hands on a piece of Kleenex.

One afternoon after a luncheon she went around the house collecting the guest towels as usual, and was very much surprised to find that one of the towels in Douglas's bathroom had been used. It was, in fact, filthy. There was no question about who had used this towel. She found Douglas sitting in a tree in the vacant lot. He was not doing anything as far as she could tell; he was just up in the tree. Mrs. Bridge approached the tree and asked him about the towel. She held it up. He gazed down at it with a thoughtful expression. Yes, he had dried his hands on it.

"These towels are for guests," said Mrs. Bridge, and felt herself unaccountably on the verge of tears.

"Well, why don't they use them then?" asked Douglas. He began to gaze over the rooftops.

"Come down here where I can talk to you. I don't like shouting at the top of my lungs."

"I can hear you okay," said Douglas, climbing a little higher.

Mrs. Bridge found herself getting furious with him, and was annoyed with herself because it was all really so trivial. Besides, she had begun to feel rather foolish standing under a tree waving a towel and addressing someone who was probably invisible to any of the neighbors who might be watching. All she could see of him were his tennis shoes and one leg. Then, too, she knew he was right, partly right in any event; even so, when you had guests you put guest towels in the bathroom. That was what everyone did, it was what she did, and it was most definitely what she intended to continue doing.

"They always just use their handkerchief or something," said Douglas moodily from high above.

"Never mind," said Mrs. Bridge. "From now on you leave those towels alone."

There was no answer from the tree.

"Do you hear me?"

"I hear you," said Douglas.

Good-by Alice

Alice Jones was now appearing every month or so, though her father came to work at the neighbors' each Saturday as usual. On those occasions when she accompanied him she would spend the morning with Carolyn, but then, about noon, she would get on the streetcar and go home by herself.

During the morning she and Carolyn would have a confidential talk, usually in Carolyn's room, that is, in the room that Carolyn and Ruth shared. Ruth was seldom at home on Saturday; nobody in the family knew where she went. So Alice Jones and Carolyn would shut the door to the room and converse in low tones or in whispers about school and clothes and friends and boys and how they intended to raise their children.

"How many are you going to have?" asked Carolyn.

"Eleven," Alice said firmly.

"Heavens!" said Carolyn. "That's certainly telling."

"What kind of talk is that?" Alice wanted to know. "How many are you going to have?"

"Two, I believe. That makes a nice family."

One Saturday at lunch time, shortly after Alice had started to the streetcar line, Carolyn said that Alice had invited her to come to a party next Saturday afternoon.

"Well, that was nice of Alice, wasn't it?" Mrs. Bridge replied, and with a tiny silver fork she ate a slice of banana from her fruit salad, and then a piece of lettuce.

"Where is the party to be?"

"At her house."

"Where does Alice live?"

"Thirteenth and Prospect."

Mrs. Bridge took up a little silver knife and began to cut a slice of peach which was rather too large to be eaten in one bite. She knew where Thirteenth and Prospect was, although she had never stopped there. It was a mixed neighborhood.

"Can I go?"

Mrs. Bridge smiled affectionately at Carolyn. "I wouldn't if I were you."

Grace Barron

Grace Barron was a puzzle and she was disturbing. She belonged in the country-club district, for Virgil was a banker, and yet she seemed dissatisfied there. Mrs. Bridge could not altogether grasp whatever it was Grace Barron was seeking, or criticizing, or saying.

Grace Barron had once said to her, "India, I've never been anywhere or done anything or seen anything. I don't know how other people live, or think, even how they believe. Are we right? Do we believe the right things?"

And on another occasion, when Mrs. Bridge had passed a nice compliment on her home, Grace replied, "Virgil spent fifty thousand dollars on this place." It had not been a boast; it had been an expression of dissatisfaction.

At luncheons, Auxiliary meetings, and cocktail parties Mrs. Bridge always found herself talking about such matters as the by-laws of certain committees, antique silver, Royal Doulton, Wedgwood, the price of margarine as compared to butter, or what the hemline was expected to do, but since Grace Barron had entered the circle she found herself fumbling for answers because Grace talked of other things—art, politics, astronomy, literature. After such a conversation Mrs. Bridge felt inadequate and confused, if a little flattered and refreshed, and on the way home she would think of what she should have said, and could have said, instead of only smiling and replying, "It does seem too bad," or, "Well, yes, I expect that's true."

Said Mr. Bridge, glancing over the edge of his evening newspaper while she was talking about Grace Barron, "Ask her if she wants one to marry her daughter."

Mrs. Bridge replied defensively, "They just have a son." She knew this was a silly remark and added hurriedly, "I suppose you're right, but—"

"If you doubt me, ask her and see what she says."

"Goodness," Mrs. Bridge said, picking up the latest *Tattler*, "suppose we drop the subject. I certainly didn't mean to provoke you so."

Yet she continued to think about many things Grace Barron had said and about Grace herself because she was different somehow. The first time she had ever seen Grace was one afternoon in October of the previous year. The sun was shining and the leaves of the trees were changing color. It was a beautiful day. The Barrons had just moved into the neighborhood and Madge Arlen, whose husband had attended high school with Virgil Barron, was going to stop by and get acquainted, and Mrs. Bridge went along. The Barrons had moved into an enormous Colonial home near Meyer Circle, and that afternoon as Mrs. Bridge and Madge Arlen drove up to the house they saw a gang of boys playing football in the street. Apparently Grace Barron was not at home because no one answered the bell; they were about to leave when one of the boys came running up from the street. He stopped and kicked the ball back to the other players, then jumped over a flower bed, and with a whoop and a wave came running straight across the lawn.

"That must be her son," Madge Arlen observed.

"His name will be mud if she catches him leaping over her flowers," said Mrs. Bridge.

They waited, a trifle critically, for him to approach. He was wearing a baggy sweatshirt, faded blue jeans, dirty white tennis shoes, and a baseball cap. He was a thin, graceful boy, about the same height as Douglas, and as he came nearer they could see that he had freckles and a snub nose. He was laughing and panting for breath.

"Hello!" he called, and at that moment they realized he was not a boy at all. It was Grace Barron.

And Mrs. Bridge recalled with equal clarity an evening when she and Grace attended an outdoor symphony. Music was one of the things Mrs. Bridge had always wanted to know more about, and so she was pleased, if startled, when Grace, whom she scarcely knew, simply telephoned one evening and asked if she would like to go to the concert in the park. They sat on folding chairs and listened, and it was like nothing else Mrs. Bridge had ever experienced. When the symphony ended, while the musicians were packing away their instruments and the conductor was autographing programs, Grace suggested they come to the next concert.

"I'd love to!" Mrs. Bridge exclaimed. "When is it?" And upon learning the date she said regretfully, "Oh, dear, the Noel Johnsons are having a few people over for cocktails—"

"That's all right," Grace interrupted. "I know how it is."

And there was an afternoon when they happened to run into each other downtown. Mrs. Bridge was looking over some new ovenware she had heard advertised on the radio. She decided not to buy, and in the course of wandering around the store she suddenly came upon Grace Barron staring fixedly at a gift item—an arrangement of tiny silver bells that revolved around an elaborate candlestick.

"Oh, isn't this tricky!" Mrs. Bridge said, having a look at the price tag. "But I think they're asking too much."

"I feel like those bells," said Grace. "Why are they turning around, India? Why? Because the candle has been lighted. What I want to say is—oh, I don't know. It's just that the orbit is so small." She resumed staring at the contrivance, which went slowly around and around and gave out a faint, exquisite tinkling.

What's Up, Señora Bridge?

Spanish was a subject she had long meant to study, and quite often she remarked to her friends that she wished she had studied it in school. The children had heard her say this, so for her birthday that year they gave her an album of phonograph records consisting of a lethargic dialogue between Señor Carreño of Madrid and an American visitor named Señora Brown. Along with the records came an attractive booklet of instructions and suggestions. Mrs. Bridge was delighted with the gift and made a joke about how she intended to begin her lessons the first thing "mañana."

As it turned out, however, she was busy the following day, and the day after because of a PTA meeting at the school, and the day after. Somehow or other more than a month passed before she found time to begin, but there came a morning when she resolved to get at it, and so, after helping Harriet with the breakfast dishes, she found her reading glasses and sat down in the living room with the instruction booklet. The course did not sound at all difficult, and the more pages she read the more engrossing it became. The instructions were clear enough: she was simply to listen to each line of dialogue and then, in the pause that followed, to repeat the part of Señora Brown.

She put the first record on the phonograph, turning it low enough so that the mailman or any delivery boys would not overhear and think she had gone out of her mind. Seated on the sofa directly opposite the machine, she waited, holding onto the booklet in case there should be an emergency.

"Buenas días, Señora Brown," the record began, appropriately enough. "Cómo está usted?"

"Buenas días, Señor Carreño," Señora Brown answered. "Muy bien, gracias. Y usted?"

The record waited for Mrs. Bridge who, however, was afraid it would begin before she had a chance to speak, and in consequence only leaned forward with her lips parted. She got up, walked across to the phonograph, and lifted the needle back to the beginning.

"Buenas días, Señora Brown. Cómo está usted?"

"Buenas días, Señor Carreño," replied Señora Brown all over again. "Muy bien, gracias. Y usted?"

"Buenas días, Señor Carreño," said Mrs. Bridge with increasing confidence. "Muy bien, gracias. Y usted?"

"Muy bien," said Señor Carreño.

Just then Harriet appeared to say that Mrs. Arlen was on the telephone. Mrs. Bridge put the booklet on the sofa and went into the breakfast room, where the telephone was.

"Hello, Madge. I've been meaning to phone you about the Auxiliary luncheon next Friday. They've changed the time from twelve-thirty to one. Honestly, I wish they'd make up their minds."

"Charlotte told me yesterday. You knew Grace Barron was ill with flu, didn't you?"

"Oh, not really! She has the worst luck."

"If it isn't one thing, it's another. She's been down since day before yesterday. I'm running by with some lemonade and thought you might like to come along. I can only stay a split second. I'm due at the hairdresser at eleven."

"Well, I'm in slacks. Are you going right away?"

"The instant the laundress gets here. That girl! She should have been here hours ago. Honestly, I'm at the end of my rope."

"Don't tell me you're having that same trouble! I sometimes think they do it deliberately just to put people out. We're trying a new one and she does do nice work, but she's so independent."

"Oh," said Madge Arlen, as if her head were turned away from the phone, "here she comes. Lord, what next?"

"Well, I'll dash right upstairs and change," said Mrs. Bridge. "I suppose the garden can wait till tomorrow." And after telling Harriet that she would be at Mrs. Barron's if anyone called, she started toward the stairs.

"Qué tal, Señora Brown?" inquired the record.

Mrs. Bridge hurried into the living room, snapped off the phonograph, and went upstairs.

Advanced Training

Appearances were an abiding concern of Mrs. Bridge, which was the reason that one evening as she saw Ruth preparing to go out she inquired, "Aren't you taking a purse, dear?"

Ruth answered in a husky voice that whatever she needed she could carry in her pockets.

Said Mrs. Bridge, "Carolyn always takes a purse."

Ruth was standing in front of the hall mirror, standing in a way that disturbed Mrs. Bridge, though she did not know precisely why, unless it could be that Ruth's feet were too far apart and her hips a little too forward. Mrs. Bridge had been trying to cure her of this habit by making her walk around the house with a book balanced on her head, but as soon as the book was removed Ruth resumed sauntering and standing in that unseemly posture.

"And you're older than Corky," Mrs. Bridge went on with a frown; and yet, looking at her elder daughter, she could not continue frowning. Ruth really was quite lovely; if only she were not so conscious of it, not so aware of people turning to look at her, for they did stop to look—men and women both—so deliberately sometimes that Mrs. Bridge grew uneasy, and could not get over the idea that Ruth, by her posture and her challenging walk, was encouraging people to stare.

"Is somebody coming by for you?"

"I'm only going to the drugstore."

"What on earth do you do in the drugstore?" asked Mrs. Bridge after a pause. "Madge Arlen told me she saw you there one evening sitting all by yourself in a booth. She said she supposed you were waiting for someone."

At this Ruth stiffened noticeably, and Mrs. Bridge wanted to ask, "Were you?"

"I really don't approve of you sitting around in drugstores," she went on, for she was afraid to ask directly if Ruth was going there to meet a boy—not afraid of asking the question, but of the answer. "And I don't believe your father would approve of it either," she continued, feeling helpless and querulous in the knowledge that her daughter was hardly listening. "Goodness, I should think you could find something else to do. What about playing with Carolyn and her friends?"

Ruth didn't bother to answer.

"I'll lend you my blue suede purse, if you like," said Mrs. Bridge hopefully, but again there was no response. Ruth was still admiring herself in the mirror.

"I shouldn't think you could carry much in those pockets."

Ruth stepped backward, narrowed her eyes, and unfastened the top button of her blouse.

"Really, you *need* some things," Mrs. Bridge remarked a trifle sharply. "And button yourself up, for goodness sake. You look like a chorus girl."

"Good night," said Ruth flatly and started for the door.

"But, dear, a lady always carries a purse!" Mrs. Bridge was saying when the door closed.

Tower

Douglas did a peculiar thing.

Instead of building a cave, or a house in a tree, as most of his friends were doing, he chose to build a tower of rubbish.

"Sounds awfully exciting," Mrs. Bridge responded somewhat absently when he first told her of his project; then, because she knew children wanted their parents to be interested in what they were doing, she asked how big it was going to be. He was vague, saying only that it was going to be the biggest tower anybody ever saw. She smiled and patted him affectionately. He looked at her for a long moment, shrugged in a singular way, and returned to the vacant lot where he intended to build the tower.

In the lot he had found some two-by-fours and a number of old bricks and half a bag of cement. He did not know where these materials had come from; he waited several days to see if they belonged to anybody. Apparently they didn't, so he claimed them. He got a shovel and went to work.

Having dug a hole about four feet deep, he lined it with brick and cement, planted the two-by-fours solidly upright, and liberally sprinkled this foundation with water. He then waited for his friends, the trash collectors, and followed their truck around the neighborhood. There was a moment between the time a rubbish barrel was rolled to the curb and the time the truck stopped for it that Douglas made good use of; he grabbed anything he thought belonged on his tower. He collected a great quantity of useful objects, and, on the side, about forty or fifty cereal boxtops, which he mailed to such places as Battle Creek, where there was a cereal factory, getting in return all kinds of prizes.

Within a week he had accumulated enough junk to keep the construction going for a long while. Half-hidden in the tall grass and wild shrubbery of the vacant lot lay a bundle of brass curtain rods which the Arlens thought were now in the city dump, a roll of electrician's tape and a bent skillet from the Pfeiffers' trash barrel, a hatchet with a splintered handle, a cigar box full of rusty nails, a broken fishing rod, several lengths of clothesline and wire, coat hangers, bottles, two apple boxes, an old raincoat and a pair of worn galoshes, a punctured inner tube, some very old golf clubs with wooden shafts, the cylinder from a lawnmower, springs from an overstuffed chair, and, among other articles, thanks again to the unconscious generosity of the Arlens, a mildewed leather suitcase.

"My!" said Mrs. Bridge, when he told her he was working on the tower, "I can see you're going to be an architect or an engineer when you grow up. Now we're having an early lunch because this is my day for bridge club, so don't run off somewhere."

Douglas said he would be in the vacant lot.

During the next week he managed to steal a full bag of powdered cement from a house going up in the next block; he broke it open after the workmen left, shoveled the powder into a wheelbarrow, and eventually managed to push the wheelbarrow into the vacant lot, where he dumped the powder in the pit and gave it a thorough watering. Thereafter he stopped mentioning his tower, and if asked what he was doing in the lot he would reply laconically that he was just playing.

With the addition of jugs and stones, tin cans, tree limbs, broken bottles, and all the other trash he could find, tied or nailed or cemented to the uprights, the tower continued to grow, until there came a Sunday morning when a man named Ewing who lived on the far side of the lot saw the tower rising above his hedge. At this point it was nearly six feet high. Ewing went around for a better look, and, discovering Douglas watching him from behind a sycamore tree, said to him, "What have you got here, my friend?"

"Nothing," replied Douglas, coming out from behind the sycamore. "It's just a tower, that's all. It isn't hurting anybody."

Having inspected the tower from all sides, Ewing turned his attention to Douglas, because it was the builder, after all, and not the building which was remarkable; and Douglas, embarrassed by the speculative eyes, picked up a length of pipe and struck the tower a resounding blow to prove it was as substantial as it looked.

Shortly thereafter Mrs. Bridge saw it too—it rose jaggedly above the fence that divided their grounds from the lot—and went out to investigate. She looked at it for a considerable period, tapping a fingernail against her teeth, and that same afternoon she said lightly to her son, "My, but that certainly is a big old tower."

Douglas thrust his hands in his pockets and gazed with a distant expression at his shoes.

"Think what would happen if it fell over ker-*plunk* and hit you square on the head," she continued, ruffling his hair, and reflecting automatically that he needed another haircut.

Douglas knew his tower would stop a truck, so he only sighed and pursed his lips.

Mrs. Bridge was not overly concerned, being under the impression he was going to become bored with the tower and would dismantle it. But about two weeks later she realized he was still working on it, because she could see a cider jug and a chicken coop wired to the top of a broken chair, and she recalled that on her last visit this chair had been on top of everything. She had assumed this chair was his throne; she remembered how he liked to play king-of-the-mountain, and possibly he only built the tower in order to have a throne. Now, wondering how much higher he meant to go, she walked out to the vacant lot for another look, and this time she remained somewhat longer. Tentatively she pushed at the tower and was troubled by its solidity. She pushed again, with her palm, and again, much harder. The tower did not sway an inch. She began to wonder whether or not he would be able to destroy his creation—assuming she could convince him it ought to be torn down.

She intended to speak to him that same afternoon, but she did not know precisely how to begin because, like the tower, he seemed to be growing out of her reach. He was becoming more than a small boy who could be coaxed this way or that; the hour was approaching when she must begin to reason with him as an adult, and this idea disturbed her. She was not certain she was equal to it. And so a few days, a week, two weeks went by, and though she had not spoken neither had she forgotten.

"Well!" she finally exclaimed, as though she had just thought of it. "I see that ugly old tower keeps getting bigger and bigger." It was, to tell the truth, quite a bit bigger. When he did not say a word, or even look at her, she wanted to grab him by the shoulders and shake loose whatever was growing inside him.

"It seems to me that a big boy like you wouldn't want to go on building a silly tower," she said, hopefully, and then he glanced at her in a way that was somehow derisive, as if he were reading her mind.

"I'll tell you what let's do!" She stooped in order to look directly into his face. "First thing after dinner we'll get some wire clippers and a hammer and a screwdriver and—well, just everything we need, and you and I together will tear it to bits. Won't that be fun?"

He turned his head away and said very softly, "No."

"No? Why not?"

After a while Douglas rubbed his nose and muttered that there was too much concrete.

"Oh, I'll bet we—" Mrs. Bridge hesitated. Her insights usually arrived too late to illuminate the situation, but this one was in time.

"You're probably right," she said, continuing with treacherous frankness, "I doubt if you or anybody else could tear it down."

She watched him almost fall into the trap. He was ready to defy her by saying he could if he wanted to, and if she could get him to say that she knew the battle would be half over. He was on the verge of it; she could see the defiance on his face and in the way he stood. But then, instead of answering, he paused to think, and Mrs. Bridge was dismayed. All her life she had been accustomed to responding immediately when anyone spoke to her. If she had been complimented she promptly and graciously thanked the speaker; or if, by chance, her opinion was asked on something, any-thing—the cost of butter, the Italian situation—no matter what, if she was asked she answered readily. Now, seeing her son with his mouth clamped shut like a turtle with a seed and his face puckered in thought, she did not know what to do. She gazed down on him expectantly.

After a long silence Douglas said, "Maybe."

And here, for the time being, the matter rested.

Sentimental Moment

Mrs. Bridge stood alone at a front window thinking of how quickly the years were going by. The children were growing up so rapidly, and her husband—she stirred uneasily. Already there was a new group of "young marrieds," people she hardly knew. Surely some time had gone by—she expected this; nevertheless she could not get over the feeling that something was drawing steadily away from her. She wondered if her husband felt the same; she thought she would ask him that evening when he got home. She recalled the dreams they used to share; she recalled with a smile how she used to listen to him speak of his plans and how she had never actually cared one way or another about his ambition, she had cared only for him. That was enough. In those days she used to think that the long hours he spent in his office were a temporary condition and that as soon as more people came to him with legal problems he would, somehow, begin spend-ing more time at home. But this was not the way it turned out, and Mrs. Bridge understood now that she would never see very much of him. They had started off together to explore something that promised to be wonder-ful, and, of course, there had been wonderful times. And yet, thought Mrs. Bridge, why is it that we haven't—that nothing has—that whatever we—?

It was raining. Thunder rumbled through the lowering clouds with a constant, monotonous, trundling sound, like furniture being rolled back and forth in the attic. In the front yard the evergreen trees swayed in the wind and the shutters rattled in the sudden rainy gusts. She noticed that a branch had been torn from the soft maple tree; the branch lay on the driveway and the leaves fluttered.

Harriet came in to ask if she would like some hot chocolate.

"Oh, no thank you, Harriet," said Mrs. Bridge. "You have some."

Harriet was so nice. And she was a good worker. Mrs. Bridge was very proud of having Harriet and knew that she would be next to impossible to replace, and yet there were times when Mrs. Bridge half wished she would quit. Why she wished this, she did not know, unless it was that with Harriet around to do all the work she herself was so often dismally bored. When she was first married she used to do the cooking and housecleaning and washing, and how she had looked forward to a few minutes of leisure! But now—how odd—there was too much leisure. Mrs. Bridge did not admit this fact to anyone, for it embarrassed her; indeed she very often gave the impression of being distracted by all the things needed to be done—phone the laundry, the grocer, take Ruth to the dentist, Carolyn to tap-dancing class, Douglas to the barber shop, and so on. But the truth remained, and settled upon her with ever greater finality.

The light snapped on in the back hall. She heard his cough and the squeak of the closet door and the familiar flapping sound of his briefcase on the upper shelf. Suddenly overwhelmed by the need for reassurance, she turned swiftly from the window and hurried toward him with an intent, wistful expression, knowing what she wanted without knowing how to ask for it.

He heard the rustle of her dress and her quick footsteps on the carpet. He was hanging up his coat as she approached, and he said, without irritation, but a trifle wearily because this was not the first time it had happened, "I see you forgot to have the car lubricated."

Nothing Spectacular

At his wife's suggestion Mr. Bridge had walked around to the vacant lot to examine the eccentric and mystifying memorial Douglas had built and which he had not yet abandoned; Mr. Bridge tried to topple it and then simply attempted to shake it. The tower did not move. Satisfied that it would not collapse while Douglas or his friends were clambering about, and that they had sense enough not to impale themselves on the outcroppings, he returned to his evening newspaper and thought no more about it.

Mrs. Bridge, however, was uneasy. She sensed that people in the neighborhood were aware of the tower. Even so, she did not become actively alarmed until a man at a cocktail party, upon being introduced to her, mentioned that he had driven over to see the tower.

"Oh, horrors!" she exclaimed as a means of registering her attitude. "Is it famous all over the city?" And though she was joking she was dead serious.

"A curious form of protest," the man replied, tucking his pipe with tobacco; then, after a sharp glance directly into her eyes, he added, "You *are* aware of the boy's motivations, are you not?"

To which she smiled politely, being somewhat confused, and made a mental note that the man had been drinking.

The next morning as soon as Douglas left for school she telephoned the fire department. Everyone called the fire department when there was a problem that defied classification. Shortly before noon a small red truck parked in front of the house and two firemen—she had never spoken to a fireman before and found the experience rather strange—two of them entered the house as though it were the most natural thing in the world, and listened to what she told them about the tower. Then they went out to have a look. Mildly amused at first, presently they were startled. However they had been called upon by housewives for many unnatural labors, and so they unhooked their tools of destruction and set to work. It took them until almost dark to turn it into a mound of rubble, but at last an area of several square yards was covered with splintered wood, broken glass, wire, great gritty chunks of lumpy concrete, and whatever else had gone into the creation of it, and the air was filled with dust as though there had been a peculiar explosion. The firemen said they would make a report of the tower and its destruction and that the lot would be cleaned up within a day or two.

Douglas, having come home a few minutes before the firemen left, stood watching them in grieved silence. Mrs. Bridge, seeing him from an upstairs window, went out to stand behind him with her hands resting on his shoulders, and occasionally rumpled his hair.

"It was just getting too big," she confided to him gently. "People were beginning to wonder."

Revolt of the Masses

The evenings were growing cooler, September was here, autumn not far to the north, and the trees rustled uneasily.

Having ordered the groceries and having spent the remainder of the morning more or less listening to the radio, and being then unable to find anything else to do, she informed Harriet—who was in the kitchen furiously smoking one cigarette after another while cutting up dates for a pudding—that she had some shopping to take care of on the Plaza and would not be home until late that afternoon. She felt somewhat guilty as she said this because in reality there was no shopping to be done, but, with the children again in school and with Harriet to do the cooking and house-keeping and with the laundress coming once a week to do the washing, Mrs. Bridge found the days were very long. She was restless and unhappy and would spend hours thinking wistfully of the past, of those years just after her marriage when a day was all too brief.

After luncheon in her favorite tearoom she decided she might as well look at candlesticks. She had been thinking of getting some new ones; this seemed as good a time as any. On her way to Bancroft's, which carried the nicest things on the Plaza, she stopped at a drugstore for a box of aspirin, then paused in front of a bookstore where her eye was caught by the title of a book in the window display: *Theory of the Leisure Class*. She experienced a surge of resentment. For a number of seconds she eyed this book with definite hostility, as though it were alive and conscious of her. She went inside and asked to see the book. With her gloves on it was difficult to turn the pages, so she handed it back to the clerk, thanked him, and with a dissatisfied expression continued to Bancroft's.

Voting

She had never gone into politics the way some women did, though she listened attentively whenever such topics as the farm surplus or public works programs were discussed at luncheons or at circle meetings; she felt her lack of knowledge and wanted to improve herself, and she often resolved to buckle down to some serious studying. But so many things kept popping up, always at the very moment she was about to begin, and then too she did not know exactly where to start. Once in a while she would be on the point of questioning her husband, but, after thinking it over, she realized she would be asking silly questions, and he was so overburdened with business problems that she did not want to distract him. Besides, there was not much she herself could accomplish.

This was how she defended herself to Mabel Ong after having incautiously let slip the information that her husband always told her how to vote.

"Don't you have a mind of your own?" Mabel demanded, and looked quite grim. "Great Scott, woman! Speak out! We've been emancipated!" She rocked back and forth, hands clasped behind her back, while she frowned at the carpet of the Auxiliary clubhouse.

"You're right, of course," Mrs. Bridge apologized, discreetly avoiding the stream of smoke from Mabel's cigarette. "But don't you find it hard to know *what* to think? There's so much scandal and fraud everywhere you turn, and I suppose the papers only print what they want us to know." She hesitated, and then spoke out boldly. "How do you make up *your* mind?"

Mabel Ong, without removing the cigarette from her lips, considered the ceiling, the carpet, and squinted critically at a Degas print on the wall, as though debating how to answer such an ingenuous question, and finally she suggested that Mrs. Bridge might begin to grasp the fundamentals by a deliberate reading of certain books, the titles of which she jotted down on the margin of a tally card. Mrs. Bridge had not heard of any of these books except one, and this one because the author had committed suicide, but she decided to read it anyway.

The lady at her favorite rental library had never heard of the book, which was somehow gratifying; even so, having resolved to read it, Mrs.

Bridge set out for the public library. Here, at last, she got it, and settled down to the deliberate reading Mabel had advised. The author's name was Zokoloff, which certainly sounded threatening, and to be sure the first chapter dealt with bribery in the circuit courts.

When she had gotten far enough along to feel capable of discussing it she left it on the hall table; however Mr. Bridge did not even notice it until it had lain there for three days. She watched him pick it up, saw his nostrils flatten as he read the title, and then she waited nervously and excitedly. He opened the book, read a few sentences, grunted, and dropped the book on the table. This was disappointing. In fact, now that there was no danger involved, she had trouble finishing the book; she thought it would be better in a magazine digest. But eventually she did finish it and returned it to the library, saying with a slight air of sophistication, "I can't honestly say I agree with it all, but he's certainly well informed."

Certain arguments of Zokoloff remained with her, and she found that the longer she thought about them the more penetrating and logical they became; surely it *was* time, as he insisted, for a change in government. She decided to vote liberal at the next election, and as time for it approached she became filled with such enthusiasm and with such great conviction and determination that she planned to discuss her new attitude with her husband. She became confident that she could persuade him to change his vote also. Politics were not mysterious after all. However, when she challenged him to discussion he did not seem especially interested; in fact he did not answer. He was studying a sheaf of legal papers and only glanced across at her with an annoyed expression. She let it go until the following evening when he was momentarily unoccupied, and this time he stared at her curiously, intently, as if probing her mind, and then all at once he snorted.

She really intended to force a discussion on election eve. She was going to quote from the book of Zokoloff. But he came home so late, so exhausted, that she had not the heart to upset him. She concluded it would be best to let him vote as he always had, and she would do as she herself wished; still, on getting to the polls, which were conveniently located in the country-club shopping district, she became doubtful and a little uneasy. And when the moment finally came she pulled the lever recording her wish for the world to remain as it was.

Complexities of Life

The elegant Lincoln her husband had given her for her birthday was altogether too long, and she drove it as prudently as she might have driven a locomotive. People were always sounding their horns at her, or turning their heads to stare when she coasted by. Because the Lincoln had been set to idle too slowly, the engine frequently died when she pulled up at an intersection, but as her husband never used the Lincoln and she herself assumed it was just one of those things about automobiles, the idling speed was never adjusted. Often she would delay a line of cars while she pressed the starter button either too long or not long enough. Knowing she was not expert she was always quite apologetic when something unfortunate happened, and did her best to keep out of everyone's way. She shifted into second gear at the beginning of every hill and let herself down the far side much more slowly than necessary.

Usually she parked in a downtown garage where Mr. Bridge rented a stall for her. She had only to honk at the doors, which would soon trundle open, after which she coasted inside, where an attendant would greet her by name, help her out, and then park the formidable machine. But in the country-club district she parked on the street, and if there were diagonal stripes she did very well, but if parking was parallel she had trouble judging her distance from the curb and would have to get out and walk around to look, then get back in and try again. The Lincoln's cushions were so soft and Mrs. Bridge so short that she was obliged to sit erect in order to see whatever was going on ahead of her. She drove with arms thrust forward and gloved hands firmly on the wheel, her feet just able to depress the pedals. She never had serious accidents, but was often seen here and there being talked to by patrolmen. These patrolmen never did anything, partly because they saw immediately that it would not do to arrest her, and partly because they could tell she was trying to do everything the way it should be done.

When parking on the street it embarrassed her to have people watch, yet there always seemed to be someone at the bus stop or lounging in a doorway with nothing to do but stare while she struggled with the wheel and started jerkily backward. Sometimes, however, there would be a nice man who, seeing her difficulty, would come around and tip his hat and ask if he might help.

"Would you, please?" she would ask in relief, and after he opened the door she would get out and wait on the curb with an attentive expression while he parked the car. It was then a problem to know whether he expected a tip or not. She knew that people who stood around on street corners did not have much money; still she did not want to offend anyone. Sometimes she would hesitantly ask, sometimes not, and whether the man would accept a quarter or not she would smile brightly up at him, saying, "Thank you so much," and having locked the Lincoln's doors she would be off to the shops.

The Hat

Douglas was now in high school, and so far as she could tell he was less of an Apache than most of his companions, for which she was grateful, but he did become unpredictable, given to fits of introspection during which he dressed quite formally and stalked about with hands behind his back, followed by a grandiose kind of good-fellowship, and it was in this latter mood that the battle of the hat took place.

She was of the opinion that at certain ages one wore certain articles of clothing—each of the girls had received a girdle on her fourteenth birthday —and she now suggested to Douglas that he was old enough to begin wearing a hat.

"I don't need a hat," he said.

"It's time you started wearing one," she replied.

"They don't feel good on my head," said Douglas.

"Your father would look awfully silly without a hat," she argued.

"Who knows?" he countered, flinging up his hands.

So it went for a period of several weeks until finally they drove downtown and picked out a hat, a very nice conservative hat. She never expected to see it on his head, but strangely enough he began to wear it everywhere. He wore it to school and while playing ball after school, and he wore it around the house and in his room at night while doing homework. Very shortly she was sick of seeing the hat, but now he would not think of going anywhere without it. Furthermore there developed, somewhere between the high school and the drugstore where he played the pinball games, the habit of wearing it on the back of his head; not only this but on the crown he pinned a glazed yellow button saying: LET'S GET ACQUAINTED!

First Babies

That summer the family was invited to the wedding of a relative named Maxwell who was a postal clerk in the nearby town of Olathe. Carolyn was the only one who wanted to attend the wedding, but because it was an obligation of sorts the entire family—except Mr. Bridge—drove to Olathe. When the bride came down the aisle they discovered the reason for the wedding.

After the ceremony they put in an appearance at the reception and then, in silence, drove home.

About three months later they received the traditional announcement concerning the birth of a child. It happened that Ruth, Carolyn, and Douglas were at home when this announcement arrived, and Mrs. Bridge, having exclaimed, in spite of her disgust, "Isn't that nice!" felt it necessary to add, "First babies are so often premature."

At this time Ruth was eighteen years old, Carolyn was sixteen, and Douglas, nobody's fool, a shrewd fourteen. A profound silence, a massive, annihilating silence, greeted her remark. Carolyn gazed out the window. Douglas became greatly interested in his fingernails. Ruth looked at

Carolyn, then at Douglas, and she seemed to be considering. Finally she said, quietly, "Oh, Mother, don't."

None of them said anything further. The Maxwells were not mentioned again.

Mademoiselle From Kansas City

It was to Carolyn, though she was younger, that Mrs. Bridge was in the habit of confiding her hopes for them all. The two were apt to sit on the edge of Carolyn's bed until quite late at night, their arms half-entwined, talking and giggling, while across the room Ruth slept her strangely restless sleep—mumbling and rolling and burying her face in her wild black hair.

Mrs. Bridge could never learn what Ruth did in the evenings, or where she went; she entered the house quietly, sometimes not long before dawn. Mrs. Bridge had always lain awake until both girls were home, and one evening during the Christmas holidays she was still downstairs reading when Carolyn returned, bringing Jay Duchesne, who was now considerably over six feet tall and was doing his best to grow a mustache. In certain lights the mustache was visible, and he was quite proud of it and stroked it constantly and feverishly, as if all it needed in order to flourish was a little affection. Mrs. Bridge liked Jay. She trusted him. There were moments when she thought she knew him better than she knew Douglas.

"What's new, Mrs. B ?" he inquired, twirling his hat on one finger. And to Carolyn, "How's for chow, kid?" So they went out to the kitchen to cook bacon and eggs while Mrs. Bridge remained in the front room with the book turned over in her lap and her eyes closed, dozing and dreaming happily, because it seemed to her that despite the difficulties of adolescence she had gotten her children through it in reasonably good condition. Later, when Duchesne roared out of the driveway—he still drove as recklessly as ever and she was still not resigned to it—she climbed the stairs, arm in arm, with Carolyn.

"Jay's voice has certainly changed," she smiled.

"He's a man now, Mother," Carolyn explained a bit impatiently.

Mrs. Bridge smiled again. She sat on the bed and watched as Carolyn pulled off the baggy sweater and skirt and seated herself at the dressing table with a box of bobby pins.

"Funny—it's so quiet," said Carolyn.

Mrs. Bridge looked out the window. "Why, it's snowing again. Isn't that nice! I just love snowy winter nights."

Large wet flakes were floating down and clasping the outside of the window, and the street light shone on the evergreen tree in the back yard.

"There goes a rabbit!" she cried, but by the time Carolyn reached the window only the tracks were visible.

"Is Daddy asleep?" Carolyn asked.

"Yes, poor man. He didn't get away from the office until after seven and insists he has to get up at five-thirty tomorrow morning."

"That's silly."

"I know, but you can't tell him anything. I've tried, goodness knows, but it never does any good."

"Why does he do it?"

"Oh," said Mrs. Bridge irritably, for the thought of it never failed to irritate her, "he insists we'll all starve to death if he doesn't."

"That'll be the day!"

Both of them were silent for a while, watching the snow descend.

"I do hope Ruth gets home soon."

"She can drop dead for all I care."

"You know I don't like you to use that expression."

Carolyn split a bobby pin on her teeth and jammed it into her curly blond hair. "Well, what's the matter with her then? Who does she think she is, anyway?" She leaned to one side and opened the cupboard that belonged to Ruth. "Look at that! Black lace bras. Mademoiselle from Kansas City."

Presently the grandfather clock in the hall chimed twice, and Mrs. Bridge, after brushing Carolyn's cheek with her lips, went downstairs and into the kitchen, where she made herself some cocoa and moodily watched the snow building up on the sill. After a while she went upstairs again, changed into her nightgown, and got into bed beside her husband. There she lay with her hands folded on the blanket while she waited for the faint noise of the front door opening and closing.

She believed she was awake but all at once, without having heard a sound, she realized someone was downstairs. She heard a gasp and then what sounded like a man groaning. The luminous hands of the bedside clock showed four-fifteen. Mrs. Bridge got out of bed, pulled on her robe, and hurried along the hall to the top of the stairs, where she took hold of the banister and leaned over, calling just loud enough to be heard by anyone in the living room, "Ruth?"

No one answered.

"Ruth, is that you?" she asked, more loudly, and there was authority in her tone. She listened and she thought some delicate noise had stopped. The dark house was silent.

"I'm coming down," said Mrs. Bridge.

"It's me," said Ruth.

"Is there anyone with you?"

"He's leaving."

And then Ruth coughed in a prolonged, unnatural way, and Mrs. Bridge knew she was coughing to conceal another noise.

"Who's there?" she demanded, unaware that she was trembling from anger and fright, but there was only the sound of the great front door opening and shutting and seconds later the crunch of auto tires on the crust of yesterday's frozen snow as whoever it was released the brake and coasted away.

A cold draft swept up the spiral staircase. Mrs. Bridge, peering down into the gloom, saw her daughter ascending. She snapped on the hall light and they met at the top step. Ruth was taking the last of the pins out of her hair. She reeked of whisky and her dress was unbuttoned. Idly she pushed by her mother and wandered along the hall. Mrs. Bridge was too shocked to do anything until Ruth was at the door of her room; there they confronted each other again, for Ruth had felt herself pursued and turned swiftly with a sibilant ominous cry. Her green eyes were glittering and she lifted one hand to strike. Mrs. Bridge, untouched by her daughter's hand, staggered backward.

Ruth Goes to New York

That was the year Ruth finally managed to graduate from high school. She was there five years and for a while they were afraid it would be six, though she had taken the easiest courses possible. Her electives were music, drawing, athletics, and whatever else sounded easy. She seldom studied, and even when she did study she did poorly. She had been a member of the swimming team and this was the only activity listed after her name in the yearbook: "member of girls' swimming team"—that and the desperate phrase "interested in dramatics." She had once tried out for a play, but gave a rather hysterical reading and failed to get the part. When she finished high school Carolyn was only one semester behind her, although they had started two years apart.

A few days after the graduation she said she was going to New York to get a job. She did not like Kansas City; she never had. She had not made many friends. She had never seemed happy or even much at ease in Kansas City.

Mrs. Bridge tried to become indignant when Ruth announced she was going to New York, but after all it was useless to argue.

"What on earth would you do in New York?" she asked, because Ruth had been unable to learn shorthand, nor could she operate a typewriter as efficiently as Douglas, who tapped out his English themes with one finger.

"Don't worry about me," Ruth said. She had grown tall and beautiful, and somehow—in the powerful arch of her nose and in her somber, barbaric eyes—she looked biblical, swarthy and violent.

"I'm putting a thousand dollars in the bank for you," said Mr. Bridge, "on one condition." This condition was that if she could not support herself by the time the money ran out she would agree to return to Kansas City. She laughed and put her arms around him, and no one in the family had seen her do this since she was a child.

Mrs. Bridge was disturbed that she did not want to go to college, being of the opinion that although one might never actually need a college degree it was always nice to have; and yet, thinking the matter over, she realized Ruth would only be wasting four years—obviously she was no student. But why New York? Why not some place closer to home?

Soon she was ready to leave. The entire family went to the station.

"You didn't forget your ticket, did you?" asked Mrs. Bridge.

"Not quite," said Ruth drily.

"Be sure to look up the Wenzells when you get there. I've already written them you're coming to New York, but of course they won't know where to find you." The Wenzells were people they had met one summer in Colorado and with whom they exchanged Christmas greetings.

"I will," said Ruth, who had no intention of getting in touch with them.

"Have a good trip," her mother said as they were embracing at the gate. "Don't forget to write. Let us know as soon as you arrive."

"Here are your traveling expenses," her father said, handing her some folded bills. "For God's sake, don't lose it. And behave yourself. If you don't, I'm coming after you."

"I can look out for myself," said Ruth.

He laughed, and his laughter rang out odd and bold, the laughter of a different man, a free and happy man, who was not so old after all. "That isn't what I said," he told her lightly, and Mrs. Bridge, glancing from one to the other, was struck by their easy companionship, as though they had gotten to know each other quite well when she was not around.

Once on the train Ruth kicked off her shoes and curled up in the seat. She unsnapped the catch of her traveling bag and reached in for a copy of *Theatre Arts* but felt a strange envelope. She knew immediately what it was—it was called a "train letter," and a generation or so ago they were given to young people who were leaving home for the first time. She withdrew her hand and sat motionless for quite a while. Tears gathered in her eyes and presently she was shaken with dry sobs, although she did not know whether she was laughing or weeping. Before long she dried her face and lighted a cigarette.

Much later Ruth took out the envelope, read the letter of advice, and seemed to see her mother seated at the Chippendale highboy with some stationery and a fountain pen, seeking to recall the guidance of another era.

Progress, Madness, Defeat

One morning Mrs. Bridge telephoned Grace Barron. The maid answered and said Mrs. Barron was in bed. Mrs. Bridge asked if she was ill. The maid didn't seem to know, saying only that she had gone to bed about noon.

This was so strange that Mrs. Bridge decided to drive over and find out what was the matter.

She was sitting up in bed wearing her favorite sweatshirt and a baseball cap and she was reading a monstrous Russian novel. Closing the book on a hairpin she said, "I'm losing my mind."

"This is the first I've heard of it," said Mrs. Bridge with a smile.

"Do stop," Grace said unhappily. "Don't be gay, India. Please, for once, don't."

"Well, it *is* rather a shocking remark."

"Life can be shocking." She took off the ball player's cap and began turning it around in her hands and frowning. "It's just that I do want to be a person. I do, I do!" Mrs. Bridge did not know what to say and presently Grace continued. "Virgil says there's something wrong with me. He says he's never known another woman in all his life who would wear a sweatshirt on the Plaza."

"Well, you do attract attention. Not that I mind, and I can't see where it's anyone else's business, and there certainly isn't any law against it."

"But I do attract attention."

"Well," Mrs. Bridge answered uneasily, "as Virgil says, you're the only one from this neighborhood who dresses as though you were going to work in the north end."

Grace nodded. "It's true. Yes, it's true."

Both of them fell silent.

"Can you tell me what happened, Grace? Being in bed is so unlike you."

"It was the washing machine's fault," she answered without a smile, and went on to explain that she and the machine had never gotten along very well— "We've always despised each other," she said—and on this day it had defied her, it had knocked and trembled, and begun tearing the clothing, and so infuriated her that she had grabbed it by one leg and tipped it over, and the water ran all over the basement. The maid, who was upstairs in the kitchen preparing lunch, heard her screaming and summoned a doctor.

Mrs. Bridge remained silent and was thoughtful, for here was someone less confident of the future than herself. An evil, a malignancy, was at work. Its nature she could not discern, though she had known of its carbuncular presence for many years. Until now, until this revelation of its existence, she had not imagined it could be more than a fanciful illness, nor that there could be other victims than herself. But her friend was ill and suffering and Mrs. Bridge, too, was afflicted. Thinking back she was able to remember moments when this anonymous evil had erupted and left as its only cicatrices a sour taste in the mouth and a wild, wild desire.

One morning she had chanced to meet Grace downtown and Grace had wanted to look around in a toy store, and so, together, Mrs. Bridge amused and puzzled by this whim, they stopped here and there. So much had changed from the years when she used to buy toys for Ruth and Carolyn and Douglas. Everything was more intricate now, more automatic. It seemed you no longer played with a toy, you operated it. Douglas used to spend hours on his knees—ruining his corduroy knickers—pushing a fire engine or a dump truck and making appropriate noises. Now, however, you simply pushed a lever and the toy ran around by itself and the sirens wailed and the lights flashed until you were able to catch the machine and stop it. And Grace had caught it and was trembling so she could hardly reverse the lever.

There was a doll, too, with its little frock tied up around its head in order to display the electronics in the abdomen. There was a booklet tied to the wrist of the doll and they had read the booklet and then Mrs. Bridge turned the doll on. The eyes began to roll, the jaw dropped, and from the loudspeaker in the stomach came a nursery rhyme, and when this ended the doll sat down and a thin, colorless liquid appeared from beneath it and trickled over the counter.

"Can you help me?" Grace was asking, but Mrs. Bridge was too depressed to speak.

Paquita de las Torres

Douglas liked the Lincoln, and he had no more than gotten his first driver's license when he began asking to borrow the car. She was glad enough to let him have it, only cautioning him to drive carefully; if she had to run an errand while he was using the Lincoln she did not mind catching a bus, and if the weather was bad she could telephone one of her friends. She often wondered where he went and what he was doing, but she did not worry much about him because he was growing to be rather conservative, which gratified her, and furthermore he seemed to be using his head more effectively than he did as a child. He was even taking a reasonable amount of interest in schoolwork. In short he was becoming a sober, self-reliant young man, a bit too mysterious, perhaps, but otherwise agreeably normal.

She was, therefore, almost startled out of her wits to encounter him on the Plaza with the wildest-looking girl in the world. He had borrowed the car to go bowling and Mrs. Bridge had later decided to go shopping for some cocktail napkins and so, quite unexpectedly, they met. The girl was a gypsy-looking business with stringy black uncombed hair, hairy brown arms jingling with bracelets, and glittering mascaraed eyes in which there was a look of deadly experience. She was wearing a sheer blouse of burnt orange silk and a tight white skirt, and Mrs. Bridge did not need a second glance to realize that was practically all.

"How do you do, Paquita?" she said, smiling neutrally, after Douglas had sullenly mumbled an introduction. The girl did not speak and Mrs. Bridge wondered if she understood English. The hairy arms and the rancid odor were almost too much for Mrs. Bridge to bear. "I hope you two are having a nice time," she said, and heard a bracelet jingle and saw Douglas and Paquita exchange a deep, knowing look.

"Dad will be home early this evening for a change, so Harriet is planning on dinner at six sharp. I hope you won't be late. It's nice to have met you, Paquita." And she could not be sure, but it seemed to her that a moment after she turned away the girl spat on the sidewalk.

On the bus going home with the cocktail napkins she tried to make sense of it. She tried to be fair. Why would he want to go bowling with someone obviously from a different high school when there were so many nice girls at Southwest? Why would he want to see this girl at all? What could they possibly have in common? Where could he have met her?

"You'd think I was poison," she said to him that evening, jokingly and very seriously, as they entered the dining room. "Why not tell us when you're beau-ing someone new? Your Dad and I are interested in knowing your friends."

Douglas, having pushed her chair in as usual, went around the table and seated himself without a word.

"Paquita certainly jingles."

"She likes bracelets," he said trenchantly.

Mr. Bridge entered, and in passing behind Douglas's chair gave him a solid, affectionate rap on the skull with his knuckles.

"Well," said Douglas, grinning, "you must have had a good day today. You make another million bucks or something?"

Mr. Bridge laughed and picked up the carving knife, and while examining the roast he said, "I hear you're turning into quite a basketball player."

"Who told you that?"

"Never mind who told me."

"Oh, I don't know," Douglas said, blushing. He played forward on the church team and was trying to make the high-school squad but so far had been unsuccessful.

"Maybe you should butter up the coach's daughter," said Mr. Bridge, busying himself with the roast.

Douglas groaned in elaborate agony. "Anyway, I don't even know if he's got a daughter. And besides, that's no way to make the team."

"Well, how else are you going to do it?"

"Oh, you have to play just the way the coach likes. I mean he likes real smooth dribbling and things like that that really aren't important. I guess I told you about our church team skunking the Southwest second team, didn't I?"

"Yes, you did. Pass your mother's plate."

"Well, doesn't it stand to reason that if we can beat the second team we ought to be at least as good as the first team? I mean, this coach has got his favorites, see? And if you aren't one of his favorites, well, you just don't have a chance."

Mr. Bridge glanced at him and said calmly, "You're joking about that, so I don't mind. But don't let me catch you whining seriously. This million dollars you referred to—if I had earned it I wouldn't have earned it from being the judge's favorite. This country operates on the principle that the more industry and intelligence a man applies to his job the more he is entitled to profit. I hope it never changes."

"Yuh, okay," Douglas muttered, trying to end the conversation before it turned into a lecture.

"Remember that."

"I will. Okay. Okay."

The telephone rang at that moment and Harriet came into the dining room to say it was for Mr. Bridge. No sooner was he out of the room when Mrs. Bridge remarked, "I saw Patty Duncan the other day. She asked how you were."

"Tell her I'm still alive and kicking."

"She's such a lovely girl. And they say she's becoming quite the pianist."

"Okay," said Douglas, who had found himself assaulted from both ends of the dinner table. "For the love of Mike, I mean can't I live my own life?"

For the remainder of the meal she said no more about the encounter on the Plaza, but it had so disturbed her that she waited up until he got in late that night.

"Were you out with Paquita?" she asked, gazing at him earnestly.

In silence, face averted, Douglas took off his leather jacket.

"Does she live around here?" Mrs. Bridge asked, following him to the closet and picking a bit of lint from his sweater.

He hung up the jacket and walked into the living room, where he took a comb from his hip pocket, stooped a little in order to see himself in the mirror, for he was now almost six feet tall and still growing—soon he would be taller than his father—and began combing his long red hair straight back in the style he had recently adopted. His hair would not lie down, it grew stubbornly in various directions, and the more he combed it the more rebellious it looked, but he would not give in and the hair would not lie down.

"You're just like your Dad," she said, observing him, and there was not only love but vexation in her tone. Douglas, scowling, combed his hair and mashed it with his palms. As soon as he lifted his hands the hairs began to rise.

"Dear," she said, having followed him from the closet. She now stood a little way in back of him, looking at his face in the mirror. He slipped the comb in his pocket and bent a look of deep hatred against the mirror.

"What is it?" he asked brutally.

"Oh, I don't know."

"Well, good night," he said and turned to go upstairs, but she reached out and caught his arm.

"Douglas, why do you want to go around with that sort of person?"

At this he jerked his arm free and went to the closet, where he got his jacket and left the house again. She remained with one hand resting on the banister and was sick with anxiety, not so much because of the girl, for she knew he would outgrow her, but because she did not want to lose his friendship. She had lost his love, she knew not why, as she had forfeited that of Ruth, and the thought of losing her son entirely was more than she could endure.

Frayed Cuffs

Ordinarily Mrs. Bridge examined the laundry that Ingrid carried up from the basement every Tuesday afternoon in a creaking wicker basket, but when she was out shopping, or at a luncheon, the job fell to Harriet, who never paid much attention to such things as missing buttons or loose elastic. Thus it was that Mrs. Bridge discovered Douglas wearing a shirt with cuffs that were noticeably frayed.

"For heaven's sake!" she exclaimed, taking hold of his sleeve. "Has a dog been chewing on this?"

He looked down at the threads as though he had never before seen them; in fact he hadn't.

"Surely you don't intend to *wear* this shirt?"

Since he was already wearing the shirt this struck him as a foolish question, but he said, "It looks perfectly okay to me."

"Why, just look at these cuffs! Anyone would think we were on our way to the poorhouse."

"So is it a disgrace to be poor?"

"No!" she cried. "But we're *not* poor!"

Sex Education

Thereafter she kept a sharp eye on the laundry, going through it piece by piece to see what needed mending, after which she separated it into three stacks: one for the master bedroom, one for the room which Ruth and Carolyn had shared and which now was Carolyn's alone, and a third for Douglas's room. One by one she carried these piles of clothing into the proper room and there divided them further, handkerchiefs, underwear, blouses, and so forth, and arranged them neatly in the proper drawers.

One afternoon she carried Douglas's laundry into his room as usual and placed it on his bed as she always did in order to sort it. She put the newly laundered shirts on top of the others in his dresser and was about to go on with her work when it occurred to her that in all likelihood he was wearing the same shirts again and again; probably the ones in the bottom of the drawer were never being worn, and with the idea of reversing the order she took them all out and beneath the final shirt she found a magazine. Although she had never before seen one like it she knew instinctively what it was.

Mrs. Bridge sank to the edge of the bed and gazed dismally at the wall, the unopened magazine in her hands. She could hear Harriet singing hymns in the kitchen while peeling green apples for a pie, and the fervency of those good shrill Christian notes caused Mrs. Bridge to feel more desolate and abandoned than ever. She closed her eyes and shook her head in disbelief. The last thing on earth she wanted was to look into this magazine, but it had to be done. She looked at one page. There was a naked woman. That was enough. She looked no more. Never in her life had she been confronted with a situation like this and she did not know what to do. She was under the impression that these magazines had been legislated against and were not available. She asked herself where she had failed. With him, as with Ruth and Carolyn, she had adroitly steered around threatening subjects; in no way had she stimulated his curiosity—quite the contrary. Where, then, had she failed? She had let him realize, without her having to say so, that there were two kinds of people in the world, and this was true, she knew, for it was what she had been taught by her father and mother.

She kept expecting Douglas to say something about the magazine—which she burned in the incinerator—but if he noticed it was gone he gave no indication. Weeks passed. She did not want to rush him. She wanted him to come to her and confess of his own free will. Carolyn was now a freshman at the university, which was located in the town of Lawrence, about forty miles distant; she often came home on week ends, but during the week she was gone, with the result that Mrs. Bridge and Douglas were sometimes the only members of the family at the dinner table. These dinners were silent and unpleasant for them both; they tended to avoid looking at each other. She waited patiently for the moment when he would give a sign—a single deep look would be enough—and she would know then that he wanted to have a talk. Still time went by and, since he made no move, she began to fasten her eyes on him. These mute invitations had a singular effect on Douglas; whenever he became conscious of her mournful, wretched gaze he would leave the house. She thought he was touched and full of remorse at the unhappiness he was causing and so she continued to gaze deeply at him whenever they were alone. However, more time went by and for some reason he failed to come to her.

One evening, therefore, she walked upstairs to his room and tapped on the door with her fingernail. The door was closed but she knew he was at his desk and that he was staring at the door. She was right, because after she had waited a few minutes she heard the chair creak and then his footsteps on the carpet. He jerked the door open and found her there smiling miserably. She glided past him into the room and to his desk where, without a word, she placed on the blotter a slim, musty pamphlet with a gray cover and sepia pages which she had gotten from a trunk in the attic. The pamphlet had a faint dried odor, like the crumbled wings of moths, and the elaborate typography related a little story about the marriage of a sperm and an ovum. On the frontispiece, beneath an attached sheet of tissue, were two circular photographs taken from laboratory slides.

He had followed her across the room and was now standing on the opposite side of the desk with his fists clenched behind his back. Seeing him so tense she thought that if she could only manage to rumple his hair as she used to do when he was a small boy everything would be all right. Calmly, and a little slyly, she began easing toward him.

Seeing that she was after him he also moved to keep the desk between them.

Words of Wisdom

A few days later on his return from high school Douglas saw, beneath the hairbrush on his dresser, a page torn from a magazine. On one side of the page was an automobile advertisement, and on the other side was a picture of an elderly Chinese gentleman called the Old Sage, together with a list of maxims:

> It is as easy to grin as to growl.
> Hatred is self-punishment.
> Rotten or decayed wood cannot be carved.
> Have no care for the future and you will sorrow for the present.
> Life is a mirror that gives back as much as it receives.
> A record is often broken when competition gets keen.
> A good cure for drunkenness is while sober to see a drunken man.
> Courage at the critical moment is half the victory.
> Words show the wit of a man, actions his meanings.
> The anvil lasts longer than the hammer.
> The pleasure of doing good is never tiresome.
> Contentment is an inexhaustible treasure.
> A handful of common sense is worth a bushel of learning.

Douglas went through these more and more rapidly. Having finished, and not knowing exactly what to do with the list, thinking she might want it back, he put it in a desk drawer and paid no further attention to it. In the days that followed their eyes occasionally met and locked, inexpressively.

He knew she was waiting for him to comment; she knew he had read the maxims.

Very Gay Indeed

Ruth did not write home as often as Mrs. Bridge had expected, nor was it possible to guess from her letters what sort of a life she was leading in New York; however she seemed to be getting along all right and did not sound unhappy. She wrote that she had moved into an apartment near the Hudson, that she was now working for a fashion magazine, and that she hoped for a promotion before long. In April she was promoted; she became an "assistant editor," whatever that meant, but it did sound important and Mrs. Bridge was very proud and let her friends know about Ruth's success. That same month they were surprised and delighted when she flew home for a visit. She had changed a great deal; she had become very sophisticated.

Carolyn came home from the university that week end, and Mrs. Bridge was struck by the difference in the girls. It was hard to believe they were sisters—Ruth so dark and sleek, and really too thin, angular, sauntering about and smoking one cigarette after another and having cocktails with her father as though she had been drinking for years; Carolyn so active and blond and determined, and rather sturdy-looking in low-heeled golfing shoes, for she had begun playing golf in high school and was now getting exceptionally good.

Ruth was undeniably more mature and Mrs. Bridge noticed an odd fact: Ruth and Douglas liked each other very much. There was no reason they should not—in fact they certainly should like each other—but she could not get over a sense of astonishment when she heard them laughing together, or saw them earnestly talking in the breakfast room, drinking pots of coffee and discussing she did not know what. They appeared to have developed a new relationship. They were no longer just brother and sister, and Mrs. Bridge felt a little thrilled and more than a little sad.

She and Ruth did not have much time alone, and all at once, so it seemed, Ruth was on the telephone checking her plane reservation to New York. On her last evening in Kansas City the two of them remained in the dining room after Douglas and Mr. Bridge had left the table. They had only a few minutes because a young man named Callaway Rugg was coming to take Ruth to a Little Theatre production of *Cyrano,* but while they were talking at the dinner table she mentioned that one of the men who worked in her office in New York was a homosexual.

"Just what do you mean, Ruth?" asked Mrs. Bridge soberly. She had picked up a spoon and was slowly stirring her coffee.

"Why, he's gay, Mother. Queer. You know."

"I'm afraid I don't know," said Mrs. Bridge.

Ruth could not tell whether her mother was serious or not. The idea of her mother not knowing was too incredible, and yet, thinking back, and having talked with Douglas about things that had happened recently, and after a long, probing look into her mother's eyes, Ruth knew her mother was speaking the truth.

Exchange of Letters

The new *Tattler* came out a few days after Ruth returned to New York and Mrs. Bridge mailed a clipping to her: "Found holidaying at the charming home of her parents, Mr. and Mrs. Walter Bridge of Crescent Heights Drive, was the lovely eldest, Ruth, now setting Gotham aflame. Scores of admirers hope the fascinating and exotic editoress-to-be won't become a permanent Manhattanite." On the back of the clipping was the conclusion of an article of advice to hostesses: ". . . jungle the natives simply peel and eat, and so should we! No more worry about knives and forks, lefthand or righthand." And below this was the first line of a quotation from Thoreau.

Mrs. Bridge wrote that Carolyn was playing golf every afternoon and had beaten one of the boys who was on the university team, that the weather in Kansas City was awfully pleasant this time of year, that some man named Genaro had telephoned just after she returned to New York but hadn't left a message, that the city was finally widening the street in front of the Junior League clubhouse, and that her visit to Kansas City had seemed awfully brief. Ruth had remarked on the graft in New York, so Mrs. Bridge wrote, "Isn't it awful there's so much graft? We have it here, too. It just makes you wonder about people."

She also mentioned what had been going on socially and what events were on the calendar. "Wednesday evening the Arlens are staging a cocktail party for Anne who's off to Europe and it sounds quite intriguing. Thursday, Madge and I are off to a recital given by some folk singer who plays the dulcimer, and then on Friday there's to be a church doing (at which a Moslem will talk!) but I'm not sure I'll be able to make it. I've been having a siege of headaches and they just don't seem to be able to make heads or tails of them. Dr. Stapp told me it's all mental but that doesn't make sense. Dr. McIntyre (he's so nice!) thinks it may be an allergy but if so I wish they'd hurry up and get together, whatever it is. Then next Monday there's a reception at Crestwood for the McKinney girls who're just back from a month at the Royal Hawaiian. That must have been grand. . . ."

Ruth chose to answer this letter one night while she was in bed with a man named Dowdey, whom she had met the previous week. She wrestled the pillow away from him and put it behind her back in order to sit up more comfortably, and with an airmail pad on her knees she began:

"The weather in New York has been lovely, but otherwise there isn't very much news. I can't stand my boss because he's an absolute tyrant, but everybody else is nice, and we're trying a new format that I like better. A man who works in the next office"—and she dropped one hand to give Dowdey a pinch on the buttocks—"has been awfully sweet although I don't know him very well yet. I haven't been going out much lately. I usually come home after work and get to bed early. It was marvelous seeing everybody in Kansas City." Here she paused and tapped the pen against her teeth, and finally added that she hoped to visit Kansas City again before long.

Dowdey, having rolled over and raised himself to one elbow, was reading the letter with his chin propped on Ruth's shoulder.

"Jus' like I aim to get back to San Antone," he said, and began kissing her throat.

"Hush," she said. "And stop. You're bothering me!"

"Come on down here and le's bother all over," said Dowdey, "on account of you can write yo' little mama in the mornin'."

"Cut that out," said Ruth. "Now cut that out!"

"Yo' mama look like you?" he asked, sliding his arms around her waist.

"She's my sister's mother!"

And as if by hearing these words she realized what she had said, Ruth touched her lover gently and looked down into his unblinking hazel eyes. She caressed the wind wrinkles of his leathery face; he became solemn and expectant.

"I'll only be a little while," she said. For a few minutes she sat with her knees drawn up to her chin and gazed across the river and the buildings on the western shore, and she was able to see her home, not as it was now, but ten years before, at a time in her life when she would never have thought to say her mother was not her own: when she had been as tall as the new evergreen trees in the yard, when her brother was a baby. Now this was gone, and it was gone forever. She wondered why she was in New York, why she would soon give herself to this man for whom she had no feeling.

"I don't think it's her fault," Ruth whispered, with her head on her knees, and when Dowdey asked what she had said she did not answer. Presently she sighed and continued with the letter, thanking her mother for sending a box of oatmeal cookies Harriet had baked, and said they were wonderful, though in truth they had arrived broken and crushed, and she had sprinkled them on the window sill for the pigeons. Having signed the letter with love, as she always did, she ordered Dowdey to open his mouth and hold out his tongue to lick the envelope.

"That all?" he asked, grinning, as she leaned across him to place the letter on the night table.

"It depends on what you mean," Ruth said. She turned out the light. When he covered her she was looking across the dark river, gravely thinking of her home.

Frozen Fruit

With Ruth gone and with Carolyn at home only an occasional week end, with Mr. Bridge continuing to spend long hours at the office, and with Douglas appearing only for meals, Mrs. Bridge found the days growing interminable; she could not remember when a day had seemed so long since the infinite hours of childhood, and so she began casting about rueful and disconsolate for some way to occupy the time. There were mornings when she lay in bed wide awake until noon, afraid to get up because there was nothing to do. She knew Harriet would take care of ordering the groceries, Harriet would take care of everything, Harriet somehow was running the house and Mrs. Bridge had the dismal sensation of knowing that she, herself, could leave town for a week and perhaps no one would get overly excited. At breakfast—lunch if she chose to call it so—she would consider the newspaper with sober apathy, sighing at the events in Europe, lethargically eating whatever Harriet prepared—toast and orange juice, chipped beef and cinnamon rolls, fruit salad, bacon and tomato sandwich, a dish of sherbet; whatever it happened to be Mrs. Bridge would eat some of it though it seemed tasteless. Summer had come again, another summer, another year.

One warm windy morning in June she could hardly open her eyes; she lay in the stuffy bedroom and listened to the wind in the trees, to the scratching of the evergreen branches against the house, and wondered if she was about to die. She did not feel ill, but she had no confidence in her life. Why should her heart keep beating? What was there to live for? Then she grew cheerful because she recalled her husband had told her to get the Lincoln waxed and polished. In fact he had told her that three weeks ago but she had not yet gotten around to it. Now, in any event, there was something to do; she would do the work herself. She would drive to the Plaza to an auto-supply store and buy a can of wax and some polish and a chamois, or whatever the salesman recommended, and she would spend the day working on the Lincoln. It had been years since she had done any work, with the exception of puttering in the garden, and it would be refreshing. But then, still in bed, she became doubtful and more reasonable. She had never attempted to polish an automobile, she knew nothing about it, nothing whatsoever, and if she should ruin the finish of the Lincoln what on earth could she say to her husband? He would be amazed and furious because it was so nonsensical; he would manage to control his temper but he would be infuriated all the same, and want to know why she had done it. Could she explain how the leisure of her life—that exquisite idleness he had created by giving her everything—was driving her insane?

However, she reflected, as she got out of bed holding a hand to her brow to prevent herself from collapsing, she could at least drive to the Plaza and wander around while the Lincoln was being polished. She could look into Bancroft's; perhaps they had some new imports. She could have a late luncheon in the tea shoppe. Surely something else would come to mind by then and soon the day would be over.

Once out of bed she felt more alive, and while getting dressed she thought of telephoning Grace Barron. Perhaps they could spend the day together. No one answered the Barrons' phone. After a few minutes she tried again with no success and then dialed Madge Arlen. The line was busy. She knew from past experience that Madge stayed on the telephone for hours, but now the Plaza idea had begun to sound exciting with or without company and she began to hurry around getting ready to go, and was annoyed with herself for having wasted the entire morning. It was fifteen minutes to one when Mrs. Bridge came downstairs. Harriet was vacuuming the hall. Mrs. Bridge signaled her to stop the machine, and when the roaring died away she said, looking quickly into her purse to see she had not forgotten anything, "I've got to run to the Plaza to have the car taken care of. It needs waxing. If anybody calls, tell them I'll be home about five."

Harriet replied that Mr. Bridge had had the car waxed and polished the previous Saturday.

Mrs. Bridge stopped and looked at her in stupefaction. "He did? I wonder why he didn't mention it."

Harriet did not say anything.

"Are you sure?" asked Mrs. Bridge.

Harriet nodded.

"Oh. Well, then," she said doubtfully, "I suppose it doesn't need to be done again. Isn't that strange? He must have forgotten to tell me." She noticed Harriet looking at her without expression, but intently, and she became embarrassed. She dropped the car keys back in her purse and slowly took off her hat. She had driven the Lincoln several times since Saturday and it was odd she had not noticed the difference.

Harriet turned on the vacuum.

After changing into more comfortable clothes Mrs. Bridge wandered to the kitchen, fixed a sandwich for herself, and sat in the breakfast room for about an hour watching the sparrows in the garden. Finally she managed to get Madge Arlen on the telephone.

"Lord, I'm glad you called!" her friend exclaimed. "I'm out of my wits for something to do."

"Come on over this minute," said Mrs. Bridge.

"Are you in the same fix?"

"I should say I am!"

And now the day took shape and Mrs. Bridge was no longer embarrassed. She had found she was not alone, and if others felt as she felt there was no reason to be depressed. The hours no longer loomed ahead; it was just another warm June day. A few minutes later Madge Arlen was coming in the front door, wearing a loose lavender gaucho blouse, chartreuse slacks, and cork wedgies that made her nearly six feet tall. She was smoking one of the English cigarettes she liked but which were now so hard to obtain. Harriet made some coffee, for Madge Arlen drank coffee all day, and they sat on the porch and talked about people they knew. Grace Barron's son, David, had been taking violin lessons for a number of years and wanted to make a career of music. His father disapproved of this and, as everyone knew, the Barrons were not getting along well. Madge Arlen mentioned that the situation was worse.

"Being a professional musician does sound exciting," Mrs. Bridge observed. "But I just wonder how practical it would be. Oh, my word, it's four o'clock already! I don't know about you, Madge, but I'm simply famished."

They went to the kitchen and Mrs. Bridge looked into the refrigerator.

"Strawberries and whipped cream?" she suggested. "These are frozen, of course. They don't really taste the same as the fresh, but they certainly are a time-saver."

Quo Vadis, Madame?

That evening, while preparing for bed, Mrs. Bridge suddenly paused with the fingertips of one hand just touching her cheek. She was seated before her dressing table in her robe and slippers and had begun spreading cold cream on her face. The touch of the cream, the unexpectedness of it—for she had been thinking deeply about how to occupy tomorrow—the swift cool touch demoralized her so completely that she almost screamed.

She continued spreading the cream over her features, steadily observing herself in the mirror, and wondered who she was, and how she happened to be at the dressing table, and who the man was who sat on the edge of the bed taking off his shoes. She considered her fingers, which dipped into the jar of their own accord. Rapidly, soundlessly, she was disappearing into white, sweetly scented anonymity. Gratified by this she smiled, and perceived a few seconds later that beneath the mask she was not smiling. All the same, being committed, there was nothing to do but proceed.

Joseph Conrad

She was wakened by the chimes of the grandfather clock in the hall. It was three or four in the morning. Her husband was sleeping easily, but gravely, as though exhausted. She awoke simultaneously with the knowledge of one morning many years before when she had been dusting the bookcase and came across an old, old red-gold volume. Taking it down she found on the flyleaf in dry, spidery script the name of Shannon Bridge, who was the uncle of her husband—an unambitious, taciturn man who had married a night-club entertainer and later died of a heart attack in Mexico, and upon whose death they had inherited a few books and charts. She had no idea what the charts were about, for she had not unrolled them, only stored them in the attic, and then one day, absently, since they were useless, she had discarded them; and as for the books, no one had read them, so far as she knew, though later she found Douglas examining them, and now at four in the morning she was lying completely awake, thinking of the time she had taken a book down from a shelf and had begun turning the brittle, yellowed pages. She stood beside the bookcase for quite a while, growing absorbed in what she read, and wandered, still reading, into the living room, where she did not look up from the book until someone called her, because she had come upon a passage which had been underlined, no doubt by Shannon Bridge, which observed that some people go skimming over the years of existence to sink gently into a placid grave, ignorant of life to the last, without ever having been made to see all it may contain; and this passage she had read once again, and brooded over it, and turned back to it again, and was thinking deeply when she was interrupted.

And Mrs. Bridge remembered now that she had risen and had said, "Yes, all right, I'm on my way," and had placed the book on the mantel, for she had intended to read further. She wondered what had interfered, where she had gone, and why she had never returned.

Psychotherapy

Mabel Ong was going to an analyst. Mrs. Bridge was surprised to learn this because Mabel in her tailored suits and with her authoritative masculine manner had always seemed the very picture of confidence. At the luncheon club not long after Dr. Foster's eloquent sermon on church attendance she found herself sitting next to Mabel, and by the time luncheon was over Mrs. Bridge was convinced that she, too, needed analysis. She had, in fact, privately thought so long before her talk with Mabel. More and more it had occurred to her that she was no longer needed. Ruth was gone, so very gone—even her letters said so little—and Carolyn was almost gone, and Douglas, though still at home, was growing so independent, more like his father every year. Soon he too would be leaving home. What would she do then? It had been a long time, she felt, since her husband truly needed her. He accepted her, and he loved her, of this she had never had a doubt, but he was accustomed to and quite unconscious of love, whereas she wanted him to think about it and to tell her about it. The promise of the past had been fulfilled: she had three fine children and her husband was wonderfully successfully. But Mrs. Bridge felt tired and ill. She wanted help.

She surmised her husband would not be sympathetic to her idea of being psychoanalyzed, so, for a number of weeks before mentioning it, she planned the conversation. She meant to open with the direct, positive, almost final statement that she was going downtown the first thing in the morning to arrange a series of appointments. That certainly ought to settle the matter—he ought to be able to understand the situation. Possibly he was going to inquire how much it would cost, and she was uneasy about this, suspecting it was going to be expensive, with the result that she avoided finding out what it would cost. After all, in spite of his complaints, she knew, and he was aware that she knew, that they had plenty of money.

She tried to imagine all his objections to her idea, but really there was nothing he could say. He would simply be forced to agree. It had been years since she had asked him for anything, no matter how slight; indeed, every once in a while he would inquire if there wasn't something she wanted—anything for the house, or for herself. No, there was nothing. It was difficult to find things to buy. She had the money, but she had already bought everything she could use, which was why she often spent an entire day shopping and came home without having bought anything except lunch, and perhaps some pastry during the afternoon.

Having solved whatever objection he might make in regard to the expense, she concluded that all she had to do was let him know her intention. She kept putting it off. She rehearsed the scene many times and it always came out satisfactorily. The difficulty lay in finding the opportunity to begin. So it was that several weeks slipped away, then one evening after supper, as they were settling themselves in the living room, she with a bag of knitting and he with the stock-market page of the newspaper, she knew the time had come. She pretended to be straightening her knitting, but she was greatly occupied with marshaling her thoughts. He always got to the heart of a matter at once, wasting no energy on preliminaries, and she had to be ready for this. Just then he lowered the paper and she was terrified that somehow he had been reading her mind. Quite often he could, and this more than anything else was the reason she found it exceedingly difficult to defend her ideas. He was glaring at the newspaper.

"Listen to this: The Central has asked the ICC to investigate the circumstances of the sale of eight hundred thousand shares of stock, owned by the Chesapeake and Ohio Railway, to Murchison and Richardson last week." He looked across the paper at her as if she were responsible.

"Well!" said Mrs. Bridge in what she thought an appropriate tone. It would be unwise to annoy him at this point, but until he made it clear whose side he was on she could not say anything specific. Her expression remained intent and neutrally expectant, as though she wanted to hear more.

"What in God's name do those people think they're doing?" he demanded sharply.

"It certainly doesn't seem right," she answered, still not certain whether the scoundrels were Central, or Chesapeake and Ohio, or Murchison and Richardson. Or, of course, he could be angry with the newspaper for having publicized it.

Mr. Bridge had taken off his glasses and was staring at her.

"I don't know a thing in the world about it, of course," she added hastily.

He resumed reading. A few minutes later he said, "Allied Chemical: up four! Great Lord! What's going on here?" After this he was quiet for a long time, coughing once, shaking the paper into shape. Mrs. Bridge, having noted it was almost time for bed, decided she must speak.

"Walter," she began in a tremulous voice, and went on rapidly, "I've been thinking it over and I don't see any way out except through analysis."

He did not look up. Minutes went by. Finally he muttered, "Australian wool is firm." And then, roused by the sound of his own voice, he glanced at her inquisitively. She gave him a stark, desperate look; it was unnecessary to repeat what she had said because he always heard everything even when he failed to reply.

"What?" he demanded. "Nonsense," he said absently, and he struck the paper into submission and continued reading.

Pineapple Bread

The following day being Thursday, Harriet's day off, Mrs. Bridge prepared supper for herself and her husband. Douglas had telephoned a few minutes after school let out to say he was at a fraternity meeting and that as soon as it was over he and a couple of friends were going to get a hamburger somewhere and then were going downtown to a track meet in the municipal auditorium.

"What about your homework?" she asked.

"Homework," he replied, giving a very final opinion of it.

"Well, I don't think you should stay out late," she answered. "After all, it's a week night."

He said he would be home early, but early could mean any hour.

"All right now, don't forget," she said. "Your grades haven't been worth boasting about."

"I'll get by," said Douglas. "Holy Cow!"

"Yes, well you just might Holy Cow yourself right out of graduating."

With that the conversation ended and she went into the kitchen to start preparing a casserole, as she had done many, many times before. She moved around the kitchen slowly. She had plenty of time. The house was so quiet that she began to think of how noisy it had been when all the children were there, how very much different everything had been, and presently, remembering the days when she used to cook the meals, she went to the cupboard where the old recipe books were stored. Harriet occasionally referred to them, but otherwise they had lain untouched for years. Mrs. Bridge began looking through them, seeing pencil notations in her own handwriting, scarcely legible any more. Her husband liked more pepper in this, no bay leaves in that—whatever he wanted and whatever he did not like was expertly registered in the margins, and as she turned through these recipes she thought how strangely intimate the faded penciled notes remained; they brought back many scenes, many sweet and private memories; they brought back youth.

Mrs. Bridge grew thoughtfully excited. A glance at the electric clock on the stove panel told her there might be time enough to alter her plans for supper. She was thinking of fixing spaghetti for him, with the special sauce he had so often said was the best in the world. She had not fixed it for years. Harriet could not sense just how long to let it simmer, and without that particular flavor to the sauce there was not much point in eating spaghetti. A quick search of the refrigerator and of the cupboards disclosed there were not the right ingredients. She found some canned sauce and thought about improvising from it, but it would not be the same. He would taste the difference. And so, regretfully, she admitted it was going to be the casserole again. Next week they would have spaghetti. A little sadly she turned on through the cookbooks, and once more she had an idea. She had come across the recipe for pineapple bread and there was time for that and she was certain they had the ingredients—not only the pineapple but the chipped pecans, the raisins—yes, yes, she could do it.

She carried the bread to the table wrapped in a towel because it was still hot from the oven, and Mr. Bridge, who, as he unfolded his napkin, had been looking at the casserole with resignation, now glanced with puzzled interest at what she was bringing him. His expression began to brighten. He smiled.

"Oh-ho!" said Mr. Bridge, rubbing his hands together. "What have we here?"

She placed it before him, too thrilled to speak, and hurried back to the kitchen for the bread knife.

"Well, well!" said he, accepting the knife, and he smacked his lips and shut his eyes for a moment to inhale the fragrance of the small plump loaf.

"Go ahead and cut it," she said to him intensely, and waited beside his chair.

The first slice fell down like a corpse and they saw bubbles of dank white dough around the pecans. After a moment of silence Mrs. Bridge covered it with the towel and carried it to the kitchen. Having disposed of the bread she untied her little ruffled apron and waited quietly until she regained control of herself.

A few minutes later she re-entered the dining room with a loaf of grocery-store bread on a silver tray. She smiled and said, "It's been a long time, I'm afraid."

"Never mind," said Mr. Bridge as he removed the lid of the casserole, and the next day he brought her a dozen roses.

Carolyn's Engagement

Time was passing more rapidly than she thought; she was almost over-come when Carolyn appeared in the middle of the week with an engage-ment ring she had gotten the night before from a thin, shaggy boy with protruding teeth whose name was Gil Davis. He was a junior at the univer-sity. He was studying business management and working part-time in the dean's office.

Mrs. Bridge, seeking a moment to recover from the shock, looked at Carolyn's ring and said, "It's an opal, isn't it?"

"Gil doesn't have much money," Carolyn explained. "He told me he thought diamonds were absurd. And you know, Mother, he's worked for everything he owns!"

She was fascinated by this. She had never known a boy who was poor. In high school she had known boys who worked during summers and some who worked after school in order to have spending money, but none of them had been forced to work in order to eat and buy clothing. "Well, I think it's lovely!" said Mrs. Bridge, squeezing her hand. "Does your father know?"

"No," said Carolyn.

"Well, I'm afraid you'd better tell him, don't you think so?"

"Why don't you call him?" Carolyn suggested.

"This isn't my engagement," replied Mrs. Bridge.

Mr. Bridge, being informed of his daughter's engagement, was outraged. He had never heard of any Gil Davis, and who did Gil Davis think he was? And as for Carolyn, there was to be no more of this ridiculous nonsense. She was to return that ring to that upstart boy, whatever his name was, and that was to be the end of the matter. Carolyn immediately burst into tears and threw her ring on the carpet. Her father had never talked to her like that before. When she returned to the university the ring was in her pocket. She had promised to give it back.

Gil Davis, being informed that his suit had been rejected, was also outraged. He was twenty years old and never before in his life had he been the cause of any trouble. He looked at the ring, he looked at Carolyn, and then he ran out of the dean's office and ran all the way to the bus station, where he bought a ticket to Kansas City. He pushed his way past the secretary who wanted to know what his business was and he walked into Mr. Bridge's private office without bothering to knock. He emerged at eight o'clock that night in company with his intended father-in-law; they ate sausage and buckwheat cakes together in a lunch wagon, both of them exhausted, and they had agreed he was going to marry Carolyn. So, for the second time, Gil Davis placed his opal ring on her finger and she wore the ring with a truculent expression.

"I know you two are going to be very happy," Mrs. Bridge said, hugging her. "I'm so relieved everything worked out all right."

Carolyn said, "You do like him, Mother, don't you?"

"Why, of course, dear! He's awfully nice. It's just that he's so different from the kind of boys you've been used to."

Gil Davis was aware of this fact; he quit the university because he saw he would need steady money and quite a lot of it as soon as he married Carolyn. He returned to his home town, which was located near the Oklahoma border in southern Kansas, and there he went to work for his uncle, who owned a dry-goods emporium. Carolyn wanted him to work in an aircraft factory where he could get overtime wages, but saw the sense of his decision when he told her his uncle was considering retirement.

The friends of Mrs. Bridge were avid for information about Carolyn's engagement.

"Is her ring a blue or a white?"

"It's a lovely opal," Mrs. Bridge replied, facing the inquiries with her best smile.

"What a nice idea!"

"It's what Carolyn was hoping for," Mrs. Bridge countered.

"I understand he's not a Kansas Citian."

"From Parallel," she replied serenely, and scored a point by not explaining where Parallel could be found.

"It sounds quite far."

"They'll be driving up for visits, I'm sure."

"What does the father do?"

He was a plumber. Mrs. Bridge had confronted herself with this fact a thousand times; there was simply no way around it. She imagined herself replying to this question, which, inevitably, would be asked, replying evasively that he was associated with a company that did household installation, and yet she knew in her heart she must speak the truth. It seemed to her that Carolyn's happiness depended on the acknowledgment of this condition, and, for better or worse, the acceptance of it.

Said Mrs. Bridge—and her throat was so constricted she was afraid the words would lodge there—"Mr. Davis is a plumber." She was astonished to see she had very nearly scored again, for she had spoken with such ease that one might almost believe everybody nowadays was marrying the sons of plumbers.

"I hear the boy is a Beta."

"Well, no. As I understand the situation, Gil is of the opinion fraternity life can be a liability."

"Oh, how true."

"And how does he stand with the draft?"

His feet were as flat as ironing boards and his teeth were bad; he had been rejected as generally unsatisfactory. There was no sense going into detail, such details as Carolyn had given, and so she replied that he had been exempted for medical reasons. She believed he had had rheumatic fever when he was a child. In any event this sounded plausible, and was acceptable.

"You say he's in Parallel now?"

Mrs. Bridge knew what was next. She nodded.

"I see. I didn't realize he'd already graduated."

"According to what Carolyn tells me, in his opinion a four-year university education is actually less worth while than a certain amount of practical experience." It had been badly put, she knew, and it was a retreat, but the business of the plumber had broken her composure.

Present From Douglas

Wedding gifts arrived. Day after day they arrived and Carolyn received enough silver to open a shop. She tore open the packages greedily and her blue eyes gleamed more brightly than the richest plate. Mrs. Bridge, meanwhile, seated at her writing table with a notebook and fountain pen, dutifully jotted down what it was and who had sent it. Carolyn would be expected to memorize this list in order to be able to thank everyone personally and specifically: she would be expected to, but would she? Mrs. Bridge was uneasy. She, herself, no matter how long it took, no matter how arduous the job, would have learned to identify every gift. She could only hope Carolyn would be as considerate.

There were a few awkward presents—a green bronze frog to be used as a doorstop, a queer desk lamp that resembled a pagoda, two or three novels and a book of Persian poetry, and from cousin Lulubelle Watts in Memphis a lifetime subscription to a magazine no one had ever heard of. There was one gift, however, worse than these. It was a present from Douglas. It was a toaster.

Douglas had delayed until the last moment because he hated to give or receive presents. He liked his sister but he did not see where spending fifteen or twenty dollars would prove he wished her happiness. In deference to custom, however, on the next to last day he decided to buy a toaster because she had said she would need one. He walked to the Plaza— "Nobody's using the Lincoln," she had said, but he replied that he felt like walking—and on the Plaza he looked them over, hands in his pockets, while a salesman demonstrated. He was shown the most elaborate toasters that money could buy, but he was not pleased. The dials were set, the pointers turned, the levers pressed, the machine plugged in, the concealed tray that collected crumbs was removed, all for his benefit, but he was not pleased. At the conclusion of the demonstration he walked across the street to a dime store and bought a primitive toaster such as his parents had had when they were first married.

No one criticized the gift. Carolyn thanked him. Mrs. Bridge exclaimed over how simple it was to operate, and indeed it was simple. Neither of them mentioned the four magnificent automatic toasters which had been delivered that same morning.

Of course the amount of money spent was not the important thing, everyone admitted that, and everyone said something really should be done to make wedding gifts more reasonable; all the same, people would want to know what Douglas had given his sister, and either Mrs. Bridge or Carolyn would be obliged to point it out. Clearly it had not cost more than two dollars. Mrs. Bridge was absolutely baffled by her son. Never in her life had she so wanted to shake him.

Carolyn Marries

To southern Kansas Carolyn moved after the ceremony and a one-week honeymoon at Excelsior Springs. Mr. Bridge had offered them a wedding trip to the Bahamas, but Gil refused, saying they would honeymoon on the money he himself had earned, so Excelsior Springs was the extent of it. Carolyn had wanted to see the Bahamas ever since she could remember. The wedding gift metamorphosed into one hundred shares of expensive, conservative stock.

Gil began working nights in order to convince his uncle that it was feasible to retire and leave the dry-goods business in his hands, the result being that Carolyn was lonely and bored, and became petulant, and frequently drove to Kansas City for the night after leaving a note pinned to the tablecloth. She would stay in her old room and, if there chanced to be a party that week end, she might remain in Kansas City until Monday. From the beginning she disliked Parallel and could not make up her mind whether she could stand living there.

"The golf course is pathetic, Mother," she said one evening. "It's a nine-hole public course—and by public I mean *anybody,* but anybody, even if they never *saw* a golf club before, can play there. I mean, really, how does Gil expect me to accomplish anything there? It'll absolutely ruin my game. The greens—there aren't any greens, Mother, they're as hard as wood and the grass is burnt to a crisp. It isn't any fun. Anybody can hit the ball three hundred yards, just about—they just go on rolling. My God! I mean, actually, Mother, you should see that place! I had no idea it would be like that."

Mrs. Bridge was extremely anxious for Carolyn to be happy. "I should think it would be nice for a change," she said.

Carolyn was not listening.

"Gil's a type, really. He *is*. He's a small-town boy, and it shows, Mother. He got simply furious when I tried to tell the barber how to cut his hair. I got so mad I wouldn't speak to him for three days."

"Dear, I wish you wouldn't argue with him."

"Listen, Mother, no man is ever going to push me around the way Daddy pushes you around."

Alice

Subsequent events proved that Carolyn and her husband had their reconciliations, no matter how brief, for she very soon was pregnant.

She drove up from Parallel one snowy afternoon and said as she came in the door, stamping snow from her galoshes, "You'll never believe this, Mother, because it's too perfectly incredible." And she said this repeatedly, as if to convince herself it was a dream. It was less than a dream, or more, depending, though she continued to exclaim for about three months, "I mean, this is just insane!"

Eventually she grew accustomed to her situation and it appeared to Mrs. Bridge that the marriage was going to work out all right. Gil and Carolyn were looking for a house in Parallel; their apartment would be too small when the baby came.

"But everything is so high," said Carolyn. They were in the kitchen. It was Harriet's day off and Mrs. Bridge was baking some oatmeal cookies to send to Ruth, and Carolyn was helping. "We want something with a decent yard," she went on, sliding a spatula under a row of hot cookies and transferring them to a towel spread on the drainboard. "And Gil insists on a dry basement. That's the first place he goes. The real-estate agent no more than has the door open when Gil heads for the basement and I'm left standing there as big as an elephant. He's gone mad on turning out salad bowls on a lathe. A friend of his has a lathe. He says it calms his nerves, and so that's why he has to have a dry basement—so it won't rust the goddamned lathe. Really, how berserk can a man go?"

Mrs. Bridge, carefully drawing a second tray of cookies from the oven, observed that there should be lots of pleasant homes in Parallel.

"Oh, there are, there are," Carolyn mumbled, "but you've got to check the neighbors."

"I don't understand what you mean."

"The niggers are moving in."

Mrs. Bridge slowly put down the tray of cookies. She did not know just what to say. Such situations were awkward. On the one hand, she herself would not care to live next door to a houseful of Negroes; on the other hand, there was no reason not to. She had always liked the colored people she had known. She still thought affectionately of her laundry woman, Beulah Mae, and worried about her, wondering if she was still alive. She had never known any Negroes socially; not that she avoided it, just that there weren't any in the neighborhood, or at the country club, or in the Auxiliary. There just weren't any for her to meet, that was all.

"That reminds me, Carolyn. You'll never guess who I bumped into the other day. Alice Jones! We got on an elevator together."

"My God! I'd absolutely forgotten that girl."

"Don't you remember how you two used to play together? You were practically inseparable. I almost had to pry you apart at lunch time."

"Did she recognize you?"

"Oh, right away."

"What's she doing?"

"She's married now and she's working as a maid in one of the downtown hotels."

"How many children does she have?"

"She didn't say."

"Does she look the same?"

"Heavens, no! She's almost as tall as Douglas and she looked so black. It's such a shame."

Carolyn became thoughtful, and finally said, "I think I'd like to see her. Which hotel is she working at?"

"I've been trying to think. I knew you'd want to see her. And she told me which one it was."

"Well, it doesn't matter, I guess. I don't know what we could say to each other, it's been so long."

"How many years has it been?"

"Quite a few," Carolyn answered, biting her lip. "It's been quite a few years, Mother."

Mrs. Bridge turned off the gas in the oven and shut the doors.

Death and Life of Grace Barron

The next morning Lois Montgomery telephoned to say that Grace Barron had committed suicide.

In the days that followed Mrs. Bridge attempted to suppress this fact. Her reasoning was that nothing could be gained by discussing it; consequently she wrote to Ruth that there was some doubt as to what had been the cause of Mrs. Barron's death but it was presumed she had accidentally eaten some tuna-fish salad which had been left out of the refrigerator overnight and had become contaminated, and this was what she told Douglas and Carolyn.

To intimate friends, to those who knew the truth, which was that Grace Barron had swallowed over fifty sleeping tablets, Mrs. Bridge talked more openly. They asked one another familiar and similar questions because, in many ways, Grace Barron was indistinguishable from anyone among them. Their problems had been hers, their position, their wealth, and the love they knew, these also had belonged to her.

"It came as such a shock," Mrs. Bridge heard herself say again and again. "It's awfully hard to believe."

She often wondered if anyone other than herself had been able to divine the motive; if so, it went unmentioned. But she herself had found it instinctively less than an instant after hearing the news: her first thought had been of an afternoon on the Plaza when she and Grace Barron had been looking for some way to occupy themselves, and Grace had said, a little sadly, "Have you ever felt like those people in the Grimm fairy tale—the ones who were all hollowed out in the back?"

Carolyn Comes Home

Sometime in the middle of the night Mrs. Bridge awoke and knew Carolyn had come home. The house was absolutely still and yet she had no doubt; rising quietly so as not to disturb her husband she pulled on her quilted satin robe, found her slippers, and went along the hall to the room where the girls had lived. Sure enough the door was closed; ordinarily it was open. Mrs. Bridge hesitated outside, listening, but heard nothing; she had expected to hear Carolyn sobbing.

"Dear, may I come in?" she asked. There was no answer, but she pushed open the door and saw Carolyn lying on the bed fully dressed with her hands clasped beneath her head. She was staring at the ceiling.

"Did you and Gil have another argument?" she asked, seating herself on the edge of the bed.

"I can't stand him," she answered after a while.

"What was it this time?"

"He hit me."

Mrs. Bridge caught her breath.

"He did," she repeated, with no apparent anger. "He slapped me so hard I lost my balance and fell down."

"You must have done something to provoke him. Didn't you?" she asked.

"Are you on his side?"

"I'm trying not to be on anyone's side, dear," she said, and reached out to stroke Carolyn's head. "It's just that I don't think Gil is that sort."

"Oh, no? If you lived with him you'd find out different." Tears had sprung into her eyes, and seeing them Mrs. Bridge felt herself ready to weep.

"Do you know what he did afterward, Mother? He tried to make it up the way men always do."

"Carolyn, there are some things about marriage that a woman has to—"

"Oh, no, don't tell me that! I don't want any part of that myth—I don't! Why, Mother, he didn't even know it was me. Do you know what I'm saying?"

"Why don't you tell me how it all started?" she replied, pulling the robe more tightly around her throat.

"It started at breakfast because I'd forgotten to get butter the day before, so he got sarcastic, and then he decided I didn't know how to feed the baby, and then he began yelling when he couldn't find his blue suit. Mother, he's been hounding me about that suit for two weeks. It's been at the cleaners and I've been so rushed with the baby and with the qualifying rounds at the club that I haven't had time to pick it up. He could have picked it up himself because he comes right by the cleaners every day, but he keeps saying that's my job. So, anyway, next he began shouting at me that if I spent less time playing golf and more—oh, hell, what's the use? I mean, anyway, after he finally went to work I thought maybe it was partly my fault and so in order to make it up to him I got a baby-sitter to come over while I went to the beauty shop to have my hair set, and they couldn't take me right away and by the time I finally got through it was late and I didn't get home till after he did because I had to pay some bills and stop at the club to see if my entry had been posted. Well, I guess you can imagine what a foul temper he was in when his dinner wasn't ready for him, and he'd called the club and they'd told him I was there, even after I'd given strict orders to say I wasn't. Well," she went on, after drawing a deep breath, "he was furious and swearing. He'd thrown clothes all over the bedroom and even jerked out some of the drawers and turned them over on the bed because he couldn't find what he wanted. I told him the stuff hadn't been washed and he knew perfectly well the washing machine was broken. I guess he expected me to hand-wash everything. I mean, really, Mother, that's what he expected."

"Well, I don't think it would hurt you to do some washing."

"Oh, Mother, honestly! All he has to do is get the machine fixed."

"Yes, I understand, dear, but perhaps if both of you were to try a little harder—"

"He said I didn't have the faintest idea what it meant to have to work."

"Why, that's absurd!"

"He said I was spoiled, Mother. Is that the truth?"

"Of course not, dear. Why should he say a thing like that? Now I'm sure everything is going to work out all right, so why don't you get some rest? You'll feel better in the morning."

"And do you know whose fault he said it was, Mother?"

Mr. Bridge Adjourns

Mrs. Bridge was caught between wanting Carolyn home again for good, and wanting the marriage to succeed. She was often frightened now that Douglas was gone. He had persuaded his father to let him join the Army before the draft caught up with him and now he was somewhere in Arizona. He wrote to her every week—cheerful, airy letters, as though he had gone camping for the summer and would be back in time for college, and she could almost believe this was true. Then, without warning, she would be struck by the actual truth and she would feel lonely and helpless, and guilty over the happiness she experienced whenever Carolyn appeared. With Carolyn in the house—even in a foul humor so that she smoked and cursed without regard for anyone else—even then Mrs. Bridge was comforted, for her presence was an arch to the past, and Mrs. Bridge never tired of dreaming of the days when the children were small, and there had been peace, and so much to anticipate.

Often she sat up with a start, and after a desperate glance at the clock she would be ashamed to learn that two or three hours had gone by while she was thinking. She had given up working at the charity center; there were more than enough volunteers, particularly among the younger women, and the staring eyes of the people on Ninth Street had begun to haunt her. She often saw them in the middle of the night, the hungry, lost people.

And she was haunted, too, by recollections as inanimate and soulless as these unfortunate people, which surrounded her with undemanding, relentless attention, like a perfect circle of question marks—incidents, for the most part, comments she had offered, replies, attitudes, trivial circumstances which by all logic should have long since passed into obscurity, but which recurred persistently to trouble her. And always, or very nearly so, she overcame these doubts; and yet, even as she arose, secure in her convictions, she was aware she had not triumphed over them, nor destroyed them, nor pacified them, but only pushed them away for a little while, like nagging children.

Douglas came home on furlough; he got out of the taxicab looking much older. There was another soldier in the taxi to whom he waved good-by.

"Who was that?" she asked.

"Fellow I met on the train," he replied briefly.

"Didn't you want to ask him in?"

"I did, but he's on his way," Douglas said, and throwing his duffel bag across one shoulder he pushed open the door and strode into the house.

"You've gained some weight," she said, and she noticed, too, that he stood erect now, and there was a frankly adult look in his eyes. The most remarkable change, however, was the fact that he was beginning to grow a mustache—a reddish burr looking somewhat like a patch of sandpaper. Mrs. Bridge thought it looked very silly, and not wanting to hurt his feelings she avoided mentioning it.

Mr. Bridge, however, was neither reticent nor considerate of Douglas's feelings.

"For the love of Mike, what's that?" he asked, on first catching sight of the new mustache, but Douglas, very much to the surprise of his mother, neither flushed in embarrassment nor dropped his eyes.

"You think you could do any better?" he solemnly replied.

Mr. Bridge laughed and clapped him solidly on the shoulder. "How about a drink before dinner, soldier?"

"I could use one," said Douglas, and away they went to the kitchen. Mrs. Bridge heard them laughing, and Harriet's shrill laughter joining in.

Although she could not understand her son she was so pleased to have him home that she continually found excuses to be near him. So it was that she knocked on his door to ask if his socks needed mending. He told her to come in and look. She entered and found him standing in front of the bathroom mirror lathering his jaw. He was not wearing a shirt, only an olive green undershirt and khaki trousers, and she noticed a metal chain around his neck that he had never worn before.

"What on earth is this?" she inquired, approaching hesitantly, full of love and tenderness.

"Dog tags," he said. He was amused.

She drew the chain up from beneath the undershirt, strangely and deeply moved to discover there was hair on his chest, and she held the tags in trembling fingers. She inquired about the data stamped on the dull brass disks, and he told her that one was his serial number, another his blood type, and so on.

"What is this 'P'?" she wanted to know.

"Protestant," he said. "I told them I was a Buddhist, but they insisted I was a Protestant."

"You did *what?*"

"We have to fill out forms all the time. Every form has a blank where you write down your religious affiliation. I always write Buddhist, but somebody always types it up Protestant. I don't know why."

"Well, for goodness' sakes, that's an awfully odd thing to write. You're not a Buddhist."

Douglas dipped his razor in the water. He was looking gently down on her in the mirror, white and foamy almost up to his eyes. She thought he looked inscrutable. She was bewildered.

"Well, I suppose you know what you're doing. Now hurry and finish shaving; Harriet will soon have dinner ready."

She expected him to shave off the mustache, but he did not, and so several days later while he was leaning against the bookcase with Omar Khayyám in hand she remarked, "You look like a perfect stranger."

Douglas glanced down at her in a friendly way and said, without having asked what she meant, that he thought he would keep his mustache nonetheless.

But next morning, seeing it across the breakfast table, she knew it would have to go. Without a word she set down her orange juice and went upstairs to his room, where, in the closet, she found his Army cap. She put this on her head, and having touched up her graying curls at the mirror she marched downstairs and into the breakfast room swinging her arms stiffly. Douglas was not there. Harriet, stacking the dishes, gazed at her in astonishment. Mrs. Bridge smiled at her bravely, and as serenely as possible under the circumstances. Just then she heard Douglas cough. It sounded as though he were in the living room. She turned around and marched through the hall and into the front room where she came to a halt in what she considered a military manner, and tried to click her heels.

"Attention, Private Bridge. March right upstairs this very minute and shave off your silly mustache."

Douglas had been looking at the photograph on the dust jacket of Dr. Foster's book of essays. He dropped the book on the sofa and crossed his arms. When it became obvious that he did not intend to speak, that he was simply waiting for her to leave, she pulled the cap from her head and stood in front of him uncertainly, rather humbly.

He was to leave from the Union Station at four o'clock the next afternoon, but a few minutes after three the telephone rang. It was Mr. Bridge's office and the secretary was on the phone. Mr. Bridge was dead. He had hurried into the office immediately after lunch and resumed work with a dictaphone. Sometime after that he rolled out of his swivel chair and sprawled on the carpet as dead as he would ever be. When the dictaphone cylinder was played they heard him say, "It appears, therefore, the defendant—" and the squeak of the swivel chair.

"It was awfully good of you," Mrs. Bridge said, standing at the half-open door, telling each visitor good-by. "Everyone has been so kind."

Letter From a Buddhist

Douglas, having exchanged telegrams with the commandant of his camp, remained in Kansas City till after the funeral. Ruth had flown home from New York and Carolyn had driven up from Parallel; both of them were struck by the change in Douglas. Ruth had no difficulty accepting him as the new head of the family, though he was nearly five years younger than she. Carolyn challenged him once or twice, halfheartedly. Neither of them expected their mother to make decisions. And to Mrs. Bridge herself it seemed natural that he should become the authority. Harriet, keenly attuned to every situation, asked Douglas if she could have a raise; he said no. From that moment on she stopped calling him by his first name and referred to him as Mr. Bridge, and his mother, hearing this for the first time, began to weep.

Soon, like birds abandoning a tree, they flew off in different directions. Ruth went back to New York, Carolyn to southern Kansas, and Douglas to the Army. The functions of the house were carried on by Harriet, and Mrs. Bridge was left alone. She often went to Auxiliary meetings, and she went shopping downtown, and to the Plaza for luncheon, and to a number of parties, but she could no longer lose herself in these activities; the past was too much with her, and so she was frequently content to stay at home, waiting for the mail, or waiting for someone to call, remotely conscious of the persistent roar of the vacuum cleaner, no longer caring if Harriet smoked in the kitchen.

When she received the first letter Douglas wrote after returning to camp she thought how intimately it resembled the letters her husband used to write when he was out of town on business. There had been something quaint about her husband, an old-fashioned inclination which had caused him to begin his letters to her with, "My dear wife . . ."

How strange that Douglas should write:

My dear Mother,

My father loved you above all else, and if he was apt to be rude or tyrannical it was because he wanted to protect you. He wanted so much for us all. He did not ever realize that what we needed was himself instead of what he could give us. On more than one occasion he and I discussed the family and its problems and in these talks I felt his constant preoccupation with your welfare after he was gone. I guess he knew he was not going to live much longer. He said he had never told you about the trouble with his heart.

There is nothing at all for you to worry about. You made him very happy during his life. I am quite certain that never once was he interested in another woman. My love to you, Mother, and to both my sisters. Tell Ruth when next you write her that I am anxious to hear from her.

Well, we have to go out on maneuvers now, but I'll write you again pretty soon.

With love, as always,
Douglas

Remembrance of Things Past

Her album provided many comforting hours. There she could find her children once again, and her husband, too. He was standing in bright sunshine with one hand on the fender of the new Reo and Carolyn was sitting on his shoulders. There was Douglas showing off the baseball bat they had given him for his birthday. And there was Ruth in her first high heels, standing pigeon-toed and earnestly determined not to fall on her face. There, too, were her friends—Grace Barron waving from the high diving board at the country-club pool, Mabel Ong outside the Auxiliary clubhouse with hands thrust in the side pockets of her tweed jacket, Madge one snowy day in a Persian lamb coat with her galoshes unzipped, and Lois Montgomery looking presidential. Mrs. Bridge wished she had taken more snapshots.

She had quite a few of the European trip she and Mr. Bridge had taken one summer. She had spent more than one enjoyable morning with a damp sponge on which to wet the mounting corners, the huge album lying open on the writing desk and the carpet all around her feet littered with negatives and with yellow drugstore envelopes. In went Trafalgar Square, Buckingham Palace, Piccadilly, the Thames, the changing of the Guard, and the ravens she had seen at the Tower of London. In went the Seine, the Arch of Triumph, an awning of Maxim's, Notre Dame, and Mr. Bridge buying the *Herald Tribune* in front of the American Express. The pictures of the Riviera had not turned out well, though she could not imagine why, unless the light meter had not been working properly; the Riviera, whenever she thought about it, seemed so foreign, really more foreign to her way of life than Paris had been. Often she remembered the cliffs, the harbor, and the shining sea.

"I don't know whether this would interest you or not," she would say to guests, picking up the album in both hands, and as she deposited it on her visitor's lap she would say, "Now, just look at them until you get bored, but for heaven's sake don't feel obliged to go through them all." And she would then hover nearby, anxious to know which pictures were being looked at. Often she would be unable to sit still; she had to look over the visitor's shoulder, reaching down now and then to say, "That's the famous old cathedral you're always hearing about." Or, "That's the ocean, of course." Or, "This was taken from the steps of the National Gallery, and right there—directly behind the man on the bicycle—is where we ate lunch."

But the pictures to which she returned most often for her own pleasure were those of her family: they evoked what she had known most intimately, and all she had loved most profoundly.

Hello?

One December morning near the end of the year when snow was falling moist and heavy for miles all around, so that the earth and the sky were indivisible, Mrs. Bridge emerged from her home and spread her umbrella. With small cautious steps she proceeded to the garage, where she pressed the button and waited impatiently for the door to lift. She was in a hurry to drive downtown to buy some Irish lace antimacassars that were advertised in the newspaper, and she was planning to spend the remainder of the day browsing through the stores because it was Harriet's day off and the house was empty—so empty.

She had backed just halfway out of the garage when the engine died. She touched the starter and listened without concern because, despite her difficulties with the Lincoln, she had grown to feel secure in it. The Lincoln was a number of years old and occasionally recalcitrant, but she could not bear the thought of parting with it, and in the past had resisted this suggestion of her husband, who, mildly puzzled by her attachment to the car, had allowed her to keep it.

Thinking she might have flooded the engine, which was often true, Mrs. Bridge decided to wait a minute or so.

Presently she tried again, and again, and then again. Deeply disappointed, she opened the door to get out and discovered she had stopped in such a position that the car doors were prevented from opening more than a few inches on one side by the garage partition, and on the other side by the wall. Having tried all four doors she began to understand that until she could attract someone's attention she was trapped. She pressed the horn, but there was not a sound. Half inside and half outside she remained.

For a long time she sat there with her gloved hands folded in her lap, not knowing what to do. Once she looked at herself in the mirror. Finally she took the keys from the ignition and began tapping on the window, and she called to anyone who might be listening, "Hello? Hello out there?"

⬦

What appears above is a much shortened version of the novel Mrs. Bridge. *The mosaic structure of the book made it possible to abridge it without losing readability or altering the basic plot and themes, but the reader should be aware that many episodes, sequences, and characters that enrich the novel have been omitted.* Mrs. Bridge *is by no means a "cult" novel— although it has never sold well, it has never been out of print—but for many middle- and upper-middle-class Americans who grew up in the suburbs in World War II there is intense identification and recognition ("My God, that's my mother exactly!"), and many find themselves buying copies for their friends. A first reaction to the book is often that it is a marvelously accurate, but bitterly satirical and perhaps even malicious, exposure of the typical complacent, ineffectual American "Mom"—the best job done on her since Philip Wylie. This effect is enhanced by what seems a cold, distant voice recounting a series of surreptitiously barbed anecdotes: the author, in collusion with the reader behind Mrs. Bridge's back, agreeing about her deficiencies. But on reconsideration, and especially on rereading, this initial reaction gives way to an appreciation of how much more complex the novel's ironic tone is. It is also a sympathetic, forgiving, and loving portrait of a very real and much individualized character. Each of the separate anecdotes could be advanced to show how the irony cuts both ways, but this is especially clear toward the end, where one finds himself commiserating with Mrs. Bridge. The episodic, family-album structure and the simple, flat style reflect Mrs. Bridge's view of her life and her family: she has it all before her in contained sequence, but she is unable to make the same sense of the parts of it that the reader does. Her trouble— and her salvation—is that she has a closed mind. There are simply no "problems," as we think of them, for Mrs. Bridge: she can have only the vaguest sense of things being not quite what she expected. She does not conceive of a choice of actions: for her there is only one right way to be or act. What seem to us unrealistic niceties and irrelevant manners are to her real values, the explicit manifestations of all her deeply held, unquestioned beliefs. Carrying a pocketbook when you go downtown and not using the towels put out for guests are not for her merely symbols of a proper way to act, but are actually themselves part of the proper way to act. Her goal for her children is "that when they were spoken of it would be in connection with their nice manners, their pleasant dispositions, and their cleanliness." What she teaches them is not to be "different from everyone else," and what she means by "everyone" is all those of her class who share her ideas of correctness and niceness. Her blind confidence in the permanent, enduring rightness of the nice way things should or ought to be prevents her from recognizing, much less adapting herself to, still less preparing her children for, the modern world of constant change. When Carolyn marries, her husband has neither the money Mr. Bridge has, nor the inclination (his is a different class expectation), to support an idle and ineffectual wife. Ruth, in overreaction to her mother's prudery, is unhappily promiscuous in New York; Mrs. Bridge, incapable of even imagining this, sends the traditional train letter, oatmeal cookies, and news items from the hometown society column. "Mobility," "choice," "flexibility"—none of the "realities" of all the sexual, cultural, and social revolutions of our times makes sense to Mrs. Bridge. While her convictions and her innocence protect her from*

270 EVAN S. CONNELL, JR.

all the not-niceness of the world, they isolate her from the one thing she cares most about, her family. The ending is a metaphor, but very moving: she is finally immobilized in the old Lincoln that Mr. Bridge gave her and that she never really learned to handle, calling out to a world that isn't there. She is locked in by her attitudes.

There is so much unreality in Mrs. Bridge's "nice" orientation that it, and she, seem obsolete, irrelevant. In reaction to this sort of upbringing, a generation of youths has grown up convinced of the opposite—that only the not-nice is "real"—and in some cases develops standards of conduct based on being dirty, unconventional, and without manners, from which, ironically, little individual deviation is allowed. What Mrs. Bridge tries to teach her children is just what she learned from her parents. In exactly such a way standards of conduct, codes of manners, and sets of attitudes have in other eras been successfully passed down within classes for generations. The complete, self-protective value system, which proposes to contain all possible answers within its own defensive world-view, is like a medieval castle, impregnable to anything alien to it, in a static, stable situation where control of power is maintained. But in these shifting, mobile, flexible times we live in now, the complete system (even when strengthened by warm family ties and by the secure status of the successful suburban household) can become more like a prison than a castle, for it isolates the individual from the possibility of communicating with the surrounding world of constant change.

JOHN UPDIKE

Incest

◇◇◇◇◇◇

"I WAS IN A MOVIE HOUSE, fairly plush, in a sort of mezzanine, or balcony. It was a wide screen. On it there were tall people—it seemed to be at a dance or at least *function*—talking and bending toward each other gracefully, in that misty technicolor Japanese pictures have. I *knew* that this was the movie version of 'Remembrance of Things Past.' I had the impression sitting there that I had been looking forward to it for a long time, and I felt slightly guilty at not being home, you know. There was a girl sitting down one row, catty-corner from me. She had a small head with a thin, rather touching neck, like Moira Lengel, but it wasn't her, or anyone we know. At any rate there was this feeling of great affection toward her, and it seemed, in the light of the movie—the movie was taking place entirely in a bright yellow ballroom, so the faces of the audience were clear—it seemed somehow that the entire chance to make my life good was wrapped up in this girl, who was strange to me. Then she was in the seat beside me, and I was giving her a back rub."

"*Uh*-oh," his wife said, pausing in her stooping. She was grazing the carpet, picking up the toys, cards, matches, and spoons scattered by their daughter Jane, a year and seven months old. Big Jane, as she had dreaded being called when they named the child, held quite still to catch what next he had to tell. Lee had begun the recitation ironically, to register his irritation with her for asking him, her own day had been so dull and wearing, to talk to tell her of *his* day. Nothing interested him less than his own day, done. It made his jaws ache, as with a smothered yawn, to consider framing one sentence about it. So, part desperation, part discipline, he had begun the account of the dream he had been careful to keep from her at breakfast. He protected his wife here, at the place where he recalled feeling his hands leave the lean girl's comforted shoulder blades and travel thoughtfully around the cool, strait, faintly ridged sides of the rib case to the always surprising boon in front—sensations momentarily more vivid in the nerves of his fingers than the immediate texture of the bamboo chair he occupied.

"Through the blouse."

"Good," she said. "Good for you both."

Jane appeared so saucy saying this he was emboldened to add a true detail: "I think I did undo her bra strap. By pinching through the cloth." To judge by his wife's expression—tense for him, as if he were bragging before company—the addition was a mistake. He hastened on. "Then we were standing in back of the seats, behind one of those walls that comes up to your chest, and I was being introduced to her father. I had the impression he was a doctor. He was rather pleasant, really: gray hair, and a firm grip. He seemed cordial, and I had a competent feeling, as if I couldn't help making a good impression. But behind this encounter—with the girl standing off to one side—there was the sadness of the movie itself continuing on the screen; the music soared; Proust's face was shown—a very young face—with the eyelids closed, and this shimmered and spun and turned into a slow pink vortex that then solidified into a huge motionless rose, filling the whole screen. And I thought, *Now I know how the book ends.*"

"How exciting, darley! It's like 'The Dream of the Rood.' " Jane resumed cleaning up after her daughter. Lee was abruptly oppressed by a belief that he had made her life harder to bear.

He said, "The girl must have been you because you're the only person I know who likes to have their back rubbed."

"You find my neck touching?"

"Well for God's sake, I can't be held accountable for the people I meet in dreams. I don't invite them." He was safe, of course, as long as they stayed away from the real issue, which was why he had told her the dream at all. "That girl means nothing to me now. In the dream obviously I was still in high school and hadn't met you. I remember sitting there and wondering, because it was such a long movie, if my mother would give me hell when I got back."

"I say, it's a very exciting dream. How far *are* you in Proust?"

" 'Sodom and Gomorrah.' " It occurred to him, what a queer mediocre thing it was, to scorn the English title yet not dare pronunciation of the French, and apropos of this self-revelation he said, "I'll never get out; I'm just the sort of person who begins Proust and can't finish. Lowest of the low. The humiliated and oppressed. Won't even tell his wife what his day was like." He changed his tone. "Which is better—to finish 'Remembrance of Things Past,' or to never begin it?"

Unexpectedly, so profound was her fatigue, she did not recognize the question as a piece of sport rhetoric, and, after a moment's thought, seriously answered, "To finish it."

Then she turned, and her lovely pale face—in photographs like a white water-smoothed stone, so little did the indentations and markings of it have harshness—lengthened, and the space between her eyebrows creased verti-cally; into the kitchen she shouted, *"Jane!* What are you *doing?"*

While they had been talking, the child had been keeping herself quiet with the sugar bowl. It was a new trick of hers, to push a chair and climb up on it; in this way a new world, a fresh stratum of things, was made available to her curiosity. The sugar bowl, plump Swedish pewter, lived casually on the counter of a waist-high cabinet, near the wall. Little Jane had taken and inverted it, and with an eerie, repetitious, patient dabbling motion had reduced the one shining Alp to a system of low ranges. She paid no attention to her mother's shout, but when her parents drew closer and sighed together, she quickly turned her face toward them as if for admiration, her chin and lips frosted. Her upper lip, when she smiled, curved like the handlebar of a bicycle. The sight of her incredibly many, perfect, blue, inturned teeth struck joy into Lee's heart.

With an audience now, little Jane accelerated her work. Her right hand, unattended by her eyes, which remained with her parents, scrabbled in a panicky way among the white drifts and then, palm down, swept a quantity onto the floor, where it hit with a sound like one stroke of a drummer's brush. On the spatter-pattern linoleum the grains of sugar were scarcely visible. The child looked down, wondering where they had gone.

"Damn you," his wife said to Lee, "you never do a damn thing to help. Now, why can't you play with her a minute? You're her father. I'm not going to clean it up." She walked out of the kitchen.

"I *do* play with her," he said, helplessly amiable (he understood his wife so well, divined so exactly what confused pain the scattered sugar caused her heart, as neatness-loving as her mother's), although he recognized that in her distraught state his keeping cheerful figured as mockery of her, one more cross to carry toward the day's end.

Lee asked his daughter, "Want to run around?"

Jane hunched her shoulders and threw back her head, her sugar-gritty teeth gleefully clenched. "Pay roun," she said, wagging her hand on her wrist.

He made the circular motion she had intended, and said, "In a minute. Now we must help poor Mommy." With two sheets of typing paper, using one as a brush and the other as a pan, he cleaned up what she had spilled on the counter, reaching around her, since she kept her position standing on the chair. Her breath floated randomly, like a butterfly, on his forearms as he swept. They seemed two conspirators. He folded the pan into a chute and returned the sugar to the bowl. Then there was the sugar on the floor—when you moved your feet, atoms of it crackled. He stooped, the two pieces of paper in his hands, knowing they wouldn't quite do.

Jane whimpered and recklessly jogged her body up and down on her legs, making the chair tip and slap the cabinet. *"Jane,"* he said.

"Pay roun," the girl whined feebly, her strength sapped by frustration.

"What?" his wife answered from the living room in a voice as cross as his. She had fought giving the baby her name, but he had insisted; there was no other woman's name he liked, he had said.

"Nothing, I was shouting at the kid. She was going to throw herself off the chair. She wants to play Round."

"Well, why don't you? She's had an awfully dismal day. I don't think we make her happy enough."

"O.K., dammit. I will." He crumpled the sheets of paper and stuffed them into the wastepaper can, letting the collected sugar fly where it would.

Round was a simple game. Jane ran from the sofa in one room to the bed in the other, through the high white double doorway, with pilasters, that had persuaded them to take the small apartment. He chased her. When his hands nicked her bottom or touched her swollen waist, she laughed wildly her double laugh, which originated deep in her lungs and ricocheted, shrill, off her palate. Lee's problem was to avoid overtaking her, in the great length of his strides, and stepping on her. When she wobbled or slowed, he clapped twice or thrice, to give her the sense of his hands right behind her ears, like two nipping birds. If she toppled, he swiftly picked her up, tickling her briefly if she seemed stunned or indignant. When she reached the bed—two low couches, box springs on short legs, set side by side and made up as one—he leapfrogged over her and fell full-length on the mattresses. This, for him, was the strenuous part of the game. Jane, finding herself between her father's ankles after the rush of his body above her head, laughed her loudest, pivoted, and ran the other way, flailing her arms, which she held so stiffly the elbows were indentations. At the sofa end of the track there could be no leapfrogging. Lee merely stopped and stood with his back toward her until the little girl calculated she dare make a break for it. Her irises swivelled in their blue whites; it was the first strategy of her life. The instant she decided to move, her bottled excitement burst forth; as she clumped precipitately toward the high white arch laughter threatened to upend her world. The game lasted until the child's bath. Big Jane, for the first time that day free of her daughter, was not hurrying toward this moment.

After four times back and forth Lee was exhausted and damp. He flopped on the bed the fifth time and instead of rising rolled onto his back. This was ruining the crease in his pants. His daughter, having started off, felt his absence behind her and halted. Her mother was coming from the kitchen, carrying washed diapers and a dust brush. Like her own mother, big Jane held a cigarette in the left corner of her mouth. Her left eye fluttered against the smoke. Lee's mother-in-law was shorter than his wife, paler, more sarcastic—very different, he had thought. But this habit was hers right down to the tilt of the cigarette and the droop of the neglected ash. Looking, Lee saw that as Jane squinted, the white skin at the outside corner of her eye crinkled finely, as dry as her mother's, and that his wife's lids were touched with the lashless, grainy, humiliated quality of the lids of the middle-aged woman he had met not a dozen times, mostly in Indianapolis where she kept a huge brick house spotlessly clean and sipped sherry from breakfast to bed. All unknowing he had married her.

Jane, as she passed him, glanced down with an untypical, sardonic, cigarette-stitched expression. By shifting his head on the pillow he could watch her in the bathroom. She turned her back to hang the diapers on a grocer's cord strung between mirror and window. This was more his Jane: the rounded shoulders, the soft and expressive back shaped like a peach of two halves; the big thighs, the narrow ankles. In the mirror her face, straining up as she attached the clothespins, showed age and pallor. It was as if there could exist a coin one side of which wears thin while the other keeps all the gloss and contour of the minting.

"Da-*tee.*" A coral flush had overspread his daughter's face; in another moment she would whimper and throw herself on the floor.

With an ostentatious groan—he didn't know which of his women he was rebuking—Lee rose from the bed and chased his daughter again. Then they played in the living room with the bolsters, two prism-shaped pieces of foam rubber that served as a back to the sofa, an uncomfortable modernist slab that could, when a relative visited, be used for sleeping. Stood on end, the stiff bolsters were about the baby's height, and little Jane hugged them like brothers, and preferred them to dolls. Though to her human-sized, they were light enough to lift. Especially she loved to unzip the skin of mongrel linen fabric and prod with her finger the grayish, buoyant flesh beneath.

Catching them at this, big Jane said, "It kills me, it just is more depressing than anything she does, the way she's always trying to undress those bolsters. Don't en*cour*age her at it."

"I don't. It's not my idea. It was *you* who took the covers to the Launderette so she saw them naked. It made a big impression. It's a state of primal innocence she wants to get them back to."

Wavering between quarrel and honest discussion—that there was a way of "talking things out" was an idea she had inherited from her father, a rigorously liberal civic leader and committeeman—she chose discussion. "It's not just those bolsters, you know. About three times a day she takes all the books out of their jackets. And spills matches in a little heap. You have no idea how much cleaning up I have to do to keep this place from looking like a pigpen. Yesterday I was in the bathroom washing my hair and when I came out she had gotten our camera open. I guess the whole roll's exposed. I put it back. Today she wanted to get the works out of the music box and threw a tantrum. And I don't know how often she brings those nasty frustrating little Chinese eggs you got her to me and says, 'Opo. Opo.' "

Reminded of the word, little Jane said, of a bolster, "Opo, opo." The zipper was stuck.

"Japanese," Lee said. "Those eggs were made in Genuine Occupied

Japan. They're antiques." The child's being balked by the zipper preyed on his nerves. He hated fiddling with things like zippers caught on tiny strips of cloth. It was like squinting into a specific detail of Hell. Further, as he leaned back on the bolsterless sofa to rest his neck against the wall, he was irritated to feel the glass-capped legs skid on the uneven floor. "It's a very healthy instinct," he went on. "She's an empiricist. She's throwing open doors long locked by superstition."

Jane said, "I looked up 'unwrapping instinct' in Spock and the only thing in the index was 'underweight.' " Her tone was listless and humorous, and for the moment this concession put the family, to Lee's mind, as right as three Japanese eggs, each inside the other.

His wife gave his daughter her bath as day turned to evening. He had to go into the bathroom himself and while there studied the scene. The child's silky body, where immersed, was of a graver tint than that of her skin smarting in air. Two new cakes of unwrapped soap drifted around her. When her mother put a washrag to her face, blinding and scratching her, her fingers turned pale green with the pressure of her grip on the edge of the tub. She didn't cry, though. "She seems to like her bath better now," he said.

"She loves it. From five on, until you come, she talks about it. Daddy. Bath. Omelet."

"Omma net," his daughter said, biting her lower lip in a smile for him.

It had become, in one of those delicate mutations of routine whereby Jane shifted duties to him, his job to feed the little girl. The child's soft mouth had been burned and she was wary; the sample bites Lee took to show her that the food was safe robbed of sharpness his appetite for his own dinner. Foreknowledge of the emotion caused in his wife by the sight of half-clean plates and half-full cups led him to complete little Jane's portion of tomato juice, omelet-with-toast, and, for dessert, applesauce. Handling the tiny cup and tiny knife and fork and spoon set his stomach slightly on edge. Though not fussy about food, he was disturbed by eating implements of improper weight or length. Jane, hidden in the kitchen, was unable to see, or if she had seen, to appreciate—for all their three years of marriage, she had a stunted awareness of his niceties—the discomfort he was giving himself. This annoyed him.

So he was unfortunately brusque with little Jane's bottle. Ideally the bottle was the happiest part of the meal. Steaming and dewy, it soared, white angel, out of the trembling pan, via Mommy's hands, with a kiss, into hers. She grabbed it, and Lee, his hand behind her head, steered her toward the bedroom and her crib.

"Nice maugham," she said, conscientiously echoing the infinity of times they had told her that the bottle was nice and warm.

Having lifted her into the crib and seen her root the bottle in her mouth, he dropped the fuzzy pink blanket over her and left quickly, gently closing the doors and sealing her into the darkness that was to merge with sleep. It was no doubt this quickness that undid the process. Though the child was drugged with heated milk, she still noticed a slight.

He suspected this at the time. When, their own meal barely begun, the crib springs creaked unmistakably, he said, "Son of a bitch." Stan Lomax, on their faint radio, was giving an account of Williams' latest verbal outrage; Lee was desperate to hear every word. Like many Americans he was spiritually dependent on Ted Williams. He asked his wife, "God damn it, doesn't that kid do anything in the day? Didn't you take her to the park? Why isn't she worn out?"

The one answer to this could be his own getting up, after a silence, and going in to wait out the baby's insomnia. The hollow goodness of the act, like a gift given to a beggar with embarrassment, infuriated his tongue: "I work like a fool all day and come home and run the kid up and down until my legs ache and I have a headache and then I can't even eat my pork chop in peace."

In the aquarium of the dark room his child's face floated spectrally, and her eyes seemed discrete pools of the distant, shy power that had put them all there, and had made these walls, and the single tree outside, showing the first stages of leaf under the yellow night sky of New York. "Do you want to go on the big bed?"

"Big—bed!"

"O.K."

"Ogay."

Adjusting to the lack of light, he perceived that the bottle, nested in a crumpled sheet, was drained. Little Jane had been standing in her crib, one foot on the edge, as in ballet school. For two weeks she had been gathering nerve for the time she would climb the crib's wall and drop free outside. He lifted her out, breathing "Ooh, *heavy*," and took her to the wide low bed made of two beds. She clung to the fuzzy blanket—with milk, her main soporific.

Beside her on the bed, he began their story. "Once upon a time, in the big, big woods—" She flipped ecstatically at the known cadence. "Now you relax. There was a tiny little creature name of Barry Mouse."

"Mouff!" she cried, and sat straight up, as if she had heard one. She looked down at him for confirmation.

"Barry Mouse," he said. "And one day when Barry Mouse was walking through the woods, he came to a great big tree, and in the top of the great big tree what do you think there was?"

At last she yielded to the insistent pressure of his hand and fell back, her heavy blond head sinking into the pillow. He repeated, "What do you think there was?"

"Owl."

"That's right. Up at the top of the tree there was an owl, and the owl said, 'I'm going to eat you, Barry Mouse.' And Barry Mouse said, 'No, no.' So Owl said, 'O.K., then why don't you *hop* on my *back* and we'll *fly* to the *moon?*' And so Barry Mouse hopped on Owl's back and away they went—"

Jane turned on her side, so her great face was an inch from his. She giggled and drummed her feet against his abdomen, solidly. Neither Lee nor his wife, who shared the one bedtime story, had ever worked out what happened on the moon. Once the owl and the mouse were aloft, their imaginations collapsed. Knowing his voice daren't stop now, when her state was possibly transitional and he felt as if he were bringing to his lips an absolutely brimful glass of liquid, he continued with some nonsense about cinnamon trees and Chinese maidens, no longer bothering to keep within her vocabulary. She began touching his face with her open mouth, a sure sign she was sleepy. "Hey," he murmured when one boneless moist kiss landed directly on his lips.

"Jane is so sleepy," he said, "because Daddy is sleepy, and Mommy is sleepy, and Bear is ssleepy, and Doll is sssleepy. . . ."

She lay quiet, her face in shadow, her fine straight yellow hair fanned across the pillow. Neither he nor his wife was blond; they had brown hair, rat color. There was little blondness in either family: just Jane's Aunt Ruth, and Lee's sister Margaret, eight years older than he and married before he had left grade school. She had been the fetching one of the children and he the bright one. So he imagined, though his parents loved them all impeccably.

Presuming his daughter asleep, he lifted himself on one elbow. She kicked his belly, rolled onto her back, and said in a voice loud with drowsiness, "Baaiy Mouff."

Stroking her strange hair, he began again, "Once upon a time, in the deep, deep woods, there lived a little creature," and this time succeeded.

As he lowered her into her crib, her eyes opened. He said, "O.K.?"

She pronounced beautifully, "O.K."

"Gee, she's practically epileptic with energy," he said, blinded by the brilliant light of the room where his wife had remained.

"She's a good child," Jane affirmed, speaking out of her thoughts while left alone rather than in answer to his remark. "Your dessert is on the table." She had kept hers intact on the sofa beside her, so they could eat their raspberry whip together. She also had beside her an orange-juice glass half full of sherry.

When the clock said 7:50, he said, "Why don't you run off to the movie? You never have any fun."

"All right," she said. "Go ahead. Go."

"No, I don't mean that. I mean you should go." Still, he smiled.

"You can go as a reward for putting her to sleep."

"Venus, I don't *want* to go," he said, without great emphasis, since at that moment he was rustling through the paper. He had difficulty finding the theatre section, and decided. "No, if you're too tired, no one will. I can't leave you. You need me too much."

"If you want to, go; don't torment me about it," she said, drawing on her sherry and staring into the *New Republic*. When she had the chance, she worked at being liberal.

"Do you think," he asked, "when Jane is sixteen, she'll go around in the back seat of Chevrolets and leave her poor old Daddy?"

"I hope so," Jane said.

"Will she have your bosom?"

"Not immediately."

He earnestly tried to visualize his daughter matured, and saw little but a charm bracelet on a slim, fair wrist. The forearms of teen-age girls tapered amazingly, toward little cages of bird bones. Charm bracelets were *démodé* already, he supposed.

Lee, committed to a long leisured evening at home, of the type that seemed precious on the nights when they had to go out and be entertained, was made nervous by its wide opportunities. He nibbled at the reading matter closest to hand—an article, "Is the Individual a Thing of the Past?" and last Sunday's comic section. At Alley Oop he checked himself and went into the kitchen. Thinking of the oatmeal cookies habitual in his parents' home, he opened the cupboard and found four kinds of sugar and seven of cereal, five infants' and two adults'. Jane was always buying some esoteric grind of sugar for a pastrymaking project, then discovering she couldn't use it. He smiled at this foible and carried his smile like an egg on a spoon into the living room, where his wife saw it but of course not the point of it, that it was in love of her. He leaned his forehead against the bookcase, by the anthology shelf, and considered all the poetry he had once read evaporating in him, a vast dying sea.

As he stood there, his father floated from behind and possessed him, occupying specifically the curved area of the jawbone. He understood perfectly why that tall stoical man had been a Mason, Booster, deacon, and Scout troop leader.

Jane, concentrating all the pleasures her day had withheld into the hour remaining before she became too dopey to think, put Bach on the record-player. As she did so, her back and arms made angles signifying to him a whole era of affection and, more, awe.

When she returned to the sofa, he asked, "What makes you so pretty?" Then, having to answer it, he said, "Childbearing."

Preoccupied with some dim speckled thinker in her magazine, she fondled the remark briefly and set it aside, mistakenly judging it to be a piece of an obscure, ill-tempered substance. He poured a little sherry for himself and struck a pose by the mantel, trying to find with his legs and shoulders angles equivalent in effect to those she had made putting on the record. As she sat there, studious, he circumscribed her, every detail, with the tidal thought *Mine, mine.* She wasn't watching. She thought she knew what to expect from him, tonight at least.

He resolved, *Later,* and, in a mood of resolution, read straight through the Jones Very section of Matthiessen's anthology. The poet's stubborn sensibility aroused a readerly stubbornness; when Lee had finished, it was too late, the hour had slipped by. By the clock it was 10:30; for his wife, it was after one. Her lids were pink. This was the sort of day when you sow and not reap.

Two hissing, clattering elves working a minor fairytale transposition, together they lifted the crib containing the sleeping girl and carried it into the living room, and shut the doors. Instead of undressing, Jane picked up odds and ends of his—spare shoes and the socks he had worn yesterday and the tie he had worn today. Next she went into the bathroom and emerged wearing a cotton nightie. In bed beside him she read a page of *Swann's Way* and fell asleep under the harsh light. He turned it off and thought furiously, the family's second insomniac. The heat of Jane's body made the bed stuffy. He hated these low beds; he lay miles below the ceiling, deep in the pit. The radiator, hidden in the window sill by his head, breathed lavishly. High above, through a net of crosses, a few stars strove where the yellow gave out. The child cried once, but, thank God, in her sleep.

He recalled what he always forgot in the interval of day, his insomnia game. Last night he had finished D in a burst of glory: Yvonne Dionne, Zuleika Dobson. He let the new letter be G. Senator Albert Gore. Benny Goodman, Constance Garnett, *David* Garnett, Edvard Grieg. Goethe was Wolfgang and Gorki was Maxim. Farley Granger, Graham Greene (or Greta Garbo, *or* George Gobel), Henry Green. I was always difficult. You kept thinking of Ilka Chase. He wrestled and turned and cursed his wife, her heedless rump way on his side. To choke the temptation to thump her awake, he padded after a glass of water, scowling into the mirror. As he returned his head to the cooled pillow, it came to him, Christian name and surname both at once: Ira Gershwin. Ira Gershwin: he savored it before proceeding. John Galsworthy, Kathryn Grayson . . . Lou Gehrig, poor devil . . .

He and Jane walked along a dirt road, in high, open-field country, like the farm owned by Mark, his mother's brother. He was glad that Jane was seeing the place, because while he was growing up it had given him a sense of wealth to have an uncle attached to a hundred such well-kept acres. His relationship with Jane seemed to be at that stage when it was important for each side of the betrothal to produce external signs of respectability. "But I am even richer," he abruptly announced. She appeared not to notice. They walked companionably but in silence, and seemed responsible for the person with them, a female their height. Lee gathered the impression, despite a veil against his eyes, that this extra girl was blond and sturdy and docile. His sense of her sullenness may have been nothing but his anxiety to win her approval, reflected; though her features were hard to make out, the emotion he bore her was precise: the coppery, gratified, somewhat adrift feeling he would get when physically near girls he adored in high school. The wind had darkened and grown purposeful.

Jane went back, though the countryside remained the same. Then he was dousing, with a lawn hose attached to the side of the house, the body of this third person. Her head rested on the ground; he held her ankles and slowly, easily turned the light, stiff mass, to wet every area. It was important that water wash over every bit of skin. He was careful; the task, like rinsing an automobile, was more absorbing than pleasant or unpleasant.

◇

John Updike is a sort of short-story laureate of the nuclear family in the nuclear age. In various stories he uses different sets of names—Jack and Clare and baby Joanne, or Robert and Joan and baby Corinne, or Ralph and Eve and unnamed baby, as well as a variety of others—but it is usually more or less the same warm, cozy three- or four-person family. He has written a dozen stories with this cast of characters, and each seems to reveal something more of the complexities of three people living together when one is a man, another is a woman, and the third is their child. In "Incest," perhaps the most analytical of all these stories, he shows us, with a poet's extended perceptions, the infinite and self-sufficient world in two rooms that contain the new, child-centered family of Lee and Big Jane and Little Jane. It is a world that has the unreality, the deliberate detail, and the multiple and private disturbing meanings of the dreams with which the story begins and ends. Each person and object, every movement or speech, the color or shape of everything, has a relation to every other thing, is a symbol of a further meaning. The three are completely bound up in and with one another. Even the game they play is "round," back and forth in the small apartment. Yet Updike shows us how distances in time (his wife sometimes looks like her mother, sometimes like the baby) and space (Lee's uncle has one hundred acres, but in his dream Lee says, "But I am even richer") are collapsed and contained in this tiny, enclosed world, intensifying the participation of each in the other's life. The writer does not create this world by his own intensity; he reports on it, describes it, makes us see how it feels to live this way. It is an ordinary world of ordinary people and furniture and actions which, because all its points of ref-

erence are within it, is experienced with extraordinary intensity. And, too, it is the intensity caused by the containment and isolation of the nuclear family that creates the constant possibility of trouble and misunderstanding: there is no privacy from one another in this world. But when things are right, the three of them exist as a closed and perfect system, "as right as three Japanese eggs, each inside the other." Sexual symbols and attitudes are constant and plentiful (the bolsters, the hose, the automobile—many others, especially in the dreams); but they do not so much evoke the horror of unnatural sexual intercourse we associate with incest as celebrate the strength and complexity of the original bonds of intimacy the taboo restrains.

HAROLD BRODKEY

The Dark Woman of the Sonnets

◇◇◇◇◇◇◇

LAURA ANDREWS was one of those tall, big-bodied young women who look so serene. Because of the way her eyes were set, deep, beneath sensible eyebrows, and because of the calm light in them, it was difficult to think of her as moody or frightened or as anything, as a matter of fact, except warm and wise. She also had a certain comic flair, which made people laugh at her even when she was upset, and when they laughed, she became frantic because she believed no one would ever understand her; and her eyes would narrow, and she would quite determinedly set out to prove just how upset she was. Not on purpose, of course, but driven, you might say, by the thought that no one was taking her suffering seriously.

It was six-thirty on a hot August day that had not gone well for Laura. She was pottering around the kitchen, glancing occasionally out the back window to keep an eye on her four-year-old daughter, Faith, who was playing in the sandbox. The third time Laura looked out the window it seemed to her there were insects in the air everywhere, and, clutching a bottle of insect repellent, she ran out and encased Faith in a thick oily film.

"Mommy, I don't like this stuff," Faith cried.

"It's good for you," Laura said absently, but after that Faith couldn't play in the sand because the sand stuck to her and made her itch; and she took to following her mother around the kitchen, clutching at her mother's skirt, and making whining noises.

This sort of thing had been going on all day.

Laura bore this nobly; she was three months pregnant, and she had told herself she must be careful not to hurt Faith's feelings now that Faith was going to be displaced. Faith was bewildered by this sudden laxity in the air and grew more and more distraught, and finally burst into tears in the middle of the kitchen. Laura despairingly offered her an orange popsicle to eat, even though she knew it would ruin the child's appetite for dinner.

At seven, Martin Andrews came up the front walk of their duplex garden apartment and he knew the minute he entered the house that something was wrong. He was a well-knit and tall young man, with a firm and enterprising face, but suddenly he looked discouraged. Through the kitchen door he saw Laura crouched beside the kitchen table, holding the popsicle out to Faith, whose face was pink and streaked with tears. The vacuum cleaner was lying in the middle of the living-room floor. Cautiously, he put down his briefcase. "Hello, everybody," he said.

"Oh, hello, dear!" Laura cried, and rose to go to him and kiss him, but Martin was opening and closing the front door to see why it stuck sometimes and sometimes opened freely. "These modern houses are put together with chewing gum," he said. "I've had a foul day." He kept his eye on the door, closing it slowly, with great care, watching it alertly. "Aha!" he said. "I see where it sticks."

He looked hollow-cheeked and cowardly, bent over by the door.

"God," Laura said. "It's shocking, the way men are so full of self-pity."

After that, Martin refused to talk to her or to tell her what had gone wrong at the office. In persecuted silence, he went upstairs and changed his clothes and put on bathing trunks. Then he and Faith played with the hose in the back yard, squirting each other and running around on the grass with noisy laughter, while Laura resentfully cooked pork chops for supper, putting out of her mind the fact that she always said that pork was indigestible when the weather was hot.

Martin put on shorts and a sports shirt, and the family had their dinner almost in silence. Faith told her father she had gone to the store with her mommy. "We had a letter from Aunt Dorothy today," Laura said at one point. Martin raised his eyebrows and said pointedly, "You're in a poisonous mood, and I'm not going to pretend you're not." Pale and haughty, Laura went to work fiercely on her pork chop, hoping that if she cut the pieces small enough they wouldn't make her sick.

Immediately after dinner, she took Faith up to bed. Outside Faith's bedroom window was the sunset, all crimson and runny. Laura laid the child in her bed, turned on the air-conditioner, and tiptoed out of the room.

She was wearing a sun dress, and suddenly she couldn't bear the sight of her bare arms. She went to her bedroom closet and got down the box of her old maternity clothes. They were wrinkled and looked faded; after all, they were four years old, and her waist hadn't enlarged enough for her to wear maternity clothes yet. Besides, she was keeping her pregnancy a secret so that it wouldn't seem so long.

She leafed through the dresses in the box and finally pulled out what had been her favorite—her dress-up outfit, with a high white collar and long sleeves, and pleats. It hung loosely on her now, and it smelled of mothballs, but she didn't care. She descended the stairs, and, in full maternity regalia, sweating, she did the dishes.

Martin was sitting in the back yard in a lawn chair drinking a highball, solitary in the suburban dusk. Laura turned out all the lights in the apartment and went outside. Down the row of apartments several of the yellow back-door lights were turned on, signifying that the occupants were secreted in their yards, leaving only that light to guide them if their phones should ring.

The evening was no cooler than the day had been. "It's so hot," she said. "I'm tired of its being so hot."

Martin drank from his highball glass. Laura watched the outline of his Adam's apple in the darkness, and then she clumsily climbed into the hammock and lay there in her maternity dress, an absurd figure, dabbing with a Kleenex at her forehead.

"I would love to hear the sound of a human voice," she said at last. "The hoofs of the rescue party, sort of."

Martin stirred in the lawn chair. "I'm sorry. I thought you liked the quiet."

Laura made a disrespectful noise, a snort. "You're angry with me and you know it."

Martin said nothing.

"A penny for your thoughts, you bastard," Laura said after a while.

Martin laughed abruptly, with obvious discomfort. "Why do you want to know? You'll only get mad at me because I wasn't thinking about you."

Laura was stabbed by that remark—by the fact that he hadn't been thinking about her. "No, I won't," she said. "Tell me."

"I was thinking about Ferguson." Ferguson was the head bookkeeper in the office.

"In August? When everyone's on vacation?" Laura said incredulously.

"Yes," Martin said, sighing, and picked up his highball glass and clinked the remnants of the ice cubes. The tinkle floated on the air, and Laura said, "Oh, do that again, Martin, please. It was so pretty."

Martin laughed and did it again. Then he lifted the glass and sucked the ice cubes into his mouth and crunched them up. The noise was strangely sharp and clear in the darkness. All the leaves were absolutely motionless.

She was still hurt because he had been thinking about his office. "You're a beast," she said, and began tearing off bits of her Kleenex and dropping them in the grass.

"Me!" Martin was startled. He had thought she was coming out of her mood and growing peaceful.

"You torture me," Laura said. "You play with my feelings. God, you must hate me!" She stretched out one arm in the darkness.

"Oh, Laura," Martin said plaintively.

"And the baby, the poor child I carry. I can feel what you're doing to it. It's all knotted up. If you only knew how unhappy it is."

"For God's sake," Martin said. "For God's sake. Laura, do you realize your so-called baby is little more than a fish at this point?"

"Oh, you're inhuman," Laura muttered. "You really are."

"And you're the dark woman of the sonnets," Martin said, plucking a handful of grass. He stood up, and, holding his glass in one hand, dropped the grass from his other onto Laura's hair. "Stop picking on me, honey," he said and went into the house. Laura lay in the hammock; the grass tickled her ear. Suddenly she was terribly frightened, and not at all sure that Martin would come back. He might get dressed and walk out of the house. He might find a woman somewhere. Laura wanted to cry, but the tears wouldn't come.

From the house, Martin called, "Laura! I can't get the ice tray unstuck!"

Laura slid off the hammock. She walked slowly, drowsily, into the house. Martin was bent over the icebox.

"I must have some disease," he said. "My fingers—Oh!" he said admiringly as Laura did something mysterious that loosened the tray in its bed.

Martin took out the tray and closed the icebox door. "I love the way you do things like that," he said. "It's really lovely to see—that flip of the wrist sort of thing. My."

"You think of me as a clown, don't you?" Laura sounded infinitely long-suffering and gentle. "I ought to wear floppy shoes and turn somersaults, I think. Would you be sorry if I never looked foolish again?"

"No, of course not," Martin said unconvincingly, as he ran hot water over the bottom of the ice tray.

"If only—" Laura folded her hands over her bosom—an absurd, perspiring figure in her balloonlike maternity dress, with the smell of mothballs emanating from her, and on her face a look of such matchless calm thoughtfulness that it was impossible to believe she was serious. "God knows, I try to be intelligent, Martin. You should respect the effort I make, if nothing else, and—" But she couldn't think of what to say next.

"Aunt Dorothy have anything to say in her letter?" Martin asked, sighting carefully as he dropped the ice cubes in his glass.

"They're going to be in town next week," Laura said wearily, turning away. "They'd like me to come in and bring Faith."

"Well, do it, then."

How sweet the silence of this hot evening was, Laura thought; it seemed to lie around the house like a great, dark cat.

"Yes, I suppose so," she murmured. "But it's so hot for a child. And she might catch something. Oh, I'm a terrible mother. I want to take her to see Aunt Dorothy, but I wouldn't take her in to see most people. I wouldn't take her in to see Cousin Eleanor, for instance. I use that child for my own purposes."

"You don't like Cousin Eleanor," Martin pointed out. He restored the ice tray to the icebox. "You do like Aunt Dorothy. I don't think that's so awful." He was careful to sound rational and friendly, but not too sympathetic, because he was afraid of what emotions sympathy might release.

"Yes, of course," Laura said, laying her hand to her cheek. "I forgot that. Sometimes I get myself all upset over nothing." She felt disappointment washing back and forth in her chest, like waves. "I think I won't take Faith, anyhow. All those diseases . . ."

"Then don't take her," Martin said. He added water to the Scotch he had already poured.

"But Aunt Dorothy will be so disappointed." Laura wrung her hands, hoping that now she was on the trail of her real unhappiness, that her quarry wasn't far ahead.

"Laura," Martin said. "Aunt Dorothy can live without Faith. So can practically everyone, except us."

Laura interrupted. "You're jealous of her," Laura said. "Oh!" she added inanely and went out the back door, across the lawn, toward the wonderful, comfortable hammock, suspended in the darkness. Martin walked behind her, and as Laura started to climb into the hammock, she felt him holding it steady for her. She sank down on the cloth and lay with her eyes closed. When she opened them, she saw Martin looking down at her. "What's wrong, lovebug?" he asked.

"I don't know," Laura said. "That's it. I just don't know. Everything seems so awful, so sad—especially me. I—I've done something awful, I suppose. I suppose it's my subconscious or something getting back at me, but I don't know why. I don't know why at all. I don't understand one thing I do."

"But you must have some idea," Martin said. "Please tell me. I promise not to get angry. Please tell me, Laura dearest. Let me help. I can't stand it when you're like this."

"Oh, it's the most dreadful feeling . . . dreadful."

Somebody in the row of garden apartments was playing the radio loudly, and the music of a string quartet swam on the heated, motionless air. Someone else had hung a Japanese lantern in another back yard, and it glowed like a frail moon among the dark leaves of the bushes and trees. And in the middle of this whole scene, Martin bent over the hammock, peering helplessly at the strange, distorted figure of his wife wrapped in that absurd maternity outfit.

"Martin, I'm no good," Laura said. "I'm a terrible person." She paused but she wasn't getting any nearer to what she felt. "I'm growing older," she whispered, "but I don't act older, and I'm ashamed." But that had nothing to do with anything, and in the darkness Laura sighed and folded her arms over her forehead, hiding her eyes. "Martin, I really don't know what's wrong. Isn't that silly?"

Martin was bent over, his arms around the entire hammock, holding

Laura to his chest. He looked very uncomfortable bent over like that, and Laura suddenly embraced his head, pressing it tight against her breast.

"You mustn't talk," Martin whispered. "If you say things, Laura, you'll start to believe them. I know you. Just don't say anything. Just lie here and relax. In the morning this feeling will go away, I promise. But I can't stand to hear you talk like this. It kills me, Laura. It really does. I think the heat's just got you down. God, I'm all distraught!" He moved his head out of her embrace and kissed her sticky cheeks. "If you knew what it does to me to hear you talk like this, you wouldn't do it."

Laura turned away; the last thing in the world she wanted was to talk about Martin.

"Listen," he said, "I have to go inside a minute. I'll be right back, and I don't want you to be upset while I'm gone."

"All right," Laura said. She smiled at him, but it was a sickly smile, and she was grateful it was dark and he couldn't see her too clearly.

Lying in the hammock, she covered her eyes with her arm and listened to Martin's footsteps moving rapidly toward the house. Then the screen door slammed and the sound died slowly on the night air.

Oh, why can't I feel better? Laura thought. Why am I unconsoled?

And quickly her mind poured forth accusations, reminding her of her temper, her foolishnesses, her selfishness. She stifled a groan and stirred on the hammock. She was low, she was terrible, she would never be able to show Martin she really loved him and wanted to be good, because her wicked nature got in the way. And she was punished for this because when he tried to console her, she didn't feel consoled. "I'll never really know how much he loves me," she thought. "There's no way I'll know. I can only suspect it." At that her tears started to flow, and it seemed to her that she had found one of the secret springs of sadness that water the whole world. She wasn't a fool to feel sad at all.

She cried mostly for Martin's sake. "Poor Martin!" she thought. "Poor Faith!" She couldn't cry for herself because she disapproved of herself so severely. "They're saddled with the most awful woman, and we'll never know how much we love each other, never, never, never." And each time she thought this, her tears flowed faster.

Martin came out of the house. He saw that the hammock was swinging gently back and forth, and he smiled. He knew at once that Laura felt better, and he was serious and proud because he had consoled her. Not that he knew what he had done; in fact, as he walked across the grass, he felt small, and awed by the mysteries of what went on between a husband and wife.

"You all right?" he whispered.

"Yes," Laura whispered tearfully.

"You want to cry on my shoulder or do you want to cry alone?"

"Alone," said Laura. "But don't go too far away." Oh, the world was sad, she thought. Oh, the separateness of people. Oh, the clumsiness of being a woman.

Martin sat in the lawn chair and drank his highball. His heart was full. And, smiling peacefully in the darkness, Laura cried.

❖

Harold Brodkey was born in Staunton, Illinois, in 1930, was educated at Harvard, and now lives in New York City. He has published only one book, a collection of stories, called First Love and Other Sorrows *(1957); but these stories have earned him a fine reputation as a writer—perhaps because of their quality of warmth, a tone not much found in other good contemporary American writers, anxious as they are to avoid any sentimentality. Of the nine stories in the book, five are about Laura: the first shows her as a college student trying to decide between a rich suitor and Martin, a poor law student; in the second she is seen with her first baby, Faith, six weeks old; then reluctantly entrusting Faith to a baby-sitter; and in the fourth she and Martin have his college roommate to dinner in their new home. The fifth is the story reprinted above; like the others, it can be read as a successful work entirely separately from the other stories, but the stories as a whole portray Laura's growing maturity.*

In "The Dark Woman of the Sonnets" Brodkey depicts the world of the young family as warm and soft and dark and loving—but it is also isolated and full of self-doubt, and perhaps because it is so tender, somehow vulnerable and precarious. As the story shows, this sense of isolation and of there being something somehow vaguely wrong is borne mostly by the young mother. She protects (with insect repellent) and appeases (with orange popsicles), coping as best she can with a world that still seems strange to her. Her family, like all the other families on this suburban block, is cut off—"secreted in their yards" from neighbors and any supportive sense of community. Like many other young couples now, she and Martin are living far away from the rest of their families: her aunts are people she sees in the city on the basis of liking them or not liking them. Small new families in the suburban middle class are without the rituals and traditions that would make such transitions as a second pregnancy seem routine. Alone, the husband and wife are unable to "console" each other, to make things seem ordinary. Such an event in a big family would be taken for granted; in a small family it seems cataclysmic. Martin is as bewildered and as confused about his role as husband and father as she is about hers of wife and mother. In an attempt to make sense of herself as mother in this family she searches through her clothes to find an appropriate costume that will invest her with some sense of ritual and continuity. Then, in her best maternity gown, "in full maternal regalia, sweating, she did the dishes." Feeling she is the only source of definition as well as of sorrow, she can find consolation only in a mystical communion with the isolation of others: "Oh, the separateness of people. Oh, the clumsiness of being a woman." Crying happily at the end, she has found "one of the secret springs of sadness that water the whole world." The story is a lyrical rendering of the mystery of the irrepressible human qualities of doubt and sorrow that find their own rituals of participation in the unity of human essence with human nature and Nature herself, the world over, despite as well as through such sociologisms as "the nuclear family."

Herzog Visits Chicago

◇◇◇◇◇◇◇◇

BEFORE HE RECEIVED Geraldine Portnoy's letter, Moses Herzog had been thinking of his house in Ludeyville, Mass., of the green Berkshires, and had wondered whether he might not, after all, take refuge there from the heat and noise of New York before he went to visit his son by his first marriage, Marco, who was at camp. But the house held problems of its own (there were problems and perplexities on all sides). Perhaps he was too excited and distracted to solve any of them. To many, his behavior seemed somewhat mad. It was not simply his inexplicable abandonment of an academic career, his divorce from Daisy, his remarriage and second divorce; not simply the fact that he had settled *for good* in the Berkshires in order to write *the* historical work which would overwhelm all other 20th-century efforts but had taken off again, with wife and child, for Chicago; it was that everything was done so impulsively, so oddly, with such an expenditure of money and emotions that cast doubts on his sanity. To him, the oddest part of it was that he should have thought so intensely about everything and seen so little of what was about him. To take the most striking instance, he had failed to see that his wife Madeleine, was in love (if love was the word for it) with his friend (if friend he had been) Valentine Gersbach.

It was not enough that Madeleine could not endure the country any more and had to continue her graduate studies at the University of Chicago; no, she insisted that the Gersbachs move to Chicago, too, and that Moses must find a job for Valentine. You couldn't leave people like the Gersbachs to rot in provincial Massachusetts. And Herzog, preoccupied, brooding Herzog, had said "Yes, of course," to all her demands, and had made all the arrangements, found a job in radio for Gersbach, who was an announcer, found a house for Phoebe Gersbach, who was a particular and fastidious housekeeper, found a school for the Gersbach boy and a kindergarten for his own little daughter, Junie. The house in Ludeyville with thousands of dollars' worth of dishes, furnishings and modern equipment was abandoned to the field mice and the moles, and Herzog, for perhaps the twentieth time, made a new start in life, teaching in Chicago. Only, when everything was settled to Madeleine's satisfaction, she put her husband out. She told him to leave. She sent him packing. It was not for several months clear to him that there was another man involved, and that that man was Valentine Gersbach, Gersbach the radio announcer, his friend, and, during the worst of his troubles, his only comforter. "Well," thought Herzog, now in New York, "if any man knew exactly what I needed to be comforted about, it was Valentine. After all, he organized the whole disaster for me." Thus everyone was settled in Chicago except Herzog. He, the only Chicagoan in the lot, was living in a cheap apartment in New York, thinking matters over, his work abandoned, his career in pieces. There are times when a man cannot defend himself from his own peculiarities. Such a time had come in the life of Moses E. Herzog.

No, he felt, he couldn't go to Ludeyville to confront what he had done there, the visible signs of his ingratitude, his squandered legacy, the money poor Papa had worked and suffered so much for, spent idly by Madeleine (with Herzog's consent). And then there was his library, damaged by mice, no doubt; they chewed the bindings of books. They loved the taste of glue.

But evidently he hadn't yet had enough of desperate impulsiveness. He was trying to calm himself; he had had enough, he thought, of heartache and sleeplessness and of frenzied confrontations when the letter from Geraldine Portnoy came and set him off again.

He kept Geraldine Portnoy's letter always on his bed table, and he picked it up now and reread it before he fell asleep. He tried to remember how he had felt when he had first read it, in Chicago, after some delay.

Dear Mr. Herzog, I am Geraldine Portnoy, Lucas Asphalter's friend. You may remember. . . . May remember? Moses read faster (the script was feminine—progressive-school printing turned cursive and the i's dotted with curious little open circles), trying to swallow the whole letter at once, turning the pages to see whether the gist of the thing was underscored anywhere. *Actually I took your course in Romantics as Social Philosophers. We differed about Rousseau and Karl Marx. I have come around to your view, that Marx expressed metaphysical hopes for the future of mankind. I took what he said about materialism far too literally.* My view! It's common, and why does she want to make me dangle like this—why doesn't she get on with it? He tried again to find the point, but all those circular open dots fell on his vision like snow and masked the message. *You probably never noticed me, but I liked you, and as a friend of Lucas Asphalter— he just adores you, he says you are just a feast of the most human qualities—I have of course heard a lot about you growing up in Lucas' old neighborhood, and how you played basketball in the Boys' Brotherhood of the Republic, in the good old Chicago days on Division Street. An uncle of mine by marriage was one of the coaches—Jules Hankin.* I think I do recall Hankin. He wore a blue cardigan, and parted his hair in the middle. *I don't want you to get me wrong. I don't want to meddle in your affairs. And I am not an enemy of Madeleine's. I sympathize with her, too. She is so vivacious, intelligent, and such a charmer, and has been so warm and frank with me. For quite a while, I admired her and as a younger woman was very pleased by her confidences.* Herzog flushed. Her confidences would include intimate details. *And as a former student, I was of course intrigued to hear of your private life, but was also surprised by her freedom and willingness to talk, and soon saw she wanted to win me over, for some reason. Lucas warned me to look out for something fishy but then any intense feeling between members of the same sex is often, and unjustly, under suspicion. My scientific background has taught me to make more cautious generalizations, and resist this creeping psychoanalysis of ordinary conduct. But she did want to win me to her side, although far too subtle to pour it on, as they say. She told me that you had very fine human and intellectual qualities, though neurotic and with an intolerable temper which often frightened her. However she added you could be great, and after two bad, loveless marriages perhaps you would devote yourself to the work you were meant to do. Emotional relationships you were not really good at. It was soon obvious that she would never have given herself to a man who lacked distinction of intelligence or feeling. Madeleine said that for the first time in her life she knew clearly what she was doing. Until now it was all confusion and there were even gaps of time she couldn't account for. In marrying you, she was in this mixup and might have remained so but for a certain break. It is extremely exciting to talk with her, she gives a sense of a significant encounter—with life—a beautiful, brilliant person with a fate of her own. Her experiences are rich, or pregnant. . . .* What is this? Herzog thought. Is she going to tell me that Madeleine is going to have a child? Gersbach's child! No! How wonderful—what luck for me. If she has a kid out of wedlock, I can petition for Junie's custody. Eagerly he devoured the rest of the page, turned over. No, Madeleine was not pregnant. She'd be far too clever to let that happen. She owed her survival to intelligence. It was part of her sickness to be shrewd. She was not pregnant, then. *I was not merely a graduate student who helped with the child, but a confidante. Your little girl is greatly attached to me, and I find her a most extraordinary child. Exceptional, really. I love Junie with more than the usual affection, far more, than one has for the children one meets in this way. I understand the Italians are supposed to be the most child-oriented culture in the West (judge by the figure of the Christ child in Italian painting), but obviously Americans have their own craze about child psychology. Everything is done for children, ostensibly. To be fair, I think Madeleine is not bad with little June, basically. She tends to be authoritarian. Mr. Gersbach, who has an ambiguous position in this household, is very amusing to the child, on the whole. She calls him Uncle Val, and I often see him giving her a piggyback, or tossing her in the air.* Here Herzog set his teeth, angry, scenting danger. *But I have to report one disagreeable thing, and I talked this over with Lucas. This is that, coming to Harper Avenue the other night, I heard the child crying. She was inside Gersbach's car, and couldn't get out, and the poor little thing was shaking and weeping. I thought she had shut herself in while playing, but it was after dark, and I didn't understand why she would be outside, alone, at bedtime.* Herzog's heart pounded with dangerous thick beats at these words. *I had to calm her, and then I found out that her Mama and Uncle Val were having a quarrel inside, and Uncle Val had taken her by the hand and led her out to the car, and told her to play a while. He shut her up and went back in the house.* I can see him mount the stairs while Junie screams in fright. I'll kill him for that—so help me, if I don't! He reread the concluding lines. *Luke says you have a right to know such things. He was going to phone, but I felt it would be upsetting and harmful to hear this over the phone. A letter gives one a chance to consider—think matters over, and reach a more balanced view. I don't think Madeleine is a bad mother, actually.*

New York could not hold him now. He had to go to Chicago to see his daughter, confront Madeleine and Gersbach. The decision was not reached; it simply arrived. He went home and changed from the new clothes in which he had been diverting himself, into an old seersucker suit. Luckily, he had not unpacked when he came back from the Vineyard. He checked the valise quickly and left the apartment. Characteristically, he was determined to act without clearly knowing what to do, and even recognizing that he had no power over his impulses. He hoped that on the plane, in the clearer atmosphere, he would understand why he was flying.

The superjet carried him to Chicago in ninety minutes, due west, almost countering the rotation of the planet and giving him an extension of afternoon and sunlight. Beneath, the white clouds were foaming. And the sun, like the spot that inoculated us against the whole of disintegrating space. He looked into the blue vacancy and at the sharp glitter of wing-borne engines. When the plane bucked, he held his lip with his teeth. Not that he feared flying, but it occurred to him that if the ship were to crash, or simply explode (as had happened over Maryland recently, when human figures were seen to spill and fall like shelled peas), Gersbach would become June's guardian. Unless Simkin tore up the will. There would also be two insurance policies, one bought by Father Herzog for his son Moshe. The stewardess offered him a drink, which he refused with a shake of the head. He felt incapable of looking into the girl's pretty, healthful face.

As the jet landed, Herzog turned back his watch. He hurried from gate 38 and down the long corridor to the auto-rental office. To identify himself, he had an American Express card, his Massachusetts driver's license, his university credentials. He himself would have been suspicious of such diverse addresses, to say nothing of the soiled, wrinkled seersucker suit worn by this applicant, Moses Elkanah Herzog; but the official who took his application, a sweet-mannered, bosomy, curly, fat-nosed little woman (even in his present stage Herzog felt moved to smile faintly), only asked whether he wanted a convertible or a hard-top. He chose the hard-top, teal blue, and drove off, trying to find his way under the greenish glare of the lamps and dusty sunlight amid unfamiliar signs. He followed the winding cloverleaf into the expressway and then joined the speeding traffic—in this zone, 60 mph. He did not know these new sections of Chicago. Clumsy, stinking, tender Chicago dumped on its ancient lake bottom; and this murky orange west, and the hoarseness of factories and trains, spilling gases and soot on the newborn summer. Traffic was heavy coming from the city, not on Herzog's side of the road, and he held the right lane looking for familiar street names. After Howard Street he was in the city proper and knew his way. Leaving the expressway at Montrose, he turned east and drove to his late father's house, a small two-story brick building, one of a row built from a single blueprint—the pitched roof, the cement staircase inset on the right side, the window boxes the length of the front-room windows, the lawn a fat mound of grass between the sidewalk and the foundation; along the curb, elms and those shabby cottonwoods with blackened, dusty, wrinkled bark, and leaves that turned very tough by midsummer. There were also certain flowers, peculiar to Chicago, crude, waxy things like red and purple crayon bits, in a special class of false-looking natural objects. These foolish plants touched Herzog because they were so graceless, so corny. He was reminded of his father's devotion to his garden, when old Herzog became a property owner toward the end of his life—how he squirted his flowers at evening with the hose and how rapt he looked, his lips quietly pleased and his straight nose relishing the odor of the soil. To right and left, as Herzog emerged from the rented hard-top, the sprinklers turned and danced, scattering bright drops, fizzing out iridescent veils. And this was the house in which Father Herzog had died a few years ago, on a summer night.

In any case, here was his late father's house in which the widow lived, Moses' very ancient stepmother, quite alone in this small museum of the Herzogs. The bungalow belonged to Moses and his brothers and sister. No one wanted it now. Shura was a multimillionaire, he made that obvious enough. Willie had gone far in his father's construction-materials business —owned a fleet of those trucks with tremendous cylinder bodies that mixed cement en route to the job where it was funneled, pumped (Moses was vague about it) into the rising skyscrapers. Helen, if her husband was not in Willie's class, was at least well off. She rarely spoke of money any more. And he himself? He had about six hundred dollars in the bank. Still, for his purposes, he had what he needed. Poverty was not his portion; unemployment, slums, the perverts, thieves, victims in court, the horror of cheap

hotels and housekeeping rooms, smelling of decay and deadly bug juice—
these were not for him. He could still take the superjet to Chicago when he
had the impulse, could rent a teal-blue Falcon, drive to the old house. Thus
he realized with peculiar clarity his position in the scale of prerogatives—
of affluence, of insolence, of untruth, if you like. And not only his position,
but when lovers quarreled they had a Lincoln Continental to shut a weeping child up in.

Face white, mouth grim, he mounted the stairs in the shadow of approaching sunset, and pressed the button. It had a crescent moon in the
middle which lighted up at night.

The chimes rang inside, those chromium tubes above the door, xylo-
phone metal, that played *Merrily We Roll Along,* all but the last two notes.
He had long to wait. The old woman, Taube, always had been slow, even
in her fifties, thorough, deliberate, totally unlike the dexterous Herzogs—
they had all inherited their father's preposterous quickness and elegance,
something of the assertiveness of that one-man march with which old
Herzog had defiantly paraded through the world. Moses was rather fond of
Taube, he told himself; perhaps to feel differently toward her would have
been too troubling. The unsteady gaze of her round prominent eyes was
possibly caused by a radical resolve to be slow, a lifelong program of delay
and stasis. Creepingly, she accomplished every last goal she set herself. She
ate, or sipped, slowly. She did not bring the cup to her mouth but moved
her lips out toward it. And she spoke very slowly, to give her shrewdness
scope. Cooked with fingers that did not grip firmly but was an excellent
cook. She won at cards, poking along, but won. All questions she asked
two or three times, and repeated the answers half to herself. With the same
slowness she braided her hair, she brushed her exposed teeth, or chopped
figs, dates, and senna leaves for her digestion. Her lip grew pendulous as
she aged and her neck gradually thickened at the shoulders so that she had
to hold her head forward somewhat. Oh, she was very old now, in her
eighties, and far from well. She was arthritic; one eye had a cataract. But
she had a clear mind. No doubt her troubles with Father Herzog, stormier
and more hot-headed and fractious as he aged, had strengthened her brain.

The house was dark, and anyone but Moses would have gone away,
assuming there was no one at home. He, however, waited, knowing she
would presently open. In his youth he had watched her take five minutes to
open a bottle of soda—an hour to spread the dough over the table when
she baked. Her strudel was like jewelers' work, and filled with red and
green gems of preserves. At last he heard her at the door. Links of brass
chain rose in the narrow opening. He saw old Taube's dark eyes, more
somber now, and more extruded. The glass winter door still separated her
from Moses. He knew it would also be locked. The old people had been
guarded and suspicious in their own house. Moreover, Moses knew the
light was behind him; he might not be recognized. And he was not the same

Moses, anyway. But, although she studied him like a stranger, she had already identified him. Her intellect was not slow, whatever else.

"Who is it?"

"It's Moses. . . ."

"I don't know you. I'm alone. Moses?"

"Tante Taube—Moses Herzog. Moshe."

"Ah—Moshe."

Slow lame fingers released the catch. The door was shut to free the links from strain, and then opened, and—merciful God!—what a face he saw, how grooved with woe and age, lined downward at the mouth. As he came in she raised feeble hands to embrace him. "Moshe! . . . Come in. I'll make a light. Shut the door, Moshe."

He found the switch and turned on the very dim bulb of the entry hall. It shed a pinkish color; the old-fashioned glass of the fixture reminded him of the vigil light in the synagogue. He shut the door on the watered fragrance of lawns as he entered. The house was close and faintly sour with furniture polish. The remembered luster was there in the faint twilit parlor—cabinets and tables, with inlaid tops, the brocaded sofa in its gleaming protective plastic, the Oriental rug, the drapes perfect and rigid on the windows with laterally rigid venetian blinds. A lamp went on behind him.

"Let me look at you," she said, coming before him. Her eyes were puffy, but steady enough. He stared at her, and tried to prevent the horror from coming into his face. He guessed that it was putting in her plates that had delayed her. She had new ones, poorly made—no arch but a straight line of teeth. Like a woodchuck, he thought. Her fingers were disfigured, with loose skin that had worked forward over the nails. But those fingertips were painted. And what changes did she see in him? "Ach, Moshe, you changed."

He limited his answer to a nod. "And how are you?"

"You see. The living dead."

"You live alone?"

"I had a woman—Bella Ockinoff from the fish store. You knowed her. But she was not clean."

"Come, Tante, sit down."

"Oh, Moshe," she said. "I can't sit, I can't stand, can't lay. Better, already, next to Pa. Pa is better off than me."

"Is it so bad?" Herzog must have betrayed more emotion than he knew, for he now found her eyes examining him rather sharply, as if she did not believe that his feeling was for her and tried to find the real source of it. Or was it the cataract that gave her that expression? He guided her to a chair, holding her arm, and sat on the plastic-covered sofa. Under the tapestry, Pierrot. Clair de Lune. Venetian moonlight. All that phony banality that oppressed him in his student days. It had no special power over him now. He was another man and had different purposes. The old woman, he saw, was trying to find what he had come for. She sensed that he was strongly agitated, missed his habitual vagueness, the proud air of abstraction in which M. E. Herzog, Ph.D., had once been clothed. *Them days is gone forever.*

"You working hard, Moshe?"

"Yes."

"Making a living?"

"Oh, yes."

The old woman bowed her head a moment. He saw the scalp, her thin gray hair. Exiguous. The organism had done all it could.

He clearly understood that she was communicating her right to live in this Herzog property, even though by staying alive she was depriving him of this remaining part of the estate.

He sat near the very spot where Father Herzog, the year before his death, had threatened to shoot him. The cause of his rage was money. Herzog was broke, and asked his father to underwrite a loan. The old man questioned him narrowly, about his job, his expenses, his child. He had no patience with Moses. At that time I was living in Philadelphia, alone, making my choice (it was no choice!) between Madeleine and Sono, my other girl friend. Perhaps he had even heard I was about to be converted to Catholicism. Someone started such a rumor. I was in Chicago then because Papa had sent for me. He wanted to tell me about the changes in his will. Day and night, he thought how he would divide his estate, and thought accordingly of each of us, what we deserved, how we would use it. At odd times, he'd telephone and tell me I had to come right away. I'd sit up all night on the train. And he'd take me into a corner and say, "I want you to hear, once and for all. Your brother Willie is an honest man. When I die, he'll do as we agreed." "I believe it, Papa."

But he lost his temper every time, and when he wanted to shoot me it was because he could no longer bear the sight of me, that look of mine, the look of conceit or proud trouble. The elite look. I don't blame him, thought Moses as Taube slowly and lengthily described her ailments. Papa couldn't bear such an expression on the face of his youngest son. I aged. I wasted myself in stupid schemes, *liberating* my spirit. His heart ached angrily because of me. And Papa was not like some old men who become blunted toward their own death. No, his despair was keen and continual. And Herzog again was pierced with pain for his father.

They had had lunch on the back porch that day, and that was where the quarrel began. It had seemed to Moses, perhaps, that he was here as a prodigal son, admitting the worst and asking for the old man's mercy, and so Father Herzog saw nothing except a stupid appeal in his son's face— incomprehensible. "Idiot!" was what the old man had shouted. "Calf!" Then he saw the angry demand underlying Moses' look of patience. "Get out! I leave you nothing! Everything to Willie and Helen! You? . . . Croak in a flophouse." Moses rising. Father Herzog shouted, "Go. And don't come to my funeral."

"All right, maybe I won't."

Too late, Tante Taube had warned him to keep silent, raising her brows —she had still had brows then. Father Herzog rose stumbling from the table, his face distorted, and ran to get his pistol.

"Go, go! Come back later. I'll call you," Taube had whispered to Moses, and he, confused, reluctant, burning, stung because his misery was not recognized in his father's house (his monstrous egotism making its peculiar demands)—he reluctantly got up from the table. "Quick, quick!" Taube tried to get him to the front door, but old Herzog overtook them with the pistol.

He cried out, "I'll kill you!" and Herzog was startled not so much by this threat, which he did not believe, as by the return of his father's strength. In his rage he recovered it briefly, though it might cost him his life. The strained neck, the grinding of his teeth, his frightening color, even the military Russian strut with which he lifted the gun—these were better, thought Herzog, than his sinking down during a walk to the store. Father Herzog was not made to be pitiful.

"Go, go," said Tante Taube. Moses was weeping then.

"Maybe you'll die first," Father Herzog shouted.

"Papa!"

Half-hearing Tante Taube's slow description of Cousin Mordecai's approaching retirement, Herzog grimly recovered the note of that cry. *Papa—Papa.* You lout! The old man in his near-demented way was trying to act out the manhood you should have had. Coming to his house with that Christianized smirk of the long-suffering son. He should have pulled the trigger. Those looks were agony to him. He deserved to be spared, in his old age.

And then there was Moses with puffy weeping eyes, in the street, waiting for his cab, while Father Herzog hastily walked up and back before these windows, staring at him in agony of spirit—yes, you got that out of him. Walking quickly there, back and forth in his hasty style, dropping his weight on the one heel. The pistol thrown down. Who knows whether Moses shortened his life by the grief he gave him? Perhaps the stimulus of anger lengthened it. He could not die and leave this half-made Moses yet.

They were reconciled the following year. And then more of the same. And then . . . death.

"Should I make a cup of tea?" said Tante Taube.

"Yes, please, I'd like that if you feel up to it. And I also want to look in Papa's desk."

"Pa's desk? It's locked. You want to look in the desk? Everything belongs to you children. You could take the desk when I die."

"No, no!" he said. "I don't need the desk itself, but I was passing from the airport and thought I'd see how you were. And now that I'm here, I'd like to have a look in the desk. I know you don't mind."

"You want something, Moshe? You took your Mamma's silver coin case the last time."

He had given it to Madeleine.

"Is Papa's watch chain still in there?"

"I think Willie took it."

He frowned with concentration. "Then what about the rubles?" he asked. "I'd like them for Marco."

"Rubles?"

"My grandfather Isaac bought Czarist rubles during the Revolution, and they've always been in the desk."

"In the desk? I surely never seen them."

"I'd like to look, while you make a cup of tea, Tante Taube. Give me the key."

"The key . . . ?" Questioning him before, she had spoken more quickly, but now she receded again into slowness, raising a mountain of dilatory will in his way.

"Where do you keep it?"

"Where? Where did I put it? Is it in Pa's dresser? Or somewheres else? Let me remember. That's how I am now, it's hard to remember. . . ."

"I know where it is," he said, suddenly rising.

"You know where it is? So where is it?"

"In the music box, where you always used to keep it."

"In the music? . . . Pa took it from there. He locked up my social-security checks when they came. He said all the money *he* should have. . . ."

Moses knew he had guessed right. "Don't bother, I'll get it," he said. "If you'll put the kettle on. I'm very thirsty. It's been a hot, long day."

He helped her to rise, holding her flaccid arm. He was having his way—a poor sort of victory and filled with dangerous consequences. Going forward without her he entered the bedroom. His father's bed had been removed. Hers stood alone with its ugly bedspread—some material that reminded him of a coated tongue. He breathed the old spice, the dark, heavy air, and lifted the lid of the music box. In this house he had only to consult his memory to find what he wanted. The mechanism released its little notes as the cylinder turned within, the small spines picking out the aria from *Figaro*. Moses was able to supply the words:

> *Nel momento*
> *Della mia cerimonia*
> *Io rideva di me*
> *Senza saperlo.*

His fingers recognized the key.

Old Taube in the dark outside the bedroom said, "Did you found it?"

He answered, "It's here," and spoke in a low, mild voice, not to make matters worse. The house was hers, after all. It was rude to invade it. He was not ashamed of this, he only recognized with full objectivity that it was not right. But it had to be done.

"Do you want me to put the kettle on?"

"No, a cup of tea I can still make."

He heard her slow steps in the passage. She was going to the kitchen. Herzog quickly made for the small sitting room. The drapes were drawn. He turned on the lamp beside the desk. In seeking the switch he tore the ancient silk of the shade, releasing a fine dust. The name of this color was old rose—he felt certain of it. He opened the cherry-wood secretary, braced the wide leaf on its runners, drawing them out from either side. Then he went back and shut the door, first making sure Taube had reached the kitchen. In the drawers he recognized each article—leather, paper, gold. Swift and tense, veins standing out on his head, and tendons on the hands, he groped, and found what he was looking for—Father Herzog's pistol. An old pistol, the barrel nickel-plated. Papa had bought it to keep on Cherry Street, in the railroad yards. Moses flipped the gun open. There were two bullets. This was it, then. He rapidly clicked it shut and put it in his pocket. There it made too large a bulge. He took out his wallet and replaced it with the gun. The wallet he buttoned in his hip pocket.

Now he began to search for those rubles. Those he found in the small compartment with old passports, ribbons sealed in wax, like gobs of dried blood. They were in a large billfold—his playthings of forty years ago. Peter the Great in a rich coat of armor, and a splendid imperial Catherine. Lamplight revealed the watermarks. Recalling how he and Willie used to play casino for these stakes, Herzog uttered one of his short laughs, then made a nest of these large bills in his pocket for the pistol. He thought it must be less conspicuous now.

"You got what you want?" Taube asked him in the kitchen.

"Yes." He put the key on the enameled metal table.

He knew it was not proper that he should think her expression sheeplike. This figurative habit of his mind crippled his judgment, and was likely to ruin him some day. Perhaps the day was near; perhaps this night his soul would be required of him. The gun weighed on his chest. But the protuberant lips, great eyes, and pleated mouth *were* sheeplike, and they warned him he was taking too many chances with destruction. Taube, a veteran survivor, to be heeded, had fought the grave to a standstill, balking death itself by her slowness. All had decayed but her shrewdness and her incredible patience; and in Moses she saw Father Herzog again, nervy and hasty, impulsive, suffering. His eye twitched as he bent toward her in the kitchen. She muttered, "You got a lot of trouble? Don't make it worser, Moshe."

"There's no trouble, Tante. I had business to take care of. . . . I don't think I can wait for tea, after all."

"I put out Pa's cup for you."

Moses drank tap water from his father's teacup.

"Good-by, Tante Taube, keep well." He kissed her forehead.

"Remember I helped you?" she said. "You shouldn't forget. Take care, Moshe."

He left by the back door; it made departure simpler. Honeysuckle grew along the rainspout, as in his father's time, and fragrant in the evening—almost too rich. Could any heart become quite petrified?

He gunned his motor at the stoplight, trying to decide which was the faster route to Harper Avenue. The new Ryan Expressway was very quick but it would land him in the thick of the traffic on West 51st Street, where people promenaded, or cruised in their cars. There was Garfield Boulevard, much better; however, he was not sure he could find his way through Washington Park after dark. He decided to follow Edens to Congress Street and Congress to the Outer Drive. Yes, that would be fastest. What he would do when he got to Harper Avenue he hadn't yet decided. Madeleine had threatened him with arrest if he so much as showed his face near the house. The police had his picture, but that was sheer bunk, bunk and paranoia, the imperiousness of imaginary powers that had once impressed him. But there was now a real matter between him and Madeleine, a child, a reality—June. Out of cowardice, sickness, fraud, by a bungling father out of a plotting bitch, something genuine! This little daughter of his! He cried out to himself as he raced up the ramp of the expressway that nobody would harm *her*. He accelerated, moving in his lane with the rest of the traffic. The thread of life was stretched tight in him. It quivered crazily. He did not fear its breaking so much as his failing to do what he should. The little Falcon was storming. He thought his speed was terrible until a huge trailer truck passed him on the right, when he realized that this was not the time to risk a traffic ticket—not with a pistol in his pocket—and lifted his foot from the pedal. Peering left and right, he recognized that the new expressway had been cut through old streets, streets he knew. He saw the vast gas tanks, crowned with lights, from a new perspective, and the rear of a Polish church with a Christ in brocades exhibited in a lighted window, like a showcase. The long curve eastbound passed over the freight yards, burning with sunset dust, rails streaking westward; next, the tunnel under the mammoth post office; next, the State Street honky-tonks. From the last slope of Congress Street the distortions of dusk raised up the lake like a mild wall crossed by bands, amethyst, murky blue, irregular silver, and a slate color at the horizon, boats hanging rocking inside the breakwater, and helicopters and small aircraft whose lights teetered overhead. The familiar odor of the fresh water, bland but also raw, reached him as he sped south. It did not seem illogical that he should claim the privilege of insanity, violence, having been made to carry the rest of it—name-calling and gossip, railroading, pain, even exile in Ludeyville. That property was to have been his madhouse. Finally, his mausoleum. But they had done something else to Herzog—unpredictable. It's not everyone who gets the opportunity to kill with a clear conscience. They had opened the way to justifiable murder. They deserved to die. He had a right to kill them. They would even know why they were dying; no explanation necessary. When he stood before them they would have to submit. Gersbach would only hang his head, with tears for himself. Madeleine would shriek and curse. Out of hatred, the most powerful element in her life, stronger by far than any other power or motive. In spirit she was his murderess, and therefore he was turned loose, he could shoot or choke without remorse. He felt in his arms and in his fingers, and to the core of his heart, the sweet exertion of strangling—horrible and sweet, an orgastic rapture of inflicting death. He was sweating violently, his shirt wet and cold under his arms. Into his mouth came a taste of copper, a metabolic poison, a flat but deadly flavor.

When he reached Harper Avenue he parked around the corner, and entered the alley that passed behind the house. Grit spilled on the concrete; broken glass and gravelly ashes made his steps loud. He went carefully. The back fences were old here. Garden soil spilled under the slats, and shrubs and vines came over their tops. Once more he saw open honey-suckle. Even rambler roses, dark red in the dusk. He had to cover his face when he passed the garage because of the loops of briar that swung over the path from the sloping roof. When he stole into the yard he stood still until he could see his way. He must not stumble over a toy, or a tool. A fluid had come into his eyes—very clear, only somewhat distorting. He wiped it away with fingertips, and blotted, too, with the lapel of his coat. Stars had come out, violet points framed in roof shapes, leaves, strut wires. The yard was visible to him now. He saw the clothesline—Madeleine's underpants and his daughter's little shirts and dresses, tiny stockings. By the light of the kitchen window he made out a sandbox in the grass, a new red sandbox with broad ledges to sit on. Stepping nearer, he looked into the kitchen. Madeleine was there! He stopped breathing as he watched her. She was wearing slacks and a blouse fastened with a broad red-leather-and-brass belt he had given her. Her smooth hair hung loose as she moved between the table and the sink, cleaning up after dinner, scraping dishes in her own style of abrupt efficiency. He studied her straight profile as she stood at the sink, the flesh under her chin as she concentrated on the foam in the sink, tempering the water. He could see the color in her cheeks, and almost the blue of her eyes. Watching, he fed his rage, to keep it steady, up to full strength. She was not likely to hear him in the yard because the storm windows had not been taken down—not, at least, those he had put up last fall at the back of the house.

He moved into the passageway. Luckily the neighbors were not at home, and he did not have to worry about their lights. He had had his look at Madeleine. It was his daughter he wanted to see now. The dining room was unoccupied—after-dinner emptiness, Coke bottles, paper napkins. Next was the bathroom window, set higher than the rest. He remembered, however, that he had used a cement block to stand on, trying to take out the bathroom screen until he had discovered that there was no storm window to replace it. The screen was still in, therefore. And the block? It was exactly where he had left it, among the lilies of the valley on the left side of the path. He moved it into place, the scraping covered by the sound of water in the tub, and stood on it, his side pressed to the building. He tried to muffle the sound of his breathing, opening his mouth. In the rushing water with floating toys his daughter's little body shone. His child! Madeleine had let her black hair grow longer, and now it was tied up for the bath with a rubber band. He melted with tenderness for her, putting his hand over his mouth to cover any sound emotion might cause him to make. She raised her face to speak to someone he could not see. Above the flow of water he heard her say something but could not understand the words. Her face was the Herzog face, the large dark eyes *his* eyes, the nose his father's, Tante Zipporah's, his brother Willie's nose, and the mouth his own. Even the bit of melancholy in her beauty—that was his mother. It was Sarah Herzog, pensive, slightly averting her face as she considered the life about her. Moved, he watched her, breathing with open mouth, his face half covered by his hand. Flying beetles passed him. Their heavy bodies struck the screen but did not attract her notice.

Then a hand reached forward and shut off the water—a man's hand. It was Gersbach. He was going to bathe Herzog's daughter! Gersbach! His waist was now in sight. He came into view stalking beside the old-fashioned round tub, bowing, straightening, bowing—his Venetian hobble, and then, with great trouble, he began to kneel, and Herzog saw his chest, his head, as he arranged himself. Flattened to the wall, his chin on his shoulder, Herzog saw Gersbach roll up the sleeves of his paisley sport shirt, put back his thick glowing hair, take the soap, heard him say, not unkindly, "Okay, cut out the monkeyshines," for Junie was giggling, twisting, splashing, dimpling, showing her tiny white teeth, wrinkling her nose, teasing. "Now hold still," said Gersbach. He got into her ears with the washrag as she screamed, cleaned off her face, the nostrils, wiped her mouth. He spoke with authority, but affectionately and with grumbling smiles and occasionally with laughter he bathed her—soaped, rinsed, dipping water in her toy boats to rinse her back as she squealed and twisted. The man washed her tenderly. His look, perhaps, was false. But he had no *true* expressions, Herzog thought. His face was all heaviness, sexual meat. Looking down his open shirt front, Herzog saw the hair-covered heavy soft flesh of Gersbach's breast. His chin was thick, and like a stone ax, a brutal weapon. And then there were his sentimental eyes, the thick crest of hair, and that hearty voice with its peculiar fraudulence and grossness. The hated traits were all there. But see how he was with June, scooping the water on her playfully, kindly. He let her wear her mother's flowered shower cap, the rubber petals spreading on the child's head. Gersbach ran fresh water on her, cumbersomely rose and opened the bath towel. Steady and thorough, he dried her, and then with a large puff he powdered her. The child jumped up and down with delight. "Okay, enough of this wild stuff," said Gersbach. "Put on those p-j's now."

She ran out. Herzog still saw faint wisps of powder, that floated over Gersbach's stooping head. His red hair worked up and down. He was scouring the tub. Moses might have killed him now. His left hand touched the gun, enclosed in the roll of rubles. He might have shot Gersbach as he methodically salted the yellow sponge rectangle with cleansing powder. There were two bullets in the chamber. . . . But they would stay there. Herzog clearly recognized that. Very softly he stepped down from his perch, and passed without sound through the yard again. He saw his child in the kitchen, looking up at Mady, asking for something, and he edged through the gate into the alley. Firing this pistol was nothing but a thought.

I seem to think because June looks like a Herzog, she is nearer to me than to them. But how is she near to me if I have no share in her life? Those two grotesque love-actors have it all. And I apparently believe that if the child does not have a life resembling mine, educated according to the Herzog standards of "heart," and all the rest of it, she will fail to become a human being. This is sheer irrationality, and yet some part of my mind takes it as self-evident. But what in fact can she learn from them? From Gersbach, when he looks so sugary, repulsive, poisonous, not an individual but a fragment, a piece broken off from the mob. To shoot him!—an absurd thought. As soon as Herzog saw the actual person giving an actual bath, the reality of it, the tenderness of such a buffoon to a little child, his intended violence turned into *theater,* into something ludicrous. He was not ready to make such a complete fool of himself. Only self-hatred could lead him to ruin himself because his heart was "broken." How could it be broken by such a pair? Lingering in the alley awhile, he congratulated himself on his luck. His breath came back to him; and how good it felt to breathe! It was worth the trip.

But he was not yet willing to call it a day. He had to have a talk with Phoebe Gersbach. It was essential. And he decided not to phone her and give her an opportunity to prepare herself, or even refuse to see him. He drove directly to Woodlawn Avenue—a dreary part of Hyde Park, but characteristic, *his* Chicago: massive, clumsy, amorphous, smelling of mud and decay and dogs; sooty façades, slabs of structural *nothing,* senselessly ornamented triple porches with huge cement urns for flowers that contained only rotting cigarette butts and other stained filth; sun parlors under tiled gables, rank areaways, gray backstairs, seamed and ruptured concrete from which sprang grass; ponderous 4x4 fences that sheltered growing weeds. And among these spacious, comfortable, dowdy apartments where liberal, benevolent people lived (this was the university neighborhood) Herzog did in fact feel at home. He was perhaps as midwestern and unfocused as these same streets. (Not so much determinism, he thought, as a lack of determining elements—the absence of a formative power.) But it was all typical, and nothing was lacking, not even the sound of roller skates awkwardly gritting on the pavement beneath new summer leaves. Two poky little girls under the green transparency of street lamps, skating in short skirts, and with ribbons in their hair.

A nervous qualm went through him now that he was at Gersbach's gate, but he mastered it and went up the walk, rang the bell. Phoebe approached quickly. She called, "Who is it?" and seeing Herzog through the glass was silent. Was she scared?

"It's an old friend," said Herzog. A moment passed, Phoebe, despite the firmness of her mouth, hesitating, eyes large-lidded beneath her bangs. "Won't you let me in?" Moses asked. His tone made refusal unthinkable. "I won't take much of your time," he said as he was entering. "We do have a few matters to discuss, though."

"Come in the kitchen, will you."

"Sure . . ." She didn't want to be surprised talking to him in the front room or overheard by little Ephraim, who was in his bedroom. In the kitchen she shut the door and asked Herzog to sit. The chair her eyes were looking at was beside the refrigerator. There he would not be seen from the kitchen window. With a faint smile he sat down. From the extreme composure of her slender face he knew how her heart must be pounding, working, even more violently than his. An orderly person, self-controlled in high degree, clean—the head nurse—she tried to maintain a businesslike look. Herzog buttoned up his jacket to make sure the butt of his gun did not show. The sight of a weapon would certainly frighten her to death.

"Well, how are you, Phoebe?"

"We're all right."

"Comfortably settled? Liking Chicago? Little Ephraim still in the Lab School?"

"Yes."

"And the Temple? I see that Val taped a program with Rabbi Itzkowitz —what did he call it? 'Hasidic Judaism, Martin Buber, *I and Thou.*' Still this Buber kick! He's very thick with these rabbis. Maybe he wants to swap wives with a rabbi. He'll work his way round from 'I and Thou' to 'Me and You'—'You and Me, Kid!' But I suppose you'd draw the line there. You wouldn't go along with everything."

Phoebe made no answer and remained standing.

"Maybe you think I'll leave sooner if you don't sit. Come, Phoebe, sit down. I promise you I haven't come to make scenes. I have only one purpose here, in addition to wanting to see an old friend. . . ."

"We're not really old friends."

"Not by calendar years. But we were so close out in Ludeyville. That is true. You have to think of duration—Bergsonian duration. We have known each other in duration. Some people are *sentenced* to certain relationships. Maybe every relationship is either a joy or a sentence."

"You earned your own sentence, if that's how you want to think about it. We had a quiet life till you and Madeleine descended on Ludeyville and forced yourself on me." Phoebe, her face thin but hot, eyelids unmoving, sat down on the edge of the chair Herzog had drawn forward for her.

"Good. Say what you think, Phoebe. That's what I want. Sit back. Don't be afraid. I'm not looking for trouble. We've got a problem in common."

Phoebe denied this. She shook her head, with a stubborn look, all too vigorously. "I'm a plain woman. Valentine is from upstate New York."

"Just a rube. Yes. Knows nothing about fancy vices from the big city. Didn't even know how to dial a number. Had to be led step by step into degeneracy by me—Moses E. Herzog."

Stiff and hesitant, she turned her body aside in her abrupt way. Then she came to a decision and turned to him again with the same abruptness. She was a pretty woman, but stiff, very stiff, bony, without self-confidence. "You never understood a thing about him. He fell for you. Adored you. Tried to become an intellectual because he wanted to help you—saw what a terrible thing you had done in giving up your respectable university position and how reckless you were, rushing out to the country with Madeleine. He thought she was ruining you and tried to set you on the right track again. He read all those books so you'd have somebody to talk to, out in the sticks, Moses. Because you needed help, praise, flattery, support, affection. It was never enough. You wore him out. It nearly killed him, trying to back you up."

"Yes . . . ? What else? Go on," said Herzog.

"It's still not enough. What do you want from him now? What are you here for? More excitement? Are you still greedy for excitement?"

Herzog no longer smiled. "Some of what you say is right enough, Phoebe. I was certainly floundering in Ludeyville. But you take the wind out of me when you say you were leading a perfectly ordinary life up there in Barrington. Until Mady and I came along with the books and the theatrical glamour, high-level mental life, scattering big-shot ideas, squandering and blowing whole ages of history. You were scared by us because we— Mady especially—gave him confidence. As long as he was only a small-time gimpy radio announcer, he might bluff at being a big shot, but you had him where you wanted him. Because he is a bluffer and a screwball, a kind of freak, but *yours*. Then he got bolder. He gave his exhibitionism scope. Quite right, I'm an idiot. You were even right to dislike me, if only because I wouldn't see what was happening and in that way put another burden on you. But why didn't you say something? You watched the whole thing going on. It went on for years, and you said nothing. I wouldn't have been so indifferent if I saw the same thing happening to you."

Phoebe hesitated to speak of this and turned even paler. She said, at last,

"It's not my fault that you refuse to understand the system other people live by. Your ideas get in the way. Maybe a weak person like me has no choice. I couldn't do anything for you. Especially last year. I was seeing a psychiatrist, and he advised me to keep away. To keep away from you, most of all from you and all your trouble. He said I wasn't strong enough, and you know it's true—I'm not strong enough."

Herzog considered this—Phoebe was weak, that was certainly the truth. He decided to get to the point. "Why don't you divorce Valentine?" he said.

"I see no reason why I should." Her voice immediately recovered strength.

"He's deserted you, hasn't he?"

"Val? I don't know why you say that! I'm not deserted."

"Where is he now—this evening? This minute?"

"Downtown. On business."

"Oh, come on, don't pull that stuff on me, Phoebe. He's living with Madeleine. Do you deny it?"

"I most certainly do. I can't imagine how you ever got such a fantastic idea."

Moses leaned with one arm against the refrigerator as he shifted in his chair and took out a handkerchief—the scrap of kitchen towel from his New York apartment. He wiped his face.

"If you would sue for divorce," he explained, "as you have every right to do, you could name Madeleine for adultery. I'd help raise the money. I'd underwrite the whole cost. I want Junie. Don't you see? Together we could nail them. You've let Madeleine drive you here and there. As if you were a nanny goat."

"That's the old devil in you talking again, Moses."

Nanny goat was a mistake; he was making her more obstinate. But, anyway, she was going to follow her own line. She'd never share any plan of his.

"Don't you want me to have custody of June?"

"I'm indifferent to that."

"You have your own war with Madeleine, I suppose," he said. "Fighting over the man. A cat fight—a female sex fight. But she'll beat you. Because she's a psychopath. I know you've got reserve strength. But she's a nut, and nuts win. Besides, Valentine doesn't want you to get him."

"I really don't understand what you're saying."

"He'll lose his value to Madeleine as soon as you withdraw. After the victory, she'll have to throw him out."

"Valentine comes home every night. He's never out late. He should be here soon. . . . When I'm even a little delayed somewhere, why, he gets frantic with worry. He phones all over the city."

"Perhaps that's hope," said Moses. "Hope disguised as concern. Don't you know how that is? If you get killed in an accident, he cries and packs up and moves in with Madeleine for good."

"That's your devil speaking again. My child is going to keep *his* father. You still want Madeleine, don't you!"

"Me? Never! All that hysterical stuff is finished. No, I'm glad to be rid of her. I don't even loathe her much anymore. And she's welcome to all she chiseled from me. She must have been banking my money all along. Okay! Let her keep it with my blessing. Bless the bitch! Good luck and good-bye. I bless her. I wish her a busy, useful, pleasant, dramatic life. Including *love.* The best people fall in love, and she's one of the best, therefore she loves this fellow. They both *love.* She's not good enough to bring up the kid, though. . . ."

If he were a wild pig, and those bangs of hers a protective hedge— Phoebe's brown eyes were as vigilant as that. And yet Moses was sorry for her. They bullied her—Gersbach and Madeleine through Gersbach. But Phoebe herself meant to win this contest. It must be inconceivable to her that one should set such modest, such minimal goals—table, market, laundry, child—and still lose the struggle. Life couldn't be as indecent as that, could it? Another hypothesis: sexlessness was her strength; she wielded the authority of the superego. Still another: she acknowledged the creative depth of modern degeneracy, all the luxuriant vices of emancipated swingers, and thus accepted her situation as a poor, neurotic, dry, unfortunate, mud-stuck, middle-class woman. To her, Gersbach was no ordinary man, and because of his richness of character, his spiritual-erotic drive, or God knows what foot-smelling metaphysics, he required two wives or more. Maybe these two women lent this piece of orange-tufted flesh to each other for widely different needs. For domestic peace.

"Phoebe," he said. "Admitting you're weak—but how weak are you? Excuse me. . . . I find this pretty funny. You have to deny *everything,* and keep up a perfect appearance. Can't you admit even a tiny bit?"

"What good would that do you?" she asked sharply. "And also, what are you prepared to do for me?"

"I? I'd help . . ." he began. But he checked himself. It was true, he couldn't offer much. He really was useless to her. With Gersbach she could still be a wife. He came home. She cooked, ironed, shopped, signed checks. Without him, she could not exist, cook, make beds. The trance would break. Then what?

"Why do you come to me, if you want custody of your daughter? Either do something by yourself, or forget it. Let me alone, now, Moses."

This, too, was perfectly just. Silent, he stared hard at her. The early and native tendency of his mind, lately acting without inhibitions, found significance in small bloodless marks on her face. As if death had tried her with his teeth and found her still unripe.

"Well, thank you for this talk, Phoebe. I'm going." He stood up. There was a softer kindliness in Herzog's expression, not often seen. Rather awkwardly he took Phoebe's hand, and she could not move fast enough to avoid his lips. He drew her closer and kissed her on the head. "You're right. This was an unnecessary visit." She freed her fingers.

"Good-bye, Moses." She spoke without looking at him. He would not get more from her than she was able to spare. ". . . You've been treated like dirt. That's true. But it's all over. You should get away. Just get away from this now."

The door was shut.

He went to spend the night with Lucas Asphalter, telephoning from a sidewalk booth to invite himself over. "I won't be in the way, will I? Have you got anybody there with you? No? I want you to do me a special favor. I can't phone Madeleine to ask to see the child. She hangs up on me as soon as she recognizes my voice. Will you call and arrange for me to pick up June tomorrow?"

"Why, of course," said Asphalter. "I'll do it now and have the answer for you when you get here. Did you just blow in, on impulse? Unplanned?"

"Thank you, Luke. Please do it now."

He left the booth, reflecting that he really must rest tonight, try to get some sleep. At the same time, he hesitated somewhat to lie down and shut his eyes; tomorrow he might not be able to recover his state of simple, free, intense realization. He therefore drove slowly, stopping at Walgreen's, where he bought a bottle of Cutty Sark for Luke and playthings for June—a toy periscope through which she could look over the sofa, around corners, a beach ball you inflated with your breath.

In front of Asphalter's house he locked the Falcon for the night, leaving Junie's gifts in the trunk. He felt certain she would love the periscope. There was much to be seen in that house on Harper Avenue. Let the child find life. The plainer the better, perhaps.

He was met on the staircase by Asphalter.

"I've been waiting for you."

"Is something wrong?" said Herzog.

"No, no, don't worry. I'm picking June up at noon tomorrow. She goes to a play school, half-days."

"Wonderful," Herzog said. "No trouble?"

"With Madeleine? None at all. She doesn't want to see you. Otherwise, you can visit with your little girl to your heart's content."

"She doesn't want me to come with a court order. Legally, she's in a dubious position, with that crook in the house. Well, let's have a look at you." They entered the apartment where the light was better. "You've a bit of a beard, Luke."

Nervously and shyly Asphalter touched his chin, looking away. He said, "I'm brazening it out."

"Compensation for the sudden unfortunate baldness?" said Herzog.

"Fighting a depression," said Asphalter. "Thought a change of image might be good . . . Excuse my pad."

Asphalter had always lived in such graduate-student filth. Herzog looked about. "If I ever have another windfall I'll buy you some bookshelves, Luke. About time you got rid of these old crates. This scientific literature is heavy stuff. But look, you've got clean sheets on the studio couch for me. This is very kind of you, Luke."

"You're an old friend."

"Thanks," said Herzog. To his surprise he found difficulty in speaking. A swift rush of feeling, out of nowhere, caught his throat. His eyes filled up. The potato love, he announced to himself. It's here. To advert to his temperament, call things by the correct name, restored his control. Self-correction refreshed him.

He said suddenly, "What happened to that bottle of Cutty Sark I brought? I need a shot."

"You need to go to sleep. You look ready to cave in."

"I don't feel bad at all," said Herzog.

"I've got some things to do, anyway. Go to sleep. I haven't finished grading all my exams."

"I guess I am folding," Moses said. "The bed looks good."

"I'll let you sleep late. Plenty of time," said Asphalter. "Good night, Moses." They shook hands.

At last he embraced his daughter, and she pressed his cheeks with her small hands and kissed him. Hungry to feel her, to breathe in her childish fragrance, to look in her face, her black eyes, touch her hair, the skin under her dress, he pressed her little bones, stammering, "Junie, sweetie. I've missed you." His happiness was painful. And she with all her innocence and childishness and with the pure, or amorous, instinct of tiny girls, kissed him on the lips, her careworn, busted, germ-carrying father.

Asphalter stood by, smiling but feeling somewhat awkward, his bald scalp perspiring, his new parti-colored beard looking hot. They were on the long gray staircase of the Museum of Science in Jackson Park. Busloads of children were entering, black and white flocks, herded by teachers and parents. The bronze-trimmed glass doors flashed in and out, and all these little bodies, blessed heads of all hues, shapes, the promise of the world to come, in the eyes of benevolent Herzog, its future good and evil, hurried in and out.

"My sweet June. Papa missed you."

"Poppy!"

"I can meet you at this spot at four P.M.," Asphalter said.

"Only three and a half hours? Where does she get off! Well, all right, I won't quarrel. I don't want any conflict. There's another day tomorrow, Luke. Thank you. I'll be here at four."

Moses carried his daughter into the museum to see the chickens hatching. "Did Marco send you a postcard, baby?"

"Yes. From the camp."

"You know who Marco is?"

"My big brother."

So Madeleine was not trying to estrange her from the Herzogs, whatever course of madness she was running.

"Have you gone down in the coal mine, here in the museum?"

"It scared me."

"Do you want to see the chickies?"

"I seen them."

"Don't you want to see them more?"

"Oh, yes. I like them. Uncle Val took me last week."

"Do I know Uncle Val?"

"Oh, Papa! You fooler." She hugged his neck, snickering.

"Who is he?"

"He's my stepfather, Papa. You *know* it."

"Is that what Mama tells you?"

"He's my stepfather."

"Was he the one who locked you up in the car?"

"Yes."

"And what did you do?"

"I was crying. But not long."

"And do you like Uncle Val?"

"Oh, yes, he's fun. He makes faces. Can you make good faces?"

"Some," he said. "I have too much dignity to make good faces."

"You tell better stories."

"I expect I do, sweetheart."

"About the boy with the stars."

So she remembered his best inventions. Herzog nodded his head, wondering at her, proud of her, thankful. "The boy with all the freckles?"

"They were like the sky."

"Each freckle was just like a star, and he had them all. The Big Dipper, Little Dipper, Orion, the Bear, the Twins, Betelgeuse, the Milky Way. His face had each and every star on it, in the right position."

"Only one star nobody knew."

"They took him to all the astronomers."

"I saw astronomers on television."

"And the astronomers said, 'Pooh, pooh, an interesting coincidence. A little freak.' "

"More. More."

"At last he went to see Hiram Shpitalnik, who was an old old old man, very tiny, with a long beard down to his feet. He lived in a hatbox. And he said, 'You must be examined by *my* grandfather.' "

"He lived in a walnut shell."

"Exactly. And all his friends were bees. The busy bee has no time for sorrow. Great-grandfather Shpitalnik came out of the shell with a telescope, and looked at Rupert's face."

"The boy's name was Rupert."

"Old Shpitalnik had the bees lift him into position, and he looked and said it *was* a real star, a new discovery. He had been watching for that star. . . . Now, here are the chicks." He held the child on the railing, to his left, so that she would not press against the pistol, wrapped in her great-grandfather's rubles. These were in his right breast pocket still.

"They're yellow," she said.

"They keep it hot and bright in there. See that egg wobble? The chick is trying to get out. Soon his bill will go through the shell. Watch."

"Papa, you don't shave at our house anymore, why not?"

He must stiffen his resistance to heartache now. A kind of necessary hardness was demanded. Otherwise it was as the savage described the piano, "You fight 'im 'e cry." In measured words he answered. "I have my razor in another place. What does Madeleine say?"

"She says you didn't want to live with us anymore."

He kept his anger from the child. "Did she? Well, I always want to be with you. I just can't."

"Why?"

"Because I'm a man, and men have to work, and be in the world."

"Uncle Val works. He writes poems and reads them to Mama."

Herzog's sober face brightened. "Splendid." She had to listen to his trash. Bad art and vice hand in hand. "I'm glad to hear it."

"He looks ooky when he says them."

"And does he cry?"

"Oh, yes."

Sentiment and brutality—never one without the other, like fossils and oil. This news is priceless. It's sheer happiness to hear it.

June had bent her head, and held her wrists to her eyes.

"What's the matter, darling?"

"Mama said I shouldn't talk about Uncle Val."

"Why?"

"She said you'd be very very angry."

"But I'm not. I'm laughing my head off. All right. We won't talk about him. I promise. Not one word."

An experienced father, he prudently waited until they reached the Falcon before he said, "I have presents for you in the trunk!"

"Oh, Papa—what did you bring!"

Against the clumsy, gray, gaping Museum of Science she looked so fresh, so new (her milk teeth and sparse freckles and big expectant eyes, her fragile neck). And he thought how she would inherit this world of great

instruments, principles of physics and applied science. She had the brains
for it. He was already intoxicated with pride, seeing another Madame Curie
in her. She loved the periscope. They spied on each other from the sides of
the car, hiding behind tree trunks and in the arches of the comfort station.
Crossing the bridge on the Outer Drive they walked by the lake. He let her
take off her shoes and wade, drying her feet afterward in his shirttail,
carefully brushing out the sand between her toes. He bought her a box of
Cracker Jack which she nibbled on the grass. The dandelions had blown
their fuses and were all loose silk; the turf was springy, neither damp as in
May nor dry and hard as in August, when the sun would scorch it. The
mechanical mower was riding in circles, barbering the slopes, raising a
spray of clippings. Lighted from the south the water was a marvelous,
fresh, heavy daylight blue; the sky rested on the mild burning horizon, clear
except toward Gary, where the dark thin pillars of the steel hearths puffed
out russet and sulphur streams of smoke. By now the lawns at Ludeyville,
uncut for two years, must be simply hayfields, and local hunters and
lovers were breaking in again, most likely, shattering windows, lighting
fires.

"I want to go to the aquarium, Papa," said June. "Mama said you
should take me."

"Oh, did she? Well, come on then."

The Falcon had grown hot in the sun. He opened the windows to cool it.
He had an extraordinary number of keys by now and must organize them
better in his pockets. There were his New York house keys, the Faculty
Men's Lounge key from the university, and the key to Asphalter's apartment, as well as several Ludeyville keys. "You must sit in the back seat,
honey. Creep in, now, and pull down your dress because the plastic is very
hot." The air from the west was drier than the east air. Herzog's sharp
senses detected the difference. In these days of near-delirium and wide-
ranging disordered thought, deeper currents of feeling had heightened his
perceptions, or made him instill something of his own into his surroundings.

"Papa, you must turn here. This is where Uncle Val always turns."

"Okay." He observed in the mirror that the slip had distressed her. She
had mentioned Gersbach again. "Hey, Pussycat," he said. "If you say
anything about Uncle Val to me, I'll never tell. I'll never ask you any
questions about him. Now don't you ever worry about it. It's all silliness.
There's nothing wrong with a few secrets."

"I know lots of them." She stood directly behind him in the back seat
and stroked his head. "Uncle Val is very nice."

"Why of course he is."

"But I don't like him. He doesn't smell good."

"Ha, ha! Well, we'll get him a bottle of perfume and make him smell
terrific."

He held her hand as they mounted the aquarium staircase, feeling himself to be the father whose strength and calm judgment she could trust. The center court of the building, whitened by the skylight, was very warm. The splashing pool and luxuriant plants and soft tropical fishy air forced Moses to take a grip on himself, to keep up his energy.

"What do you want to see first?"

"The big turtles."

They went up and down the obscure gold and green alleys.

"This fast little fish is called the humuhumuu-ele-ele, from Hawaii. This slithering beast is the stingray and has teeth and venom in its tail. And these are lampreys, related to hagfish, they fasten their sucker mouths on other fish and drink until they kill them. Over there you see the rainbow fish. No turtles in this aisle, but look at those great things at the end. Sharks?"

"I saw the dolphins at Brookfield," said June. "They wear sailor hats, ring a bell. They can dance on their tails and play basketball."

Herzog picked her up and carried her. These children's outings, perhaps because they were pervaded with so much emotion, were always exhausting. Often, after a day with Marco, Moses had to put a cold compress on his eyes and lie down. It seemed his fate to be the visiting father, an apparition who faded in and out of the children's lives. But this peculiar sensitivity about meeting and parting had to be tamed. Such trembling sorrow—he tried to think what term Freud had for it: partial return of repressed traumatic material, ultimately traceable to the death instinct?— should not be imparted to children, not that tremulous lifelong swoon of death. This same emotion, as Herzog the student was aware, was held to be the womb of cities, heavenly as well as earthly, mankind being unable to part with its beloved or its dead in this world or the next. But to Moses E. Herzog as he held his daughter in his arms, looking through aqueous green at the lampreys and smooth sharks with their fanged bellies, this emotion was nothing but tyranny.

"*There* is the turtle!" June shouted. The thing rose from the depths of the tank in its horny breastplate, the beaked head lazy, the eyes with aeons of indifference, the flippers slowly striving, pushing at the glass, the great scales pinkish yellow, or on the back, bearing beautiful lines, black curved plates mimicking the surface tension of water. It trailed a fuzz of parasitic green.

For comparison they went back to the Mississippi River turtles in the pool at the center; their sides were red-straked; they dozed on their logs and paddled in company with catfish over a bottom shaded by ferns, strewn with pennies.

The child had now had enough, and so had her father. "I think we'll go and get you a sandwich. It's lunchtime," he said.

They left the parking lot carefully enough, Herzog later thought. He was a circumspect driver. But getting his Falcon into the main stream of traffic he should perhaps have reckoned with the long curve from the north on which the cars picked up speed. A little Volkswagen truck was on his tail. He touched the brakes, meaning to slow up and let the other driver pass. But the brakes were all too new and responsive. The Falcon stopped short and the small truck struck it from behind and rammed it into a utility pole. June screamed and clutched at his shoulders as he was thrown forward, against the steering wheel. The kid! he thought; but it was not the kid he had to worry about. He knew from her scream that she was not hurt, only frightened. He lay over the wheel, feeling weak, radically weak; his eyes grew dark; he felt that he was losing ground to nausea and numbness. He listened to June's screams but could not turn to her. He notified himself that he was passing out, and he fainted away.

They spread him out on the grass. He heard a locomotive very close—the Illinois Central. And then it seemed somewhat farther off, blundering in the weeds across the Drive. His vision at first was bothered by large blots, but these dwindled presently to iridescent specks. His pants had worked themselves up. He felt a chill in his legs.

"Where's June? Where's my daughter?" He raised himself and saw her between two Negro policemen, looking at him. They had his wallet, the Czarist rubles, and the pistol, of course. There it was. He closed his eyes again. He felt the nausea return as he considered what he had gotten himself into. "Is she all right?"

"She's okay."

"Come here, Junie." He leaned forward and she walked into his arms. As he felt her, kissed her scared face, he had a sharp pain in his ribs. "Papa lay down for a minute. It's nothing." But she had seen him lying on this grass. Stretched limp, looking dead, probably, while the cops went through his pockets. His face felt bloodless, hollow, stiff, its sensations intensely reduced, and this frightened him. From the pricking of his hair at the roots he thought it must be turning white all at once. The police were giving him a few minutes to come to himself. The blue light of the squad car flashed, revolving. The driver of the small truck was staring at him, angry. A little beyond, the grackles were walking, feeding, the usual circle of lights working flexibly back and forth about their black necks. Over his shoulder Herzog was aware of the Field Museum. If only I were a mummy in that cellar! he thought.

The cops had him. Their silent looks gave him this information. Because he was holding Junie they waited; they might not be too rough with him just yet. Already stalling for time, he acted more dazed than he really felt. The cops could be very bad, he had seen them at work. But that was in the old days. Perhaps times had changed. There was a new Commissioner. He had sat close to Orlando Wilson at a Narcotics Conference last year. They had shaken hands. Of course it wasn't worth mentioning; anyway, nothing would antagonize these two big Negro cops more than hints of influence. For them, he was part of today's haul, and with his rubles, the gun, he couldn't hope that they would simply let him go. And there was the teal-blue Falcon crumpled against the utility pole. The traffic rushing by, the road with its blazing cars.

"You Moses?" the older of the two Negroes asked. There it was—that note of deadly familiarity that you heard only when immunity was lost.

"Yes, I'm Moses."

"This your chile?"

"Yes—my little girl."

"You better put your handkercher to your head. You got a little cut, Moses."

"Is that so?" This explained the pricking under his hair. Unable to locate his handkerchief, he unknotted his silk tie and folded it, pressed the broad end to his scalp. "Nothing to it," he said. The child had hidden her head in his shoulder. "Sit down by Papa, sweetheart. Sit on the grass right next to me. Papa's head hurts a little." She obeyed. Her docility, her feeling for him, what seemed to him the wise, tender sense of the child, her sympathy, moved him, pressed his guts. He put a protective, wide, eager hand on her back. Sitting forward, he held the tie to his scalp.

"You got the permit for this gun, Moses?" The cop pursed his large lips as he waited for the answer, brushing the small bristles of his moustache upward with his fingernail. The other policeman spoke with the driver of the Volkswagen truck, who was wildly angry. Sharp-faced, his nose sharp and red, he was glaring at Moses, saying, "You're going to take that guy's license away, aren't you?" Moses thought, I'm in bad because of the pistol, and this fellow wants to pour it on. Warned by this indignation, Herzog held his own feelings in.

"I asked you once, I ask you again, Moses, you got a permit?"

"No sir, I haven't."

"Two bullets in here. Loaded weapon, Moses."

"Officer, it was my father's gun. He died, and I was taking it back to Massachusetts." His answers were as brief and patient as he could make them. He knew he would have to repeat his story, over and over.

"What's this money here?"

"Worthless, officer. Like Russian Confederate money. Stage money. Another souvenir."

Not devoid of sympathy, the policeman's face also expressed a fatigued skepticism. He was heavy-lidded, and on his silent, thick mouth there was a sort of smile. Well—the variety of oddities, alibis, inventions, fantasies the police ran into every day. . . . Herzog, making his reckonings as intelligently as he could, though he had a heavy weight of responsibility and dread inside him, believed it might not be so easy for this cop to type him. There were labels to fit him, naturally, but a harness cop like this would not be familiar with them. Even now there was possibly some tinge of pride in this reflection, so tenacious was human foolishness. "Lord, let the angels praise thy name. Man is a foolish thing, a foolish thing. Folly and sin play all his game. . . ."

Herzog's head ached and he could remember no more verses. He lifted the tie from his scalp. No sense in letting it stick; it would pull away the clot. June had put her head in his lap. He covered her eyes from the sun.

"We have to diagram this accident." The copper in his shiny pants squatted beside Herzog. From his fat, bulging hips his own gun hung low. Its brown butt of cross-hatched metal and the cartridge belt looked very different from Father Herzog's big, clumsy Cherry Street revolver. "I don't see the title of this Falcon, here."

The small car was staved in at both ends, the hood gaping like a mussel shell. The engine itself could not be damaged much; no fluids had trickled out. "It's rented. I picked it up at O'Hare. The papers are in the glove compartment," said Herzog.

"We got to get these facts, here." The policeman opened a folder and began to mark the thick paper of a printed form with his yellow pencil. "You come out of this parking lot—what speed?"

"I was creeping. Five, eight miles an hour—I just nosed out."

"You didn't see this fellow coming?"

"No. The curve was hiding him, I suppose. I don't know. But he was right on my bumper when I got into the lane." He bent forward, trying to change his position and ease the pain in his side. He had already arranged with his mind to disregard it. He stroked June's cheek. "At least she wasn't hurt," he said.

"I just lifted her out the back window. The door got jammed. I looked her over. She's okay." The moustached Negro frowned, as if to make plain that he did not owe Herzog—a man with a loaded gun—any explanations whatever. For it was the possession of this clumsy horse pistol with two cartridges, not the accident, that would be the main charge against him.

"I'd have blown my brains out if anything happened to her."

The squatting cop, to judge by his silence, had no concern with what Moses might have done. To speak of any use of the revolver, even against himself, was not very smart. But he was still somewhat stunned and dizzy, brought down, as he pictured it, from his strange, spiraling flight of the last few days; and the shock, not to say desperation of this sudden drop. His head still swam. He decided that this foolishness must stop, or things would go even worse. Running to Chicago to protect his daughter, he almost killed her. Coming to offset the influence of Gersbach, and to give her the benefit of his own self—man and father, et cetera—what did he do but bang into a pole. And then the child saw him dragged out fainting, cut on the head, the revolver and the rubles sliding from his pocket. No, weakness, or sickness, with which he had copped a plea all his life (alternating with arrogance), his method of preserving equilibrium—the Herzog gyroscope—had no further utility. He seemed to have come to the end of *that*.

The driver of the Volkswagen utilities truck, in a green jumper, was giving his account of the accident. Moses tried to make out the letters stiched in yellow thread over his pocket. Was he from the gas company? No telling. He was laying the whole guilt on him, of course. It was very inventive—creative. The story deepened every moment. Oh, the grandeur of self-justification, thought Herzog. What genius it brought out in these mortals, even the most red-nosed. The ripples in this fellow's scalp followed a different pattern from the furrows in his forehead. You could make out his former hairline by this means. A certain number of skimpy hairs remained.

"He just cut out in front of me. No signal, nothing. Whyn't you give him the drunk test? That's drunken driving."

"Well, now, Harold," the older Negro said. "What was your speed?"

"Why, Jesus! I was way below the limit."

"A lot of these company drivers like to give private cars the business," said Herzog.

"First he cut in front, then he slammed his brake."

"You mashed him pretty hard. That means you were crowdin' him."

"That's right. Looks like to me . . ." The senior policeman pointed two, three, five times with the rubber tip of his pencil before he spoke another word; he made you consider the road. "Looks to me, you were pushin' him, Harold. He couldn't get in the next lane so he thought he'd slow and give you a chance to pass. Hit the brake too hard, and you clobbered him. I see from the staple marks on your license you already got two moving violations."

"That's right, and that's why I've been extra careful."

God keep this anger from burning up your scalp, Harold. A very unbecoming red color, and all ridges, like a dog's palate.

"Looks like to me, if you hadn't been on top of him, you wouldn't have hit him so flush. You'd a tried to turn, and got him on the right. Got to write you a ticket, Harold."

Then, to Moses, he said, "I got to take you in. You gonna be booked for misdemeanor."

"This old gun?"

"Loaded. . . ."

"Why, it's nothing. I have no record—never been booked."

They waited for him to get to his feet. Sharp-nosed, the Volkswagen-truck driver knitted his ginger brows at him and, under his red, angry stare, Herzog stood and then picked up his daughter. She lost her barrette as he lifted her. Her hair came free beside her cheeks, quite long. He could not bend again to hunt for the tortoise-shell clip. The door of the squad car, parked on a slope, opened wide for him. He could now feel for himself what it was like to be in custody. No one was robbed, no one had died. Still he felt the heavy, deadly shadow lying on him. "And this is just like you, Herzog," he said to himself. He could not escape self-accusation. For this big, nickel-plated pistol, whatever he had vaguely intended yesterday to do with it, he should have left today in the flight bag under Asphalter's sofa. When he had put on his jacket in the morning and felt the awkward weight on his chest, then and there he might have stopped being quixotic.

"What are we going to do about this Falcon?" he asked the police. He stopped. But they pushed him on, saying, "Don't worry about that. We'll take care of it."

He saw the tow truck coming up with its crane and hook. It too had the blue light spinning above its cab.

"Listen," he said, "I have to get this kid home."

"She'll get home. She ain't in no danger."

"But I'm supposed to turn her over at four."

"You got almost two hours."

"But isn't this going to take longer than an hour? I'd certainly appreciate it if you'd let me look after her first."

"Get goin', Moses. . . ." Grimly kind, the senior patrolman moved him along.

"She hasn't eaten lunch."

"You in worse shape than she is. Come on, now."

He shrugged and crumpled the stained necktie, letting it drop at the roadside. The cut was not serious; it had stopped bleeding. He handed June in, and when he was seated in the fiery heat of the blue plastic rear, he took her on his lap and explained, "We're going for a ride, darling." She nodded and was silent. Her face was tearless, clouded, and this was far worse. It hurt him. It tore his heart. As if Madeleine and Gersbach weren't enough, *he* had to come running with his eager love and excitement, hugging, kissing, periscopes, anxious emotions. She had to see him bleeding from the head. His eyes smarted, and he shut them with thumb and forefinger. The doors slammed. The motor gave a raw snort and raced smoothly, and the dry, rich summer air began to flow in, flavored with exhaust gas. It aggravated his nausea like a forced draft. When the car left the lake front he opened his eyes on the yellow ugliness of 22nd Street. He recognized the familiar look of summer damnation. Chicago! He smelled the hot reek of chemicals and inks coming from the Donnelley plant. And here was South State Street; here movie distributors used to hang their garish posters: Tom Mix plunging over a cliff; now it's only a smooth empty street where they sell glassware to bars. The car finally stopped. As if he had come to police headquarters in a rocking boat, over the water, he wavered when he got out on the sidewalk.

They handed his daughter out to him and escorted them to the elevator, which seemed roomy enough for a squadron. Two men who had been pinched—two other men in custody—went up with him. This was 11th and State. He remembered it. Dreadful here. Armed men came in, got out. As he was ordered, he followed the stout Negro policeman with the huge hands and wide hips down the corridor. Others walked behind him.

He and June were taken into a big but close room, and he was being booked by another Negro policeman, a sergeant. He was well along in years, smoothly wrinkled. His creases were extruded, not internal. His color was dark yellow, Negro gold. He conferred with the arresting police-man and then looked at the gun, took out the two bullets, whispered more questions to the cop in shiny pants who bent down to whisper secretly.

"Okay, you," he then said to Moses. He put on his Ben Franklin spec-tacles, two colonial tablets in thin gold frames. He took up his pen.

"Name?"

"Herzog—Moses."

"Middle initial?"

"E. Elkanah."

"Address?"

"Not living in Chicago."

The sergeant, fairly patient, said again, "Address?"

"Ludeyville, Mass., and New York City. Well, all right. Ludeyville, Massachusetts. No street number."

"This your chile?"

"Yes, sir. My little daughter June."

"Where does she live?"

"Here in the city, with her mother, on Harper Avenue."

"You divorced?"

"Yes, sir. I came to see the child."

"I see. You want to put her down?"

"No, officer—sergeant," he corrected himself, smiling agreeably.

"You're bein' booked, Moses. You weren't drunk, were you? Did you have a drink today?"

"I had one last night, before I went to sleep. Nothing today. Do you want me to take an alcohol test?"

"It won't be necessary. There's no traffic charge against you. We're booking you on account of this gun."

Herzog pulled down his daughter's dress.

"It's just a souvenir. Like the money."

"What kind of dough is this?"

"It's Russian, from World War I."

"Just empty your pockets, Moses. Put your stuff down so's I can check it over."

Without protest, he laid down his money, his notebooks, pens, the hand-kerchief, his pocket comb, and his keys.

"Seems to me you've got a mess of keys, Moses."

"Yes, sir, but I can identify them all."

"That's okay. There's no law against keys, exceptin' if you're a burglar."

"The only Chicago key is this one with the red mark on it. It's the key to my friend Asphalter's apartment. He's supposed to meet me at four o'clock, by the Rosenwald Museum. I've got to get her to him."

"Well, it ain't four, and you ain't goin' anywhere yet."

"I'd like to phone and head him off. Otherwise, he'll stand waiting."

"Well, now, Moses, why ain't you bringin' the kid straight back to her mother?"

"You see . . . we're not on speaking terms. We've had too many scraps."

"Appears to me you might be scared of her."

Herzog was briefly resentful. The remark was calculated to provoke him. But he couldn't afford to be angry now. "No, sir, not exactly."

"Then maybe she's scared of you."

"This is how we arranged it, with a friend to go between. I haven't seen the woman since last autumn."

"Okay, we'll call your buddy and the kid's mama, too."

Herzog exclaimed, "Oh, don't call her!"

"No?" The sergeant gave him an odd smile, and rested for a moment in his chair as if he had gotten from him what he wanted. "Sure, we'll bring her down here and see what she's got to say. If she's got a complaint in against you, why, it's worse than just illegal possession of firearms. We'll have you on a bad charge, then."

"There isn't any complaint, sergeant. You can check that in the files without making her come all this way. I'm the support of this child, and never miss a check. That's all Mrs. Herzog can tell you."

"Who'd you buy this revolver from?"

There it was again, the natural insolence of the cops. He was being goaded. But he kept himself steady.

"I didn't buy it. It belonged to my father. That and the Russian rubles."

"You're just sentimental?"

"That's right. I'm a sentimental s.o.b. Call it that."

"You sentimental about these here, too?" He tapped each of the bullets, one, two. "All right, we'll make those phone calls. Here, Jim, write the names and numbers."

He spoke to the copper who had brought Herzog in. He had been standing by, fat-cheeked, teasing the bristles of his moustache with his nail, pursing his lips.

"You may as well take my address book, the red one there. Bring it back, please. My friend's name is Asphalter."

"The other's name is Herzog," said the sergeant. "On Harper Avenue, ain't it?"

Moses nodded. He watched the heavy fingers turning the pages of his Parisian leather address book with its scribbles and blots.

"It'll put me in bad if you notify the child's mother," he said, making a last attempt to persuade the sergeant. "Why wouldn't it be the same to you if my friend Asphalter came here?"

"Go on, Jim."

The Negro marked the places with red pencil, and went. Moses made a special effort to keep a neutral look—no defiance, no special pleading, nothing of the slightest personal color. He remembered that he once believed in the appeal of a direct glance, driving aside differences of position, accident, one human being silently opening his heart to another. The recognition of essence by essence. He smiled inwardly at this. Sweet dreams, those! If he tried looking into his eyes, the sergeant would throw the book at him. So Madeleine was coming. Well, let her come. Perhaps that was what he wanted after all, a chance to confront her. Straight-nosed and pale, he looked intently at the floor. June changed her position in his arms, stirring the pain in his ribs. "Papa's sorry, sweetheart," he said. "Next time we'll go see the dolphins. Maybe the sharks were bad luck."

"You can sit down if you want," said the sergeant. "You look a little weak in the legs, Moses."

"I'd like to phone my brother to send his lawyer. Unless I don't need a lawyer. If I have to post a bond . . ."

"You'll have to post one, but I can't say how big, yet. Plenty of bondsmen settin' here." He motioned with the back of the hand, or with a wag of his wrist, and Moses turned and saw all sorts of people ranged behind him, along the walls. In fact, there were two men, he now noticed, loitering near, bondsmen by their natty appearance. He neutrally recognized that they were sizing him up as a risk. They had already seen his plane ticket, his keys, pens, rubles, and his wallet. His own car, wrecked on the Drive, would have secured a small bond. But a rented car? A man from out of state, in a dirty seersucker, no necktie? He didn't look good for a few hundred bucks. If it's no more than that, he reflected, I can probably swing it without bothering Will, or Shura. Some fellows always make a nice impression. I never had that ability. Due to my feelings. A passionate heart, a bad credit risk. Asked to make this practical judgment on myself, I wouldn't make it any differently.

His hands were clasped about his daughter's heart, which was beating quickly and lightly.

"Now, Moses, why you been carryin' a loaded gun? To shoot somebody?"

"Of course not. And, please, sergeant, I don't like the kid to hear such things."

"You the one that brought it along, not me. Maybe you just wanted to scare somebody. You sore at somebody?"

"No, sergeant, I was only going to make a paperweight of it. I forgot to take out the bullets, but that's because I don't know much about guns so it didn't occur to me. Will you let me make a phone call?"

"By and by. I ain't ready to. Sit down while I take care of other business. You sit and wait for the kid's mama to come."

"Could I get a container of milk for her?"

"Give Jim, here, two bits. He'll fetch it."

"With a straw, eh, June? You'd like to drink it with a straw." She nodded and Herzog said, "Please, a straw with it, if you don't mind."

"Papa?"

"Yes, June."

"You didn't tell me about the most-most."

For an instant he did not remember. "Ah," he said, "you mean that club in New York where people are the most of everything."

"That's the story."

She sat between his knees on the chair. He tried to make more room for her. "There's this association that people belong to. They're the most of every type. There's the hairiest bald man, and the baldest hairy man."

"The fattest thin lady."

"And the thinnest fat woman. The tallest dwarf and the smallest giant. They're all in it. The weakest strong man, and the strongest weak man. The stupidest wise man and the smartest blockhead. Then they have things like crippled acrobats, and ugly beauties."

"And what do they do, Papa?"

"On Saturday night they have a dinner-dance. They have a contest."

"To tell each other apart."

"Yes, sweetheart. And if you can tell the hairiest bald man from the baldest hairy man, you get a prize."

Bless her, she enjoyed her father's nonsense, and he must amuse her. She leaned her head on his shoulder and smiled, drowsy, with small teeth.

The room was hot and close. Herzog, sitting off to one side, took in the case of the two men who had come up in the elevator with him. A pair of plainclothesmen giving testimony—the Vice Squad, he soon realized. They had brought a woman too. He hadn't noticed her before. A prostitute? Yes, obviously, for all her respectable middle-class airs. In spite of his own troubles, Herzog looked on and found himself listening keenly. The plainclothesman was saying, "They were having a hassle in this woman's room."

"Sip your milk, June dear," said Herzog. "Is it cold? Drink it nice and easy, darling."

"You heard them from the corridor?" said the sergeant. "What's it about?"

"This fellow was yelling about a pair of earrings."

"What about earrings? The ones she's wearing? Where'd you get them?"

"I bought them. From him. It was just business."

"On payments, which you didn't make."

Moses watched with interest, whispering occasionally to the child to divert her attention. The woman looked oddly familiar, despite her smeary makeup, emerald eye shadow, dyed hair, the thickening pride of her nose. He wanted very much to ask her a question. Had she attended McKinley High School? Did she sing in the Glee Club? Me too! Don't you remember? Herzog? Herzog who gave the class oration—who spoke on Emerson?

"Papa, the milk won't come."

"Because you've chewed the straw. Let's get the kinks out of it."

"We got to get out of here, sergeant," said the jewel salesman. "We got people waiting for us."

The wives! thought Herzog. The wives were waiting!

"You two fellows related?"

The jewel salesman said, "He's my brother-in-law, just visiting from Louisville."

The wives, one of them a sister, were waiting. And he, too, Herzog, was waiting, light-headed with anticipation. Could this really be Carlotta from the Glee Club who sang the contralto solo in *Once More with Joy* (from Wagner)? It was not impossible.

At this moment Madeleine arrived. She came in, saying, "Where is my child!" Then she saw June on Herzog's lap and crossed the room quickly. "Come here to me, baby!" She lifted the milk container and put it aside, and took up the girl in her arms. Herzog felt the blood beating in his eardrums, and a great pressure at the back of the head. It was necessary that Madeleine should see him, but her look was devoid of intimate recognition. Coldly she turned away, her brow twitching. "Is the child all right?" she said.

The sergeant motioned to the Vice Squad to make way. "She's fine. If she had even a scratch on her we'd have taken her to Michael Reese." Madeleine examined June's arms, her legs, felt her with nervous hands. The sergeant beckoned to Moses. He came forward, and he and Mady faced each other across the desk.

She wore a light-blue linen suit and her hair fell loose behind her. The word to describe her conduct was *masterful*. Her heels had made a commanding noise clearly audible in this buzzing room. Herzog took a long look at her blue-eyed, straight, Byzantine profile, the small lips, the chin that pressed on the flesh beneath. Her color was deep, a sign with her that consciousness was running high. He thought he could make out a certain thickening in her face—incipient coarseness. He hoped so. It was only right that some of Gersbach's grossness should rub off on her. Why shouldn't it? He observed that she was definitely broader behind.

"Is this the girl's daddy, lady?"

Madeleine still refused to grant him a look of recognition. "Yes," she said, "I divorced him. Not long ago."

"Does he live in Massachusetts?"

"I don't know where he lives. It's none of my business."

Herzog marveled at her. He could not help admiring the perfection of
her self-control. She never hesitated. When she took the milk from Junie
she knew precisely where to drop the container, though she had been only
an instant in the room. By now she had certainly made an inventory of all
the objects on the desk, including the rubles, and gun, of course. She had
never seen it, but she could identify the Ludeyville keys by the round
magnetic clasp of the ring, and she would realize the pistol belonged to
him. He knew her ways so well, all her airs, her patrician style, the tic of
her nose, the crazy clear hauteur of the eyes. As the sergeant questioned
her, Moses, in his slightly dazed but intense way, was unable to restrain
associations. That personal sweet-and-sour fragrance of hers, and her fire-
blue eyes, her spiky glances and her small mouth ready with any wickedness would never again have the same power over him. Still, it gave him a
headache merely to look at her. The pulses in his skull were quick and
regular, like the tappets of an engine beating in their film of dark oil. He
saw her with great vividness—the smoothness of her breast, bared by the
square-cut dress, the smoothness of her legs, Indian brown. Her face,
especially the forehead, was altogether too smooth, too glabrous for his
taste. The whole burden of her severity was carried there. She had what the
French called le front bombé; in other terms, a pedomorphic forehead.
Ultimately unknowable, the processes behind it. See, Moses? We don't
know one another. Even that Gersbach, call him any name you like—
charlatan, psychopath, with his hot phony eyes and his clumsy cheeks, with
the folds. He was unknowable. And I myself, the same. But hard ruthless
action taken against a man is the assertion by evildoers that he is fully
knowable. They put me down, ergo, they claimed final knowledge of
Herzog. They knew me! And I hold with Spinoza (I hope he won't mind)
that to demand what is impossible for any human being, to exercise power
where it can't be exercised, is tyranny. Excuse me, therefore, sir and
madame, but I reject your definitions of me. Ah, this Madeleine is a
strange person, to be so proud but somehow not quite clean—so beautiful
but distorted by rage—such a mixed mind of pure diamond and Woolworth glass. And Gersbach who sucked up to me. For the symbiosis of it.
Symbiosis and trash. And she, as sweet as cheap candy, and just as reminiscent of poison as chemical sweet acids. But I make no last judgment.
That's for them, not me. I came to do harm, I admit. But the first blood-
shed was mine, and so I'm out of this now. Count me out. Except in what
concerns June. But for the rest, I withdraw from the whole scene as soon
as I can. Good-bye to all.

"Well, he give you hard time?" Herzog who had been listening sub-
liminally heard the sergeant put this question.

He said tersely to Madeleine, "Watch it, if you please. Let's not have
unnecessary trouble."

She ignored this. "He bothered me, yes."

"He make any threats?"

Herzog waited, tense, for her reply. She would consider the support money—the rent. She was canny, a superbly cunning, very canny woman. But there was also the violence of her hatred, and that hatred had a fringe of insanity.

"No, not directly to me. I haven't seen him since last October."

Madeleine's color was very high. Her throat flushed, like pink—like rose quartz, and the curious tinge had come into her eyes. He knew what this moment was to her—happiness!

"Do you recognize this gun?" The sergeant held it in his yellow palm, turning it over with delicate fingers like a fish—a perch.

The radiance of her look as it rested on the gun was deeper than any sexual expression he had ever seen on her face. "It's his, isn't it?" she said. "The bullets, too?" He recognized the hard clear look of joy in her eyes. Her lips were pressed shut.

"He had it on him. Do you know it?"

"No, but I'm not surprised."

Moses was watching June now. Her face was clouded again; she seemed to frown.

"Did you ever file a complaint against Moses, here?"

"No," said Mady. "I didn't actually do that." She took a sharp breath. She was about to plunge into something.

"Sergeant," said Herzog. "I told you there was no complaint. Ask her if I've ever missed a single support check."

Madeleine said, "I did give his photograph to the Hyde Park police."

He warned her that she was going too far. "Madeleine!" he said.

"Shut up, Moses," said the sergeant. "What was that for, lady?"

"In case he prowled around the house. To alert them."

Herzog shook his head, partly at himself. He had made the kind of mistake today that belonged to an earlier period. As of today it was no longer characteristic. But he had to pay an earlier reckoning. When will you catch up with yourself! he asked himself. When will that day come!

"Did he ever prowl?"

"He was never seen, but I know damn well he did. He's a jealous man and a troublemaker. He has a terrible temper."

"You never signed a complaint, though?"

"No. But I expect to be protected from any sort of violence."

Her voice went up sharply, and as she spoke, Herzog saw the sergeant take a new look at her, as if he were beginning to make out her haughty peculiarities at last. He picked up the Ben Franklin glasses with the tablet-shaped lenses. "There ain't going to be any violence, lady."

Yes, Moses thought, he's beginning to see how it is. "I never intended to use that gun except to hold papers down," he said.

Madeleine now spoke to Herzog for the first time, pointing with a rigid finger to the two bullets and looking him in the eyes. "One of those was for me, wasn't it!"

"You think so? I wonder where you get such ideas? And who was the other one for?" He was quite cool as he said this, his tone was level. He was doing all he could to bring out the hidden Madeleine, the Madeleine he knew. As she stared at him her color receded and her nose began to move very slightly. She seemed to realize that she must control her tic and the violence of her stare. But by noticeable degrees her face became very white, her eyes smaller, stony. He believed he could interpret them. They expressed a total will that he should die. This was infinitely more than ordinary hatred. It was a vote for his nonexistence, he thought. He wondered whether the sergeant was able to see this. "Well, who do you think that second imaginary shot was for?"

She said no more to him, only continued to stare in the same way.

"That'll be all now, lady. You can take your child and go."

"Good-bye June," said Moses. "You go home now. Papa'll see you soon. Give us a kiss, now, on the cheek." He felt the child's lips. Over her mother's shoulder, June reached out and touched him, "God bless you," he added, as Madeleine strode away. "I'll be back."

"I'll finish bookin' you now, Moses."

"I've got to post bond? How much?"

"Three hundred. American, not this stuff."

"I wish you'd let me make a call."

As the sergeant silently directed him to take one of his own dimes, Moses still had the time to note what a powerful police-face he had. He must have Indian blood—Cherokee, perhaps, or Osage; an Irish ancestor or two. His sallow gold skin with heavy seams descending, the austere nose and prominent lips for impassivity, and the many separate, infinitesimal gray curls on his scalp for dignity. His rugged fingers pointed to the phone booth.

Herzog was tired, dragged out, as he dialed his brother, but far from downcast. For some reason he believed he had done well. He was running true to form, yes; more mischief; and Will would have to bail him out. Still, he was not at all heavyhearted but, on the contrary, felt rather free. Perhaps he was too tired to be glum. That may have been it, after all—the metabolic wastes of fatigue (he was fond of these physiological explanations; this one came from Freud's essay on Mourning and Melancholia) made him temporarily lighthearted, even gay.

"Yes."

"Will Herzog in?"

Each instantly recognized the other's voice.

"Mose!" said Will.

Herzog could do nothing about the feelings stirred by hearing Will. They came to life suddenly at hearing the old tone, the old name. He loved Will,

Helen, even Shura, though his millions had made him remote. In the confinement of the metal booth the sweat burst out instantly on his neck.

"Where've you been, Mose? The old woman called last night. I couldn't sleep afterward. Where are you?"

"Elya," said Herzog, using his brother's family name, "don't worry. I haven't done anything serious, but I'm down at Eleventh and State."

"At Police Headquarters?"

"Just a minor traffic accident. No one hurt. But they're holding me for three hundred bucks bond, and I haven't got the money on me."

"For heaven's sake, Mose. Nobody's seen you since last summer. We've been worried sick. I'll be right down."

He waited in the cell with two other men. One was drunk and sleeping in his soiled skivvies. The other was a Negro boy, not old enough to shave. He wore a fawn-colored expensive suit and brown alligator shoes. Herzog said hello, but the boy chose not to answer. He stuck to his own misery, and looked away. Moses was sorry for him. He leaned against the bars, waiting. The wrong side of the bars—he felt it with his cheek. And here were the toilet bowl, the bare metal bunk, and the flies on the ceiling. This, Herzog realized, was not the sphere of *his* sins. He was merely passing through. Out in the streets, in American society, that was where he did his time. He sat down calmly on the bunk. Of course, he thought, he'd leave Chicago immediately, and he'd come back only when he was ready to do June good, genuine good. No more of this hectic, heart-rent, theatrical window-peering; no more collision, fainting, you-fight-'im-'e-cry encounters, confrontations. The drone of trouble coming from the cells and corridors, the bad smell of headquarters, the wretchedness of faces, the hand that turned the key of no better hope than the hand of this stuporous sleeper in his urine-stained underpants—the man who had eyes, nostrils, ears, let him hear, smell, see. The man who had intellect, heart, let him consider.

His brother observed, as they were leaving police headquarters, "You don't seem too upset."

"No, Will."

Above the sidewalk and the warm evening gloom the sky carried the long gilt rails of jets, and the jumbled lights of honky-tonks, just north of 12th Street, were already heaving up and down, a pale pass in which the street seemed to end.

"How do you feel?"

"I feel fine," said Herzog. "How do I look?"

His brother said discreetly, "You could do with a little rest. Why don't we stop and have you looked at by my doctor?"

"I don't think that's necessary. This small cut on my head stopped bleeding almost immediately."

"But you've been holding your side. Don't be a fool, Mose."

Will was an undemonstrative man, substantial, shrewd, quiet, shorter than his brother but with thicker, darker hair. In a family of passionately expressive people as Father Herzog and Aunt Zipporah, Will had developed a quieter, observant, reticent style.

"How's the family, Will—the kids?"

"Fine . . . What have you been doing, Moses?"

"Don't go by appearances. There's less to worry about than meets the eye. I'm really in very good shape. Do you remember when we got lost at Lake Wandatega? Floundering in the slime, cutting our feet on those reeds? That was really dangerous. But this is nothing."

"What were you doing with that gun?"

"You know I'm no more capable of firing it at someone than Papa was. You took his watch chain, didn't you? I remembered those old rubles in his drawer and then I took the revolver too. I shouldn't have. At least I ought to have emptied it. It was just one of those dumb impulses. Let's forget it."

"All right," said Will. "I don't mean to embarrass you. That's not the point."

"I know what it is," Herzog said. "You're worried." He had to lower his voice to control it. "I love you too, Will."

"Yes, I know that."

"But I haven't behaved very sensibly. From your standpoint . . . Well, from any reasonable standpoint. I brought Madeleine to your office so you could see her before I married her. I could tell you didn't approve. I didn't approve of her myself. And she didn't approve of me."

"Why did you marry her?"

"God ties all kinds of loose ends together. Who knows why! He couldn't care less about my welfare, or my ego, that thing of value. All you can say is, 'There's a red thread spliced with a green, or blue, and I wonder why.' And then I put all that money into the house in Ludeyville. That was simply crazy."

"Perhaps not," said Will. "It is real estate, after all. Have you tried to sell it?" Will had great faith in real estate.

"To whom? How?"

"List it with an agent. Maybe I'll come and look it over."

"I'd be grateful," said Herzog. "I don't think any buyer in his right mind would touch it."

"But let me call Doctor Ramsberg, Mose, and have him examine you. Then come home and have some dinner with us. It would be a treat for the family."

"When could you come to Ludeyville?"

"I've got to go to Boston next week. Then Muriel and I were going out to the Cape."

"Come by way of Ludeyville. It's close to the turnpike. I'd consider it a tremendous favor. I have to sell that house."

"Have dinner with us, and we can talk about it."

"Will—no. I'm not up to it. Just look at me. I'm stinking dirty, and I'd upset everyone. Like a lousy lost sheep." He laughed. "No, some other time when I'm feeling a little more normal. I look as if I'd just arrived in this country. A D.P. Just as we arrived from Canada at the Old Baltimore and Ohio Station. On the Michigan Central. God, we were filthy with the soot."

William did not share his brother's passion for reminiscence. He was an engineer and technologist, a contractor and builder; a balanced, reasonable person, he was pained to see Moses in such a state. His lined face was hot, uneasy; he took a handkerchief from the inner pocket of his well-tailored suit and pressed it to his forehead, his cheeks, under the large Herzog eyes.

"I'm sorry, Elya," said Moses, more quietly.

"Well——"

"Let me straighten myself up a bit. I know you're concerned about me. But that's just it. I'm sorry to worry you. I really am all right."

"Are you?" Will sadly looked at him.

"Yes, I'm at an awful disadvantage here—dirty, foolish, just bailed out. It's just ridiculous. Everything will look a lot different in the East, next week. I'll meet you in Boston, if you like. When I've got myself in better order. There's nothing you can do now but treat me like a jerk—a child. And that's not right."

"I'm not making any judgments on you. You don't have to come home with me, if that embarrasses you. Although we're your own family. . . . But there's my car, across the street." He gestured toward his dark-blue Cadillac. "Just come along to the doctor so I can be sure you weren't hurt in the accident. Then you can do what you think best."

"All right. Fair enough. There's nothing wrong. I'm sure of it."

He was not entirely surprised, however, to learn that he had a broken rib. "No lung puncture," the doctor said. "Six weeks or so in tape. And you'll need two or three stitches in your head. That's the whole story. No heavy lifting, straining, chopping, or other violent exercise. Will tells me you're a country gentleman. You've got a farm in the Berkshires? An estate?"

The doctor with grizzled backswept hair and small keen eyes looked at him with thin-lipped amusement.

"It's in bad repair. Miles from a synagogue," said Herzog.

"Ha, your brother likes to kid," Dr. Ramsberg said. Will faintly smiled. Standing with folded arms he favored one heel, somewhat like Father Herzog, and had a bit of the old man's elegance but not his eccentricities. He had no time for such stuff, thought Herzog, running a big business. No great interest in it. Other things absorb. He's a good man, a very good man. But there's a strange division of functions that I sense, in which I am the specialist in . . . in spiritual self-awareness; or emotionalism; or ideas; or nonsense. Perhaps of no real use or relevance except to keep alive primordial feelings of a certain sort. He mixes grout to pump into these new highrisers all over town. He has to be political, and deal, and wangle and pay off and figure tax angles. All that Papa was inept in but dreamed he was born to do. Will is a quiet man of duty and routine, has his money, position, influence, and is just as glad to be rid of his private or "personal" sides. Sees me spluttering fire in the wilderness of this world, and pities me no doubt for my temperament. Under the old dispensation, as the stumbling, ingenuous, burlap Moses, a heart without guile, in need of protection, a morbid phenomenon, a modern remnant of otherworldliness— under that former dispensation I would need protection. And it would be gladly offered by him—by the person who "knows-the-world-for-what-it-is." Whereas a man like me has shown the arbitrary withdrawal of proud subjectivity from the collective and historical progress of mankind. And that is true of lower-class emotional boys and girls who adopt the aesthetic mode, the mode of rich sensibility. Seeking to sustain their own version of existence under the crushing weight of *mass*. What Marx described as that "material weight." Turning this thing, "my personal life," into a circus, into gladiatorial combat. Or tamer forms of entertainment. To make a joke of your "shame," your ephemeral dimness, and show why you deserve your pain. The white modern lights of the small room were going round, wheeling. Herzog himself felt that he was rotating with them as the doctor wound the medicinal-smelling tapes tightly about his chest. Now, to get rid of all such falsehoods. . . .

"I have an idea my brother could do with some rest," said Will. "What's your opinion, doctor?"

"He looks as if he's been going pretty hard, that's true."

"I'm going to spend a week at Ludeyville," Moses said.

"What I mean is complete rest—bed rest."

"Yes, I know I seem to be in a state. But it's not a bad state."

"Still," said Herzog's brother, "you worry me."

A loving brute—a subtle, spoiled, loving man. Who can make use of him? He craves use. Where is he needed? Show him the way to make his sacrifice to truth, to order, to peace. Oh, that mysterious creature, that Herzog! Awkwardly taped, helped into his wrinkled shirt by brother Will.

He reached his country place the following afternoon, after taking a plane to Albany, from there the bus to Pittsfield, and then a cab to Ludeyville. Asphalter had given him some Tuinal the night before. He slept deeply and was feeling perfectly fine, despite his taped sides.

The house was two miles beyond the village, in the hills. Beautiful, sparkling summer weather in the Berkshires, the air light, the streams quick, the woods dense, the green new. As for birds, Herzog's acres seemed to have become a sanctuary. Wrens nested under the ornamental scrolls of the porch. The giant elm was not quite dead, and the orioles lived in it still. Herzog had the driver stop in the mossy roadway, boulder-lined. He couldn't be sure the house was approachable. But no fallen trees blocked the path, and although much of the gravel had washed down in thaws and storms, the cab might easily have gotten through. Moses, however, didn't mind the short climb. His chest was securely armored in tape and his legs were light. He had bought some groceries in Ludeyville. If hunters and prowlers had not eaten it, there was a supply of canned goods in the cellar. Two years ago he had put up tomatoes and beans and raspberry preserves, and before leaving for Chicago he had hidden his wine and whisky. The electricity of course was turned off, but perhaps the old hand pump could be made to work. There was always cistern water to fall back on. He could cook in the fireplace; there were old hooks and trivets—and here (his heart trembled) the house rose out of weeds, vines, trees, and blossoms. Herzog's folly! Monument to his sincere and loving idiocy, to the unrecognized evils of his character, symbol of his Jewish struggle for a solid footing in the White Anglo-Saxon Protestant America. I too have done my share of social climbing, he thought, with hauteur to spare, defying the Wasps, who, because the Government gave much of this continent away to the railroads, stopped boiling their own soap circa 1880, took European tours, and began to complain of the Micks and the Spicks and the Sheenies. What a struggle I waged!—left-handed but fierce. But enough of that— here I am. How marvelously beautiful it is today. He stopped in the overgrown yard, shut his eyes in the sun, against flashes of crimson, and drew in the odors of catalpa bells, soil, honeysuckle, wild onions, and herbs. Either deer or lovers had lain in this grass near the elm, for it was flattened. He circled the house to see whether it was much damaged. There were no broken windows. All the shutters, hooked from within, were undisturbed. Only a few of the posters he had put up warning that this property was under police protection had been torn down. The garden was a thick mass of thorny canes, roses and berries twisted together. It looked too hopeless —past regretting. He would never have the strength to throw himself into such tasks again, to hammer, paint, patch, splice, prune, spray. He was here only to look things over.

The house was as musty as he had expected. He opened a few windows and shutters in the kitchen. The debris of leaves and pine needles, webs, cocoons, and insect corpses he brushed away. What was needed, immediately, was a fire. He had brought matches. One of the benefits of a riper age was that you became clever about such things—foresightful. Of course he had a bicycle—he could ride to the village to buy what he had forgotten. He had even been smart enough to set the bike on its saddle, to spare the tires. There was not much air in them, but they'd get him down to the Esso station. He carried in a few pine logs, kindling, and started a small blaze first, to make sure of the draft. Birds or squirrels might have nested in the flues. But then he remembered that he had climbed out on the roof to fasten wire mesh over the chimneys—part of his frenzy of efficient toil. He laid on more wood. The old bark dropped away and disclosed the work of insects underneath—grubs, ants, long-legged spiders ran away. He gave them every opportunity to escape. The black, dry branches began to burn with yellow flames. He heaped on more logs, secured them with the andirons, and continued his examination of the house.

The canned food had not been touched. There were fancy goods bought by Madeleine (always the best of everything), S. S. Pierce terrapin soup, Indian pudding, truffles, olives, and then grimmer-looking victuals bought by Moses himself at Army-surplus sales—beans, canned bread, and the like. He made his inventory with a sort of dreamy curiosity about his onetime plan for solitary self-sufficiency—the washer, dryer, the hot-water unit, pure white and gleaming forms into which he had put his dead father's dollars, ugly green, laboriously made, tediously counted, divided in agony among the heirs.

Herzog's present loneliness did not seem to count because it was so consciously cheerful. It was odd, the tour he made through his property. In his own room he found the ruins of his scholarly enterprise strewn over the desk and the shelves. The windows were so discolored as to seem stained with iodine, and the honeysuckles outside had almost pulled the screens down. The books, muslin-covered, were undisturbed. He lifted the cloth and glanced at them with no special interest. Visiting the little bathroom, he was entertained to see the lavish fittings Madeleine had bought at Sloane's, scalloped silver soap dishes and flashing towel racks too heavy for the plaster, even after they were fastened with toggle bolts. They were drooping now. The shower stall, for Gersbach's convenience—the Gersbachs had had no shower in Barrington—was thoughtfully equipped with a handrail. "If we're going to put it in, let's make it so Valentine can use it," Mady had said. Ah, well—Moses shrugged. A strange odor in the toilet bowl attracted his notice next, and raising the wooden lid he found the small beaked skulls and other remains of birds who had nested there after the water was drained, and then had been entombed by the falling lid. He looked grimly in, his heart aching somewhat at this accident. There must be a broken window in the attic, he inferred from this, and other birds nesting in the house. Indeed, he found owls in his bedroom, perched on the red valances, which they had streaked with droppings. He gave them every opportunity to escape, and, when they were gone, looked for a nest. He found the young owls in the large light fixture over the bed. Unwilling to disturb these flat-faced little creatures, Herzog pulled the mattress of his marriage bed into June's room.

He opened more windows, and the sun and country air at once entered. He was surprised to feel such contentment . . . contentment? Whom was he kidding, this was joy! For perhaps the first time he felt what it was to be free from Madeleine. Joy! His servitude was ended, and his heart released from its grisly heaviness and encrustation. Nothing more than the fact of her absence was simply sweetness and lightness of spirit. To her, at 11th and State, it had been happiness to see him in trouble, and to him, in Ludeyville, it was a delicious joy to have her removed from his flesh, like something that had stabbed his shoulders, his groin, made his arms and his neck lame and cumbersome. Those strange lights, Herzog's brown eyes, so often overlaid with the film or protective chitin of melancholy, the by-product of his laboring brain, shone again.

It cost him some effort to turn over the mattress on the floor of June's old room. He had to move aside some of her cast-off toys and kiddie furniture, a great stuffed blue-eyed tiger, the potty chair, a red snowsuit, perfectly good. Herzog, lying under the open window with the sun in his face, rested on the mattress. Over him the great trees, the spruces in the front yard, showed their beautiful jaggedness and sent down the odor of heated needles and gum.

Despite the hours he spent in the open he believed he still looked pale. Perhaps this was because the mirror of the bathroom door into which he stared in the morning reflected the massed green of the trees. No, he did not look well. His excitement must be a great drain on his strength, he thought. And then there was the persistently medicinal smell of the tapes on his chest to remind him that he was not quite well. After the second or third day he stopped the sleeping on the second floor. He didn't want to drive the owls out of the house and leave a brood to die in the old fixture with the triple brass chain. It was bad enough to have those tiny skeletons in the toilet bowl. He moved downstairs, taking with him a few useful articles, an old trench coat and rain hat, his boots made to order at Gokey's in St. Paul—marvelous, flexible, handsome snakeproof boots; he had forgotten that he had them. In the storeroom he made other interesting discoveries, photographs of the "happy days," boxes of clothing, Madeleine's letters, bundles of canceled checks, elaborately engraved wedding announcements, and a recipe book belonging to Phoebe Gersbach. The photographs were all of him. Madeleine had left those behind, taking the others. Interesting—her attitude. Among the abandoned dresses were her expensive maternity outfits. The checks were for large sums, and many of these were paid to cash. Had she secretly been saving? He wouldn't put it past her. The announcements made him laugh; Mr and Mrs Pontritter were giving their daughter in marriage to Mr Moses E Herzog Ph D.

In one of the closets he found a dozen or so Russian books under a painter's dropcloth. He read a few pages of Rozanov's *Solitaria*. Then he looked over the paint situation—old brushes, thinners, evaporated, crusted buckets. There were several cans of enamel, and Herzog thought, What if I should paint up the little piano? I could send it out to Chicago, to Junie. The kid is really highly musical. As for Madeleine, she'll have to take it in, the bitch, when it's delivered, paid for. She can't send it back. The green enamel seemed to him exactly right, and he wasted no time but found the most usable brushes and set himself to work, full of eagerness, in the parlor. He painted the lid of the piano with absorption; the green was light, beautiful, like summer apples.

The enamel covered well but it would probably need a second coat, and he might not have enough paint for that. Putting down the brush, he gave the piano lid time to dry, considering how to get the instrument out of here. He couldn't expect one of the giant interstate vans to climb this hill. He would have to hire Tuttle from the village to come in his pick-up truck. The cost would amount to something like a hundred dollars, but he must do everything possible for the child, and he had no serious problems about money. Will had offered him as much as he needed to get through the summer. This was just what she needed, just what he should send her, he thought, a piano, a green piano, the green of Ludeyville, a piano from the Berkshires.

❖

Saul Bellow was born of Russian parents in Lachine, Quebec, in 1915, grew up in Chicago, attended the University of Chicago, was graduated from Northwestern University in 1937, did graduate work at the University of Wisconsin, has lectured and taught at the University of Minnesota, Princeton, New York University, Bard, the University of Puerto Rico, and now is back at the University of Chicago. He has twice been awarded Guggenheim fellowships and has twice won the National Book Award for fiction. Although he has published critical essays and short stories, edited the influential literary periodical The Noble Savage, *and has had several plays produced, Bellow's very great reputation, as perhaps the foremost American writer, derives almost entirely from his six novels. The first,* Dangling Man (1944) *a short novel in the form of a diary kept by a man waiting to be drafted, was startlingly original among the World War II novels and has served as a prototype for much fiction by others. The second,* The Victim (1947), *was on the theme of responsibility and told of a man plagued by a faint obligation to another, with whom he virtually exchanges roles as victim; it revealed much about the pervasiveness of guilt and anxiety in our times, and it too has had a great influence on the work of other writers. Neither of these carefully wrought, introspective novels gave any hint of the methods of the third book,* The Adventures of Augie March

(1953), a big, long, far-ranging, picaresque novel, episodic and sprawling. Bellow next published a very short novel, or long story, Seize the Day *(1956), telling of a man who is at an utterly empty point in his life, but whose commonality with humanity is movingly asserted at the end. For the perfect control with which it expresses the modern theme of alienation, many cite* Seize the Day *as Bellow's finest work and as perhaps the central story of our time. In his fifth book,* Henderson the Rain King *(1959), Bellow surprised again; for it is a wildly inventive novel, recounting the adventures of a rich, giant, bumbling American in Africa. With publication of his most recent novel,* Herzog *(1964), Bellow achieved a resounding critical and public success. The excerpt comprising "Herzog Visits Chicago" reads very satisfactorily of itself, almost as a novella, and indicates some of the emotional and intellectual range of the work, but it should not substitute for a reading of the whole novel.*

"Herzog Visits Chicago" reveals a lot, explicitly and implicitly, about changing patterns in family life in this country, and specifically about the new institution of divorce. Divorce, today so common in America, is now thought to be, like marriage, a matter of choice, simply a decision to be made by an individual to preserve or regain personal "happiness" or "fulfillment." This new easiness about divorce is part of the modern affluent mobility-opportunity syndrome, and it reflects the expectation that marriage will carry the burden for the personal "adjustment" of the two adults involved. In other times, marriage was a social contract, with religious overtones, involving family and property and community, and therefore not subject to the whims or "ideas" or personal qualities or conditions of the husband and wife. A good deal of Herzog's trouble stems from clinging to traditional attitudes after the breakup of his typically modern marriage. As wandering academics, he and Madeleine are not subject to pressures from any community. There is little or no family involved on either side: Herzog expects to be part of warm, loving Jewish family life, but as a professional intellectual he has cut himself off so completely from his relatives as to seem a stranger to them. And of course he has married a girl who is not of his religion, his "race," or his class: except that they are both intellectuals and compatible sexually, they have little in common. And a marriage based on sex and commonly held ideas is vulnerable to new ideas and new sexual partners, as Madeleine shows when she puts Herzog out, simply ending the marriage as a matter of choice. But this makes no sense to Herzog-the-family-man, Herzog-the-putter-up-of-shutters, the father of precious children. His trained intellect, his broad learning, his deep perceptions and intense thoughts about everything haven't helped him to see what was going on about him in his marriage, nor do they help him now to come to terms with his divorce. The meaning of divorce in America seems about to disappear under the blanket of statistics spread by our great bureaucracy, showing how commonplace it is. Modern American writers have contributed

more than their share individually to these statistics, but in their stories about divorce—and it sometimes seems each writer has written at least one—they have done much to make the meaning clear as experience rather than as statistic. They show us that divorce of this modern sort, based on choice rather than dire necessity, still brings with it a deep sense of personal failure—immense self-doubt, not only of one's self as an object of love, but of one's whole plan for life—and unless one has, like Madeleine, new ideas, a new partner, new plans, he is liable, like Herzog, to go through an unsettled, anxious period in which nothing seems to have much purpose. Our times are anyway anxious and unsettled times for many Americans, and the prevalence of divorce in this country now ought to be considered both a symptom and a cause.

HERBERT GOLD

Dance of the Divorced

✧✧✧✧✧✧✧

FRANK AND CYNTHIA had been acquainted for years, but were not friends. They had been propelled out of their separate marriages at almost the same time, although for different reasons; therefore, how natural for them to keep each other company now that both were in New York. "Honey, I understand. I sure do. Now let me tell you about the money from the other end. . . ."

Their love affair, which was not *truly* a love affair, could not last very long. They talked, talked, talked; they clung to each other and touched each other's soul. After a few months they went their separate ways. As bitterness about the resented spouse subsided, they each wearied of that first comfort of shame and chagrin. They wished they had not exchanged so many confessions; it was still marital—these fears and complaints over dinner, this passionate recompense for old slights and miseries. Their tender longing for each other was first too delicate, timorous; then too fierce, despairing. Remaining friends, all their talents for contempt exhausted by their destroyed marriages, they embarked on separate adventures which they felt had no apparent relevance to the conjugal walls within which they had been so long enclosed.

They guarded for each other that secret indulgence which the lucky divorced sometimes keep for their former husbands or wives. Nice Frank, nice Cynthia. It had not been True Love, but it had been Nice. They climbed over the wall into the distant world. They parted in peace. If only marriage could go so peaceably.

Frank had a Madison Avenue specialty—he wrote for several magazines that series of mournful letters which is machined out to delinquent subscribers. "*You* need to keep on being informed of the fast-moving events in our changing world. . . . *We* feel a neighborly obligation to keep on sending you. . . ."

Since he could perform much of this neighborly labor on the typewriter in his high-ceilinged studio room, he had time without undue strain during

339

the first year of his freedom to explore a folk singer, a Polish fur model, a Rorschach analyst, and an assistant to a Broadway producer. In his own mind he measured his true freedom from the weekend when, painfully, with regret and good hope, Cynthia and he had decided to find their fresh chances elsewhere.

"But you really don't remind me of my wife," he assured her. "You're a pal."

"But you're not like my husband at all, not a bit," she promised him.

"No, I have the brooding dark eyes and the long, sensitive fingers of the composer of heartfelt circulation letters."

"Oh, shush, Frank." And she touched him fondly. "These hands will play the violin once more."

They smiled. They agreed. "It's for the best," one of them may have said (or perhaps both of them merely thought). "I'll call you. We'll have lunches."

"Yes, call me. I'll always be glad to hear, Frank."

For several months he did not see her; then their orbits crossed briefly— he was with the folk singer, she with a music publisher; then they faded away from each other into the Manhattan winter. Driving home late up the East Side highway, he always thought of her—she had an apartment over- looking the river at 79th Street. And when the folk singer was forgotten, all but her names (she had two of them, real and stage, and, somehow, her daughter bore a third), Frank still remembered that evening when Cynthia and he had been reunited briefly, at the music publisher's penthouse. Since Cynthia's first husband had washed out of Alcoholics Anonymous before he got his wings, Frank found it mystifying that she could be attracted to a man who got so drunk at his own party. Too neat. She was much too intelligent not to find the parallel troubling. On the other hand, almost all unhappy men flee toward drink, and men without steadiness in love are always unhappy, so who could just automatically reject a man because he drank, when she might eventually make him happy and stop the waste?

He tried to see things this sentimental way, both sentimental and calcu- lating, as some like it; but she looked tired, and he couldn't see things this way. He was relieved when he heard from her directly—he asked her to lunch the next week, inquired, pried—that the music publisher was al- ready a thing of the past. She had another friend now. But she felt that there was no point in telling Frank about him now.

He agreed. No real point. Dance of the divorced.

The seasons rolled away. My God, he thought, meeting her on the street again, it's been two years now; and not two years from the time he left his wife, but two years since Cynthia and he had given it up. But she looked lovely, cool and slightly more plump in a light, old-fashioned dress of soft, clinging silk. She was not dressing like a Manhattan career girl these days. "Have lunch?"

"I suppose," she said.

"Today? Tomorrow?"

"No, not tomorrow. Soon. Don't name a day; call me."

She was putting him off! He now looked beneath the healthy plumpness to find that she was very tired; there was an eruption of permanent fatigue —eyes, mouth. Her smile seemed worn at the bright edge of lipstick. Can a mouth really change so fast? Her slightly heavy way of walking, toes turned out, was accentuated by the new weight—but still that delicate, high-bridged nose, that peacefully questing face, that patient, girlish hope in the eyes of a woman with one child already learning to read and another in kindergarten.

"It's been so long," he complained.

"Well, you know, old friends. . . . No hurry, Frank."

She would not let him name a time to meet her; again their orbits intersected at a party. Across most of a couch another drunk lay in tow. Tears abruptly filled Frank's eyes, and he turned away, sneezing. Pure selfishness, he thought. I have no right! It was because he remembered one of their long breakfast ceremonials after a tender, confiding night. He had been out of coffee in the morning. She had telephoned to make sure that her elder boy was getting off to nursery school all right, and then, while he shaved, she found everything, eggs and toast and orange marmalade and tea. Tea for breakfast. Spooned heaps of marmalade laced across the toast.

"Veddy Briddish," he had said. "You mean no more coffee?"

"Veddy. Not even instant, my friend."

After breakfast she had asked if he thought her five-year-old really understood about mommy's not sleeping at home. For sure the maid understood, which was not the same thing. He reassured her that she was doing the best she could.

They had taken good comfort, kissed, and parted, smiling.

Now she took one drunk after another. She had no right to repeat her husband. Why not repeat Frank, if she had to repeat? *He* was not that kind of feeble unconscientious objector to life. But, on the other hand, neither the folk singer nor the fur model nor anyone else had the steady gaze of Cynthia; none of them ever made tea for breakfast with such playful ceremony, or made tea for breakfast at all (of course, Frank seldom ran out of coffee). Memory of Cynthia did not protect him from argumentative bitches, foolish dolls, scented calculating machines—all those creatures with too much vanity and not enough pride. Cynthia was prideful, had dismissed vanity, yet had not taught him much.

Perhaps Frank had no right to feel such anger. But no argument against anger could spoil it, and Frank held his anger tight in his fist. He liked it; he liked his righteous nails in his righteous palm. Ah-*choo!* A sneeze, not tears.

Anyway, Cynthia's newest drunk was called Sam Rogers, and he had a sports-car agency in Queens. He used to be in advertising, and had started his new life by driving a rebuilt Rolls to district meetings. His most recent achievement was to put a Corvette motor in a classic MG chassis. Speedy Gonzales, Frank thought, over-working transmissions is his chief delight. Someplace he had a wife with garden chairs and a complete wash-and-wear closet and a subscription to *Better Homes and Gardens,* and he wanted to leave her for Cynthia, provided she bought garden furniture and wash-and-wear and a more advanced view of house decoration and architecture. What the devil was on Cynthia's mind? A career of rapid cornering, surliness over brake linings, ecstatic moments of getting into high gear in six seconds?

This time she consented to have lunch with him; he insisted.

He covered her hand with his. "Will these hands ever play the violin again?"

"What? Who?"

Old jokes between them. She did not remember. He went straight on.

"What is it with you, Cynthia? A character like that—Buck Rogers!— you *know* what I mean. Excuse my incoherence. Pent up and all that."

"Periods," she said vaguely. "You're excused."

"What?"

"You asked to be excused, Frank. I'm excusing you."

"OK, OK."

"But all right. Periods in a woman's life. He's nice to me. Sam."

"He needs me," Frank mimicked sadly.

"I never said that."

"But it's what you think. That's the power of the weak. They need you. The souses of New York need you!"

She colored as if slapped, flaming at the cheeks, a bluish white around the eyes and mouth, but she did not reply. She knew the value of her steady gaze and used it. Was there some underground explosion between Cynthia and her drunk that Frank had not been able to match in their careworn, conjugal, subsiding consolation together? Was all this angry protest merely envy for something he could never give her because he drank too little, needed her not enough? He did not demand her aid head-on, only sideways, incidentally, unlike those spoiled, overfilial boys. Was that their secret? At any rate, he took satisfaction from her flush and was undefeated by her eyes.

"A woman gets drunk in public," he said, "everyone is ashamed for her, men think she's a clod, a baggage. But a slob of a man gets drunk and there's a crowd of women who want to protect him, take care of him, the poor, sensitive, smelly kid. Help him sleep it off. Certain kinds of girls."

"You think more of looks—men do. We don't care so much about enlarged pores, spaces between the teeth, even empty spaces in the character. We like to fill them. Sure, I need to be needed by somebody, Frank, and whatever he may do that seems wrong in your eyes, Sam knows how to need me. . . ."

There was no good in this discussion. They were mouthing angry clichés from ten thousand analyses, an unclimbed mountain of graduate term papers. Still, no matter what they said above the food, when he ate with Cynthia there always seemed to be a fine crisp crust on bread and real butter. Crunch-crunch into breadsticks over lunch with unhappy, tired, pretty Cynthia. Having escaped from a nightmare of marriage, Frank still dreamed that eternal male dream of domesticity—good bed warmth, bacon frying in a well-watched pan on Sunday morning, the happy clutch of little children saying, "Dada." The dream was more real than this anxious babble, which made his jaw itch where his skin opened under the after-shave lotion; the dream was close in a pleasant lunch in one of those East Side Italian restaurants. It was three o'clock in the afternoon, and quiet, and a fine crisp crust on the bread, and real butter—again crunch-crunch. Submissive, she, too, took a breadstick, smiling.

"You make them look so good."

"I like."

"You have an infectious appetite. You make me want to share. I shouldn't—my figure."

"Eating doesn't make anybody fat. Listen to my theory. Eating feeds the metabolism, gives it strength to burn up calories, the more you eat the thinner you get. If you eat enough, you'll die of starvation. That's my Theory of Svelte Snackery. Just try to pronounce it and you'll lose five pounds."

She smiled and lifted a crisp, buttered breadstick in tribute.

Silence; then down they slipped once more. He insisted; he nagged.

"Don't tie yourself to Sam Rogers! You marry that creep, it'll be just like last time, only the second one has to be worse."

She was not really surprised by his rapid change of mood; the smile remained, though it seemed to show more teeth.

"Worse? I don't have the benefit of so many theories. But now at least I know what to expect in a broken marriage."

"Cynthia! I don't even like you to make jokes like that." And wanted to add, but didn't: You are good at so many things, but not at joking. Instead, he said, "You know, when you want to say something funny, you always signal it by blushing."

"Yes."

"You blush often."

"I suppose."

"Oh," he cried in deep distress, "just don't! Don't marry him! You can do so much better!"

"You really think I can live by calculations like that?" She did not blush now, it was no joke. Her face stiffened with a cold, explaining anger.

"Yes, I can float and meet more interesting men, maybe nicer men. Bouncing like a cork, parties and plays and trying to get a cab in the rain at one in the morning when everyone else in the world is trying to get the same damn cab. But it's just bouncing and floating. I'm thirty. I can do better and better each year for a couple of years. And then? *And then, Frank?*"

He had no answer.

"So I'll marry Sam and he won't drink so much. If he does, I'll hide the bottles. Sure, I like taking care of a man. I admit it. The best way I can. I know it about myself. Knowledge is power, yes? That's health?"

Frank gave up. The good was gone from the breadsticks and the sweet butter and the coffee which followed; his metabolism was no fun.

"Well, just promise not to do anything rash for a while," he said.

"All right. Nothing rash until November, when Sam will have his divorce. OK? Also I'll try not to resent you for talking to me like this."

"I was just going to ask you that, for later, you know, when you need someone to resent."

She tapped her forehead. "The old intuition. I knew. Worth millions on the open market, maybe more."

They separated at the sidewalk and shook hands very formally. They were separated before they shook hands, but he watched her hurrying off in the crowd from Third to Lexington Avenue, walking rather stiffly—the lady-knows-gentleman-watches-from-behind walk. Lady thinks about gentleman.

What her intuition had not told her was something which Frank knew by mere chatter—they would meet that evening at a large cocktail party given by a cigarette company's top copywriter to celebrate his discovery of extra bubbles and other qualities in its newer, finer filter. A friend of Frank's happened to tell him that Cynthia would be there. He walked across Central Park to the East Side later that October day; he watched the fading rose of a departed sun staining the sky and the musical spires and towers of Manhattan. He felt as tense and expectant as if . . . as if. . . . Well, he knew that the proper thing would be to avoid Cynthia for a time after their conversation at lunch. She would probably consider it a breach of tact. Scuffing leaves, he breathed the damp chill of the park and calmed his quaking, cowardly, inquisitive heart. He would see what came of him. In Manhattan a man can bury his disgraces from everyone but himself, who hardly counts.

At the party Sam Rogers was worse than ever. Probably he felt dragged out of place by Cynthia and was taking his revenge. A tall, florid, blotched complainer he was; a whining, handsome, purposeful drunk. He rang the note of cool disdain, complicated by a slow sway on his heels, to drive home the inside dope that he was a solid citizen with an automobile agency in Queens. He had given up the knife-grinders of Madison Avenue; he only came around now and then to congratulate himself by examining these museum dummies.

"It's not exactly un-American—hell, I used to be like that myself—it's just without *roots,*" said Sam Rogers. "Me, I got an agency—cars, not words—out on the Island." He hardly spoke to Cynthia, but Frank understood that his performance was largely for her sake, and she was thinking: Poor Sam. He needs so much help. Poor Sam. You have to be terribly lonely for years to be so eager to step on people before they step on you.

And Frank was thinking, as he watched her anxious glance keeping track of Sam: Those who handed us psychology like an ice-cream cone have a lot to answer for. He must remember to warn his children: Never take Freud from a stranger.

Sam was working hard. He was imagining a glorious fight which would expose the corruption of Manhattan as contrasted with the rural innocence and purity of Queens. To a narrow-breasted designer of shoes he said, "*You* can wear Ivy League suits, they're made by people like you for people like you—no shoulders." The young man drew himself up, his mouth flickered in a cold smile, he moved off. Unpersistent Sam was not following him. He had something new to try on someone else.

When Frank looked at Cynthia on the other side of the room, sitting with a book of photographs, trying to look busy, busily white and miserable, he felt Sam's drunken rudeness flying straight at her. They had a reason between them, some pain and destruction, and this elegant girl with the high, straight nose and wide, white forehead was taking it without protest.

Frank strode across the room and said to her, "Hello, Cynthia. I'm leaving now. May I take you home? Let's get out of here."

"Oh."

"Let's go, Cynthia. Let's have some coffee."

"Oh. Oh. You know I can't."

"Cynthia."

"Please. I can't."

He shrugged helplessly. He met two friends leaving, and on the way down the stairway his friends burst into laughter at something foolish he said. He asked if he resembled somebody named G. Willikers, because a lot of people were looking at him these days and saying, "Gee Willikers!" Nervous, liquored, popping laughter. Frank looked up at the second floor where the party was going on, and at Cynthia standing at the open French window, watching him, wringing her hands in that most primitive gesture of sorrow, as if she thought they were laughing at something he had said about her. Frank turned without a word and went running back up the stairs to her.

"I was just making jokes because I was sad."

"All right. I know."

"Why won't you go home with me, Cynthia?"

"I can't. I have to stay. What else can I do?" Sam Rogers was glaring at the two of them from the other side of the room, but for a moment his pride prevented his crossing. His inflamed eyes blinked angry warnings at them. He sprawled along a couch to look around someone who got in his way.

"Oh, Cynthia," Frank said, "take anything else. *Anything*. Even take me."

"Are you serious? You don't mean it."

The words had slipped out, and now he thought about what he had said and watched the colors changing in her very serious, frightened face. Red; more red; white.

"We know too much, Frank. We wouldn't even fight enough."

"Enough, but not too much."

"Maybe," she said.

"Yes, Cynthia? Yes? I *mean* it now."

"Yes, maybe you mean it. We're idiots. Idiots. Can we just go, and pick up my coat tomorrow?"

⬦

Herbert Gold was born in Lakewood, Ohio, in 1924, served in the Army in World War II, has a B.A. and an M.A. from Columbia University, and now lives in San Francisco. His short stories and novels have won him virtually all the grants and awards going: he spent two years in Paris on a Fulbright fellowship and a year in Haiti as a Buenos Aires Convention fellow; he has had a Guggenheim fellowship and a Hudson Review *fellowship and has won an O. Henry prize and an award from the National Institute of Arts and Letters; he has been a judge of the National Book Awards and several times was an American delegate to the Formentor Prize Conference; and he has had a Ford Foundation Theater fellowship to work at the San Francisco Actors' Workshop. He has visited or taught at many colleges and universities, including Cornell, Iowa, Brandeis, Western Reserve, Wayne State. His stories have appeared in* The New Yorker, The Atlantic, Harper's, The Saturday Evening Post, Playboy, Hudson Review, *and all sorts of other magazines. He has written nearly fifty stories; fourteen of them are collected in* Love and Like *(1960). He has also published seven novels:* The Birth of a Hero *(1951),* The Prospect Before Us *(1954),* The Man Who Was Not With It *(1956),* The Optimist *(1959),* Therefore Be Bold *(1960),* Salt *(1963), and* Fathers *(1967). Also, he has published a book of his essays,* The Age of Happy Problems *(1962), and edited two anthologies:* Fiction of the Fifties *(1959) and* First Person Singular: Essays for the Sixties *(1963). He is, both as an essayist and as a fiction writer, very much in touch with the times, very much "with it." Yet in some of his very best fiction, in his famous "The Heart of the Artichoke" and in other good stories, and in some of his novels, especially in* Therefore Be Bold *and* Fathers, *he has written about the past, at least his childhood past, and most effectively about his father and his own relations with him. This aspect of his fiction depicts the warm love and the humor and the authority of a first-generation Jewish immigrant family, and the secure (albeit they were Depression hard times), almost oppressively close-knit life centered around a family-owned grocery store in Cleveland. Often in his fiction he makes a telling contrast, explicitly or implicitly, between the warmth and security of those scenes and the cold lack of communication and love, the chaos and the insecurity, of modern life. Varying themes are developed as he portrays varying modern worlds he knows: the unsettled life of Americans living abroad, everywhere from Paris to Haiti; restless young couples teaching at midwestern campuses; the bizarre, dope-ridden world of the traveling carnival; the semisophisticated world of the professional people—artists or admen or publishers—in New York City; or the hip, swinging world of the Beat and semi-Beat in San Francisco and Los Angeles. And often, inevitably, he has written about divorce —most famously perhaps in "Love and Like," but in many other stories and novels. And usually we see the same contrast made: longing for the warmth and security and tenderness of marriage, the way things were; this put in direct confrontation with an unblinking, unsparing depiction of how impossibly different is the way things are now.*

This thematic contrast underlies "Dance of the Divorced." Gold shows in this story how ritualistic, how almost like going through the patterned steps of a dance, can be the behavior of formerly married men and women trying to find their way back to the way things once were. Divorce brings neither new life nor real freedom to either Frank or Cynthia, although they seem to seek it. Frank steps out into the obligatory sleeping-around with an assortment of other partners, identified by their occupation for the most part. Cynthia is attracted, as so many divorced people are said to be, by a sequence of people with the same characteristics as the first spouse. Much of Cynthia's and Frank's emotion, when they are together and when they are apart, goes toward an effort not so much to recapture the past as somehow to reshape it successfully. Their longing is not really for one another specifically, as much as it is for a return to the married state. Frank has his "dream of domesticity": warm bed, bacon frying, happy children saying "Dada." Cynthia knows how much she needs someone to need her. What makes it possible for them to get together at the end is that they've managed, by their dancing, to make one another the symbol of a new, better *past. They have, in their equally sorrowful, failed conditions, a reality for one another that is similar to the reality of their former spouses—and again, their dance enhances this. Just after their divorces they had their period of "marriage"—an affair, but "it was still marital" how they were together, and they were careful this time to part amiably. "They guarded for each other that secret indulgence which the lucky divorced sometimes keep for their former husbands or wives." Their coming-together at the end, back to their pseudo-marriage that ended so nicely and was really very pleasant, is not so much a new marriage as a reconciliation. They've stepped forward into the future, then back into the past; they've touched, then parted; whirled around; then come together again. It is just as if they had been partners in the first place.*

GRACE PALEY

Two Short Sad Stories from a Long and Happy Life

◇◇◇◇◇◇◇

1. *The Used-Boy Raisers*

THERE WERE TWO HUSBANDS disappointed by eggs.

I don't like them that way either, I said. Make your own eggs. They sighed in unison. One man was livid; one was pallid.

There isn't a drink around here, is there? asked Livid.

Never find one here, said Pallid. Don't look; driest damn house. Pallid pushed the eggs away, pain and disgust his escutcheon.

Livid said, Now really, isn't there a drink? Beer? he hoped.

Nothing, said Pallid, who'd been through the pantries, closets, and re-frigerators looking for a white shirt.

You're damn right, I said. I buttoned the high button of my powder-blue duster. I reached under the kitchen table for a brown paper bag full of an embroidery which asked God to Bless Our Home.

I was completing this motto for the protection of my sons, who were also Livid's. It is true that some months earlier, from a far place—the British plains in Africa—he had written hospitably to Pallid; I do think they're fine boys, you understand. I love them too, but Faith is their mother and now Faith is your wife. I'm so much away. If you want to think of them as yours, old man, go ahead.

Why, thank you, Pallid had replied, airmail, overwhelmed. Then he implored the boys, when not in use, to play in their own room. He made all efforts to be kind.

Now as we talked of time past and upon us, I pierced the ranch house that nestles in the shade of a cloud and a Norway maple, just under the golden script.

Ha-ha, said Livid, dripping coffee on his pajama pants, you'll never guess whom I met up with, Faith.

Who? I asked.

Saw your old boy friend Clifford at the Green Coq. He looks well. One thing must be said, he addressed Pallid, she takes good care of her men.

True, said Pallid.

How is he? I asked coolly. What's he doing? I haven't seen him in two years.

Oh, you'll never guess. He's marrying. A darling girl. She was with him. Little tootsies, little round bottom, little tummy—she must be twenty-two, but she looks seventeen. One long yellow braid down her back. A darling girl. Stubby nose, fat little underlip. Her eyes put on in pencil. Shoulders down like a dancer . . . slender neck. Oh, darling, darling.

You certainly observed her, said Pallid.

I have a functioning retina, said Livid. Then he went on. Better watch out, Faith. You'd be surprised, the dear little chicks are hatching out all over the place. All the sunny schoolgirls rolling their big black eyes. I hope you're really settled this time. To me, whatever is under the dam is in another county; however, in my life you remain an important person historically, he said. And that's why I feel justified in warning you. I must warn you. Watch out, sweetheart! he said, leaning forward to whisper harshly and give me a terrible bellyache.

What's all this about? asked Pallid innocently. In the first place, she's settled . . . and then she's still an attractive woman. Look at her.

Oh yes, said Livid, looking. An attractive woman. Magnificent, sometimes.

We were silent for several seconds in honor of that generous remark.

Then Livid said, Yes, magnificent, but I just wanted to warn you, Faith.

He pushed his eggs aside finally and remembered Clifford. A mystery wrapped in an enigma . . . I wonder why he wants to marry.

I don't know, it just ties a man down, I said.

And yet, said Pallid seriously, what would I be without marriage? In luminous recollection—a gay dog, he replied.

At this moment the boys entered: Richard the horse thief and Tonto the crack shot.

Daddy! they shouted. They touched Livid, tickled him, unbuttoned his pajama top, whistled at the several gray hairs coloring his chest. They tweaked his ear and rubbed his beard the wrong way.

Well, well, he cautioned. How are you boys, have you been well? You look fine. Sturdy. How are your grades? he inquired. He dreamed that they were just up from Eton for the holidays.

I don't go to school, said Tonto. I go to the park.

I'd like to hear the child read, said Livid.

Me. I can read, Daddy, said Richard. I have a book with a hundred pages.

Well, well, said Livid. Get it.

I kindled a fresh pot of coffee. I scrubbed cups and harassed Pallid into opening a sticky jar of damson-plum jam. Very shortly, what could be read, had been, and Livid, knotting the tie strings of his pants vigorously, approached me at the stove. Faith, he admonished, that boy can't read a tinker's damn. Seven years old.

Eight years old, I said.

Yes, said Pallid, who had just remembered the soap cabinet and was rummaging in it for a pint. If they were my sons in actuality as they are in everyday life, I would send them to one of the good parochial schools in the neighborhood where reading is taught. Reading. St. Bartholomew's, St. Bernard's, St. Joseph's.

Livid became deep purple and gasped. Over my dead body. *Merde,* he said in deference to the children. I've said, yes, you may think of the boys as your own, but if I ever hear they've come within an inch of that church, I'll run you through, you bastard. I was fourteen years old when in my own good sense I walked out of that grotto of deception, head up. You sonofa-bitch, I don't give a damn how *au courant* it is these days, how gracious to be seen under a dome on Sunday. . . . Shit! Hypocrisy. Corruption. Cave dwellers. Idiots. Morons.

Recalling childhood and home, poor Livid writhed in his seat. Pallid listened, head to one side, his brows gathering the onsets of grief.

You know, he said slowly, we iconoclasts . . . we free-thinkers . . . we latter-day masons . . . we idealists . . . we dreamers . . . we are never far from our nervous old mother, the Church. She is never far from us.

Wherever we are, we can hear, no matter how faint, her hourly bells, tolling the countryside, reverberating in the cities, bringing to our civilized minds the passionate deed of Mary. Every hour on the hour we are startled with remembrance of what was done for us. FOR US.

Livid muttered in great pain. Those bastards, oh oh oh, those contempti-ble, goddamnable bastards. Do we have to do the nineteenth century all over again? All right, he bellowed, facing us all, I'm ready. That Newman!

He turned to me for approval.

You know, I said, this subject has never especially interested me. It's your little dish of lava.

Pallid spoke softly, staring past the arched purple windows of his soul. I myself, although I lost God a long time ago, have never lost faith.

What the hell are you talking about, you moron? roared Livid. I have never lost my love for the wisdom of the Church of the World. When I go to sleep at night, I inadvertently pray. I also do so when I rise. It is not to God, it is to that unifying memory out of childhood. The first words I ever wrote were: What are the sacraments? Faith, can you ever forget your old grandfather intoning Kaddish? It will sound in your ears forever.

Are you kidding? I was furious to be drawn into their conflict. Kaddish? What do I know about Kaddish? Who's dead? You know my opinions perfectly well. I believe in the Diaspora, not only as a fact but a tenet. I'm against Israel on technical grounds. I'm very disappointed that they decided to become a nation in my lifetime. I believe in the Diaspora. After all, they *are* the chosen people. Don't laugh. They really are. But once they're huddled in one little corner of a desert, they're like anyone else: Frenchies, Italians, temporal nationalities. Jews have one hope only—to remain a remnant in the basement of world affairs—no, I mean something else—a splinter in the toe of civilizations, a victim to aggravate the conscience.

Livid and Pallid were astonished at my outburst, since I rarely express my opinion on any serious matter but only live out my destiny, which is to be, until my expiration date, laughingly the servant of man.

I continued. I hear they don't even look like Jews any more. A bunch of dirt farmers with no time to read.

They're your own people, Pallid accused, dilating in the nostril, clenching his jaw. And they're under the severest attack. This is not the time to revile them.

I had resumed my embroidery. I sighed. My needle was now deep in the clouds which were pearl gray and late afternoon. I am only trying to say that they aren't meant for geographies but for history. They are not supposed to take up space but to continue in time.

They looked at me with such grief that I decided to consider all sides of the matter. I said, Christ probably had all that trouble—now that you mention it—because he knew he was going to gain the whole world but he forgot Jerusalem.

When you married us, said Pallid, and accused me, didn't you forget Jerusalem?

I never forget a thing, I said. Anyway, guess what. I just read somewhere that England is bankrupt. The country is wadded with installment paper.

Livid's hand trembled as he offered Pallid a light. Nonsense, he said. That's not true. Nonsense. The great British Island is the tight little fist of the punching arm of the Commonwealth.

What's true is true, I said, smiling.

Well, I said, since no one stirred, do you think you'll ever get to work today? Either of you?

Oh, my dear, I haven't even seen you and the boys in over a year. It's quite pleasant and cozy here this morning, said Livid.

Yes, isn't it? said Pallid, the surprised host. Besides, it's Saturday.

How do you find the boys? I asked Livid, the progenitor.

American, American, rowdy, uncontrolled. But you look well, Faith. Plumper, but womanly and well.

Very well, said Pallid, pleased.

But the boys, Faith. Shouldn't they be started on something? Just lining up little plastic cowboys. It's silly, really.

They're so young, apologized Pallid, the used-boy raiser.

You'd both better go to work, I suggested, knotting the pearl-gray late-afternoon thread. Please put the dishes in the sink first. Please. I'm sorry about the eggs.

Livid yawned, stretched, peeked at the clock, sighed. Saturday or no, alas, my time is not my own. I've got an appointment downtown in about forty-five minutes, he said.

I do too, said Pallid. I'll join you on the subway.

I'm taking a cab, said Livid.

I'll split it with you, said Pallid.

They left for the bathroom, where they shared things nicely—shaving equipment, washstand, shower, and so forth.

I made the beds and put the aluminum cot away. Livid would find a hotel room by nightfall. I did the dishes and organized the greedy day; dinosaurs in the morning, park in the afternoon, peanut butter in between, and at the end of it all, to reward us for a week of beans endured, a noble rib roast with little onions, dumplings and pink applesauce.

Faith, I'm going now, Livid called from the hall. I put my shopping list aside and went to collect the boys, who were wandering among the rooms looking for Robin Hood. Go say goodbye to your father, I whispered.

Which one? they asked.

The real father, I said. Richard ran to Livid. They shook hands manfully. Pallid embraced Tonto and was kissed eleven times for his affection.

Goodbye now, Faith, said Livid. Call me if you want anything at all. Anything at all, my dear. Warmly with sweet propriety he kissed my cheek. Ascendant, Pallid kissed me with considerable business behind the ear.

Goodbye, I said to them.

I must admit that they were at last clean and neat, rather attractive, shiny men in their thirties, with the grand affairs of the day ahead of them. Dark night, the search for pleasure and oblivion were well ahead. Goodbye, I said, have a nice day. Goodbye, they said once more, and set off in pride on paths which are not my concern.

2. A Subject of Childhood

At home one Saturday and every Saturday, Richard drew eight-by-eleven portraits of stick men waving their arms. Tonto held a plastic horse in his hand and named it Tonto because its eyes were painted blue as his had been. I revised the hem of last year's dress in order to be up to the minute, chic, and *au courant* in the midst of spring. Strangers would murmur, "Look at her, isn't she wonderful? Who's her couturier?"

Clifford scrubbed under the shower, singing a Russian folk song. He rose in a treble of cold water to high C, followed by the scourging of the flesh. At last after four hots and three colds, he was strong and happy and he entered the living room, a steaming emanation. His face was round and rosy. He was noticeably hairless on the head. What prevented rain and shower water from running foolishly down his face? Heavy dark down-sloping brows. Beneath these his eyes were round and dark, amazed. This Clifford, my close friend, was guileless. He would not hurt a fly and he was a vegetarian.

As always, he was glad to see us. He had wrapped a large sun-bathing towel around his damp body. "Behold the man!" he shouted, and let the towel fall. He stood for a moment, gleaming and pleasant. Richard and Tonto glanced at him. "Cover yourself, for God's sakes, Clifford," I said.

"Take it easy, Faith," he called to the ear of reason. "The world is changing." Actually propriety did not embarrass him. It did not serve him. He peeked from behind the rubber plant where his pants, under and over, were heaped. When he reappeared, snapped and buttoned, he said, "Wake up, wake up. What's everyone slouching around for?" He poked Richard in the tummy. "A little muscle tone there, boy. Wake up."

Richard said, "I want to draw, Clifford."

"You can draw any time. I'm not always here. Draw tomorrow, Rich. Come on—fight me, boy. Fight. Come on . . . let's go, get me. You better get started, Richy, 'cause I'm gonna really punch you one. Here I come, ready or not!"

"Here *I* come," said Tonto, dropping his horse, and he whacked Clifford hard across the kidneys.

"Who did that?" asked Clifford. "What boy did that?"

"Me, me," said Tonto, jumping up and down. "Did I hurt you bad?"

"Killed me, yes sir, yes you did, and now I'm going to get *you*." He whirled. "I'm going to tickle you, that's what." He raised Tonto high above his head, a disposable item, then pitched him into the air-foam belly of the couch.

Richard tiptoed with the Teddy bear to a gentle rise, the sofa cushion, from which he crowned Clifford three times.

"Oh, I'm getting killed," cried Clifford. "They're all after me. They're very rough." Richard kicked him in the shin. "That's it," said Clifford. "Get it out! Get it all out! Boys! Out! Out!"

Tonto spit right into his eye. He wiped his cheek. He feinted and dodged the Teddy bear that was coming down again on his bowed head. Tonto leaped onto his back and got hold of his ears. "Ouch," said Clifford.

Richard found a tube of rubber cement in the bookcase and squirted it at Clifford's hairy chest.

"I'm wild," said Richard. "I am, I'm wild."

"So am I," said Tonto. "I'm the wildest boy in the whole park." He tugged at Clifford's ears. "I'll ride you away. I'm an elephant boy."

"He's a lazy camel," screamed Richard. "Bubbles, I want you to work."

"Pretend I'm the djinn," said Tonto in a high wail. "Giddap, Clifford."

"Me, me, me," said Richard, sinking to the floor. "It's me. I'm a poison snake," he said, slithering to Clifford's foot. "I'm a poison snake," he said, resting his chin on Clifford's instep. "I'm a terrible poison snake," he swore. Then he raised his head like the adder he is, and after a prolonged hiss, with all his new front teeth, he bit poor Clifford above the bone, in his Achilles' heel, which is his weak left ankle.

"Oh no, oh no . . ." Clifford moaned, then folded neatly at all joints.

"Mommy, Mommy, Mommy," cried Richard, for Clifford fell, twelve stone, on him.

"Oh, it's me," screamed Tonto, an elephant boy thrown by his horse, headlong into a trap of table legs.

And he was the one I reached first. I hugged him to my lap. "Mommy," he sobbed, "my head hurts me. I wish I could get inside you." Richard lay, a crushed snake in the middle of the floor, without breath, without tears, angry.

Well, what of Clifford? He had hoisted his sorrowful self into an armchair and lay there lisping on a bloody tongue which he himself had bitten, "Faith, Faith, the accumulator, the accumulator!"

Bruised and tear-stricken, the children agreed to go to bed. They forgot to say it was too early to nap. They forgot to ask for their bears. They lay side by side and clutched each other's thumb. Here was the love that myth or legend has imposed on brothers.

I re-entered the living room where Clifford sat, a cone like an astrologer's hat on his skin-punctured place. Just exactly there, universal energies converged. The stationary sun, the breathless air in which the planets swing were empowered now to make him well, to act, in their remarkable art, like aspirin.

"We've got to have a serious talk," he said. "I really can't take those kids. I mean, Faith, you know yourself I've tried and tried. But you've done something to them, corrupted their instincts in some way or other. Here we were, having an absolutely marvelous time, rolling around making all kinds of free noise, and look what happened—like every other time, someone got hurt. I mean I'm really hurt. We should have all been relaxed. Easy. It should have been all easy. Our bodies should have been so easy. No one should've been hurt, Faith."

"Do you mean it's my fault you all got hurt?"

"No doubt about it, Faith, you've done a rotten job."

"Rotten job?" I said.

"Lousy," he said.

I gave him one more chance. "Lousy?" I asked.

"Oh my god! Stinking!" he said.

Therefore, the following—a compendium of motivations and griefs, life to date:

Truthfully, Mondays through Fridays—because of success at work—my ego is hot; I am a star; whoever can be warmed by me, I may oblige. The flat scale stones of abuse that fly into that speedy atmosphere are utterly consumed. Untouched, I glow my little thermodynamic way.

On Saturday mornings in my own home, however, I face the sociological law called the Obtrusion of Incontrovertibles. For I have raised these kids, with one hand typing behind my back to earn a living. I have raised them all alone without a father to identify themselves with in the bathroom like all the other little boys in the playground. Laugh. I was forced by inclement management into a yellow-dog contract with Bohemia, such as it survives. I have stuck by it despite the encroachments of kind relatives who offer ski pants, piano lessons, tickets to the rodeo. Meanwhile I have serviced Richard and Tonto, taught them to keep clean and hold an open heart on the subjects of childhood. We have in fact risen mightily from toilets in the hall and scavenging in great cardboard boxes at the Salvation Army for underwear and socks. It has been my perversity to do this alone, except for the one year their father was living in Chicago with Claudia Lowenstill and she was horrified that he only sent bicycles on the fifth birthday. A whole year of gas and electricity, rent and phone payments followed. One day she caught him in the swiveling light of truth, a grand figure who took a strong stand on a barrel of soapsuds and went down clean. He is now on the gold coast of another continent, enchanted by the survival of clandestine civilizations. Courts of kitchen drama cannot touch him.

All the same, I gave Clifford one more opportunity to renege and be my friend. I said, "Stinking? I raised them lousy?"

This time he didn't bother to answer because he had become busy gathering his clothes from different parts of the room.

Air was filtering out of my two collapsing lungs. Water rose, bubbling to enter, and I would have died of instantaneous pneumonia—something I never have heard of—if my hand had not got hold of a glass ash tray and, entirely apart from my personal decision, flung it.

Clifford was on his hands and knees looking for the socks he'd left under the armchair on Friday. His back was to me; his head convenient to the trajectory. And he would have passed away a blithering idiot had I not been blind with tears and only torn off what is anyway a vestigial ear lobe.

Still, Clifford is a gentle person, a consortment of sweet dispositions. The sight of all the blood paralyzed him. He hulked, shuddering; he waited on his knees to be signaled once more by Death, the Sheriff from the Styx.

"You don't say things like that to a woman," I whispered. "You damn stupid jackass. You just don't say anything like that to a woman. Wash yourself, moron, you're bleeding to death."

I left him alone to tie a tourniquet around his windpipe or doctor himself according to present-day plans for administering first aid in the Great Globular and Coming War.

I tiptoed into the bedroom to look at the children. They were asleep. I covered them and kissed Tonto, my baby, and "Richard, what a big boy you are," I said. I kissed him too. I sat on the floor, rubbing my cheek on Richard's rubbly fleece blanket until their sweet breathing in deep sleep quieted me.

A couple of hours later Richard and Tonto woke up picking their noses, sneezing, grumpy, then glad. They admired the ticktacktoes of Band-Aid I had created to honor their wounds. Richard ate soup and Tonto ate ham. They didn't inquire about Clifford, since he had a key which had always opened the door in or out.

That key lay at rest in the earth of my rubber plant. I felt discontinued. There was no one I wanted to offer it to.

"Still hungry, boys?" I asked. "No, sir," said Tonto. "I'm full up to here," leveling at the eyes.

"I'll tell you what," I came through with a stunning notion. "Go on down and play."

"Don't shove, miss," said Richard.

I looked out the front window. Four flights below, armed to the teeth, Lester Stukopf waited for the enemy. Carelessly I gave Richard this classified information. "Is he all alone?" asked Richard.

"He is," I said.

"O.K., O.K." Richard gazed sadly at me. "Only, Faith, remember, I'm going down because I feel like it. Not because you told me."

"Well, naturally," I said.

"Not me," said Tonto.

"Oh, don't be silly, you go too, Tonto. It's so nice and sunny. Take your new guns that Daddy sent you. Go on, Tonto."

"No, sir, I hate Richard and I hate Lester. I hate those guns. They're baby guns. He thinks I'm a baby. You better send him a picture."

"Oh, Tonto——"

"He thinks I suck my thumb. He thinks I wet my bed. That's why he sends me baby guns."

"No, no, honey. You're no baby. Everybody knows you're a big boy."

"He is not," said Richard. "And he does so suck his thumb and he does so wet his bed."

"Richard," I said, "Richard, if you don't have anything good to say, shut your rotten mouth. That doesn't help Tonto, to keep reminding him."

"Goodbye," said Richard, refusing to discuss, but very high and first-born. Sometimes he is nasty, but he is never lazy. He returned in forty-five seconds from the first floor to shout, "As long as he doesn't wet my bed, what do I care?"

Tonto did not hear him. He was brushing his teeth, which he sometimes does vigorously seven times a day, hoping they will loosen. I think they are loosening.

I served myself hot coffee in the living room. I organized comfort in the armchair, poured the coffee black into a white mug that said MAMA, tapped cigarette ash into a ceramic hand-hollowed by Richard. I looked into the square bright window of daylight to ask myself the sapping question: What is man that woman lies down to adore him?

At the very question mark Tonto came softly, sneaky in socks, to say, "I have to holler something to Richard, Mother."

"Don't lean out that window, Tonto. Please, it makes me nervous."

"I have to tell him something."

"No."

"Oh yes," he said. "It's awful important, Faith. I really *have* to."

How could I permit it? If he should fall, everyone would think I had neglected them, drinking beer in the kitchen or putting eye cream on at the vanity table behind closed doors. Besides, I would be bereaved forever. My grandmother mourned all her days for some kid who'd died of earache at the age of five. All the other children, in their own municipal-pension and federal welfare years, gathered to complain at her deathside when she was ninety-one and heard her murmur, "Oh, oh, Anita, breathe a little, try to breathe, my little baby."

With tears in my eyes I said, "O.K., Tonto, I'll hold onto you. You can tell Richard anything you have to."

He leaned out onto the air. I held fast to one thick little knee. "Richie," he howled. "Richie, hey, Richie!" Richard looked up, probably shielding his eyes, searching for the voice. "Richie, hey, listen, I'm playing with your new birthday-present army fort and all them men."

Then he banged the window shut as though he knew nothing about the nature of glass and tore into the bathroom to brush his teeth once more in triumphant ritual. Singing through toothpaste and gargle, "I bet he's mad," and in lower key, "He deserves it, he stinks."

"So do you," I shouted furiously. While I sighed for my grandmother's loss, he had raised up his big mouth against his brother. "You really stink!"

"Now listen to me. I want you to get out of here. Go on down and play. I need ten minutes all alone. Anthony, I might kill you if you stay up here."

He reappeared, smelling like peppermint sticks at Christmas. He stood on one foot, looked up into my high eyes, and said, "O.K., Faith. Kill me."

I had to sit immediately then, so he could believe I was his size and stop picking on me.

"Please," I said gently, "go out with your brother. I have to think, Tonto."

"I don't wanna. I don't have to go anyplace I don't wanna," he said. "I want to stay right here with you."

"Oh, please, Tonto, I have to clean the house. You won't be able to do a thing or start a good game or anything."

"I don't care," he said. "I want to stay here with you. I want to stay right next to you."

"O.K., Tonto. O.K. I'll tell you what, go to your room for a couple of minutes, honey, go ahead."

"No," he said, climbing onto my lap. "I want to be a baby and stay right next to you every minute."

"Oh, Tonto," I said, "please, Tonto." I tried to pry him loose, but he put his arm around my neck and curled up right there in my lap, thumb in mouth, to be my baby.

"Oh, Tonto," I said, despairing of one solitary minute. "Why can't you go play with Richard? You'll have fun."

"No," he said, "I don't care if Richard goes away, or Clifford. They can go do whatever they wanna do. I don't even care. I'm never gonna go away. I'm gonna stay right next to you forever, Faith."

"Oh, Tonto," I said. He took his thumb out of his mouth and placed his open hand, its fingers stretching wide, across my breast. "I love you, Mama," he said.

"Love," I said. "Oh love, Anthony, I know."

I held him so and rocked him. I cradled him. I closed my eyes and leaned on his dark head. But the sun in its course emerged from among the water towers of downtown office buildings and suddenly shone white and bright on me. Then through the short fat fingers of my son, interred forever, like a black and white barred king in Alcatraz, my heart lit up in stripes.

♦

Grace Paley was born in the Bronx in 1922, attended New York public schools, Hunter College, and New York University, and now lives in New York City. Her first and so far only published book is The Little Disturbances of Man *(1959), a collection of short stories. Her stories are sometimes of Jewish family life in the past, but more often of modern life and often concerned with problems of divorce, remarriage, absent husbands, errant lovers. Not only is the subject matter contemporary, but so is the tone—mocking, wryly glib, always humorous—a tone that nevertheless somehow manages never to be at odds with the often genuinely poignant situations and characters she creates.*

In "Two Short Sad Stories from a Long and Happy Life" we see some of the little disturbances of man that are in fact the life problems of mod-

ern, educated, middle-class mothers. The mother, Faith, is here the all-powerful "patriarch" because she is the one who takes on the responsibility for the family. She derives her insistence on the importance of "family" from her Jewish grandmother. And she sees family, as she sees the Jews, as "the chosen people": they may not be supposed to take up space, but they must continue in time. She finds, however, that the men in her life are more concerned with their own feelings and with manners and matters of place than with what to her are the real "subjects of childhood"—love, honor, dignity, and imagination. Pallid and Livid, husbands both, fathers both, are in agreement about everything, from eggs to razors to the arguability of schooling and raising "used boys," whom they see as objects belonging to the household. Emancipated through her pride in her own work, where she is "a star," in her own body, which is "magnificent, sometimes," Faith is still traditional in her expectations for family life. She embroiders her motto, she will cook the big meal, and she has always organized "the greedy day." She can get by, she can cope with Bohemia and the Salvation Army baskets, and "she takes good care of her men," as they themselves say. But she cannot answer "the sapping question: What is man that woman lies down to adore him?" Certainly he is not the family patriarch. He is, for her, a variety of "humours"—that is, either Pallid or Livid or "a consortment of sweet dispositions" (Clifford). They in turn have become objects in her household where she is the continuing force for cohesion and love, for survival in the city. The men are hers to keep clean and neat, and hers in "the dark night, the search for pleasure and oblivion." She sees her destiny to be "until my expiration date, laughingly, the servant of man." She does not put herself forward in a militant feminist manner; she holds no brief for herself as a professional woman or as an intellectual. "I rarely express my opinion on any serious matter," she says; and when the husbands set out together with "the grand affairs of the day ahead of them," she knows that those "are not my concern." Because she has children, the men in her life are all past, present, or potential fathers, a role they define intellectually but for which, because of divorce, they have no real responsibility. Livid, the "real" father, is "enchanted by the survival of clandestine civilizations" but cannot deal with "the courts of kitchen drama" at home. Pallid implores the boys "when not in use, to play in their own room." Clifford attempts to present a masculine image, but when the roughhouse gets too much for him, complains: "It should all have been easy." Only Faith, objective and amused by the whole situation, including her own passionate involvement, can afford to see the failures of family life as short sad stories, little disturbances, in a long and happy life.

JAMES PURDY

Don't Call Me by My Right Name

◇◇◇◇◇◇◇

HER NEW NAME was Mrs. Klein. There was something in the meaning that irritated her. She liked everything about her husband except his name and that had never pleased her. She had fallen in love with him before she found out what his name was. Once she knew he was Klein, her disappointment had been strong. Names do make a great difference, and after six months of marriage she found herself still not liking her name. She began using more and more her maiden name. Then she always called herself on her letters Lois McBane. Her husband seldom saw the mail arrive so perhaps he did not know, and had he known she went by her old name he might not have cared enough to feel any particular hurt.

Lois Klein, she often thought as she lay next to her husband in bed. It is not the name of a woman like myself. It does not reflect my character.

One evening at a party when there had been more drinking for her than usual, she said offhand to him in the midst of some revelry: "I would like you to change your name."

He did not understand. He thought that it was a remark she was making in drink which did not refer to anything concrete, just as once she had said to him, "I want you to begin by taking your head off regularly." The remark had meant nothing, and he let it pass.

"Frank," she said, "you must change your name, do you hear? I cannot go on being Mrs. Klein."

Several people heard what it was she said, and they laughed loudly so that Lois and Frank would hear them appreciating the remark.

"If you were all called Mrs. Klein," she said turning to the men who were laughing, "you would not like to be Mrs. Klein either."

Being all men, they laughed harder.

"Well, you married him, didn't you," a man said, "and we guess you will have to keep his name."

"If he changed his name," another of the men said, "what name would you have him change it to?"

Frank put his hand on her glass, as though to tell her they must go home, but she seized the glass with his hand on it and drank quickly out of it.

"I hadn't thought what name I did want," she said, puzzled.

"Well, you aren't going to change your name," Frank said. "The gentlemen know that."

"The gentlemen do?" she asked him. "Well, I don't know what name I would like it changed to," she admitted to the men.

"You don't look much like Mrs. Klein," one of the men said and began to laugh again.

"You're not friends!" she called back at them.

"What are we, then?" they asked.

"Why don't I look like Mrs. Klein?" she wanted to know.

"Don't you ever look in the mirror?" one of the men replied.

"We ought to go, Lois," her husband said.

She sat there as though she had heard the last of the many possible truths she could hear about herself.

"I wonder how I will get out of here, Frank," she said.

"Out of where, dear?" he wondered. He was suddenly sad enough himself to be dead, but he managed to say something to her at this point.

"Out of where I seem to have got into," she told him.

The men had moved off now and were laughing among themselves. Frank and Lois did not notice this laughter.

"I'm not going to change my name," he said, as though to himself. Then turning to her: "I know it's supposed to be wrong to tell people when they're drunk the insane whim they're having is insane, but I am telling you now and I may tell the whole room of men."

"I have to have my name changed, Frank," she said. "You know I can't stand to be tortured. It is too painful and I am not young anymore. I am getting old and fat."

"No wife of mine would ever be old or fat," he said.

"I just cannot be Mrs. Klein and face the world."

"Anytime you want me to pull out is all right," he said. "Do you want me to pull out?"

"What are you saying?" she wanted to know. "What did you say about pulling out?"

"I don't want any more talk about your changing your name or I intend to pull up stakes."

"I don't know what you're talking about. You know you can't leave me. What would I do, Frank, at my age?"

"I told you no wife of mine is old."

"I couldn't find anybody now, Frank, if you went."

"Then quit talking about changing our name."

"*Our* name? I don't know what you mean by *our* name."

He took her drink out of her hand and when she coaxed and whined he struck her not too gently over the mouth.

"What was the meaning of that?" she wanted to know.

"Are you coming home, Mrs. Klein?" he said, and he hit her again. Her lip was cut against her teeth so that you could see it beginning to bleed.

"Frank, you're abusing me," she said, white and wide-eyed now, and as though tasting the blood slightly with the gin and soda mix.

"Mrs. Klein," he said idiotically.

It was one of those fake dead long parties where nobody actually knows anybody and where people could be pushed out of windows without anybody's being sure until the morrow.

"I'm not going home as Mrs. Klein," she said.

He hit her again.

"Frank, you have no right to hit me just because I hate your name."

"If you hate my name what do you feel then for me? Are you going to act like my wife or not?"

"I don't want to have babies, Frank. I will not go through that at my age. Categorically not."

He hit her again so that she fell on the floor, but this did not seem to surprise either her or him because they both continued the conversation.

"I can't make up my mind what to do," she said, weeping a little. "I know of course what the safe thing is to do."

"Either you come out of here with me as Mrs. Klein, or I go to a hotel room alone. Here's the key to the house," he said, and he threw it on the floor at her.

Several of the men at the party had begun to notice what was really going on now. They thought that it was married clowning at first and they began to gather around in a circle, but what they saw had something empty and stiff about it that did not interest and yet kept one somehow watching. For one thing, Mrs. Klein's dress had come up and exposed her legs, which were not beautiful.

"I can't decide if I can go on with his name," she explained from the floor position to the men.

"Well, it's a little late, isn't it, Mrs. Klein," one of the men said in a sleepy voice.

"It's never too late, I don't suppose, is it?" she inquired. "Oh, I can't believe it is even though I feel old."

"Well, you're not young," the same man ventured. "You're too old to be lying there."

"My husband can't see my point of view," she explained. "And that is why he can't understand why his name doesn't fit me. I was unmarried too long, I suppose, to suddenly surrender my own name. I have always been known professionally and socially under my own name and it is hard to change now, I can tell you. I don't think I can go home with him unless he lets me change my name."

"I will give you just two minutes," Mr. Klein said.

"For what? Only two minutes for what?" she cried.

"To make up your mind what name you are going out of here with."

"I know, men," she said, "what the sensible decision is, and tomorrow, of course, when I'm sober I will wish I had taken it."

Turning to Frank Klein, she said simply, "You will have to go your way without me."

He looked hurriedly around as though looking for an exit to leave by, and then he looked back to her on the floor as though he could not come to a decision.

"Come to your senses," Frank Klein said unemphatically.

"There were hundreds of Kleins in the telephone directory," she went on, "but when people used to come to my name they recognized at once that I was the only woman going under my own special name."

"For Jesus Christ's sake, Lois," he said, turning a peculiar green color.

"I can't go with you as Mrs. Klein," she said.

"Well, let me help you up," he said.

She managed to let him help her up.

"I'm not going home with you, but I will send you in a cab," he informed her.

"Are you leaving me?" she wanted to know.

He did not know what to say. He felt anything he said might destroy his mind. He stood there with an insane emptiness on his eyes and lips.

Everyone had moved off from them. There was a silence from the phonograph and from the TV set which had both been going at the same time. The party was over and people were calling down to cabs from all the windows.

"Why won't you come home with me?" she said in a whisper.

Suddenly he hurried out the door without waiting for her.

"Frank!" she called after him, and a few of the men from the earlier group came over and joked with her.

"He went out just like a boy, without any sense of responsibility," she said to them without any expression in her voice.

She hurried on out too, not waiting to put her coat on straight.

She stood outside in the fall cold and shivered. Some children went by dressed in Hallowe'en costumes.

"Is she dressed as anybody?" one of the children said pointlessly.

"Frank!" she began calling. "I don't know what is happening really," she said to herself.

Suddenly he came up to her from behind a hedge next to where she was standing.

"I couldn't quite bring myself to go off," he said.

She thought for a minute of hitting him with her purse which she had remembered to bring, but she did nothing now but watch him.

"Will you change your name?" she said.

"We will live together the way we have been," he said not looking at her.

"We can't be married, Frank, with that name between us."

Suddenly he hit her and knocked her down to the pavement.

She lay there for a minute before anything was said.

"Are you conscious?" he said crouching down beside her. "Tell me if you are suffering," he wanted to know.

"You have hurt something in my head, I think," she said, getting up slightly on one elbow.

"You have nearly driven me out of my mind," he said, and he was making funny sounds in his mouth. "You don't know what it means to have one's name held up to ridicule like this. You are such a cruel person, Lois."

"We will both change our names, if you like," she said.

"Why do you torture me?" he said. "Why is it you can't control your power to torture?"

"Then we won't think about it, we will go home," she said, in a cold comforting voice. "Only I think I am going to be sick," she warned.

"We will go home," he said in a stupid voice.

"I will let you call me Mrs. Klein this one evening, then tomorrow we will have a good talk." At the same moment she fell back on the walk.

Some young men from the delicatessen who had been doing inventory came by and asked if there was anything they could do.

"My wife fell on the walk," he said. "I thought she was all right. She was talking to me just a moment ago."

"Was it your wife, did you say?" The younger man leaned down to look at her.

"Mrs. Klein," Frank replied.

"You are Mr. Klein, then?"

"I don't understand," the older of the two young men said. "You don't look somehow like her husband."

"We have been married six months."

"I think you ought to call a doctor," the younger man said. "She is bleeding at the mouth."

"I hit her at a party," Frank said.

"What did you say your name was?" the older man asked.

"Mr. Klein. She is Mrs. Klein," Frank told them.

The two men from the delicatessen exchanged looks.

"Did you push her?" the one man asked.

"Yes," Frank said. "I hit her. She didn't want to be Mrs. Klein."

"You're drunk," the one man ventured an opinion.

Lois suddenly came to. "Frank, you will have to take me home," she said. "There is something wrong with my head. My God," she began to scream, "I am in awful pain."

Frank helped her up again.

"Is this your husband?" the one man asked.

She nodded.

"What is your name?" he wanted to know.

"It's none of your business," she said.

"Are you Mrs. Klein?" he asked.

"No," Lois replied, "I don't happen to be Mrs. Klein."

"Come on, J. D., we can't get mixed up in this," the younger man said. "Whatever the hell their names are."

"Well, I'm not Mrs. Klein, whoever you are," she said.

Immediately then she struck Frank with the purse and he fell back in surprise against the building wall.

"Call me a cab, you cheap son of a bitch," she said. "Can't you see I'm bleeding?"

◇

James Purdy was born in Ohio, attended the University of Chicago, worked in Latin America for the U.S. Office of Education and did illustrative drawings for his first books, the collection Don't Call Me by My Right Name *and the novella* 63: Dream Palace, *which he published privately in 1956. These works were later reprinted in* Color of Darkness (1961); *and more stories, as well as two short plays, appear in* Children Is All (1961). *He has written four novels:* Malcolm (1959), *featuring an immobilized bench sitter like Jacob Horner;* The Nephew (1960), *an unsparing look under the surface of life in a small town in America;* Cabot Wright Begins (1964), *about a "moral" rapist in a "corrupt" American society; and* Eustace Chisholm and the Works (1967), *about frightening goings-on in a boardinghouse in Chicago in the Depression. All of Purdy's work has a macabre quality, something of the appallingly convincing projection of reality that occurs in an unpleasant dream. In conversations between characters, for instance, which is the form a great many of his stories take, the people always talk slightly off the point, in a way that is both quite realistic—for Purdy has a fine "ear" for the aimlessness of dialogue—and also somehow frighteningly surrealistic, with the innuendo that some other significance— perhaps even a sinister significance—lurks behind even the most commonplace remark.*

In "Don't Call Me by My Right Name," Purdy shows us the urban non-

family in its social habitat, the drinking party. In a marriage based on love without family, individual identity is likely to be in conflict with family role. Mrs. Klein has lost her own sense of her own "professional and social" uniqueness and become one of "hundreds of Kleins in the telephone directory." It would make sense to be Mrs. Klein if she had children, but she is "too old for that." It does not mean anything, she feels, to be a wife under these circumstances. She and Mr. Klein speak to each other in blows that cause pain but seem strangely unrelated to the problem. There is not even a sense of feminine and masculine roles here; both are brutal, stupid, and somehow neuter people, newly related by marriage in a way that seems distasteful and meaningless to them. But they are together. There is no alternative, no lack of love; there is even a weird companionship in the drinking and slugging matches, and they go "home" together. There seems to be no more reason to leave each other than to stay together. Certainly "family" does not seem the right name for such a bond, but it is the only connection these two people have. As is becoming increasingly common in an increasingly urbanized world, the identifying relationships with other members of a large family or with neighbors in a community—the relationships that would help to tell Mrs. Klein who she is and what is expected of her—are simply not available.

PHILIP L. GREENE

One of You Must Be
Wendell Corey

◇◇◇◇◇◇◇

LIL WAGNER'S MARRIAGE was on the rocks when I first met her. She was at a point where her need for spiritual renewal came from Erich Fromm. *"The Art of Loving,"* she said to me with conviction, "if I had known before I met Ben, if I could have talked with my analyst before he went to California. . . ." The Fromm revelation came to me in a surprised voice. Lil's constant seizing of the obvious and investing it with wonder—another secret uncovered to reward her with a new life—kept her in a perpetual cycle of desire, rapt discovery, and flat-eyed disillusionment. Lil was always a cultural idea away. This caused an impasse between her and Ben, who was always on the frontier of an idea. This situation made for a most satisfactory lesion. They knew what was wounding them. Ben was all modernity, in the vanguard of good causes, always in control of the intellectual apparatus rigged for him by the monopolists of the mid-city mind—*Dissent, Commentary*, the *New Leader*. "Can't you see," he said to me once, while Lil was looking vacantly out of the window onto Waverly Place, "that the social mobility of the new class depends on the morality of the cash nexus." Lil said, "Oh, shit," and walked out of the room. Ben stared after her, looked back at me, and went on. "Take Weber's view of the Protestant ethic and update it to give the petit bourgeoisie its function under the new capitalism. What do you have? The little man with just enough illusions to keep him morally bankrupt forever. I mentioned this to my analyst, and do you know what he said? 'Don't you think you're hiding behind all this, Ben.' "

Lil's doctor had called Ben's doctor to discuss a possible separation—this at the suggestion of Lil, who had thrown herself at the mercy of a new idea: why shouldn't the transferents involve themselves directly in the transferers' problems. When Ben found a place on Hudson Street over a wholesale meat market and refused to put a phone in, Lil's mother sent him a telegram: "Lil wants to try again. Please call." Ben called. Possessed with the idea of effecting a moral sacrifice—he wanted it desperately—he persuaded Lil to a reconciliation. That night, Ben told me later with embarrassing ingenuousness, they got into bed, and he couldn't get an erection. He cried. Lil laughed at him, and he hit her in the face, once, a short, open-handed slap. She screamed at him, "You can punch, but you can't screw, you lousy fat louse."

Shortly after that at a gathering at Marsha Weinstein's house she told me in a drawn voice that she had given up sex for yogurt and carrot juice. Marsha, her best friend, was a ballet dancer when she was not working part-time for Secretaries Anonymous. Marsha's three abortions had taken the limber out of her legs, which were running to fat, and she had recommended the Health Shoppe on Madison Avenue right around the corner from her analyst. Lil had decided to move in with Marsha, the reconciliation with Ben a washout. Larry Jonas, Marsha's new man, was in Washington doing a study of pressure groups and would not be back for a while. Larry had been Lil's boy friend, so she felt a vicarious renewal with Larry in staying at Marsha's. Larry had been good to her, but after two years of indecision, she found Ben at a party given by Murray Abramson, whose book, *Existential Psychodynamics,* had stirred the psychological community. Murray had studied at the W. A. White school with Ben before Ben decided to go into his father's medical supply business. Lil told me that Ben was the warmest, brightest, tenderest man she had ever met. "I never knew about social consciousness before I met Ben," she said. Ben had admired Larry's work with the American Civil Liberties Union and knew too that Larry was sleeping with Lil, so that he found the usurpation of Larry's girl a moral problem painful enough to engage him full time. "I knew something was wrong," Lil said, "the night Ben took me home from Murray's party, but he told me later that he was discussing the problem with his doctor. He had a premature ejaculation; he came all over my dress before I had time to take it off. He said the Larry problem was a projection of an infantile regression, a kind of Oedipal return, since he had always thought of Larry as a kind of father figure."

The marriage had gone on like that for four years, deteriorating steadily. Toward the end, I was having dinner at the Cookery with Merle Jonas, Larry's kid brother. We had just come from Max Lerner's third lecture at The New School where Lerner brilliantly illustrated his thesis of the dynamics of American pluralism by showing the bipolar attitude of the nation at large toward abortion, a topic Merle continued with great expertise, over a cookeryburger. "Marsha has had three—one in Jersey, one in Puerto Rico, and one right here on Fifth Avenue. Lerner is right because this problem epitomizes the indigenous moral strength of the American people. In the face of official sanctions against it, there is a remarkable pragmatic will operating."

When Merle told me that Marsha was having some people over and that Lil would be there, I accepted the invitation. I was at loose ends myself and Lil had looked plaintively neurotic the last time I had seen her. I knew that her health-food phase was temporary, and I hoped I might be just the thing to renew her contact with love. She was leaning heavily on her new Frommian world view. Merle had to pick up Tibby Barrett, Lil's old roommate at Oswego State College, who had recently arrived from Goshen and had taken a one and a half on Jane Street just around the corner from the old cat and dog store that was being torn down to make way for a luxury apartment, one of a number around the West Village that were following an artist motif. The Van Gogh and The Rembrandt had already been built. The new one was called The Picasso Arms. Tibby was doing research at *Newsweek*. Merle, who was writing advertising copy, met her for lunch every day in front of the library lions.

When we arrived at Marsha's Lil was sitting on the couch between Murray Abramson and his wife Lisa, who greeted me with a warm voice edged with a Hungarian accent. She was finishing her work at the White school. Murray and Lisa were planning to start a husband-and-wife group therapy experiment. As the husband-and-wife doctor team they would take only husband-and-wife teams as patients. Murray's chapter on existential therapy for marital groups had been published as an article in the *Saturday Evening Post*. When Marsha came in with a tray of stuffed mushrooms she announced that Larry had just called and would be arriving from Washington any minute. Over drinks Lil posed the problem of pre-non-post-extra-marital relations to Murray. Murray, with Lisa counterpointing in soft Hungarian, suggested that behavioral patterns weren't subject to moral judgments, only analysis and clarification. Lil was overwhelmed by the simple logic of Murray's position. Larry arrived, kissed Marsha and Lil, and added that Murray's view could be applied to the law; in fact his trip to Washington had shown that the sociological carry-over into law had in effect reduced the moral difficulties of law immeasurably. Murray said that he didn't think of sex as sociological. "Sociology is what happens after the behaviorists get finished. Understanding human actions, especially group action, is the psychologists' business. The sociologist puts down in his notebook the kind of hors d'oeuvres served in a group. For the sociologist the great question is: are we or are we not a stuffed mushroom group?"

Then Murray introduced a game called "Psychology." "Someone goes out of the room," he explained, "one of the group is 'it,' and the person excluded is called back and must identify the one chosen by a series of associational questions. For example, you might ask: 'If this person was a fruit, what kind would he be, or if he was on a desert island, what five books would he take.' The same question is asked of all, so there are conflicting answers. Through the pattern of responses the person who is 'it' can be guessed."

Everything went along all right until Lil went out. She asked: "If this person was a movie actor who would he be?" Merle was "it." Merle is a kind of relaxed kid, Crosbyish, who surprises occasionally with sharp

Spencer Tracy-like perceptions. Everybody gave Lil a tough time, saying things like Mickey Rooney, Donald O'Connor, Jack Lemmon, when Lil came out with a crazy remark: "One of you must be Wendell Corey."

That stopped the show. Murray guffawed. "You mean all of us must be Wendell Corey. How is that for a group label?"

Tibby asked in her bright, flat upstate accent, "Who is Wendell Corey?"

"I was 'it,'" said Merle, "and I see myself as Gerard Philipe. Wendell Corey never made love to anybody. Always that sour, pinched face, like he's getting ready to take a crap any minute."

"Maybe that's how Lil sees the world," Murray said, "constipated non-lovers." Murray thought that was funny, but Lisa gave him a stony look.

"I saw Jimmy Stewart in Washington," Larry said, "with some finky right-wing group. You know, the Hollywood hero acting out the role of patriot. It made me sick."

"But nobody answered the question," Marsha said. "Who is Merle? I vote for James Mason."

"I hear he is Jewish," Lil said. Murray really broke up on that one.

"What's so funny?" Lil asked. She was beginning to get sore.

Larry said, "Murray has a big anti-Jewish complex. He is the only analyst in New York who refuses Jewish patients. He even married a shikse."

Lisa smiled. "But I really think Jewish. He must be out of luck."

We finally decided that Merle was Anthony Franciosa, and stopped for coffee and cake. Murray picked it up again at the table, "You are not playing the game right. If you want to show what impression people have of others why not ask some dangerous questions. It's only in discomfort that we find emotional truth. Here's one: If somebody was drowning would this person jump in, call for help, or run away? Or, even better, if this person had a perverse habit, what would it be? That's a good one, because the responder would reveal his own tastes in perversion."

Everybody boldly agreed and I felt then that there really was a difference between intellectual life in the city and the wasteland of suburbia. Murray went out to be the guesser, and we decided on Tibby Barrett as "it," since most of us knew her slightly and it would lessen our personal embarrassment. Murray popped the question about perversion and we went around.

Lisa, sitting in Marsha's Saarinen Womb Chair, was first. She blushed a little, thought for a while, and then said: "If this person had a perverse habit, I would say he likes to smell armpits."

"Not much of a perversion," said Murray. "You know what Freud says about the olfactory sense and primitive man's delight in all smells."

"But this is twentieth-century civilized man," said Lisa. "Who today likes to handle and smell his own excretion?"

Larry, who was next, said loudly, "As a matter of fact, that was going to be my statement about our person, that he likes to smell human feces."

Tibby was next. I figured this was pretty rough stuff for a closed-in upstater, but she came out with a lulu. It almost broke up the game. "If this person was a female and had a perverse habit," she said matter-of-factly, "it would be wearing athletic supporters. Jock straps, you know."

"That's nothing more than locker-room transvestism," said Murray, "but I'll guess it is you Tibby, because everybody else in the room sees you as anal-oriented. You at least know yourself."

"What does that mean?" asked Merle.

"Probably she thinks she harbors homosexual feelings, and the way to defeat them is to talk about them," answered Murray.

At this point, Lil, who had been crouching in the corner of the couch, said, "I think this whole business is perverse. How everybody enjoys it."

"Verbal sublimation may be a way of ridding oneself of a compulsion neurosis toward societally taboo sex feelings," said Lisa.

"But where is love in all this?" asked Lil.

Larry said, "As an old Stalinist friend would say: love is a romantic excrescence of bankrupt bourgeois capitalism."

Everybody laughed, and right in the middle, Tibby farted. "Oops," she said, and before she could blush we doubled up with laughter. Except Lil.

"I think it's a stupid game. Let's talk about something else." But that finished it. We were all ready to go home.

"Now that Larry is back are you going to stay?" I asked Lil. I offered to take her to my place. She agreed and as soon as we got home she showered and went right to sleep. I thought she was faking it, but when I jostled her, she murmured, "Mommy," and began to snore a little.

I told Ben the story some days later. He was back over the meat market on Hudson Street. "You know," he said, "Lil is really all right. I mean that Marsha Weinstein crowd, I hate it." He stared soupily at a glass of warm Scotch. "I read an article in this week's *Reporter* about the fragmented man. This guy said, I think it was Oscar Jones, who wrote that study of the light-skinned Negro as *the* symbol of the alienated man. He's up at Columbia in C. Wright Mills' place. Wasn't that a tragic thing? Anyway, Jones discussed the possibility that we have lost a real work tradition and are seeking substitute gratification through the arts. He calls it cultural tunneling, whereby the true emotions of man, work-directed, have gone underground, so we seek love, not in sex, but in the movies, 'sex's blessed surrogate' he said. Maybe if I make it with Lil again I'll get job satisfaction too. Does that make sense?"

I said that it did, but I wondered why he didn't comment on Lil's sleeping in my bed. I asked him. "Well," he said, "you're no real threat the way Larry Jonas is. I haven't been able to satisfy Lil, so you may be my blessed surrogate."

"But she fell asleep," I said, thinking how nice it would have been to take her in her sleep.

A few days later Ben told me that he and Lil were going to try again and invited me to dinner to celebrate the reconciliation. When I arrived Lil was on the floor in leotards, practicing a leg-raising exercise she learned from Marsha. The "Ode to Joy" was storming out of the record player. Ben was whistling in the bathroom. "I've got a part-time job as a dental assistant," Lil said, as she kept exercising, and then, jumping up, she whispered, "We have decided to try for a baby."

Ben walked in wiping his face with a towel and boomed, "Say, did Lil tell you that we decided to try for a baby?" Lil flashed an angry look at him. He went on. "I looked around me, at all the people I know in the Village, and nobody has a family. Maybe they think it's a concession to middle-class attitudes, but it occurred to me that barrenness extirpates life. Listen to the Beethoven. It sings out the triumph of life, but without the child-bearing function man is deracinated, absolutely deracinated. Have a drink."

Lil looked at him, the light going out of her eyes. "Why must you always intellectualize everything? I want a baby because it will be the fruit of me, mine, yours, ours. Don't feelings have a place anywhere?"

"Of course they do. That's what I was trying to say. There must be a return to feeling and away from the highbrow dissection of everything. I can't even read *Dissent* any more. Doesn't Murray say in his book that the existential moment is truly realized in the coital act?"

"Good God, Murray is forty-five years old, Lisa is his third wife, and do you see any kids around the house?"

"What do you know?" Ben gulped his drink. "Murray can't have babies, for goodness sake."

"I don't believe it."

"He is sterile. S-T-E-R-I-L-E. Sterile."

I thought of Murray, wavy-haired, graying at the temples, the image of Jeff Chandler, poor guy, as a psychoanalyst. I didn't believe Ben either.

"But he is," Ben said. "He told me so at the White school. Why do you think he was interested in asking those questions about perversity? He is capable of intercourse, but he knows the guilt-anxiety of the act, and he chooses wayward acts as a kind of self-mutilating penance to his libido. I think those were his exact words to me."

Dinner went along aimlessly and I left shortly after. Ben had put on a John Cage record, and Lil was in the kitchen washing the floor. As I closed the door I heard him come into the kitchen. "Come on, Lil, get off the floor."

The next week I met Merle at Lerner's fourth lecture on American pluralism, this time the dichotomy between our Puritan adherence to monogamy on the one hand, and the new culture's rampant extra-maritalism on the other, a split which carried directly into the political arena. Lerner explained that the only way our statesmen could exorcise private guilt is by being supermoral in our foreign policy. He called it the Dulles syndrome. I wanted to pursue the point over a cookery-split, their ice cream special, but Merle broke in. "I wasn't listening. I broke up with Tibby last week."

"You don't look like you're collapsing over it," I said.

"I'm not. I'm puzzled more by an eerie feeling I have. I might as well tell you because you'll find out soon enough. A few days after the break I ran into Lil at the 8th Street Bookstore. She was looking haggard. The thing with Ben was over, but she said what disturbed her was the fact that she had been riding on the wings of a new idea, and her wings had been clipped. She did look like a fallen bird. She wanted a baby. That was the answer. She knew it. She spoke to her doctor and all he could say was, 'Do you really want it?' 'I don't know what I want,' she answered, and he said, 'Tell me what you think.' She talked a lot. She lies down now, you know, but she came out depressed. I told her about Tibby and me, and a strange, desperate look came over her. 'Come up to my place and we'll talk,' she said, and before I knew it, although I really knew it, we were in bed. 'I want a baby. I want a baby,' she kept repeating. She was too hysterical for any honest screwing, and we ended up drinking coffee in the kitchen. The thing that bothers me is that she was Larry's girl for quite a while. I mean, he is my older brother."

I asked him if he wanted the affair, and he shrugged. "Who knows what I want? The thing with Tibby went sour overnight. Really. We didn't even have a fight. She said, 'I'm moving out,' and I said O.K. I'm not like that. I like to analyze a relationship; that's half the fun. But the lights went out, that's all. So I look at Lil. I mean she probably can be good in bed if she works at it. But she is sick. And there is Larry. And maybe Ben with his crazy moral views will get sore. I like Ben. He was the first guy to give me a sense of social consciousness. I spoke to Marsha this morning and she insisted that I see a doctor. So her analyst arranged for an appointment with a man he recommends. Do you know him? Talcott Weingarten. He's a Sullivanian. I thought of going to Murray, but Marsha laughed. 'You are naive, Merle. You don't go to your friends. He knows too much about you.' I thought that was a funny remark, but I let it go."

I called Ben that night. He was back again at Hudson Street, and he had put a phone in, because, he said, "Who am I kidding? Artificial means of severing communications won't work. I have got to make the break from the inside."

"Why are you breaking?" I asked.

"Actually I'm not. As a matter of fact, for the first time in my life I feel a real spiritual renewal. Why don't you come over and see."

When I got to his place I saw demolition notices on all the stores. A new luxury building was going up. This one, a big placard announced, was going to be called The Titian Terrace. When I walked in, Tibby was sitting in a sling chair, holding a copy of *Civilization and Its Discontents*. "It's all in here," she said with a straight face. "He says I'm in trouble because I'm using sex as a sublimation for sex." I laughed and Ben greeted me.

"She really means that Freud is a fraud. Tibby is the answer to all neuroses. She is the incarnation of the love instinct."

"You mean the sex instinct," I offered.

"No, the love instinct. Lil didn't have it. I've been looking for the direct woman all my life. Look at her in the flesh." He went to her and kissed her.

"Ben thinks I am the embodiment of Marilyn Monroe and Jean Harlow. He is cute. I think I'm a quiet Bette Davis. Freud says it's a reaction formation. I refuse to accept my image of myself. I think he's cute too."

Ben said, "You see what I mean. She has insight, a native gift. She is the master of the innocuous apothegm. 'He's cute too.' Could Lil ever say anything like that?"

I said I thought she could. But Ben answered that it didn't matter, and launched into a recital of Tibby's virtues, while Tibby kept looking at him with bemused detachment. After the last breakup with Lil, Ben said he felt like committing suicide, but despite his despondency he knew that suicide was a failure of moral commitment. He had gone to the Cedar Street Bar for a drink, and Tibby was sitting at a table in the back. She told him about her break with Merle, and suggested that they try something together. She meant it as a joke, but Ben said why not. Tibby moved in that night, and Ben had his first successful love-making in months.

"Do you know what it is to make real love?" he said. "I told my doctor that it was a bourgeois myth kept alive for the sake of promoting wish-fulfilling fantasies and to keep the advertising business going. Did you see that piece in *Commentary* on 'Eros as Money-Making Myth'? It may be true, but nobody has ever seen the archetypal force of the pure, private act. It is positively prelapsarian." Just then Tibby farted.

"Oops," she said, and I noticed that she had learned not to blush as she had done at Marsha's.

Ben turned on her. "What kind of a stupid thing is that to do?"

"I had gas," Tibby said.

About a month later I met Larry and Marsha coming out of the 8th Street Playhouse. *Paths of Glory* was playing. "Film-making of the highest order," Larry said, "absolutely devastating exposure of the military mind. But why cast that right-wing bastard Menjou I can't understand." Marsha thought Larry looked like Kirk Douglas without the cleft. We went to the Limelight for capuccino.

"There's Wilder Benjamin, the movie critic of the *Voice*," Marsha said. "Do you know that he was Lil's first boy friend in the Village?"

"Can you believe it," Larry said, "Ben and Lil are together again. Lil's fling with Merle lasted about a week. Merle came to me and told me that my image haunted the bedroom. He couldn't even get an erection."

"And Ben," Marsha added, "had a terrible fight with Tibby. He accused

her of lacking any distinction as a human being. He said he couldn't live
with a girl so obtuse about the world around her. So Lil and Ben are back
together, and they have decided to attend Murray's husband-and-wife
therapy team. They are not going to think about a baby for a while.
Murray recommended that Lil go back to dancing classes with me in order
to get back to her primal self."

Although it was late when I left them, I wandered over to the Cedar
Street Bar thinking that despite the problems people seem to have, they
were alive to the possibilities of existence. It was almost closing time. Two
fairies were standing at the bar having a furious argument. The only other
person was Tibby.

She was sitting at a table in the corner, looking disconsolate. "I just
broke up with Ben," she said, before I could sit down. I ordered two beers,
and after a quiet cigarette I asked her if she would like to stay at my place.
She agreed.

◇

Philip L. Greene was born in Brooklyn in 1924, attended Lowell Tech-
nological Institute and New York University, has been an editor of Venture, *and is now an assistant professor of English at Adelphi College. The*
above story, which originally appeared in the spring, 1965, issue of Partisan
Review, *was his first published story.*

"One of You Must Be Wendell Corey" is not a glimpse into the future,
in the sense of being science fiction; nor is it a burlesque or caricature,
although the tone is satiric; it is the way some people do live now, exag-
gerated only slightly. How these people live is not so much a projection
of some of the tendencies we've been talking about as it is a projection
beyond *them: they live in what is really a post-industrial society; they have*
refashioned anonymous urban life into something resembling life in a small
community where everyone is related to everyone else; they are beyond
the wave of divorce, for only occasionally do they legalize their "relation-
ships" with one another; they are beyond the hung-up stage where an indi-
vidual may be immobilized by an older-fashioned sense that action should
be taken only according to real emotion or real conviction and that respon-
sibility must be assumed for its consequences. They are even beyond the
stage of the nuclear family, having created a crazy kind of extended family
of their own, a "kinship system" that would be an anthropologist's night-
mare. This kinship system is somewhat like—except for the sexual "switch-
ies" played in this case—the kind of pseudo-extended "occupational family"
that is becoming more and more common. The mobility, both social and
geographical, made necessary by modern life often separates small families

*from their real relatives, with whom they may have little in common any-
way. Families now find their "courtesy" aunts and uncles and cousins not in
old family friends and neighbors as in days past, but in recently acquired
close friendships with people their own age, often supported by occupational
ties and commonly held interests. Common sense tells us, however, that
life as described in this story can't represent the future pattern of family
life in America: if so, it would have a short future. Besides, it is too abhorrent to contemplate. So let us say simply that this is upper-bohemian life
in a big city and try to ignore that this life seems to have evolved as a
result of two so-called "revolutions" that are still supposed to be sweeping
America—the sexual revolution and the cultural revolution—carried
through to their ultimate absurd post-revolutionary anarchy. At any rate,
the story shows us how entwined the cultural and the sexual have become,
not simply among sandled Hippies but among people of the professional
class described in the story. Every one of them is in the grip of his own
intellectuality. Lil will occasionally ask some foolishly sensible question
like "Where is love in all this?" or "Don't feelings have a place anywhere?"
but from the very first lines of the story (her marriage "on the rocks . . .
her need for spiritual renewal came from Erich Fromm['s]* The Art of
Loving"), she is always shown "riding on the wings of a new idea." Even
she has an entirely idea-oriented "perpetual cycle of desire, rapt discovery
and flat-eyed disillusionment." The ideas these people live by are not permanent, traditional convictions, internalized and deeply held; they are simply a putting-into-practice of the newest interesting intellectual conception
that they come across in their studies or in their reading or at a party. Ben
decides he and Lil should have a baby because it occurs to him that "barrenness extirpates life." He doesn't commit suicide because "suicide was a
failure of moral commitment." Merle regrets the abruptness of his breakup
with Tibby because "I like to analyze a relationship; that's half the fun."
Ideas substitute for convictions and emotions; intellectuality and awareness
substitute for responsibility. They enthusiastically agree with Murray when
he tells them that "behavioral patterns weren't subject to moral judgments,
only analysis and clarification." They are caught in psychologism: being
able to name their behavior and being aware of what they are doing, they
can feel that not only are they doing nothing wrong, but that by their ex-
plorations and enthusiasms they are actively seeking solutions to their
problems. But their awareness never gets them anywhere; it leads only to
re-evaluation, new ideas, new diets and exercises, new analyses of self and
society. Toward the end, when the narrator is going to the Cedar Street Bar,
he thinks that despite the problems these people seem to have, they are
"alive to the possibilities of existence." The reader feels that now that it
is "almost closing time" they seem close to having exhausted all the possible
combinations of existence within their group. But when the narrator asks
Tibby to come live with him, the story ends with the words: "She agreed."*

The choice of verb makes clear that she is assenting as if it were an idea that had been proposed to her. Not just one of them is Wendell Corey, they all are Wendell Coreys: faceless actors playing out roles written for them according to the ideas of others.

❖

There seems to be a great distance of time and space between the world described in "The Family Meadow" and the world described in "One of You Must Be Wendell Corey." It is important to realize that there are perhaps only one hundred miles between the Jersey meadow of the first story and the Greenwich Village of the last—not far at all in American terms. But it is even more important to realize that the actions of the two stories may be presumed to be taking place at the same time: in contemporary America people live simultaneously in ways that are ages apart. The diversity of American life is still awesome, and that must be appreciated. But other realizations cannot be escaped. One is that this diversity of our lives is ironically and sadly disappearing just at a time when the mobility and fluidity of modern life are making it possible for more Americans to experience it—and somewhat as a result of that mobility. Also, one is forced to realize that the direction of change in America is away from the world of the family meadow, already encroached on by development houses, and toward an urban world that may unfortunately be not too unlike that described in the last story. Changes in the family are related to changes in the community which are related to changes in occupational patterns: as change occurs, there is a back-and-forth cause and effect relationship between all these elements of our life. The stories in the next section show the effects on the individual and on the family of change in our relationship to the place in which we live . . .

The Way We Live Now

IN COMMUNITIES

*The American idea of "community" is the small town: tree-lined streets,
corner drugstore, high-school band, civic meetings in the town hall, fireworks on the Fourth of July—the noisy, happy authentic technicolor River
City, Iowa, of* The Music Man. *Even in black and white such towns still
exist, of course; but few are now independent of the influence of a large
city; and, as is well known, the effect of "urban sprawl" and "megalopolis"
is to consume them geographically. Even small towns that have preserved
their geographical integrity are within the grip of our evolving mass society.
Automobiles and superhighways have erased the identity of small towns as
train stops. Giant shopping centers financed by nationwide chain stores
have removed commercial activity from the centers of towns to the outskirts between them. Local governments and schools depend on power
structures and funds managed at state and federal levels. Few towns are
independent of the economy as a whole, and the "local" industry may be
closed down by orders from a "home" office two thousand miles away.
Mass communications provide the same information and entertainment via
network television all across the land. Thus has taken place the "eclipse
of community" in America, at least of community as a small town.*

*Reflecting this, contemporary fiction seldom shows community-as-a-
whole, except when it deals—as it in fact often and successfully does—
with such "total communities" as insane asylums, old-age homes, and hospitals. That aspect of a story or novel which is its "setting," the place where
the action occurs, will be carefully rendered by the author so as to enhance
and add meaning to the whole purpose of the story. But place as such is
seldom now a main subject of fiction, as "the wilderness," say, might have
been considered one of James Fenimore Cooper's main subjects, or "The
South" one of Faulkner's. When contemporary writers do write directly of
community or place, it tends to be of the past, in some varying degree, if
only the past of childhood. William Humphrey, for instance, writes brilliantly of Texas, but never of it more recently than thirty years ago; Saul
Bellow's description of childhood in the ghetto, in* The Adventures of Augie
March, *is a classic of its kind. And most writers at one time or another
have set a story or a passage in a novel in their home town; but even if the*

379

story is not deliberately dated in the past it will seem so. Anyone not know-ing this country (if such there be, and he can read) and reading contem-porary American fiction would have the quite accurate impression of a rural past and an urban present. But the strictly country-to-city movement of the early years of industrialization seems to have given way to a drift in and out of cities which changes with age and occupation, achieving a sort of stable neither-nor compromise in the suburbs.

The stories that follow reflect this movement, as the stories in the pre-vious section moved from the "old" extended family to the "new" patterns in family life. Again it should be noted, however, that the "history" of change is occurring as of this moment. The rural world of the early stories and the urban and suburban worlds of the later ones are all part of the way that we live now.

THOMAS WILLIAMS

Goose Pond

◇◇◇◇◇◇◇

ROBERT HURLEY'S WIFE died in September, and by the middle of October
he had more or less settled everything. His son and daughter were both
married and lived far away from New York; his son in Los Angeles, his
daughter in Toledo. They came East for the funeral and each wanted him
to come and visit. "I'm not about to retire. I won't be an old man in a guest
room," he told them, knowing the great difference between the man he
looked at fifty-eight and the man he felt himself to be. It had taken Mary
six months to die, and during the last few of those months he began quietly
to assume many of her symptoms. The doctors noticed it and understood,
but his children, accustomed to a father who had always been to them a
common-sense, rather unimaginative figure, were shocked by his loss of
weight, by a listlessness as unlike him, as unsettling to them as if the earth's
rotation had begun to slow down.

But he would do no visiting, even though his business did not need him.
"I know what visiting is," he wrote to his son. "I don't do it very well.
Please don't call so much. You know how to write letters." "Daddy," his
daughter said, long distance. "The children are crazy to have their grandfather come and see them."

And he thought, there is one place I would like to go, and there are no
children I know there: "I'm going to New Hampshire, to Leah."

"All by yourself? What for?" She began to get excited, almost hysterical.
He could see her biting her lower lip—a habit of her mother's. Afterwards
she would be calling Charles in Los Angeles.

"I was born there. Your mother and I lived there before you were born.
Do I need any other reason? It's October. Anyway, I'll be back in a couple
of weeks."

"But, Daddy, we felt that you shouldn't be alone. . . ."

"I haven't been alone for thirty years," he said. "I want to try it again.
Now go back to whatever you were doing. I can hear a baby crying in your

house. Go take care of it. I'm going to stay with the Pedersens. Do you remember the old people in the big house on the mountain? If they still take boarders, that's where I'll be." *If they're still alive,* he thought. He wanted to walk in the woods again, but he had other reasons. The sight of his grandchildren, the hundred times a day when their small disasters caused screaming, tears; he couldn't stand it. They were always about to hurt themselves, they nearly fell so many times. They had so many deadly years to make. Automobiles, knives, leukemia, fire. . . . On the afternoon of the funeral he had watched his granddaughter, Ann, and suddenly he saw her having his wife's senseless pain, saw her crying not because of a bumped knee, but at more serious wounds. And the Pedersens? They were so old, they had somehow escaped, and as he remembered them they lived dried-up and careful, in a kind of limbo. He would go to the Pedersens, on Cascom Mountain.

Nana fussed with the Edison lamp, turning the white flame up in the mantle, moving the broad base across the crack made by the table leaf; then with the side of her hand she wiped the shiny surface of the table where it had been. The light shone past the tinted shade, up the glass chimney and sharpened her old face, made her glasses glint for a second until she moved away, tall and always busy, her small eyes always alert. She rarely sat down, and even then seemed poised, ready for busy duty. The old man settled himself cautiously, as he did now, one piece at a time. Nana had his zither out of its case, the light just right, made sure he had his hearing aid, his pick, and ash tray near. In spite of his age, he smoked cigarettes.

Back in the shadows, between a lacy, drooping vine and the narrow window, Nana's older sister, blue dress and high black shoes, composed and fragile face, sat in a rocker and never spoke. Nana herself was seventy-nine. For forty years she had bossed the seven-mile trek down to Leah in the late fall, back up the mountain again to this high old house in the spring. It was Nana who dealt with the world, who shut the windows when it rained, herded great-grandchildren when the family came in the summer, locked the house for the winter. In a few weeks they would be going down to their small apartment in Leah, to take their chances on another winter.

The old man tuned his zither, humming in a dry, crackly falsetto and turning his wrench as he picked the short strings. Tuned against the windy old voice, the crisp notes of the zither were startling, clear and metallic. There seemed to be no connection between the voice and the sounds of the strings, as if the old man heard other notes, the sounds of memory to check his instrument against.

"German *concert* zither," Nana said proudly, still hovering over the lamp. She rearranged his cigarettes, the coffee cup. She spoke from behind him, "He don't hear so good," nodding vigorously. "But he got the hearing aid." She pointed into his ear, where the pink button shone like a flower against brown freckles. "He don't wear it all the time, like he should." She moved quickly away on some sudden errand, and the old man looked up and winked at Hurley.

"Sometimes it makes too much noise," he said, smiling benevolently at his wife. She began to move the table. "It's all right. It's all right!" he said. In his fifty years in America he had mastered the sounds of English, but the rhythms of his speech were Scandinavian. "I'm going to play first a Norwegian song."

Nana poised herself upon a chair, folded her hands firmly, set herself for a moment and then began energetically to smooth her apron down her long thighs. The old lady against the wall stopped rocking. It always startled Hurley when, out of her silent effacement, she responded.

The old man bent over his zither, his shiny face as ruddy as a baby's. His mottled, angular fingers worked over the strings; he swayed back and forth to keep time and snorted, gave little gasps and grunts he evidently did not hear himself, in time with the music. Beneath, occasionally overcoming the sibilant, involuntary breaths, the music was poignantly clear, ordered, cascading, vivid as little knives in the shadowy room. At the end they all applauded, and the old man bowed, very pleased.

That night Hurley climbed the staircase that angled around the central chimney, an oil lamp to light his way, and entered his cold room in moonlight almost as bright as the lamp, but colder, whiter against the lamp's yellow. Two little windows looked down across the old man's garden— "Mostly for the deer," the old man had said of it—then over the one still-mown pasture left to the farm, down the long hills silvery in moonlight to Lake Cascom in the valley, white among black surrounding spruce. Behind, on the other side of the house, he could feel the dark presence of Cascom Mountain.

He wondered if it would be a night for sleep. He was tired enough. In the last few days he had taken many of the familiar trails, especially following those that he remembered led through hardwood. Although the leaves had turned and mostly fallen, here or there one tree flamed late among the bare ones, catching light and casting it in all directions as if it were an orange or soft-red sun. He stopped often in the woods, surprised by each molten maple branch, even the smallest bright veins of each leaf golden and precious against a gnarled black trunk or the green twilight of a spruce grove. He walked carefully, resting often, sampling the few cold, sweet apples from the abandoned mountain trees, eating Nana's sandwiches a little at a time. He wanted the day to last as long as possible. At night he thought of his wife.

The high, sloping bed was wide and lonesome as a field of snow. During his wife's illness he could not sleep in their own bed, but slept every night on a studio couch where he could reach the sides, hold himself down, remember exactly where he was and why she was not beside him. If he woke in the night and for a second forgot, he had to learn over again from the beginning that Mary was going to die. It was always the first time over again, when they had left the doctor (the poor doctor, according to Mary) at the cancer hospital and walked together to Grant's Tomb. Mary finally said, "You know? They should pay a man a thousand dollars a minute for having to say those words."

Then the inevitable sequence of hours came through his mind, one after the other, until the afternoon when she was not so brave any more and shook her head back and forth as if to throw off the plastic tube that went into her nose and down, jiggling the clamps and the bottle on its hanger. Tears rolled from the outside corners of her drowned eyes and she cried pettishly, "Help me, help me."

She had taken pain better than most, was better at taking it by far than her husband or her children. When she had the compound fracture of her wrist she had been the calm one, the strong one. And he thought, *My God, how much pain she must have if she is caused to do this—if it is Mary who is caused to do this. . . .*

As they cut nerves, cutting off pain in little bits and pieces, it was as if they cut off her life, too, by shreds—the pain, the possibility of it forever gone; the life forever gone. But new pain took the place of the old. She lived for six months and died almost weightless, ageless, the little lines and wrinkles of her familiar body smoothed as if by a filling pulp. Her arms turned to thin tubes, her forehead waxed as taut, as translucent as a yellow apple. Her eyes, before the final cutting, watched him, blameful as a beaten child's. She whined for help: "What is happening to me?" And being a man only, he could stand, and stand, and stand, helpless at the foot of her crank-operated bed, the simple handle drawing his eyes, mocking, it seemed to him, telling him to crank, to grasp the handle in his strong hands and crank, sweat at it, crank faster and harder, crank until she is well again.

He turned and his hand touched the firm, virginal pillow next to his. The linen smelled country new, of washdays and clotheslines.

At midnight he heard what he first supposed to be a hundred dogs barking in the distance, and as the barking changed on the wind he suddenly knew, in exactly the same way he had known in his childhood, that it was the Canada geese flying over, low here because of the height of the land, streaming over in the darkness. *Lorlorn, lorlorn, lorlorn,* the geese called to each other as they passed. He ran to the window—remembering an old excitement, feet numb on the cold boards—but the geese did not cross the moon. He remembered them well enough that way: the long wavering files of geese, necks thrust out straight, dark wings arching tirelessly on their long journey over the guns, through all the deadly traps set for them—the weather, the ice, the hunting animals and the traitor decoys.

Each one its own warm life deep in the cold sky, and they called to each other, kept close and on course together, facing with disciplined bravery that impossible journey.

He came awake in the indeterminate time when night was breaking and the small windows were luminous squares upon the wall. He lay on his back and watched the light grow, the corners arrange themselves and the moldings darken, wondering at a curved shape above the closet door. As the morning increased (he heard pans banging down in the kitchen, Nana's sharp morning voice) he finally saw that the curved shape was a bow hung on pegs. This room evidently had been a young boy's during the summer: a huge fungus platter hung between the windows, and in the back of the closet he had found a fly rod enmeshed in kinky leader. Nana had missed a trout hook crusted with dried worm, stuck high on a curtain.

Before he went downstairs he remembered the bow, took it down and, wondering at the easy memories of his youth, strung it. He instinctively placed the lower end against the inside of his right foot, his left hand slid easily up the wood with the string lightly guided by his finger tips. The string vibrated tautly, and he remembered, too, how a bow seemed lighter after being strung, the tense pressure communicating energy to the arm. He estimated the pull at sixty pounds—quite a powerful bow.

"Oh, you found the bow'n' arrow!" Nana said when he came into the kitchen with it. "You going to shoot? Say, how did you cock it?"

He placed the bow against his foot, pulled with his right hand and pushed with the heel of his left hand, his fingers working the string out of the notch.

"Nobody could fix it. The children going crazy they couldn't shoot, nobody could cock it," Nana said admiringly.

"Do you have any arrows?"

The old man had decided to listen. "In the umbrella stand is some arrows," he said, and Nana rushed out after them. After breakfast she insisted they all go out and watch him shoot, and he was surprised at his own excitement when he fitted the nock of one of the warped target arrows to the string. He drew and loosed the arrow across the thirty yards between the driveway and the barn. *Whap* as the arrow hit the silvery, unpainted wood of the barn and stuck, quivering. A cloud of swallows streamed out of a sashless window, and shreds of dusty hay fell from between the boards. The old people were impressed.

As he drew his second arrow the bow split apart above the grip. Arrow, string, half the bow fell loosely over his arms.

"Ooooh!" the old people sighed. "The wood was too old," the old man said. "It all dries up and it got no give to it."

"I'll get you another one," Hurley said. They shushed him up, said it wasn't any good, that nobody could cock it anyway. But later when he drove his Drive-Ur-Self Chevrolet down into Leah for groceries and the mail, he stopped in at Follansbee's hardware store.

Old Follansbee remembered him from the times he and Mary had come up to ski, possibly not from the earlier time when Follansbee was a young man working in his father's store and Hurley was a boy.

"Do for you?" Old Follansbee's bald head (once covered with black, bushy hair, parted in the middle) gleamed softly, approximately the same color and texture as his maple roll-top desk.

"I'd like to buy a bow—and some arrows," Hurley added in order to specify what kind of bow he meant. In Leah he had always been constrained to come immediately to the point. The old man led him to the sporting-goods corner where rifles and shotguns, fish poles and outboard motors, knives, rubber boots, decoys, pistols lay in cases on counters, hung on racks. He remembered this part of the store and the objects he had fallen in love with as a boy. No girl had meant as much to him at fifteen as had the beautiful angular lines of a Winchester model 62, .22 pump. He even remembered the model number, but from this distance he wondered how a number could have meant so much.

He tried out a few of the pretty, too-modern bows until he found one that seemed to have the same pull as the one he had broken.

"That one's glass," Old Follansbee said. "My boy says it don't want to break."

"Glass? It's made of glass?"

"Correct. Strange, ain't it? What they can do these days? You'll want some arrows, did you say?"

He bought two arrows. When he'd pulled the one out of the barn it came apart in his hands, split all the way up the shaft. He decided to replace it with two, even though he knew the New Hampshire way was to resent such prodigality. He bought a leather arm guard and finger tabs; then he saw the hunting arrows. The slim, three-bladed heads suggested Indians and his youth. The target arrows, beside them, seemed to have no character, no honest function. He bought two hunting arrows and, under old Follansbee's suspicious conventional eye, a bow hunting license, feeling like a child who had spent his Sunday-school money on a toy.

At the post office he found a joint communiqué from his worried children. "We have decided that it would be best. . . ." the words went. He sent two identical telegrams: *Having wonderful time. Tend your business. Love, Dad.* They all believe in the therapy of youth—in this case, grandchildren. He couldn't think of a way to tell them that he loved them all too much.

Nana and the old man walked with him as far as the ledges at the top of the wild orchard, careful in their white tennis shoes. Nana stood splay-footed on the granite, queen of the hill, and surveyed the valley, the advancing forest with a disapproving eye.

"I see Holloways is letting their north pasture go back," she said, shaking her head. She had seen whole hills go back to darkness, many fine houses fall into their cellar holes. She turned toward Hurley accusingly, he being from the outside and thus responsible for such things. "You got to pay money to have them take the hay!"

"Tell me it's cheaper to buy it off the truck," the old man said. "But I told them it don't grow on trucks." He stood beside his tall wife, in his baggy pants and old mackinaw. His new tennis shoes were startlingly white. "I call this 'the hill of agony,'" he said, winking at Hurley.

"You see where the deer come down to eat our garden?" Nana said, pointing to the deer trails through the apple trees. "We tell the game warden to shoot. Nothing. They hang bangers in the trees. All night, 'Bang! Bang!' Nobody can sleep."

"Neither could the deer. They stayed up all night and et my lettuce," the old man said. He laughed and whacked his thigh.

"You shoot me a nice young deer," Nana said. "I make mincemeat, roasts, nice sausage for your breakfast."

He had tried to tell them that he didn't want to shoot anything with the bow, just carry it. Could he tell them that it gave a peculiar strength to his arm, that it seemed to be a kind of dynamo? When he was a boy in these same woods he and his friends had not been spectators, but actors. Their bows, fish poles, skis, rifles had set them apart from the mere hikers, the summer people.

"I won't be back tonight unless the weather changes," he said. The sun was warm on the dry leaves, but the air was crisply cool in the shadows. He said good-by to the old people, took off his pack and waited on the ledges to see them safely back to the house below, then unrolled his sleeping bag and rolled it tighter. The night before he had noticed on his geodetic map a small, five-acre pond high in the cleft between Cascom and Gilman mountains. It was called Goose Pond, and he seemed to remember having been there once, long ago, perhaps trout fishing. He remembered being very tired, yet not wanting to leave; he remembered the cattails and alders and a long beaver dam, the pond deep in a little basin. He was sure he could follow the brook that issued from the pond—if he could pick the right one from all the little brooks that came down between Gilman and Cascom.

His pack tightened so that it rode high on his back, he carried his bow and the two hunting arrows in one hand. He soon relearned that arrows pass easily through the brush only if they go point first.

Stopping often to rest he climbed past the maples into ground juniper and pine, hearing often the soft explosions of partridge, sometimes seeing them as they burst up and whistled through the trees. He passed giant beeches crossing their noisy leaves, then walked silently through softwood until he came to a granite knob surrounded by stunted, wind-grieved hemlock. To the northwest he could see the Presidential Range, but Leah, the lake and the Pedersens' farm were all out of sight. He ate a hard-boiled egg and one of the bittersweet wild apples he had collected on the way. The wind was delightfully cool against his face, but he knew his sweat would soon chill. At two o'clock the sun was fairly low in the hard blue sky—whole valleys were in shadow below.

He took out his map. He had crossed three little brooks, and the one he could hear a short way ahead must be Goose Pond's overflow. By the sound it was a fair-sized brook. When he climbed down through the hemlock and saw it he was sure. White water angled right and left, dropping over boulders into narrow sluices and deep, clear pools. He knelt down and lowered his head into the icy water. His forehead turned numb, as if it were made of rubber. A water beetle darted to the bottom. A baby trout flashed green and pink beside a stone. It was as if he were looking through a giant lens into an alien world, where life was cold and cruel, and even the light had a quality of darkness about it. Odd little sticks on the bottom were the camouflaged larvae of insects, waiting furtively to hatch or to be eaten. Fish hid in the shadows under stones, their avid little mouths ready to snap. He shuddered and raised his head—a momentary flash of panic, as if some carnivorous animal with a gaping mouth might come darting up to tear his face.

Following the brook, jumping from stone to stone, sometimes having to leave it for the woods in order to get around tangles of blowdown or waterfalls, he came suddenly into the deep silence of the spruce, where the channel was deep. In the moist, cathedral silence of the tall pillars of spruce he realized how deafening the white water had been. The wind stirred the tops of the trees and made the slim trunks move slowly, but could not penetrate the dim, yet luminous greenness of the place.

And he saw the deer. He saw the face of the deer beside a narrow tree, and for a moment there was nothing but the face: a smoky-brown eye deep as a tunnel, it seemed, long delicate lashes, a black whisker or two along the white-shaded muzzle. The black nose quivered at each breath, the nostrils rounded. Then he began to follow the light-brown line, motionless and so nearly invisible along the back, down along the edge of the white breast. One large ear turned slowly toward him. It was a doe, watching him carefully, perfect in the moment of fine innocence and wonder—a quality he suddenly remembered—the expressionless readiness of the deer. But other instincts had been working in him. He hadn't moved, had breathed slowly, put his weight equally on both legs. The light sharpened as if it had been twilight and the sun had suddenly flashed. Every detail—the convolutions of the bark on the trees, tiny twigs, the fine sheen of light on each hair of the doe, each curved, precious eyelash—became vivid and distinct. Depth grew, color brightened; his hunter's eyes became painfully efficient, as if each needlelike detail pierced him. The world became polarized on the axis of their eyes. He was alone with the doe in a green world that seemed to cry for rich red, and he did not have time to think: it was enough that he sensed the doe's quick decision to leave him. An onyx hoof snapped, her white flag rose and the doe floated in a slow arc, broadside to him, clear of the trees for an endless second. He watched down the long arrow, three blades moved ahead of the doe and at the precise moment all tension stopped; his arms, fingers, eyes and the bow were all one instrument. The arrow sliced through the deer.

Her white flag dropped. Gracefully, in long, splendid leaps, hoofs stabbing the hollow-sounding carpet of needles, the doe flickered beyond the trees. One moment of crashing brush, then silence. A thick excitement rose like fluid into his face, his arms seemed to grow to twice their normal size, become twice as strong. And still his body was governed by the old, learned patterns. He walked silently forward and retrieved his bloody arrow, snapped the feathers alive again. The trail was a vivid line of jewels, brighter than the checkerberries against their shiny green leaves, unmistakable. He rolled the bright blood between his fingers as he slowly moved forward. He must let the doe stop and lie down, let her shock-born strength dissipate in calm bleeding. Watching each step, figuring out whole series of steps, of brush bendings in advance, he picked the silent route around snags and under the blowdown.

In an hour he had gone a hundred yards, still tight and careful, up out of the spruce and onto a small rise covered with birch and poplar saplings. The leaves were loud underfoot and, as he carefully placed one foot, the doe rose in front of him and crashed downhill, obviously weak, staggering against the whippy birch. A fine mist of blood sprayed at each explosion of breath from the holes in her ribs. He ran after her, leaping over brush, running along fallen limbs, sliding under low branches that flicked his cheeks like claws. His bow caught on a branch and jerked him upright. After one impatient pull he left it. He drew his knife. The brown shape ahead had disappeared, and he dove through the brush after it, witch hobble grabbing at his legs.

The doe lay against a stump, one leg twitching. He knelt down and put one hard arm around her neck and, not caring for the dangerous hoofs, the spark of life, raised the firm, warm neck against his chest and, sighing, stabbed carefully into the sticking place. Blood was hot on the knife and on his hand.

He rolled over into the leaves, long breaths bending him, making his back arch. His shirt vibrated over his heart, his body turned heavy and pressed with unbelievable weight into the earth. He let his arms melt into the ground, and a cool, lucid sadness came over his flesh.

He made himself get up. In order to stand he had to fight gravity, to use all his strength—a quick fear for his heart. His joints ached and had begun to stiffen. He must keep moving. Shadows were long and he had much to do before dark. He followed the blood trail back and found his bow and one arrow. He limped going back down the hill; at a certain angle his knees tended to jackknife, as if gears were slipping.

He stood over the clean body of the doe, the white belly snowy against brown leaves. One hind leg he hooked behind a sapling, and he held the other with his knee as he made the first long incision through the hair and skin, careful not to break the peritoneum. He ran the incision from the breast to the tail, then worked the skin back with his fingers before making the second cut through the warm membrane, the sticky blue case for the stomach and entrails. He cut, and the steamy innards rolled unbroken and still working out onto the ground. A few neat berries of turd rattled on the leaves. He cut the anus and the organs of reproduction clear of the flesh, then found the kidneys and liver and reached arm-deep into the humid chest cavity, the hot smell of blood close in his nostrils, and removed the yellow lungs in handfuls. Then he pulled out the dark-red heart. Kidneys, liver and heart he wrapped carefully in his sandwich wrappings, then rose and painfully stretched. Goose Pond lay just below; he could see a flicker of water through the skein of branches, and there he would make camp.

With his belt looped around the neck and front hoofs, he slid the doe down toward the pond. It was dusk by the time he found a dry platform of soft needles beneath a hemlock, next to the water. The doe had become stiff enough so that he could hang it in a young birch, head wedged in a fork. He spread his sleeping bag, tried it for roots and stones, and found none. The last high touch of sun on the hill above him had gone; he had even prepared ground for a fire when he realized that he had no energy left, no appetite to eat the liver of the doe.

Darkness had settled in along the ground, but the sky was still bright; one line of cirrus clouds straight overhead still caught orange sunlight. Across the silver water the alder swamp was jet black, and the steep hill rose behind, craggy with spruce. A beaver's nose broke water and even, slow circles spread across the pond. The dark woods filled with cold, and one of his legs began to jerk uncontrollably. He took off his boots and slid into his sleeping bag.

The doe was monstrous, angular against the sky, her neck stretched awkwardly, head canted to one side. The black hole in her belly gaped empty. He drew his sleeping bag up around his face.

If he were twenty again he would be happy. To have shot a deer with a bow—he'd be a hero, a woodsman, famous in Leah. How it would have impressed Mary! She would have said little about it—she went to great lengths never to flatter him; her compliments had been more tangible, seldom in words. He must think of something else. The world was too empty. The cold woods, the darkening water were empty. He was too cold, too tired to manipulate his thoughts. And the progression of hours began again. Mary's eyes watched him, deep in sick hollows. How could her flesh turn so brown? Why could he do nothing to stop the pain? She watched him, in torment, her frail body riven, cut beyond endurance. The disease had killed her bravery with pain and left her gruesomely alive, without dignity, whimpering like a spoiled brat, asking for help she should have known did not exist. And he stood by and watched, doing nothing. Nothing. He was not a man to do nothing. *Mary, did I do nothing to help you?*

He heard, far away, the lonely cry of the Canada geese. He was alone, hidden in the blind night, high on the stony mass of Cascom Mountain.

And then they came in, circling, calling to each other above the doubtful ground. Perhaps they had seen the reflected circle of fading sky, or remembered; generations remembering that geese had rested safely in the high pond and found food there. The scouts came whistling on their great wings, searching and listening. They sent their messages back to the flock waiting above, then planed down, braking, smeared the water with wind and came to rest in a flash of spray. The flock circled down after, careless now it was safe, honking gaily, giving the feeding call prematurely, echoing the messages of the leaders and landing masters. "Come in, come down and rest," they seemed to call, until everyone had landed safely. Then the voices grew softer, less excited, and only an occasional word drifted across the water.

Robert Hurley lay in the warm hollow of his sleeping bag, where the hours had stopped. He thought for a moment of the doe's death, and of his knife. The geese spoke softly to each other on the water—a small splash, a flutter of wings and the resting, contented voices in the deep basin of the pond. As sleep washed over him he seemed to be among them; their sentinels guarded him. When they had rested well they would rise and continue the dangerous journey down the world.

⟡

Thomas Williams was born in Duluth in 1926, attended schools in Minnesota, New York City, and New Hampshire, served in the Army of Occupation in Japan, earned his B.A. and M.A. at the University of New Hampshire, studied in Paris for a year, worked at the Iowa Writers' Workshop, and then returned again to New Hampshire, where he teaches writing at the university. His first novel was Ceremony of Love *(1955), about American soldiers in Japan; since then most of his work has been set in a New Hampshire locale. This includes the second and third novels,* Town Burning *(1959) and* The Night of Trees *(1961), and several of the stories in his collection,* A High New House *(1963). His fiction successfully develops many sorts of scenes and themes and characters, but in the passages of his novels and his stories dealing with men hunting, or in some other direct relation with Nature, his prose takes on the subtlety and density of poetry, each natural descriptive detail charged with meaning. He is capable of descriptive-symbolic passages at least the equal of the best of Thomas Hardy's.*

In "Goose Pond" we see some of the uses to which the actuality of direct experience of Nature and the symbol of Nature can still be put by modern fiction in an increasingly urbanized world. Americans' longing for the rural is akin to a yearning for the past, and Robert Hurley's decision to return to Leah after his wife's death is an entirely natural, if unconscious, desire to go again to the place of his birth and youth in search of renewal. In the last line of the story it is implied that he will "rise and continue," but the story is no sentimental expression of clichés about the soothing powers of gentle Mother Nature. On the contrary, menace is everywhere in the story, and Robert Hurley sees it all. He doesn't go to live with his children's families because he can't bear to see the dangers surrounding his grandchildren, "always about to hurt themselves . . . so many deadly years to make . . . automobiles, knives, leukemia, fire. . . ." Even at the Pedersens', the fragile old people who are so careful and beyond life, the notes of the zither are "vivid as little knives in the shadowy room." The geese that he hears in the night must make "their long journey over the guns, through all the deadly traps set for them—the weather, the ice, the hunting animals and the traitor decoys." The old bow breaks, the arrow shatters, the new bow is made of glass—everything is fragile, threatened. In the small brook pond "life was cold and cruel": larvae wait "to hatch or to be eaten"; fish hide, but with "their avid little mouths ready to snap." It is shown to Hurley—a dozen times and in a dozen ways—that all life, including human life, is subject to natural law, and as such, is an "impossible journey." He himself becomes somehow a part of natural law when he kills the deer. The graphic description of the cleaning of the deer is counterposed in the story to the graphic account of his wife's cruel death by cancer. Both descriptions may make a sensitive reader squirm, but a point of the story is that both events are a natural part of life and must be accepted as such. Again, Nature is not sentimentalized in the story: quite the opposite. Nor does the story reflect the pessimism of the Naturalism school. Nature is shown as cruel, but as naturally so, not evilly so. Its beauty is as much emphasized as its savagery—one is a part of the other. Nature has the power to heal gently and the power to kill savagely—both are natural aspects of life. From the beautiful passage at the end, when Hurley is about to sleep at the pondside and the geese come in, it is to be understood that as a result of his day he will rest better. This is of course not simply because of his fatigue, for this was discounted earlier when we were shown his vain attempts to exhaust himself sufficiently to fall asleep without having to relive the agony of his wife's death. It is important that as he is about to sleep *"he thought for a moment of the doe's death, and of his knife."* He has a better understanding of how all-pervasive and entirely natural are both death and the cruelty of life, and through that understanding comes a better acceptance of what has happened in his life. Having rested well, he will, like the geese, *"rise and continue the dangerous journey down the world."* The possibility of such a direct and meaningful experience of Nature has always been part of the American heritage, but the opportunity seems to be passing. It is not to be equated with family camping trips, a run around the lake in an outboard, an afternoon on a suburban golf course, or most of the other ways Americans conduct their pursuits of leisure outdoors. Whether this kind of direct communication, or communion, with the natural cycles of life may be necessary for men or not, it is clear that most of us have deprived ourselves of it as we live now.

R. V. CASSILL

The Father

◇◇◇◇◇◇◇◇

THIS BEGAN MANY YEARS AGO. Since its origin was from an accident and since many of the consequences would never be duplicated, it may stand as a unique little history without much relation to the fated march of public events or the destinies of most people.

It began on a March morning when Cory Johnson was shelling corn in the crib on his farm. He had a rattletrap old sheller that he was rather proud of. Some of its parts—the gears and the rust-pitted flywheel bored for a hand crank—had come from a machine in use on this farm for longer than Cory had lived. But he had rebuilt the frame and replaced the shelling spikes inside. He had rigged an electric motor and a system of belts to run the apparatus after the REA brought the wires out on this mail route west of Boda.

The sheller worked well enough. When there was no load of corn hitting the spikes, the rising and falling hum of the motor and the sibilance of the belts on the pulley faces were reasonably quiet. Of course, when corn was actually being shelled, a deafening racket filled this solid-walled room in the corner of the slatted crib.

Cory thought he was alone on the farm at this hour. His wife had taken all three children with her in the Model A. The two older boys were in school and would not come home until late afternoon. His wife hoped to drive into Boda to see her parents if the roads had not thawed too badly. She meant to take Bobbie, the youngest boy, along with her. Probably those two would not be back much before noon.

Cory liked being alone on his place. The job he had laid out for himself this morning was not pressing. At midmorning he would go to the house for coffee and cold pancakes with jelly. While he ate the snack he meant to listen to a science program broadcast daily from the station of the state university. He liked science. In his rural isolation he believed—then, early in the thirties, almost a full century after it began to dominate the life of the western world—that science was "the coming thing."

As he fell into the rhythm of it, he was enjoying his work as much as he ever had. The warming day, which would probably take the bottom out of the gravel roads between here and town before it was through, permitted him to take off his sheepskin coat. He was warm enough in a sweater as long as he kept busy, and for a good hour he worked without pause, bringing tin bushels full of corn from a pile in the slatted corncrib and feeding it into the machine.

While the ears ran down the trough to the hopper, Cory sometimes watched the throat of the outlet where the shelled grains poured into gunnysacks. Mostly the grains flowed out in a brisk, placid stream, but now and then above the main flow some single grains would leap like fast, yellow sparks from a grinding wheel. There was of course nothing extraordinary in the maverick behavior of these grains. They were the ones that had caught somehow between the cobs and the whirling spikes just long enough for elastic and centrifugal forces to build up, then hurl them like bullets ricocheting out the metal chute that filled the sacks. Still, their unpredictable flight suggested mysteries beyond the fringe of his experience. He had read in *Popular Science Monthly* where some Jap had invented a centrifugal machine gun. It pleased him mildly to think he was watching the principle of the gun being demonstrated by the apparatus he had put together. In another issue of the same magazine he had seen a photograph of electrons leaping through the dark of an experimental chamber, and though these pictures had showed no more than the scratch of a white line across a black rectangle, it pleased him to believe that electrons *really* looked like these hard-flung, zinging grains of corn.

Once that morning when Cory went out into the main storage bins of the crib to fill his bushels, he heard the electric motor change pitch. I*t*; normal whine became a level, unpleasant hum. The slap and hiss of the driving belts had stopped. The motor was no longer turning over, and he had better shut down the current quickly before the armature burned out.

As he skipped for the door, the motor began to run again. A belt whistled on an immobilized pulley.

He saw his four-year-old son Bobbie standing beside the fly wheel with his gloved hand raised to the gear reduction. The boy's face was turned back over his sheepskin collar, and he was grinning the not quite honest grin he often showed when caught doing something destructive and forbidden—he grinned as if trying to minimize his offense.

Cory thought the boy had pushed a cob into the gears, experimentally, and thus had stopped the whole complex of machinery cold.

Then with a hawking scream that scalded his throat and the inside of his nose with bile, Cory called his wife's name. The boy's hand was in the gears. Down the fringed and starred cuff of his glove, blood was oozing briskly onto his sleeve and down the sleeve to the hem of his coat.

Cory had turned the power off and knelt with the boy in his arms by the time his wife ran from the car she had just parked.

As pain returned to the shocked nerves of the hand, the boy's grin merely enlarged until his mouth stood in a ridged O like the corolla of a white flower. He was now shrieking incessantly in fear and pain. He danced in his father's arms and jerked and jerked to free his hand. Urine bubbled through his overalls and mixed with the blood under his boots.

"Daddy'll get you out," Belle Johnson shouted in the boy's face.

"Daddy, Daddy, Daddy, Daddy," she moaned to Cory, depending like the child on his act to save them.

"Hold'm," Cory said. He vaulted the machine and knocked the belt from the drive shaft, vaulted back and set his shoulder to a spoke of the fly-wheel. When the gears moved, the boy shrieked louder and fainted.

"I'll take the sonofabitch apart," Cory said. He looked under the motor table for his toolbox. He remembered having put it in the trunk of the car. He was not sure whether he had left it there or had taken it out later in the barn.

"Daddy, he's swallowing his tongue," Belle said.

Cory put a finger and thumb in the boy's mouth. It was like putting them into an electric socket with the current on. The strength of the curling tongue seemed greater than any he could force into his own hand.

It took him five seconds to secure the tongue and press his wife's nails into it. He believed it had taken two or three minutes.

Sweat was blinding him. He thought the boy might die if he did not hurry, but he caught himself staring with revulsion at the machine, taking time to blame himself not only for the failure to enclose the gears in a safety box, but for making anything so ugly and rough—for presuming to do something that only factory technicians working for pay could do right.

He fished out his jackknife and cut away the blood-sopped glove from the jammed hand. He thought it possible that the jersey might have cushioned the bones at least. What he saw looked like boiled and shredded chicken in which a bad cook had left bits of gristle and bone.

"Daddy, his mouth is turning blue," Belle said.

"All right. Hold onto him. Hold him tight," Cory said.

He took a dark-bladed hatchet from its hanging place on the wall. There was not much room for it between the gears and the bottom of the hopper. With a three-inch blow he clipped the hand just above the wristbone.

"Get a tourniquet on him. I'll get the car," he told his wife.

The doctor in Boda, young Doctor Grant, said that Cory had done a pretty good job of amputation, all things considered.

"Bobbie probably never even felt what you did," Doctor Grant said, with his clean, pink-nailed fingers resting on Cory's sleeve. "There was quite a little shock. Naturally. But if his hand was so badly mangled you couldn't get it free, you can be sure that's where the shock came from. Say, it didn't take you long to get him in here to me," he said with an encouraging gleam of admiration in his eyes.

"No," Cory said, "I just didn't pay any attention to the mudholes. I came through the bad stretch the other side of the bridge doing about sixty-five, I guess."

The doctor laughed quite loudly. "I'll bet you jumped that Model A right over the bad spots."

Now that he knew his boy was going to be all right—which at the moment meant that he was going to live—Cory felt an unaccountable but decent pride in his behavior after the accident. By God, he had held back nothing. He had ripped the guts out of his Model A, coming in from the farm in just seventeen minutes. By God, he had seen the mail carrier—the mail carrier, mind you—out beside his car studying the mire of gravel and standing water in the low spot beyond the creek and probably deciding it had thawed too bad for him to get the mail through. Now Cory could remind himself—what he wouldn't bend the doctor's ear with—that Belle had shouted from the back seat to go around the longer way by Hopewell Church when he took it on his own shoulders to give this way a try. He hated to think what might have happened if he had stuck the car in deep there, a mile and a quarter from town. And for a minute or two it had been touch-and-go with the mud geysering over his windshield and the car skidding always to the left against his pull on the steering wheel. He had seen the face of the mail carrier through a muddy window, puckered in disbelief, almost in awe, as he watched the Model A churn past him.

The car was still fishtailing uncontrollably when Cory took her up the bridge approach. The whipping rear end grazed half the girders of the span before he got her straightened. The rear bumper was gone and somewhere along the line he'd overtaxed the transmission so he couldn't get her shifted down from high when he had to wait for a truck to cross at the Boda stop sign. He killed the motor then and ran three blocks to the doctor's office with the boy in his arms and Belle unable to keep up with him. And made it in time.

In time. In time. In time. The thought quieted the thudding of his heart.

"I don't think there's enough loss of blood to worry us," Doctor Grant said. "The tourniquet worked very nicely." Doctor Grant was only concerned—just a little—about the effects of shock, he said. He wanted to drive the boy over to the hospital in the county seat as soon as he had seen two more patients. He wanted to make sure Bobbie had his strength built up "before I finish the job for you," as he put it to Cory, with a wink of complicity. The Johnsons could ride along in the doctor's car. Belle could hold the little fellow in her lap, and everything would be arranged so one of them could stay all night with him in the hospital.

In the meantime, while his parents waited, the boy was sleeping in one of the doctor's examination rooms. He had been given morphine. Everything seemed to be under control. The orderly flow of circumstance had resumed again.

Cory opened a magazine, there in the doctor's waiting room—not so much because he thought he could read anything just now as because he wanted some shield behind which to hide until he came to terms with himself. Most importantly, he had to choke down the boisterous, excessive pride that had come on the rebound of his relief. He kept wanting to grin when he thought of the mail carrier's face. But if he couldn't help grinning, no one ought to see him do it. Then, too, he might want to pray out some of his thanksgiving that the roads hadn't been too bad, that Doctor Grant knew his business; and so on. Cory was still religious in crisis, though in normal times he lived by the opinion that "a lot of people went too far" with the religious business.

"Cory?"

He heard Belle's whisper like something whispering to him out of the past—like his mother come to wake him for a fine day in summer after vacation from school had begun and he could enjoy himself helping *his* daddy around the farm.

He looked up from the magazine. Belle's face was so pale he was frightened for her. Her blue eyes looked black against her ghostly skin.

"Daddy," she said, "don't feel too bad. You had to do it."

Of course it would have occurred to him sooner or later, without any prompting from Belle, that he and he alone was guilty for the loss of Bobbie's hand.

Since Cory would rather—if wishes had anything to do with the matter —have given his own hand, the way the guilt came to present itself was especially hard for him to master.

The point wasn't his negligence. As his father-in-law said, "There's a great many dangerous things around a farm, Cory. There always will be for kids."

"I know it," Cory said. "There's got to be machinery and animals and the pony that Joe and Gordon ride. You take the windmill tower for an example. I've caught Joe and Gordon up there I don't know how many times. They might any time fall and break their necks. Or the fan's going and they stick their heads up through the platform. Pfffttt!"

The older man extended the rhythm of agreement. "That's a fact, and you know Belle, when she was little, one time I nearly toppled a horse tank I was loading right onto her." He shuddered even now.

"Ah, but Dad, you held it," Belle recalled.

"I did," her father said. "And I paddled you for it when I saw you were safe. And I always remembered what a scare I had. But the point is that accidents just happen, Cory. After all, that's what the word *accident* means."

"Yeah, it does," Cory said.

The conversation was one of a great many that took place in the spring and summer after Bobbie lost his hand. They amounted to a kind of informal funeral, commemorating and at the same time draining away the immediate emotions of loss. It appeared, even to Cory, that it did him good to speak of the accident. He found no difficulty in saying man to man, man to wife, father to children—even to Bobbie—that an accident was something that just happened. Cory knew as well as any man that this was so.

Though he said many times that he could shoot himself for not having put a safety box around those gears on the sheller, this negligence was not the point that proved most crucial, either.

"You should have done that," his father-in-law said once when Cory lamented the absence of such a guard. "Well, we go on and try to make up for our past mistakes, and it does seem kind of sad to lock the door after the horse is gone, but that's what we do. I notice you took some rungs out of the ladder up the windmill."

"And Gordon climbed it the other night anyway," Belle said. "Shinnied right up the frame and had to yell for Cory to come and get him off."

They laughed and Cory laughed with them. Yes. Just to go on living he had to accept the likelihood of accidents, particularly where boys were involved, and he could do that.

But it wasn't the accidental part of Bobbie's misfortune that settled permanently into Cory's mind, freezing it to a pattern of distress. What he could never face—could never understand—was that he was guilty in taking that hatchet down from its hanging place on the wall and cutting off his son's hand.

"You had to do it," Belle said. She was willing to repeat this assurance whenever she thought it would help.

It never helped. Cory knew he'd had to do it. But necessity was no excuse at all for the guilt that rode him. The more he rehearsed his motives, the less important they seemed in comparison with the immortal act. If it was only bad luck that had put him in a situation where he had no choice, still, that luck was *his*. The guilt seemed to reside in that simple fact.

"It's like if I'd been someone else, not any part of this awful thing would have happened," he said to Belle.

Now that her emotions had resumed their normal level, she was almost as much amused as concerned at this odd way of putting it. She probably thought he was fishing for sympathy, and though she didn't mind sympathizing with him all he wanted, she didn't know how to offer the right response to his fancy. She said, "Sure. Sure. If you were someone else you wouldn't have this farm. You wouldn't have your nice kids. You wouldn't be stuck with me. Well, that's all a pipe dream, old man. You're stuck with all of us, and we'll get along. You know we will. Bobbie's a brave little guy. We might just thank God he was always left-handed."

"I know we'll get along," Cory said.

"You shouldn't punish yourself this way, because there's nothing to punish yourself for."

"I know that too."

"Then don't get depressed like this."

He had not spoken from depression, but from guilt. He knew well enough what depression was. He was depressed in those years of the thirties when the drought took most of his corn crop two years in succession; when he let himself be cheated in buying a secondhand car that turned out to have a cracked block; when he had trouble with his gallstones and had to cripple around all one winter; when his oldest boy, Joe, had trouble with his high-school studies and went off to join the Navy; when Belle's father, a man who'd been so good to Cory and his family and so dear to Bobbie, died of cancer; when the war came and Joe was out there at Pearl Harbor, where the Japs dropped on them with their newfangled weapons, and so many didn't have a chance on the anchored ships.

Year by year there were things to depress him. Big things and little things. And through the same years there'd been good times and times of satisfaction when he *wasn't* depressed. Take the summer he'd put the family in the car and driven them out to Yellowstone Park. That trip was a pure satisfaction. He couldn't remember a thing wrong with it.

Easily he remembered the good winters when he and Gordon were teaching Bobbie to hunt with them. They would load the dogs in the back seat of the car and drive over to the creek bottom to look for rabbits, quail, or pheasants. Cory had his pump gun. Gordon and Bobbie "shared" the single-shot .410 that had been bought for Joe when he turned twelve. Off they'd mush through the snow and broken cornstalks, trying to keep up with the badly trained dogs, joking and trading insults like three men—or three boys, it didn't matter which. Once, Cory'd knocked down three cock pheasants from a rising covey. Bobbie clapped his mitten to the side of his head and howled in admiration and disbelief. "Purty good, for an old man," he yelled over the snow. "Purty good."

"Even if you did get more than the limit," Gordon put in. "You going to tell the game warden I shot one of them?"

What he'd seen in the boys' eyes that afternoon was unmistakable and worth treasuring—just standing there in the snow with the dead birds around them, the boys being proud of their old man. It was like the male satisfaction he'd felt the day he took Bobbie in through the mud to the doctor's. In time. Only now the boys were here to share and mirror back the lonely pride of his manhood.

There had also been the good times—not to mention *all* the blessings of the years—when Joe came home on boot leave; when prices picked up in thirty-nine and the same year Belle had another boy, Cory, Jr.; and when they got the first letter from Joe after Pearl Harbor saying he was all right.

The good things and the bad things of an ordinary farmer's life had happened to him. He had responded to them like an ordinary man, with satisfaction or depression.

But the guilt he endured was something else. It seemed to have a life of its own, to be almost a distinct life he lived when his ordinary life gave him the opportunity.

Weeks, months, years went by in which he forgot that he was guilty. During those periods he got quite used to Bobbie's disfigurement, as if it were a condition that had always existed, one intended by nature.

Fortunately, Bobbie wasn't the boy to feed on sympathy. He managed. As far as his parents could tell, he was a happier boy than Joe had been.

Cory watched without sentimentality as his maimed son grew up. But when the awareness of his guilt came back in one of its cyclic manifestations, he found that it had not diminished with time. After ten years it was as keen and lively as it had been that morning in Doctor Grant's office when Belle had unintentionally announced it to him.

An assortment of events served, through the years, to recall it, the way symptoms in the throat announce the approach of a general systemic infection.

For example, there was Bobbie's fight in the school yard when he was in the second grade.

Cory saw most of the mix-up. Driving homeward from an errand in Boda, he and Gordon stopped to pick up Bobbie from his play after school. From where the car was parked, they could see some boys darting back and forth beyond the schoolhouse, dodging, turning, skidding in the grass, swinging at each other in what seemed to be a game of tag. Then Glen Horstman chased Bobbie down into the corner by the well. Bobbie backed into the hedge separating the school yard from a cornfield. He sparred away the jabs and pokes the bigger boy aimed at him. It looked as if both boys were laughing breathlessly, having a lot of fun.

They saw Glen Horstman feint a kick and follow the feint with a blow of his fist that started Bobbie's nose bleeding. Bobbie signaled that he'd had enough: *Lay off. I surrender.*

Glen kept punching. He had knocked Bobbie to the ground and was sitting on him when Gordon leaped the ditch and went running to the rescue.

Laggardly, Cory followed. He was only a few steps from the car when he saw Gordon chase Glen into the schoolhouse.

"Gordon!" he commanded.

Gordon stopped on the wooden stairs by the door and turned. His face was quizzical and angry. "Why, I'll just knock *him* around a little bit," he said.

"No you won't," Cory told him. "You and Bobbie come on and get in the car now. Bobbie'd better wash his face at the pump."

"But he's bigger than Bobbie," Gordon said. He blushed because he did not want to mention that Bobbie lacked one hand to use in self-defense.

"Get in the car!" Cory shouted.

All the way home from the schoolhouse, Gordon sat in incredulous, wounded silence. Bobbie, though, was talkative enough. He wasn't in any pain from his beating. He wasn't really mad at Glen Horstman. Now that it was over, the fight seemed to him a pure entertainment.

But that, as Gordon's silence implied, was not all that must be taken into account. On almost any other day he would have been there at school to protect his brother. At least, without his father's inexplicable attitude to reckon with, he would have known what he ought to do tomorrow.

After supper, Gordon went to his mother about what had happened. She, in turn, spoke furiously to Cory as soon as the boys were in bed.

"I think I'd just better get on the telephone and find out from his teacher if this has ever happened before—the kids picking on Bobbie. I won't have it. Just because he's crippled—"

"Aw, Belle, that wasn't why Glen done it. They was playing and he got carried away."

"Playing? Gordon said he hit Bobbie with his fist. He was sitting on him, pounding his head, and you didn't . . ." She didn't say what Cory should have done that he had omitted, but she shook her head bitterly. The more she thought, the more worked up she got.

"Well, you go ahead and call the teacher if you want to put your nose in it," Cory growled.

"I *will* put my nose in it," she said, "and you'd better go over to the Horstmans' place and have a little talk with Glen's dad, because I don't intend to have this kind of thing going on, whatever you intend."

"But Bobbie wouldn't want—"

"You can drive me over and sit in the car while I go in and have it out with them," she raged. "You can sit in the car if you're scared to tell Ralph Horstman we want this stopped."

The Horstman farm was less than a two-mile drive. Through the spring night and the murmur of a rainy wind, Cory drove slowly, telling himself that of course Belle was right. He sighed heavily and thought he'd want his friends who lived around him to come and tell him about it if one of his boys had done a wrong. But he seldom felt so uneasy about anything as he did walking in under the elms of the Horstman yard and knocking at the screen door of the back porch.

"He what? Glen done *what?*" Ralph Horstman bellowed. He grabbed Cory's shoulder and dragged him in from the back porch to the kitchen. "When'd he do that? This afternoon?" Horstman's throat began to swell rhythmically. He seemed to be growing taller and broader. "Mama, give Cory a cup of coffee or—or some *beer!*" he shouted to his wife. Then he fled the kitchen, pounding up the stairway from the living room like a plow horse frenzied in a burning building.

Cory and Mrs. Horstman heard the thump of a body dumped from its bed onto the floor and then a long, sleepy, uninterrupted wail, accompanied irregularly by the sound of slaps. In a minute Mrs. Horstman ran upstairs, too.

More slaps then. A more complicated sound of struggle began as the woman tried to mediate. Again and again, like the boom of outraged justice itself, Ralph Horstman's voice shouted, "He hit li'l Bobbie!"

After the condemnation, the smack of a hand on a rump, and then the woman's plea, seeming only to convince her husband that she had not understood the enormity of the offense. "But he hit li'l Bobbie!"

Downstairs Cory listened in what he could no longer doubt was envy. He knew well enough what he had no wish and no way of explaining to Gordon or Belle—that when he had seen Glen Horstman's fist bring blood from Bobbie's nose, he had felt a merciless identification with the aggressor. He had been unmanned by the recognition.

He had not wanted Bobbie hurt. No! He had never wanted Bobbie hurt, but he had seen his own act reenacted and known himself as powerless to prevent the pain as before.

But Glen Horstman, because he was a little boy, could be punished for what was, after all, a small offense. Cory, for his immeasurably greater offense, could expect no such squaring of accounts.

Afterward, each time his guilt flared in his face, he had to endure it in the same way until, mysteriously, it faded in his mind again—not dead, not even eroded by the remorse he had paid for it, merely waiting to be wakened again and endured again like an operation submitted to without anesthetic because, though he was guilty, no one owed him punishment.

He was punished. In the last year of the war, Gordon had just been drafted and sent to Fort Bragg when Joe was killed near Okinawa. By that time Joe was a seaman first class serving on a destroyer escort. The DE was on picket duty about seventy miles east of Buckner Bay when it was attacked by a George fighter. The attack occurred near sundown. A broad highway of gold and choppy crimson opened away from the little ship toward the west. The fighter came down this road like an erratic spark of gallantry and panic, hurled without conscious aim. The big ring sights on Joe's 20-mm. cannon must have circumscribed the sun itself as he swung it over to defend the ship. The fighter struck just abaft and below the bridge. The ship lived for several hours more, time enough for the survivors to be transferred to a destroyer. None of Joe's shipmates saw him or his body after the attack.

When the news came to the Johnson farm, Cory wept like any father bereft. And his tears were partly tears of relief, for it seemed to him in the first debility of sorrow that this extravagant punishment might, at last, pay off his guilt. It was not even in his heart to protest that the payment was too great, though he saw no equivalence between the hand he had taken from one child and the life he must now yield helplessly back to darkness. If he was quits, he must be satisfied.

But when his grief diminished and his strength returned, Cory saw that whatever had happened to Joe had nothing to do with his old guilt, which was neither increased nor minimized by Joe's death. What little religion Cory had kept through the years melted with this discovery. Religion seemed foolish to him now, a windy pretense at linking things that had no real connection. The issue was between himself and a chaos to which only a fool would pray.

He had nothing with which to replace religion. His irregular and shallow enthusiasm for science had long since vanished of its own inanity. Besides, though science had once seemed to him "the coming thing," he had never been notified that science might pretend to explain what he thirsted terribly to know. It had been fun to read about the novelties science discovered. He had got bored. That was all.

In his whole life, as he could look back at it now, only one condition had given meaning to his work and the depressions or satisfactions that went with it. That condition was his fatherhood. Even if he had fathered his boys more or less accidentally, in lust, in lukewarm fondness for his wife, his fatherhood had come to be more than the sum of days and of forgotten wishes. Before anything else, he was a father—and it was against this definition of himself that he had been forced to strike that day in the corncrib.

Belle died in 1950. Cory wept for her, too; envied her, too, for he suspected she must have carried through life some secret, like his, of undiminishable guilt for rebellion against the self that time and accident had given her. But now she was free of it.

They said Cory's mind began to fail him after Belle's death.

His mind was working better than ever—and he understood that was what his family and Doctor Grant *meant,* though they had to express themselves by an exact inversion of the truth.

If they had said he was troublesome and a bit frightening to live with, he could have agreed straightforwardly. But they needed more than that. Like most people, they needed a shallow burrow of "reasons" and "explanations" because they dared not deal with a sheer, objective fact. He could no longer live on their sort of explanations, but he sympathized with them. So he said, Yes, he reckoned his mind was going back on him. He didn't want to be a trouble to them, and if he couldn't straighten up by himself, he would certainly do what Doctor Grant recommended. He would go to the asylum "for a while." In the meantime, while they gave him a chance, he wanted to carry on his share of the work on the farm.

In this period there were five of the family living together there. Cory, Bobbie and his wife Lucy, and their little boy Ed (after Lucy's father), and Cory, Jr. Between them, Bobbie and Cory, Jr., could just about take care of the farm work. Bobbie had been to Ag school at the state university and he was a fine manager, very good with bookwork and planning ahead about the crops and machinery and soil, and figuring how they could afford the new things they needed. Farm work was more and more a matter of business brains these days, and he was sure that Bobbie was all right in that department.

Bobbie had got himself a new device to use for a right hand, too, now that they could afford it. There had been so much more money coming in during and after the war! Now you take Joe, Cory would tell himself, we just couldn't have afforded to send him to the university, Mother and I, back when he might have wanted to go. Then, quicker than anyone else could have reminded him that Joe was not a great one for study or using his brain, Cory would throw in that very qualification and go on: Yes, but things are getting so well-organized that they can take a boy who's not so bright to begin with and kind of guide him over the hurdles and give him remedial work and guide him into the right niche and he does all right! This was the way Cory's mind went on and on in an endless series of examinations and connections. His mind was far from failing. It dealt with more all the time, and, insofar as the mind alone was concerned, it was dealing more effectively. The sickness was elsewhere.

What Bobbie had was too grand and clever to be called a hook, though he good-humoredly called it that on weekdays. On Sunday, for fun, he called it a prosthesis. It was really three hooks and a bar, all with a bright chromium finish that twinkled wonderfully in the May morning sun when the young man swung himself up on the tractor seat and headed out to the fields, while Lucy held little Ed and waved to him from the back door.

It was so strange, sometimes, to Cory to see that shiny batch of levered claws on the baby's back when Bobbie was holding him—as at the homecoming picnic in Boda when there was a crowd and the Johnsons drove in to see all their old friends come back to this hick town. Gordon was with them, too, on that occasion, visiting a week from his job in Seattle, where he'd remained with an opportunity after the service.

That *thing* on the baby's back would look just as firm and tender as a human hand. Odd how Bobbie could use it to caress with sometimes, as if it were alive, though of course it had no sense of touch. It could express feeling though it had none. The only time the baby minded being touched with it was in cold weather. But Cory's thoughts were often busy on conjectures as to whether the baby *ought* to mind being touched by the lifeless thing. No end to considerations involved there.

With his prosthesis Bobbie could manage nearly any chore on the farm. No doubt if worst came to worst, everything could be handled without hired help if Cory went away. But Cory had made his place, now that the boys were taking over so much, by doing the dirty and menial jobs that their machinery still left undone. True, they had a milker, and even Cory, Jr., could handle the milking of their twelve cows without complaining he had been put upon. Someone still had to shovel up after the stock. The boys rented a corn picker from the elevator in Boda for the corn shucking. Someone had to drive the tractor into town through a November rain to get the picker and see that it got back on schedule. Cory always did jobs like that.

Doctor Grant didn't like it much that Cory should make himself into a nigger—that was his word—for the boys. As he saw it, this was another symptom of Cory's mental deterioration. But the doctor's opinion on this account was only one way of looking at it, and Cory was very well aware of this.

He realized that quite aside from any help he gave with the work or any hardship he imposed on Lucy by giving her another mouth to cook for, he *worried* his family.

He was sorry for this, but deliberately he went ahead with his alarming and aberrant courses. In the winter of 1952 he spent part of every day in the corncrib, where he was reconstucting the corn sheller that used to stand in the corner room. He scoured the neighborhood and the junk piles around Boda for old parts. He rebuilt the wooden frame where the electric motor had sat. He drilled bolt holes in the concrete floor he and Gordon had poured back in wartime when they junked the old sheller. He begged some secondhand lumber from the people who had moved onto the Horstman farm, not wanting to spend any more good money than he had to on his "foolishness."

It took Bobbie less than a week to figure out what his father was doing —a little longer to decide to intervene. Then one morning he made a point of sauntering down to the crib and entering the room where his father was hammering and sweating.

"What you up to?" Bobbie said. "I thought since I didn't have much to do this morning, maybe I could . . ."

The brightness and pretense—from both sides—faded quickly enough. A reckless pity shone from Bobbie's face. He wet his lips.

"Dad, you're making that sheller again, isn't that it?"

"Well, Bobbie, yeah, I thought I'd run her up again and see if maybe I could improve the design. Like you say, there's not too awful much work to be done these days, though maybe I ought to be down at the barn having a look at that loader Cory broke last summer." He started to leave the room.

Bobbie stopped him. "I didn't mean that, Dad. You don't have to work every minute. But—but, it seems kind of useless for you to be making a sheller."

"Yeah, it does."

"Then—"

"It kind of—"

"Dad, Lucy and I've been talking and we want you to, well, go out to Seattle and see Gordon awhile. You keep saying it would cost too much, and Seattle's a big place if you don't want to stay with Gordon. Look, I'm going to come right out with it. Lucy and I don't feel right for having called Doctor Grant in on you. Doctors don't know everything. But a family is different, and I know that Gordon would want you to come."

"—kind of helps me think things out," Cory said mildly, touching the homely machine he was building. "I'm not a hand like you are to put things down on paper or in words, either, and if I can build something to see, that helps with my brain work."

Bobbie gritted his teeth. "But you're thinking about things you ought to leave alone," he said. He held up his claw, glittering and lightly sweating in the cold room. "You're brooding about *this* again. For my sake, leave it alone. You think all my life I've blamed you somehow and I haven't. Can't you believe me when I say it? You *saved* my life and everyone knows that."

"I don't know," Cory said. "Maybe there was some other way to do it."

"*Was!*" The horror of that exploded syllable stood with them like the angel of death. What had been in time was not, any longer, in time. The past was unalterable, and yet they could not shake from their minds the illusion of free choice.

"I've had a good life," Bobbie said—as if that bore on the enigma that Cory wrestled. He might have had *another* life if his father had been the man to find another means of saving him. "What more could I want? I've been happy," Bobbie said.

"I know, son," Cory answered. "What I'll do, I'll get the pickup this afternoon and carry this junk down in the east forty and dump it. Guess I'd better save the lumber and use it for kindling."

Bobbie snarled in his frustration. "You don't have to do *that*, Dad. You don't have to do anything I tell you or anything for my sake. That's the point. Don't you get it?"

"Sure I see what you mean," Cory said. "I wasn't thinking about how you—and Lucy, I suppose—would feel about this contraption. Now let's just walk up to the house for some coffee and I'll tell Lucy I'm sorry I started it."

Bobbie said, "Maybe you'd better not mention it to her."

"All right," Cory said. "Whatever you think is best."

The next morning he was working on the sheller again. He had got to the point of installing the gears and covering them with a steel safety box.

Probably his queer behavior and his family's concern with it had been going on longer than he realized. Because they cared for him they would have taken what pains they could not to let him notice their precautions. Noting their few failures to be discreet was like seeing an advance guard of rats begin to invade the farm. Experience had convinced him that if you saw only the signs of depredation, that meant there were ten rats around your buildings. If you saw one rat, that meant a hundred. If you saw two together, a thousand, probably.

Now, to all his other considerations, he added the task of measuring the impressions he made each day on Lucy, Bobbie, and Cory, Jr. Like a stock-market gambler he read the daily quotations of his stock with them. Better this afternoon. Low and worried this week. Cautious. Desperate. Better. Better. The same.

They could not bring themselves to wound him by flat and final decisions in his behalf. If Bobbie had really insisted, Cory would have packed and gone to Seattle. Probably he would never have come back from that city.

At the same time, he realized that he confused their impressions by the very act of measuring them. And if their sanity wavered to the magnetism of his craziness—as he saw it did—then how could he trust them for reliable guidance, even in what he ought to do?

He understood, sometime during 1953, that they had been cautioned by Doctor Grant—or another authority they might have consulted at Grant's recommendation—to be on the lookout for a suicide attempt. He knew this first by subtle signs, as he would have known about a family of rats in the corncrib before he saw the first darting black shape and prepared for a campaign of poison and traps. The subtle signs were followed by a blunder so loving and crude it made him weep.

One morning he found that his straight razor had disappeared from the cabinet in the bathroom and had been replaced with an electric shaver. The exchange had been made just one week before Christmas, and he knew the electric gadget had been bought as a present for him. In their anxiety they had been unable to wait.

He picked up the shaver without hesitation. He accepted whatever Lucy and Bobbie (or was it Lucy alone, weaker in her fear, who had made the switch?) thought had to be done. He put the plug into an outlet and set the humming head to his cheek. He saw his cowed eyes under the windburnt sag of lids. It seemed to him his courage was not adequate to his pity.

"Father," he said, as he used to pray in the time he had not taken religion seriously enough to reject it. "Father." He heard no distinct syllables, but a shapeless groan.

The futility of their gesture seemed unendurable. They had taken his razor—didn't these children know that, on a farm, as Belle's Dad had put it, the means to harm were never lacking? He supposed they had hidden away the shells for his pump gun, too, though he had not bothered to check for some time. Odds and ends of rope had probably been gathered from the barn and outbuildings (by Bobbie, careful not to let on to Cory, Jr., why he was being so neat these days). They probably timed his comings and goings, not to permit him to be too long alone. And what good would all that do if he could claim the right to kill himself?

To put their minds at ease he wanted to go to them now and tell them how he had once determined to do away with himself and why that was all past. The occasion had come soon after Joe's death. The absence of the coffin from the funeral services had served as a reminder of the absence of justice due from the empty heavens. That had been more than eight years ago. No one had worried then about gathering up ropes from the sheds, garage, or barn.

He had put a rope around his neck one morning before anyone else was out of bed, standing by the square opening in the floor of the haymow. There was enough light at that hour to show the churchlike vaulting of rafters in the empty mow. Nothing had ever tempted him more seductively than the black square in front of his toes.

But he had taken the rope off with the slow deliberation of a judge—not for a moment assuming that he was granting himself reprieve, but that in all solemnity he was refusing it. Self-execution was inappropriate to his guilt.

Well—of course he must not go to the children and tell them what he remembered of that morning. He was poor with words; he was more likely to scare them than to appease them. They weren't prepared to understand that what he had sentenced himself to that morning in the barn was *to think*. Under that sentence, he was obliged to respect all the problems raised whenever he was rash enough to solve one of them.

He had to think, though it was not easy for him. It was not easy to rid the farm of a pestilence of rats, either, but, again and again through his years on this place, he had set himself the task of poisoning and trapping creatures who had over him the advantages of number, secrecy, and natures that recognized no obligation except to exist. He supposed there had never been a day when the farm was free of rats. Yet, by unwavering persistence he had thinned the rat population again and again to the point at which it was tolerable.

It wasn't easy for him to get ahead of the problem he now presented to his anxious children, but he set himself to find how to make it easier for them.

Through that spring and much of the following summer he appeared to be succeeding. The cycles of compulsive thought that had made him careless of his behavior since Belle's death sped faster—of necessity—as they seemed to settle down into the tranquillity of age. Once upon a time he would have refused to believe himself capable of the nimble calculations that now became a commonplace.

He gave up working on the sheller in the corncrib—because he had now got the whole material apparatus in his mind, from the grain of old wood to the bolts that fastened the electric motor to its bench, the pulleys and flywheel and their weight, strength, appearance, sound, and speed—all of this so completely transposed into an image that he could set the machine going in his imagination whenever he wanted. While he helped his youngest son with homework, or went over the accounts with Bobbie, or listened attentively to Lucy's frets about her new pregnancy, another part of his mind could repeat the crucial morning of his life.

So his family thought him better. They said he was "more himself" than he had been for years. They noticed how he gave up a share of the meanest work to each of his boys. Sometimes now he talked voluntarily of going to visit Gordon.

They were glad, again, to invert the truth. He saw that this second inversion did not cancel out the first—when they had believed him mad— but only made it incalculably more difficult to encompass, as if an already insoluble labyrinth should suddenly open out into its duplicate.

World without end, the world of thought that seemed bent on returning to some safe, lost starting point; but the prospect of its difficulty neither cheered nor daunted him. While he had strength of mind, he would go on as best he could, pretending that he was a juggler, an explorer, an acrobat, though he was only a big-footed farmer. At least he had learned to pace himself in his pursuit of multiplying complications. He had learned not to try too much at once. He was glad to think this adjusted pace—whether it meant success or failure to him—comforted his family.

One night in late summer he reached the end of thought. He had not foreseen (as a man with greater original gifts might have) that there could be an end of it. But there it was, confronting him. What had been a constantly accelerating series of wheels within wheels, wheels begetting wheels, a spinning and a spiraling that multiplied and exploded toward the ultimate horizons—all that was frozen in an instant into what seemed to him an immense sphere of light, motionless, achieved.

On the night it happened he was alone on the farm except for his grandson, who was sleeping upstairs. At suppertime Lucy had said with unusual petulance that she probably wouldn't get to go anywhere again for months or see any of their friends. The new baby was due soon. She would be tied down permanently after its arrival, so why didn't Bobbie take her anyplace any more?

Since he had been working hard in the hayfield all day, Bobbie might have snapped back at her. But Cory smoothed things over. He suggested that they drive through Boda to the county seat and find a place to dance or go to a movie. He was kind of tired himself, but would be glad to bathe Ed and read him a story and let him watch TV awhile before he went to bed.

Then Cory, Jr., had popped up and said he wanted to go along, too, and again there had been the threat of friction that Cory had to deflate judiciously. Why didn't young Cory ride just as far as Boda, he suggested, and drop off there to see some of his buddies? He could stay all night with Mickey Carnahan if he wanted, as a reward for working so well all day.

Cory had eased them away smoothly. The three young people left the farm after supper in a jolly mood. Young Ed had turned out to be no trouble at all. He nodded in front of the TV and went to bed early.

It was still not altogether dark when Cory took his cigar onto the screen porch to sit on the glider and do some thinking. On quiet evenings, left alone, he felt able to catch up on the arrears in his thought.

The night was faintly oppressive, though mild. He could hear the tree frogs dinning in the yard and the chug of the pump down by the barn. He heard the intermittent traffic of his neighbors going in late to Boda or the county seat, most of them traveling the new blacktop.

He thought about the highway and his neighbors and the way things had changed and the way things had been before. He thought, without emotion, of the difference between the blacktop and the muddy gravel he had charged through the day he cut off Bobbie's hand. Then he thought of the real sheller that had caused the accident and of the imaginary sheller that had duplicated it in his mind. And presently he was sure as could be that the sheller he imagined was run by the same principles that had run the sheller made of wood and steel. His creation and he were indistinguishable.

With that realization he reached the end of thought, knowing neither good nor evil but only guilt. The tree frogs, perhaps, continued their monotonous, hysterical song in the dark leaves around him. There may have been a continuing traffic on the roads and the sound of the pump's piston beating back and forth in its imprisoning cylinder. He did not hear them. Whatever existed was silent and motionless. Eternal. As it had been and as it would be when time ended.

In that silence he rose from the soft glider and let himself out the screen door onto the grass of the yard. He walked, without needing a light, to the shed by the back gate. The motion of his body was fluent and easy, but he felt nothing. It seemed to him that he was constituted of the same material as Bobbie's well-wrought hook and had been able, like it, to express love without the ability of knowing it. (The proposition was the same if exactly reversed: to know love without the ability to express it.) The only passion remaining was for a justice that would bring a man in phase with the total equilibrium of the night.

From the shed he took a short ax and went upstairs to his grandson's bedroom. He came down a little later without it.

He sat in the glider and relit his cigar. After a while he found himself straining to hear the tree frogs. To hear anything. Because he was not dead he had to break the motionless, soundless sphere of the thoughtless universe. He needed a noise to start him thinking again.

It was peaceful enough not to think—just to suck on the sweet cigar and let it all go up in a gentle exhalation. But he had to resume, if he could, the pain of thought so he could review what he had done in that silence when the sound of machinery stopped.

He had to plan the right way to present his act, or all those folks who relied on explanations would refuse to believe him sane. If they did not believe him sane, they would not punish him for this repetition of his guilt, and if he could not trick those who ought to love him into responsibility for a just punishment, then there was no hope for him in all this vast gleam of silence.

✧

R. V. Cassill was born in Cedar Falls, Iowa, in 1919, holds B.A. and M.A. degrees from the State University of Iowa, spent 1953 in Paris as a Fulbright Fellow and 1954 in New York City on a Rockefeller grant. For many years off and on he has taught fiction at the Iowa Writers' Workshop, but he has taught as well at the University of Washington, Columbia, The New School, and Purdue and is now at Brown. He has published four novels: The Eagle on the Coin *(1954),* Clem Anderson *(1961),* Pretty Leslie *(1963), and* The President *(1964). He has published more than fifty short stories, some of them collected in* The Father *(1965) and* The Happy Marriage *(1966). Although all Cassill's work is neglected in proportion to its merit, the greatest discrepancy is between the small readership of* Clem Anderson *and its very great excellence. A long and complex but very readable novel, it recounts the whole life of a vigorous and gifted writer, from midwestern childhood through fame and fortune to disintegration by despair and drink, the two enemies that seem eventually to do most of our good American writers in. In no sense merely a composite, the story of Clem Anderson nevertheless epitomizes the peculiarly destructive effect this country has on its serious writers—whether in rejecting their work or in accepting it doesn't seem to matter.*

"The Father" begins with a disclaimer: since the story began with an accident that happened some time ago, it stands as only "a unique little history without much relation to the fated march of public events or the destinies of most people." Accepting this more or less at face value, we still find a typical chronicle of an ordinary farm family from the Depression years, through World War II and the prosperity that followed, right up to times that may be considered approximately contemporary. As such, it is a compelling rural Gothic tale, showing how isolation and solitary brooding in the rural community lead an ordinary man to a shocking act of madness. However, the effect of this story is much deeper than that of a unique incident, and the author's disclaimer may be read as a flag to warn

the reader of a deeper intention. The corn sheller is not just a piece of potentially dangerous farm equipment. It is part of Cory's dreams about the magic world of science that he reads about in magazines. Through the machine that he has made he participates in a world of "electrons" and Japanese "centrifugal machine guns." There is nothing sinister in it, nor is there any real failure in Cory's handling of the accident when it happens. He acts as an isolated farmer and father must act, brutally and swiftly to the purpose, and he saves the boy's life. It is only after it is all over, when "everything seemed to be under control" and "the ordinary flow of circumstances had resumed again" and Belle says, "Daddy, don't feel too bad, you had to do it"—only then does Cory realize that "he and he alone was guilty for the loss of Bobbie's hand." The pride he felt in having done so well what a father had to do in an emergency was not only irrelevant but entirely unequal to "the point" of his guilt, the guilt that "settled permanently" into his mind. It was as creator, father, of the machine that he was guilty of the loss of his son's hand. It is his infatuation with science, which he later realizes is beyond his grasp, and his pride in the machine he has created, but which he has not been able to control, that comprise the sources of his guilt. This father, then, stands somewhat in the position of modern man, a creator in two worlds: that of his own family, set securely in the traditions of his rural past, living by the same kinds of work and belief as his neighbors; and also that world of science and machines, of the "science program broadcast daily from the station of the state university" and of the "factory technicians working for pay." The rest of the story is spent in remorseless and painstaking accumulation of evidence to show that the institutions of the first of these worlds—religion, family, community, and so forth—are not adequate to deal with guilt for the creations of the second. The machine that took Bobbie's hand lives again in the hook that replaces it. Cory is thus responsible for having created in his boy a man who is part machine, who in fact accepts a prosthesis of stainless steel as a natural part of his normal life as a rational, college-educated farmer. Cory's mind, with its "unwavering persistence" and "nimble calculations," is perfectly adequate to the tasks of his traditional community and serves him well enough in his war against the rats. It is inadequate to the sentence he imposes on himself "to think." He does not, in fact, "think" his way out of his insoluble dilemma; what he does is reach "the end of thought." He recreates the sheller in his mind and gets it working again so that "his creation and he were indistinguishable," thus enabling himself to commit the terrible act of "justice" that is a "repetition of his guilt" (not for having severed Bobbie's hand, but for once before having built the machine) and for which his only hope is that he will, finally, receive "a just punishment." Anyone who will reread the story, especially the last several pages, paying attention not only to the various direct references to machinery but also to all the imagery and language associated with science and calculations of various sorts, will see clearly that Cory's story is not "a unique little history without much relation to . . . the destinies of most people." It has an important relation to our belief in the beauty and power and importance and usefulness of a scientific technology of machines, and to our disillusion and distrust, our guilt, now that we find we are unable to control them. Cassill shows us that this guilt can drive Man to an act of ultimate destructive violence, an act of almost inconceivable madness, arrived at by some crazy idea of "rationality" and "justice." He shows us this not in the city nor on the assembly line nor in any of the places where the direct pressures of urban industrialized life might have been blamed. He shows us this happening in what city dwellers tend to think of as the idyllic world of homely sanity and certainty, the world of our recent rural past, where families and communities absorbed their misfits and absolved those who erred, a world whose conventions and institutions and beliefs are here shown to be unequal to the needs of men who, like Cory, insist on taking responsibility for their own creations.

FRANK ROONEY

Cyclists' Raid

◇◇◇◇◇◇◇◇

JOEL BLEEKER, owner and operator of the Pendleton Hotel, was adjusting the old redwood clock in the lobby when he heard the sound of the motors. At first he thought it might be one of those four-engine planes on the flights from Los Angeles to San Francisco which occasionally got far enough off course to be heard in the valley. And for a moment, braced against the steadily approaching vibrations of the sound, he had the fantastic notion that the plane was going to strike the hotel. He even glanced at his daughter, Cathy, standing a few feet to his right and staring curiously at the street.

Then with his fingers still on the hour hand of the clock he realized that the sound was not something coming down from the air but the high, sputtering racket of many vehicles moving along the ground. Cathy and Bret Timmons, who owned one of the two drugstores in the town, went out onto the veranda but Bleeker stayed by the clock, consulting the railroad watch he pulled from his vest pocket and moving the hour hand on the clock forward a minute and a half. He stepped back deliberately, shut the glass case and looked at the huge brass numbers and the two ornate brass pointers. It was eight minutes after seven, approximately twenty-two minutes until sundown. He put the railroad watch back in his pocket and walked slowly and incuriously through the open doors of the lobby. He was methodical and orderly and the small things he did every day—like setting the clock—were important to him. He was not to be hurried—especially by something as elusively irritating as a sound, however unusual.

There were only three people on the veranda when Bleeker came out of the lobby—his daughter Cathy, Timmons, and Francis LaSalle, co-owner of LaSalle and Fleet, Hardware. They stood together quietly, looking, without appearing to stare, at a long stern column of red motorcycles coming from the south, filling the single main street of the town with the noise of a multitude of pistons and the crackling of exhaust pipes. They could see now that the column was led by a single white motorcycle which when it came abreast of the hotel turned abruptly right and stopped. They saw too that the column without seeming to slow down or to execute any elaborate movement had divided itself into two single files. At the approximate second, having received a signal from their leader, they also turned right and stopped.

The whole flanking action, singularly neat and quite like the various vehicular formations he remembered in the Army, was distasteful to Bleeker. It recalled a little too readily his tenure as a lieutenant colonel overseas in England, France, and finally Germany.

"Mr. Bleeker?"

Bleeker realized the whole troop—no one in the town either then or after that night was ever agreed on the exact number of men in the troop— had dismounted and that the leader was addressing him.

"I'm Bleeker." Although he hadn't intended to, he stepped forward when he spoke, much as he had stepped forward in the years when he commanded a battalion.

"I'm Gar Simpson and this is Troop B of the Angeleno Motorcycle Club," the leader said. He was a tall, spare man and his voice was coldly courteous to the point of mockery.

"We expect to bivouac outside your town tonight and we wondered if we might use the facilities of your hotel. Of course, sir, we'll pay."

"There's a washroom downstairs. If you can put up with that—"

"That will be fine, sir. Is the dining room still open?"

"It is."

"Could you take care of twenty men?"

"What about the others?"

"They can be accommodated elsewhere, sir."

Simpson saluted casually and, turning to the men assembled stiffly in front of the hotel, issued a few quiet orders. Quickly and efficiently, the men in the troop parked their motorcycles at the curb. About a third of the group detached itself and came deferentially but steadily up the hotel steps. They passed Bleeker who found himself maneuvered aside and went into the lobby. As they passed him, Bleeker could see the slight converted movement of their faces—though not their eyes, which were covered by large green goggles—toward his daughter Cathy. Bleeker frowned after them but before he could think of anything to say, Simpson, standing now at his left, touched his arm.

"I've divided the others into two groups," he said quietly. "One group will eat at the diner and the other at the Desert Hotel."

"Very good," Bleeker said. "You evidently know the town like a book. The people too. Have you ever been here before?"

"We have a map of all the towns in this part of California, sir. And of course we know the names of all the principal hotels and their proprietors. Personally, I could use a drink. Would you join me?"

"After you," Bleeker said.

He stood watching Simpson stride into the lobby and without any hesitation go directly to the bar. Then he turned to Cathy, seeing Timmons and LaSalle lounging on the railing behind her, their faces already indistinct in the plummeting California twilight.

"You go help in the kitchen, Cathy," Bleeker said. "I think it'd be better if you didn't wait on tables."

"I wonder what they look like behind those goggles," Cathy said.

"Like anybody else," Timmons said. He was about thirty, somewhat coarse and intolerant and a little embarrassed at being in love with a girl as young as Cathy. "Where did you think they came from? Mars?"

"What did they say the name of their club was?" Cathy said.

"Angeleno," LaSalle said.

"They must be from Los Angeles. Heigh-ho. Shall I wear my very best gingham, citizen colonel?"

"Remember now—you stay in the kitchen," Bleeker said.

He watched her walk into the lobby, a tall slender girl of seventeen, pretty and enigmatic, with something of the brittle independence of her mother. Bleeker remembered suddenly, although he tried not to, the way her mother had walked away from him that frosty January morning two years ago saying, "I'm going for a ride." And then the two-day search in the mountains after the horse had come back alone and the finding of her body—the neck broken—in the stream at the foot of the cliff. During the war he had never really believed that he would live to get back to Cathy's mother and after the war he hadn't really believed he would be separated from her—not again—not twice in so short a time.

Shaking his head—as if by that motion he could shed his memories as easily as a dog sheds water—Bleeker went in to join Gar Simpson who was sitting at a table in the barroom. Simpson stood politely when Bleeker took the opposite chair.

"How long do you fellows plan to say?" Bleeker asked. He took the first sip of his drink, looked up, and stared at Simpson.

"Tonight and tomorrow morning," Simpson said.

Like all the others he was dressed in a brown windbreaker, khaki shirt, khaki pants, and as Bleeker had previously observed wore dark calf-length boots. A cloth and leather helmet lay on the table beside Simpson's drink, but he hadn't removed his flat green goggles, an accouterment giving him and the men in his troop the appearance of some tropical tribe with enormous semi-precious eyes, lidless and immovable. That was Bleeker's first impression and, absurd as it was, it didn't seem an exaggeration of fancy but of truth.

"Where do you go after this?"

"North." Simpson took a rolled map from a binocular case slung over his shoulder and spread it on the table. "Roughly we're following the arc of an ellipse with its southern tip based on Los Angeles and its northern end touching Fresno."

"Pretty ambitious for a motorcycle club."

"We have a month," Simpson said. "This is our first week but we're in no hurry and we're out to see plenty of country."

"What are you interested in mainly?"

"Roads. Naturally, being a motorcycle club—you'd be surprised at the rate we're expanding—we'd like to have as much of California as possible opened up to us."

"I see."

"Keeps the boys fit too. The youth of America. Our hope for the future." Simpson pulled sternly at his drink and Bleeker had the impression that Simpson was repressing, openly, and with pride, a vast sparkling ecstasy.

Bleeker sat and watched the young men in the troop file upstairs from the public washroom and stroll casually but nevertheless with discipline into the dining room. They had removed their helmets and strapped them to their belts, each helmet in a prescribed position to the left of the belt-buckle but—like Simpson—they had retained their goggles. Bleeker wondered if they ever removed the goggles long enough to wash under them and, if they did, what the flesh under them looked like.

"I think I'd better help out at the tables," Bleeker said. He stood up and Simpson stood with him. "You say you're from Troop B? Is that right?"

"Correct. We're forming Troop G now. Someday—"

"You'll be up to Z," Bleeker said.

"And not only in California."

"Where else for instance?"

"Nevada—Arizona—Colorado—Wyoming."

Simpson smiled and Bleeker, turning away from him abruptly, went into the dining room where he began to help the two waitresses at the tables. He filled water glasses, set out extra forks, and brought steins of beer from the bar. As he served the troop, their polite thank yous, ornate and insincere, irritated him. It reminded him of tricks taught to animals, the animals only being allowed to perform under certain obvious conditions of security. And he didn't like the cool way they stared at the two waitresses, both older women and fixtures in the town and then leaned their heads together as if every individual thought had to be pooled and divided equally among them. He admitted, after some covert study, that the twenty men were really only variations of one, the variations, with few exceptions, being too subtle for him to recognize and differentiate. It was the goggles, he decided, covering that part of the face which is most noteworthy and most needful for identification—the eyes and the mask around the eyes.

Bleeker went into the kitchen, pretending to help but really to be near

Cathy. The protective father, he though ironically, watching his daughter cut pie and lay the various colored wedges on the white blue-bordered plates.

"Well, Daddy, what's the verdict?" Cathy looked extremely grave but he could see that she was amused.

"They're a fine body of men."

"Uh-huh. Have you called the police yet?"

He laughed. "It's a good thing you don't play poker."

"Child's play." She slid the last piece of blueberry pie on a plate. "I saw you through the door. You looked like you were ready to crack the Siegfried line—single-handed."

"That man Simpson."

"What about him?"

"Why don't you go upstairs and read a book or something?"

"Now, Daddy—you're the only professional here. They're just acting like little tin soldiers out on a spree."

"I wish to God they were made of tin."

"All right. I'll keep away from them. I promise." She made a gesture of crossing her throat with the thin edge of a knife. He leaned over and kissed her forehead, his hand feeling awkward and stern on her back.

After dinner the troop went into the bar, moving with a strange co-ordinated fluency that was both casual and military and sat jealously to-gether in one corner of the room. Bleeker served them pitchers of beer and for the most part they talked quietly together, Simpson at their center, their voices guarded and urgent as if they possessed information which couldn't be disseminated safely among the public.

Bleeker left them after a while and went upstairs to his daughter's room. He wasn't used to being severe with Cathy and he was a little embarrassed by what he had said to her in the kitchen. She was turning the collars of some of his old shirts, using a portable sewing machine he had bought her as a present on her last birthday. As he came in she held one of the shirts comically to the floor lamp and he could see how thin and transparent the material was. Her mother's economy in small things, almost absurd when compared to her limitless generosity in matters of importance, had been one of the family jokes. It gave him an extraordinary sense of pleasure, so pure it was like a sudden inhalation of oxygen, to see that his daughter had not only inherited this tradition but had considered it meaningful enough to carry on. He went down the hall to his own room without saying anything further to her. Cathy was what he himself was in terms which could mean absolutely nothing to anyone else.

He had been in his room for perhaps an hour, working on the hotel accounts and thinking obliquely of the man Simpson, when he heard, faintly and apparently coming from one direction, the sound of singing.

He got up and walked to the windows overlooking the street. Standing there, he thought he could fix the sound farther up the block toward Cunningham's bar. Except for something harsh and mature in the voices it was the kind of singing that might be heard around a Boy Scout campfire, more rhythmic than melodic and more stirring than tuneful. And then he could hear it almost under his feet, coming out of the hotel lobby and making three or four people on the street turn and smile foolishly toward the doors of the veranda.

Oppressed by something sternly joyous in the voices, Bleeker went downstairs to the bar, hearing, as he approached, the singing become louder and fuller. Outside of Simpson and the twenty men in the troop there were only three townsmen—including LaSalle—in the bar. Simpson, seeing Bleeker in the door, got up and walked over to him, moving him out into the lobby where they could talk.

"I hope the boys aren't disturbing you," he said.

"It's early," Bleeker said.

"In an organization as large and selective as ours it's absolutely necessary to insist on a measure of discipline. And it's equally necessary to allow a certain amount of relaxation."

"The key word is selective, I suppose."

"We have our standards," Simpson said primly.

"May I ask just what the hell your standards are?"

Simpson smiled. "I don't quite understand your irritation, Mr. Bleeker."

"This is an all-year-round thing, isn't it? This club of yours?"

"Yes."

"And you have an all-year-round job with the club?"

"Of course."

"That's my objection, Simpson. Briefly and simply stated, what you're running is a private army." Bleeker tapped the case slung over Simpson's shoulder. "Complete with maps, all sorts of local information, and of course a lobby in Sacramento."

"For a man who has traveled as widely as you have, Mr. Bleeker, you display an uncommon talent for exaggeration."

"As long as you behave yourselves I don't care what you do. This is a small town and we don't have many means of entertainment. We go to bed at a decent hour and I suggest you take that into consideration. However, have your fun. Nobody here has any objections to that."

"And of course we spend our money."

"Yes," Bleeker said. "You spend your money."

He walked away from Simpson and went out onto the veranda. The singing was now both in front and in back of him. Bleeker stood for a moment on the top steps of the veranda looking at the moon, hung like a slightly soiled but luminous pennant in the sky. He was embarrassed by his outburst to Simpson and he couldn't think why he had said such things.

Private army. Perhaps, as Simpson had said, he was exaggerating. He was a small-town man and he had always hated the way men surrendered their individuality to attain perfection as a unit. It had been necessary during the war but it wasn't necessary now. Kid stuff—with an element of growing pains.

He walked down the steps and went up the sidewalk toward Cunningham's bar. They were singing there too and he stood outside the big plate-glass window peering in at them and listening to the harsh, pounding voices colored here and there with the sentimentalism of strong beer. Without thinking further he went into the bar. It was dim and cool and alien to his eyes and at first he didn't notice the boy sitting by himself in a booth near the front. When he did, he was surprised—more than surprised, shocked— to see that the boy wasn't wearing his goggles but had placed them on the table by a bottle of Coca-Cola. Impulsively, he walked over to the booth and sat across from the boy.

"This seat taken?"

He had to shout over the noise of the singing. The boy leaned forward over the table and smiled.

"Hope we're not disturbing you."

Bleeker caught the word "disturbing" and shook his head negatively. He pointed to his mouth, then to the boy and to the rest of the group. The boy too shook his head. Bleeker could see that he was young, possibly twenty-five, and that he had dark straight hair cut short and parted neatly at the side. The face was square but delicate, the nose short, the mouth wide. The best thing about the boy, Bleeker decided, were his eyes, brown perhaps or dark gray, set in two distorted ovals of white flesh which contrasted sharply with the heavily tanned skin on the cheeks, forehead and jaws. With his goggles on he would have looked like the rest. Without them he was a pleasant young man, altogether human and approachable.

Bleeker pointed to the Coca-Cola bottle. "You're not drinking."

"Beer makes me sick."

Bleeker got the word "beer" and the humorous gulping motion the boy made. They sat exchanging words and sometimes phrases, illustrated always with a series of clumsy, groping gestures until the singing became less coherent and spirited and ended finally in a few isolated coughs. The men in the troop were moving about individually now, some leaning over the bar and talking in hoarse whispers to the bartender, others walking unsteadily from group to group and detaching themselves immediately to go over to another group, the groups usually two or three men constantly edging away from themselves and colliding with and being held briefly by others. Some simply stood in the center of the room and brayed dolorously at the ceiling.

Several of the troop walked out of the bar and Bleeker could see them standing on the wide sidewalk looking up and down the street—as contemptuous of one another's company as they had been glad of it earlier. Or not so much contemptuous as unwilling to be coerced too easily by any authority outside themselves. Bleeker smiled as he thought of Simpson and the man's talk of discipline.

"They're looking for women," the boy said.

Bleeker had forgotten the boy temporarily and the sudden words spoken in a normal voice startled and confused him. He thought quickly of Cathy —but then Cathy was safe in her room—probably in bed. He took the watch from his vest pocket and looked at it carefully.

"Five minutes after ten," he said.

"Why do they do that?" the boy demanded. "Why do they have to be so damned indecent about things like that? They haven't got the nerve to do anything but stare at waitresses. And then they get a few beers in them and go around pinching and slapping—they—"

Bleeker shivered with embarrassment. He was looking directly into the boy's eyes and seeing the color run under the tears and the jerky pinching movement of the lids as against something injurious and baleful. It was an emotion too rawly infantile to be seen without being hurt by it and he felt both pity and contempt for a man who would allow himself to display such a feeling—without any provocation—so nakedly to a stranger.

"Sorry," the boy said.

He picked up the green goggles and fitted them awkwardly over his eyes. Bleeker stood up and looked toward the center of the room. Several of the men turned their eyes and then moved their heads away without seeming to notice the boy in the booth. Bleeker understood them. This was the one who could be approached. The reason for that was clear too. He didn't belong. Why and wherefore he would probably never know.

He walked out of the bar and started down the street toward the hotel. The night was clear and cool and smelled faintly of the desert, of sand, of heated rock, of the sweetly-sour plants growing without water and even of the sun which burned itself into the earth and never completely withdrew. There were only a few townsmen on the sidewalk wandering up and down, lured by the presence of something unusual in the town and masking, Bleeker thought, a ruthless and menacing curiosity behind a tolerant grin. He shrugged his shoulders distastefully. He was like a cat staring into a shadow the shape of its fears.

He was no more than a hundred feet from the hotel when he heard—or thought he heard—the sound of automatic firing. It was a well-remembered sound but always new and frightening.

Then he saw the motorcycle moving down the middle of the street, the exhaust sputtering loudly against the human resonance of laughter, catcalls, and epithets. He exhaled gently, the pain in his lungs subsiding with his breath. Another motorcycle speeded after the first and he could see four or five machines being wheeled out and the figures of their riders leaping into the air and bringing their weight down on the starting pedals. He was aware too that the lead motorcycles, having traversed the length of the street had turned and were speeding back to the hotel. He had the sensation of moving—even when he stood still—in relation to the objects heading toward each other. He heard the high unendurable sound of metal squeezing metal and saw the front wheel of a motorcycle twist and wobble and its rider roll along the asphalt toward the gutter where he sat up finally and moved his goggled head feebly from side to side.

As Bleeker looked around him he saw the third group of men which had divided earlier from the other two coming out of a bar across the street from Cunningham's, waving their arms in recognizable motions of cheering. The boy who had been thrown from the motorcycle vomited quietly into the gutter. Bleeker walked very fast toward the hotel. When he reached the top step of the veranda, he was caught and jostled by some five or six cyclists running out of the lobby, one of whom fell and was kicked rudely down the steps. Bleeker staggered against one of the pillars and broke a fingernail catching it. He stood there for a moment, fighting his temper, and then went into the lobby.

A table had been overthrown and lay on its top, the wooden legs stiffly and foolishly exposed, its magazines scattered around it, some with their pages spread face down so that the bindings rose along the back. He stepped on glass and realized one of the panes in the lobby door had been smashed. One of the troop walked stupidly out of the bar, his body sagging against the impetus propelling him forward until without actually falling he lay stretched on the floor, beer gushing from his mouth and nose and making a green and yellow pool before it sank into the carpet.

As Bleeker walked toward the bar, thinking of Simpson and of what he could say to him, he saw two men going up the stairs toward the second floor. He ran over to intercept them. Recognizing the authority in his voice, they came obediently down the stairs and walked across the lobby to the veranda, one of them saying over his shoulder, "Okay, pop, okay—keep your lid on." The smile they exchanged enraged him. After they were out of sight he ran swiftly up the stairs, panting a little, and along the hall to his daughter's room.

It was quiet and there was no strip of light beneath the door. He stood listening for a moment with his ear to the panels and then turned back toward the stairs.

A man or boy, any of twenty or forty or sixty identical figures, goggled and in khaki, came around the corner of the second-floor corridor and put his hand on the knob of the door nearest the stairs. He squeezed the knob gently and then moved on to the next door, apparently unaware of Bleeker. Bleeker, remembering not to run or shout or knock the man down, walked over to him, took his arm and led him down the stairs, the arm unresisting, even flaccid, in his grip.

Bleeker stood indecisively at the foot of the stairs, watching the man walk automatically away from him. He thought he should go back upstairs and search the hall. And he thought too he had to reach Simpson. Over the noise of the motorcycles moving rapidly up and down the street he heard a crash in the bar, a series of drunken elongated curses, ending abruptly in a small sound like a man's hand laid flatly and sharply on a table.

His head was beginning to ache badly and his stomach to sour under the impact of a slow and steady anger. He walked into the bar and stood staring at Francis LaSalle—LaSalle and Fleet, Hardware—who lay sprawled on the floor, his shoulders touching the brass rail under the bar and his head turned so that his cheek rubbed the black polished wood above the rail. The bartender had his hands below the top of the bar and he was watching Simpson and a half a dozen men arranged in a loose semi-circle above and beyond LaSalle.

Bleeker lifted LaSalle, who was a little dazed but not really hurt, and set him on a chair. After he was sure LaSalle was all right he walked up to Simpson.

"Get your men together," he said, "And get them out of here."

Simpson took out a long yellow wallet folded like a book and laid some money on the bar.

"That should take care of the damages," he said. His tongue was a little thick and his mouth didn't quite shut after the words were spoken but Bleeker didn't think he was drunk. Bleeker saw too—or thought he saw— the little cold eyes behind the glasses as bright and as sterile as a painted floor. Bleeker raised his arm slightly and lifted his heels off the floor but Simpson turned abruptly and walked away from him, the men in the troop swaying at his heels like a pack of lolling hounds. Bleeker stood looking foolishly after them. He had expected a fight and his body was still poised for one. He grunted heavily.

"Who hit him?" Bleeker motioned toward LaSalle.

"Damned if I know," the bartender said. "They all look alike to me."

That was true of course. He went back into the lobby, hearing LaSalle say, weakly and tearfully, "Goddam them—the bastards." He met Campbell, the deputy sheriff, a tall man with the arms and shoulders of a child beneath a foggy, bloated face.

"Can you do anything?" Bleeker asked. The motorcycles were racing up and down the street, alternately whining and backfiring and one had jumped the curb and was cruising on the sidewalk.

"What do you want me to do?" Campbell demanded. "Put 'em all in jail?"

The motorcycle on the sidewalk speeded up and skidded obliquely into a plate-glass window, the front wheel bucking and climbing the brick base beneath the window. A single large section of glass slipped edge-down to the sidewalk and fell slowly toward the cyclist who, with his feet spread and kicking at the cement, backed clumsily away from it. Bleeker could feel the crash in his teeth.

Now there were other motorcycles on the sidewalk. One of them hit a parked car at the edge of the walk. The rider standing astride his machine beat the window out of the car with his gloved fists. Campbell started down the steps toward him but was driven back by a motorcycle coming from his left. Bleeker could hear the squeal of the tires against the wooden riser at the base of the steps. Campbell's hand was on his gun when Bleeker reached him.

"That's no good," he yelled. "Get the state police. Ask for a half a dozen squad cars."

Campbell, angry but somewhat relieved, went up the steps and into the lobby. Bleeker couldn't know how long he stood on the veranda watching the mounting devastation on the street—the cyclist racing past store windows and hurling, presumably, beer bottles at the glass fronts; the two, working as a team, knocking down weighing machines and the signs in front of the motion picture theater; the innumerable mounted men running the angry townspeople, alerted and aroused by the awful sounds of damage to their property, back into their suddenly lighted homes again or up the steps of his hotel or into niches along the main street, into doorways, and occasionally into the ledges and bays of glassless windows.

He saw Simpson—or rather a figure on the white motorcycle, helmeted and goggled—stationed calmly in the middle of the street under a hanging lamp. Presumably, he had been there for some time but Bleeker hadn't seen him, the many rapid movements on the street making any static object unimportant and even, in a sense, invisible. Bleeker saw him now and he felt again that spasm of anger which was like another life inside his body. He could have strangled Simpson then, slowly and with infinite pride. He knew without any effort of reason that Simpson was making no attempt to control his men but waiting rather for that moment when their minds, subdued but never actually helpless, would again take possession of their bodies.

Bleeker turned suddenly and went back into the lobby as if by that gesture of moving away he could pin his thoughts to Simpson, who, hereafter, would be responsible for them. He walked over to the desk where Timmons and Campbell, the deputy, were talking.

"You've got the authority," Timmons was saying angrily. "Fire over their heads. And if that doesn't stop them—"

Campbell looked uneasily at Bleeker. "Maybe if we could get their leader—"

"Did you get the police?" Bleeker asked.

"They're on their way," Campbell said. He avoided looking at Timmons and continued to stare hopefully and miserably at Bleeker.

"You've had your say," Timmons said abruptly. "Now I'll have mine."

He started for the lobby doors but Campbell, suddenly incensed, grabbed his arm.

"You leave this to me," he said. "You start firing a gun—"

Campbell's mouth dropped and Bleeker, turning his head, saw the two motorcycles coming through the lobby doors. They circled leisurely around for a moment and then one of them shot suddenly toward them, the goggled rider looming enormously above the wide handlebars. They scattered, Bleeker diving behind a pillar and Campbell and Timmons jumping behind the desk. The noise of the two machines assaulted them with as much effect as the sight of the speeding metal itself.

Bleeker didn't know why in the course of watching the two riders he looked into the hall toward the foot of the stairway. Nor did it seem at all unreasonable that when he looked he should see Cathy standing there. Deeply, underneath the outward preoccupation of his mind, he must have been thinking of her. Now there she was. She wore the familiar green robe, belted and pulled in at the waist and beneath its hem he could see the white slippers and the pink edge of her nightgown. Her hair was down and he had the impression her eyes were not quite open although, obviously, they were. She looked, he thought, as if she had waked, frowned at the clock, and come downstairs to scold him for staying up too late. He had no idea what time it was.

He saw—and of course Cathy saw—the motorcycle speeding toward her. He was aware that he screamed at her, too. She did take a slight backward step and raise her arms in a pathetic warding gesture toward the inhuman figure on the motorcycle but neither could have changed—in that dwarfed period of time and in that short, unmaneuverable space—the course of their actions.

She lay finally across the lower steps, her body clinging to and equally arching away from the base of the newel post. And there was the sudden, shocking exposure of her flesh, the robe and the gown torn away from the leg as if pushed aside by the blood welling from her thigh. When he reached her there was blood in her hair too and someone—not Cathy—was screaming into his ears.

After a while the doctor came and Cathy, her head bandaged and her leg in splints, could be carried into his office and laid on the couch. Bleeker sat on the edge of the couch, his hand over Cathy's, watching the still white face whose eyes were closed and would not, he knew, open again. The doctor, after his first examination, had looked up quickly and since Bleeker too had been bent over Cathy, their heads had been very close together for a moment. The doctor had assumed, almost immediately, his expression of professional austerity but Bleeker had seen him in that moment when he had been thinking as a man, fortified of course by a doctor's knowledge, and Bleeker had known then that Cathy would die but that there would be also this interval of time.

Bleeker turned from watching Cathy and saw Timmons standing across the room. The man was—or had been—crying but his face wasn't set for it and the tears, points of colorless, sparkling water on his jaws, were unexpectedly delicate against the coarse texture of his skin. Timmons waved a bandaged hand awkwardly and Bleeker remembered, abruptly and jarringly, seeing Timmons diving for the motorcycle which had reversed itself, along with the other, and raced out of the lobby.

There was no sound now either from the street or the lobby. It was incredible, thinking of the racket a moment ago, that there should be this utter quietude, not only the lack of noise but the lack of the vibration of movement. The doctor came and went, coming to bend over Cathy and then going away again. Timmons stayed. Beyond shifting his feet occasionally he didn't move at all but stood patiently across the room, his face toward Cathy and Bleeker but not, Bleeker thought once when he looked up, actually seeing them.

"The police," Bleeker said sometime later.

"They're gone," Timmons said in a hoarse whisper. And then after a while, "They'll get 'em—don't worry."

Bleeker saw that the man blushed helplessly and looked away from him. The police were no good. They would catch Simpson. Simpson would pay damages. And that would be the end of it. Who could identify Cathy's assailant? Not himself, certainly—nor Timmons nor Campbell. They were all alike. They were standardized figurines, seeking in each other a willful loss of identity, dividing themselves equally among one another until there was only a single mythical figure, unspeakably sterile and furnishing the norm for hundreds of others. He could not accuse something which didn't actually exist.

He wasn't sure of the exact moment when Cathy died. It might have been when he heard the motorcycle, unbelievably solitary in the quiet night, approaching the town. He knew only that the doctor came for the last time and that there was now a coarse, heavy blanket laid mercifully over Cathy. He stood looking down at the blanket for a moment, whatever he was feeling repressed and delayed inside him, and then went back to the lobby and out onto the veranda. There were a dozen men standing there looking up the street toward the sound of the motorcycle, steadily but slowly coming nearer. He saw that when they glanced at each other their faces were hard and angry but when they looked at him they were respectful and a little abashed.

Bleeker could see from the veranda a number of people moving among the smashed store-fronts, moving, stopping, bending over and then straightening up to move somewhere else, all dressed somewhat extemporaneously and therefore seeming without purpose. What they picked up they put down. What they put down they stared at grimly and then picked up again. They were like a dispossessed minority brutally but lawfully discriminated against. When the motorcycle appeared at the north end of the street they looked at it and then looked away again, dully and seemingly without resentment.

It was only after some moments that they looked up again, this time purposefully, and began to move slowly toward the hotel where the motorcycle had now stopped, the rider standing on the sidewalk, his face raised to the veranda.

No one on the veranda moved until Bleeker, after a visible effort, walked down the steps and stood facing the rider. It was the boy Bleeker had talked to in the bar. The goggles and helmet were hanging at his belt.

"I couldn't stand it any longer," the boy said. "I had to come back."

He looked at Bleeker as if he didn't dare look anywhere else. His face was adolescently shiny and damp, the marks, Bleeker thought, of a proud and articulate fear. He should have been heroic in his willingness to come back to the town after what had been done to it but to Bleeker he was only a dirty little boy returning to a back fence his friends had defaced with pornographic writing and calling attention to the fact that he was afraid to erase the writing but was determined nevertheless to do it. Bleeker was revolted. He hated the boy far more than he could have hated Simpson for bringing this to his attention when he did not want to think of anything or anyone but Cathy.

"I wasn't one of them," the boy said. "You remember, Mr. Bleeker. I wasn't drinking."

This declaration of innocence—this willingness to take blame for acts which he hadn't committed—enraged Bleeker.

"You were one of them," he said.

"Yes. But after tonight—"

"Why didn't you stop them?" Bleeker demanded loudly. He felt the murmur of the townspeople at his back and someone breathed harshly on his neck. "You were one of them. You could have done something. Why in God's name didn't you do it?"

"What could I do?" the boy said. He spread his hands and stepped back as if to appeal to the men beyond Bleeker.

Bleeker couldn't remember, either shortly after or much later, exactly what he did then. If the boy hadn't stepped back like that—if he hadn't raised his hand. . . . Bleeker was in the middle of a group of bodies and he was striking with his fists and being struck. And then he was kneeling on the sidewalk, holding the boy's head in his lap and trying to protect him from the heavy shoes of the men around him. He was crying out, protesting, exhorting, and after a time the men moved away from him and someone helped him carry the boy up the steps and lay him on the veranda.

When he looked up finally only Timmons and the doctor were there. Up and down the street there were now only shadows and the diminishing sounds of invisible bodies. The night was still again as abruptly as it had been confounded with noise.

Some time later Timmons and the doctor carried the boy, alive but terribly hurt, into the hotel. Bleeker sat on the top step of the veranda, staring at the moon which had shifted in the sky and was now nearer the mountains in the west. It was not in any sense romantic or inflamed but coldly clear and sane. And the light it sent was cold and sane and lit in himself what he would have liked to hide.

He could have said that having lost Cathy he was not afraid any longer of losing himself. No one would blame him. Cathy's death was his excuse for striking the boy, hammering him to the sidewalk, and stamping on him as he had never believed he could have stamped on any living thing. No one would say he should have lost Cathy lightly—without anger and without that appalling desire to avenge her. It was utterly natural—as natural as a man drinking a few beers and riding a motorcycle insanely through a town like this. Bleeker shuddered. It might have been all right for a man like Timmons who was and would always be incapable of thinking what he— Joel Bleeker—was thinking. It was not—and would never be—all right for him.

Bleeker got up and stood for a moment on the top step of the veranda. He wanted, abruptly and madly, to scream his agony into the night with no more restraint than that of an animal seeing his guts beneath him on the ground. He wanted to smash something—anything—glass, wood, stones— his own body. He could feel his fists going into the boy's flesh. And there was that bloody but living thing on the sidewalk and himself stooping over to shield it.

After a while, aware that he was leaning against one of the wooden pillars supporting the porch and aware too that his flesh was numb from being pressed against it, he straightened up slowly and turned to go back into the hotel.

There would always be time to make his peace with the dead. There was little if any time to make his peace with the living.

⋄

Frank Rooney was born in Kansas City in 1913, moved to Los Angeles in 1925, went into the Army in 1941, went to New York City in 1945, and now lives in Mamaroneck, New York, with his wife and children. He has published five novels: Courts of Memory *(1954),* Heel of Spring *(1956),*

McGinnis Speaks *(1960)*, The Great Circle *(1962)*, *and* The Shadow of God *(1967)*, *but his best-known work is still probably "Cyclists' Raid,"* *which after its original appearance in* Harper's *in January, 1951, was made into a celebrated movie,* The Wild One, *with Marlon Brando. For those who want to see them, there are always available ironic disparities between the fine achievement of modern fiction and its generally glum reputation; consider, for instance, what follows. "Cyclists' Raid" was reprinted in an anthology of pieces from* Harper's *immediately in front of an article that appeared in the magazine in November, 1951, ten months after "Cyclists' Raid." The article, called "The Trouble with Books Today," said that the fiction "of our time is in the doldrums . . . [because authors] have in these difficult times lost that clarity of vision which is a pre-requisite to successful literary composition." It is difficult to imagine what greater "clarity of vision" can be expected of a fiction writer than sixteen years ago to have given so vivid and dramatic a rendering of what has since become a cliché subject of magazine and newspaper reportage—and as we shall see, the story suggests meanings and ambiguities of the situation that are not to be found in the journalistic accounts.*

In "Cyclists' Raid" we see a small town invaded, its integrity violated, by an anonymous horde from a neighboring large city. The small town, part of the American ideal of what community is, or should be, is composed of persons whose individuality and identity are known to one another —by name, by business, by address, by family—and oppressive as this may sometimes seem, it is this knowing of one another as individuals which establishes the sense of unity and integrity that comprise the sense of community. Of all the cities in America, Los Angeles most epitomizes the opposite of this. The motorcyclists from Los Angeles have neither individuality nor community, and for the sake of a sense of the latter, they surrender all chance for the former. The point-of-view character in the story, Joel Bleeker, hates the cyclists even before they've harmed him, because "he was a small-town man and he had always hated the way men surrendered their individuality to attain perfection as a unit." He sees that "they were standardized . . . seeking in each other a willful loss of identity." By masking themselves with goggles and uniforming themselves in khaki and by executing precision movements they achieve through personal anonymity a group unity to substitute for the loss of the meaningful community of individuals. They find community, too, in their drunkenness and violence. When at the end the lone cyclist returns to town and is beaten and stomped by the townsmen (even Bleeker wants "to smash something— anything"), it is clear that they have not only violated the town but also corrupted it to their own kind of anonymous violence, meaningless and unremembered. The story was an early, accurate depiction of a specific social disruption of life in California, but it may be that some of its success rests in a broader implication it may have to all contemporary American readers. It may be that the story seems not perhaps a symbol but an analogy of the rape, followed by contagion, of the American small town by the dreaded anonymity, standardization, and violence of urban life. In fact, the story suggests clearly the ambiguities of the "innocent" position of the small town in its confrontation with the forces of a large city. The town welcomes the money the motorcyclists bring because it is not economically independent, just as small towns welcome large industrial plants and army bases as a source of income. Both the town and the cyclists are left-overs, rejects of an urbanized society in which "community" can no more be defined by a club of free-roving like-minded men than by a cluster of stores and houses that calls itself a town. Both are victims (the innocent daughter and the innocent cyclist who returns) of a lack of community; both the town and the cyclists respond to their loss of function in the larger urban community with unreasonable violence. In the confrontation of the cyclists and the town we see not so much the rape of one by the other as the weakness and failure, the vulnerability of both as pseudo-communities lacking the integrity and control which both believe they have achieved.

ROBERT HENDERSON

The Intruder

◇◇◇◇◇◇◇◇

MY NAME IS NEIL WAINWRIGHT, and I am a teacher. Professor of history. Sixteenth century. Married. Thirty-four years married. Wife's name: Elizabeth. One married daughter: Ann. I haven't seen Ann in nearly ten months. It seems too long. I live in a place I've loved for seventeen years, in a block off lower Fifth Avenue that has trees, and grace, and quiet people. This apartment is a rambling duplex, and I am writing not in my own workroom but in a small room upstairs.

Tonight Elizabeth is at a concert with friends and I am alone, searching for something that I have not yet been able to define. Something—well, faceless. I've said "panic" to myself all week, but that is just a dodge. I know it. What lies *back* of panic is the question.

I keep writing, running along, and I am reluctantly aware that behind me is the window through which someone entered this room one warm night last April. Is that what I am looking for? Perhaps. Yes, that night must be the starting place. And was it because of that intrusion, though it wasn't much in itself, that I came to the room tonight? I think so.

It really is rather a ridiculous little room. It makes no sense, has no coherence, though it can start memories up like rabbits. Ann is in it, so to speak. It was her room for three years before she went to college, and she left a few tokens. High-school texts; a clay model she made of her poodle which is quite good. She was only thirteen. The proportions are rough, maybe, but the thing is alive.

On the daybed is one of Elizabeth's handbags. She used to leave a row of them there—she often dresses in this room—but since that night in April she generally keeps them out of sight. The burglar went through them, and afterward they seemed unclean to her. She brushed and rubbed them half the next afternoon. Then there are filing cases and stacks of big envelopes, all full of work I finished long ago. Cards I made out in Gloucestershire and other places. On the table in front of me is a round smooth, honey-colored stone. I picked it up in a meadow in Greece. It's not a fragment of anything that I know of, though it could be. I just believed that it must have been there when the temples were. With some things you don't have to care too much about verification. They connect. Besides, the Greeks aren't my field, and I can imagine them to suit myself.

So, begin with the burglar—or at least with the burglary, for I never saw him. Elizabeth saw a shape. Our bedroom door is next to the door of this room. The night was warm. We had put on the air conditioner, which, of course, made a sound in the room. Opposite the bedroom door is another door giving on an outer stairway. Elizabeth heard someone moving and groping in the little hall between. She thought I had got up and was ill or confused, and she called to me, and I woke up and answered from the bed beside hers. The stair door opened, and a man slipped out, and it closed behind him. All I saw, half awake, was a burst of light and the return of the dark; and then Elizabeth screamed.

I jumped for the door—a hero—but listened before I opened it. There was no sound, and no one was outside. No one was on the staircase. I shut and locked the door and put on the hall light. Elizabeth was standing in the middle of the bedroom. She is almost as tall as I am, but she seemed quite small. I could see her shaking. So was I. We just looked at each other, and then, at the same moment, hurried into Ann's room—this room.

The window was open, though not very wide. He must have been agile; he had come in over a row of potted plants on the sill. The handbags on the bed had been thrown about. There had been money in only one of them—a few dollars. Nothing else seemed to be gone. We went downstairs and I called the police, who came quickly. They looked around, asked questions, and left, and we waited there awhile without saying that what we were waiting for was dawn. When it came, we went upstairs, and before going back to bed, looked into the room again. I closed the window, feeling an odd distaste at touching it. Elizabeth found a few nickels and dimes on the bed and table, and then a little red coin purse lying in a corner of the hall. I picked up a large number of burnt matches from the rug. He had been lighting matches—for how long?—a dozen feet away from us while we slept.

Now it suddenly seems strange that that was all there was to it. It happened half a year ago, and this room is still always *that* room. Worse things—terrible things—have happened to peaceful people. A man happens to jostle another man and is followed and stabbed to death with a broken bottle. A woman rings for her elevator and finds her husband in it, shot through the heart. But this place is not the street, or some alien corner of town. It is where Elizabeth and I live—where we and Ann have lived, full of certainty—and it was entered by stealth, invaded in darkness by someone silent and faceless.

Certainty. I suppose that may be the word I am reaching for at the moment. How do you write down what the place you live in is to you? Seventeen years' worth of the growth of certainties. That's enough to lay a soft luster over the rooms and the furniture and us. It didn't always exist, either; there have been changes and storms—even here, at first. But this apartment lies at the physical heart of a kind of enclave, a haven. The Avenues at each end are busy, but our block is apart and knows it. When you turn into the block, you feel as if you had entered a private place, come through a gate. It has legends of ghosts in old town houses, and other minor traditions. It even has a tame beggar—a tall, watery, middle-aged man with a foolish smile, who turns up each spring and cruises the block once or twice a day during the good weather. He pets the dogs and picks up a few coins. People tolerate him. He isn't around *too* much, and he's part of the scene.

No one seems to move away. Some of the neighbors get up a caroling session at Christmas. We've never joined in, but it is extremely pleasant to hear. So yes, it is a scene where certainties develop. For instance, the certainty of things in balance—weatherproof, watertight. The certainty of safety.

Elizabeth and I didn't sleep any more that morning, and the rest of the day was out of kilter, though we pretended it wasn't. We would catch ourselves speaking low and listening to nothing. We weren't afraid. There was nothing to be afraid of. But I know I felt displaced, or somehow guilty of defilement, and I resented it. I gave two lectures. I wanted to cancel the second and get back home, but what for? To startle Elizabeth? I had bolts put on the doors, which did seem sensible. I fitted a two-by-four into the upper frame of that window—I told myself I did it to calm Elizabeth—and ordered a special window lock. And then, going through the room while she was cleaning handbags, I saw a smudge of black at the edge of the rug. It was sticky. We hadn't been talking much about the burglar, so I didn't point it out, but I knew that the roof next door was newly tarred, and I saw smears of black on our gutter. Later, I found a grimy empty match packet under this table. He was hard to exorcise. We had been asked out to dinner that night. When we got home and were preparing for bed, I saw Elizabeth absently look back of several doors. As I came out of the bathroom, she was closing the one to the staircase. "There's some of that tar on the landing," she said offhandedly, and we went to bed without turning on the air conditioner, though the night was warm again.

The window lock came in less than a week, and I put it on, myself. It seemed more than just a device to secure a window—more like a promise that the nights, and days, would be as they always had been. The window is a dormer, with triangles of wall on either side. I installed the lock to the left of the frame and tightened it, and as I turned away I saw a clear handprint high on the right-hand wall. He was not gone yet. I scrubbed it off at once, and never told Elizabeth it had been there.

Perhaps, because of later events, I am dwelling too much on how upset we were—perhaps I am even magnifying it, but I think not. At any rate, that is what happened. We tried to forget the intruder, but for a long time untethered pronouns would keep slipping into the talk—just "he" or "him" or "his." "He must be small," Elizabeth would say, out of the blue; or, "I wish I could know who he is, or *what* he is." She seemed to need to give him a face and a definition. It bothered her that he might be someone she had passed on the street, and she began to scrutinize all grocers' boys and repairmen.

Between then and now, a secretary has been shot down at her desk in a college office, no one know why—no one but the person who shot her. A quiet, elderly woman has been strangled for two dollars and thirty cents in a great hive of a building not far from here. A middle-aged teacher has been raped and killed in her own hallway. These are the incidents that happen to come to mind at the moment; there have been a hundred others, and, in a way, our burglar has been guilty of them all.

I used to walk everywhere on this island, sometimes with Elizabeth, sometimes alone, often at night. We would stay up prowling small bars or penny arcades, or the Washington Market. Once we waited all night to go out on the Brooklyn Bridge at dawn. "The whole thing belongs to you, doesn't it?" Elizabeth said, as we stood looking back at the skyline. I had just been given some sort of promotion, and that was why she said it. I like to recall how her face looked.

I love to be in strange sections of Manhattan, to turn a corner and come unexpectedly on trees, or a glimpse of a ship. I love the way darkness comes into the streets, while the sun still burns on the windows of a building that has, itself, turned dusty red. And such things as I am putting down here used to add up to a curious contentment. Lively but casual. Free. One recent winter, there was such a snow that no cars were allowed on the streets, and people poured outdoors and wandered in them. Neighbors became friends. The goodness of the city was boundless. I guess I did know better, but that was how it seemed.

Well, not now. For a while, Elizabeth gathered a small bouquet of suspects. I don't think she really believed in them herself, but she needed them. She remembered a skinny painter who had once worked in our building. She tried to believe that the block beggar was a burglar's lookout, though even she wouldn't argue that he could have made the climb to this window. Later, she recalled that when the man who picked up our laundry had been ill, a lithe little Puerto Rican had taken his place.

And as Elizabeth narrowed the field, I widened it. Before long, I had stopped thinking about one man. "He" had become "they," and I was conscious of all the stealthy and violent men. Facelessness became a multiplicity of faces. And now I think I am coming to one of the things I was afraid I would find out: All of the faces, or most of them, were dark. Black, or at least swarthy. I think I pretended they weren't. I tried to blur the picture or dismiss it. I had never yet confronted prejudice in myself; it was something I was not supposed to have. But the faces were dark. After a while, some of the faces changed. Pale ones crept in. Addicts. Sick boys. Crazy ones. Drifters from the Bowery, or from the South or West. "They" come from everywhere; they *are* everywhere, and they are of all complexions. But most of the faces were dark for quite a while. Eventually they blurred, and violence grew anonymous again. A climate. A component of the air. Every so often you read of a stone thrown through a window of a commuter train; a commuter has an eye put out on his way home. Done by the climate. A young girl, going home at night from a graduation party, is picked off by a sniper from some anonymous roof.

But even home is not always safe. One is aware of that in spite of new locks and bars. Elizabeth is not safe. I sometimes wonder what I would have done if I had wakened and found the man there in the bedroom with us. I don't know. I believe I would have tackled him somehow, but only out of confusion or shock, or because it would seem incumbent on me in Elizabeth's presence. That is the only way I do anything brave—under pressure or grimly. Something is expected of me, or expected by myself. Mostly I try to evade the need—and I am evading now. I am stalling. I do not want to face the fears I have for Elizabeth. Too explicit pictures come to the edge of vision sometimes, and I deny them, refuse them entry. One day when Ann was four, she was playing outside with a part-time maid, who left her for a short while. I went out, just by chance, and saw a squat, unshaven man with her. He scuttled away. I thought she had never looked so tiny. She said he was nice—he had promised to buy her candy and take her to a park, and I can feel again, now, the sensation in my belly. They would have been gone around the corner in a minute, and I have never let myself imagine beyond that.

Well, I am not going to imagine what harm could come to Elizabeth. I want no harm at all to come to her, and there must be other ways of thinking this through. For instance, start with the old stone, there, that came from Greece. There is more clinging to it than a doubtful antiquity. When I brought it home, it was also a kind of token, a private promise that wherever I went afterward, Elizabeth would go too. It has been a paperweight in here for a dozen years, but that is how it got here. I've kept the promise. It has been easy.

That Greek meadow is a shallow green cup that tilts to the edge of a high cliff beside the Aegean Sea. I could see islands, I remember. I went there in search of presences. I was also there because I had ruined Elizabeth's plans for a summer on Cape Cod by banging off to do research in Naples, and then going on to Greece just to show her that I could. Independence. Rubbing it in. We quarreled too much, in those days. I was always snatching at traveling grants and fellowships to get away. I liked to put on a bit of swagger, for one thing, and I could never enjoy it around home. I liked to wear jaunty old soft-brimmed hats and carry a blackthorn cane, and look appraisingly at people. I don't suppose they took much notice, but I thought they did.

Elizabeth and I were very far apart by that summer. We scarcely wrote, and I was miserable from June until late August. But I hung around there in that meadow all my last afternoon in Greece, turning this stone in my hand and feeling no presence except hers. I grew peculiarly happy, and somehow I made peace with myself and, in my mind, with her. I don't know how I managed it—effect of the pale-gold light, the sea; maybe, after all, the other presences. Or else I felt that I deserved a reward for having been so miserable. Now that I was going home, I calculated that I didn't even need to be forgiven. And I forgave Elizabeth for her part in all our wars. I meant it, and with love.

Yes, but there was so little to forgive. Even tonight, when there is nothing whatever left of those old quarrels, they seem immeasurably sad and wasteful. She would plunge into some needless piece of housework afterward. At midnight, her hair flying, she would passionately wax the kitchen floor. (Her hair is very fine and light, and it has always flown a little.) I thought then that she was showing me how put-upon she was, but now I know she was also setting her house in order against the time when order would come back to it. She has always longed for order.

She has found it. We have it. That was a turning-point summer. The battles stopped. They never were the large part of our life, only the worst part. We've traveled; the fellowships still come, and the college is generous with time. But getting back here, to Manhattan and to this smaller island of our own within it, has always been at least as good as going away. Certainty and order. I haven't been to Greece again, but someday we will go there. We will try to find some presences. I think Elizabeth will feel at home with them, and they with her. *Nothing* must happen to her.

So, then—what does lie back of panic? What is the deep source? That is what I've told myself I was looking for, chiefly, and all these matters of fear and love may add up to part of the answer, but not to all of it. Now I had better set down quickly what happened that night last week.

I went to an evening meeting uptown. I sometimes carry my blackthorn cane at night, and I had it with me. Coming home, I wasn't able to get a cab, so I took the subway. I got off at Fourteenth Street, walked down Sixth Avenue, and turned into our block, and a man stepped out of the shadows around a tree directly in front of me and stood blocking my path. I was badly startled, and I swung and pushed at him with the cane in an awkward, womanish way, but he didn't speak, just loomed there. And then—and I assume this was panic—I hit him with the heavy end of it, and he went down. It happened fast. I will have to try to remember at what point I recognized him. This is crucial. It was our foolish beggar. For a minute or so I was sure that I had killed him. I felt as if I might be drowning.

It was panic and it wasn't. That day, some boys with knives had run loose on a subway platform, cutting two men and a girl selected at random. Nothing really untoward had happened on my own train, but a man—yes, a Negro; and yes, I do know now that this must have mattered to me, at least a little—had been across the car, talking to himself and swaying and lurching, and watching me, but he had stayed there. And the beggar is white.

I didn't want to touch him, though I thought I must. If Elizabeth had been there, of course I would have. Everything would have been different. He moved and grunted and sat up. He was facing away from me, and I walked backward to the corner, where there is a police call box. The man got up. He went east slowly without looking around, staggering a good deal. I called the police and reported an injured derelict wandering in this block. By then, he was gone in the darkness, but a police car came and drove slowly down the block, and stopped near Fifth Avenue. I had waited just around the corner on Sixth, and now I followed at a distance. The car stood a while. I suppose they picked him up. They left, and when I walked down there, the block was empty.

There it is. A ludicrous affair with an unspeakably shabby ending. A nineteenth-century caning in the streets. A twentieth-century panic. But something besides panic swung the cane, for before I hit him hard, I recognized him. And I hit him more than once. I don't say that I could have stopped my arm. But—I have to say—I *wanted* to hit him.

No—not *him*, I suppose. He is harmless. I never for a moment thought otherwise. He was only going to try to wheedle a small donation. He stands and simpers at you before he comes to the point. I knew him, but at the same time, he was—well, faceless. Irrelevant in himself, but suddenly one of *them*. I may have been defending myself, my ordered life, from them, but I know that just for a few seconds there, I joined them. I can't say what's fear and what's hate—they are all but synonymous. But I know you can get a lot said with a few swings of a blackthorn cane, and then you have to figure out what it was.

I will find some anonymous way to make amends to him. I would like to think I could face him, but this is an evening for at least approximate truth. I can find him. He has not been back, but I saw him from a taxi yesterday, in a seedy block of rooming houses and small stores, shambling along as usual, smiling his silly smile. He seemed all right. But why did I remain anonymous *then?* Cowardice? No. No, no—not really. I just didn't want to get mixed up in a mess. Well, I have *never* wanted to be mixed up with anyone but Elizabeth and Ann and a few friends, or anything but my work and selected pleasures. But for a long time now, Elizabeth and I have been caught up inescapably in the climate, the violent air. The intruder came, and in a sense, he stayed. In this room. In our lives. In me.

Yes. There it is, at last. In me. And in me all along. Sleeping, but there. Fear that had no call to stir out of doors, becoming hate, in all the good years. The faces were dark because of something in me. Something embedded. I have been thinking of that stealthy little man as an invader, but perhaps he is more of a resident, after all. Sometimes, when Elizabeth lies awake, I can guess that she is listening, more than half expecting him to come back. But now I know that he has been here all the while. We may never really exorcise him, but we must try.

⬦

Robert Henderson was born in Chicago in 1906, graduated from the University of Illinois in 1928, and has worked at The New Yorker *as a fiction editor for many years. He has published one book,* The Enameled Wishbone *(1963), a collection of "familiar essays" originally published in* The New Yorker.

"The Intruder" is a very explicit story about the effects of the fear of anonymous violence that has become so prevalent, especially in our large cities, but to some extent in all areas of the country. The terror of urban living constantly recurs as the subject of modern stories: Hortense Calisher's "The Scream on 57th Street," John Updike's "A Gift from the City," and Irwin Shaw's "Noises in the City" are three successful stories on the theme, but there are many. Strangely, most of these stories show that the fear is in each case quite groundless—often, as in "The Intruder," there is no real danger—but the fear is nevertheless very real. It has become the "climate" of the city, a "component of the air," as the professor-narrator of this story realizes. He believes he has established "certainty and order" in his life, after a period of uncertainty and disorder; he lives a quiet, separate life on a quiet street, an enclave; he has a nodding acquaintance with some of the neighbors, but he doesn't want to be involved with them. If community as such has something to do with knowing who people are and with being part of a network of responsibility and dependency, then he is clearly shown as being without community. The social organization of a large city is so vast and impersonal that personal involvement can easily be avoided. That is one of the advantages of urban living, especially for such a detached intellectual. But the other side of the matter is that the individual who is without knowledge or responsibility in the community,

who is not a part of a neighborhood or ghetto, is powerless and without protection. Knowing no one, it is necessary to fear everyone. Fear is of a violence that is anonymous, of "them," of all the dangerous strangers, the different, the unknown, the alien, the unplaceable and untraceable, the hidden, the dark, the unseen. When the burglar intrudes into the narrator's ordered and independent world, he stays only a few moments; but it is sufficient to leave traces of himself and his act—not just in the apartment but within the narrator. The intruder becomes "resident"; he so inhabits the Wainwrights' life that they "may never really exorcise him." For it is shown that fear and violence, panic and hate, are but opposite aspects of the same emotions. When the narrator canes the beggar toward the end, it may be a nineteenth-century act, but it is as a result of "a twentieth-century panic." It is an act of panic, but it is also an act of hate; it is an act of fear, but it is also an act of violence. Where there is a climate of violence the most frightened people become capable of fearsome acts—and violence is "a component of the air" in many other places we live now than just New York City and Dallas.

MARK HARRIS

The Self–Made Brain

Surgeon

✧✧✧✧✧✧✧

I ORDERED the illumination extinguished in the power pole, but on the
following day the cruising Streetlight Bench replaced it. It was the Electrical Overhead who referred me to the Streetlight Bench, again I ordered
the illumination extinguished, but the Fire Department took issue, one
Inspector Mahaffey there, complaining that he required the light, it illuminated the alarm box on the corner. Not enough co-operation, too much
efficiency, men are double-barreled. I arranged with the Streetlight Bench
for an independent circuit, they installed it in the ground at the base of the
pole. A buried brook ran underneath the sidewalk. It emptied in the
reservoir. I could kick on the power pole with my foot when I went home,
or off, however I desired. Several nights I went home very late, I was
constantly afraid, the neighborhood was unfamiliar to me.

Complaints were initiated in the neighborhood when the light was observed extinguished, and I observed in the dark beside the pole. But where
else could I have stood? From any other point I could not have obtained a
full view.

It was not Mr. Kayzee who initiated complaint, for he is not a man
frightened by much. He possessed no gun, while his door he long ago took
down off the hinges, so at night when he quits he drops and lashes a tarp,
that's all. The hinges are there, but no door hanging, yet he has never been
broken or entered.

His own illumination is all interior, except his beer sign, which throws a
little blue light on the sidewalk. Late at night, when the fog blew in, it shone
blue on the particles of the fog, and when the wind was right I could hear
the foghorns. It was cold. Sometimes, when all was very quiet, I could hear
his beer sign buzz, and yet I don't see how I could have heard it as far
away as the power pole, but I thought I could. I became accustomed to the
noises.

What you don't hear. Imagine if you could see as well as hear. I could hear the water running in the buried brook underneath my feet, babies crying and people arguing, dogs or cats barking or wailing, cars starting, doors slamming, brakes or honking, people whistling or singing, pianos or trumpets playing or blowing, bells ringing, radio or television, hammering or repairing. It is a great neighborhood for repairing, do it yourself. A man was repairing dents in bodies, one Lionel Hefley, age 44, residence 615 Twelfth, he was a moonlighter, he didn't really need the money but he needed the hammering. Nobody complained. Somebody shouted out a window one night: "Hefley, for Christ's sake, go to bed," then I heard the window slam, but it wasn't a peeve or beef, it wasn't anger, it is an understanding neighborhood, he needed the hammering. He was a patient of Mr. Kayzee's. Then little by little all around you the lights go out.

Sometimes he forgot to turn his beer sign off. He lives over his shop, when he switched his lights on upstairs he remembered his beer sign and came back down again. The mind is not such a mystery. If he had a patient he went in the back room. One night I went around the corner and down the alley, but I could not see in, nor was there entry or access there, although the Fire Department claimed that escapement was not impeded, one Inspector Farmholder there. What was he thinking? It was a small window, and I scraped it, but it was painted brown and blue on the inside, triangles all crisscross, and I could not see in, nor hear in.

One Mrs. Marinda Marveaux was a patient at that time, a housewife, age 24, residence 55 San Pedro, I stood aside when she left, the rear of the Marveaux house faces the rear of Mr. Kayzee's premises. Complaint was initiated by one Armand Marveaux, her husband. Another patient was his alleged bookkeeper, one Miss Denise Willerts, age 18, residence 689 Twelfth, a student at the Washby Office Machines School & Sales. Another patient was one Lionel Hefley aforementioned.

Never was a job more lonely or depressing, it was too little to do for the hours, standing and observing nothing happening. It is a quiet neighborhood, night after night, go out and buy a loaf of bread, a half a dozen slices of meat for the pail tomorrow, two cans of beer for bedtime. Where is such a life leading? I was so depressed, talking out loud under the pole was next in store for me, babies cry, people die, one night there was a wake for one Mrs. Theresa McQuinn, age 78, deceased, residence 714 Twelfth. Mr. Kayzee closed early and attended the wake, babies cry, people die, get up, and go to work, everybody waiting for some piece of luck to carry them out of the neighborhood. In front of Mr. Kayzee's store they were always talking, the word I could hear was "Money." Yet when will such a piece of luck float by, and for who? You can try to promote your luck, you can bet the horses, fly to Reno for the weekend, hunt for your Lucky Dollar in the newspaper numbers, you can drink or take a pill, but half the ways of promoting your luck are illegal or harmful to your health, and the harder you promote it the thinner your lines become, you lose patience, your habits become irregular, you become irked and irritated. Finally you lose your job. Most of them figured it was luck enough to be working. You can borrow, you can gamble, but you can't really win, or even if you win you won't be satisfied, for winning once is only half of winning twice, in the end the regular life is best, come home, eat your dinner, put the kids to bed, read the papers, look at the television, go out and buy two cans of beer, come home and drink it, argue with the wife, turn out the lights, and go to sleep. It is that kind of a neighborhood, just the noises, not much.

He was born over the store. He was named Hopkins in honor of one Hopkins, deceased, who held the first mortgage on the store for his father. His father's name was full of k's and z's, such as Kzotszki, a foreign name, and when he was a young man he took out the k's and z's and called himself Kayzee. It was clever. I inquired of one M. J. Cavendish, age 84, retired, of 802 Twelfth (back): "What kind of a boy was Mr. Kayzee?"

He replied: "He was a studious boy, read books and ate fruit in the front of the store."

"Was he given to cutting up frogs and such?" I inquired. Information to this effect was divulged by Mr. Marveaux, complainant.

"Yes," replied Mr. Cavendish, "he was given to cutting up frogs and such. The boys all caught frogs in the buried brook. It ran diagonal to what is now called Twelfth. The boys caught frogs and the Kzotszki boy cut them up with a knife. He ate fruit and read books and cut up frogs and such."

In the old war he served in a medical detachment, 1917-1918, carrying, bandaging, and nursing. Following his military career he continued his career in his father's store to date, The Rite-By Market, 696 Twelfth.

Once every night I crossed the street and entered, purchasing a cigar. Cigarettes I kept lighting up and illuminating myself, maybe it was how I was observed, whereas a cigar could remain dead in my mouth for long periods of time and avoid illuminating myself. At that time I smoked three packages of cigarettes daily, I was on the verge of a nervous collapse. Once I cashed a small check, five dollars.

He always wore a white coat, and it was always clean, the sleeves turned back neatly one turn at the wrists. He wore a badge of blue and gold three inches in diameter, like an election button, it was a joke.

U.S. OFFICIAL
taxpayer

Every night he threw the coat in the hamper, the final action before turning out the lights, pinned the badge on the new coat, except on Thursday night he also set the hamper on the sidewalk prior to dropping and lashing the tarp. The liner of the hamper was removed on Friday morning by one Owen Segret, age 27, driver for the Pacific Linen Supply Company.

The coats bore no stains or questionable matter other than ordinary, the pockets contained nothing informative, sometimes a coin or a register receipt. Segret returned the coins, if any, each following Friday when he replaced the new liner.

His books were kept by his alleged bookkeeper, one Miss Denise Willerts aforementioned. In addition to Miss Willerts he was assisted by his wife, one Dorothy, age 59, residence same. She was formerly a nurse at Letterman Army Hospital, 1951-1956, and elsewhere. Also by a delivery boy, one Warren Ponce, age 15, residence 685 Twelfth, the boy and the girl are relations. I can't describe how. Her mother and Ponce's father were formerly husband and wife, their marriage terminated, the wives exchanged husbands, the husbands exchanged residences. It was the second exchange, since prior to the termination of their marriages Mr. and Mrs. Willerts were married to each other, and Mr. and Mrs. Ponce also. The Willerts girl and the Ponce boy now reside again with their natural parents. Eight other children are also issue, residing at 685 and 689, three born to Mrs. Ponce and living with same (two by Mr. Ponce, one by Mr. Willerts), while five were born to Mrs. Willerts (three by Mr. Willerts, two by Mr. Ponce), all eight now resident with their natural parents except August Willerts, age 14, resident in the Ponce residence, 685. Mr. Willerts was arraigned but never tried for alleged attempt to defraud, June 1946, in connection with a litigation involving multiple disability claims for alleged internal injuries suffered in a collision of two machines at the intersection of Junipero Serra and St. Francis Circle *de facto* unoccupied when alleged collision occurred. He was represented by one Carlo Minna, age 57, an attorney, residence 113 San Pedro, also attorney for Mr. Kayzee.

In addition he employs one Alvin (Monk) Kuhnle Jr., age 38, a painter seasonally employed, residence 134 San Pedro, who paints items and prices and occasional interior surfaces, who painted the blue door leading to Mr. Kayzee's alleged storage room, who painted the window in blue and brown triangles within, and who paints the numerous signs or decorations such as MY MIND IS MADE UP. DON'T CONFUSE ME WITH FACTS or DON'T CRITICIZE YOUR WIFE. LOOK WHO SHE MARRIED or LOVE YOUR ENEMY. IT'LL DRIVE HIM CRAZY. These are the simple wisdom of ages. Kuhnle receives groceries and sundries in lieu of rates or wages. He was arrested in January 1953, for petty pilfer of the poorbox of the Church of Our Lady of Mercy, San Pedro at Thirteenth, charges were not preferred, he was represented by one Mr. Minna aforementioned and released in Mr. Kayzee's recognizance.

Except in the case of Kuhnle he pays standard rates or wages to Miss Willerts and Warren Ponce, withholding withholding taxes and Social Security deductions according to law, and $599 to his wife *per annum,* whereby he claims her as an itemized business expenditure while also retaining her as a dependent exemption, it is legal.

Nothing was illegal. He possesses authorization to sell beer, wine, liquor, or one or all and has no record of violation, possesses a Fire-Sanitation permit to burn trash during daylight hours in an approved receptacle, permit to encumber pedestrian right-of-way with cardboard or light wood cartons or crates or other pending removal by scavenger service, and permit to maintain storage space at the rear of his establishment not to impede escapement. I ordered a Fire examination of the alleged storage space, one Inspector Farmholder there, but he failed to observe contents as I directed, reporting only "adequate escapement." Co-operation is difficult. Persons in high stations are often negligent or indifferent.

I made numerous inquiries of nonperishable salesmen or truckmen dealing in such goods as bottled or canned beverages, packaged cereals or desserts or cake mixings, inquiring: "Does your business with Mr. Kayzee differ in any way from your business with other grocers operating establishments similar in size or kind?" I gained helpful information from all, especially one Jack Schindler, age 48, a salesman-truckman employed by the Twin Peaks Bottling & Distributing Company.

"I am forced to call daily on Mr. Kayzee," he replied, "whereas I don't call daily on anybody else."

"How do you account for this?" I inquired.

"Because he'll stock shelves or refrigerator facilities," replied Mr. Schindler, "but he won't stock storage."

"Why won't he stock storage?" I inquired.

"Because he's not a progressive businessman," replied Mr. Schindler.

"Doesn't he do a good business?" I inquired. Then I stated: "He lives."

"You're asking a tricky-type question," replied Mr. Schindler. "He does a marginal business, he owns the building, he eats off his shelves, sure. Sure, he *lives*."

"But he has a storage room," I stated, and then inquired: "Why doesn't he use his storage room?"

"Because he performs brain surgery back there," replied Mr. Schindler. He laughed. Over the freezer was a sign painted by Kuhnle aforementioned in the old English style: BRAIN SURGERY PERFORMED ON PREMISES. ALL WORK GUARANTEED.

Everybody knew so. It was a joke in the neighborhood. Who cares? Anything goes, everything and anything is taken for granted, it was no surprise I became depressed. Consider the neighborhood. It is a neighborhood of churches, including the Church of Our Lady of Mercy, San Pedro at Thirteenth, the largest Church in the Diocese, and yet you will hear a great deal of criticism of the Priests. All persons follow politics but do not trust the politicians. It is heavy with the residences of municipal workers, Police or Fire or other, and yet the Department is not respected. It is a Union district, and yet the leaders of labor are not respected. The taverns are full, illegal betting is freely solicited, graft and corruption are everywhere, violations exist, scores of residents draw unemployment but will not work though bodily able, it is a neighborhood joke. Scores of residents draw disability but are not sick, respectable physicians sign statements, and everybody knows but nobody tells. The outstanding industry of the area is minding your own business. Information is difficult to develop. I saw children smoking on the street, the adults turned their backs. I heard vile language from women and children. Do my own children do this, does the wife swear outside the house?

Whereas when I was a boy the future was arranged, my father allowed me my way, but never too much, I swore on the street but nobody heard me, I smoked under the stairway, we respected our elders, or if anybody heard me or saw me it was definitely by chance. I ran around a little, I fought a little, I pinched a stick of candy here or there, an article of fruit, I cut school, I window-peeped, I sneaked into ball parks and films, we all did. I wrote my name in the municipal cement. But we never doubted the future was arranged, and when the time came we settled down.

The more I stood there the more depressed I became. I wore dark clothes. I surveyed his premises from across the street beneath the power pole. For three nights I stood there late, while after the first few nights I became almost too depressed to remain, sometimes I kicked the power pole on and went home early, though I put in far short of the hours.

His knives depressed me, he was always slicing fruit, the blades reflected from his interior lighting. He sliced a little, he laid the knives down carefully for a customer, he wiped his hands on his coat, rang up the money, and picked up the knives again. Over the bread and pastries was a sign: ANYONE WHO REMAINS CALM IN THE MIDST OF ALL THIS CONFUSION SIMPLY DOESN'T UNDERSTAND THE SITUATION, but he was calm, there was no confusion, his hands were steady. He sharpened his knives on a whetstone, and when he spoke he spoke slow, and he was calm, a deep thinker. MAKE SURE BRAIN IS ENGAGED BEFORE PUTTING MOUTH IN GEAR.

On the east wall is a large sign:

GOOD RULES FOR BUSINESS MEN

1. Don't worry; don't overbuy; don't go security.
2. Keep your vitality up; keep insured; keep sober; keep cool; keep your dignity.
3. Stick to chosen pursuits, but not to chosen methods.
4. Be content with small beginnings and develop them.
5. Be wary of dealing with unsuccessful men.
6. Be cautious, but when a bargain is made stick to it.
7. Keep down expenses, but don't be stingy.
8. Make friends, but not favorites.
9. Don't take new risks to retrieve old losses.
10. Stop a bad account at once.
11. Make plans ahead, but don't make them in cast iron.
12. Don't tell what you are going to do until you have done it.
13. Speak up, for dignity is more than dollars.

Mr. Kayzee discovered these rules in the front of his Daily Reminder, a black book I examined, showing Domestic and Foreign Postage Rates, Table of Days Between Two Dates, Actual Rate of Income, Distances and Mail Time Between Cities in the United States, Distances and Mail Time to Foreign Cities from San Francisco, Common Stains and How to Remove Them, Rates of Interest in All States, Actual Time in Use in the Largest Cities of the World when it is Noon in San Francisco, Rules for Computing Interest, Points of Constitutional Law, Weights and Measures, Explanation of Weather Bureau Flag Signals, Help in Case of Accident, Approximate Weight of Substances, Presidents of the United States, Nicknames and Flowers of the States, Supervisors of the City of San Francisco, Assemblymen of the State of California, Population of Principal Cities, Legal Holidays in Various States, and other necessary information.

2

Complaint was initiated by one Armand Marveaux aforementioned, age 33, a plasterer, residence 55 San Pedro. San Pedro is only three blocks long, running parallel to Twelfth between Twelfth and Thirteenth, blocked at the east end by the reservoir, and at the west by the Nun Convent adjacent to the Church. The rear of the Marveaux house faces the rear of Mr. Kayzee's premises as aforementioned, she crossed her garden, jumped over a rock wall there, it was not high, afterward returning the same way and entering her own house by her own rear door. She was in love with Mr. Kayzee, afterward she loved her husband again, all was proper, it was only transference. San Pedro was known in former times as Vivian Lane, honoring a noted prostitute, one Vivian. Certain older residents of the neighborhood still refer to it as Vivian Lane, such as Mr. Cavendish aforementioned. They are incorrect. Complainant complained that his grocer, one Hopkins Kayzee, was engaged in alleged illegal or illicit relationships with his wife, one Marinda, in the storage room of the latter's premises and was performing alleged illegal or illicit brain surgery upon the head of same.

I was at that time assigned to Convention Protection. "We are the Nation's foremost Convention City, boasting splendid luxury hotels, unexcelled fine restaurants, a wide variety of sophisticated nocturnal amusements and daylight summit vistas, an average Summer temperature of 65 degrees (Fahrenheit), the world's largest International Airport, and a Cosmopolitan Atmosphere blended with a Frontier Tradition whose spirit encourages mature restraint as the better alternative to an unrealistic strict enforcement." It was the height of my depression.

I worked hotels and demonstration or display rooms with an old friend of mine, Archie Wilson. He also depressed me. Some months prior, coming home one night, he was attacked by hoodlums, his gun was stolen, he was beaten, his assailants were never apprehended. Requesting a change, I drew for a partner a young man of little experience, one Robert (Bob) McFee. Our work was limited to report. We were permitted to detain or arrest pickpockets or confederates only. McFee took it in stride, everything and anything he took for granted, and yet a college man. Is this the respect my children will be taught in college? We reported or observed, but we could not take action, we could only survey. Whereas with an arrest here or an arrest there it could have been cleaned up entirely, Convention Protection done away with forever, but it wasn't done, the idea being allow it to be professional but prevent it from being organized, let girls work, let card players work, only keep it in singles or pairs and off the telephones, keep pimps or heavy operations out. What were we doing? Do you wish your city to be no more than a protected operation? You will attract to it the dregs of civilization from Reno, Vegas, Denver, or other points.

When I awoke I inquired: "How can I face another day?"

The wife replied: "Let it pass, it's the summer season," while McFee took the same position, stating: "Let it pass, you're already an ulcer type, let it pass, let it pass."

"How can I see and not speak?" I inquired.

"Who would you speak to?" the wife inquired, then stating: "Limiting and containing is all you can do, accept it, it's the summer season," until I bottled it up inside me but could not release it, for who could be spoken to. She was right. "Speak up, for dignity is more than dollars." Men cannot always speak up. Men shoot themselves in the head in the locker room, it is a common occurrence.

Lt. Kline said a little rest would do me wonders, he gave me a week away, we left the children with my mother, the wife and I flew to Reno. We allotted one hundred dollars to the slots, we attended the nude shows, we slept in a hotel, we approached the end of our allotted money on several occasions, we hit, we were rich again, we laughed, but I wouldn't live there. When I returned Lt. Kline stated it was better for me to work slowly, relax a little, avoid tension, keep to myself. "What's this?" the Lt. inquired. He laughed. "Whose wife? The grocer's wife or complainant's wife? Investigate the back room, work slow, relax a little, avoid tension, is it a storage room, or what is it?"

Complainant is the father of three children, Marilyn, Lucinda, and Marilinda. I rang the bell, the children and the dog came running, laughing or barking, and Marveaux himself behind them. I stated my business. "Finally you came," stated Mr. Marveaux, walking out on the porch and chasing the children back inside. Then he himself went inside, coming out again wearing an orange leather jacket, and he zippered it up. In those days I never forgot anything, if a man wore a jacket and zippered it up it remained in my mind, my mind was a storage room of useless small facts, whereas I was out of touch with the big pattern of things. After he zippered up his jacket we walked down San Pedro and around the corner. "What right has any man got," inquired Mr. Marveaux, "to be tampering with another man's wife's ways?"

"No right," I replied.

"When your wife goes to the grocery store," inquired Mr. Marveaux, "do you expect the grocer to be asking her all kinds of questions or making her all kinds of suggestions regarding her sexual activities with her husband?"

"Certainly not," I replied.

"A grocer is a grocer," stated Mr. Marveaux, "a grocery store is a grocery store." We crossed Twelfth and stood under the light of the power pole, his hair was cut in sideburns, he smoked Oasis cigarettes and his jacket was illuminated, shining orange. It was called The Rite-By Market. "Don't you think a grocery store is a grocery store?" inquired Mr. Marveaux. "Is he permitted to call himself a brain surgeon?"

"We must know the facts," I stated, and then inquired: "Does he actually call himself a brain surgeon?"

"He performs brain surgery," replied Mr. Marveaux.

I inquired: "He actually cuts people's heads open with a knife?"

"He tampered with my wife's sexual attitudes," replied Mr. Marveaux.

"He cut open your wife's head with a *knife?*" I inquired.

"It was brain surgery," he stated. "He shifted around her brain, causing her to alter her image of herself by brain surgery."

"With a knife?" I inquired, then stated: "If it was a knife she would have come home bleeding. Answer me," then inquiring again: "A *knife?*"

"Go read the sign," he replied. "See the knives."

I crossed the street, he remained where he was. I entered the store, I bought a package of cigarettes. Over the freezer was the sign aforementioned: BRAIN SURGERY PERFORMED ON PREMISES. ALL WORK GUARANTEED, and in his hands a knife, he was slicing an apple. He put down the knife, he placed his apple on the scale, he gave me my cigarettes, rang my money, gave me change. Then he picked up the knife and the apple again. I went back across the street and leaned against the power pole again. "It's just a joke," I stated.

"It's no joke," he stated. "He made a regular sexual fiend out of her. She was just an ordinary girl, after six years you don't suddenly develop along the lines of a sexual fiend unless somebody's been tampering with your attitudes. It was surgery."

"With a *knife?*" I inquired.

"Formerly it was now and then, take it or leave it, *comme ci, comme ça,* my background is French. She's also of French background."

"Answer me. Did she come home *bleeding?*"

"She came home a fiend. 'Where are you going?' It's seven o'clock. 'I'm going down to The Rite-By for a loaf of bread.' It's eight o'clock. It's nine o'clock. I'm all alone. Where is she? 'Where have you been?' 'I went down to The Rite-By for a loaf of bread.' 'Since when does it take two hours to buy a loaf of bread?' 'He was slicing it. It was unsliced bread.' "

"Slicing it with what?" I inquired.

"A knife."

"Was she bleeding when she came home?"

"It was brain surgery."

"You can't leave the house," I stated, "at seven o'clock and have brain surgery and walk in at nine and not be bleeding."

"She never walked in, she ran in, she leaped in my arms after six years, she loved me, I was tired, I'm a plasterer all day. She had a new image of herself. Formerly she was who she was, now she is Marinda Marveaux, French lady of the night. 'Where have you been?' 'I've been in the back of the store with Mr. Kayzee.' 'Doing what?' 'Receiving brain surgery.' Everybody in the neighborhood is having brain surgery in the back of Mr. Kayzee. Ask around. Read the sign."

"Mr. Marveaux," I stated, "brain surgery is a job done by medicine men of long experience and training in many colleges, and you bleed. You lie around unconscious for many hours afterward, and they send you a big bill." Then I inquired: "Does Mr. Kayzee send you a bill?"

"Only for groceries," he replied. He leaned against the power pole, thinking of Mr. Kayzee. "He's a very fair dealer. I like him. He has done wonders for the wife."

"Then why did you issue complaint?" I inquired.

"I didn't issue complaint," he replied.

"You called the police," I stated.

"Well, it's all right now," he stated. Again he leaned, thinking, and soon he stated further: "I withdraw complaint. I'm not complaining any more."

It was Wednesday. Thursday I ordered the illumination extinguished in the power pole, but Friday the cruising Streetlight Bench replaced it. Monday they installed the independent circuit, I could kick it off or on with my foot, however I desired. The cigars depressed me. The noises depressed me. The water in the buried brook depressed me, flowing, flowing, flowing, flowing, babies crying, people dying, I could feel it in the vibrations of my feet. It never ended. I began going crazy from depression. It became foggy at night, and the people were a blur, sometimes it was difficult to view the movement or motion within his store. What was I accomplishing?

Miss Willerts, Mrs. Marveaux, and Mr. Hefley were patients on the first three nights of the week, Monday, Tuesday, and Wednesday. Thursday I went home early. I was cold. Friday night I cashed a small check, five dollars. He took the check and placed it in his pocket still wet. "Will that be all?" he inquired. I bought a cigar, that was all. "That will be all," I replied, and he stated: "I thank you very kindly." I turned around and started out, he further stating: "Oh, by the way Mr. Cop, last night you forgot to kick the power pole back on."

"What power pole?" I inquired. Then I stated: "You're crazy, Mr.," and I continued walking. Yet why deny it? I had made many inquiries, I was illuminated by cigarettes, one way or another it was bound to get back to him, it was how the neighborhood is, he is appreciated, he extends credit and courtesies of every sort, he has lived all his life in the neighborhood, raised his children there, maintains his property, respects the peace, such a man is respected in that neighborhood or any other. I stated: "You've got no license to dispense."

He stated: "Maybe you're crazy, too."

"O.K." I bent my head, I removed my hat, it was a joke. "Here's my brain. Cut." He laughed, I laughed a little also, he dropped and lashed his tarp and turned out the lights. "Don't forget your beer sign," I stated. He went back and turned out his beer sign, in his hand was his knife. In the storage room he took off his white coat, unpinning his badge, then pinning it on a fresh coat. The room was dark, his coat was white, he turned his lamp toward the window, and it shone against the triangles brown and blue. Behind him was a shelf of books made of crates standing side by side.

"What's the tapecorder for?" I inquired.

"To talk in," he replied. "I record their lives."

"Play me a life. Play me Mrs. Marinda Marveaux."

"I erased her," he stated. "Tapes are expensive. She is a woman who expected perfection, but men are not perfect, men are double-barreled, smoke if you wish." He turned the tapecorder on, a small red light shone, the spools went around and around, reflecting on the ceiling. In former times I was hypnotized by the spools going around and around, but later I did not mind them.

"Turn it off," I ordered. He turned it off.

He gave me a sheet of paper, *Good Rules for Business Men.* "This is all I dispense," he stated. "This is all I dispensed her, these are the simple wisdom of the ages. I recommend especially Number 13, speak up, for people must tell their troubles to one another, they discover their own mind with help, the mind is not such a mystery. They cannot pay much. Poor people cannot go downtown to the high-priced men. Accept the world, it's a low-income neighborhood."

I inquired, "This is all you dispensed her?"

"That's all," he replied. "We discussed the imperfections of her husband, which are numerous, but also his qualities, which are also numerous, he is steadily employed, he does not drink, he does not gamble, and he beat her only once in six years."

"You've got no license or authority to dispense," I stated.

"Why not eat your apple?" he inquired. He ran a small electric heater, the room grew gradually warmer, the heater switched off, the hour still was early, I agreed to eat my apple.

I inquired: "Where can I wash my apple?" He took me to a lavatory adjoining, it was clean but cool, I washed my apple, it was good to return to the warm room again. "Since when," I inquired, "does it take two hours to dispense a sheet of paper? Tuesday night she entered your store at 7:09, you turned out your lights, you entered this room, she departed at 9:11."

"We also talked," he replied.

"Where was she?" I inquired.

"Sitting where you are," he replied. I was in a leather chair.

"Did she sit or did she lie back flat?" I inquired, for the chair leaned back for comfort.

"*Comme ci, comme ça,*" he replied. "However she desired."

"Where were you?" I inquired.

"I was right here," he replied.

It was a comfortable chair, my head rested on a barber-pillow, I leaned back, I sliced my apple, while outside the wind blew fog down the alley. "Go ahead and eat it," he ordered. "Enjoy something. An apple is an apple, don't be so cautious, the health of the apple overpowers the germs. Why are you so cautious? You screw the cap on your pen too tight, your pen clips too tight in your pocket, your writing is extremely small and cautious, your hat is a half a size too small, it leaves a red mark on your forehead. Do you think the world is lying in wait to steal your fountain pen?" He informed me that in former times he also was an extremely cautious man. He spoke in a soft, steady voice, I loosened my shoes, I loosened my tie, I smoked cigarettes. In those days I smoked three packages daily. We discussed smoking. When I was a boy I smoked cigarettes under the stairway, I thought nobody saw me, but Mr. Kayzee suggested that the smoke drifted up, I was observed by my father and others, I agreed it was a possible theory.

"Take off your coat," he advised. "Take off your gun, too." He possessed no gun, and he inquired whether I had ever shot a man or not. I replied that I did not know, for I shot into the shadows twice after Archie Wilson was attacked by hoodlums unknown. He inquired whether he might hear the story of Archie Wilson in the tapecorder, I agreed, the red light shone and the spools went around and around on the ceiling. Upon later occasions I heard my own voice on the tape. My voice grew stronger in later weeks, I became less depressed.

The hour grew later and later, and the wind died, but I did not leave, although it soon was midnight, and I became afraid, stating: "I cannot go, you must at least walk me to my machine, the hour is late and the neighborhood is unfamiliar to me."

"There is no reason to be afraid," he stated.

"Even in a machine a man is not safe," I stated. "You dare not even stop at the light at certain intersections, they are on you in a minute. Our own municipal streets are no longer even safe."

"The front page of the papers," he stated, "is not the story. Don't be afraid."

"I'm not afraid," I stated.

"Good," he replied, "because there is little to be afraid of."

"Then walk with me," I stated, but he refused. I could not go, I could not stay. What could I do? "You do not know the number of crimes committed every night, we are under-staffed, we are not respected, we are without power, young thugs are running wild, attorneys defend them, the judiciary is far too lenient, social workers bleed their hearts out, the boy had a bad beginning, excuse and forgive, meanwhile they leave court in a stolen machine full of billiard balls in high stockings, the streets are not safe, I cannot go," yet he refused to go with me. He unlashed his tarp and lifted it, and we stood on the sidewalk in front of the shop.

"Cross," he stated, "and kick on your power pole, walk to your machine, do not run, and drive home," but still I could not do as he directed. The wind was down, I lit a cigarette. "Consider," he stated, "that you were observed smoking under the stairway, not only by your father but by all the neighborhood. You were loved and protected by your neighborhood, although you thought it was filled with enemies. But the truth is, let a thief enter, let a man be lewd or molest a child, let a man assault, and the neighborhood will rise and crush him, then or now or anywhere or anytime, the neighborhood defends itself. The police are few, the residents are many, the neighborhood is its own Department, it cures or mends, it regulates itself. There is some danger tonight, but there was always some danger every night, not more and not less, so cross."

I did as he advised, and I continued afterward for some time until my depression faded away. We said goodnight, I crossed the street, I kicked the power pole back on, I walked to my machine, I drove home, I advised Lt. Kline on the following day complainant withdrew complaint, I ordered the independent circuit discontinued, I resumed Convention Protection at that time.

◇

Mark Harris was born in Mount Vernon, New York, in 1922, received his B.A. and M.A. from the University of Denver and his Ph.D. from the University of Minnesota, and for many years has taught writing at San Francisco State. He has published a biography of Vachel Lindsay, City of Discontent *(1952), and a book about Richard Nixon's California campaign,* Mark The Glove Boy *(1964).* Trumpet to the World *(1946) was his first novel;* Something About a Soldier *(1957) is a comical novel about an odd-ball GI;* Wake Up Stupid *(1959) is a very funny novel in letter form. He is perhaps best known for his three books "in the Henry Wiggen man-ner":* The Southpaw *(1953),* Bang the Drum Slowly *(1956), and* Ticket for a Seamstitch *(1957). These are warm and pleasant baseball novels narrated by Henry Wiggen, a savvy, comical pitcher who writes books "corrected" by Mark Harris. A good deal of the fun of them rests in the amusing language that emerges. In thus constructing a special vernacular that is at once original, realistic, and functional, Harris is in the original tradition of American fiction, a tradition that is not much exploited by other contemporary writers.*

In "The Self-Made Brain Surgeon" we see this same good use of an original language—in this case a development of the policeman's report-book style. Like many officials and bureaucrats, the Convention Protection cop—the narrator—has fallen under the spell of his own officialese; and because his job and training have been to report on illegalities and crime, it is difficult for him to think or see much of anything else. He is a moral man, and because of the limitations put on his job—the idea is not to eradicate vice, but to protect it and its customers, to "allow it to be professional but prevent it from being organized"—he has become distressed and disturbed. He is unable to see that now he is confronted not with sin-loving conventioneers far from home but with a more or less permanent community that operates in a peculiar way. The conception of urban community that he gradually and inadvertently reveals is entirely different from that presented in "The Intruder." Here there is no anonymous violence—not only no violence but no anonymity. There may be no money and much irregularity (the Willerts-Ponce marriages, for instance), but the poor have dignity and learn to love and are not afraid. "Graft and corruption are everywhere, violations exist," but "nothing was illegal." The people take guidance from the "Brain Surgeon," Kayzee, a sort of modern urban intellectual version of the small-town, homespun philosopher David Harem—a cracker-barrel, fruit-slicing wise man whose father had the grocery store before him and who needs no locks on his door. The neighborhood itself is a combination small town and nostalgic ghetto, where everybody knows everybody and they all get along. It is a noisy neighborhood, a neighborhood of repairing and do-it-yourself. "It is a neighborhood of churches . . . yet you will hear a great deal of criticism of the Priests." "All persons follow politics but do not trust the politicians." Again, it is the small-town ideal: a community of individuals. The people stand around chatting about money in front of the store—cynical, lazy, easygoing, shifty, but harmless people, who wouldn't be too out of place in an operetta. Nobody has money, nobody needs money, because "the regular life is best." No doubt such neighborhoods as this still exist in America, just as small towns still exist. No doubt there are still neighborhoods of which one can say, as Kayzee does of this: "Let a man assault, and the neighborhood will rise and crush him, then or now or anywhere or anytime, the neighborhood defends itself." But the newspapers tell us of neighborhoods where sixty-five neighbors will hear the screams of a woman being murdered and no one will even phone the police (out of fear of becoming "involved") much less "rise and crush" the murderer. Harris' neighborhood makes for a funny story, and it is perceptive about the way officials automatically confuse poor neighborhoods with criminal neighborhoods. But it does not so much represent a typical urban neighborhood as a nostalgic idea of an urban neighborhood of the past that is typically sought out by the uncommitted who have no regular life, no congenial atmosphere of tolerance and freedom in the places where they live. It is the "Bohemian Ideal" as imagined by the work-a-day middle class, cheated of romance. It bears roughly the same relation to urban life that the pastoral ideal bears to rural life. As an idyllic, romantic conception of "The Lost Community" we nostalgically yearn for, the story represents a meaningful expression of something that's missing from how we live now.

ROY BONGARTZ

Twelve Chases on West Ninety-ninth Street

◇◇◇◇◇◇◇

EVERYBODY is running in New York; "the pace is fast," they say. What they are doing is chasing one another. Every one of them is either after somebody or running away from somebody. Once in a while, one of them manages, with careful timing, to do both at the same time. But on the upper West Side, between Broadway and Riverside Drive, the timing is only fair. On the 300 block of West Ninety-ninth Street, the residents chase each other up and down the steep hill that rises from the Drive to West End Avenue, and then, between chases, they rest, and sit on the front stoops or lean out of their windows and passively absorb the chaotic racket and motion of dogs, children, cats, fire engines, police cars, garbage trucks, moving vans, blocked and klaxoning cars, and rusty-wheeled grocery carts. Beat-up two-toned cars with North Carolina plates and cracked safety glass in the side windows park in broken brown-bottle glass. Everything is cracked, knocked in, busted on West Ninety-ninth. Two buildings on opposite sides of the street in the middle of the block are Negro rooming houses, one high-class and one low-class. The other buildings on the block exclude Negroes but are open to examples of all the other groups that exist. When the people there chase, they usually pick out someone of their own type to go after; it is a rare sight to see a white chasing a Negro, or a Negro chasing a white. Even the children scattered about in front of the buildings ordinarily chase within their own groups. In one way, these barriers were attacked when a Negro named Ray fell twelve feet from a porch railing into a concrete-floored cellarway and broke his neck.

Ray lives in the low-class rooming house, where a torn, flapping canvas marquee proclaims its name—the Ritz. Across the street, the high-class rooming house, unnamed, displays only a neat red-lettered sign—"NO

LOITERING IN THIS DOORWAY." The sign is obeyed, and altogether that building sustains a higher tone of amenities. Screams and violent threats are unusual, and among all the residents there is clear evidence of good taste in bathrobes and other nightdress, as everyone on the block can see when a fire breaks out in the basement or in one of the rooms and firemen rout the inhabitants out into the night. (Within one year, five fires broke out in one rooming house. In the whole of the 300 block, there were over two dozen.) The nightdress and other comparisons can be made among the residents even though direct, inter-building, man-to-man relationships are, as has been noted, rare.

There is no way to examine all of these people at a given moment so as to come up with a truthful and complete account of what is going on here. All that can be done is to take a sample of, say, three of these people: a wide-brim-hatted man in his late forties named Benny, who runs an inefficient parking lot; a very thin young woman named Flo, with good-looking dark eyes; and a young cop who actually lives in the Bronx but has made himself at home in the neighborhood. Broken-necked Ray does not figure in the sample, but he is in this scene nevertheless; all those people on the block, forever riding up and down in the elevators or wandering up to Broadway twenty times a day for small, obscure purposes—all those people are in it. The trouble, of course, is that nobody stays put in this slice-of-life 300 block; people are forever leaking out at each end of it (and sometimes, as with the local juvenile delinquents, they cut out of the scene laterally, via the rooftops). Never mind. We have, all lined up, Benny, Flo, and the cop. These three sample people, taken as chasers and also as chased, can work into an arithmetical maximum of twelve relationships, twelve chases.

What is the thin-limbed young woman Flo doing on West Ninety-ninth Street this Saturday evening, arguing with Benny out in front of his apartment building? She doesn't even live on this street; she lives on Amsterdam Avenue. (Nothing is perfect; of the three sample 300-block people, two of them live elsewhere. It's nowhere *near* perfect.) Flo is a waitress in the Crosstown Bar, on West Ninety-sixth Street, another world.

"Come on up," Benny says. "Come on, Flo. I thought you wanted to come up."

Flo looks out to the cars streaming along the Henry Hudson Parkway but doesn't focus her eyes on them. She's thinking. She says, "Don't rush me. You're always in a hurry."

"Already I know you over a year and I'm in a hurry?"

"Yes, you're in a hurry."

There they go, they're chasing now. Flo is going up the hill toward Broadway. She heads for the Cake Masters bakery to pick up a loaf of seeded rye with which eventually to carry out a secret plan to end Chase

No. 1 by making sandwiches up in Benny's so-called studio apartment (where the stove is on top of the refrigerator). As she goes into the bakery, she sweeps a glance over the throng of beanbag women customers, all under five feet tall, scarves over their hair, jumping up and down waving exploding coins in their fists, and she hears a strong, oily-voiced baritone singing out from somewhere in a ululating vibrato. Flo takes a pink ticket from the Takacheck machine just inside the door and glances at her number—44. She compares this with the changing number in the frame behind the counter—3. Flo, although of a stolid, unimaginative nature, has nevertheless absorbed from the circuslike variety in the city around her a certain resiliency when she finds herself in untoward situations, so that at first she hardly remarks the presence of a singer in the Cake Masters. This is a long-faced, rheumy-eyed singer with thatchy brown hair and bony red wrists and unstable lips, a gawky, sentimental bakery singer, with good strong lungs. "My Yiddishe Momme" and "When Irish Eyes Are Smiling" he sings while Flo waits for her number to come up. When it does, she whispers to the baker, "Why is he singing?" The baker replies loudly, embarrassing Flo, "He wants to sing, let him sing, why shouldn't he sing?" He gazes in amused speculation into Flo's handsome dark eyes. "Let him *sing,* he wants to sing." All the jolting little women are asking each other the same question, "Why is he singing?" Flo thinks, If he is singing, he must want money. She whispers to the baker, "But does he want money?" The baker smiles at her and says, "Give him money, you got too much. He's singing. He asks nothing." Flo at this point begins to suspect a kind of existence beyond her own, but then she leaves the bakery with the rye bread, and the process is interrupted. Flo, almost unchanged, now returns to the 300 block, late for the chase with Benny.

Chase No. 1 continues. Benny is again chasing Flo up that 300-block hill, Flo running awkwardly on spike heels, jerkily twisting her elbows as she goes. Her lips are tight as she flounces past the open doorway of the Ritz, where the lounging Negroes eye her implacably. As she clicks past, she shoots a sharp look at them, a chastising what-are-*you*-looking-at look, but they don't mind the look; they have seen Flo before and they have seen her look before, too. At the Cake Masters, we discovered Flo to be of a square state of mind, yet ready to consider giving a bakery singer a tip for singing she did not enjoy (though she would remember it). Here she is now giving Benny a hard time, giving the Negroes a cold eye, flouncing up the hill like a girl of no substance, like some floppy suburban teen-ager. She gives Benny a hard time but she doesn't turn him off altogether, as one ought to expect. Flo, who insists on a bakery singer giving an account of himself, insists on logic and rightness. When one considers Benny's over-ripe gambit to Flo six months ago (a blizzardy evening, and Benny emboldened by a rare excess of ambition: "Say, young lady, how about taking in a show after you get off work, and before that maybe some Chinese food at the Gung Ho?"), it is clear that Flo should have frozen him solid. But that is not what Flo did; she accepted him, conditionally, accepted a little of him. She goes on up past the areaway of an apartment house and stops. Benny runs up to her, and Chase No. 1 ends, statistically, at least. Flo is going to come to his apartment. Benny opens his hands outward in a gesture of hopeless generosity—anything-you-say-is-O.K.-by-me. Now Flo wonders why she ever set foot in this 300 block. Benny is too old and his nose is too big and he talks too loud. But she had nothing better to do.

"Come on up for a little while," Benny persists.

Flo realizes that going with Benny means nothing to her one way or the other. She is altogether uninvolved with him. "No," she says, her lips forming the word completely by chance; it could just as easily have been "yes" or "green." This refusal is so unemotional that Benny receives it unquestioningly. He turns and heads for home.

Chase No. 2 takes up as Flo uncertainly retraces her steps and follows Benny down the hill. They go Indian file, loping along. Just before the Ritz entrance, Flo hears a groan, and stops. She looks around. The Negroes on the steps of the Ritz are watching her. Benny, sensing he is no longer being chased, turns around. All the figurants turn to stone momentarily until the next groan releases them. High above them, his elbows leaning on a blue-and-white striped pillow on the window ledge, a sallow-cheeked old man, immutable Cro-Magnon street watcher, gazes down, drawing no conclusions, one sight worth another—fat woman with shopping cart, nimble-footed television-set repossessors, jingling Good Humor man, busted Negro. Flo looks in every direction, trying to trace that groan, and notices this old man in his window, unblinkingly eying her, a gargoyle cemented to his window ledge. There is another groan. Flo peers down into a cellarway between the sidewalk and the wall of the Ritz. A man is lying down there.

She runs down the narrow stairs to him, and Benny runs up and peers over the railing at her, then looks up at the porch railing from which the man has fallen. Flo kneels beside the fallen Negro. "Where are you hurt?" she demands. The Negro mumbles. "Are you all right?" she demands more loudly.

"Of course he isn't all right," Benny interrupts. "He fell from way up here. We better call a cop."

Flo tugs at the Negro's arm. The Negro lies in sooty wetness. "Gimme a drink," he says. Flo clicks up the stairs and runs in her rag-doll run to the Ritz Negroes and commands in her thin voice, "Get some blankets, there's a man hurt down here!" Heads appear in Ritz windows, lounging Negroes stir, faces press against windows of parked cars; the gargoyle turns his head away from his late-afternoon-sun watching. Negroes clatter into the cellarway to help their fallen comrade, now moaning and cursing, as busy thin-legged Flo and useless wide-brimmed Benny run off (No. 3) to find a cop.

Flo runs blindly down West End Avenue, Benny protesting that they should go on over to Broadway. He will protest all his life; he has created a protesting existence for himself with this dark-haired, sharp-chinned girl— Benny the follower, the whiner, the pleader, would-be seducer of a Ninety- sixth Street waitress, operator of lousy parking lot. He cannot even catch a cop to save a busted Negro that his girl found, Benny himself never having noticed a single fallen human being in all his humdrum life. ("But if somebody would just let me know what I'm supposed to do," Benny is always complaining, and shrugging, his hands outstretched in that gesture of facile generosity.) Then he puts his hand in the side pocket of his checked jacket, where he can feel the silky, grainy texture of some crum- pled dollar bills. He thinks, Maybe I will give this money to the Negro. But Benny won't actually give the money, because later he will decide the city will take care of the Negro.

Flo finds the cop, who follows her back to the Ritz and descends to kneel, in his turn, beside the fallen Negro. "How do you feel, buddy?" says the cop.

The Negro pronounces barely audible curses, velvet-caressing curses, in a sad, rambling, uninterested voice, as if someone else were doing his cursing for him and was falling asleep at the task. "Sons of bitches," he murmurs, "gimme a drink ma wine, man." He passes out, then passes in again.

The cop tests the articulation of the man's arms and legs. "How does that feel, buddy?" No answer.

Above, Benny and Flo and many Negro neighbors peer down, the Ne- groes according a preferred vantage point to Benny and Flo because of their central role in the diversion. Benny stands back, suddenly impatient of this intrusion into his plans by fallen Negro and co-chasing, which any- way is done with. The victim is being attended by a city official. Good, thinks Benny, grasping Flo's arm, but even after a year she still acts as if he were a stranger molesting her. Has he not taken this girl to the Gung Ho, to movies at the Midtown, to Pizza Burger Pete's? Yet a little favor, a little friendliness like coming up to his place for a drink and sandwiches, be- comes impossible. Benny now imagines the soft light of dusk in his room becoming dimmer; the two of them hear pigeons cooing, and the clapping of car tires over manhole covers, and the hum of weekend motorists on the Henry Hudson Parkway. But the cop shouts up at Flo, "Call an ambu- lance!"

Benny sees it is his and Flo's duty to call the ambulance, because they had called the cop in the first place. So now the cop is bringing them *his* troubles, chasing (No. 4) *them* with orders and demands. It is *their* fallen Negro now. But that's not true, Benny thinks protestingly. Still, nobody in the crowd offers to take the job from them, and Flo has already gone into the Ritz to telephone. Benny follows, as he follows all his life, to no purpose. Imperious Flo calls the ambulance: "Come right away! Man hurt,

West Ninety-ninth." Negro residents crowd the doorway and the stairs and stare at Flo, who returns to the railing above the cellarway; the people make room for her. There is enough residue of respect for Benny, as Flo's associate, to warrant him a place at the railing as well. The ambulance arrives; two wiry Puerto Rican interns jump out, clatter out a stretcher, and exchange bursts of Spanish. They, too, test his bones and joints. Ray curses them in his phenomenally soft voice. The interns grab his shoulders and lift him up; Ray screams in a cruel, hopeless spasm, and they edge him onto their stretcher. Flo pulls away from the cellarway, and a Negro next to her says, "Thanks a lot for helping." She says, "I just hope those guys don't kill him." She goes off toward Broadway without looking back, and a few minutes later Benny follows.

The Negroes watch Benny depart as if he were the mayor of West Ninety-ninth Street—the mayor of West Ninety-ninth Street who has lost his girl. He sees the cop about to get into a police cruiser at the top of the hill. Benny chases (No. 5) him to ask where Flo might have gone—if she has gone to the police station to make a report, or something. Benny gets no information here, and goes on up to the end of the 300 block before the cop yells after him and chases (No. 6) him calling, "Hey, wait a minute." He wants to know the exact time the victim was found in the cellarway. But even this small usefulness Benny cannot produce. His watch is not working—not wound, probably, or just clogged. The cop lets him go. Benny gazes along the street hoping for the sight of a black skirt, thin legs. If it hadn't been for the cop, I could have caught her, he thinks. Still, the cop *had* come to him for information—important information. He glows a bit. He crosses West End Avenue and goes down to Albert's Liquor Store, source of Ray-toppling Gallo. Benny tells the proprietor of having found the busted Negro—"Probably saved his life," he boasts. A general conversation ensues on the subject of hard falls. Benny is looking for the girl, but he buys a bottle of J. W. Dant anyway.

Flo returns to the 300 block, where the Negroes welcome her. "Let the lady pass," they cry. After a round-the-world trip along escaping-from-Benny West End Avenue up to 100th Street, and then down unknown who-are-those-people-in-the-window-watching 300 block of 100th Street, she comes with relief into the safe, known world, past the firemen's memorial, to Ninety-ninth Street. She knows she has found a home away from home in this place where the ambulance she had summoned has only just rolled away with damaged Negro aboard, Ray enthroned inside with Puerto Rican attendant cooling him with a palm fan, Ray waving a hand to all faithful subjects outside, and these Negroes, having been blessed by Ray, and by his rescue mollified, now retreat into their welcome-to-the-North furnished cages in the Ritz. Flo looks up at the façade of the Ritz, the bottles of beer, cartons of orange juice, cans of evaporated milk littering the sills. It's not good enough, she thinks, mumbles aloud; she isn't precisely sure what that means. The rooming house is included, and so is Benny, and Ray falling down drunk into the cellarway is in it, too. Somebody is responsible, she thinks; the nearest representative of organizing forces is that cop. So she chases (No. 7) off after him. She wants to make a general complaint.

Up the hill she goes. "Where's that cop?" she asks her new Negro neighbors. "Where's the cop?" the Negroes repeat to one another. A tall Negro girl in a thin red flower-printed dress, with a gold cap over one front tooth, and auburn-dyed hair, and high Indian cheekbones, grins at Flo and says, "What do you want that cop for, honey? Can we help you some way?" But Flo clicks up the street alone. She finds the cop leaning on the police car door. "That ambulance took an hour to arrive," she complains.

The cop says, "Lady, anybody in this whole city calls in with even a stomach ache, anything, we got to rush to him, and you can figure it takes a lot of ambulances, a city this size, and this being Saturday, and a hot Saturday, with people out in the parks and in the streets. We get a lot of calls, and there's just so many ambulances to go around. That boy there, he'll be all right."

"What is your name?" Flo demands, these being the only words she can think of by way of explaining that she really wants to saddle him with the responsibility of having made none of it good enough; the dirty hot street not good enough, the hot-roast-beef and steam-table-pastrami waitress job not good enough, soggy-brained Ray fallen in that cellarway not good enough, and Benny—my God, Benny, he's not good enough, either—But that isn't the cop's fault, none of it is the cop's fault, leave him alone, the poor guy; this won't be his only case today. "Never mind," she tells him, and goes off toward Broadway.

The cop says something to his colleagues in the police car and then follows (No. 8) Flo across West End Avenue. She passes a group of Haitians, shadowy French phrases echoing up and down the 200 block. The cop catches up. "If you want my name, I'll give it to you," he tells her challengingly. "Never mind," says Flo. "I didn't mean to bother you again."

Benny returns to the 300 block with his bottle of bourbon and stops to talk with a Ritz resident, a tall, gangling Negro with a beret, Charlie Chan mustache, and thick-lensed horn-rimmed glasses, who says, "Ray he fell right off this railing like a sack of meal and nobody heard him till you came along, he could have died down there you hadn't heard him call out and then go on down there to see what it was." Benny modestly shakes his head; he doesn't know what to say, and he wonders why Flo has run out on him like this. Why could he never get the girl to come home with him? Why? Nothing worked out. He returns to the chase.

The cop is leaning on the door of the synagogue at the corner of West End Avenue; he raises an indolent finger at Benny. "Who is that girl friend of yours?"

"Ah," Benny replies, pained, the memory of her too much for him to communicate in a word. He wants to put out his two hands there in front of him like *that* and force her to appear—right there where he can take hold of her. Women always have somewhere else to go, Benny thinks.

"She wanted to take down my name," the cop says aggressively.

"So what do you want me to do about it?" says Benny.

"Well, what does she want with my name? She going to report me?" asks the cop.

"I don't know what she's going to do. Me, I'm the last person you should ask what she's going to do. You want to talk to her again? I'll tell you something. *I'd* like to talk to her."

"Let's find her," the cop suggests. They go off together, looking for her, an unspoken threat eating into the cop's silver-badge mind, his chief receiving an unfounded report of neglect of duty or of cruelty to fallen Negro, as if *he* had pushed the Negro into the cellarway. The cop and Benny (the lover) go after (No. 9) Flo and find her in a drugstore on Broadway having a Coke.

"I won't report you for it," she tells the cop, having decided that the cop is slightly responsible for nothing being good enough; he deserves a little needling. (And here is Benny again, she thinks.)

"For *what?*" says the cop. "What won't you report me for?"

Flo won't tell him what it is. She won't tell the cop what he wants to know, nor will she go up to Benny's place for the drinks and sandwiches. It is too late to do that, though she has nothing else to do. Her plans lead through a white blank into tomorrow's table-waiting at the Crosstown Bar, unless, by good fortune, another fallen citizen should be lying in her path for her to retrieve. "I don't want to know your name," she tells the cop, absolving him and then sending both him and Benny away as if she owns the drugstore. The cop goes out, ready for a quiet stand in front of the cigar store half a block down Broadway, where life is both more colorful and more peaceful than on the cross streets.

Benny goes out with him. They get only to the corner before Flo chases (No. 10) after them. "What hospital did that hurt man go to?" she asks the cop.

"Roosevelt Hospital," he replied.

Benny says, "What, you still worried about that fellow? He'll get the best care in the world, best care in the world. Right, Officer?"

The cop says, "Do me a favor, the next time you hear something like that, somebody groaning, take my advice, just keep on walking, save yourself a lot of trouble."

"But he would have died," Flo protests.

"They never die," the cop says. "You can't kill them as easy as that."

He goes off and leaves outraged Flo in the incapable hands of Benny, who is wondering how he is going to make off with her, how to make the most of her anger. "Come on up to my place and cool off a little," he suggests. Flo is indecisive. A chink appears in her armor. Patience, thinks Benny. But I'll put my foot in it again, thinks Benny, remembering the time he had brought her some carnations while she was at work and she had stared at them as if she had never seen a flower before in her life, saying, "I don't like carnations!" Another time, during a walk in Riverside Park, he had grasped her hand in what was supposed to be an affectionate gesture, but he had done it too abruptly, it had been too grabby there in the dusk of the park, and she had simply been scared, briefly but sharply. All he had ever succeeded in doing was to wait until she finished work so as to take her to a movie. Now he has two cases of beer in his kitchen, and this bottle of bourbon. He is all ready for her. They walk together down West Ninety-ninth, past the two Chinese laundries, Benny keeping his mouth shut for fear of ruining everything. She's not the only broad in this town, he tries to convince himself. Springily he walks along, clapping his perforated brown-and-white shoes down on the concrete. Anyway, he thinks, he is *with* Flo. She isn't looking at him, doesn't adjust her pace to his—he can sense that, he is not insensitive to such tips of bad news. "Bought some *bourbon*," he says tantalizingly, pulling the neck of the bottle from his coat pocket so that she may see it. "Good for you," she says. There is no use in his kidding himself, he thinks; she is lost to him. What has happened, he wonders. She was on her way up to his place, then a man falls into a cellarway, and now she might as well be on another planet. Suddenly Flo is talking to him: "I'll have a drink with you; let's go to a bar somewhere." Benny understands nothing at all. They turn back, he takes her arm, and they go to a bar at 100th Street and Broadway to have Manhattans. Before they finish their first round, Benny orders another. Flo sighs a why-did-I-start-*this* sigh. Later, outside, Benny tries to pull her along with him; she resists, becomes angry, and then Benny becomes ugly and drags her a little way down Broadway. "Waste of *time!*" he shouts at her. Flo jerks away and runs down the street, past the cop, who calls out, "Where's the fire?" She stops, points accusingly, and she and the cop, in unrehearsed concert, move toward oncoming, lumbering Benny, on his way into another of his inconsequential disasters. Benny turns away from them, from secure and civilized Broadway, and runs (No. 11) down West Ninety-ninth Street, heading for home.

On the 300 block the old-man gargoyle leans on his pillowed elbows and gazes, with the stone lions in the cornices, blankly down to the warm asphalt of the darkened street. Empty garbage cans, one inside another like Dixie cups, are piled up before each building; a broken lamppost leans stupidly at the end of the street, and abruptly, with all the others on the street, it lights up. Benny walks along disgruntled, wondering what to do with his bourbon and his cold beer. Only three residents of the Ritz are on the stoop now. One is the whiskered, bereted one, who looks up and says formally, "Evening."

Benny pulls himself out of his vindictive trance, stops, and says, "Any word about our friend?"

"Busted his neck," says the bereted one. "What they said there at the hospital. We called. He ought to be all right, though."

"That's pretty rough," says Benny. "Well, I hope he——he comes out of it, comes through it all right."

"We hope so, too."

"Well, good night," Benny says uneasily. The three residents all reply, "Good night." Benny goes on down the hill.

When he gets to his building, he looks back to the Ritz marquee flapping in the warm wind, then gazes out at the red neon Spry sign on the Jersey shore. Then, as if chasing were the easiest thing in the world, he thinks his way back up (No. 12) to Broadway, where Flo, like a wise guy, has called the cop on him—*him*, Benny, who is greeted good evening by all the people on the street. And she already *agreed* to come up here, he says to himself once more. What did that busted Negro have to do with them? But now he knows how to handle her; he sees himself, as in a dream, striding right up to Flo and that cop, and he hands the cop a five-dollar bill. Thank you, Copper, he says. You've done your duty, Copper. Then Benny takes the girl's arm, and the two of them stroll along the street, everybody saying hello, and then they go up to his place and open up that bottle of bourbon.

◇

Roy Bongartz was born in Providence in 1924, brought up in Dayton, edu-cated at Miami University (Ohio) and at universities in Grenoble, Paris, Mexico City, and Biarritz; after an assortment of jobs and an amount of traveling unusual even among footloose modern American writers, he has returned to live in Rhode Island. He has published many short stories in many magazines, but only one collection. Called Twelve Chases on West Ninety-ninth Street *(1965), it comprises twelve stories, many of which first appeared in* The New Yorker, *recounting the further adventures of Benny and Flo and some of the other characters in the title story.*

The "Twelve Chases on West Ninety-ninth Street" are seen through a sort of sociological framework of "three sample people" worked into "an arithmetical maximum of twelve relationships, twelve chases." This is be-cause, as the omniscient-author narrator says, "There is no way to examine all of these people at a given moment so as to come up with a truthful and complete account of what is going on here." The limitations imposed by his point of view are matched by the limitations of the people and the life on "this slice-of-life 300 block." The only constant is change: "nobody stays put." And yet "when the people there chase," even the children, they all "chase within their own groups." Nothing really happens to change things or make things better, although "in one way, these barriers were attacked" by the action of the story, by what happens when Ray falls. The arithmetical model is appropriate in several ways: it gives a precise, arbitrary, and anonymous tone to the narration, presented as an abstraction, an inevitability that can make sense only in terms of this particular "sample" on this particular day; yet the arithmetical model still represents "all those people on the block, forever riding up and down in the elevators or wandering up to Broadway twenty times a day for small obscure purposes—all these people are in it." In direct opposition to Mark Harris' idealized, coherent, responsible Bohemia, or to the small-town, just-out-of-sight window watchers who know every passerby's state of mind as well as his business. Bongartz gives us this: "a sallow-cheeked old man, immutable Cro-Magnon street watcher, gazes down, drawing no conclusions, one sight worth another —fat woman with shopping cart, nimbled-footed television-set repossessors, jingling Good Humor man, busted Negro." There is no Self-Made Brain Surgeon straightening out affairs in this neighborhood. It isn't even a neighborhood: on the 300 block the two Negro rooming houses are different from each other and from all the other buildings on the block, and West Ninety-sixth Street, where Flo works, is "another world." The action of the story for a few brief moments ignites a flicker of community in this area where no one knows anyone else or what anyone else is doing. For at least this one chase, the 300 block becomes a "safe, known world" for Flo, because she has acted responsibly in it, summoning the ambulance for Ray. It is the very sense of having been responsible that makes her think, "It's not good enough," meaning the whole scene, including her "would-be seducer," Benny. But there are no intellectual problems of depression or identity or purpose here either. Nobody gets what he wants, but nobody is on the verge of a nervous breakdown. The scale of human values and events is small, but the applications, the indications of what it is like to be one of the chasers in this kind of urban non-community where "everything is cracked, knocked in, busted," are extensive. The block stands for many areas in many cities, where neither the Bohemian Ideal nor the ghetto coherence is present: chaotic, jumbled, purposeless, but highly defined. It stands for them, but like all of them it is entirely singular.

JOHN CHEEVER

The Country Husband

◇◇◇◇◇◇◇

TO BEGIN at the beginning the airplane from Minneapolis in which
Francis Weed was traveling East ran into heavy weather. The sky had been
a hazy blue, with the clouds below the plane lying so close together that
nothing could be seen of the earth. Then mist began to form outside the
windows, and they flew into a white cloud of such density that it reflected
the exhaust fires. The color of the cloud darkened to gray, and the plane
began to rock. Francis had been in heavy weather before, but he had never
been shaken up so much. The man in the seat beside him pulled a flask out
of his pocket and took a drink. Francis smiled at his neighbor, but the man
looked away; he wasn't sharing his painkiller with anyone. The plane had
begun to drop and flounder wildly. A child was crying. The air in the cabin
was overheated and stale, and Francis' left foot went to sleep. He read a
little from a paper book that he had bought at the airport, but the violence
of the storm divided his attention. It was black outside the ports. The
exhaust fires blazed and shed sparks in the dark, and, inside, the shaded
lights, the stuffiness, and the window curtains gave the cabin an atmosphere of intense and misplaced domesticity. Then the lights flickered and
went out. You know what I've always wanted to do?" the man beside
Francis said suddenly. "I've always wanted to buy a farm in New Hampshire and raise beef cattle." The stewardess announced that they were
going to make an emergency landing. All but the children saw in their
minds the spreading wings of the Angel of Death. The pilot could be heard
singing faintly, "I've got sixpence, jolly, jolly sixpence. I've got sixpence to
last me all my life. . . ." There was no other sound.

The loud groaning of the hydraulic valves swallowed up the pilot's song,
and there was a shrieking high in the air, like automobile brakes, and the
plane hit flat on its belly in a cornfield and shook them so violently that an
old man up forward howled, "Me kidneys! Me kidneys!" The stewardess
flung open the door, and someone opened an emergency door at the back,

letting in the sweet noise of their continuing mortality—the idle splash and smell of a heavy rain. Anxious for their lives, they filed out of the doors and scattered over the cornfield in all directions, praying that the thread would hold. It did. Nothing happened. When it was clear that the plane would not burn or explode, the crew and the stewardess gathered the passengers together and led them to the shelter of a barn. They were not far from Philadelphia, and in a little while a string of taxis took them into the city. "It's just like the Marne," someone said, but there was surprisingly little relaxation of that suspiciousness with which many Americans regard their fellow-travelers.

In Philadelphia, Francis Weed got a train to New York. At the end of that journey, he crossed the city and caught, just as it was about to pull out, the commuting train that he took five nights a week to his home in Shady Hill.

He sat with Trace Bearden. "You know, I was in that plane that just crashed outside Philadelphia," he said. "We came down in a field . . ." He had traveled faster than the newspapers or the rain, and the weather in New York was sunny and mild. It was a day in late September, as fragrant and shapely as an apple. Trace listened to the story, but how could he get excited? Francis had no powers that would let him re-create a brush with death—particularly in the atmosphere of a commuting train, journeying through a sunny countryside where already, in the slum gardens, there were signs of harvest. Trace picked up his newspaper, and Francis was left alone with his thoughts. He said good night to Trace on the platform at Shady Hill and drove in his secondhand Volkswagen up to the Blenhollow neighborhood, where he lived.

The Weeds' Dutch Colonial house was larger than it appeared to be from the driveway. The living room was spacious and divided like Gaul into three parts. Around an ell to the left as one entered from the vestibule was the long table, laid for six, with candles and a bowl of fruit in the center. The sounds and smells that came from the open kitchen door were appetizing, for Julia Weed was a good cook. The largest part of the living room centered around a fireplace. On the right were some bookshelves and a piano. The room was polished and tranquil, and from the windows that opened to the west there was some late-summer sunlight, brilliant and as clear as water. Nothing here was neglected; nothing had not been burnished. It was not the kind of household where, after prying open a stuck cigarette box, you would find an old shirt button and a tarnished nickel. The hearth was swept, the roses on the piano were reflected in the polish of the broad top, and there was an album of Schubert waltzes on the rack. Louisa Weed, a pretty girl of nine, was looking out the western windows. Her younger brother Henry was standing beside her. Her still younger brother, Toby, was studying the figures of some tonsured monks drinking beer on the polished brass of the wood box. Francis, taking off his hat and putting down his paper, was not consciously pleased with the scene; he was not that reflective. It was his element, his creation, and he returned to it with that sense of lightness and strength with which any creature returns to his home, "Hi, everybody," he said. "The plane from Minneapolis . . ."

Nine times out of ten, Francis would be greeted with affection, but tonight the children are absorbed in their own antagonisms. Francis has not finished his sentence about the plane crash before Henry plants a kick in Louisa's behind. Louisa swings around, saying, "*Damn* you!" Francis makes the mistake of scolding Louisa for bad language before he punishes Henry. Now Louisa turns on her father and accuses him of favoritism. Henry is always right; she is persecuted and lonely; her lot is hopeless. Francis turns to his son, but the boy has justification for the kick—she hit him first; she hit him on the ear, which is dangerous. Louisa agrees with this passionately. She hit him on the ear, and she *meant* to hit him on the ear, because he messed up her china collection. Henry says that this is a lie. Little Toby turns away from the wood box to throw in some evidence for Louisa. Henry claps his hand over little Toby's mouth. Francis separates the two boys but accidentally pushes Toby into the wood box. Toby begins to cry. Louisa is already crying. Just then, Julia Weed comes into that part of the room where the table is laid. She is a pretty, intelligent woman, and the white in her hair is premature. She does not seem to notice the fracas. "Hello, darling," she says serenely to Francis. "Wash your hands, every-one. Dinner is ready." She strikes a match and lights the six candles in this vale of tears.

This simple announcement, like the war cries of the Scottish chieftains, only refreshes the ferocity of the combatants. Louisa gives Henry a blow on the shoulder. Henry, although he seldom cries, has pitched nine innings and is tired. He bursts into tears. Little Toby discovers a splinter in his hand and begins to howl. Francis says loudly that he has been in a plane crash and that he is tired. Julia appears again, from the kitchen, and, still ignoring the chaos, asks Francis to go upstairs and tell Helen that every-thing is ready. Francis is happy to go; it is like getting back to headquarters company. He is planning to tell his oldest daughter about the airplane crash, but Helen is lying on her bed reading a *True Romance* magazine, and the first thing Francis does is to take the magazine from her hand and remind Helen that he has forbidden her to buy it. She did not buy it, Helen replies. It was given to her by her best friend, Bessie Black. Everybody reads *True Romance*. Bessie Black's father reads *True Romance*. There isn't a girl in Helen's class who doesn't read *True Romance*. Francis ex-presses his detestation of the magazine and then tells her that dinner is ready—although from the sounds downstairs it doesn't seem so. Helen follows him down the stairs. Julia has seated herself in the candlelight and spread a napkin over her lap. Neither Louisa nor Henry has come to the table. Little Toby is still howling, lying face down on the floor. Francis speaks to him gently: "Daddy was in a plane crash this afternoon, Toby. Don't you want to hear about it?" Toby goes on crying. "If you don't come to the table now, Toby," Francis says, "I'll have to send you to bed without any supper." The little boy rises, gives him a cutting look, flies up the stairs to his bedroom, and slams the door. "Oh dear," Julia says, and starts to go after him. Francis says that she will spoil him. Julia says that Toby is ten pounds underweight and has to be encouraged to eat. Winter is coming, and he will spend the cold months in bed unless he has his dinner. Julia goes upstairs. Francis sits down at the table with Helen. Helen is suffering from the dismal feeling of having read too intently on a fine day, and she gives her father and the room a jaded look. She doesn't understand about the plane crash, because there wasn't a drop of rain in Shady Hill.

Julia returns with Toby, and they all sit down and are served. "Do I have to look at that big, fat slob?" Henry says, of Louisa. Everybody but Toby enters into this skirmish, and it rages up and down the table for five minutes. Toward the end, Henry puts his napkin over his head and, trying to eat that way, spills spinach all over his shirt. Francis asks Julia if the children couldn't have their dinner earlier. Julia's guns are loaded for this. She can't cook two dinners and lay two tables. She paints with lightning strokes that panorama of drudgery in which her youth, her beauty, and her wit have been lost. Francis says that he must be understood; he was nearly killed in an airplane crash, and he doesn't like to come home every night to a battlefield. Now Julia is deeply committed. Her voice trembles. He doesn't come home every night to a battlefield. The accusation is stupid and mean. Everything was tranquil until he arrived. She stops speaking, puts down her knife and fork, and looks into her plate as if it is a gulf. She begins to cry. "Poor Mummy!" Toby says, and when Julia gets up from the table, drying her tears with a napkin, Toby goes to her side. "Poor Mummy," he says. "Poor Mummy!" And they climb the stairs together. The other children drift away from the battlefield, and Francis goes into the back garden for a cigarette and some air.

It was a pleasant garden, with walks and flower beds and places to sit. The sunset had nearly burned out, but there was still plenty of light. Put into a thoughtful mood by the crash and the battle, Francis listened to the evening sounds of Shady Hill. "Varmints! Rascals!" old Mr. Nixon shouted to the squirrels in his bird-feeding station. "Avaunt and quit my sight!" A door slammed. Someone was playing tennis on the Babcocks' court; someone was cutting grass. Then Donald Goslin, who lived at the corner, began to play the "Moonlight Sonata." He did this nearly every night. He threw the tempo out the window and played it *rubato* from beginning to end, like an outpouring of tearful petulance, lonesomeness, and self-pity—of everything it was Beethoven's greatness not to know. The music rang up and down the street beneath the trees like an appeal for love, for tenderness aimed at some lonely housemaid—some fresh-faced, homesick girl from Galway, looking at old snapshots in her third-floor room. "Here, Jupiter, here, Jupiter," Francis called to the Mercers' retriever. Jupiter crashed through the tomato vines with the remains of a felt hat in his mouth.

Jupiter was an anomaly. His retrieving instincts and his high spirits were out of place in Shady Hill. He was as black as coal, with a long, alert, intelligent, rakehell face. His eyes gleamed with mischief, and he held his head high. It was the fierce, heavily collared dog's head that appears in heraldry, in tapestry, and that used to appear on umbrella handles and walking sticks. Jupiter went where he pleased, ransacking wastebaskets, clotheslines, garbage pails, and shoe bags. He broke up garden parties and tennis matches, and got mixed up in the processional at Christ Church on Sunday, barking at the men in red dresses. He crashed through old Mr. Nixon's rose garden two or three times a day, cutting a wide swath through the Condesa de Sastagos, and as soon as Donald Goslin lighted his barbecue fire on Thursday nights, Jupiter would get the scent. Nothing the Goslins did could drive him away. Sticks and stones and rude commands only moved him to the edge of the terrace, where he remained, with his gallant and heraldic muzzle, waiting for Donald Goslin to turn his back and reach for the salt. Then he would spring onto the terrace, lift the steak lightly off the fire, and run away with the Goslins' dinner. Jupiter's days were numbered. The Wrightsons' German gardener or the Farquarsons' cook would soon poison him. Even old Mr. Nixon might put some arsenic in the garbage that Jupiter loved. "Here, Jupiter, Jupiter!" Francis called, but the dog pranced off, shaking the hat in his white teeth. Looking in at the windows of his house, Francis saw that Julia had come down and was blowing out the candles.

Julia and Francis Weed went out a great deal. Julia was well liked and gregarious, and her love of parties sprang from a most natural dread of chaos and loneliness. She went through her morning mail with real anxiety, looking for invitations, and she usually found some, but she was insatiable, and if she had gone out seven nights a week, it would not have cured her of a reflective look—the look of someone who hears distant music—for she would always suppose that there was a more brilliant party somewhere else. Francis limited her to two week-night parties, putting a flexible interpretation on Friday, and rode through the weekend like a dory in a gale. The day after the airplane crash, the Weeds were to have dinner with the Farquarsons.

Francis got home late from town, and Julia got the sitter while he dressed, and then hurried him out of the house. The party was small and pleasant, and Francis settled down to enjoy himself. A new maid passed the drinks. Her hair was dark, and her face was round and pale and seemed familiar to Francis. He had not developed his memory as a sentimental faculty. Wood smoke, lilac, and other such perfumes did not stir him, and his memory was something like his appendix—a vestigial repository. It was not his limitation at all to be unable to escape the past; it was perhaps his limitation that he had escaped it so successfully. He might have seen the maid at other parties, he might have seen her taking a walk on Sunday afternoons, but in either case he would not be searching his memory now. Her face was, in a wonderful way, a moon face—Norman or Irish—but it was not beautiful enough to account for his feeling that he had seen her before, in circumstances that he ought to be able to remember. He asked Nellie Farquarson who she was. Nellie said that the maid had come through an agency, and that her home was Trénon, in Normandy—a small place with a church and a restaurant that Nellie had once visited. While Nellie talked on about her travels abroad, Francis realized where he had seen the woman before. It had been at the end of the war. He had left a replacement depot with some other men and taken a three-day pass in Trénon. On their second day, they had walked out to a crossroads to see the public chastisement of a young woman who had lived with the German commandant during the Occupation.

It was a cool morning in the fall. The sky was overcast, and poured down onto the dirt crossroads a very discouraging light. They were on high land and could see how like one another the shapes of the clouds and the hills were as they stretched off toward the sea. The prisoner arrived sitting on a three-legged stool in a farm cart. She stood by the cart while the mayor read the accusation and the sentence. Her head was bent and her face was set in that empty half smile behind which the whipped soul is suspended. When the mayor was finished, she undid her hair and let it fall across her back. A little man with a gray mustache cut off her hair with shears and dropped it on the ground. Then, with a bowl of soapy water and a straight razor, he shaved her skull clean. A woman approached and began to undo the fastenings of her clothes, but the prisoner pushed her aside and undressed herself. When she pulled her chemise over her head and threw it on the ground, she was naked. The women jeered; the men were still. There was no change in the falseness or the plaintiveness of the prisoner's smile. The cold wind made her white skin rough and hardened the nipples of her breasts. The jeering ended gradually, put down by the recognition of their common humanity. One woman spat on her, but some inviolable grandeur in her nakedness lasted through the ordeal. When the crowd was quiet, she turned—she had begun to cry—and, with nothing on but a pair of worn black shoes and stockings, walked down the dirt road alone away from the village. The round white face had aged a little, but there was no question but that the maid who passed his cocktails and later served Francis his dinner was the woman who had been punished at the crossroads.

The war seemed now so distant and that world where the cost of partisanship had been death or torture so long ago. Francis had lost track of the men who had been with him in Vésey. He could not count on Julia's discretion. He could not tell anyone. And if he had told the story now, at the dinner table, it would have been a social as well as a human error. The people in the Farquarsons' living room seemed united in their tacit claim that there had been no past, no war—that there was no danger or trouble in the world. In the recorded history of human arrangements, this extraordinary meeting would have fallen into place, but the atmosphere of Shady Hill made the memory unseemly and impolite. The prisoner withdrew after passing the coffee, but the encounter left Francis feeling languid; it had opened his memory and his senses, and left them dilated. He and Julia drove home when the party ended, and Julia went into the house. Francis stayed in the car to take the sitter home.

Expecting to see Mrs. Henlein, the old lady who usually stayed with the children, he was surprised when a young girl opened the door and came out onto the lighted stoop. She stayed in the light to count her textbooks. She was frowning and beautiful. Now, the world is full of beautiful young girls, but Francis saw here the difference between beauty and perfection. All those endearing flaws, moles, birthmarks, and healed wounds were missing, and he experienced in his consciousness the moment when music breaks glass, and felt a pang of recognition as strange, deep, and wonderful as anything in his life. It hung from her frown, from an impalpable darkness in her face—a look that impressed him as a direct appeal for love. When she had counted her books, she came down the steps and opened the car door. In the light, he saw that her cheeks were wet. She got in and shut the door.

"You're new," Francis said.

"Yes. Mrs. Henlein is sick. I'm Anne Murchison."

"Did the children give you any trouble?"

"Oh, no, no." She turned and smiled at him unhappily in the dim dashboard light. Her light hair caught on the collar of her jacket, and she shook her head to set it loose.

"You've been crying."

"Yes."

"I hope it was nothing that happened in our house."

"No, no, it was nothing that happened in your house." Her voice was bleak. "It's no secret. Everybody in the village knows. Daddy's an alcoholic, and he just called me from some saloon and gave me a piece of his mind. He thinks I'm immoral. He called just before Mrs. Weed came back."

"I'm sorry."

"Oh, *Lord!*" She gasped and began to cry. She turned toward Francis, and he took her in his arms and let her cry on his shoulder. She shook in his embrace, and this movement accentuated his sense of the fineness of her flesh and bone. The layers of their clothing felt thin, and when her shuddering began to diminish, it was so much like a paroxysm of love that Francis lost his head and pulled her roughly against him. She drew away. "I live on Belleview Avenue," she said. "You go down Lansing Street to the railroad bridge."

"All right." He started the car.

"You turn left at that traffic light. . . . Now you turn right here and go straight on toward the tracks."

The road Francis took brought him out of his own neighborhood, across the tracks, and toward the river, to a street where the near-poor lived, in houses whose peaked gables and trimmings of wooden lace conveyed the purest feelings of pride and romance, although the houses themselves could not have offered much privacy or comfort, they were all so small. The street was dark, and, stirred by the grace and beauty of the troubled girl, he seemed, in turning into it, to have come into the deepest part of some submerged memory. In the distance, he saw a porch light burning. It was the only one, and she said that the house with the light was where she lived. When he stopped the car, he could see beyond the porch light into a dimly lighted hallway with an old-fashioned clothes tree. "Well, here we are," he said, conscious that a young man would have said something different.

She did not move her hands from the books, where they were folded, and she turned and faced him. There were tears of lust in his eyes. Determinedly—not sadly—he opened the door on his side and walked around to open hers. He took her free hand, letting his fingers in between hers, climbed at her side the two concrete steps, and went up a narrow walk through a front garden where dahlias, marigolds, and roses—things that had withstood the light frosts—still bloomed, and made a bittersweet smell in the night air. At the steps, she freed her hand and then turned and kissed him swiftly. Then she crossed the porch and shut the door. The porch light went out, then the light in the hall. A second later, a light went on upstairs at the side of the house, shining into a tree that was still covered with leaves. It took her only a few minutes to undress and get into bed, and then the house was dark.

Julia was asleep when Francis got home. He opened a second window and got into bed to shut his eyes on that night, but as soon as they were shut—as soon as he had dropped off to sleep—the girl entered his mind, moving with perfect freedom through its shut doors and filling chamber after chamber with her light, her perfume, and the music of her voice. He was crossing the Atlantic with her on the old *Mauretania* and, later, living with her in Paris. When he woke from his dream, he got up and smoked a cigarette at the open window. Getting back into bed, he cast around in his mind for something he desired to do that would injure no one, and he thought of skiing. Up through the dimness in his mind rose the image of a mountain deep in snow. It was late in the day. Wherever his eyes looked, he saw broad and heartening things. Over his shoulder, there was a snow-filled valley, rising into wooded hills where the trees dimmed the whiteness like a sparse coat of hair. The cold deadened all sound but the loud, iron clanking of the lift machinery. The light on the trails was blue, and it was harder than it had been a minute or two earlier to pick the turns, harder to judge—now that the snow was all deep blue—the crust, the ice, the bare spots, and the deep piles of dry powder. Down the mountain he swung, matched his speed against the contours of a slope that had been formed in the first ice age, seeking with ardor some simplicity of feeling and circumstance. Night fell then, and he drank a Martini with some old friend in a dirty country bar.

In the morning, Francis' snow-covered mountain was gone, and he was left with his vivid memories of Paris and the *Mauretania*. He had been bitten gravely. He washed his body, shaved his jaws, drank his coffee, and missed the seven-thirty-one. The train pulled out just as he brought his car to the station, and the longing he felt for the coaches as they drew stubbornly away from him reminded him of the humors of love. He waited for the eight-two, on what was now an empty platform. It was a clear morning; the morning seemed thrown like a gleaming bridge of light over his mixed affairs. His spirits were feverish and high. The image of the girl seemed to put him into a relationship to the world that was mysterious and enthralling. Cars were beginning to fill up the parking lot, and he noticed that those that had driven down from the high land above Shady Hill were white with hoarfrost. This first clear sign of autumn thrilled him. An express train—a night train from Buffalo or Albany—came down the tracks between the platforms, and he saw that the roofs of the foremost cars were covered with a skin of ice. Struck by the miraculous physicalness of everything, he smiled at the passengers in the dining car, who could be seen eating eggs and wiping their mouths with napkins as they traveled. The sleeping-car compartments, with their soiled bed linen, trailed through the fresh morning like a string of rooming-house windows. Then he saw an extraordinary thing; at one of the bedroom windows sat an unclothed woman of exceptional beauty, combing her golden hair. She passed like an apparition through Shady Hill, combing and combing her hair, and Francis followed her with his eyes until she was out of sight. Then old Mrs. Wrightson joined him on the platform and began to talk.

"Well, I guess you must be surprised to see me here the third morning in a row," she said, "but because of my window curtains I'm becoming a regular commuter. The curtains I bought on Monday I returned on Tuesday, and the curtains I bought Tuesday I'm returning today. On Monday, I got exactly what I wanted—it's a wool tapestry with roses and birds—but when I got them home, I found they were the wrong length. Well, I exchanged them yesterday, and when I got them home, I found they were still the wrong length. Now I'm praying to high Heaven that the decorator will have them in the right length, because you know my house, you *know* my living-room windows, and you can imagine what a problem they present. I don't know what to do with them."

"I know what to do with them," Francis said.

"What?"

"Paint them black on the inside, and shut up."

There was a gasp from Mrs. Wrightson, and Francis looked down at her to be sure that she knew he meant to be rude. She turned and walked away from him, so damaged in spirit that she limped. A wonderful feeling enveloped him, as if light were being shaken about him, and he thought again of Venus combing and combing her hair as she drifted through the Bronx. The realization of how many years had passed since he had enjoyed being deliberately impolite sobered him. Among his friends and neighbors, there were brilliant and gifted people—he saw that—but many of them, also, were bores and fools, and he had made the mistake of listening to them all with equal attention. He had confused a lack of discrimination with Christian love, and the confusion seemed general and destructive. He was grateful to the girl for this bracing sensation of independence. Birds were singing —cardinals and the last of the robins. The sky shone like enamel. Even the smell of ink from his morning paper honed his appetite for life, and the world that was spread out around him was plainly a paradise.

If Francis had believed in some hierarchy of love—in spirits armed with hunting bows, in the capriciousness of Venus and Eros—or even in magical potions, philters, and stews, in scapulae and quarters of the moon, it might have explained his susceptibility and his feverish high spirits. The autumnal loves of middle age are well publicized, and he guessed that he was face to face with one of these, but there was not a trace of autumn in what he felt. He wanted to sport in the green woods, scratch where he itched, and drink from the same cup.

His secretary, Miss Rainey, was late that morning—she went to a psychiatrist three mornings a week—and when she came in, Francis wondered what advice a psychiatrist would have for him. But the girl promised to bring back into his life something like the sound of music. The realization that this music might lead him straight to a trial for statutory rape at the county courthouse collapsed his happiness. The photograph of his four children laughing into the camera on the beach at Gay Head reproached him. On the letterhead of his firm there was a drawing of the Laocoön, and the figure of the priest and his sons in the coils of the snake appeared to him to have the deepest meaning.

He had lunch with Pinky Trabert. At a conversational level, the mores of his friends were robust and elastic, but he knew that the moral card house would come down on them all—on Julia and the children as well—if he got caught taking advantage of a babysitter. Looking back over the recent history of Shady Hill for some precedent, he found there was none.

There was no turpitude; there had not been a divorce since he lived there; there had not even been a breath of scandal. Things seemed arranged with more propriety even than in the Kingdom of Heaven. After leaving Pinky, Francis went to a jeweler's and bought the girl a bracelet. How happy this clandestine purchase made him, how stuffy and comical the jeweler's clerks seemed, how sweet the women who passed at his back smelled! On Fifth Avenue, passing Atlas with his shoulders bent under the weight of the world, Francis thought of the strenuousness of containing his physicalness within the patterns he had chosen.

He did not know when he would see the girl next. He had the bracelet in his inside pocket when he got home. Opening the door of his house, he found her in the hall. Her back was to him, and she turned when she heard the door close. Her smile was open and loving. Her perfection stunned him like a fine day—a day after a thunderstorm. He seized her and covered her lips with his, and she struggled but she did not have to struggle for long, because just then little Gertrude Flannery appeared from somewhere and said, "Oh, Mr. Weed . . ."

Gertrude was a stray. She had been born with a taste for exploration, and she did not have it in her to center her life with her affectionate parents. People who did not know the Flannerys concluded from Gertrude's behavior that she was the child of a bitterly divided family, where drunken quarrels were the rule. This was not true. The fact that little Gertrude's clothing was ragged and thin was her own triumph over her mother's struggle to dress her warmly and neatly. Garrulous, skinny, and unwashed, she drifted from house to house around the Blenhollow neighborhood, forming and breaking alliances based on an attachment to babies, animals, children her own age, adolescents, and sometimes adults. Opening your front door in the morning, you would find Gertrude sitting on your stoop. Going into the bathroom to shave, you would find Gertrude using the toilet. Looking into your son's crib, you would find it empty, and, looking further, you would find that Gertrude had pushed him in his baby carriage into the next village. She was helpful, pervasive, honest, hungry, and loyal. She never went home of her own choice. When the time to go arrived, she was indifferent to all its signs. "Go home, Gertrude," people could be heard saying in one house or another, night after night. "Go home, Gertrude. It's time for you to go home now, Gertrude." "You had better go home and get your supper, Gertrude." "I told you to go home twenty minutes ago, Gertrude." "Your mother will be worrying about you, Gertrude." "Go home, Gertrude, go home."

There are times when the lines around the human eye seem like shelves of eroded stone and when the staring eye itself strikes us with such a wilderness of animal feeling that we are at a loss. The look Francis gave the little girl was ugly and queer, and it frightened her. He reached into his pocket—his hands were shaking—and took out a quarter. "Go home,

Gertrude, go home, and don't tell anyone, Gertrude. Don't—" He choked and ran into the living room as Julia called down to him from upstairs to hurry and dress.

The thought that he would drive Anne Murchison home later that night ran like a golden thread through the events of the party that Francis and Julia went to, and he laughed uproariously at dull jokes, dried a tear when Mabel Mercer told him about the death of her kitten, and stretched, yawned, sighed, and grunted like any other man with a rendezvous at the back of his mind. The bracelet was in his pocket. As he sat talking, the smell of grass was in his nose, and he was wondering where he would park the car. Nobody lived in the old Parker mansion, and the driveway was used as a lovers' lane. Townsend Street was a dead end, and he could park there, beyond the last house. The old lane that used to connect Elm Street to the riverbanks was overgrown, but he had walked there with his children, and he could drive his car deep enough into the brushwoods to be concealed.

The Weeds were the last to leave the party, and their host and hostess spoke of their own married happiness while they all four stood in the hallway saying good night. "She's my girl," their host said, squeezing his wife. "She's my blue sky. After sixteen years, I still bite her shoulders. She makes me feel like Hannibal crossing the Alps."

The Weeds drove home in silence. Francis brought the car up the driveway and sat still, with the motor running. "You can put the car in the garage," Julia said as she got out. "I told the Murchison girl she could leave at eleven. Someone drove her home." She shut the door, and Francis sat in the dark. He would be spared nothing then, it seemed, that a fool was not spared: ravening lewdness, jealousy, this hurt to his feeling that put tears in his eyes, even scorn—for he could see clearly the image he now presented, his arms spread over the steering wheel and his head buried in them for love.

Francis had been a dedicated Boy Scout when he was young, and, remembering the precepts of his youth, he left his office early the next afternoon and played some round-robin squash, but, with his body toned up by exercise and a shower, he realized that he might better have stayed at his desk. It was a frosty night when he got home. The air smelled sharply of change. When he stepped into the house, he sensed an unusual stir. The children were in their best clothes, and when Julia came down, she was wearing a lavender dress and her diamond sunburst. She explained the stir: Mr. Hubber was coming at seven to take their photograph for the Christmas card. She had put out Francis' blue suit and a tie with some color in it, because the picture was going to be in color this year. Julia was lighthearted at the thought of being photographed for Christmas. It was the kind of ceremony she enjoyed.

Francis went upstairs to change his clothes. He was tired from the day's work and tired with longing, and sitting on the edge of the bed had the effect of deepening his weariness. He thought of Anne Murchison, and the physical need to express himself, instead of being restrained by the pink lamps of Julia's dressing table, engulfed him. He went to Julia's desk, took a piece of writing paper, and began to write on it. "Dear Anne, I love you, I love you, I love you . . ." No one would see the letter, and he used no restraint. He used phrases like "heavenly bliss," and "love nest." He salivated, sighed, and trembled. When Julia called him to come down, the abyss between his fantasy and the practical world opened so wide that he felt it affect the muscles of his heart.

Julia and the children were on the stoop, and the photographer and his assistant had set up a double battery of floodlights to show the family and the architectural beauty of the entrance to their house. People who had come home on a late train slowed their cars to see the Weeds being photographed for their Christmas card. A few waved and called to the family. It took half an hour of smiling and wetting their lips before Mr. Hubber was satisfied. The heat of the lights made an unfresh smell in the frosty air, and when they were turned off, they lingered on the retina of Francis' eyes.

Later that night, while Francis and Julia were drinking their coffee in the living room, the doorbell rang. Julia answered the door and let in Clayton Thomas. He had come to pay her for some theater tickets that she had given his mother some time ago, and that Helen Thomas had scrupulously insisted on paying for, though Julia had asked her not to. Julia invited him in to have a cup of coffee. "I won't have any coffee," Clayton said, "but I will come in for a minute." He followed her into the living room, said good evening to Francis, and sat awkwardly in a chair.

Clayton's father had been killed in the war, and the young man's fatherlessness surrounded him like an element. This may have been conspicuous in Shady Hill because the Thomases were the only family that lacked a piece; all the other marriages were intact and productive. Clayton was in his second or third year of college, and he and his mother lived alone in a large house, which she hoped to sell. Clayton had once made some trouble. Years ago, he had stolen some money and run away; he had got to California before they caught up with him. He was tall and homely, wore hornrimmed glasses, and spoke in a deep voice.

"When do you go back to college, Clayton?" Francis asked.

"I'm not going back," Clayton said. "Mother doesn't have the money, and there's no sense in all this pretense. I'm going to get a job, and if we sell the house, we'll take an apartment in New York."

"Won't you miss Shady Hill?" Julia asked.

"No," Clayton said. "I don't like it."

"Why not?" Francis asked.

"Well, there's a lot here I don't approve of," Clayton said gravely.

"Things like the club dances. Last Saturday night, I looked in toward the end and saw Mr. Granner trying to put Mrs. Minot into the trophy case. They were both drunk. I disapprove of so much drinking."

"It was Saturday night," Francis said.

"And all the dovecotes are phony," Clayton said. "And the way people clutter up their lives. I've thought about it a lot, and what seems to me to be really wrong with Shady Hill is that it doesn't have any future. So much energy is spent in perpetuating the place—in keeping out undesirables, and so forth—that the only idea of the future anyone has is just more and more commuting trains and more parties. I don't think that's healthy. I think people ought to be able to dream big dreams about the future. I think people ought to be able to dream great dreams."

"It's too bad you couldn't continue with college," Julia said.

"I wanted to go to divinity school," Clayton said.

"What's your church?" Francis asked.

"Unitarian, Theosophist, Transcendentalist, Humanist," Clayton said.

"Wasn't Emerson a transcendentalist?" Julia asked.

"I mean the English transcendentalists," Clayton said. "All the American transcendentalists were goops."

"What kind of job do you expect to get?" Francis asked.

"Well, I'd like to work for a publisher," Clayton said, "but everyone tells me there's nothing doing. But it's the kind of thing I'm interested in. I'm writing a long verse play about good and evil. Uncle Charlie might get me into a bank, and that would be good for me. I need the discipline. I have a long way to go in forming my character. I have some terrible habits. I talk too much. I think I ought to take vows of silence. I ought to try not to speak for a week, and discipline myself. I've thought of making a retreat at one of the Episcopalian monasteries, but I don't like Trinitarianism."

"Do you have any girl friends?" Francis asked.

"I'm engaged to be married," Clayton said. "Of course, I'm not old enough or rich enough to have my engagement observed or respected or anything, but I bought a simulated emerald for Anne Murchison with the money I made cutting lawns this summer. We're going to be married as soon as she finishes school."

Francis recoiled at the mention of the girl's name. Then a dingy light seemed to emanate from his spirit, showing everything—Julia, the boy, the chairs—in their true colorlessness. It was like a bitter turn of the weather.

"We're going to have a large family," Clayton said. "Her father's a terrible rummy, and I've had my hard times, and we want to have lots of children. Oh, she's wonderful, Mr. and Mrs. Weed, and we have so much in common. We like all the same things. We sent out the same Christmas card last year without planning it, and we both have an allergy to tomatoes, and our eyebrows grow together in the middle. Well, good night."

Julia went to the door with him. When she returned, Francis said that Clayton was lazy, irresponsible, affected, and smelly. Julia said that Francis seemed to be getting intolerant; the Thomas boy was young and should be given a chance. Julia had noticed other cases where Francis had been short-tempered. "Mrs. Wrightson has asked everyone in Shady Hill to her anniversary party but us," she said.

"I'm sorry, Julia."

"Do you know why they didn't ask us?"

"Why?"

"Because you insulted Mrs. Wrightson."

"Then you know about it?"

"June Masterson told me. She was standing behind you."

Julia walked in front of the sofa with a small step that expressed, Francis knew, a feeling of anger.

"I did insult Mrs. Wrightson, Julia, and I meant to. I've never liked her parties, and I'm glad she's dropped us."

"What about Helen?"

"How does Helen come into this?"

"Mrs. Wrightson's the one who decides who goes to the assemblies."

"You mean she can keep Helen from going to the dances?"

"Yes."

"I hadn't thought of that."

"Oh, I knew you hadn't thought of it," Julia cried, thrusting hilt-deep into this chink of his armor. "And it makes me furious to see this kind of stupid thoughtlessness wreck everyone's happiness."

"I don't think I've wrecked anyone's happiness."

"Mrs. Wrightson runs Shady Hill and has run it for the last forty years. I don't know what makes you think that in a community like this you can indulge every impulse you have to be insulting, vulgar, and offensive."

"I have very good manners," Francis said, trying to give the evening a turn toward the light.

"Damn you, Francis Weed!" Julia cried, and the spit of her words struck him in the face. "I've worked hard for the social position we enjoy in this place, and I won't stand by and see you wreck it. You must have understood when you settled here that you couldn't expect to live like a bear in a cave."

"I've got to express my likes and dislikes."

"You can conceal your dislikes. You don't have to meet everything head-on, like a child. Unless you're anxious to be a social leper. It's no accident that we get asked out a great deal! It's no accident that Helen has so many friends. How would you like to spend your Saturday nights at the movies? How would you like to spend your Sundays raking up dead leaves? How would you like it if your daughter spent the assembly nights sitting at her window, listening to the music from the club? How would you like it—"

He did something then that was, after all, not so unaccountable, since her words seemed to rise up between them a wall so deadening that he gagged: He struck her full in the face. She staggered and then, a moment later, seemed composed. She went up the stairs to their room. She didn't slam the door. When Francis followed, a few minutes later, he found her packing a suitcase.

"Julia, I'm very sorry."

"It doesn't matter," she said. She was crying.

"Where do you think you're going?"

"I don't know. I just looked at a timetable. There's an eleven-sixteen into New York. I'll take that."

"You can't go, Julia."

"I can't stay. I know that."

"I'm sorry about Mrs. Wrightson, Julia, and I'm—"

"It doesn't matter about Mrs. Wrightson. That isn't the trouble."

"What is the trouble?"

"You don't love me."

"I do love you, Julia."

"No, you don't."

"Julia, I do love you, and I would like to be as we were—sweet and bawdy and dark—but now there are so many people."

"You hate me."

"I don't hate you, Julia."

"You have no idea of how much you hate me. I think it's subconscious. You don't realize the cruel things you've done."

"What cruel things, Julia?"

"The cruel acts your subconscious drives you to in order to express your hatred of me."

"What, Julia?"

"I've never complained."

"Tell me."

"You don't know what you're doing."

"Tell me."

"Your clothes."

"What do you mean?"

"I mean the way you leave your dirty clothes around in order to express your subconscious hatred of me."

"I don't understand."

"I mean your dirty socks and your dirty pajamas and your dirty underwear and your dirty shirts!" She rose from kneeling by the suitcase and faced him, her eyes blazing and her voice ringing with emotion. "I'm talking about the fact that you've never learned to hang up anything. You just leave your clothes all over the floor where they drop, in order to humiliate me. You do it on purpose!" She fell on the bed, sobbing.

"Julia, darling!" he said, but when she felt his hand on her shoulder she got up.

"Leave me alone," she said. "I have to go." She brushed past him to the closet and came back with a dress. "I'm not taking any of the things you've given me," she said. "I'm leaving my pearls and the fur jacket."

"Oh, Julia!" Her figure, so helpless in its self-deceptions, bent over the suitcase made him nearly sick with pity. She did not understand how desolate her life would be without him. She didn't understand the hours that working women have to keep. She didn't understand that most of her friendships existed within the framework of their marriage, and that without this she would find herself alone. She didn't understand about travel, about hotels, about money. "Julia, I can't let you go! What you don't understand, Julia, is that you've come to be dependent on me."

She tossed her head back and covered her face with her hands. "Did you say that *I* was dependent on *you?*" she asked. "Is that what you said? And who is it that tells you what time to get up in the morning and when to go to bed at night? Who is it that prepares your meals and picks up your dirty clothes and invites your friends to dinner? If it weren't for me, your neckties would be greasy and your clothing would be full of moth holes. You were alone when I met you, Francis Weed, and you'll be alone when I leave. When Mother asked you for a list to send out invitations to our wedding, how many names did you have to give her? Fourteen!"

"Cleveland wasn't my home, Julia."

"And how many of your friends came to the church? Two!"

"Cleveland wasn't my home, Julia."

"Since I'm not taking the fur jacket," she said quietly, "you'd better put it back into storage. There's an insurance policy on the pearls that comes due in January. The name of the laundry and the maid's telephone number —all those things are in my desk. I hope you won't drink too much, Francis. I hope that nothing bad will happen to you. If you do get into serious trouble, you can call me."

"Oh, my darling, I can't let you go!" Francis said. "I can't let you go, Julie!" He took her in his arms.

"I guess I'd better stay and take care of you for a little while longer," she said.

Riding to work in the morning, Francis saw the girl walk down the aisle of the coach. He was surprised; he hadn't realized that the school she went to was in the city, but she was carrying books, she seemed to be going to school. His surprise delayed his reaction, but then he got up clumsily and stepped into the aisle. Several people had come between them, but he could see her ahead of him, waiting for someone to open the car door, and then, as the train swerved, putting out her hand to support herself as she crossed the platform into the next car. He followed her through that car and halfway through another before calling her name—"Anne! Anne!"—but she didn't turn. He followed her into still another car, and she sat down in an aisle seat. Coming up to her, all his feelings warm and bent in her direction, he put his hand on the back of her seat—even this touch warmed him—and, leaning down to speak to her, he saw that it was not Anne. It was an older woman wearing glasses. He went on deliberately into another car, his face red with embarrassment and the much deeper feeling of having his good sense challenged; for if he couldn't tell one person from another, what evidence was there that his life with Julia and the children had as much reality as his dreams of iniquity in Paris or the litter, the grass smell, and the cave-shaped trees in Lovers' Lane?

Late that afternoon, Julia called to remind Francis that they were going out for dinner. A few minutes later, Trace Bearden called. "Look, fellar," Trace said. "I'm calling for Mrs. Thomas. You know? Clayton, that boy of hers, doesn't seem able to get a job, and I wondered if you could help. If you'd call Charlie Bell—I know he's indebted to you—and say a good word for the kid, I think Charlie would—"

"Trace, I hate to say this," Francis said, "but I don't feel that I can do anything for that boy. The kid's worthless. I know it's a harsh thing to say, but it's a fact. Any kindness done for him would backfire in everybody's face. He's just a worthless kid, Trace, and there's nothing to be done about it. Even if we got him a job, he wouldn't be able to keep it for a week. I know that to be a fact. It's an awful thing, Trace, and I know it is, but instead of recommending that kid, I'd feel obligated to warn people against him—people who knew his father and would naturally want to step in and do something. I'd feel obliged to warn them. He's a thief . . ."

The moment this conversation was finished, Miss Rainey came in and stood by his desk. "I'm not going to be able to work for you any more, Mr. Weed," she said. "I can stay until the seventeenth if you need me, but I've been offered a whirlwind of a job, and I'd like to leave as soon as possible."

She went out, leaving him to face alone the wickedness of what he had done to the Thomas boy. His children in their photograph laughed and laughed, glazed with all the bright colors of summer, and he remembered that they had met a bagpiper on the beach that day and he had paid the piper a dollar to play them a battle song of the Black Watch. The girl would be at the house when he got home. He would spend another evening among his kind neighbors, picking and choosing dead-end streets, cart tracks, and the driveways of abandoned houses. There was nothing to mitigate his feeling—nothing that laughter or a game of softball with the children would change—and, thinking back over the plane crash, the Farquarsons' new maid, and Anne Murchison's difficulties with her drunken father, he wondered how he could have avoided arriving at just where he was. He was in trouble. He had been lost once in his life, coming back from a trout stream in the north woods, and he had now the same bleak realization that no amount of cheerfulness or hopefulness or valor or perseverance could help him find, in the gathering dark, the path that he'd lost. He smelled the forest. The feeling of bleakness was intolerable, and he saw clearly that he had reached the point where he would have to make a choice.

He could go to a psychiatrist, like Miss Rainey; he could go to church and confess his lusts; he could go to a Danish massage parlor in the West Seventies that had been recommended by a salesman; he could rape the girl or trust that he would somehow be prevented from doing this; or he could get drunk. It was his life, his boat, and, like every other man, he was made to be the father of thousands, and what harm could there be in a tryst that would make them both feel more kindly toward the world? This was the wrong train of thought, and he came back to the first, the psychiatrist. He had the telephone number of Miss Rainey's doctor, and he called and asked for an immediate appointment. He was insistent with the doctor's secretary—it was his manner in business—and when she said that the doctor's schedule was full for the next few weeks, Francis demanded an appointment that day and was told to come at five.

The psychiatrist's office was in a building that was used mostly by doctors and dentists, and the hallways were filled with the candy smell of mouthwash and memories of pain. Francis' character had been formed upon a series of private resolves—resolves about cleanliness, about going off the high diving board or repeating any other feat that challenged his courage, about punctuality, honesty, and virtue. To abdicate the perfect loneliness in which he had made his most vital decisions shattered his concept of character and left him now in a condition that felt like shock. He was stupefied. The scene for his *miserere mei Deus* was, like the waiting room of so many doctor's offices, a crude token gesture toward the sweets of domestic bliss: a place arranged with antiques, coffee tables, potted plants, and etchings of snow-covered bridges and geese in flight, although there were no children, no marriage bed, no stove, even, in this travesty of a house, where no one had ever spent the night and where the curtained windows looked straight onto a dark air shaft. Francis gave his name and address to a secretary and then saw, at the side of the room, a policeman moving toward him. "Hold it, hold it," the policeman said. "Don't move. Keep your hands where they are."

"I think it's all right, officer," the secretary began. "I think it will be—"

"Let's make sure," the policeman said, and he began to slap Francis' clothes, looking for what—pistols, knives, an icepick? Finding nothing, he went off, and the secretary began a nervous apology: "When you called on the telephone, Mr. Weed, you seemed very excited, and one of the doctor's patients has been threatening his life, and we have to be careful. If you want to go in now?" Francis pushed open a door connected to an electrical chime, and in the doctor's lair sat down heavily, blew his nose into a handkerchief, searched in his pockets for cigarettes, for matches, for something, and said hoarsely, with tears in his eyes, "I'm in love, Dr. Herzog."

It is a week or ten days later in Shady Hill. The seven-fourteen has come and gone, and here and there dinner is finished and the dishes are in the dish-washing machine. The village hangs, morally and economically, from a thread; but it hangs by its thread in the evening light. Donald Goslin has begun to worry the "Moonlight Sonata" again. *Marcato ma sempre pianissimo!* He seems to be wringing out a wet bath towel, but the housemaid does not heed him. She is writing a letter to Arthur Godfrey. In the cellar of his house, Francis Weed is building a coffee table. Dr. Herzog recommended woodwork as a therapy, and Francis finds some true consolation in the simple arithmetic involved and in the holy smell of new wood. Francis is happy. Upstairs, little Toby is crying, because he is tired. He puts off his cowboy hat, gloves, and fringed jacket, unbuckles the belt studded with gold and rubies, the silver bullets and holsters, slips off his suspenders, his checked shirt, and Levis, and sits on the edge of his bed to pull off his high boots. Leaving this equipment in a heap, he goes to the closet and takes his space suit off a nail. It is a struggle for him to get into the long tights, but he succeeds. He loops the magic cape over his shoulders and, climbing onto the footboard of the bed, he spreads his arms and flies the short distance to the floor, landing with a thump that is audible to everyone in the house but himself.

"Go home, Gertrude, go home," Mrs. Masterson says. "I told you to go home an hour ago, Gertrude. It's way past your suppertime, and your mother will be worried. Go home!" A door on the Babcocks' terrace flies open, and out comes Mrs. Babcock without any clothes on, pursued by her naked husband. (Their children are away at boarding school, and their terrace is screened by a hedge.) Over the terrace they go and in at the kitchen door, as passionate and handsome a nymph and satyr as you will find on any wall in Venice. Cutting the last of the roses in her garden, Julia hears old Mr. Nixon shouting at the squirrels in his bird-feeding station. "Rapscallions! Varmints! Avaunt and quit my sight!" A miserable cat wanders into the garden, sunk in spiritual and physical discomfort. Tied to its head is a small straw hat—a doll's hat—and it is securely buttoned into a doll's dress, from the skirts of which protrudes its long, hairy tail. As it walks, it shakes its feet, as if it had fallen into water.

"Here, pussy, pussy, pussy." Julia calls.

"Here, pussy, here, poor pussy!" But the cat gives her a skeptical look and stumbles away in its skirts. The last to come is Jupiter. He prances through the tomato vines, holding in his generous mouth the remains of an evening slipper. Then it is dark; it is a night where kings in golden suits ride elephants over the mountains.

◈

John Cheever was born in Quincy, Massachusetts, in 1912, was educated at Thayer Academy, has lived in New York City, New Hampshire, West-chester, and Italy, and now lives in Ossining, New York. His work won him a Guggenheim fellowship in 1951, the National Institute of Arts and Letters award in literature in 1956, and the National Book Award in 1958. He has published two novels, The Wapshot Chronicle *(1957) and* The Wapshot Scandal *(1963). But he is best known for his short stories, which have been collected in* The Way Some People Live *(1943),* The Enormous Radio *(1953),* The Housebreaker of Shady Hill *(1958),* Some People, Places, and Things That Will Not Appear in My Next Novel *(1961), and* The Brigadier and the Golf Widow *(1964). His work has been successful: he has made money from it and he has had a good readership, both in* The New Yorker, *where most of his work usually appears, and in the books, and he has had his share of awards. But his work has suffered a neglect of a particular kind: it has not been given the attention of the academic critics, whose consideration of a writer seems now to be the necessary first step toward establishing him as a classic. This will not matter in the long run, for Cheever's novels and stories may prove to be the work that future his-torians of this period turn to first for both a depiction and expression of our times. The stories in* The Enormous Radio, *for instance, will show forever how life is in a New York City apartment house; and his Wapshot family chronicle ranges widely in the middle-class American world.*

In "The Country Husband" and in the other stories in The Housebreaker of Shady Hill, *Cheever shows us how an upper-middle-class suburb tem-pers the behavior and emotions of individuals who live there. Shady Hill has tolerance, but it is a world in which the truly exceptional or extraordi-nary has no place. The close encounter with death in the airplane crash that begins the story cannot even be told in Shady Hill; it has no place or meaning or relevance there. Francis' daughter, for instance, "doesn't un-derstand about the plane crash, because there wasn't a drop of rain in Shady Hill." To tell anyone of having seen the Farquarsons' maid punished at the crossroads as a collaborator "would have been a social as well as a human error," because "the people in the Farquarsons' living room seemed united in their tacit claim . . . that there was no danger or trouble in the world." Minor idiosyncrasies are tolerated in Shady Hill: old Mr. Nixon, for instance, can shout all he wants in his crazy way at the squirrels in his bird-feeding station. And minor transgressions are overlooked: Mr. Granner's attempt to put Mrs. Minot into the trophy case, both drunk, is all right, because "it was Saturday night." The mores of Shady Hill are "robust and elastic," but that is "at the conversational level"; Francis knows that "the moral card house would come down" on him if he were "caught taking advantage of a babysitter." What Cheever so perfectly does is manage both to show his characters and their situations as foolish and ludicrous and yet to develop them with sympathy and warmth. A middle-aged husband's love for a babysitter may be absurd and "typical," but it is also painful, joyful, "natural." This opposition is implicit in every incident or detail in the story and is the basis of the various kinds of symbol and imagery that are used. Throughout the story Cheever makes the confrontation of the ancient myths and heroic legends with situations of modern life that has served so many modern writers: Eliot in "Sweeney Among the Nightingales," for instance, or Joyce in* Ulysses. *The letterhead of Francis' firm has a drawing of the Laocoön, and when it seems to him to have "the deepest meaning" we smile that he should think of himself, in the toils of love for a babysitter, in those terms. There are many other such references: to Venus and Eros and love philters and to the Rockefeller Center Atlas, "shoulders bent under the weight of the world." When the Weeds leave a party and the host says of the hostess, "She makes me feel like Hannibal crossing the Alps," the image is preposterous, yet it is returned to for another meaning in the last line of the story. It is in this last section, after the line space, that all the threads of meaning and symbol in the story are drawn together; like the last section of* The Great Gatsby, *it seems that no matter how often one reads these paragraphs some hitherto unnoticed excellence appears. Jupiter, of course, has a fittingly central place: we are meant to think of the myths of Zeus' loves in contrast with Francis' love, as well as the character of the rakehell, mischievous, fierce, and proud dog himself. Jupiter is disruptive in Shady Hill, an anomaly; and "Jupiter's days were numbered." Toby's myths are modern ones: he changes from a cowboy outfit to a space suit with a magic cape but flies only "the short distance to the floor." The cat's animality is buttoned into a doll's dress, its long, hairy tail in skirts. Mr. Babcock chasing Mrs. Babcock make "as passionate and handsome a nymph and satyr as you will find on any wall in Venice." The effect is of a modern frieze, the life of Shady Hill frozen in action in this tableau. The meaning and metaphor recall Keats' "Ode on a Grecian Urn." Cheever has taken the comic in modern life and shown how sad it is, taken the sadness and shown how comic it is. He has made order out of the absurd chaos of modern life. He has taken the truth about the way we live and somehow made beauty out of it. To be stinting in praise of this piece of work simply because it is contemporary would be to miss the very point of what it has to say to us: that within our own times great beauty can be found.*

⬦⬦

The stories in this section have not been chosen to show how community works or is structured as a whole; what they have been concerned with is how the individual stands in relation to his community or his lack of it. Full of violence as some of these stories may be, they scarcely reflect how much modern fiction is concerned with this subject. If what this fiction reflects is an accurate insight into our times and how we feel about them, then it is more than clear that whatever "community" used to mean in American life—a place of safety and sanctuary, a source of identity and security—it now means very nearly the opposite. Violence would seem to have no place in the dynamics of urbanized, bureaucratized mass society, where constant conflict and struggle for status and power take place within a context of being nice, pleasant, easy, and relaxed—cool and "Compozed." But violence in the nice society undoubtedly does have a relation to the boredom and powerlessness of those who are at the bottom of this indus- trial-bureaucratic heap. At any rate, the eclipse of community in America— from the loss of the small town ideal to the fragmentation of the urban ghetto to the failure of the suburban compromise—can be seen to have con- tributed, in the same way as the breaking-up of the normal family structures contributed, to the unsettled condition of the individual we were concerned with in the first section.

The geographical mobility required by the way people now work for pay has been something of a force in this breaking-up of community and in even more direct ways is responsible for the lack of sense of self that is apparently so typical of our times. It is obvious that all the effects of these changes in our patterns of family life and community life are interrelated with the effects of changes in the occupational patterns of how we live . . .

The Way We Live Now

AT WORK

Changes in the patterns of occupation in American life have been even more radical and rapid than changes in the family and the community. It is estimated that in the early nineteenth century four-fifths of those Americans who worked were self-employed; by 1940, only about one-fifth were, and we know that the rate of change has accelerated since World War II. The classic texts in economic and social history have shown the changes worked on the American social character by the successive shifts of emphasis in occupation involved in the transition from pioneer to farmer to merchant to blue collar factory worker to white collar office worker, and in recent years there have been many analyses of the character of the evolving bureaucratic man. The way most Americans now work—separated not only from the means of production but also from home and community and a sense of the meaning of their work—exists as a direct result of the urbanization, industrialization, and bureaucratization of the society. Machines, of course, now save human labor by doing most of the manufacturing of things; but they produce so much of so many things that a good deal more human labor must go into selling and distributing and accounting for it all. There is not less work as a result of industrialization, but more. But even as the American economy as a whole continues to grow and to become more complex, the importance of work in the life of any one man seems to be diminishing, and in a number of ways. It takes up fewer hours of the day, fewer days of the week, and less of a total lifetime, and thus is less effective in defining who or what a man is. The competition for status and the indispensability of specialization mean that more and more training is required for more and more "professions," which means that men go to work later while compulsory retirement provides an early cutoff point at the other end of their career. The bureaucratic mode of technical efficiency does not require, in fact cannot use, a total involvement in the job to be done; the human factor must always be subordinate to and shaped by the mechanics of efficiency. This means that only a man in a policy-making position of power, or one who can afford to work independently, is in the position to have his work define his life and self. For the rest of us there is very little sense of the importance of what we actually

490

do at work and very little relationship between the sense of our own skills and the ultimate product of our work. Nor has identification with the company really substituted for identification with the craft: white-collar jobs tend to be interchangeable from one corporation to another, and moving up is often accomplished by moving over into another organization. Since rank and power within the organization mean more than the job done, what you do is far less important than how your job ranks.

As a result of this across-the-board diminishment in the time, skill, energy, involvement, and meaning in the work people do for pay, a great deal more time, skill, involvement, energy, and meaning go into how they spend their leisure. We now have the time to develop special leisure skills and find a sense of meaning and importance and identification in sports, crafts, arts, hobbies, and do-it-yourself. Corporations sponsor bowling leagues for their workers, demand country-club skills and community leadership from their executives. People nowadays tend to work as hard at their leisure as at their job. And where a man used once to be almost primarily known—and take his own sense of his identity—from his occupation, nowadays it may be that we are on the verge of an era in which a man will be known to others—and find his deepest sense of his self—in the choices he makes in the use of his leisure.

The four stories that follow show the effects on the individual of four sorts of work, starting with something rather like the pioneering work of the American past and running through to something like the purely bureaucratic work of the American future. Again it should be emphasized that these stories have not been chosen to reflect an historical development of occupational patterns, nor do they indicate the great variety of ways in which people earn a living. They do show, however, some of the ways in which our expectations about what work means in our lives have changed, and are still changing.

ARTHUR MILLER

The Misfits

◇◇◇◇◇◇◇◇

WIND BLEW DOWN from the mountains all night. A wild river of air swept and swirled across the dark sky and struck down against the blue desert and hissed back into the hills. The three cowboys slept under their blankets, their backs against the first upward curve of the circling mountains, their faces toward the desert of sage. The wind and its tidal washing seethed through their dreams and when it stopped there was a lunar silence that caused Gay Langland to open his eyes. For the first time in three nights he could hear his own breathing and in the new hush he looked up at the stars and saw how clear and bright they were. He felt happy and slid himself out of his blankets and stood up fully dressed.

On the silent plateau between the two mountain ranges Gay Langland was the only moving thing. He turned his head and then his body in a full circle, looking into the deep blue sky for sign of storm. He saw that it would be a good day and a quiet one. He walked a few yards from the two other sleepers and wet the sandy ground. The excitement of the stillness was awakening his body. He returned and lit the bundle of dry sage he had gathered last night, dropped some heavier wood on the quick flames, perched the blackened coffee pot on the stones surrounding the fire-bed, and sat on one heel staring at the fresh orange embers.

Gay Langland was forty-five years old, but as limber as he had ever been in his life. The light of his face brightened when there were things to do, a nail to straighten, an animal to size-up, and it dimmed when there was nothing in his hands, and his eyes then went sleepy. When there was something to be done in a place he stayed there, and when there was nothing to be done he went from it. He had a wife and two children less than a hundred miles from here whom he had not seen in more than three years. She had betrayed him and did not want him, but the children were naturally better off with their mother. When he felt lonely for them all he thought of them lovingly, and when the feeling passed it went unsettled, without leaving him with any question as to what he might do to bring them all back together again. He had been born and raised on rangeland, and he did not know that anything could be undone that was done, any more than falling rain could be stopped in mid-air. And he had a smile and a look in his face that was in accordance. His forehead was evenly tracked with deep ridges, as though his brows were always raised a little expectantly, slightly surprised, a little amused, and his mouth friendly. His ears stuck out, as they often do with little boys or young calves and he had a boy's turned-up snub nose. But his skin was browned by the wind, and his small eyes looked and saw and, above all, were trained against showing fear.

Gay Langland looked up from the fire at the sky and saw the first delicate stain of pink. He went over to the sleepers and shook Guido Racanelli's arm. A grunt of salutation sounded in Guido's head but he remained on his side with his eyes shut. "The sumbitch died off," Gay said to him. Guido listened, motionless, his eyes shut against the firelight, his bones warm in his fat. Gay wanted to shake him again and wake him but in the last two days he had come to wonder whether Guido was not secretly considering not flying at all. The plane's engine was rattling its valves and one shock absorber was weak. Gay had known the pilot for years and he knew and respected his moods. Flying up and down these mountain gorges within feet of the rock walls was nothing you could pressure a man to do. But now that the wind had died Gay hoped very much that Guido would take off this morning and let them begin their work.

He got to his feet and again glanced skywards. Then he stood there thinking of Roslyn. And he had a strong desire to have money in his pocket that he had earned himself when he came to her tonight. The feeling had been returning again and again that he had somehow passed the kidding point, and that he had to work again and earn his way as he always had before he met her. Not that he didn't work for her, but it wasn't the same. Driving her car, repairing her house, running errands—all that stuff wasn't what you would call work. Still, he thought, it was too. Yet, it wasn't either.

He stepped over to the other sleeper and shook him. Perce Howland opened his eyes.

"The sumbitch died, Perce," Gay said.

Perce's eyes looked toward the heavens and he nodded. Then he slid out of his blankets and walked past Gay and stood wetting the sand, breathing deeply as in sleep. Gay always found him humorous to watch when he woke up. Perce walked into things and sometimes stood wetting his own boots. He was a little like a child waking up, and his eyes now were still dreamy and soft.

Gay called over to him, "Better'n wages, huh Perce?"

"Damn right," Perce muttered, and returned to the fire rubbing his skin against his clothes.

Gay kneeled by the fire again, scraping hot coals into a pile and setting the frying pan over them on stones. He could pick up hot things without feeling pain. Now he moved an ember with his finger.

"You make me nervous doing that," Perce said, looking down over his shoulder.

"Nothin' but fire," Gay said, pleased.

They were in silence for a moment, both of them enjoying the brightening air. "Guido goin' up?" Perce asked.

"Didn't say. I guess he's thinkin' about it."

"Be light pretty soon," Perce warned.

He glanced off to the closest range, and saw the purple rocks rising in their mystery toward the faintly glowing stars. Perce Howland was twenty-two, hipless and tall, and he stood there as effortlessly as the mountains he was looking at, as though he had been created there in his dungarees, with the tight plaid shirt and the three-button cuffs, the broad-brimmed beige hat set back on his blond head, and his thumbs tucked into his belt so his fingers could touch the engraved belt buckle with his name spelled out under the raised figure of the bucking horse. It was his first bucking horse prize and he loved to touch it when he stood waiting, and he liked to wait.

Perce had known Gay Langland for only five weeks, and Guido for three days. He had met Gay in a Bowie bar, and Gay had asked him where he was from and what he was doing and he had told Gay his story, which was the usual for most of the rodeo riders. He had come on down from Nevada, as he had done since he was sixteen, to follow the local rodeos and win some money riding bucking horses, but this trip had been different, because he had lost the desire to go back home again.

They had become good friends that night when Gay took him to Roslyn's house to sleep, and when he woke in the morning he had been surprised that an educated Eastern woman should have been so regular and humorous and interested in his opinions. So he had been floating around with Roslyn and Gay Langland, and they were comfortable to be with; Gay mostly, because Gay never thought to say he ought to be making something of his life. Gay made him feel it was all right to go from day to day and week to week. Perce Howland did not trust anybody too far and it was not necessary to trust Gay because Gay did not want anything of him or try to manipulate him. He just wanted a partner to go mustanging, and Perce had never done anything like that and he wanted to see how it was. And now he was here, sixty miles from the nearest town, seven thousand feet up in the air, and for two days waiting for the wind to die so the pilot could take off into the mountains where the wild horses lived.

Perce looked out toward the desert which was beginning to show its silent horizon. "Bet the moon looks like this if anybody could get there."

Gay Langland did not answer. In his mind he could feel the wild horses grazing and moving about in the nearby mountains and he wanted to get to them. Indicating Guido Racanelli, he said, "Give him a shake, Perce. The sun's about up."

Perce started over to Guido who moved before Perce reached him. "Gettin' light, Guido," Perce said.

Guido Racanelli rolled upright on his great behind, his belly slung over his belt, and he inspected the brightening sky in the distance as though some personal message were out there for him. The pink reflected light brightened his face. The flesh around his eyes was white where the goggles protected his face, and the rest of his skin was burned brown by wind. His silences were more profound than the silences of others because his cheeks were so deep, like the mellon-half cheeks of a baboon which curve forward from the mouth. Yet, they were hard cheeks, as hard as his great belly. He looked like a jungle bird now, slowly turning his head to inspect the far-away sky, a serious bird with a brown face and white eyes. His head was entirely bald. He took off his khaki army cap and rubbed his fingers into his scalp.

Gay Langland stood up and walked to him and gave him his eggs and thick bacon on a tin plate. "Wind died, Guido," Gay said, standing there and looking down at the pilot.

"It doesn't mean much what it did down here." Guido pointed skyward with his thumb. "Up there's where it counts."

"Ain't no sign of wind up there," Gay said. Gay's eyes seemed amused. He did not want to seem committed to a real argument. "We got no more eggs, Guido," he warned.

Guido ate.

Now the sky flared with true dawn like damp paper suddenly catching fire. Perce and Gay sat down on the ground facing Guido and they all ate their eggs.

The shroud of darkness quickly slipped off the red truck which stood a few yards away. Then, behind it, the little plane showed itself. Guido Racanelli ate and sipped his coffee, and Gay Langland watched him with a weak smile and without speaking. Perce blinked contentedly at the brightening sky, slightly detached from the other two. He finished his coffee and slipped a chew of tobacco into his mouth and sucked on it.

It was a pink day now all around the sky.

Gay Langland made a line in the sand between his thighs and said, "You goin' up, Guido?" He looked at Guido directly and he was still smiling.

Guido thought for a moment. He was older, about fifty. His pronunciation was unaccountably Eastern, with sharp R's. He sounded educated sometimes. He stared off toward the squat little plane. "Every once in a while I wonder what the hell it's all about," he said.

"What is?" Gay asked.

Perce watched Guido's face, thoroughly listening.

Guido felt their attention and spoke with ease and comfort. He still stared past them at the plane. "I got a lousy valve. I know it, Gay."

"Been that way a long time, Guido," Gay said, with sympathy.

"I know," Guido said. They were not arguing but searching now. "And we won't hardly get twenty dollars apiece out of it—there's only four or five horses back in there."

"We knew that, Guido," Gay said. They were in sympathy with each other.

"I might just get myself killed, for twenty dollars."

"Hell, you know them mountains," Gay said.

"You can't see wind, Gay," the pilot said.

Gay knew now that Guido was going up right away. He saw that Guido had just wanted to get all the dangers straight in his mind so he could see them and count them; then he would go out against them.

"You're flying along in and out of those passes and then you dive for the sons of bitches, and just when you're pulling up some goddam gust presses you down and there you are."

"I know," Gay said.

There was silence. Guido sipped his coffee, staring off at the plane. "I just wonder about it every once in a while," the pilot said.

"Well hell," Perce Howland said, "it's better than wages."

"You damn right it is, Perce," the pilot said thoughtfully.

"I seen guys get killed who never left the ground," Perce said.

The two older men knew that his father had been killed by a bull long ago and that he had seen his father die. He had had his own arms broken in rodeos and a Brahma bull had stepped on his chest. "One rodeo near Salinas I see a fella get his head snapped right clear off his chest by a cable busted. They had this cable drawin' horses up onto a truck. I seen his head rolling away like a bowlin' ball. Must've roll twenty-five yards before it hit a fence post and stopped." He spat tobacco juice and turned back to look at Guido. "It had a moustache. Funny thing, I never knowed that guy had a moustache. Never noticed it. Till I see it stop rolling and there it was, dust all over the moustache."

"That was a dusty moustache," Gay said, grinning against their deepening morbidity.

They all smiled. Then time hung for a moment as they waited. And at last Guido shifted onto one buttock and said, "Well, let's get gassed up."

Guido leaned himself to one side with his palm on the ground, then got to his feet by moving in a circle around this palm, and stood up. Gay and Perce Howland were already moving off toward the truck, Perce heisting up his dungarees over his breakfast-full stomach, and the older Gay more sprightly and intent. Guido stood holding one hand open over the fire, watching them loading the six enormous truck tires onto the bed of the truck. Each tire had a twenty-foot length of rope wired to it, and at the end of each rope was a loop. Before they swung the tires onto the truck, Gay inspected the ropes to be sure they were securely knotted to the tires, and the loops open and ready for throwing.

Guido blinked against the warming sun, watching the other two, then he looked off to his right where the passes were, and the fingers of his mind felt around beyond those passes into the bowls and hollows of the mountains where last week he had spotted the small herd of wild horses grazing. Now he felt the lightness he had been hoping to feel for three days, the good sense of wanting to fly. For three days he had kept away from the plane because the careless feeling had been itching at him, the feeling which he always thought would lead him to his death. About five weeks ago he had come up to this desert with Gay Langland and he had chased seven mustangs out of the mountains. But that time he had dived to within a foot of the mountain side, and afterward, as they sat around the fire eating dinner, Guido had had the feeling that he had made that deep dive so he could die. And the thought of his dead wife had come to him again, and the other thought that always came into his mind with her dead face. It was the wonderment, the quiet pressing-in of the awareness that he had never wanted a woman after she had been buried with the still-born baby beside her in the graveyard outside Bowie. Seven years now he had waited for some real yearning for woman, and nothing at all had come to him. It pleasured him to know that he was free of that, and it sometimes made him careless in the plane, as though some great bang and a wreckage would make him again what he had been. By now he could go a week through Bowie and in an odd moment recall that he hadn't even looked at a girl walking by, and the feeling of carelessness would come on him, a kind of loose gaiety, as though everything was comical. Until he had made that dive and pulled out with his nose almost scraping the grass, and he had climbed upward with his mouth hanging open and his body in a sweat. So that through these past three days up here he had refused to let himself take off until the wind had utterly died, and he had clung to moroseness. He wanted to take off in the absolute grip of his own wits, leaving nothing to chance, and now there was no wind at all, and he felt he had pressed the lightness and the gaiety out of his mind. He left the dying fire and walked past Gay and Perce and down the gentle slope to the plane looking like a stout, serious football coach before the kick-off.

He glanced over the fuselage and at the bald doughnut tires and he loved the plane. Again, as always, he looked at the weakened starboard shock absorber which no longer held its spread and let the plane stand tilted a little to one side, and told himself that it was not serious. He heard the truck motor starting, and he unfastened the knots of the ropes holding the plane to the spikes driven into the desert floor. Then the truck pulled up, and young Perce Howland dropped off and went over to the tail handle, gripped it, lifted the tail off the ground and swung her around so she faced out across the endless desert and away from the mountains. Then they unwound the rubber hose from the gas drum on the truck and stuck the nozzle into the gas tank behind the engine, and Perce turned the pump crank.

Guido then walked around the wing and over to the cockpit whose right door was folded down, leaving the inside open to the air. He reached in and took out his ripped leather flight jacket and got into it. Perce stood leaning against the truck fender now, grinning. "That sure is a ventilated type jacket, Guido," he said.

Then Guido said, "I can't get my size any more." The jacket had one sleeve off at the elbow, and the dried leather was split open down the back, showing the lamb's wool lining. He had bombed Germany in this jacket long ago. He reached in behind the seat and took out a goggle case, slipped his goggles out, replaced the case, set his goggles securely on his face, and reached in again and took out a shotgun pistol and three shells from a little wooden box beside his seat. He loaded the pistol and laid it carefully under his seat. Then he got into the cockpit, sat in his seat, drew the strap over his belly and buckled it. Meantime Gay had taken his position before the propeller.

Guido called through the open doorway of the cockpit, "Turn her over, Gay-boy!"

Gay stepped up to the propeller, glanced down behind his heels to be sure no stone waited to trip him when he stepped back, and pulled down on the blade and hopped back watchfully.

"Give her another!" Guido called in the silence.

Gay stepped up again, again glancing around his heels, and pulled the blade down. The engine inhaled and exhaled and they could all hear the oily clank of her inner shafts turning loosely.

"Ignition on, Gay-boy!" Guido called, and threw the switch.

This time Gay inspected the ground around him even more carefully, and pulled his hatbrim down tighter on his head. Perce stood leaning on the truck's front fender, spitting and chewing, his eyes softly squinted against the brazen sun. Gay reached up and pulled the propeller down and jumped back. A puff of smoke floated up from the engine ports.

"Goddam car gas," Guido said. "Ignition on. Go again, Gay-boy!" They were buying low octane to save money.

Gay again stepped up to the propeller, swung the blade down, and the engine said its "Chaaahh!" and the ports breathed white smoke into the morning air. Gay walked over to Perce and stood beside him watching. The fuselage shuddered and the propeller turned into a wheel, and the dust blew pleasantly from behind the plane and toward the mountains. Guido gunned her and she tumbled toward the open desert, bumping along over the sage clumps and crunching whitened skeletons of cattle killed by the winter. The stiff-backed plane grew smaller, shouldering its way over the broken ground, and then its nose turned upward and there was space between the doughnut tires and the desert, and lazily it climbed, turning back the way it had come. It flew over the heads of Perce and Gay, and Guido waved down, a stranger now, fiercely goggled and wrapped in leather, and they could see him exposed to the waist, turning from them to look through the windshield at the mountains ahead of him. The plane flew away, climbing smoothly, losing itself against the orange and purple walls that vaulted up from the desert to hide from the cowboy's eyes the wild animals they wanted for themselves.

They would have at least two hours before the plane flew out of the mountains driving the horses before it, so they washed the three tin plates and the cups and stored them in the aluminum grub box. If Guido did find horses they would break camp and return to Bowie tonight, so they packed up their bedrolls with sailors' tidiness and laid them neatly side by side on the ground. The six great truck tires, each with its looped rope coiled within, lay in two piles on the bed of the truck. Gay Langland looked them over and touched them with his hand and stood for a moment trying to think if there was anything they were leaving behind. He jumped up on the truck to see that the cap was screwed tight on the gas drum which was lashed to the back of the cab up front, and it was. Then he hopped down to the ground and got into the cab and started the engine. Perce was already sitting there with his hat tipped forward against the yellow sunlight pouring through the windshield. A thin and concerned border collie came trotting up as Gay started to close his door and he invited her into the cab. She leaped up and he snugged her into the space between the clutch and the left wall of the cab. "Damn near forgot Belle," he said, and they started off.

Gay owned the truck and he wanted to preserve the front end which he knew could be twisted out of line on broken ground. So he started off slowly. They could hear the gas sloshing in the drum behind them outside. It was getting warm now. They rode in silence staring ahead at the two-track trail they were following across the bone-cluttered sagebrush. Thirty miles ahead stood the lava mountains which were the northern border of this desert, the bed of a bowl seven thousand feet up, a place no one ever saw excepting the few cowboys searching for stray cattle every few months. People in Bowie, sixty miles away, did not know of this place. There were the two of them and the truck and the dog, and now that they were on the move they felt between them the comfort of purpose and their isolation, and Perce slumped in his seat blinking as though he would go to sleep again, and Gay smoked a cigarette and let his body flow from side to side with the pitching of the truck. There was a moving cloud of dust in the distance toward the left, and Gay said, "Antelope," and Perce tipped his hat back and looked. "Must be doin' sixty," he said, and Gay said, "More.

I chased one once and I was doin' more than sixty and he lost me." Perce shook his head in wonder and they turned to look ahead again.

After he had thought a while Perce said, "We better get over to Largo by tomorrow if we're gonna get into that rodeo. They's gonna be a crowd trying to sign up for that one."

"We'll drive down in the morning," Gay said.

"I'll have to see about gettin' me some stock."

"We'll get there early tomorrow; you'll get stock if you come in early."

"Like to win some money," Perce said. "I just wish I get me a good horse down there."

"They be glad to fix you up, Perce. You're known pretty good around there now. They'll fix you up with some good stock," Gay said. Perce was one of the best bronc riders and the rodeos liked to have it known he would appear.

Then there was silence. Gay had to hold the gear shift lever in high or it would slip out into neutral when they hit bumps. The transmission fork was worn out, he knew, and the front tires were going too. He dropped one hand to his pants pocket and felt the four silver dollars he had from the ten Roslyn had given him when they had left her days ago.

As though he had read Gay's mind, Perce said, "Roslyn would've liked it up here. She'd liked to have seen that antelope, I bet." Perce grinned as both of them usually did at Roslyn's Eastern surprise at everything they did and saw and said.

"Yeah," Gay said, "she likes to see things." Through the corner of his eye he watched the younger man who was looking ahead with a little grin on his face. "She's a damned good sport, old Roslyn," Gay said.

"Sure is," Perce Howland said. And Gay watched him for any sign of guile, but there was only a look of glad appreciation. "First woman like that I ever met," the younger man said.

"They's more," Gay said. "Some of them Eastern women fool you sometimes. They got education but they're good sports. And damn good *women* too, some of them."

There was a silence. Then the younger man asked, "You get to know a lot of them? Eastern women?"

"Ah, I get one once in a while," Gay said.

"Only educated women I ever know, they was back home near Teachers College. Students. Y'know," he said, warming to the memory, "I used to think, hell, education's everything. But when I saw the husbands some of them got married to—schoolteachers and everything, why I don't give them much credit. And they just as soon climb on a man as tell him good morning. I was teachin' them to ride for a while near home."

"Just because a woman's educated don't mean much. Woman's a woman," Gay said. The image of his wife came into his mind. For a moment he wondered if she were still living with the same man he had beaten up when he discovered them together in a parked car six years ago.

"You divorced?" Perce asked.

"No. I never bothered with it," Gay said. It always surprised him how Perce said just what was on his mind sometimes. "How'd you know I was thinkin' of that?" he asked, grinning with embarrassment. But he was too curious to keep silent.

"Hell, I didn't know," Perce said.

"You're always doin' that. I think of somethin' and you go ahead and say it."

"That's funny," Perce said.

They rode on in silence. They were nearing the middle of the desert where they would turn east. Gay was driving faster now because he wanted to get to the rendezvous and sit quietly waiting for the plane to appear. He held onto the gear shift lever and felt it trying to spring out of high and into neutral. It would have to be fixed. The time was coming fast when he would need about fifty dollars or sell the truck, because it would be useless without repairs. Without a truck and without a horse he would be down to what was in his pocket.

Perce spoke out of the silence. "If I don't win Saturday I'm gonna have to do something for money."

"Goddam, you always say what's in my mind."

Perce laughed. His face looked very young and pink. "Why?"

"I was just now thinkin'," Gay said, "what I'm gonna do for money."

"Well, Roslyn give you some," Perce said.

He said it innocently, and Gay knew it was innocent, and yet he felt angry blood moving into his neck. Something had happened in these five weeks and Gay did not know for sure what it was. Roslyn had taken to calling Perce cute and now and again she would bend over and kiss him on the back of the neck when he was sitting in the living room chair, drinking with them.

Not that that meant anything in itself, because he'd known Eastern women before who'd do something like that and it was just their way. Especially college graduate divorced women. What he wondered at was Perce's way of hardly even noticing what she did to him. Sometimes it was like he'd already had her and could ignore her the way a man will who knows he's boss. But then Gay thought it might just be that he really wasn't interested, or maybe that he was keeping cool in deference to Gay.

Again Gay felt a terrible longing to earn money working. He sensed the bottom of his life falling if it turned out Roslyn had really been loving this boy beside him. It had happened to him once before with his wife but this frightened him more and he did not know exactly why. Not that he couldn't do without Roslyn. There wasn't anybody or anything he couldn't do without. She was about his age and full of laughter that was not laughter and gaiety that was not gaiety and adventurousness that was labored, and he knew all this perfectly well even as he laughed with her and was high with her in the bars and rodeos. He had only lived once, and that was when he had had his house and his wife and his children. He knew the difference, but you never kept anything and he had never particularly thought about keeping anything or losing anything. He had been all his life like Perce Howland sitting beside him now, a man moving on or ready to. It was only when he discovered his wife with a stranger that he knew he had had a stake to which he had been pleasurably tethered. He had not seen her or his children for years, and only rarely thought about any of them. Any more than his father had thought of him very much after the day he had gotten on his pony, when he was fourteen, to go to town from the ranch, and had kept going into Montana and stayed there for three years. He lived in this country as his father did and it was the same endless range wherever he went and it connected him sufficiently with his father and his wife and his children. All might turn up sometime in some town or at some rodeo where he might happen to look over his shoulder and see his daughter or one of his sons, or they might never turn up. He had neither left anyone nor not-left as long as they were all alive on these ranges, for everything here was always beyond the furthest shot of vision and far away, and mostly he had worked alone or with one or two men between distant mountains anyway.

In the distance now he could see the shimmering wall of the heat waves rising from the clay flatland they wanted to get to. Now they were approaching closer and it opened to them beyond the heat waves, and they could see once again how vast it was, a prehistoric lakebed thirty miles long by seventeen miles wide, couched between the two mountain ranges. It was a flat, beige waste without grass or bush or stone where a man might drive a car at a hundred miles an hour with his hands off the wheel and never hit anything at all. They drove in silence. The truck stopped bouncing as the tires rolled over harder ground where there were fewer sage clumps. The waves of heat were dense before them and they drove through them as through dreams of watery cascades. Now the truck rolled smoothly and they were on the clay lakebed and when they had gone a few hundred yards onto it Gay pulled up and shut off the engine. The air was still in a dead, sunlit silence. When he opened his door he could hear a squeak in the hinge he had never noticed before. When they walked around out here they could hear their shirts rasping against their backs and the brush of a sleeve against their trousers.

They stood on the clay ground which was as hard as concrete, and turned to look the way they had come. They looked back toward the mountains at whose feet they had camped and slept, and scanned their ridges for Guido's plane. It was too early for him and they made themselves busy taking the gas drum off the truck and setting it a few yards away on the ground because they would want the truck bed clear when the time came to run the horses down. Then they climbed up and sat inside the tires with their necks against the tire beads and their legs hanging over.

Perce said, "I sure hope they's five up in there."

"Guido saw five, he said."

"He said he wasn't sure if one wasn't only a colt," Perce said.

Gay let himself keep silence. He felt he was going to argue with Perce. He watched Perce through the corner of his eye, saw the flat, blond cheeks and the strong, lean neck and there was something tricky about Perce now. "How long you think you'll be stayin' around here, Perce?" he asked.

They were both watching the distant ridges for a sign of the plane.

"Don't know," Perce said, and spat over the side of the truck. "I'm gettin' a little tired of this, though."

"Well, it's better than wages, Perce."

"Hell yes. Anything's better than wages."

Gay's eyes crinkled. "You're a real misfit, boy."

"That suits me fine," Perce said. They often had this conversation and savored it. "Better than workin' for some goddam cow outfit buckarooin' so somebody else can buy gas for his Cadillac."

"Damn right," Gay said.

"Hell, Gay, you are the most misfitted man I ever saw and you done all right."

"I got no complaints," Gay said.

"I don't want nothin' and I don't want to want nothin'."

"That's the way, boy."

Gay felt closer to him again and he was glad for it. He kept his eyes on the ridges far away. The sun felt good on his shoulders. "I think he's havin' trouble with them sumbitches up in there."

Perce stared out at the ridges. "Ain't two hours yet." Then he turned to Gay. "These mountains must be cleaned out by now, ain't they?"

"Just about," Gay said. "Just a couple small herds left. Can't do much more around here."

"What you goin' to do when you got these cleaned out?"

"Might go North, I think. Supposed to be some big herds in around Thighbone Mountain and that range up in there."

"How far's that?"

"North about a hundred miles. If I can get Guido interested."

Perce smiled. "He don't like movin' around much, does he?"

"He's just misfitted like the rest of us," Gay said. "He don't want nothin'." Then he added, "They wanted him for an airline pilot flyin' up into Montana and back. Good pay too."

"Wouldn't do it, huh?"

"Not Guido," Gay said, grinning. "Might not like some of the passengers, he told them."

Both men laughed and Perce shook his head in admiration for Guido. Then he said, "They wanted me take over the riding academy up home. I thought about that. Two hundred a month and board. Easy work too. You don't hardly have to ride at all. Just stand around and see the customers get satisfied and put them girls off and on."

He fell silent. Gay knew the rest. It was the same story always. It brought him closer to Perce and it was what he had liked about Perce in the first place. Perce didn't like wages either. He had come on Perce in a bar where the boy was buying drinks for everybody with his rodeo winnings, and his hair still clotted with blood from a bucking horse's kick an hour earlier. Roslyn had offered to get a doctor for him and he had said, "Thank you kindly. But I ain't bad hurt. If you're bad hurt you gonna die and the doctor can't do nothin', and if you ain't bad hurt you get better anyway without no doctor."

Now it suddenly came upon Gay that Perce had known Roslyn before they had met in the bar. He stared at the boy's profile. "Want to come up North with me if I go?" he asked.

Perce thought a moment. "Think I'll stay around here. Not much rodeoin' up North."

"I might find a pilot up there, maybe. And Roslyn drive us up in her car."

Perce turned to him, a little surprised. "Would she go up there?"

"Sure. She's a damn good sport," Gay said. He watched Perce's eyes which had turned interested and warm.

Perce said, "Well, maybe; except to tell you the truth, Gay, I never feel comfortable takin' these horses for chicken feed."

"Somebody's goin' to take them if we don't."

"I know," Perce said. He turned to watch the far ridges again. "Just seems to me they belong up there."

"They ain't doin' nothin' up there but eatin' out good cattle range. The cow outfits shoot them down if they see them."

"I know," Perce said.

"They don't even bother takin' them to slaughter. They just rot up there if the cow outfits get to them."

"I know," Perce said.

There was silence. Neither bug nor lizard nor rabbit moved on the great basin around them and the sun warmed their necks and their thighs. Gay said, "I'd a soon sell them for riding horses but they ain't big enough, except for a kid. And the freight on them's more than they're worth. You saw them—they ain't nothin' but skinny horses."

"I just don't know if I'd want to see like a hundred of them goin' for chicken feed, though. I don't mind like five or six, but a hundred's a lot of horses. I don't know."

Gay thought. "Well, if it ain't this it's wages. Around here anyway." He was speaking of himself and explaining himself.

"I'd just as soon ride buckin' horses and make out that way, Gay." Perce turned to him. "Although I might go up North with you. I don't know."

"Roslyn wouldn't come out here at first," Gay said, "but soon as she saw what they looked like she stopped complainin' about it. You didn't hear her complainin' about it."

"I ain't complainin', Gay. I just don't know. Seems to me God put them up there and they belong up there. But I'm doin' it and I guess I'd go on doin' it. I don't know."

"Sounds to me like the newspapers. They want their steaks, them people in town, but they don't want castration or branding or cleanin' wild horses off the ranges."

"Hell, man, I castrated more bulls than I got hairs on my head," Perce said.

"I better get the glasses," Gay said, and slid out of the tire in which he had been lounging and off the truck. He went to the cab and reached in and brought out a pair of binoculars, blew on the lenses, mounted the truck, and sat on a tire with his elbows resting on his knees. He put the glasses to his eyes and focused them. The mountains came up close with their pocked, blue hides. He found the pass through which he believed the plane would come and studied its slopes and scanned the air above it. Anger was still warming him. "God put them up there!" Why, Christ, God put everything everywhere. Did that mean you couldn't eat chickens, for instance, or beef? His dislike for Perce was flowing into him again.

They heard the shotgun off in the sky somewhere and they stopped moving. Gay narrowed his eyes and held the binoculars perfectly still.

"See anything?" Perce asked.

"He's still in the pass, I guess," Gay said.

They sat still, watching the sky over the pass. The moments went by. The sun was making them perspire now, and Gay wiped his wet eyebrows with the back of one hand. They heard the shotgun again from the general sky. Gay spoke without lowering the glasses: "He's probably blasting them out of some corner."

Perce quickly arched out of his tire. "I see him," he said quickly. "I see him glintin', I see the plane."

It angered Gay that Perce had seen the plane first without glasses. In the glasses Gay could see it clearly now. It was flying out of the pass, circling back and disappearing into the pass again. "He's got them in the pass now. Just goin' back in for them."

"Can you see them?" Perce asked.

"He ain't got them in the clear yet. He just went back in for them."

Now through his glasses he could see moving specks on the ground where the pass opened onto the desert table. "I see them," he said. He counted, moving his lips. "One, two, three, four. Four and a colt."

"We gonna take the colt?" Perce asked.

"Hell, can't take the mare without the colt."

Perce said nothing. Then Gay handed him the glasses. "Take a look."

Gay slid off the truck bed and went forward to the cab and opened its door. His dog lay shivering on the floor under the pedals. He snapped his fingers and she warily got up and leaped down to the ground and stood there quivering as she always did when wild horses were coming. He watched her sit and wet the ground, and how she moved with such care and concern and fear, sniffing the ground and moving her head in slow motion and setting her paws down as though the ground had hidden explosives everywhere. He left her there and climbed onto the truck and sat on a tire beside Perce, who was still looking through the glasses.

"He's divin' down on them. God, they sure can run."

"Let's have a look," Gay said and reached out and Perce handed him the glasses, saying, "They're comin' on fast."

Gay watched the horses in the glasses. The plane was starting down toward them from the arc of its climb. They swerved as the roaring motor came down over them, lifted their heads, and galloped faster. They had been running now for over an hour and would slow down when the plane had to climb after a dive and the motor's noise grew quieter. As Guido climbed again Gay and Perce heard a shot, distant and harmless, and the shot sped the horses on again as the plane took time to bank and turn. Then, as they slowed, the plane returned over them, diving down over their backs, and their heads shot up again and they galloped until the engine's roar receded over them. The sky was clear and lightly blue, and only the little plane swung back and forth across the desert like the glinting tip of a magic wand, and the horses came on toward the vast stripped clay bed where the truck was parked.

The two men on the truck exchanged the glasses from time to time. Now they sat upright on the tires waiting for the horses to reach the edge of the lakebed when Guido would land the plane and they would take off with the truck. And now the horses stopped.

"They see the heat waves," Gay said, looking through the glasses. He could see the horses trotting with raised, alarmed heads along the edge of the barren lakebed which they feared because the heat waves rose from it like liquid in the air, and yet their nostrils did not smell water and they dared not move ahead onto unknowable territory. The plane dived down on them and they scattered but would not go forward onto the lakebed from the cooler, sage-dotted desert behind them. Now the plane banked high in the air and circled out behind them over the desert and banked again and came down within yards of the ground and roared in behind them almost at the height of their heads, and as it passed over them, rising, the men on the truck could hear the shotgun. Now the horses leaped forward onto the lakebed all scattered and heading in different directions, and they were only trotting, exploring the ground under their feet and the strange, superheated air in their nostrils. Gradually, as the plane wound around the sky to dive again they closed ranks and slowly galloped shoulder to shoulder out onto the borderless lakebed. The colt galloped a length behind with its nose nearly touching the mare's long silky tail.

"That's a big mare," Perce said. His eyes were still dreamy and his face was calm, but his skin had reddened.

"She's a bigger mare than usual up here, ya," Gay said.

Both men watched the little herd now, even as they got to their feet on the truck. There was the big mare, as large as any full-grown horse, and both of them downed their surprise at the sight of her. They knew the mustang herds lived in total isolation and that inbreeding had reduced them to the size of large ponies. The herd swerved now and they saw the stallion. He was smaller than the mare but still larger than any they had brought down before. The other two horses were small, the way mustangs ought to be.

The plane was coming down for a landing now. Gay and Perce Howland moved to the forward edge of the truck's bed where a strap of white webbing was strung at hip height between two stanchions protruding upward from sockets at the corners of the truck. They drew another web strap from one stanchion to the other and stood inside the two. Perce tied the back strap to his stanchion. Then they turned around inside their harness and each reached into a tire behind him and drew out a coil of rope whose ends hung in a loop. They glanced out on the lakebed and saw Guido taxiing toward them, and they stood waiting for him. He cut the engine twenty yards from the truck and leaped out of the open cockpit before the plane had halted. He lashed the tail of the plane to a rope which was attached to a spike driven into the clay, and trotted over to the truck lifting his goggles off and stuffing them into his torn jacket pocket. Perce and Gay called out laughingly to him but he seemed hardly to have seen them. His face was puffed with preoccupation. He jumped into the cab of the truck and the collie dog jumped in after him and sat on the floor, quivering. He started the truck and roared ahead across the flat clay into the watery waves of heat.

They could see the herd standing still in a small clot of dots more than two miles off. The truck rolled smoothly and in the cab Guido glanced at the speedometer and saw it was past sixty. He had to be careful not to turn over and he dropped back to fifty-five. Gay on the right front corner of the truck bed and Perce Howland on the left, pulled their hats down to their eyebrows and hefted the looped ropes which the wind was threatening to coil and fowl in their palms. Guido knew that Gay Langland was a good roper and that Perce was unsure, so he headed for the herd's left in order to come up to them on Gay's side of the truck if he could. This whole method—the truck, the tires, the ropes, and the plane—were Guido's invention and once again he felt the joy of having thought of it all. He drove with both heavy hands on the wheel and his left foot ready over the brake pedal. He reached for the shift lever to feel if it were going to spring out of gear and into neutral but it felt tight and if they did not hit a bump he could rely on it. The herd had started to walk but it stopped again now and the horses were looking at the truck, ears raised, necks stretched up and forward. Guido smiled a little. They looked silly to him standing there, but he knew and pitied them their ignorance.

The wind smashed against the faces of Perce and Gay standing on the truck bed. The brims of their hats flowed up and back from a low point in front, and their faces were dark red. They saw the horses watching their approach at a standstill. And as they roared closer and closer they saw that this herd was beautiful.

Perce Howland turned his head to Gay who glanced at him at the same time. There had been much rain this spring and this herd must have found good pasture. They were well-rounded and shining. The mare was almost black and the stallion and the two others were deep brown. The colt was curly-coated and had a gray sheen. The stallion dipped his head suddenly and turned his back on the truck and galloped. The others turned and clattered after him with the colt running alongside the mare. Guido pressed down on the gas and the truck surged forward, whining. They were a few yards behind the animals now and they could see the bottoms of their hoofs, fresh hoofs that had never been shod. They could see the full manes flying and the thick and long black tails that would hang down to their fetlocks when they were still. The truck was coming abreast of the mare now and beside her the others galloped with only a loud ticking noise on the clay. It was a gentle tacking clatter for they were light-footed and unshod. They were slim-legged and wet after running almost two hours in this alarm, but as the truck drew alongside the mare and Gay began twirling his loop above his head, the whole herd wheeled away to the right and Guido jammed the gas pedal down and swung with them, but they kept galloping in a circle and he did not have the speed to keep abreast of them so he slowed down and fell behind them a few yards until they would straighten out and move ahead again. And they wheeled like circus horses, slower now, for they were at the edge of their strength, and suddenly Guido saw a breadth between the stallion and the two browns and he sped in between, cutting the mare off at the left with her colt. Now the horses stretched, the clatter quickened. Their hind legs flew straight back and their necks stretched low and forward. Gay whirled his loop over his head and the truck came up alongside the stallion whose lungs were hoarsely screaming with exhaustion and Gay flung the noose. It fell on the stallion's head, and with a whipping of the lead Gay made it fall over his neck. The horse swerved away to the right and stretched the rope until the tire was pulled off the truck bed and dragged along the hard clay. The three men watched from the slowing truck as the stallion, with startled eyes, pulled the giant tire for a few yards, then leaped up with his forelegs in the air and came down facing the tire and trying to back away from it. Then he stood still, heaving, his hind legs dancing in an arc from right to left and back again as he shook his head in the remorseless noose.

As soon as he was sure the stallion was secure, Guido scanned the lakebed and without stopping turned sharply left toward the mare and the colt which were trotting idly together by themselves. The two browns were already disappearing toward the north but Guido knew they would halt soon because they were tired, while the mare might continue to the edge of the lakebed and back into her familiar hills where the truck could not follow. He straightened the truck and jammed down the gas pedal. In a minute he was straight on behind her and he drew up on her left side because the colt was running on her right. She was very heavy, he saw, and he wondered now if she was a mustang at all. As he drove alongside her his eye ran across her flanks, seeking out a brand, but she seemed unmarked. Then through his right window he saw the loop flying out and down over her head, and he saw her head fly up, and then she fell back. He turned to the right, braking with his left boot, and he saw her dragging a tire and coming to a halt, with the free colt watching her and trotting beside her very close. Then he headed straight ahead across the flat toward two specks, which rapidly enlarged until they became the two browns, which were at a standstill and watching the oncoming truck. He came in between them and as they galloped, Perce on the left roped one and Gay roped the other almost at the same time. And Guido leaned his head out of his window and yelled up at Perce, who was on the truck bed on his side. "Good boy!" he hollered, and Perce let himself return an excited grin, although there seemed to be some trouble in his eyes.

Guido made an easy half circle and headed back to the mare and the colt and in a few minutes he slowed to a halt some twenty yards away and got out of the cab. The dog remained sitting on the floor of the cab, her body shaking all over.

The three men approached the mare. She had never seen a man and her eyes were wide in fear. Her rib cage stretched and collapsed very rapidly and there was a trickle of blood coming out of her nostrils. She had a heavy dark brown mane, and her tail nearly touched the ground. The colt with dumb eyes shifted about on its silly bent legs, trying to keep the mare between itself and the men, and the mare kept shifting her rump to shield the colt from them.

They wanted now to move the noose higher up on the mare's neck because it had fallen on her from the rear and was tight around the middle of her neck, where it could choke her if she kept pulling against the weight of the tire. They had learned from previous forays that they could not leave a horse tied that way without the danger of suffocation, and they wanted them alive until they could bring a larger truck from Bowie and load them on it.

Gay was the best roper so Perce and Guido stood by as he twirled a noose over his head, then let it fall open softly, just behind the forefeet of the mare. They waited for a moment, then approached her and she backed a step. Then Gay pulled sharply on the rope, and her forefeet were tied together. Then with another rope Gay lass'd her hind feet and she swayed and fell to the ground on her side. Her body swelled and contracted, but she seemed resigned. The colt stretched its nose to her tail and stood there as the men came to the mare and spoke quietly to her, and Guido bent down and opened the noose and slipped it up under her jaw. They inspected her for a brand but she was clean.

"Never see a horse that size up here," Gay said to Guido.

Guido stood there looking down at the great mare.

Perce said, "Maybe wild horses was all big once," and he looked to Guido for confirmation.

Guido bent and sat on his heels and opened the mare's mouth, and the other two looked in with him. "She's fifteen if she's a day," Gay said, and to Perce he said, "She wouldn't be around much longer anyway."

"Ya, she's old," Perce agreed, and his eyes were filled with thought.

Guido stood up and the three went back to the truck. Perce hopped up and sat on the truck bed with his legs dangling, and Gay sat in the cab with Guido. They drove across the lakebed to the stallion and stopped, and the three of them approached him.

"Ain't a bad lookin' horse," Perce said.

They stood inspecting the horse for a moment. He was standing still now, heaving for breath and bleeding from the nostrils. His head was down, holding the rope taut, and he was looking at them with his deep brown eyes that were like the lenses of enormous binoculars. Gay got his rope ready in his hand. "He ain't nothin' but a misfit," he said, "except for some kid. You couldn't run cattle with him and he's too small for a riding horse."

"He is small," Perce conceded. "Got a nice neck, though."

"Oh, they're nice *lookin'* horses, some of them," Guido said. "What the hell you goin' to do with them, though? Cost more to ship them anywhere than they'd bring."

Gay twirled the loop over his head, and they spread out around the stallion. "They're just old misfit horses, that's all," he said, and he flung the rope behind the stallion's forelegs and the horse backed a step and he drew the rope and the noose bit into the horse's lower legs drawing them together, and the horse swayed but would not fall.

"Take hold," Gay called to Perce, who ran around the horse and grabbed onto the rope and held it taut. Then Gay went back to the truck, got another rope, returned to the rear of the horse, and looped his hind legs. But the stallion would not fall.

Guido stepped closer to push him over, but the horse swung his head and showed his teeth and Guido stepped back. "Pull on it!" Guido yelled to Gay and Perce, and they pulled on their ropes to trip the stallion, but he righted himself and stood there bound by the head to the tire and his feet by the two ropes which the men held. Then Guido hurried over to Perce and took the rope from him and walked with it toward the rear of the horse and pulled hard. The stallion's forefeet slipped back, and he came down on his knees and his nose struck the clay ground and he snorted as he struck, but he would not topple over and stayed there on his knees as though he were bowing to something, with his nose propping up his head against the ground and his sharp bursts of breath blowing up dust in little clouds under his nostrils. Now Guido gave the rope back to young Perce Howland, who held it taut, and he came up alongside the stallion's neck and laid his hands on the side of the neck and pushed and the horse fell over onto his flank and lay there, and like the mare, when he felt the ground against his body he seemed to let himself out and for the first time his eyes blinked and his breath came now in sighs and no longer fiercely. Guido shifted the noose up under the jaw, and they opened the ropes around his hoofs and when the horse felt his legs free he first raised his head curiously and then clattered up and stood there looking at them, from one to the other, blood dripping from his nostrils and a stain of deep red on both dusty knees.

For a moment the three men stood watching him to be sure he was tightly noosed around the neck. Only the clacking of the truck's engine sounded on the enormous floor between the mountains, and the wheezing inhale of the horse and his blowing out of air. Then the men moved without hurrying to the truck, and Gay stored his two extra ropes behind the seat of the cab and got behind the wheel with Guido beside him, and Perce climbed onto the back of the truck and lay down facing the sky, and made a pillow with his palms under his head.

Gay headed the truck south toward where they knew the plane was, although it was still beyond their vision. Guido was slowly catching his breath and now he lighted a cigarette, puffed it, and rubbed his left hand into his bare scalp. He sat gazing out the windshield and the side window. "I'm sleepy," he said.

"What you reckon?" Gay asked.

"What you?" Guido said. He had dust in his throat and his voice sounded high and almost girlish.

"That mare might be six hundred pounds."

"I'd say about that, Gay," Guido agreed.

"About four hundred apiece for the browns and a little more for the stallion."

"That's about the way I figured."

"What's that come to?"

Guido thought. "Nineteen hundred, maybe two thousand," he said.

They fell silent, figuring the money. Two thousand pounds at six cents a pound came to a hundred and twenty dollars. The colt might make it a few dollars more, but not much. Figuring the gas for the plane and the truck, and twelve dollars for their groceries, they came to the figure of a hundred dollars for the three of them. Guido would get forty-five dollars, since he had used his plane, and Gay would get thirty-five including the use of his truck, and Perce Howland, if he agreed, as he undoubtedly would, had the remaining twenty.

They fell silent after they had said the figures, and Gay drove in thought. Then he said, "We should've watered them last time. They can pick up a lot of weight if you let them water."

"Yeah, let's be sure to do that," Guido said.

They knew they would as likely as not forget to water the horses before they unloaded them at the dealer's lot in Bowie. They would be in a hurry to unload and to be free of the horses, and only later, as they were doing now, would they remind themselves that by letting the horses drink their fill they could pick up another fifteen or twenty dollars in added weight. They were not thinking of the money any more, once they had figured it, and if Perce were to object to his smaller share they would both hand him a five or ten dollar bill or more if he wanted it.

Gay stopped the truck beside the plane at the edge of the lakebed. The tethered horses were far away now, except for the mare and her colt, which stood in clear view less than half a mile off. Guido opened his door and said to Gay, "See you in town. Let's get the other truck tomorrow morning."

"Perce wants to go over to Largo and sign up for the rodeo tomorrow," Gay said. "Tell ya—we'll go in and get the truck and come back here this afternoon. Maybe we bring them in tonight."

"All right, if you want to. I'll see you boys tomorrow," Guido said, and he got out and stopped for a moment to talk to Perce. "Perce?" he said.

Perce propped himself up on one elbow and looked down at him. He looked very sleepy. Guido smiled. "You sleeping?"

Perce's eyelids almost seemed swollen and his face was indrawn and troubled. "I was about to," he said.

Guido let the reprimand pass. "We figure about a hundred dollars clear. Twenty all right for you?"

"Ya, twenty's all right," Perce said, blinking heavily. He hardly seemed to be listening.

"See you in town," Guido said, and turned and waddled off to the plane, where Gay was already standing with his hands on the propeller blade. Guido got in and Gay swung the blade down and the engine started immediately. Guido waved to Gay and Perce who raised one hand slightly from the truck bed. Guido gunned the plane, and trundled off and into the sky, and the two men on the ground watched as it flew toward the mountains and away.

Now Gay returned to the truck and as he started to climb in behind the wheel he looked at Perce who was still propped up on one elbow and he said, "Twenty all right?" And he said this because he thought Perce looked hurt.

"Heh? Ya, twenty's all right," Perce answered. Then he let himself down from the truck bed and Gay got behind the wheel. Perce stood beside the truck and wet the ground while Gay waited for him. Then Perce got into the cab and they drove off.

The mare and her colt stood between them and the sage desert toward which they were heading. Perce stared out the window at the mare, and he saw that she was watching them apprehensively but not in real alarm, and the colt was lying upright on the clay, its head nodding slightly as though it would soon fall asleep. Perce looked long at the colt as they approached and he thought about it waiting there beside the mare, unbound and free to go off, and he said to Gay, "Ever hear of a colt leave a mare?"

"Not that young a colt," Gay said. "He ain't goin' nowhere." And he glanced to look at Perce.

They passed the mare and colt and left them behind and Perce laid his head back and closed his eyes. His tobacco swelled out his left cheek and he let it soak there.

Now the truck left the clay lakebed and it pitched and rolled on the sage desert. They would return to their camp and pick up their bedrolls and cooking implements, and then drive to the road which was almost fifteen miles beyond the camp across the desert.

"Think I'll go back to Roslyn's tonight," Gay said.

"Okay," Perce said and did not open his eyes.

"We can pick them up in the morning and then take you down to Largo."

"Okay," Perce said.

Gay thought about Roslyn. She would probably razz them about all the work they had done for a few dollars, saying they were too dumb to figure in their labor time and other hidden expenses. To hear her, sometimes they hadn't made any profit at all. "Roslyn going to feel sorry for the colt," Gay said, "so might as well not mention it."

Perce opened his eyes, and with his head resting on the back of the seat he looked out the window at the mountains. "Hell, she feeds that dog of hers canned dogfood, doesn't she?"

Gay felt closer to Perce again and he smiled. "Sure does."

"Well what's she think is in the can?"

"She knows what's in the can."

"There's wild horses in the can," Perce said, almost to himself.

They drove in silence for a while. Then Perce said, "That's what beats me."

After a few moments Gay said, "You comin' back to Roslyn's with me or you gonna stay in town?"

"I'd just as soon go back with you."

"Okay," Gay said. He felt good about going into her cabin now. There would be her books on the shelves he had built for her, and they would have some drinks, and Perce would fall asleep on the couch, and they would go into the bedroom together. He liked to come back to her after he had worked, more than when he had only driven her here and there or just stayed around her place. He liked his own money in his pocket. And he tried harder to visualize how it would be with her and he thought of himself being forty-six soon, and then nearing fifty. She would go back East one day, he knew, maybe this year, maybe next. He wondered again when he would begin turning gray and how he would look with gray hair, and he set his jaw against the picture of himself gray and an old man.

Perce spoke, sitting up in his seat. "I want to phone my mother. Damn, I haven't called her all year." He stared out the window at the mountains. He had the memory of how the colt looked and he wished it would be gone when they returned in the morning. Then he said, "I got to get to Largo tomorrow and register."

"We'll go," Gay said.

"I could use a good win," he said. He thought of five hundred dollars now, and of the many times he had won five hundred dollars. "You know something, Gay?" he said.

"Huh?"

"I'm never goin' to amount to a damn thing." Then he laughed. He was hungry, and he laughed without restraint for a moment and then laid his head back and closed his eyes.

"I told you that first time I met you, didn't I?" Gay grinned. He felt the mood coming on for some drinks at Roslyn's.

Then Perce spoke. "That colt won't bring two dollars anyway. What you say we just left him there?"

"Why you know what he'd do?" Gay said. "He'd just follow the truck right into town."

"I guess he would at that," Perce said. He spat a stream of juice out the window.

They reached the camp in twenty minutes and loaded the three bedrolls and the aluminum grub box in the truck and drove on toward Bowie. After they had driven for fifteen minutes without speaking, Gay said he wanted to go North very soon for the hundreds of horses that were supposed to be in the mountains there. But Perce Howland had fallen fast asleep beside him. Gay wanted to talk about that expedition because as they neared Bowie he began to visualize Roslyn razzing them again, and it was clear to him that he had somehow failed to settle anything for himself; he had put in three days for thirty-five dollars and there would be no way to explain it so it made sense, and it would be embarrassing. And yet he knew that it had all been the way it ought to be even if he could never explain it to her or anyone else. He reached out and nudged Perce, who opened his eyes and lolled his head over to face him. "You comin' up to Thighbone with me, ain't you?"

"Okay," Perce said, and went back to sleep.

Gay felt more peaceful now that the younger man would not be leaving him. He drove in contentment.

The sun shone hot on the beige plain all day. Neither fly nor bug nor snake ventured out on the waste to molest the four horses tethered there, or the colt. They had run nearly two hours at a gallop, and as the afternoon settled upon them they pawed the hard ground for water, but there was none. Toward evening the wind came up, and they backed into it and faced the mountains from which they had come. From time to time the stallion caught the smell of the pastures up there, and he started to walk toward the vaulted fields in which he had grazed; but the tire bent his neck around, and after a few steps he would turn to face it and leap into the air with his forelegs striking at the sky, and then he would come down and be still again.

With the deep blue darkness the wind blew faster, tossing their manes and flinging their long tails in between their legs. The cold of night raised the colt onto its legs and it stood close to the mare for warmth. Facing the southern range five horses blinked under the green glow of the risen moon, and they closed their eyes and slept. The colt settled again on the hard ground and lay under the mare.

In the high hollows of the mountains the grass they had cropped this morning straightened in the darkness. On the lusher swards, which were still damp with the rains of spring, their hoofprints had begun to disappear. When the first pink glow of another morning lit the sky the colt stood up, and as it had always done at dawn it walked waywardly for water. The mare shifted and her bone hoofs ticked the clay. The colt turned its head and returned to her and stood at her side with vacant eye, its nostrils sniffing the warming air.

❖

Arthur Miller was born in New York City in 1915, educated at the University of Michigan, and now lives in Connecticut. He is of course most well known for his popular and award-winning plays: All My Sons *(1947),* Death of a Salesman *(1949),* The Crucible *(1953),* A View from the Bridge *(1955),* After the Fall *(1964), and* Incident at Vichy *(1965). But he had published a successful novel,* Focus, *in 1945; and from time to time in the*

1950s and 1960s stories of his appeared in magazines, collected in 1967 under the title I Don't Need You Any More. *He also did the screenplay of the celebrated film made of "The Misfits," which appeared in its original short-story version, reprinted above, in* Esquire *in 1957.*

Much of the meaning of "The Misfits" is developed through the sustained analogy drawn between the men and the horses. The parallels are so clear as to preclude much explication: virtually everything that is said of the one applies as well to the other, whether it be the comments in dialogue or the author's exposition. One observation, made by Perce as he and Gay and Guido stand watching the big mare, should be singled out as more or less central. "Maybe wild horses was all big once," he says. The point is being made that the age when these three men could have been big is past; such skills and virtues as they possess had value only when America still had a frontier. They have energy, strength, and enterprise, hand-skill, ingenuity, and resourcefulness, courage, independence, and initiative—the very qualities that are regularly cited as characteristically American, the supposed national attributes that built a great nation from a wilderness. But these qualities have no commercial or social value in the new world of "wages" and—as we shall see in the stories that follow—often act now to the detriment of their possessor. The men skillfully use such modern mechanical devices as the truck and the airplane, but they use them like cow ponies. They have an affinity with the land and with nature, but it is not their own land, and they cultivate nothing, accumulate nothing. Their abilities in capturing and subduing wild horses—which once would have been so useful—are now put to use for entertainment (Perce's rodeo riding) or for a despised purpose (canned horsemeat for pet dogs). The story makes clear that, like the mustangs, there are few men of this sort left. The older man, Gay, acts as a kind of model for the younger, Perce, and takes reassurance from the emulation. But it is an uneasy, temporary relationship; and none of the three men has any effect in perpetuating his kind. Even Gay, who has children, is absent from his home and plays no role in their upbringing. The most giant forces in American life—urbanization and industrialization—are at work against these men, but they feel that they themselves are their own worst enemy. And in a way they are right, for their independence of spirit militates against their survival. Constant frustration has already made them somewhat listless and degenerate. In an increasingly standardized society they will be increasingly conspicuous misfits and will disappear in favor of temperaments better adjusted to the times. The situation demonstrates dramatically how changes in the instrumental cultural forces quickly achieve changes in the social character of a nation.

Joe, The Vanishing American

IF WALTER had not been so desperately anxious to go away to college he might never have been able to stick it out those first few weeks at the factory. His father, once district sales manager for a bankrupt sewing-machine concern, had come down in the world and was now a continually uneasy clerk in the branch office of a usury outfit called the Friendly Finance Corporation; his mother, who had borne Walter late in life, clung jealously to the fading prestige conferred on her by her many beneficences on behalf of the Ladies' Guild.

Walter had never done anything harder than shovel the neighbors' snowy driveways and sell magazines to reluctant relatives. But the night of his graduation from high school his father grunted in a choked voice that there was no money to send him to college. Walter swore to himself that he would get a college education if he had to rob a bank. At the commence-ment exercise a classmate had told him that you could get a job at the new auto assembly plant if you said on your application that you had worked as a garage mechanic. While his parents rocked creakily, proud but miserable, on the porch glider, Walter mounted the narrow steps to his little room and sat down at his desk. If he could work steadily at the plant for a year he ought to be able to save several thousand dollars even after contributing his share of the household expenses. Without saying a word to his parents, he went to the plant the following morning and filled out an application blank. Three days later he received a telegram asking him to report for work at 6:30 A.M.

When he returned, grey and exhausted, from his first long day in the body shop to which he had been assigned, Walter found his mother sitting in the parlor and sobbing into a handkerchief. She raised her eyes at the slamming of the door and stared at him in horror.

"Look at you!" she cried, and immediately Walter knew that her first shock was at the way he *looked,* not at how he must have *felt.* Nevertheless Walter felt it his filial duty to explain that he would not have to march past the neighbors in greasy coveralls, but could wear sport clothes to work and change at the plant; furthermore, he hinted, when his mother was preparing his sandwiches for the next day's lunch, he could just as easily carry them in a little paper sack as in a metal lunchbox.

His father, keeping them company in the kitchen, took a different tack, and even blustered a little about the advantages of working for a huge corporation.

"I don't see why Walter couldn't have started with something more pleasant," his mother said plaintively, smoothing mayonnaise across white bread. "In an office he could at least use his brains."

"Don't kid yourself," her husband replied. "There's no shame attached to factory work any more. Besides, Walter has a darned good chance to advance if he shows them the stuff he's got."

Implicit in all this was his parents' fear that Walter had started down a dead-end street, and their own shame at not having been able to send him away to college. Anxious not to inflame their feelings, Walter refrained from defending his decision; even if he were only to point out that he would be making big money, it would be a direct insult to his father, who at fifty-nine was making only five dollars a week more than his son. So he put the case negatively.

"There's just no place else around," he said, "that would pay me anything like what I'm going to be making at the auto plant."

"The boy is right, Mother," his father said decisively, much to Walter's satisfaction. "You're doing the smart thing, Walter."

Thus challenged at home, Walter had no alternative but to grit his teeth and swear to himself that nothing would make him quit until he had reached his goal. Like a groggy but game boxer, he measured out his future not with the end of the fight in view, for that would have been too far away, but rather in terms of more immediate accomplishments: his first automatic nickel raise at the end of four weeks, his second automatic nickel raise at the end of eight weeks, his acceptance as a permanent employee at the end of ninety days, and most of all his listing as a metal-finisher, which would mean that he would be in the highest-paid group in the plant and that he would be recognized as a skilled worker, a man who had made the grade.

His surroundings meant nothing to Walter, who had not expected that the factory would look like an art gallery; but the work, and the conditions under which he had to do it, were a nightmare of endless horror from which Walter sometimes thought, stumbling wearily out of the plant after ten hours of unremitting anguish, he would one day awaken with a scream. It was not simply that the idea of working on an endless succession of auto bodies as they came slowly but ineluctably rolling down the assembly line like so many faceless steel robots was both monotonous and stupefying, or that the heavy work of finding bumps and dents in them, knocking them out and filing them down, was in itself too exhausting.

No, it was the strain of having to work both fast and accurately, with the foreman standing over him and glaring through his thick-lensed glasses, that made Walter dread the beginning of each day. Under the best of conditions, he figured, he had three and a half minutes to complete his metal-finishing work from the time he started a job on his line to the time it reached the platform and was swung off on hooks toward the bonderizing booth. If he began at the very beginning, as soon as the inspector had indicated bad spots with a stump of chalk, circling hollows and x-ing high spots, he could finish before the job reached the final inspector at the far end of the line—unless the dents were too deep or too numerous, in which case he was still madly pounding and filing, squatting and straining with the sweat running down his temples and his cheekbones while the solder-flower worked next to him in a tangle of rubber hose, melting lead and a blazing gun with a flame so hot that it scorched dry the running sweat on his face, and the final inspector stood over him, imperturbably chalking newly discovered hollows and pimples in the infuriating metal. Then he would straighten up from his hopeless effort and with a despairing glance at the impassive pickup man, who had to finish what he had left undone, he would hurry back down the line, praying to dear God that the next car—he did every third one—would be in fairly decent condition.

Worst of all were the times when he would hear a piercing whistle and would look up from the damnable dent at which he had been rapping blindly with the point of his file to see Buster the foreman all the way past the platform, waving angrily with his cigar. Hurrying from his unfinished work to his punishment, Walter would try to steel himself against what he knew was coming, but it was no use.

"You call yourself a metal man?" Buster would ask, stuffing the cigar between his teeth with an angry snap. "You want to get metal-finisher's pay and you let a job like that go through?" His eyes glinting with rage behind his thick spectacles, Buster would gesticulate at one of Walter's cars, freshly speckled with chalk marks as it swung in the air. "Get going on it!"

And Walter would hurl himself at the job, dashing the sweat from his brow with the back of his gloved hand and filing away in a clumsy fury.

By the time he had somehow or other repaired what he had left undone, he would find on hastening back to the line that he was far behind once again in his regular work, so far behind that it might take him the better part of an hour to gradually work his way back on the line to where he really belonged, safe for the moment from shouted complaints.

Inevitably the men around him had suggestions as to how Walter might better his condition. Of the two other metal-finishers who worked on the line with him, one was a dour, fattish man, a leader in the opposition of the local union and disgusted because it did nothing to provide security for probationary employees like Walter.

"I'll tell you something else. There's countries where a bright young hard-working fellow like you, that wants to go to college, doesn't have to waste the best years of his life in factory work just to save the money for college fees. He gets sent right through school and the government foots the bills. All he has to do is show that he's got the stuff and his future is secure."

Walter allowed that this sounded fine, although "having the stuff" sounded uncomfortably like his father's eulogies of life in America, but he could not see what practical good it did him here and now—unless he was supposed to get satisfaction from the bitterness of knowing that in mysterious other countries his opposite numbers were better off than he.

The third metal-finisher, a lean efficient sardonic man, had been listening silently to this talk of free college careers. He put his wiry hand inside his open-necked khaki shirt, scratched the coarse curling hair below his throat, and laughed aloud.

"What's the matter?" asked his fattish colleague suspiciously.

"You think your propaganda's going to change this boy's ideas about the other side of the world when everything here tells him he's got it so good?" He tapped the fat man on the shoulder with the butt end of his file as patronizingly as if he were patting him on the head. "Even if he has to suffer for his education in a way that shouldn't be necessary, he's free. He can blunder around and maybe even learn something that isn't listed in the college catalogues. Those poor kids you want him to envy, they may be getting their college for nothing, but they're paying a higher price for it than this fellow ever will. And the sad part is that most of them probably don't even know what the price is." And he turned back to his work without giving the fat man a chance to reply.

Fortunately for the three of them, the fat metal-finisher was transferred. He was only replaced, however, by an intense worker with two vertical wrinkles between his brows, who watched Walter's ineffectual work with growing impatience. At last he could stand it no more.

"In this game, kid, the knack of it is in the speed. The speed," he said fiercely, "and the way you concentrate on the job. If you're going to fumble around and just bitch about your mistakes, you'll be a long time getting straightened out." He greeted his own badly dented job, rolling toward them, with a smile of genuine pleasure. "Size it up quick, pick out the worst dents, and get going on them right away. Leave the high spots for last—the pickup men don't mind doing them."

The third man, the grey-haired cynic whom everyone liked but no one seemed to know, had been listening quietly, with a strange, mild grin on his long and youthful face. He put a stick of chewing gum in his mouth, ruminated for a moment, and said: "What you really want is for him to enjoy his work, Orrin. Might be more practical if you'd get down and actually show him how to do it. Here, hold on a minute, Walter."

Walter had been squatting on his haunches before the wheel-housing of his job, blindly pounding with a hammer at his hidden screwdriver, trying hopelessly to punch a hole underneath so that with the screwdriver he could dig out a deep dent as the others did, trying so hopelessly that as he smashed the hammer against his left hand, missing the butt end of the screwdriver, he had to squeeze his eyes to keep the tears from starting forth.

"Give me that screwdriver."

Handing up the tool to the laconic man, Walter noticed for the first time that he bore an unusual tattoo, faded like an old flag, on his right forearm: an American eagle, claws gripping his wrist, beak opened triumphantly at the elbow—you could almost hear it screaming. Without a word the man took the screwdriver and swiftly pressed it to a grinding wheel, fashioning a beveled point.

"Try it now."

Walter stuck the screwdriver under the car, rapped at it smartly several times—*bang!* it was through and resting against the outer skin of the car, just at the very dent. Gratefully, he turned to the grey-haired man, but he was gone, like a mirage.

There was something miragelike about him, anyway. He drove to and from work alone, he never engaged in small talk, he never hung around with a group at lunch hour or before work, he kept a paper book in the hip pocket of his khaki trousers, and always when he was not concentrating on his own work, when he was watching Walter or listening to the others handing him advice, he had that mocking irreligious smile on his long narrow youthful face. What was more, his cold blue eye seemed always to be on Walter, sizing him up, watching not so much his work, as everyone else did, but his temperament and his personality. It made him uncomfortable.

Gradually Walter began to sort out the other men around him, the ones who had more common reality in their talk and their tastes. Most companionable of them all was Kevin, the former rural school teacher, now an immigrant hook-man. His accent was so delightful, his turns of speech so happy, that Walter engaged the towering redhead in conversation at every opportunity.

"Hey, Kevin," he shouted at him one day, "how old were those kids you taught in County Kerry?"

"Ah, Walter," Kevin sighed, showing his long white teeth as he spoke, "they weren't *all* such children. If you were to see some of the older girls—quite well developed, they were. Oh, how shameful if they had known what was passing through their schoolmaster's mind!"

Kevin laughed at the memory, Walter at the picture the big fellow conjured up of countryside lust; he turned around and there was the grey-haired metal-finisher, smiling too, but so coldly you would have thought him a scientist observing a successful experiment. It was chilling, and yet not wholly unpleasant. In a way that he could not define, Walter felt that he was being judged and approved.

This third man, reserved and anonymous as ever, continued to observe him as Walter chatted not only with Kevin and the second metal-finisher, but with all of the other men on their line. Conversation was necessarily shouted and fragmentary, but Walter was astonished at how intimacies could be revealed in the course of a few phrases:

"A man's a fool to get married."

"Grab the overtime while you can. In the auto industry you never know when you'll be laid off."

"Happiest time of my life was when I was in the army."

"Only reason I'm here is because I was too stupid to learn a trade."

"I came here out of curiosity, but my curiosity's all used up."

"My wife says if I quit I'll have a better chance to line up a construction job."

"Walter, don't turn out like those college men who can tell you how to do everything but can't do a damn thing themselves."

The only one to rebuff Walter's friendly overtures was Pop, the seamy-faced little inspector with a rooster's ruff of yellowing white hair that rose and tumbled down over his forehead, and sunken old lips from which depended miraculously a heavy, unlit cigar. Wizened, pale and bloodless, he regarded Walter, for no apparent reason, with bottomless contempt. With a little cap perched sideways on his Niagara of a head like a precarious canoe, and a soft brown cloth knotted about the hand with which he probed Walter's work for defects and omissions, he seemed to Walter like some strange and hateful gnome.

"Kids like you," he said in a dry and rusty monotone, "they come and go. Twenty-three years I'm here, and I seen a million like you. Not steady, not reliable, don't want to learn, just out for fun. You'll never make a metal man."

I don't want to be a metal man, Walter wanted to reply; I just want to make my money and get out of here. But this was, he knew, just what Pop was goading him to say, so he held his tongue. A moment later he was glad that he had, for he was startled to hear the third metal-finisher address him.

"Pop is an exception," he said, bending over Walter's car and scrubbing at it with his sandpaper as he spoke. "By and large there is a democracy of age in the factory. Men who have been here since before you were born fought for a union contract guaranteeing equal treatment for you. Ninety days after you start you get the same wage as a worker who's been on the job nineteen years. A man twice your age will treat you as a working partner and an adult. Where else is that true?"

"Yes," Walter replied angrily, "but Pop—"

"He's got reason to be bitter. Some day I'll tell you why."

He straightened up abruptly and walked away to his own job. But the words he had used reverberated in Walter's mind. Who was he, with his young-old face and his expressions like "democracy of age"? Walter asked, but no one seemed to know. Some said he was a seaman and adventurer, and his big tattoo was pointed to as proof, for he had been heard to state himself that he had acquired it in Lourenço Marques; but others, who had themselves come to the assembly line from rural homesteads, were positive from clues he had let fall that he had formerly been an itinerant farm laborer; and there were even those who swore that he was really an educated man, a kind of college professor amusing himself by slumming among them.

Whoever he was, for the time he had nothing more to say. But Walter felt his presence, for he was always ready to lend a hand, always laconically helpful, always silently observing and listening.

One day the younger inspector at the beginning of the line, blowing genial clouds of illegal pipe smoke, gave Walter some frank and cynical advice.

"Been listening to the bosses talking about you, buddy." He took the pipe from his mouth and formed a fat smoke ring. "Want to know what's wrong with what you're doing?"

"I guess so," said Walter dully.

"You try too hard. You're trying to do a good job—that's the worst thing you can do."

Walter stared in bewilderment at the inspector. "But why?"

"They're interested in pulling production. If you're going to be running up and down the line all day trying to make every job perfect, you're just going to get in people's way. What the bosses will do is, they'll look for an excuse to fire you before your probationary period is up, or else they'll stick you in a routine lower-paying job."

"Then . . ."

"I've been here ten years. Believe me," he drew on his pipe once again and smiled disarmingly, "they're not interested in making good cars, they're interested in making cars. You know what production means? Volume. And you know what they hired you for? To camouflage, not to get rid of every flaw. Hide them so they don't show up after the car's been through paint, so the customer doesn't see them at the dealer's, and you'll get along great."

"Camouflage them how?"

"With your sandpaper. With the grinding wheel. If you hit them up and down and then across, final inspection will never know what's underneath. Make it look good, and confusing. Be a camouflage artist and the bosses'll very seldom bother you."

Walter could not help laughing. "Listen, how could you stand it here for ten years? Every day I think maybe I ought to get out and look for something else."

"For six years," the inspector said pleasantly, "I was like you. This was going to be just temporary until I found something with a real future. It took me six years to realize that I was going to be spending the rest of my life here—it's like breaking in a wild horse, only with a human being it takes longer. I got married, had three kids, now I'm building a home near the plant. So I make the best of it, I take it easy, and I have as much fun as I can, and I hate to see a guy like you breaking his back all for nothing."

Bending over his work, Walter raised his file and heard the inspector's final shot, lightly enough intended but bearing its own weight of bitterness and resignation: "You'd be surprised how many fellows I've heard talking just like you, couldn't stand the work, going to quit any day, and now they're five- and ten-year men, starting to think about retirement benefits."

Walter could not clarify in his own mind what it was about the inspector's attitude that increased his desperation, not until his silent partner eased up to him from nowhere and said quietly, "Kind of terrified you, didn't he?"

"Not exactly terrified."

"Just the same, it's no fun to be doing time and to be told that your sentence just might turn out to be indefinite. Then if you've got a good imagination you can see yourself gradually getting used to it, even getting to like the routine, so that one day follows another and the first thing you know the wrinkles are there and the kids are grown up and you don't know where it's all gone to, your life."

Walter felt himself shuddering. Was it from the blower overhead that he felt his hot sweat turning cold and drying on his face? He said, "I suppose you have to be cynical if you're going to stay here."

"Day after day your life becomes a joke without any point, a trick that you play on yourself from punching in to punching out."

"But that's only if you're an imaginative or a sensitive person."

For the first time, the man's angular face hardened. "Don't you think somebody like that inspector had his ambitions? Don't you think he still has his man's pride? Did you ever figure the cost of the job in terms of what it does to the personality of a clever intelligent fellow like him? He says if you're going to be trapped you might as well make the best of it, and by his lights he may be right. Anyway don't be too quick to blame him—he probably never had the opportunity to save money and go off to college."

No one had ever, not ever in eighteen years, talked to Walter in such a way. He would never again be able to look at a man like the inspector without compassion. Even at home in the evening with his father, whom he could no longer talk to about anything but baseball or the weather (although they both tried clumsily to broach other more serious topics), Walter found that he was viewing this desolate man not just as his father but as a man who had his own miseries; and this, he knew, was a part of growing up that could not have come about as it had without the influence of his strange friend in the factory.

More and more as the weeks passed and exhaustion was gradually overcome by vitality, only to be transformed into monotony, Walter came to feel that only this man could explain the real meaning of the assembly line. But he remained aloof, insubstantial as a ghost. The more he held to himself, the more Walter was piqued, and determined to make the ghost speak.

At last one day he ventured to demand: "Say, what does that tattoo of yours stand for, that big bird?"

The man smiled with one side of his mouth. "That old bird is the American eagle." He raised his arm briefly, flexed it, and let it fall to his side. "It's screaming with rage at what's happened to the republic."

"What *has* happened?"

"Where are the guts? Where's the drive? In a place like this a man's life goes down the drain like scummy water."

"But you're working here too," Walter said boldly.

The man shook his head slowly, with such finality that there was something elemental about the gesture. "I'm not a settled-down man, I'm just passing through."

Walter cleared his throat. "I don't even know your name."

"Why should you? Instead of learning names, we refer to the fellow with the bad teeth, or the guy with the blue coveralls. When I work next to a man for months and learn that his wife is being operated on for cancer of the breast and still don't know his name, it tells me something not just about him and me, but about the half-connections that are all the factory allows you in the way of friendships."

"The old-timers are clubby enough, but everybody else claims they're here for a limited time. The place is so big and everything seems so temporary that I suppose we don't feel the need of introducing ourselves."

The older man looked at Walter somberly. "No one who comes here wants to admit that the place has any real connection with his real life. He has to say that he is just putting in his time here, and so no matter how friendly he is by nature he has to think of the people around him as essentially strangers, men whom he can't even trouble to say goodbye to when he quits or gets laid off."

"But *your* name—"

"Call me Joe."

Walter pursued him: "Every third guy on the line must be named Joe. Joe what?"

He smiled again, his long Yankee countenance creasing in a cold grin. "Joe, the vanishing American." And he turned his back on Walter and bent to his work as the line resumed its endless progress.

But he was a curious man, a nosy man, and he was there, listening and leering, when Walter found a minute to respond without cursing to a bitter remark of Pop's. Walter turned on him with the anger he had managed to suppress when speaking to the old inspector.

"It's easy for you to stand there and laugh. You think you're better than anybody else in the shop."

Joe hitched up his khaki trousers and replied with deliberate anger, "I never claimed that. I just read a little more and ponder a little more than the average fellow. That's why I don't laugh at them, I feel sorry for them. If I'm a little freer, I've had to make sacrifices for it—no dependents, no ties." He added cryptically, "They punish you one way or they punish you another way."

Walter did not quite understand, but it struck him that these remarks were a prelude to farewell. He asked uneasily, "You're not going to quit?"

"One of these days. Maybe the weather will turn, or I'll hear of something else, or I'll have words with Buster . . ." He added with somewhat more warmth, "But I'll be back—if not here, some place like here. You won't though. That's why I hope you won't forget what it was like for the people who made the things you'll be buying."

Walter cried indignantly: "How could I? How could I ever forget?" It seemed to him that the thick scurf of silver through which he shuffled as he worked, the glittering waste of lead filings and melted sticks, were so many needles, each carrying its stinging injection of memory—of sweat, exhaustion, harrying, feverish haste, and stupid boredom.

"You forget worse things, don't you? Pain, and even death? You'll think back on the days when you were slaving away to save money for college, and they'll strike you as comical, maybe even romantic."

"God forbid!" Walter laughed. And yet he had suddenly a shivery foretaste of a future beyond the one of which he daydreamed as he worked.

When the siren screamed the end of their nine and a half hours Walter hurled his file and apron into his toolbox and trotted down the aisle toward the time clock. Turning the corner of the body shop office just as its lights were extinguished, he ran headlong into the iron antennae of a fork truck and cried aloud with pain as the metal plate struck his shinbone. Tottering backwards, Walter was suddenly gripped by the forearm and pulled erect. He turned gratefully and found himself staring into the eyes of Joe.

Smarting with soreness and embarrassment, Walter demanded aggressively, "I suppose that's what you want me to remember!"

A faint stubble glinted along Joe's narrow cheeks. Greying like his iron hair, it aged him as it grew. He scraped his hand across it wearily and replied quietly, "Never mind the machinery. Remember the men. The men make the machines, and they make their own tragedies too. Once your own life gets easier, you'll take it for granted not only that theirs must be easier too, but that they deserve what they get anyway, that some law of natural selection has put you up where you are and them down where they are."

They had reached the clock bay where they took their place meekly in line, waiting to punch out, shuffling forward every few seconds while they spoke in low voices. Around them a swarm of men surged toward freedom —noisy boys with laughter to spare for the evening, haggard weary men in their forties, surly powerful black men in stained coveralls and scrawny brown men chattering in Spanish, vacant-faced fools with slack jaws and dangling hands, shrewd-eyed men fingering their union contract books, composing their campaign leaflets, and computing their chances of election to positions that would lift them out of the work routine.

"Why do they stay?"

"They're trapped, that's why. They say everybody's supposed to be, one way or another, but it's worse to be stuck here. Spending your life on the production line means counting out the minutes, being grateful that Mondays go fast because you're rested, and hating Tuesdays because the week is so long. It means that you're paying off forever on all the things you've been pressured into buying by getting up every day in order to do something you'd never, never think of doing if it was a matter of choice. It means never having anything to look forward to in all of your working life." Joe took his card from the rack, clicked it in the time clock, and with a wave of his hand was gone.

What was happening, as Walter woke daily to the dawn's dull alarm and went from the still house through the newly washed streets to the waiting assembly line, was that his self-pity, so strong that the page blurred before him when he lay in bed reading himself to sleep, was altering into a maturer concern with the fate of others who could not, like himself, set a term to their labor.

He began to question the men on the line with him, one after another, to find out how many of them felt as he did about what they were doing for a living. More sure of himself with every passing hour, he moved up and down the line, demanding, whenever there was a moment, an answer to his insistent question: "Do you think anybody likes coming in here to work?"

"Everybody does one day a week—payday," said the solder-flower.

"Not even the bosses," said the deck-fitter. "Do you think anybody with sense would knock himself out in this dirt and noise if it wasn't for the money?"

And the door-fitter said wryly, "Do you know what this kind of work is?

It's colored man's work. Why, even the colored men are smartening up—they turn up their noses at it too, unless they get strapped."

Saddened and bewildered by this last comment, Walter turned away from the man who had made it, and who had punctuated his bitter remark with a series of thunderous blows on a door that he was fitting. Only Orrin, the second metal-finisher, grudgingly admitted that the work was a challenge to him, that the pay was fair, and that there were worse jobs. Behind them all, long-jawed Joe, caught up with his work as usual, stood casually beveling his screwdriver.

"I hear you've been taking a little poll," he said to Walter.

"What's it to you?" Walter asked truculently. He was in no mood to be mocked.

With apparent irrelevance, Joe replied by demanding, "How come you fixed on being an engineer?"

Walter was taken aback. "Why, that's where everybody says the future is."

"That's not reason enough for a fellow to struggle and sweat to get to college. Damn it, doesn't anybody go out and do what he wants to any more? I'm not saying you wouldn't make a good engineer, or that it wouldn't be fine for a change to have some engineers who care as much about people as they do about gadgets. But supposing you find out after you get to college that you want to spend your time learning something useless—are you going to leave yourself open for it?"

"Boy, you sure are free with advice."

Joe looked at him gravely. His long sad jaw had the hint of a smile. "The men on the line like you, Walter. They don't think you're just nosy when you ask questions. They think you're one of them, and in a good way you are. Maybe that's why I've got hopes for you."

Walter fought hard against the influence of the older man, whose crabbed and subversive outlook was so foreign to everything Walter had been taught, but he was forced to admit to himself that more and more he was seeing the factory through Joe's cold discerning eyes; and he began to fear that if Joe were ever to leave, the plant would have no real existence other than as a money-producing nightmare. Not only was there no one else really to talk to about it, but Joe had forced Walter to try to formulate his emerging ideas in an adult and comprehensible way.

"The worst thing about the assembly line is what it does to your self-respect," he said to Joe early one morning as they squatted on their haunches, waiting for the starting siren. "It's hard to keep from feeling like a fool when you know that everybody looks down on what you're doing, even the men who are doing it themselves."

Joe hung his hammer and metal spoon from the brass hook at his belt. "The big pitch has always been that we're a practical people, that we've proved to all the impractical European dreamers that production can serve people. But instead people are serving production. Look how frightened, how hysterical the bosses get when the line stops—they can't afford to figure what it costs *you* to keep it moving—they only know they've got a production quota. Of course when sales resistance starts building up and they put the cork back in themselves, they give you just the opposite story. Who can blame the poor slob in the middle for suspecting that the whole setup is really as nutty as a fruitcake, and for feeling ashamed of himself for being caught up in it?"

"All right," Walter challenged him. "Who's crazy? You, me, the guys around us, or the board of directors?"

"Anybody who gets suckered into believing that there's anything real behind the billboards they put up to get the show on the road, so that he commits himself to buying the billboard pictures by selling his life on the installment plan. I sympathize with any joker who begins to suspect that the whole world is against him, that he's the victim of a huge conspiracy organized to make his car fall apart before it's been paid off. Doesn't life in the factory seem to be deliberately designed to lower your own self-esteem? What happens when you're knocking down a dent? If you rap it too hard from the inside, you have to file it down that much more, and you hate yourself for it. If you don't rap it hard enough you only find out after it's moved on down the line, and then you have to hurry up and wallop it again. In either case you hate yourself instead of hating the car, or the invisible man that started up the line." He laughed briefly in anticipation of what he was about to add. "It's like the man that hits his thumb with a hammer while he's hanging a picture—only here he keeps hitting his thumb because they're moving the wall as fast as the union will let them. Who does he yell at every time that ball peen comes down on his nail? Himself."

"I wonder," Walter said slowly, "how many people actually feel that way."

"More than you can count. It's always safe to figure that if you feel something, the world must be full of people who feel the same way. Every sensible man realizes as he gets older that his feelings aren't unique. After all, that's the basis of the best art: the fact that you recognize yourself in it, and all those inner experiences that you'd thought no one else but you could know."

Walter was willing to recognize that he was not the only one to cringe when Buster called him back on a badly done job, to swear at himself for the mistakes that made him fall behind, to realize how he was being trapped into swearing at himself and deflecting his anger from what he did to the way he did it. But it was hard for him to believe that there were others who felt as intensely as he did, who beat their heads against the bars as he did, who dreamed of sunlight and freedom as he did, even though Joe tried to persuade him that the difference was often one of degree, or of his being able to express his feelings in a way that others couldn't. This was one of the questions that Walter was eager to argue with Joe, who moved from one extreme position to another, always mocking, always challenging him to learn what he stood for and to defend it like a man.

"You know something," Walter burst out impetuously one day, "I don't know what I would have done here without you."

Instead of laughing, or belittling this praise, Joe's face darkened. The next morning he was not on the line.

By the third day of his absence Walter was beginning to feel as though it had all been a dream, as though he were slipping once again into the awful pit of loneliness, exhaustion and self-doubting despair. As a last resort he sought out the men on the line to learn what they thought of Joe.

"He's irresponsible," said Pop.

"He's the kind of guy that just don't care," said the younger inspector. "No wife, no kids, no wonder he can take off three days without worrying about getting a reprimand or getting fired."

"He knows his work," said Orrin grudgingly. "I don't know where he learned it, but he did. Just the same, he takes off. You can't *afford* to take off like that nowadays, not if you want to hold down a job."

On the fourth day he came back. He told no one where he had been. "Am I glad to see you!" Walter exclaimed—but Joe merely indicated, with a cold grin and a turn of his tattooed arm, that from time to time things came up that were more important than the making of automobiles. He did not set to work, but almost immediately was engaged in serious talk with Buster the foreman and with the union shop steward. The two were arguing vigorously, but suddenly Joe cut them off simply by lifting his hand. He said something very briefly, shoved his hands into his pockets, and the discussion was finished.

To Walter's amazement, he came back to the line, picked up his toolbox, and nodded casually to him.

"I just quit, Walter," he said. "Going to hit the road."

"But—"

"You'll make out all right, no matter what you do. I don't even have to wish you good luck."

Then he was off down the aisle, on his way to the tool crib and the plant police and the parking lot and God alone knew where after that, without so much as a handshake or an inclination of his lean frame. Suddenly Walter remembered something: "Hey!" he shouted. But Joe—if he heard him— did not turn around and soon was out of sight.

You never told me about Pop, he wanted to tell Joe, you never answered all the questions I was going to ask you—but even if Joe had not gone for good, Walter would not have known how to say to him all the things that should have been said, the words of gratitude and self-confidence.

When the relief man came a few minutes later to give him a twelve-minute break, he hurried to the bathroom. There, just beyond the big circular sink that could accommodate half a dozen men, he could see out the tilted window to the vast parking lot.

The dull winter light was gloomy and deceptive, and so vague was the air that the dark ranks of massed automobiles were no more than darker blurs against the background of the grey metal fencing and the lowering sky. One of the cars moved, or was it his imagination? But no, the red tail-light dimmed, glowed, dimmed. Joe, the vanishing American, was swinging out of the lot and away from the production line, out of Walter's life and into someone else's, out of the present and into what lay beyond the gate. He was leaving the future to Walter, who now at last could wave his farewell, with his face pressed to the cool window as he watched the little light disappearing from view.

Then he washed the sweat from his face and returned to his work.

◇

Harvey Swados was born in Buffalo in 1920, educated at the University of Michigan, and has taught writing at the State University of Iowa, New York University, and San Francisco State College. He now lives in Valley Cottage, New York, with his wife and three children and teaches at Sarah Lawrence. He has published three novels, Out Went the Candle *(1955),* False Coin *(1960), and* The Will *(1963); three collections of short stories,* On the Line *(1957), nine connected stories of life in an automobile plant, from which the above story is taken,* Nights in the Gardens of Brooklyn *(1961) and* A Story for Teddy—and Others *(1965); and a collection of essays,* A Radical's America *(1962). He has won many awards for his work—a* Hudson Review *fellowship, the Sidney Hillman Award, a Guggenheim fellowship, a grant in literature by the National Academy of Arts and Letters—yet none of his books has sold as many as five thousand copies.*

In "Joe, The Vanishing American," Swados indicts the assembly line for destroying individuality in America, not only for turning out mass-produced commodities that have indirectly contributed so much to the standardization of our lives, but also for its direct dehumanizing and depersonalizing effect on the individual worker on the line. As the younger inspector tells Walter, using a simile reminiscent of the previous story, the assembly line breaks down the worker's individuality and independence "like breaking in a wild horse, only with human beings it takes longer." Production is supposed to serve people, as Joe says; "but instead people are serving production." The assembly line destroys any sense of pride in craft or initiative not only because, as is well known, it is a kind of manufacturing in which the individual worker sees only a meaninglessly small part of the process of creation, but also because speed and not excellence is the essence. "You try too hard," Walter is told. "You're trying to do a good job . . . trying to make every job perfect." All that excellence on the job can do is to slow down the line. The line is so dehumanizing that few of the workers will risk their identity near it. Joe explains this: "No one who comes here wants to admit that the place has any real connection with his real life. He has to say that he is just putting in his time here." And eventually the line beats down even the individual's will to leave: men who come on the line to work briefly stay on the rest of their working lives. It is this that makes Joe's mysterious disappearance so meaningful at the end. Joe is not so much a shadowy figure as a mythical one. He—like the three misfits —pays a price for his freedom, for like them he is without wife, children, possessions, "obligations," or future. He is of the vanishing breed of independent and free-thinking Americans who come and go as they please. They are vanishing, it seems, because as the price they must pay for their freedom goes higher, the opportunities to make some use of it become fewer.

THOMAS BERGER

Reinhart Goes to Work

◇◇◇◇◇◇◇◇

REINHART saw half his rumpled self, clear, in the toilet mirror; unseen beneath the Army shirt was the life preserver of useless flesh about his waist. The last time he had bathed, now a dim memory, he had soaped arms the color and consistency of uncooked bratwurst, and his pectorals had sagged like a woman's.

The figure he cut nowadays was unusual for a man who until six months before had been blond and pink and muscled as Hitler's prescription for the *Herrenmensch*. Reinhart was no longer even blond; what sprang from an untended crewcut grew snot-mottled and here and there dark with grease. To get away from the psychiatrists he had been forced to replace one kind of pride with another; thus his honorable discharge, which breathed no hint of how his service had ended; and thus his will, which was nonexistent.

On the other hand, he could be a bright man again almost instantly: bath, shave, clean clothes, haircut being a matter of hours; and regular work with the dumbbells would sculpture the old Reinhart from the flab in a mere month. If he so chose. For his will had not really been destroyed but just lay dormant. He delighted in his capacity for alternation, believing that it made him more human than your ordinary *homme moyen sensual* who stayed the same from cradle to grave. Not to mention that it gave some point to freedom of choice: he knew the differences between options, had experienced being a fop, then a slob. He had also been exposed to a host of other things in the British Isles and occupation Germany, and was certain he had at least dreamt of most philosophies. In his time he had been both sane and mad. The only trouble at the moment was in what he wanted to *be*. But he might decide that as early as the morrow.

Reinhart had always had a feeling that something would turn up, from nowhere would come money or women or adventure and even an old friend, that is, an *opportunity;* Christ, it was the richest and most powerful country in the world, and you every day read about vagrants picked off

Adapted from *Reinhart in Love,* by Thomas Berger. Copyright © 1962 by Thomas Berger and reprinted by permission of The Dial Press, Inc.

park benches and made movie stars and John T. Nobody whose name was pulled from a hopper to win radio lotteries worth thousands—

But for several weeks now he had been with Maw & Dad and still hadn't seen a *person* since he returned.

Civilian life had more terrors than even he, who seldom knew a sanguine anticipation, dreamed of. Add to this the distinct impression he had that in America it wasn't serious, either—because all tragedies here seemed to be specific rather than generic; mad little private hopelessnesses—and you had his dilemma. Which need not be permanent, however, because he would go back to college in June, when the next term started, in a year or so get a crash-program BA majoring in Vagueness, be instantly hired for the young-executive training by Whirlpool Inc., the great detergents empire of southern Ohio, and issued a wife, sedan, and six-room cottage from their stockroom and whatever the quota in kids. Living to a smooth old age, and a clean one owing to the employes' discount on soap, in time retiring to a dotage of home-workshop puttering and a bland diet for his ulcers, he would finally and unobtrusively turn up his toes, leaving behind the means for his delinquents to accept the obligations of maturity and in their time follow suit.

Who did he think *he* was? as Maw always asked.

A fat man, for one. He hadn't yet got around to using his weights, which he couldn't locate; he suspected they had been sold during the iron shortage.

Lathering with the old GI-issue brush, Reinhart heard a sound outside the door not unlike what he supposed obsolete novelists meant by "a scratching in (or *on* or *at*) the wainscot," whatever that was. Couldn't be Maw, who would have split the wood. He asked Dad in, thinking it would please him to be recognized unseen.

And surely it did; yet the old fellow showed worry behind his good manners, saying "Thank you, Carlo, I don't want to intrude, but. . ."

"Be my guest." Reinhart indicated the toilet seat in its green chenille envelope, and Dad went there and sat.

"Carlo, I was wondering—look here, why don't you use my gear? Seen it?" He rose and in the linen closet found an enormous giftbox of men's toiletries, matched: powder and lotion and scalp-goo, a blade for corns, nailclippers, rotary mower for nose-hair, and a paste to allay underarm offending. "Your aunt's Xmas idea for me. Pearls in front of swine. I wish you would use it. I don't."

Pointing to his own porcine face in the mirror, Reinhart asked: "Why then cast it in front of me?"

"Good-looking fellow like you?" His father in embarrassment leaned against the toilet tank behind, agitating its heavy lid, and the Epsom-salts and bicarbonate jars thereon made their clinking remarks. "Fellow with all the advantages?"

"Tell you what was on my mind," he apprehensively changed the subject. "Now, no criticism intended, it goes without saying, but I was contemplating what you figure on doing till school starts. Because I know you'll be taking advantage of the GI Bill, full tuition paid and in addition this generous emollient per the month of expenses. A *wonderful opportunity,* and one never before vouchfaced to the American veteran. . . . You *will* take advantage of this wonderful opportunity?"

Dad attended patiently on Reinhart's deliberate opening of the tap—the son refused to assent before the plumbing did; at last scalding his finger, Carlo nodded.

"Righto," agreed Dad. "But till the onset of the summer session, if I have sized you up, with all your pep you can't stand laying around the house. Mentioned my calculation to Claude Humbold today, and as you might expect, that good-hearted man—who thinks almost as much of you as your mother—well, to put it in a word, he's ready to make you an offer."

Reinhart left the Nirvana of the hot washrag and asked, with open pores: "For what, Dad?"

"A job, Carlo. Or rather, if I know him, a position. Till college starts and even then, maybe, for late-afternoon and Saturday morning, ess etera, ess etera."

Reinhart had never concealed his distaste for Humbold, having nothing particular against the man but everything in general.

"Ah, Dad, you never give up. You've been throwing that bastard at me all my life. I cut his grass and washed his car, and he beat my price down ten cents less than I got from anybody else. I walked the rotten dog he had before Popover, which tore my cuff, and Humbold simply laughed when I told him. Before I left for college you had me go see Humbold, I'll never know why, because he left school in the eighth grade and is, so he told me, an enemy of higher education who could buy up the entire faculty of the Municipal University from his petty cash." Reinhart milked the water from his shaving brush and tossed it into the medicine cabinet between tincture of merthiolate and cocoa-butter suppositories, feeling a pain the latter could never assuage. "You are the Mahatma Gandhi to my British Empire, Dad, and I see your strength but don't get the moral behind it."

Dad showed him a back of rumpled shirt and baggy seat, handkerchief three-quarters out of the rear left pocket, cuffs scouring the floor and frayed where the shoe heels bit them.

"Okay, okay, okay." Dad's voice issued from the little end of a megaphone, and his expiration seemed imminent.

Now Reinhart, with his overdeveloped sympathies, felt why couldn't he once do something for the old man? Gritting his teeth, he could probably survive in the job till June and the beginning of the summer term at the university. He had to trust that Dad would understand the sacrifice being made for him. He also believed it might do him, Reinhart, good by doing him bad, which was a principle he had worked out some time before and told to a friend in Germany on the night they got into a certain trouble resulting in the death of two men, including the friend, and his own psychoneurotic difficulties. It had taken him until this moment to really get well, which he did now at once when he realized—as how few people do! hence the widespread disaffection—that the mere formulation of a principle has absolutely no effect on existence *in re;* which, for example, is why you'll look forever to find a good Christian.

He went to the phone book, found the realtor's number, dialed it, and soon heard a competent female voice in his ear. He asked for his enemy and was icily resisted, the secretary being one of those persons who confuse intermediary with principal positions. He had to invent a house he wished to buy; even then, in ignorance he put the price too low: five thousand dollars, what he recalled his parents had paid for their bungalow years ago; one forgot that inflation grew by leaps and bounders like Humbold.

"*Five?*" sneered the secretary. "Say, who is this? All our listings are in restricted neighborhoods—"

To his own delighted surprise, Reinhart heard himself answer harshly: "Madam, I suggest you let me talk to someone in authority. I am Conrad Fluellen, regional director of the Federal Bureau of Investigation and I said *twenty*-five."

Soon a man who must have been Humbold came upon the wire, though Reinhart hardly recognized the voice, so wheedling had it gone. He decided he had begun on the wrong foot, and quietly hung up. He would report personally to the office.

The least he could do was travel in dignity. He phoned for a taxi—in an impulse of Bohemianism, the Negro one. When at length it appeared—an aged Chrysler with a yellow roof and body of asymmetrical checkers, belching blue smoke and making odd groans at the tailpipe—in the driver's seat sat a Negro Reinhart had known in high school. He wore semi-official cab clothes: cap with a sweatband of wicker, his jacket had epaulets and the pocket was compartmented for pencils; but Reinhart knew him well enough. The reverse, however, was not true: see one Caucasian, see them all.

The Negro hopped out and opened the rear door, which was more than a white taximan would have, but then he proceeded to do another peculiar thing: cheat on the distance by taking the longest way, up around the end of the suburbs, where a sallow woman scratched the start of a garden; down to the other extremity, where some Slav with an enormous family all boys sold waste paper and rusty iron, then plunged to the eastern limits and its railroad of abandoned boxcars.

Now Reinhart never said a word until they finally stopped before the mock fieldstone exterior of Humbold's one-story office at the edge of the business district. Over the years he had never learned how to remonstrate with a malefactor face to face; between his indignation and its expression always rose the specter of his own corrupt person; he feared damaging countercharges.

Thus now he could only say with veiled sarcasm: "Thanks for the tour."

The Negro answered: "We aim to please." He left the taxi, slipped between its forward bumper and the rear one of a bloated auto parked ahead, probably Humbold's, and opened Reinhart's door. He announced the fare as thirty-five cents. It slowly became apparent to Reinhart, who tipped him the remainder of a half-dollar, that this cab like all suburban taxis went by zone charges rather than meters. The ride had cost him under five cents a mile, and he just wished he had been intelligent enough to enjoy it.

To boot, the Negro returned the tip, explaining that he was owner-driver, not wage-slave, and Reinhart thanked him, and he rejoined "Yours truly," and drove away.

Expecting the resistance of a compressed-air device, Reinhart thrust too hard against the glass door to the office. It swept back, hit some hidden elastic stop, and came forward with great velocity. Was he struck? No, deft fellow, he performed a neat evasion, but the door's wind raised the papers from the secretary's desk and whirled them to the floor.

"I'm terribly sorry," he said, secretly resentful. Since the inconvenience must occur repeatedly, he supposed it was artfully arranged to happen, to put the caller at an immediate disadvantage. On the other hand, he was thrilled he understood it, that within his first moment on the premises he had divined one of the subtleties of modern business.

"Not at all," the secretary answered malignantly. "You're not sorry at all. Neither are you really the regional director of the FBI." She was actually as young as he, but in her clothing and make-up pretended not to be, wearing the tight under-armor and pungent perfume of a middle-aged woman simulating youth, as well as conspicuous junk jewelry. She stared so caustically at Reinhart as he crept about fetching papers that he believed his fly must be open. Coughing as a cover, he checked it, and it wasn't; but he regretted not having bought a new suit, for at his right hip was a considerable moth hole through which protruded a corner of his olive-drab drawers.

"You don't want to do anything for *us*," the secretary charged. "You want *us* to do something for *you*." She wet on her tongue the end of a purple-taloned finger and pressed it upon her glossy knee.

"Got a runner?" Reinhart asked sympathetically, trying to ingratiate himself, for he foresaw that working with or near this girl would be abrasive unless he could, metaphorically speaking, refasten her brassiere strap from the tightest to the loosest connection.

She swung her legs into the cavity provided for them below the desk. "You don't look like an Italian, but you have Roman eyes." She bit her lips, which were small but full and permanently drooped in exigence. Every so often she widened her gray eyes and then squinted, at which times the point of her little nose was depressed and the back of her brown bob seemed to lift like the behind of a chicken in flight.

She was really kind of cute, and Reinhart turned on for her his winning grin. He fundamentally liked all girls, especially those who worked in an office and took it seriously; a woman's life being ever threatened with disorder—for example, at least once a month—he found both delightful and touching a secretary's illusion she had hers arranged.

"How did you know it was me?" he asked, meaning the counterfeit Fed, and she understood. He also liked clever people, or tried to.

"I remember voices like a sensitive person remembers slights." This was perhaps too clever, and she meant it to be, and flipped both her pretty, insolent head and the switch of an intercom, reporting: "Mr. Humbold, a person to see you." Dirty with static, a reply was metallically audible: *"Hen or rooster?"* Miss X answered: "Rooster," and superciliously pointed coxcomb Reinhart to the private door.

Humbold, sitting behind a blond desk, next to a rubber plant in a bamboo-wrapped urn, lost no time in demonstrating his disappointment; nor could the gravel in his voice be blamed on static any longer; he had a throatful of saliva and was too lazy or arrogant to clear it. Frankly, Reinhart would never understand such a person, and thus at a moment which called for strength had only weakness to offer. On the other hand, perhaps the weakness was just as good, since Humbold would not permit the offering of anything. It was *his* office, *his* secretary, and shortly Reinhart discovered that he himself was owned by Humbold, having hypnotically assented to an oral indenture which he failed to hear properly except for the wage terms, which were extraordinarily generous: sixty-five dollars a week.

Reinhart was suddenly rich; at the same time, he felt distinctly deprived of something he had with him when he entered the office. He studied his employer, to see if he had taken it.

Humbold wore his trousers very high to cover his wide belly; the end of his gaudy necktie was secured under the waistband of his pants, and a golden safety pin fastened his tie to his shirt, which was white with a white figure, looking at which you were sure your vision was failing. He wore a pin at the collar as well: conspicuous consumption, for the collar was also button-down. In his shirt pocket, fastened to an isinglass liner bearing on its fold an advertisement for his own business, he carried a matched pen and pencil of silver with onyx topknots, though no cigars. His face was smooth as a bladder and as fat, but harder. He had unusually long and loose earlobes; like a turkey's wattles, they continued to move when he did no more than stare. His eyes were smaller than the muzzles of his shotgun nose.

"O.K., bud," said Humbold, "never had a job? You ain't paid for gawking."

"Excuse me." Reinhart collected himself—which was what had turned out to be missing—and asked: "Mr. Humbold—"

"Call me Claude," said the boss.

"I just wanted to be sure you knew who I was."

"No danger of that," jeered Humbold. "You just flush when I pull the chain. Your daddy called me every day. I done a lot for your old man, and I'll do more, though ten years younger than him. I'm *making* this job for you, bud, there being no opening. Everything I got, I built for myself." He touched the knot of his tie with a hand wearing two rings, a watch, a manicure, and hair fine as a baby's. "Now get to your work."

"Just what would that be?" Reinhart asked, choosing this moment to sit upon a chair of metal tubing.

"Well it ain't sitting!" cried Humbold. "Bud, you ain't one to appreciate opportunity. A man give me a opportunity like this and I'd have his bidniss inside a year." He rose, impudently rejecting the swivel chair with his large hams. His face grew so amiable as to appear imbecilic: his eyes vanished, his ears grew, his teeth showed, and his tongue dangled. Rube-like, he sauntered to Reinhart and squeezed his hand as if it were a cow's udder. He doffed an imaginary straw hat and droned: "Take a piece of propitty off muh hans? You an me'll mosey later to take a look at whut I got fuh sale, but fust we drink a bourbon and branch water?"

Humbold came out of his role and explained: "That technique is for the city type, contrary to what you might think. You always be different from the client. What a man buying a property *don't* want is for the salesman to be no more than him. Now if you get a hick, you act hoity-toity and then show a property near a exclusive golf club, tell him everybody in the neighborhood eats supper in a Tuxedo and set their dogs on Baptists. Get the point? You always work *against the grain.*"

Humbold returned to the other side of the room, where two different kinds of his own calendars were hung, turned, put a twist on his hip, and waltzed back like a fruit.

"The mosth darling little place," he lisped, "that you'll *dearly* love! . . . The approach for a crude, physical type with a mousey wife. You have to watch he don't belt you, but you'll make a real hit with the little woman. On the other hand, you get a sissy, you lay on the threat: you start by hurting his hand when you shake. You belch, sneeze, spit, and pee in a deserted hallway. You pull him inta some tough saloon and show only slum properties near a factory where the air stinks."

It had taken Reinhart all this while to understand that he was being hired as a real-estate man, and he was very gloomy about it, disliking nothing more than houses and lots, dreaming invariably of palaces in parks on the one hand and urban apartments on the other. For a moment he hated Dad for having had to do him this favor.

"Never," said Humbold, "sell a man what he wants!"

"Why?" Reinhart asked. "Why are people like that?" For if Humbold said they were, they were; he did not challenge his employer, the one man hereabouts who had made an unqualified success and was worth, they said, six figures, and continued to live in the same neighborhood as Reinhart's parents only because he had the biggest house there.

Contrary to what his employe expected, Humbold looked pleased at the query and answered ecstatically: "Because that's not what they want!" He plunged into a closet and brought out the jacket to his pin-striped suit, a fawn-colored topcoat, and a kind of Confederate cavalry hat of light gray with a narrow black band. From the lapel of his jacket sprouted a crimson feather-duster boutonniere, apropos of the predominant color, in a mélange of others, in his necktie. An Alp of white handkerchief rose from his breast pocket. He cocked his hat and cried to Reinhart: "Let's move out, bud!"

Struggling into his old trenchcoat, Reinhart followed Humbold through the outer office and past the secretary. Their air swept her correspondence to the floor again. She shook her little fist at Reinhart, and he stopped to make things right. "Bud!" shouted Humbold, half through the street door, admitting a March wind that mocked any efforts at reorder. "Step lively before it gets away!"

"Before what does?" Reinhart screamed into the wind. He was now outdoors. Humbold, already in his eight-cylinder Gigantic, started the engine. The vehicle began to move as Reinhart caught the door handle, and he had to run alongside for half a block before a red light halted it and he could enter.

The boss played the pushbuttons of the radio as if it were an organ, producing a mishmash of sound. At last he settled for a rancorous raving about a deodorant: *You're a dirty pig unless you use Dream Mist.*

He thrust his face down into his coat and alternately sniffed at both armpits. "Why," he then answered, "whajuh think? Life!"

By the end of Reinhart's first working day he had had a triumph, a feature of which was that suddenly after all these years he ceased to think of Humbold as an enemy.

Humbold was generous—irrespective of the sixty-five per week, which was not exactly a salary but an estimate of what Reinhart could earn by making sales, fair enough. He had driven first to Gents' Walk, the local clothiers, and got Reinhart reoutfitted from sole to scalp (or, as Humbold put it, "from corns to dandruff"), charging it to his own account, the squaring up to come from his employe's future earnings.

Humbold was egalitarian: he vigorously pressed Reinhart to dress after his, Humbold's, fashion; and while the apprentice politely rejected the pinstripes, the aurora borealis neckties, and any kind of hat, he did appreciate the boss's selfless concern—your typical employer would rather have striven to maintain the distinctions. (Gents' wasn't where Reinhart would have gone on his own; yet he managed to find a harmless brown sports jacket, gray flannels, cordovan-dyed oxfords which might or might not run in the rain, and a single-breasted gabardine raincoat which might or might not shed it; he gave his old clothes to the halitosic clerk to burn. "I'll package them and send them to MISSIONARY, in care of your local post-master," said the clerk. "An appeal in which your neighborhood clothiers are cooperating, to cover the nakedness of certain tribes in New South Wales.")

Humbold had authority: he operated his great car as if it were a chariot fitted with hub-scythes and the pedestrians were Roman infantry. Walking, Reinhart had always condemned such driving; he saw now how the grass could be green in one's own yard. He felt, if not power, at least his adjacency to it. Their next call was to a gas station, where Humbold flashed a credit card and a herd of lackeys swarmed over the vehicle and filled it and cajoled it and laved it with a variety of their fluids, and stood in platoon formation, saluting, as the Gigantic at length blasted off, just miss-ing a fox terrier with his nose at the tail of another upon the edge of the blacktop.

Humbold had esprit: they roared towards a couple of "live ones," which was to say, clients, people in the market for a house, and the boss already had the scent of prey in his big nostrils; he increased the volume of the radio and whistled through his teeth in accompaniment to the musical commercials; he sideswept his hat brim like an Anzac; he ground two sticks of gum between his molars and winced as if in some excruciatingly sweet pain.

"Keep your eye on me, bud," he said. "It's worth a college course."

Since the boss was going to this trouble over him, Reinhart believed it was only fair to advise: "Which reminds me, sir—"

Humbold buried him in an avalanche of derision. "Sir! That went out with Tom Thumb golf and near-beer, bud. You never make a dollar calling 'sir' like a Limey butler. To a client, I repeat, you got to be boss. And as to me"—on a shaded avenue, going fifty, he suddenly squashed the brakes, which hurled Reinhart against the dashboard and permitted a woman to wheel a baby carriage across the street in the middle of the block; or rather, she was forced to cross by Humbold's sweeping arm; it was doubt-ful whether she had really wanted to—"as to me," Humbold repeated, then parenthetically told Reinhart to snap out of it, the dashboard would break sooner than his head, and accelerated forward, waving his hat at the woman. "As to me, everybody calls me Claude, but nobody forgets who pays the bills."

He shot past a stop sign onto an arterial highway, greeting with one raised finger, as if in the schoolroom signal of Number One, the motorcycle cop hiding behind the billboard there, among the early poison ivy. Reinhart cracked his neck to turn and read what wind and weather, or a cunning vandal, had made more eloquent:

CHOICE PROPERTIES SEE HUMBOLD REAL

He decided there was little point in hastily telling the boss he could work only until school started, since at this moment culture seemed irrelevant even to himself. Uncomfortable in his new clothes, he drew a cigarette and punched the dashboard lighter, which instantly glowed like a witch's eye.

"No boy no!" cried Humbold, at the same time gunning off the highway onto a washboard dirt road, the Gigantic much bumpier than the ads, with their photos taken in stroboscopic light at the Gigantic Torture Test Track, Dearborn, Mich., admitted. "Stamp out the King Brothers!"

By the time Reinhart had puzzled this through—he was really very pleased to have been able to: Smo King and Drin King—they had drawn up on the village green, only it was mud, of a cannibal village, only instead of shrunken heads diapers were everywhere hanging out to dry on sagging lines between the huts, which were made of corrugated iron rather than palm fronds, and the children who burst ululating upon him and the boss were white beneath the dirt.

Humbold broke a passage by flinging a handful of nickels in another direction, saying to Reinhart: "When I was a boy, you could buy off a kid with a penny. I made it my bidniss to be completely nauseating and soon I had more cents than anybody." He asked nothing for his wit, however, and didn't smile himself, but rather studied his shoe-tips in annoyance, which were gathering a film of dust as they padded toward the nearest Quonset.

A respectful half-step behind, Reinhart asked, trying to be professional: "Is this hot territory?"

But he learned that you either knew the jargon or not, simulation was ill advised. Thus Humbold answered as if he had been questioned on the weather: "Temperate."

"Sorry," Reinhart said, and he lowered his voice, for they were almost at the door of the hut. "I mean, this place looks pretty low-class. Are there many clients here who could afford a house?"

Humbold banged the door, the same rusty metal as the siding, with his foot. Instantly it was opened by a skinny young man in eyeglasses, a T-shirt, and an expression of ancient apology. Humbold seized his hand and under the guise of shaking it performed a neat judo type of throw which lifted the man from his threshold and literally dropped him on Reinhart.

"Meet Bobby Clendellan."

Ah, thought Reinhart while helping Clendellan settle shakily on his own two feet, the strong-arm technique. But this fellow didn't seem effeminate, only confused and guilty, other things entirely.

Humbold retrieved poor Clendellan before Reinhart could do too much for him, and holding him by the scruff of his T-shirt, finally answered Reinhart's earlier question: "Can these jokers afford a house? Bud, this is Vetsville, these boys got all them benefits from a grateful country. Ain't that right, Bobby?"

Clendellan adjusted his glasses back of the ears, while looking cravenly through their lenses at Reinhart. He said: "I was a yeoman in the Navy."

"He killed two regulations and wounded a fountain pen," said Humbold. He propelled Clendellan into the hut, patting his slack behind. "Go get your ball and chain and your deductions, if they haven't been eaten up by the vermin in this dump: I got a nice place to show you."

Clendellan poked his head out the door again, and called to Reinhart: "I had limited service because of bad vision."

"That's quite all right," Reinhart answered grandly. He waved the client to his errand.

While they waited, Humbold pawed the ground like a bull and snorted, to maintain his role, but *sotto voce* he advised his apprentice: "A fairly uncommon case, noncombatants being usually the tough ones, with paratroopers and Marines being soft and easy to work."

"I get it," said Reinhart. "Noncombatant service is more like civil life than combat is, and—"

"Wrong, bud. All wrong. Just the opposite: life, real life, is exactly like the fighting, except in the latter you use guns and therefore don't destroy as many people. But if you already had your combat one place, you don't want it in another. . . . The present client is the black sheep, the foul ball, of the moneybags clan who own among other items the Clendellan Building in the city. He lives here like a goat while his family could buy the state from their petty cash. You figure out why?"

"Because he wants to Make His Own Way," whispered Reinhart.

"Absolutely incorrect," the boss said, beheading his gum ball again and again with chipmunked incisors and restoring it with the tongue. "Because he's a Commonist." He let that soak in for a moment, but it didn't faze Reinhart, who had been in Berlin with the real Russians. "Or a Fachist," Humbold continued. "I don't know which, whatever kind of crank it is who likes to live like a nigger when he ain't one. That's seldom a real nigger, by the way. Say bud, do you have a politics?"

"Not so's you can notice," Reinhart answered, sure at last he had said the right thing.

But Humbold turned away in chagrin and punched the side of the hut. Something fell from the wall within and broke, and Clendellan's contrite voice was heard: "Be with you in a minute. We're changing the baby's diapers." Perhaps because they didn't answer, he came to the door and explained to Reinhart: "I was stationed at the Norfolk Naval Base throughout my service, which is how I could raise a family."

Reinhart shrugged cynically.

Humbold removed his big hat and extended it, with the hole upwards, in supplication. "All right, then. Can you at least pretend to be a Red?"

"I'm sorry, Claude. I thought we always went against the grain."

"With the men, bud, the men. Look." He literally buttonholed Reinhart —or tried to, but in fact the lapel slot on the new jacket was still sewn shut; Humbold settled for a grip on the notch. "Your job is the wife."

Reinhart felt himself blush in involuntary, anticipatory lasciviousness; his id, or whatever it was, always made its own translation of remarks that linked him with a woman no matter what the intended relation. Humbold however noticed nothing amiss. He was almost a foot shorter than his assistant, but didn't admit it. This was another reason why Reinhart had begun not to dislike him: Humbold was superior to details unless they had a practical application to an immediate purpose. For example, he would never mention Reinhart's size until he wanted someone beaten up.

"You got it?" asked the boss.

"I think so."

Humbold frowned, looking like a rubber ball being pinched. "That's not the right comeback. Be positive, defiant, overbearing, never welch. When you are asked 'You got it?' answer 'Better than you!' "

"Even to you?"

"Especially to me, bud. Who you think's paying you?" Humbold found a handkerchief beneath his coat and snapping it at his shoes in the way a towel is used to sting someone's bare body, cleared them of dust. "O.K.," he said, "now try it. *Got it?*"

Because the boss held the handkerchief as if he would give him a taste of it for failure to comply, Reinhart counterfeited a heavy, sneering insolence that made his stomach curdle, replying: "Better than you, goddammit!" He felt ill and hoped he musn't have to do this frequently.

"There's one thing I won't stand for," Humbold asseverated. "And that is a foul mouth. Clean it up, bud, or you're out of a good opportunity. No taking of the Lord's name in vain; no friendship towards the King Brothers; no suggestiveness about the fair sex. Just listen to your Dutch Uncle Dudley. Remember you wouldn't be in this world without your dear old mother. Write to her frequently, boy. Worship your God in your own way, and go to the church of your choice this Sunday. I say so even to a Jew, for in the eyes of the Big Boy upstairs we are all even as children. He's the greatest bidnissman of them all, bud, and knows a bad property when he eyes one. Don't forfeit your Big Commission."

When Reinhart, more or less sincerely, said: "You know, Claude, you would have made a great preacher," he saw he had at last pushed the right pedal. Humbold uttered no sound, struck no attitude; rather, his eyes disappeared in true humility, he briefly locked arms with his employe in that old knight's embrace where each fellow clasps the other's biceps, and said: "You'll make a great bidnissman, bud, in time."

And there came upon Reinhart in this barren March afternoon a portent of imminent glory, a kind of Star of Bethlehem in whose radiance he saw himself as Henry Ford Reinhart, emperor of the clangorous assembly lines; or Woolworth Reinhart, seated on a mountain of small coins; and finally, John D. Reinhart, withered, digestion ruined, dining on milk and crackers, tipping dimes, his mouth like an empty purse and his purse like a full mouth, not the worst kind of dotage. And for years he had hated business in general and Humbold in particular; we don't know how the other half lives.

"Bandits approaching at three o'clock," warned Humbold, using his left fist as an intercom; his right presumably on the rudder, he banked towards the hut, from which Clendellan emerged with an armload of baby and extra swathings. Another child, of about two and a half feet—Reinhart was no good at computing age—a girl, and malicious of expression, walked alongside her papa clutching the seam of his chinos. Behind this group, carrying nothing, shuffled a little man in the garb and make-up of a silent-movie comedian, baggy of pants, saggy of shirt, unbarbered, with a face white as flour and hair black as night.

Of course Reinhart knew all along this little Chaplin was a woman and Clendellan's wife, but it was part of the strategy he was swiftly formulating that he pretend otherwise. He saw in astonishment that the boss had turned on a gross gallantry, bowing with fingers to his gut.

"Humbold," Mrs. Clendellan said, a description rather than a greeting.

Straightening, Humbold imperiously signaled the attendance of Reinhart. "My assistant, to take the kids off your hands."

"They're not on mine. Are you myopic?"

"No mam," said the boss. "I speak with all respect." He appealed mutely to Reinhart and back-pedaled to the side of Clendellan, where the girl fetched him a kick in the shins, which could have done little damage considering her height, but Reinhart saw his pride was wounded and marveled at it.

Reinhart himself was now unnerved at a situation that had thrown his boss, and was desperately planning to speak in the character agreed upon—he tried to think of something favorable to say about the Soviet Union—when Mrs. Clendellan shook his hand with incredible strength for so small a woman and said: "I'm Alice."

"My name is Carlo Reinhart. How do you do, madam."

She smiled and slid her grip to his big forearm. "You can drop the feudal designations, Carlo. I'm Alice, and I've been a worker in my time, too: the five-and-ten housewares section. What kind of wage does this reactionary pay you?"

"Oh, a very decent one." For a moment Reinhart thought he discerned a basically attractive woman disguised somewhere within the little creature kneading his arm, and thought oh what a pity, and there was a catch in his voice.

Mrs. Clendellan interpreted it otherwise.

"Strength!" she said, in both sympathy and triumph, and moved her grasp to his upper arm, which was indeed as high as she could reach and it must have been awkward to walk in that manner, for all this while the party was proceeding towards Humbold's car.

The word, however, had to the apprentice a certain Fascist connotation; perhaps after all Claude had been correct in his strange assessment of the Clendellans. So Reinhart answered it with: "Through Joy!" and opened the rear door of the automobile. Frankly he didn't care what they were.

He struggled briefly with Mrs. C. over who helped whom into the car. At last he won, and she clambered in giving him a view of the back of her slacks, from which no valuable data were gained, for they were too baggy to show the shape of her bottom. When he got in, however, he ascertained that her hip was very firm, for she pressed it against his and otherwise sat close enough to allow for three more passengers, though only one came: the small daughter, with a final kick at Humbold, swarmed like a chimpanzee over the backrest of the front seat and violently embraced Reinhart with all her extremities, sharp little kneecap in his ear, little paws in his nostrils, etc., screaming "I love you, big giant!"

Now if Reinhart was flattered, he was also embarrassed, not towards the titular head of this clan—for Clendellan's weak eyes were watery with approval, looking back over the baby's transparent scalp; it was clear his women were seldom pleased—but towards the boss, whose face he could see through the small fingers passionately clawing at his own.

Money? Ah no, it wasn't money which your true businessman lusted after. Reinhart all at once knew this and became a professional in one fell insight. It was love. Humbold looked ghastly, being deprived of it. On the other hand, Reinhart had never liked him more, and wondered if the boss would eventually see that his assistant's success was also his own.

For the nonce, anyway, Claude did not. He backed off the mud flat as listless as a grazing water buffalo and droned slowly along the highway hugging the right shoulder so close Reinhart feared he might sever a progression of Burma-Shave verses: IN THIS VALE—OF TOIL AND SIN—YOUR HEAD GROWS BALD—BUT NOT YOUR CHIN.

Tiny Margaret—for that was her name; she said it again and again as she climbed Reinhart's chest and sat upon his head, with one foot in the breast pocket of his jacket: "I'm Margaret Clendellan and I love the giant, I'm Margaret," etc.—little Margaret swung her weight diagonally forward, taking Reinhart's neck along with it perforce, which brought her to the rear adjacency of Humbold's fat shoulders, from which it was even for her short arm a simple maneuver to play streetcar conductor with the boss's earlobe and order: "Make it go!"

There was no love lost between mother and daughter—at the moment they contested over Reinhart, with Margaret, being spryer, holding the edge; though Mrs. C. had somehow wormed one dirty saddle oxford between his new shoes—but Clendellan's frau now contributed her heckle to the same cause.

"Why do you drive so hearselike, Humbold? Surely you must be an honorary sheriff."

"Yes mam," answered naïve Claude, making feeble efforts to free his ear, helpless as the infant in Clendellan's arms, who as a matter of fact was quite self-reliant and had begun to menace Humbold with a blue-and-white rattle, egged on by a proud, no longer cringing dad. "I'm also a big donor to the Police Retirement Fund."

"An overweight one, anyway," rejoined Alice Clendellan, making no move towards the wallet, with all his courtesy cards dangling like an open concertina, which Humbold had pushed over the backrest while steering with one hand. To save the boss's face, Reinhart thought *he* might take it, but was outmoved by little Margaret, who tore the celluloid insert from the billfold and swiftly destroyed its contents.

For Reinhart it was a further insight into the character of both Humbold and business in general to see that when the damage was discovered the boss brightened—the point was, he at last had got a response he could understand—and he actually gave his Stonewall Jackson hat to Margaret, suggesting she tear it to shreds. Some of the old lilt returned to his voice, and he speeded up to forty.

But as anybody could have told him, sanctioned destruction is not the same thing at all. Margaret not only declined; she replaced the hat upon his head and waged no further aggression against him.

Well, so it went all afternoon: the family just couldn't resist Reinhart and just couldn't stand Humbold. Claude continued to wilt until he seemed to have changed roles with Clendellan. By the time they stopped at the third house, the latter had got so far as to punch Humbold in the back and say: "I don't think we'll even bother to get out for this turkey."

The irony was that the houses looked to Reinhart like very good buys. He had assumed Humbold would try to do the Clendellans dirty, but no: the first two had been sound bungalows on Presbyterian streets. This one, a block from the northeastern corner of the town line, was old brick shaded by elms; its back yard after fifty feet became an apple orchard; and instead of your modern type of garage, with its vile bleakness, here stood a little green shed which would conceal a car without looking as if it did. Yet this was what Clendellan termed a turkey and declined to consider.

Reinhart believed everybody present save himself was fighting some kind of war which had nought to do with buying or selling a house. He understood the justice of Humbold's preparatory comments. The only trouble was that even so the boss had lost every engagement; and he certainly couldn't be happy about an assistant who had won them to no purpose. Reinhart therefore contrived an excellent, if he did say so himself, intrigue. On the long taxi ride to the office, he had noticed, in the southern district where the Slav kept his junk, a real abomination: a kind of junior tenement of four stories, absurdly distant from the town center for a multiple dwelling, built purposely as a slum, with garbage cans for a yard and a miniature Gobi as a park, where degenerates molested children, children tortured cats, and the latter ate songbirds, while rodents ran with impunity. The building was occupied by emigrés from Kentucky, who had come north to work in the factories and were, despite their salaries, forever indigent; they were also the very same people Reinhart had seen there ever since he was a boy—apparently they never grew older; he swore the urchin eating dirt from a flowerpot had been his schoolfellow in the third grade.

Anyway, this horror of a residence wore a sign on which, under an overlay of misspelled references to the reproductive and excretory activities of Homo sapiens, one could read FOR SALE (and ignore the legend some depraved wag had penciled in beneath: *my Sister*).

Reinhart's plan was this: disingenuously to offer the tenement to the Clendellans, by so doing to shock them into a reasonable attitude towards Claude and the decent properties he had been showing all afternoon.

The best feature was that not even Claude himself understood the scheme. When Reinhart suggested they drive south, the boss pouted. The baby reached over and ran a finger up his spread nose, and its father chuckled idiotically.

Freeing his air, Claude also liberated some of the spleen which had been building up in him for hours: "That's a dumb idea, you. Dumb, dumb, dumb." He abused the driving controls and started up with a thrust that threw Reinhart, Alice, and Margaret together into one amorphous monster with six limbs. Though this far from displeased the girls, they both struggled loose and made their demands, one in tinwhistle coloratura, the other in malignant contralto: they either went where Reinhart said or home.

Humbold furiously drove right to the tenement, which in addition to its other deficiences stood upon a dead-end street, where he had the greatest trouble reversing the Gigantic and finally was forced to bull, tanklike, into the curb, crumbling it.

He punched his hat, and said sardonically: "This is a waste of time, unless you want to buy the Tenderloin."

"What's the Tenderloin?" asked Clendellan.

But his wife already knew. She leaned across Reinhart's lap—and he began quickly to think she wasn't so bad a dish—and counted the windows in the façade of the building, all broken, some masked with cardboard.

"Something definitely could be made of it," Alice crooned. A cadaverous woman with Medusa hair stared back at her from the second-floor front. On the eroded entrance steps a small boy plucked at his convex navel, which was bare between pants tops and shirt-end. Leaning from the window, the woman advised him: "Don't run with them boys if they kick the shit out'n you." He seemed grateful for the counsel and having drifted along by the trash cans began to break bottles on the sidewalk.

Now it was no surprise to Reinhart that these people cared for one another, but both the Clendellans were much impressed and pursed their lips, while Claude snorted crudely and revved the engine.

"Off we go," he said. "I got to take a shower."

Little Margaret shoved past her mother and, hanging from the car with her feet in Reinhart's face, called to the boy: "I love you, tiny midget!" He replied with a fantastically vivid obscenity for such a small child, who would as yet have only known it as hearsay, absolutely enchanting Margaret, who leaped out and embraced him. He punched at her nose and missed; in no time at all her half-nelson had him grounded.

"Looks like Maggie's making a hit," Clendellan told the infant in his arms, and each bubbled at the other.

"Humbold, I may as well inform you now," said Mrs. Clendellan. "if we buy this building it will be on the following terms: Mr. Reinhart will get the commission."

Claude laughed hysterically and started to drive off. "Oh no, mam, you wouldn't joke so mean with me."

"Reverse this bison!" she ordered. "Try no Cossack tactic on me!" Clendellan tried to add a word, probably affirmative, but she anyway shouted him down.

"Mam," pleaded Humbold, showing a confusion ever ready to become chagrin. "You're a great little kidder but nobody'd purchase the Tenderloin. The town will condemn it next month and—"

"And hurl this underdeveloped population into the street?"

He nodded sadistically. "The owner would unload it maybe for eighteen five, with the rats thrown in. That proves something, being next door to selling it for the nails. The plumbing rusted out in '43; in every room there's muck knee-high like after a flood; the Hunky in his junkyard burns rubber continually; the roof's like cheesecloth; no tomcat's got nerve to enter the cellar where the vermin are big as Shetland ponies; you can't light a match but what the whole shebang would go up like excelsior soaked in fuel oil. And the neighborhood is type Z zoning; they could build a gas works next door."

But before he had finished, the three remaining Clendellans had swarmed from the car and into the tenement, the baby of course willy-nilly though he displayed the greatest interest, babbling merrily.

"Tell um I refuse to come," whispered Humbold as he frustrated Reinhart's apology and pushed him after them.

Reinhart was determined to apologize to someone, though, feeling responsible for this grotesquerie which had got out of control, but it took him ever so long just to catch up with them, who cut through the building as if it were a cantaloupe. When he did, Alice said with the inevitable bodily contact (under the mask of discretion, for a host of natives stood nearby gawking and scratching): "I think you've made yourself a sale!"

His protest was lost as they dashed upstairs. In passing, the baby scraped some filth from the banister and smeared it on its dad. With an effort Reinhart could see how they might fit in as tenants if not as landlords, and began to tell himself: Why not, old fellow, ride with the current?

Clendellan called to Alice, who climbed faster than he: "What does eighteen five mean?"

"Eighteen thousand, five hundred dollars. You can get it from your family."

"Of course that means we'll have to eat dinner with them."

"All right," said Alice, marching fearlessly into the darkened second-story hallway which smelled of faeces and far worse, "I won't say a word about Labor just this once."

An insolent rat, a street-corner bum of his breed, swaggered out of the abandoned carton that was his poolroom and sneered at her. She clattered a tomato can at him, saying: "Your days are numbered, Chiang Kai-shek." Losing face, he slunk away.

When they all returned to Humbold's car, where the realtor sat piecing together the remnants of his private documents, Alice threw herself into Reinhart's arms.

"Happy, dear?" asked her husband, depositing the baby, now foul from the tenement, on Humbold's blond upholstery.

"Aroused!" She pulled Reinhart after her into the back seat and gave him a kiss that was a sort of horror.

"Wonderful!" said Clendellan, and to Claude: "We'll take it."

No sooner had Reinhart fetched in Margaret from the walk—applying quick artificial respiration to her little friend—than the boss, who had not wanted to sell the building, had produced papers in triplicate, got his clients' signatures and a deposit for good faith, and barreled back to Vetsville at ninety.

"You planned the whole thing, didn't you?" Reinhart asked admiringly when they were again in Humbold's office.

"But," said the boss, "it was better you didn't catch on till after. You might have blown the deal." He put away his hat and topcoat, which were all over tiny black handprints.

"Claude, you are an artist."

Humbold's right eye vanished in deprecation. "Tell you what I am gonna do, bud. I'm going to make a bidnessman out of you if it kills me, and I'm going to start right out on the square by giving you a full week's commission for your work this P.M. Figure your sixty-five already earned with four days left to go. Now why don't you take off home and tell your daddy you're doing all right? He worries you'll turn bum."

"Thanks, boss."

"Claude."

"Thanks, Claude."

"Yours sincerely, bud."

Reinhart closed the door and went into the outer office, where the secretary was painting a new mouth.

"So you sold the Tenderloin," she asked, "and think you're pretty big. The next thing I know you'll be getting fresh. Well, hands off: I'm engaged."

"No," said Reinhart, "I just tagged along. But what I still can't understand is how Claude was so sure I would suggest going there."

She opened her purse and pitched the lipstick down its gullet. Her penciled brows climbing, she whispered: "Brother, how dumb can you get? He's been trying to peddle that for five years and always carries the Agreement to Buy with him. . . . What are you getting, half the commission?"

"I don't know anything about that," Reinhart said pridefully, meaning everything. "But he's giving me my whole week's salary for whatever it was I did."

"Now that's fair," she cried, though still whispering. "He makes nine and a quarter and gives you sixty-five." Her cute little chicken-rump head danced in scorn. "Who's ever going to marry somebody so weak-minded? Not Genevieve Raven!"

Reinhart was not in the least affected by her peevishness, which he believed to be a standard item in an office girl's kit, so he bade her goodbye till the morrow and left, being careful with the door. Yet, in a moment he popped back, and the wind came with him.

"Who in the devil is Genevieve Raven?"

"*Me!*" she screamed.

◇

Thomas Berger was born in Ohio in 1924, educated at the University of Cincinnati and at Columbia, and now lives in Palisades, New York. He was in the U.S. Army of Occupation in Berlin after World War II, and his first novel, Crazy in Berlin *(1958), tells of Carlo Reinhart's adventures in that same situation. It is an extravagantly funny and bitterly satirical book, hard on Americans and Germans alike, and it set the tone for its sequel,* Reinhart in Love *(1962), which tells of Reinhart's travails after he returns to America and from which "Reinhart Goes to Work" is excerpted. His third novel is a thoroughly unique work; called* Little Big Man *(1964), it purports to be the memoirs of one Jack Crabb, who was captured and raised by Indians, who lived to be one hundred and eleven years old, who during that time had the fortune or misfortune to have been present at most every famous event in the history of the West and to have known most every famous man of that time, and who gives the lowdown on what really happened and what those men were really like. It presents a new view of American history, to say the least, and it is of course comic and satiric; yet the book is said to be meticulously accurate in its details and entirely true to the real, unromanticized spirit of those times. There is a fourth novel, much shorter, a strange sort of murder story, called* Killing Time *(1967).*

In Reinhart in Love, *Berger's conscious intention was to create an alternative Ohio to Sherwood Anderson's. In fact, however, what he seems more truly to have done is re-create Sinclair Lewis' Midwest, bringing it up to date with our bizarre postwar times. Like Lewis, he uses caricature and exaggeration as his methods for getting at how things are, and his modern material seems even better suited than Lewis' to these methods. Berger uses as his point-of-view figure Carlo Reinhart, a giant, gentle man, an open-eyed, open-mouth modern Candide, who drifts into a series of increasingly loony adventures. Each character he meets talks out of his own peculiar bag, in a language and with motivations that are idiosyncratic yet somehow typical—that strange mixture of the ordinary and the extraordinary which can still be found on the fringes and at the very center of small-town life in America. Claude Humbold is one such figure, and like Babbitt he is a projection of the contemporary "bidnessman" with a curious set of ethics and a great line of somehow original clichés. "Never sell a man what he wants! . . . Because that's not what they want!" says Humbold, his salesman's psychology instinctively fathoming the subtle paradoxes of modern motivational research methods. But he is generous and egalitarian and has authority and esprit—and these qualities are set out in separate paragraphs, although admittedly somewhat ambiguously. A line like "The Big Boy upstairs . . . [is] the greatest bidnessman of them all" sounds like Babbitt under the influence of Norman Vincent Peale, but there is really more reverence in it than commercialism. For, as Reinhart quickly perceives: "Money? Ah no, it wasn't money which your true businessman lusted after . . . it was love." In the very different days that Lewis satirized—Babbitt was published in 1922—small-town, small-time businessmen were basic in the American social economy. But now they are an embattled minority, and any one of them needs to have his whole heart and soul behind his operation. Claude Humbold's very name suggests the humbleness and humility behind the boldness. He, like the misfits and the vanishing American, Joe, is part of the vanishing breed of individualists. What any "normal" American would do these days is what Reinhart plans to do when he finishes college: "be instantly hired for the young-executive training by Whirlpool Inc., the great detergents empire of southern Ohio, and issued a wife, sedan, and six-room cottage from their stockroom. . . ."*

JOHN HEFFRON PORTER

The Pale Virgins
Shrouded in Snow

◇◇◇◇◇◇◇

"THIS GUY who was once a lifeguard and then got a job buying old gold from door to door never knew why they tapped him for the job, unless perhaps the one man they'd always wanted was just the kind of moon-face he happened to be, with a twenty-mile stare like you," said Scotty, grinning at Mr. Ennis across the desk in the disorderly donkey's-hide office they shared at S & D talking a mile a minute, either because one of Scotty's talking jags had just come over him or because he guessed the long yaddity-yaddity Mr. Ennis had listened to that morning over the phone, and to which he had answered only "Uh," came from the rubbery lips of his lawyer announcing that Mr. Ennis' wife had finally got custody of the kid, a long, thin drink of water called Nicky who used to go down to the Village with his father to listen to Eddie Condon's jam sessions in a long silence broken only when the little boy shook his head and, in his squeaking treble, said "Solid, Jack."

"Anyway, there he was," said Scotty, "shaken hands with, clopped on the back, bonded, asking the *yentas* of Brooklyn if they happened to have any old gold, exhibiting his good faith with a small pair of scales and a bottle of aqua regia, before he'd had time to tell them there, in the office, he'd give it a whirl. He knocked them dead from the start, staggering back up the three flights to the office with a briefcase bulging with old wedding rings he'd had to help them pry loose from their fingers, watches, brooches, fountain pens, buttons, picture frames, and believe it or not, from the darker purlieus of Brownsville, gold inlays of every conceivable size and shape and plenty of big, solid, fourteen-carat gold teeth. It got to be a regular routine, 'Any gold teeth, today, lady, you're not living on pork chops,' and the time I was going to tell you about, this tall, tan, terrific number, like they used to say on the marquee of the old Paradise Club a spade girl in a peach-colored kimono that just waved in the breeze, said,

'No, honey, ah ain't got no gole to sell, but ah sho got something else you genlemen likes,' and he did. It got to be that some streets he couldn't touch twice or he'd have taken out all the profits in trade, so he got home hot as a pistol and raging for whisky. He was the guy I told you about, who picked up this nurse his gang shagged that swabbed them each, *faute de mieux*, I suppose, with silver nitrate, and when they got back to the bar wouldn't touch a drop of anything but lime coke with a cherry. 'I don't think it's nice for girls to go smelling of whiskey,' she said. What a build the guy had, moonface and all. He was the best handball player in Coney."

"But the rich who have pocketed their winnings, why are they so glum?" said Mr. Ennis, in whose mind the phrase had been running since he read it.

And all that Mr. Ennis had had to do to make Scotty tilt that lean Jimmy Walker face to one side and take off was to look up from the dog-food advertisement he was writing and on which, among the doodles, he had ballooned in only the one word "arf" and say, not so much to Scotty as to the cold, yellow afternoon: "What are we doing here?"

Mr. Ennis listened to Scotty without speaking a word or hearing himself say any. To Scotty, the Little King, as he thought of Ennis, the little man who might have been sitting behind a ticket window labeled "Mr. Ennis" to annoy the anonymity, seemed to be listening not with his ears at all but with the slightly exophthalmic, batrachian, lipoid eyes that occasionally peered up from a pad and stared at Scotty and having regarded the after-noon for a moment—or, on a terrace three floors below, the Powers models in their furs and violets catching for ten minutes the unseasonable sunlight of early March, wet and with a smell of spring, just as likely to make the pavements bloom with hurdy-gurdy waltzes as to blur the build-ings with an unseasonable mist of snow—looked down at the pad again. There was the hanged man. There were matchstick men climbing staircases that ascended through the sea. There was, recognizably, Louis, the Art Director, smoking a reefer on the fire escape, twelve feet tall. And Craig, the Account Executive, with the utterly unbelievable little bottles in his hand, sniffing in a stable, happy among horses.

Suddenly onto the windowsill there settled a pigeon whose flutter and feathers, iridescent as oil on a sheet of stagnant water, drew Mr. Ennis' attention to the window again. In the yellow light of an imagined beach, sea-crabs scuttled through the sand. The light was yellow where the actual sunshine cut like a spade across the street, though far away, where pres-ently Mr. Ennis could watch the evening hang, it was misty blue. And into the light of the terrace, three floors below, a man came straddling with a red and green beach chair already opened, looking like a wooden lobster cradled in his arms. He set it down, gently, and into a tube at the back of the chair he inserted a little parasol with fringe. Then the man looked up for a moment at the overcast from which wisps of sunlight protruded like straws sticking down through the boards of a hayloft, and went indoors.

While Mr. Ennis watched, he felt rather than heard Scotty's voice go on. Then another man came out and helped the first one look at the weather. While they were craning their necks at the sky, a third man waddled out with a beach chair and placed it opposite the other one and then the three men went into a huddle, the first man shrugging his shoulders and, with his elbows against his chest, spreading his hands out wide, the palms turned up, in the classic gesture of doubt or indifference or despair. And then, as Mr. Ennis grew tired of watching, Scotty's voice, saying ". . . and not only in Brooklyn but on any man's court, except for the fact that Moon-face was too god-damned lazy to do anything but sun himself on the beach all day," came fading in, as if he and Mr. Ennis were in a train that had just that minute roared out of a tunnel.

"And guzzle whisky from a Coke bottle," said Scotty, "which made him about as useful a lifeguard as if he'd been a barrel of Schenley's Reserve. That's how one of the girls got drowned, when Lippy had taken off from the tower and was being pursued by song birds at ten thousand feet. But oh what a lovely big son of a bitch he was, with the slow, easy walk of a cat and a way of ambling all over the court that fooled the hell out of you until you noticed that wherever the ball was, there was Lippy first, cuffing it back like a panther I saw in the Bronx Zoo, taking a crack at its cub. Good enough, by God and by Jesus, to lick a guy who turned out to be State Champion, though you couldn't get Lippy into any of the matches if you goosed him with a red-hot poker, either because he was too lazy, or indifferent, or perhaps because the only courts he liked were the ones I used to use myself out there on the edge of Coney where you don't have to ask the way to the ocean to take a dip. Anyway, that's all he did when he wasn't sucking whisky from a Coke bottle up on the tower, play handball and mostly lie in the sun without saying a word for hours except to ask for a light, even if there was a bull session among the local thinkers, one of whom now writes for *Partisan Review* and lectures at Columbia, where I, too, became cultured and refined, and one of whom, before he got his in the back of the head with a sawed-off shotgun, rose high in the chicken rackets in Long Island City."

Out on the terrace, the two beach chairs, with now a third one added since Mr. Ennis had looked away, were arranged for conversation and the three men stood at the far edge of the terrace studying the chairs through frames of fingers. One of the men was tall and slightly bent, as if the weight of his tremendously heavy, black-rimmed glasses pulled him forward, and when, presently, the three men walked off the terrace in a body, the first man bowed the tall one through the open door then quickly stepped inside, himself, leaving the terrace abandoned to the three bright beach chairs in the muddy light.

"And that was the life," said Scotty, "for one whose pulse ran slow and easy, pillowing the head on the warm, maternal sand, and, on duty or off, watching the whale-backed waves as green as Sandwich glass curl in and up until they shattered onto the beach in a glint of spray, from early spring through fall, until, when winter came, it was time for Lippy to hole up in the Half Moon Hotel where the mere presence of his animal spirits was a great consolation to the fat lady and the midgets who used to make that their home. Sunbathe and drink, play handball and watch the waves, that was all Lippy did until the dame got drowned in front of his tower, which was only a minor shock to his system, though, in spite of being Lippy, he was fired on the spot, until a few minutes after the event the late bather turned out to be Nola, his private piece, and for all I know, though I am skeptical in these affairs, his own dear darling. It hit him hard and he stayed hard hit, quite possibly because he was too lazy a man to break in another piece, except of course for an occasional quickie with the mice they used to pick up at the Legion dances where, as a matter of fact, he'd first latched onto Nola when she was just fourteen, though tall for her age, and with fake working papers was holding down a responsible job wearing a G-string in Salvador Dali's Dream of Venus at the World's Fair."

"Hello, Bill," said Scotty, as Craig strode in, wearing his invisible cavalry boots, and Mr. Ennis added: "I was telling Scot about the Dream of Venus at the World's Fair. Did you attend?"

"I was in the ro-day-o," said Craig, in his faint, flat Texas drawl, pressing the palm of his hand like a suction cup on Mr. Ennis' desk—"You got that booklet, Scotty? I'd like to go over it in my office for a minute"—"and if you bastards haven't anything better to do that account's going out the window."

"The rich who have pocketed their winnings, why are they so glum?" said Mr. Ennis.

"Think of all the buttons you'd have to sew on ladies' underwear to make the dough we pay you," said Craig, with his heavy, almost audible wink.

"We rich who have pocketed our winnings, we think of that," said Mr. Ennis.

Craig grinned and jingled the change in his pocket and turning on his heel marched out of the office, and Scotty, who had got up and brushed by the hat-rack on which he had hung his velvet-collared topcoat, his white silk scarf, and his homburg, said, "Keep it on an even keel," and fell in by Craig's side. A few feet from the door, Craig stopped and turned around and coming back to the entrance, said: "Oh, by the way, I just heard about Gwen. If there's anything I can do . . ."

"You might let me catch you in bed with her," said Mr. Ennis, "so I can get custody of the kid. But it won't be any fun. It hasn't been any fun for me for twenty years."

"You should worry," said Craig, trying to keep a harsh note of envy out of his voice, "with all the women you've got on the string," and gave Mr. Ennis another wink. Leaving the door open, Craig strode down the long red-carpeted hall under the glowing neon tube, always on dress parade, erect, stamping along with his bracket legs and his feet just slightly spread to keep the invisible spurs from catching, the great hams surging under his coattails, until he and Scotty turned into the foot of the staircase almost half a block away and went out of sight toward the row of offices with the Spanish grillwork doors one flight above.

And now as they walk along the hallway, thought Mr. Ennis, they pass a man who makes a half-salute, grinning, and saying "Hi!" and Scotty says: "How's it, keed, how's it?" wondering which one of the eight hundred employees that might have been, and then they come into Craig's office where Craig sits down at his desk and with a studied pretense of having to search among the dry rattle of pencils and paper clips, grunts, a satisfied smile spread all over his face, and fishes up the two unbelievable little bottles so that he can give Scotty his latest lecture on the effects of feeding and not feeding whole wheat to dogs. No, thought Mr. Ennis, no. There is not any man like that. He turned away from the neon-glowing hall to write on his pad and then look at the terrace again.

The three men had come back, one of them now wrestling a camera on a tripod whose supports trailed after it like legs, long, thin and broken. He set the camera up in an angle of the terrace and, making a bow from which he didn't straighten, sighted through a camera lens at the group of beach chairs a few paces away. For a moment he stood there adjusting the camera, while the other two men gesticulated at one another and looked up at the sky, and then the tall man in the dark-framed glasses came and peered through the camera and, standing up, shook his head slowly from side to side. The first man moved the camera imperceptibly to the left. The tall man nodded abruptly; the first man made a beckoning gesture to the third who, waiting by the door now, like a man in a silent movie, called inside; and out onto the terrace in the gentle, wavering, buttercup-yellow light there walked three girls apparently naked under their glossy, brown fur coats.

At a nod from the assistant photographer, they slipped off their coats and piled them onto the balustrade, and shivering in their short two-piece bathing suits sat down and stretched out each on one of the beach chairs under the gaudy, fringed umbrellas while the tall man prepared to take their pictures.

"Look," said Mr. Ennis, swiveling his chair around as Scotty walked into the room a few minutes later, "just look at that."

"Do you know what that man keeps in his desk?" asked Scotty, walking over to the window. "Have you got the faintest idea of what Bill Craig keeps in the middle drawer of his desk?"

"Sure," said Mr. Ennis. "We rich who keep vials of dog dung in our desks, why are we so glum? Just look at that."

"OK." said Scotty, "O.K., you saw the dead horse in the bathtub first. O.K. Who are your friends?"

"Just look," said Mr. Ennis. "Just look at them there."

"Jesus," said Scotty, looking down at the three models in the chill wavering undersea light, offering their long, lovely bodies to the camera's eye, "Jesus Christ. What are they selling now?"

"Girls," said Mr. Ennis.

"All right," said Scotty, disgustedly, "bleed. But what the hell are we, the Mayo Brothers? Can you tap? Can you imitate three Hawaiians playing the guitar? Would you rather be keeping Bill Craig out of jail for not curbing himself? Would you rather be up at Columbia, lecturing not on art, God forbid, but on metallurgy in the time of Donne? Did I ever tell you how Lippy got a job buying gold from the housewives of Brooklyn?

"He was broken up badly when his Nola gurgled and sank, and, brother, there was a loss to humanity. I love the human face and I love the human body and I do not believe that I have ever seen a more lovesome thing than Nola Krinsky, not since she drowned in eight feet of water at Coney Island these eleven years past. She would have made these cookies," he said, pointing down to the terrace, "look like mannequins in Macy's window because she moved as if she had the bones of a bird, with no more thought of how you saw her, and she had the long, narrow waist and the tangerine tits and the golden hair framing a little face with ivory curves and wide green eyes that no one has seen since Aphrodite came laughing out of the foam of the sea. And Lippy saw her there at the Legion dance, chewing gum with her girl friends in a corner, shy because she was only fourteen and felt that her job was silly. Lippy took her out on the floor without saying a word and did the big apple until Auld Lang Syne when he took her back to her mother who'd been sitting on the stoop of a brownstone in Williamsburg with a watch in her hand, wondering if it was going to be all right, since ten. But Lippy figured let *his* mother worry, and the next time he was off duty at the beach he went out to the Fair, past those fantastical statues, whipped cream bronzed over, and came to the Dream of Venus where sure enough he found Nola Krinsky floating in a tank of water surrounded by rubber cows and things and wearing nothing but a G-string so the world could admire what God had wrought. When Nola came out the side door at two that morning, she was guarded by four guys from the show, one on each side and one fore and aft, as if they still had hopes and figured that a girl who floats around like that is going to meet up with some pretty tough propositioning as soon as she steps onto dry land, but the minute they saw the way she looked at Lippy and the way Lippy *looked,* the four of them blew. She never went home again, and she never went back to the show. That was for Lippy. I've never doped it out to this day how Lippy squared it with her mother or with the cops, but that was in another country. Possibly they do these things better in Williamsburg. Anyway, she was Lippy's girl for two years and then that was that, and Lippy, who had lost all his enjoyments save an occasional bounce and the bottle, fled from them who onetime did him seek and had to look for an inland occupation. He went into a place that said 'Employment Agency' two flights up, but Lippy in his trance walked three, right into this gold-buying outfit I told you about, and the next thing he knew he was establishing an all-time record bringing 'em rings and gold teeth, until a year later he joined the Marines. What happened to him since I don't know, because I lost touch with Lippy and the old stamping ground, but some day I'll bunk into him some place and he'll ask me for a light.

"I think that even the great Charles Saunders Santiago Peirce got his doctrine of Tychistic Agapism, or love and chance, right out of the bottle, and the crystal ball clouds over when you ask it, please, how Lippy came to be buying gold or you to sit here staring or those girls down there to be offering their tender little lettuces to the cold March air."

Mr. Ennis looked away from Scotty as soon as he stopped, and Scotty, glancing down at the models again, thought rather dejectedly that you might as well talk to the wall as try to get a rise out of Ennis, though perhaps it was mostly because his sad stories turned out to be funny, and the funny ones sad.

The models were still stretched out in the beach chairs, shivering between pictures, then, when the photographer was ready to shoot, holding still in their lazy poses and producing their wide, white smiles. The gray, fleeing clouds, grown thicker now, moved slowly across the face of the sun and for a few minutes no sunlight at all fell onto the terrace. The models got up, stiff-legged, to fetch their coats and lying down on the beach chairs again held the coats over themselves like blankets while they and the men from the studio watched for a rift in the sky.

Scotty, who had a date with a client at three, decided to call it a day and got up, yawning, and stretched, and said to Mr. Ennis: "Better put out some smudge pots yonder, Pops; that's delicate, that is, and it freezes fast." Then, as if in pantomime, he drew his white silk scarf across his neck and let it slither down on either side in rapid, rustling folds, and put on his topcoat, lifting the collar just under the turn of the scarf and set his homburg straight on his head, stuck a cigarette into the corner of his mouth, and nodded to Mr. Ennis. It ought to be sunny, he thought, sunny and sharp with good shadows on things, and, standing in the doorway, looked at the window.

The day had turned a warm yellow again, so surprisingly that Scotty said to Mr. Ennis: "By Jesus, it did!" before he saw the first few flakes of snow whirl slowly from the gauzy sky.

As Scotty stood there, the snow fell faster, until, in the time it took him to strike a match for his cigarette, the room was darkened and the world outside the window flecked with white and gray. Silvery and shadowed in the streaks of light, the flakes came thicker now. Snow drifted lightly down the windless gulf between the buildings, blurring the fractured outline of the roofs.

Scotty stepped to the window to look down at the girls and there they were, still stretched out on the beach chairs under the gaudy green, red and white umbrellas, their coats on the floor beside them, gazing up at the sky with such utter amazement that Scotty thought he could see the snowflakes melt on their wide open mouths. It looked as if snow would be falling forever and the girls in their flimsy suits forever gaping at snow. Scotty turned to Mr. Ennis, and Mr. Ennis for the first time in weeks was laughing, laughing so hard that he shook and the water ran out of his eyes and he clung helplessly to the frame of the window pointing to the girls on the terrace.

Scotty sighed with relief, and bowing low to Mr. Ennis, twice, with his hands behind him, said: "I thank you, my father thanks you, my cousins thank you, and hope you will catch us again," and giving his homburg a little tap walked out of the office.

◇

John Heffron Porter was born in White Plains in 1913, has his B.A. from Antioch and an M.A. from Columbia, worked in advertising for many years, then taught English at Barnard, Sarah Lawrence, and Wagner, and now lives in New York City, where he is working on a novel.

"The Pale Virgins Shrouded in Snow" is like a scene in a play or a curtain raiser in which various little actions and distractions are played off against the man who cannot laugh—until he finally does and the bit is over. At first it is hard to determine whose story is being told: perhaps Mr. Ennis' immovable glumness is just a setting for the long central fantasy-memoir of Lippy the lifeguard, the buyer of gold; if not, why does it take up so much of the story? The whole effect is as of one of Saul Steinberg's drawings, an elaborately scrambled fantasy, none of which turns out to be extraneous or unrelated to the central theme. The theme in this story is the absurd and incidental nature of work. Lippy's story is an embroidered analogy of Mr. Ennis' situation, and although he does not react to it, it provides the framework for his ability to see the absurdity of his own occupation in the wonderfully ridiculous sight of the cold March snow falling on the amazed girls being photographed in bathing suits on a balcony three stories below his office. Scotty in this story performs the function of Joe, the vanishing American: he points out the essential quality of the occupation. "The rich who have pocketed their winnings" in an ad agency are not trapped in heavy, senseless labor on the assembly line with no chance of doing better, but their sense of the personal degradation of their work is proportionately greater because they have been to college, have "creative" talents, and are in their work by choice. The account executive with his

cavalry officer's manners and the vials of dog dung in his desk, Lippy's fourteen-year-old girl "holding down a responsible job wearing a G-string in Salvador Dali's Dream of Venus at the World's Fair," the photographers with their camera and beach chairs and the fur-coated girls, even Scotty with his white silk scarf and his homburg on his way to meet the client—there is no way to make any of this seem like work unless absurdity is admitted as central. This doesn't mean that it is without skill. The photographers are shown to be precise and skillful; Scotty, walking down the hall, demonstrates the essential skills of differential ritual greeting in the office. The account executive sniffing his vials and lecturing on the scientific effects of whole wheat on dog digestion is practicing the equally essential skill of expertise and presentation of "the facts." Advertising is one of many industries whose "products" are only adjuncts to something that people will buy; thus its employees are denied the dignity of the definition of their work as the production of something necessary or useful. Nor is any ideal of service or benefit to mankind being served. Listening to jazz with his son in Greenwich Village is what has meaning for Mr. Ennis, and Scotty knows that therefore Mr. Ennis must be made to see that the answer to "what are we doing here?" is this: We are making a living the only way it can be made, the world being what it is, as an amusing pastime. Once it becomes a game, played as Scotty plays it, with a certain amount of flair and pleasure in his own style, it can be tolerated; as Scotty says, "Would you rather be up at Columbia, lecturing not on art, God forbid, but on metallurgy in the time of Donne?" When specialization and professionalization are carried to such extremes, what makes selling dog food any more ridiculous than anything else? The bureaucratic world of government agencies and big business and giant industries has an aura of power and unbelievable scale and reach around the geographic world, beyond it even. But the actual day-to-day work done in any particular office tends to be more and more meaningless to the man who does it. When money is not a problem, people have time to wonder about the meaning of life; they don't often find it on the job unless, as some hold, absurdity is the meaning of life.

⬦–⬦

In the four stories in this section we have seen some of the ways in which the work a man does defines some aspects of his social character and ignores others; there is a consistent thread of longing to coordinate personal dignity and pride in personal skills with what the world will pay for, a longing that is consistently frustrated by the unbelievable scale—in the architectural sense of the necessary proportional relationship of parts to the whole—of work that is based on the precise and indefatigable arbitrary rationality of mass production powered by superhuman energies. Man can no longer pit his skills against the wild forces of Nature, except for the amusement of others, in rodeos; when he works directly for the machine, on the production line, his skills are defined by the speed and standards of value of the entire mechanical process of that production, not by his special part in it; the enterprising independent entrepreneur is reduced to marginal single transactions with marginal people; finally, work as the skillful use of art and language, as in advertising, supports man's sense of his own value only through the very human ability to recognize the absurdity of it and maintain an efficient and dignified, amused distance from it. The essential and hardest part of work for pay nowadays seems to be the ability to see it as unrelated to individual value and yet necessary to the support of the individual and his massive American society.

◇–◇–◇

The stories in the first of these four sections showed the condition of the individual who finds himself "alone" in the troubled situation of not being able to act in any way that seems sensible or important to him, not struggling with the external forces of society and his fellow man, but denying them any ascription of ultimate truth or value. The subsequent three sections on family, community, and work served to "explain" to some extent how the individual came to be the way he was shown to be in the first section. The pattern seems to be a dual and simultaneous breaking down of traditional modes and forming of new modes to serve specific new situations. There would also seem to be a qualitative difference between the new and the old: the old family and community and work systems of behavior and belief had, still have, a feeling of permanent moral value; while the new, taken up on a pragmatic and tentative basis, are invested with very little conviction of their permanence or moral value. This would seem to be an effect of the central experience of the individual in this climate of constant change—an experience of distance from his institutions and from himself.

Part II presents stories that show how some contemporary fiction writers see changes and confusions in the way people used to be differentiated by religion, race, and class as also contributing to the individual's difficulties in knowing who he is or how to act.

Differentiations

and

Confusions

IN RELIGION—JEWISH CONFLICTS
IN ASSIMILATION

·

IN RACE—THE VISIBLE NEGRO

·

IN CLASS—MINUTE DISTINCTIONS
IN THE MIDDLE

Part Two

DIFFERENTIATIONS AND CONFUSIONS

With change *the only constant, and with standardization of the rule, ways of differentiating among men by religion, race, and class are not as meaningful in America today as they once were. A man does not necessarily hold to the religion of his childhood any more than he spends his whole life in the house or even the town where he grew up. The new, post-World War II mobility has brought with it great freedom of choice for most Americans, and this freedom, and all the choices involved within it, have been both blessing and burden. Certainly the possibility of moving away from the binding definition of the identifying group into which he had been born meant new opportunity for the man who was able to remake his life along new patterns. But the old definitions of religion, race, and class often provided identity and security. The man who had experienced prejudice because of his religion might have taken strength from his faith in it; the man who experienced discrimination because of his race might have found warmth and companionship in the racial ghetto; and the man who experienced exploitation because of his class might have taken consolation from the very rigidity of the class structure which imposed apparently inevitable limits on his aspirations. In the new suburbs, where most of America's growth occurred after the war, distinctions according to religion, race, and class of origin tended to be less important than more subtle and confusing differentiations according to "image" or "style"—defined by patterns of consumption, leisure, language, and so forth. In such a situation the struggle for status and prestige is carried on in a bewildering variety of ways: almost every activity becomes an opportunity for judging one's own claims for prestige against another's. The possibility of choice brings with it the competitive necessity of choice, and the lack of traditional guidelines coupled with a profusion of expert advice often results in a sense of insecurity and stress and a feeling of personal loss and inadequacy. It becomes not so much a matter of conflicting ways of life dictated by the absolute values of established religions or classes, as it does a matter of a constant state of individual inner tension between the polar necessities of being like everyone else and yet unique, a tension made doubly difficult by the fact that everyone else is in the same dilemma.*

565

Conflict in cultural assimilation has always been a theme of American fiction; in the years after the waves of immigration, when nationality of origin was a major basis of differentiation among people, what we may call Melting Pot Fiction traditionally dramatized a family conflict: the first generation's clinging to Old Country ways versus the younger generation's taking up American ways. Contemporary fiction reflects more subtle and more general problems. When differentiations break down, individuals experience not only a loss of sense of belonging but a loss of sense of identity, with attendant loneliness and confusion about what is allowed for them or expected of them. The willingness to conform is frustrated by the lack of clear-cut goals. Conformity for the sake of being ."just like everyone else" when no one else is anything very inspiring ceases to be a goal in itself. And contemporary fiction, as we have seen and shall see, is constantly celebrating the struggles of individuals who resist conformity. The dread of becoming more and more like everyone else is now almost as prevalent as the older fear of being too different. This is cause for rejoicing, no doubt; but it can as well be the cause of frustration and bitterness to those virtually outside our society who have been told that the differences no longer exist but who know from how they live that the prejudice, the discrimination, and the exploitation are now only more subtle and more confusing. If the freedom of choice involved in the new mobility seems unsettling to many Americans, to be denied that freedom must be far more intolerable still.

Differentiations and Confusions

IN RELIGION—JEWISH CONFLICTS IN
ASSIMILATION

*The two most conspicuous developments in modern religion—the Ecumeni-
cal Movement and the so-called "God Is Dead" Movement—both reflect
diminishment in religious faith: for differences in religious belief are not
easily reconciled when those beliefs are strongly held; and whatever else
God's death may represent, it is obviously a analogy to Man's loss of faith.
Decades ago, fiction expressed the emotional and ethical implications to
the individual of loss of faith, although the theologians and news magazines
would now have us believe in the death of God as news. Contemporary
standards of morality are of course quite at odds with the teachings of any
church. Churches thus threatened with the loss of their traditional dual
roles, as centers of worship and as forces in socialization, have sought (as
threatened bureaucratic organizations always do) to find other justifications
for their offices. Catholic priests, Protestant ministers, and Jewish rabbis
increasingly make common cause, not only with one another, but with
nonclergical social workers, in entirely nondevotional "good works"—ranging from teen-age dances in church basements to civil rights demonstrations
hundreds of miles from their home parish. Loss of faith in religion and
loss of guidance from church no doubt contribute to the individual's feeling
of being somehow alone and adrift today, but the real cause of these effects
is as much social as religious. Religious beliefs intensely held by a group,
and separate and distinct from those of another group, contributed to the
individual's sense of his own identity as a member of his group: they were
a component of the structure of social organization. As the belief dimin-
ishes, the structure disintegrates, contributing further to social disorganization. Thus, contemporary fiction dealing with conflicts in the area of religion
is now not so likely to be concerned with a crisis of faith, as with a crisis
of identity.*

*For a number of reasons, the stories that follow show contemporary con-
flicts in religious identity in terms of only one situation: that of the Jew in
America. One reason for this is that, granted limited space, it is obviously
useful to limit the stories to one area for purposes of depth and comparison.
A more real reason is that there was really no other choice: the religious*

567

identity of such a once-distinctive group as the Irish-Catholics, for instance, fell into the melting pot along with their national identity, even before one of their number, John F. Kennedy, became the very epitome of modern American ideals. But the most important reason for our choice of stories is that over the last few decades those American writers who are Jews seem to have been writing brilliantly. In this connection one always hears the names of Saul Bellow, Bernard Malamud, Philip Roth, Norman Mailer, and Bruce Jay Friedman, but there are dozens of other excellent American Jewish writers (some mentioned in the Appendix), many of whom have found the central situations and themes of their fiction in the American Jew's conflicts in regard to cultural assimilation. Jews, as much as any of the other groups that have come to America, have felt a pride in their cultural identity and have fought hard against losing it. Their fiction documents the conflicts and regrets involved in moving from a highly differentiated world with stylized traditions to the standardized American world where individual differences are supposed to be a matter of choice. There has always been a dialogue in Jewish literature over preserving Jewish racial and religious identity in the diaspora; and whether the fruitfulness of that theme for fiction, or the traditional Jewish concern with education and achievement, is responsible for the so-called "Jewish renaissance" in contemporary American writing, no one seems able to say.

At any rate, the sampling of stories that follows does no real justice to all the fine fiction that is available in this area. But it should be noted that the very fact of the existence of this literature—instead of, for instance, an Irish-Catholic literature about conflicts that no longer exist—shows once again how fiction both expresses or "springs from" the actual problems and conflicts of our society and also illuminates the consequences to the individual of how we live.

ISAAC BASHEVIS SINGER

A Wedding in Brownsville

◇◇◇◇◇◇◇

THE WEDDING had been a burden to Dr. Solomon Margolin from the very
beginning. True, it was to take place on a Sunday, but Gretl had been right
when she said that was the only evening in the week they could spend
together. It always turned out that way. His responsibilities to the community made him give away the evenings that belonged to her. The Zionists
had appointed him to a committee; he was a board member of a Jewish
scholastic society; he had become co-editor of an academic Jewish quarterly. And though he often referred to himself as agnostic and even an
atheist, nevertheless for years he had been dragging Gretl to Seders at
Abraham Mekheles', a *Landsman* from Sencimin. Dr. Margolin treated
rabbis, refugees, and Jewish writers without charge, supplying them with
medicines and, if necessary, a hospital bed. There had been a time when he
had gone regularly to the meetings of the Senciminer Society, had accepted
positions in their ranks, and had attended all the parties. Now Abraham
Mekheles was marrying off his youngest daughter, Sylvia. The minute the
invitation arrived, Gretl had announced her decision: she was not going to
let herself be carted off to a wedding somewhere out in the wilds of
Brownsville. If he, Solomon, wanted to go and gorge himself on all kinds of
greasy food, coming home at three o'clock in the morning, that was his
prerogative.

Dr. Margolin admitted to himself that his wife was right. When would he
get a chance to sleep? He had to be at the hospital early Monday morning.
Moreover he was on a strict fat-free diet. A wedding like this one would be
a feast of poisons. Everything about such celebrations irritated him now:
the Anglicized Yiddish, the Yiddishized English, the ear-splitting music
and unruly dances. Jewish laws and customs were completely distorted;
men who have no regard for Jewishness wore skullcaps; and the reverend
rabbis and cantors aped the Christian ministers. Whenever he took Gretl to
a wedding or Bar Mitzvah, he was ashamed. Even she, born a Christian,

could see that American Judaism was a mess. At least this time he would be spared the trouble of making apologies to her.

Usually after breakfast on Sunday, he and his wife took a walk in Central Park, or, when the weather was mild, went to the Palisades. But today Solomon Margolin lingered in bed. During the years, he had stopped attending the functions of the Senciminer Society; meanwhile the town of Sencimin had been destroyed. His family there had been tortured, burned, gassed. Many Senciminers had survived, and, later, come to America from the camps, but most of them were younger people whom he, Solomon, had not known in the old country. Tonight everyone would be there: the Senciminers belonging to the bride's family and the Tereshpolers belonging to the groom's. He knew how they would pester him, reproach him for growing aloof, drop hints that he was a snob. They would address him familiarly, slap him on the back, drag him off to dance. Well, even so, he had to go to Sylvia's wedding. He had already sent out the present.

The day had dawned, gray and dreary as dusk. Overnight, a heavy snow had fallen. Solomon Margolin had hoped to make up for the sleep he was going to lose, but unfortunately he had waked even earlier than usual. Finally he got up. He shaved himself meticulously at the bathroom mirror and also trimmed the gray hair at his temples. Today of all days he looked his age: there were bags under his eyes, and his face was lined. Exhaustion showed in his features. His nose appeared longer and sharper than usual; there were deep folds at the sides of his mouth. After breakfast he stretched out on the living-room sofa. From there he could see Gretl, who was standing in the kitchen, ironing—blonde, faded, middle-aged. She had on a skimpy petticoat, and her calves were as muscular as a dancer's. Gretl had been a nurse in the Berlin hospital where he had been a member of the staff. Of her family, one brother, a Nazi, had died of typhus in a Russian prison camp. A second, who was a Communist, had been shot by the Nazis. Her aged father vegetated at the home of his other daughter in Hamburg, and Gretl sent him money regularly. She herself had become almost Jewish in New York. She had made friends with Jewish women, joined Hadassah, learned to cook Jewish dishes. Even her sigh was Jewish. And she lamented continually over the Nazi catastrophe. She had her plot waiting for her beside his in that part of the cemetery that the Senciminers had reserved for themselves.

Dr. Margolin yawned, reached for the cigarette that lay in an ashtray on the coffee table beside him, and began to think about himself. His career had gone well. Ostensibly he was a success. He had an office on West End Avenue and wealthy patients. His colleagues respected him, and he was an important figure in Jewish circles in New York. What more could a boy from Sencimin expect? A self-taught man, the son of a poor teacher of Talmud? In person he was tall, quite handsome, and he had always had a way with women. He still pursued them—more than was good for him at his age and with his high blood pressure. But secretly Solomon Margolin had always felt that he was a failure. As a child he had been acclaimed a prodigy, reciting long passages of the Bible and studying the Talmud and Commentaries on his own. When he was a boy of eleven, he had sent for a Responsum to the rabbi of Tarnow who had referred to him in his reply as "great and illustrious." In his teens he had become a master in the *Guide for the Perplexed* and the Kuzari. He had taught himself algebra and geometry. At seventeen he had attempted a translation of Spinoza's *Ethics* from Latin into Hebrew, unaware that it had been done before. Everyone predicted he would turn out to be a genius. But he had squandered his talents, continually changing his field of study; and he had wasted years in learning languages, in wandering from country to country. Nor had he had any luck with his one great love, Raizel, the daughter of Melekh the watchmaker. Raizel had married someone else and later been shot by the Nazis. All his life Solomon Margolin had been plagued by the eternal questions. He still lay awake at night trying to solve the mysteries of the universe. He suffered from hypochondria and the fear of death haunted even his dreams. Hitler's carnage and the extinction of his family had rooted out his last hope for better days, had destroyed all his faith in humanity. He had begun to despise the matrons who came to him with their petty ills while millions were devising horrible deaths for one another.

Gretl came in from the kitchen.

"What shirt are you going to put on?"

Solomon Margolin regarded her quietly. She had had her own share of troubles. She had suffered in silence for her two brothers, even for Hans, the Nazi. She had gone through a prolonged change of life. She was tortured by guilt feelings toward him, Solomon. She had become sexually frigid. Now her face was flushed and covered with beads of sweat. He earned more than enough to pay for a maid, yet Gretl insisted on doing all the housework herself, even the laundry. It had become a mania with her. Every day she scoured the oven. She was forever polishing the windows of their apartment on the sixteenth floor and without using a safety belt. All the other housewives in the building ordered their groceries delivered, but Gretl lugged the heavy bags from the supermarket herself. At night she sometimes said things that sounded slightly insane to him. She still suspected him of carrying on with every female patient he treated.

Now husband and wife sized each other up wryly, feeling the strangeness that comes of great familiarity. He was always amazed at how she had lost her looks. No one feature had altered, but something in her aspect had given way: her pride, her hopefulness, her curiosity. He blurted out:

"What shirt? It doesn't matter. A white shirt."

"You're not going to wear the tuxedo? Wait, I'll bring you a vitamin."

"I don't want a vitamin."

"But you yourself say they're good for you."

"Leave me alone."

"Well, it's your health, not mine."

And slowly she walked out of the room, hesitating as if she expected him to remember something and call her back.

2

Dr. Solomon Margolin took a last look in the mirror and left the house. He felt refreshed by the half-hour nap he had had after dinner. Despite his age, he still wanted to impress people with his appearance—even the Senciminers. He had his illusions. In Germany he had taken pride in the fact that he looked like a *Junker,* and in New York he was often aware that he could pass for an Anglo-Saxon. He was tall, slim, blond, blue-eyed. His hair was thinning, had turned somewhat gray, but he managed to disguise these signs of age. He stooped a little, but in company was quick to straighten up. Years ago in Germany he had worn a monocle and though in New York that would have been too pretentious, his glance still retained a European severity. He had his principles. He had never broken the Hippocratic Oath. With his patients he was honorable to an extreme, avoiding every kind of cant; and he had refused a number of dubious associations that smacked of careerism. Gretl claimed his sense of honor amounted to a mania. Dr. Margolin's car was in the garage—not a Cadillac like that of most of his colleagues—but he decided to go by taxi. He was unfamiliar with Brooklyn and the heavy snow made driving hazardous. He waved his hand and at once a taxi pulled over to the curb. He was afraid the driver might refuse to go as far as Brownsville, but he flicked the meter on without a word. Dr. Margolin peered through the frosted window into the wintry Sunday night but there was nothing to be seen. The New York streets sprawled out, wet, dirty, impenetrably dark. After awhile, Dr. Margolin leaned back, shut his eyes, and retreated into his own warmth. His destination was a wedding. Wasn't the world, like this taxi, plunging away somewhere into the unknown toward a cosmic destination? Maybe a cosmic Brownsville, a cosmic wedding? Yes. But why did God—or whatever anyone wanted to call Him—create a Hilter, a Stalin? Why did He need world wars? Why heart attacks, cancers? Dr. Margolin took out a cigarette and lit it hesitantly. What had they been thinking of, those pious uncles of his, when they were digging their own graves? Was immorality possible? Was there such a thing as the soul? All the arguments for and against weren't worth a pinch of dust.

The taxi turned onto the bridge across the East River and for the first time Dr. Margolin was able to see the sky. It sagged low, heavy, red as glowing metal. Higher up, a violet glare suffused the vault of the heavens.

Snow was sifting down gently, bringing a winter peace to the world, just as it had in the past—forty years ago, a thousand years ago, and perhaps a million years ago. Fiery pillars appeared to glow beneath the East River; on its surface, through black waves jagged as rocks, a tugboat was hauling a string of barges loaded with cars. A front window in the cab was open and icy gusts of wind blew in, smelling of gasoline and the sea. Suppose the weather never changed again? Who then would ever be able to imagine a summer day, a moonlit night, spring? But how much imagination—for what it's worth—does a man actually have? On Eastern Parkway the taxi was jolted and screeched suddenly to a stop. Some traffic accident, apparently. The siren on a police car shrieked. A wailing ambulance drew nearer. Dr. Margolin grimaced. Another victim. Someone makes a false turn of the wheel and all a man's plans in this world are reduced to nothing. A wounded man was carried to the ambulance on a stretcher. Above a dark suit and blood-spattered shirt and bow tie the face had a chalky pallor; one eye was closed, the other partly open and glazed. Perhaps he, too, had been going to a wedding, Dr. Margolin thought. He might even have been going to the same wedding as I. . . .

Some time later the taxi started moving again. Solomon Margolin was now driving through streets he had never seen before. It was New York, but it might just as well have been Chicago or Cleveland. They passed through an industrial district with factory buildings, warehouses of coal, lumber, scrap iron. Negroes, strangely black, stood about on the sidewalks, staring ahead, their great dark eyes full of a gloomy hopelessness. Occasionally the car would pass a tavern. The people at the bar seemed to have something unearthly about them, as if they were being punished here for sins committed in another incarnation. Just when Solomon Margolin was beginning to suspect that the driver, who had remained stubbornly silent the whole time, had gotten lost or else was deliberately taking him out of his way, the taxi entered a thickly populated neighborhood. They passed a synagogue, a funeral parlor, and there, ahead, was the wedding hall, all lit up, with its neon Jewish sign and Star of David. Dr. Margolin gave the driver a dollar tip and the man took it without uttering a word.

Dr. Margolin entered the outer lobby and immediately the comfortable intimacy of the Senciminers engulfed him. All the faces he saw were familiar, though he didn't recognize individuals. Leaving his hat and coat at the checkroom, he put on a skullcap and entered the hall. It was filled with people and music, with tables heaped with food, a bar stacked with bottles. The musicians were playing an Israeli march that was a hodgepodge of American jazz with Oriental flourishes. Men were dancing with men, women with women, men with women. He saw black skullcaps, white skullcaps, bare heads. Guests kept arriving, pushing their way through the crowd, some still in their hats and coats, munching hors d'oeuvres, drinking schnapps. The hall resounded with stamping, screaming, laughing, clapping. Flash bulbs went off blindingly as the photographers made their rounds. Seeming to come from nowhere, the bride appeared, briskly sweeping up her train, followed by a retinue of bridesmaids. Dr. Margolin knew everybody, and yet knew nobody. People spoke to him, laughed, winked, and waved, and he answered each one with a smile, a nod, a bow. Gradually he threw off all his worries, all his depression. He became half-drunk on the amalgam of odors: flowers, sauerkraut, garlic, perfume, mustard, and that nameless odor that only Senciminers emit. "Hello, Doctor!" "Hello, Schloime-Dovid, you don't recognize me, eh? Look, he forgot!" There were the encounters, the regrets, the reminiscences of long ago. "But after all, weren't we neighbors? You used to come to our house to borrow the Yiddish newspaper!" Someone had already kissed him: a badly shaven snout, a mouth reeking of whiskey and rotten teeth. One woman was so convulsed with laughter that she lost an earring. Margolin tried to pick it up, but it had already been trampled underfoot. "You don't recognize me, eh? Take a good look! It's Zissl, the son of Chaye Beyle!" "Why don't you eat something?" "Why don't you have something to drink? Come over here. Take a glass. What do you want? Whiskey? Brandy? Cognac? Scotch? With soda? With Coca-Cola? Take some, it's good. Don't let it stand. So long as you're here, you might as well enjoy yourself." "My father? He was killed. They were all killed. I'm the only one left of the entire family." "Berish the son of Feivish? Starved to death in Russia—they sent him to Kazakhstan. His wife? In Israel. She married a Lithuanian." "Sorele? Shot. Together with her children." "Yentl? Here at the wedding. She was standing here just a moment ago. There she is, dancing with that tall fellow." "Abraham Zilberstein? They burned him in the synagogue with twenty others. A mound of charcoal was all that was left, coal and ash." "Yosele Budnik? He passed away years ago. You must mean Yekele Budnik. He has a delicatessen store right here in Brownsville—married a widow whose husband made a fortune in real estate."

"*Lechayim*, Doctor! *Lechayim*, Schloime-Dovid! It doesn't offend you that I call you Schloime-Dovid? To me you're still the same Schloime-Dovid, the little boy with the blond side-curls who recited a whole tractate of the Talmud by heart. You remember, don't you? It seems like only yesterday. Your father, may he rest in peace, was beaming with pride. . . ." "Your brother Chayim? Your Uncle Oyzer? They killed everyone, everyone. They took a whole people and wiped them out with German efficiency: *gleichgeschaltet!*" "Have you seen the bride yet? Pretty as a picture, but too much make-up. Imagine, a grandchild of Reb Todros of Radzin! And her grandfather used to wear two skullcaps, one in front and one in back." "Do you see that young woman dancing in the yellow dress? It's Riva's sister—their father was Moishe the candlemaker. Riva herself? Where all the others ended up: Auschwitz. How close we came ourselves! All of us are really dead, if you want to call it that. We were exterminated, wiped out. Even the survivors carry death in their hearts. But it's a wedding, we should be cheerful." "*Lechayim*, Schloime-Dovid! I would like to congratulate you. Have you a son or a daughter to marry off? No? Well, it's better that way. What's the sense of having children if people are such murderers?"

3

It was already time for the ceremony, but someone still had not come. Whether it was the rabbi, the cantor, or one of the in-laws who was missing, nobody seemed able to find out. Abraham Mekheles, the bride's father, rushed around, scowled, waved his hand, whispered in people's ears. He looked strange in his rented tuxedo. The Tereshpol mother-in-law was wrangling with one of the photographers. The musicians never stopped playing for an instant. The drum banged, the bass fiddle growled, the saxophone blared. The dances became faster, more abandoned, and more and more people were drawn in. The young men stamped with such force that it seemed the dance floor would break under them. Small boys romped around like goats, and little girls whirled about wildly together. Many of the men were already drunk. They shouted boasts, howled with laughter, kissed strange women. There was so much commotion that Solomon Margolin could no longer grasp what was being said to him and simply nodded yes to everything. Some of the guests had attached themselves to him, wouldn't move, and kept pulling him in all directions, introducing him to more and more people from Sencimin and Tereshpol. A matron with a nose covered with warts pointed a finger at him, wiped her eyes, called him Schloimele. Solomon Margolin inquired who she was and somebody told him. Names were swallowed up in the tumult. He heard the same words over and over again: die, shot, burned. A man from Tereshpol tried to draw him aside and was shouted down by several Senciminers calling him an intruder who had no business there. A latecomer arrived, a horse and buggy driver from Sencimin who had become a millionaire in New York. His wife and children had perished, but, already, he had a new wife. The woman, weighted with diamonds, paraded about in a low-cut gown that bared a back, covered with blotches, to the waist. Her voice was husky. "Where did she come from? Who was she?" "Certainly no saint. Her first husband was a swindler who amassed a fortune and then dropped dead. Of what? Cancer. Where? In the stomach. First you don't have anything to eat, then you don't have anything to eat with. A man is always working for the second husband." "What is life anyway? A dance on the grave." "Yes, but as long as you're playing the game, you have to abide by the rules." "Dr. Margolin, why aren't you dancing? You're not among strangers. We're all from the same dust. Over there you weren't a doctor. You were only Schloime-Dovid, the son of the Talmud teacher. Before you know it, we'll all be lying side by side."

Margolin didn't recall drinking anything but he felt intoxicated all the same. The foggy hall was spinning like a carousel; the floor was rocking. Standing in a corner, he contemplated the dance. What different expressions the dancers wore. How many combinations and permutations of being, the Creator had brought together here. Every face told its own story. They were dancing together, these people, but each one had his own philosophy, his own approach. A man grabbed Margolin and for a while he danced in the frantic whirl. Then, tearing himself loose, he stood apart. Who was that woman? He found his eye caught by her familiar form. He knew her! She beckoned to him. He stood baffled. She looked neither young nor old. Where had he known her—that narrow face, those dark eyes, that girlish smile? Her hair was arranged in the old manner, with long braids wound like a wreath around her head. The grace of Sencimin adorned her—something he, Margolin, had long since forgotten. And those eyes, he was in love with those eyes and had been all his life. He half smiled at her and the woman smiled back. There were dimples in her cheeks. She too appeared surprised. Margolin, though he realized he had begun to blush like a boy, went up to her.

"I know you—but you're not from Sencimin?"

"Yes, from Sencimin."

He had learned that voice long ago. He had been in love with that voice.

"From Sencimin—who are you, then?"

Her lips trembled.

"You've forgotten me already?"

"It's a long time since I left Sencimin."

"You used to visit my father."

"Who was your father?"

"Melekh the watchmaker."

Dr. Margolin shivered.

"If I'm not out of my mind then I'm seeing things."

"Why do you say that?"

"Because Raizel is dead."

"I'm Raizel."

"You're Raizel? Here? Oh my God, if that's true—then anything is possible! When did you come to New York?"

"Some time ago."

"From where?"

"From over there."

"But everyone told me that you were all dead."

"My father, my mother, my brother Hershl . . ."

"But you were married!"

"I was."

"If that's true, then anything is possible!" repeated Dr. Margolin, still shaken by the incredible happening. Someone must have purposely deceived him. But why? He was aware there was a mistake somewhere but could not determine where.

"Why didn't you let me know? After all . . ."

He fell silent. She too was silent for a moment.

"I lost everything. But I still had some pride left."

"Come with me somewhere quieter—anywhere. This is the happiest day of my life!"

"But it's night . . ."

"Then the happiest night! Almost—as if the Messiah had come, as if the dead had come to life!"

"Where do you want to go? All right, let's go."

Margolin took her arm and felt at once the thrill, long forgotten, of youthful desire. He steered her away from the other guests, afraid that he might lose her in the crowd, or that someone would break in and spoil his happiness. Everything had returned on the instant: the embarrassment, the agitation, the joy. He wanted to take her away, to hide somewhere alone with her. Leaving the reception hall, they went upstairs to the chapel where the wedding ceremony was to take place. The door was standing open. Inside, on a raised platform stood the permanent wedding canopy. A bottle of wine and a silver goblet were placed in readiness for the ceremony. The chapel with its empty pews and only one glimmering light was full of shadows. The music, so blaring below, sounded soft and distant up here. Both of them hesitated at the threshold. Margolin pointed to the wedding canopy.

"We could have stood there."

"Yes."

"Tell me about yourself. Where are you now? What are you doing?"

"It is not easy to tell."

"Are you alone? Are you attached?"

"Attached? No."

"Would you never have let me hear from you?" he asked. She didn't answer.

Gazing at her, he knew his love had returned with full force. Already, he was trembling at the thought that they might soon have to part. The excitement and expectancy of youth filled him. He wanted to take her in his arms and kiss her, but at any moment someone might come in. He stood beside her, ashamed that he had married someone else, that he had not personally confirmed the reports of her death. "How could I have suppressed all this love? How could I have accepted the world without her? And what will happen now with Gretl?—I'll give her everything, my last cent." He looked round toward the stairway to see if any of the guests had started to come up. The thought came to him that by Jewish law he was not married, for he and Gretl had had only a civil ceremony. He looked at Raizel.

"According to Jewish law, I'm a single man."

"Is that so?"

"According to Jewish law, I could lead you up there and marry you."

She seemed to be considering the import of his words.

"Yes, I realize . . ."

"According to Jewish law, I don't even need a ring. One can get married with a penny."

"Do you have a penny?"

He put his hand to his breast pocket, but his wallet was gone. He started searching in his other pockets. Have I been robbed? he wondered. But how? I was sitting in the taxi the whole time. Could someone have robbed me here at the wedding? He was not so much disturbed as surprised. He said falteringly:

"Strange, but I don't have any money."

"We'll get along without it."

"But how am I going to get home?"

"Why go home?" she said, countering with a question. She smiled with that homely smile of hers that was so full of mystery. He took her by the wrist and gazed at her. Suddenly it occurred to him that this could not be his Raizel. She was too young. Probably it was her daughter who was playing along with him, mocking him. For God's sake, I'm completely confused! he thought. He stood bewildered, trying to untangle the years. He couldn't tell her age from her features. Her eyes were deep, dark, and melancholy. She also appeared confused, as if she, too, sensed some discrepancy. The whole thing is a mistake, Margolin told himself. But where exactly was the mistake? And what had happened to the wallet? Could he have left it in the taxi after paying the driver? He tried to remember how much cash he had had in it, but was unable to. "I must have had too much to drink. These people have made me drunk—dead drunk!" For a long time he stood silent, lost in some dreamless state, more profound than a narcotic trance. Suddenly he remembered the traffic collision he had witnessed on Eastern Parkway. An eerie suspicion came over him: Perhaps he had been more than a witness? Perhaps he himself had been the victim of that accident! That man on the stretcher looked strangely familiar. Dr. Margolin began to examine himself as though he were one of his own patients. He could find no trace of pulse or breathing. And he felt oddly deflated as if some physical dimension were missing. The sensation of weight, the muscular tension of his limbs, the hidden aches in his bones, all seemed to be gone. It can't be, it can't be, he murmured. Can one die without knowing it? And what will Gretl do? He blurted out:

"You're not the same Raizel."

"No? Then who am I?"

"They shot Raizel."

"Shot her? Who told you that?"

She seemed both frightened and perplexed. Silently she lowered her head like someone receiving the shock of bad news. Dr. Margolin continued to ponder. Apparently Raizel didn't realize her own condition. He had heard of such a state—what was it called? Hovering in the World of Twilight. The Astral Body wandering in semi-consciousness, detached from the flesh, without being able to reach its destination, clinging to the illusions and vanities of the past. But could there be any truth to all this superstition? No, as far as he was concerned, it was nothing but wishful thinking. Besides, this kind of survival would be less than oblivion. "I am most probably in a drunken stupor," Dr. Margolin decided. "All this may be one long hallucination, perhaps a result of food poisoning. . . ."

He looked up, and she was still there. He leaned over and whispered in her ear:

"What's the difference? As long as we're together."

"I've been waiting for that all these years."

"Where have you been?"

She didn't answer, and he didn't ask again. He looked around. The empty hall was full, all the seats taken. A ceremonious hush fell over the audience. The music played softly. The cantor intoned the benedictions. With measured steps, Abraham Mekheles led his daughter down the aisle.

TRANSLATED BY CHANA FAERSTEIN AND ELIZABETH POLLET

◇

Of all the successful American Jewish writers, Isaac Bashevis Singer has most retained his connection with the Jewish traditions and resisted assimilation into American life. Born in Poland in 1904, he came to this country in 1935, the year his vast chronicle novel, The Family Moskat, *was published in Yiddish. Since then he has worked on* The Jewish Daily Forward, *a Yiddish language newspaper that has regularly published his prolific output of stories and sketches. Singer has been fortunate in his translators— among them have been Saul Bellow, Isaac Rosenfield, and Cecil Hemley, and there have been many others devoted to his work—and his short stories have appeared in English in three volumes:* Gimpel the Fool (1957), The Spinoza of Market Street (1961), *and* Short Friday (1964). *In these three volumes only two stories ("Alone," a strange tale of a man alone in a Miami Beach hotel, and "A Wedding in Brownsville") deal with American life. All his novels, including the recent ones,* The Magician of Lublin (1960), The Slave (1962), *and* The Manor (1967), *have their setting in Poland in centuries past. Besides being almost entirely historical, his subjects and methods are distinctive for other qualities: often his short fiction resembles folktales, moral fables, usually set in small rural Jewish villages in remote times when superstitions seemed real; they tell of men and women inhabited by spirits, returning from the dead, or being bedeviled by witches, demons, and imps.*

So although the story "A Wedding in Brownsville" is more or less unique in Singer's work in that it is about American life today, it has at least two elements that are typical of his fiction: use of the supernatural, and at least the memory of village life in Poland in years past. The story permits (but barely) the realistic reading that all that happens at the end is due to "a drunken stupor" or "one long hallucination." But most certainly Singer wants us to believe that Dr. Margolin, killed in an accident in a taxicab on his way to a wedding, nevertheless continues right on through the unfamiliar, gloomy, strange, and unearthly streets of Brooklyn, to arrive at the wedding, greet old friends from the village of his youth, and meet again "his one great love," Raizel, the daughter of Melekh the watchmaker, who "had married someone else and later been shot by the Nazis." If a man gets up from the dead, why shouldn't he meet whomever he wants? Throughout the story, it has been made clear the distaste the Doctor feels for the "mixed" life he leads in America, married to a faded blonde, whose brother had been a Nazi but who "herself had become almost Jewish in New York. She had made friends with Jewish women, joined Hadassah, learned to cook Jewish dishes. Even her sigh was Jewish." "Even she . . ." the Doctor thinks, "could see that American Judaism was a mess." "The Anglicized Yiddish, the Yiddishized English. . . . Jewish laws and customs were completely distorted; men who have no regard for Jewishness wore skullcaps; and the reverend rabbis and cantors aped the Christian ministers." The story reflects a yearning for the past, for the "pure" life of the small Jewish village in Poland in the old days. The symbol of that yearning, and the symbol as well of the Doctor's youthful hopes and talents, before he had "wasted years in learning languages, in wandering from country to country," is the beautiful girl Raizel, with whom in death he is finally reunited.

BERNARD MALAMUD

The Jewbird

◇◇◇◇◇◇◇◇

THE WINDOW was open so the skinny bird flew in. Flappity-flap with its frazzled black wings. That's how it goes. It's open, you're in. Closed, you're out and that's your fate. The bird wearily flapped through the open kitchen window of Harry Cohen's top-floor apartment on First Avenue near the lower East River. On a rod on the wall hung an escaped canary cage, its door wide open, but this black-type longbeaked bird—its ruffled head and small dull eyes, crossed a little, making it look like a dissipated crow—landed if not smack on Cohen's thick lamb chop, at least on the table, close by. The frozen foods salesman was sitting at supper with his wife and young son on a hot August evening a year ago. Cohen, a heavy man with hairy chest and beefy shorts; Edie, in skinny yellow shorts and red halter; and their ten-year-old Morris (after her father)—Maurie, they called him, a nice kid though not overly bright—were all in the city after two weeks out, because Cohen's mother was dying. They had been enjoying Kingston, New York, but drove back when Mama got sick in her flat in the Bronx.

"Right on the table," said Cohen, putting down his beer glass and swatting at the bird. "Son of a bitch."

"Harry, take care with your language," Edie said, looking at Maurie, who watched every move.

The bird cawed hoarsely and with a flap of its bedraggled wings—feathers tufted this way and that—rose heavily to the top of the open kitchen door, where it perched staring down.

"Gevalt, a pogrom!"

"It's a talking bird," said Edie in astonishment.

"In Jewish," said Maurie.

"Wise guy," muttered Cohen. He gnawed on his chop, then put down the bone. "So if you can talk, say what's your business. What do you want here?"

"If you can't spare a lamb chop," said the bird, "I'll settle for a piece of herring with a crust of bread. You can't live on your nerve forever."

"This ain't a restaurant," Cohen replied. "All I'm asking is what brings you to this address?"

"The window was open," the bird sighed; adding after a moment, "I'm running. I'm flying but I'm also running."

"From whom?" asked Edie with interest.

"Anti-Semeets."

"Anti-Semites?" they all said.

"That's from who."

"What kind of anti-Semites bother a bird?" Edie asked.

"Any kind," said the bird, "also including eagles, vultures, and hawks. And once in a while some crows will take your eyes out."

"But aren't you a crow?"

"Me? I'm a Jewbird."

Cohen laughed heartily. "What do you mean by that?"

The bird began dovening. He prayed without Book or tallith, but with passion. Edie bowed her head though not Cohen. And Maurie rocked back and forth with the prayer, looking up with one wide-open eye.

When the prayer was done Cohen remarked, "No hat, no phylacteries?"

"I'm an old radical."

"You're sure you're not some kind of a ghost or dybbuk?"

"Not a dybbuk," answered the bird, "though one of my relatives had such an experience once. It's all over now, thanks God. They freed her from a former lover, a crazy jealous man. She's now the mother of two wonderful children."

"Birds?" Cohen asked slyly.

"Why not?"

"What kind of birds?"

"Like me. Jewbirds."

Cohen tipped back in his chair and guffawed. "That's a big laugh. I've heard of a Jewfish but not a Jewbird."

"We're once removed." The bird rested on one skinny leg, then on the other. "Please, could you spare maybe a piece of herring with a small crust of bread?"

Edie got up from the table.

"What are you doing?" Cohen asked her.

"I'll clear the dishes."

Cohen turned to the bird. "So what's your name, if you don't mind saying?"

"Call me Schwartz."

"He might be an old Jew changed into a bird by somebody," said Edie, removing a plate.

"Are you?" asked Harry, lighting a cigar.

"Who knows?" answered Schwartz. "Does God tell us everything?"

Maurie got up on his chair. "What kind of herring?" he asked the bird in excitement.

"Get down, Maurie, or you'll fall," ordered Cohen.

"If you haven't got matjes, I'll take schmaltz," said Schwartz.

"All we have is marinated, with slices of onion—in a jar," said Edie.

"If you'll open for me the jar I'll eat marinated. Do you have also, if you don't mind, a piece of rye bread—the spitz?"

Edie thought she had.

"Feed him out on the balcony," Cohen said. He spoke to the bird. "After that take off."

Schwartz closed both bird eyes. "I'm tired and it's a long way."

"Which direction are you headed, north or south?"

Schwartz, barely lifting his wings, shrugged.

"You don't know where you're going?"

"Where there's charity I'll go."

"Let him stay, papa," said Maurie. "He's only a bird."

"So stay the night," Cohen said, "but no longer."

In the morning Cohen ordered the bird out of the house but Maurie cried, so Schwartz stayed for a while. Maurie was still on vacation from school and his friends were away. He was lonely and Edie enjoyed the fun he had, playing with the bird.

"He's no trouble at all," she told Cohen, "and besides his appetite is very small."

"What'll you do when he makes dirty?"

"He flies across the street in a tree when he makes dirty, and if nobody passes below, who notices?"

"So all right," said Cohen, "but I'm dead set against it. I warn you he ain't gonna stay here long."

"What have you got against the poor bird?"

"Poor bird, my ass. He's a foxy bastard. He thinks he's a Jew."

"What difference does it make what he thinks?"

"A Jewbird, what a chuzpah. One false move and he's out on his drumsticks."

At Cohen's insistence Schwartz lived out on the balcony in a new wooden birdhouse Edie had bought him.

"With many thanks," said Schwartz, "though I would rather have a human roof over my head. You know how it is at my age. I like the warm, the windows, the smell of cooking. I would also be glad to see once in a while the *Jewish Morning Journal* and have now and then a schnapps because it helps my breathing, thanks God. But whatever you give me, you won't hear complaints."

However, when Cohen brought home a bird feeder full of dried corn, Schwartz said, "Impossible."

Cohen was annoyed. "What's the matter, crosseyes, is your life getting too good for you? Are you forgetting what it means to be migratory? I'll bet a helluva lot of crows you happen to be acquainted with, Jews or otherwise, would give their eyeteeth to eat this corn."

Schwartz did not answer. What can you say to a grubber yung?

"Not for my digestion," he later explained to Edie. "Cramps. Herring is better even if it makes you thirsty. At least rainwater don't cost anything." He laughed sadly in breathy caws.

And herring, thanks to Edie, who knew where to shop, was what Schwartz got, with an occasional piece of potato pancake, and even a bit of soupmeat when Cohen wasn't looking.

When school began in September, before Cohen would once again suggest giving the bird the boot, Edie prevailed on him to wait a little while until Maurie adjusted.

"To deprive him right now might hurt his school work, and you know what trouble we had last year."

"So okay, but sooner or later the bird goes. That I promise you."

Schwartz, though nobody had asked him, took on full responsibility for Maurie's performance in school. In return for favors granted, when he was let in for an hour or two at night, he spent most of his time overseeing the boy's lessons. He sat on top of the dresser near Maurie's desk as he laboriously wrote out his homework. Maurie was a restless type and Schwartz gently kept him to his studies. He also listened to him practice his screechy violin, taking a few minutes off now and then to rest his ears in the bathroom. And they afterwards played dominoes. The boy was an indifferent checker player and it was impossible to teach him chess. When he was sick, Schwartz read him comic books though he personally disliked them. But Maurie's work improved in school and even his violin teacher admitted his playing was better. Edie gave Schwartz credit for these improvements though the bird pooh-poohed them.

Yet he was proud there was nothing lower than C minuses on Maurie's report card, and on Edie's insistence celebrated with a little schnapps.

"If he keeps up like this," Cohen said, "I'll get him in an Ivy League college for sure."

"Oh I hope so," sighed Edie.

But Schwartz shook his head. "He's a good boy—you don't have to worry. He won't be a shicker or a wifebeater, God forbid, but a scholar he'll never be, if you know what I mean, although maybe a good mechanic. It's no disgrace in these times."

"If I were you," Cohen said, angered, "I'd keep my big snoot out of other people's private business."

"Harry, please," said Edie.

"My goddamn patience is wearing out. That crosseyes butts into everything."

Though he wasn't exactly a welcome guest in the house, Schwartz gained

a few ounces although he did not improve in appearance. He looked bedraggled as ever, his feathers unkempt, as though he had just flown out of a
snowstorm. He spent, he admitted, little time taking care of himself. Too
much to think about. "Also outside plumbing," he told Edie. Still there was
more glow to his eyes so that though Cohen went on calling him crosseyes
he said it less emphatically.

Liking his situation, Schwartz tried tactfully to stay out of Cohen's way,
but one night when Edie was at the movies and Maurie was taking a hot
shower, the frozen foods salesman began a quarrel with the bird.

"For Christ sake, why don't you wash yourself sometimes? Why must
you always stink like a dead fish?"

"Mr. Cohen, if you'll pardon me, if somebody eats garlic he will smell
from garlic. I eat herring three times a day. Feed me flowers and I will smell
like flowers."

"Who's obligated to feed you anything at all? You're lucky to get herring."

"Excuse me, I'm not complaining," said the bird. "You're complaining."

"What's more," said Cohen, "even from out on the balcony I can hear
you snoring away like a pig. It keeps me awake at night."

"Snoring," said Schwartz, "isn't a crime, thanks God."

"All in all you are a goddamn pest and free loader. Next thing you'll
want to sleep in bed next to my wife."

"Mr. Cohen," said Schwartz, "on this rest assured. A bird is a bird."

"So you say, but how do I know you're a bird and not some kind of a
goddamn devil?"

"If I was a devil you would know already. And I don't mean because
your son's good marks."

"Shut up, you bastard bird," shouted Cohen.

"Grubber yung," cawed Schwartz, rising to the tips of his talons, his long
wings outstretched.

Cohen was about to lunge for the bird's scrawny neck but Maurie came
out of the bathroom, and for the rest of the evening until Schwartz's bedtime
on the balcony, there was pretended peace.

But the quarrel had deeply disturbed Schwartz and he slept badly. His
snoring woke him, and awake, he was fearful of what would become of
him. Wanting to stay out of Cohen's way, he kept to the birdhouse as much
as possible. Cramped by it, he paced back and forth on the balcony ledge,
or sat on the birdhouse roof, staring into space. In the evenings, while
overseeing Maurie's lessons, he often fell asleep. Awakening, he nervously
hopped around exploring the four corners of the room. He spent much time
in Maurie's closet, and carefully examined his bureau drawers when they
were left open. And once when he found a large paper bag on the floor,
Schwartz poked his way into it to investigate what possibilities were. The
boy was amused to see the bird in the paper bag.

"He wants to build a nest," he said to his mother.

Edie, sensing Schwartz's unhappiness, spoke to him quietly.

"Maybe if you did some of the things my husband wants you, you would get along better with him."

"Give me a for instance," Schwartz said.

"Like take a bath, for instance."

"I'm too old for baths," said the bird. "My feathers fall out without baths."

"He says you have a bad smell."

"Everybody smells. Some people smell because of their thoughts or because who they are. My bad smell comes from the food I eat. What does his come from?"

"I better not ask him or it might make him mad," said Edie.

In late November Schwartz froze on the balcony in the fog and cold, and especially on rainy days he woke with stiff joints and could barely move his wings. Already he felt twinges of rheumatism. He would have liked to spend more time in the warm house, particularly when Maurie was in school and Cohen at work. But though Edie was good-hearted and might have sneaked him in in the morning, just to thaw out, he was afraid to ask her. In the meantime Cohen, who had been reading articles about the migration of birds, came out on the balcony one night after work when Edie was in the kitchen preparing pot roast, and peeking into the bird-house, warned Schwartz to be on his way soon if he knew what was good for him. "Time to hit the flyways."

"Mr. Cohen, why do you hate me so much?" asked the bird. "What did I do to you?"

"Because you're an A-number-one trouble maker, that's why. What's more, whoever heard of a Jewbird? Now scat or it's open war."

But Schwartz stubbornly refused to depart so Cohen embarked on a campaign of harassing him, meanwhile hiding it from Edie and Maurie. Maurie hated violence and Cohen didn't want to leave a bad impression. He thought maybe if he played dirty tricks on the bird he would fly off without being physically kicked out. The vacation was over, let him make his easy living off the fat of somebody else's land. Cohen worried about the effect of the bird's departure on Maurie's schooling but decided to take the chance, first, because the boy now seemed to have the knack of studying—give the black bird-bastard credit—and second, because Schwartz was driving him bats by being there always, even in his dreams.

The frozen foods salesman began his campaign against the bird by mixing watery cat food with the herring slices in Schwartz's dish. He also blew up and popped numerous paper bags outside the birdhouse as the bird slept, and when he had got Schwartz good and nervous, though not enough to leave, he brought a full-grown cat into the house, supposedly a gift for little Maurie, who had always wanted a pussy. The cat never stopped springing up at Schwartz whenever he saw him, one day managing to claw out several of his tailfeathers. And even at lesson time, when the cat was usually excluded from Maurie's room, though somehow or other he quickly found his way in at the end of the lesson, Schwartz was desperately fearful of his life and flew from pinnacle to pinnacle—light fixture to clothes-tree to door-top—in order to elude the beast's wet jaws.

Once when the bird complained to Edie how hazardous his existence was, she said, "Be patient, Mr. Schwartz. When the cat gets to know you better he won't try to catch you any more."

"When he stops trying we will both be in Paradise," Schwartz answered. "Do me a favor and get rid of him. He makes my whole life worry. I'm losing feathers like a tree loses leaves."

"I'm awfully sorry but Maurie likes the pussy and sleeps with it."

What could Schwartz do? He worried but came to no decision, being afraid to leave. So he ate the herring garnished with cat food, tried hard not to hear the paper bags bursting like fire crackers outside the birdhouse at night, and lived terror-stricken closer to the ceiling than the floor, as the cat, his tail flicking, endlessly watched him.

Weeks went by. Then on the day after Cohen's mother had died in her flat in the Bronx, when Maurie came home with a zero on an arithmetic test, Cohen, enraged, waited until Edie had taken the boy to his violin lesson, then openly attacked the bird. He chased him with a broom on the balcony and Schwartz frantically flew back and forth, finally escaping into his birdhouse. Cohen triumphantly reached in, and grabbing both skinny legs, dragged the bird out, cawing loudly, his wings wildly beating. He whirled the bird around and around his head. But Schwartz, as he moved in circles, managed to swoop down and catch Cohen's nose in his beak, and hung on for dear life. Cohen cried out in great pain, punched the bird with his fist, and tugging at its legs with all his might, pulled his nose free. Again he swung the yawking Schwartz around until the bird grew dizzy, then with a furious heave, flung him into the night. Schwartz sank like stone into the street. Cohen then tossed the birdhouse and feeder after him, listening at the ledge until they crashed on the sidewalk below. For a full hour, broom in hand, his heart palpitating and nose throbbing with pain, Cohen waited for Schwartz to return but the broken-hearted bird didn't.

That's the end of that dirty bastard, the salesman thought and went in. Edie and Maurie had come home.

"Look," said Cohen, pointing to his bloody nose swollen three times its normal size, "what that sonofabitchy bird did. It's a permanent scar."

"Where is he now?" Edie asked, frightened.

"I threw him out and he flew away. Good riddance."

Nobody said no, though Edie touched a handkerchief to her eyes and Maurie rapidly tried the nine times table and found he knew approximately half.

In the spring when the winter's snow had melted, the boy, moved by a memory, wandered in the neighborhood, looking for Schwartz. He found a dead black bird in a small lot near the river, his two wings broken, neck twisted, and both bird-eyes plucked clean.

"Who did it to you, Mr. Schwartz?" Maurie wept.

"Anti-Semeets," Edie said later.

⬦

Bernard Malamud was born in Brooklyn in 1914, educated at Erasmus Hall and the City College of New York, received an M.A. in literature from Columbia, has lived in Rome, taught at Oregon State University for years, and now teaches at Bennington College. He has published four novels: The Natural *(1952), a comic fantasy with a baseball background;* The Assistant *(1957), a story of love and guilt, set in a small neighborhood grocery shop;* A New Life *(1961), a sad and farcical story of sexual intrigue and English Department intrigue at a western state university; and* The Fixer *(1966), a story of injustice and anti-Semitism in Tsarist Russia. And he has published two collections of short stories:* The Magic Barrel *(1958), and* Idiots First *(1963). His work, often both comic and sad, sometimes very realistic, sometimes very symbolic and fantastic, always moving and meaningful, has won him a great variety of awards: a Ford Foundation grant, a Rockefeller grant, a* Partisan Review *fellowship, the Rosenthal Award of the National Institute of Arts and Letters, and others—including the National Book Award twice, in 1959 for* The Magic Barrel *and in 1966 for* The Fixer.

The mixture of styles Malamud uses in "The Jewbird"—sometimes the artfully simple language of the Jewish fable or the village folktale, and sometimes the slangy, modern Jewish-American idiom—is directly and usefully related to the story's central subject: conflict between "old ways" and "new ways." Schwartz, the Jewbird, of course expresses the old ways: he is more European than American, and to some extent he represents the older, first generation of Jewish immigrants fleeing oppression ("I'm running," he says. "I'm flying but I'm also running."). Cohen, and to a lesser extent his family, represent the new ways: Americanized, their preoccupation is with their boy, Maurie, and his future. The first part of the story satirizes both of these conflicting ways as it contrasts them. Cohen is a frozen-food salesman, of all things; Schwartz eats only the ritual, traditional Jewish foods. When Schwartz gently keeps Maurie working at his violin and his studies, in keeping with Jewish traditions of scholarship, Cohen sees the improvements in terms of maybe getting the kid into an Ivy League college. Schwartz is religious, praying "without Book or tallith, but with passion"; Cohen doesn't even bow his head during the prayer. Schwartz repre-

*sents an unwanted presence, an aged, sour-smelling, unassimilated grand-
parent, in the tiny apartment of this family one of whose own grandparents
is sick in her own apartment in the Bronx. Cohen keeps urging Schwartz to
migrate—whether north to the Bronx or south to Miami Beach with the
other old people doesn't matter to him. His family, he feels, will do better
without this old Jewbird radical with his warmth, wit, scholarship, tradition,
and religion. When Cohen finally takes the broom to Schwartz, the brutality
of the scene is muted by the emphasis on the bird qualities of Schwartz,
rather than on his qualities as an old man; nevertheless, the mood of the
story shifts dramatically at this point. When Edie tells Maurie at the end
that it was "Anti-Semeets" who destroyed Mr. Schwartz, several ironies
are at work; but the central point being made by the story is quite clear:
the modern Jew becomes himself a destructive anti-Semite when he turns
against his own tradition.*

LEO SKIR

Other Chanukahs

◇◇◇◇◇◇◇

IT WAS THE FIRST NIGHT of Chanukah. I had been working in the Columbia Library that day, on a paper for my History of the English Language class, which paper was to be on a line of Chaucer, chosen by the student. The line was to be translated into modern English, a phonetic transcription to be given of both lines, and the history of each word-change was to be given. For my line I had chosen:

"I have, God woot, a large feeld to ere."

Being a Columbia alumnus, I have the privilege of a stack card, which means that I cannot take the books home. That day, as always, I found reading in the stacks a suffocating experience. The pronunciation guide to Chaucer had been printed, oddly enough, in Stockholm.

I was to meet Ariela at eight down in Washington Square Park before the session of the Country Folk Dance Society. It was our last session before she would leave for her winter vacation in Palm Beach.

Before going home for supper and a shave and shower (Ariela is very particular about those things), I called my parents to wish them a happy Chanukah.

"Where are you phoning from?" my mother said. She always asks this. I always phone from outside my apartment so she won't know I have the phone connected.

"From the library," I said.

"It doesn't sound like a library to me," she said.

"The phones are in a hallway," I said. "Sometimes when people want to get out of studying for a little while they come into the hallway and smoke and laugh."

"Are you in a bar?" she said.

"No," I said, "a library."

"What are you doing tonight?" my mother said.

"Studying," I said.

I have real paranoid feelings about my mother's being able to tell where I really am at any time, her apparent stupidity being, to my deranged senses, only the fumbling put on by a professional blind man.

"Why don't you come to the house tonight?" Mother said. "Daddy's expecting you." (The reader will note that this was the first indication I had that I was either invited or expected.)

"I'm sorry Mother," I said. "I can't."

"If you can't, you can't," mother said, with the air of Hagar being driven into the desert. "I was just thinking tonight how nice it would be to have the whole family together for Chanukah."

"Well, I'm really sorry," I said (what wonderful villainous hypocrisy! Where did I learn it! Probably Ariela, she is an accomplished liar).

"Do you think you can come Friday night," she said, "and spend *Shabbos* with us? You could put on your little pee-jays and we'd open up the couch and you could sleep over."

"I'd love to," I said, "but I can't. Look, I have to get out of the phone booth. Goodbye."

Now, the reader, reading this, has come to an immediate misunderstanding of the situation. He sees me as the younger iconoclastic son, having no respect or love for the ancient ceremonies.

Nothing could be further from the truth. I am exceedingly fond of holidays of any sort, and had, as a matter of fact, been reading about just that period of Jewish history in Tcherikover's *Hellenistic Civilization and the Jews,* which had recently come out in English. (It was originally published in Hebrew.)

Let us suppose that I had accepted my mother's invitation.

For the sake of those readers who are not quite sure just what Chanukah is, and what happens during it, I will explain. Chanukah is the celebration of the successful revolt of the Jews against the Syrian-Hellenistic overlordship of Antiochus IV. The rebels were able to chase the Syrians out of the country and they restored the Temple, which had been converted to paganism, to its purity. They were called the Maccabees, after Judah, the leader of the band of brothers who led the rebellion. They were in time to establish the Hasmonean dynasty, whose fate is detailed in Moshe Shamir's *The King of Flesh and Blood* (wonderful novel!).

The central miracle (the only one) of Chanukah is the following. When the Temple was recaptured, they put holy oil in the lamp. But it was only enough for one day. It would be eight days before the new batch of pure oil could be produced. But during those eight days the oil, which was only enough for *one* day, continued to burn. To celebrate this miracle, the holiday of Chanukah lasts eight days, and during each day a larger number of candles is lit, one the first day, two the second, three the third, etc. Gifts of money and candy are given out, and games are to be played. The holiday food is potato *latkes* (pancakes). Often, in the Temples in a neighborhood, Chanukah plays are given.

Now:

I come into the house, having brought along the Tcherikover book to show my father. The Tcherikover version of the Maccabee revolution is quite a different story from that told in the Bible in Maccabees I. Tcherikover, in a very clever reconstruction, based only on internal contradictions in that text, suspects that the Hellenistic rulers had not originally violated the people's religious principles, but their later harshness, essentially not religious but political, had been brought about by the need to curb a fanatical high-orthodox Jewish group which had rebelled against the Syrian rule.

Well, of course I am never going to be able to say anything like this to my father, it being impossible in my parents' house to say five continuous sentences on any general subject.

Let us make the attempt:

I: "I've been reading an interesting book about the Hasmonean period."

Dad: "It looks very good. I'd like to read it sometime." My father's spastic existence is such that he has been unable to read any prolonged prose narrative for many years now, his diet being only the New York *Times*. It is his peculiar illusion that he has a great interest in and appetite for history, and that if he had the time he would devote himself to reading history books. The reading of the *Times* he takes as a sign of his vital interest in current history.

I say, "Tcherikover thinks that the Jews brought their troubles on themselves, that the rule of the Hellenistic rulers was, in all probability, lenient, at least in regard to religion."

Dad: "Let me look at it." He takes the book and looks at it.

Dad: "It's got nice print. How much did you pay for it?"

I: "It's only $2.50. It was one of my yearly selections from the Jewish Publication Society."

Dad: "Only two-fifty? I can't afford to get a book for two-fifty. Mother and I don't go around buying books."

This is true. The only books they have bought recently have been paperback editions of —*Lolita* and *Lady Chatterley's Lover:* both of which my father said were "full of street language." Why he and my mother, who disapprove of "filth" in literature, had selected, during an entire year, only two books, both suspected of obscenity, I leave as a question for cultural historians.

Dad has handed the Tcherikover book back to me. The reader will note that the discussion has left the Hasmonean period and Hellenism completely and has evolved into that operation for which my father and mother were ordained, namely the remedial treatment of pathological features in my makeup.

"Don't you buy a lot of throw-away books and magazines?" Dad asks.

"What's a throw-away book?" I ask.

"Oh you know what I mean," he says, "those paperbacks!"

"Yes, I buy them," I say, "but I don't buy them to throw away. I buy them to read."

"Couldn't you get them out of the library?" he says.

Like all people who have never had a desire to read a specific book, he is absolutely certain that any book one might wish to read is immediately obtainable in the local library. For some reason I have never told him that this is not so.

He has returned the book to me, and I, distracted by his discourse, which had, as was inevitable, become trained on me, like the rays from a cathode tube upon a patient, have made the mistake of putting the book on the coffee table instead of in my lap, as is my custom.

No sooner have I put it on the coffee table than Mother comes in with a cocktail glass full of tomato juice and puts the glass on the book. Mother regards any horizontal book as either a coaster or a hot-plate.

"Mother," I say, "please take the tomato juice off my book."

"Oh," Mother says, "is that your book? I thought it was one of ours. The juice is for you. I don't want you to get too hungry before dinner. Wait, I'll get a coaster."

The coaster turns out to be a napkin with the words, *Aincha Glad You Came?* printed on it.

"How do you like these napkins?" Mother asks.

"They're wonderful," I say.

"I bought them in a store," she says, "I thought they'd be nice if you have guests and you want to give them cocktails before dinner."

Now, there is not in the house any gin, vermouth, shaker, cherries, onions, olives, or any of the possible ingredients of a cocktail, nor does my mother know how to make a cocktail, nor has she ever served cocktails.

"That's a good idea," I say.

Now we go into supper. The reader will remember that the holiday is celebrated by the lighting of the Chanukah lights. Three blessings are said on this first night:

Blessed art thou, O Lord, our God, Ruler of the world who hast sanctified us by Thy commandments and hast bidden us to kindle the Chanukah lights.

Blessed art Thou, O Lord, our God, Ruler of the world, who didst wondrous things for our fathers, at this season in those days.

Blessed art Thou, O Lord, our God, Ruler of the world, who hast granted us life and hast sustained us to celebrate this joyous festival.

The dinner is a perfectly ordinary dinner, ordinary, that is, qua Mother. If it were anyone else, one might find it curiously deficient. My mother is unable to prepare and serve an entire meal of soup, salad, meat, vegetables, and dessert. I must admit that I sympathize with her, that to prepare all these foods and use all those dishes and silverware, which must be washed afterward, *is* an ordeal, and I can imagine many possible alternatives. To mention only two: having foods which do not need to be cooked, such as cold sliced meats, which can be served in sandwiches, and even to have paper plates—or again, to go out to a restaurant.

But, of course, a restaurant is *not,* as my mother has pointed out, one's own home, and of course, as she adds, "You never know what you're getting in a restaurant."

"Do you like chicken?" Mother says. "I bought it in the store. It's as soft as butter. You could cut it with a butter knife. Here! I want you to have a piece of my breast. It's as soft as butter."

A piece of chicken is deposited in my plate.

"Did you light the lamp?" I ask Mother.

"I went to the store today," she says, "and they were all out of candles. But I took out the lamp. I know you like the lamp."

(These are all imaginings since I did not go to my parents' house on that night, or on any of the eight nights of Chanukah.)

"Wasn't there any store in the neighborhood that had candles?" I ask.

Of course there would be. Rockaway in this section is almost all Jewish, and even if she could not have gotten them, I could have bought some in Manhattan. There are also no potato pancakes.

"Are there any *latkes?*" I ask Mother.

"I know you like them," Mother says, "but it's silly making them for only three people. It's so much trouble cutting up the potatoes, and my hands are bad."

What could I possibly say? That I wanted her to spend time scraping her fingers in a grater so that I could have the pleasure of eating potato *latkes* for a minute or so?

I guess Mother is the other side of the miracle. Instead of the oil which burnt for eight days rather than one, we have the woman who goes to the store and finds that there aren't any candles in stock, and instead of Hannah and her seven sons (all of them, even the youngest, he a tiny child, faced martyrdom and horrible tortures rather than bow to pagan idols), we have Mother who finds that a company of three is under the Critical Mass for which the *latkes* can be prepared.

After supper my father reads the New York *Times* and watches the news on television. Then he falls asleep. Before I leave they give me some *Chanukah* gelt, Chanukah money, which has always been given in the same way, my mother suggesting it and then, in front of me, discussing the amount with Dad, this conversation being held in Yiddish. It was the only time that Yiddish was spoken, since I did not understand Yiddish.

So it can be seen that when Mother invited me to supper on Chanukah, it was not because she was desirous of my participation in any particular feast or ceremony, or even that she wanted to see me.

What was it that she wanted?

Her speech is not to be compared with communication but more to be likened to the gasping of a fish out of water, and with her I always felt that same pity one would feel for the fish, the desire to put it in water. *But—* (how many times I have asked myself this question) *Where Was That Element Where She Would Be At Home?* Neither at Chanukah nor Christmas, Passover nor Easter! She, who had served as homemaker and as nurse for my father in his office, which was in our home, had never been either. If she dies before me and I call to mind her image, it will always be as the composite of these two occupations, she in her white nurse's uniform in the kitchen, carefully turning over the lamb chops in the broiler, or opening the refrigerator to get out the cole slaw, each operation being in some way pitifully clumsy, and I, watching her, knowing that the cooking smells would reach the waiting room, feeling shame for her clumsiness and her lack of professionalism in her nurse's capacity, and also—shame (which I feel now in writing this) for my contempt for her—but having before me my father's example, feeling somehow that the acceptance of these faults of hers, even the passive toleration of them, was dangerous, and that their quantity being legion and they, the faults themselves, being as it were, united, one would find oneself their subject.

But still, as I on this first night of Chanukah went down in the subway train to meet Ariela (who would be standing near the statue of Garibaldi in Washington Square Park), I felt bad—that I had deserted her—as if somehow, I possessed the key, or enchantment, and could, with some word or action, wake her up and take her—where? Some place where Chanukah was celebrated! In Israel, during the Mandate, on Chanukah, a series of relay racers carried a torch from Modein (where the revolt of the Maccabees had started) to Jerusalem.

When I was eight years old, in 1941, and they were putting on a Chanukah play at the Shaari Zedek in my neighborhood, I had gone to the casting session and told them that I wanted to be Judah Maccabee. But I was too young, it seemed, and was offered only the part of one of the fiddlers of King Antiochus, which I refused. I didn't know how to play the fiddle, I told them.

They had explained to me that these were toy fiddles and it didn't matter.

And *I* said, that repulsive as the idea of real fiddling was to me, fake fiddling seemed even worse. I would not be a fake fiddler.

I was finally offered what the director said was a part in the chorus. There was, in effect, no chorus. The entire cast lined up was a chorus, and the show consisted simply of each member stepping forward in turn, explaining in a short, sung quatrain, who he was (or in the case of the king's three musicians, who they were) and having their lines repeated by the rest. I was the only one who was not someone.

"You have the biggest part," the director explained to me, "You sing everything."

I stared at her wondering, first, if she believed what she was saying, and then, after dismissing this as impossible, whether this lie was one she found acceptable to all eight-year-olds and whether I, in not accepting it, would prove some sort of maverick.

I said nothing and stayed through the rehearsal that Sunday afternoon, walking home moodily through the dirty slush-snow afterward, wondering how I could tell my parents of my defeat. Of course, when I did tell them, they saw nothing wrong with being in the chorus.

But the next Sunday, when the play was given, I did not go to Sunday school. I had a cold, one of the many which filled each winter of my ciildhood, and I told my parents I had to stay home.

I sat there and thought about the play, hating the play, hating the director. The play was a *comedy* and anyone in his right mind could see that the story of the Maccabees was not a comedy! One of the Maccabees had been killed, crushed underneath an elephant! What a silly play! How glad I was that I had not dignified it with my presence!

And then Dad had come back.

He had gone to the Temple and sat through the entire play! And when it was finished, he had gone backstage where the father of one of the boys who had been in the play was distributing gifts to all the members of the cast. To the boys he gave Indian headdresses, a paper strip in which colored chicken feathers had been inserted. My father had told him that his son had been in the play but had not been able to come, and the man had given Dad an Indian headdress to give me.

Which headdress he now held in his hand.

The wind whistled in the tree outside my window. Few Brooklyn homes had trees outside their windows. I lived opposite a small park which even had a real hillock on which children could sled in winter. That hillock was to be leveled the following winter and the tree outside my window was to fall during the 1941 hurricane.

Now, the eight-year-old Leo only felt discomfort at the coldness of the winter room and also—how odd—at the fact that his father had exposed him. He, Leo, had absented himself from the play, dismissed it entirely, and his father, possessed, had attended the play.

My father had, has, the most genial of open-faced, childlike smiles, which smile he now presented along with the paper Indian headdress. I stared at him, wondering why he was not indignant at the childishness of the play, or bored at being distracted from his own, more vital concerns, and was pleased by this absurd headdress, which was, so obviously, not the proper gift for Chanukah.

"How is it that they let you backstage when you weren't in the play?" I said, staring at the red cherry-flavored cough medicine in the bottle beside my bed.

This recollection of the eight-year-old Leo was the first Leo story.

I have never felt the shames of childhood less valid than those which follow later. Often myself a victim of shames and regrets, I would find it salutary to remember these former occasions in order to show myself that my present worries would in time appear in a similar diminutive form.

At fourteen I was attending a private school in Brooklyn. It was called Olympus. At one time it had been restricted, but it had let in Jews during the Depression, and now the Children of Israel had conquered it, and although there was still Chapel each Monday, during which we sang "Holy, Holy, Holy," the institution was as much a part of Judah as the threshing floor of the Jebusite.

Now:

On a September morning of 1946, the fourteen-year-old Leo was sitting on a swinging couch on the roof garden of his apartment house. He had brought up his biology textbook and also a small notebook and a pencil.

His mother (I will now switch to the first person to preserve the illusion of veracity), my mother had told me to sit in the sun and I had at first obediently done so, but I found that it was simply quite impossible to read in the sun and had transferred myself to the other side of the roof, which was shaded by an awning. This side was a bit chilly but much more comfortable. Sitting there I had the oddest feeling that my mother would be coming up to the roof and would question me as to why, having taken the trouble to get up there, I now was sitting in the shade, and this thought—that I was disobedient—took away the pleasure I would have felt at the peace of being on the roof and in an environment that I liked. It almost seemed to work itself out into a chemicphysical equation:

Too much sun $+$ approval $=$ Coolness $-$ approval.

My general conclusion was that Life, as far as I had seen it, seemed to consist of imbalance and discomfort. I wondered on this conclusion for a while and also questioned whether I, knowing only one life, my own, could say that life was happy or unhappy. How could I, being unable, by definition, to be someone else, know if the life of anyone was happier or sadder, or more or less comfortable than mine? I thought on this matter for a while, but, as always with myself, felt my logic was inferior to my intuition. I also thought that there was certainly, for me, the criteria of my life prior to these moments.

It was then that my non-performance of the role of Judah Maccabee came to me, and, sitting on the swinging couch on that Brooklyn rooftop, I wrote the story in my notebook and then looked at it, wondering if the words—which resembled, of course, the ordinary words of notes taken in biology classes and letters and such—were really that magic thing called a story, the sort of thing that (magic possibility!) could appear in print.

When I came downstairs at noon, my parents were getting ready to go to the Bronx to visit our relatives. My brother, Stanley, couldn't go because he was meeting the boys for baseball practice. After our lunch, which was fishcakes and spaghetti, we went outside, and it was then, unable to contain myself, that I told my parents about the story I had written.

They were very angry.

By now we were outside the house, the black-painted, cast-iron, quatrefoil doors had closed behind us, and we were going toward the Pontiac.

"You must be crazy, mister," my father said, his angry face, red with anger, being almost, it would seem, the counterpart of the happy smiling face he had presented the day he returned with the chicken-feather Chanukah headdress. "Are you planning to hand that into school?"

"Yes," I said, "for the school magazine."

"Give it to me!" he said.

"No," I said.

"You heard me," he said. "Give it to me!"

"Why?" I said.

"Are you going to give it to me?" he said, "Or am I going to have to make you?"

"Please Abe," my mother said. "Not in the street. You can get it from him in the car. Leo, let's go to the car."

My father placed his fists on his hips. He is a short man and it was only at such times as these, when he felt that he had to assert his authority, that he looked ridiculous and ineffectual. I think, at that moment, and often later, I would give in to him, not out of fear of his countenance, but out of the desire to sustain his illusion of power.

"Are you going to give it to me *now?*" he said.

"Please Abe—" said my mother, "you'll get it from him in the car. Leo, darling, get in the back of the car."

"No!" my father said. "Now!"

"Here," I said.

I handed him the notebook and he tore out the two pages with the story. Standing there in the street, his legs separated like those of the Colossus of Rhodes (Richard Halliburton says they were not separated, this being, *bien entendu*, too undignified a posture for a statue), he tore the sheets into pieces, and then, being neat, went to the sewer grating at the corner and threw them in.

He had not read the story.

"What's wrong?" I said.

"You're asking me what's wrong!" my father said. "You don't see anything crazy in that?"

"No," I said.

"It's a Jewish thing," my father said. "They wouldn't be interested in a thing like that. You start talking about Chanukah to them and they'll think you're crazy."

"Most of the kids in the school are Jewish," I said, "and the Gentile kids might possibly be interested in a Jewish holiday. Catholics write books about Catholic holidays and Jews read them!"

"No, silly!" my father said. "It's a Christian country and you're going to a Christian school. If you want to write about Chanukah, you write for a Jewish magazine in a Jewish school."

"We should have sent him to a yeshiva," my mother said, and turned her head around to the back to face me, "Would you like that? to go to a yeshiva and wear a skullcap? Would you like that? We'll send you to the yeshiva on Eastern Parkway and you can wear a skullcap!"

She turned around again.

The car went through the Bedford-Stuyvesant district, which I had been seeing that morning from the rooftop, and onto the Williamsburg Bridge.

My parents were during this time repeating their complaints about my behavior. It is apparently the nature of those complaints that, since they follow irremediable wrongs, which cannot be caught up and righted, they, the complaints, must have circular and eternal paths like those of the sinners in Dante's hell driven forever by their passions. But whereas my faults were evident to me only in their consequences, the complaints, which kept at their heels, were all too audible. They would only cease when I was outside their orbit which, at that time, in the back seat of the Pontiac, was not possible.

To distract myself I looked out the window and down below. Through the grating which made the road surface of the bridge, the waters of the East River appeared far below.

*The Parable of the Fishes.**

The Romans had decreed that the people of Israel should no longer occupy themselves with Torah.

And during that time Pappos ben Judah came and found Rabbi Akiba holding great assemblies and studying Torah.

Ben Judah said to Akiba:

"Akiba, are you not afraid of the Roman government?"

To which Akiba replied:

"I will tell you a parable. A fox was walking along the bank of a stream, and saw some fishes gathering together to move from one place to another. He said to them, 'From what are you fleeing?' They answered: 'From nets which men set for us.' And the fox said: 'Why not come on the dry land?' To which the fish replied: 'And they say you are the wisest of animals! If we are afraid in our life-element, how much more so in our death-element?'

"So also it is with us: If now while we sit and study Torah, in which it is written, 'For that is thy life, and the length of thy days' (Deut. XXX, 20), we are in such a plight, how much more so if we neglect it."

Some time after he said this, the Rabbi was arrested by the Romans. He

* Adapted from Montefiore's *A Rabbinic Anthology.*

died a horrible death, skinned alive, his flesh torn off with hot metal combs.

The Williamsburg Bridge on the Manhattan side ends at Delancey Street. Dad stopped at a traffic light outside Ratner's.

"Would you like to live here?" my father said. "If you live here you could go to a yeshiva and wear *pais*. Is that the way you'd like to live? Huh?"

"Please, Abe," my mother said, "think about your heart. You can't kill yourself over him."

My father turned around (he was still stopped at the red light so that the car was not moving), and said, "When you're in Rome, you do what the Romans do!"

The fourteen-year-old Leo had cringed in the back of the car, tears starting to his eyes. . . .

"What are you looking at?" said Ariela.

We had been walking along Greenwich Avenue to the dance meeting, and I had stopped outside the window of an antique shop, staring at two metal combs which were beside a set of glass beads. They were curling iron combs, with insulated handles. In the parking lot beside the shop stood an old abandoned Pontiac, battered as if someone had beaten it. The rear window facing me was broken. I would have been afraid to look inside the car.

◇

Leo Skir was born in Brooklyn in 1932, has a B.A. from Columbia and an M.A. from New York University, and lives in New York City. His novel, Leo the Zionist, *will be published shortly; but "Other Chanukahs," which originally appeared in* Commentary *magazine in March, 1965, is part of another novel he is planning, which will be called* boychick.

The opening scene in "Other Chanukahs" presents the typical generational conflict between the bright college student whose daily world of reference includes Columbia, Stockholm, Washington Square, Palm Beach, and Chaucer and the suspicious telephone voice of deserted provincial motherhood recalling the otherworldly intellectual to his inescapable ties with a vexed and indigestible childhood. But Leo's revolt against parental attitudes is more than a simple denial of their ways: he feels that his parents have neglected their Jewish traditions and, in their desire for total assimilation into American ways, have deprived him of his heritage. His father tears up Leo's first version of his Chanukah story because "it's a Jewish thing" and of no interest or value in a Christian school in a Christian country. Throughout the story there recurs the simile that the Jew separated from his religion and tradition is like a fish out of water. Leo sees his mother's inabilities in these terms and asks: "But—*(how many times I have asked myself this question)* Where Was That Element Where She Would Be At Home? *Neither at Chanukah nor Christmas, Passover nor Easter!" Caught between two traditions, at home in neither element, she seems to him helpless and ineffective. She buys cocktail napkins for which she has no use, but she can't even "find" the candles for Chanukah and she says, ". . . it's silly making [latkes] for only three people" when she has never made a whole dinner in her life. She uses both Jewish and American customs at the conversational level, as interesting fantasies and justifications in her hybrid, neither-nor life. This infuriates the scholarly, intellectual Leo, whose interest in Jewish traditions is based on a much deeper knowledge of the history of his people and his religion but who is equally irreligious because he seeks from it not salvation but an identity, an idea of who he is, or at least of what role he should play. He remembers that when the play director told the eight-year-old Leo, "You have the biggest part. You sing everything," that what this really meant to him was, "I was the only one who was not someone." Leo searches not just for a resolution of these Jewish-Christian confusions, but for a satisfaction of his own sense of specialness: he wants a heroic role. He is very demanding, full of self-pity not only because he is unable to find a role as either martyr or hero, but also because he hates finding himself contemptuous of his family—for whom, in good Jewish tradition, he would love to feel the filial devotion of the Orthodox son. He is tortured by his own self-imposed role of unfulfilled martyr to a Jewish mother who can't even keep Chanukah.*

Defender of the Faith

◇◇◇◇◇◇◇◇

IN MAY OF 1945, only a few weeks after the fighting had ended in Europe, I was rotated back to the States, where I spent the remainder of the war with a training company at Camp Crowder, Missouri. Along with the rest of the Ninth Army, I had been racing across Germany so swiftly during the late winter and spring that when I boarded the plane, I couldn't believe its destination lay to the west. My mind might inform me otherwise, but there was an inertia of the spirit that told me we were flying to a new front, where we would disembark and continue our push eastward—eastward until we'd circled the globe, marching through villages along whose twisting, cobbled streets crowds of the enemy would watch us take possession of what, up till then, they'd considered their own. I had changed enough in two years not to mind the trembling of the old people, the crying of the very young, the uncertainty and fear in the eyes of the once arrogant. I had been fortunate enough to develop an infantryman's heart, which, like his feet, at first aches and swells but finally grows horny enough for him to travel the weirdest paths without feeling a thing.

Captain Paul Barrett was my C.O. in Camp Crowder. The day I reported for duty, he came out of his office to shake my hand. He was short, gruff, and fiery, and—indoors or out—he wore his polished helmet liner pulled down to his little eyes. In Europe, he had received a battlefield commission and a serious chest wound, and he'd been returned to the States only a few months before. He spoke easily to me, and at the evening formation he introduced me to the troops. "Gentlemen," he said, "Sergeant Thurston, as you know, is no longer with this company. Your new first sergeant is Sergeant Nathan Marx, here. He is a veteran of the European theater, and consequently will expect to find a company of soldiers here, and not a company of *boys*."

I sat up late in the orderly room that evening, trying halfheartedly to solve the riddle of duty rosters, personnel forms, and morning reports.

The Charge of Quarters slept with his mouth open on a mattress on the floor. A trainee stood reading the next day's duty roster, which was posted on the bulletin board just inside the screen door. It was a warm evening, and I could hear radios playing dance music over in the barracks. The trainee, who had been staring at me whenever he thought I wouldn't notice, finally took a step in my direction.

"Hey, Sarge—we having a G.I. party tomorrow night?" he asked. A G.I. party is a barracks cleaning.

"You usually have them on Friday nights?" I asked him.

"Yes," he said, and then he added, mysteriously, "that's the whole thing."

"Then you'll have a G.I. party."

He turned away, and I heard him mumbling. His shoulders were moving, and I wondered if he was crying.

"What's your name, soldier?" I asked.

He turned, not crying at all. Instead, his green-speckled eyes, long and narrow, flashed like fish in the sun. He walked over to me and sat on the edge of my desk. He reached out a hand. "Sheldon," he said.

"Stand on your feet, Sheldon."

Getting off the desk, he said, "Sheldon Grossbart." He smiled at the familiarity into which he'd led me.

"You against cleaning the barracks Friday night, Grossbart?" I said. "Maybe we shouldn't have G.I. parties. Maybe we should get a maid." My tone startled me. I felt I sounded like every top sergeant I had ever known.

"No, Sergeant." He grew serious, but with a seriousness that seemed to be only the stifling of a smile. "It's just—G.I. parties on Friday night, of all nights."

He slipped up onto the corner of the desk again—not quite sitting, but not quite standing, either. He looked at me with those speckled eyes flashing, and then made a gesture with his hand. It was very slight—no more than a movement back and forth of the wrist—and yet it managed to exclude from our affairs everything else in the orderly room, to make the two of us the center of the world. It seemed, in fact, to exclude everything even about the two of us except our hearts.

"Sergeant Thurston was one thing," he whispered, glancing at the sleeping C.Q., "but we thought that with you here things might be a little different."

"We?"

"The Jewish personnel."

"Why?" I asked, harshly. "What's on your mind?" Whether I was still angry at the "Sheldon" business, or now at something else, I hadn't time to tell, but clearly I was angry.

"We thought you—Marx, you know, like Karl Marx. The Marx Brothers. Those guys are all—M-a-r-x. Isn't that how *you* spell it, Sergeant?"

"M-a-r-x."

"Fishbein said—" He stopped. "What I meant to say, Sergeant—" His face and neck were red, and his mouth moved but no words came out. In a moment, he raised himself to attention, gazing down at me. It was as though he had suddenly decided he could expect no more sympathy from me than from Thurston, the reason being that I was of Thurston's faith, and not his. The young man had managed to confuse himself as to what my faith really was, but I felt no desire to straighten him out. Very simply, I didn't like him.

When I did nothing but return his gaze, he spoke, in an altered tone. "You see, Sergeant," he explained to me, "Friday nights, Jews are supposed to go to services."

"Did Sergeant Thurston tell you you couldn't go to them when there was a G.I party?"

"No."

"Did he say you had to stay and scrub the floors?"

"No, Sergeant."

"Did the Captain say you had to stay and scrub the floors?"

"That isn't it, Sergeant. It's the other guys in the barracks." He leaned toward me. "They think we're goofing off. But we're not. That's when Jews go to services, Friday night. We have to."

"Then go."

"But the other guys make accusations. They have no right."

"That's not the Army's problem, Grossbart. It's a personal problem you'll have to work out yourself."

"But it's un*fair.*"

I got up to leave. "There's nothing I can do about it," I said.

Grossbart stiffened and stood in front of me. "But this is a matter of *religion,* sir."

"Sergeant," I said.

"I mean 'Sergeant,' " he said, almost snarling.

"Look, go see the chaplain. You want to see Captain Barrett, I'll arrange an appointment."

"No, no. I don't want to make trouble, Sergeant. That's the first thing they throw up to you. I just want my rights!"

"Damn it, Grossbart, stop whining. You have your rights. You can stay and scrub floors or you can go to shul—"

The smile swam in again. Spittle gleamed at the corners of his mouth. "You mean church, Sergeant."

"I mean shul, Grossbart!"

I walked past him and went outside. Near me, I heard the scrunching of a guard's boots on gravel. Beyond the lighted windows of the barracks, young men in T shirts and fatigue pants were sitting on their bunks, polishing their rifles. Suddenly there was a light rustling behind me. I turned and saw Grossbart's dark frame fleeing back to the barracks, racing to tell his

Jewish friends that they were right—that, like Karl and Harpo, I was one of them.

The next morning, while chatting with Captain Barrett, I recounted the incident of the previous evening. Somehow, in the telling, it must have seemed to the Captain that I was not so much explaining Grossbart's position as defending it. "Marx, I'd fight side by side with a nigger if the fella proved to me he was a man. I pride myself," he said, looking out the window, "that I've got an open mind. Consequently, Sergeant, nobody gets special treatment here, for the good *or* the bad. All a man's got to do is prove himself. A man fires well on the range, I give him a weekend pass. He scores high in P.T., he gets a weekend pass. He *earns* it." He turned from the window and pointed a finger at me. "You're a Jewish fella, am I right, Marx?"

"Yes, sir."

"And I admire you. I admire you because of the ribbons on your chest. I judge a man by what he shows me on the field of battle, Sergeant. It's what he's got *here,*" he said, and then, though I expected he would point to his chest, he jerked a thumb toward the buttons straining to hold his blouse across his belly. "Guts," he said.

"O.K., sir. I only wanted to pass on to you how the men felt."

"Mr. Marx, you're going to be old before your time if you worry about how the men feel. Leave that stuff to the chaplain—that's his business, not yours. Let's us train these fellas to shoot straight. If the Jewish personnel feels the other men are accusing them of goldbricking—well, I just don't know. Seems awful funny that suddenly the Lord is calling so loud in Private Grossman's ear he's just got to run to church."

"Synagogue," I said.

"Synagogue is right, Sergeant. I'll write that down for handy reference. Thank you for stopping by."

That evening, a few minutes before the company gathered outside the orderly room for the chow formation, I called the C.Q., Corporal Robert LaHill, in to see me. LaHill was a dark, burly fellow whose hair curled out of his clothes wherever it could. He had a glaze in his eyes that made one think of caves and dinosaurs. "LaHill," I said, "when you take the formation, remind the men that they're free to attend church services *whenever* they are held, provided they report to the orderly room before they leave the area."

LaHill scratched his wrist, but gave no indication that he'd heard or understood.

"LaHill," I said, *"church.* You remember? Church, priest, Mass, confession."

He curled one lip into a kind of smile; I took it for a signal that for a second he had flickered back up into the human race.

"Jewish personnel who want to attend services this evening are to fall out in front of the orderly room at 1900," I said. Then, as an afterthought, I added, "By order of Captain Barrett."

A little while later, as the day's last light—softer than any I had seen that year—began to drop over Camp Crowder, I heard LaHill's thick, inflectionless voice outside my window: "Give me your ears, troopers. Toppie says for me to tell you that at 1900 hours all Jewish personnel is to fall out in front, here, if they want to attend the Jewish Mass."

At seven o'clock, I looked out the orderly-room window and saw three soldiers in starched khakis standing on the dusty quadrangle. They looked at their watches and fidgeted while they whispered back and forth. It was getting dimmer, and, alone on the otherwise deserted field, they looked tiny. When I opened the door, I heard the noises of the G.I. party coming from the surrounding barracks—bunks being pushed to the walls, faucets pounding water into buckets, brooms whisking at the wooden floors, cleaning the dirt away for Saturday's inspection. Big puffs of cloth moved round and round on the windowpanes. I walked outside, and the moment my foot hit the ground I thought I heard Grossbart call to the others, "Ten-*hut!*" Or maybe, when they all three jumped to attention, I imagined I heard the command.

Grossbart stepped forward. "Thank you, sir," he said.

" 'Sergeant,' Grossbart," I reminded him. "You call officers 'sir.' I'm not an officer. You've been in the Army three weeks—you know that."

He turned his palms out at his sides to indicate that, in truth, he and I lived beyond convention. "Thank you, anyway," he said.

"Yes," a tall boy behind him said. "Thanks a lot."

And the third boy whispered, "Thank you," but his mouth barely fluttered, so that he did not alter by more than a lip's movement his posture of attention.

"For what?" I asked.

Grossbart snorted happily. "For the announcement. The Corporal's announcement. It helped. It made it—"

"Fancier." The tall boy finished Grossbart's sentence.

Grossbart smiled. "He means formal, sir. Public," he said to me. "Now it won't seem as though we're just taking off—goldbricking because the work has begun."

"It was by order of Captain Barrett," I said.

"Aaah, but you pull a little weight," Grossbart said. "So we thank you." Then he turned to his companions. "Sergeant Marx, I want you to meet Larry Fishbein."

The tall boy stepped forward and extended his hand. I shook it. "You from New York?" he asked.

"Yes."

"Me, too." He had a cadaverous face that collapsed inward from his cheekbone to his jaw, and when he smiled—as he did at the news of our communal attachment—revealed a mouthful of bad teeth. He was blinking his eyes a good deal, as though he were fighting back tears. "What borough?" he asked.

I turned to Grossbart. "It's five after seven. What time are services?"

"Shul," he said, smiling, "is in ten minutes. I want you to meet Mickey Halpern. This is Nathan Marx, our sergeant."

The third boy hopped forward. "Private Michael Halpern." He saluted.

"Salute officers, Halpern," I said. The boy dropped his hand, and, on its way down, in his nervousness, checked to see if his shirt pockets were buttoned.

"Shall I march them over, sir?" Grossbart asked. "Or are you coming along?"

From behind Grossbart, Fishbein piped up. "Afterward, they're having refreshments. A ladies' auxiliary from St. Louis, the rabbi told us last week."

"The chaplain," Halpern whispered.

"You're welcome to come along," Grossbart said.

To avoid his plea, I looked away, and saw, in the windows of the barracks, a cloud of faces staring out at the four of us. "Hurry along, Grossbart," I said.

"O.K., then," he said. He turned to the others. "Double time, *march!*"

They started off, but ten feet away Grossbart spun around and, running backward, called to me, "Good *shabbus,* sir!" And then the three of them were swallowed into the alien Missouri dusk.

Even after they had disappeared over the parade ground, whose green was now a deep blue, I could hear Grossbart singing the double-time cadence, and as it grew dimmer and dimmer, it suddenly touched a deep memory—as did the slant of the light—and I was remembering the shrill sounds of a Bronx playground where, years ago, beside the Grand Concourse, I had played on long spring evenings such as this. It was a pleasant memory for a young man so far from peace and home, and it brought so many recollections with it that I began to grow exceedingly tender about myself. In fact, I indulged myself in a reverie so strong that I felt as though a hand were reaching down inside me. It had to reach so very far to touch me! It had to reach past those days in the forests of Belgium, and past the dying I'd refused to weep over; past the nights in German farmhouses whose books we'd burned to warm us; past endless stretches when I had shut off all softness I might feel for my fellows, and had managed even to deny myself the posture of a conqueror—the swagger that I, as a Jew, might well have worn as my boots whacked against the rubble of Wesel, Münster, and Braunschweig.

But now one night noise, one rumor of home and time past, and memory plunged down through all I had anesthetized, and came to what I suddenly remembered was myself. So it was not altogether curious that, in search of more of me, I found myself following Grossbart's tracks to Chapel No. 3, where the Jewish services were being held.

I took a seat in the last row, which was empty. Two rows in front of me sat Grossbart, Fishbein, and Halpern, holding little white Dixie cups. Each row of seats was raised higher than the one in front of it, and I could see clearly what was going on. Fishbein was pouring the contents of his cup into Grossbart's, and Grossbart looked mirthful as the liquid made a purple arc between Fishbein's hand and his, In the glaring yellow light, I saw the chaplain standing on the platform at the front; he was chanting the first line of the responsive reading. Grossbart's prayer book remained closed on his lap; he was swishing the cup around. Only Halpern responded to the chant by praying. The fingers of his right hand were spread wide across the cover of his open book. His cap was pulled down low onto his brow, which made it round, like a yarmulke. From time to time, Grossbart wet his lips at the cup's edge; Fishbein, his long yellow face a dying light bulb, looked from here to there, craning forward to catch sight of the faces down the row, then of those in front of him, then behind. He saw me, and his eyelids beat a tattoo. His elbow slid into Grossbart's side, his neck inclined toward his friend, he whispered something, and then, when the congregation next responded to the chant, Grossbart's voice was among the others. Fishbein looked into his book now, too; his lips, however, didn't move.

Finally, it was time to drink the wine. The chaplain smiled down at them as Grossbart swigged his in one long gulp, Halpern sipped, meditating, and Fishbein faked devotion with an empty cup. "As I look down amongst the congregation"—the chaplain grinned at the word—"this night, I see many new faces, and I want to welcome you to Friday-night services here at Camp Crowder. I am Major Leo Ben Ezra, your chaplain." Though an American, the chaplain spoke deliberately—syllable by syllable, almost— as though to communicate, above all, with the lip readers in his audience. "I have only a few words to say before we adjourn to the refreshment room, where the kind ladies of the Temple Sinai, St. Louis, Missouri, have a nice setting for you."

Applause and whistling broke out. After another momentary grin, the chaplain raised his hands, palms out, his eyes flicking upward a moment, as if to remind the troops where they were and Who Else might be in attendance. In the sudden silence that followed, I thought I heard Grossbart cackle, "Let the goyim clean the floors!" Were those the words? I wasn't sure, but Fishbein, grinning, nudged Halpern. Halpern looked dumbly at him, then went back to his prayer book, which had been occupying him all through the rabbi's talk. One hand tugged at the black kinky hair that stuck out under his cap. His lips moved.

The rabbi continued. "It is about the food that I want to speak to you for a moment. I know, I know, I know," he intoned, wearily, "how in the mouths of most of you the *trafe* food tastes like ashes. I know how you gag, some of you, and how your parents suffer to think of their children eating foods unclean and offensive to the palate. What can I tell you? I can only say, close your eyes and swallow as best you can. Eat what you must to live, and throw away the rest. I wish I could help more. For those of you who find this impossible, may I ask that you try and try, but then come to see me in private. If your revulsion is so great, we will have to seek aid from those higher up."

A round of chatter rose and subsided. Then everyone sang "Ain Kelohainu"; after all those years, I discovered I still knew the words. Then, suddenly, the service over, Grossbart was upon me. "Higher up? He means the General?"

"Hey, Shelly," Fishbein said, "he means God." He smacked his face and looked at Halpern. "How high can you go!"

"Sh-h-h!" Grossbart said. "What do you think, Sergeant?"

"I don't know," I said. "You better ask the chaplain."

"I'm going to. I'm making an appointment to see him in private. So is Mickey."

Halpern shook his head. "No, no, Sheldon——"

"You have rights, Mickey," Grossbart said. "They can't push us around."

"It's O.K.," said Halpern. "It bothers my mother, not me."

Grossbart looked at me. "Yesterday he threw up. From the hash. It was all ham and God knows what else."

"I have a cold—that was why," Halpern said. He pushed his yarmulke back into a cap.

"What about you, Fishbein?" I asked. "You kosher, too?"

He flushed. "A little. But I'll let it ride. I have a very strong stomach, and I don't eat a lot anyway." I continued to look at him, and he held up his wrist to reinforce what he'd just said; his watch strap was tightened to the last hole, and he pointed that out to me.

"But services are important to you?" I asked him.

He looked at Grossbart. "Sure, sir."

" 'Sergeant.' "

"Not so much at home," said Grossbart, stepping between us, "but away from home it gives one a sense of his Jewishness."

"We have to stick together," Fishbein said.

I started to walk toward the door; Halpern stepped back to make way for me.

"That's what happened in Germany," Grossbart was saying loud enough for me to hear. "They didn't stick together. They let themselves get pushed around."

I turned. "Look, Grossbart. This is the Army, not summer camp."

He smiled. "So?"

Halpern tried to sneak off, but Grossbart held his arm.

"Grossbart, how old are you?" I asked.

"Nineteen."

"And you?" I said to Fishbein.

"The same. The same month, even."

"And what about him?" I pointed to Halpern, who had by now made it safely to the door.

"Eighteen," Grossbart whispered. "But like he can't tie his shoes or brush his teeth himself. I feel sorry for him."

"I feel sorry for all of us, Grossbart," I said, "but just act like a man. Just don't overdo it."

"Overdo what, sir?"

"The 'sir' business, for one thing. Don't overdo that," I said.

I left him standing there. I passed by Halpern, but he did not look at me. Then I was outside, but, behind, I heard Grossbart call, "Hey, Mickey, my *leben,* come on back. Refreshments!"

"Leben!" My grandmother's word for me!

One morning a week later, while I was working at my desk, Captain Barrett shouted for me to come into his office. When I entered, he had his helmet liner squashed down so far on his head that I couldn't even see his eyes. He was on the phone, and when he spoke to me, he cupped one hand over the mouthpiece. "Who the hell is Grossbart?"

"Third platoon, Captain," I said. "A trainee."

"What's all this stink about food? His mother called a goddam congressman about the food." He uncovered the mouthpiece and slid his helmet up until I could see his bottom eyelashes. "Yes, sir," he said into the phone. "Yes, sir. I'm still here, sir. I'm asking Marx, here, right now—"

He covered the mouthpiece again and turned his head back toward me. "Lightfoot Harry's on the phone," he said, between his teeth. "This congressman calls General Lyman, who calls Colonel Sousa, who calls the Major, who calls me. They're just dying to stick this thing on me. Whatsa matter?" He shook the phone at me. "I don't feed the troops? What the hell is this?"

"Sir, Grossbart is strange—" Barrett greeted that with a mockingly indulgent smile. I altered my approach. "Captain, he's a very orthodox Jew, and so he's only allowed to eat certain foods."

"He throws up, the congressman said. Every time he eats something, his mother says, he throws up!"

"He's accustomed to observing the dietary laws, Captain."

"So why's his old lady have to call the White House?"

"Jewish parents, sir—they're apt to be more protective than you expect. I mean, Jews have a very close family life. A boy goes away from home, sometimes the mother is liable to get very upset. Probably the boy mentioned something in a letter, and his mother misinterpreted."

"I'd like to punch him one right in the mouth," the Captain said. "There's a goddam war on, and he wants a silver platter!"

"I don't think the boy's to blame, sir. I'm sure we can straighten it out by just asking him. Jewish parents worry—"

"*All* parents worry, for Christ's sake. But they don't get on their high horse and start pulling strings—"

I interrupted, my voice higher, tighter than before. "The home life, Captain, is very important—but you're right, it may sometimes get out of hand. It's a very wonderful thing, Captain, but because it's so close, this kind of thing . . ."

He didn't listen any longer to my attempt to present both myself and Lightfoot Harry with an explanation for the letter. He turned back to the phone. "Sir?" he said. "Sir—Marx, here, tells me Jews have a tendency to be pushy. He says he thinks we can settle it right here in the company. . . . Yes, sir. . . . I *will* call back, sir, soon as I can." He hung up. "Where are the men, Sergeant?"

"On the range."

With a whack on the top of his helmet, he crushed it down over his eyes again, and charged out of his chair. "We're going for a ride," he said.

The Captain drove, and I sat beside him. It was a hot spring day, and under my newly starched fatigues I felt as though my armpits were melting down onto my sides and chest. The roads were dry, and by the time we reached the firing range, my teeth felt gritty with dust, though my mouth had been shut the whole trip. The Captain slammed the brakes on and told me to get the hell out and find Grossbart.

I found him on his belly, firing wildly at the five-hundred-feet target. Waiting their turns behind him were Halpern and Fishbein. Fishbein, wearing a pair of steel-rimmed G.I. glasses I hadn't seen on him before, had the appearance of an old peddler who would gladly have sold you his rifle and the cartridges that were slung all over him. I stood back by the ammo boxes, waiting for Grossbart to finish spraying the distant targets. Fishbein straggled back to stand near me.

"Hello, Sergeant Marx," he said.

"How are you?" I mumbled.

"Fine, thank you. Sheldon's really a good shot."

"I didn't notice."

"I'm not so good, but I think I'm getting the hang of it now. Sergeant, I don't mean to, you know, ask what I shouldn't—" The boy stopped. He was trying to speak intimately, but the noise of the shooting forced him to shout at me.

"What is it?" I asked. Down the range, I saw Captain Barrett standing up in the jeep, scanning the line for me and Grossbart.

"My parents keep asking and asking where we're going," Fishbein said. "Everybody says the Pacific. I don't care, but my parents— If I could relieve their minds, I think I could concentrate more on my shooting."

"I don't know where, Fishbein. Try to concentrate anyway."

"Sheldon says you might be able to find out."

"I don't know a thing, Fishbein. You just take it easy, and don't let Sheldon—"

"I'm taking it easy, Sergeant. It's at home—"

Grossbart had finished on the line, and was dusting his fatigues with one hand. I called to him. "Grossbart, the Captain wants to see you."

He came toward us. His eyes blazed and twinkled. "Hi!"

"Don't point that rifle!" I said.

"I wouldn't shoot you, Sarge." He gave me a smile as wide as a pumpkin, and turned the barrel aside.

"Damn you, Grossbart, this is no joke! Follow me."

I walked ahead of him, and had the awful suspicion that, behind me, Grossbart was *marching,* his rifle on his shoulder, as though he were a one-man detachment. At the jeep, he gave the Captain a rifle salute. "Private Sheldon Grossbart, sir."

"At ease, Grossman." The Captain sat down, slid over into the empty seat, and, crooking a finger, invited Grossbart closer.

"Bart, sir. Sheldon Gross*bart.* It's a common error." Grossbart nodded at me; *I* understood, he indicated. I looked away just as the mess truck pulled up to the range, disgorging a half-dozen K.P.s with rolled-up sleeves. The mess sergeant screamed at them while they set up the chow-line equipment.

"Grossbart, your mama wrote some congressman that we don't feed you right. Do you know that?" the Captain said.

"It was my father, sir. He wrote to Representative Franconi that my religion forbids me to eat certain foods."

"What religion is that, Grossbart?"

"Jewish."

" 'Jewish, *sir,' "* I said to Grossbart.

"Excuse me, sir, Jewish, sir."

"What have you been living on?" the Captain asked. "You've been in the Army a month already. You don't look to me like you're falling to pieces."

"I eat because I have to, sir. But Sergeant Marx will testify to the fact that I don't eat one mouthful more than I need to in order to survive."

"Is that so, Marx?" Barrett asked.

"I've never seen Grossbart eat, sir," I said.

"But you heard the rabbi," Grossbart said. "He told us what to do, and I listened."

The Captain looked at me. "Well, Marx?"

"I still don't know what he eats and doesn't eat, sir."

Grossbart raised his arms to plead with me, and it looked for a moment as though he were going to hand me his weapon to hold. "But, Sergeant—"

"Look, Grossbart, just answer the Captain's questions," I said sharply.

Barrett smiled at me, and I resented it. "All right, Grossbart," he said. "What is it you want? The little piece of paper? You want out?"

"No, sir. Only to be allowed to live as a Jew. And for the others, too."

"What others?"

"Fishbein, sir, and Halpern."

"They don't like the way we serve, either?"

"Halpern throws up, sir. I've seen it."

"I thought *you* throw up."

"Just once, sir. I didn't know the sausage was sausage."

"We'll give menus, Grossbart. We'll show training films about the food, so you can identify when we're trying to poison you."

Grossbart did not answer. The men had been organized into two long chow lines. At the tail end of one, I spotted Fishbein—or, rather, his glasses spotted me. They winked sunlight back at me. Halpern stood next to him, patting the inside of his collar with a khaki handkerchief. They moved with the line as it began to edge up toward the food. The mess sergeant was still screaming at the K.P.s. For a moment, I was actually terrified by the thought that somehow the mess sergeant was going to become involved in Grossbart's problem.

"Marx," the Captain said, "you're a Jewish fella—am I right?"

I played straight man. "Yes, sir."

"How long you been in the Army? Tell this boy."

"Three years and two months."

"A year in combat, Grossbart. Twelve goddam months in combat all through Europe. I admire this man." The Captain snapped a wrist against my chest. "Do you hear him peeping about the food? Do you? I want an answer, Grossbart. Yes or no."

"No, sir."

"And why not? He's a Jewish fella."

"Some things are more important to some Jews than other things to other Jews."

Barrett blew up. "Look, Grossbart. Marx, here, is a good man—a goddam hero. When you were in high school, Sergeant Marx was killing Germans. Who does more for the Jews—you, by throwing up over a lousy piece of sausage, a piece of first-cut meat, or Marx, by killing those Nazi bastards? If I was a Jew, Grossbart, I'd kiss this man's feet. He's a goddam hero, and *he* eats what we give him. Why do you have to cause trouble is what I want to know! What is it you're buckin' for—a discharge?"

"No, sir."

"I'm talking to a wall! Sergeant, get him out of my way." Barrett swung himself back into the driver's seat. "I'm going to see the chaplain." The engine roared, the jeep spun around in a whirl of dust, and the Captain was headed back to camp.

For a moment, Grossbart and I stood side by side, watching the jeep. Then he looked at me and said, "I don't want to start trouble. That's the first thing they toss up to us."

When he spoke, I saw that his teeth were white and straight, and the sight of them suddenly made me understand that Grossbart actually did have parents—that once upon a time someone had taken little Sheldon to the dentist. He was their son. Despite all the talk about his parents, it was hard to believe in Grossbart as a child, an heir—as related by blood to anyone, mother, father, or, above all, to me. This realization led me to another.

"What does your father do, Grossbart?" I asked as we started to walk back toward the chow line.

"He's a tailor."

"An American?"

"Now, yes. A son in the Army," he said, jokingly.

"And your mother?" I asked.

He winked. "A *ballabusta*. She practically sleeps with a dustcloth in her hand."

"She's also an immigrant?"

"All she talks is Yiddish, still."

"And your father, too?"

"A little English. 'Clean,' 'Press,' 'Take the pants in.' That's the extent of it. But they're good to me."

"Then, Grossbart—" I reached out and stopped him. He turned toward me, and when our eyes met, his seemed to jump back, to shiver in their sockets. "Grossbart—you were the one who wrote that letter, weren't you?"

It took only a second or two for his eyes to flash happy again. "Yes." He walked on, and I kept pace. "It's what my father *would* have written if he had known how. It was his name, though. *He* signed it. He even mailed it. I sent it home. For the New York postmark."

I was astonished, and he saw it. With complete seriousness, he thrust his right arm in front of me. "Blood is blood, Sergeant," he said, pinching the blue vein in his wrist.

"What the hell *are* you trying to do, Grossbart?" I asked. "I've seen you eat. Do you know that? I told the Captain I don't know what you eat, but I've seen you eat like a hound at chow."

"We work hard, Sergeant. We're in training. For a furnace to work, you've got to feed it coal."

"Why did you say in the letter that you threw up all the time?"

"I was really talking about Mickey there. I was talking *for* him. He would never write, Sergeant, though I pleaded with him. He'll waste away to nothing if I don't help. Sergeant, I used my name—my father's name—but it's Mickey, and Fishbein, too, I'm watching out for."

"You're a regular Messiah, aren't you?"

We were at the chow line now.

"That's a good one, Sergeant," he said, smiling. "But who knows? Who can tell? Maybe you're the Messiah—a little bit. What Mickey says is the Messiah is a collective idea. He went to Yeshiva, Mickey, for a while. He says *together* we're the Messiah. Me a little bit, you a little bit. You should hear that kid talk, Sergeant, when he gets going."

"Me a little bit, you a little bit," I said. "You'd like to believe that, wouldn't you, Grossbart? That would make everything so clean for you."

"It doesn't seem too bad a thing to believe, Sergeant. It only means we should all *give* a little, is all."

I walked off to eat my rations with the other noncoms.

Two days later, a letter addressed to Captain Barrett passed over my desk. It had come through the chain of command—from the office of Congressman Franconi, where it had been received, to General Lyman, to Colonel Sousa, to Major Lamont, now to Captain Barrett. I read it over twice. It was dated May 14, the day Barrett had spoken with Grossbart on the rifle range.

> Dear Congressman:
>
> First let me thank you for your interest in behalf of my son, Private Sheldon Grossbart. Fortunately, I was able to speak with Sheldon on the phone the other night, and I think I've been able to solve our problem. He is, as I mentioned in my last letter, a very religious boy, and it was only with the greatest difficulty that I could persuade him that the religious thing to do—what God Himself would want Sheldon to do—would be to suffer the pangs of religious remorse for the good of his country and all mankind. It took some doing, Congressman, but finally he saw the light. In fact, what he said (and I wrote down the words on a scratch pad so as never to forget), what he said was "I guess you're right, Dad. So many millions of my fellow-Jews gave up their lives to the enemy, the least I can do is live for a while minus a bit of my heritage so as to help end this struggle and regain for all the children of God dignity and humanity." That, Congressman, would make any father proud.
>
> By the way, Sheldon wanted me to know—and to pass on to you—the name of a soldier who helped him reach this decision: SERGEANT NATHAN MARX. Sergeant Marx is a combat veteran who is Sheldon's first sergeant. This man has helped

Sheldon over some of the first hurdles he's had to face in the Army, and is in part responsible for Sheldon's changing his mind about the dietary laws. I know Sheldon would appreciate any recognition Marx could receive.

Thank you and good luck. I look forward to seeing your name on the next election ballot.

Respectfully,
Samuel E. Grossbart

Attached to the Grossbart communiqué was another, addressed to General Marshall Lyman, the post commander, and signed by Representative Charles E. Franconi, of the House of Representatives. The communiqué informed General Lyman that Sergeant Nathan Marx was a credit to the U.S. Army and the Jewish people.

What was Grossbart's motive in recanting? Did he feel he'd gone too far? Was the letter a strategic retreat—a crafty attempt to strengthen what he considered our alliance? Or had he actually changed his mind, via an imaginary dialogue between Grossbart *père* and Grossbart *fils?* I was puzzled, but only for a few days—that is, only until I realized that, whatever his reasons, he had actually decided to disappear from my life; he was going to allow himself to become just another trainee. I saw him at inspection, but he never winked; at chow formations, but he never flashed me a sign. On Sundays, with the other trainees, he would sit around watching the noncoms' softball team, for which I pitched, but not once did he speak an unnecessary word to me. Fishbein and Halpern retreated, too—at Grossbart's command, I was sure. Apparently he had seen that wisdom lay in turning back before he plunged over into the ugliness of privilege undeserved. Our separation allowed me to forgive him our past encounters, and, finally, to admire him for his good sense.

Meanwhile, free of Grossbart, I grew used to my job and my administrative tasks. I stepped on a scale one day, and discovered I had truly become a noncombatant; I had gained seven pounds. I found patience to get past the first three pages of a book. I thought about the future more and more, and wrote letters to girls I'd known before the war. I even got a few answers. I sent away to Columbia for a Law School catalogue. I continued to follow the war in the Pacific, but it was not my war. I thought I could see the end, and sometimes, at night, I dreamed that I was walking on the streets of Manhattan—Broadway, Third Avenue, 116th Street, where I had lived the three years I attended Columbia. I curled myself around these dreams and I began to be happy.

And then, one Saturday, when everybody was away and I was alone in the orderly room reading a month-old copy of the *Sporting News,* Grossbart reappeared.

"You a baseball fan, Sergeant?"

I looked up. "How are you?"

"Fine," Grossbart said. "They're making a soldier out of me."

"How are Fishbein and Halpern?"

"Coming along," he said. "We've got no training this afternoon. They're at the movies."

"How come you're not with them?"

"I wanted to come over and say hello."

He smiled—a shy, regular-guy smile, as though he and I well knew that our friendship drew its sustenance from unexpected visits, remembered birthdays, and borrowed lawn-mowers. At first it offended me, and then the feeling was swallowed by the general uneasiness I felt at the thought that everyone on the post was locked away in a dark movie theater and I was here alone with Grossbart. I folded up my paper.

"Sergeant," he said, "I'd like to ask a favor. It is a favor, and I'm making no bones about it."

He stopped, allowing me to refuse him a hearing—which, of course, forced me into a courtesy I did not intend. "Go ahead."

"Well, actually it's two favors."

I said nothing.

"The first one's about these rumors. Everybody says we're going to the Pacific."

"As I told your friend Fishbein, I don't know," I said. "You'll just have to wait to find out. Like everybody else."

"You think there's a chance of any of us going East?"

"Germany?" I said. "Maybe."

"I meant New York."

"I don't think so, Grossbart. Offhand."

"Thanks for the information, Sergeant," he said.

"It's not information, Grossbart. Just what I surmise."

"It certainly would be good to be near home. My parents—you know." He took a step toward the door and then turned back. "Oh, the other thing. May I ask the other?"

"What is it?"

"The other thing is—I've got relatives in St. Louis, and they say they'll give me a whole Passover dinner if I can get down there. God, Sergeant, that'd mean an awful lot to me."

I stood up. "No passes during basic, Grossbart."

"But we're off from now till Monday morning, Sergeant. I could leave the post and no one would even know."

"I'd know. You'd know."

"But that's all. Just the two of us. Last night, I called my aunt, and you should have heard her. 'Come—come,' she said. 'I got gefilte fish, *chrain*— the works!' Just a day, Sergeant. I'd take the blame if anything happened."

"The Captain isn't here to sign a pass."

"You could sign."

"Look, Grossbart—"

"Sergeant, for two months, practically, I've been eating *trafe* till I want to die."

"I thought you'd made up your mind to live with it. To be minus a little bit of heritage."

He pointed a finger at me. "You!" he said. "That wasn't for you to read."

"I read it. So what?"

"That letter was addressed to a congressman."

"Grossbart, don't feed me any baloney. You *wanted* me to read it."

"Why are you persecuting me, Sergeant?"

"Are you kidding!"

"I've run into this before," he said, "but never from my own!"

"Get out of here, Grossbart! Get the hell out of my sight!"

He did not move. "Ashamed, that's what you are," he said. "So you take it out on the rest of us. They say Hitler himself was half a Jew. Hearing you, I wouldn't doubt it."

"What are you trying to do with me, Grossbart?" I asked him. "What are you after? You want me to give you special privileges, to change the food, to find out about your orders, to give you weekend passes."

"You even talk like a goy!" Grossbart shook his fist. "Is this just a weekend pass I'm asking for? Is a Seder sacred, or not?"

Seder! It suddenly occurred to me that Passover had been celebrated weeks before. I said so.

"That's right," he replied. "Who says no? A month ago—and I was in the field eating hash! And now all I ask is a simple favor. A Jewish boy I thought would understand. My aunt's willing to go out of her way—to make a Seder a month later. . . ." He turned to go, mumbling.

"Come back here!" I called. He stopped and looked at me. "Grossbart, why can't you be like the rest? Why do you have to stick out like a sore thumb?"

"Because I'm a Jew, Sergeant. I *am* different. Better, maybe not. But different."

"This is a war, Grossbart. For the time being *be* the same."

"I refuse."

"What?"

"I refuse. I can't stop being me, that's all there is to it." Tears came to his eyes. "It's a hard thing to be a Jew. But now I understand what Mickey says—it's a harder thing to stay one." He raised a hand sadly toward me. "Look at *you*."

"Stop crying!"

"Stop this, stop that, stop the other thing! *You* stop, Sergeant. Stop closing your heart to your own!" And, wiping his face with his sleeve, he ran out the door. "The least we can do for one another—the least . . ."

An hour later, looking out the window, I saw Grossbart headed across the field. He wore a pair of starched khakis and carried a little leather ditty bag. I went out into the heat of the day. It was quiet; not a soul was in sight except, over by the mess hall, four K.P.s sitting around a pan, sloped forward from their waists, gabbing and peeling potatoes in the sun.

"Grossbart!" I called.

He looked toward me and continued walking.

"Grossbart, get over here!"

He turned and came across the field. Finally, he stood before me.

"Where are you going?" I asked.

"St. Louis. I don't care."

"You'll get caught without a pass."

"So I'll get caught without a pass."

"You'll go to the stockade."

"I'm *in* the stockade." He made an about-face and headed off.

I let him go only a step or two. "Come back here," I said, and he followed me into the office, where I typed out a pass and signed the Captain's name, and my own initials after it.

He took the pass and then, a moment later, reached out and grabbed my hand. "Sergeant, you don't know how much this means to me."

"O.K.," I said. "Don't get in any trouble."

"I wish I could show you how much this means to me."

"Don't do me any favors. Don't write any more congressmen for citations."

He smiled. "You're right. I won't. But let me do something."

"Bring me a piece of that gefilte fish. Just get out of here."

"I will!" he said. "With a slice of carrot and a little horse-radish. I won't forget."

"All right. Just show your pass at the gate. And don't tell *anybody*."

"I won't. It's a month late, but a good Yom Tov to you."

"Good Yom Tov, Grossbart," I said.

"You're a good Jew, Sergeant. You like to think you have a hard heart, but underneath you're a fine, decent man. I mean that."

Those last three words touched me more than any words from Grossbart's mouth had the right to. "All right, Grossbart," I said. "Now call me 'sir,' and get the hell out of here."

He ran out the door and was gone. I felt very pleased with myself; it was a great relief to stop fighting Grossbart, and it had cost me nothing. Barrett would never find out, and if he did, I could manage to invent some excuse. For a while, I sat at my desk, comfortable in my decision. Then the screen door flew back and Grossbart burst in again. "Sergeant!" he said. Behind him I saw Fishbein and Halpern, both in starched khakis, both carrying ditty bags like Grossbart's.

"Sergeant, I caught Mickey and Larry coming out of the movies. I almost missed them."

"Grossbart—did I say tell no one?" I said.

"But my aunt said I could bring friends. That I should, in fact."

"*I'm* the Sergeant, Grossbart—not your aunt!"

Grossbart looked at me in disbelief. He pulled Halpern up by his sleeve. "Mickey, tell the Sergeant what this would mean to you."

Halpern looked at me and, shrugging, said, "A lot."

Fishbein stepped forward without prompting. "This would mean a great deal to me and my parents, Sergeant Marx."

"No!" I shouted.

Grossbart was shaking his head. "Sergeant, I could see you denying me, but how you can deny Mickey, a Yeshiva boy—that's beyond me."

"I'm not denying Mickey anything," I said. "You just pushed a little too hard, Grossbart. *You* denied him."

"I'll give him my pass, then," Grossbart said. "I'll give him my aunt's address and a little note. At least let him go."

In a second, he had crammed the pass into Halpern's pants pocket. Halpern looked at me, and so did Fishbein. Grossbart was at the door, pushing it open. "Mickey, bring me a piece of gefilte fish, at least," he said, and then he was outside again.

The three of us looked at one another, and then I said, "Halpern, hand that pass over."

He took it from his pocket and gave it to me. Fishbein had now moved to the doorway, where he lingered. He stood there for a moment with his mouth slightly open, and then he pointed to himself. "And me?" he asked.

His utter ridiculousness exhausted me. I slumped down in my seat and felt pulses knocking at the back of my eyes. "Fishbein," I said, "you understand I'm not trying to deny you anything, don't you? If it was my Army, I'd serve gefilte fish in the mess hall. I'd sell *kugel* in the PX, honest to God."

Halpern smiled.

"You understand, don't you, Halpern?"

"Yes, Sergeant."

"And you, Fishbein? I don't want enemies. I'm just like you—I want to serve my time and go home. I miss the same things you miss."

"Then, Sergeant," Fishbein said, "why don't you come, too?"

"Where?"

"To St. Louis. To Shelly's aunt. We'll have a regular Seder. Play hide-the-matzoh." He gave me a broad, black-toothed smile.

I saw Grossbart again, on the other side of the screen.

"Pst!" He waved a piece of paper. "Mickey, here's the address. Tell her I couldn't get away."

Halpern did not move. He looked at me, and I saw the shrug moving up his arms into his shoulders again. I took the cover off my typewriter and made out passes for him and Fishbein. "Go," I said. "The three of you."

I thought Halpern was going to kiss my hand.

That afternoon, in a bar in Joplin, I drank beer and listened with half an ear to the Cardinal game. I tried to look squarely at what I'd become involved in, and began to wonder if perhaps the struggle with Grossbart wasn't as much my fault as his. What was I that I had to *muster* generous feelings? Who was I to have been feeling so grudging, so tight-hearted? After all, I wasn't being asked to move the world. Had I a right, then, or a reason, to clamp down on Grossbart, when that meant clamping down on Halpern, too? And Fishbein—that ugly, agreeable soul? Out of the many recollections of my childhood that had tumbled over me these past few days I heard my grandmother's voice: "What are you making a *tsimmes?*" It was what she would ask my mother when, say, I had cut myself while doing something I shouldn't have done, and her daughter was busy bawling me out. I needed a hug and a kiss, and my mother would moralize. But my grandmother knew—mercy overrides justice. I should have known it, too. Who was Nathan Marx to be such a penny pincher with kindness? Surely, I thought, the Messiah himself—if He should ever come—won't niggle over nickels and dimes. God willing, he'll hug and kiss.

The next day, while I was playing softball over on the parade ground, I decided to ask Bob Wright, who was noncom in charge of Classification and Assignment, where he thought our trainees would be sent when their cycle ended, in two weeks. I asked casually, between innings and he said, "They're pushing them all into the Pacific. Shulman cut the orders on your boys the other day."

The news shocked me, as though I were the father of Halpern, Fishbein, and Grossbart.

That night, I was just sliding into sleep when someone tapped on my door. "Who is it?" I asked.

"Sheldon."

He opened the door and came in. For a moment, I felt his presence without being able to see him. "How was it?" I asked.

He popped into sight in the near-darkness before me. "Great, Sergeant." Then he was sitting on the edge of the bed. I sat up.

"How about you?" he asked. "Have a nice weekend?"

"Yes."

"The others went to sleep." He took a deep, paternal breath. We sat silent for a while, and a homey feeling invaded my ugly little cubicle; the door was locked, the cat was out, the children were safely in bed.

"Sergeant, can I tell you something? Personal?"

I did not answer, and he seemed to know why. "Not about me. About

Mickey. Sergeant, I never felt for anybody like I feel for him. Last night I heard Mickey in the bed next to me. He was crying so, it could have broken your heart. Real sobs."

"I'm sorry to hear that."

"I had to talk to him to stop him. He held my hand, Sergeant—he wouldn't let it go. He was almost hysterical. He kept saying if he only knew where we were going. Even if he knew it *was* the Pacific, that would be better than nothing. Just to know."

Long ago, someone had taught Grossbart the sad rule that only lies can get the truth. Not that I couldn't believe in the fact of Halpern's crying; his eyes *always* seemed red-rimmed. But, fact or not, it became a lie when Grossbart uttered it. He was entirely strategic. But then—it came with the force of indictment—so was I! There are strategies of aggression, but there are strategies of retreat as well. And so, recognizing that I myself had not been without craft and guile, I told him what I knew. "It is the Pacific."

He let out a small gasp, which was not a lie. "I'll tell him. I wish it was otherwise."

"So do I."

He jumped on my words. "You mean you think you could do something? A change, maybe?"

"No, I couldn't do a thing."

"Don't you know anybody over at C. and A.?"

"Grossbart, there's nothing I can do," I said. "If your orders are for the Pacific, then it's the Pacific."

"But Mickey—"

"Mickey, you, me—everybody, Grossbart. There's nothing to be done. Maybe the war'll end before you go. Pray for a miracle."

"But—"

"Good night, Grossbart." I settled back and was relieved to feel the springs unbend as Grossbart rose to leave. I could see him clearly now; his jaw had dropped, and he looked like a dazed prizefighter. I noticed for the first time a little paper bag in his hand.

"Grossbart." I smiled. "My gift?"

"Oh, yes, Sergeant. Here—from all of us." He handed me the bag. "It's egg roll."

"Egg roll?" I accepted the bag and felt a damp grease spot on the bottom. I opened it, sure that Grossbart was joking.

"We thought you'd probably like it. You know—Chinese egg roll. We thought you'd probably have a taste for—"

"Your aunt served egg roll?"

"She wasn't home."

"Grossbart, she invited you. You told me she invited you and your friends."

"I know," he said. "I just reread the letter. *Next* week."

I got out of bed and walked to the window. "Grossbart," I said. But I was not calling to him.

"What?"

"What are you, Grossbart? Honest to God, what are you?"

I think it was the first time I'd asked him a question for which he didn't have an immediate answer.

"How can you do this to people?" I went on.

"Sergeant, the day away did us all a world of good. Fishbein, you should see him, he *loves* Chinese food."

"But the Seder," I said.

"We took second best, Sergeant."

Rage came charging at me. I didn't sidestep. "Grossbart, you're a liar!" I said. "You're a schemer and a crook. You've got no respect for anything. Nothing at all. Not for me, for the truth—not even for poor Halpern! You use us all—"

"Sergeant, Sergeant, I feel for Mickey. Honest to God, I do. I *love* Mickey. I try—"

"You try! You feel!" I lurched toward him and grabbed his shirt front. I shook him furiously. "Grossbart, get out! Get out and stay the hell away from me. Because if I see you, I'll make your life miserable. *You understand that?*"

"Yes."

I let him free, and when he walked from the room, I wanted to spit on the floor where he had stood. I couldn't stop the fury. It engulfed me, owned me, till it seemed I could only rid myself of it with tears or an act of violence. I snatched from the bed the bag Grossbart had given me and, with all my strength, threw it out the window. And the next morning, as the men policed the area around the barracks, I heard a great cry go up from one of the trainees, who had been anticipating only his morning handful of cigarette butts and candy wrappers. "Egg roll!" he shouted. "Holy Christ, Chinese goddam egg roll!"

A week later, when I read the orders that had come down from C. and A., I couldn't believe my eyes. Every single trainee was to be shipped to Camp Stoneman, California, and from there to the Pacific—every trainee but one. Private Sheldon Grossbart. He was to be sent to Fort Monmouth, New Jersey. I read the mimeographed sheet several times. Dee, Farrell, Fishbein, Fuselli, Fylypowycz, Glinicki, Gromke, Gucwa, Halpern, Hardy, Helebrandt, right down to Anton Zygadlo—all were to be headed West before the month was out. All except Grossbart. He had pulled a string, and I wasn't it.

I lifted the phone and called C. and A.

The voice on the other end said smartly, "Corporal Shulman, sir."

"Let me speak to Sergeant Wright."

"Who is this calling, sir?"

"Sergeant Marx."

And, to my surprise, the voice said, *"Oh!"* Then, "Just a minute, Sergeant."

Shulman's *"Oh!"* stayed with me while I waited for Wright to come to the phone. Why *"Oh!"*? Who was Shulman? And then, so simply, I knew I'd discovered the string that Grossbart had pulled. In fact, I could hear Grossbart the day he'd discovered Shulman in the PX, or in the bowling alley, or maybe even at services. "Glad to meet you. Where you from? Bronx? Me, too. Do you know So-and-So? And So-and-So? Me, too! You work at C. and A.? Really? Hey, how's chances of getting East? Could you do something? Change something? Swindle, cheat, lie? We gotta help each other, you know. If the Jews in Germany . . ."

Bob Wright answered the phone. "How are you, Nate? How's the pitching arm?"

"Good. Bob, I wonder if you could do me a favor." I heard clearly my own words, and they so reminded me of Grossbart that I dropped more easily than I could have imagined into what I had planned. "This may sound crazy, Bob, but I got a kid here on orders to Monmouth who wants them changed. He had a brother killed in Europe, and he's hot to go to the Pacific. Says he'd feel like a coward if he wound up Stateside. I don't know, Bob—can anything be done? Put somebody else in the Monmouth slot?"

"Who?" he asked cagily.

"Anybody. First guy in the alphabet. I don't care. The kid just asked if something could be done."

"What's his name?"

"Grossbart, Sheldon."

Wright didn't answer.

"Yeah," I said. "He's a Jewish kid, so he thought I could help him out. You know."

"I guess I can do something," he finally said. "The Major hasn't been around here for weeks. Temporary duty to the golf course. I'll try, Nate, that's all I can say."

"I'd appreciate it, Bob. See you Sunday." And I hung up, perspiring.

The following day, the corrected orders appeared: Fishbein, Fuselli, Fylypowycz, Glinicki, Gromke, Grossbart, Gucwa, Halpern, Hardy . . . Lucky Private Harley Alton was to go to Fort Monmouth, New Jersey, where, for some reason or other, they wanted an enlisted man with infantry training.

After chow that night, I stopped back at the orderly room to straighten out the guard-duty roster. Grossbart was waiting for me. He spoke first.

"You son of a bitch!"

I sat down at my desk, and while he glared at me, I began to make the necessary alterations in the duty roster.

"What do you have against me?" he cried. "Against my family? Would it kill you for me to be near my father, God knows how many months he has left to him?"

"Why so?"

"His heart," Grossbart said. "He hasn't had enough troubles in a lifetime, you've got to add to them. I curse the day I ever met you, Marx! Shulman told me what happened over there. There's no limit to your anti-Semitism, is there? The damage you've done here isn't enough. You have to make a special phone call? You really want me dead!"

I made the last few notations in the duty roster and got up to leave. "Good night, Grossbart."

"You owe me an explanation!" He stood in my path.

"Sheldon, you're the one who owes explanations."

He scowled, "To *you?*"

"To me, I think so—yes. Mostly to Fishbein and Halpern."

"That's right, twist things around. I owe nobody nothing, I've done all I could do for them. Now I think I've got the right to watch out for myself."

"For each other we have to learn to watch out, Sheldon. You told me yourself."

"You call this watching out for me—what you did?"

"No. For all of us."

I pushed him aside and started for the door. I heard his furious breathing behind me, and it sounded like steam rushing from an engine of terrible strength.

"*You'll* be all right," I said from the door. And, I thought, so would Fishbein and Halpern be all right, even in the Pacific, if only Grossbart continued to see—in the obsequiousness of the one, the soft spirituality of the other—some profit for himself.

I stood outside the orderly room, and I heard Grossbart weeping behind me. Over in the barracks, in the lighted windows, I could see the boys in their T shirts sitting on their bunks talking about their orders, as they'd been doing for the past two days. With a kind of quiet nervousness, they polished shoes, shined belt buckles, squared away underwear, trying as best they could to accept their fate. Behind me, Grossbart swallowed hard, accepting his. And then, resisting with all my will an impulse to turn and seek pardon for my vindictiveness, I accepted my own.

Philip Roth was born in Newark, New Jersey, in 1933, educated at Bucknell, has an M.A. from the University of Chicago, has taught writing at Iowa and Princeton, now lives in New York City. His first book, published in 1957, called Goodbye, Columbus, *consisted of the title novella and five short stories. It is unusual for a young writer to be able to have a collection of stories published before he has written a novel, but these stories had been much admired when they appeared in magazines. The book, given a Houghton Mifflin Literary Fellowship award, was hailed by reviewers as marking the appearance of an exceptionally vigorous new talent, was bought and read enthusiastically by the public, and went on to win the National Book Award. The novella, "Goodbye, Columbus," and most of the stories were directly concerned with cultural conflicts of Jews in varying degrees of assimilation into American life. His second book,* Letting Go *(1962), was only partially concerned with these themes; a big novel, it recounts the experiences of several characters in and out of the academic world in New York and in the Midwest. His second novel,* When She Was Good *(1967), hasn't a single Jewish character in it and is set in a midwestern town called Liberty Center in the present. Roth's work, then, has taken a direction opposite Malamud's: instead of going back into a Jewish past, it has gone forward into an American present.*

In reading "Defender of the Faith" it is important to see that the story is about Nathan Marx, not Sheldon Grossbart. When the story was published in The New Yorker *(April, 1959), Roth was accused by many readers of having confirmed an anti-Semitic stereotype in his portrayal of Grossbart. In an interesting article, "Writing About Jews," in* Commentary *(December, 1963), defending his work from this and other charges, Roth wrote of "Defender of the Faith": "The story is about one man who uses his own religion, and another's uncertain conscience, for selfish ends; but mostly it is about this other man, the narrator, who because of the ambiguities of being a member of his particular religion, is involved in a taxing, if mistaken, conflict of loyalties." The conflict may appear to be between Sheldon Grossbart and the U.S. Army: for the Army is the very epitome of the structured-but-homogenous bureaucracy, where the only differences acknowledged and the only privileges accorded are on the basis of rank; and Grossbart, for self-serving and hypocritical reasons, is constantly asserting his differentness as a Jew in order to obtain privileges to which he is not entitled. This serves as a useful dramatic situation for the story, but the real conflict takes place within the consciousness of Sergeant Marx. What "happens" in the story happens to Sergeant Marx; he is the point-of-view character and the one on whom the events of the story's action have an effect. At the beginning of the story his heart has been hardened by years of combat in Europe: "I had changed enough in two years not to mind the trembling of the old people, the crying of the very young, the uncertainty and fear in the eyes of the once arrogant. I had been fortunate enough to develop an infantryman's heart, which, like his feet, at first aches and swells but finally grows horny enough for him to travel the weirdest paths without feeling a thing." He is accepted and assimilated, a hero, a man with "guts," who not only plays ball with the way things are but pitches for the non-coms. But the war "had shut off all softness I might feel for my fellows." Grossbart and Fishbein and especially Halpern evoke "home and time past, and memory plunged down through all I had anesthetized, and came to what I suddenly remembered was myself." And then, "in search of more of me," he follows them to shul. The various episodes of the story continue to soften his infantryman's heart, as he is repeatedly reminded of the warmth and tenderness of his Jewish family upbringing and of the rituals of his religion and its holy days. The fact that Grossbart corrupts and exploits all these aspects of Jewish family and faith gradually strengthens rather than weakens Marx's remembrance of their true meanings. It is not "vindictiveness," as Marx fears, that motivates his action at the end; in fact, it is quite the opposite, for that action shows that Marx is now capable again of feeling and of taking actions from his feelings. Grossbart accuses him—"There's no limit to your anti-Semitism, is there?"—but it is not anti-Semitism that motivates Marx; again, it is just the opposite. He did it, as he tells Grossbart, "for all of us." He has arranged to have Grossbart the finagler continue to protect the unassimilable—Fishbein the obsequious peddler and Halpern the soft spiritual scholar. But more importantly, Marx has at the end accepted his own "fate," which was to have acted as "defender of the faith," a role he would never have thought possible for himself at the beginning of the story.*

Eli, the Fanatic

◇◇◇◇◇◇◇

Lᴇᴏ ᴛᴢᴜᴛᴇᴚ stepped out from back of a white column to welcome Eli Peck. Eli jumped back, surprised; then they shook hands and Tzuref gestured him into the sagging old mansion. At the door Eli turned, and down the slope of lawn, past the jungle of hedges, beyond the dark, untrampled horse path, he saw the street lights blink on in Woodenton. The stores along Coach House Road tossed up a burst of yellow—it came to Eli as a secret signal from his townsmen: "Tell this Tzuref where we stand, Eli. This is a modern community, Eli, we have our families, we pay taxes . . ." Eli, burdened by the message, gave Tzuref a dumb, weary stare.

"You must work a full day," Tzuref said, steering the attorney and his briefcase into the chilly hall.

Eli's heels made a racket on the cracked marble floor, and he spoke above it. "It's the commuting that's killing," he said, and entered the dim room Tzuref waved open for him. "Three hours a day . . . I came right from the train." He dwindled down into a harp-backed chair. He expected it would be deeper than it was and consequently jarred himself on the sharp bones of his seat. It woke him, this shiver of the behind, to his business. Tzuref, a bald shaggy-browed man who looked as if he'd once been very fat, sat back of an empty desk, halfway hidden, as though he were settled on the floor. Everything around him was empty. There were no books in the bookshelves, no rugs on the floor, no draperies in the big casement windows. As Eli began to speak Tzuref got up and swung a window back on one noisy hinge. "May and it's like August," he said, and with his back to Eli, he revealed the black circle on the back of his head. The crown of his head was missing! He returned through the dimness—the lamps had no bulbs—and Eli realized all he'd seen was a skullcap. Tzuref struck a match and lit a candle, just as the half-dying shouts of children at play rolled in through the open window. It was as though Tzuref had opened it so Eli could hear them.

"Aah, now," he said. "I received your letter."

Eli poised, waiting for Tzuref to swish open a drawer and remove the letter from his file. Instead the old man leaned forward onto his stomach, worked his hand into his pants pocket, and withdrew what appeared to be a week-old handkerchief. He uncrumpled it; he unfolded it; he ironed it on the desk with the side of his hand. "So," he said.

Eli pointed to the grimy sheet which he'd done over word-by-word with his partners, Lewis and McDonnell. "I expected an answer," Eli said. "It's a week."

"It was so important, Mr. Peck, I knew you would come."

Some children ran under the open window and their mysterious babble —not mysterious to Tzuref, who smiled—entered the room like a third person. Their noise caught up against Eli's flesh and he was unable to restrain a shudder. He wished he had gone home, showered and eaten dinner, before calling on Tzuref. He was not feeling as professional as usual—the place was too dim, it was too late. But down in Woodenton they would be waiting, his clients and neighbors. He spoke for the Jews of Woodenton, not just himself and his wife.

"You understood?" Eli said.

"It's not hard."

"It's a matter of zoning . . ." and when Tzuref did not answer, but only drummed his fingers on his lips, Eli said, "We didn't make the laws . . ."

"You respect them."

"They protect us . . . the community."

"The law is the law," Tzuref said.

"Exactly!" Eli had the urge to rise and walk about the room.

"And then of course"—Tzuref made a pair of scales in the air with his hands—"the law is not the law. When is the law that is the law not the law?" He jiggled the scales. "And vice versa."

"Simply," Eli said sharply. "You can't have a boarding school in a residential area." He would not allow Tzuref to cloud the issue with issues. "We thought it better to tell you before any action is undertaken."

"But a house in a residential area?"

"Yes. That's what residential means." The DP's English was perhaps not as good as it seemed at first. Tzuref spoke slowly, but till then Eli had mistaken it for craft—or even wisdom. "Residence means home," he added.

"So this is my residence."

"But the children?"

"It is their residence."

"*Seventeen* children?"

"Eighteen," Tzuref said.

"But you *teach* them here."

"The Talmud. That's illegal?"

"That makes it school."

Tzuref hung the scales again, tipping slowly the balance.

"Look, Mr. Tzuref, in America we call such a place a boarding school."

"Where they teach the Talmud?"

"Where they teach period. You are the headmaster, they are the students."

Tzuref placed his scales on the desk. "Mr. Peck," he said, "I don't believe it . . ." but he did not seem to be referring to anything Eli had said.

"Mr. Tzuref, that is the law. I came to ask what you intend to do."

"What I *must* do?"

"I hope they are the same."

"They are." Tzuref brought his stomach into the desk. "We stay." He smiled. "We are tired. The headmaster is tired. The students are tired."

Eli rose and lifted his briefcase. It felt so heavy packed with the grievances, vengeances, and schemes of his clients. There were days when he carried it like a feather—in Tzuref's office it weighed a ton.

"Goodbye, Mr. Tzuref."

"Sholom," Tzuref said.

Eli opened the door to the office and walked carefully down the dark tomb of a corridor to the door. He stepped out on the porch and, leaning against a pillar, looked down across the lawn to the children at play. Their voices whooped and rose and dropped as they chased each other round the old house. The dusk made the children's game look like a tribal dance. Eli straightened up, started off the porch, and suddenly the dance was ended. A long piercing scream trailed after. It was the first time in his life anyone had run at the sight of him. Keeping his eyes on the lights of Woodenton, he headed down the path.

And then, seated on a bench beneath a tree, Eli saw him. At first it seemed only a deep hollow of blackness—then the figure emerged. Eli recognized him from the description. There he was, wearing the hat, that hat which was the very cause of Eli's mission, the source of Woodenton's upset. The town's lights flashed their message once again: "Get the one with the hat. What a nerve, what a nerve . . ."

Eli started towards the man. Perhaps he was less stubborn than Tzuref, more reasonable. After all, it was the law. But when he was close enough to call out, he didn't. He was stopped by the sight of the black coat that fell down below the man's knees, and the hands which held each other in his lap. By the round-topped, wide-brimmed Talmudic hat, pushed onto the back of his head. And by the beard, which hid his neck and was so soft and thin it fluttered away and back again with each heavy breath he took. He was asleep, his sidelocks curled loose on his cheeks. His face was no older than Eli's.

Eli hurried towards the lights.

The note on the kitchen table unsettled him. Scribblings on bits of paper had made history this past week. This one, however, was unsigned.

"Sweetie," it said, "I went to sleep. I had a sort of Oedipal experience with the baby today. Call Ted Heller."

She had left him a cold soggy dinner in the refrigerator. He hated cold soggy dinners, but would take one gladly in place of Miriam's presence. He was ruffled, and she never helped that, not with her infernal analytic powers. He loved her when life was proceeding smoothly—and that was when she loved him. But sometimes Eli found being a lawyer surrounded him like quicksand—he couldn't get his breath. Too often he wished he were pleading for the other side; though if he were on the other side, then he'd wish he were on the side he was. The trouble was that sometimes the law didn't seem to be the answer, *law* didn't seem to have anything to do with what was aggravating everybody. And that, of course, made him feel foolish and unnecessary . . . Though that was not the situation here—the townsmen had a case. But not *exactly,* and if Miriam were awake to see Eli's upset, she would set about explaining his distress to him, understanding him, forgiving him, so as to get things back to Normal, for Normal was where they loved one another. The difficulty with Miriam's efforts was they only upset him more; not only did they explain little to him about himself or his predicament, but they convinced him of *her* weakness. Neither Eli nor Miriam, it turned out, was terribly strong. Twice before he'd faced this fact, and on both occasions had found solace in what his neighbors forgivingly referred to as "a nervous breakdown."

Eli ate his dinner with his briefcase beside him. Halfway through, he gave in to himself, removed Tzuref's notes, and put them on the table, beside Miriam's. From time to time he flipped through the notes, which had been carried into town by the one in the black hat. The first note, the incendiary:

To whom it may concern:
Please give this gentleman the following: Boys shoes with rubber heels and soles.

5 prs size 6c
3 prs size 5c
3 prs size 5b
2 prs size 4a
3 prs size 4c
1 pr size 7b
1 pr size 7c

Total 18 prs. boys shoes. This gentleman has a check already signed. Please fill in correct amount.

L. TZUREF
Director, Yeshivah of
Woodenton, N.Y.
(5/8/48)

"Eli, a regular greenhorn," Ted Heller had said. "He didn't say a word. Just handed me the note and stood there, like in the Bronx the old guys who used to come around selling Hebrew trinkets."

"A Yeshivah!" Artie Berg had said. "Eli, in Woodenton, a Yeshivah! If I want to live in Brownsville, Eli, I'll live in Brownsville."

"Eli," Harry Shaw speaking now, "the old Puddington place. Old man Puddington'll roll over in his grave. Eli, when I left the city, Eli, I didn't plan the city should come to me."

Note number two:

> Dear Grocer:
>
> Please give this gentleman ten pounds of sugar. Charge it to our account, Yeshivah of Woodenton. NY—which we will now open with you and expect a bill each month. The gentleman will be in to see you once or twice a week.
>
> L. Tzuref, Director
> (5/10/48)

P.S. Do you carry kosher meat?

"He walked right by my window, the greenie," Ted had said, "and he nodded, Eli. He's my *friend* now."

"Eli," Artie Berg had said, "he handed the damn thing to a *clerk* at Stop N' Shop—and in that hat yet!"

"Eli," Harry Shaw again, "it's not funny. Someday, Eli, it's going to be a hundred little kids with little *yamalkahs* chanting their Hebrew lessons on Coach House Road, and then it's not going to strike you funny."

"Eli, what goes on up there—my kids hear strange sounds."

"Eli, this is a modern community."

"Eli, we pay taxes."

"Eli."

"Eli!"

"*Eli!*"

At first it was only another townsman crying in his ear; but when he turned he saw Miriam, standing in the doorway, behind her belly.

"Eli, sweetheart, how was it?"

"He said no."

"Did you see the other one?" she asked.

"Sleeping, under a tree."

"Did you let him know how people feel?"

"He was sleeping."

"Why didn't you wake him up? Eli, this isn't an everyday thing."

"He was tired!"

"Don't shout, please," Miriam said.

" 'Don't shout. I'm pregnant. The baby is heavy.' " Eli found he was getting angry at nothing she'd said yet; it was what she was going to say.

"He's a very heavy baby the doctor says," Miriam told him.

"Then sit *down* and make my dinner." Now he found himself angry about her not being present at the dinner which he'd just been relieved that she wasn't present at. It was as though he had a raw nerve for a tail, that he kept stepping on. At last Miriam herself stepped on it.

"Eli, you're upset. I understand."

"You *don't* understand."

She left the room. From the stairs she called, "I do, sweetheart."

It was a trap! He would grow angry knowing she would be "understanding." She would in turn grow more understanding seeing his anger. He would in turn grow angrier . . . The phone rang.

"Hello," Eli said.

"Eli, Ted. So?"

"So nothing."

"Who is Tzuref? He's an American guy?"

"No. A DP. German."

"And the kids?"

"DP's too. He teaches them."

"What? What subjects?" Ted asked.

"I don't know."

"And the guy with the hat, you saw the guy with the hat?"

"Yes. He was sleeping."

"Eli, he sleeps with the *hat?*"

"He sleeps with the hat."

"Goddam fanatics," Ted said. "This is the twentieth century, Eli. Now it's the guy with the hat. Pretty soon all the little Yeshivah boys'll be spilling down into town."

"Next thing they'll be after our daughters."

"Michele and Debbie wouldn't look at them."

"Then," Eli mumbled, "you've got nothing to worry about, Teddie," and he hung up.

In a moment the phone rang. "Eli? We got cut off. We've got nothing to worry about? You worked it out?"

"I have to see him again tomorrow. We can work something out."

"That's fine, Eli. I'll call Artie and Harry."

Eli hung up.

"I thought you said *nothing* worked out." It was Miriam.

"I did."

"Then why did you tell Ted *something* worked out?"

"It did."

"Eli, maybe you should get a little more therapy."

"That's enough of that, Miriam."

"You can't function as a lawyer by being neurotic. That's no answer."

"You're ingenious, Miriam."

She turned, frowning, and took her heavy baby to bed.

The phone rang.

"Eli, Artie. Ted called. You worked it out? No trouble?"

"Yes."

"When are they going?"

"Leave it to me, will you, Artie? I'm tired. I'm going to sleep."

In bed Eli kissed his wife's belly and laid his head upon it to think. He laid it lightly, for she was that day entering the second week of her ninth month. Still, when she slept, it was a good place to rest, to rise and fall with her breathing and figure things out. "If that guy would take off that crazy hat. I know it, what eats them. If he'd take off that crazy hat everything would be all right."

"What?" Miriam said.

"I'm talking to the baby."

Miriam pushed herself up in bed. "Eli, please, baby, shouldn't you maybe stop in to see Dr. Eckman, just for a little conversation?"

"I'm fine."

"Oh, sweetie!" she said, and put her head back on the pillow.

"You know what your mother brought to this marriage—a sling chair and a goddam New School enthusiasm for Sigmund Freud."

Miriam feigned sleep, he could tell by the breathing.

"I'm telling the kid the truth, aren't I, Miriam? A sling chair, three months to go on a *New Yorker* subscription, and *An Introduction to Psychoanalysis*. Isn't that right?"

"Eli, must you be aggressive?"

"That's all you worry about, is your insides. You stand in front of the mirror all day and look at yourself being pregnant."

"Pregnant mothers have a relationship with the fetus that fathers can't understand."

"Relationship my ass. What is my liver doing now? What is my small intestine doing now? Is my island of Langerhans on the blink?"

"Don't be jealous of a little fetus, Eli."

"I'm jealous of your island of Langerhans!"

"Eli, I can't argue with you when I know it's not me you're really angry with. Don't you see, sweetie, you're angry with yourself."

"You and Eckman."

"Maybe he could help, Eli."

"Maybe he could help you. You're practically lovers as it is."

"You're being hostile again," Miriam said.

"What do you care—it's only *me* I'm being hostile towards."

"Eli, we're going to have a beautiful baby, and I'm going to have a perfectly simple delivery, and you're going to make a fine father, and there's absolutely no reason to be obsessed with whatever is on your mind. All we have to worry about—" she smiled at him "—is a name."

Eli got out of bed and slid into his slippers. "We'll name the kid Eckman if it's a boy and Eckman if it's a girl."

"Eckman Peck sounds terrible."

"He'll have to live with it," Eli said, and he went down to his study where the latch on his briefcase glinted in the moonlight that came through the window.

He removed the Tzuref notes and read through them all again. It unnerved him to think of all the flashy reasons his wife could come up with for his reading and rereading the notes. "Eli, why are you so *preoccupied* with Tzuref?" "Eli, stop getting *involved*. Why do you think you're getting *involved*, Eli?" Sooner or later, everybody's wife finds their weak spot. His goddam luck he had to be neurotic! Why couldn't he have been born with a short leg?

He removed the cover from his typewriter, hating Miriam for the edge she had. All the time he wrote the letter, he could hear what she would be saying about his not being *able* to let the matter drop. Well, her trouble was that she wasn't *able* to face the matter. But he could hear her answer already: clearly, he was guilty of "a reaction formation." Still, all the fancy phrases didn't fool Eli: all she wanted really was for Eli to send Tzuref and family on their way, so that the community's temper would quiet, and the calm circumstances of their domestic happiness return. All she wanted were order and love in her private world. Was she so wrong? Let the world bat its brains out—in Woodenton there should be peace. He wrote the letter anyway:

Dear Mr. Tzuref:

Our meeting this evening seems to me inconclusive. I don't think there's any reason for us not to be able to come up with some sort of compromise that will satisfy the Jewish community of Woodenton and the Yeshivah and yourself. It seems to me that what most disturbs my neighbors are the visits to town by the gentleman in the black hat, suit, etc. Woodenton is a progressive suburban community whose members, both Jewish and Gentile, are anxious that their families live in comfort and beauty and serenity. This is, after all, the twentieth century, and we do not think it too much to ask that the members of our community dress in a manner appropriate to the time and place.

Woodenton, as you may not know, has long been the home of well-to-do Protestants. It is only since the war that Jews have been able to buy property here, and for Jews and Gentiles to live beside each other in amity. For this adjustment to be made, both Jews and Gentiles alike have had to give up some of their more extreme practices in order not to threaten or offend the other. Certainly such amity is to be desired. Perhaps if such conditions had existed in prewar Europe, the persecution of the Jewish people, of which you and those 18 children have been victims, could not have been carried out with such success—in fact, might not have been carried out at all.

Therefore, Mr. Tzuref, will you accept the following conditions? If you can, we will see fit not to carry out legal action against the Yeshivah for failure to comply with township Zoning ordinances No. 18 and No. 23. The conditions are simply:

1. The religious, educational, and social activities of the Yeshivah of Woodenton will be confined to the Yeshivah grounds.

2. Yeshivah personnel are welcomed in the streets and stores of Woodenton provided they are attired in clothing usually associated with American life in the 20th century.

If these conditions are met, we see no reason why the Yeshivah of Woodenton cannot live peacefully and satisfactorily with the Jews of Woodenton—as the Jews of Woodenton have come to live with the Gentiles of Woodenton. I would appreciate an immediate reply.

> Sincerely,
> ELI PECK, Attorney

Two days later Eli received his immediate reply:

> Mr. Peck:
> The suit the gentleman wears is all he's got.
> Sincerely,
> LEO TZUREF, Headmaster

Once again, as Eli swung around the dark trees and onto the lawn, the children fled. He reached out with his briefcase as if to stop them, but they were gone so fast all he saw moving was a flock of skullcaps.

"Come, come . . . ." a voice called from the porch. Tzuref appeared from behind a pillar. Did he *live* behind those pillars? Was he just watching the children at play? Either way, when Eli appeared, Tzuref was ready, with no forewarning.

"Hello," Eli said.

"Sholom."

"I didn't mean to frighten them."

"They're scared, so they run."

"I didn't do anything."

Tzuref shrugged. The little movement seemed to Eli strong as an accusation. What he didn't get at home, he got here.

Inside the house they took their seats. Though it was lighter than a few evenings before, a bulb or two would have helped. Eli had to hold his briefcase towards the window for the last gleamings. He removed Tzuref's letter from a manila folder. Tzuref removed Eli's letter from his pants pocket. Eli removed the carbon of his own letter from another manila folder. Tzuref removed Eli's first letter from his back pocket. Eli removed the carbon from his briefcase. Tzuref raised his palms. ". . . It's all I've got . . ."

Those upraised palms, the mocking tone—another accusation. It was a crime to keep carbons! Everybody had an edge on him—Eli could do no right.

"I offered a compromise, Mr. Tzuref. You refused."

"Refused, Mr. Peck? What is, is."

"The man could get a new suit."

"That's all he's got."

"So you told me," Eli said.

"So I told you, so you know."

"It's not an insurmountable obstacle, Mr. Tzuref. We have stores."

"For that too?"

"On Route 12, a Robert Hall—"

"To take away the one thing a man's got?"

"Not take away, *replace.*"

"But I tell you he has nothing. *Nothing.* You have that word in English? *Nicht? Gornisht?*"

"Yes, Mr. Tzuref, we have the word."

"A mother and a father?" Tzuref said. "No. A wife? No. A baby? A little ten-month-old baby? No! A village full of friends? A synagogue where you knew the feel of every seat under your pants? Where with your eyes closed you could smell the cloth of the Torah?" Tzuref pushed out of his chair, stirring a breeze that swept Eli's letter to the floor. At the window he leaned out, and looked, beyond Woodenton. When he turned he was shaking a finger at Eli. "And a medical experiment they performed on him yet! That leaves nothing, Mr. Peck. Absolutely nothing!"

"I misunderstood."

"No news reached Woodenton?"

"About the suit, Mr. Tzuref. I thought he couldn't afford another."

"He can't."

They were right where they'd begun. "Mr. Tzuref!" Eli demanded. *"Here?"* He smacked his hand to his billfold.

"Exactly!" Tzuref said, smacking his own breast.

"Then we'll buy him one!" Eli crossed to the window and, taking Tzuref by the shoulders, pronounced each word slowly. "We-will-pay-for-it. All right?"

"Pay? What, diamonds!"

Eli raised a hand to his inside pocket, then let it drop. Oh stupid! Tzuref, father to eighteen, had smacked not what lay under his coat, but deeper, under the ribs.

"Oh . . ." Eli said. He moved away along the wall. "The suit is all he's got then."

"You got my letter," Tzuref said.

Eli stayed back in the shadow, and Tzuref turned to his chair. He swished Eli's letter from the floor, and held it up. "You say too much . . . all this reasoning . . . all these conditions . . ."

"What can I do?"

"You have the word 'suffer' in English?"

"We have the word suffer. We have the word law too."

"Stop with the law! You have the word suffer. Then try it. It's a little thing."

"They won't," Eli said.

"But you, Mr. Peck, how about you?"

"I am them, they are me, Mr. Tzuref."

"Aach! You are us, we are you!"

Eli shook and shook his head. In the dark he suddenly felt that Tzuref might put him under a spell. "Mr. Tzuref, a little light?"

Tzuref lit what tallow was left in the holders, Eli was afraid to ask if they couldn't afford electricity. Maybe candles were all they had left.

"Mr. Peck, who made the law, may I ask you that?"

"The people."

"No."

"Yes."

"Before the people."

"No one. Before the people there was no law." Eli didn't care for the conversation, but with only candlelight, he was being lulled into it.

"Wrong," Tzuref said.

"We make the law, Mr. Tzuref. It is our community. These are my neighbors. I am their attorney. They pay me. Without law there is chaos."

"What you call law, I call shame. The heart, Mr. Peck, the heart is law! God!" he announced.

"Look, Mr. Tzuref, I didn't come here to talk metaphysics. People use the law, it's a flexible thing. They protect what they value, their property, their well-being, their happiness—"

"Happiness? They hide their shame. And you, Mr. Peck, you are shame-less?"

"We do it," Eli said, wearily, "for our children. This is the twentieth century . . ."

"For the goyim maybe. For me the Fifty-eighth." He pointed at Eli. "That is too old for shame."

Eli felt squashed. Everybody in the world had evil reasons for his actions. Everybody! With reasons so cheap, who buys bulbs. "Enough wisdom, Mr. Tzuref. Please. I'm exhausted."

"Who isn't?" Tzuref said.

He picked Eli's papers from his desk and reached up with them. "What do you intend for us to do?"

"What you must," Eli said. "I made the offer."

"So he must give up his suit?"

"Tzuref, Tzuref, leave me be with that suit! I'm not the only lawyer in the world. I'll drop the case, and you'll get somebody who won't talk compromise. Then you'll have no home, no children, nothing. Only a lousy black suit! Sacrifice what you want. I know what I would do."

To that Tzuref made no answer, but only handed Eli his letters.

"It's not me, Mr. Tzuref, it's them."

"They are you."

"No," Eli intoned, "I am me. They are them. You are you."

"You talk about leaves and branches. I'm dealing with under the dirt."

"Mr. Tzuref, you're driving me crazy with Talmudic wisdom. This is that, that is the other thing. Give me a straight answer."

"Only for straight questions."

"Oh, God!"

Eli returned to his chair and plunged his belongings into his case. "Then, that's all," he said angrily.

Tzuref gave him the shrug.

"Remember, Tzuref, you called this down on yourself."

"*I* did?"

Eli refused to be his victim again. Double-talk proved nothing.

"Goodbye," he said.

But as he opened the door leading to the hall, he heard Tzuref.

"And your wife, how is she?"

"Fine, just fine." Eli kept going.

"And the baby is due when, any day?"

Eli turned. "That's right."

"Well," Tzuref said, rising. "Good luck."

"You know?"

Tzuref pointed out the window—then, with his hands, he drew upon himself a beard, a hat, a long, long coat. When his fingers formed the hem they touched the floor. "He shops two, three times a week, he gets to know them."

"He *talks* to them?"

"He sees them."

"And he can tell which is my wife?"

"They shop at the same stores. He says she is beautiful. She has a kind face. A woman capable of love . . . though who can be sure."

"He talks about *us,* to *you?"* demanded Eli.

"You talk about us, to her?"

"Goodbye, Mr. Tzuref."

Tzuref said, "Sholom. And good luck—I know what it is to have children. Sholom," Tzuref whispered, and with the whisper the candles went out. But the instant before, the flames leaped into Tzuref's eyes, and Eli saw it was not luck Tzuref wished him at all.

Outside the door, Eli waited. Down the lawn the children were holding hands and whirling around in a circle. At first he did not move. But he could not hide in the shadows all night. Slowly he began to slip along the front of the house. Under his hands he felt where bricks were out. He moved in the shadows until he reached the side. And then, clutching his briefcase to his chest, he broke across the darkest spots of the lawn. He aimed for a distant glade of woods, and when he reached it he did not stop, but ran through until he was so dizzied that the trees seemed to be running beside him, fleeing not towards Woodenton but away. His lungs were nearly ripping their seams as he burst into the yellow glow of the Gulf station at the edge of town.

"Eli, I had pains today. Where were you?"

"I went to Tzuref."

"Why didn't you call? I was worried."

He tossed his hat past the sofa and onto the floor. "Where are my winter suits?"

"In the hall closet. Eli, it's May."

"I need a strong suit." He left the room, Miriam behind him.

"Eli, talk to me. Sit down. Have dinner. Eli, what are you doing? You're going to get moth balls all over the carpet."

He peered out from the hall closet. Then he peered in again—there was a zipping noise, and suddenly he swept a greenish tweed suit before his wife's eyes.

"Eli, I love you in that suit. But not now. Have something to eat. I made dinner tonight—I'll warm it."

"You've got a box big enough for this suit?"

"I got a Bonwit's box, the other day. Eli, *why?"*

"Miriam, you see me doing something, let me do it."

"You haven't eaten."

"I'm *doing* something." He started up the stairs to the bedroom.

"Eli, would you please tell me what it is you want, and why?"

He turned and looked down at her. "Suppose this time you give me the reasons *before* I tell you what I'm doing. It'll probably work out the same anyway."

"Eli, I want to help."

"It doesn't concern you."

"But I want to help *you*," Miriam said.

"Just be quiet, then."

"But you're upset," she said, and she followed him up the stairs, heavily, breathing for two.

"Eli, what now?"

"A shirt." He yanked open all the drawers of their new teak dresser. He extracted a shirt.

"Eli, batiste? With a tweed suit?" she inquired.

He was at the closet now, on his knees. "Where are my cordovans?"

"Eli, why are you doing this so compulsively? You look like you *have* to do something."

"Oh, Miriam, you're supersubtle."

"Eli, stop this and talk to me. Stop it or I'll call Dr. Eckman."

Eli was kicking off the shoes he was wearing. "Where's the Bonwit box?"

"Eli, do you want me to have the baby right *here!*"

Eli walked over and sat down on the bed. He was draped not only with his own clothing, but also with the greenish tweed suit, the batiste shirt, and under each arm a shoe. He raised his arms and let the shoes drop onto the bed. Then he undid his necktie with one hand and his teeth and added that to the booty.

"Underwear," he said. "He'll need underwear."

"Who!"

He was slipping out of his socks.

Miriam kneeled down and helped him ease his left foot out of the sock. She sat with it on the floor. "Eli, just lie back. Please."

"Plaza 9-3103."

"What?"

"Eckman's number," he said. "It'll save you the trouble."

"Eli—"

"You've got that goddam tender 'You need help' look in your eyes, Miriam, don't tell me you don't."

"I don't."

"I'm not flipping," Eli said.

"I know, Eli."

"Last time I sat in the bottom of the closet and chewed on my bedroom slippers. That's what I did."

"I know."

"And I'm not doing that. This is not a nervous breakdown, Miriam, let's get that straight."

"Okay," Miriam said. She kissed the foot she held. Then, softly, she asked, "What *are* you doing?"

"Getting clothes for the guy in the hat. Don't tell me why, Miriam. Just let me do it."

"That's all?" she asked.

"That's all."

"You're not leaving?"

"No."

"Sometimes I think it gets too much for you, and you'll just leave."

"What gets too much?"

"I don't *know*, Eli. Something gets too much. Whenever everything's peaceful for a long time, and things are nice and pleasant, and we're expecting to be even happier. Like now. It's as if you don't think we *deserve* to be happy."

"Damn it, Miriam! I'm giving this guy a new suit, is that all right? From now on he comes into Woodenton like everybody else, is that all right with you?"

"And Tzuref moves?"

"I don't even know if he'll take the suit, Miriam! What do you have to bring up moving!"

"Eli, I didn't bring up moving. Everybody did. That's what everybody wants. Why make everybody un*happy?* It's even a law, Eli."

"Don't tell me what's the law."

"All right, sweetie. I'll get the box."

"I'll get the box. Where is it?"

"In the basement."

When he came up from the basement, he found all the clothes neatly folded and squared away on the sofa: shirt, tie, shoes, socks, underwear, belt, and an old gray flannel suit. His wife sat on the end of the sofa, looking like an anchored balloon.

"Where's the green suit?" he said.

"Eli, it's your loveliest suit. It's my favorite suit. Whenever I think of you, Eli, it's in that suit."

"Get it out."

"Eli, it's a Brooks Brothers suit. You say yourself how much you love it."

"Get it out."

"But the gray flannel's more practical. For shopping."

"Get it out."

"You go overboard, Eli. That's your trouble. You won't do anything in moderation. That's how people destroy themselves."

"I do *everything* in moderation. That's my trouble. The suit's in the closet again?"

She nodded, and began to fill up with tears. "Why does it have to be *your* suit? Who are you even to decide to give a suit? What about the others?" She was crying openly, and holding her belly. "Eli, I'm going to have a baby. Do we need all *this?*" and she swept the clothes off the sofa to the floor.

At the closet Eli removed the green suit. "It's a J. Press," he said, looking at the lining.

"I hope to hell he's happy with it!" Miriam said, sobbing.

A half hour later the box was packed. The cord he'd found in the kitchen cabinet couldn't keep the outfit from popping through. The trouble was there was too much: the gray suit *and* the green suit, an oxford shirt as well as the batiste. But let him have two suits! Let him have three, four, if only this damn silliness would stop! And a hat—of course! God, he'd almost forgotten the hat. He took the stairs two at a time and in Miriam's closet yanked a hatbox from the top shelf. Scattering hat and tissue paper to the floor, he returned downstairs, where he packed away the hat he'd worn that day. Then he looked at his wife, who lay outstretched on the floor before the fireplace. For the third time in as many minutes she was saying, "Eli, this is the real thing."

"Where?"

"Right under the baby's head, like somebody's squeezing oranges."

Now that he'd stopped to listen he was stupefied. He said, "But you have two more weeks . . ." Somehow he'd really been expecting it was to go on not just another two weeks, but another nine months. This led him to suspect, suddenly, that his wife was feigning pain so as to get his mind off delivering the suit. And just as suddenly he resented himself for having such a thought. God, what had he become! He'd been an unending bastard towards her since this Tzuref business had come up—just when her pregnancy must have been most burdensome. He'd allowed her no access to him, but still, he was sure, for good reasons: she might tempt him out of his confusion with her easy answers. He could be tempted all right, it was why he fought so hard. But now a sweep of love came over him at the thought of her contracting womb, and his child. And yet he would not indicate it to her. Under such splendid marital conditions, who knows but she might extract some promise from him about his concern with the school on the hill.

Having packed his second bag of the evening, Eli sped his wife to Woodenton Memorial. There she proceeded not to have her baby, but to lie hour after hour through the night having at first oranges, then bowling balls, then basketballs, squeezed back of her pelvis. Eli sat in the waiting room, under the shattering African glare of a dozen rows of fluorescent bulbs, composing a letter to Tzuref.

> Dear Mr. Tzuref:
>   The clothes in this box are for the gentleman in the hat. In a life of sacrifice what is one more? But in a life of no sacrifices even one is impossible. Do you see what I'm saying, Mr.

Tzuref? I am not a Nazi who would drive eighteen children who are probably frightened at the sight of a firefly, into homelessness. But if you want a home here, you must accept what we have to offer. The world is the world, Mr. Tzuref. As you would say, what is, is. All we say to this man is change your clothes. Enclosed are two suits and two shirts, and everything else he'll need, including a new hat. When he needs new clothes let me know.

We await his appearance in Woodenton, as we await friendly relations with the Yeshivah of Woodenton.

He signed his name and slid the note under a bursting flap and into the box. Then he went to the phone at the end of the room and dialed Ted Heller's number.

"Hello."

"Shirley, it's Eli."

"Eli, we've been calling all night. The lights are on in your place, but nobody answers. We thought it was burglars."

"Miriam's having the baby."

"At home?" Shirley said. "Oh, Eli, what a fun-idea!"

"Shirley, let me speak to Ted."

After the ear-shaking clatter of the phone whacking the floor, Eli heard footsteps, breathing, throat-clearing, then Ted. "A boy or a girl?"

"Nothing yet."

"You've given Shirley the bug, Eli. Now she's going to have *our* next one at home."

"Good."

"That's a terrific way to bring the family together, Eli."

"Look, Ted, I've settled with Tzuref."

"When are they going?"

"They're not exactly going, Teddie. I settled it—you won't even know they're there."

"A guy dressed like 1000 B.C. and I won't know it? What are you thinking about, pal?"

"He's changing his clothes,"

"Yeah, to what? Another funeral suit?"

"Tzuref promised me, Ted. Next time he comes to town, he comes dressed like you and me."

"What! Somebody's kidding somebody, Eli."

Eli's voice shot up. "If he says he'll do it, he'll do it!"

"And, Eli," Ted asked, "he said it?"

"He said it." It cost him a sudden headache, this invention.

"And suppose he doesn't change, Eli. Just suppose. I mean that *might* happen, Eli. This might just be some kind of stall or something."

"No," Eli assured him.

The other end was quiet a moment. "Look, Eli," Ted said, finally, "he changes. Okay? All right? But they're still up there, aren't they? *That* doesn't change."

"The point is you won't know it."

Patiently Ted said, "Is this what we asked of you, Eli? When we put our faith and trust in you, is that what we were asking? We weren't concerned that this guy should become a Beau Brummell, Eli, believe me. We just don't think this is the community for them. And, Eli, we isn't me. The Jewish members of the community appointed me, Artie, and Harry to see what could be done. And we appointed you. And what's happened?"

Eli heard himself say, "What happened, happened."

"Eli, you're talking in crossword puzzles."

"My wife's having a baby," Eli explained, defensively.

"I realize that, Eli. But this is a matter of zoning, isn't it? Isn't that what we discovered? You don't abide by the ordinance, you go. I mean I can't raise mountain goats, say, in my backyard—"

"This isn't so simple, Ted. People are involved—"

"People? Eli, we've been through this and through this. We're not just dealing with people—these are religious fanatics is what they are. Dressing like that. What I'd really like to find out is what goes on up there. I'm getting more and more skeptical, Eli, and I'm not afraid to admit it. It smells like a lot of hocus-pocus abracadabra stuff to me. Guys like Harry, you know, they think and they think and they're afraid to admit what they're thinking. I'll tell you. Look, I don't even know about this Sunday school business. Sundays I drive my oldest kid all the way to Scarsdale to learn Bible stories . . . and you know what she comes up with? This Abraham in the Bible was going to kill his own *kid* for a sacrifice. She gets nightmares from it, for God's sake! You call that religion? Today a guy like that they'd lock him up. This is an age of science, Eli. I size people's feet with an X-ray machine, for God's sake. They've disproved all that stuff, Eli, and I refuse to sit by and watch it happening on my own front lawn."

"Nothing's happening on your front lawn, Teddie. You're exaggerating, nobody's sacrificing their kid."

"You're damn right, Eli—I'm not sacrificing mine. You'll see when you have your own what it's like. All the place is, is a hideaway for people who can't face life. It's a matter of *needs*. They have all these superstitions, and why do you think? Because they can't face the world, because they can't take their place in society. That's no environment to bring kids up in, Eli."

"Look, Ted, see it from another angle. We can convert them," Eli said, with half a heart.

"What, make a bunch of Catholics out of them? Look, Eli—pal, there's a good healthy relationship in this town because it's modern Jews and

Protestants. That's the point, isn't it, Eli? Let's not kid each other, I'm not Harry. The way things are now are fine—like human beings. There's going to be no pogroms in Woodenton. Right? 'Cause there's no fanatics, no crazy people—" Eli winced, and closed his eyes a second—"just people who respect each other, and leave each other be. Common sense is the ruling thing, Eli. I'm for common sense. Moderation."

"Exactly, exactly, Ted. I agree, but common sense, maybe, says make this guy change his clothes. Then maybe—"

"Common sense says that? Common sense says to me they go and find a nice place somewhere else, Eli. New York is the biggest city in the world, it's only 30 miles away—why don't they go there?"

"Ted, give them a chance. Introduce them to common sense."

"Eli, you're dealing with *fanatics*. Do they display common sense? Talking a dead language, that makes sense? Making a big thing out of suffering, so you're going oy-oy-oy all your life, that's common sense? Look, Eli, we've been through all this. I don't know if you know—but there's talk that *Life* magazine is sending a guy out to the Yeshivah for a story. With pictures."

"Look, Teddie, you're letting your imagination get inflamed. I don't think *Life's* interested."

"But I'm interested, Eli. And we thought you were supposed to be."

"I am," Eli said, "I am. Let him just change the clothes, Ted. Let's see what happens."

"They live in the medieval ages, Eli—it's some superstition, some *rule.*"

"Let's just *see,*" Eli pleaded.

"Eli, every day—"

"One more day," Eli said. "If he doesn't change in one more day . . ."

"What?"

"Then I get an injunction first thing Monday. That's that."

"Look, Eli—it's not up to me. Let me call Harry—"

"You're the spokesman, Teddie. I'm all wrapped up here with Miriam having a baby. Just give me the day—them the day."

"All right, Eli. I want to be fair. But tomorrow, that's all. Tomorrow's the judgment day, Eli, I'm telling you."

"I hear trumpets," Eli said, and hung up. He was shaking inside—Teddie's voice seemed to have separated his bones at the joints. He was still in the phone booth when the nurse came to tell him that Mrs. Peck would positively not be delivered of a child until the morning. He was to go home and get some rest, he looked like *he* was having the baby. The nurse winked and left.

But Eli did not go home. He carried the Bonwit box out into the street with him and put it in the car. The night was soft and starry, and he began to drive the streets of Woodenton. Square cool windows, apricot-colored, were all one could see beyond the long lawns that fronted the homes of the townsmen. The stars polished the permanent baggage carriers atop the station wagons in the driveways. He drove slowly, up, down, around. Only his tires could be heard taking the gentle curves in the road.

What peace. What incredible peace. Have children ever been so safe in their beds? Parents—Eli wondered—so full in their stomachs? Water so warm in its boilers? Never. Never in Rome, never in Greece. Never even did walled cities have it so good! No wonder then they would keep things just as they were. Here, after all, were peace and safety—what civilization had been working toward for centuries. For all his jerkiness, that was all Ted Heller was asking for, peace and safety. It was what his parents had asked for in the Bronx, and his grandparents in Poland, and theirs in Russia or Austria, or wherever else they'd fled to or from. It was what Miriam was asking for. And now they had it—the world was at last a place for families, even Jewish families. After all these centuries, maybe there just had to be this communal toughness—or numbness—to protect such a blessing. Maybe that was the trouble with the Jews all along—too soft. Sure, to live takes guts . . . Eli was thinking as he drove on beyond the train station, and parked his car at the darkened Gulf station. He stepped out, carrying the box.

At the top of the hill one window trembled with light. What *was* Tzuref doing up there in that office? Killing babies—probably not. But studying a language no one understood? Practicing customs with origins long forgotten? Suffering sufferings already suffered once too often? Teddie was right —why keep it up! However, if a man chose to be stubborn, then he couldn't expect to survive. The world is give-and-take. What sense to sit and brood over a suit. Eli would give him one last chance.

He stopped at the top. No one was around. He walked slowly up the lawn, setting each foot into the grass, listening to the shh shhh shhhh his shoes made as they bent the wetness into the sod. He looked around. Here there was nothing. Nothing! An old decaying house—and a suit.

On the porch he slid behind a pillar. He felt someone was watching him. But only the stars gleamed down. And at his feet, off and away, Woodenton glowed up. He set his package on the step of the great front door. Inside the cover of the box he felt to see if his letter was still there. When he touched it, he pushed it deeper into the green suit, which his fingers still remembered from winter. He should have included some light bulbs. Then he slid back by the pillar again, and this time there was something on the lawn. It was the second sight he had of him. He was facing Woodenton and barely moving across the open space towards the trees. His right fist was beating his chest. And then Eli heard a sound rising with each knock on the chest. What a moan! It could raise hair, stop hearts, water eyes. And it did all three to Eli, plus more. Some feeling crept into him for whose deepness he could find no word. It was strange. He listened—it did not hurt to hear this moan. But he wondered if it hurt to make it. And so, with only stars to hear, he tried. And it did hurt. Not the bumble-bee of noise that turned at the back of his throat and winged out his nostrils. What hurt buzzed down. It stung and stung inside him, and in turn the moan sharpened. It became a scream, louder, a song, a crazy song that whined through the pillars and blew out to the grass, until the strange hatted creature on the lawn turned and threw his arms wide, and looked in the night like a scarecrow.

Eli ran, and when he reached the car the pain was only a bloody scratch across his neck where a branch had whipped back as he fled the greenie's arms.

The following day his son was born. But not till one in the afternoon, and by then a great deal had happened.

First, at nine-thirty the phone rang. Eli leaped from the sofa—where he'd dropped the night before—and picked it screaming from the cradle. He could practically smell the hospital as he shouted into the phone, "Hello, yes!"

"Eli, it's Ted. Eli, he *did* it. He just walked by the store. I was opening the door, Eli, and I turned around and I swear I thought it was you. But it was him. He still walks like he did, but the clothes, Eli, the clothes."

"Who?"

"The greenie. He has on man's regular clothes. And the suit, it's a beauty."

The suit barreled back into Eli's consciousness, pushing all else aside. "What color suit?"

"Green. He's just strolling in the green suit like it's a holiday. Eli . . . is it a Jewish holiday?"

"Where is he now?"

"He's walking straight up Coach House Road, in this damn tweed job. Eli, it worked. You were right."

"We'll see."

"What next?"

"We'll see."

He took off the underwear in which he'd slept and went into the kitchen where he turned the light under the coffee. When it began to perk he held his head over the pot so it would steam loose the knot back of his eyes. It still hadn't when the phone rang.

"Eli, Ted again. Eli, the guy's walking up and down every street in town. Really, he's on a tour or something. Artie called me, Herb called me. Now Shirley calls that he just walked by our house. Eli, go out on the porch you'll see."

Eli went to the window and peered out. He couldn't see past the bend in the road, and there was no one in sight.

"Eli?" He heard Ted from where he dangled over the telephone table. He dropped the phone into the hook, as a few last words floated up to him—"Eliyousawhim. . . ?" He threw on the pants and shirt he'd worn the night before and walked barefoot on to his front lawn. And sure enough, his apparition appeared around the bend: in a brown hat a little too far down on his head, a green suit too far back on the shoulders, an unbuttoned-down button-down shirt, a tie knotted so as to leave a two-inch tail, trousers that cascaded onto his shoes—he was shorter than that black hat had made him seem. And moving the clothes was that walk that was not a walk, the tiny-stepped shlumpy gait. He came round the bend, and for all his strangeness—it clung to his whiskers, signaled itself in his locomotion—he looked as if he belonged. Eccentric, maybe, but he belonged. He made no moan, nor did he invite Eli with wide-flung arms. But he did stop when he saw him. He stopped and put a hand to his hat. When he felt for its top, his hand went up too high. Then it found the level and fiddled with the brim. The fingers fiddled, fumbled, and when they'd finally made their greeting, they traveled down the fellow's face and in an instant seemed to have touched each one of his features. They dabbed the eyes, ran the length of the nose, swept over the hairy lip, until they found their home in the hair that hid a little of his collar. To Eli the fingers said, *I have a face, I have a face at least.* Then his hand came through the beard and when it stopped at his chest it was like a pointer—and the eyes asked a question as tides of water shifted over them. *The face is all right, I can keep it?* Such a look was in those eyes that Eli was still seeing them when he turned his head away. They were the hearts of his jonquils, that only last week had appeared—they were the leaves on his birch, the bulbs in his coach lamp, the droppings on his lawn: those eyes were the eyes in his head. They were his, he had made them. He turned and went into his house and when he peeked out the side of the window, between shade and molding, the green suit was gone.

The phone.

"Eli, Shirley."

"I saw him, Shirley," and he hung up.

He sat frozen for a long time. The sun moved around the windows. The coffee steam smelled up the house. The phone began to ring, stopped, began again. The mailman came, the cleaner, the bakery man, the gardener, the ice cream man, the League of Women Voters lady. A Negro woman spreading some strange gospel calling for the revision of the Food and Drug Act knocked at the front, rapped the windows, and finally scraped a half-dozen pamphlets under the back door. But Eli only sat, without underwear, in last night's suit. He answered no one.

Given his condition, it was strange that the trip and crash at the back door reached his inner ear. But in an instant he seemed to melt down into the crevices of the chair, then to splash up and out to where the clatter had been. At the door he waited. It was silent, but for a fluttering of damp little leaves on the trees. When he finally opened the door, there was no one there. He'd expected to see green, green, green, big as the doorway, topped by his hat, waiting for him with those eyes. But there was no one out there, except for the Bonwit's box which lay bulging at his feet. No string tied it and the top rode high on the bottom.

The coward! He couldn't do it! He couldn't!

The very glee of that idea pumped fuel to his legs. He tore out across his back lawn, past his new spray of forsythia, to catch a glimpse of the bearded one fleeing naked through yards, over hedges and fences, to the safety of his hermitage. In the distance a pile of pink and white stones— which Harriet Knudson had painted the previous day—tricked him. "Run," he shouted to the rocks, "run, you . . ." but he caught his error before anyone else did, and though he peered and craned there was no hint anywhere of a man about his own size, with white, white, terribly white skin (how white must be the skin of his body!) in cowardly retreat. He came slowly, curiously, back to the door. And while the trees shimmered in the light wind, he removed the top from the box. The shock at first was the shock of having daylight turned off all at once. Inside the box was an eclipse. But black soon sorted from black, and shortly there was the glassy black of lining, the coarse black of trousers, the dead black of fraying threads, and in the center the mountain of black: the hat. He picked the box from the doorstep and carried it inside. For the first time in his life he *smelled* the color of blackness: a little stale, a little sour, a little old, but nothing that could overwhelm you. Still, he held the package at arm's length and deposited it on the dining room table.

Twenty rooms on a hill and they store their old clothes with me? What am I supposed to do with them? Give them to charity? That's where they came from. He picked up the hat by the edges and looked inside. The crown was smooth as an egg, the brim practically threadbare. There is nothing else to do with a hat in one's hands but put it on, so Eli dropped the thing on his head. He opened the door to the hall closet and looked at himself in the full-length mirror. The hat gave him bags under the eyes. Or perhaps he had not slept well. He pushed the brim lower till a shadow touched his lips. Now the bags under his eyes had inflated to become his face. Before the mirror he unbuttoned his shirt, unzipped his trousers, and then, shedding his clothes, he studied what he was. What a silly disappointment to see yourself naked in a hat. Especially in that hat. He sighed, but could not rid himself of the great weakness that suddenly set on his muscles and joints, beneath the terrible weight of the stranger's strange hat.

He returned to the dining room table and emptied the box of its contents: jacket, trousers, and vest (*it* smelled deeper than blackness). And under it all, sticking between the shoes that looked chopped and bitten, came the first gleam of white. A little fringed serape, a gray piece of semi-underwear, was crumpled at the bottom, its thready border twisted into itself. Eli removed it and let it hang free. What is it? For warmth? To wear beneath underwear in the event of a chest cold? He held it to his nose but it did not smell from Vick's or mustard plaster. It was something special, some Jewish thing. Special food, special language, special prayers, why not special BVD's? So fearful was he that he would be tempted back into wearing his traditional clothes—reasoned Eli—that he had carried and buried in Woodenton everything, including the special underwear. For that was how Eli now understood the box of clothes. The greenie was saying, Here, I give up. I refuse even to be tempted. We surrender. And that was how Eli continued to understand it until he found he'd slipped the white fringy surrender flag over his hat and felt it clinging to his chest. And now, looking at himself in the mirror, he was momentarily uncertain as to who was tempting who into what. Why *did* the greenie leave his clothes? Was it even the greenie? Then who was it? And why? But Eli, for Christ's sake, in an age of science things don't happen like that. Even the goddam pigs take drugs . . .

Regardless of who was the source of the temptation, what was its end, not to mention its beginning, Eli, some moments later, stood draped in black, with a little white underneath, before the full-length mirror. He had to pull down on the trousers so they would not show the hollow of his ankle. The greenie, didn't he wear socks? Or had he forgotten them? The mystery was solved when Eli mustered enough courage to investigate the trouser pockets. He had expected some damp awful thing to happen to his fingers should he slip them down and out of sight—but when at last he jammed bravely down he came up with a khaki army sock in each hand. As he slipped them over his toes, he invented a genesis: a G.I.'s present in 1945. Plus everything else lost between 1938 and 1945, he had also lost his socks. Not that he had lost the socks, but that he'd had to stoop to accepting these, made Eli almost cry. To calm himself he walked out the back door and stood looking at his lawn.

On the Knudson back lawn, Harriet Knudson was giving her stones a second coat of pink. She looked up just as Eli stepped out. Eli shot back in again and pressed himself against the back door. When he peeked between the curtain all he saw were paint bucket, brush, and rocks scattered on the Knudsons' pink-spattered grass. The phone rang. Who was it—Harriet Knudson? Eli, there's a Jew at your door. *That's me.* Nonsense, Eli, I saw him with my own eyes. *That's me, I saw you too, painting your rocks pink.* Eli, you're having a nervous breakdown again. Jimmy, Eli's having a nervous breakdown again. Eli, this is Jimmy, hear you're having a little breakdown, anything I can do, boy? Eli, this is Ted, Shirley says you need help. Eli, this is Artie, you need help. Eli, Harry, you need help you need help . . . The phone rattled its last and died.

"God helps them who help themselves," intoned Eli, and once again he stepped out the door. This time he walked to the center of his lawn and in full sight of the trees, the grass, the birds, and the sun, revealed that it was he, Eli, in the costume. But nature had nothing to say to him, and so stealthily he made his way to the hedge separating his property from the field beyond and he cut his way through, losing his hat twice in the underbrush. Then, clamping the hat to his head, he began to run, the threaded tassels jumping across his heart. He ran through the weeds and wild flowers, until on the old road that skirted the town he slowed up. He was walking when he approached the Gulf station from the back. He supported himself on a huge tireless truck rim, and among tubes, rusted engines, dozens of topless oil cans, he rested. With a kind of brainless cunning, he readied himself for the last mile of his journey.

"How are you, Pop?" It was the garage attendant, rubbing his greasy hands on his overalls, and hunting among the cans.

Eli's stomach lurched and he pulled the big black coat round his neck.

"Nice day," the attendant said and started around to the front.

"Sholom," Eli whispered and zoomed off towards the hill.

The sun was directly overhead when Eli reached the top. He had come by way of the woods, where it was cooler, but still he was perspiring beneath his new suit. The hat had no sweatband and the cloth clutched his head. The children were playing. The children were always playing, as if it was that alone that Tzuref had to teach them. In their shorts, they revealed such thin legs that beneath one could see the joints swiveling as they ran. Eli waited for them to disappear around a corner before he came into the open. But something would not let him wait—his green suit. It was on the porch, wrapped around the bearded fellow, who was painting the base of a pillar. His arm went up and down, up and down, and the pillar glowed like white fire. The very sight of him popped Eli out of the woods onto the lawn. He did not turn back, though his insides did. He walked up the lawn, but the children played on; tipping the black hat, he mumbled, "Shhh . . . shhhh," and they hardly seemed to notice.

At last he smelled paint.

He waited for the man to turn to him. He only painted. Eli felt suddenly that if he could pull the black hat down over his eyes, over his chest and belly and legs, if he could shut out all light, then a moment later he would be home in bed. But the hat wouldn't go past his forehead. He couldn't kid himself—he was there. No one he could think of had forced him to do this.

The greenie's arm flailed up and down on the pillar. Eli breathed loudly, cleared his throat, but the greenie wouldn't make life easier for him. At last, Eli had to say "Hello."

The arm swished up and down; it stopped—two fingers went out after a brush hair stuck to the pillar.

"Good day," Eli said.

The hair came away; the swishing resumed.

"Sholom," Eli whispered and the fellow turned.

The recognition took some time. He looked at what Eli wore. Up close, Eli looked at what he wore. And then Eli had the strange notion that he was two people. Or that he was one person wearing two suits. The greenie looked to be suffering from a similar confusion. They stared long at one another. Eli's heart shivered, and his brain was momentarily in such a mixed-up condition that his hands went out to button down the collar of his shirt that somebody else was wearing. What a mess! The greenie flung his arms over his face.

"What's the matter . . ." Eli said. The fellow had picked up his bucket and brush and was running away. Eli ran after him.

"I wasn't going to hit . . ." Eli called. "Stop . . ." Eli caught up and grabbed his sleeve. Once again, the greenie's hands flew up to his face. This time, in the violence, white paint spattered both of them.

"I only want to . . ." But in that outfit Eli didn't really know what he wanted. "To talk . . ." he said finally. "For you to look at me. Please, just *look* at me . . ."

The hands stayed put, as paint rolled off the brush onto the cuff of Eli's green suit.

"Please . . . please," Eli said, but he did not know what to do. "Say something, speak *English,*" he pleaded.

The fellow pulled back against the wall, back, back, as though some arm would finally reach out and yank him to safety. He refused to uncover his face.

"Look," Eli said, pointing to himself. "It's your suit. I'll take care of it."

No answer—only a little shaking under the hands, which led Eli to speak as gently as he knew how.

"We'll . . . we'll moth-proof it. There's a button missing"—Eli pointed —"I'll have it fixed. I'll have a zipper put in . . . Please, please—just look at me . . ." He was talking to himself, and yet how could he stop? Nothing he said made any sense—that alone made his heart swell. Yet somehow babbling on, he might babble something that would make things easier between them. "Look . . ." He reached inside his shirt to pull the frills of underwear into the light. "I'm wearing the special underwear, even . . . Please," he said, *"please, please, please"* he sang, as if it were some sacred word. "Oh, *please* . . ."

Nothing twitched under the tweed suit—and if the eyes watered, or twinkled, or hated, he couldn't tell. It was driving him crazy. He had dressed like a fool, and for what? For this? He reached up and yanked the hands away.

"There!" he said—and in that first instant all he saw of the greenie's face were two white droplets stuck to each cheek.

"Tell me—" Eli clutched his hands down to his sides—"Tell me, what can I do for you, I'll do it . . ."

Stiffly, the greenie stood there, sporting his two white tears.

"Whatever I can do . . . Look, look, what I've done *already*." He grabbed his black hat and shook it in the man's face.

And in exchange, the greenie gave him an answer. He raised one hand to his chest, and then jammed it, finger first, towards the horizon. And with what a pained look! As though the air were full of razors! Eli followed the finger and saw beyond the knuckle, out past the nail, Woodenton.

"What do you want?" Eli said. "I'll bring it!"

Suddenly the greenie made a run for it. But then he stopped, wheeled, and jabbed that finger at the air again. It pointed the same way. Then he was gone.

And then, all alone, Eli had the revelation. He did not question his understanding, the substance or the source. But with a strange, dreamy elation, he started away.

On Coach House Road, they were double-parked. The Mayor's wife pushed a grocery cart full of dog food from Stop N' Shop to her station wagon. The President of the Lions Club, a napkin around his neck, was jamming pennies into the meter in front of the Bit-in-Teeth Restaurant. Ted Heller caught the sun as it glazed off the new Byzantine mosaic entrance to his shoe shop. In pinkened jeans, Mrs. Jimmy Knudson was leaving Halloway's Hardware, a paint bucket in each hand. Roger's Beauty Shoppe had its doors open—women's heads in silver bullets far as the eye could see. Over by the barbershop the pole spun, and Artie Berg's youngest sat on a red horse, having his hair cut; his mother flipped through *Look*, smiling: the greenie had changed his clothes.

And into this street, which seemed paved with chromium, came Eli Peck. It was not enough, he knew, to walk up one side of the street. That was not enough. Instead he walked ten paces up one side, then on an angle, crossed to the other side, where he walked ten more paces, and crossed back. Horns blew, traffic jerked, as Eli made his way up Coach House Road. He spun a moan high up in his nose as he walked. Outside no one could hear him, but he felt it vibrate the cartilage at the bridge of his nose.

Things slowed around him. The sun stopped rippling on spokes and hubcaps. It glowed steadily as everyone put on brakes to look at the man in black. They always paused and gaped, whenever he entered the town. Then in a minute, or two, or three, a light would change, a baby squawk, and the flow continue. Now, though lights changed, no one moved.

"He shaved his beard," Eric the barber said.

"Who?" asked Linda Berg.

"The . . . the guy in the suit. From the place there."

Linda looked out the window.

"It's Uncle Eli," little Kevin Berg said, spitting hair.

"Oh, God," Linda said, "Eli's having a nervous breakdown."

"A nervous breakdown!" Ted Heller said, but not immediately. Immediately he had said "Hoooly . . ."

Shortly, everybody in Coach House Road was aware that Eli Peck, the nervous young attorney with the pretty wife, was having a breakdown. Everybody except Eli Peck. He knew what he did was not insane, though he felt every inch of its strangeness. He felt those black clothes as if they were the skin of his skin—the give and pull as they got used to where he bulged and buckled. And he felt eyes, every eye on Coach House Road. He saw headlights screech to within an inch of him, and stop. He saw mouths: first the bottom jaw slides forward, then the tongue hits the teeth, the lips explode, a little thunder in the throat, and they've said it: Eli Peck Eli Peck Eli Peck Eli Peck. He began to walk slowly, shifting his weight down and forward with each syllable: E–li–Peck–E–li–Peck–E–li–Peck. Heavily he trod, and as his neighbors uttered each syllable of his name, he felt each syllable shaking all his bones. He knew who he was down to his marrow— they were telling him. Eli Peck. He wanted them to say it a thousand times, a million times. He would walk forever in that black suit, as adults whispered of his strangeness and children made "Shame . . . shame" with their fingers.

"It's going to be all right, pal . . ." Ted Heller was motioning to Eli from his doorway. "C'mon, pal, it's going to be all right . . ."

Eli saw him, past the brim of his hat. Ted did not move from his doorway, but leaned forward and spoke with his hand over his mouth. Behind him, three customers peered through the doorway. "Eli, it's Ted, remember Ted . . ."

Eli crossed the street and found he was heading directly towards Harriet Knudson. He lifted his neck so she could see his whole face.

He saw her forehead melt down to her lashes. "Good morning, Mr. Peck."

"Sholom," Eli said, and crossed the street where he saw the President of the Lions.

"Twice before . . ." he heard someone say, and then he crossed again, mounted the curb, and was before the bakery, where a delivery man charged past with a tray of powdered cakes twirling above him. "Pardon me, Father," he said, and scooted into his truck. But he could not move it. Eli Peck had stopped traffic.

He passed the Rivoli Theater, Beekman Cleaners, Harris' Westinghouse, the Unitarian Church, and soon he was passing only trees. At Ireland Road he turned right and started through Woodenton's winding streets. Baby carriages stopped whizzing and creaked—"Isn't that . . ." Gardeners held their clipping. Children stepped from the sidewalk and tried the curb. And Eli greeted no one, but raised his face to all. He wished passionately that he had white tears to show them . . . And not till he reached his own front lawn, saw his house, his shutters, his new jonquils, did he remember his wife. And the child that must have been born to him. And it was then and there he had the awful moment. He could go inside and put on his clothes and go to his wife in the hospital. It was not irrevocable, even the walk wasn't. In Woodenton memories are long but fury short. Apathy works like forgiveness. Besides, when you've flipped, you've flipped—it's Mother Nature.

What gave Eli the awful moment was that he turned away. He knew exactly what he could do but he chose not to. To go inside would be to go halfway. There was more . . . So he turned and walked towards the hospital and all the time he quaked an eighth of an inch beneath his skin to think that perhaps he'd chosen the crazy way. To think that he'd *chosen* to be crazy! But if you chose to be crazy, then you weren't crazy. It's when you didn't choose. No, he wasn't flipping. He had a child to see.

"Name?"

"Peck."

"Fourth floor." He was given a little blue card.

In the elevator everybody stared. Eli watched his black shoes rise four floors.

"Four."

He tipped his hat, but knew he couldn't take it off.

"Peck," he said. He showed the card.

"Congratulations," the nurse said, ". . . the grandfather?"

"The father. Which room?"

She led him to 412. "A joke on the Mrs.?" she said, but he slipped in the door without her.

"Miriam?"

"Yes?"

"Eli."

She rolled her white face towards her husband. "Oh, Eli . . . Oh, Eli."

He raised his arms. "What could I do?"

"You have a son. They called all morning."

"I came to see him."

"Like *that!*" she whispered harshly. "Eli, you can't go around like that."

"I have a son. I want to see him."

"Eli, why are you doing this to me!" Red seeped back into her lips. *"He's* not your fault," she explained. "Oh, Eli, sweetheart, why do you feel guilty about everything? Eli, change your clothes. I forgive you."

"Stop forgiving me. Stop understanding me."

"But I love you."

"That's something else."

"But, sweetie, you *don't* have to dress like that. You didn't do anything. You don't have to feel guilty because . . . because everything's all right. Eli, can't you see that?"

"Miriam, enough reasons. Where's my son?"

"Oh, please, Eli, don't flip now. I need you now. Is that why you're flipping—because I need you?"

"In your selfish way, Miriam, you're very generous. I want my son."

"Don't flip now. I'm afraid, now that he's out." She was beginning to whimper. "I don't know if I love him, now that he's out. When I look in the mirror, Eli, he won't be there . . . Eli, Eli, you look like you're going to your own funeral. Please, can't you leave well enough *alone?* Can't we just have a family?"

"No."

In the corridor he asked the nurse to lead him to his son. The nurse walked on one side of him, Ted Heller on the other.

"Eli, do you want some help? I thought you might want some help."

"No."

Ted whispered something to the nurse; then to Eli he whispered, "Should you be walking around like this?"

"Yes."

In his ear Ted said, "You'll . . . you'll frighten the kid . . ."

"There," the nurse said. She pointed to a bassinet in the second row and looked, puzzled, to Ted. "Do I go in?" Eli said.

"No," the nurse said. "She'll roll him over." She rapped on the enclosure full of babies. "Peck," she mouthed to the nurse on the inside.

Ted tapped Eli's arm. "You're not thinking of doing something you'll be sorry for . . . are you, Eli? Eli—I mean you know you're still Eli, don't you?"

In the enclosure, Eli saw a bassinet had been wheeled before the square window.

"Oh, Christ. . . ." Ted said. "You don't have this Bible stuff on the brain—" And suddenly he said, "You wait, pal." He started down the corridor, his heels tapping rapidly.

Eli felt relieved—he leaned forward. In the basket was what he'd come to see. Well, now that he was here, what did he think he was going to say to it? I'm your father, Eli, the Flipper? I am wearing a black hat, suit, and fancy underwear, all borrowed from a friend? How could he admit to this reddened ball—*his* reddened ball—the worst of all: that Eckman would shortly convince him he wanted to take off the whole business. He couldn't admit it! He wouldn't do it!

Past his hat brim, from the corner of his eye, he saw Ted had stopped in a doorway at the end of the corridor. Two interns stood there smoking, listening to Ted. Eli ignored it.

No, even Eckman wouldn't make him take it off! No! He'd wear it, if he chose to. He'd make the kid wear it! Sure! Cut it down when the time came. A smelly hand-me-down, whether the kid liked it or not!

Only Teddie's heels clacked; the interns wore rubber soles—for they were there, beside him, unexpectedly. Their white suits smelled, but not like Eli's.

"Eli," Ted said, softly, "visiting time's up, pal."

"How are you feeling, Mr. Peck? First child upsets everyone. . . ."

He'd just pay no attention; nevertheless, he began to perspire, thickly, and his hat crown clutched his hair.

"Excuse me—Mr. Peck. . . ." It was a new rich bass voice. "Excuse me, rabbi, but you're wanted . . . in the temple." A hand took his elbow, firmly; then another hand, the other elbow. Where they grabbed, his tendons went taut.

"Okay, rabbi. Okay okay okay okay okay okay. . . ." He listened; it was a very soothing word, that okay. "Okay okay everything's going to be okay." His feet seemed to have left the ground some, as he glided away from the window, the bassinet, the babies. "Okay easy does it everything's all right all right—"

But he rose, suddenly, as though up out of a dream, and flailing his arms, screamed: *"I'm the father!"*

But the window disappeared. In a moment they tore off his jacket—it gave so easily, in one yank. Then a needle slid under his skin. The drug calmed his soul, but did not touch it down where the blackness had reached.

❖

It is easier to see in "Eli, The Fanatic" than it was in "Defender of the Faith" that the important conflict in the story takes place in the consciousness of the narrator, and that however interesting may be the situational conflict of the narrative (in this case: the assimilated, "new," "American" Jews of the suburb of Woodenton versus the unassimilated, "old," "European" Jews of the yeshiva of Woodenton), that conflict is to some extent secondary. There are as well two central subjects in the story—identity and law—and the two are worked together to say something complex about conformity. All this is shaped by the voice and mind of the point-of-view character, Eli Peck, in such a way that while it permits some useful ambiguity as to whether or not he is insane, it nevertheless makes clear the essential rightness of the crazy position he finds himself in at the end. Explication can't really demonstrate, but only suggest, how complexly and successfully all these elements are made to work together. At the beginning of the story Eli's identity is that of a lawyer. He "stands for" or "represents" his clients, the Jews of Woodenton, and he tells Tzuref: "I am them, they are me." Yet this role of lawyer stifles him, "surrounded him like quicksand—he couldn't get his breath." And the law doesn't seem to take into account the ambiguities ("too often he wished he were pleading for the other side") or the emotions ("law didn't seem to have anything to do with what was aggravating everybody") involved in this conflict. The trouble with the situation is, as is brought out in Eli's conversations about law with Tzuref, that the law of the land (the zoning code), which the Woodenton Jews are using to evict the yeshiva Jews, is in direct conflict with moral law, the law of the heart and of God, which forbids that the safety and security of the suburb be denied the poor displaced persons and demands that sanctuary and welcome be extended to them, especially by members of their own religion. Feeling the pull of the moral law, Eli tries to disassociate himself from his clients' heartlessness: "It's not me, Mr. Tzuref, it's them," he says. And when Tzuref reminds him of what he'd said at first, he reaffirms: "No. I am me. They are them." When, instead of the promised law suit, he presents them with his green tweed suit, it is to some extent an attempt to convey some J. Press conformity to the representative of the yeshiva Jews; but more importantly the act symbolizes his giving up of his identity as the representative of the Woodenton Jews. Eli, caught between the two laws, the law of the land and the law of the heart (his suburb versus his God), doesn't know where he stands, and this brings about his breakdown. His identity is split, as is shown in the scene where, in the black suit, he confronts the greenie in his green suit: "The recognition took some time. He looked at what Eli wore. Up close, Eli looked at what he wore. And then Eli had the strange notion that he was two people." Then, when he walks the streets of Woodenton in the black suit, "he knew what he did was not insane, though he felt every inch of its strangeness." As he walks, every syllable of his name is emphasized by his neighbors' whispers and by the movements of the clothes themselves: "E-li-Peck-E-li-Peck-E-li-Peck." Hearing every syllable of his name, "he knew who he was down to his marrow." He is not just asserting his identity as a Jew, he is emphasizing his differentness from the homogenous, assimilated Jews of Woodenton, who have forgotten the moral laws of their religion. And perhaps he is demonstrating, too, his differentness, his uniqueness, his strangeness as an individual man. The necessity to conform will prevail later ("Eckman would shortly convince him he wanted to take off the whole business"), for to be different is to be crazy and to be outside the law in the modern land of psychoanalysts and zoning codes. As at the end of the previous story, Sergeant Nathan Marx unexpectedly finds himself accepting his "fate" to be the "defender of the faith," so now Eli, with some of the same ruefulness, reluctance, and surprise, accepts the inevitability of his role, to be a "fanatic." Both of these stories seem to confirm a point made in the introduction to this section: that fiction having to do with religion in our time is more likely to be concerned with a crisis of identity than with a crisis of faith.

BRUCE JAY FRIEDMAN

When You're Excused

You're Excused

◇◇◇◇◇◇◇

HAVING A GALLSTONE REMOVED at the age of thirty-seven almost frightened Mr. Kessler to death, and after he was healed up, he vowed he would get into the best shape of his life. He joined a local sports club called Vic Tanny's, and for six months took workouts every other night of the week, missing only three sessions for Asian flu. When one of his workouts came due on the eve of Yom Kippur, holiest day of the Jewish year, Mr. Kessler, who usually observed important religious holidays, said to his wife, "I've come to need these workouts and my body craves them like drugs. It's medicine and when I miss one I get edgy and feel awful. It doesn't make any difference that this is the most important holiday of all. I've got to go tonight. It's part of the religion that if you're sick you're excused from synagogue. It's in one of the psalms."

Mrs. Kessler was a woman of deep religious conviction but slender formal training. Her husband, as a result, was able to bully her around with references to obscure religious documents. Once he mentioned the psalms, rebuttal was out of the question, and she could only say, "All right, as long as it's in there."

Mr. Kessler did a great deal of aimless walking through the house for the rest of the day. His four-year-old son asked him, "Are any pirates good?" and Mr. Kessler said, "I don't feel like talking pirates." When the dark came and it was time for the gym, Mr. Kessler said to his wife, "All right, it isn't in the psalms, but it's in the religion somewhere, and it doesn't make any difference that it's such an important holiday. If you're excused, you're excused. That goes for Columbus Day and Washington's Birthday and if the Japs attack Pearl Harbor again, you're excused on that day, too. In fact, as a matter of principle, you're *especially* excused on Yom Kippur."

Mr. Kessler got his gym bundle together and his wife walked him to the driveway. "It seems dark and religious out here," she said.

"Nonsense," said Mr. Kessler.

He opened the door of his car and then said, "All right, I admit I'm not confident. I started to imagine there was a squadron of old rabbis prowling the streets taking down the names of Jews who were going off to gyms. When the railroad whistle sounded, I thought it was a ram's horn, and the wind tonight is like the wail of a thousand dying ghetto holdouts. But I've got to go there even if I just take a quick workout and skip my steambath. It's too bad it's Yom Kippur and I admit that's throwing me a little, but if you're excused you're excused. On Yom Kippur or *double* Yom Kippur."

Mr. Kessler got behind the wheel and his young son hollered down from an open window, "Can a giant find you if you hide?"

"No giants when important things are going on," said Mr. Kessler, swinging out of the driveway and driving into the night.

Fifteen minutes later, he parked his car outside the gym and swept inside. He walked past the blonde receptionist who called out, "Where's your wife?" and Mr. Kessler said, "She only came that once, and you know damned well her hips are past help. Why do you have to ask me that every time I come in here?"

He undressed in the locker room and gave his street clothing to Rico, the tiny attendant, who blew his nose and said, "I've got a cold, but I'm glad. It's good to have one. Guys come in here to lose colds and I'm glad to have one all year round. When you have a cold, you're always taking care of yourself and that's good."

Mr. Kessler said, "I never said anything to you before because I know you're supposed to be a charming old character, but you're an idiot. It's not good to have a cold. It's better not to have a cold. Any time. I just want to take a fast workout and go home and be in the house. I don't want to kid around."

Upstairs, in the workout room, a man with a thin body was lying on the floor in an awkward position, lifting a barbell in an unnatural movement. "Do you want to know this one?" the man asked. "It's the best exercise in the gym, getting a muscle no one else bothers with. It's right in the center of the arm and you can't see it. Its function is to push out all the other muscles. You don't have very much of a build while you're getting it started, but once she's going, all the other muscles shoot out and you look like an ape."

"I don't have time for any new exercises tonight," said Mr. Kessler. "I just want to get in and get out. Besides, I don't like the kind of body you have."

Mr. Kessler did a few warm-up exercises and then picked up a pair of light dumbbells to work his biceps. A handsome and heavily perspired young man with large shoulders came over and said, "Whew, it certainly is rough work. But when I was sixteen, I only weighed 110 and I said to myself, 'I'm going to look like something.' So each night, after working in dad's filling station, I began to lift stuff in the family garage, getting to the point where I really had a nice build and then, in later years, joining up here. I vowed I would never again look like nothing."

"What makes you think that's such an exciting story?" said Mr. Kessler. "I've heard it a thousand times. I think *you* told it to me once and I don't want to hear it again as long as I live."

"What's eating you?" asked the handsome man.

"I just want to get in and get out and not hear any dull stories," said Mr. Kessler. He went over to a rowing machine, but a sparse-haired man who was doing vigorous waist-twisting Alpine calisthenics blocked his way. "Why don't you do those at home?" said Mr. Kessler. "You're in my way. I've seen you in here and you never use any of the equipment. You only do calisthenics and you're crazy to come here to do them. What are you, showing off?"

"I just like to do them here," said the man and let Mr. Kessler get at the rowing machine. Looking up at the clock, Mr. Kessler did half a dozen rows and then leaped up and caught the high bar, swinging back and forth a few times. A police sergeant who took clandestine workouts during duty hours came by and said, "Your lats are really coming out like honeys."

"Oh, really?" said Mr. Kessler. "Can you see the delts from back there?"

"Beauties," said the sergeant. "Both beauties."

"Thank you for saying that," said Mr. Kessler, swinging easily on the bar. "I can really feel them coming out now. I don't know why, but your saying they're coming out like honeys made me feel good for the first time tonight. I was rushing through my workout because we have this big holiday tonight and I felt guilty, but now I'm going to stay up here awhile. Six months ago I was sick with a bad gallstone and told everyone that if you're sick your only obligation is to yourself. Ahead of kids, your wife and the synagogue. Now I feel good up here and I'm not rushing. This is where I should be. I don't care if it's Yom Kippur or if the mayor's been killed by a bird turd."

"I don't say I follow all your arguments," said the sergeant, "but your lats are up like honeys. I'll tell that to any man here in the gym, straight to his face."

"Thank you for feeling that way," said Mr. Kessler, dropping from the bar now and taking his place on a bench for some leg-raises. Sharing the bench with him was a tiny, dark-haired man with powerful forearms.

"It pays to work your forearms," said the little man. "You get them pumped up real good and even the big bastards will run."

"I'm one of the big bastards," said Mr. Kessler. "You can't tell because I'm sitting down."

"I couldn't see that," said the little man.

"It's all right," said Mr. Kessler. "It's just that maybe you ought to tell that story to a little bastard."

"I'm not telling it to anyone," said the little man.

Mr. Kessler did his legs and then went over to the board for some sit-ups. A man with a large head came over and said, "You look awfully familiar. From a long time ago."

"Public school," said Mr. Kessler, rising to shake hands with the man. "Your name is Block and your father was an attorney."

"Accountant," said the man. "But you're right about Block."

"You lived in the rooming house and there was something else about you. How come you're not in synagogue tonight?"

"I don't observe," said the man. "We never did. This is my first workout here."

"I do observe, but I was sick and I figure I'm excused. A long time ago I remember an old man in the temple didn't have to fast because his stomach was on the fritz. That was orthodox and I figure if he was excused, I'm certainly excused. I was feeling bad for awhile but not any more. If you're sick it doesn't matter if it's Yom Kippur or even if they make up a day holier than Yom Kippur. If you're excused, you're excused. What the hell *was* it about you?"

"I'd like to take off a little around the waist and pack some on the shoulders."

"I know," said Mr. Kessler. *"Blockhead. They used to call you Blockhead. That's it, isn't it?"*

"I don't like it now any more than I did then," said the man with the big head.

"Yes, but I just wanted to get it straight," said Mr. Kessler. "A thing like that can nag you."

Mr. Kessler did ten sets of sit-ups, and when he had worked up a good sweat, he went downstairs and showered. The massage room was empty and Mr. Kessler said to the attendant, "I want a massage. It doesn't matter that I've never had one before and that I associate it with luxury and extravagance. I want one. When I came in here I was going to get right out, but there's a principle involved. We have this big holiday, very big, but you're either excused from it or you're not. And I am. I was pretty sick."

"If I had the towel concession, I'd have it made," said the masseur, oiling up Mr. Kessler's body. "You can't make it on rubs alone. You've got to have rubs and rags."

"It's crazy that they're all sitting out there bent over in prayer and I'm in here, but when you're proving a point, sometimes things look ridiculous."

"If you have any influence at all," said the masseur, "try to get me towels. I can't make it on rubs alone."

Music poured into the gym now, and Mr. Kessler hummed along to several early Jerome Kern tunes. His massage at an end, he got up from the table, showered, and then, as he dressed, told Rico, the locker room attendant, "I'm all tingling. I knew this was the right thing to do. Next year I'll be in the temple all bent over like they are, but I did the right thing tonight."

"All you need is a cold," said Rico.

"You know how I feel about that remark," said Mr. Kessler.

Upstairs, Mr. Kessler smiled at the blonde receptionist who grabbed him and began to lead him in a cha-cha across the front office. "I don't do this with girls," said Mr. Kessler, falling into step, "and I'm going right home. You have a pony-tail and I can hardly stand that."

"Where's your wife?" asked the girl, going off into a complicated cha-cha break that flustered Mr. Kessler.

"You ask me that all the time," said Mr. Kessler, picking up the beat again and doing primitive arm motions. "Look, it doesn't matter about her hips. Don't you understand a man can be in love with a woman with any size hips? Where's my wife, you ask? What do we need her for?"

"Do you want to go dancing?" asked the girl.

"I told you I don't do things with girls," said Mr. Kessler. "I shouldn't even be carrying on here in the lobby. What's your name?"

"Irish," said the girl.

"Irish?" said Mr. Kessler. "Do you have to be named the most gentile name there is? They're all out there wailing and beating their breasts for atonement and I'm with an Irish. But I've got to ask myself if it would be better if you were an Inge. I'm not doing anything wrong and even if I am it doesn't make any difference that I'm doing it tonight. I'm either excused or I'm not excused. I'm finished early and I'll go for about twenty minutes."

The girl put on a sweater and walked ahead of Mr. Kessler to his car. He started the motor and she said, "I don't want to dance just yet. I'd rather that you park somewhere and make love to me."

"I can't stand it when the girl says a thing like that," said Mr. Kessler. "That drives me out of my mind. Look, it was all right in there in the gym, but I'm feeling a little funny out here in the night air. As though I'm wandering around somewhere in the goddamned Sinai. But that's just the kind of thing I've got to fight. I don't think there'll be anyone behind the Chinese restaurant now. All we're going to do is fool around a little, though."

The lights in the Chinese restaurant's parking field were dark when they got there and Mr. Kessler stopped the car and put his head into the receptionist's blonde hair and bit her ear. "You smell young. About that ear bite, though. I just feel that as long as I'm being so honest about Yom Kippur I can't do anything dishonest at all. The ear bite isn't mine. That is, it's just something I do. A long time ago, before my wife got big-hipped, we took a Caribbean cruise and she danced on deck with a Puerto Rican public relations man named Rodriguez. She acted funny after that and finally told me it was because he'd aroused her. I got it out of her that it was because he'd bitten her ear. I can't use an ear bite on her, of course, but I've been dying to try one out and that's why I worked it in."

"Really make love to me," the receptionist whispered, putting herself against Mr. Kessler.

"There'll only be some light fooling around," said Mr. Kessler. "Do you know what the hell night this is? Uh oh. The voice you have just heard was that of the world's worst hypocrite. Am I proving anything if I just do some elaborate kissing about the neck and shoulders? A man is either excused or he's not excused. Oh, Jesus, you're wearing boyish-type underwear. You would be wearing something along those lines. That did it," he said, and fell upon her.

After a while, she said, "Now that you've had me, I want us to dance slowly knowing that you've had me."

"You're suggesting crazy things," said Mr. Kessler. "I'm calling my wife before I do any more of them."

They drove to a filling station and Mr. Kessler dialed his number and said, "I thought I'd get in and get out, but the car's broken. It's in the differential."

"You know I don't know what that is," said Mrs. Kessler. "It's like telling me something is in the psalms."

"The garage has to run out and get some parts," he said.

"Do you feel funny about what you did?" asked Mrs. Kessler.

"I didn't do anything," he said. "Everybody forgets how sick I was. When you're sick, the religion understands."

Mr. Kessler hung up and the receptionist showed him the way to a dancing place. It was a cellar called Tiger Sam's, catering to Negroes and whites and specializing in barbecued ham hocks. They danced awhile and the receptionist said she was hungry. "I am, too," said Mr. Kessler. "It's going to be tough getting down that first bite because I know the fast isn't over until sundown tomorrow night, but it's about time I stopped thinking that way. I forget how sick I was."

The receptionist said she wanted the ham hocks, and Mr. Kessler said, "I confess I've had the urge to try them, but they're probably the most un-kosher things in the world. I'm starting in again. Wouldn't I just be the most spineless man in America if I ordered eggs and told them to hold the hocks? I'll have the hocks."

When he had finished eating, Mr. Kessler began drinking double shots of bourbon until he slid off his stool and fell into the sawdust.

"I've gone past that point where I should have stopped. I only hope I don't get sentimental and run off into a synagogue. It's here where my heart starts breaking for every Jew who ever walked with a stoop and cried into a prayerbook. That's just the kind of thing I've got to watch, though. It would be the best medicine in the world for me if an old Jewish refugee woman just happened to stumble in here by accident. Just so I could fail to hug and kiss her and apologize to her for all the world's crimes. And that would be that and I'd have proven that number one I was sick and number two when you're sick you're excused and number three when you're excused you're really excused."

A young Negro with a dancer's grace in his body came over, bowed to Mr. Kessler in the sawdust and said, "I'm Ben and should like to try the meringue with your lovely blonde companion. With your permission."

Mr. Kessler said it was all right and stayed in the sawdust while the two danced closely and primitively to a Haitian rhythm. Two Negro musicians sat on stools above Mr. Kessler. One handed another double bourbon down to him and said, "Like happy Yom Kippur, dad."

"I can't get to my feet," said Mr. Kessler. "You think that's funny and sort of like a jazz musician's joke, but it so happens I am Jewish. I ought to let you have it in the guts, but the point is even jokes shouldn't bother me if I'm excused from the holiday. If I got upset and let you have it in the guts, it would show that I really haven't excused myself."

One of the musicians dangled a toilet bowl deodorizer in front of Mr. Kessler's nose while the other howled.

"I don't know where this fits into anything," said Mr. Kessler, "but I'm not going to get upset or start feeling sentimental."

The Negro named Ben came back now with his arm around the receptionist's waist and said, "I wonder if you two would join me at my apartment. I'm having a do there and am sure you'll love Benny's decor."

The two musicians carried Mr. Kessler out to a Sunbeam convertible and put him on the floor of the rear seat, slipping in above him. The receptionist got in alongside Ben, who drove to Harlem. The two musicians kept the deodorizer in Mr. Kessler's face. "I suppose you've got a reason for that," he said from the floor, as they howled in the night air and kept pushing it against his nose.

When the car stopped, Mr. Kessler said, "I can walk now," and stumbled along behind the four as they mounted the steps of a brownstone. Ben knocked on the door, two light raps and a hard one, and a powerful pale-skinned man in leotards opened the door quickly to a huge single room, divided by a purple curtain. It was done in the style of a cave and there were bits of African sculpture on shelves, along with campaign pictures of New York's Governor Harriman. A film flashed on one wall, demonstrating Martha Graham ballet techniques, and some forty or fifty Negro-white couples in leotards stood watching it in the haze of the room, some assuming ballet poses along with the dancers. Ben got leotards for the new arrivals and led them behind the purple curtain so they could change.

There, a man in a silk dressing gown sat reading *Popular Mechanics* on a divan shaped like a giant English muffin. Ben introduced him to Mr. Kessler and the receptionist as "Tor," his roommate, a noted anthropologist. "Why do I have to get into leotards?" asked Mr. Kessler as the receptionist and the two Negro musicians began to slip into theirs and the anthropologist looked on. "I'll bet my new Vic Tanny's body won't look bad in them, though." After he had changed, there was a scuffle outside the curtain. The film had stopped suddenly, fixing Martha Graham on the screen with one leg on the practice bar. Several couples were screaming. A police officer was on the floor, and Ben said to Mr. Kessler, "Get his legs. He came up here and got stuck and we've got to get him out."

"I've never committed a crime," said Mr. Kessler, smoothing his leotards and taking the policeman's legs. Something wine-colored and wet was on the officer's breast pocket. "What do you mean he got stuck? I don't want to be carrying him if he got stuck."

They stumbled down the stairs with him and then walked several blocks in the blackness, finally propping the officer's body against an ashcan.

"I don't know about leaving him against an ashcan," said Mr. Kessler. "This is one thing I'm sorry I had to do tonight. Not because it's tonight especially, but because I wouldn't want to do it any night. But if I had to do it at all, I suppose I'm glad it was tonight. Why should I worry about doing this on Yom Kippur? I can see worrying about it in general, but not because it's tonight. Not if I'm supposed to be excused."

They went back to the party. The film was off now and couples were dancing wildly in the murk to a three-man combo, each of whom was beating a bongo. They were hollering out a song in which the only lyrics were, "We're a bongo combo," repeated many times. One of the Negro musicians put a slim cigarette in Mr. Kessler's mouth and lit it. "Hey, wait a minute," said Mr. Kessler. "I know what kind of cigarette this is. I may have always had a yen to just try a puff of one, but that's one thing I'm absolutely not doing tonight. Not because it's tonight. I'd resist even more if it were just an ordinary night. In fact, the reason I haven't spit it out already is I want to show I'm not afraid of Yom Kippur. It's working already." Mr. Kessler sat down peacefully in the middle of perfumed, dancing, frenzied feet. "My senses are sharpened. I read that's what's supposed to happen." He saw the curtain part momentarily. Holding the anthropologist's purple dressing gown toreador style, the blonde receptionist, nude now, stood atop the English muffin. The noted Swede charged forward, making bull-like passes at her, one finger against each ear. A Negro girl with full lips leaned down and caught Mr. Kessler's head to her pistol-like bosoms, holding him there, senses sharpened, for what seemed like a season, and then Ben came whirling by in a series of *West Side Story* leaps, chucking him flirtatiously under the chin and then kissing him wetly in the ear. Mr. Kessler got to his knees and screamed, "J'ACCUSE. That isn't what I mean. What I mean is I'M EXCUSED, I'M EXCUSED," but no one heard him and he fell unconscious.

When he awakened, Ben and the two Negro musicians were helping him behind the wheel of his own car. Ben tapped the blonde receptionist on the behind and she slid in beside Mr. Kessler.

"We enjoyed your company terribly much," said Ben, and the two musicians howled. "Hope you enjoyed the decor and the Ivy League entertainment."

"What time is it?" Mr. Kessler asked the girl when the Negroes had driven off.

"Almost morning," said the receptionist.

"Well, at least they're out," said Mr. Kessler.

"Who's out of where?" she asked.

"The Jews are out of synagogue," said Mr. Kessler.

"I want you to meet my brothers," she said. "Maybe we can have a few beers before the sun comes up."

"The holiday is still on, but the important part is over," said Mr. Kessler. "Then tonight it's all over."

The receptionist showed Mr. Kessler the way to her white frame house. "I was divorced two years ago," she said. "Now I live with my two brothers. They're a hell of a lot of fun and I was lucky to have them."

The night was breaking when they got to the house. The receptionist introduced Mr. Kessler to the two brothers, both of whom were tall and freckled. The oldest brother served cans of beer for all, and when they had finished the beers, began to open a crate of grapefruits. "Our sales manager sent these back from the South," he said. "Aren't they honeys?" He picked up one of the grapefruits and rolled it to his younger brother, who fielded it like a baseball and threw it back. "You grabbed that one like Tommy Henrich," said the older brother, rolling it back. The younger brother picked it up, made a little skipping motion and flung it back again. "Hey, just like Johnny Logan," said the older one. He rolled it once again and when he got it back, said, "That was Marty Marion."

"Or 'Phumblin' Phil' Weintraub," said Mr. Kessler.

The brothers stopped a second and then the older brother rolled the grapefuit again. "George Stirnweiss," he hollered when his brother pegged it to him. He rolled it. He got it back. "Just like Bobby Richardson," he said.

"Or 'Phumblin' Phil' Weintraub," said Mr. Kessler.

"Who's that?" asked the older brother.

"That's it," said Mr. Kessler. He got to his feet with fists clenched and walked toward the older brother.

"You never should have said that," said Mr. Kessler.

"I didn't say anything," said the boy.

"Oh yes you did," said Mr. Kessler, through clenched teeth. "Maybe I went to Vic Tanny's and shacked up with a girl named Irish and got drunk and ate barbecued ham hocks. Maybe I hid a dead cop and smoked marijuana and went to a crazy party and got kissed by a Negro homosexual ballet dancer. But I'm not letting you get away with something like that."

He flew at the older brother now, knocked him down and began to tear at his ear. "He was all-hit-no-field and he played four years for the Giants in the early forties and faded when the regular players got out of service AND NO SON OF A BITCH IS GOING TO SAY ANYTHING ABOUT POOR 'PHUMBLIN' PHIL' WEINTRAUB ON YOM KIPPUR!"

The younger brother and the girl tugged at him with fury and finally dislodged him, but not before a little piece of the ear had come off. Then Mr. Kessler smoothed his leotards and went sobbing out the door.

"I may have been excused," they heard him call back in the early morning, "but I wasn't that excused."

❖

Bruce Jay Friedman was born in New York City in 1930, attended the University of Missouri, worked for many years as a magazine editor, and now lives on Long Island with his family. His first novel was Stern *(1962), a book that was at once extraordinarily funny and extraordinarily bitter.* Stern *is a city man, and he has trouble enough adjusting to life in the suburbs; when a neighbor is rude to his wife and calls his kid a "kike" he is obsessed with the idea that he must do something about it, but for the greater part of the book he is incapable of action. His second novel,* A Mother's Kisses *(1964), was a comedy, portraying a Jewish mother somewhat in the mode of Auntie Mame. He has published two collections of short stories:* Far from the City of Class *(1963) and* Black Angels *(1966). He has also edited an anthology called* Black Humor *(1963) and is often associated with that so-called school of bitter humorists, along with such other American writers as Joseph Heller, Thomas Pynchon, and Terry Southern.*

In "When You're Excused You're Excused," Friedman uses one of the most effective "black humor" methods: achieving serious social criticism by extending the clichés and hypocrisies of contemporary life to the point where their absurdity is clear. This is what Heller did in Catch 22 *and what Southern did in* Dr. Strangelove. *Kessler's absurd hypocrisy is extended and extended and extended. He himself sums up all he has done at the end, when out of guilt or remorse or whatever, he suddenly decides he must stand up for the religion he has so violated. The culminating absurdity is that all he can find to defend is a baseball player (a baseball player!)*

with a Jewish name, which name he had to bring up three times himself and no one ever attacked. Yet Kessler's reaction is not in itself suddenly absurd—it is a familiar enough example of the form class and ethnic loyalty takes in a mass society: everyone can "believe" in the superiority of a sports hero and defend him to strangers, without being labeled by his belief. Having acted as a fanatic defender of the faith, Kessler can go home righteously indignant, no longer "excused" from being Jewish.

HERBERT WILNER

Dovisch in the Wilderness

❖❖❖❖❖❖❖

CALL ME DOVISCH, another wanderer survived to tell a story.

I mean it. Since I saw you last Wednesday, I had an American misadventure—a preposterous, outrageous, comic misadventure, if you will, but a thoroughly *American* one. I find myself obligated to share it with you, a class in American Literature, Early Period. Yes, I know what you are here for: I announced last week that this hour was set aside to talk with you about your final examination. Thus come all the bright faces at eight in the morning at the end of May in yet another spring in a part of California that has only weather and no climate, thus no season, hence no time. Except finals time. What kinds of questions will Dovisch ask on his final exam? A short route to a high grade to know beforehand the kind of questions. So no one is absent today. Perfect attendance for the first time in—how many weeks?

Nevertheless, I shall share this experience with you. I promise it will be preparation enough for your finals. I share it with you fresh and unrehearsed, because it didn't end till two o'clock this very morning. Six hours ago. No, that's not right. Today is for a flyer, but it is also for facts. My colleagues would remind me: dates, figures, facts—toughness. At the bottom of all knowledge and every wisdom, a fact. It is the gossip of the corridors, what my colleagues accuse me of. And some of you have heard it in the corridors, or over coffee, or in your other classes. I know how they accuse me, leavening it with an intolerable affection: Dovisch, the rainbow-maker. So the hard fact of it is that my misadventure did not come to its end at two this morning. It continues still, because I am obligated to share it with you, and I am going to share it with you, delicacies notwithstanding. And you will not learn from it because you will not see the immediate profit to yourselves because you will not imagine it can have anything to do with your final exam. You begin already to put down your ballpoint pens, to close your notebooks, and on some of your faces I see that smile reserved for moments like this when you know I am about to go the long way around. There goes Dovisch again, the rainbow-maker on another flyer. Students of Early American Literature, Section 2, listen to me. Take notes. My little misadventure *is* your finals. And then I begin, Dovisch fashion, accented by way of the Bronx, inflected a little by a history somewhat older than the American, the inflection slightly exaggerated this morning.

I went last week to Pyramid Lake. I went alone after my last class on Wednesday, I went in my car. I curse cars every day of my life, but I went to Pyramid Lake to be alone, to hold conversations with no one, so the car was a matter of free choice. For those of you not from this part of the country, know that Pyramid Lake is thirty miles north and slightly east of Reno. It is thirty miles long and ten miles wide. I went to Pyramid Lake to test myself in the experience of solitude and isolation. I had four whole days to spend there. It will come to some of you as no surprise that I had never in all my life sustained a period, however brief, of true solitude. Isolation, yes—isolation always—but not solitude. So the four days, seized from my work and my family, seemed time enough for a deliberate test. I took a sleeping bag, which I preferred to buy for the occasion rather than borrow from a colleague. I know too well not their unwillingness to lend but their looks upon lending. Dovisch in a sleeping bag? I took a sweater, a flannel shirt, changes of socks, and so forth; also canned fruits and a can opener, and boxes of zwieback borrowed from my daughter. I have a credit card, so I needed no money even for gas. I took fifty cents for bridge tolls, and no more. And my checkbook. I must explain this.

I did not start out intending to make things difficult. I wanted, if possible, to experience joy in my solitude, not hardship. Thus my food arrangement. I was not going to test self-reliance in the form of survival. That's not what Emerson meant. Thoreau either. I was going to test solitude, in which self-reliance was a mere consequence. I can't fish. I have never in my life gone fishing. And if I did fish and caught a fish, I could not trust myself to build a fire. And if I caught a fish and built a fire, I would have had to have brought along the fishing equipment. Also a pot for cooking. No, I was altogether less encumbered with the canned fruits, and I admit a fondness for sweet syrups and a distaste for fish. I must insist upon the fact that I went responsibly to Pyramid Lake for pleasure, not hardship. I left out money not because I sneer at it. I am Puritan enough to know its grace. But in my wallet it would remind me always of purchase, and that would imply some other person who sells, and though he might through all my stay be absent, the money in my wallet would be an emblem of his implication in my life and a diminishment of my solitude. I took the checkbook because solitude is the essence of responsibility and has nothing in common with thoughtlessness. I have a wife and four little children. There are emergencies in such a world. I will soon tell you of some of them.

Be advised also that I took no books, magazines or newspapers. I took no paper and no writing implements. I must correct again the easy assumption some of you begin to make that I went to Pyramid Lake on a merely literary impulse borrowed from those very books I refused to take. "Life is our dictionary," Emerson said, *American Scholar,* 1837, and you imagine I set aside books the better to experience real life. It is not what Emerson meant. It is not what I intended. He wanted us to possess and not to be possessed by what we read. Reading was an extension of the active life by which he challenged all Americans. For my own part, I disavowed books because they implicate a voice roaring at me, a diminishment of solitude. I disavowed writing. It implicates my untalented efforts to roar at someone else. Another diminishment. You see—I tried to be practical in everything.

So, directly to it. The time goes. This is our last meeting. I must get it all in. I tell you, I see America now. I can open my fist and watch it dance. Rainbows, Dovisch, rainbows. Facts, dates—

I arrived at Pyramid Lake on Wednesday at five-thirty in the evening, having traveled east to find the West. I went through Reno and then north. Motels, restaurants, gas stations, domiciles for the divorced, the divorcing, the gamblers. Scarlet letters in every face, branded in the flesh. The un-epic frontier of our present time. Then northward through the desert mountains. Sagebrush and female slopes and hollows. Late sunlight shifting colors, purple and violet and blue and a flare of red, shimmering, shifting. Mountains shifting in the light. The windshield dances. A curve in the road, a descent, and there to the right, below the lowering line of the desert mountain, Pyramid Lake. Brilliant even for a polished stone. Water polished by water. A table top in a naked world. Not a tree. Not a cloud. The whole lake in one turn of the head. A great belt of not quite water under a balloon of sky. Into which enters, into that universe of silence, the *phtt phtt* of the old Plymouth, inside of which is Dovisch, Professor of American Literature. Specialist in Emerson; seminars offered also, for a touch of the old country, in Dostoevski. Inside of Dovisch, before this naked world all in silence, the heart empties with a gush, a roar reaching into the corners of *our* Promised Land.

Terrifying landscape. Perfection for solitude. I must impress you with it through *my* eyes, but I have no power for such description. From where would I get it? Born forty-two years ago in the Bronx, Simon Dovisch, second son to Morris and Esther Dovisch, immigrants from Russia, that eastern world tilting off Europe, related also to uncles of Oriental countenance to make a boy wonder from which angle the wanderers first began to wander, to cohabit with what strange ancestors along the way. Raised on the fourth floor rear, sharing his brother's room with a view opening to other windows on the fourth floor with coal-smoked bricks between, and raised in the streets, down there on the dark concrete bottom of what *your* Whitman called the clefts of streets, raised to games of ball, at which he was inept, and among the squealings and the yawpings of those to whom solitude would be death and for whom isolation was a way of life. Who learned sex on the corners under lampposts and fumbled at its practice in night-time backyards and on tenement roofs, filled with it by a guilt the whole tribe of Mathers could not have endured because it derived from the shame of poverty and not from a mere redemptive sin. So with much to prove through the years, and with books already the only means of his demonstrations. Immersed then, drowning in the vivid American history: splashed and drenched with Pilgrims and Puritans and Quakers, Revolutionists and Rationalists, fur trappers and Indians too, poets and novelists and cowboys and presidents, prairies and mountains and deserts and oceans, gleaned, all of it, from black type on a white page, millions of pages by a light bulb on the fourth floor rear in the Bronx. Later in libraries. Here now, on the Western shore, a Professor of American Literature.

That literature beginning, as I have told you, in a bitter romance with God for the possession by His grace of an endless wealth of wilderness to be ravished in love, goaded into the love of primitive instincts, and shamed by those instincts into savagery itself, which is the worship of the thing. So they found emblems of it everywhere, the thing: witches, kites and keys, scarlet letters, a whale, a ferry, a river, things celebrated by the very prophets who saw the doom in them. And all the while even the most ignorant of them learning in their blood what Dovisch from the Bronx, professing American literature, cannot infuse into the blood, melt down the books how he will.

Things. Things. Things. To fish, to hunt, to build a house, to farm, to conduct a business, to predict a season. To name a tree, to name a flower, to name a fish, a bird, to control a single practical art—to repair, say, a car, a damned cursed old Plymouth. Things. Things. In them resides the power of all description.

Dovisch alone at Pyramid Lake, in a naked world of silence, seeking solitude, testing whether he can so late in life experience it at all, in order to understand by experience one of the conditions of what he teaches.

Students, I take pride in telling you I remained at the lake all my allotted time. You must understand what it was for me if you are to share my experience of what came to pass at the end of it. That first night. Arrivals are stunning. Impressions are immediate. You never know again all that lives in the first encounter. And now, a mere four days later, I cannot recover those first minutes of coming upon the lake. Because none of what followed—

Look. I did this the first day. I arrived in the evening at five-thirty. I drove on. I did not want to stay where the highway came directly to the lake. There was something like a diner there. Hot dogs, soda, so forth. Closed and deserted, it could nevertheless be a point of gathering. I follow the lake road some miles farther. The sun glaring. Barren everywhere. I park the car. I open a can of stewed pears, a box of zwiebacks, and I have my supper at the lake. I sit and stare. Dovisch alone. Later, the sun going down. A dish of flame. Thoughts of my dear family in our friendly life-insurance-company housing project. Thoughts of my students, of you. Thoughts of America. Then a chill, the sudden cold. I put on my flannel shirt, my sweater. The growing darkness. I prepare the sleeping bag. Ah, that first night of trying to sleep in that wretched sack. Smile all you want, but one thing all of you can learn from the Bronx is the nature of a true mattress. Here at the lake, rocks and stones underneath. And I told them in the shop where I purchased the sleeping bag. Look at me, I told them. A tall man, feet like canoes. Ample room, ample room, he assured me. American entrepreneurs. The human contact gone, the cash register, everything. But I was too big for the bag, the bag too small for me. In physical discomfort begins the wilderness of imaginings. The enemy of sleep.

In the total darkness, in the universe of silence, what else, what vast night life crawls and slithers here? Snakes? Rattlers? Spiders? Tarantulas? Calm yourself, Dovisch! Achieve solitude. I ransack such knowledge as I have of flora and fauna. Miserable knowledge. I could have written all that I knew on a part of one zwieback and have made a supper of the part remaining. So I confess. The first night was full of imagined horrors. I have from a cockroach childhood on the fourth floor a loathing of crawling things.

You can imagine, then, the depths of my self-contempt when I commenced to believe I would not even make it through the first night. Not only the lumps and clumps of stones beneath me, but the wretched sleeping bag too small. Not only the stones and the sleeping bag, but my eyeglasses too. If the stones and the bedding should keep me awake, I should at least enjoy the stars. When in his life did Dovisch sleep with stars? But with his eyeglasses off, who could see the stars? With his eyeglasses on, how sleep at all? And if the stones and the sleeping bag and the eyeglasses were not enough, comes now the wild imaginings of crawling things. Thoughts, then, of retreating to the car. It was not that much of a cheat on my idea of solitude, but something in me argued against it as a mere disguise for an early withdrawal. Besides, if a crawling thing had made its way into the car while I had unloaded? Wouldn't that be worse? The crawling thing and myself made natural enemies by being confined together in an artificial compartment. Wouldn't the thing then seek artificial revenge on me, whereas it might in the open space,with a whole Western desert in which to conduct its slithering life, might it not merely crawl away from me as a nuisance to be avoided? Ultimately, I resigned myself. In the middle of the night I offered myself the following proposition. If it was my fate to succumb to a venomous bite, if a snake or a spider with thousands of square barren miles to crawl in chooses the few inches of my exposed face, then God's will be done. I surrendered. I can report to you I overcame my imaginings. Ultimately, I slept.

Came then the first of my pink dawns at the lake. Morning is when I am awake and there is a dawn in me, said Thoreau, echoes Dovisch now, who ordinarily, by old Bronx habit and by way of avoiding noisy children in the morning, leads the Dostoevski life of the underground world after the midnight hour when the soul, losing God, finds the psychiatrist. Let me summarize those blessed days. Let me give you the light and the tone and the angle. You squirm. You ask yourselves: of what relevance? Is there at least a story? But the story is also the arrangements for the story. Didn't the writers we have studied arrange? Didn't Hawthorne? Didn't Melville?

Know then that I sat for long hours in the sun-bright places at the side of the lake. Then I walked for miles along the rim of the water, my pants rolled, feet naked, naked head to the naked sun. My eye grew accustomed to naked distance. My mind thereafter sought relief from panoramic registrations. It ordered my eyes to closer recognitions. I forced myself to look for long, uninterrupted sequences at nearer things. At pebbles, rocks, pools of water, boulders that were porous, at the pores of boulders, at brush; at silence itself I looked and listened. I spent a whole hour tossing one pebble into shallow water, retrieving it each time. I spent a whole hour watching a large bird flying high in great circles—watching me, perhaps. Crow, eagle, hawk, falcon—who am I to know the names of birds? For a whole hour we were hundreds of feet apart, but eyeball to eyeball. And I knew its great power of sight compared to my weakness of vision. Easy then to make factual what I have told you again and again as mere surmise: the object seen is in the image of the eyes, not the object. Never again ask me, where is it—the Oversoul? Of what size, what shape? Know then what I mean when I ask in turn: of what size and shape is your eye?

Look—picture my days at Lake Pyramid this way. Know that my days were symmetrical. Know that I lived inside them with great precision. Picture me there from up close as a tall, gross-featured, big-footed, clumsy man, alien to where he stood and what he gazed at, reddening in the sun, his hidden heart slipping into the thrill of un-isolation. Picture him there from afar as but another sparrow in the great void, not without a little grace, a small addition of human design against the barren mountains overlooking the blue and stony water under the height of sky. Hear me whistling Mozart melodies into the Nevada air.

Students, in this landscape so strange to me, I learned how I loved the great, secret, mythical history of my country. Yes, *my* country too. Removed by the solitude itself from all isolation, I would have laid down my life for my country's secret heart. Yes, Dovisch on a flyer, but fly with me if you can. Solitude is the experience of the idea itself. It is the racial nostalgia reducing the baggage of our life's factuality—even the fourth floor rear and its crazy summons to books. But in the thingness of time, the idea vanishes. It had to be lost. Long before cars and jets and bombs and rockets. Lost even as far back as whaling time, as *Walden* time, as *Leaves of Grass* time. But history is the aspiration as well as the loss.

The idea and the fact and the emblem between. I could not wait to get back to share some of this with you in the beginning of this hour, to give you a particle of my new feeling. But how would I say it, since it was itself only another idea? More Dovisch rainbows. But fate waited. Nothing is wasted. My misadventure waited. The facts themselves waited. So—the arrangements made and the story at last.

My time was up, and I threw my litter into the car. I left not one trace of my presence there. The bird who had watched me was long since gone. Would its eyes remember Dovisch? Who knows? It was Sunday. It was yesterday. It was two in the afternoon. I was exuberant. I had stayed out my time. I had learned. Which of you cannot by now picture Dovisch in his exuberance? I almost could not find my car keys. Trembling fingers fumbling in pockets. The beginning of panic. Voluntary solitude is one thing, but who am I to confront an enforced one? Calm, calm, I urged myself. There were the keys in the glove compartment, where I had with good forethought left them. The return home then.

I turn the key. I press the pedal. Nothing. A little *erk-erk* noise in the big silence, and then nothing. Calm, calm, I urge myself. First the fuel. But how should it be the fuel when I had filled up in Truckee with just such a precaution in mind? I am almost afraid to look. If there was a leak and in three days it all ran out, where should I walk now for gas? I turn the key and look. Plenty of fuel. The needle almost to the three-quarters. It was a mistake. A clumsiness of the fingers. My excitement to get home. To see you here this morning, to tell. Again, then, on the pedal. Again nothing. *Erk-erk-erk,* and nothing more. In the middle of nowhere with a car that won't start on a Sunday afternoon, with a lecture class to meet on the next morning, having promised, given my word to review for the finals, not to mention a devoted family, the oldest child only seven, but who knows already how to worry. Calm yourself. A voice into the panic, into the silence, into another *erk-erk,* another and another. I ransack such facts as I have gathered of cars that will not start. Another zwieback full. Gathered from the general mechanic atmosphere and previous car catastrophes, like old people in hospitals who know their organs in proportion to the number of survived diseases therein. So a car that won't start: wet spark plugs? How could that be in a desert? Once with an old Studebaker there was trouble with the vacuum advance. A vacuum advance. Who could remember what it was? Where in the engine would I find it? Once with an old Ford there was trouble with a voltage regulator. Again, who knows where such a thing is to be found in an engine? Would you believe me when I confess I do not even know what voltage is? I would tell you back what you tell me of the Oversoul. I can't see it, so why should I believe in it? Is a voltage regulator something to believe in? Tinker Toys for children. Apparatus. But if the ignorance derived from a lack of faith should cost you your life in a desert? or attendance at your job? or the peace of mind of your family? There's the rub.

So smile at me and my car pickle. Do you pause ever to count up all the things to which you have delivered faith and are ignorant of? Girls here who drive cars to campus. Do you know what makes them go? Gasoline. Is that an answer? Then food alone would keep alive a dying man. Do you know, when you press a button, why the elevator should go up or down to the designated floor and not through the top of the building or through the bottom of the cellar? Do you know why an airplane should fly? Why these senseless tubes in the ceiling should light up when I press a button? Not to mention computers. Or X-rays. Or a radio. Or television. Listen—our Benjamin Franklin, whom I treated so scantily in the first semester. Sandwiched between Puritans and Emerson, who could afford to pause there? But who would deny that he was one of those who lived with his feet on the ground? That I despise the man is another story.

The battery. Of course I thought of the battery. Three days and I had not once used the car. But the battery was only three months old and the guarantee was for eighteen. So go cash in a guarantee at Pyramid Lake. A million eighteen-month batteries, and Dovisch gets the lemon. Another old story. The question was a push. Where could I find another car to push me in that sand and sage where I had pulled mine off the road? Calm. Calm. Perhaps not the whole battery. A cable connection, perhaps. I too had heard of such things. For luck I try once more. *Erk-erk,* and then nothing. I open the hood. I see the battery and the cables thereto, one with the plus and one with the minus. What all that means, I never knew. Gingerly, I touch the wires. My heart leaps. Indeed, one seems loose. I turn a little, and it tightens. I rush back to the car, turn the ignition. *Erk-erk,* nothing more. I go out again. Again with the cables—pinching, stroking, prodding, pushing, punching at last, punching the senseless cable, the stupid battery, and for good measure the hot fender. *Erk-erk.*

Listen—the hour flies. To make it short: I need a push, and the solitude is over for me, but not for where I am. To walk then and return in a car with help. I take the keys. I walk. I walk and walk. At last a sign. Four miles to Nixon. It is already an hour since I first tried to start the car. Three o'clock now and who ever heard of Nixon? A community, a hamlet, and people nevertheless. Nixon in an hour, I assure myself, and perhaps a car I can flag down along the way before then. I am a good walker, an old Manhattan tramper. A deep breath for fortitude, and off I go, driven by hatred of cars, hurried by my anxiety about driving at night on highways.

There is no time to give you the hike in the hot desert sun. Fill in as you will. All history is incomplete. Only imagine the anger, the distress, the reasonable panic. The sweat, the dust. The beginning of trees, an oasis. A cool head, says Melville, betrays an icy heart. The sight at last of a car on the highway. I get out in the lane. Exultant, I wave my arms. How lucky that I so soon see a car! Would you believe it that they nearly ran me down? A gang of boys, maybe college boys, car-tinkerers. Maybe any one of them could have helped me. Am I innocent to believe any one of them would have, if I had had the opportunity to explain to him what it was all about? But can I make a speech to a rocket? Seventy, eighty miles an hour they went past me, swerving into the other lane in the last minute, and at the same time I leaped into a thicket of sage on my side. One of them had the gall to stick his head out the window and shake a fist at me.

I brushed myself off and resumed walking. Only then did I think for the first time of the appearance I presented to others. Since the Wednesday morning of my departure, I had not shaved. My nose and forehead, I knew from old experience, would be shining like a McIntosh apple—sunburn. My khaki pants were some other color now, and no end of wrinkles everywhere from struggles with the undersized sleeping bag. My T-shirt smeared from where I leaned under the hood of the car, and my hands all dirt and grease from playing with the battery cable. What sort of welcome could I expect at the first house I came to? Bedraggled and begrimed, how would I be received on someone's property uninvited on a Sunday afternoon?

Came then the first house. Not a house, a shack. Albeit under a few trees and with a porch, and before the porch not one but three cars. Not a person in sight. Behind the dwelling place, on a small slope, cows, cattle—it was not then the time to discriminate. But on the other side of the road, another shack, and only one car. I decided for that one. Three cars on a Sunday before such a small dwelling place means company, visitors. Not, it seemed to me, an encouraging atmosphere for a plea of distress, a call for help. I crossed the road, noticing the newness of the car. A shack to live in, but a new car for leaving and returning. Another small porch. Three, four steps, the wood answering back to my feet. Good, I tell myself: for the door to the right of the steps is half open, and the noise of my approach forewarns them I don't come in stealth. Outside the brilliant sun; inside, all dark. And already a foul odor. Better that way, I encourage myself. Poverty and even filth will be less offended by my own appearance. I knock, not timidly, not too loudly. Good luck to you here, Dovisch, I announce to myself, implore. Then I tell myself at once: Ask only to use the telephone, to call the nearest service station.

There is no answer to my knocking. I knock again, somewhat louder. I wait. No answer. There is the odor, definitely foul, reminiscent for me of dark corners in schoolyards, of relief stations on certain desolate subway stops. Also sounds—a chair scraping, perhaps. But no footsteps, no speech. I call out: "Anyone at home?" And that, in four days' time, is the first spoken language I have addressed to a listener. Do you know the experience of separation from your own voice? I thought: Should I push the door open the rest of the way or knock again? I push. Not vigorously—politely. The light from outside floods in. They are standing there blinking at the light, watching me.

A man and a woman. Puerto Ricans, I tell myself. No, Mexicans. What would Puerto Ricans be doing there? Short and thick and swarthy, wide foreheads, wide noses, like Gauguins—but no sparkle: sullen, suspicious. They keep blinking at the light. They look at me, and they look at each other. Dark black hair, both of them. The man in a sort of crew cut, but not cut down enough. The hairs standing up like quills, and greasy. The woman's too, but lank, uncombed. He wears dungarees and one of those faded blue worker's-farmer's shirts, also denim. She is bare-armed in a dress that merely hangs from her, that needs a belt, a collar, a something. Will they even understand English, I wonder, as I begin my introduction, my explanation, my need.

Students, I am not a good reporter, not a good observer to begin with. Furniture I am blind to. I can stare at stuff in the house of a stranger or friend and not remember the very next day what was there. But did you need to be Henry James or even Dreiser to stand where I stood yesterday afternoon on the threshold of that shack (no one had yet invited me in) and not know at once as you tried to explain your predicament that there could be no telephone in such a place? Perhaps there was not even electricity. Between the two of them, where they stood, there was a little table of skinny legs—a bridge table—piled with dishes and beer cans, and on the table was a thick, half-burned candle. So you see how I had to shift my explanation toward a plea for direct help. What I do remember is a pot-bellied stove with a tilted flue, clothes on hooks on one of the walls, and in a corner, by itself, nothing near it, like a museum piece, a single contour chair on those pipe legs. Sears, Roebuck modern. Red yet.

So—were they, in all those exchanges of looks between them, understanding a word of what I said about my car, my plight, my explanation of and apology for my ragged appearance? I must confess I said nothing of my professional occupation. Instinctively I imagined it would make no impression, or it would actually run a risk. Anywhere in Europe it would have been my first announcement. Put that in your notebooks and make of it what you will. I ended with a mention of my children and my wife, and the worry my absence from dinner tonight would cause them until I could get the car started to find a telephone. Did they understand? Another exchange of looks between them. Then at last the man speaks. One word.

"Sunday."

No accent, least of all a Mexican accent. But with spitefulness. That haughtiness of the permanently deprived addressing the temporarily deprived.

"Yes, Sunday," I said. "My wife alone on a Sunday and worrying that something has happened to me. The accidents on highways these days." I look toward the woman. I have, you noticed, dropped the plea of children. I get the impression this is a childless place. Who can guess what resentments it causes? Again the exchange of looks between them. Except for the turning of their heads and the blinking of their eyes, they remain all the while motionless. And I am still only on the threshold. He talks again. Two words now.

"How much?" he says.

"How much what?" I ask him. I look again at the woman. I am forced to say she was ugly. That stoop, that arch and thickness between the shoulder blades. The filthy hair. That sullenness, that stupefaction of face. She looks again at the man.

"Sunday," he repeats. "You pay how much?"

"How much do you want?" I say.

"How much do you give?" he asks.

"How much do you get paid an hour?" I ask him.

No response. Like wood. Nevertheless, in fairness, in fact, though I am but a poor businessman, I do admit the bargain is on his side, and, humanity apart, the right too. I cannot conceive of what I intruded upon between those two, but I am the intruder, and in need.

"Ten dollars if you get the car to start," I tell him.

Again the looks back and forth. This time a little perceptible heightening of effect. The impact of ten dollars in this place, in these lives.

"Fifteen," he says. "Fifteen for the car to start."

I smile to him, I shrug. All this from the threshold still. The smile and shrug of my people for centuries with their backs against the wall. "It will take you," I tell him, "ten minutes to get there, two minutes to push, ten minutes to get back. But all right, fifteen."

"Ten anyway," he says.

"Fifteen is all right," I say. "I made a bargain. I gave my word."

"Ten anyway," he repeats. The woman moves now for the first time. She scratches.

"Anyway what?" I ask him.

"If the car don't start, ten dollars anyway."

Bitter, money-sucking pessimist! Go romanticize peasants. What could I do? I agree. I refuse to contemplate the possibility that the car should not start. What could be wrong with it after bringing me all this way here without incident and sitting there undisturbed for four days, what else but a battery?

And so then to his car, the key for which he removes from a chain around his neck inside his shirt. Can you imagine? And though it was parked right outside his shack, the doors were locked. Well, I do not make much of it. Who is really to blame him? A brand-new Chevy with red-leather seats. What efforts it took to buy it, the labors now to keep paying for it. Did he come all the way from Mexico—under what hardships?—to live here—in what alienation?—and not have some chrome glitter of our ways rub off on him? So let Professor Dovisch sweat blood with the old Plymouth that won't start and let the laborer of the shack have his firebox that he was driving now a wild seventy miles an hour. Compensation,

Emerson called it. It was also a source of reassurance. When they drive like maniacs. They know all about cars.

He had nothing to say to me. We sat the first minute in silence. There was almost a foot between us in height—the advantage on my side. I must say it helped me to contemplate with a little less anxiety the financial arrangement I had made—the fact that I would have to pay with a check, and somewhere find a pen, and commence with identifications. And what would he make of such identifications? American Association of University Professors, Modern Language Association, New England Historical Society. He would have to settle for the gasoline credit card.

I mentioned at the beginning of the hour that I would tell my misadventure despite certain indelicacies. Let me say, then, that in the man's car on the way back to the lake and to my own car, whether from understandable tension or from the unrelieved diet of stewed fruits, whatever it was, my stomach commenced now to emit noises. To cover the awkwardness, though I had determined I could be as sullenly silent as my companion, I began to speak.

"My name is Simon Dovisch," I say to him.

He nods. No handshake. Nothing.

"And your name is——?" I ask.

"Mike," he says.

"Mike what?" I press him. Why should I alone be the vulnerable one? Why should I have given away everything and he nothing?

"Mike," he repeats. Nothing more, and stares straight ahead. A profile, I am forced to say, that looks as if it got finished off with a bang from a flat shovel.

"This is an impressive country," I remark. I confess a twinge for the stuffy ambiguity of the word I chose. "A beautiful country," I correct myself. No answer. I try again. "The kind of country," I observe, "in which, for four days, you might say, we were almost neighbors." Like a stone he sits behind the wheel, not even a blink of the eyes. An elbow on his door where the window is open, the arm up, the fingers drumming on the roof. With one hand seventy miles an hour, seventy-five. What else can I try with him in this simple way that's demanded of decent human exchange? Can I offer a hint of what I was doing at the lake? How would he understand it? From where do human connections come anyway? Must language always fail except among the limited few who have formed a corporation to study from it, but also without connection and only until finals time, and then the corporation dissolved, finished? Am I committed forever to my alienation? Is it my fault, or the others'? Who was alien in the car that I should talk and he shouldn't answer and that ten inches between us should be a whole Mississippi? Do I make mistakes not knowing country ways? Is there a right subject for conversation with him that I have not the instinct for? The colors on the hills? Or even Reno: gambling?

Or something personal—a compliment to his car? Or something more manly, albeit speculative, about the common labor before us of starting my car, and by which, if he would respond, I could sneakily test his air of authority over such matters as batteries and vacuum advances? Or something historical, as, for instance, not too long ago Indians had lived here?

Indians!

I had no sooner shaped the word in my head when my eyes gave it back again, in type, recollected all at once from the road map I had used on the way up. Near Lake Pyramid, Nixon. Printed next to Nixon, each word under the other inside the lines designating borders of the allotted land, the words: Pyramid Lake Piute Indian Reservation. An Indian! Not a Puerto Rican, not a Mexican—a Piute Indian. Simon Dovisch in a car in the Far West with an American Indian.

"You're an Indian!" I exclaimed.

Students of American Literature, Early Period. I call on you to appreciate that moment. I am not one of those who hides his faults. I leave myself open. I do not hedge on the personal if it will but throw a particle of light on the common subject. But I call on you now to admit with me, would I, am I the one to shout out, "You're an Indian!" and mean it as a curse? What was it if not plain and unchecked Dovisch enthusiasm? A joy for an unexpected enthusiasm, this embodied experience, new at least to me, of meeting and traveling and about to labor with an American Indian—Piute. Could I have meant anything but a form of my own congratulation for his identity? Did he have to, at seventy-five miles an hour, slam on the brakes? Did he have to nearly kill us both, the car screaming and squealing and twisting on the highway and not stopping till I had jammed one hand on my side of the dash trying to brace myself and skinned an elbow on the door handle? Did he have to turn on me then and show his teeth in a snarl God meant only for creatures of the jungle who go on four feet with heads turned down? He holds out his hand to me.

"Five dollars till here," he repeats.

"What's the matter?" I plead. "What did you do that for?"

"Five dollars till here," he repeats.

I can feel the heat of his eyes, and though I have done nothing I dare not look at them.

"You could have killed us," I say, and thought to say, Do you run a taxi, the mileage and fare and destination based on unfounded resentments along the way? Bending my wrist, rubbing the elbow on my thigh, I try to explain. But how? Can I bring him into the exuberance out of which I spoke? Can I tell him that, on the contrary, I love Indians? How shall I love Indians? I never met an Indian before. And if he who sat there snarling at me with his hand out was a prototype of his race, or even his tribe, why should I pretend to love them?

To make it short, I apologized. I had said nothing for which I had to be guilty, but there was no other way. On top of the apology, I offered five dollars more. Twenty now to get the car started. Thus Dovisch, the rainbow-maker, is also a man of bribes. That flicker appeared in his eyes again. We resumed. This time I chose silence. Dovisch, I told myself, let the facts stand for themselves, their own essence toward their own emblem.

Come we at last to my car, there as I had left it, hood up, no one else in sight, a forlorn object: a machine which doesn't work. Immediately, then, another disagreement. I want him to push. He wants to look. I explain how it could be nothing but the battery. He looks under the hood. I look with him. He orders me into the car.

"Start it," he says.

What do I know of cars to quarrel with him? Perhaps he is a man of craft, after all. But if I could start it, would I have walked all those miles to find him, Indian or not? Into the car then, the hood up before my vision like a metal wing. My head out the window to hear signals from a body I no longer see. "Start it," he says. Again, *erk-erk.* "Stop it," he says. "The battery?" I suggest. "A push?" I plead. "Start it," he says. And this time a variation, an *erk-erk* with a gasp at the end, an asthma. Nevertheless, a slight improvement, a promise. I see him now come past my side of the car on the way to his. His face, as he passes, a mask of sullenness and resentment. I get out to follow.

"You know now what it is?" I ask him. "Is it the battery? Are you going to push?"

He stops with his hand on the door of the trunk and looks up at me. If it was not a hostile look, then call me Natty Bumppo. If it is the way of his people, then too bad they learned no written language. They would have left us a great literature, for they are melancholy enough. If it was merely his own way, then my heart goes out to the woman, ugly or not, he lives with in the shack.

"Fix," he says to me, leaning over the trunk. Nothing else. Then opens the trunk and rummages inside and walks off, going around me without another word, holding in his hand some kind of tool that I tell you did not inspire confidence. Too big to be a scissors, too small to be a shears, not a screwdriver, not a wrench, but almost a pliers. I follow after him. I try to summon control and decency, also a little command, and yet a degree of deference for the unhappy incident on the way here with him. Helplessness for my ignorance and plight—that, I didn't need to summon.

"Would you mind telling me what's wrong with my car and what you are going to do now?"

Delicacy set aside, the last part of my question was addressed not to his ear but to his behind. He was already gone, altogether under the hood, his body draped over its insides like a dungaree rag. Should such a man inspire confidence in the ignorant and dependent? Who's to say? Doctors also will probe and prod with gadgets on your own body and tell you nothing. But I must confess I had no confidence. Call it the prejudice of a provincial man. God knows I regard mechanical work as toy-tinkering, a skill on the idiot level of man's capacity. But to each his own, and from each, nevertheless, a kind of emanation, manifesting the essence of the work itself, the man at or in his work. Thus a professor of sociology, say, shall be known by his bow tie and pipe, and the smack of brightness in his face, like an insult. And the true professor of literature, by the weariness of spirit. And so with auto mechanics. Also an essence. Was it that he lacked the boyish gleam of the eyes you see in the born mechanic let loose before an automobile, a refrigerator, a clock, an anything in need of repair? Was it his sullenness alone? Was it the strange implement he carried as a tool? Was it merely, finally— face it, Dovisch—my own bigoted preconception that an Indian and an engine make for no better combination than Dovisch and an engine do, admitting, as I face it, that I hold myself above such a combination and hold him not up to it? And on top of it an Indian who might be bent on spite for what he ineradicably regarded as name-calling?

I squatted down to see better what he was up to. It was already four o'clock. The instrument he carried, I could see now. He had placed it on top of the engine. All covered with rust, between a wire cutter and a pliers. He was head down into the engine, grunting, his hands, both of them, pulling at something, yanking. Was this a part of a skillful operation?

"What are you doing?" I shouted. "What are you pulling on like that?"

You must understand I was still not used to talking. How much opportunity had he given me? It was the unmodulated sound of my sudden voice that frightened him into snapping his head back. He banged it against the hood. Then he turned his head toward me, a side of his face against the engine, his eyes all white, with terror, or anger—who knows? But his hands kept on pulling. And then I heard something snap. It was as clear as a bone fracture in total silence. He began inching out of the engine, his arms working now, hauling, the way a sailor pulls in rope, a housewife a clothesline. And coming out after him, draping over the engine and then coiling on the desert floor, was half the insides of my car. Who knew a car had such insides? Bowels, I tell you. A regular vascular system. Wires and wires, black ones and red ones, and then a piece of tubing, and a piece of hose, and more wires, and some sort of chain. And he kept on hauling it all out, backing off further and further from the car and hauling it, his own face now a picture of surprise. You can imagine the horror with which I regarded this performance. From where could I find voice and words to tell him what I felt?

"Madman!" I cried, "Spiteful lunatic! You have ruined my car. Look at what you did! You have pulled out all the insides. It is all there on the ground. My car will never go again."

Let me not make it a big thing, the feelings I endured. Suffice it to say I wanted to punch him. Instead, I pulled at my hair. You see, it was more than my car he destroyed. It was the whole sense of my experience, of belonging—all that I had fought for in my solitude in those terrified nights, the silent days. What recourse now? Salvage what? Was it for the car alone that there passed now, at last, some expression on his face? He glanced at me and then looked at the heap of car guts at his feet, his small eyes widening and his heavy mouth falling open in an uncomplicated look of— what shall I call it?—astonishment?

Students, listen—you are free to leave. I can't keep you, those of you due for another fifty-minute injection somewhere else—Geology, Speech for the Classroom Teacher, Spinoza. I have used up all my time, a lecturer and not a storyteller. Some could go directly in, but for Dovisch, layer by layer. Because aliveness itself is the crisis. But you know the end of the story. Here I am. I got back. Go, those who need to; stay, those who can. If I haven't come yet to that last layer which opens on at least the conditions of your final exam, then add up consequences as you will. Not a threat, not a bribe—another fact. Facts are facts. Leave your term papers here, those who go.

So, then—half of you gone. More than half. Let it be so. I will not, for all that, change my style. A picture is also a picture, and a picture we made then, Dovisch and Mike the Piute. It's hard to believe it happened only yesterday. The time for it seems to have been histories ago. The two of us soon to become three, and then four and five if I may count that passive Cleopatra whose description you can relay to your fellow students who walked out.

See us then on the highway, car chained to car, Dovisch in the old Plymouth pulled by the Indian in the new Chevy, having removed a chain from his trunk and lashed us bumper to bumper. Crawling now on the highway toward Reno that follows the Truckee River along the valley in the desert through the purple-shifting hills in the growing twilight. Fancy diction, but we were on our way by my command to find an open gas station. The guts of my car stuffed back under the hood. And me staring with constant hot and maybe tearing eyes at the constant backside of the head in front that belongs to him who pulls. Always twenty feet away. And Dovisch ponders. And now I say a curse upon the analytic mind. That it kept me from resigning myself to my recognition. Which spoke this way to me, the recognition—which is the beginning of all compassion. Said to me then: Wherefore not peace in this peaceful place, albeit you are being hauled? The man who hauls you, is it not a labor for him as felt with pain as it would be if he hauled you with his back instead of an engine? Regard the slope of his shoulder that crowns his back. Heaped with humility which is born out of remorse for the harm he did me that might have been done to revenge a mere word I spoke that he imagined was a name I called him. All the old stuff: pride and defeat and foolishness and sorrow, and damage too. From Russia to the Bronx, and from God knows where to Indian Reservation, Nixon, Nevada—an old story. A shack and slop jars and beer cans, a sputtered candle and a contour chair—red. And a woman to live with made ugly not by nature (what woman is ever by nature ugly?) but by deprivation, designation, contamination. But then is it my fault? I plead. A Simon-come-lately to this total land, and a stranger altogether to this specific place. But for him who calls himself Mike, how shall it not be in some part my fault? For if Dovisch is a rainbow-maker, why shouldn't the mind of the other have some license to abstract? So resign then, Dovisch, to this moment given to you as a gift, and feel for him who pulls you in the desert as though he pulled you on his back. The aspiration and the loss. But comes the needling analytic fact. A question. Does he pull me for the money? Not as we are stretched and held as men across the rack of his chain, but for twenty dollars? And if it is for money, do I owe money to him who wrecked my car? And if my car is wrecked and I need some other way of getting home, does he owe me? And if he owes me, is it money? Can I collect?

With such questions the sweet elegy of dependent journey is done with, finished. Arrive we then, after miles, at the gas station, my mouth sour, the time now almost five. In two seconds flat my benefactor is out the door, has the cars unchained, and with two words justifies all the cruelty of my analysis. His hand out and his back to the station: "Fifteen dollars." See what he was up to. Because I had raised from fifteen to twenty the amount I would pay him for starting the car, he raised from ten to fifteen the amount I should pay him for not only *not* starting my car, but for destroying it. At least wait, I reply acidly. At least see what happens here. No answer. A glance toward the station, and a nervousness of face. The wide mouth twitches a little. He shifts from foot to foot, a thick, arrogant body. He holds the chain, the main length of it coiling on the asphalt, and a foot or two of it hanging from his hands. Like a weapon. This I need now to cap my quiet intention—bloody violence.

There is only one attendant I can see at this small station, a Negro. Yes, a Negro. Am I responsible for the racial distribution of Nevada? He is watching us as soon as we arrive, and he is still watching, leaning against the window of the office—whatever you call it where they keep the money and the oil. He wears one of those one-piece things from the Army. His arms are folded on his chest. I said he looks at *us*. He looks at the Chevy, and he looks at the back of the Indian. There is a charge, a tension to how he looks. Even from where I stand, I can feel its current. This, too, I need: petty anthropological animosities. He gives no sign, the attendant, that he will come to us. He leans there, arms folded, glaring.

"Listen," I say to the Indian. "I solicited your help. What you did, I invited. I understand that. What your motives were, that's for a debating society. Some other time. Now, whether I pay you ten dollars or fifteen,

I need first to get squared away. Surely you can wait five minutes, since, as a result of your help, I might have to wait until tomorrow. Now let me pass."

I walk around him. I walk to the attendant. I summarize the situation. I ask him finally for the use of his telephone for a long distance call, collect. I need to eliminate my own anxiety for what will soon be a worried wife. I need to have the time and latitude to do whatever has to be done. There is the nagging problem of money. Not only that I don't have cash and I might confront skepticism about a check. But the checking account itself now at the end of the month will take just so much for the repair of a cursed car. Know then that all the time I told my story and endured my fears, the attendant never once looked at me. He looked always at the other one. At his back, because the Indian hadn't turned. I repeated my immediate need. I raised my voice to repeat it. "May I use your phone? It's an emergency. Can't you people see that? My wife——" Then the Indian turned. Then the attendant moved. He came off the window. He dropped his arms to his side. Over his breast pocket in red embroidery, the name Wilbur. A lean man with a sharp moustache and ears back on his head as though they had been sewed. A little pointed also. A regular Donatello. Not a word to me. Once a glance. A slightest turning of the head and a shot with the eyes. He takes two steps forward.

"You gonna get off? You gonna beat it?" Not to me. To the Indian. The Indian looks back at him.

"I got money now," the Indian says. "I got fifteen dollars from him."

The attendant takes two more steps. "The boss says *you* come back here, even if you have fifteen hundred dollars, I keep you off. You getting offa here?"

"No boss here now," says the Indian.

"Piute, me and you together makes me boss."

I run up to him. "Wilbur, I told you. My wife. I need to use your phone."

Now he spins on me. Movements like a boxer. "I call you Mister, you call me same. You don't hear me callin' you first-name basis."

Another one. In the middle of nowhere Dovisch flushes out these advocates of niceties. That I'm the one in the human crisis, that they ignore.

"Look—"

"I already looked. I see a Piute haulin' a tramp in here that—"

"Now just you wait a minute."

"—ain't too smart either. 'Cause you hired a guy to fix your car that went and wrecked your car that likely pulled a wire on it in the first place some night you were snorin' away out there and now you got to pay him for it."

"Liar!"

Not the Indian's protest. Mine. If the Indian at that moment took himself to be insulted, I can't report. He merely stood there, his back almost on the door of his car, the chain still hanging from his hands. Once he turned his head to look down the road. Otherwise he looked at the attendant. Not yet with plain hatred. Something worse. His face, his whole body pinched with watching and waiting. And the Negro, arrested from his walking toward the other one by what he had stopped to tell me, was arrested still by the epithet I had impulsively flung out at him. I had to. I didn't intend by it to take sides in whatever miserable history the two of them had made together. How, anyway, could I have been on the side of the one who had done me so much harm? But to believe that the harm had been done even before I saw it? To believe that it had been done so that I couldn't see it? While I slept and dreamt, overcoming fears of animals and crawling things? While I made blueprints for an architecture of ideas about my country? It was more than I could bear. Picture now the Negro himself frozen to the spot. Confused for the moment. Confronting suddenly a second enemy. Diverted from the one idea of the Indian which was obviously all his mind could hold from the first moment he saw the cars.

So I apologized. Why not? What pride did I have at stake here? I asked once more for the use of the telephone. I called him Mister. I told him he could call me Simon. I told him all right, he could forget the telephone. Would he at least look at my car? Would he try to repair my car?

"This ain't no mechanic place," he says. "On Sunday I pump gas," he says. "I don't need no lookin' in your car," he says. "He got his hands on it, you can send it back to Detroit. Take it to a dump. Maybe you get something for the tires."

"To a dump? Listen, let me call my wife. Let me——"

"Boss says nobody use the phone."

"But this is an emer——"

Enter once more the Indian. Hear again the voice of love. Two words spoken with a flatness you cannot make out of speech with two such words. Not on the spot. It takes centuries. Spoken with the mouth, it goes along the ground the way a snake moves.

"Cotton picker," he says.

Good-bye Negro attendant. Like a track star, like a shot: back to the office and in the door and then out the door with a yard of iron bar in his hands they use for tires, running with it over his shoulder behind his head. Good God, murder! I say to myself as he runs past me, and I see the Indian turn sideways and brace his legs and let out two more feet of the chain and raise it to the height of his shoulder and almost close his eyes, as if he prepared himself to lash out when his hearing told him to and not his vision. Or else thinking of it as a kind of foregone conclusion, a suicide, and who wants to greet his own death with wide-open eyes? They will murder each other, I say to myself, or out loud—who knows?—and begin to close my own eyes and raise my hands to my ears to keep out the sounds of iron and bone. I raise my shoulders and lower my head and almost turn away—waiting, waiting. Nothing. The attendant has stopped in his tracks a little better than the chain length away. His iron bar is still raised. They confront each other, their chests heaving as though they had already fought. Their faces twisted with fear and hatred—nostrils and lips. Dark skin and darker skin. A madness here.

What goes through my mind, frozen there? I turn lunatic myself. I analyze: What did the Indian mean? Why did he choose that time to fling his curse? Was he on my side? Was I back again to his remorse for my plight that made him empty his sac of venom at the attendant's refusal to allow me the telephone? Or was it the mere overflow of hatred that drowned his need, his claim, his greed—whatever you want to call his idea of the fifteen, the ten dollars he could get from me? Because what he chose to say he must surely have known would provoke what it did.

So picture us. Make the tableau. It was not there for me then, but I see it now. Off the highway a little gas station with two yellow pumps and a small office. A dot in a desert country. One way with the road is back to the lake and the Indian Reservation. The other way is to Reno. The dry, tough land—Bible land—and the shifting, shimmering mountains and the miraculous stony water. Sunday at five P.M. When even solitude itself ceases to have value and all men past thirty should be home—shack, palace, or insurance-company housing project—in the tumultuous retreat of family. Picture, then, that neighbor of a bird I had looking down with hawk vision at that spot of a gas station in that vast empty land, seeing three alien specks of men inside that spot on the vast land, all of them motionless, waiting, not for the consolations of an alien man to a more alien man to the most alien of men, but for murder.

Come down from there and the bird and see it with Dovisch, who, lugging the Bronx with him, thus Europe too, finds in man himself all the universe. Dovisch looking at the other two, also men, poised with implements of murder. The hatred in their faces, which is the willingness to murder, dreadful to see. And dreadful to see, also, the fear in each face for his own murder, which is all that holds them back. Muscles in the hands, in the faces, too tight to be too long held back. Dovisch saying to himself: Outsider, alien—did you start this? Did you bring it on? But a moment for panic, not questions. Finished with analyzing. In panic, to the drowning man, the pictures, the fantasies. Picture Dovisch, then, picturing salvation. To be out of there. To be back with family, with books, back here in this classroom with you. Then cries out to himself: To hell with books! To give it all, his whole kingdom, for one skill: to repair a car. Picture him staring in dread at the two men who begin at last to put the slightest pinwheel of motion into the tableau, making half circles about each other across the diameter they still fear to diminish, the weapons poised. And see Dovisch making fantasy as he looks, seeing himself in a Disney rescue, rushing to

the car, opening the hood, the flash of Ben Franklin hands and the resto-
ration of wires, tubes, hoses, chains, and in an instant in the car, the car
starting, and Dovisch, all in the same timeless Disney instant, lowering the
window and calling out I don't understand you. I never understood you.
The lake was a lie. Gentlemen, good-bye!

Picture finally what I did do, a madman equal to them. Between an iron
bar and an iron chain, and between the savage intentions born out of the
heartache of their own isolations, strides Dovisch. In dirty clothes, in a
four-day beard, off a diet of zwieback and stewed fruits, and in a celebration of or recoil from the hot blood of abstract insights, with his arms
outstretched, one for each of them so that they could have fractured his
wrists at a single impulse, offering for peace what he has taken from his
wallet: identification cards. And a brief illustrating lecture that must have
gone something like this:

"Madmen, what are you doing? You are going to kill each other. For
what? Listen, I am no tramp. That I don't belong here, I grant you. But not
a tramp. Are you Russians that you tell everything from a man's clothing?
See—here. Take the cards. Look. Identification. I'm Simon Dovisch, Professor of American Literature. See this one—The New England Historical
Society. And this one—The Modern Language Association. This one, too,
from my university—Simon Dovisch, Ph.D. That's Doctor of Philosophy.
Take them. Read them. Put away the chain. Put down the bar. I only came
here to recover something I lost that I never had. Take them, please! Read!
Study! Peace!"

I have returned to tell you they put down their weapons. They looked at
me as though I alone were the one madman, and they looked at the cards I
held out the way I would have looked at tarantulas held out to me. But
they took them. And they looked at them. And they looked at each other.
And then at the cards again, turning them this way and that. And then they
spoke to me. The Negro says, "I ain't afraid of him." The Indian says, "I
pulled you. You pay fifteen dollars."

Nobody heard the new car come until it parked behind my Plymouth. I
ran to it.

"You have to help me!" I begged to the window.

Right then, on the spot, I didn't notice, but now I can tell you. A
Cadillac, white like the whale itself, and as long, and with fins and flukes
too. Behind the wheel, lowering the window so he could hear me, this—
what shall I call him? What is the term I have heard you people use against
yourselves—WASP? White Anglo-Saxon Protestant? Well, I have never
used it. I deplore it. It is your own form of Bronx snobbery injected from
behind. I use it now as a shortcut from your own shorthand. I would say,
rather, that he was a papermonger. Insurance, banking, credit, stocks, even
publishing, even a registrar in a college—except for the Cadillac. Anything
by which the management of the entity itself, people or things, is accom-

plished by the avoidance of the person or thing. The paper accomplishes. So I say a papermonger to describe a face. And if you say to me a man's work does not describe his face, I say to you it is because you haven't begun to work. In his fifties he was, with silver hair, a Palm Springs sunburn, a straight nose like a knife blade, a tight mouth, a light-gray suit. Later I would notice the transparent film of nail polish. But much before that—indeed, a moment after I noticed him—I would notice who sat beside him, the Cleopatra I promised some while back to describe to you for the envy of your fellow students who have abandoned us.

I asked him to help me. What I then, at the first moment of his arrival, like salvation itself (yes, I confess, I was grateful at once that it came in all the pompous authority of a Cadillac)—what I then told him I can't now recall. It would have had such phrases in it as "destroyed my car," "my wife will be frantic," "murdering each other," "Professor of American Literature," "only my checkbook," "four days at the lake," "fruits and zwieback," "excuse my appearance"—and so forth. He looked at me only once while I was talking, the look of a long moment, of taking someone in. Then he never looked at me again. Dovisch summarized. But his face was alert and firm, and I must confess my heart went to calmness, rubbed and soothed by this stranger's—who in all other circumstances would have been so inimical to me—by his Cadillacs of certainty. Came then the gas-station attendant to the car. Edges me from the window. Makes an at-your-service smile.

"Fill 'er up?"

"Just a minute," says the stranger, like a slap across the face. And turns to the Cleopatra beside him and says, "Go ahead. Use it, now that we've stopped." She makes a reply I can't hear, and he says, "Yes, here. It won't kill you." Her door opens and she walks to the office.

I promised a description. Say only that she was no older than some of you here. Say also that she could not have been his daughter. Even a blind man could sense that right away—an essence. And let me say her hair was beautiful, and her own color, blond, like sunlight. And almost no makeup, makeup only on the eyes, but a quality in the face of something between good health and a frost that made the face more blatant than all the sticks and paints and rouges in Woolworth's could have. She wore a white dress —bare arms, bare back, bare shoulders—and was as tanned as he was. Listen—we are, what is left of us, a mixed group here. Propriety is a value. Furthermore, my place here before the room and behind the desk is a position of trust. A prig is a bore, but a libertine is a coward. Suffice it to say that what she wore she filled; what she filled she wore. And say also that her walk to the office and whatever rest room she would find there was a short parade under the desert sky. The attendant watched her, the Indian watched her, I watched her. Only the stranger himself did not watch her.

When she disappeared, I edged at the attendant, nudged him from the window, and began again with the stranger on my baggage of miserable phrases.

"Yes," he said, and cut me off. He opened the door and got out. A trim man. Squash and swimming twice a week at the athletic club. Also a wedding ring. You may wonder that I notice it after my admission of my incapacity to observe. I say then, given the *mise en scène*, wait till you are forty-two. He addresses the attendant.

"Fill it with super. The oil's all right. Check the water." Then to me: "I'll take you as far as Sacramento. You can get a bus there. I'll give you the fare."

I am broken by his kindness; also with my own resentment. I mention my car, a badge of ruined shame beside his great white whale.

"You have no choice. It's Sunday." He turns to the attendant, who is already pumping gas, wiping windows. "You have this man's car towed to a mechanic tomorrow. Leave it here overnight."

"I can't do that. My boss—"

"Tell your boss a letter from my office will cancel his franchise. Tell him I can have this place closed in twenty-four hours."

So—an oil man.

The attendant stares at him, wipes the windows. End of debate. God in His wisdom, seeing my troubles, sends me not an Emerson, not a Thoreau, not even a Franklin, but a regular James Bond—or his father. Comes then the Indian, not to me, but to the stranger, and still dragging his length of chain.

"He owes me fifteen dollars," he says.

I looked once to the attendant. Will he go again for his iron bar that he had placed against the pump with the arrival of the Cadillac? No. He stops his cleaning of the windows to watch the outcome. His face is full of pleasure and deliverance. The stranger gets out of the whale, stretches his legs, turns to me. He inquires of details. I give him details. You understand that the moral situation behind my business arrangement with the Indian is now complex. Yes, I hired him to start the car. But I stipulated for a push. The surgery was his idea. In sum, my answer to the stranger is yes and no. Shakes his head, then, the silver-haired stranger. Obviously ambiguities are outside his territory. He turns to the Indian. One sentence. A question.

"What's the name of the Indian Commissioner here?"

Exit the Indian, trailing the length of his chain. Smile on the face of the attendant as wide as vengeance. The Indian, my so-to-speak neighbor of four days, tearing off in a lamentable assertion from his exhaust pipe and a shouted obscenity one can barely hear. But for me, before he shut the door of his car, he reserved a special look: accusation, betrayal, or some secret shared—who knows? Reenters now from the Palace of Fine Arts, Miss America. Another parade. Dovisch rejoins the staring. A polite walking aside by the stranger and his possession. Hushed conference. Looks from

her toward me. Dovisch shrugs. And now a look for me from the attendant, even a laying on of hands, at least a finger on the shoulder, a warm
smile. But for what?

So now a trio in the car, myself in the back, the deep, black-leather seats
of a Cadillac. Another first for Dovisch. The stranger starts the car. No
erk-erk here. The power of God's chosen continent in the turn of a key.
Which he turns off again.

"You want to make that call home?" he asks. She turns and regards me.
That mere flesh could hurl such challenge. Another old story.

"No need now," I reply.

Off then to Sacramento. Good-bye, old Plymouth. Dovisch from the rear
murmurs gratitudes. Stranger from the front in brief disclaimers. Pays
respects to higher education and learning. "They ought to raise salaries,"
he concludes. Dovisch deeper into the corner, arms over chest, bottom lip
out. A long and uneventful journey back, if you exclude from eventfulness
the growing frequency of exchanges of hot glances in the front seat, the
sliding of thighs. Dovisch stares out the window. An intruder, yes, an
isolate always, but not yet a *voyeur*.

The misadventure, then, almost at an end, but not quite. I said at the
beginning that I did not get home until two A.M. Wherefore, then, you
should ask, all the consumed time? Departing a little past five P.M. yesterday, it is not nine hours to home. Know, then, that two hours were spent in
Sacramento waiting for the bus. Know that two hours *before* that was spent
in front of a motel. Dovisch pacing like a patrolman, waiting for the two of
them to get done with the business that is now the national pastime all the
way from the Bronx to where we were now on the Western side of the
Sierras. A factory of Hester Prynnes sewing night and day couldn't keep up
with the scarlet letters needed here. It was also from the stranger—let me
credit him with his deservings—a gesture as well as a need. The need for
him, with her; the gesture for me. Having rescued, having saved me, having
as much as said to me: Aren't you lucky that I came along instead of
another Professor of American Literature? The stranger says now: So eat a
little crow. Do I need to spell it out? Can't you see the rainbow finished
now? Poor, thingless Dovisch is the emblem itself.

In Sacramento, after long silence in the car, the beauty asleep and the
stranger quiet, and even Dovisch in a surfeit of his own, speaks now the
stranger, out of nowhere addressing me.

"I took a course in Lit. once. Never knew what he was talking about."

Pronounced, of course, before the bus station, when there is time for
Dovisch to retort with nothing more than another "Thanks" because the
stranger turns now to put in my hand the money that is the bus fare home.
Dovisch closing the door lightly, not to wake the dozing Cleopatra. Good-
bye, Prince of the Silver Hair and Master of All Situations. Then to the bus
and the wooden bench in this midnight depository of transportation and

breakage. Home then to keep up his wife all night in a rehearsal of what I have told you now. Checking with her wise soul the relevance of it all for your final exam. When I make rainbows and take my flyers, she is there, bless her days, like a shining thing. And checking with her all night, too, on remaining ambiguities. Today's schedule, for instance, for the return to that American Bible landscape to retrieve my car. And my identification cards. Which means, this afternoon, another visit to that shack and the Indian. Or to let it go. Let him paste the one I gave him on the wall somewhere. Paste it over the red chair. Whichever one I gave him, let him be an honorary member of the society. And let it suffice, too, for my own resignation. Enough can be too much. And even too much is inadequate. Endure, endure—and not the least of it now, I confess frankly, is that half of you should walk out in the middle of all this Dovisch vulnerability, prior commitments notwithstanding. Well, I am not altogether drowned. I have my own survival weapons. Ishmael and his floating coffin, Dovisch and his final exam.

Listen, leave me your term papers on the way out. Your final exam? Only this. A critical appraisal of my original intention and of what befell me. Include a moral estimate of the characters involved. Answer to the question of lawful and human guilt. Discuss deprivation. Also rescue. And don't neglect the car. Support all your assessments with liberal reference to as many of the works we have studied this semester as will shed particles of light on such dark problems. References to be factual (God bless all my colleagues) and ideational (you know, rainbows).

That's all. Dovisch is finished. I'll see you at our finals.

❖

Herbert Wilner was born in Brooklyn, in 1925, has a B.A. from Brooklyn College, an M.A. from Columbia, a Ph.D. from the University of Iowa, and has taught English at Yale and writing at San Francisco State College. He has published some ten stories, collected in Dovisch in the Wilderness and Other Stories *(1968), and one novel,* All the Little Heroes *(1966).*

In "Dovisch in the Wilderness," Wilner puts the Jewish and American traditions in direct confrontation, for meaning as well as humor. The structure of the story, a lecture, is a projection of a common situation: many Jewish intellectuals (as do most of the writers in this volume, in fact) teach in colleges and universities throughout the country, and as likely as not teach American literature. Many stories and novels have exploited the confrontations implicit in this situation: Bernard Malamud's A New Life, *Leslie Fiedler's* The Last Jew in America, *and Jack Ludwig's* Confusions, *all set on campuses in the West, are only three examples of what has be-*

come virtually a subgenre in our literature, like the subgenre of the faculty couple abroad for a year on a grant. But "Dovisch in the Wilderness" goes beyond the basic situation to establish, within the lecture frame, a sequence of episodes that is contrasted, in terms of incident and symbol as well as theme, with the great classics of American literature: Thoreau's Walden, *Melville's* Moby Dick, *Mark Twain's* Huckleberry Finn, *Cooper's* Leatherstocking Tales, *Emerson, Whitman, Hawthorne—the whole lot. But again, the confrontation is played for meaning as well as laughs. Dovisch's account of his adventures is framed within the experiences of American history and the reading of American literature, but that tradition is in turn framed within a larger older tradition; his narration, as he says, mocking more than his own voice, is "inflected a little by a history somewhat older than the American." In his attempt to re-create for himself the direct experience of isolation and solitude, which has always been a major theme in American literature, Dovisch on the shores of Pyramid Lake reminds one not only of Thoreau at Walden Pond (and all the other classic American figures on their rafts or whaling ships or on the prairie or in the forest), but also of the great deranged prophets of the Old Testament alone in the Biblical wilderness. Dovisch out there with his canned fruit, in his ill-fitting sleeping bag, staring up at stars he can't see without his glasses, is a comic conception, the humor evoked in the same way that the phrase "a Jewish cowboy" is supposed automatically to evoke a smile. The story makes great use of this conjunction of opposites for humor, but it is far from being the only one used in the story. The American Indian, the noble red man, the gentle companion of the wilderness, is redescribed in modern terms. So is the humble, fearful, fun-loving Negro, gentle companion of long trips downriver on a raft. So, too, is the basic American type, the WASP: he is still master of the situation (now as a papermonger rather than a Deerslayer), but he is seen to have an attitude entirely different from the traditional reverence of the purity of womankind found in most heroes of American classics. And the countryside as a whole is redrawn, or reversed: where once it was civilization threatened by the wilderness (as, for instance, the small Puritan settlement in* The Scarlet Letter *is ringed round by the savage forest), now it is wilderness threatened by civilization (Pyramid Lake still there, but surrounded by the encroachments of highways, diners, automobiles). But the wilderness has always figured as a usefully paradoxical symbol in American literature—representing both savagery and innocence— and the story plays off these ambiguities. Now, too, there has been an end to innocence: "a factory of Hester Prynnes sewing night and day couldn't keep up with the scarlet letters needed here." This story, as much perhaps as any other in the book, seems to need either pages of annotation and explication and appreciation, or to need none at all. One sympathizes with Dovisch's students, who are given it as a final exam. It rewards many readings. Ultimately—and ironically—the reader may come to feel that ludi-*

crously "different" as Dovisch makes himself appear, he is himself as close as modern man can realistically be—in both his innocence in the story and his fervor in the lecture—to the original American frontier-Puritan tradition.

❖❖

From the idealized life of the Polish ghetto built around love and scholarship it is a long way to Dovisch's class on American literature, early period, and the Jew as Puritan intellectual reconquering the frontier-wilderness of culturally revolting America with ideas, not facts. These Jewish writers writing about Jews in America show us how and why religion no longer discriminates among us. They speak for our sense of loss in no longer having the rights and wrongs of life all spelled out for us. They show us how religion has become a suitable aspect of life-style, something that's "good for you," like the fresh air of the suburbs (as long as it isn't too old-fashioned or outlandish)—a loyalty to be preserved and stood up for, in baseball players, for instance. They show us how fitting-in with American middle-class success patterns has meant discarding valued aspects of religious culture, and how this results in the loss of sense of personal uniqueness based on an internalized, all-encompassing ideology. The road beyond religious persecution requires the traveler to know who he is and what he is doing, where he came from and where it is important to go.

There are undoubtedly many situations in which Jews in America suffer the effects of discrimination, but we don't need this morning's news that twenty per cent of next year's select Harvard freshmen will be Jewish to understand that Jews are no longer a hopelessly oppressed "race." They are eminently successful Americans because they have been able to profit from a tradition that has held them together in the oppressed ghettos of the world: a combination of sensitivity, intellectuality, warmth, and, above all, humor (folk, ironic, or "black") which comprises an approach to these times that virtually guarantees great achievement—qualities that have enabled Jewish writers most accurately to reflect and express our times and thus make an invaluable contribution to our understanding of them.

Negroes in America, as we will see in the following stories, face a tragically different situation.

Differentiations and Confusions

IN RACE—THE VISIBLE NEGRO

Discrimination is the key word here—making a distinction, recognizing a difference. By itself "discrimination" is the mark of the sensitive intelligence, but it is so altered by the addition of "against" as to refer then to the means of making an arbitrarily distinguishable difference a stigma for persecution. If we were allowed but one example to prove the difference between an ideology—ours, of equality and opportunity for all—and the living dynamics of a society, the history of the Negro in America would suffice. (For some of the same reasons that we chose only stories about Jews in the section on "religion," we have limited this section on "race" to stories about Negroes; but it is obvious that American Indians, Mexicans, Asians, Puerto Ricans, and others have also suffered the effects of discrimination in ways that are similar to and different from the Negro.) It is clear that although the civil rights of equality and opportunity before the law are essential prerequisites, they do not by themselves solve the problems of daily living for Negroes, much less guarantee their hopes for an ordinary American future. The basic reason is that Negroes are different from other races and nationalities that have come to this country. They are different, first of all, because they came as slaves (except the West Indian Negroes, who have become part of the Negro elite) rather than as bond servants, debtors, ne'er-do-wells, and religious fanatics like so many of our other ancestors. Slavery, however, is only a legal definition of ownership which was overturned by law a hundred years ago. The difference that remains is skin color and other secondary physical characteristics. This is the crucial difference between the Negro and white ingredients in our melting pot: their addition to the flavor does not become an ineffable essence, a memory of a former distinct difference; but like coarsely ground pepper, it remains highly visible in the finished soup. This means that in the various social processes of exclusion that occur in the building of power and elite classes, it has always been easy to exclude Negroes. Aside from the "separate" (and therefore unequal) solution, the only ways Negroes can attain practical equality (as a race, not as individual exceptions) are either by the breeding-out of their recognizable physical differences (another aspect of

698

eliteness among Negroes is degree of whiteness) or by the recognition by whites and Negroes of these distinguishable physical attributes as valuable in themselves. Both solutions are viewed negatively by whites, the first as "miscegenation," the second as "Black Power." Both are made difficult by lack of educational and economic opportunities. Unlike the Jews, who have such opportunities and can change their distinguishing names and noses and adopt the elite religions and life styles, and thus not only melt in but rise to the top in a few generations, the Negroes have a much longer and more difficult road to follow in order to lose their racial stigma and become plain, ordinary Americans.

For these reasons, and some others, there has been no "Negro renaissance" in contemporary American fiction to compare with the "Jewish renaissance" we remarked on earlier. There are at least a half-dozen Jewish writers in the absolutely first rank of American writing today, and there are dozens of others whose potential or achievement places them not far behind. Only two really first-rate Negro writers can be named—Ralph Ellison and James Baldwin—and the ranks behind them are almost empty. To mention the names of Ronald Fair, Ernest J. Gaines, Chester Himes, Claude Brown, William Melvin Kelley, Paule Marshall, and John Williams is to stretch and virtually exhaust the list of Negroes from whom we can expect literary fiction of significant interest. It is not that Negroes are not writing or being published; but aside from Ellison and Baldwin, they have not yet produced the kind of writing that satisfies the complex contemporary literary tastes and sensibilities. This situation will of course change soon, but up to this time it seems that the dialects and situations of Negro life have provided the Negro writer with the kind of material that is translatable only into a direct recounting of or protest against the sordid or subtle facts of his oppression. This is all perhaps by way of explaining that two of the stories in this section are by Jewish writers and one is by a southern white woman.

RALPH ELLISON

Prologue to Invisible Man

❖❖❖❖❖❖❖

I AM AN INVISIBLE MAN. No, I am not a spook like those who haunted Edgar Allan Poe; nor am I one of your Hollywood-movie ectoplasms. I am a man of substance, of flesh and bone, fiber and liquids—and I might even be said to possess a mind. I am invisible, understand, simply because people refuse to see me. Like the bodiless heads you see sometimes in circus sideshows, it is as though I have been surrounded by mirrors of hard, distorting glass. When they approach me they see only my surroundings, themselves, or figments of their imagination—indeed, everything and anything except me.

Nor is my invisibility exactly a matter of a bio-chemical accident to my epidermis. That invisibility to which I refer occurs because of a peculiar disposition of the eyes of those with whom I come in contact. A matter of the construction of their *inner* eyes, those eyes with which they look through their physical eyes upon reality. I am not complaining, nor am I protesting either. It is sometimes advantageous to be unseen, although it is most often rather wearing on the nerves. Then too, you're constantly being bumped against by those of poor vision. Or again, you often doubt if you really exist. You wonder whether you aren't simply a phantom in other people's minds. Say, a figure in a nightmare which the sleeper tries with all his strength to destroy. It's when you feel like this that, out of resentment, you begin to bump people back. And, let me confess, you feel that way most of the time. You ache with the need to convince yourself that you do exist in the real world, that you're a part of all the sound and anguish, and you strike out with your fists, you curse and you swear to make them recognize you. And, alas, it's seldom successful.

One night I accidentally bumped into a man, and perhaps because of the near darkness he saw me and called me an insulting name. I sprang at him, seized his coat lapels and demanded that he apologize. He was a tall blond man, and as my face came close to his he looked insolently out of his blue eyes and cursed me, his breath hot in my face as he struggled. I pulled his chin down sharp upon the crown of my head, butting him as I had seen the West Indians do, and I felt his flesh tear and the blood gush out, and I yelled, "Apologize! Apologize!" But he continued to curse and struggle, and I butted him again and again until he went down heavily, on his knees, profusely bleeding. I kicked him repeatedly, in a frenzy because he still uttered insults though his lips were frothy with blood. Oh yes, I kicked him! And in my outrage I got out my knife and prepared to slit his throat, right there beneath the lamplight in the deserted street, holding him in the collar with one hand, and opening the knife with my teeth—when it occurred to me that the man had not *seen* me, actually; that he, as far as he knew, was in the midst of a walking nightmare! And I stopped the blade, slicing the air as I pushed him away, letting him fall back to the street. I stared at him hard as the lights of a car stabbed through the darkness. He lay there, moaning on the asphalt; a man almost killed by a phantom. It unnerved me. I was both disgusted and ashamed. I was like a drunken man myself, wavering about on weakened legs. Then I was amused: Something in this man's thick head had sprung out and beaten him within an inch of his life. I began to laugh at this crazy discovery. Would he have awakened at the point of death? Would Death himself have freed him for wakeful living? But I didn't linger. I ran away into the dark, laughing so hard I feared I might rupture myself. The next day I saw his picture in the *Daily News,* beneath a caption stating that he had been "mugged." Poor fool, poor blind fool, I thought with sincere compassion, mugged by an invisible man!

Most of the time (although I do not choose as I once did to deny the violence of my days by ignoring it) I am not so overtly violent. I remember that I am invisible and walk softly so as not to awaken the sleeping ones. Sometimes it is best not to awaken them; there are few things in the world as dangerous as sleepwalkers. I learned in time though that it is possible to carry on a fight against them without their realizing it. For instance, I have been carrying on a fight with Monopolated Light & Power for some time now. I use their service and pay them nothing at all, and they don't know it. Oh, they suspect that power is being drained off, but they don't know where. All they know is that according to the master meter back there in their power station a hell of a lot of free current is disappearing somewhere into the jungle of Harlem. The joke, of course, is that I don't live in Harlem but in a border area. Several years ago (before I discovered the advantages of being invisible) I went through the routine process of buying service and paying their outrageous rates. But no more. I gave up all that, along with my apartment, and my old way of life: That way based upon the fallacious assumption that I, like other men, was visible. Now, aware of my invisibility, I live rent-free in a building rented strictly to whites, in a section of the basement that was shut off and forgotten during the nineteenth century, which I discovered when I was trying to escape in the night from Ras the Destroyer. But that's getting too far ahead of the story, almost to the end, although the end is in the beginning and lies far ahead.

The point now is that I found a home—or a hole in the ground, as you will. Now don't jump to the conclusion that because I call my home a "hole" it is damp and cold like a grave; there are cold holes and warm holes. Mine is a warm hole. And remember, a bear retires to his hole for the winter and lives until spring; then he comes strolling out like the Easter chick breaking from its shell. I say all this to assure you that it is incorrect to assume that, because I'm invisible and live in a hole, I am dead. I am neither dead nor in a state of suspended animation. Call me Jack-the-Bear, for I am in a state of hibernation.

My hole is warm and full of light. Yes, *full* of light. I doubt if there is a brighter spot in all New York than this hole of mine, and I do not exclude Broadway. Or the Empire State Building on a photographer's dream night. But that is taking advantage of you. Those two spots are among the darkest of our whole civilization—pardon me, our whole *culture* (an important distinction, I've heard)—which might sound like a hoax, or a contradiction, but that (by contradiction, I mean) is how the world moves: Not like an arrow, but a boomerang. (Beware of those who speak of the *spiral* of history; they are preparing a boomerang. Keep a steel helmet handy.) I know; I have been boomeranged across my head so much that I now can see the darkness of lightness. And I love light. Perhaps you'll think it strange that an invisible man should need light, desire light, love light. But maybe it is exactly because I *am* invisible. Light confirms my reality, gives birth to my form. A beautiful girl once told me of a recurring nightmare in which she lay in the center of a large dark room and felt her face expand until it filled the whole room, becoming a formless mass while her eyes ran in bilious jelly up the chimney. And so it is with me. Without light I am not only invisible, but formless as well; and to be unaware of one's form is to live a death. I myself, after existing some twenty years, did not become alive until I discovered my invisibility.

That is why I fight my battle with Monopolated Light & Power. The deeper reason, I mean: It allows me to feel my vital aliveness. I also fight them for taking so much of my money before I learned to protect myself. In my hole in the basement there are exactly 1,369 lights. I've wired the entire ceiling, every inch of it. And not with fluorescent bulbs, but with the older, more-expensive-to-operate kind, the filament type. An act of sabotage, you know. I've already begun to wire the wall. A junk man I know, a man of vision, has supplied me with wire and sockets. Nothing, storm or flood, must get in the way of our need for light and ever more and brighter light. The truth is the light and light is the truth. When I finish all four walls, then I'll start on the floor. Just how that will go, I don't know. Yet when you have lived invisible as long as I have you develop a certain ingenuity. I'll solve the problem. And maybe I'll invent a gadget to place my coffee pot on the fire while I lie in bed, and even invent a gadget to warm my bed—like the fellow I saw in one of the picture magazines who made himself a gadget to warm his shoes! Though invisible, I am in the great American tradition of tinkers. That makes me kin to Ford, Edison and Franklin. Call me, since I have a theory and a concept, a "thinker-tinker." Yes, I'll warm my shoes; they need it, they're usually full of holes. I'll do that and more.

Now I have one radio-phonograph; I plan to have five. There is a certain acoustical deadness in my hole, and when I have music I want to *feel* its vibration, not only with my ear but with my whole body. I'd like to hear five recordings of Louis Armstrong playing and singing "What Did I Do to Be so Black and Blue"—all at the same time. Sometimes now I listen to Louis while I have my favorite dessert of vanilla ice cream and sloe gin. I pour the red liquid over the white mound, watching it glisten and the vapor rising as Louis bends that military instrument into a beam of lyrical sound. Perhaps I like Louis Armstrong because he's made poetry out of being invisible. I think it must be because he's unaware that he *is* invisible. And my own grasp of invisibility aids me to understand his music. Once when I asked for a cigarette, some jokers gave me a reefer, which I lighted when I got home and sat listening to my phonograph. It was a strange evening. Invisibility, let me explain, gives one a slightly different sense of time, you're never quite on the beat. Sometimes you're ahead and sometimes behind. Instead of the swift and imperceptible flowing of time, you are aware of its nodes, those points where time stands still or from which it leaps ahead. And you slip into the breaks and look around. That's what you hear vaguely in Louis' music.

Once I saw a prizefighter boxing a yokel. The fighter was swift and amazingly scientific. His body was one violent flow of rapid rhythmic action. He hit the yokel a hundred times while the yokel held up his arms in stunned surprise. But suddenly the yokel, rolling about in the gale of boxing gloves, struck one blow and knocked science, speed and footwork as cold as a well-digger's posterior. The smart money hit the canvas. The long shot got the nod. The yokel had simply stepped inside of his opponent's sense of time. So under the spell of the reefer I discovered a new analytical way of listening to music. The unheard sounds came through, and each melodic line existed of itself, stood out clearly from all the rest, said its piece, and waited patiently for the other voices to speak. That night I found myself hearing not only in time, but in space as well. I not only entered the music but descended, like Dante, into its depths. And *beneath the swiftness of the hot tempo there was a slower tempo and a cave and I entered it and looked around and heard an old woman singing a spiritual as full of Weltschmerz as flamenco, and beneath that lay a still lower level on which I saw a beautiful girl the color of ivory pleading in a voice like my mother's as she stood before a group of slaveowners who bid for her naked body, and below that I found a lower level and a more rapid tempo and I heard someone shout:*

"Brothers and sisters, my text this morning is the 'Blackness of Blackness.'"

And a congregation of voices answered: "That blackness is most black, brother, most black . . ."

"In the beginning . . ."

"At the very start," they cried.

". . . there was blackness . . ."

"Preach it . . ."

". . . and the sun . . ."

"The sun, Lawd . . ."

". . . was bloody red . . ."

"Red . . ."

"Now black is . . ." the preacher shouted.

"Bloody . . ."

"I said black is . . ."

"Preach it, brother . . ."

". . . an' black ain't . . ."

"Red, Lawd, red: He said it's red!"

"Amen, brother . . ."

"Black will git you . . ."

"Yes, it will . . ."

". . . an' black won't . . ."

"Naw, it won't!"

"It do . . ."

"It do, Lawd . . ."

". . . an' it don't."

"Halleluiah . . ."

". . . It'll put you, glory, glory, Oh my Lawd, in the WHALE'S BELLY."

"Preach it, dear brother . . ."

". . . an' make you tempt . . ."

"Good God a-mighty!"

"Old Aunt Nelly!"

"Black will make you . . ."

"Black . . ."

". . . or black will un-make you."

"Ain't it the truth, Lawd?"

And at that point a voice of trombone timbre screamed at me, "Git out of here, you fool! Is you ready to commit treason?"

And I tore myself away, hearing the old singer of spirituals moaning, "Go curse your God, boy, and die."

I stopped and questioned her, asked her what was wrong.

"I dearly loved my master, son," she said.

"You should have hated him," I said.

"He gave me several sons," she said, "and because I loved my sons I learned to love their father though I hated him too."

"I too have become acquainted with ambivalence," I said. "That's why I'm here."

"What's that?"

"Nothing, a word that doesn't explain it. Why do you moan?"

"I moan this way 'cause he's dead," she said.

"Then tell me, who is that laughing upstairs?"

"Them's my sons. They glad."

"Yes, I can understand that too," I said.

"I laughs too, but I moans too. He promised to set us free but he never could bring hisself to do it. Still I loved him . . ."

"Loved him? You mean . . .?"

"Oh yes, but I loved something else even more."

"What more?"

"Freedom."

"Freedom," I said. "Maybe freedom lies in hating."

"Naw, son, it's in loving. I loved him and give him the poison and he withered away like a frost-bit apple. Them boys woulda tore him to pieces with they homemade knives."

"A mistake was made somewhere," I said, "I'm confused." And I wished to say other things, but the laughter upstairs became too loud and moan-like for me and I tried to break out of it, but I couldn't. Just as I was leaving I felt an urgent desire to ask her what freedom was and went back. She sat with her head in her hands, moaning softly; her leather-brown face was filled with sadness.

"Old woman, what is this freedom you love so well?" I asked around a corner of my mind.

She looked surprised, then thoughtful, then baffled. "I done forgot, son. It's all mixed up. First I think it's one thing, then I think it's another. It gits my head to spinning. I guess now it ain't nothing but knowing how to say what I got up in my head. But it's a hard job, son. Too much is done happen to me in too short a time. Hit's like I have a fever. Ever' time I starts to walk my head gits to swirling and I falls down. Or if it ain't that, it's the boys; they gits to laughing and wants to kill up the white folks. They's bitter, that's what they is . . ."

"But what about freedom?"

"Leave me 'lone, boy; my head aches!"

I left her, feeling dizzy myself. I didn't get far.

Suddenly one of the sons, a big fellow six feet tall, appeared out of nowhere and struck me with his fist.

"What's the matter, man?" I cried.

"You made Ma cry!"

"But how?" I said, dodging a blow.

"Askin' her them questions, that's how. Git outa here and stay, and next time you got questions like that, ask yourself!"

He held me in a grip like cold stone, his fingers fastening upon my windpipe until I thought I would suffocate before he finally allowed me to go. I stumbled about dazed, the music beating hysterically in my ears. It was dark. My head cleared and I wandered down a dark narrow passage, thinking I heard his footsteps hurrying behind me. I was sore, and into my being had come a profound craving for tranquillity, for peace and quiet, a state I felt I could never achieve. For one thing, the trumpet was blaring and the rhythm was too hectic. A tom-tom beating like heart-thuds began drowning out the trumpet, filling my ears. I longed for water and I heard it rushing through the cold mains my fingers touched as I felt my way, but I couldn't stop to search because of the footsteps behind me.

"Hey, Ras," I called. "Is it you, Destroyer? Rinehart?"

No answer, only the rhythmic footsteps behind me. Once I tried crossing the road, but a speeding machine struck me, scraping the skin from my leg as it roared past.

Then somehow I came out of it, ascending hastily from this underworld of sound to hear Louis Armstrong innocently asking,

> *What did I do*
> *To be so black*
> *And blue?*

At first I was afraid; this familiar music had demanded action, the kind of which I was incapable, and yet had I lingered there beneath the surface I might have attempted to act. Nevertheless, I know now that few really listen to this music. I sat on the chair's edge in a soaking sweat, as though each of my 1,369 bulbs had every one become a klieg light in an individual setting for a third degree with Ras and Rinehart in charge. It was exhausting—as though I had held my breath continuously for an hour under the terrifying serenity that comes from days of intense hunger. And yet, it was a strangely satisfying experience for an invisible man to hear the silence of sound. I had discovered unrecognized compulsions of my being—even though I could not answer "yes" to their promptings. I haven't smoked a reefer since, however; not because they're illegal, but because to *see* around corners is enough (that is not unusual when you are invisible). But to hear around them is too much; it inhibits action. And despite Brother Jack and all that sad, lost period of the Brotherhood, I believe in nothing if not in action.

Please, a definition: A hibernation is a covert preparation for a more overt action.

Besides, the drug destroys one's sense of time completely. If that happened, I might forget to dodge some bright morning and some cluck would run me down with an orange and yellow street car, or a bilious bus! Or I might forget to leave my hole when the moment for action presents itself.

Meanwhile I enjoy my life with the compliments of Monopolated Light & Power. Since you never recognize me even when in closest contact with me, and since, no doubt, you'll hardly believe that I exist, it won't matter if you know that I tapped a power line leading into the building and ran it into my hole in the ground. Before that I lived in the darkness into which I was chased, but now I see. I've illuminated the blackness of my invisibility —and vice versa. And so I play the invisible music of my isolation. The last statement doesn't seem just right, does it? But it is; you hear this music simply because music is heard and seldom seen, except by musicians. Could this compulsion to put invisibility down in black and white be thus an urge to make music of invisibility? But I am an orator, a rabble rouser —Am? I *was*, and perhaps shall be again. Who knows? All sickness is not unto death, neither is invisibility.

I can hear you say, "What a horrible, irresponsible bastard!" And you're right. I leap to agree with you. I am one of the most irresponsible beings that ever lived. Irresponsibility is part of my invisibility; any way you face it, it is a denial. But to whom can I be responsible, and why should I be, when you refuse to see me? And wait until I reveal how truly irresponsible I am. Responsibility rests upon recognition, and recognition is a form of agreement. Take the man whom I almost killed: Who was rsponsible for that near murder—I? I don't think so, and I refuse it. I won't buy it. You can't give it to me. *He* bumped *me, he* insulted *me*. Shouldn't he, for his own personal safety, have recognized my hysteria, my "danger potential"? He, let us say, was lost in a dream world. But didn't *he* control that dream world—which, alas, is only too real!—and didn't *he* rule me out of it? And if he had yelled for a policeman, wouldn't I have been taken for the offending one? Yes, yes, yes! Let me agree with you, I was the irresponsible one; for I should have used my knife to protect the higher interests of society. Some day that kind of foolishness will cause us tragic trouble. All dreamers and sleepwalkers must pay the price, and even the invisible victim is responsible for the fate of all. But I shirked that responsibility; I became too snarled in the incompatible notions that buzzed within my brain. I was a coward . . .

But what did *I* do to be so blue? Bear with me.

❖

Ralph Ellison was born in Oklahoma City in 1914, studied music at Tuskegee Institute from 1933 to 1936, then came to New York City, where he met Richard Wright, who influenced him to write fiction. He has taught literature or writing at Bard College and the University of Chicago and is now writer-in-residence at Rutgers University. He has won many awards and fellowships for his work, including the National Book Award in 1952. This was for his first novel, Invisible Man, *the only one he has published so far, although parts of a second have appeared in magazines. He has also published a collection of his essays,* Shadow and Act *(1964).* Invisible Man *was instantly acknowledged a brilliant book when it was published, and it is now well on its way toward a reputation as an American classic. The title refers to a central theme of the book, that the Negro, so easily discriminated against in a white society because his skin color makes him so highly visible, at the same time suffers from being socially invisible, unrecognized as an ordinary man. He is "socially visible" to his fellow white man only as a problem or an exception. Ellison is himself a further extension of this paradox. He has not associated himself with the militant "rabble-rousing" aspects of "the Negro problem" in order to remain "free" to be what he is: a man of letters, a writer and intellectual. He refuses to be a Negro writer in the sense of the Negro baseball star or singer or congressman. The faith he keeps now is with his own talents and the life he has made for himself. He insists on being an exceptional writer, not simply an exceptional Negro.*

In "The Prologue" we see the argument of the book sketched out as a defense of Ellison's strategy: he retreats from the untenable position of being socially invisible as a Negro by adopting the ultra-visible, though hidden and isolated, position of the writer. The prologue begins with an act of senseless violence, an act that will appear to be anonymous violence to the other man, for the narrator realizes that "the man had not seen me, actually." It is the same sort of anonymous violence that haunted the dreams of the professor in "The Intruder," but it is used here, oppositely, to show just how brutalizing is the realization of his own invisibility—of being "a figure in a nightmare . . . a phantom in other people's minds"—how frightening the recognition of his own anonymity can be to a flesh and blood man. It is the ultimate in identity loss, as his "hibernation" appears to be the ultimate in immobilization. But he is making his fight against "the sleepwalkers" who do not recognize him as a man by draining off power from "Monopolated Light and Power," to light his underground room with 1,369 light bulbs, because "light confirms my reality, gives birth to my form." By "light" he means the light of truth: "Nothing, storm or flood, must get in the way of our need for light and ever more and brighter light. The truth is the light and light is the truth." Invisible Man *is rich with meanings, and they cannot all be considered at once, but it is clear that there is at least one other meaning to this act, beyond simply providing light and truth to confirm his reality and identity. For "Monopolated Light and Power" clearly suggests the monopoly that the white intellectual establishment and academic community have held on knowledge and truth, on light, as a*

*source of power. And the narrator is draining off this power during his
"hibernation" toward a future use. He is careful to say: "A hibernation is
a covert preparation for a more overt action." During this hibernation, by
way of a reefer and Louis Armstrong's "What Did I Do to Be so Black
and Blue?," he relives the history of his race, comparing it to Dante's descent into the depths of Hell. This journey through time and space is essential to the Negro intellectual, even though it tempts him to act: "At first
I was afraid; this familiar music had demanded action, the kind of which I
was incapable, and yet had I lingered there beneath the surface I might
have attempted to act." It is essential because through it "I had discovered unrecognized compulsions of my being . . . this compulsion to put
invisibility down in black and white." He is, he says, "one of the most irresponsible beings that ever lived. Irresponsibility is part of my invisibility; any way you face it, it is a denial." Yet it is by this very denial
of overt action that he arrives at the "warm hole" that is full of light from
which as an invisible man, both Negro and writer, he has produced a supreme act of responsibility: a book that tells what it is to be a Negro. By
his own conduct and through his book, by providing identity and humanity
where there was only anonymity, Ellison has done much to make the sleepwalkers open their eyes, and has done much to make the invisible man
visible.*

IVAN GOLD

The Nickel Misery of George Washington Carver Brown

◇◇◇◇◇◇◇◇

THE DAY that Carver Brown fell backward from the freshly painted pinnacle of failure (setting even for him a new low) was the day before Thanksgiving Day: it dawned in frozen reds and blues, without portent. Between the sleep-smelling barracks and the temporary security of the mess hall he was called upon to face three minor crises, indisputable sources of discomfort, but nothing like harbingers because they had all happened to him before. In the crowded latrine his towel disappeared as he groped for it blind, soapy-eyed; back at his bunk his bootlaces had become tightly knotted, his blankets were wet, his mattress on the floor; as (having to repair the damage) the last man to appear at the reveille formation, he naturally attracted the attention of Corporal Cherry, who sliced off the open button of his field-jacket pocket with a straight razor and ordered him to replace (and button) it before entering the mess hall. Unstrung as Carver was by all three incidents he would not have said that they surprised him. They represented, at the five-and-one-half-week point, the sum and definition of his military experience, foreshadowed (on the day before Thanksgiving) nothing more than the status quo, another day of continual low-key persecution.

Weeks later, when Carver's mother had keened away the sharper edges of her grief, she would say that on that day (and on the three days previous, too) at precisely one-forty in the afternoon she had felt pass through her back and spine murderous unforgettable pain, as if a fat hand had brought her to a great giddy height and slammed her from it to the ground, but Carver was possessed of no such (real or imagined) extrasensory power; received no indication on Wednesday or at any time previous that his luck had totally left him until that fractionary instant (and perhaps not even then) when there was nothing else to believe. The frigid bloody sun lofted into the cloud-streaked, quickening sky, the second platoon scattered before the first, third and fourth because Wednesday breakfast was their turn to queue up first outside the mess hall, and Carver Brown, who enjoyed food, stamped, shuffled and whined completely in character into the barracks to hunt in the chaos of his foot locker tray for his sewing kit. He had made this early-morning search a dozen times before.

The second platoon's athletic dash toward breakfast left still another in its wake a non-competitor (whom it would have out-distanced anyway). This was Roger Hines, the group's least agile man. At the command to fall out he took a long awkward step out of the first squad and continued toward the barracks while the trainees jostled and raced behind him to the mess hall. Eating was not foremost in his mind. Copper-tinted and frail, he had a terrible brittle quality, his stooped, skinny form warning Touch me and break me, and since the second day of the fourth week, when he tripped while double-timing and twisted his ankle, he existed in a state approaching grace, an accepted member of the so-called fifth platoon. This was the three-man fringe group allowed to straggle to the training areas at its own pace behind the company proper because of leg trouble—a man who had broken both a year ago on an obstacle course and spent most of the time since shuttling between various basic-training units and the post hospital; a man who contracted in the Army (and almost overcame) polio, eighteen months before, and claimed wistfully, in the twilight of his military career, to be awaiting early separation; and most recently Hines, his ankle not now seriously injured nor even when he fell, but its job done, italicizing what his body and bearing should have thundered from the start: that here, in this brittle, silent twenty-six-year-old, was nothing less than a great potential tragedy. Given an hour of crisis and not the slack time following the Korean truce; a sixteen-week infantry training regimen in place of this abbreviated, almost token program for men being groomed for non-combatant duty in the Signal Corps; given, in other words, the military context in which even gratuitous brutality commands an aura of necessity —Hines might conceivably have had it. But he had been drafted at the right time, sent to the right place, come by the right injury, and his luck was going to hold.

Only Brown was in the barracks as Hines hobbled down the center aisle: Brown sitting on his bunk and sewing with a frantic clumsiness, still wearing the jacket, mumbling furious regional epithets about the character of Corporal Cherry that might have offended Hines at a less urgent time. Brown's presence alone was enough to disturb him, yet he knew he would be lucky to have to cope with no other distractions: the handful of trainees who might give up their early-breakfast privilege to fuss around their areas, or worse, use the latrine. His heart pounding under the field jacket, Hines reached the end of the center aisle without the barracks door slamming behind him, ducked with his rifle into the empty latrine, placed the weapon between the wall and his commode, and grabbed at the buckle of his pants. For roughly twenty seconds he defeated himself by ignoring the hard-won privacy to concentrate on the prospect of its imminent dissolution, but he heard no footsteps, and the sound of no door, and Carver's mumbling blended finally with the troop noises outside and he was on the point of achieving a kind of success when the saccharine whine broke into his ear:

"Man, why that mother always pick on me?"

He had not even heard him, neither stop his mumbling nor approach; he had built up for the first time in seven miserable weeks the kind of insulation he guessed he would have to have if he was ever going to learn to manage in what could at best be a delicate temporary privacy (for it was mad to expect him to cope with the rushed early-morning shoulder-to-shoulder public performance, men lined up heckling, urging haste), and all the insulation had done was prevent him from composing himself for what he should have learned by now was the inevitable failure. Because someone always came in. He would have to wait until tonight, after lights out, and even then until the last diehard poker players and letter writers were gone from the latrine. He had waited painfully the night before, only to discover that Brown's tormentors were on the prowl: men deferring sleep until Brown crawled noisily beneath his blankets, then yanking him out, smothering his protests, dragging him to to the shower room, administering the traditional GI shower. So last night too had been a failure. His insides convoluted strangely, dipped against the sudden shock of Brown's materialization. He felt sick with frustration, carrying a poisonous weight of a thousand pounds. He wished for absolutely nothing now but that he had heard the boy's approach.

"Man, why everybody always pick on me?" Brown repeated. He continued to work on the field jacket, his chin scraping his chest, the low, plump body half in and out of the commode room, his eyes crossed on the needle and thread. "There's three hundred boys in this company, they all screwups, why that Cherry and everybody always pick on me?"

Because you're built for guilt, you black fool, Roger thought. He couldn't move to wipe himself.

"Copperhaid, you smart," Carver went on. "Where you from anyhow, New York? You see how they wet my blanket this mornin' after somebody take my towel? How that Cherry pull out that razor before daylight and try to cut off my haid? Why they do that to me, Copperhaid? Why they mess with me instead of you and everybody else?"

"I have no idea," Roger said harshly, in the strident tones he had used all his life as a substitute for communication. Loud and with perfect diction in love, hate, and neutrality. It set off in the latrine the other's soft, accented whine. "And my name isn't Copperhead. It's Hines, Roger B."

Carver glanced behind him in response to the tone, although he was standing with his rump against the wall. "But everbody call you that," he protested. "Ever damn body."

"My name is Hines," Roger said loudly, "and that is the only name I answer to. Any other I've acquired since being in the Army because of the color of my skin I feel privileged to ignore." He would have retracted that; pinned insanely here to an unreal toilet seat by a dumb suffering son of the South, telling him things he could not even bring himself to write home about this nightmarish time, even to his wife.

Above the fat cheeks Carver's eyes grew wide. His mouth hung slack between laughter and surprise. Abruptly he discarded the suppliant's role for its opposite, and he said, "You's all confused," slipping the needle into his pocket and easing (across from Hines) onto a lidless commode. "You think us boys call you Copperhaid because you a nigrah? Naw, man. You look like a damn snake," Carver said, guffawed suddenly and doubled over onto himself, the top of his head inches from Roger's knees. And straightened at once, with a look of joy. "It just the way your face sits, man, all tight across the bone like that. The way you don't seem to have no ears. All the blood gone out of your mouth. Nothin' to do with bein' a nigrah, man, you just resembles a snake, that's all. You unnerstan'?" His interest was all directed toward Roger now; he had forgotten himself. "Some boy tells me you from New York, Copperhaid. Where y'all live at, Hahlem?"

And still Hines could not rise; to leave or (better, but a dream) collect the power in one hundred thirty pounds and smash this fat-cheeked, persecuted, black-faced boy—this was the court fool, the butt, the door mat of the company, baiting him, Hines, one of the few who left him alone while hating him with a ferocity his tormentors could never muster—this was his *worst enemy* sitting there grinning fully clothed on a toilet seat touching-distance away, not even dimly aware that he flirted with what would never become disaster. It was almost too much to bear.

"Why . . . don't . . . you . . . get . . . some . . . breakfast," Hines said, and again Brown felt tempted to look over his shoulder to see who Copperhead was talking to.

"Plenty of time," Carver said. "If I can't be in there first, I just as quick be last. That way Copul Cherry maybe be out and I don't have so much worryin' to do. You live in that Hahlem, man?"

"My home is in Syracuse," Hines said.

"Where that at? A boy tell me you go to *college* up North. That right, man?"

"Yes!" Hines almost shouted. Where I learned what I was born to fear and hate and hoped to God would never meet except where I had to every day in my own spoiled insides.

Two trainees, through with breakfast, walked into the washroom. Despair made him brave, and he grabbed at the toilet paper. The situation could only grow worse, and he would rise.

Suddenly Carver began to whine once more, leaning toward him.

"Then you must be pretty smart, Copperhaid. Maybe you can say why everbody in this here company pick on Georgia Brown?"

"Because you like it and you want them to," Roger said, and stood jerkily and trembling and looked straight ahead at the bare wall over Carver's clipped round head and pulled up and buckled his pants. He reached for his rifle and limped out hurriedly, not stopping to wash his hands. But it came anyway (as he had magically known it would), Brown's voice, reaching after and transfixing him, nailing him to his own cross a foot or two from freedom:

"Damn, Copperhaid, if you ain't just buttoned up the longest sonbitch I ever seen."

Only Cherry, Sergeant Braun, and Mentor, the mess sergeant, were at the cadre table when Brown sidled in at the door. Cherry sat at the end of the table, facing the entrance, Braun to his right. Mentor was opposite Cherry, his back to the door. Brown looked over warily, but the corporal's big-jawed face was down into his coffee mug. Brown took a step toward the table anyway, then changed his mind, reached for a tray and went over to the serving line. Sergeant Braun glanced at Cherry, but he didn't have to. Cherry waited until the second man had two strips of fatty bacon suspended over Carver's tray.

"Brown!"

The boy wheeled and the fried eggs leaped from his tray and skittered along the floor. "Aww!" Carver said.

The mess sergeant spun around on the bench. "Goddamn," he said. *"God*damn. And here we just got through workin' our tails to the bone GIin' the floor last night. Buddy, you're going to clean that up, along about now. And eat 'em if you want to. Because right there are your eggs for this mornin'. If this ain't the asskissinist bunch of trainees," he appealed to Braun. "Pick 'em up. Then go on back out and get a mop," he said to Brown.

"In a minute, sergeant," Cherry said. "I want him over here."

"Well, let him pick up the damn eggs before the captain or somebody comes in and breaks their neck," Mentor said.

"You heard him," Cherry said. But Carver was already on his knees, trying to coax the eggs (one yolk miraculously intact) with knife and fork back onto his tray, trying desperately not to compound the damage; succeeding, and only the moist outline and a figure eight of yellow remained on the concrete floor. He approached the cadre mess table with the tray held out in front of him, the edge of it pressing into his belly, and in five seconds his face ran the gamut, a dash, a pinch of everything. He was having trouble (an old problem) in forming an attitude.

Cherry looked up at him. "Now you see," he said gently. "If you had come right over to me like I told you to do at reveille and showed me your button and *then* went about getting your breakfast, you wouldn't have got all shook up and dropped your fried eggs and picked up any extra duty tonight. And I *know* you got better things to do with your time at night than fuss around the mess hall."

"Nobody say nothin' 'bout no extra duty, man," Carver said.

"Brown, when a man eats in the Army, it's a holy time. His mind and body has got to be free and completely at rest. There is positively no one messing with the troops at mealtime. That's how I can guarantee Sergeant Mentor don't mean for you to clean up his floor now, but he would like to see you back here around six o'clock tonight."

"He'll mop that crud up now," Mentor said. "If you send him back here tonight to help out the poor KP's, nobody's kickin'.'"

"You hear that, Brown? The sergeant has got you both ways. There's no pleasing some people. Suppose you take them dirty eggs out of my face and let me see that button now."

"Copul, I thought I'd clean my rifle tonight," Carver begged. "It's been a long while since I got that mother all stripped down and oiled and all. Y'all remember you had me in the mess hall every day last week. It's sewed real good, copul," he said, as Cherry's hand reached ominously for his jacket pocket.

"Well, now, you don't have to be no expert sewer," Cherry said reasonably, lifting the flap and tugging at the button, once. "Just so long as she's nice and tight and always closed. You know me and my razor are getting pretty tired of cutting it off damn near every morning. You ever think of it that way?"

Carver had narrowed it now (a way to feel), the whine doing battle wit'. no more than a tentative gaiety.

"Copul, you ain't got to cut anyhow. If you just go and *tell* Carver 'bout that button, you see how fast I get the mother closed. But the way everybody take on after me in barracks I just don't have time to worry 'bout it. You know what they done last night? They pull me out of baid and give me another GI shower, and they just give one to me day before yesterday. And when I get back to baid, don't you know I'm short-sheeted? And got to strip the sonbitch down and make it up in the dark? And this mornin' . . . ."

"All right, young soldier," Braun cut in. "You get that floor cleaned up and put something in your belly. And not stand here pissing and moaning all day. We march out in five minutes."

"Yes suh," Carver said, secure in (warmed by) the knowledge that the field first sergeant was teasing him. Didn't the man's wrist watch, resting face upward on the table, allow twenty minutes before the fall-in whistle blew? "Carver's goin' in half a second to fetch a mop. I just got to make sure that Copul Cherry know that if he sends me out to the kitchen tonight I ain't never goin' to get. . . ."

"Move out!" Braun yelled, half-rising, and Carver moved out, whining, on his lips the corpse of a smile.

From the rear of the hall where he lingered over coffee, Tom Frazier watched what (from that remove) was little more than a pantomime, an interracial dumbshow set in motion by Cherry's sharp summons, and closed by Braun's overresonant dismissal, and highlighted by the short (soundless) arc the eggs described on the way to the floor. He had to have a theory if he was not going to be ashamed of the way this type of incident still had the power to amuse him, and over the weeks he had developed one, of a middling complexity, and just possibly true. It held that while Carver Brown was a scapegoat, a Christ-figure, and a clown, he was none of these things because he was a black man. His color had no bearing on the continuous round of double-pronged persecution (in which Frazier— while admitting his interest—played no part); he was simply the unfortunate heir to certain transcendent morbid qualities which made him a convenient receptacle for and a symbol of corporate guilt and suffering.

This was the theory (briefly put) that Frazier had to have. He required it because he was a militant egalitarian; he had become this only recently, against considerable odds, and he would not tolerate his slightest backsliding; not until (later: after the fall) it no longer had to go by that name.

It was not a bad theory, but it took (to Frazier's mind) some shoring up, because he noticed a great deal. He did not miss Brown's field-hand shuffle, his telltale wool, his ridiculous speech; he was even aware of the broad piece of irony staged at reveille two or three times a week by Corporal Cherry, when he brandished his outsized razor (which he had come by earlier in the cycle through confiscation from a since-court-martialed, lithe, violent, altogether unhumorous Negro boy) and slashed at Brown's jacket: he noticed these things, and he was obliged to dispose of them. The razor was simply the form the persecution took in the hands of someone like Cherry; while no doubt a less subtle bigotry did play a part, as in the case of someone like Griever, a Tennessee mountaineer; but these were merely *effects,* existing (within the larger framework) alongside more congenial evidence: as for example Brown's frequent discomfort at the hands of trainees (and cadre too) who hailed from large cities in the North, or at the hands of the grinning Negro cook out in the kitchen with whom Brown jockeyed, at that moment, for custody of an idle mop, seeming to have almost gained it, to have teased it free, until the cook tired of the game and sent him on principle to fetch one from the mop rack outside—his blackness no more explained Brown's role in Charlie Company than the coloration of the limping Hines accounted for his being spared this kind of misery; it explained, in other words, nothing at all. So Tom Frazier lingered over coffee in the mess hall, and allowed himself to be mildly (but watchfully) amused.

He was a tall, athletic Southerner who had been expelled (as he would later, in part, tell Hines) from a fraternity for being apprehended (during Homecoming Week) hosting a Negress in the fraternity president's bedroom. The expulsion had turned his thinking into strange and unaccustomed channels, but he tracked these channels down tenaciously (with no backsliding) because he had that kind of mind. He was drafted not long after the incident, and while he professed a strong distaste for military service, he enjoyed having to cope with the challenges and the inconvenience of the six weeks up to here; and he had gained time (and an excellent set of situations) in which to test his fresh convictions. He wished only that he might have been assigned to a Northern camp, but, with luck, this too might come in time.

He was about to leave (Brown was busy mopping the floor, and only Mentor sat at the cadre table now) when Hines walked into the mess hall, removed the helmet liner from his flat, fuzzed top, and reached for a coffee cup. So Frazier put off leaving for a while and watched the snake-faced copper boy limp up the aisle. And tried to draw him with his eyes. But Hines (moving deliberately, almost in slow motion, gentling his brittle, damaged bones) jerked his downcast eyes from table to table and sat down at the first empty one, half the distance between Frazier and the serving line. Frazier stared at the brown tapering fingers as they wormed a cigarette from the field-jacket pocket and trembled in the lighting it, watched Hines inhale with all of his body, suck the smoke deep into the translucency of him, visibly almost into his belly, and then lower his face to the oversized coffee mug and lock his fingers around its bulk; and he decided to try once again to make contact, although he had been rebuffed by the fellow in the six weeks a half-dozen times. He picked up his helmet liner, his empty tray, and he covered the ground from table to table in long rapid strides.

In reaching across his chest for the cigarette, Hines glanced up and collided briefly with the wall of Frazier's eyes. He actually felt their impact; so he lowered his gaze to the flame's kind glare, slitted his eyes for the journey down to the black smoking drink, and told himself that Frazier was not looking at him, could not be, because he had no reason to; that if he was looking at him (if he had a reason), it would probably mean a confrontation, further distress, and he had already (by breakfast) filled his quota for the day. So when he sensed the form beside him, nothing remained but to gulp the scalding coffee (yet barely diminish it) and burn himself.

"Morning, Hines; mind if I join you?"

But he was on his feet, the corner of the table knifing between them, Frazier still bulking above him, like an adult over a child. "I . . . was . . . just . . . leaving," Hines said.

"Christ, man, you just came in. Why don't you sit tight and we'll chat for a while. Do you make it all right till noon with only black coffee for a breakfast?"

"I was just leaving," Hines said loudly. "I'm sorry."

"Nothing to be sorry about," Frazier said, but the boy was already on the move, a wounded quarry, scuttling down the aisle.

"That old Northern hospitality," Frazier said quietly, aloud. "Just like you read about. Why I believe we'll converse yet, you unsociable so and so," and followed Hines rapidly to the exit, caught and passed him wordlessly as somewhere in the half-light Braun's whistle blew shrilly, three long blasts, beginning the day.

It took anywhere from fifteen to twenty-five days for a company to learn to the last man of Corporal Cherry's unique means of supplementing his income, a group alertness determining the interval, *esprit de corps,* and the soundness of communication lines. He was circumspect, and taciturn, and there was nothing public about the money-making situation, although at first glance the opposite seemed true. The three hundred-odd men lay in neat rows on their backs in the training area, each engrossed in the taut private world of the particular exercise, regarding fixedly (depending on their stamina, the angle's acuteness) toes, crotch or sky, and the nature of Cherry's activity in an exerciser's immediate vicinity was not (at first) carefully observed, even by the object of such attention. A man could not help but be aware (although L-shaped, concentrating) of the looming presence of a member of the cadre, and when Cherry bent to him he expected his position to be manually adjusted, or at least to be reprimanded; Cherry would occasionally accommodate, but more often he straightened in silence, leaving the trainee bewildered until the end of the exercise when the man stood, dusted himself off, and reached to the ground for his ID tag and keys—and nothing more. By the time even the most alert group discovered (to the last man) the most effective means of coping with the corporal (you left your change in the barracks, in your foot locker), he had added to a given month's pay check between twenty and thirty dollars.

The group of which Carver Brown was a member adhered to the norm in this respect, contributed twenty-seven dollars in small denominations over the first twelve working days and then abruptly wised up, much more rapidly than they should have, almost as if someone had hung a notice on the company bulletin board, *You will bring no change out onto the training field.* Although a cycle rarely yielded more than (even as much as) this one had, it had never done so quite so fast, and the complete, sudden stoppage left Cherry disgruntled and mystified. But the Army being what it was, he had no recourse but silence.

Cherry had taken a bullet in the left buttock in Korea, not far from his spine, had emerged from the well-intentioned but necessarily imperfect medical setup somewhere behind the lines with a slight permanent limp which rendered him unfit for further combat duty, but did not otherwise inconvenience him, and he had been sent to fill the niche of shaper-of-men at the basic-training camp. The life suited him. Disappointments, like the present one, were rare, and more serious irritations rarer still. There had been the need to scrub down the barracks after the last cycle because the captain had been dissatisfied with the departed trainees' cleaning job, and had held the cadre responsible—but this was just. Cherry (a corporal with a combat record) had not relished the work—cleaning and mopping up after these men who were something even less than subordinates, a race apart—but he had not questioned its equity. It would teach the cadre not to make the same mistake next time. (He had not made the mistake at all—his building was the only one of the four which had passed inspection, but the captain ordered him in to work with the others, mentioning collective responsibility.) If these gold-bricking weak-kneed civilian people headed for the Signal Corps thought they had it made for these eight weeks as well as the time after, they were probably right—but they would not have it as made as they thought. He had seen to that through the two and one-half cycles up to here, and, after the recent mandatory housecleaning, the rest of the noncoms would probably see to it too. Cherry disliked none of the trainees so much as the idea of them, the knowledge of what they were going out into (and what not) and he treated them all with the same impartiality, except when a man begged for, demanded the only kind of attention he had to give, as had Brown. Even here, he enjoyed Brown, he had nothing personally against Brown. Cherry hated no man.

Yet that Wednesday morning he was to come close to it, striding through the ranks of L-shaped men, straightening buckling legs and barking commands, believing himself reconciled by now, the sixth week, to the empty pockets and the bare earth, but learning in an instant how wrong he was as somewhere behind him the coins jingled, clattered, and kept coming with jack-pot regularity; he spun to the ground and witnessed the end of it, the last few striking the clay surface and wobbling away from the rest, the stumpy boy turning his head on its cushion of interlaced fingers and uttering a noise of anguish—Brown. A lame cat, he glided over a straining form as the instructor called, "Keep it going, five more reps now, one-two-three-four—" met Brown's shocked, pleading eye for only the time this took, bent to scoop before the exercise ended and stopped, halfway down.

Pennies lay by Brown. Copper and silver ones, dull ones and shining; some rolling still but most piled neatly in the shadow of his thigh, a modest hill of money, pennies. Terrified and silent, Brown implored from his place on the ground, his fingers twitching beneath his head, his eyes wide, his body still. Cherry straightened empty-handed, and the flush crept upward from his jaw.

"Brown, you son of a bitch. . . ."

From the platform came the command to rise. Carver struggled to his feet with all the rest, but "Attention!" was too much to ask: his chin inched forward onto his chest, his eyes struggled to focus on the pile. Cherry kicked it then. He dug the boot of his good leg into the heart of the mound and sent the money flying as from the platform came the command, "Rest!", and Brown with a wild look started to sink to the ground.

"Stand up!" Cherry screamed.

"Copul, that my *money* there you. . . ."

"I said stand up! Does this here look like the PX? You see something out here you going to buy?"

"Copul, that fifty cent I got till payday, why you kick it that way, man?"

"Don't 'man' me, buddy," Cherry said furiously; "I want to know if you think there's something humorous in bringing fifty pennies out here?" seeking the source of his anger, to explain it by unmasking malicious intent, although he knew the boy would not dare. "Every goddamn body else seems to know we leave our money in the barracks when we go out to train. You need an engraved invitation?"

"Copul, listen. Lemme tell you why. I was in the haid this mornin' talkin' to Copperhaid—y'all know who Copperhaid is, that skinny nigrah boy—and when I come back out to my area, some of the boys has took off with my two locks and I can't even close up my uniforms and my foot locker neither, and all I could carry was my money, so I took it along out here. I know some of the boys talk in the barracks about some cadreman he take all your money if you lose it out here, but it wasn't safe no place else. I can't even get no tooth paste till payday, Copul Cherry."

"Somebody took your locks?"

"Sure did, copul," Carver said.

"If you'd had them lockers locked, that couldn't have happened now, could it?"

"Naw, suh. But I had to open them mothers for my sewin' kit."

"Well, now, that's pretty much toughtit. Brown, you didn't bring those lousy pennies out here just to piss me off, did you?"

"Naw, copul."

"I seem to be pissed off anyway, don't I? And I'm thinking if it gets any worse you'll be in the kitchen on extra detail every day until the end of the cycle, and never smell another week-end pass."

"Copul Cherry, excuse me but I ain't never been on pass yet. They always askin' me one of the genul orders 'fore they give one to me, and them genul orders too long for Carver to remember. Y'all had me on extra duty ever Saturday since basic began, anyway. If I can just get my hands on that fifty cent. . . ."

"Brown, you listen to me. You're the lowest form of gold-bricking excuse for a soldier I have ever seen in all my time. If you bend for one—not fifty but one—of those goddamn coins you're going to be working a twenty-day from here to the end and everything up to now will seem like a Sunday picnic. You'll hope you were dead, you know what I mean? Now drop to the ground and do your push-ups like the rest of these gold-bricks and *remember what I said*," and kicked at a coin in reach and turned away in disgust; the fat, perspiring, active face seemed an inch away from tears. Or was it joy?

Pennies! He limped away furiously while Carver quivered in self-pity and indignation, thinking If I don't have money I might as well be daid (but knowing better than to scrabble behind Cherry's back or even snatch at the coin or two within reach). Why that mother always got to pick on me.

Sergeant-First-Class William Divino, a twenty-eight-year-old combat veteran, awoke in high spirits on the day before Thanksgiving and retained this feeling throughout the sluggish, workday morning, which did not nec-essarily imply the top-level functioning of his creative powers. In fact, the opposite might have been true: it took him, in high spirits, almost three hours to hammer out and smooth the doggerel he would probably have hammered out and smoothed, feeling down at the mouth, in half that time, so that not until the class on booby traps and mines, the lesson in squad tactics, the chaplain's assault on pornography were all history did he feel ready to commit to public performance and scrutiny the verses inspired by the event he had witnessed (strolling a rank or two behind) some three hours before. The event itself might have damaged the good feeling (hastening thereby its own commemoration), but today it did not. While there was no gainsaying, there was also no speeding up the need for song. With the ready-made melodies frozen into perpetuity more through the demands of folk-lore than military need or desire, Sergeant Divino marched his third platoon homeward for the noon break, a cooperative, hungry bunch, suited at least as well for choral work as soldiering, respond-ing heartily to his alternating bass and falsetto, the greatest quantity of sound issuing from the five or ten who had been eyewitnesses, the trainees who could boast that they were there:

"There's pennies all over the field."	"You're right!"
"There's pennies all over the field."	"You're right!"
"Pick 'em up,"	"One two!"
"Pi-ick 'em up,"	"Three four!"
"Kick 'em around,"	"One two three four, three four!"

Scowling magnificently, his craggy face guaranteeing mayhem, Divino stormed up and down the outside file. "Dress it up. Sound off like you own a pair. Castellani, get in step. *Change step, you dumb wop.* Green, you're bouncin' . . . still bouncin', Green. . . . *Green, stop your bouncin'!*" "Can't help it, sarge, damn boots too tight," the tall boy replied, from the security of an inner marching column. Divino's breath poured onto him from across the man's face on the outer file: "No talkin' in ranks, you dumb bunny, just hold down the motherin' bouncin'," and he guffawed suddenly, no invitation to continued infraction but a measure of forgiveness, malice, good will, and cakewalked in step back to the center of the moving platoon. He was a thick and powerful man, a little under six feet tall, a missing left ring finger all that stood between him and a kind of physical perfection. He was also a skilled, butter-jointed clown.

"Lemme hear it, you bunch of Wacs."

"O Brown had a pocket of cash,"	"You're right!"
"O Brown had a pocket of cash,"	"You're right!"
"Pick it up,"	"One two!"
"Pi-ick it up,"	"Three four!"
"Kick it around,"	"One two three four, three four!"

Up front a few in the know strained for a look at Cherry, marching his group twenty yards ahead, but he gave no sign that he understood or cared. Divino never looked. He had them bawl the verses all the way back to the company area, riding over the more conventional cadence-counting of the three other platoons, and silenced them as they swung into position, behind the orderly room.

The company marked time until the three stragglers, the fifth platoon, limped in and into their respective parent groups, and Sergeant Braun appeared on the steps. He halted them, and gave them "At ease," regarded his realm for a moment, and smiled.

"Gentlemen. It's a real pleasure to see your bright shining faces. This morning, administrative duties on behalf of our absent first sergeant, laid up in the hospital, kept me from joining you in the field, where a field first sergeant is paid to be; they will also do so this afternoon. Yet you all know that in spirit I am out there with you, keeping an eye on each individual uncooperative ass. Behave accordingly. When you get out on that obstacle course this afternoon, do your finest work, because rumors exist to the effect that the battalion commander will be in the area. If he is not pleased with what he sees, he hops on the captain, who has no choice but to hop on me. This is what we know as the chain of command. In my turn I am forced to hop on the platoon sergeants, who then give the business to their platoons. So who gets it in the end? That's correct. You ream yourselves when you put out less than your best. This is the thought I would like to leave you with. Now I disremember which platoon is supposed to eat first Wednesday lunch, and I know I can't trust you people to remind me, so what we are going to do is stand at attention for a while, and the sharpest-looking platoon is going into that mess hall first, and so on down the line. Atennshut!"

A bristling, palpable silence gripped the field. Braun removed a clipper from his pocket and worked on his nails for a minute or so. Finally he looked up, and threw a quick glance at each platoon.

"You're all looking pretty good out there, you four platoons, with some individual exceptions, and I want you to look at least that good in this Saturday's parade. I would say from here that the embattled second platoon, under the guidance of Corporal Cherry, is our winner for today, followed by the first, fourth and third. Second, first, fourth and third. There is the order for the meal. At ease! I have a message here from the old man, which is to bring your smiling faces back around these steps at twenty to one, for a little talk on a subject dear to everyone's heart. Right after mail call. That is all I have for you. Attennneshut! First platoon, fall out. . . ." With a flourish he cupped his hand behind his ear and cocked his head toward the second platoon. "Do I detect a voice or more raised in protest? A second platooner anxious to know why he winds up eating last, even though Sergeant Braun just told him he is eating first? The reason is that our friend George Washington Brown turned his ugly face for a sneak peek up here right after I got finished telling you how nice and soldierly you looked. While you were still supposed to be at attention. Now this goes by the name of idle curiosity. You all know you've got to have every man doing his best, because one bad apple spoils the bunch, as they say. Fourth platoon, fall out! Divino's platoon, the sloppiest as usual, you're eating third today through the grace of God, fall out! Second platoon, go!" and spun around, and walked back into the orderly room. The brief drama he set in motion below would not have surprised him.

"You son of a bitch," said Griever, a wide blond from Tennessee. "You cain't stand still fo' a minute, can you. You got to move yo' ugly face. We'll drum up a little somethin' fo' you to move around about after lights out tonight."

"Man," Carver whined, "I never *moved*. That Sahgt Braun, he lyin' to you." His face worked violently under the impact of thought. "That chow the same five ten minutes later anyhow. What difference who eat first?" He was jostled by two more of the men he lived with, walking toward the mess hall. They regarded him with hate, threatened vengeance. They passed.

"Shee-it," Carver mumbled. He dug a boot heel into the earth. "Tonight still a long way off. I ain't even goin' to worry 'bout it."

When Captain Palmer appeared on the orderly-room steps promptly at twelve-forty to give an extemporaneous talk on social disease, he found he had a live audience, delighted to have put an unscheduled meal of C-rations behind it, bound by a collective grumbling as well as anticipation for the holiday, susceptible to and even eager for communications from above. He was a lean twenty-six-year-old Virginian with sharp, delicate features and sun-colored hair, concealed now beneath the white helmet liner, set low over his eyes. He was a college-trained ROTC officer, but his origins were buried under three long years of military abrasion and blood: he owned an excellent war record, and he was no stranger to command.

This would be the third company he had run through since being sent to Georgia, and while a basic-training unit brought its unique problems, required a shift in the delicate balance between cajoling and force with which one handled a combat outfit, he had succeeded in mastering these new techniques to his own satisfaction.

"Do you men *like* basic training?" he began, in the thin, reedy voice he had trained to carry, and good-naturedly imputed the proper meaning to the good-natured, garbled, answering roar. "Is this the best damn outfit in the best damn camp in the United States?" The catechismic roar, "With the best damn cadre?" The roar. "And the best damn mess hall?" The roar changed in character, increased in volume, and Palmer raised his hands. "Any of you men want turkey tomorrow? And cranberry sauce? If you do, you've got to give Sergeant Mentor and his cooks a little breathing space. C-rations today only mean that you chow down that much better tomorrow. Does that make sense?" The crowd replied. "Let me hear you now—anybody out there who *likes* turkey and cranberry sauce?" The wild animal roar.

To the rear of the crowd, almost detached from it, Roger Hines, laden with contempt, watched the mad mob display. He wished fervently that Palmer would get to the point, deliver whatever idiotic message he had summoned the company to hear, so that Hines could move off into the shade of the barracks and rest for the minutes remaining to the noon hour. He would not be able (even after Palmer dismissed them) to drag his perspiring, weary body into the barracks and plump down on his bed, as he longed to do. The barracks were off limits during the noon hour. The urge to inspect might grip the captain at any time during the course of an afternoon (went the rationale), and a barrack had always to retain its buffed, dusted symmetry. Of course (Hines thought bitterly) violations resulting from the full-scale invasion which took place shortly before the men marched out (if the heat held) to permit the replacing of field jackets —the heel marks, the dirt, the beds nudged out of line—were easily distinguished by a U.S. Army captain from other, illicit untidiness; naturally (thought Hines) Palmer could identify outrages perpetrated during the legal assault and weighed, in his evaluation, only the dirt remaining . . . but he derived only minimum comfort from his irony. Pure malice, nothing else, accounted for the thousand stupid, niggling rules that contrived to make his life a misery. It staggered him to think of the brain power devoted to being asinine.

He watched Palmer's thin lips move soundlessly in the distance, and he wiped his forehead with his sleeve. It was hot . . . as brutally hot now as it had been cold in the predawn morning, and he had known that it would be—but the knowledge was never enough. To be jolted from sleep by the sudden flood of light and the CQ's bark; to be compelled to abandon the cultivated warmth beneath the two blankets in the double set of underwear and face the unheated barracks: these were shocks it required his entire being to withstand. While others shed the extra socks and the longjohns and hopped about for warmth, while others dressed rapidly and trapped what heat remained in their bodies, Hines, numb with cold, stepped stiff and dreamy into his fatigues, still clad in the winter (over summer) underwear, unable to deal efficiently, in the clasp of the frigid Georgia morning, with the fact of the sweaty Georgia noon, although he conceived of it; he simply was not able to calculate the suffering.

While his mind wandered thus within the soundproofed halls of his unhappiness, the captain's speech unfolded, and was well attended. The subject of gonorrhea, and of the five fresh cases reported in the company, was not without interest, and almost everyone paid close attention to the commanding officer's exhortations. He made it plain that he was not happy with the fresh outbreak, not so much because it tarnished the company's record—which was worth taking into consideration—but because of the downright unwholesomeness of this disease. He did not believe it necessary, as he put it, to "get the clap in order to have a good time." There were pro-kits available in the orderly room, there was a clean, decent club or two in town, but best of all, for recreation, there was the post beer hall. He could restrict them all to the post until the end of the eight weeks, starting with the holiday tomorrow, but he did not like to do that. He preferred to trust them. He had found that (once warned) his boys could be trusted. Besides, not only did they risk incurring his displeasure through disobedience, but ". . . Dorothy wouldn't like it. She wouldn't like it a little bit if I had to tell her that some more of my boys have gone into town and come back all fouled up, no good to the company, no good to themselves. She's a pretty sensitive gal, and she's upset by information like that. So think of Dorothy, and think of me, those of you who go into town. Have fun, but keep yourselves clean, and keep the record of Charlie Company the same way. Are there any questions?"

It was Frazier (for not many else would dare) who popped his large calloused hand into the air and queried, in the broad accents and at the top of his voice: "Now just who in Jesus Christ's name is Daaaathey, suh?" and earned the captain's hard, bright-eyed stare; but the acne-ravaged face was the face of someone wanting desperately to know.

"Dorothy happens to be my wife, soldier. I thought I had mentioned that before. Are there any other questions?" But there were none. Sergeant Braun called the company to attention, and released them, to idle away what remained of the noon hour. The captain returned inside.

"His wife," Frazier said meditatively, for the immediate few. The accent was nowhere apparent now. "I thought he meant the Dorothy I knew, that little old clapped-up Atlanta whore," and moved off purposefully, knifing through the slowly dispersing crowd, in the wake of Roger Hines, who moved crablike toward sanctuary.

Hines limped around to the side of the barracks and lowered himself in its shadow. He slipped out of his field jacket, laid it across his knees, and dug his shoulder blades into the wall. He shut his eyes. At once he opened them, sensing the intruder, and his stomach dipped in fear and anger as Frazier dropped to his knees and swung into position beside him.

"Doesn't he make your belly crawl?" Frazier said. "That patronizing so-and-so. 'Dorothy wouldn't like it. *Daaathy* wouldn't like it.' Who gives a shit what Dorothy likes? Of all the ways to appeal to a group of men to avoid the clap, that has to be the guaranteed worst. Dorothy! That paternal son of a bitch. Not only do we have Marse lookin' after us poor old disease-prone field hands, but Missy, too. . . . Did you know that Palmer was from Virginia?"

"I had no idea," Roger said loudly.

"A son of the Southland," Frazier said and produced a slow, confidential smile. "Like me. And Griever. With certain differences. . . . Who do you reckon has contracted the dread disease?"

"I have no idea," Roger said, and watched an image of himself rise lightly to its feet, stretch casually, and stride off sweat-free and unconcerned, into the sunlight; himself did not move.

"No idea," Frazier echoed. "I don't either but I can guess pretty well where they got it. The Mayfair. Julian's. The Star. You been to town yet, Hines?"

"No."

Frazier produced a pack of cigarettes and offered one to Hines, who shook his head. Frazier lit his own. They sat side by side, their backs pressed against the boards. Frazier's face was turned toward Hines, who stared out in front of him, at some point in the grass, his glasses dangling from his hand. The flat tan profile did look reptilian, Frazier thought, but helpless (less a copperhead than a garter snake, or a frog), and he felt a faint twinge of disgust, but he did not turn away. "You're not missing much. A desiccated, soldier-hating hick town is all it is. I've been in only once myself. I usually get a lift into Atlanta over a week end. There's a nice little town. It's a hundred-fifty-mile drive, but it's worth the trouble. Takes your mind off this military horseshit for a while. Have you. . . ."

"I have never been to Atlanta either," Hines broke in. "I have never left the post. I don't intend to. Look, is there anything I can do for you? Is there something you want?"

"Is there anything you. . . ." Frazier craned forward, and tried, without success, to meet Hines's eyes. "No, mister. There's nothing I can think of you can do for me. Nor is there a goddamn thing I want." He paused. "You know, you are about as unfriendly a cuss as I have ever met. You talk like a damn adding machine."

Still staring at nothing, Hines fell forward onto his knees, brought his uninjured leg forward, and prepared to rise.

Frazier's hand shot out and gripped his arm.

"No, look, Hines, I'm sorry I said that. It's the damn heat, makes a dumb rebel like me forget his manners. Maybe it affects you the same way. Why don't you just sit tight, and let's chat a while."

With a dull, pained look, Hines brought his eyes to the hammy hand that clutched his biceps, the thumb and forefinger not quite meeting around the bunched green cloth of his sleeve. Frazier looked at it too. Slowly, elaborately, he removed his hand, but did not otherwise move. Hines remained on his knees, poised; his eyes were still glued to that spot on his upper arm. It takes as much energy right now to stay as to go, he thought; but he did not move. The apology hung new and sticky between them, as if to have insulted him and then recanted gave Frazier a hold he could have achieved no other way. He felt he had to remain now, although he dreaded the encounter not less—more. He replaced his glasses and propelled himself awkwardly backward. His helmet liner clunked on the tops of his frames, and his back banged into the wall.

"I noticed you noticing the ring!" Frazier said. He flashed the fingers of the offending hand, and for the first time Hines saw the school ring. I noticed no ring, he thought, but held his peace.

"Jefferson College. Best four years of my life. You know, they pulled me off KP here one afternoon to do some typing in the orderly room, and I got a look at the company records. A pre-signal group is supposed to be hand-picked for brains over brawn, but I counted five college graduates in the whole damn company. Three besides you and me. That's probably why I'm always busy sniffin' around for somebody to talk to. A whole company of crackers and Brooklyn boys is pretty rough on a snob like me. That's why I come messin' with you every once in a while, although it's pretty obvious you like your privacy."

Hines remained silent.

"The Army's not much of a place for privacy," Frazier went on. "Or any of the other comforts. My idea is that while I'm hooked I'll give it all I've got for the two lousy years, but I feel only pity for the poor bastards that join up, whatever their reasons. Things can never be that bad. Take that Brown. I got a look at his record, too. He's an eighteen-year-old enlistee, lives about fifty miles from here. He probably joined so he could get the hell out of Georgia. Naturally he winds up down here, being shit all over, and with his kind of luck he'll pull a permanent assignment in the South. He's a rare bird, though. I figure it would be the same for him anywhere. What do you make of him?"

"What?"

"That Brown. What do you make of him?"

Hines made a quick-jerking movement with his shoulders, and continued to stare straight ahead. Frazier was seriously annoyed, but he masked it; he would have to force it a little now.

"I've got a theory about that boy. Not a theory, just a couple of ideas. I maintain he's got a special quality, something that begs to be kicked around, if you know what I mean, and the capacity to seem to enjoy it, after it happens. This makes him a pretty handy item to have around a basic-training camp. On the one hand he makes it easy for the cadre—he's a symbol of the company, and therefore a handy whipping boy. They lay into him whenever anything goes wrong, or even when nothing does, just to keep the company on its toes. On the other hand, the men ride him because they've got to ride somebody, and here's this fella who is askin' for it. So he's not only our lightning rod, he's also our punching bag, gettin' it from both ends. It's like he went around wearin' a sign sayin' 'Kick me.' The point is, it's not a racial thing. I've noticed Negroes hop on him as often as anybody else. Northerners too, like Braun and Cherry. I'm inclined to believe it's got nothing to do with his color at all. Do you go along with that?"

Still Hines did not speak. You're built for guilt, you black fool, he had thought to himself that morning, trapped on the toilet seat by the man he had maligned by labeling him the worst enemy (for his worst enemy was the man he had until today so carefully, instinctively avoided, the man who pinioned and tormented him with such elaborate civility now). You're built for guilt you black fool because you are foolish, and black, and there is no deadlier combination and somewhere in here might lie a modicum of (intellectual) agreement with what Frazier had said, but he would never probe for it now. He shrugged a second time.

So Frazier marshaled his patience, and shifted his ground. His irritation was intense, but he was determined to elicit some response. To simply have Hines listening to him (once his goal) was no longer enough.

"Tell me, Hines, have you ever been South before?"

"No."

"Don't you have any curiosity about what it might be like in town?"

Hines turned to him for the first time. He met Frazier's blue, violent, impatient eyes, belying the mildness of his tone, and the sudden surge of anger melted to fear, and hardened again. All right! he thought. If it is something he wants so bad.

"I happen to be a Negro," Hines said loudly. "I have no curiosity about what it would be like to go into town."

Frazier smiled. "Well, now I know you're a Negro," he said. "Give me that much credit. I thought for that reason, as an *educated* Negro, you would want to go in and have a look around. In order to get the picture. I would take you in myself, if you could stand my company."

"What picture are you talking about?"

Frazier looked surprised. "What picture? The racial picture. Seeing firsthand what a man has to put up with in the South if he happens to be a black man. What you probably meet up with from time to time yourself. Don't tell me you haven't run into prejudice up North? Or in the Army?"

"Very little," Hines said. "Virtually none." He removed the liner, and drew his sleeves across the drops of sweat that stood out along the hairline. The long wool underwear itched unbearably. He looked at his watch, but it would not save him: ten minutes remained to the lunch hour. He decided to save himself. "I think I'm going to take a walk," Hines said.

"Wait!" Frazier said. "Let me just tell you something about myself. I see you're tense, and there's no need to be. Do you know what I was at college? Nothin' but a glad-handin', bird-brained fraternity boy, right into my senior year, and then one day the roof came down. I still couldn't tell you how or why it happened. There I was, boozin', and generally raisin' hell and not givin' a damn, and then there I was dropped from my fraternity for soundin' off against the bias clauses in the charter, damn near kicked out of school, losin' all my friends, and receivin' all kinds of strikin' notes in my mailbox. I just woke up knowin' one day, in spite of everythin' I'd ever been taught, that the Negro was as good as me, or would be, given half the chance, and if the sons of bitches I grew up with wanted to call me nigger lover, well frig 'em, I learned to take it as a compliment. I took sides in a fracas or two . . . hell, I won't bore you with the details. I was drafted soon after, and here I am, talkin' to you. Rather, tryin' to. I can understand your reservations, but now you know. That all makes some difference, doesn't it?"

"Yes," said Hines.

"You're from New York, aren't you?"

"Yes."

"That makes you the first Northern Negro I've ever had the opportunity to talk to. Although I've been doin' most of the talkin'. I've been thinkin' of settlin' in New York, after my discharge. Sever connections with the Dark Ages, in a manner of speakin'. Maybe get some kind of job workin' with race relations. Tell me a little somethin' about the life up there."

There has to be some basis, some fact or facts from which he takes off, thought Hines. He cannot have created, wholly from malice, such a sickly, elaborate lie.

"I see you're interested in the Negro Problem," Hines said.

"Why, hell, yes. Haven't I just been. . . ."

"I don't happen to share your interest."

"What?"

"I said I don't happen to share your interest. I have no desire to listen to your theories on Brown, or on anything else. No doubt it's rare and admirable for you to take such an interest. It's also excellent that you feel the need to broaden your horizons, and get the Northern Negro's point of view. Well, I must tell you you've chosen badly. I went to school with a brilliant boy from Chicago, a Phi Beta Kappa as black as the night, with racial consciousness and theories up to here, one of which was that you were obliged to reclaim individual white Southerners where you found them, and that's the man you want a conversation with. But so far fate has been kind.

I have no intention of going into town and be treated as something different from a human being, although I suspect you might enjoy seeing that. I have no desire to be considered representative of a so-called ethnic group I feel no allegiance for. I have no stomach for being patronized, as you're patronizing me now. You've made a mistake. Whatever it is you want, you'd do better to look someplace else."

Frazier knew that this was not the case. He had what he wanted right here.

"If every Negro was as sensitive as you are," he said reasonably, "y'all might just as well clear some timberland and run up a flag. I'm not Uncle-Tommin' you, Hines, although you seem to have got that impression. I'm talkin' to you man to man. You can't help bein' what you are, you know that, but there's no need being ashamed of it, either. That's what the damn fight's about. Equal opportunity for all, regardless. When you say you're not interested in the Negro Problem, well now that's a lot of shit. You people have got to quit runnin' to extremes; bein' so damn conscious of your color that you think of nothin' else, or tryin' to pretend there's no difference between black and white at all. The point is the difference is there all right, but it shouldn't matter. Shit, Hines, I didn't mean to hurt your feelings, and I sure as hell wasn't Uncle-Tommin' you as you seem to think. I was only interested in gettin' your slant on things."

"You have it," Roger said. He struggled to his feet and stared down at Frazier. "You have my slant. I want to be left alone. If there is one thing that interests me less than the Negro Problem, it's you. My only concern is how to cope with the Army. I don't need your help and I don't want your interest. So for the few weeks that are left, please find someone else to chase around and interview, and leave me alone."

While his usual pre-cut, strident delivery marked this speech, and his expression hardly changed, Hines's frail body trembled; for a second Frazier thought the boy might attack him, and he had to fight a smile. He could murder him, break him like a black, withered branch—and he would. But Hines made no such move. Frazier tipped the liner back onto his head and said, "Take care of your leg now, you wouldn't want it to get any worse than it already is," and Hines turned suddenly, wrenched himself around and started for the front of the barracks, limping more heavily than he needed to; for Frazier's benefit? he wondered bitterly; his own? and loathing them both as he stepped out into the bright, merciless sunlight.

Around the corner from this painful private conversation Divino frolicked before an eager, sizable audience, his own men mostly, with a few interested additions from other platoons. He clowned with a limber marionette fierceness, a puppet gone loose and unstrung with humor and jerked now by its own residual showmanship, spinning and buckling and roaring and miming through the complex comic routines it seemed he

would have needed to rehearse for, recruiting from the ranks indiscriminately as he re-required them the "volunteers," the sometimes willing and
the more often wary (but the only risk that any ran was ridicule). On week
ends he had his favorites (packing the Ford full with them Saturday noon
and sparing them the inconvenience of the bus ride into town—foregoing
the dollar a head other car-owning cadre charged, but screening applicants
with a lot more care), but never in the field, and so in the field during a
break, or during lunch hour, he could admit to his bias (rather glory in it)
and lose nothing but gain (if he had made this calculation) in stature and
appeal. This was one of the few comic devices he repeated during the
course of any cycle, the one he repeated now, cutting short a highly successful imitation of Sergeant Braun to lean suddenly backward and propel
his maimed left hand into the air and rotate it lethargically clockwise in a
limp-wristed parody of the military "Assemble!", but there was no
mockery in his face or tone:

"All wops assemble on me! Assemble! Assemble! All wops assemble!"
in the voice of command they knew could dissolve at once into lisp or
laugh or ladylike plea, as he charged up the barracks steps and waited at a
height to be obeyed. Five men pushed to the front of the crowd to join the
three already there. All of them had, at one time or another, been chauf-
feured by him into town, and six of them were members of his platoon.

"Now, you wops," he began. ". . . We all wops here?"

About half of the fifty men chorused jocular yeas and nays.

"All right. I want to know if you hear that dripping? That's my ass
bleeding for you. This here is no place for wops, especially if they have a
little character. A wop with character should be doing midnight push-ups
around the clock and collecting his twenty-six-a-week job insurance and
not be out here soldiering. The Army was made for men, not wops. But I
want you all to get something straight. We all wops here? I want you to
know that a wop gets a fair shake in Divino's platoon. Not that a wop
won't soldier, and not that a wop won't sweat, but he gets taken care of.
On the other hand, every ass which is not a wop ass is in a sling. I'm going
to jump it and I'm going to stomp it. It gets no favors and it probably gets
persecuted. This is the message. Any questions? Any of you dumb wop
bunnies got any questions?"

Somebody did. Somebody spotted a shuffling, muttering Brown (freshly
risen from the grass where Griever had sprawled him) moving aimlessly
toward the bleachers, about thirty yards out from Divino's group, and
somebody said, "Ask Brown is he a wop?" with an oily anticipation and
Divino, unpredictable, complied. He brought his hands to his mouth and he
megaphoned *"Brown!"*

The boy twisted to the sound his black mask of fear, and (when he saw
from whom it came) indignation. He would not allow Divino to join (at
this late date) the ranks of his persecutors, the one cadreman who had not,

in six weeks, taken advantage of (or created) the opportunity to molest
him. "Come on now, damn you mother, you messed your chance up long
before," he whispered righteously. "It too late in the day for you to start to
pick on me now." With sudden hopelessness, despairing of his internal
logic the moment he had worked it out, as he had been forced that morning
to waive the hope of marshaling an external one, to squeeze in the latrine
from the boy he thought he could talk to (for Copperhead was not only
bright, he was a Negro, too) only a worthless, a lying reply. Man, he *didn't*
like to be always picked on (like Copperhead said), this was no help, this
was nothing but a lie. Yet here he was about to be tripped up again (and
from a brand-new source) minutes after lifting himself from the floor. All
he wanted was to walk out to the bleachers to sit still until Braun's whistle
blew, to be left by himself, and he didn't move or speak for fully five
seconds after the sergeant's sharp command: "Brown, come double-timin'
up here."

"If you don't mind, Sahgt Divina, I got myself enough trouble right
now."

"Get your miserable tail on up here!"

So then at a shuffling trot, mouth working, face lowered, Brown moved
up to and through the crowd which opened for him until he stood at the
bottom step at a form of attention and Divino, hands on cartridge belt and
legs spread wide, looked at him from above.

Divino's wild laugh burst into the new silence, and as suddenly was
gone. Then the sergeant was not standing but sitting on the top step,
leaning toward Brown, speaking conversationally so that the back rows had
to crowd in and strain to hear:

"Carver, we got a little problem here that requires your expert help. You
a wop?"

"What you mean?"

"I mean are you a wop," Divino said softly. "Like me and most of these
other gentlemen here. Are you a wop is what I mean."

"Sahgt, I don't know," Carver whined. "I ain't never thought none about
it."

"Well you start thinking now," Divino said gently.

"Theah ain't no nigger wops," Griever said scornfully. He had ambled
over to join the fun, and pushed up front, when Divino hailed Brown.

The sergeant stared for some seconds at the newcomer; then rose wearily
from the top stair, removed his helmet liner, and placed it over his heart.
His exaggerated, imperfect accent did more for the calculated effect than a
flawless one could have. "Now, Tennessee, suppose yo keep yo cotton-
pickin' opinions locked up inside yo cotton-pickin' face. Unless yo want
you dumb rebel ass down here on the floor givin' me twenty-five. *Why,
goddamit, man, you all ain't even in my platoon!"* He leveled his left index
finger at Griever in this devastating revelation. Then he seemed to forget
Griever, and stared at his fist. He opened it slowly, and held it out before

his face, the hand so carefully concealed for almost six weeks that only three of the trainees ever knew, spread his fingers wide, and raised them over his head. With his right hand he replaced the helmet liner, and then rested the hand on the shoulder of Brown.

"Gentlemen, have you got any idea where Sergeant Divino's ring finger is? Anybody got any ideas?" If any man did, he held his peace. "I see I got to tell you. I left it in Korea, fighting the common enemy, where all the jackoffs go. Sergeant Braun has already notified you jackoffs where you go if you don't shape up. You go to Korea to fight the common enemy and protect democracy, like I say. I been there. I froze my ass in winter and I broiled it in summer and I got out in one piece and I killed my share of gooks, but I left the live ones a souvenir. So hear this. The next jackoff who pops off about who is a wop and who ain't, which jackoff ain't even in my platoon, is going to wish he was stationed right now in his underwear on the thirty-eighth parallel, because that's how hot I intend to make it for him. Is that understood? Now Brown, one more time, are you a wop?"

He was prepared now, having sniffed in Divino's attitude the possibility of reprieve, a situation different from the blind alleys he was accustomed to (with Cherry and the others) where the contact itself was as good as the persecution: he had researched, holding his body rigid as he turned his head so as not to disturb Divino's hand on his shoulder, and he had inquired (with little hope), and had miraculously received a reply (while Divino enlarged on his missing digit) from the boy behind. So he thought he knew the issue now (a wop was an "Eyetalian"), and he thought he had a chance.

"Sahgt," he said, "my folks was never wops, but I b'lieve I might be a wop at heart."

Divino swept off his orange liner and slammed it against the railing. Brown recoiled. "There ain't no wops at heart except *wops!*" Divino roared. "You understand that, mother? Now I get the impression you don't even know what a wop is because I just heard you askin' that goofball behind. I'm going to inform you what makes a wop, and then you're going to make up your mind. Either you are one or you ain't. And if you ain't. . . ." The threat dissolved into high, demoniac laughter, in which the crowd joined. Divino's audience had doubled since he summoned Brown. He did not ignore it. He talked to be heard by the back rows now, although right at Brown:

"Now listen good. You're walkin' down a motherin' street at two o'-motherin'-clock in the morning. It's dark as a coal miner's ass; you ain't never seen it this dark. You got no idea where you are, you can't get off this street, you don't know how you're gonna get home. It ain't quiet. All around you in the dark you hear strange noises, people whisperin' or yellin' in gook, except once in a while you can make out your name. Now are you scared, or ain't you?"

There was, he decided dolefully, no right reply. He was in as much trouble (contrary to his earlier impression) as if Cherry were doing the baiting, or Griever, or Braun. Maybe more. He couldn't understand Divino at all. It made as much sense as anything else to give a direct, honest reply.

"Man, you right I'm scared," he said. "I never liked it in the dark."

"Good!" Divino said. "Good, you're scared. Now listen. All at once a door opens on that dark street, and there is a nice warm piece of light where there wasn't none before. And back in there your shiverin', shakin' tail beholds a clean double bed with the covers turned back and a long cool rye and ginger and a wide-screen television set. And into the ee-luminated doorway blockin' your vision pops a big fat momma. . . . You like a big fat momma, Brown?"

"Yes, sahgt," Brown said morosely. He wondered vaguely what color that big fat momma might be, and felt a sharp new twinge of fear.

But Divino said, "Good. You're doing fine. Well, now, Momma knows when you're about to come pussyfootin' down that dark street because you're so scared you give off a stink, and she's lookin' out for you anyway. And she looks at you and she gives you the finger and the big hip and she says, 'Gohge Wash'ton Cahver Brown, honey, you my man. You's my tub-thumpin' dickslingin' happiness man. Listen to me, sugah. You all have wandered smack onto Crud Alley, out of which hardly a man leaves alive because that is the way things are run heah. Y'all got a very slim chance to excape which all depends on how quick you decide to cut a chogy because th' impohtant thing is speed, but theah ain't no guarantees, even if you was to start leavin' ten minutes ago. Y'all in a peck o'trouble, honey, and I want you to stop in heah and try to fohget it for a while,' and she opens that housecoat, Brown, and damn if she is wearin' a motherin' thing in the way of ladies' underwear. You with me up to here, you dumb bunny?"

"I understand, sahgt," Brown said.

"All right. So you got a problem. Because just then a red light flashes on down the road a piece, and it says 'This Way To The Exit' and it flashes off again. And it flashes on. Then it flashes off. Now that light wasn't there before, and maybe it will never be there again, and you know your chances of gettin' out are slim anyway because Fat Momma told you so. You're breathin' hard. You look at Fat Momma. She looks at you. You look at the sign. It blinks back at you. You're sweatin'. You're thinkin'. You got a big decision to make. All right, Brown, what's it gonna be?"

"How you mean, sahgt?"

"What you mean how I mean? You dumb bunny, you gonna slip it to the lady between the clean sheets like she is askin' or you gonna tuck it between your chicken legs and haul ass for the exit sign?"

He was dumb, but he was not that dumb. This time he read the signs. He knew well what Divino wanted him to say, but he still did not know what would happen to him if he said it—whether Divino was on his side or was his enemy, like the rest. But if the sergeant was out to get him, he reasoned, he would get him no matter what; oddly, this line of thought soothed him. He would tell the sergeant what the sergeant so obviously wanted to hear.

"Sahgt Divina, I guess I'd just as soon knock off that piece," and recoiled again as Divino's hand shot toward him, but only to clap him on the shoulder just before Divino shouted at the crowd:

"Look at him! A true-blue wop! A wop's wop. Right?" To the first few rows: "Graziano? Boccia? He's a wop, ain't he? You a wop, ain't you, Brown?"

"I guess so, sahgt."

"You *guess* so? You *guess* so! Get down there and give me ten, you mother." And when Brown dropped to the ground and laboriously began the push-ups Divino straddled him, and just then caught sight of Cherry, exiting from the mess hall. So he leapt back up the stairway and stood looking down at Brown.

"Don't get up!" Divino roared. "You done your ten like a girl scout, but don't get up till we count the small change. Castelli, what's that fell out of that man's pocket?" while Cherry limped easily toward the orderly room.

"Nothin', sarge."

"Pennies! Did you say pennies? Brown, you jackoff, troublemaking sonofabitch, did you bring pennies out here onto the training field for me to bend for with my war wounds?" Divino whooped like a man in battle or pain, changed it to a high staccato giggle while Carver trembled below him and Cherry stopped finally, turned his head, and winged the hate over the yards like a shaft of light coning from his eyes.

So Divino breathed it. He stopped the noisemaking, and the antics, and he breathed it, what he had elicited for the second, the fifth, or the thousandth time. It was all he wanted now or ever from the Cherrys, the knowledge he was limned in spades for them (Divino!) to know they knew that from the civilian crazy core of him he hated their souls. Needing no crisis, no confrontation, no mundane test of strength (because he knew they feared him, would always fear him, and needed one less); he needed only this periodic (and mutual) affirmation of their polarity: that on a barren bloody peninsula blasting gooks with no names he could muster no love for, or in a basic-training camp crapping on people he sweated and created for eight weeks, Divino was Divino, Cherry was Cherry, and being in the Army changed nothing important, did not shape the guts of a man.

So once again he had it on record, where he had to have it, and he made no more noise. He spun the instant Cherry did, and he disappeared into the barracks, leaving Brown stretched face to the ground and the disappointed crowd to wait for Braun's whistle, and he stalked into the latrine and he urinated, neatly and accurately, for he knew the captain planned to inspect the barracks that afternoon.

They screw their own, he thought. The image of the clean, delicate, wiry

Captain Palmer burned through him now, and himself on hands and knees beside two corporals, three sergeants, and two other Sfc's, scrubbing amidst a sea of suds at a wooden barracks floor while Palmer hovered briefly and scolded and warned it would happen again, oh, yes, men, with all the stripes and ribbons and purple hearts they had between them it would happen again if in future a group was allowed to move on with dust on the rifle racks and an ink spot on the floor—scrubbing the barracks floor and choking on it, a far more damaging indignity than being shot at even (because that was what you were there for): they screw their own, he thought, and then he amended: that's only statistics, they screw everybody and their own are around longer; this the link between the Palmers and the Cherrys and the Browns and his own general unsuitability. And suddenly after six crazy years he *knew* it, there in the latrine, that the battle was over; that it was not enough for him (and never was) for the Cherrys to know that he was there; that when Palmer called him down in a week's time for the token reenlistment talk Sfc Divino would say, Captain, I'm twenty-eight years old, unskilled, I have nine fingers, and I'm bugging out back to my home town of Ohio to look for a job. Because I can deal with the Cherrys, and if not for the Cherrys maybe put up with the Palmers, but with the combination, no—there is no way to educate that pig except to kill him and there's no way to educate you, Captain, unless it's maybe to quit on you and make damn sure you know the reason why.

"*Screw everybody!*" he yelled suddenly, startling the barracks orderly who lay on his bed, in a half doze, near the door. "Get off that rack and pull it tight," Divino shouted at him. "You ain't no privileged character. Don't you know the old man is gonna inspect shit out of this place this afternoon?"

"You bet, sarge," the boy said nervously, but to Divino's back and the slam of the door. From the orderly-room steps Braun's whistle tweeted shrilly, the platoons assembled, and here began the unorthodox, ill-fated conclusion to the Wednesday afternoon.

Q7 loomed tall and complex over all of the low-slung, less ominous field, the whole brilliant in the afternoon sunlight under coats of fresh orange paint, uniformly applied. Signal Corps orange covered even the rapidly rotating legs (maintaining-one's-footing-on) set in Q7's foreshortened shadow, decorated the barrel-sized iron pipes through which the trainees would crawl, brightened all except the barbed wire strewn at random in the jump pit, and the hempen rope descending at a forty-five-degree angle from the top of Q7 and attached to an orange pole fifteen feet from the floor (this device providing the trainees with an option, having met the first half of Q7's challenge, on the means of returning to the ground). Repairs and refinements had accompanied the paint job, part of a major base-wide overhaul completed only that morning, and Captain Palmer's was the first unit called upon to cope with the course in all its refurbished glory.

Q7 naturally caused most trainee comment, a centrally located Brobdingnagian ladder, rungs five feet apart, gaudy pinnacle lost in the black blinding sunlight; to some a bona fide obstacle, to others a challenge, a lark to the few. Frazier mocked it; he was a monkey in high places. Hines, who had been excused, limped belatedly on the scene behind the two other members of the fifth platoon, regarded it briefly, gave thanks once more for his injured ankle, lowered himself in the shade of an evergreen, and tried to think about time: basic training would be over in two and a half weeks (he only half believed it), he would be granted a leave, and he would go on home.

The eight-man cadre dispersed itself strategically over the width of the field, determined to maintain order and enforce honesty, but a form of chaos reigned. There were too many obstacles and there were too many men going through. It was possible for the enterprising lazy, by combining adroit footwork with a moment of facile inattention, to move around and past an obstacle rather than over or through it, to join the disorderly queue which had just completed it, and move on to the next; or, in some cases, if an obstacle appeared particularly congenial, to double back on one's tracks and repeat it, for a good part of the training period. Thus it happened that Carver Brown, muttering but sharp-eyed, outfoxed Divino who was supposed to see that anyone who came his way took a running leap across the barbed-wire-strewn jump pit (Brown shuffled around it), crawled four times at his leisure through the thirty-foot pipes (and was apprehended the fifth time by the sergeant in charge, who imagined—and was appropriately vexed—that he had caught Brown trying to sneak through for a second time), avoided scaling a fifteen-foot wall which had no handholds, and spent a considerable portion of his time coping with his balance on the rapidly rotating logs. But when carried inevitably to the base of Q7, he was too outraged to scheme. He would not even concede that it was something he wished to avoid, this nightmare of height and risk and ridiculous unfunctional labor; he would not even honor it by subterfuge, and head down he charged past its base (ignoring even its underside where grouped briefly those who had most recently completed the descent), moving blindly, laterally, back toward the beginning, toward the sidelines, toward rest, toward at the very worst scraping his belly on the earthbound ragged insides of the orange pipes once more. And he would have made it too— would have seen confirmed (what he had just learned from Divino) that he could abandon fear and caution and still escape punishment, just as a thousand times in the past six weeks he had mobilized caution and fear in usually vain efforts to avoid it; that there was no sense in and no way of predicting anything in the mothering Army—because Cherry gazed skyward at the moment Carver fled, upward past the creeping climbing succession of figures, fighting the glare with hands over helmet liner and checking on Frazier's whoop of contempt and power as he straddled the topmost rung; looking up (Cherry) because the whoop could have meant that someone was in trouble up there, too. So it was not Cherry but Griever who shaped what was to come, one of many who saw and were amused by or else resented Brown's flight from what some of them feared and almost all were taxed by, it was Griever who yelled after him in the unmistakable accents of the land where both were born: "Brown, you buggin' out again? Trot yo' ass back here and up this thing!" And even that didn't stop him (because he knew it as the voice of Griever, who wielded a different kind of power), although it slowed him down, and Cherry caught him; Cherry sprung silently after him at a lightfooted limp and spun him around. The corporal didn't speak. He balled the back of the boy's sweat-drenched T-shirt in his fist and dragged and pushed him toward the waiting, growing crowd.

It was a reflex, not a plea: "Copul Cherry, naw!" in Q7's hot, odd-shaped shadow, touching distance from the bottom rung. Familiar ruddy fear replaced his indignation, flushing him clean, yet he did not really believe that he would have to climb the monstrous thing. Only his body knew: it quivered as never in the cool black mornings when the white man's razor flashed before his eyes in a cruel burlesque he was not even aware of, as it never did when he was faced by the venom of Griever, or the torments of Braun, as it had never reacted before. Elaborately Cherry released his hold on the sweatshirt and put Brown away from him like a slug, a thing picked crawling from his flesh, his mask of unfeigned disgust having its effect on the watchers, but completely lost on Brown.

" 'Copul Cherry, naw!' " Cherry mimed fiercely. "Naw, copul, don't make my shiverin' shakin' bugout ream-my-buddy yellow tail go climbin' up that big old ladder. Let everybody else do it, not me. You are a cowardly, worthless, cheating sonofabitch, you *hear* me, Brown? You been under my skin ever since this cycle began, you're not fitten to be a soldier. If I have to take any more shit from you I'm gonna puke all over the field. Now move out. Climb. Hand over foot. Foot over hand. We'll all be down here rootin' for you. Climb."

"When I'm up high my haid spins, copul, I mean it now I never was no good at gettin' up onto high places evah since I was a baby I fell off a porch and opened my haid took twelve stitches. Copul Cherry, please I'll KP ever night for you and straighten up my area. . . . Shit, man, I can't climb that motherin' thing."

One man laughed. The rest were carried blankly, smoothly, on the music of the whine. Q7 stood bare, the last man having chosen the rope-pole route and shimmied to the ground. Behind Brown the crowd swelled, some men approaching for their second turn.

"Climb," Cherry said.

"Copul, if you listen. . . ."

"Climb," Cherry said. "I'm giving you a direct order. I've stopped my playing around. You know what a direct order is, you've learned that much. So you go ahead and climb."

"Copul, I'll never make it. . . ."

"Climb!" Cherry screamed. He sneered at Brown's recoil, but abruptly altered his tone. "Concentrate on what you're doin' at all times. Don't look up and don't look down. Keep your eyes glued to the individual rung you are working on and move. Now move out! Move out, you chicken bastard! Move out!" And he was not even sure that Cherry had not taken a step toward him; he was ten feet off the ground reaching for the third orange block before he realized he had begun the ascent and scrambled up still another before his momentum went, and he looked below him at the up-turned sun-drenched faces, and started back down.

"Don't come down!" Cherry shouted. "Go on up! You're doin' fine. Climb, climb, climb, or I will cut your chicken heart out," Cherry sing-songed, reaching into his pocket, "I just sharpened it this morning." And Brown did climb, clambered upward, to his own shock and surprise, driven now not by unchanneled fear but the image of Cherry's razor, catching the sunlight (although he had never seriously considered that the corporal would cut him before). He climbed, using to good advantage the vertical center strut, suddenly deliberate and almost cool, talking himself up a rung and then a rung more, watching his hands (but not his legs), hand, leg, hand until finally above him was one orange rung, and above that was space, and broad sunwashed sky. There was no longer anything to reach for; he had a moment of panic, shut his eyes tight, and it passed. "Man, this is the top," he said aloud. "You done come to the top. Don't look down, Brown," he sang to himself. "Start on down, Brown, down Brown, to the motherin' bottom," he sang, and from below came a rich cry: "Atta boy, wop," and it moved him, hands gripping the center strut which extended a yard past the topmost rung; he thought that Sahgt Divina, he not such a bad old mother, he don't give George Washington hardly ever no trouble at all, anxiety flicking at him suddenly as he saw the need for different techniques, a new approach, in the matter of coming down. I got to kneel first, it suddenly occurred to him and slowly he inched his hands along the top beam, leaving it reluctantly, with great care, for the center pole, began to bend his knees, the left one pressed firmly against the strut and then (like a sonbitchin' ghost, he thought, not wondering how Cherry, with only his hands, was able or needed to achieve the banshee megaphone effect when he had heard Divino's voice only seconds before sounding loud and clear): "Browwwwwn. Yoooo don't come dowwwwwn yet. Stay right there. Yooo climb ooooover the top and you come dowwwwwn on the ooooother siiiide, the oooother siiide, Browwwwn. Ooooover the top. No goddamn cheeeeting, you understand? Do it right now or your ass is miiine, you hear me Browwwwn?"

Please, you mother fucker, Brown said to himself, and brought his right knee down flush with his left, his hands above his head and off to the left clutching at the center bar, a tableau of anguish, or prayer.

The echoic quality had gone. "Brown, I'm coming up. I'm on the way up and I'm going to toss you over the top if you don't straighten up and do it by yourself. Get up off your knees. Don't look down. I'm climbin' up to get you. You feel it shakin'? You feel the pole shakin', Brown?"

He thought he felt the pole shaking. Sweat dribbled off his forehead and ran into his eyes. "Naw!" he yelled. "Don't you come up! I'm standin' up!" He felt giddy with shouting, although he knew with a strange certainty that he would not fall. Just hold tight, man, he said to himself. You keep your arms wrapped round that center pole nothing gonna happen, and he blinked the sweat out of his eyes, pulled himself slowly erect, and once again over Q7's summit he faced the blue, naked sky.

"Oooover the top," came the ghostly voice from below; wasn't it closer now? Wasn't Cherry on the way up to make sure that he obeyed "I *tole* you not to come up," Carver blubbered, and out of the sickening fear of Cherry behind him, and the expanse above (but Cherry behind him) he distilled enough crazy courage to work his hands once more above his head, to bear down on the flat smooth surface of the topmost bar, to pull and kick himself onto the summit—and he crouched there, clutching the yard-long extension of the center pole, all handholds below him, straddling the rung as Frazier had (in triumph) only moments before. From below came scattered cheers and ripples of applause. He heard them, and he knew what they were for: they were plaudits for Cherry, who even now scrambled up the ladder, five yards from him, a yard away, a foot away, and he sought the corporal, suddenly rigid with fear—down a rung, then two, then three, then drawn irresistibly in relief and terror he plunged his vision into the upturned faces, the pink and green (speckled with orange) sea. Naw! He shut his eyes. Almost immediately he opened them again, peered out past the training field, past the road, over the tops of giant firs and onto another road, a half-mile distant, where a doll-sized unit marched in ragged formation, rifles aslant, complete with its own limping stragglers, its own fifth platoon. Oh, Lawd! Carver said, I didn't mean to be up this high, and glued shut his eyes. He smacked his cheek into the grained wood, released his hold on the center strut, and gripped the surface with quivering forearms and thighs. He bruised the numb, fatty, uncomprehending flesh, ground the skin convulsively from the left side of his face, slavered, and suddenly relaxed, awaiting the conclusion of the dream.

Roger Hines did not move from his leafy shelter, the fir's concealing shade, but he craned forward and upward, caught his lower lip between his teeth, and amazed himself. *If he broke his foolish neck there would be much less unpleasantness then,* he thought, and rebuked himself at once, severely, and with a great deal of surprise. But it was easier then: *If he fell there would be lots less pressure then. Less stupidity, less viciousness; the two remaining weeks might see this place a country club,* and once again inflicted a reprimand, experienced a guiltless rush of surprise. I shouldn't feel this way, he thought, and stopped feeling any way; his eyes traveled the length of the ladder, from the pressing eager crowd upward to the motionless clutching Carver (the highest part of him his green protruding rump, a study in fear) and focused there.

"That boy is crucified up there," Frazier said aloud. "He *is* paying for the sins of Charlie Company." He looked around—was it possible that someone within earshot might be worthy of the conceit?—but no one had heard. What had happened to that stinking Hines, who would barely admit that he was alive? Was he taking all this in? It was he (with his bogus injury and phony detachment) who should be cringing and moaning at the top of the tower. Frazier searched the upturned faces of the crowd while Cherry bellowed through his paws, "Come on dowwwn, Browwwwn, all your friends waitin' on you down here," and Frazier gave it up finally and stared instead at the immobile animal sixty feet above the ground.

Divino performed a little jig, standing on the underside of the ladder, directly opposite Cherry, his hand gripping the bottom rung. He too stared into the sky. "You'd better go fetch him, corporal," Divino said. "It appears his belly is glued," and laughed a wild man's laugh which could have fooled no man who saw his eyes. Cherry ignored him. He backed off and shouted again, louder than before, and succeeded in disrupting Carver's dream.

"Come on down, you chicken bastard. I'm giving you three seconds to start coming down."

"Lawd, shut up that noisy sonbitch," Carver mumbled, from lips pressed out of shape against the grain.

"Maybe he's a cat," Divino suggested. "He can haul ass up a tree when he has to, but he don't have no notion how to come down. Now you got to call the fire department." The few who heard joined tentatively in his maniacal laughter.

The color went from Cherry's face. His eyes never left Brown as he unbuttoned his fatigue shirt and shucked out of it, took off his helmet liner. With a cat's grace, and its speed, he ascended Q7, embraced the supine Carver at the summit with consummate gentleness, talked lovingly into his ear, pried loose his hold, enveloped him with his presence, and brought him, guided him, carried him down. The crowd held its breath, and then cheered. On the ground again, disturbed, Carver sought to resume his jarred garbled dream. Cherry brought him to his feet. He would have slapped him if he had to, but Brown's eyes were wide. The left side of his face was scraped almost raw.

"You damn right you ain't gonna faint now," Cherry said. "You son of a bitch you just committed a court-martial offense, you know that?"

"I'm tired," Carver mumbled.

"You been messin' around and messin' around and makin' this company look like hell right from the beginnin' and lousin' up my platoon in particular, but you really stepped into it just now, soldier, you disobeyed a direct order and I'm gonna see it gets you ten years."

Brown wet his chin and rolled his eyes, from an older, more potent fear.

"I'm puttin' it to you now. You're getting another chance to go up this here ladder and come back down the right way, under your own power. Not to be carried down by a man with a game leg. Up, and down, and you're off my shitlist, that fast. You don't have no choice, buddy, I'm orderin' you up one more time."

"I can't sleep," Brown said.

"Whaaat? You can't do what? Why you lowlife bugout yellow trouble-making ugly sneaky crawling son of a bitch. You want to sleep? You want to sleep for the next twenty years in the stockade? I'm warning you. Climb!"

Called him everything but a nigger, Frazier thought. Even in that particular moment of stress. I have been right about it all the time.

What are they doing to him now, Hines wondered. He's down off it. I can't see a thing.

You got to kill them or quit on them, thought Divino. But you cannot kill them *and* quit on them. You cannot have it both ways.

Brown dreamed that Cherry shook him, and dragged him closer to the ladder, but he experienced no terror. Even when he began to climb he was not afraid, although he was surprised: you do any motherin' thing in a dream. Halfway up he misstepped and swayed forward through the bars, caught himself with a lazy drunken agility, twisted his body and (one at a time) his hands, and continued the ascent on the wrong, the other side. A few men cheered, with half a heart. Cherry fought for himself. "Now that was all right. You just saved yourself the trouble of crawlin' over the top. Hit the top and start comin' down," fighting the need to add "You hear me, Brown?" He lowered his head and this time caught Divino's beetling bright-eyed stare—raised his eyes in time to see Brown ignore instructions once again, and with a smooth, nonstop movement hoist himself onto Q7's top crossbar and once more straddle it, in reverse position this time, and lower his right cheek to the familiar comfort of the grain.

"He's gonna shave the other side now," Divino said. "He's shaping up. What a crazy wop. Come on down, wop," Divino called; but no one heard.

"All right," Cherry yelled. "Don't go to sleep up there one more time." He strove for volume only. "If I got to come up for you again. . . ." His voice gave out on the threat, and he hawked away the soreness. He sucked in his breath and held it, for the boy had begun to move: he raised himself slowly to his knees and lifted his arms and thought calmly if you reach for the pole Carver and hold tight nothin gonna happen, even in a motherin' dream, extended his arms off to the left where (on his first ascent) the center strut had been, closed his fingers, wrists, forearms on air, came lazily, lopsided to a crouch and toppled from the tower.

A few men yelled, "Look out!" but this was a warning, while he was still on the rise, groping for the pole, so that the descent was made in an eerie silence which he smashed himself on the four-foot orange hurdle that broke his back, caroming from here into the jump pit (the perils of which he had so recently avoided), slicing his contorted puffy face on the exposed barbed wire, and it was with the blood the noise began. Cherry did not contribute; was not among the first to race toward Brown's crumpled form; did just begin to move in that direction when he turned (realizing too late) to the hand gripping his shoulder and received two blows, a four-fingered fist at his temple and a whole one smashing with devastating effect into the base of his throat; while Frazier remained rooted for a moment, too: he stood on his toes and looked wildly around (while the object of his search was staggering from tree to tree on the perimeter, being sick on the move) and finally had to settle for an exasperated shout directed over the heads of the scampering heedless forms: *"Where is that antisocial Northern nigger? Is he still above it all now?"*

❖

Ivan Gold was born in New York City in 1932, has degrees from Columbia University and the School for Oriental and African Studies of the University of London, has lived in Japan, England, Sweden, and Spain, and now lives in New York. He has published only one book, Nickel Miseries *(1963), a collection of only five titles, but each of the four others was as original and nearly as effective as the story reprinted above.*

In "The Nickel Misery of George Washington Carver Brown" Ivan Gold presents the persecution and death of a man and offers the question: Who was responsible? The story shows how difficult it is to tell if the responsibility belongs to the system, to the victim himself, to the participants in the persecution, or to the observers who took no action. The Army system as such cannot be "right" or "wrong" in any moral sense: its rules and its methods of training men can be judged only as efficient or inefficient. And in the case of Brown, the inefficiency of the system in not making him a soldier cannot even be proved, for one Brown broken at the foot of a training tower may be more efficient for the Army's purpose than a live Brown on the battlefield endangering the lives of others with his fear and ineptitude. One of the purposes of discipline in the bureaucratic Army system is to internalize necessary patterns of behavior so that uniform, predictable results can be achieved without constant supervision. All, except Brown, abide by the spoken and unspoken rules of this complex organization; the episode of the pennies is a case in point, an example of the way in which secret rules of a particular bureaucratic system are taught and learned. Such subtleties are beyond Brown. A Negro "boy" coming out of the paternalistic system in the rural South, he has no way of grasping a situation in which he is not given direct orders. As he says to Corporal Cherry, if he'd just told *him to button his shirt pocket, he would have done it. The Army system, again like any modern bureaucratic system, requires each individual to find a role for himself, an identity or* persona *somewhere between the Army's ranks of undifferentiated followers-of-rules and his own concealed actual self. The others have found such roles for themselves, which allows them to perform their necessary duties and still maintain a sense of private individuality. But Brown, always caught between his hopes and his fears, has trouble "forming an attitude," never knows what kind of response or mode will work for him. Always either whining or joking, he can only project himself as either victim or clown, and his vacillating is interpreted by infuriated authority as either laughing at an order or complaining about a reprieve. Since he can never catch on to what is expected of him, his current fault becomes his manner of repairing his last fault: the GI shower of the night before leads to the button, which leads to the eggs, which leads on— eventually and inevitably—to the "freshly painted pinnacle of failure," the tower. But Brown's troubles really began, as Hines says, way back when he was born, "foolish and black, and there is no deadlier combination." It is just this deadly combination that Hines, by good luck and perseverance, has avoided. When Brown asks Hines why the company picks on him, his fellow Negro offers neither advice nor sympathy but says angrily, "Because you like it and you want them to." Brown denies this to himself later, for no man* wants *to be a victim; but he does think of himself as a victim (as being picked on), and it is at any rate too late for him now to establish any other role. It is necessary for both Hines and Frazier, if they are to preserve their own adopted roles, to believe that the scapegoat role is natural to Brown. Hines has chosen the role of the invisible Negro: he has, like the copperhead, a protective and concealing skin color that makes him less visible and noticeable than Brown; he uses this and his sprained ankle to stay out of trouble. ("Copperhead" was also the name for Confederate sympathizers in the North during the Civil War.) Hines cannot allow Frazier to involve him in discussions of Brown's situation, because any admission of common cause with Brown would be a direct threat to Hines's mode of survival, not simply an abstract intellectual position as it is with Frazier. For Frazier adopts a liberal enough role, but it is as a detached observer, theorizer, interpreter. He has to convince himself that Brown is being perse-*

cuted not because he is black but because he is a natural victim—otherwise Frazier's "fresh set of convictions" about the rights of Negroes would have to be tested. Sergeant Divino's role is that of the clown who is not a victim: his clowning mocks Cherry and Palmer and the others who comprise the regular Army system he hates, and it dissociates him from them. The elaborate hypothetical question he sets up to determine whether Brown is a "wop" is a kind of black parable, establishing the common humanity of all men. But Divino, even though he seemed more nearly free of the system than the others, is unable to assume responsibility for Brown or to protect him. He has the "divine" immunity of the clown, an individual mode he has created for himself, and it cannot be transferred to Brown any more than can the "invisible" immunity Hines has created for his own protection. For once again: Brown is both foolish and black.

After the "accident" Divino blames the nearest symbol of the system, lashing out at Cherry, and Frazier accuses Hines in the final lines; but the story has clearly shown that no one man—not Brown himself, not Hines or Frazier or Divino, not even Cherry or Griever, not the company as a whole, not the ineffectual captain and not the system—is singly to blame. It might seem that Gold, following the Jewish tradition of responsibility for fellow victims, is singling out the "copperhead" Hines, blaming him (through Frazier's accusations) for his "fifth platoon" attitude of holding himself apart from Brown and all that Brown represents. But, within each man's possibilities for action as Gold defines them, there are no more purposeful villains than purposeful heroes in this story. Perhaps the deepest tragedy made manifest by Brown's death occurs from the reader's sense that the iron law of dramatic inevitability devolves in modern times no longer from "the Gods" or from "Nature" (human or otherwise), but from the dreadful limitations put on man's possibilities for individual responsibility and individual action within a complex, all-inclusive bureaucratic system, requiring absolute obedience to impersonal, apparently arbitrary rules, the sole justification for which is the bureaucratic ideal itself: "efficiency." Again, though, it is not wholly the system that is presented as "to blame" —indeed, the story is not really about blame or guilt as such, but on a more general theme about the relation of responsibility to victimization. For if the roles of each of the characters were extended by interpretation, it would be clear how each plays an ever larger part in a story that always remains the same: Brown representing not only the persecuted Negro in the South, but the Negro in general, and finally all victimized men; Hines representing the failure of responsibility through self-preservation not only of the northern Negro but of the educated Negro, and finally of all educated men who hold themselves apart; Frazier representing the failed responsibility not only of the liberal southerner but of all liberals who fail to help, and finally of all those who hold humane beliefs but never act on them; Divino, as a fellow "wop," not only representing the failure of denigrated ethnic minorities to make common cause, but finally showing perhaps the failure of any man or all men of whatever sort to assume responsibility for every other man. The story thus stands as a little closed model of the perplexing relation between persecution and victimization on the one hand and responsibility on the other. It presents the dynamics of interrelationships between "victims," "persecutors," "bystanders," and "system" in a way that may be seen to be "eternal" and to apply to all cases of persecution, not just this one. But it does this by creating an entirely real experience of a specific set of characters in a fully realized time and place. In thus evoking a specific experience, with a meaning that is unique to the story and yet somehow has implications that are more general, this story—as much perhaps as any story in this anthology —thus does just what fiction ought to do.

JAMES BALDWIN

Sonny's Blues

◇◇◇◇◇◇◇◇

I READ ABOUT IT in the paper, in the subway, on my way to work. I read it, and I couldn't believe it, and I read it again. Then perhaps I just stared at it, at the newsprint spelling out his name, spelling out the story. I stared at it in the swinging lights of the subway car, and in the faces and bodies of the people, and in my own face, trapped in the darkness which roared outside.

It was not to be believed and I kept telling myself that, as I walked from the subway station to the high school. And at the same time I couldn't doubt it. I was scared, scared for Sonny. He became real to me again. A great block of ice got settled in my belly and kept melting there slowly all day long, while I taught my classes algebra. It was a special kind of ice. It kept melting, sending trickles of ice water all up and down my veins, but it never got less. Sometimes it hardened and seemed to expand until I felt my guts were going to come spilling out or that I was going to choke or scream. This would always be at a moment when I was remembering some specific thing Sonny had once said or done.

When he was about as old as the boys in my classes his face had been bright and open, there was a lot of copper in it; and he'd had wonderfully direct brown eyes, and great gentleness and privacy. I wondered what he looked like now. He had been picked up, the evening before, in a raid on an apartment downtown, for peddling and using heroin.

I couldn't believe it: but what I mean by that is that I couldn't find any room for it anywhere inside me. I had kept it outside me for a long time. I hadn't wanted to know. I had had suspicions, but I didn't name them, I kept putting them away. I told myself that Sonny was wild, but he wasn't crazy. And he'd always been a good boy, he hadn't ever turned hard or evil or disrespectful, the way kids can, so quick, so quick, especially in Harlem. I didn't want to believe that I'd ever see my brother going down, coming to nothing, all that light in his face gone out, in the condition I'd already seen so many others. Yet it had happened and here I was, talking about algebra to a lot of boys who might, every one of them for all I knew, be popping off needles every time they went to the head. Maybe it did more for them than algebra could.

I was sure that the first time Sonny had ever had horse, he couldn't have been much older than these boys were now. These boys, now, were living as we'd been living then, they were growing up with a rush and their heads bumped abruptly against the low ceiling of their actual possibilities. They were filled with rage. All they really knew were two darknesses, the darkness of their lives, which was now closing in on them, and the darkness of the movies, which had blinded them to that other darkness, and in which they now, vindictively, dreamed, at once more together than they were at any other time, and more alone.

When the last bell rang, the last class ended, I let out my breath. It seemed I'd been holding it for all that time. My clothes were wet—I may have looked as though I'd been sitting in a steam bath, all dressed up, all afternoon. I sat alone in the classroom a long time. I listened to the boys outside, downstairs, shouting and cursing and laughing. Their laughter struck me for perhaps the first time. It was not the joyous laughter which— God knows why—one associates with children. It was mocking and in- sular, its intent to denigrate. It was disenchanted, and in this, also, lay the authority of their curses. Perhaps I was listening to them because I was thinking about my brother and in them I heard my brother. And myself.

One boy was whistling a tune, at once very complicated and very simple, it seemed to be pouring out of him as though he were a bird, and it sounded very cool and moving through all that harsh, bright air, only just holding its own through all those other sounds.

I stood up and walked over to the window and looked down into the courtyard. It was the beginning of the spring and the sap was rising in the boys. A teacher passed through them every now and again, quickly, as though he or she couldn't wait to get out of that courtyard, to get those boys out of their sight and off their minds. I started collecting my stuff. I thought I'd better get home and talk to Isabel.

The courtyard was almost deserted by the time I got downstairs. I saw this boy standing in the shadow of a doorway, looking just like Sonny. I almost called his name. Then I saw that it wasn't Sonny, but somebody we used to know, a boy from around our block. He'd been Sonny's friend. He'd never been mine, having been too young for me, and, anyway, I'd never liked him. And now, even though he was a grown-up man, he still hung around that block, still spent hours on the street corners, was always high and raggy. I used to run into him from time to time and he'd often work around to asking me for a quarter or fifty cents. He always had some real good excuse, too, and I always gave it to him, I don't know why.

But now, abruptly, I hated him. I couldn't stand the way he looked at me, partly like a dog, partly like a cunning child. I wanted to ask him what the hell he was doing in the school courtyard.

He sort of shuffled over to me, and he said, "I see you got the papers. So you already know about it."

"You mean about Sonny? Yes, I already know about it. How come they didn't get you?"

He grinned. It made him repulsive and it also brought to mind what he'd looked like as a kid. "I wasn't there. I stay away from them people."

"Good for you." I offered him a cigarette and I watched him through the smoke. "You come all the way down here just to tell me about Sonny?"

"That's right." He was sort of shaking his head and his eyes looked strange, as though they were about to cross. The bright sun deadened his damp dark brown skin and it made his eyes look yellow and showed up the dirt in his kinked hair. He smelled funky. I moved a little away from him and I said, "Well, thanks. But I already know about it and I got to get home."

"I'll walk you a little ways," he said. We started walking. There were a couple of kids still loitering in the courtyard and one of them said good-night to me and looked strangely at the boy beside me.

"What're you going to do?" he asked me. "I mean, about Sonny?"

"Look. I haven't seen Sonny for over a year, I'm not sure I'm going to do anything. Anyway, what the hell *can* I do?"

"That's right," he said quickly, "ain't nothing you can do. Can't much help old Sonny no more, I guess."

It was what I was thinking and so it seemed to me he had no right to say it.

"I'm surprised at Sonny, though," he went on—he had a funny way of talking, he looked straight ahead as though he were talking to himself—"I thought Sonny was a smart boy, I thought he was too smart to get hung."

"I guess he thought so too," I said sharply, "and that's how he got hung. And now about you? You're pretty goddamn smart, I bet."

Then he looked directly at me, just for a minute. "I ain't smart," he said. "If I was smart, I'd have reached for a pistol a long time ago."

"Look. Don't tell *me* your sad story, if it was up to me, I'd give you one." Then I felt guilty—guilty, probably, for never having supposed that the poor bastard *had* a story of his own, much less a sad one, and I asked, quickly, "What's going to happen to him now?"

He didn't answer this. He was off by himself some place. "Funny thing," he said, and from his tone we might have been discussing the quickest way to get to Brooklyn, "when I saw the papers this morning, the first thing I asked myself was if I had anything to do with it. I felt sort of responsible."

I began to listen more carefully. The subway station was on the corner, just before us, and I stopped. He stopped, too. We were in front of a bar and he ducked slightly, peering in, but whoever he was looking for didn't seem to be there. The juke box was blasting away with something black and bouncy and I half watched the barmaid as she danced her way from the juke box to her place behind the bar. And I watched her face as she laughingly responded to something someone said to her, still keeping time to the music. When she smiled one saw the little girl, one sensed the doomed, still-struggling woman beneath the battered face of the semi-whore.

"I never *give* Sonny nothing," the boy said finally, "but a long time ago I come to school high and Sonny asked me how it felt." He paused, I couldn't bear to watch him, I watched the barmaid, and I listened to the music which seemed to be causing the pavement to shake. "I told him it felt great." The music stopped, the barmaid paused and watched the juke box until the music began again. "It did."

All this was carrying me some place I didn't want to go. I certainly didn't want to know how it felt. It filled everything, the people, the houses, the music, the dark, quicksilver barmaid, with menace; and this menace was their reality.

"What's going to happen to him now?" I asked again.

"They'll send him away some place and they'll try to cure him." He shook his head. "Maybe he'll even think he's kicked the habit. Then they'll let him loose"—he gestured, throwing his cigarette into the gutter. "That's all."

"What do you mean, that's *all?*"

But I knew what he meant.

"I *mean,* that's *all.*" He turned his head and looked at me, pulling down the corners of his mouth. "Don't you know what I mean?" he asked, softly.

"How the hell *would* I know what you mean?" I almost whispered it, I don't know why.

"That's right," he said to the air, "how would *he* know what I mean?" He turned toward me again, patient and calm, and yet I somehow felt him shaking, shaking as though he were going to fall apart. I felt that ice in my guts again, the dread I'd felt all afternoon; and again I watched the barmaid, moving about the bar, washing glasses, and singing. "Listen. They'll let him out and then it'll just start all over again. That's what I mean."

"You mean—they'll let him out. And then he'll just start working his way back in again. You mean he'll never kick the habit. Is that what you mean?"

"That's right," he said, cheerfully. "*You* see what I mean."

"Tell me," I said at last, "why does he want to die? He must want to die, he's killing himself, why does he want to die?"

He looked at me in surprise. He licked his lips. "He don't want to die. He wants to live. Don't nobody want to die, ever."

Then I wanted to ask him—too many things. He could not have answered, or if he had, I could not have borne the answers. I started walking. "Well, I guess it's none of my business."

"It's going to be rough on old Sonny," he said. We reached the subway station. "This is your station?" he asked. I nodded. I took one step down. "Damn!" he said, suddenly. I looked up at him. He grinned again. "Damn it if I didn't leave all my money home. You ain't got a dollar on you, have you? Just for a couple of days, is all."

All at once something inside gave and threatened to come pouring out of me. I didn't hate him any more. I felt that in another moment I'd start crying like a child.

"Sure," I said. "Don't sweat." I looked in my wallet and didn't have a dollar, I only had a five. "Here," I said. "That hold you?"

He didn't look at it—he didn't want to look at it. A terrible closed look came over his face, as though he were keeping the number on the bill a secret from him and me. "Thanks," he said, and now he was dying to see me go. "Don't worry about Sonny. Maybe I'll write him or something."

"Sure," I said. "You do that. So long."

"Be seeing you," he said. I went on down the steps.

And I didn't write Sonny or send him anything for a long time. When I finally did, it was just after my little girl died, he wrote me back a letter which made me feel like a bastard.

Here's what he said:

Dear brother,

You don't know how much I needed to hear from you. I wanted to write you many a time but I dug how much I must have hurt you and so I didn't write. But now I feel like a man who's been trying to climb up out of some deep, real deep and funky hole and just saw the sun up there, outside. I got to get outside.

I can't tell you much about how I got here. I mean I don't know how to tell you. I guess I was afraid of something or I was trying to escape from something and you know I have never been very strong in the head (smile). I'm glad Mama and Daddy are dead and can't see what's happened to their son and I swear if I'd known what I was doing I would never have hurt you so, you and a lot of other fine people who were nice to me and who believed in me.

I don't want you to think it had anything to do with me being a musician. It's more than that. Or maybe less than that. I can't get anything straight in my head down here and I try not to think about what's going to happen to me when I get outside again. Sometime I think I'm going to flip and *never* get outside and sometime I think I'll come straight back. I tell you one thing, though, I'd rather blow my brains out than go through this again. But that's what they all say, so they tell me. If I tell you when I'm coming to New York and if you could meet me, I sure would appreciate it. Give my love to Isabel and the kids and I was sure sorry to hear about little Gracie. I wish I could be like Mama and say the Lord's will be done, but I don't know it seems to me that trouble is the one thing that never does get stopped and I don't know what good it does to blame it on the Lord. But maybe it does some good if you believe it.

Your brother,
Sonny

Then I kept in constant touch with him and I sent him whatever I could and I went to meet him when he came back to New York. When I saw him many things I thought I had forgotten came flooding back to me. This was because I had begun, finally, to wonder about Sonny, about the life that Sonny lived inside. This life, whatever it was, had made him older and thinner and it had deepened the distant stillness in which he had always moved. He looked very unlike my baby brother. Yet, when he smiled, when we shook hands, the baby brother I'd never known looked out from the depths of his private life, like an animal waiting to be coaxed into the light.

"How you been keeping?" he asked me.

"All right. And you?"

"Just fine." He was smiling all over his face. "It's good to see you again."

"It's good to see you."

The seven years' difference in our ages lay between us like a chasm: I wondered if these years would ever operate between us as a bridge. I was remembering, and it made it hard to catch my breath, that I had been there when he was born; and I had heard the first words he had ever spoken. When he started to walk, he walked from our mother straight to me. I caught him just before he fell when he took the first steps he ever took in this world.

"How's Isabel?"

"Just fine. She's dying to see you."

"And the boys?"

"They're fine, too. They're anxious to see their uncle."

"Oh, come on. You know they don't remember me."

"Are you kidding? Of course they remember you."

He grinned again. We got into a taxi. We had a lot to say to each other, far too much to know how to begin.

As the taxi began to move, I asked, "You still want to go to India?"

He laughed. "You still remember that. Hell, no. This place is Indian enough for me."

"It used to belong to them," I said.

And he laughed again. "They damn sure knew what they were doing when they got rid of it."

Years ago, when he was around fourteen, he'd been all hipped on the idea of going to India. He read books about people sitting on rocks, naked, in all kinds of weather, but mostly bad, naturally, and walking barefoot through hot coals and arriving at wisdom. I used to say that it sounded to me as though they were getting away from wisdom as fast as they could. I think he sort of looked down on me for that.

"Do you mind," he asked, "if we have the driver drive alongside the park? On the west side—I haven't seen the city in so long."

"Of course not," I said. I was afraid that I might sound as though I were humoring him, but I hoped he wouldn't take it that way.

So we drove along, between the green of the park and the stony, lifeless elegance of hotels and apartment buildings, toward the vivid, killing streets of our childhood. These streets hadn't changed, though housing projects jutted up out of them now like rocks in the middle of a boiling sea. Most of the houses in which we had grown up had vanished, as had the stores from which we had stolen, the basements in which we had first tried sex, the rooftops from which we had hurled tin cans and bricks. But houses exactly like the houses of our past yet dominated the landscape, boys exactly like the boys we once had been found themselves smothering in these houses, came down into the streets for light and air and found themselves encircled by disaster. Some escaped the trap, most didn't. Those who got out always left something of themselves behind, as some animals amputate a leg and leave it in the trap. It might be said, perhaps, that I had escaped, after all, I was a school teacher; or that Sonny had, he hadn't lived in Harlem for years. Yet, as the cab moved uptown through streets which seemed, with a rush, to darken with dark people, and as I covertly studied Sonny's face, it came to me that what we both were seeking through our separate cab windows was that part of ourselves which had been left behind. It's always at the hour of trouble and confrontation that the missing member aches.

We hit 110th Street and started rolling up Lenox Avenue. And I'd known this avenue all my life, but it seemed to me again, as it had seemed on the day I'd first heard about Sonny's trouble, filled with a hidden menace which was its very breath of life.

"We almost there," said Sonny.

"Almost." We were both too nervous to say anything more.

We live in a housing project. It hasn't been up long. A few days after it was up it seemed uninhabitably new, now, of course, it's already rundown.

It looks like a parody of the good, clean, faceless life—God knows that people who live in it do their best to make it a parody. The beat-looking grass lying around isn't enough to make their lives green, the hedges will never hold out the streets, and they know it. The big windows fool no one, they aren't big enough to make space out of no space. They don't bother with the windows, they watch the TV screen instead. The playground is most popular with the children who don't play at jacks, or skip rope, or roller skate, or swing, and they can be found in it after dark. We moved in partly because it's not too far from where I teach, and partly for the kids; but it's really just like the houses in which Sonny and I grew up. The same things happen, they'll have the same things to remember. The moment Sonny and I started into the house I had the feeling that I was simply bringing him back into the danger he had almost died trying to escape.

Sonny has never been talkative. So I don't know why I was sure he'd be dying to talk to me when supper was over the first night. Everything went fine, the oldest boy remembered him, and the youngest boy liked him, and Sonny had remembered to bring something for each of them; and Isabel, who is really much nicer than I am, more open and giving, had gone to a lot of trouble about dinner and was genuinely glad to see him. And she's always been able to tease Sonny in a way that I haven't. It was nice to see her face so vivid again and to hear her laugh and watch her make Sonny laugh. She wasn't, or, anyway, she didn't seem to be, at all uneasy or embarrassed. She chatted as though there were no subject which had to be avoided and she got Sonny past his first, faint stiffness. And thank God she was there, for I was filled with that icy dread again. Everything I did seemed awkward to me, and everything I said sounded freighted with hidden meaning. I was trying to remember everything I'd heard about dope addiction and I couldn't help watching Sonny for signs. I wasn't doing it out of malice. I was trying to find out something about my brother. I was dying to hear him tell me he was safe.

"Safe!" my father grunted, whenever Mama suggested trying to move to a neighborhood which might be safer for children. "Safe, hell! Ain't no place safe for kids, nor nobody."

He always went on like this, but he wasn't, ever, really as bad as he sounded, not even on weekends, when he got drunk. As a matter of fact, he was always on the lookout for "something a little better," but he died before he found it. He died suddenly, during a drunken weekend in the middle of the war, when Sonny was fifteen. He and Sonny hadn't ever got on too well. And this was partly because Sonny was the apple of his father's eye. It was because he loved Sonny so much and was frightened for him. It doesn't do any good to fight with Sonny. Sonny just moves back, inside himself, where he can't be reached. But the principal reason that they never hit it off is that they were so much alike. Daddy was big and rough and loud-talking, just the opposite of Sonny, but they both had—that same privacy.

Mama tried to tell me something about this, just after Daddy died. I was home on leave from the army.

This was the last time I ever saw my mother alive. Just the same, this picture gets all mixed up in my mind with pictures I have of her when she was younger. The way I always see her is the way she used to be on a Sunday afternoon, say, when the old folks were talking after the big Sunday dinner. I always see her wearing pale blue. She'd be sitting on the sofa. And my father would be sitting in the easy chair, not far from her. And the living room would be full of church folks and relatives. There they sit, in chairs all around the living room, and the night is creeping up outside, but nobody knows it yet. You can see the darkness growing against the windowpanes and you hear the street noises every now and again, or maybe the jangling beat of a tambourine from one of the churches close by, but it's real quiet in the room. For a moment nobody's talking, but every face looks darkening, like the sky outside. And my mother rocks a little from the waist, and my father's eyes are closed. Everyone is looking at something a child can't see. For a minute they've forgotten the children. Maybe a kid is lying on the rug, half asleep. Maybe somebody's got a kid in his lap and is absent-mindedly stroking the kid's head. Maybe there's a kid, quiet and big-eyed, curled up in a big chair in the corner. The silence, the darkness coming, and the darkness in the faces frightens the child obscurely. He hopes that the hand which strokes his forehead will never stop—will never die. He hopes that there will never come a time when the old folks won't be sitting around the living room, talking about where they've come from, and what they've seen, and what's happened to them and their kinfolk.

But something deep and watchful in the child knows that this is bound to end, is already ending. In a moment someone will get up and turn on the light. Then the old folks will remember the children and they won't talk any more that day. And when light fills the room, the child is filled with darkness. He knows that every time this happens he's moved just a little closer to that darkness outside. The darkness outside is what the old folks have been talking about. It's what they've come from. It's what they endure. The child knows that they won't talk any more because if he knows too much about what's happened to *them,* he'll know too much too soon, about what's going to happen to *him.*

The last time I talked to my mother, I remember I was restless. I wanted to get out and see Isabel. We weren't married then and we had a lot to straighten out between us.

There Mama sat, in black, by the window. She was humming an old church song, *Lord, you brought me from a long ways off.* Sonny was out somewhere. Mama kept watching the streets.

"I don't know," she said, "if I'll ever see you again, after you go off from here. But I hope you'll remember the things I tried to teach you."

"Don't talk like that," I said, and smiled. "You'll be here a long time yet."

She smiled, too, but she said nothing. She was quiet for a long time. And I said, "Mama, don't you worry about nothing. I'll be writing all the time, and you be getting the checks. . . ."

"I want to talk to you about your brother," she said, suddenly. "If anything happens to me he ain't going to have nobody to look out for him."

"Mama," I said, "ain't nothing going to happen to you *or* Sonny. Sonny's all right. He's a good boy and he's got good sense."

"It ain't a question of his being a good boy," Mama said, "nor of his having good sense. It ain't only the bad ones, nor yet the dumb ones that gets sucked under." She stopped, looking at me. "Your Daddy once had a brother," she said, and she smiled in a way that made me feel she was in pain. "You didn't never know that, did you?"

"No," I said, "I never knew that," and I watched her face.

"Oh, yes," she said, "your Daddy had a brother." She looked out of the window again. "I know you never saw your Daddy cry. But *I* did—many a time, through all these years."

I asked her, "What happened to his brother? How come nobody's ever talked about him?"

This was the first time I ever saw my mother look old.

"His brother got killed," she said, "when he was just a little younger than you are now. I knew him. He was a fine boy. He was maybe a little full of the devil, but he didn't mean nobody no harm."

Then she stopped and the room was silent, exactly as it had sometimes been on those Sunday afternoons. Mama kept looking out into the streets.

"He used to have a job in the mill," she said, "and, like all young folks, he just liked to perform on Saturday nights. Saturday nights, him and your father would drift around to different places, go to dances and things like that, or just sit around with people they knew, and your father's brother would sing, he had a fine voice, and play along with himself on his guitar. Well, this particular Saturday night, him and your father was coming home from some place, and they were both a little drunk and there was a moon that night, it was bright like day. Your father's brother was feeling kind of good, and he was whistling to himself, and he had his guitar slung over his shoulder. They was coming down a hill and beneath them was a road that turned off from the highway. Well, your father's brother, being always kind of frisky, decided to run down this hill, and he did, with that guitar banging and clanging behind him, and he ran across the road, and he was making water behind a tree. And your father was sort of amused at him and he was still coming down the hill, kind of slow. Then he heard a car motor and that same minute his brother stepped from behind the tree, into the road, in the moonlight. And he started to cross the road. And your father started to run down the hill, he says he don't know why. This car was full of white men. They was all drunk, and when they seen your father's brother they let out a great whoop and holler and they aimed the car straight at him. They was having fun, they just wanted to scare him, the way they do sometimes, you know. But they was drunk. And I guess the boy, being drunk, too, and scared, kind of lost his head. By the time he jumped it was too late. Your father says he heard his brother scream when the car rolled over him, and he heard the wood of that guitar when it give, and he heard them strings go flying, and he heard them white men shouting, and the car kept on a-going and it ain't stopped till this day. And, time your father got down the hill, his brother weren't nothing but blood and pulp."

Tears were gleaming on my mother's face. There wasn't anything I could say.

"He never mentioned it," she said, "because I never let him mention it before you children. Your Daddy was like a crazy man that night and for many a night thereafter. He says he never in his life seen anything as dark as that road after the lights of that car had gone away. Weren't nothing, weren't nobody on that road, just your Daddy and his brother and that busted guitar. Oh, yes. Your Daddy never did really get right again. Till the day he died he weren't sure but that every white man he saw was the man that killed his brother."

She stopped and took out her handkerchief and dried her eyes and looked at me.

"I ain't telling you all this," she said, "to make you scared or bitter or to make you hate nobody. I'm telling you this because you got a brother. And the world ain't changed."

I guess I didn't want to believe this. I guess she saw this in my face. She turned away from me, toward the window again, searching those streets.

"But I praise my Redeemer," she said at last, "that He called your Daddy home before me. I ain't saying it to throw no flowers at myself, but, I declare, it keeps me from feeling too cast down to know I helped your father get safely through this world. Your father always acted like he was the roughest, strongest man on earth. And everybody took him to be like that. But if he hadn't had *me* there—to see his tears!"

She was crying again. Still, I couldn't move. I said, "Lord, Lord, Mama, I didn't know it was like that."

"Oh, honey," she said, "there's a lot that you don't know. But you are going to find it out." She stood up from the window and came over to me. "You got to hold on to your brother," she said, "and don't let him fall, no matter what it looks like is happening to him and no matter how evil you gets with him. You going to be evil with him many a time. But don't you forget what I told you, you hear?"

"I won't forget," I said. "Don't you worry, I won't forget. I won't let nothing happen to Sonny."

My mother smiled as though she were amused at something she saw in my face. Then, "You may not be able to stop nothing from happening. But you got to let him know you's *there*."

Two days later I was married, and then I was gone. And I had a lot of things on my mind and I pretty well forgot my promise to Mama until I got shipped home on a special furlough for her funeral.

And, after the funeral, with just Sonny and me alone in the empty kitchen, I tried to find out something about him.

"What do you want to do?" I asked him.

"I'm going to be a musician," he said.

For he had graduated, in the time I had been away, from dancing to the juke box to finding out who was playing what, and what they were doing with it, and he had bought himself a set of drums.

"You mean, you want to be a drummer?" I somehow had the feeling that being a drummer might be all right for other people but not for my brother Sonny.

"I don't think," he said, looking at me very gravely, "that I'll ever be a good drummer. But I think I can play a piano."

I frowned. I'd never played the role of the older brother quite so seriously before, had scarcely ever, in fact, *asked* Sonny a damn thing. I sensed myself in the presence of something I didn't really know how to handle, didn't understand. So I made my frown a little deeper as I asked: "What kind of musician do you want to be?"

He grinned. "How many kinds do you think there are?"

"Be *serious*," I said.

He laughed, throwing his head back, and then looked at me. "I *am* serious."

"Well, then, for Christ's sake, stop kidding around and answer a serious question. I mean, do you want to be a concert pianist, you want to play classical music and all that, or—or what?" Long before I finished he was laughing again. "For Christ's *sake*, Sonny!"

He sobered, but with difficulty. "I'm sorry. But you sound so—*scared!*" and he was off again.

"Well, you may think it's funny now, baby, but it's not going to be so funny when you have to make your living at it, let me tell you *that*." I was furious because I knew he was laughing at me and I didn't know why.

"No," he said, very sober now, and afraid, perhaps, that he'd hurt me, "I don't want to be a classical pianist. That isn't what interests me. I mean"—

he paused, looking hard at me, as though his eyes would help me to understand, and then gestured helplessly, as though perhaps his hand would help—"I mean, I'll have a lot of studying to do, and I'll have to study *everything*, but, I mean, I want to play *with*—jazz musicians." He stopped. "I want to play jazz," he said.

Well, the word had never before sounded as heavy, as real, as it sounded that afternoon in Sonny's mouth. I just looked at him and I was probably frowning a real frown by this time. I simply couldn't see why on earth he'd want to spend his time hanging around nightclubs, clowning around on bandstands, while people pushed each other around a dance floor. It seemed—beneath him, somehow. I had never thought about it before, had never been forced to, but I suppose I had always put jazz musicians in a class with what Daddy called "good-time people."

"Are you *serious?*"

"Hell, *yes*, I'm serious."

He looked more helpless than ever, and annoyed, and deeply hurt.

I suggested, helpfully: "You mean—like Louis Armstrong?"

His face closed as though I'd struck him. "No. I'm not talking about none of that old-time, down home crap."

"Well, look, Sonny, I'm sorry, don't get mad. I just don't altogether get it, that's all. Name somebody—you know, a jazz musician you admire."

"Bird."

"Who?"

"Bird! Charlie Parker! Don't they teach you nothing in the goddamn army?"

I lit a cigarette. I was surprised and then a little amused to discover that I was trembling. "I've been out of touch," I said. "You'll have to be patient with me. Now. Who's this Parker character?"

"He's just one of the greatest jazz musicians alive," said Sonny, sullenly, his hands in his pockets, his back to me. "Maybe *the* greatest," he added, bitterly, "that's probably why *you* never heard of him."

"All right," I said, "I'm ignorant. I'm sorry. I'll go out and buy all the cat's records right away, all right?"

"It don't," said Sonny, with dignity, "make any difference to me. I don't care what you listen to. Don't do me no favors."

I was beginning to realize that I'd never seen him so upset before. With another part of my mind I was thinking that this would probably turn out to be one of those things kids go through and that I shouldn't make it seem important by pushing it too hard. Still, I didn't think it would do any harm to ask: "Doesn't all this take a lot of time? Can you make a living at it?"

He turned back to me and half leaned, half sat, on the kitchen table. "Everything takes time," he said, "and—well, yes, sure, I can make a living at it. But what I don't seem to be able to make you understand is that it's the only thing I want to do."

"Well, Sonny," I said, gently, "you know people can't always do exactly what they *want* to do——"

"*No,* I don't know that," said Sonny, surprising me. "I think people *ought* to do what they want to do, what else are they alive for?"

"You getting to be a big boy," I said desperately, "it's time you started thinking about your future."

"I'm thinking about my future," said Sonny, grimly. "I think about it all the time."

I gave up. I decided, if he didn't change his mind, that we could always talk about it later. "In the meantime," I said, "you got to finish school." We had already decided that he'd have to move in with Isabel and her folks. I knew this wasn't the ideal arrangement because Isabel's folks are inclined to be dicty and they haven't especially wanted Isabel to marry me. But I didn't know what else to do. "And we have to get you fixed up at Isabel's."

There was a long silence. He moved from the kitchen table to the window. "That's a terrible idea. You know it yourself."

"Do you have a *better* idea?"

He just walked up and down the kitchen for a minute. He was as tall as I was. He had started to shave. I suddenly had the feeling that I didn't know him at all. He stopped at the kitchen table and picked up my cigarettes. Looking at me with a kind of mocking, amused defiance, he put one between his lips. "You mind?"

"You smoking already?"

He lit the cigarette and nodded, watching me through the smoke. "I just wanted to see if I'd have the courage to smoke in front of you." He grinned and blew a great cloud of smoke to the ceiling. "It was easy." He looked at my face. "Come on, now. I bet you was smoking at my age, tell the truth."

I didn't say anything but the truth was on my face, and he laughed. But now there was something very strained in his laugh. "Sure. And I bet that ain't all you was doing."

He was frightening me a little. "Cut the crap," I said. "We already decided that you was going to go and live at Isabel's. Now what's got into you all of a sudden?"

"*You* decided it," he pointed out. "*I* didn't decide nothing." He stopped in front of me, leaning against the stove, arms loosely folded. "Look, brother. I don't want to stay in Harlem no more, I really don't." He was very earnest. He looked at me, then over toward the kitchen window. There was something in his eyes I'd never seen before, some thoughtfulness, some worry all his own. He rubbed the muscle of one arm. "It's time I was getting out of here."

"Where do you want to *go,* Sonny?"

"I want to join the army. Or the navy, I don't care. If I say I'm old enough, they'll believe me."

Then I got mad. It was because I was so scared. "You must be crazy. You goddamn fool, what the hell do you want to go and join the *army* for?"

"I just told you. To get out of Harlem."

"Sonny, you haven't even finished *school*. And if you really want to be a musician, how do you expect to study if you're in the *army?"*

He looked at me, trapped, and in anguish. "There's ways. I might be able to work out some kind of deal. Anyway, I'll have the G.I. Bill when I come out."

"If you come out." We stared at each other. "Sonny, please. Be reasonable. I know the setup is far from perfect. But we got to do the best we can."

"I ain't learning nothing in school," he said. "Even when I go." He turned away from me and opened the window and threw his cigarette out into the narrow alley. I watched his back. "At least, I ain't learning nothing you'd want me to learn." He slammed the window so hard I thought the glass would fly out, and turned back to me. "And I'm sick of the stink of these garbage cans!"

"Sonny," I said, "I know how you feel. But if you don't finish school now, you're going to be sorry later that you didn't." I grabbed him by the shoulders. "And you only got another year. It ain't so bad. And I'll come back and I swear I'll help you do *whatever* you want to do. Just try to put up with it till I come back. Will you please do that? For me?"

He didn't answer and he wouldn't look at me.

"Sonny. You hear me?"

He pulled away. "I hear you. But you never hear anything *I* say."

I didn't know what to say to that. He looked out of the window and then back at me. "OK," he said, and sighed. "I'll try."

Then I said, trying to cheer him up a little, "They got a piano at Isabel's. You can practice on it."

And as a matter of fact, it did cheer him up for a minute. "That's right," he said to himself. "I forgot that." His face relaxed a little. But the worry, the thoughtfulness, played on it still, the way shadows play on a face which is staring into the fire.

But I thought I'd never hear the end of that piano. At first, Isabel would write me, saying how nice it was that Sonny was so serious about his music and how, as soon as he came in from school, or wherever he had been when he was supposed to be at school, he went straight to that piano and stayed there until suppertime. And, after supper, he went back to that piano and stayed there until everybody went to bed. He was at the piano all day Saturday and all day Sunday. Then he bought a record player and started playing records. He'd play one record over and over again, all day long sometimes, and he'd improvise along with it on the piano. Or he'd play one section of the record, one chord, one change, one progression, then he'd do it on the piano. Then back to the record. Then back to the piano.

Well, I really don't know how they stood it. Isabel finally confessed that it wasn't like living with a person at all, it was like living with sound. And the sound didn't make any sense to her, didn't make any sense to any of them—naturally. They began, in a way, to be afflicted by this presence that was living in their home. It was as though Sonny were some sort of god, or monster. He moved in an atmosphere which wasn't like theirs at all. They fed him and he ate, he washed himself, he walked in and out of their door; he certainly wasn't nasty or unpleasant or rude, Sonny isn't any of those things; but it was as though he were all wrapped up in some cloud, some fire, some vision all his own; and there wasn't any way to reach him.

At the same time, he wasn't really a man yet, he was still a child, and they had to watch out for him in all kinds of ways. They certainly couldn't throw him out. Neither did they dare to make a great scene about that piano because even they dimly sensed, as I sensed, from so many thousands of miles away, that Sonny was at that piano playing for his life.

But he hadn't been going to school. One day a letter came from the school board and Isabel's mother got it—there had, apparently, been other letters but Sonny had torn them up. This day, when Sonny came in, Isabel's mother showed him the letter and asked where he'd been spending his time. And she finally got it out of him that he'd been down in Greenwich Village, with musicians and other characters, in a white girl's apartment. And this scared her and she started to scream at him and what came up, once she began—though she denies it to this day—was what sacrifices they were making to give Sonny a decent home and how little he appreciated it.

Sonny didn't play the piano that day. By evening, Isabel's mother had calmed down but then there was the old man to deal with, and Isabel herself. Isabel says she did her best to be calm but she broke down and started crying. She says she just watched Sonny's face. She could tell, by watching him, what was happening with him. And what was happening was that they penetrated his cloud, they had reached him. Even if their fingers had been a thousand times more gentle than human fingers ever are, he could hardly help feeling that they had stripped him naked and were spitting on that nakedness. For he also had to see that his presence, that music, which was life or death to him, had been torture for them and that they had endured it, not at all for his sake, but only for mine. And Sonny couldn't take that. He can take it a little better today than he could then but he's still not very good at it and, frankly, I don't know anybody who is.

The silence of the next few days must have been louder than the sound of all the music ever played since time began. One morning, before she went to work, Isabel was in his room for something and she suddenly realized that all of his records were gone. And she knew for certain that he was gone. And he was. He went as far as the navy would carry him. He finally sent me a postcard from some place in Greece and that was the first I knew that Sonny was still alive. I didn't see him any more until we were both back in New York and the war had long been over.

He was a man by then, of course, but I wasn't willing to see it. He came by the house from time to time, but we fought almost every time we met. I didn't like the way he carried himself, loose and dreamlike all the time, and I didn't like his friends, and his music seemed to be merely an excuse for the life he led. It sounded just that weird and disordered.

Then we had a fight, a pretty awful fight, and I didn't see him for months. By and by I looked him up, where he was living, in a furnished room in the Village, and I tried to make it up. But there were lots of people in the room and Sonny just lay on his bed, and he wouldn't come downstairs with me, and he treated these other people as though they were his family and I weren't. So I got mad and then he got mad, and then I told him that he might just as well be dead as live the way he was living. Then he stood up and he told me not to worry about him any more in life, that he *was* dead as far as I was concerned. Then he pushed me to the door and the other people looked on as though nothing were happening, and he slammed the door behind me. I stood in the hallway, staring at the door. I heard somebody laugh in the room and then the tears came to my eyes. I started down the steps, whistling to keep from crying, I kept whistling to myself, *You going to need me, baby, one of these cold, rainy days.*

I read about Sonny's trouble in the spring. Little Grace died in the fall. She was a beautiful little girl. But she only lived a little over two years. She died of polio and she suffered. She had a slight fever for a couple of days, but it didn't seem like anything and we just kept her in bed. And we would certainly have called the doctor, but the fever dropped, she seemed to be all right. So we thought it had just been a cold. Then, one day, she was up, playing, Isabel was in the kitchen fixing lunch for the two boys when they'd come in from school, and she heard Grace fall down in the living room. When you have a lot of children you don't always start running when one of them falls, unless they start screaming or something. And, this time, Grace was quiet. Yet, Isabel says that when she heard that *thump* and then that silence, something happened in her to make her afraid. And she ran to the living room and there was little Grace on the floor, all twisted up, and the reason she hadn't screamed was that she couldn't get her breath. And when she did scream, it was the worst sound, Isabel says, that she'd ever heard in all her life, and she still hears it sometimes in her dreams. Isabel will sometimes wake me up with a low, moaning, strangled sound and I have to be quick to awaken her and hold her to me and where Isabel is weeping against me seems a mortal wound.

I think I may have written Sonny the very day that little Grace was buried. I was sitting in the living room in the dark, by myself, and I suddenly thought of Sonny. My trouble made his real.

One Saturday afternoon, when Sonny had been living with us, or, anyway, been in our house, for nearly two weeks, I found myself wandering aimlessly about the living room, drinking from a can of beer, and trying to work up the courage to search Sonny's room. He was out, he was usually out whenever I was home, and Isabel had taken the children to see their grandparents. Suddenly I was standing still in front of the living room window, watching Seventh Avenue. The idea of searching Sonny's room made me still. I scarcely dared to admit to myself what I'd be searching for. I didn't know what I'd do if I found it. Or if I didn't.

On the sidewalk across from me, near the entrance to a barbecue joint, some people were holding an old-fashioned revival meeting. The barbecue cook, wearing a dirty white apron, his conked hair reddish and metallic in the pale sun, and a cigarette between his lips, stood in the doorway, watching them. Kids and older people paused in their errands and stood there, along with some older men and a couple of very tough-looking women who watched everything that happened on the avenue, as though they owned it, or were maybe owned by it. Well, they were watching this, too. The revival was being carried on by three sisters in black, and a brother. All they had were their voices and their Bibles and a tambourine. The brother was testifying and while he testified two of the sisters stood together, seeming to say, amen, and the third sister walked around with the tambourine outstretched and a couple of people dropped coins into it. Then the brother's testimony ended and the sister who had been taking up the collection dumped the coins into her palm and transferred them to the pocket of her long black robe. Then she raised both hands, striking the tambourine against the air, and then against one hand, and she started to sing. And the two other sisters and the brothers joined in.

It was strange, suddenly, to watch, though I had been seeing these street meetings all my life. So, of course, had everybody else down there. Yet, they paused and watched and listened and I stood still at the window. *"Tis the old ship of Zion,"* they sang, and the sister with the tambourine kept a steady, jangling beat, *"it has rescued many a thousand!"* Not a soul under the sound of their voices was hearing this song for the first time, not one of them had been rescued. Nor had they seen much in the way of rescue work being done around them. Neither did they especially believe in the holiness of the three sisters and the brother, they knew too much in the way of rescue work being done around them, knew where they lived, and how. The woman with the tambourine, whose voice dominated the air, whose face was bright with joy, was divided by very little from the woman who stood watching her, a cigarette between her heavy, chapped lips, her hair a cuckoo's nest, her face scarred and swollen from many beatings, and her black eyes glittering like coal. Perhaps they both knew this, which was why, when, as rarely, they addressed each other, they addressed each other as Sister. As the singing filled the air the watching, listening faces underwent a change, the eyes focusing on something within; the music seemed to soothe a poison out of them; and time seemed, nearly, to fall away from the sullen, belligerent, battered faces, as though they were fleeing back to their first condition, while dreaming of their last. The barbecue cook half shook his head and smiled, and dropped his cigarette and disappeared into his joint. A man fumbled in his pockets for change and stood holding it in his hand impatiently, as though he had just remembered a pressing appointment further up the avenue. He looked furious. Then I saw Sonny, standing on the edge of the crowd. He was carrying a wide, flat notebook with a green cover, and it made him look, from where I was standing, almost like a schoolboy. The coppery sun brought out the copper in his skin, he was very faintly smiling, standing very still. Then the singing stopped, the tambourine turned into a collection plate again. The furious man dropped in his coins and vanished, so did a couple of the women, and Sonny dropped some change in the plate, looking directly at the woman with a little smile. He started across the avenue, toward the house. He has a slow, loping walk, something like the way Harlem hipsters walk, only he's imposed on this his own halfbeat. I had never really noticed it before.

I stayed at the window, both relieved and apprehensive. As Sonny disappeared from my sight, they began singing again. And they were still singing when his key turned in the lock.

"Hey," he said.

"Hey, yourself. You want some beer?"

"No. Well, maybe." But he came up to the window and stood beside me, looking out. "What a warm voice," he said.

They were singing *If I could only hear my mother pray again!*

"Yes," I said, "and she can sure beat that tambourine."

"But what a terrible song," he said, and laughed. He dropped his notebook on the sofa and disappeared into the kitchen. "Where's Isabel and the kids?"

"I think they went to see their grandparents. You hungry?"

"No." He came back into the living room with his can of beer. "You want to come some place with me tonight?"

I sensed, I don't know how, that I couldn't possibly say no. "Sure. Where?"

He sat down on the sofa and picked up his notebook and started leafing through it. "I'm going to sit in with some fellows in a joint in the Village."

"You mean, you're going to play, tonight?"

"That's right." He took a swallow of his beer and moved back to the window. He gave me a sidelong look. "If you can stand it."

"I'll try," I said.

He smiled to himself and we both watched as the meeting across the way broke up. The three sisters and the brother, heads bowed, were singing *God be with you till we meet again.* The faces around them were very quiet. Then the song ended. The small crowd dispersed. We watched the three women and the lone man walk slowly up the avenue.

"When she was singing before," said Sonny, abruptly, "her voice reminded me for a minute of what heroin feels like sometimes—when it's in your veins. It makes you feel sort of warm and cool at the same time. And distant. And—and sure." He sipped his beer, very deliberately not looking at me. I watched his face. "It makes you feel—in control. Sometimes you've got to have that feeling."

"Do you?" I sat down slowly in the easy chair.

"Sometimes." He went to the sofa and picked up his notebook again. "Some people do."

"In order," I asked, "to play?" And my voice was very ugly, full of contempt and anger.

"Well"—he looked at me with great, troubled eyes, as though, in fact, he hoped his eyes would tell me things he could never otherwise say— "they *think* so. And *if* they think so—!"

"And what do *you* think?" I asked.

He sat on the sofa and put his can of beer on the floor. "I don't know," he said, and I couldn't be sure if he were answering my question or pursuing his thoughts. His face didn't tell me. "It's not so much to *play*. It's to *stand* it, to be able to make it at all. On any level." He frowned and smiled: "In order to keep from shaking to pieces."

"But these friends of yours," I said, "they seem to shake themselves to pieces pretty goddamn fast."

"Maybe." He played with the notebook. And something told me that I should curb my tongue, that Sonny was doing his best to talk, that I should listen. "But of course you only know the ones that've gone to pieces. Some don't—or at least they haven't *yet* and that's just about all *any* of us can say." He paused. "And then there are some who just live, really, in hell, and they know it and they see what's happening and they go right on. I don't know." He sighed, dropped the notebook, folded his arms. "Some guys, you can tell from the way they play, they on something *all* the time. And you can see that, well, it makes something real for them. But of course," he picked up his beer from the floor and sipped it and put the can down again, "they *want* to, too, you've got to see that. Even some of them that say they don't—*some,* not all."

"And what about you?" I asked—I couldn't help it. "What about you? Do *you* want to?"

He stood up and walked to the window and remained silent for a long time. Then he sighed. "Me," he said. Then: "While I was downstairs before, on my way here, listening to that woman sing, it struck me all of a sudden how much suffering she must have had to go through—to sing like that. It's *repulsive* to think you have to suffer that much."

I said: "But there's no way not to suffer—is there, Sonny?"

"I believe not," he said and smiled, "but that's never stopped anyone from trying." He looked at me. "Has it?" I realized, with this mocking look, that there stood between us, forever, beyond the power of time or forgiveness, the fact that I had held silence—so long!—when he had needed human speech to help him. He turned back to the window. "No, there's no way not to suffer. But you try all kinds of ways to keep from drowning in it, to keep on top of it, and to make it seem—well, like *you*. Like you did something, all right, and now you're suffering for it. You know?" I said nothing. "Well you know," he said, impatiently, "why *do* people suffer? Maybe it's better to do something to give it a reason, *any* reason."

"But we just agreed," I said, "that there's no way not to suffer. Isn't it better, then, just to—take it?"

"But nobody just takes it," Sonny cried, "that's what I'm telling you! *Everybody* tries not to. You're just hung up on the *way* some people try—it's not *your* way!"

The hair on my face began to itch, my face felt wet. "That's not true," I said, "that's not true. I don't give a damn what other people do, I don't even care how they suffer. I just care how *you* suffer." And he looked at me. "Please believe me," I said, "I don't want to see you—die—trying not to suffer."

"I won't," he said, flatly, "die trying not to suffer. At least, not any faster than anybody else."

"But there's no need," I said, trying to laugh, "is there? in killing yourself."

I wanted to say more, but I couldn't. I wanted to talk about will power and how life could be—well, beautiful. I wanted to say that it was all within; but was it? or, rather, wasn't that exactly the trouble? And I wanted to promise that I would never fail him again. But it would all have sounded —empty words and lies.

So I made the promise to myself and prayed that I would keep it.

"It's terrible sometimes, inside," he said, "that's what's the trouble. You walk these streets, black and funky and cold, and there's not really a living ass to talk to, and there's nothing shaking, and there's no way of getting it out—that storm inside. You can't talk it and you can't make love with it, and when you finally try to get with it and play it, you realize *nobody's* listening. So *you've* got to listen. You got to find a way to listen."

And then he walked away from the window and sat on the sofa again, as though all the wind had suddenly been knocked out of him. "Sometimes you'll do *anything* to play, even cut your mother's throat." He laughed and looked at me. "Or your brother's." Then he sobered. "Or your own." Then: "Don't worry. I'm all right now and I think I'll *be* all right. But I can't forget—where I've been. I don't mean just the physical place I've been, I mean where I've *been*. And *what* I've been."

"What have you been, Sonny?" I asked.

He smiled—but sat sideways on the sofa, his elbow resting on the back, his fingers playing with his mouth and chin, not looking at me. "I've been something I didn't recognize, didn't know I could be. Didn't know anybody could be." He stopped, looking inward, looking helplessly young, looking old. "I'm not talking about it now because I feel *guilty* or anything like that—maybe it would be better if I did, I don't know. Anyway, I can't really talk about it. Not to you, not to anybody," and now he turned and faced me. "Sometimes, you know, and it was actually when I was most *out* of the world, I felt that I was in it, that I was *with* it, really, and I could play or I didn't really have to *play,* it just came out of me, it was there. And I don't know how I played, thinking about it now, but I know I did awful things, those times, sometimes, to people. Or it wasn't that I *did* anything to them—it was that they weren't real." He picked up the beer can; it was empty; he rolled it between his palms: "And other times—well, I needed a fix, I needed to find a place to lean, I needed to clear a space to *listen*—and I couldn't find it, and I went crazy, I did terrible things to *me,* I was terrible *for* me." He began pressing the beer can between his hands, I watched the metal begin to give. It glittered, as he played with it, like a knife, and I was afraid he would cut himself, but I said nothing. "Oh well. I can never tell you. I was all by myself at the bottom of something, stinking and sweating and crying and shaking, and I smelled it, you know? *my* stink, and I thought I'd die if I couldn't get away from it and yet, all the same, I knew that everything I was doing was just locking me in with it. And I didn't know," he paused, still flattening the beer can, "I didn't know, I still *don't* know, something kept telling me that maybe it was good to smell your own stink, but I didn't think that *that* was what I'd been trying to do—and—who can stand it?" and he abruptly dropped the ruined beer can, looking at me with a small, still smile, and then rose, walking to the window as though it were the lodestone rock. I watched his face, he watched the avenue. "I couldn't tell you when Mama died—but the reason I wanted to leave Harlem so bad was to get away from drugs. And then, when I ran away, that's what I was running from—really. When I came back, nothing had changed, *I* hadn't changed, I was just—older." And he stopped, drumming with his fingers on the windowpane. The sun had vanished, soon darkness would fall. I watched his face. "It can come again," he said, almost as though speaking to himself. Then he turned to me. "It can come again," he repeated. "I just wanted you to know that."

"All right," I said, at last. "So it can come again. All right."

He smiled, but the smile was sorrowful. "I had to try to tell you," he said.

"Yes," I said. "I understand that."

"You're my brother," he said, looking straight at me, and not smiling at all.

"Yes," I repeated, "yes. I understand that."

He turned back to the window, looking out. "All that hatred down there," he said, "all that hatred and misery and love. It's a wonder it doesn't blow the avenue apart."

We went to the only nightclub on a short, dark street, downtown. We squeezed through the narrow, chattering, jam-packed bar to the entrance of the big room, where the bandstand was. And we stood there for a moment, for the lights were very dim in this room and we couldn't see. Then, "Hello, boy," said a voice and an enormous black man, much older than Sonny or myself, erupted out of all that atmospheric lighting and put an arm around Sonny's shoulder. "I been sitting right here," he said, "waiting for you."

He had a big voice, too, and heads in the darkness turned toward us.

Sonny grinned and pulled a little away, and said, "Creole, this is my brother. I told you about him."

Creole shook my hand. "I'm glad to meet you, son," he said, and it was clear that he was glad to meet me *there,* for Sonny's sake. And he smiled, "You got a real musician in *your* family," and he took his arm from Sonny's shoulder and slapped him, lightly, affectionately, with the back of his hand.

"Well. Now I've heard it all," said a voice behind us. This was another musician, and a friend of Sonny's, a coal-black, cheerful-looking man, built close to the ground. He immediately began confiding to me, at the top of his lungs, the most terrible things about Sonny, his teeth gleaming like a lighthouse and his laugh coming up out of him like the beginning of an earthquake. And it turned out that everyone at the bar knew Sonny, or almost everyone; some were musicians, working there, or nearby, or not working, some were simply hangers-on, and some were there to hear Sonny play. I was introduced to all of them and they were all very polite to me. Yet, it was clear that, for them, I was only Sonny's brother. Here, I was in Sonny's world. Or, rather: his kingdom. Here, it was not even a question that his veins bore royal blood.

They were going to play soon and Creole installed me, by myself, at a table in a dark corner. Then I watched them, Creole, and the little black man, and Sonny, and the others, while they horsed around, standing just below the bandstand. The light from the bandstand spilled just a little short of them and, watching them laughing and gesturing and moving about, I had the feeling that they, nevertheless, were being most careful not to step into that circle of light too suddenly: that if they moved into the light too suddenly, without thinking, they would perish in flame. Then, while I watched, one of them, the small, black man, moved into the light and crossed the bandstand and started fooling around with his drums. Then—being funny and being, also, extremely ceremonious—Creole took Sonny by the arm and led him to the piano. A woman's voice called Sonny's name and a

few hands started clapping. And Sonny, also being funny and being ceremonious, and so touched, I think, that he could have cried, but neither
hiding it nor showing it, riding it like a man, grinned, and put both hands
to his heart and bowed from the waist.

Creole then went to the bass fiddle and a lean, very bright-skinned
brown man jumped up on the bandstand and picked up his horn. So there
they were, and the atmosphere on the bandstand and in the room began to
change and tighten. Someone stepped up to the microphone and announced
them. Then there were all kinds of murmurs. Some people at the bar
shushed others. The waitress ran around, frantically getting in the last
orders, guys and chicks got closer to each other, and the lights on the
bandstand, on the quartet, turned to a kind of indigo. Then they all looked
different there. Creole looked about him for the last time, as though he
were making certain that all his chickens were in the coop, and then
he—jumped and struck the fiddle. And there they were.

All I know about music is that not many people ever really hear it. And
even then, on the rare occasions when something opens within, and the
music enters, what we mainly hear, or hear corroborated, are personal,
private, vanishing evocations. But the man who creates the music is hearing something else, is dealing with the roar rising from the void and imposing order on it as it hits the air. What is evoked in him, then, is of another
order, more terrible because it has no words, and triumphant, too, for that
same reason. And his triumph, when he triumphs, is ours. I just watched
Sonny's face. His face was troubled, he was working hard, but he wasn't
with it. And I had the feeling that, in a way, everyone on the bandstand
was waiting for him, both waiting for him and pushing him along. But as I
began to watch Creole, I realized that it was Creole who held them all
back. He had them on a short rein. Up there, keeping the beat with his
whole body, wailing on the fiddle, with his eyes half closed, he was listening
to everything, but he was listening to Sonny. He was having a dialogue with
Sonny. He wanted Sonny to leave the shoreline and strike out for the deep
water. He was Sonny's witness that deep water and drowning were not the
same thing—he had been there, and he knew. And he wanted Sonny to
know. He was waiting for Sonny to do the things on the keys which would
let Creole know that Sonny was in the water.

And, while Creole listened, Sonny moved, deep within, exactly like
someone in torment. I had never before thought of how awful the relationship must be between the musician and his instrument. He has to fill it, this
instrument, with the breath of life, his own. He has to make it do what he
wants it to do. And a piano is just a piano. It's made out of so much wood
and wires and little hammers and big ones, and ivory. While there's only so
much you can do with it, the only way to find this out is to try; to try and
make it do everything.

And Sonny hadn't been near a piano for over a year. And he wasn't on much better terms with his life, not the life that stretched before him now. He and the piano stammered, started one way, got scared, stopped; started another way, panicked, marked time, started again; then seemed to have found a direction, panicked again, got stuck. And the face I saw on Sonny I'd never seen before. Everything had been burned out of it, and, at the same time, things usually hidden were being burned in, by the fire and fury of the battle which was occurring in him up there.

Yet, watching Creole's face as they neared the end of the first set, I had the feeling that something had happened, something I hadn't heard. Then they finished, there was scattered applause, and then, without an instant's warning, Creole started into something else, it was almost sardonic, it was *Am I Blue*. And, as though he commanded, Sonny began to play. Something began to happen. And Creole let out the reins. The dry, low, black man said something awful on the drums, Creole answered, and the drums talked back. Then the horn insisted, sweet and high, slightly detached perhaps, and Creole listened, commenting now and then, dry, and driving, beautiful and calm and old. Then they all came together again, and Sonny was part of the family again. I could tell this from his face. He seemed to have found, right there beneath his fingers, a damn brand-new piano. It seemed that he couldn't get over it. Then, for awhile, just being happy with Sonny, they seemed to be agreeing with him that brand-new pianos certainly were a gas.

Then Creole stepped forward to remind them that what they were playing was the blues. He hit something in all of them, he hit something in me, myself, and the music tightened and deepened, apprehension began to beat the air. Creole began to tell us what the blues were all about. They were not about anything very new. He and his boys up there were keeping it new, at the risk of ruin, destruction, madness, and death, in order to find new ways to make us listen. For, while the tale of how we suffer, and how we are delighted, and how we may triumph is never new, it always must be heard. There isn't any other tale to tell, it's the only light we've got in all this darkness.

And this tale, according to that face, that body, those strong hands on those strings, has another aspect in every country, and a new depth in every generation. Listen, Creole seemed to be saying, listen. Now these are Sonny's blues. He made the little black man on the drums know it, and the bright, brown man on the horn. Creole wasn't trying any longer to get Sonny in the water. He was wishing him Godspeed. Then he stepped back, very slowly, filling the air with the immense suggestion that Sonny speak for himself.

Then they all gathered around Sonny and Sonny played. Every now and again one of them seemed to say, amen. Sonny's fingers—filled the air with life, his life. But that life contained so many others. And Sonny went all the way back, he really began with the spare, flat statement of the opening phrase of the song. Then he began to make it his. It was very beautiful because it wasn't hurried and it was no longer a lament. I seemed to hear with what burning he had made it his, with what burning we had yet to make it ours, how we could cease lamenting. Freedom lurked around us and I understood, at last, that he could help us to be free if we would listen, that he would never be free until we did. Yet, there was no battle in his face now. I heard what he had gone through, and would continue to go through until he came to rest in earth. He had made it his: that long line, of which we knew only Mama and Daddy. And he was giving it back, as everything must be given back, so that, passing through death, it can live forever. I saw my mother's face again, and felt, for the first time, how the stones of the road she had walked on must have bruised her feet. I saw the moonlit road where my father's brother died. And it brought something else back to me, and carried me past it. I saw my little girl again and felt Isabel's tears again, and I felt my own tears begin to rise. And I was yet aware that this was only a moment, that the world waited outside, as hungry as a tiger, and that trouble stretched above us, longer than the sky.

Then it was over. Creole and Sonny let out their breath, both soaking wet, and grinning. There was a lot of applause and some of it was real. In the dark, the girl came by and I asked her to take drinks to the bandstand. There was a long pause, while they talked up there in the indigo light and after awhile I saw the girl put a Scotch and milk on top of the piano for Sonny. He didn't seem to notice it, but just before they started playing again, he sipped from it and looked toward me, and nodded. Then he put it back on top of the piano. For me, then, as they began to play again, it glowed and shook above my brother's head like the very cup of trembling.

◇

James Baldwin was born in Harlem in 1924, was graduated from De Witt Clinton High School, lived in Paris for nearly ten years, and now divides his time between Paris and New York. He has won a Eugene F. Saxton Memorial Trust award, a Rosenwald fellowship, a Guggenheim fellowship, a National Institute of Arts and Letters fellowship, a Partisan Review *fellowship, and a Ford Foundation grant-in-aid. He has published three novels:* Go Tell It on the Mountain *(1953),* Giovanni's Room *(1956), and* Another Country *(1962); and a collection of short stories,* Going to Meet the Man *(1965). In recent years he has written much nonfiction, essays and reportage of various sorts for magazines, and these pieces have been collected in:* Notes of a Native Son *(1956),* Nobody Knows My Name *(1961), and* The Fire Next Time *(1963).*

In "Sonny's Blues" Baldwin contrasts the two ways the Negro has of escaping from the trap that a white society has made of his life: rising up or breaking out. He uses two brothers to present, or represent, these two ways; and while they are to some extent types, they are certainly not wholly so. He assigns the more routinely accepted way to his point-of-view character, which permits explanation of alteration, thus preparing for a reconciliation of attitudes at the end. The narrator is somewhat square, a schoolteacher, married and with children, in all ways a responsible sort of man. His is the way of rising up: he has been able to rise somewhat above the squalid Harlem streets where he and Sonny were raised, but he still lives in Harlem and daily sees the plight of the boys he teaches: "they were growing up with a rush and their heads bumped abruptly against the low ceiling of their actual possibilities." Escape by breaking out of this trapped life by crime or by marijuana and heroin is antithetical to his responsible nature; but he understands clearly the frustrations of the boys, and says of heroin: "Maybe it did more for them than algebra could." A good deal of the meaning of the story is implicit in that simple-sounding, somewhat comic statement. Sonny tries the heroin escape but is busted; he is hipper, wilder, less responsible than the narrator. He is likened to their father's brother, who was killed by white men—suggesting the continuity of this duality in the Negro reaction to oppression and exploitation by whites. When the narrator brings Sonny home from prison, he reflects, "The moment Sonny and I started into the house I had the feeling that I was simply bringing him back into the danger he had almost died trying to escape." But Sonny finds another way out besides heroin—out of Harlem and out of the trap it represents. The ending is foreshadowed by the sidewalk revival meeting and the warm evocative tones of the woman singer: "her voice reminded me for a minute of what heroin feels like sometimes," says Sonny; and as the narrator watches the bystanders, "the music seemed to soothe a poison out of them." The ending, when the narrator finally hears Sonny play and "understands," may be a bit too Hollywood-finale for some readers—too much a daydream of parental understanding and approval of the artistic-bohemian life—but for others it is effective, and it serves to achieve a synthesis of the two ways that had seemed to be in conflict. "Freedom lurked round us," says the narrator, "and I understood, at last, that he could help us to be free if we would listen, that he would never be free until we did." Sonny's blues give expression to the Negro's plight and help him to overcome his traditional situation by comprehending it—not simply evading it. And Baldwin seems to say that the responsible family man and schoolteacher, the middle-class Negro who finds his aspirations and attitudes within the norms of white middle-class respectability, lacks a vision and an understanding that the artist, writer or musician can provide, if his people will only listen. The life of the artist, the jazz musician in this case, while it may sacrifice respectability, allows Sonny to be himself and say what he has to say. Its dangers are those of the night world—drugs and drink and no settled home. But they take Sonny into a world that has its own way of judging a man and honoring those who, like Sonny, are good at what they do and have something to say. It may be a dark world, but it is a world where color doesn't matter.

FLANNERY O'CONNOR

Everything That Rises Must Converge

❖❖❖❖❖❖❖

HIS DOCTOR had told Julian's mother that she must lose twenty pounds on account of her blood pressure, so on Wednesday nights Julian had to take her downtown on the bus for a reducing class at the Y. The reducing class was designed for working girls over fifty, who weighed from 165 to 200 pounds. His mother was one of the slimmer ones, but she said ladies did not tell their age or weight. She would not ride on the buses by herself at night since they had been integrated, and because the reducing class was one of her few pleasures, necessary for her health, and *free,* she said Julian could at least put himself out to take her, considering all she did for him. Julian did not like to consider all she did for him, but every Wednesday night he braced himself and took her.

She was almost ready to go, standing before the hall mirror, putting on her hat, while he, his hands behind him, appeared pinned to the door frame, waiting like Saint Sebastian for the arrows to begin piercing him. The hat was new and had cost her seven dollars and a half. She kept saying, "Maybe I shouldn't have paid that for it. No, I shouldn't have. I'll take it off and return it tomorrow. I shouldn't have bought it."

Julian raised his eyes to heaven. "Yes, you should have bought it," he said. "Put it on and let's go." It was a hideous hat. A purple velvet flap came down on one side of it and stood up on the other; the rest of it was green and looked like a cushion with the stuffing out. He decided it was less comical than jaunty and pathetic. Everything that gave her pleasure was small and depressed him.

She lifted the hat one more time and set it down slowly on top of her head. Two wings of gray hair protruded on either side of her florid face, but her eyes, sky-blue, were as innocent and untouched by experience as they must have been when she was ten. Were it not that she was a widow who had struggled fiercely to feed and clothe and put him through school and who was supporting him still, "until he got on his feet," she might have been a little girl that he had to take to town.

"It's all right, it's all right," he said. "Let's go." He opened the door himself and started down the walk to get her going. The sky was a dying violet and the houses stood out darkly against it, bulbous liver-colored monstrosities of a uniform ugliness though no two were alike. Since this had been a fashionable neighborhood forty years ago, his mother persisted in thinking they did well to have an apartment in it. Each house had a narrow collar of dirt around it in which sat, usually, a grubby child. Julian walked with his hands in his pockets, his head down and thrust forward and his eyes glazed with the determination to make himself completely numb during the time he would be sacrificed to her pleasure.

The door closed and he turned to find the dumpy figure, surmounted by the atrocious hat, coming toward him. "Well," she said, "you only live once and paying a little more for it, I at least won't meet myself coming and going."

"Some day I'll start making money," Julian said gloomily—he knew he never would—"and you can have one of those jokes whenever you take the fit." But first they would move. He visualized a place where the nearest neighbors would be three miles away on either side.

"I think you're doing fine," she said, drawing on her gloves. "You've only been out of school a year. Rome wasn't built in a day."

She was one of the few members of the Y reducing class who arrived in hat and gloves and who had a son who had been to college. "It takes time," she said, "and the world is in such a mess. This hat looked better on me than any of the others, though when she brought it out I said, 'Take that thing back. I wouldn't have it on my head,' and she said, 'Now wait till you see it on,' and when she put it on me, I said, 'We-ull,' and she said, 'If you ask me, that hat does something for you and you do something for the hat, and besides,' she said, 'with that hat, you won't meet yourself coming and going.'"

Julian thought he could have stood his lot better if she had been selfish, if she had been an old hag who drank and screamed at him. He walked along, saturated in depression, as if in the midst of his martyrdom he had lost his faith. Catching sight of his long, hopeless, irritated face, she stopped suddenly with a grief-stricken look, and pulled back on his arm. "Wait on me," she said. "I'm going back to the house and take this thing off and tomorrow I'm going to return it. I was out of my head. I can pay the gas bill with that seven-fifty."

He caught her arm in a vicious grip. "You are not going to take it back," he said. "I like it."

"Well," she said. "I don't think I ought . . ."

"Shut up and enjoy it," he muttered, more depressed than ever.

"With the world in the mess it's in," she said, "it's a wonder we can enjoy anything. I tell you, the bottom rail is on the top."

Julian sighed.

"Of course," she said, "if you know who you are, you can go anywhere." She said this every time he took her to the reducing class. "Most of them in it are not our kind of people," she said, "but I can be gracious to anybody. I know who I am."

"They don't give a damn for your graciousness," Julian said savagely. "Knowing who you are is good for one generation only. You haven't the foggiest idea where you stand now or who you are."

She stopped and allowed her eyes to flash at him. "I most certainly do know who I am," she said, "and if you don't know who you are, I'm ashamed of you."

"Oh hell," Julian said.

"Your great-grandfather was a former governor of this state," she said. "Your grandfather was a prosperous landowner. Your grandmother was a Godhigh."

"Will you look around you," he said tensely, "and see where you are now?" and he swept his arm jerkily out to indicate the neighborhood, which the growing darkness at least made less dingy.

"You remain what you are," she said. "Your great-grandfather had a plantation and two hundred slaves."

"There are no more slaves," he said irritably.

"They were better off when they were," she said. He groaned to see that she was off on that topic. She rolled onto it every few days like a train on an open track. He knew every stop, every junction, every swamp along the way, and knew the exact point at which her conclusion would roll majestically into the station: "It's ridiculous. It's simply not realistic. They should rise, yes, but on their own side of the fence."

"Let's skip it," Julian said.

"The ones I feel sorry for," she said, "are the ones that are half white. They're tragic."

"Will you skip it?"

"Suppose we were half white. We would certainly have mixed feelings."

"I have mixed feelings now," he groaned.

"Well, let's talk about something pleasant," she said. "I remember going to Grandpa's when I was a little girl. Then the house had double stairways that went up to what was really the second floor—all the cooking was done on the first. I used to like to stay down in the kitchen on account of the way the walls smelled. I would sit with my nose pressed against the plaster and take deep breaths. Actually the place belonged to the Godhighs but your grandfather Chestny paid the mortgage and saved it for them. They were in reduced circumstances," she said, "but reduced or not, they never forgot who they were."

"Doubtless that decayed mansion reminded them," Julian muttered. He never spoke of it without contempt or thought of it without longing. He had seen it once when he was a child before it had been sold. The double stairways had rotted and been torn down. Negroes were living in it. But it remained in his mind as his mother had known it. It appeared in his dreams regularly. He would stand on the wide porch, listening to the rustle of oak leaves, then wander through the high-ceilinged hall into the parlor that opened onto it and gaze at the worn rugs and faded draperies. It occurred to him that it was he, not she, who could have appreciated it. He preferred its threadbare elegance to anything he could name and it was because of it that all the neighborhoods they had lived in had been a torment to him—whereas she had hardly known the difference. She called her insensitivity "being adjustable."

"And I remember the old darky who was my nurse, Caroline. There was no better person in the world. I've always had a great respect for my colored friends," she said. "I'd do anything in the world for them and they'd . . ."

"Will you for God's sake get off that subject?" Julian said. When he got on a bus by himself, he made it a point to sit down beside a Negro, in reparation as it were for his mother's sins.

"You're mighty touchy tonight," she said. "Do you feel all right?"

"Yes I feel all right," he said. "Now lay off."

She pursed her lips. "Well, you certainly are in a vile humor," she observed. "I just won't speak to you at all."

They had reached the bus stop. There was no bus in sight and Julian, his hands still jammed in his pockets and his head thrust forward, scowled down the empty street. The frustration of having to wait on the bus as well as ride on it began to creep up his neck like a hot hand. The presence of his mother was borne in upon him as she gave a pained sigh. He looked at her bleakly. She was holding herself very erect under the preposterous hat, wearing it like a banner of her imaginary dignity. There was in him an evil urge to break her spirit. He suddenly unloosened his tie and pulled it off and put it in his pocket.

She stiffened. "Why must you look like *that* when you take me to town?" she said. "Why must you deliberately embarrass me?"

"If you'll never learn where you are," he said, "you can at least learn where I am."

"You look like a—thug," she said.

"Then I must be one," he murmured.

"I'll just go home," she said. "I will not bother you. If you can't do a little thing like that for me . . ."

Rolling his eyes upward, he put his tie back on. "Restored to my class," he muttered. He thrust his face toward her and hissed, "True culture is in the mind, the *mind,*" he said, and tapped his head, "the mind."

"It's in the heart," she said, "and in how you do things and how you do things is because of who you *are.*"

"Nobody in the damn bus cares who you are."

"I care who I am," she said icily.

The lighted bus appeared on top of the next hill and as it approached, they moved out into the street to meet it. He put his hand under her elbow and hoisted her up on the creaking step. She entered with a little smile, as if she were going into a drawing room where everyone had been waiting for her. While he put in the tokens, she sat down on one of the broad front seats for three which faced the aisle. A thin woman with protruding teeth and long yellow hair was sitting on the end of it. His mother moved up beside her and left room for Julian beside herself. He sat down and looked at the floor across the aisle where a pair of thin feet in red and white canvas sandals were planted.

His mother immediately began a general conversation meant to attract anyone who felt like talking. "Can it get any hotter?" she said and removed from her purse a folding fan, black with a Japanese scene on it, which she began to flutter before her.

"I reckon it might could," the woman with the protruding teeth said, "but I know for a fact my apartment couldn't get no hotter."

"It must get the afternoon sun," his mother said. She sat forward and looked up and down the bus. It was half filled. Everybody was white. "I see we have the bus to ourselves," she said. Julian cringed.

"For a change," said the woman across the aisle, the owner of the red and white canvas sandals. "I come on one the other day and they were thick as fleas—up front and all through."

"The world is in a mess everywhere," his mother said. "I don't know how we've let it get in this fix."

"What gets my goat is all those boys from good families stealing automobile tires," the woman with the protruding teeth said. "I told my boy, I said you may not be rich but you been raised right and if I ever catch you in any such mess, they can send you on to the reformatory. Be exactly where you belong."

"Training tells," his mother said. "Is your boy in high school?"

"Ninth grade," the woman said.

"My son just finished college last year. He wants to write but he's selling typewriters until he gets started," his mother said.

The woman leaned forward and peered at Julian. He threw her such a malevolent look that she subsided against the seat. On the floor across the aisle there was an abandoned newspaper. He got up and got it and opened it out in front of him. His mother discreetly continued the conversation in a lower tone but the woman across the aisle said in a loud voice, "Well that's nice. Selling typewriters is close to writing. He can go right from one to the other."

"I tell him," his mother said, "that Rome wasn't built in a day."

Behind the newspaper Julian was withdrawing into the inner compartment of his mind where he spent most of his time. This was a kind of mental bubble in which he established himself when he could not bear to be a part of what was going on around him. From it he could see out and judge but in it he was safe from any kind of penetration from without. It was the only place where he felt free of the general idiocy of his fellows. His mother had never entered it but from it he could see her with absolute clarity.

The old lady was clever enough and he thought that if she had started from any of the right premises, more might have been expected of her. She lived according to the laws of her own fantasy world, outside of which he had never seen her set foot. The law of it was to sacrifice herself for him after she had first created the necessity to do so by making a mess of things. If he had permitted her sacrifices, it was only because her lack of foresight had made them necessary. All of her life had been a struggle to act like a Chestny without the Chestny goods, and to give him everything she thought a Chestny ought to have; but since, said she, it was fun to struggle, why complain? And when you had won, as she had won, what fun to look back on the hard times! He could not forgive her that she had enjoyed the struggle and that she thought *she* had won.

What she meant when she said she had won was that she had brought him up successfully and had sent him to college and that he had turned out so well—good looking (her teeth had gone unfilled so that his could be straightened), intelligent (he realized he was too intelligent to be a success), and with a future ahead of him (there was of course no future ahead of him). She excused his gloominess on the grounds that he was still growing up and his radical ideas on his lack of practical experience. She said he didn't yet know a thing about "life," that he hadn't even entered the real world—when already he was as disenchanted with it as a man of fifty.

The further irony of all this was that in spite of her, he had turned out so well. In spite of going to only a third-rate college, he had, on his own initiative, come out with a first-rate education; in spite of growing up dominated by a small mind, he had ended up with a large one; in spite of all her foolish views, he was free of prejudice and unafraid to face facts. Most miraculous of all, instead of being blinded by love for her as she was for him, he had cut himself emotionally free of her and could see her with complete objectivity. He was not dominated by mother.

The bus stopped with a sudden jerk and shook him from his meditation. A woman from the back lurched forward with little steps and barely escaped falling in his newspaper as she righted herself. She got off and a large

Negro got on. Julian kept his paper lowered to watch. It gave him a certain satisfaction to see injustice in daily operation. It confirmed his view that with a few exceptions there was no one worth knowing within a radius of three hundred miles. The Negro was well dressed and carried a briefcase. He looked around and then sat down on the other end of the seat where the woman with the red and white canvas sandals was sitting. He immediately unfolded a newspaper and obscured himself behind it. Julian's mother's elbow at once prodded insistently into his ribs. "Now you see why I won't ride on these buses by myself," she whispered.

The woman with the red and white canvas sandals had risen at the same time the Negro sat down and had gone further back in the bus and taken the seat of the woman who had got off. His mother leaned forward and cast her an approving look.

Julian rose, crossed the aisle, and sat down in the place of the woman with the canvas sandals. From this position, he looked serenely across at his mother. Her face had turned an angry red. He stared at her, making his eyes the eyes of a stranger. He felt his tension suddenly lift as if he had openly declared war on her.

He would have liked to get in conversation with the Negro and to talk with him about art or politics or any subject that would be above the comprehension of those around them, but the man remained entrenched behind his paper. He was either ignoring the change of seating or had never noticed it. There was no way for Julian to convey his sympathy.

His mother kept her eyes fixed reproachfully on his face. The woman with the protruding teeth was looking at him avidly as if he were a type of monster new to her.

"Do you have a light?" he asked the Negro.

Without looking away from his paper, the man reached in his pocket and handed him a packet of matches.

"Thanks," Julian said. For a moment he held the matches foolishly. A No Smoking sign looked down upon him from over the door. This alone would not have deterred him; he had no cigarettes. He had quit smoking some months before because he could not afford it. "Sorry," he muttered and handed back the matches. The Negro lowered the paper and gave him an annoyed look. He took the matches and raised the paper again.

His mother continued to gaze at him but she did not take advantage of his momentary discomfort. Her eyes retained their battered look. Her face seemed to be unnaturally red, as if her blood pressure had risen. Julian allowed no glimmer of sympathy to show on his face. Having got the advantage, he wanted desperately to keep it and carry it through. He would have liked to teach her a lesson that would last her a while, but there seemed no way to continue the point. The Negro refused to come out from behind his paper.

Julian folded his arms and looked stolidly before him, facing her but as if he did not see her, as if he had ceased to recognize her existence. He visualized a scene in which, the bus having reached their stop, he would remain in his seat and when she said, "Aren't you going to get off?" he would look at her as at a stranger who had rashly addressed him. The corner they got off on was usually deserted, but it was well lighted and it would not hurt her to walk by herself the four blocks to the Y. He decided to wait until the time came and then decide whether or not he would let her get off by herself. He would have to be at the Y at ten to bring her back, but he could leave her wondering if he was going to show up. There was no reason for her to think she could always depend on him.

He retired again into the high-ceilinged room sparsely settled with large pieces of antique furniture. His soul expanded momentarily but then he became aware of his mother across from him and the vision shriveled. He studied her coldly. Her feet in little pumps dangled like a child's and did not quite reach the floor. She was training on him an exaggerated look of reproach. He felt completely detached from her. At that moment he could with pleasure have slapped her as he would have slapped a particularly obnoxious child in his charge.

He began to imagine various unlikely ways by which he could teach her a lesson. He might make friends with some distinguished Negro professor or lawyer and bring him home to spend the evening. He would be entirely justified but her blood pressure would rise to 300. He could not push her to the extent of making her have a stroke, and moreover, he had never been successful at making any Negro friends. He had tried to strike up an acquaintance on the bus with some of the better types, with ones that looked like professors or ministers or lawyers. One morning he had sat down next to a distinguished-looking dark brown man who had answered his questions with a sonorous solemnity but who had turned out to be an undertaker. Another day he had sat down beside a cigar-smoking Negro with a diamong ring on his finger, but after a few stilted pleasantries, the Negro had rung the buzzer and risen, slipping two lottery tickets into Julian's hand as he climbed over him to leave.

He imagined his mother lying desperately ill and his being able to secure only a Negro doctor for her. He toyed with that idea for a few minutes and then dropped it for a momentary vision of himself participating as a sympathizer in a sit-in demonstration. This was possible but he did not linger with it. Instead, he approached the ultimate horror. He brought home a beautiful suspiciously Negroid woman. Prepare yourself, he said. There is nothing you can do about it. This is the woman I've chosen. She's intelligent, dignified, even good, and she's suffered and she hasn't thought it *fun*. Now persecute us, go ahead and persecute us. Drive her out of here, but remember, you're driving me too. His eyes were narrowed and through the indignation he had generated, he saw his mother across the aisle, purple-faced, shrunken to the dwarflike proportions of her moral nature, sitting like a mummy beneath the ridiculous banner of her hat.

He was tilted out of his fantasy again as the bus stopped. The door opened with a sucking hiss and out of the dark a large, gaily dressed, sullen-looking colored woman got on with a little boy. The child, who might have been four, had on a short plaid suit and a Tyrolean hat with a blue feather in it. Julian hoped that he would sit down beside him and that the woman would push in beside his mother. He could think of no better arrangement.

As she waited for her tokens, the woman was surveying the seating possibilities—he hoped with the idea of sitting where she was least wanted. There was something familiar-looking about her but Julian could not place what it was. She was a giant of a woman. Her face was set not only to meet opposition but to seek it out. The downward tilt of her large lower lip was like a warning sign: DON'T TAMPER WITH ME. Her bulging figure was encased in a green crepe dress and her feet overflowed in red shoes. She had on a hideous hat. A purple velvet flap came down on one side of it and stood up on the other; the rest of it was green and looked like a cushion with the stuffing out. She carried a mammoth red pocketbook that bulged throughout as if it were stuffed with rocks.

To Julian's disappointment, the little boy climbed up on the empty seat beside his mother. His mother lumped all children, black and white, into the common category, "Cute," and she thought little Negroes were on the whole cuter than little white children. She smiled at the little boy as he climbed on the seat.

Meanwhile the woman was bearing down upon the empty seat beside Julian. To his annoyance, she squeezed herself into it. He saw his mother's face change as the woman settled herself next to him and he realized with satisfaction that this was more objectionable to her than it was to him. Her face seemed almost gray and there was a look of dull recognition in her eyes, as if suddenly she had sickened at some awful confrontation. Julian saw that it was because she and the woman had, in a sense, swapped sons. Though his mother would not realize the symbolic significance of this, she would feel it. His amusement showed plainly on his face.

The woman next to him muttered something unintelligible to herself. He was conscious of a kind of bristling next to him, a muted growling like that of an angry cat. He could not see anything but the red pocketbook upright on the bulging green thighs. He visualized the woman as she had stood waiting for her tokens—the ponderous figure, rising from the red shoes upward over the solid hips, the mammoth bosom, the haughty face, to the green and purple hat.

His eyes widened.

The vision of the two hats, identical, broke upon him with the radiance of a brilliant sunrise. His face was suddenly lit with joy. He could not believe that Fate had thrust upon his mother such a lesson. He gave a loud chuckle so that she would look at him and see that he saw. She turned her eyes on him slowly. The blue in them seemed to have turned a bruised purple. For a moment he had an uncomfortable sense of her innocence, but it lasted only a second before principle rescued him. Justice entitled him to laugh. His grin hardened until it said to her as plainly as if he were saying aloud: Your punishment exactly fits your pettiness. This should teach you a permanent lesson.

Her eyes shifted to the woman. She seemed unable to bear looking at him and to find the woman preferable. He became conscious again of the bristling presence at his side. The woman was rumbling like a volcano about to become active. His mother's mouth began to twitch slightly at one corner. With a sinking heart, he saw incipient signs of recovery on her face and realized that this was going to strike her suddenly as funny and was going to be no lesson at all. She kept her eyes on the woman and an amused smile came over her face as if the woman were a monkey that had stolen her hat. The little Negro was looking up at her with large fascinated eyes. He had been trying to attract her attention for some time.

"Carver!" the woman said suddenly. "Come heah!"

When he saw that the spotlight was on him at last, Carver drew his feet up and turned himself toward Julian's mother and giggled.

"Carver!" the woman said. "You heah me? Come heah!"

Carver slid down from the seat but remained squatting with his back against the base of it, his head turned slyly around toward Julian's mother, who was smiling at him. The woman reached a hand across the aisle and snatched him to her. He righted himself and hung backwards on her knees, grinning at Julian's mother. "Isn't he cute?" Julian's mother said to the woman with the protruding teeth.

"I reckon he is," the woman said without conviction.

The Negress yanked him upright but he eased out of her grip and shot across the aisle and scrambled, giggling wildly, onto the seat beside his love.

"I think he likes me," Julian's mother said, and smiled at the woman. It was the smile she used when she was being particularly gracious to an inferior. Julian saw everything lost. The lesson had rolled off her like rain on a roof.

The woman stood up and yanked the little boy off the seat as if she were snatching him from contagion. Julian could feel the rage in her at having no weapon like his mother's smile. She gave the child a sharp slap across his leg. He howled once and then thrust his head into her stomach and kicked his feet against her shins. "Be-have," she said vehemently.

The bus stopped and the Negro who had been reading the newspaper got off. The woman moved over and set the little boy down with a thump between herself and Julian. She held him firmly by the knee. In a moment he put his hands in front of his face and peeped at Julian's mother through his fingers.

"I see yoooooooo!" she said and put her hand in front of her face and peeped at him.

The woman slapped his hand down. "Quit yo' foolishness," she said, "before I knock the living Jesus out of you!"

Julian was thankful that the next stop was theirs. He reached up and pulled the cord. The woman reached up and pulled it at the same time. Oh my God, he thought. He had the terrible intuition that when they got off the bus together, his mother would open her purse and give the little boy a nickel. The gesture would be as natural to her as breathing. The bus stopped and the woman got up and lunged to the front, dragging the child, who wished to stay on, after her. Julian and his mother got up and followed. As they neared the door, Julian tried to relieve her of her pocketbook.

"No," she murmured, "I want to give the little boy a nickel."

"No!" Julian hissed. "No!"

She smiled down at the child and opened her bag. The bus door opened and the woman picked him up by the arm and descended with him, hanging at her hip. Once in the street she set him down and shook him.

Julian's mother had to close her purse while she got down the bus step but as soon as her feet were on the ground, she opened it again and began to rummage inside. "I can't find but a penny," she whispered, "but it looks like a new one."

"Don't do it!" Julian said fiercely between his teeth. There was a streetlight on the corner and she hurried to get under it so that she could better see into her pocketbook. The woman was heading off rapidly down the street with the child still hanging backward on her hand.

"Oh little boy!" Julian's mother called and took a few quick steps and caught up with them just beyond the lamppost. "Here's a bright new penny for you," and she held out the coin, which shone bronze in the dim light.

The huge woman turned and for a moment stood, her shoulders lifted and her face frozen with frustrated rage, and stared at Julian's mother. Then all at once she seemed to explode like a piece of machinery that had been given one ounce of pressure too much. Julian saw the black fist swing out with the red pocketbook. He shut his eyes and cringed as he heard the woman shout, "He don't take nobody's pennies!" When he opened his eyes, the woman was disappearing down the street with the little boy staring wide-eyed over her shoulder. Julian's mother was sitting on the sidewalk.

"I told you not to do that," Julian said angrily. "I told you not to do that!"

He stood over her for a minute, gritting his teeth. Her legs were stretched out in front of her and her hat was on her lap. He squatted down and looked her in the face. It was totally expressionless. "You got exactly what you deserved," he said. "Now get up."

He picked up her pocketbook and put what had fallen out back in it. He picked the hat up off her lap. The penny caught his eye on the sidewalk and he picked that up and let it drop before her eyes into the purse. Then he stood up and leaned over and held his hand out to pull her up. She remained immobile. He sighed. Rising above them on either side were black apartment buildings, marked with irregular rectangles of light. At the end of the block a man came out of a door and walked off in the opposite direction. "All right," he said, "suppose somebody happens by and wants to know why you're sitting on the sidewalk?"

She took the hand and, breathing hard, pulled heavily up on it and then stood for a moment, swaying slightly as if the spots of light in the darkness were circling around her. Her eyes, shadowed and confused, finally settled on his face. He did not try to conceal his irritation. "I hope this teaches you a lesson," he said. She leaned forward and her eyes raked his face. She seemed trying to determine his identity. Then, as if she found nothing familiar about him, she started off with a headlong movement in the wrong direction.

"Aren't you going on to the Y?" he asked.

"Home," she muttered.

"Well, are we walking?"

For answer she kept going. Julian followed along, his hands behind him. He saw no reason to let the lesson she had had go without backing it up with an explanation of its meaning. She might as well be made to understand what had happened to her. "Don't think that was just an uppity Negro woman," he said. "That was the whole colored race which will no longer take your condescending pennies. That was your black double. She can wear the same hat as you, and to be sure," he added gratuitously (because he thought it was funny), "it looked better on her than it did on you. What all this means," he said, "is that the old world is gone. The old manners are obsolete and your graciousness is not worth a damn." He thought bitterly of the house that had been lost for him. "You aren't who you think you are," he said.

She continued to plow ahead, paying no attention to him. Her hair had come undone on one side. She dropped her pocketbook and took no notice. He stooped and picked it up and handed it to her but she did not take it.

"You needn't act as if the world has come to an end," he said, "because it hasn't. From now on you've got to live in a new world and face a few realities for a change. Buck up," he said, "it won't kill you."

She was breathing fast.

"Let's wait on the bus," he said.

"Home," she said thickly.

"I hate to see you behave like this," he said. "Just like a child. I should be able to expect more of you." He decided to stop where he was and make her stop and wait for the bus. "I'm not going any farther," he said, stopping. "We're going on the bus."

She continued to go on as if she had not heard him. He took a few steps and caught her arm and stopped her. He looked into her face and caught his breath. He was looking into a face he had never seen before. "Tell Grandpapa to come get me," she said.

He stared, stricken.

"Tell Caroline to come get me," she said.

Stunned, he let her go and she lurched forward again, walking as if one leg were shorter than the other. A tide of darkness seemed to be sweeping her from him. "Mother!" he cried. "Darling, sweetheart, wait!" Crumpling, she fell to the pavement. He dashed forward and fell at her side, crying, "Mamma, Mamma!" He turned her over. Her face was fiercely distorted. One eye, large and staring, moved slightly to the left as if it had become unmoored. The other remained fixed on him, raked his face again, found nothing and closed.

"Wait here, wait here!" he cried and jumped up and began to run for help toward a cluster of lights he saw in the distance ahead of him. "Help, help!" he shouted, but his voice was thin, scarcely a thread of sound. The lights drifted farther away the faster he ran and his feet moved numbly as if they carried him nowhere. The tide of darkness seemed to sweep him back to her, postponing from moment to moment his entry into the world of guilt and sorrow.

❖

Flannery O'Connor was born in Savannah in 1925, graduated from the Georgia State College for Women in 1945, studied writing at Iowa for two years, lived in New York City, then Connecticut, then returned to Milledgeville, Georgia, in 1950. Her work has won many awards, including Ford Foundation and Kenyon Review *fellowships, and first prize in the O. Henry short story collections in 1956 and 1963. There are two novels,* Wise Blood *(1952) and* The Violent Bear It Away *(1960), and two collections of stories,* A Good Man Is Hard to Find *(1955) and* Everything That Rises Must Converge *(1965). Her work is often cited as belonging to the Southern Gothic tradition, and it is true that violent incidents and grotesque characters do recur in it; but there is always great meaning in the incident and great humanity in the characters. Her work must be included in any anthology intended to show how very excellent American fiction has been in our times, but doing this somewhat misrepresents the future. No matter what is achieved in the years to come, the excellence will be less than we had every right to expect: for Flannery O'Connor died in 1964, when she was thirty-nine.*

In "Everything That Rises Must Converge" we have a wonderfully ironic view of two sets of mothers and sons, one white and one black, risen from a widely different past of slavery, decadence, and no money to converge on a desegregated bus in a present full of pride and dignity, topped by two identical, hopelessly ridiculous purple and green hats. The two women, apparently so different from each other, are the same in many ways. Their shared sense of the past of slavery is of course interpreted differently by each. Julian's mother uses the glorification of her family's slave-owning past to define her sense of who she is now; she has used it to give herself the courage to support her son and send him to college, and to ignore the poverty and ugliness of her present way of life. "Her eyes, sky-blue, were as innocent and untouched by experience as they must have been when she was ten." This innocence is what keeps her defenses impervious to a present that she cannot accept because it would mean giving up the identity and the security of the past which keep her going. It is the same innocence of the present and remembrance of the past that made the Reconstruction possible, and her achievement is implicitly likened to it. The sources of her strength are those of the South as a whole. But she makes the mistake of dealing with integration as she has dealt with poverty and widowhood and the loss of the old mansion—as if it hadn't happened. One point of the story is that the South as a whole should not make the same mistake. The behavior of the Negro mother, similarly, is implicitly likened to that of the Negro in the South in general. She sees every gesture of genteel "graciousness" as a reminder, which it clearly is, of the degradations and humiliations of her own past. Her present pride and dignity depend on her ability to reject every act that could be associated with it. The vehemence of her rejection of the patronizing penny is directly related to her powerlessness to change any other aspects of her present situation. The sons—the four-year-old in his Tyrolean hat and Julian in his tie and college education—are each a symbol to his mother of her feeling that "she had enjoyed the struggle and that she thought she had won." The failure of Julian's "sympathy" and "complete objectivity" toward Negroes should not be misinterpreted as a southern writer's reaction to northern oversimplification of the Negro-white problem in the South. Julian represents a southern point of view, a modern attitude that is right about recognizing what has happened in the present, but he is wrong—in fact shows a failure of the very sympathy and objectivity he is so proud of—in his emotional disgust with the innocence and blindness that gave his mother strength to rebuild their life. He sees the ugliness of it, but this makes him retreat into "a kind of mental bubble in which he established himself when he could not bear to be a part of what was going on around him." He takes no identity or security or strength whatsoever from the past, but longs for it secretly—and it is a past that he has not simply lost, but never actually knew. He knows that he is "too intelligent to be a success" and that there is "no future ahead of him." He is unable to make sense of either his mother or the Negro woman or to prevent the collision of the rising forces they represent. The ending is strong, but the matter-of-factness, the accuracy of detail with which the rest of the story is done, makes it believable. It is an act of violence, of the sort one often finds in Flannery O'Connor's stories, but just as the humanity of these grotesque women in their hideous hats has been revealed to us, so is the meaning of the violent act. The author is telling us that the modern intelligent southerner, educated and supported by a struggle in the past, must break out of his "mental bubble," must overcome his disgust and impatience with the past, must use his "sympathy" and "objectivity" for more than token acts, and must somehow take action to prevent the collision of converging rising forces, so that the Negro, after an equally difficult struggle in the present, will not be so enraged at every intimation of the past as to destroy what little of its blind strength remains. The story is told in human terms and is not an allegory; but another point of the story may be that if the southerner is unable to prevent this destructive convergence it will mark the South's "entry into the world of guilt and sorrow."

JOHN A. WILLIAMS

Son in the Afternoon

◇◇◇◇◇◇◇

IT WAS HOT. I tend to be a bitch when it's hot. I goosed the little Ford over Sepulveda Boulevard toward Santa Monica until I got stuck in the traffic that pours from L.A. into the surrounding towns. I'd had a very lousy day at the studio.

I was—still am—a writer and this studio had hired me to check scripts and films with Negroes in them to make sure the Negro moviegoer wouldn't be offended. The signs were already clear one day the whole of American industry would be racing pell-mell to get a Negro, showcase a spade. I was kind of a pioneer. I'm a *Negro* writer, you see. The day had been tough because of a couple of verbs—slink and walk. One of those Hollywood hippies had done a script calling for a Negro waiter to slink away from the table where a dinner party was glaring at him. I said the waiter should walk, not slink, because later on he becomes a hero. The Hollywood hippie, who understood it all because he had some colored friends, said that it was essential to the plot that the waiter slink. I said you don't slink one minute and become a hero the next; there has to be some consistency. The Negro actor I was standing up for said nothing either way. He had played Uncle Tom roles so long that he had become Uncle Tom. But the director agreed with me.

Anyway . . . hear me out now. I was on my way to Santa Monica to pick up my mother, Nora. It was a long haul for such a hot day. I had planned a quiet evening: a nice shower, fresh clothes, and then I would have dinner at the Watkins and talk with some of the musicians on the scene for a quick taste before they cut to their gigs. After, I was going to the Pigalle down on Figueroa and catch Earl Grant at the organ, and still later, if nothing exciting happened, I'd pick up Scottie and make it to the Lighthouse on the Beach or to the Strollers and listen to some of the white boys play. I liked the long drive, especially while listening to Sleepy Stein's show on the radio. Later, much later of course, it would be home, back to Watts.

So you see, this picking up Nora was a little inconvenient. My mother was a maid for the Couchmans. Ronald Couchman was an architect, a good one I understood from Nora who has a fine sense for this sort of thing; you don't work in some hundred-odd houses during your life without getting some idea of the way a house should be laid out. Couchman's wife, Kay, was a playgirl who drove a white Jaguar from one party to another. My mother didn't like her too much; she didn't seem to care much for her son, Ronald, junior. There's something wrong with a parent who can't really love her own child, Nora thought. The Couchmans lived in a real fine residential section, of course. A number of actors lived nearby, character actors, not really big stars.

Somehow it is very funny. I mean that the maids and butlers knew everything about these people, and these people knew nothing at all about the help. Through Nora and her friends I knew who was laying whose wife; who had money and who *really* had money; I knew about the wild parties hours before the police, and who smoked marijuana, when, and where they got it.

To get to Couchman's driveway I had to go three blocks up one side of a palm-planted center strip and back down the other. The driveway bent gently, then swept back out of sight of the main road. The house, sheltered by slim palms, looked like a transplanted New England Colonial. I parked and walked to the kitchen door, skirting the growling Great Dane who was tied to a tree. That was the route to the kitchen door.

I don't like kitchen doors. Entering people's houses by them, I mean. I'd done this thing most of my life when I called at places where Nora worked to pick up the patched or worn sheets or the half-eaten roasts, the battered, tarnished silver—the fringe benefits of a housemaid. As a teen-ager I'd told Nora I was through with that crap; I was not going through anyone's kitchen door. She only laughed and said I'd learn. One day soon after, I called for her and without knocking walked right through the front door of this house and right on through the living room. I was almost out of the room when I saw feet behind the couch. I leaned over and there was Mr. Jorgensen and his wife making out like crazy. I guess they thought Nora had gone and it must have hit them sort of suddenly and they went at it like the hell-bomb was due to drop any minute. I've been that way too, mostly in the spring. Of course, when Mr. Jorgensen looked over his shoulder and saw me, you know what happened. I was thrown out and Nora right behind me. It was the middle of winter, the old man was sick and the coal bill three months overdue. Nora was right about those kitchen doors: I learned.

My mother saw me before I could ring the bell. She opened the door. "Hello," she said. She was breathing hard, like she'd been running or something. "Come in and sit down. I don't know *where* that Kay is. Little Ronald is sick and she's probably out gettin' drunk again." She left me then and trotted back through the house, I guess to be with Ronnie. I hated the combination of her white nylon uniform, her dark brown face and the wide streaks of gray in her hair. Nora had married this guy from Texas a few years after the old man had died. He was all right. He made out okay. Nora didn't have to work, but she just couldn't be still; she always had to be doing something. I suggested she quit work, but I had as much luck as her husband. I used to tease her about liking to be around those white folks. It would have been good for her to take an extended trip around the country visiting my brothers and sisters. Once she got to Philadelphia, she could go right out to the cemetery and sit awhile with the old man.

I walked through the Couchman home. I liked the library. I thought if I knew Couchman I'd like him. The room made me feel like that. I left it and went into the big living room. You could tell that Couchman had let his wife do that. Everything in it was fast, dart-like, with no sense of ease. But on the walls were several of Couchman's conceptions of buildings and homes. I guess he was a disciple of Wright. My mother walked rapidly through the room without looking at me and said, "Just be patient, Wendell. She should be here real soon."

"Yeah," I said, "with a snootful." I had turned back to the drawings when Ronnie scampered into the room, his face twisted with rage.

"Nora!" he tried to roar, perhaps the way he'd seen the parents of some of his friends roar at their maids. I'm quite sure Kay didn't shout at Nora, and I don't think Couchman would. But then no one shouts at Nora. "Nora, you come right back here this minute!" the little bastard shouted and stamped and pointed to a spot on the floor where Nora was supposed to come to roost. I have a nasty temper. Sometimes it lies dormant for ages and at other times, like when the weather is hot and nothing seems to be going right, it's bubbling and ready to explode. "Don't talk to *my* mother like that, you little—!" I said sharply, breaking off just before I cursed. I wanted him to be large enough for me to strike. "How'd you like me to talk to *your* mother like that?"

The nine-year-old looked up at me in surprise and confusion. He hadn't expected me to say anything. I was just another piece of furniture. Tears rose in his eyes and spilled out onto his pale cheeks. He put his hands behind him, twisted them. He moved backwards, away from me. He looked at my mother with a "Nora, come help me" look. And sure enough, there was Nora, speeding back across the room, gathering the kid in her arms, tucking his robe together. I was too angry to feel hatred for myself.

Ronnie was the Couchman's only kid. Nora loved him. I suppose that was the trouble. Couchman was gone ten, twelve hours a day. Kay didn't stay around the house any longer than she had to. So Ronnie had only my mother. I think kids should have someone to love, and Nora wasn't a bad sort. But somehow when the six of us, her own children, were growing up we never had her. She was gone, out scuffling to get those crumbs to put into our mouths and shoes for our feet and praying for something to happen so that all the space in between would be taken care of. Nora's affection for us took the form of rushing out into the morning's five o'clock blackness to wake some silly bitch and get her coffee; took form in her trudging five miles home every night instead of taking the streetcar to save money to buy tablets for us, to use at school, we said. But the truth was that all of us liked to draw and we went through a writing tablet in a couple of hours every day. Can you imagine? There's not a goddamn artist among us. We never had the physical affection, the pat on the head, the quick, smiling kiss, the "gimmee a hug" routine. All of this Ronnie was getting.

Now he buried his little blond head in Nora's breast and sobbed.

"There, there now," Nora said. "Don't you cry, Ronnie. Ol' Wendell is just jealous, and he hasn't much sense either. He didn't mean nuthin'."

I left the room. Nora had hit it of course, hit it and passed on. I looked back. It didn't look so incongruous, the white and black together, I mean. Ronnie was still sobbing. His head bobbed gently on Nora's shoulder. The only time I ever got that close to her was when she trapped me with a bearhug so she could whale the daylights out of me after I put a snowball through Mrs. Grant's window. I walked outside and lit a cigarette. When Ronnie was in the hospital the month before, Nora got me to run her way over to Hollywood every night to see him. I didn't like that worth a damn. All right, I'll admit it: it did upset me. All that affection I didn't get nor my brothers and sisters going to that little white boy who, without a doubt, when away from her called her the names he'd learned from adults. Can you imagine a nine-year-old kid calling Nora a "girl," "our girl"? I spat at the Great Dane. He snarled and then I bounced a rock off his fanny. "Lay down, you bastard," I muttered. It was a good thing he was tied up.

I heard the low cough of the Jaguar slapping against the road. The car was throttled down, and with a muted roar it swung into the driveway. The woman aimed for me. I was evil enough not to move. I was tired of playing with these people. At the last moment, grinning, she swung the wheel over and braked. She bounded out of the car like a tennis player vaulting over a net.

"Hi," she said, tugging at her shorts.

"Hello."

"You're Nora's boy?"

"I'm Nora's son." Hell, I was as old as she was; besides, I can't stand "boy."

"Nora tells us you're working in Hollywood. Like it?"

"It's all right."

"You must be pretty talented."

We stood looking at each other while the dog whined for her attention. Kay had a nice body and it was well tanned. She was high, boy, was she high. Looking at her, I could feel myself going into my sexy bastard routine; sometimes I can swing it great. Maybe it all had to do with the business inside. Kay took off her sunglasses and took a good look at me. "Do you have a cigarette?"

I gave her one and lit it. "Nice tan," I said. Most white people I know think it's a great big deal if a Negro compliments them on their tans. It's a large laugh. You have all this volleyball about color and come summer you can't hold the white folks back from the beaches, anyplace where you can get some sun. And of course the blacker they get, the more pleased they are. Crazy. If there is ever a Negro revolt, it will come during the summer and Negroes will descend upon the beaches around the nation and paralyze the country. You can't conceal cattle prods and bombs and pistols and police dogs when you're showing your birthday suit to the sun.

"You like it?" she asked. She was pleased. She placed her arm next to mine. "Almost the same color," she said.

"Ronnie isn't feeling well," I said.

"Oh, the poor kid. I'm so glad we have Nora. She's such a charm. I'll run right in and look at him. Do have a drink in the bar. Fix me one too, will you?" Kay skipped inside and I went to the bar and poured out two strong drinks. I made hers stronger than mine. She was back soon. "Nora was trying to put him to sleep and she made me stay out." She giggled. She quickly tossed off her drink. "Another, please?" While I was fixing her drink she was saying how amazing it was for Nora to have such a talented son. What she was really saying was that it was amazing for a servant to have a son who was not also a servant. "Anything can happen in a democracy," I said. "Servants' sons drink with madames and so on."

"Oh, Nora isn't a servant," Kay said. "She's part of the family."

Yeah, I thought. Where and how many times had I heard *that* before?

In the ensuing silence, she started to admire her tan again. "You think it's pretty good, do you? You don't know how hard I worked to get it." I moved close to her and held her arm. I placed my other arm around her. She pretended not to see or feel it, but she wasn't trying to get away either. In fact she was pressing closer and the register in my brain that tells me at the precise moment when I'm in, went off. Kay was very high. I put both arms around her and she put both hers around me. When I kissed her, she responded completely.

"Mom!"

"Ronnie, come back to bed," I heard Nora shout from the other room. We could hear Ronnie running over the rug in the outer room. Kay tried to get away from me, push me to one side, because we could tell that Ronnie knew where to look for his Mom: he was running right for the bar, where we were. "Oh, please," she said, "don't let him see us." I wouldn't let her push me away. "Stop!" she hissed. "He'll *see* us!" We stopped struggling just for an instant, and we listened to the echoes of the word *see*. She gritted her teeth and renewed her efforts to get away.

Me? I had the scene laid right out. The kid breaks into the room, see, and sees his mother in this real wriggly clinch with this colored guy who's just shouted at him, see, and no matter how his mother explains it away, the kid has the image—the colored guy and his mother—for the rest of his life, see?

That's the way it happened. The kid's mother hissed under her breath. "You're *crazy!*" and she looked at me as though she were seeing me or something about me for the very first time. I'd released her as soon as Ronnie, romping into the bar, saw us and came to a full, open-mouthed halt. Kay went to him. He looked first at me, then at his mother. Kay turned to me, but she couldn't speak.

Outside in the living room my mother called, "Wendell, where are you? We can go now."

I started to move past Kay and Ronnie. I felt many things, but I made myself think mostly, *There you little bastard, there.*

My mother thrust her face inside the door and said, "Good-bye, Mrs. Couchman. See you tomorrow. 'Bye, Ronnie."

"Yes," Kay said, sort of stunned. "Tomorrow." She was reaching for Ronnie's hand as we left, but the kid was slapping her hand away. I hurried quickly after Nora, hating the long drive back to Watts.

❖

John A. Williams was born in 1925 in Jackson, Mississippi, raised in Syracuse, New York, has his B.A. from the University of Syracuse and did graduate work there, and now lives in New York City. He has published four novels: The Angry Ones *(1960),* Night Song *(1961),* Sissie *(1963), and* The Man Who Cried I Am *(1967). He has also written three nonfiction books:* Africa, Her History, Lands and People *(1963);* The Protectors *(1964), about the U.S. Narcotics Bureau and published under a pseudonym; and* This Is My Country Too *(1965), an account of a journey he took across the United States for* Holiday *magazine in 1963. He has also edited an anthology of prose, poetry, and fiction on Negro themes, published origi-nally as* The Angry Black *(1962) and revised as* Beyond the Angry Black *(1967).*

In "Son in the Afternoon" we see another pair of Negro and white mothers and sons, but the situation is nevertheless startlingly different from that in Flannery O'Connor's "Everything That Rises Must Converge." This time we see the story, not from the point of view of the white son, but from that of the grown, successful, independent Negro son. He talks hip, moves fast, and has a successful social and professional life of his own. Yet again the past rises up to complicate things. The resentments of a childhood in which his mother's love and time were spent on white children in order to keep her own family going are still there, aggravated now by the brattish character of the white boy and the irresponsible character of his good-looking mother. Wendell's revenge is so perfectly suited to the hurts he has suffered that it has the quality of all those things people dream of saying and doing only after they realize they have reacted too mildly to an insulting situation. This daydream quality of the story is one indication of its slickness, another is the pseudo-hardboiled tone of the narration; thus, some of what the story reveals is inadvertent: the daydream of the perfect revenge. But the story also knowingly and revealingly puts into direct confrontation variations of the two archetypal kinds of Negro-white relations: basically "mammy" and "pinktoes." The first has of course been the traditional and only approved interracial love relation historically in America. Now, as economic leveling makes this relationship less common, it is also becoming somewhat suspect, by whites finally, as well as by Negroes, as being patronizing and exploitative and perhaps not as natural as it always seemed. "Pinktoes," as defined by Chester Himes in a preamble to his novel of that title, "is a term of indulgent affection applied to white women by Negro men, and sometimes conversely by Negro women to white men, but never adversely by either." It assumes sexual attraction. This relationship has been forbidden by law as miscegenation in many parts of America, and historically and traditionally it has been socially forbidden throughout the country. Now, in a parallel, or at least seesaw kind of change, it is becoming more common as the mammy relation grows less common, and similarly is considered not as unnatural as it once was. But, up to and into our changing times, the mammy relation has been approved and open and visible; and the pinktoes relation has been forbidden, hidden, invisible. In the variations on these two stereotypes of Negro-white love in this story, we see how the first causes the second, how the second is a resentful reaction to the exclusion that is one effect of the first. Kay has been excluded from Ronnie's love, as she has been from his room by Nora as she puts him to bed; Wendell recognizes that his reaction to Nora's love for Ronnie is jealousy. The pinktoes attraction between Kay and Wendell is for both of them something of an instrument of revenge and guilt, completely lacking the responsibility and affection of true adult love (whether interracial or otherwise) and lacking even the mutual devotion and dependence of the mammy love between Nora and Ronnie. Neither of these two kinds of relationship seems to have done much toward solving the Negro-white problem in America, partially perhaps because of the exclusivity of both. Mammy love has often incurred resentment among excluded Negroes, as shown here; and besides it too often happens that the white child's love for his Negro mammy remains within the parent-child axis, simply reversing later in life to a master-"boy" relationship, a kind of affectionate paternalism that considers all Negroes to be children. The pinktoes relationship is also exclusive, of course, and causes resentment and anger, for a great variety of not very good reasons, among those excluded of both races. A pinktoes relation that is not, as it is in this case, built on a reaction pattern of resentment and guilt is of course a different matter, and the stability and success of interracial marriages based on mature responsibility on both sides will in time do much to diminish the disapproval and antagonism of both races. For centuries in America the roles Negroes and whites played in this drama, interchanging the roles of parents and children, were socially and economically determined. Now, as the story makes clear, the rules have been changed, and both Negro and white should stop playing it as a game, sometimes playing grown-up parent and sometimes irresponsible child, and finally be willing to make contact with each other as adults.

BERNARD MALAMUD

Black Is My Favorite Color

◇◇◇◇◇◇◇

CHARITY SWEETNESS sits in the toilet eating her two hardboiled eggs while I'm having my ham sandwich and coffee in the kitchen. That's how it goes only don't get the idea of ghettoes. If there's a ghetto I'm the one that's in it. She's my cleaning woman from Father Divine and comes in once a week to my small three-room apartment on my day off from the liquor store. "Peace," she says to me, "Father reached on down and took me right up in Heaven." She's a small person with a flat body, frizzy hair, and a quiet face that the light shines out of, and Mama had such eyes before she died. The first time Charity Sweetness came in to clean, a little more than a year and a half, I made the mistake to ask her to sit down at the kitchen table with me and eat her lunch. I was still feeling not so hot after Ornita left but I'm the kind of a man—Nat Lime, forty-four, a bachelor with a daily growing bald spot on the back of my head, and I could lose frankly fifteen pounds—who enjoys company so long as he has it. So she cooked up her two hardboiled eggs and sat down and took a small bite out of one of them. But after a minute she stopped chewing and she got up and carried the eggs in a cup in the bathroom, and since then she eats there. I said to her more than once, "Okay, Charity Sweetness, so have it your way, eat the eggs in the kitchen by yourself and I'll eat when you're done," but she smiles absentminded, and eats in the toilet. It's my fate with colored people.

Although black is still my favorite color you wouldn't know it from my luck except in short quantities even though I do all right in the liquor store business in Harlem, on Eighth Avenue between 110th and 111th. I speak with respect. A large part of my life I've had dealings with Negro people, most on a business basis but sometimes for friendly reasons with genuine feeling on both sides. I'm drawn to them. At this time of my life I should have one or two good colored friends but the fault isn't necessarily mine. If they knew what was in my heart towards them, but how can you tell that to anybody nowadays? I've tried more than once but the language of the heart either is a dead language or else nobody understands it the way you speak it. Very few. What I'm saying is, personally for me there's only one human color and that's the color of blood. I like a black person if not because he's black, then because I'm white. It comes to the same thing. If I wasn't white my first choice would be black. I'm satisfied to be white because I have no other choice. Anyway, I got an eye for color. I appreciate. Who wants everybody to be the same? Maybe it's like some kind of a talent. Nat Lime might be a liquor dealer in Harlem, but once in the jungle in New Guinea in the Second War, I got the idea when I shot at a running Jap and missed him, that I had some kind of a talent, though maybe it's the kind where you have a marvelous idea now and then but in the end where do they come to? After all, it's a strange world.

Where Charity Sweetness eats her eggs makes me think about Buster Wilson when we were both boys in the Williamsburg section of Brooklyn. There was this long block of run-down dirty frame houses in the middle of a not-so-hot white neighborhood full of pushcarts. The Negro houses looked to me like they had been born and died there, dead not long after the beginning of the world. I lived on the next street. My father was a cutter with arthritis in both hands, big red knuckles and swollen fingers so he didn't cut, and my mother was the one who went to work. She sold paper bags from a second-hand pushcart in Ellery Street. We didn't starve but nobody ate chicken unless we were sick or the chicken was. This was my first acquaintance with a lot of black people and I used to poke around on their poor block. I think I thought, brother, if there can be like this, what can't there be? I mean I caught an early idea what life was about. Anyway I met Buster Wilson there. He used to play marbles by himself. I sat on the curb across the street, watching him shoot one marble lefty and the other one righty. The hand that won picked up the marbles. It wasn't so much of a game but he didn't ask me to come over. My idea was to be friendly, only he never encouraged, he discouraged. Why did I pick him out for a friend? Maybe because I had no others then, we were new in the neighborhood, from Manhattan. Also I liked his type. Buster did everything alone. He was a skinny kid and his brothers' clothes hung on him like worn-out potato sacks. He was a beanpole boy, about twelve, and I was then ten. His arms and legs were burnt out matchsticks. He always wore a brown wool sweater, one arm half unraveled, the other went down to the wrist. His long and narrow head had a white part cut straight in the short woolly hair, maybe with a ruler there, by his father, a barber but too drunk to stay a barber. In those days though I had little myself I was old enough to know who was better off, and the whole block of colored houses made me feel bad in the daylight. But I went there as much as I could because the street was full of life. In the night it looked different, but it's hard to tell a cripple in the dark. Sometimes I was afraid to walk by the houses when they were dark and quiet. I was afraid there were people looking at me that

I couldn't see. I liked it better when they had parties at night and every-body had a good time. The musicians played their banjos and saxophones and the houses shook with the music and laughing. The young girls, with their pretty dresses and ribbons in their hair, caught me in my throat when I saw them through the windows.

But with the parties came drinking and fights. Sundays were bad days after the Saturday night parties. I remember once that Buster's father, also long and loose, always wearing a dirty gray Homburg hat, chased another black man in the street with a half-inch chisel. The other one, maybe five feet high, lost his shoe and when they wrestled on the ground he was already bleeding through his suit, a thick red blood smearing the sidewalk. I was frightened by the blood and wanted to pour it back in the man who was bleeding from the chisel. On another time Buster's father was playing in a crap game with two big bouncy red dice, in the back of an alley between two middle houses. Then about six men started fist-fighting there, and they ran out of the alley and hit each other in the street. The neigh-bors, including children, came out and watched, everybody afraid but nobody moving to do anything. I saw the same thing near my store in Harlem, years later, a big crowd watching two men in the street, their breaths hanging in the air on a winter night, murdering each other with switch knives, but nobody moved to call a cop. I didn't either. Anyway, I was just a young kid but I still remember how the cops drove up in a police paddy wagon and broke up the fight by hitting everybody they could hit with big nightsticks. This was in the days before LaGuardia. Most of the fighters were knocked out cold, only one or two got away. Buster's father started to run back in his house but a cop ran after him and cracked him on his Homburg hat with a club, right on the front porch. Then the Negro men were lifted up by the cops, one at the arms and the other at the feet, and they heaved them in the paddy wagon. Buster's father hit the back of the wagon and fell, with his nose spouting very red blood, on top of three other men. I personally couldn't stand it, I was scared of the human race so I ran home, but I remember Buster watching without any expression in his eyes. I stole an extra fifteen cents from my mother's pocketbook and I ran back and asked Buster if he wanted to go to the movies. I would pay. He said yes. This was the first time he talked to me.

So we went more than once to the movies. But we never got to be friends. Maybe because it was a one-way proposition—from me to him. Which includes my invitations to go with me, my (poor mother's) movie money, Hershey chocolate bars, watermelon slices, even my best Nick Carter and Merriwell books that I spent hours picking up in the junk shops, and that he never gave me back. Once he let me go in his house to get a match so we could smoke some butts we found, but it smelled so heavy, so impossible, I died till I got out of there. What I saw in the way of furniture I won't mention—the best was falling apart in pieces. Maybe we went to the movies all together five or six matinees that spring and in the summertime, but when the shows were over he usually walked home by himself.

"Why don't you wait for me, Buster?" I said. "We're both going in the same direction."

But he was walking ahead and didn't hear me. Anyway he didn't answer.

One day when I wasn't expecting it he hit me in the teeth. I felt like crying but not because of the pain. I spit blood and said, "What did you hit me for? What did I do to you?"

"Because you a Jew bastard. Take your Jew movies and your Jew candy and shove them up your Jew ass."

And he ran away.

I thought to myself how was I to know he didn't like the movies. When I was a man I thought, you can't force it.

Years later, in the prime of my life, I met Mrs. Ornita Harris. She was standing by herself under an open umbrella at the bus stop, crosstown 110th, and I picked up her green glove that she had dropped on the wet sidewalk. It was in the end of November. Before I could ask her was it hers, she grabbed the glove out of my hand, closed her umbrella, and stepped in the bus. I got on right after her.

I was annoyed so I said, "If you'll pardon me, Miss, there's no law that you have to say thanks, but at least don't make a criminal out of me."

"Well, I'm sorry," she said, "but I don't like white men trying to do me favors."

I tipped my hat and that was that. In ten minutes I got off the bus but she was already gone.

Who expected to see her again but I did. She came into my store about a week later for a bottle of scotch.

"I would offer you a discount," I told her, "but I know you don't like a certain kind of a favor and I'm not looking for a slap in the face."

Then she recognized me and got a little embarrassed.

"I'm sorry I misunderstood you that day."

"So mistakes happen."

The result was she took the discount. I gave her a dollar off.

She used to come in about every two weeks for a fifth of Haig and Haig. Sometimes I waited on her, sometimes my helpers, Jimmy or Mason, also colored, but I said to give the discount. They both looked at me but I had nothing to be ashamed. In the spring when she came in we used to talk once in a while. She was a slim woman, dark but not the most dark, about thirty years I would say, also well built, with a combination nice legs and a good-size bosom that I like. Her face was pretty, with big eyes and high cheek bones, but lips a little thick and nose a little broad. Sometimes she didn't feel like talking, she paid for the bottle, less discount, and walked out. Her eyes were tired and she didn't look to me like a happy woman.

I found out her husband was once a window cleaner on the big build-ings, but one day his safety belt broke and he fell fifteen stories. After the funeral she got a job as a manicurist in a Times Square barber shop. I told her I was a bachelor and lived with my mother in a small three-room apartment on West Eighty-third near Broadway. My mother had cancer, and Ornita said she was very sorry.

One night in July we went out together. How that happened I'm still not so sure. I guess I asked her and she didn't say no. Where do you go out with a Negro woman? We went to the Village. We had a good dinner and walked in Washington Square Park. It was a hot night. Nobody was surprised when they saw us, nobody looked at us like we were against the law. If they looked maybe they saw my new lightweight suit that I bought yester-day and my shiny bald spot when we walked under a lamp, also how pretty she was for a man of my type. We went in a movie on West Eighth Street. I didn't want to go in but she said she had heard about the picture. We went in like strangers and we came out like strangers. I wondered what was in her mind and I thought to myself, whatever is in there it's not a certain white man that I know. All night long we went together like we were chained. After the movie she wouldn't let me take her back to Harlem. When I put her in a taxi she asked me, "Why did we bother?"

For the steak, I wanted to say. Instead I said, "You're worth the bother."

"Thanks anyway."

Kiddo, I thought to myself after the taxi left, you just found out what's what, now the best thing is forget her.

It's easy to say. In August we went out the second time. That was the night she wore a purple dress and I thought to myself, my God, what colors. Who paints that picture paints a masterpiece. Everybody looked at us but I had pleasure. That night when she took off her dress it was in a furnished room I had the sense to rent a few days before. With my sick mother, I couldn't ask her to come to my apartment, and she didn't want me to go home with her where she lived with her brother's family on West 115th near Lenox Avenue. Under her purple dress she wore a black slip, and when she took that off she had white underwear. When she took off the white underwear she was black again. But I know where the next white was, if you want to call it white. And that was the night I think I fell in love with her, the first time in my life though I have liked one or two nice girls I used to go with when I was a boy. It was a serious proposition. I'm the kind of a man when I think of love I'm thinking of marriage. I guess that's why I am a bachelor.

That same week I had a holdup in my place, two big men—both black —with revolvers. One got excited when I rang open the cash register so he could take the money and he hit me over the ear with his gun. I stayed in the hospital a couple of weeks. Otherwise I was insured. Ornita came to see me. She sat on a chair without talking much. Finally I saw she was uncomfortable so I suggested she ought to go home.

"I'm sorry it happened," she said.

"Don't talk like it's your fault."

When I got out of the hospital my mother was dead. She was a wonderful person. My father died when I was thirteen and all by herself she kept the family alive and together. I sat shive for a week and remembered how she sold paper bags on her pushcart. I remembered her life and what she tried to teach me. Nathan, she said, if you ever forget you are a Jew a goy will remind you. Mama, I said, rest in peace on this subject. But if I do something you don't like, remember, on earth it's harder than where you are. Then when my week of mourning was finished, one night I said, "Ornita, let's get married. We're both honest people and if you love me like I love you it won't be such a bad time. If you don't like New York I'll sell out here and we'll move someplace else. Maybe to San Francisco where nobody knows us. I was there for a week in the Second War and I saw white and colored living together."

"Nat," she answered me, "I like you but I'd be afraid. My husband woulda killed me."

"Your husband is dead."

"Not in my memory."

"In that case I'll wait."

"Do you know what it'd be like—I mean the life we could expect?"

"Ornita," I said, "I'm the kind of a man, if he picks his own way of life he's satisfied."

"What about children? Were you looking forward to half-Jewish polka dots?"

"I was looking forward to children."

"I can't," she said.

Can't is can't. I saw she was afraid and the best thing was not to push. Sometimes when we met she was so nervous that whatever we did she couldn't enjoy it. At the same time I still thought I had a chance. We were together more and more. I got rid of my furnished room and she came to my apartment—I gave away Mama's bed and bought a new one. She stayed with me all day on Sundays. When she wasn't so nervous she was affectionate, and if I know what love is, I had it. We went out a couple of times a week, the same way—usually I met her in Times Square and sent her home in a taxi, but I talked more about marriage and she talked less against it. One night she told me she was still trying to convince herself but she was almost convinced. I took an inventory of my liquor stock so I could put the store up for sale.

Ornita knew what I was doing. One day she quit her job, the next day she took it back. She also went away a week to visit her sister in Philadelphia for a little rest. She came back tired but said maybe. Maybe is maybe so I'll wait. The way she said it it was closer to yes. That was the winter two years ago. When she was in Philadelphia I called up a friend of mine from the Army, now CPA, and told him I would appreciate an invitation for an evening. He knew why. His wife said yes right away. When Ornita came back we went there. The wife made a fine dinner. It wasn't a bad time and they told us to come again. Ornita had a few drinks. She looked relaxed, wonderful. Later, because of a twenty-four hour taxi strike I had to take her home on the subway. When we got to the 116th Street station she told me to stay on the train, and she would walk the couple of blocks to her house. I didn't like a woman walking alone on the streets at that time of the night. She said she never had any trouble but I insisted nothing doing. I said I would walk to her stoop with her and when she went upstairs I would go back to the subway.

On the way there, on 115th in the middle of the block before Lenox, we were stopped by three men—maybe they were boys. One had a black hat with a half-inch brim, one a green cloth hat, and the third wore a black leather cap. The green hat was wearing a short coat and the other two had long ones. It was under a street light but the leather cap snapped a six-inch switchblade open in the light.

"What you doin' with this white son of a bitch?" he said to Ornita.

"I'm minding my own business," she answered him, "and I wish you would too."

"Boys," I said, "we're all brothers. I'm a reliable merchant in the neighborhood. This young lady is my dear friend. We don't want any trouble. Please let us pass."

"You talk like a Jew landlord," said the green hat. "Fifty a week for a single room."

"No charge fo' the rats," said the half-inch brim.

"Believe me, I'm no landlord. My store is 'Nathan's Liquors' between Hundred Tenth and Eleventh. I also have two colored clerks, Mason and Jimmy, and they will tell you I pay good wages as well as I give discounts to certain customers."

"Shut your mouth, Jewboy," said the leather cap, and he moved the knife back and forth in front of my coat button. "No more black pussy for you."

"Speak with respect about this lady, please."

I got slapped on my mouth.

"That ain't no lady," said the long face in the half-inch brim, "that's black pussy. She deserve to have evvy bit of her hair shave off. How you like to have evvy bit of your hair shave off, black pussy?"

"Please leave me and this gentleman alone or I'm gonna scream long and loud. That's my house three doors down."

They slapped her. I never heard such a scream. Like her husband was falling fifteen stories.

I hit the one that slapped her and the next I knew I was lying in the gutter with a pain in my head. I thought, goodbye, Nat, they'll stab me for sure, but all they did was take my wallet and run in three different directions.

Ornita walked back with me to the subway and she wouldn't let me go home with her again.

"Just get home safely."

She looked terrible. Her face was gray and I still remembered her scream. It was a terrible winter night, very cold February, and it took me an hour and ten minutes to get home. I felt bad for leaving her but what could I do?

We had a date downtown the next night but she didn't show up, the first time.

In the morning I called her in her place of business.

"For God's sake, Ornita, if we got married and moved away we wouldn't have that kind of trouble that we had. We wouldn't come in that neighborhood any more."

"Yes, we would. I have family there and don't want to move anyplace else. The truth of it is I can't marry you, Nat. I got troubles enough of my own."

"I coulda sworn you love me."

"Maybe I do but I can't marry you."

"For God's sake, why?"

"I got enough trouble of my own."

I went that night in a cab to her brother's house to see her. He was a quiet man with a thin mustache. "She gone," he said, "left for a long visit to some close relatives in the South. She said to tell you she appreciate your intentions but didn't think it will work out."

"Thank you kindly," I said.

Don't ask me how I got home.

Once on Eighth Avenue, a couple of blocks from my store, I saw a blind man with a white cane tapping on the sidewalk. I figured we were going in the same direction so I took his arm.

"I can tell you're white," he said.

A heavy colored woman with a full shopping bag rushed after us.

"Never mind," she said, "I know where he live."

She pushed me with her shoulder and I hurt my leg on the fire hydrant. That's how it is. I give my heart and they kick me in my teeth.

"Charity Sweetness—you hear me?—come out of the goddamn toilet!"

"Black Is My Favorite Color" is in many ways a rough story: rough in technique and tone for so controlled a writer as Malamud; and on a rough,

touchy subject—the difficult, controversial relationship between Negroes and Jews. James Baldwin has written about this question at least twice: in "The Harlem Ghetto" in Notes of a Native Son, *and in "Negroes are Anti-Semitic Because They're Anti-White" in* The New York Times Magazine. *Baldwin points out that many of the merchants in Harlem are Jewish and they exploit their Negro customers. He says: "The Jew is singled out by Negroes not because he acts differently from other white men, but because he doesn't." But the Negro ghetto present has great poignancy for the literate, successful Jew, for whom it is symbolic of his own ghetto past. And it is also attractive as a free-and-easy place, "where the action is," directly opposite to the restraints imposed by Jewish culture and religion. In two earlier stories in this anthology "I Look Out For Ed Wolfe" and "When You're Excused You're Excused"—the voyage to Harlem figures as part of the escape from and the search for the Jewish self, and it is against this background that "Black Is My Favorite Color" should be read.*

Malamud tells his story from the bittersweet, humorous point of view of a Jewish bachelor who is "in the liquor store business in Harlem." Charity Sweetness eating her hard-boiled eggs in the bathroom is a marvelously ludicrous image of Nat Lime's sense of being excluded from the simplest kind of shared life with his "favorite color." The blacks have decreed no commensality and, as the story later explains, no connubium—even when love is possible (as with Nat and Ornita), even when there are places (Greenwich Village) and people (Nat's CPA buddy and wife) that accept the mixed couple happily and easily. Nat and Ornita are nice, ordinary people, but no world-beaters. Because he has grown up in a Jewish ghetto next door to a Negro ghetto that was even worse off ("ghetto" American-style, segregated not by walls but by socioeconomic deprivation and immobility), Nat feels that he is "going in the same direction" as Buster Wilson, the Negro boy he treats and takes to the movies. But Buster finally hits him in the teeth and curses him out, just as do the three Negroes who see him walking Ornita home at night on 115th Street. That finishes Nat and the ghetto for Ornita, who leaves "for a long visit to some close relatives in the South." The story-argument ends with another Negro, "a blind man with a white cane," whom irrepressible Nat again figures must be "going in the same direction." But even the blind man can tell Nat is white, and a colored woman, who claims to know where the blind man lives, pushes Nat away and into a fire hydrant. This sets up the rationale for his final cry to Charity Sweetness to "come out of that goddamn toilet." "I give my heart," he says, "and they kick me in my teeth."

Nat's difficulty, of course, is that "heart," a wonderful and prominent Jewish concern, has nothing to do with how Negroes feel about white men, and especially Jews. Take Nat, "Nat Lime": his name does not seem to belong to any particular nationality or race; he has changed his neighborhood, and not to Harlem, either; he only makes his living from, or off,

Negroes in Harlem. As his mother told him, "If you ever forget you are a Jew a goy will remind you." But the goyim-Negroes who do remind him and despise him for his Jewishness are not turning against a fellow ghetto sharer who loves and wants to help them. They are reacting in a very natural way to the particular kind of white man who has risen from the ghetto by making money from it—the Jewish landlord and merchant. There is no possibility of choice involved here for Nat; as a successful white man he is part of the socioeconomic structure that keeps Negroes in their ghettos. Heart doesn't get them out. To the Negro, still locked in, Nat's love is like having a man come and stand on your stomach while pleading with you to take his hand and get out of the gutter. Naturally, you'd rather knock him off your belly first. The point is that the liberal white man, Jew or not Jew, cannot expect to earn love, salve his guilt, and take responsibility for his fellow black man by an individual reassurance of love. This kind of offer is the same sort of some-of-my-best-friends-are-Jews implied acceptance of another's inferior status by claiming personal exception to it. As Ornita has her brother tell Nat, "she appreciate your intentions but didn't think it will work out."

JAMES BALDWIN

The Man Child

◇◇◇◇◇◇◇

As THE SUN began preparing for her exit, and he sensed the waiting night, Eric, blond and eight years old and dirty and tired, started homeward across the fields. Eric lived with his father, who was a farmer and the son of a farmer, and his mother, who had been captured by his father on some far-off, unblessed, unbelievable night, who had never since burst her chains. She did not know that she was chained anymore than she knew that she lived in terror of the night. One child was in the churchyard, it would have been Eric's little sister and her name would have been Sophie: for a long time, then, his mother had been very sick and pale. It was said that she would never, really, be better, that she would never again be as she had been. Then, not long ago, there had begun to be a pounding in his mother's belly, Eric had sometimes been able to hear it when he lay against her breast. His father had been pleased. I *did that,* said his father, big, laughing, dreadful, and red, and Eric knew how it was done, he had seen the horses and the blind and dreadful bulls. But then, again, his mother had been sick, she had had to be sent away, and when she came back the pounding was not there anymore, nothing was there anymore. His father laughed less, something in his mother's face seemed to have gone to sleep forever.

Eric hurried, for the sun was almost gone and he was afraid the night would catch him in the fields. And his mother would be angry. She did not really like him to go wandering off by himself. She would have forbidden it completely and kept Eric under her eye all day but in this she was overruled: Eric's father liked to think of Eric as being curious about the world and as being daring enough to explore it, with his own eyes, by himself.

His father would not be at home. He would be gone with his friend, Jamie, who was also a farmer and the son of a farmer, down to the tavern. This tavern was called The Rafters. They went each night, as his father said, imitating an Englishman he had known during a war, to *destruct The*

Rafters, sir. They had been destructing The Rafters long before Eric had kicked in his mother's belly, for Eric's father and Jamie had grown up together, gone to war together, and survived together—never, apparently, while life ran, were they to be divided. They worked in the fields all day together, the fields which belonged to Eric's father. Jamie had been forced to sell his farm and it was Eric's father who had bought it.

Jamie had a brown and yellow dog. This dog was almost always with him; whenever Eric thought of Jamie he thought also of the dog. They had always been there, they had always been together: in exactly the same way, for Eric, that his mother and father had always been together, in exactly the same way that the earth and trees and the sky were together. Jamie and his dog walked the country roads together, Jamie walking slowly in the way of country people, seeming to see nothing, head slightly bent, feet striking surely and heavily on the earth, never stumbling. He walked as though he were going to walk to the other end of the world and knew it was a long way but knew that he would be there by morning. Sometimes he talked to his dog, head bent a little more than usual and turned to one side, a slight smile playing about the edges of his granite lips; and the dog's head snapped up, perhaps he leapt upon his master, who cuffed him down lightly, with one hand. More often he was silent. His head was carried in a cloud of blue smoke from his pipe. Through this cloud, like a ship on a foggy day, loomed his dry and steady face. Set far back, at an unapproachable angle, were those eyes of his, smoky and thoughtful, eyes which seemed always to be considering the horizon. He had the kind of eyes which no one had ever looked into—except Eric, only once. Jamie had been walking these roads and across these fields, whistling for his dog in the evenings as he turned away from Eric's house, for years, in silence. He had been married once, but his wife had run away. Now he lived alone in a wooden house and Eric's mother kept his clothes clean and Jamie always ate at Eric's house.

Eric had looked into Jamie's eyes on Jamie's birthday. They had had a party for him. Eric's mother had baked a cake and filled the house with flowers. The doors and windows of the great kitchen all stood open on the yard and the kitchen table was placed outside. The ground was not muddy as it was in winter, but hard, dry, and light brown. The flowers his mother so loved and so labored for flamed in their narrow borders against the stone wall of the farmhouse; and green vines covered the grey stone wall at the far end of the yard. Beyond this wall were the fields and barns, and Eric could see, quite far away, the cows nearly motionless in the bright green pasture. It was a bright, hot, silent day, the sun did not seem to be moving at all.

This was before his mother had had to be sent away. Her belly had been beginning to grow big, she had been dressed in blue, and had seemed—that day, to Eric—younger than she was ever to seem again.

Though it was still early when they were called to table, Eric's father and Jamie were already tipsy and came across the fields, shoulders touching, laughing, and telling each other stories. To express disapproval and also, perhaps, because she had heard their stories before and was bored, Eric's mother was quite abrupt with them, barely saying, "Happy Birthday, Jamie" before she made them sit down. In the nearby village church bells rang as they began to eat.

It was perhaps because it was Jamie's birthday that Eric was held by something in Jamie's face. Jamie, of course, was very old. He was thirty-four today, even older than Eric's father, who was only thirty-two. Eric wondered how it felt to have so many years and was suddenly, secretly glad that he was only eight. For today, Jamie *looked* old. It was perhaps the one additional year which had done it, this day, before their very eyes—a metamorphosis which made Eric rather shrink at the prospect of becoming nine. The skin of Jamie's face, which had never before seemed so, seemed wet today, and that rocky mouth of his was loose; loose was the word for everything about him, the way his arms and shoulders hung, the way he sprawled at the table, rocking slightly back and forth. It was not that he was drunk. Eric had seen him much drunker. Drunk, he became rigid, as though he imagined himself in the army again. No. He was old. It had come upon him all at once, today, on his birthday. He sat there, his hair in his eyes, eating, drinking, laughing now and again, and in a very strange way, and teasing the dog at his feet so that it sleepily growled and snapped all through the birthday dinner.

"Stop that," said Eric's father.

"Stop what?" asked Jamie.

"Let that stinking useless dog alone. Let him be quiet."

"Leave the beast alone," said Eric's mother—very wearily, sounding as she often sounded when talking to Eric.

"Well, now," said Jamie, grinning, and looking first at Eric's father and then at Eric's mother, "it *is* my beast. And a man's got a right to do as he likes with whatever's his."

"That dog's got a right to bite you, too," said Eric's mother, shortly.

"This dog's not going to bite me," said Jamie, "he knows I'll shoot him if he does."

"That dog knows you're not going to shoot him," said Eric's father. "Then you *would* be all alone."

"All alone," said Jamie, looked around the table. "All alone." He lowered his eyes to his plate.

Eric's father watched him. He said, "It's pretty serious to be all alone at *your* age." He smiled. "If I was you, I'd start thinking about it."

"I'm thinking about it," said Jamie. He began to grow red.

"No, you're not," said Eric's father, "you're dreaming about it."

"Well, goddammit," said Jamie, even redder now, "it isn't as though I haven't tried!"

"Ah," said Eric's father, "that was a *real* dream, that was. I used to pick *that* up on the streets of town every Saturday night."

"Yes," said Jamie, "I bet you did."

"I didn't think she was as bad as all that," said Eric's mother, quietly. *"I liked her. I was surprised when she ran away."*

"Jamie didn't know how to keep her," said Eric's father. He looked at Jamie and chanted: *"Jamie, Jamie, pumkin-eater, had a wife and couldn't keep her!"* At this, Jamie at last looked up, into the eyes of Eric's father. Eric laughed again, more shrilly, out of fear. Jamie said:

"Ah, yes, you can talk, you can."

"It's not my fault," said Eric's father, "if you're getting old—and haven't got anybody to bring you your slippers when night comes—and no pitter-patter of little feet—"

"Oh, leave Jamie alone," said Eric's mother, "he's *not* old, leave him alone."

Jamie laughed a peculiar, high, clicking laugh which Eric had never heard before, which he did not like, which made him want to look away and, at the same time, want to stare. "Hell, no," said Jamie, "I'm not old. I can still do all the things we used to do." He put his elbows on the table, grinning. "I haven't ever told you, have I, about the things we used to do?"

"No, you haven't," said Eric's mother, "and I certainly don't want to hear about them now."

"He wouldn't tell you anyway," said Eric's father, "he knows what I'd do to him if he did."

"Oh, sure, sure," said Jamie, and laughed again. He picked up a bone from his plate. "Here," he said to Eric, "why don't you feed my poor mistreated dog?"

Eric took the bone and stood up, whistling for the dog; who moved away from his master and took the bone between his teeth. Jamie watched with a smile and opened the bottle of whiskey and poured himself a drink. Eric sat on the ground beside the dog, beginning to be sleepy in the bright, bright sun.

"Little Eric's getting big," he heard his father say.

"Yes," said Jamie, "they grow fast. It won't be long now."

"Won't be long *what?*" he heard his father ask.

"Why, before he starts skirt-chasing like his Daddy used to do," said Jamie. There was mild laughter at the table in which his mother did not join; he heard instead, or thought he heard, the familiar, slight, exasperated intake of her breath. No one seemed to care whether he came back to the table or not. He lay on his back, staring up at the sky, wondering—wondering what he would feel like when he was old—and fell asleep.

When he awoke his head was in his mother's lap, for she was sitting on the ground. Jamie and his father were still sitting at the table; he knew this from their voices, for he did not open his eyes. He did not want to move or speak. He wanted to remain where he was, protected by his mother, while the bright day rolled on. Then he wondered about the uncut birthday cake. But he was sure, from the sound of Jamie's voice, which was thicker now, that they had not cut it yet; or if they had, they had certainly saved a piece for him.

"—ate himself just as full as he could and then fell asleep in the sun like a little animal," Jamie was saying, and the two men laughed. His father—though he scarcely ever got as drunk as Jamie did, and had often carried Jamie home from The Rafters—was a little drunk, too.

Eric felt his mother's hand on his hair. By opening his eyes very slightly he would see, over the curve of his mother's thigh, as through a veil, a green slope far away and beyond it the everlasting, motionless sky.

"—she was a no-good *bitch,*" said Jamie.

"She was beautiful," said his mother, just above him.

Again, they were talking about Jamie's wife.

"Beauty!" said Jamie, furious. "Beauty doesn't keep a house clean. Beauty doesn't keep a bed warm, neither."

Eric's father laughed. "You were so—poetical—in those days, Jamie," he said. "Nobody thought you cared much about things like that. I guess she thought you didn't care, neither."

"I cared," said Jamie, briefly.

"In fact," Eric's father continued, "I *know* she thought you didn't care."

"How do you know?" asked Jamie.

"She told me," Eric's father said.

"What do you mean," asked Jamie, "what do you mean, she told you?"

"I mean just that. She told me."

Jamie was silent.

"In those days," Eric's father continued after a moment, "all you did was walk around the woods by yourself in the daytime and sit around The Rafters in the evenings with me."

"You two were always together then," said Eric's mother.

"Well," said Jamie, harshly, "at least that hasn't changed."

"Now, you know," said Eric's father, gently, "it's not the same. Now I got a wife and kid—and another one coming—"

Eric's mother stroked his hair more gently, yet with something in her touch more urgent, too, and he knew that she was thinking of the child who lay in the churchyard, who would have been his sister.

"Yes," said Jamie, "you really got it all fixed up, you did. You got it all—the wife, the kid, the house, and all the land."

"I didn't steal your farm from you. It wasn't my fault you lost it. I gave you a better price for it than anybody else would have done."

"I'm not blaming you. I know all the things I have to thank you for."

There was a short pause, broken, hesitantly, by Eric's mother. "What I don't understand," she said, "is why, when you went away to the city, you didn't *stay* away. You didn't really have anything to keep you here."

There was the sound of a drink being poured. Then, "No. I didn't have nothing—*really*—to keep me here. Just all the things I ever knew—all the things—*all* the things—I ever cared about."

"A man's not supposed to sit around and mope," said Eric's father, wrathfully, "for things that are over and dead and finished, things that can't *ever* begin again, that can't ever be the same again. That's what I mean when I say you're a dreamer—and if you hadn't kept on dreaming so long, you might not be alone now."

"Ah, well," said Jamie, mildly, and with a curious rush of affection in his voice, "I know you're the giant-killer, the hunter, the lover—the real old Adam, that's you. I know you're going to cover the earth. I know the world depends on men like you."

"And you're damn right," said Eric's father, after an uneasy moment.

Around Eric's head there was a buzzing, a bee, perhaps, a blue-fly, or a wasp. He hoped that his mother would see it and brush it away, but she did not move her hand. And he looked out again, through the veil of his eyelashes, at the slope and the sky, and then saw that the sun had moved and that it would not be long now before she would be going.

"—just like you already," Jamie said.

"You think my little one's like me?" Eric knew that his father was smiling—he could almost feel his father's hands.

"Looks like you, walks like you, talks like you," said Jamie.

"*And* stubborn like you," said Eric's mother.

"Ah, yes," said Jamie, and sighed. "You married the stubbornest, most determined—most selfish—man I know."

"I didn't know you felt that way," said Eric's father. He was still smiling.

"I'd have warned you about him," Jamie added, laughing, "if there'd been time."

"Everyone who knows you feels that way," said Eric's mother, and Eric felt a sudden brief tightening of the muscle in her thigh.

"Oh, *you*," said Eric's father, "I know *you* feel that way, women like to feel that way, it makes them feel important. But," and he changed to the teasing tone he took so persistently with Jamie today, "I didn't know my fine friend, Jamie, here—"

It was odd how unwilling he was to open his eyes. Yet, he felt the sun on him and knew that he wanted to rise from where he was before the sun went down. He did not understand what they were talking about this afternoon, these grown-ups he had known all his life; by keeping his eyes closed he kept their conversation far from him. And his mother's hand lay on his head like a blessing, like protection. And the buzzing had ceased, the bee, the blue-fly, or the wasp seemed to have flown away.

"—if it's a boy this time," his father said, "we'll name it after you."

"That's touching," said Jamie, "but that really won't do me—or the kid—a hell of a lot of good."

"Jamie can get married and have kids of his own any time he decides to," said Eric's mother.

"No," said his father, after a long pause, "Jamie's thought about it too long."

And, suddenly, he laughed and Eric sat up as his father slapped Jamie on the knee. At the touch, Jamie leaped up, shouting, spilling his drink and overturning his chair, and the dog beside Eric awoke and began to bark. For a moment, before Eric's unbelieving eyes, there was nothing in the yard but noise and flame.

His father rose slowly and stared at Jamie. "What's the matter with you?"

"What's the matter with me!" mimicked Jamie. "What's the matter with me? What the hell do you care what's the matter with me! What the hell have you been riding me for all day like this? What do you want? What do you *want?*"

"I want you to learn to hold your liquor for one thing," said his father, coldly. The two men stared at each other. Jamie's face was red and ugly and tears stood in his eyes. The dog, at his legs, kept up a furious prancing and barking. Jamie bent down and, with one hand, with all his might, slapped his dog, which rolled over, howling, and ran away to hide itself under the shadows of the far grey wall.

Then Jamie stared again at Eric's father, trembling, and pushed his hair back from his eyes.

"You better pull yourself together," Eric's father said. And, to Eric's mother. "Get him some coffee. He'll be all right."

Jamie set his glass on the table and picked up the overturned chair. Eric's mother rose and went into the kitchen. Eric remained sitting on the ground, staring at the two men, his father and his father's best friend, who had become so unfamiliar. His father, with something in his face which Eric had never before seen there, a tenderness, a sorrow—or perhaps it was, after all, the look he sometimes wore when approaching a calf he was about to slaughter—looked down at Jamie where he sat, head bent, at the table. "You take things too hard," he said. "You always have. I was only teasing you for your own good."

Jamie did not answer. His father looked over to Eric, and smiled.

"Come on," he said. "You and me are going for a walk."

Eric, passing on the side of the table farthest from Jamie, went to his father and took his hand.

"Pull yourself together," his father said to Jamie. "We're going to cut your birthday cake as soon as me and the little one come back."

Eric and his father passed beyond the grey wall where the dog still whimpered, out into the fields. Eric's father was walking too fast and Eric stumbled on the uneven ground. When they had gone a little distance his father abruptly checked his pace and looked down at Eric, grinning.

"I'm sorry," he said. "I guess I said we were going for a walk, not running to put out a fire."

"What's the matter with Jamie?" Eric asked.

"Oh," said his father, looking westward where the sun was moving, pale orange now, making the sky ring with brass and copper and gold—which, like a magician, she was presenting only to demonstrate how variously they could be transformed—"Oh," he repeated, "there's nothing wrong with Jamie. He's been drinking a lot," and he grinned down at Eric, "and he's been sitting in the sun—you know, his hair's not as thick as yours," and he ruffled Eric's hair, "and I guess birthdays make him nervous. Hell," he said, "they make me nervous, too."

"Jamie's *very* old," said Eric, "isn't he?"

His father laughed. "Well, Butch, he's not exactly ready to fall into the grave yet—he's going to be around awhile, is Jamie. Hey," he said, and looked down at Eric again, "you must think I'm an old man, too."

"Oh," said Eric, quickly, "I know you're not as old as Jamie."

His father laughed again. "Well, thank you, son. That shows real confidence. I'll try to live up to it."

They walked in silence for awhile and then his father said, not looking at Eric, speaking to himself, it seemed, or to the air: "No, Jamie's not so old. He's not as old as he should be."

"How old *should* he be?" aked Eric.

"Why," said his father, "he ought to be his age," and, looking down at Eric's face, he burst into laughter again.

"Ah," he said, finally, and put his hand on Eric's head again, very gently, very sadly, "don't you worry now about what you don't understand. The time is coming when you'll have to worry—but that time hasn't come yet."

Then they walked till they came to the steep slope which led to the railroad tracks, down, down, far below them, where a small train seemed to be passing forever through the countryside, smoke, like the very definition of idleness, blowing out of the chimney stack of the toy locomotive. Eric thought, resentfully, that he scarcely ever saw a train pass when he came here alone. Beyond the railroad tracks was the river where they sometimes went swimming in the summer. The river was hidden from them now by the high bank where there were houses and where tall trees grew.

"And this," said his father, "is where your land ends."

"What?" said Eric.

His father squatted on the ground and put one hand on Eric's shoulder. "You know all the way we walked, from the house?" Eric nodded. "Well," said his father, "that's your land."

Eric looked back at the long way they had come, feeling his father watching him.

His father, with a pressure on his shoulder made him turn; he pointed:

"And over there. It belongs to you." He turned him again. "And that," he said, "that's yours, too."

Eric stared at his father. "Where does it end?" he asked.

His father rose. "I'll show you that another day," he said. "But it's further than you can walk."

They started walking slowly, in the direction of the sun.

"When did it get to be mine?" asked Eric.

"The day you were born," his father said, and looked down at him and smiled.

"My father," he said, after a moment, "had some of this land—and when he died, it was mine. He held on to it for me. And I did my best with the land I had, and I got some more. I'm holding on to it for you."

He looked down to see if Eric was listening. Eric was listening, staring at his father and looking around him at the great countryside.

"When I get to be a real old man," said his father, "even older than old Jamie there—you're going to have to take care of all this. When I die it's going to be yours." He paused and stopped; Eric looked up at him. "When you get to be a big man, like your Papa, you're going to get married and have children. And all this is going to be theirs."

"And when *they* get married?" Eric prompted.

"All this will belong to *their* children," his father said.

"Forever?" cried Eric.

"Forever," said his father.

They turned and started walking toward the house.

"Jamie," Eric asked at last, "how much land has *he* got?"

"Jamie doesn't have any land," his father said.

"Why not?" asked Eric.

"He didn't take care of it," his father said, "and he lost it."

"Jamie doesn't have a wife anymore, either, does he?" Eric asked.

"No," said his father. "He didn't take care of her, either."

"And he doesn't have any little boy," said Eric—very sadly.

"No," said his father. Then he grinned. "But I have."

"*Why* doesn't Jamie have a little boy?" asked Eric.

His father shrugged. "Some people do, Eric, some people don't."

"Will I?" asked Eric.

"Will you what?" asked his father.

"Will I get married and have a little boy?"

His father seemed for a moment both amused and checked. He looked down at Eric with a strange, slow smile. "Of course you will," he said at last. "Of course you will." And he held out his arms. "Come," he said, "climb up. I'll ride you on my shoulders home."

So Eric rode on his father's shoulders through the wide green fields which belonged to him, into the yard which held the house which would hear the first cries of his children. His mother and Jamie sat at the table talking quietly in the silver sun. Jamie had washed his face and combed his hair, he seemed calmer, he was smiling.

"Ah," cried Jamie, "the lord, the master of this house arrives! And bears on his shoulders the prince, the son, and heir!" He described a flourish, bowing low in the yard. "My lords! Behold your humble, most properly chastised servant, desirous of your—compassion, your love, and your forgiveness!"

"Frankly," said Eric's father, putting Eric on the ground, "I'm not sure that this is an improvement." He looked at Jamie and frowned and grinned. "Let's cut that cake."

Eric stood with his mother in the kitchen while she lit the candles—thirty-five, one, as they said, to grow on, though Jamie, surely, was far past the growing age—and followed her as she took the cake outside. Jamie took the great, gleaming knife and held it with a smile.

"Happy Birthday!" they cried—only Eric said nothing—and then Eric's mother said, "You have to blow out the candles, Jamie, before you cut the cake."

"It looks so pretty the way it is," Jamie said.

"Go ahead," said Eric's father, and clapped him on the back, "be a man."

Then the dog, once more beside his master, awoke, growling, and this made everybody laugh. Jamie laughed loudest. Then he blew out the candles, all of them at once, and Eric watched him as he cut the cake. Jamie raised his eyes and looked at Eric and it was at this moment, as the suddenly blood-red sun was striking the topmost tips of trees, that Eric had looked into Jamie's eyes. Jamie smiled that strange smile of an old man and Eric moved closer to his mother.

"The first piece for Eric," said Jamie, then, and extended it to him on the silver blade.

That had been near the end of summer, nearly two months ago. Very shortly after the birthday party, his mother had fallen ill and had had to be taken away. Then his father spent more time than ever at The Rafters; he and Jamie came home in the evenings, stumbling drunk. Sometimes, during the time that his mother was away, Jamie did not go home at all, but spent the night at the farm house; and once or twice Eric had awakened in the middle of the night, or near dawn, and heard Jamie's footsteps walking up and down, walking up and down, in the big room downstairs. It had been a strange and dreadful time, a time of waiting, stillness, and silence. His father rarely went into the fields, scarcely raised himself to give orders to his farm hands—it was unnatural, it was frightening, to find him around the house all day, and Jamie was there always, Jamie and his dog. Then one day Eric's father told him that his mother was coming home but that she would not be bringing him a baby brother or sister, not this time, nor in any time to come. He started to say something more, then looked at Jamie who was standing by, and walked out of the house. Jamie followed him slowly, his hands in his pockets and his head bent. From the time of the birthday party, as though he were repenting of that outburst, or as though it had frightened him, Jamie had become more silent than ever.

When his mother came back she seemed to have grown older—old; she seemed to have shrunk within herself, away from them all, even, in a kind of storm of love and helplessness, away from Eric; but, oddly, and most particularly, away from Jamie. It was in nothing she said, nothing she did—or perhaps it was in everything she said and did. She washed and cooked for Jamie as before, took him into account as much as before as a part of the family, made him take second helpings at the table, smiled good night to him as he left the house—it was only that something had gone out of her familiarity. She seemed to do all that she did out of memory and from a great distance. And if something had gone out of her ease, some-thing had come into it, too, a curiously still attention, as though she had been startled by some new aspect of something she had always known. Once or twice at the supper table, Eric caught her regard bent on Jamie, who, obliviously, ate. He could not read her look, but it reminded him of that moment at the birthday party when he had looked into Jamie's eyes. She seemed to be looking at Jamie as though she were wondering why she had not looked at him before; or as though she were discovering, with some surprise, that she had never really liked him but also felt, in her weariness and weakness, that it did not really matter now.

Now, as he entered the yard, he saw her standing in the kitchen door-way, looking out, shielding her eyes against the brilliant setting sun.

"Eric!" she cried, wrathfully, as soon as she saw him. "I've been looking high and low for you for the last hour. You're getting old enough to have some sense of responsibility and I wish you wouldn't worry me so when you know I've not been well."

She made him feel guilty at the same time that he dimly and resentfully felt that justice was not all on her side. She pulled him to her, turning his face up toward hers, roughly, with one hand.

"You're filthy," she said, then. "Go around to the pump and wash your face. And hurry, so I can give you your supper and put you to bed."

And she turned and went into the kitchen, closing the door lightly be-hind her. He walked around to the other side of the house, to the pump.

On a wooden box next to the pump was a piece of soap and a damp rag. Eric picked up the soap, not thinking of his mother, but thinking of the day gone by, already half asleep: and thought of where he would go tomorrow. He moved the pump handle up and down and the water rushed out and wet his socks and shoes—this would make his mother angry, but he was too tired to care. Nevertheless, automatically, he moved back a little. He held the soap between his hands, his hands beneath the water.

He had been many places, he had walked a long way and seen many things that day. He had gone down to the railroad tracks and walked beside the tracks for awhile, hoping that a train would pass. He kept telling himself that he would give the train one more last chance to pass; and when he had given it a considerable number of last chances, he left the railroad bed and climbed a little and walked through the high, sweet meadows. He walked through a meadow where there were cows and they looked at him dully with their great dull eyes and moo'd among each other about him. A man from the far end of the field saw him and shouted, but Eric could not tell whether it was someone who worked for his father or not and so he turned and ran away, ducking through the wire fence. He passed an apple tree, with apples lying all over the ground—he wondered if the apples belonged to him, if he were still walking on his own land or had gone past it—but he ate an apple anyway and put some in his pockets, watching a lone brown horse in a meadow far below him nibbling at the grass and flicking his tail. Eric pretended that he was his father and was walking through the fields as he had seen his father walk, looking it all over calmly, pleased, knowing that everything he saw belonged to him. And he stopped and pee'd as he had seen his father do, standing wide-legged and heavy in the middle of the fields; he pretended at the same time to be smoking and talking, as he had seen his father do. Then, having watered the ground, he walked on, and all the earth, for that moment, in Eric's eyes, seemed to be celebrating Eric.

Tomorrow he would go away again, somewhere. For soon it would be winter, snow would cover the ground, he would not be able to wander off alone.

He held the soap between his hands, his hands beneath the water; then he heard a low whistle behind him and a rough hand on his head and the soap fell from his hands and slithered between his legs onto the ground.

He turned and faced Jamie, Jamie without his dog.

"Come on, little fellow," Jamie whispered. "We got something in the barn to show you."

"Oh, did the calf come yet?" asked Eric—and was too pleased to wonder why Jamie whispered.

"Your Papa's there," said Jamie. And then: "Yes. Yes, the calf is coming now."

And he took Eric's hand and they crossed the yard, past the closed kitchen door, past the stone wall and across the field, into the barn.

"But *this* isn't where the cows are!" Eric cried. He suddenly looked up at Jamie, who closed the barn door behind them and looked down at Eric with a smile.

"No," said Jamie, "that's right. No cows here." And he leaned against the door as though his strength had left him. Eric saw that his face was wet, he breathed as though he had been running.

"Let's go see the cows," Eric whispered. Then he wondered why he was whispering and was terribly afraid. He stared at Jamie, who stared at him.

"In a minute," Jamie said, and stood up. He had put his hands in his pockets and now he brought them out and Eric stared at his hands and began to move away. He asked, "Where's my Papa?"

"Why," said Jamie, "he's down at The Rafters, I guess. I have to meet him there soon."

"I have to go," said Eric. "I have to eat my supper." He tried to move to the door, but Jamie did not move. "I have to go," he repeated, and, as Jamie moved toward him the tight ball of terror in his bowels, in his throat, swelled and rose, exploded, he opened his mouth to scream but Jamie's fingers closed around his throat. He stared, stared into Jamie's eyes.

"That won't do you any good," said Jamie. And he smiled. Eric struggled for breath, struggled with pain and fright. Jamie relaxed his grip a little and moved one hand and stroked Eric's tangled hair. Slowly, wondrously, his face changed, tears came into his eyes and rolled down his face.

Eric groaned—perhaps because he saw Jamie's tears or because his throat was so swollen and burning, because he could not catch his breath, because he was so frightened—he began to sob in great, unchildish gasps. "Why do you hate my father?"

"I love your father," Jamie said. But he was not listening to Eric. He was far away—as though he were struggling, toiling inwardly up a tall, tall mountain. And Eric struggled blindly, with all the force of his desire to live, to reach him, to stop him before he reached the summit.

"Jamie," Eric whispered, "you can have the land. You can have all the land."

Jamie spoke, but not to Eric: "I don't want the land."

"I'll be your little boy," said Eric. "I'll be your little boy forever and forever and forever—and you can have the land and you can live forever! Jamie!"

Jamie had stopped weeping. He was watching Eric.

"We'll go for a walk tomorrow," Eric said, "and I'll show it to you, all of it—really and truly—if you kill my father I can be your little boy and we can have it all!"

"This land," said Jamie, "will belong to no one."

"Please!" cried Eric, "oh, please! Please!"

He heard his mother singing in the kitchen. Soon she would come out to look for him. The hands left him for a moment. Eric opened his mouth to scream, but the hands then closed around his throat.

Mama, Mama.

The singing was further and further away. The eyes looked into his, there was a question in the eyes, the hands tightened. Then the mouth began to smile. He had never seen such a smile before. He kicked and kicked.

Mama. Mama. Mama. Mama. Mama.

Far away, he heard his mother call him.

Mama.

He saw nothing, he knew that he was in the barn, he heard a terrible breathing near him, he thought he heard the sniffling of beasts, he remembered the sun, the railroad tracks, the cows, the apples, and the ground. He thought of tomorrow—he wanted to go away again somewhere tomorrow. *I'll take you with me,* he wanted to say. He wanted to argue the question, the question he remembered in the eyes—wanted to say, *I'll tell my Papa you're hurting me.* Then terror and agony and darkness overtook him, and his breath went violently out of him. He dropped on his face in the straw in the barn, his yellow head useless on his broken neck.

Night covered the countryside and here and there, like emblems, the lights of houses glowed. A woman's voice called, "Eric! Eric!"

Jamie reached his wooden house and opened his door; whistled, and his dog came bounding out of darkness, leaping up on him; and he cuffed it down lightly, with one hand. Then he closed his door and started down the road, his dog beside him, his hands in his pockets. He stopped to light his pipe. He heard singing from The Rafters, then he saw the lights; soon, the lights and the sound of singing diminished behind him. When Jamie no longer heard the singing, he began to whistle the song that he had heard.

◇

When James Baldwin's long, personal, polemical essay, The Fire Next Time, *appeared in* The New Yorker, *readers of that magazine were astounded and shocked to find, running along in thin columns of type between the slick advertisements for expensive products, such a direct and powerful exposition of the anger and hate the Negro feels for the white man. Even though there is not a single Negro character in "The Man Child," the story is another expression of this same anger and hate.*

"The Man Child" appears in Baldwin's collection of stories called Going to Meet the Man, *and "The Man" in Negro parlance is, of course, "The White Man." The "Man Child" of the title is, then, in this context, "the son of the white man." It also has other connotations, including that of "the inheritor," the man child through which a man's future is established, and hence, in even more general terms, the future itself. The story should be read as a cautionary tale, a warning from the Negro to the white man. Jamie is given Baldwin's own first name. It is also the name of Nigger Jim, who accompanied Huck Finn on the idyllic trip down the Mississippi on a raft; and in this connection it should be noticed that the name of the*

tavern where Jamie and Eric's father used to drink and pal around so much together is called "The Rafters." Leslie Fiedler's notorious interpretation of the Huck Finn–Nigger Jim trip (and the other interracial excursions in the American fiction classics) as expressing homosexual attraction between the races probably has some relevance here and suggests a supplementary reading of the story, which we will consider in a moment. Jamie has lost his wife and his land, which is now owned by Eric's father, and has nothing. He is told by Eric's father that it is his own fault, that he must settle down and become more serious and responsible—an analogy to all the things white men have for centuries told Negroes in order to justify their deprivation. At the birthday dinner, Eric's father prods and teases Jamie just as Jamie teases the dog at his feet to make it growl and snap. Throughout the story Jamie's relation to the dog is used as a parallel to Eric's father's relation to him—and by extension to the white man's relation to the Negro throughout history. It is made clear that Eric's mother will bear no other children: Eric is to be the only inheritor. As his father walks over their land with Eric, he explains how it has been handed down from his father and how Eric will pass it on to his children and so on—"forever," as Eric says. But what Baldwin warns is: "This land will belong to no one!" A great black darkness will descend on it, sometime just as the sun sets. We will rise up and throttle your future. No matter how friendly you may seem to have been with us (singing and drinking in the tavern, and together on the raft, and since childhood), you have nevertheless dispossessed us, and we will take a terrible revenge. The story is imperfectly wrought, and although the allegory is concealed, it is far from subtle. It suffers greatly by comparison with the other rural Gothic tale of murder of a child on a farm that we considered earlier, R. V. Cassill's "The Father." Also, the tone of this story is somewhat hysterical or high-pitched, intimating the supplementary meaning: an expression of an even more general anger at those who marry and manage to keep their wives and have children and own property and live settled lives. This second interpretation may devolve as an expression of Baldwin's own irregular circumstances. The first interpretation, however, is the strongest possible expression of his feelings as a Negro: a strong statement of his race's refusal to be dispossessed "forever."

◇–◇

The problem of "race" for Negroes is like the problem of age for the elderly: it cannot be reversed or ignored, and the exceptional person tends to prove the rule of discrimination. The stories in this section have shown how differentiation by skin color brings about the highly visible–therefore invisible paradox; how the urban educated Negro can avoid the ranks of persecu-

tion in a highly bureaucratized Army situation while the rural uneducated Negro cannot; how city life offers conflicting kinds of self-realization; how the situation of the Negro in the South is inseparable from its history; how a more or less conscious resentment of his history of exclusions affects the conduct of a relatively successful Negro in his relations with whites; how a common history of racial oppression fails to make common cause for white Jews and black Negroes; how Negro hatred of whites is an expression of the realization of their disinheritance as Americans. While there are many kinds of racial discrimination, even of racial success, not covered here, one thing is clear: Negroes are still suffering from a kind of differentiation that is entirely different from the kinds of prejudice defined by religion or nationality of origin. It's unlike all the other differences among Americans with which Negroes also contend—differences of wealth, political power, education, occupation, opportunity.

For those Americans who do not suffer from the ineradicable differentiations of race, age, or sex, and think of themselves as securely "middle class," there seems to be another process of differentiation at work, one that depends not on broad categorical exclusions but on the minutiae of life styles, explored in the section that follows.

Differentiations and Confusions

IN CLASS—MINUTE DISTINCTIONS
IN THE MIDDLE

There is an argument—one that we do not propose to enter—about whether class as such—good, old-fashioned socioeconomic class, upper and middle and lower—is a relevant or useful description of the patterns and divisions of American life, and even about whether it exists at all in America today. Like personality typologies, it has the disadvantage of saying at once too much and too little about any individual assigned to any particular type; but like almost any typology, class has a sort of instinctive, recognizable thumbnail truth about it that makes it a concept difficult to discard. Surely societies in other eras were more structured, less fluid than ours; class distinctions were then more distinct; fewer qualifications had to be made when defining them. In America today we are more likely to think of differences in people in terms of their occupation, their upbringing, what part of the country they come from, all their manners and attitudes and consumption patterns, their education, their income—in terms, that is, of a bewildering multiplicity of differences, some large, some small, some important, some trivial. Yet all these qualities can be conceived as constituting class, as being determined by class, and also as being the very qualities by which a person is assigned to a class. The trouble seems to be in finding enough class divisions or names to accommodate a sufficient number of different people to constitute a class mode. Slice it as thin as one can—into upper, upper-middle, middle-middle, lower-middle, lower, with certain helpful pseudo-classes like "celebrity" and "bohemian" on the side—there still doesn't seem to be any way to divide up the country's population on a purely socioeconomic basis. It sometimes seems that it is at least as useful to start with one aspect of things and then see what other traits and characteristics associate with basic divisions in that aspect—as, for instance, the differences between the blue collar class of workers and the white collar class; or the differences between the highbrows, the upper-middle brows, the lower-middle brows, and the lowbrows; or between urbanites, suburbanites, and exurbanites. Yet there seem to be as many aspects to class as there are to personality, and simply to establish a great number of scales by which to measure class does not finally tell us much about a person. It may finally be that, again like personality, there are as many different classes as there are different people, each in a "class" of his own.

As our oft-cited forces of urbanization, industrialization, and bureau-cratization work to decrease the differences among Americans from any particular region or income group or social level, it is nevertheless true that each individual American's experience today is of more encounters with a greater variety of people, people more unlike himself, than ever before. In any one day we may deal with in business or be introduced to socially more persons more unlike ourselves than many of our grandfathers might have met in a whole lifetime. Thus, in American life, just as social classes as such may be said to be breaking down, the differences among people seem every day to be more conspicuous. It is this infinite variety in the middle that causes so much confusion among people of different back-grounds attempting to work with one another or to live with one another. In another era they most likely would not even have met; or if they did, there would have been a prescribed code of behavior for them to adopt with one another. Now they are expected to operate out of the assumption that everyone is the same. America purports to be a classless society, and those who understand this to mean that it is a land without differences must expect to be confused in their relations with others.

The purely *upper class* and the purely *lower class do not figure in this analysis; although they of course exist, it is to some extent outside the province of how we live now. The upper class as such seems to consist of ways of life as different as old ladies in rocking chairs in Newport and their powerful, wealthy statesmen-sons on the one hand, and the café society jet-setters with their celebrity and artistic associations on the other. The purely lower class in America today seems to live in a variety of separate, powerless excluded cultures, in poverty pockets and racial ghettos that are almost entirely outside the fabric of American life as the rest of us know it. The main connection either of these classes has with the rest of us is through some sort of* interview—*either that of the journalist in the case of the rich, or the social worker in the case of the poor. They both live in different lands that we inquire about from time to time.*

"Class fiction" as such has usually been associated with those who wrote about extremes of upper or lower: John Steinbeck's Grapes of Wrath *or* Cannery Row, *for instance, about the poor; J. P. Marquand's* The Late George Apley *about the rich. Such fiction is concerned mostly with the effects of having money and position and power, or with the effects of not having them. To some extent it is a different subject, concerned as it is with the often rigid and unchanging sets of definitions about the way these people must or should live. The central experience in such fiction tends to be the difficulties of changing a set of strict rules or of breaking through a set of limited possibilities; only some minor differences and deviations are acceptable, as merely eccentric. Much more revealing about the way most*

of us live now is the fiction that tries to deal with the misconceptions and uncertainties and confusions that occur as a result of ignoring or not recognizing the multiplicity of differences among people that exist in the great muddling pot in the middle. Even here, however, stories that center around class distinctions don't seem to have the vision and imagination and soaring language of much other good contemporary fiction. They seem to have a kind of leaden circumstantiality, an emphasis on clothes and eating habits and the kind of car owned, which weighs the story down in "insightful list-making." The picky accuracy of the fiction of John O'Hara is a well-known example. When the attributes and motivations of a class of people are the determining factors and chief interest in what happens in a story, the unique qualities of the individual characters become less important. In most great fiction, no matter how accurate and insightful the rendering of class distinctions, the characters remain in our memories as specific and unique individuals, not as representatives of a class. Contrary to those who maintain that the novel is an art form having to do with facts, and contrary to those who maintain that the novel is dying as a form because it is based on manners and social differences and these differences are disappearing—contrary to all such clichés with wrong reasons for wrong conclusions, the obvious must be stated: class distinctions, although of course almost always an essential aspect of setting and characterization, has never been one of the great themes of fiction.

ELIZABETH HARDWICK

The Classless Society

◇◇◇◇◇◇◇

WILLARD NESBITT marked his place in *The Power Elite* with a match-stick and put the book on the table beside his reading chair. Nesbitt was a handsome man, with a brisk, trim, lecturing air about him both in and out of his classroom. He was a professor of American history at the University of Chicago and well known beyond that for his books, his round-table discussions, his articles in the Sunday *Times*. He was clever, had easy, rather flippant manners, and treated the academic world as if he were just passing through on his way to, perhaps, the State Department or the United Nations. Hidden in his sensible heart was the desire to run sometime for the Senate, like Paul Douglas.

Nesbitt put down his book with an ambiguous sigh. He found it very difficult to like anything with his whole mind. He was always being disappointed, even in the best. Laurence Olivier's Hotspur turned out to be not quite as vigorous as he had heard it was; David Oistrakh's violin playing left him with a sense of imperfection hard to define; he had expected there would be a lot more in Dr. Jones' biography of Freud than he found; and he thought there might well be a lot less on every subject from Arnold Toynbee. Professor Nesbitt rejoiced in his failure to concur with the common opinion; he cherished his dissents and worked to refine and elaborate them as if they were a piece of historical composition always going to press. When he said, hesitating and smiling slyly, that de Tocqueville's "Democracy in America" was immensely readable and would cause less trouble if thought of as a sort of poem, his students were charmed by his impudence. The theme that went the campus rounds, year in and year out, about Nesbitt was that whether one liked him or not, he was at least alive.

Henrietta, Willard's wife, looked up from the crossword puzzle in the *New Statesman & Nation*. The Nesbitts were expecting guests for dinner—Henrietta's cousin Dodo Babcock, and a colleague of Willard's, Clarence Anderson. The Nesbitts had known Anderson for five or six years. They invited him every year to several cocktail parties and small dinners, and yet they did not especially like him. The invitations were sometimes to be laid at the door of Clarence's condition of bachelorhood but more often to something demanding and disturbing in the man himself. Willard, if a number of months had passed without his making any special effort over Anderson, would begin to experience a feeling of unease, of neglectfulness vaguely dangerous to his own well-being. Anderson's themes were a devotion to academic life and a claim to be a nature molded by the habit of idealism and disinterestedness. He played upon these themes gently enough, but with assurance, leaving his auditors with the feeling of having been accused of something less than perfection.

"I dread seeing Dodo tonight, somehow," Henrietta said.

"All that branch of your Babcock relations fills me with gloom," Willard answered. "They have suffered the most fantastic collapse. The strain seems to have undergone a queer fatigue, as even metals are said to do. Or so I've heard."

"Metals?" Henrietta said sharply.

Willard went on, in a musing tone, "There is an element of mystery about this generation of Babcocks. They present with a good deal of clarity the ancient debate between environment and heredity. Their parents were so gay and rich, and the children are so melancholy and undistinguished. They haven't even got money."

"Yes, they do seem rather languid," Henrietta agreed. "John and Evelyn have tried them all and given them up, though I think they admit that young Perry is good fun upon occasion." John and Evelyn were Henrietta's brother and sister-in-law.

"But they think Perry's wife is awful. I distinctly remember Evelyn's saying that," Willard offered.

"I believe she thought it was *Dudley* Babcock's wife who was so awful," Henrietta said.

"Each in her own way, perhaps."

Henrietta Nesbitt had been born a Babcock. In Chicago, the name of this family rang out with a clear and beautiful glory. The founder of the family had made a fortune in the copper mines of the West; copper sons had married Chicago meat-packing daughters. Henrietta's branch of the family had never been as rich as Dodo Babcock's branch. Now both branches were of unexceptional means, though among the more distant cousins there were still Babcocks of large fortune.

Willard Nesbitt took pride in making no use of Henrietta's connection with the great and famous Babcock family. This was not the act of spiritual renunciation he sometimes imagined, since there was not a great deal of personal advantage to be gained from the connection; the advantage, such as it was, was purely aesthetic. Willard, straining to keep the proper degree of faith with what he described as his own "fabulously simple" beginnings, felt that the absence of material benefit from his marriage gave him the right—even the duty—to make creative use of his special knowledge, through Henrietta, of the decline of certain members of what he liked to call "the ruling class." On an intimate and yet ironic note, he sometimes declared he was less fascinated by the living Babcock fortune than by the dead one—those riches gone like a dear person, or buried by destiny like a once thriving village crushed by disaster. The financial decay of some of Henrietta's relatives served Nesbitt as fresh fact from which theories might be drawn.

"It's damned risky having Clarence Anderson to meet poor Dodo Babcock," Willard said, with a sigh.

"Do you suppose he'll be wearing his black loafers with the tassels on them?" Henrietta said.

"Of course, and God knows what to match. These English teachers are all Cockneys at heart, secretly in love with Princess Margaret."

"Poor Dodo," Henrietta said. "She has a faded regality, but her housekeeping is like a Puerto Rican's."

" 'Faded regality'—monstrous phrase. Probably accurate."

"Don't you like Clarence Anderson at all?" Henrietta asked lazily. "If not, why do you see him?"

"I always expect him to be something like Thorstein Veblen. You know, he's Norwegian, and from one of those states out there—Nebraska, I think."

"He probably does go in for 'pecuniary emulation'—or whatever Veblen called it," Henrietta said, with a smile. Nesbitt had been educating Henrietta for all the years of their marriage, but he did this without earnestness, because he was proud of his wife's somewhat destructive natural brightness and not ashamed of her ignorance. The frightfully poor education of the well-bred society lady was a topic they often discussed. If Henrietta thought, as Zola is said to have thought, that Charlemagne lived and flourished around the fifteenth century—well that was amusing. With her frightening gift for mockery, her disarming self-confidence, she at least did not have to talk cant, and that was worth all the education in the world. Or usually worth it. Willard had had occasion to feel Henrietta's bite sink into some sensitive spot of his own being.

"It certainly is hard to make the grade with you," Henrietta said, after a pause.

"Well, some few do at last succeed with me, but rare is the bird that meets with your unqualified praise," Willard answered in his most affectionate voice.

"Don't be ridiculous. . . . Please don't be over Dodo's head tonight. It's bad manners."

"But it is impossible not to be over Dodo's head. I thought manners was the art of the possible—or is that politics?"

"It can be cow-milking, for all I know. Dodo has her own peculiar backwardness—that I admit, since one must. But she's not stupid."

"I like old Dodo," Willard said, retreating hastily. (Henrietta did not like to be pushed the whole way in her condemnation of her family. Sometimes, if they drank too many Martinis before dinner, she would turn upon Willard and say, with profound intent, "You know nothing whatsoever about people with money and power. That you can go about all over the country, and on television, sounding off on the subject completely amazes me!")

"Do you think Dodo will be annoyed that we haven't asked someone more fancy than Clarence?" Henrietta wondered. "It's been such a long time since we've had her over I feel a little stingy not to be making it more of an occasion. One of the ways in which Dodo is absolutely unique is that you can't flatter her by intellectual appeal, so Clarence *as a mind* won't mean a thing to her. She's an old-fashioned girl—money and position speak louder to her than all the artistic or cultural honors in the world. Mother, for instance, is quite different. When we asked her to our cocktail party for that dull friend of Albert Schweitzer's, she was beside herself with joy and excitement."

"Actually, there is no one in Chicago fancier than Clarence Anderson when you come right down to it."

The Nesbitts had a four-room walkup apartment near the university. The place was brownish, shabby, comfortable, stuffed with books and periodicals—all of which indicated, like a workman's toolbox in a hallway, the life of the occupant. At the Nesbitts', there were also a few surprises, the most surprising and important of which was a huge abstraction done in the manner of Jackson Pollock. "By a very gifted young Chicago painter, a friend of ours," Willard would say by way of identification. The Jackson Pollock disciple had turned out to be a disappointment to the Nesbitts. He seemed to be becoming less known rather than more, but they did not take down the picture and store it in the basement, as the museums do. To be snobbish about Chicago painters seemed to them ludicrous and dull, like protesting about baseball or television. Among their other possessions were a magnificent silver tray, nearly as large as the abstraction, and a badly restored portrait of "Aunt Mag Pierce," by Sully, which hung with careful negligence in a not very light corner of the dining room, flanked on one side by a Medici print of Uccellos' "Cavalry Battle" and on the other side by a disc of hammered copper brought from Istanbul.

Just after Henrietta went to the bedroom to smooth her hair, the street doorbell rang. "There they are!" she called out. "Or at least there Clarence is. Dodo is probably still at home looking for her change purse or coloring her nails."

Willard opened the door and saw that Clarence had arrived first, but

Dodo was just behind him on the stairs, calling up to him wistfully, "We are both going to the same place. Of course, I couldn't have known."

Clarence had a rather controlled and faraway expression on his face. He loathed being patronized by the Nesbitts. He thought himself much more popular, serious, and clever than they; in his opinion, Willard was something of a charlatan, and Henrietta came under his suspicion as impertinent and shallow. Since he harbored these disparaging thoughts, the feeling he had that the Nesbitts, even at their friendliest, were somehow snubbing him made him rage with irritation and resentment. His dream was that he might get the jump on the Nesbitts—in some subtle, fascinating, and morally plausible way soar above them. That was the desperate hope behind his cool and stiff expression when the door opened.

Willard, seeing that Clarence *was* wearing his black loafers with the tassels on them, smiled and bowed. An amused and condescending look came involuntarily over his face—just the look that Clarence detested, and called "the hard-hearted Nesbitt smile."

When Dodo joined them, Willard said, "I don't know whether Henrietta told you that her cousin Dodo Babcock was dining with us tonight. And here she is."

"How do you do?" Dodo said, calmly inspecting Clarence. "I came by taxi for fear of being late. I hope I'm not."

"You're in perfect time," Willard said. Dodo was impressive in a dress of purple silk and a little cape of black broadtail. She did not look smart— the cape was worn in spots and the dress was not new—but she did have, resting upon the solid foundation of her privileged childhood, an awesome tranquillity, a quaintly pure and steadfast self-confidence. Her gaze was fresh, open-eyed, and self-esteeming, in the manner of a family portrait.

Clarence felt tricked and uncertain when he recognized the clear tremble of interest that flowed through him as he was presented to Dodo. He had not expected a relative of Henrietta's, an unmarried lady, clearly near his own age of thirty-eight. His mind, always painfully alerted by piercing longings, and his flirtatious heart leaped up to greet the complications and possibilities of the situation. He smiled, carefully measuring his gallantry.

"Dodo, darling, how are you!" Henrietta said gaily, coming out of her bedroom in a hurry as her guests entered, acting as if she had not expected them so soon. Henrietta hated to give the impression of being ready and waiting for anyone, and this led her to assume a flustered and brightly rushed air when guests arrived, even though she was, behind the busyness, prompt, efficient, and quite prepared to receive them. "You two have been introduced, I gather," she added, smiling brilliantly at Clarence and giving him her hand.

"You're looking awfully well," Clarence said, deciding to pay Henrietta, rather than Dodo, his first quietly uttered compliment.

"I wish I could believe you," Henrietta replied, smiling mischievously at

Clarence's way of feeling out a situation, as if he were a diplomat among an inscrutable, tricky people.

Clarence Anderson was not a lighthearted man, and when he took a notion to denounce someone, his nature forced him to assume a moralistic tone. This tone was quite in contrast to the way of the Nesbitts, who went in, simply and indefatigably, for the kind of impudence and gossip they judged to be amusing. Clarence never mentioned the defect of an acquaintance without clearly showing the poor, faulty person's character to be morally inferior to his own. When he used the word "dull," he did not mean to lament a lack of sprightliness so much as to expose a sluggish, self-loving soul, remarkably different from his own vigorous, light openness of feeling. With his impatient, moralizing bent, Clarence was a powerful enemy. Clarence's enmity was, like the Nesbitts' insults, purely verbal. He did not wish to effect a deterioration in his antagonist's circumstances so much as to cause everyone to think of his victim precisely as he did. If he thought someone charmingly foolish or harmlessly inane, he was not satisfied until the whole world acknowledged this foolishness or inanity. It was an agony to him that there might exist an intelligent person who knew his circle of friends and yet saw the various members of it in a light opposed to his own. To insist on his own view was, to his mind, "telling the truth." Stubbornly he repudiated the tolerant, careless opinion, and with a great show of idealism and objectivity he corrected it. This readiness to speak out led Clarence to imagine that others spoke out also, and when he was praised, as he often was by timid, well-mannered people, he took the praise as genuine and unmixed, and found much pleasure in it.

"I'll go first. I'd love a Martini, pet," Henrietta said, leading the way into the living room. She sat down, crossing her long, handsome legs, of which she was very vain. She wore high heels, which would have been painful if her delight in the way they showed her legs to advantage had not mysteriously made her nearly unconscious of any such pain. For the rest, she was passable in appearance—round nose, brown face, good teeth, and graying brown hair, difficult to manage.

"I'm very fond of gin myself," Dodo said thoughtfully. "I suppose one shouldn't say a thing like that, but I do think a gin drink is awfully good before dinner. God himself wouldn't drink it afterward."

"And what about you, Anderson?" Willard said abruptly. "You aren't to feel committed by the ready Martini pitcher."

"I don't feel committed, but I'll take one nevertheless. It would be a great deprivation to have to forgo what I really prefer."

Clarence was as clerical-suited as Nesbitt was brown-tweeded. This evening, Willard was dressed with even more than his usual sportiness: he was wearing an old jacket with suède patches on the elbows. Clarence immediately analyzed the patched jacket as a form of condescension toward himself. He marked it down against Willard as inverted snobbery. Clarence had, by his quickness to spot pretension, succeeded in turning quite a few people against the Nesbitts. He had made Willard's intellectual arrogance appear flimsy and ersatz. "What, in the long run, has Nesbitt written?" often passed Clarence's lips. As for Henrietta's connection with the Babcock family, Clarence sometimes made its very existence seem open to question, or, if admitted, a peculiar and interesting handicap, a disqualifying affliction.

When Willard saw Clarence's red bow tie and inky sack suit, he felt a gush of irritation, even though he knew that this was the way Clarence would and did dress, with a reasonable sort of up-to-dateness and appropriateness, as economically and neatly achieved as a little suburban house, with its breezeway, utility room, and dining area. Nesbitt wanted Clarence, as he said, to be, like Thorstein Veblen, a radical from the Western plains, and Clarence, in turn, thought Nesbitt should go around with a sign on his back that read, "Born in Akron, Ohio, of simple, decent stock. Undergraduate at Wayne, connection with Harvard on graduate level *only,* wife from minor branch of well-known Chicago family—the poor side."

Clarence smiled quietly at Dodo Babcock, and she returned his smile with equal quiet and composure. Dodo tended toward redness, even down to the girlish flush of her cheeks. Her hair was touched with auburn lights, her eyebrows were a scanty reddish brown, and her hands, pink as a shell, lay beautifully and languidly in her purple silk lap. In her face, there was the mark of a charming immaturity, of expectation still to be fulfilled, and a suggestion of hurt feelings—proud, disdainful chagrin, such as one finds in those for whom history is fully dramatized in the story of their own fate. A reactionary, of course, Clarence thought, but amiably, forgivingly.

"Well," Willard said, with a short laugh, waiting for the conversation to begin.

After a pause, Clarence said, "Did you know that idiot G. B. Cooper was being sent to Baghdad by the Ford Foundation? I have no doubt scholars, even bone-lazy ones like Cooper, can benefit from the advantages of foreign travel, but—"

"Baghdad. That's pretty foreign indeed," Dodo said vaguely.

"Exactly," Clarence said. "There is something exorbitant—monstrous —about these foundation affairs. They go beyond what anyone would expect. In the long run, I am most bothered by the details—the luxurious, preposterous details. Wife and children and Chevrolet all sent, free of charge, to Baghdad!"

"G. B. Cooper? I can't quite place him," Willard said.

"He's the most slavish follower of T. S. Eliot in America—perhaps in the world, for all I know. The whole—the whole, mind you—of his professional attitude comes out of 'Tradition and the Individual Talent.' I doubt he has read a critical work before or since."

"That doesn't seem quite enough baggage, somehow," Henrietta suggested.

"Wife, children, and car sent to Baghdad," Clarence repeated. "It's an unnerving thought. For quantity, lavishness, excess, trust our dear, huge America!"

"I bet they wish they had some quantity in Baghdad," Dodo said, nodding coquettishly.

Everyone smiled. "Have you ever applied for Baghdad yourself, Clarence?" Henrietta asked.

"God, no!" Clarence replied with heat.

"Or some more plausible place?" Willard added.

"To be perfectly frank," Clarence said, delighted to be able to state his position, "I have not applied for Baghdad, or Istanbul, or even London, the love of my life. I can't feel deeply needed in the Near East. I am astonished at those who can, and full of admiration for them. Trucking over the world with only my treasured Victorian prose to offer the fellahin —Cardinal Newman and Ruskin in the Garden of Allah? One must keep some sense of what is fitting. As for London, I am too full of gratitude and private feelings of reverence to want to go dashing over there, my pockets full of money, to tell them what they already know, or to do work they've already done."

"That's excessive. Your conscientiousness is out of control," Henrietta said, with a clear trace of ill-humor.

One of Clarence's "positions" was a refusal to apply for grants, fellowships, easy posts. Whether this attitude came from a fear of failure, even Willard, an inveterate and successful getter of grants, project funds, and endowments, was uncertain. Clarence had a way of suggesting that since he could never be entirely sure his researches would be of clear value to the world, it would be personally fraudulent for him to accept—indeed, to seek—generous sums. He preferred to let his lonely little bark move under its own sail.

Clarence continued, "When I was at Oxford in '54, there was quite a bit of fun poked at American scholars and their foreign studies and lectures and cushy positions. It is easy enough to dismiss that as envy, but I think it is more serious—or less serious. I mean I truly believe one can maintain that all manner of stupid, incompetent, repetitious work is being done by our American scholars, and at an expense that staggers the imagination!"

Willard poured a second Martini for everyone. Then he settled back in his chair and, smiling maliciously at Clarence's flushed, eager face, said, "What you people never seem to realize is that these foundations literally —*literally,* mind you—have more money than they can spend. To look upon the few thousand one may get for teaching as something that must in the purest, most competitive sense be earned is sheer conceit!" With a modest, self-deprecating laugh, he added, "This thing is bigger than any of us. Of course, you aren't married, Anderson, and so perhaps you are allowed more perfection and chastity than the rest of us. Without undeserved honors and unearned foundation funds, how on earth could I keep my son Clark at Groton, where he is dreadfully and expensively out of place?"

Clarence knew well that Willard Nesbitt did not think of himself as the recipient of undeserved honors and unearned funds. It was enraging that by this insincere show of cynicism Nesbitt could make him seem to be guilty of false piety and pretentious scrupulosity.

"Groton?" Dodo said vaguely. "I wonder if Clark sees anything of Babcock Van der Veen, who is also there. You remember—he's old Cousin Jimmy's nephew."

"That I couldn't possibly say, dear," Henrietta answered. "Boys of Clark's age are very odd. They seem to fear nothing so much as their blood relations." Henrietta's smile for Dodo was just a little too brilliant, too sweet. All of Henrietta's pride and her habit of condescension came together in the smile. Her arrogance was of the enduring, comfortable kind, and came from her sheer and bold delight in being who she was. She felt she and Dodo had something no deprivation or failure could erase; beyond that, everything was trimming, superstructure. It was a pleasure to feel herself clever, to be married to a well-known man, but these were truly to be described as pleasure, not as the very foundation of her personal well-being or her belief in herself. Henrietta's tendency to patronize was just as real and unmanageable as her family pride. She was tolerant of Dodo as a fellow-Babcock but also superior to her cousin's helpless pale eyes, her innocence of intellect, her bald and uncomplicated assumptions. She felt that Dodo's imagination declined to supply the facts relating to her true situation.

Turning suddenly to Clarence, Dodo asked, in her thrilling and beautiful voice, "Did you admire Adlai Stevenson terribly?"

Clarence blushed. He longed to resent Dodo as a foolish woman, but when his intense powers of observation revealed to him the ambivalence of the Nesbitts' presentation of their cousin, the way they at once displayed and gently mocked her, he felt hopelessly drawn to her—allied even to her complacency and childishness.

"Yes, yes, I must say I did—quite a lot. He seemed to me a remarkable man," Clarence answered. "And I am not ashamed to admit that I cherished his literacy. It is a mistaken notion that one can think without words." He did not smile, he did not adopt his moralizing, rebuking tone. He treated, or pretended to treat, Dodo's question with deep and puzzling seriousness. Also, he was curious to know how this creature might express herself on the subject of politics and whether she might not discomfit her hosts. Clarence secretly suspected Willard and Henrietta of political dishonesty. He believed they were more conservative than they appeared, more willing to compromise with the status quo than they admitted.

"I dislike Adlai Stevenson terribly," Dodo offered. Willard laughed indulgently, but she appeared unaware of the meaning of this laugh, which was designed to stop the free expression of her political notions. "I know quite a few people who know him personally. The idea seems to be that he is very superficial."

"Are you a great partisan of Eisenhower, then?" Clarence said, bending politely toward Dodo and waiting gallantly for her reply.

"I am indeed. I love him. Terribly," Dodo said, with her great pale-eyed earnestness.

Henrietta coughed. "A perfectly atrocious dinner is awaiting us," she said. "I have my part-time maid here this evening. She was a short-order cook—for the White Tavern or some such place."

At that moment, a moon-faced colored woman appeared and said, "O.K."

They went into the dining room and settled themselves under the Sully portrait of "Aunt Mag Pierce" and the disc of hammered copper. Willard had trouble with the wine bottle, but when the cork was at last extracted, he said, "The wine is not superb, that I grant you. But it is just good enough to resent being on the same program with the overdone lamb that is as sure to follow as the night the day."

"Do you remember Hélène, Mummy's wonderful Swiss cook?" Dodo said wistfully. She was incorrigibly reminiscent. The disposition came upon her with the regularity of a stutter.

"I do remember her, dear, and a painful memory it is, at the moment," Henrietta replied.

During the meal, Clarence observed Dodo—trained the heavy ammunition of his mind upon her, as if he were a general besieging an undefended shepherdess on her lonely hill. At the same time, he was careful to conceal the wild unruliness of his natural curiosity. Dodo was, he saw, of a savage invincibility and bitter composure. She lived, waiting patiently and proudly, like an old deposed tribal chieftain indolently dreaming of a hopeless return to power and dignity. "I passed our old house recently," she said, accepting a second potato. "Can you imagine, the old red draperies—the velvet ones with gold braid—are still hanging, even after all these years! It's an awful thought—insulting, somehow. I felt, looking at those dingy curtains behind the smeared windows, as if some part of my past were still in the house, rotting away. It's a rooming house, or so I gather from the looks of the place. Milk cartons on every window ledge, miserable faces peering out of the windows, dirty, torn shades in the room that used to be mine. Do you remember the dressing table with the pink brocade skirt I was so fond of, Hennie?" Dodo coughed, reproaching fate and adversity. Henrietta gave a melancholy sigh in honor of the old, decaying red brick mansion and the memory of gold service plates, four butlers, and the little Babcocks, pale and fair and spoiled.

"Let it all go! I couldn't care less!" Dodo suddenly exclaimed. "I miss having someone to wash out my underwear more than I miss our marble entrance hall. Money, not beauty, is what I mourn." To her, it was more tedious to have to wash a coffee cup than to be forced to wear a tattered dinner dress. In these preferences Dodo showed a clear and terrifying grasp of reality. She understood that the dirty coffee cup represented an effort. A frayed dress was simply itself. It did not ask anything of her except the nerve to wear it, and that nerve Dodo had in abundance.

Clarence did not speak during this nostalgic moment. His silences were ordinarily well considered; there was a lurking, impressive withholding of approval in them. He knew when to let other people worry for fear they might be making fools of themselves; with a deep and greedy sense of drama he could sit nodding attentively and send a chill of apprehension through the speaker. In this case, though, his silence was not malicious, for, in truth, Clarence found Dodo endlessly engaging. His sensibility, his scholarly discipline, his obstinacy—it was almost a form of genius the way he could bring all these to bear upon the thin, reddish woman sitting across from him. He felt, somehow, a vague but genuine sympathy with this frayed and yet luxurious person. Already he was busily informing his conscience that Dodo had an honesty, a candor, and a rigid simplicity of emotion that he found more elegant and admirable than Henrietta's cleverness. Dodo was certainly not smart, and she was not kind. She was profoundly incapable of that greatness of sacrifice or purity of feeling at whose throne Clarence worshipped and in whose name he criticized and sighed over most of his acquaintances. But Clarence decided to find Dodo majestically produced, gloriously out of date, even historically significant. No, not that, not significant, he amended his thoughts, but socially expressive in a small and interesting way. She was ridiculous, like many a genuine article; she was a Chicago Babcock, helpless, proud, paralyzed by her self-esteem and bemused by the decline of her fortunes. Her clear eyes and pink skin reminded him of portraits of German princesses. Her long, pale fingernails were adorned with coral polish; on one haughty finger there was a splendid emerald ring, telling of days past and lost treasure hoards. There was a runner in her stocking, and affecting thinness to her ankles, a whiff of sachet clinging to the dress of purple silk.

Clarence was, he liked to say, "some kind of a Socialist." Still, he did not approve of what he called "Socialist provincialism"; he freely admitted the possibility of charm, the capacity for suffering, in all classes. Thus, it was almost to his credit, he believed, to take a tolerant, worldly view of Dodo.

As a young girl, Dodo had spent several years in Italy, living in an expensive *pensione* in Florence. She never managed to meet the eligible Englishman who should have entered her life, conquering her with his vanity and his pedigree. She did not even manage to return to America with an attractive, penniless Italian of noble birth. It was not that she sought and did not find. She did not seek and was not found. Dodo had studied singing, but her interest in singing had gradually declined, leaving as a mark of its previous existence only a quantity of vehement opinion. As her passion for the art and the hopes of her youth diminished, they had been replaced by dissatisfaction with other voices and with modern music. Now, at dinner at the Nesbitts', she found her days as a voice student another topic for reminiscence. "I was a mezzo," she explained, giving to the middle register in which nature had placed her voice a romantic, elusive significance. Then, with the authority of a retired diva, she turned and said to Clarence with dazzling irrelevance, " 'The Rake's Program,' or whatever that phony concoction was called—I couldn't, and never shall, find the courage to hear it through. Nowadays you can put anything over by a little publicity in the right places. The Russians, in my opinion, have no feeling for the voice. They understand only the violin."

Clarence listened, and allowed an expression of gentle amusement to pass over his features. He thought there was considerable beauty in the clarity of Dodo's chagrined countenance.

"Dodo, dear," Willard said as they left the table, "your intransigence in this other-directed world we live in is a delightful curiosity."

"I can't imagine what you mean," Dodo said, smiling girlishly. "I simply state my opinion. Nothing very original about that."

Willard Nesbitt did not like to offer his guests alcohol after dinner, and so at his parties there was always this period of pause and hesitation, and even a bit of discomfort, because his guests were likely to wonder suddenly if Nesbitt did not regret the whole affair. And he did, indeed, often give the clearest indication that he wished the evening were over. By not drinking after dinner, Willard managed to avoid dull, headachy mornings and lazy, worthless days. His ambitions were limitless; there was not enough time for all he wanted to do. His abrupt seizures of boredom and restlessness were symptoms of his ambition and of his sense that time was running out and fame fickle and hard to command. He enjoyed social life, and yet he felt himself best suited to the formal occasion, to the meetings and councils of public life, to an existence of decisions, addresses, cameras, and microphones. He had had all too much of the unbuttoned, cozy, secure little world of the university.

Nesbitt's restlessness, as the evening went on, offended Clarence, who took it for what it was, since he understood his colleague very well, and yet felt an exception should be made in his own case. His sense of personal affront was quickly translated into a generalization: Nesbitt's longing for the world stage was an example of the increasing commercialization and superficiality of academic life.

Clarence, a bachelor and only thirty-eight, was nevertheless a lover of things as they once were. Everything seemed to him to have been subtly degraded, from the quality of bread to the high-school curriculum. Violent feelings of disappointment, exhausting worries about the future of culture, had a fierce dominion over Clarence's existence. He was so fully and abjectly under the tyranny of these feelings that the feelings themselves were in his own mind mistaken for "work." When he was angry with a colleague, defeated in a committee meeting, dismayed by the poor preparation of the students, these experiences seemed to him to be his job. They were much too devastating and severe for him to take lightly. In judging his extremity of emotion, he found it simply an example of his greater diligence and dedication, his superiority to the mechanics being turned out by the graduate schools. Clarence cared, he suffered, he worried. Nesbitt's Under-Secretary of State airs and his desire to be an important figure in the intellectual world seemed to his critic, Clarence, to be a slighting of the great career of education.

Across the room, cool and smiling, sat Dodo Babcock. That schizophrenic, dangerous serenity, Clarence thought. Childishness, indifference, greed, and empty vanity; Clarence counted them off on his fingers—the faults of upper-class women. Yet out of nowhere came the answer that he had the opposite qualities in superabundance. He was careful, liberal, idealistic, and so the arrogant, self-loving, little-girl character of Dodo appealed to him. He tilted his head so that he might overhear what she was saying to Henrietta without interrupting his own conversation with a drowsy-looking Willard.

"This heavy reliance on Freud may prove embarrassing a few decades from now—even one decade from now," Clarence was saying. "I don't think people quite realize the extent of this influence. It is like a gas that has mixed into the natural atmosphere. Of course, a great mind and great work would make incalculable differences in special fields—in this case, in psychology and character analysis. But history, sociology, religion, architecture! I am reminded of the seriousness with which the Victorians took phrenology."

"You can't honestly mean to imply the two things are comparable in any sense," Willard said, languidly taking a cigarette from a Chinese box on the table.

"No, I certainly do not. I think Freud is immense, don't mistake me. But still, some of the details, some of the literalness, the use to which he has been put, disturbs me. Even the greatest intellectual events are often distorted by overearnest followers. There are fashions, exaggerations, mistakes here, as elsewhere. We don't know exactly what will remain, after all, of Freudianism—what its real contribution will turn out to be."

"Naturally, naturally," Willard said, without enthusiasm.

Clarence heard Henrietta say to Dodo, "Your parents were truly glamorous, and I am not one to use that word lightly."

"Daddy was the most wonderful person I have ever known," Dodo said.

"He was strong, clever, good-natured. He knew how to have a good time, how to be gay, how to give people pleasure." It seemed to Clarence that Dodo blushed when she saw him looking at her.

"Who are you?" Dodo suddenly said to him. "Are you terribly brilliant, and all that?"

"Yes. I must confess I am." Clarence replied, with an elaborate flourish of self-mockery. "I am very frightening with my great brilliance."

Dodo did not laugh. She was as free of irony as a doll. A mind like that. Clarence thought giddily, lives by sheer superstition. Dodo's eyes remained upon him. She was archaic, quaint, and yet not really eccentric. Clarence decided it would be agreeable if she turned out to love Jane Austen, or even Trollope. But his sanity soon returned and he sullenly reminded himself that privileged persons no longer had hobbies like Jane Austen. Daddy Babcock would never have spent an evening—or an hour—with Roman history. The Babcocks' culture, such as it was, was thin and vulgar, and prodigiously indolent. Clarence's irritation mounted, but it did not center on Dodo so much as on her group—or what was once her group. Dodo's haughty, grim helplessness saved her. The old purple dress and the runner in her stocking somehow brought her back to the possible. At least she was a failure! And at the same time a challenge, subtly touching the vein of competition that throbbed in Clarence's soul. The smile Dodo gave him was sweet, hesitant, wondering. He observed that he and she were not at ease with each other, and this signified to him the possibility of sexual drama—the painful and promising period of courtship and discovery. Clarence felt bold. He said, in a harsh, uncaring voice, "Do you like chamber music, Miss Babcock?"

"I adore it," Dodo said, clasping her hands and looking at Willard and Henrietta as if she had scored a triumph and meant to be congratulated. They gave no sign of encouragement, but Dodo let the disappointment pass. She did not know that though she had been asked with Clarence for the evening, she was not particularly asked to admire him.

"Would you like to go with me to hear three fine instrumentalists perform some trios next week?" said Clarence. "The 'Archduke,' for one, and some Mozart, I think. The full program escapes me."

"I'd adore it," Dodo said.

"Good!" Clarence said.

Henrietta looked at him with a twisted grin. Willard coughed. Clarence now felt he could leave the Nesbitts to their post-mortem conversation. He could leave dramatically, on his own terms, giving as fit payment for the evening's invitation the little bit of confusion, wonder, and mystery that his determination to continue the friendship with Dodo meant for the Nesbitts. Looking at his watch, he exclaimed gaily that it was a quarter to eleven. With great gentleness and delicacy, he offered Dodo a taxi ride, which she accepted. The Nesbitts were quiet.

At the door, Clarence took his time. He paused reflectively, to round out his conversation with Willard. "There is certainly a question of just how much encouragement we want to give the new era in education, which I have called the Divinity School Era," he said slowly. "I, for one, am not absolutely certain that it is an advance on the Teachers College Age."

"Perhaps not," Willard said limply. "The only thing that can be said for it is that a lot of persons will be forced to take New Testament Greek."

"Some comfort but not enough," Clarence said, giving his arm to Dodo and disappearing down the stairs.

Alone, the Nesbitts were crestfallen. "That was sort of boring," Henrietta said. She poured herself a brandy and shrugged when Willard refused one.

"Clarence is terribly irritating," Willard said savagely. "Somehow, I keep forgetting just how provoking his personality can be. He's too cold and at the same time too intense—a tiresome, disturbing combination. I don't know why I ever had the dull idea of having him here. We didn't even *owe* him! Of course, no one owes him, because he never invites anyone."

"What did you think of Dodo?" Henrietta said, dreamily sipping her brandy. "She seemed delighted with Clarence—at least delighted for *her*. She's not very demonstrative, but the poor girl is susceptible. *Quite,* I can tell you."

"I thought Dodo was the same," Willard said crossly. "But I must say that if she is attracted to Clarence, then she has deteriorated since the last time I saw her. She used to have more sense. It would be absolutely unbearable if that ass Anderson started to escort Dodo about. I thought it was very speedy of him to make the engagement for that damned concert right here, the first meeting."

"I don't know that I agree," Henrietta said, her eyes glinting mischievously. The brandy was having its effect. "Dodo is lonely. She must be. And Clarence is plausible to a degree that is positively frightening."

"He'd only be using that foolish Dodo to vex us. I know him! I don't relish the idea of Clarence as a part of the family, let me tell you—not even as a part by nothing more than friendship with Dodo. Not even that! The whole thing is exasperating!"

"Just exactly why, pet?" Henrietta insisted, with a bit of hoarseness, giving her husband that look of bone-and-blood superiority he had learned to dread. "Dodo is not likely to marry anyone—at least so far as I can predict. You can never tell about what are called the middle years, though. Of course, she turned down a number of quite soundly eligible persons in her very young days. And don't you forget it!"

"Why should I forget it?"

"Well, I mean her situation, her single blessedness, is due to a certain overreaching of ambition and expectation at an early date. It is not that she was unmarriageable, by any means. You never know what odd person—what shy girl—will turn out to be difficult to please in the most outrageous and inexplicable way. Her sister Jeannine, a great beauty and wildly popular, was not like that at all. She married at twenty-one, and while Emory is perfectly sweet, he's nothing to write home about so far as money, birth, personal charm, or even achievement is concerned!"

"Poor Emory!" Willard said. He was extremely annoyed with Henrietta. If anything, she disliked Clarence more than he did!

"I'd loathe having Clarence Anderson seeing a lot of Dodo. Simply loathe it," Henrietta continued, gathering steam. "He is not a bijou. Not for my money."

"Maybe that is exactly what he is, at least to some people. Ugh!" Willard said.

"But, loathe it as I would," Henrietta went on briskly, "I think, from their point of view, they might have a pleasant time together occasionally. Concerts, little dinners, a play. Not too frequently, just once in a while."

"You've got it all worked out. Anyone would think you were directing them in a movie."

Henrietta was hardly listening. "I always think of poor Dodo in the theatrical way I last saw her on her own ground, in that dreary, soiled little flat of hers. It's a frightful place, and somehow made all the worse because of bits of heavenly things here and there, all chipped and dusty and battered. The final tableau was wonderful: there was Dodo in an ancient wrapper eating a sandwich of canned meat, sitting under the portrait of Grandfather Perry Babcock, who made three million out West before he was twenty-five—all those years ago."

"Clarence will adore that note, I assure you. Nothing will escape him, and his additions to the scene will be epical. If he chooses to do so, he can manage to turn Dodo's poverty into a great spiritual principle. A sort of Christian Socialist impulse will be found to lie behind the waste and poor management."

"Darling," Henrietta interrupted, "there's one thing I believe should be cleared up. By your standards and Clarence's, Dodo isn't poor! She has, unearned, at least three or four thousand dollars a year. Unearned and for life, bar the revolution. That isn't *poor,* really. It's just poor to Dodo."

"Yes, I suppose she has something," Willard conceded irritably. "But, with her, what is unearned is all there is. She couldn't *earn* her carfare. That three or four thousand is all she'll ever have. With taxes, and so on, I can imagine Dodo feels pretty strapped and worries quite a bit about the future."

"How do you know that's all she'll ever have? You have much less imagination than our dear Clarence."

"How do you know Clarence has imagination about what Dodo will have—or has, for that matter?"

Henrietta lit a cigarette and resumed with a knowledgeable air, "At least, Clarence wouldn't be so positive about a thing like that. He wouldn't consider Dodo or her prospects mummified. Don't forget, Mr. Professor, rich people, well-connected people, are always inheriting a little bit here and there. Sometimes more than a little bit will come from an utterly unexpected source—and a greater delight human society cannot offer. Yet sometimes from an expected source nothing comes, or much less than might have. That scars your very soul, believe me. . . . But don't count out any Babcock while a single branch of the family is as filthy rich as Uncle Wink!"

Henrietta was soaring into her most lofty sphere. "In the thirties, when all the so-called clever people were making so much fun of Ford and Rockefeller and Uncle Wink, I felt, without daring to utter it, that times would change, the swing would come. Right now, I don't know a single damned sociologist who wouldn't be beside himself with joy at the thought of dining with Uncle Wink and Aunt Bea! And the conversation would be a lot more diverting than what one hears at the Faculty Club, I can assure you. I don't deny that it would be different—lighter—but that light sort of thing can, in its own way, be original and interesting. And, above all, gay! God, the charm of a sense of gaiety!"

These aggrieved moods appalled Willard. He felt defenseless, embarrassed, accused. Henrietta struck this note only when she had had too much to drink, and the mood and the language—even the feelings—vanished with the return to full sobriety. And yet how distressing the words were, how resentful, how disappointed and unpredictable! Just beneath the surface of Henrietta's amiable, witty, and nervous temperament lay this sewer of narrowness and disillusion. Willard shrank from the moments when it was exposed to him. He hated himself for having clumsily allowed himself to be somehow paired with Clarence Anderson in Henrietta's intoxicated dialogue. Her grudging, preaching, outlandish statements seemed to be meant for both men alike. It was a relief to know that in the morning she would mercilessly make fun of Clarence and praise her husband.

Henrietta was reaching her big scene. She began, as usual, to repeat her refrain. "I find myself overcome with admiration for you academic people—"

"Really, dear?" Willard injected in a vanishing voice.

"Yes, utter admiration. How you talk about things with such godlike assurance! How you give forth on matters you have never experienced! Ideas flow like wine—everything out of books and other people's lectures, nothing from actual life! People write *books* on the psychology of the upper classes who have only read other books on the upper classes, or on the peasants—it's all the same—or on Negroes, any subject you like. There is always someone with the courage to talk or write on any topic under the sun. The brave teacher is always to be found!" Her voice dropped. "And now I suppose our good friend Clarence will join you in the fascinating analysis of the great Middle Western fortunes—in the authoritative statement on the Chicago robber barons!"

Willard shivered. He picked up his book, kissed Henrietta on the cheek, and retired to his bedroom. Thoughts and dreams of Clarence Anderson tormented his sleep.

❖

Elizabeth Hardwick was born in Lexington, Kentucky, and educated at the University of Kentucky, came to New York City in the early 1940s, has lived in Boston and abroad but is now back in New York; married to the poet Robert Lowell, she is an advisory editor of The New York Review of Books *and teaches at Barnard. She has written many short stories that have appeared in the major magazines, but they have not yet been collected. She has published two novels:* The Ghostly Lover *(1945), and* The Simple Truth *(1955). In recent years her work has been literary essays; these are collected in* A View of My Own *(1962).*

In "The Classless Society" the author is of course mocking her title: a good deal of the talk in the story is about class, and all that happens is as a result of it. But what are the classes involved? It would be simple to say that the Babcock cousins are upper class, while the two professors are middle class, and that not recognizing this is what causes all the confusion. But there seems to be more to it. A Bostonian or Philadelphian, for instance, might not think that any Chicago family could be really upper class, certainly not one whose fortune was founded on the fact that "copper sons had married Chicago meat-packing daughters." Dodo has come from the wealthy branch of this family, but she is powerless—even helpless—and relatively poor. Henrietta comes from a poor branch of the family, but she is married to a man who is well known, who ranks high in academia, and is on the edge of the prestigious and influential intellectual establishment. But Nesbitt's own origins are "fabulously simple," presumably no grander than those of Clarence Anderson, whom Nesbitt looks down on, but whose intellectual integrity is presented as greater. If the standard, straightforward aspects of socioeconomic class—power, prestige, birth, and wealth—don't sort this foursome out, neither do such subtler considerations as "style" or confidence, or education and intelligence and "brow." Clothes seem, as usual, to reveal more than they actually may. Clarence in his black tasseled loafers, Nesbitt wearing his tweed jacket with the suede patches, Dodo in her tattered purple silk dinner dress—all are wearing clothes that to some extent inevitably reflect their social background; but the clothes are also used to state their individuality and assert their self-confidence, for they do not believe them to be "uniforms," like blue jeans for Beatniks and gray

flannel for organization men. The Nesbitts' casualness, which should indi-
cate confidence, seems calculated and arranged: there is a "careful negli-
gence" with which their possessions are displayed, and they are deliberately
offhand about the "perfectly atrocious dinner." Dodo is the one who seems
to have the most real confidence: "resting upon the solid foundation of her
privileged childhood," she has "an awesome tranquillity, a quaintly pure
and steadfast self-confidence." Yet Clarence, who is least secure of them
all, is attracted by her "helplessness," because "at least she is a failure."
And she is the least intelligent, or at any rate the least educated of the lot.
Yet in this academic environment, that seems not really to matter; for
Nesbitt is proud of, or at least not ashamed of, his wife's ignorance, repre-
senting as it does "the frightfully poor education of the well-bred society
lady." How they stand in relation to one another is very complicated and
confusing, deliberately presented as such—not only to any class-conscious
sociologist who might have been unfortunate enough to be in the room,
but to themselves. For they are all very conscious of these matters, and
keep trying to score points in what much resembles an ultra-subtle game
of lifemanship or one-upmanship. Each conjectures about the other, trying
to fit the other into the nice little typology he has prepared for him. It is
not so much that each is trying to put the other down, but that each wants
the other to conform to his own estimates. Nesbitt is the one with most to
lose in this game, and he loses disastrously. He patronizes everyone out-
rageously—not only Clarence and poor Dodo and his wife, but also de
Tocqueville. He gets his comeuppance. Not only does Clarence make points
on him by going off with Dodo, but Henrietta also takes the opportunity
to patronize and lecture him, with "that look of bone-and-blood superiority
he had learned to dread." It is made clear at the beginning that this is
something she has done before, and by the end we easily see why this is an
experience he is anxious to avoid. For him, or indeed for any of these
individualized and differentiated people, it is not as pleasant to live in a
classless society as it would seem it ought to be. Because of the lack of
clear-cut definitions, prestige and status are never final, can never be taken
for granted. No one can rest easy.

MALCOLM WOOD

What Really Matters

❖❖❖❖❖❖❖

I ASK MYSELF, will I be living in a place like home, with Formica and chromium in the kitchen? Or will the drainboard be made of little, six-sided tiles like the Kirkbroads' had? Aurelia Kirkbroad would say, "Dope, it really doesn't matter."

The tiles were white, with an occasional blue one. Frank Farrell says those tiles were in style about fifty years ago. According to Farrell, the experts believe that practically everything stays in your mind, and you can fish it up if circumstances are right. It can work the other way, too. Important things can be pushed way to the *back* of your mind. I once overheard Doctor Kirkbroad say I was a "cool customer" and "very sharp." He said some other things. His remarks pushed me toward this joint, in a way, though it's more complicated than that. But until recently I never let myself think about that period at the Kirkbroads.

You can see why I like talking to Frank Farrell. He's the librarian here at the Correction Center. You can mention a little thing to him, like these six-sided tiles, and it may lead to something interesting. Farrell is about forty, with a red moustache that wiggles when he talks.

It was the fifteenth of September, three years ago, that I pulled my Olds 88 alongside the hitching post in front of the Kirkbroads' house. That hitching post's an antique. The whole house is an antique—a three-story, shingled place with stained glass above the front door and sleeping porches out back like the older farmhouses out home. The carriage house had been converted into a garage, with overhead doors and a concrete apron. Whenever Eric Kirkbroad came home from Yale it was a three-car family—four, counting mine. It was a quiet neighborhood because after school most of the kids were away taking music lessons, or French lessons, or exercising their horses—not that the Kirkbroads had horses. They went in for sail-boats.

I'd come into the city to start junior college, and I'd been invited to live with the Kirkbroads. I went up and used the door knocker. Nothing happened. I knocked harder. There was a scraping sound above, then a clatter like a Great Dane charging downstairs and a bang against the door. The door was thrown open and a frail, white-faced girl frowned at me. This was my cousin, Aurelia Kirkbroad. At the time she was seventeen, a year younger than myself. Her eyes were large and her eyebrows pinched together in a scowl. She seemed to be thinking hard all the time.

"I'm Ken Sprague," I said.

Aurelia kept frowning.

"You don't remember me. I just came in from Mesaville———"

"Hey, of course!" Aurelia's face changed for a moment as if someone had pulled on a bulb. "I'm Aurelia. Do you remember the time I visited?"

I nodded. "You played at helping me with the chores, and they paid you for it. It made me sore."

Aurelia grinned switfly, then looked out at my Olds. "That your heap?"

"Yeah."

She frowned at the Olds. "We were expecting you," she said. "Come on, I'll help you bring in your stuff."

She carried in some cartons and she got interested in my record collection. "Gosh," she said, "I never heard of these people. Who's Eldred Haines?"

"Just a band leader. He was popular a couple years ago."

"Can we listen to some of these after dinner?"

"Listen to them now."

She shook her head. "I've got to study and do some practicing. That's why I can't entertain you or anything. Is that all right? Just poke around on your own. You're practically part of the family. The others will be home in a while."

I wasn't exactly worried about meeting the family, or how to act at dinner. I'd lettered in basketball at Mesaville and I was secretary of the Corinthian Club, and the group of guys I went with were the elite. Still, there had been an attitude around home that the Kirkbroads were above us. Long before, when Aunt Eliza first married Kirkbroad and ran off to England, he was a broke, unsuccessful actor. But somehow Kirkbroad had become a Doctor of Philosophy, and a college professor, and he wrote books.

I think I expected that every night the Kirkbroads' dinners would be like my stepmother's dinners when she invited in company to show off something new. After we moved from the ranch into Mesaville, my stepmother was always remodeling, and buying new drapes, and getting more appliances. We had a refrigerator and freezer, naturally. And an electric stove, an electric rotisserie, a garbage disposal, a dishwasher, a washer-dryer, an ironer and mangle, a humidifier, and all sorts of little things like a waffle iron and a sandwich grill and an electric skillet. We had three TV's. I guess we lived about as well as anyone around Mesaville.

Aunt Eliza came home in her station wagon, and she reminded me so much of Dad that I felt comfortable. Same bushy eyebrows and square jaw. Even her small wrists and knotty forearms were like Dad's. I suppose those arm muscles came from squeezing the clay around on her potter's wheel.

Gail, three years older than Aurelia and two years older than me, came in next from the university with her arms full of books. Classes at the university had already begun. Gail had a beat-up Volkswagen of her own. She was short, with a good figure—kind of dumpy, though—and cool, gray eyes. We shook hands and she said, "Say, you're *handsome,* Kenneth. You could be a bobby-sox idol. That wave of blond hair is quite a touch." She winked. She wasn't being unfriendly, and certainly not flirtatious. I was a lot taller than she was, naturally, but she made me feel like a kid.

Gail disappeared and a door right near us in the hall opened suddenly. Kirkbroad was standing there. Apparently he'd been in his study all afternoon, ignoring everything that went on. "What time is it, Liz? My watch stopped," he said to Aunt Eliza. He was a small, bald-headed guy with rimless glasses and a bent-down pipe in the side of his mouth. He wore old moccasins, baggy pants that were riddled with holes from pipe embers, and one of those button sweaters that baggage agents wear. "I thought I heard a strange voice," he said. His eyes looked at me like a couple of gun barrels.

"This is Kenneth, Alex," said Aunt Eliza.

"Kenneth? Let's see, whose nephew are you?"

"Yours," said Aunt Eliza.

"Never mind, Liz. I mean, which side of the family?"

"He's Holman's boy," said Aunt Eliza.

"Ah! From out on the ranch."

"Well—"

"Kenneth, don't be offended," said Aunt Eliza. "Alex has five nephews and nieces on his own side of the family, and seven on mine."

"What time is it?" asked Kirkbroad again.

I said that it was six-thirty. I wondered if we were ever going to have dinner.

"Go up and pour the sherry," said Aunt Eliza to Kirkbroad. To me she said, "We have dinner at seven-fifteen."

Kirkbroad climbed the stairs. I looked through magazines in the living room. I could hear the skinny sound of Aurelia practicing the oboe. Aunt Eliza went out in the kitchen and then followed Kirkbroad upstairs. I learned later that one of the porches on the third floor looked over the trees and across the bay toward some mountains. Aunt Eliza and Kirkbroad had fixed up the porch with greenery and comfortable chairs, and just the two of them drank sherry wine up there before dinner every night.

Every single night the Kirkbroads had table wine with dinner. Also different kinds of bread, undercooked vegetables, and meat that was practically raw. The salad was a main course. They never had a regular dessert —just cheese and fruit. After dinner they always brought out an Italian machine and made bitter coffee right at the table.

That first night I told them the latest about home. They didn't realize that Dad had acquired more acreage and hired a full-time dairy manager, or that we'd moved into Mesaville. I explained that Dad spends his time now on beef brokerage. I described our new house casually, and let them know we have a Chrysler Imperial. "Heck, Kenneth," said Aurelia. "I thought you'd be able to teach me where to find eggs, and how to skin a frog. You don't sound like a farm boy at all anymore."

"The country has caught up with the city," I said. "Everybody has television now. Most of my friends have their own cars. My best friend has a new Thunderbird."

I didn't suspect that all this bragging was backfiring. With me the Kirkbroads were already covering up, as if they were wearing masks. But with themselves they were fantastically outspoken. That first night, out of a clear sky, Gail said, "I forgot to tell you, Mother. Last weekend Max and I stayed at the cabin."

Aurelia jerked her head and stared at Gail. Aunt Eliza went on serving up beets, very cool. Kirkbroad was pouring himself wine, and he paused for an instant and looked at Gail with raised eyebrows.

"What happened to the original plan?" asked Aunt Eliza.

"Florence and I were supposed to stay at the cabin, and Max was going to sleep on the boat. But when Florence called home, her mother said she had to come right back, her father was in the hospital."

"What's the matter with him?"

"Ulcers, I guess. Florence took the bus."

"I'm a little surprised at Max," said Kirkbroad.

"It was *my* idea," said Gail. "I insisted. I didn't want to stay in the cabin alone. The papers have been full of stories about rural punks breaking into summer places and terrorizing people. Max was against staying, but I made him."

"It might have been better to come home," said Aunt Eliza.

Gail looked grim. Aurelia said, "Don't be paleolithic, Mother. Let's face it. Any boy and girl can do anything practically anytime they want." Aunt Eliza winced. "All they have to do is go somewhere and park."

"Perhaps you had better stay out of this," said Kirkbroad.

"The subject interests me deeply," said Aurelia.

Everyone smiled.

"We *couldn't* come back," said Gail. "We had to gather our sea urchins on the low tide in the morning."

There was a silence. The older Kirkbroads seemed to be considering whether to probe this delicate matter further, and Gail seemed to be defying them quietly. It was Aurelia who said, "Max *could* have slept on the boat and left you at the motel in Vista Del Mar."

"I suppose we could have done that," said Gail. She darted an icy look at Aurelia, then looked steadily at her father.

Kirkbroad studied the lamb roast. Then he said, "Hereafter, that would be a better way, Gail."

Gail made no reply. It was clear she had deliberately not said a word about whether she and this Max had slept together or separately.

Everybody ate the rare lamb and Kirkbroad offered wine again. Aurelia and I took a little. Then Aurelia said in her grown-up way, "I raised an issue that nobody has acknowledged." (Aurelia talked this way. She was a senior at a girl's prep school where all the kids took Latin and two other languages, and extra math. She liked it.) "Isn't the business of chaperones completely obsolete? I don't date much, but even *I've* had a dozen opportunities to do anything I wanted. I'm talking about parking somewhere in a car. Aren't you just trying to avoid seeing the problem? Or are you worried about *your* reputation if someone sees your daughter and a man coming out of your summer cabin some morning?"

Kirkbroad said, "Aurelia, your mother and I simply want to discourage thoughtless behavior."

Aunt Eliza said in a calm, definite voice, "Making love in an automobile must be a furtive, awkward business—for the girl especially. I should think it would be humiliating. Perhaps it takes place, but this doesn't mean you, or any other young girls, should therefore feel perfectly free to spend whole weekends in summer cabins with men."

"In other words," said Aurelia, "you don't care what happens as long as it's not satisfying, and you don't know about it."

This set Aunt Eliza back, but only for a moment. "Aurelia," she snapped, "I'll be perfectly glad to hear about any humiliating and sordid experiences you may have."

Everyone laughed. Kirkbroad said, "You know by now that we want you girls to enjoy the pleasures of sex *after* you're married. Quite apart from pregnancy and disease, sexual experiments probably damage a person's capacity for a satisfying sexual partnership when the person does marry. I suspect many divorces are caused by the young people's confusion about sex . . . from too much *bad* experience before marriage."

"Authority!" snorted Aurelia. She turned to me. "You see, Kenneth? Around here issues aren't settled by the Bible, or tradition, or science. All issues are settled by Alexander S. Kirkbroad, Ph.D."

"I haven't settled the issue," said Kirkbroad. "You and Gail will have to resolve it for yourselves. In the meantime, don't take your boyfriends to the cabin for any more weekends. We can't control everything you do, but we can discourage certain patterns and encourage others."

Aurelia sipped her wine and muttered into the glass, "Hypocritical, bourgeois tyrant." She winked at me.

During dessert the Kirkbroads got into a terrible argument over whether Bobby Kennedy had been pro-McCarthy. At one point Aurelia got up from the table in a fury and hurled her napkin on the floor. Even Aunt Eliza got mad enough to swear. Later I realized that they enjoyed arguments, and that it was usually matters of "principle"—often politics—that got them worked up.

Upstairs in my room Gail said, "Gosh Kenneth, where did you get all the clothes?" We put on some records and they immediately got interested in my Latin Rhythm albums. For the next hour I actually had some fun. I taught both Gail and Aurelia the Cha-cha, the mambo, and the samba. They didn't know any real dances, but they had plenty of rhythm. We opened the door into the hall and I'd dance with one sister until she was exhausted, and then I'd take on the other. I was more used to it. Finally Gail sprawled out on the bed on top of my sport coats and said, "I'm pooped." Aurelia was leaning against the wall. She let her feet slide out until she'd slipped to a sitting position on the floor. She looked around again at my stuff and said, "Criminee, Kenneth. Don't you have *any* books?"

I made some excuse about not having any books, and Aurelia and Gail went back to their rooms. I felt like watching TV, but I hadn't seen a set in the house. I went out and cruised around in my car for a while. I dragged a '57 Plymouth and took him easy. I found a drive-in and had a milk shake and fries. Then I went back to the Kirkbroads. Aunt Eliza told me to help myself from the refrigerator and I found a cold chicken leg and ate it. Up in the hall I could hear violin music coming from Aurelia's radio and no sound from Gail's room. I went in my room and turned out the lights and listened to ROKC, which was the station I and this redhead I'd been going with always listened to. I thought about her. I was lonesome already. Later I heard that right after I left Mesaville she started going with some older guy who had an Impala convertible.

During those weeks, miserable as I was, I had respect for the Kirk-broads. Of course it's natural to respect people who have money, but it wasn't just the money. They always tried to cut me in on things—parties, and plays, and eating out at restaurants sometimes. But it wasn't just their hospitality, either. They all lived with the gas pedal right on the floor. They worked like maniacs, and they had fun—their kind of fun, at least. On a Friday night they might all go to a Chinese restaurant and then to a play or a concert. Afterward they'd sit in a coffeehouse listening to folk music and arguing about the play, or about some book, until one-thirty or two o'clock. Did they ever sleep late in the morning? Never. They'd be off to the library, or a biology field trip, or a Young People's Symphony rehearsal, which Aurelia played in. Aunt Eliza would start thumping on her pottery right after breakfast, if it was Sunday, no matter how late they'd been up the night before, Kirkbroad and Aurelia would leave the house at eight o'clock for a sailboat race.

They had their problems. Gail had migraine headaches, and I got the impression she'd had some sort of breakdown once. Aunt Eliza was a chain smoker, so you can figure she was under plenty of strain. Kirkbroad could be sarcastic, really cruel. When they had their terrible arguments over some "principle," you could tell they were sore at each other underneath. And Aurelia talked about her "depressions." I think she was serious one night in the kitchen when she said to Gail, "Do you ever get the rotten feeling that deep down you're superficial?" That broke everyone up. You should have seen the grin come over Aurelia's face when she realized she'd said something really funny.

In many ways I admired the Kirkbroads, yes. But I didn't like them. How could I? Aurelia once told me I was a lousy driver. For once she leveled with me. I was furious. I could drive better than that whole family put together. And I found out that this boyfriend of Gail's, Max, was a Jew. His name was Fishbein or something like that. He was a skinny little guy with a big Adam's apple and glasses. I didn't get it. Gail was a good-looking chick. Naturally he was smart, and he had a sense of humor, but I never felt he had much use for me.

Max was a Jew, and Aurelia's best girlfriend at school was Negro, which reminds me of something else. I made one friend at the junior college, a guy named Tom who was in two of my classes. All he had was a '52 Plymouth, but he was saving for a Corvette. He was good-looking—tall and blond, kind of like Paul Newman. One Saturday night Aurelia and Gail were showing far-out movies in the big room in the basement, and having a kind of party. They asked me to bring my records in case people wanted to dance afterward. They said I could invite some friends. I invited a girl I'd gotten to know in geology that was good enough looking and stacked. She had fun at the party, all right. She made it plain that it was my cousins and their friends that she thought were so terrific. But I had fun myself. When we came in, Aurelia announced to the whole crowd, "Here's my favorite cousin, Kenneth!" I was grinning. "Isn't that the greatest grin you ever saw?" said Aurelia, and Gail said, "Every night at dinner, Kenneth's smile makes me feel better."

Anyway, this Tom came to the party. He didn't bring a girl, and Aurelia's best friend Melanie, the Negro girl, had come by herself. So Tom stuck close to her. Maybe I'd given him the wrong impression of the Kirkbroads by telling him how they talked about sex and the kind of plays they went to. During the evening he whispered to me that this chick Melanie reminded him of Lena Horne, and maybe she would change his luck. I don't know exactly what happened. He took her home. The next afternoon Aurelia said to me, "Where in hell did you find that boy Tom?"

"He's just a guy from school," I said. "What happened?"

"Never mind. But I'd rather you didn't bring *him* around again."

I asked again what had happened.

"I said never mind. It was pretty traumatic for Melanie, that's all. He isn't very bright."

I must have looked worried, because Aurelia said, "Don't sulk, Kenneth. It wasn't your fault." Whatever it was, I figured Aurelia and Gail really did blame me.

Tom and I both had trouble with the same English instructor. That was another thing. I was doing well in geology, only fair in world history, and poorly in French and especially in English. The first composition was supposed to be about something you knew. I wrote on "What To Do If Your Car Burns Oil." I got an A for content, and a D for grammar and spelling. After that we worked on business letters and I got C's. Then we read this play, *Death of a Salesman,* and had to write about it. I really worked on that paper, looking up all the spelling in the dictionary. This time I got a C on grammar and spelling and an F for content. The instructor wrote on the front, "Incredibly superficial. Are you naïve or callous?" This seemed pretty snotty to me. I didn't understand what he meant, but I wasn't going to ask *him.* I showed the paper to Aurelia.

She read it and a pained expression came over her face. She tried not to show it. When she'd finished reading she looked out the window. She was only seventeen, but believe me, she was smart. Finally she said, "Somehow you missed the point, Kenneth. You're supposed to *like* Willy Loman, and sympathize with him in spite of his faults. Arthur Miller would blame Willy's phony dream, not Willy."

"How can you like a liar?" I asked. "He was weak, and a failure, and he wouldn't admit it. He ruined his two boys."

We had a long argument. Since then I've read *Death of a Salesman* again, and a lot of other books besides. Frank Farrell has a record of the actual play in the Correction Center library and I listened to that with earphones. I guess I *was* pretty naïve. I have different ideas about a lot of things now. But it's funny: When you get to telling things that happened, you feel the way you felt back *then,* even if you've changed since. I can still get mad at that snotty English instructor. And I remember that in some ways I enjoyed that argument with Aurelia. It was the first time I ever got worked up about a book. But when it was all over, I felt ignorant, and a little as if I'd been kicked in the belly.

I started playing things super-cool. I made it a point not to start a conversation, never to say anything enthusiastic and definite, because if it turned out stupid, I'd be stuck. "Don't act, *re*act," was my rule. When I was sure of my ground, I'd make some comment that was funny. But I couldn't blast around, saying and doing anything that popped into my head like the Kirkbroads did. For kicks I hung around with Tom at the Broadway Bowl. We'd both practically quit studying. Sometimes on Friday night we picked up quail at the roller rink. Naturally I said nothing about this at the Kirkbroads.

Everything came to a head down at the vacation place. The Kirkbroads called it a "cabin." What a laugh. It was on a hill above the ocean and had enough room to sleep twenty people. Besides a couple of bedrooms and two big dormitory sleeping rooms (one for boys, one for girls) there was a new kitchen, a deck, and a living room with a fireplace.

I agreed to go because, as usual, the Kirkbroads urged me as if they meant it. Aurelia and Gail were inviting friends I hadn't met, as well as out-of-towners that would be there for the sailboat race on Saturday. You always figure there may be one new chick that will go for you. I day-dreamed about a brunette who would like my dancing, and be interested in basketball, and maybe have a sports car of her own. Does a person ever get daydreams out of his head?

First of all, nobody would ride down with me. They all had explanations: Gail was going with Max in his brand new M.G.; Aurelia had to take food and extra bedding in the station wagon; Melanie and Aurelia's other friends had their own cars, or wanted to go in the station wagon to sing; and they all objected that my Olds didn't have any seat belts. That whole bunch was fanatic about seat belts. They probably all believed Aurelia's line about me driving too fast. I could have ridden in the station wagon myself, but I knew I'd feel kind of helpless down there without my own car.

When I arrived at Vista Del Mar it was a bright blue day with a hard wind blowing. The surf was huge. Offshore there were millions of white-caps. I located the "cabin," but nobody was there—just cars and boat trailers. On the door was a note.

> Kenneth:
> Come down to the harbor before 1:15. Urgent!
> Aurelia

Aurelia and Melanie were alongside the dock in a little sailboat that wasn't as long as my car. The sails looked tremendous and were making a terrific noise flapping in the wind. Other little boats were bobbing around and banging against the floats, and several were already flying across the harbor practically tipped over.

Aurelia hollered at me, "Can you swim?" I nodded. "I need a heavy crew," she said.

I looked at all the ropes going this way and that, none of which I understood. I looked out at the water. The waves were about six feet high, even inside the breakwater. None of the little boats had capsized—yet. Aurelia said, "Don't come unless you *want* to, Kenneth. Melanie will come."

"Can't three of us go?"

"The rules only allow two."

There was Aurelia in her yellow oil-skins, no bigger than a minute, with her little pinched girl's face. She was raring to get out there. I couldn't chicken.

Melanie's slicker was too small, and Aurelia warned I'd get soaked and frozen. She urged me again to back out if I wanted. I climbed into the boat, and just my weight made it sink way down on one side. Aurelia showed me where to sit. "You'll have to do everything I tell you, Kenneth, and don't do *anything* I don't tell you. Here, put this on." When I'd buckled the life jacket, Melanie shoved us off. Aurelia tightened some ropes and shouted, "Wahoo!" The sails stopped flapping. In the sudden silence the boat leaned way over and began streaking across the water. The first big wave we came to we went *through*. Water crashed over me like I'd dived through a surf.

I sat up on the high side and leaned back over the water like Aurelia told me. I guess my weight did help hold the boat down. Then we'd change course, and I'd have to scramble over to the other side, scraping myself, cracking my shins, getting fouled up in the ropes. Aurelia would holler, "Take up on the jib sheet! Slack off the centerboard pennant!" "Whataya mean?" I'd holler. Then she'd translate into English. There was a terrific mess, with all the boats running toward each other, and then the starting gun went off.

Let's not talk about the next hour. I guess we were out in front right from the first. We ploughed one direction and then another, working toward markers I couldn't even see, me scrambling and ducking the boom. Waves kept breaking over us. I was scared. The cold made me shake as if I were having a fit. Aurelia kept looking back at the other boats and grinning like a fiend. Looking at me once, she whooped, "Poor Kenneth! You're really out of your element. But I love you. You're so *heavy!*"

So we won the race. I shivered for hours. Everyone kept congratulating Aurelia, and I realized that we were mostly racing against men, not just kids and girls. You had to admire her. Someday I might try sailing myself if there wasn't so much complicated stuff to learn. Aurelia kept saying, "Congratulate *Kenneth!* He was a terrific crew, and he'd never been out before."

"How do you like sailing?" the person would ask. "I was frozen and scared to death," I would say, which usually got a laugh. I can see that sailing is a great sport, but for me at the time, the whole thing was a drag. Among other things I ruined a good pair of slacks.

It was a mixed party. Aurelia's friends were mostly seventeen and eighteen. Gail's and Max's friends were in their early twenties. Then there was an uncle and his wife. He was a dentist, and they were about fifty. Then there was a biologist friend of Max's and his wife, who were about thirty-five. They had two tiny kids. It was a complete hodgepodge, and everyone still had fun. Now take my own family, and people out in Mesaville. I've thought about it. Nobody out there thinks of having fun except with people their own age. It's because they're always hiding things from each other. The kids cover up what they really do and think; the parents hide everything important from the kids; and parents *and* kids hide things from the grandparents. With the Kirkbroads nobody covered up anything. Since everyone's so relaxed, they can have fun without thinking anything about it.

I didn't have any fun. Before dinner everyone drank wine and beer and got a little high. Then they had an enormous mess of spaghetti. Afterward hardly anyone thought of drinking, which might have made them want to dance. (I'd brought my records.) Instead they built a fire and began singing. There were two guitar players, and everyone kept singing one song after another—folk songs, foreign songs, old pop songs. Not all of them knew all the songs, but most of them knew most of them. I watched their lips. I hardly knew any of those songs.

Then they got excited about "The Game," they called it. They chose up two teams and wrote the names of books on scraps of paper. Then a member of one team had to act out the title so that his own team (they hadn't seen the scrap of paper) could guess what the book was. They timed how long it took. The whole game was invented for the know-it-alls to show off. There was one redheaded friend of Max's who drove me crazy. He was *always* guessing, and about half the time he was right. When it was his turn to act, he just held up three fingers. "Three words?" asked Aurelia. He nods, and holds up three fingers again. "Third word?" asked Melanie. He nodded. Then he acted like he was shooting a gun. Aurelia said instantly, *"The Great Gatsby!"*

"Right."

"Eleven seconds!" says the dentist, who had been keeping time. Everyone laughed and clapped.

I never made one single guess. When it was my turn to act, my face and arms and legs felt like they were made of cement. I picked out a piece of paper and it said *"Oedipus Rex."* At that time I'd never heard of it. I went over to the other team and asked them to whisper how to pronounce it. This redheaded guy made a kind of concealed sneer. But it was Melanie, Aurelia's friend, who said, "Books aren't Kenneth's strong point. He thought *Death of a Salesman* was just about a slob who didn't know how to sell."

Everybody gets a big belly laugh. I was too paralyzed to act out anything. I could have killed Aurelia. After about a minute of agony I gave the piece of paper back and sat down. I kept my eyes on my shoes. When the rest of them decided to take a midnight swim (they were crazy: it was almost November and the water was freezing), I put my suitcase in the Olds and took off.

I did one stupid thing. I came to a back road called Eucalyptus Cañon Road and I remembered Max saying his new M.G. had broken down and he and Gail had walked the last two miles to the cabin. I went up that way and sure enough, I found the M.G. parked on a shoulder. I hated Max for having that car. It was a bright red. He didn't appreciate it. He was a graduate student and made good money working in some laboratory. He just went down and bought the car one day like he was buying razor blades.

I removed the fancy FM radio and locked it in my trunk. The road was completely deserted. Then I took my pocket-knife and ripped the top a couple times. Then I got in my car and worked over the left side of that M.G. with the end of my bumper. This made a racket and brought me to my senses. I decided I'd better go back to the cabin and cover up.

They were all coming up from the beach, whooping and hollering. Even the dentist. I realized they'd gone in nude, but nothing wild or sexy. Now they were going to make popcorn and coffee and all that wholesome jazz. I kidded around a little and acted natural. I stayed away from Aurelia because she had that apologizing look in her eye. Then I took a long shower and went to bed early. I didn't sleep much. At daybreak I got up and left a note on the kitchen table saying I'd promised to visit Tom, who'd gone home for the weekend to a nearby town.

I never found Tom because his last name was Johnson, and there were about forty Johnsons in the book. So I drove fifty miles to another town that has Sunday drag races, but there weren't any that Sunday. I bought some steel wool and rubbed the red paint off my bumper and I threw the radio into a ditch. I began just cruising around, all the time thinking about things. That valley country was depressing. The squash and cabbage had just been harvested and the fields looked like they'd been blasted in a war. At one point I considered going down the highway at ninety miles an hour until I hit something. I was still way out in the country when my fuel pump conked.

By the time I hitched back to the Kirkbroads it was after three A.M., and I slept through until the middle of Monday afternoon. Aunt Eliza was in the kitchen when I got up. She fixed me a sandwich and some broth, and I told her my car was broken down. She said the station wagon was broken too, that something was dragging on the street. I said I'd look at it.

First I went downtown and bought a rebuilt fuel pump. Then I crawled under the station wagon, and sure enough, a muffler bracket was rusted out. All it needed was a little wire. I was still under there, wiring it up, when Gail's VW rolled into the garage. You'd think they would have

858　　　　　　　MALCOLM WOOD

noticed me under the station wagon: I guess my own car not being parked out front fooled them.

Old man Kirkbroad was driving. As soon as he turned off the VW ignition I could hear him perfectly. They all just sat there finishing the conversation, the way people do before they get out of a car.

"Quit condemning yourself, Aurelia," Kirkbroad was saying. "You and Gail did your best. Anyway, I suspect you're exaggerating."

"He was about to crack, I tell you. . . ." It was Aurelia's voice from the back seat of the VW. "You should have seen his eyes. I tried to talk to him but he kept slipping away. Melanie feels terrible. The minute she said it, she wanted to cut her tongue out."

"You don't *know* it was Kenneth that wrecked Max's car," said Kirkbroad. "Even if we knew, we wouldn't do anything. It's pretty understandable. I tried to warn you girls that first week. It has nothing to do with Kenneth's I.Q., or his other natural gifts. I suspect he's a cool customer, and very sharp. But here's a kid who has been something of a big shot in a small town. He comes to live with us, and what does he find? He doesn't know anything about books, he doesn't know anything about real music, or tide zone animals, or international affairs, or sailboats, or politics—or anything else we care about. No matter what goes on around here, Kenneth comes in last. He's about nineteen years behind. The things he does know about, we look down on."

"That's an awfully depressing analysis," said Gail.

"Perhaps. But it's an enormous gulf."

"I thought about buying a Model A," said Aurelia, "and having Kenneth soup it up for me. Then he'd be an expert on something. But I don't really want a Model A anymore. I got over that."

A door opened and Kirkbroad got out. His crummy moccasins were about four feet from my head. He went out of the garage. I could see the girls' feet as they got out on the other side. Aurelia said, "Keys, Gail. I've got to pick up Mother's groceries."

"Use the station wagon. I'm going back to the campus," said Gail.

"I can't. There's supposed to be something loose underneath."

Aurelia's beat-up sneakers came around to the side of the station wagon. Suddenly she kneeled down. There she was, looking right in my face. She gave a big gasp, naturally. After she'd stood up again she said, "Come out from there, Kenneth. Really! I don't think that was very fair. . . ."

I didn't get into any conversations. I just gathered all my stuff together and called a cab. Forty-five minutes later I checked in at the Y.M.C.A. That was the last I saw, probably ever will see, of the Kirkbroads.

I turned out to be very sharp, all right. I went to another city and got a job helping a guy with a used-car lot. I washed cars, answered the phone, made small repairs. After a while he let me sell. He reamed me on commissions, but I made pretty good dough. Eventually I realized twenty percent of his cars were hot—faked motor numbers, forged registrations, payoffs at the vehicle bureau. I dropped a hint to the kid who was delivering this stuff from out of state, and eventually a guy named Ludwig Bohm offered me a deal. "We have an organization," he says. "You got to start at the bottom."

I started at the bottom, and I was picked up on my first run. Bohm hadn't told me the trunk was full of arts and crafts—license plates made from welding together phony numbers from stolen plates that had been cut up.

They sent me here, which hasn't been bad. For a while I was in a daze. But I got to reading more and more books. First I just read mysteries and science fiction. But in the library I'd recognize authors and books from hearing the Kirkbroads argue. One book would lead to another. I read a book by Steinbeck I liked, so then I read all of Steinbeck's books. Same thing with Dostoevski. The more I read, the more I talked about books with Frank Farrell. He's the librarian with the red handlebar moustache. Farrell is definitely not a phony. He helped me file my parole application and he has actually lined up a job for me. I'm going to work for a friend of his who has a book store in Kansas City, Missouri.

The main thing Farrell did was to make me think about what kind of kid I'd been and what kind of life to try for outside. Farrell is a lot like old man Kirkbroad. He sees things very clear and he calls a spade just that. After I trusted Farrell, he questioned me about everything before I was convicted. For a long time I hadn't thought about the Kirkbroads, for instance, but when I finally started, I remembered plenty, as you can see.

A thing that hit me hardest was that Kirkbroad was mostly right. That guy was deep. I thought he wasn't noticing me at all.

It's funny how I've built up the Kirkbroads in my mind. I'll never see them again, but if I did go back there, they'd probably accept me. They're like Frank Farrell. They could believe that an ex-con still has a chance. But out home in Mesaville? I'm finished out there.

Naturally I realize I'll never be in the Kirkbroads' league. Kirkbroad would say I'm twenty-two years behind now. But I'm not so sure. I mentioned wondering about Formica or old tiles on the drainboard after I get out, remember? Actually I'll rent a furnished room and cook on a hot plate. I may not even own a car. I may save my money and go back to college eventually. Some people say that nobody ever really changes, but I am personally convinced that that's baloney.

◈

Malcolm Wood was born in Denver in 1924 and has degrees from Harvard and the University of California; he now lives in California with his family, teaching humanities at the California College of Arts and Crafts in Oak-

land. He has published many short stories in various magazines but has not yet published a collection of them or a novel.

In "What Really Matters" Malcolm Wood presents a much less complex confrontation of classes than we saw in "The Classless Society." The Kirkbroads seem to belong to the same upper-brow academic class as the Nesbitts, but they seem much less driven and more relaxed, less pretentious. They appear to enjoy their way of life, and it seems natural to them. It clearly seems so, at least in retrospect, to the narrator, Kenneth, a young man of what must be something like the ordinary middle-middle class who has been brought up according to what seem to him entirely different ways and different values. This conflict of life styles is the central subject of the story, is perfectly clear anyway, and is hammered home in the explanation that Kenneth overhears Mr. Kirkbroad give in the garage. Certain insights into specific class differences made in the story are perceptive: how in Kenneth's middle class "nobody thinks of having fun except with people their own age . . . because they're always hiding things from each other"; how cars are important almost to the point of providing identity in the lower of the two classes but in the other appear to serve only as a means of getting from one place to another. Most of the details of the story— from the differing kitchen drainboards to the differing attitudes about sex— seem accurate and well observed. That the Kirkbroads' manner and style may be at all calculated or affected, may be conforming to simple upper-brow reverse snobbism (Volkswagenism), isn't considered at all by the narrator. He is entirely shaken by this new set of "values" and resolves to make them his own. It may be that the author also believes that the Kirkbroads' values are the true ones and their style of life the best; it may be that the reader does too. At any rate, exposure of this sort to another entirely different way of life and system of values in our geographically and socially mobile society is becoming increasingly common. Kenneth's violent reaction and conversion may seem a bit precipitous, but young people today are thought to be especially susceptible to the impact of new ideas, and few of them have sufficiently deep conviction about the principles behind their own upbringing to stand by them for very long.

RICHARD YATES

The Best of Everything

❖❖❖❖❖❖❖

NOBODY EXPECTED Grace to do any work the Friday before her wedding. In fact, nobody would let her, whether she wanted to or not.

A gardenia corsage lay in a cellophane box beside her typewriter—from Mr. Atwood, her boss—and tucked inside the envelope that came with it was a ten-dollar gift certificate from Bloomingdale's. Mr. Atwood had treated her with a special shy courtliness ever since the time she necked with him at the office Christmas party, and now when she went in to thank him he was all hunched over, rattling desk drawers, blushing and grinning and barely meeting her eyes.

"Aw, now, don't mention it, Grace," he said. "Pleasure's all mine. Here, you need a pin to put that gadget on with?"

"There's a pin that came with it," she said, holding up the corsage. "See? A nice white one."

Beaming, he watched her pin the flowers high on the lapel of her suit. Then he cleared his throat importantly and pulled out the writing panel of his desk, ready to give the morning's dictation. But it turned out there were only two short letters, and it wasn't until an hour later, when she caught him handing over a pile of dictaphone cylinders to Central Typing, that she realized he had done her a favor.

"That's very sweet of you, Mr. Atwood," she said, "but I do think you ought to give me all your work today, just like any oth—"

"Aw, now, Grace," he said. "You only get married once."

The girls all made a fuss over her too, crowding around her desk and giggling, asking again and again to see Ralph's photograph ("Oh, he's *cute!*"), while the office manager looked on nervously, reluctant to be a spoilsport but anxious to point out that it was, after all, a working day.

Then at lunch there was the traditional little party at Schrafft's—nine women and girls, giddy on their unfamiliar cocktails, letting their chicken à la king grow cold while they pummeled her with old times and good wishes. There were more flowers and another gift—a silver candy dish for which all the girls had whisperingly chipped in.

Grace said "Thank you" and "I certainly do appreciate it" and "I don't know what to say" until her head rang with the words and the corners of her mouth ached from smiling, and she thought the afternoon would never end.

Ralph called up about four o'clock, exuberant. "How ya doin', honey?" he asked, and before she could answer he said, "Listen. Guess what I got?"

"I don't know. A present or something? What?" She tried to sound excited, but it wasn't easy.

"A bonus. Fifty dollars." She could almost see the flattening of his lips as he said "fifty dollars" with the particular earnestness he reserved for pronouncing sums of money.

"Why, that's lovely, Ralph," she said, and if there was any tiredness in her voice he didn't notice it.

"Lovely, huh?" he said with a laugh, mocking the girlishness of the word. "Ya *like* that, huh Gracie? No, but I mean I was really surprised, ya know it? The boss siz, 'Here, Ralph,' and he hands me this envelope. He don't even crack a smile or nothin', and I'm wonderin', what's the deal here? I'm getting fired here, or what? He siz, 'G'ahead, Ralph, open it.' So I open it, and then I look at the boss and he's grinning a mile wide." He chuckled and sighed. "Well, so listen, honey. What time ya want me to come over tonight?"

"Oh, I don't know. Soon as you can, I guess."

"Well listen, I gotta go over to Eddie's house and pick up that bag he's gonna loan me, so I might as well do that, go on home and eat, and then come over to your place around eight-thirty, nine o'clock. Okay?"

"All right," she said. "I'll see you then, darling." She had been calling him "darling" for only a short time—since it had become irrevocably clear that she was, after all, going to marry him—and the word still had an alien sound. As she straightened the stacks of stationery in her desk (because there was nothing else to do), a familiar little panic gripped her: she couldn't marry him—she hardly even *knew* him. Sometimes it occurred to her differently, that she couldn't marry him because she knew him too well, and either way it left her badly shaken, vulnerable to all the things that Martha, her roommate, had said from the very beginning.

"Isn't he funny?" Martha had said after their first date. "He says 'terlet.' I didn't know people really said 'terlet.' " And Grace had giggled, ready enough to agree that it *was* funny. That was a time when she had been ready to agree with Martha on practically anything—when it often seemed, in fact, that finding a girl like Martha from an ad in the *Times* was just about the luckiest thing that had ever happened to her.

But Ralph had persisted all through the summer, and by fall she had begun standing up for him. "What don't you like about him, Martha? He's perfectly nice."

"Oh, everybody's perfectly nice, Grace," Martha would say in her college voice, making perfectly nice a faintly absurd thing to be, and then she'd look up crossly from the careful painting of her fingernails. "It's just that he's such a little—a little *white worm*. Can't you see that?"

"Well, I certainly don't see what his *complexion* has to do with—"

"Oh God, *you* know what I mean. Can't you see what I *mean*? Oh, and all those friends of his, his Eddie and his Marty and his George with their mean, ratty little clerks' lives and their mean, ratty little. . . . It's just that they're all *alike*, those people. All they ever say is 'Hey, wha' happen t'ya Giants?' and 'Hey, wha' happen t'ya Yankees?' and they all live way out in Sunnyside or Woodhaven or some awful place, and their mothers have those damn little china elephants on the mantelpiece." And Martha would frown over her nail polish again, making it clear that the subject was closed.

All that fall and winter she was confused. For a while she tried going out only with Martha's kind of men—the kind that used words like "amusing" all the time and wore small-shouldered flannel suits like a uniform; and for a while she tried going out with no men at all. She even tried that crazy business with Mr. Atwood at the office Christmas party. And all the time Ralph kept calling up, hanging around, waiting for her to make up her mind. Once she took him home to meet her parents in Pennsylvania (where she never would have dreamed of taking Martha), but it wasn't until Easter time that she finally gave in.

They had gone to a dance somewhere in Queens, one of the big American Legion dances that Ralph's crowd was always going to, and when the band played "Easter Parade" he held her very close, hardly moving, and sang to her in a faint, whispering tenor. It was the kind of thing she'd never have expected Ralph to do—a sweet, gentle thing—and it probably wasn't just then that she decided to marry him, but it always seemed so afterwards. It always seemed she had decided that minute, swaying to the music with his husky voice in her hair:

> "I'll be all in clover
> And when they look you over
> I'll be the proudest fella
> In the Easter Parade. . . ."

That night she had told Martha, and she could still see the look on Martha's face. "Oh, Grace, you're not—surely you're not *serious*. I mean, I thought he was more or less of a *joke*—you can't really mean you want to—"

"Shut up! You just shut up, Martha!" And she'd cried all night. Even now she hated Martha for it; even as she stared blindly at a row of filing cabinets along the office wall, half sick with fear that Martha was right.

The noise of giggles swept over her, and she saw with a start that two of the girls—Irene and Rose—were grinning over their typewriters and pointing at her. *"We* saw ya!" Irene sang. *"We* saw ya! Mooning again, huh Grace?" Then Rose did a burlesque of mooning, heaving her meager breasts and batting her eyes, and they both collapsed in laughter.

With an effort of will Grace resumed the guileless, open smile of a bride. The thing to do was concentrate on plans.

Tomorrow morning, "bright and early," as her mother would say, she would meet Ralph at Penn Station for the trip home. They'd arrive about one, and her parents would meet the train. "Good t'see ya, Ralph!" her father would say, and her mother would probably kiss him. A warm, homely love filled her: *they* wouldn't call him a white worm; *they* didn't have any ideas about Princeton men and "interesting" men and all the other kinds of men Martha was so stuck-up about. Then her father would probably take Ralph out for a beer and show him the paper mill where he worked (and at least Ralph wouldn't be snobby about a person working in a paper mill, either), and then Ralph's family and friends would come down from New York in the evening.

She'd have time for a long talk with her mother that night, and the next morning, "bright and early" (her eyes stung at the thought of her mother's plain, happy face), they would start getting dressed for the wedding. Then the church and the ceremony, and then the reception (Would her father get drunk? Would Muriel Ketchel sulk about not being a bridesmaid?), and finally the train to Atlantic City, and the hotel. But from the hotel on she couldn't plan any more. A door would lock behind her and there would be a wild, fantastic silence, and nobody in all the world but Ralph to lead the way.

"Well, Grace," Mr. Atwood was saying, "I want to wish you every happiness." He was standing at her desk with his hat and coat on, and all around her were the chattering and scraping-back of chairs that meant it was five o'clock.

"Thank you, Mr. Atwood," She got to her feet, suddenly surrounded by all the girls in a bedlam of farewell.

"All the luck in the world, Grace."

"Drop us a card, huh Grace? From Atlantic City?"

"So long, Grace."

"G'night, Grace, and listen: the best of everything."

Finally she was free of them all, out of the elevator, out of the building, hurrying through the crowds to the subway.

When she got home Martha was standing in the door of the kitchenette, looking very svelte in a crisp new dress.

"Hi, Grace. I bet they ate you alive today, didn't they?"

"Oh no," Grace said. "Everybody was—real nice." She sat down, exhausted, and dropped the flowers and the wrapped candy dish on a table. Then she noticed that the whole apartment was swept and dusted, and the dinner was cooking in the kitchenette. "Gee, everything looks wonderful," she said. "What'd you do all this for?"

"Oh, well, I got home early anyway," Martha said. Then she smiled, and it was one of the few times Grace had ever seen her look shy. "I just thought it might be nice to have the place looking decent for a change, when Ralph comes over."

"Well," Grace said, "it certainly was nice of you."

The way Martha looked now was even more surprising: she looked awkward. She was turning a greasy spatula in her fingers, holding it delicately away from her dress and examining it, as if she had something difficult to say. "Look, Grace," she began. "You do understand why I can't come to the wedding, don't you?"

"Oh, sure," Grace said, although in fact she didn't, exactly. It was something about having to go up to Harvard to see her brother before he went into the Army, but it had sounded like a lie from the beginning.

"It's just that I'd hate you to think I— well, anyway, I'm glad if you do understand. And the other thing I wanted to say is more important."

"What?"

"Well, just that I'm sorry for all the awful things I used to say about Ralph. I never had a right to talk to you that way. He's a very sweet boy and I—well, I'm sorry, that's all."

It wasn't easy for Grace to hide a rush of gratitude and relief when she said, "Why, that's all right, Martha, I—"

"The chops are on fire!" Martha bolted for the kitchenette. "It's all right," she called back. "They're edible." And when she came out to serve dinner all her old composure was restored. "I'll have to eat and run," she said as they sat down. "My train leaves in forty minutes."

"I thought it was *tomorrow* you were going."

"Well, it was, actually," Martha said, "but I decided to go tonight. Because you see, Grace, another thing—if you can stand one more apology —another thing I'm sorry for is that I've hardly ever given you and Ralph a chance to be alone here. So tonight I'm going to clear out." She hesitated. "It'll be a sort of wedding gift from me, okay?" And then she smiled, not shyly this time but in a way that was more in character—the eyes subtly averted after a flicker of special meaning. It was a smile that Grace— through stages of suspicion, bewilderment, awe, and practiced imitation— had long ago come to associate with the word "sophisticated."

"Well, that's very sweet of you," Grace said, but she didn't really get the point just then. It wasn't until long after the meal was over and the dishes washed, until Martha had left for her train in a whirl of cosmetics and luggage and quick goodbyes, that she began to understand.

She took a deep, voluptuous bath and spent a long time drying herself, posing in the mirror, filled with a strange slow excitement. In her bedroom, from the rustling tissues of an expensive white box, she drew the prizes of her trousseau—a sheer nightgown of white nylon and a matching negligee —put them on, and went to the mirror again. She had never worn anything like this before, or felt like this, and the thought of letting Ralph see her like this sent her into the kitchenette for a glass of the special dry sherry Martha kept for cocktail parties. Then she turned out all the lights but one and, carrying her glass, went to the sofa and arranged herself there to wait for him. After a while she got up and brought the sherry bottle over to the coffee table, where she set it on a tray with another glass.

When Ralph left the office he felt vaguely let down. Somehow, he'd expected more of the Friday before his wedding. The bonus check had been all right (though secretly he'd been counting on twice that amount), and the boys had bought him a drink at lunch and kidded around in the appropriate way ("Ah, don't feel too bad, Ralph—worse things could happen"), but still, there ought to have been a real party. Not just the boys in the office, but Eddie, and *all* his friends. Instead there would only be meeting Eddie at the White Rose like every other night of the year, and riding home to borrow Eddie's suitcase and to eat, and then having to ride all the way back to Manhattan just to see Gracie for an hour or two. Eddie wasn't in the bar when he arrived, which sharpened the edge of his loneliness. Morosely he drank a beer, waiting.

Eddie was his best friend, and an ideal best man because he'd been in on the courtship of Gracie from the start. It was in this very bar, in fact, that Ralph had told him about their first date last summer: "Ooh, Eddie—what a paira *knockers!*"

And Eddie had grinned. "Yeah? So what's the roommate like?"

"Ah, you don't want the roommate, Eddie. The roommate's a dog. A snob, too, I think. No, but this *other* one, this little *Gracie*—boy, I mean, she is *stacked.*"

Half the fun of every date—even more than half—had been telling Eddie about it afterwards, exaggerating a little here and there, asking Eddie's advice on tactics. But after today, like so many other pleasures, it would all be left behind. Gracie had promised him at least one night off a week to spend with the boys, after they were married, but even so it would never be the same. Girls never understood a thing like friendship.

There was a ball game on the bar's television screen and he watched it idly, his throat swelling in a sentimental pain of loss. Nearly all his life had been devoted to the friendship of boys and men, to trying to be a good guy, and now the best of it was over.

Finally Eddie's stiff finger jabbed the seat of his pants in greeting. "Whaddya say, sport?"

Ralph narrowed his eyes to indolent contempt and slowly turned around. "Wha' happen ta you, wise guy? Get lost?"

"Whaddya—in a hurry a somethin'?" Eddie barely moved his lips when he spoke. "Can't wait two minutes?" He slouched on a stool and slid a quarter at the bartender. "Draw one, there, Jack."

They drank in silence for a while, staring at the television. "Got a little bonus today," Ralph said. "Fifty dollars."

"Yeah?" Eddie said. "Good."

A batter struck out; the inning was over and the commercial came on. "So?" Eddie said, rocking the beer around in his glass. "Still gonna get married?"

"Why not?" Ralph said with a shrug. "Listen, finish that, willya? I wanna get a move on."

"Wait awhile, wait awhile. What's ya hurry?"

"C'mon, willya?" Ralph stepped impatiently away from the bar. "I wanna go pick up ya bag."

"Ah, bag schmagg."

Ralph moved up close again and glowered at him. "Look, wise guy. Nobody's gonna *make* ya loan me the goddamn bag, ya know. I don't wanna break ya *heart* or nothin'—"

"Arright, arright, arright. You'll getcha bag. Don't worry so much." He finished the beer and wiped his mouth. "Let's go."

Having to borrow a bag for his wedding trip was a sore point with Ralph; he'd much rather have bought one of his own. There was a fine one displayed in the window of a luggage shop they passed every night on their way to the subway—a big, tawny Gladstone with a zippered compartment on the side, at thirty-nine, ninety-five—and Ralph had had his eye on it ever since Easter time. "Think I'll buy that," he'd told Eddie, in the same offhand way that a day or so before he had announced his engagement ("Think I'll marry the girl"). Eddie's response to both remarks had been the same: "Whaddya—crazy?" Both times Ralph had said, "Why not?" and in defense of the bag he had added, "Gonna get married, I'll *need* somethin' like that." From then on it was as if the bag, almost as much as Gracie herself, had become a symbol of the new and richer life he sought. But after the ring and the new clothes and all the other expenses, he'd found at last that he couldn't afford it; he had settled for the loan of Eddie's, which was similar but cheaper and worn, and without the zippered compartment.

Now as they passed the luggage shop he stopped, caught in the grip of a reckless idea. "Hey wait awhile, Eddie. Know what I think I'll do with that fifty-dollar bonus? I think I'll buy that bag right now." He felt breathless.

"Whaddya—crazy? Forty bucks for a bag you'll use maybe one time a year? Ya crazy, Ralph. C'mon."

"Ah—I dunno. Ya think so?"

"Listen, you better *keep* ya money, boy. You're gonna *need* it."

"Ah—yeah," Ralph said at last. "I guess ya right." And he fell in step with Eddie again, heading for the subway. This was the way things usually turned out in his life; he could never own a bag like that until he made a better salary, and he accepted it—just as he'd accepted without question, after the first thin sigh, the knowledge that he'd never possess his bride until after the wedding.

The subway swallowed them, rattled and banged them along in a rocking, mindless trance for half an hour, and disgorged them at last into the cool early evening of Queens.

Removing their coats and loosening their ties, they let the breeze dry their sweated shirts as they walked. "So, what's the deal?" Eddie asked. "What time we supposed to show up in this Pennsylvania burg tomorra?"

"Ah, suit yourself," Ralph said. "Any time in the evening's okay."

"So whadda we do then? What the hell can ya *do* in a hillbilly town like that, anyway?"

"Ah, I dunno," Ralph said defensively. "Sit around and talk, I guess; drink beer with Gracie's old man or somethin'; I dunno."

"Jesus," Eddie said. "Some weekend. Big, big deal."

Ralph stopped on the sidewalk, suddenly enraged, his damp coat wadded in his fist. "Look, you bastid. Nobody's gonna *make* ya come, ya know—you or Marty or George or any a the rest of 'em. Get that straight. You're not doin' *me* no favors, unnastand?"

"Whatsa matta?" Eddie inquired. "Whatsa matta? Can'tcha take a joke?"

"Joke," Ralph said. "You're fulla jokes." And plodding sullenly in Eddie's wake, he felt close to tears.

They turned off into the block where they both lived, a double row of neat, identical houses bordering the street where they'd fought and loafed and played stickball all their lives. Eddie pushed open the front door of his house and ushered Ralph into the vestibule, with its homely smell of cauliflower and overshoes. "G'wan in," he said, jerking a thumb at the closed living-room door, and he hung back to let Ralph go first.

Ralph opened the door and took three steps inside before it hit him like a sock on the jaw. The room, dead silent, was packed deep with grinning, red-faced men—Marty, George, the boys from the block, the boys from the office—everybody, all his friends, all on their feet and poised motionless in a solid mass. Skinny Maguire was crouched at the upright piano, his spread fingers high over the keys, and when he struck the first rollicking chords they all roared into song, beating time with their fists, their enormous grins distorting the words:

> "Fa he's a jally guh fella
> Fa he's a jally guh fella
> Fa he's a jally guh fell-ah
> That nobody can deny!"

Weakly Ralph retreated a step on the carpet and stood there wide-eyed, swallowing, holding his coat. *"That nobody can deny!"* they sang, *"That nobody can deny!"* And as they swung into the second chorus Eddie's father appeared through the dining-room curtains, bald and beaming, in full song, with a great glass pitcher of beer in either hand. At last Skinny hammered out the final line:

"That—no—bod—dee—can—dee—nye!"

And they all surged forward cheering, grabbing Ralph's hand, pounding his arms and his back while he stood trembling, his own voice lost under the noise. "Gee, fellas—thanks. I—don't know what to—thanks, fellas. . . ."

Then the crowd cleaved in half, and Eddie made his way slowly down the middle. His eyes gleamed in a smile of love, and from his bashful hand hung the suitcase—not his own, but a new one: the big, tawny Gladstone with the zippered compartment on the side.

"Speech!" they were yelling. *"Speech! Speech!"*

But Ralph couldn't speak and couldn't smile. He could hardly even see.

At ten o'clock Grace began walking around the apartment and biting her lip. What if he wasn't coming? But of course he was coming. She sat down again and carefully smoothed the billows of nylon around her thighs, forcing herself to be calm. The whole thing would be ruined if she was nervous.

The noise of the doorbell was like an electric shock. She was halfway to the door before she stopped, breathing hard, and composed herself again. Then she pressed the buzzer and opened the door a crack to watch for him on the stairs.

When she saw he was carrying a suitcase, and saw the pale seriousness of his face as he mounted the stairs, she thought at first that he knew; he had come prepared to lock the door and take her in his arms. "Hello, darling," she said softly, and opened the door wider.

"Hi, baby." He brushed past her and walked inside. "Guess I'm late, huh? You in bed?"

"No." She closed the door and leaned against it with both hands holding the doorknob at the small of her back, the way heroines close doors in the movies. "I was just—waiting for you."

He wasn't looking at her. He went to the sofa and sat down, holding the suitcase on his lap and running his fingers over its surface. "Gracie," he said, barely above a whisper. "Look at this."

She looked at it, and then into his tragic eyes.

"Remember," he said, "I told you about that bag I wanted to buy? Forty dollars?" He stopped and looked around. "Hey, where's Martha? She in bed?"

"She's gone, darling," Grace said, moving slowly toward the sofa. "She's gone for the whole weekend." She sat down beside him, leaned close, and gave him Martha's special smile.

"Oh yeah?" he said. "Well anyway, listen. I said I was gonna borrow Eddie's bag instead, remember?"

"Yes."

"Well, so tonight at the White Rose I siz, 'C'mon, Eddie, let's go home pick up ya bag.' He siz, 'Ah, bag schmagg.' I siz, 'Whatsa matta?' but he don't say nothin', see? So we go home to his place and the living-room door's shut, see?"

She squirmed closer and put her head·on his chest. Automatically he raised an arm and dropped it around her shoulders, still talking. "He siz, 'G'ahead, Ralph, open the door.' I siz, 'Whatsa deal?' He siz 'Never mind, Ralph, open the door.' So I open the door, and oh Jesus." His fingers gripped her shoulder with such intensity that she looked up at him in alarm.

"They was all there, Gracie," he said. "All the fellas. Playin' the piana, singin', cheerin'—" His voice wavered and his eyelids fluttered shut, their lashes wet. "A big surprise party," he said, trying to smile. "Fa me. Can ya beat that, Gracie? And then—and then Eddie comes out and—Eddie comes out and hands me this. The very same bag I been lookin' at all this time. He bought it with his own money and he didn't say nothin', just to give me a surprise. 'Here, Ralph,' he siz. 'Just to let ya know you're the greatest guy in the world.' " His fingers tightened again, trembling. "I cried, Gracie," he whispered. "I couldn't help it. I don't think the fellas saw it or anything, but I was cryin'." He turned his face away and worked his lips in a tremendous effort to hold back the tears.

"Would you like a drink, darling?" she asked tenderly.

"Nah, that's all right, Gracie. I'm all right." Gently he set the suitcase on the carpet. "Only, gimme a cigarette, huh?"

She got one from the coffee table, put it in his lips and lit it. "Let me get you a drink," she said.

He frowned through the smoke. "Whaddya got, that sherry wine? Nah, I don't like that stuff. Anyway, I'm fulla beer." He leaned back and closed his eyes. "And then Eddie's mother feeds us this terrific meal," he went on, and his voice was almost normal now. "We had *steaks;* we had French-fried *potatas"*—his head rolled on the sofa-back with each item of the menu—"lettuce-and-tomato *salad, pickles, bread, butter*—everything. The works."

"Well," she said. "Wasn't that nice."

"And afterwards we had ice cream and coffee," he said, "and all the beer we could drink. I mean, it was a real spread."

Grace ran her hands over her lap, partly to smooth the nylon and partly to dry the moisture on her palms. "Well, that certainly was nice of them," she said. They sat there silent for what seemed a long time.

"I can only stay a minute, Gracie," Ralph said at last. "I promised 'em I'd be back."

Her heart thumped under the nylon. "Ralph, do you—do you like this?"

"What, honey?"

"My negligee. You weren't supposed to see it until—after the wedding, but I thought I'd—"

"Nice," he said, feeling the flimsy material between thumb and index finger, like a merchant. "Very nice. Wudga pay fa this, honey?"

"Oh—I don't know. But do you like it?"

He kissed her and began, at last, to stroke her with his hands. "Nice," he kept saying. "Nice. Hey, I like this." His hand hesitated at the low neckline, slipped inside and held her breast.

"I do love you, Ralph," she whispered. "You know that, don't you?"

His fingers pinched her nipple, once, and slid quickly out again. The policy of restraint, the habit of months was too strong to break. "Sure," he said. "And I love you, baby. Now you be a good girl and get ya beauty sleep, and I'll see ya in the morning. Okay?"

"Oh, Ralph. Don't go. Stay."

"Ah, I promised the fellas, Gracie." He stood up and straightened his clothes. "They're waitin' fa me, out home."

She blazed to her feet, but the cry that was meant for a woman's appeal came out, through her tightening lips, as the whine of a wife: "Can't they wait?"

"Whaddya—*crazy?*" He backed away, eyes round with righteousness. She would *have* to understand. If this was the way she acted before the wedding, how the hell was it going to be afterwards? "Have a *heart,* willya? Keep the fellas waitin' *tonight?* After all they done fa *me?*"

After a second or two, during which her face became less pretty than he had ever seen it before, she was able to smile. "Of course not, darling. You're right."

He came forward again and gently brushed the tip of her chin with his fist, smiling, a husband reassured. " 'At's more like it," he said. "So I'll see ya, Penn Station, nine o'clock tomorra. Right, Gracie? Only, before I go—" he winked and slapped his belly. "I'm fulla beer. Mind if I use ya terlet?"

When he came out of the bathroom she was waiting to say goodnight, standing with her arms folded across her chest, as if for warmth. Lovingly he hefted the new suitcase and joined her at the door. "Okay, then, baby," he said, and kissed her. "Nine o'clock. Don't forget, now."

She smiled tiredly and opened the door for him. "Don't worry, Ralph," she said. "I'll be there."

◈

*Richard Yates was born in Yonkers, New York, in 1926, served in the
Army in World War II, later worked for newspapers, and has written several screenplays; he has taught writing at Columbia, The New School, and
at the Writers' Workshop at the State University of Iowa. He has received
many awards for his work, among them a Guggenheim fellowship and an
Academy of Arts and Letters award. He has published one novel,* Revolutionary Road *(1961), not a historical novel as the title sounds, but actually
very revealing and relevant to our times.* Revolutionary Road *is a suburban
avenue, and the novel is of a modern suburban middle-class marriage that
disintegrates under the impact of all the forces at work against it. Yates
has also published a collection of eleven short stories called* Eleven Kinds
of Loneliness *(1962), each a poignant illustration of the difficulties individuals experience in communicating their emotions to one another in modern life.*

*In "The Best of Everything," confusion about class differences figures
as the villain of the story, shaking the confidence of a young couple already
very skittish about getting married. The difficulty occurs, as it did in the
previous two stories, with people from different backgrounds not being able
to deal with the implications of those differences. It is not the difference
between Ralph and Grace that is important, but the difference between
Grace and her roommate, Martha. Grace has met Martha only recently,
not through a party or through work—for they would not be likely to meet
in such ways—but through an advertisement in* The New York Times, *in
the way that people alone in the city sometimes find another to share an
apartment. Grace falls under the influence of this girl, who in education
and social status is several notches above her. But it is difficult for Grace
to assume Martha's values and attitudes when she hasn't shared her background. She is naturally uncomfortable with the Princetonians and other
"interesting" men she meets through Martha, nearly flounders (the "crazy
business" with her boss, for instance), then gives in and agrees to marry
Ralph. Martha is accurate in her descriptions of Ralph and his friends,
although certainly very unkind; but she has a wrong conception about
Grace and fails to see that Grace and Ralph are not really unsuited to each
other. Grace's parents see nothing funny about Ralph; he and her father
go out and drink beer. Beer versus "sherry wine" could virtually stand as
symbols of the class conflict involved in the story. Under Martha's influence, Grace forgets how powerful are the bonds of beer and buddies to
men in Ralph's (and her) class. And again under Martha's influence, and
also the influence of the sherry, she puts on the sheer negligee and assumes
a more liberal attitude toward premarital sex than prevails in her own (and*

Ralph's) class—at least toward the girl one is going to marry. (This more open and permissive attitude toward sex was one of the differences Kenneth noted between his own upbringing and the relatively more upper-class upbringing of the Kirkbroad girls in "What Really Matters.") It is important not to misread the crucial scene at the end, where Ralph leaves her in her seductive negligee to return to his beer-and-buddies party, a ritualistic send-off that is important and strengthening to him and which he had bitterly missed at the beginning of the story. It is not to be understood that he is brute and unfeeling, latently homosexual, or anything like that. He is merely conforming to a pattern of behavior that is customary and proper as he and those like him see it. Grace, following the different practices of a different class, offering herself to him before their marriage in accordance with rites strange to him, is the one who has acted improperly. Confusions about such patterns of behavior are increasingly common as susceptible people more frequently nowadays are exposed to the influence of those who are not like themselves and are attracted to ways that have not traditionally been their own.

J. F. POWERS

The Forks

◇◇◇◇◇◇◇

THAT SUMMER when Father Eudex got back from saying Mass at the orphanage in the morning, he would park Monsignor's car, which was long and black and new like a politician's, and sit down in the cool of the porch to read his office. If Monsignor was not already standing in the door, he would immediately appear there, seeing that his car had safely returned, and inquire:

"Did you have any trouble with her?"

Father Eudex knew too well the question meant, Did you mistreat my car?

"No trouble, Monsignor."

"Good," Monsignor said, with imperfect faith in his curate, who was not a car owner. For a moment Monsignor stood framed in the screen door, fumbling his watch fob as for a full-length portrait, and then he was suddenly not there.

"Monsignor," Father Eudex said, rising nervously, "I've got a chance to pick up a car."

At the door Monsignor slid into his frame again. His face expressed what was for him intense interest.

"Yes? Go on."

"I don't want to have to use yours every morning."

"It's all right."

"And there are other times." Father Eudex decided not to be maudlin and mention sick calls, nor be entirely honest and admit he was tired of busses and bumming rides from parishioners. "And now I've got a chance to get one—cheap."

Monsignor, smiling, came alert at *cheap*.

"New?"

"No, I wouldn't say it's new."

Monsignor was openly suspicious now. "What kind?"

"It's a Ford."

"And not new?"

"Not new, Monsignor—but in good condition. It was owned by a retired farmer and had good care."

Monsignor sniffed. He *knew* cars. "V-Eight, Father?"

"No," Father Eudex confessed. "It's a Model A."

Monsignor chuckled as though this were indeed the damnedest thing he had ever heard.

"But in very good condition, Monsignor."

"You said that."

"Yes. And I could take it apart if anything went wrong. My uncle had one."

"No doubt." Monsignor uttered a laugh at Father Eudex's rural origins. Then he delivered the final word, long delayed out of amusement. "It wouldn't be prudent, Father. After all, this isn't a country parish. You know the class of people we get here."

Monsignor put on his Panama hat. Then, apparently mistaking the obstinacy in his curate's face for plain ignorance, he shed a little more light. "People watch a priest, Father. *Damnant quod non intelligunt.* It would never do. You'll have to watch your tendencies."

Monsignor's eyes tripped and fell hard on the morning paper lying on the swing where he had finished it.

"Another flattering piece about that crazy fellow. . . . There's a man who might have gone places if it weren't for his mouth! A bishop doesn't have to get mixed up in all that stuff!"

Monsignor, as Father Eudex knew, meant unions, strikes, race riots—all that stuff.

"A parishioner was saying to me only yesterday it's getting so you can't tell the Catholics from the Communists, with the priests as bad as any. Yes, and this fellow is the worst. He reminds me of that bishop a few years back—at least he called himself a bishop, a Protestant—that was advocating companionate marriages. It's not that bad, maybe, but if you listened to some of them you'd think that Catholicity and capitalism were incompatible!"

"The Holy Father——"

"The Holy Father's in Europe, Father. Mr. Memmers lives in this parish. I'm his priest. What can I tell him?"

"Is it Mr. Memmers of the First National, Monsignor?"

"It is, Father. And there's damned little cheer I can give a man like Memmers. Catholics, priests, and laity alike—yes, and princes of the Church, all talking atheistic communism!"

This was the substance of their conversation, always, the deadly routine in which Father Eudex played straight man. Each time it happened he seemed to participate, and though he should have known better he justified his participation by hoping that it would not happen again, or in quite the same way. But it did, it always did, the same way, and Monsignor, for all his alarums, had nothing to say really and meant one thing only, the thing he never said—that he dearly wanted to be, and was not, a bishop.

Father Eudex could imagine just what kind of bishop Monsignor would be. His reign would be a wise one, excessively so. His mind was made up on everything, excessively so. He would know how to avoid the snares set in the path of the just man, avoid them, too, in good taste and good conscience. He would not be trapped as so many good shepherds before him had been trapped, poor souls—caught in fair-seeming dilemmas of justice that were best left alone, like the first apple. It grieved him, he said, to think of those great hearts broken in silence and solitude. It was the worst kind of exile, alas! But just give him the chance and he would know what to do, what to say, and, more important, what not to do, not to say—neither yea nor nay for him. He had not gone to Rome for nothing. For him the dark forest of decisions would not exist; for him, thanks to hours spent in prayer and meditation, the forest would vanish as dry grass before fire, his fire. He knew the mask of evil already—birth control, indecent movies, salacious books—and would call these things by their right names and dare to deal with them for what they were, these new occasions for the old sins of the cities of the plains.

But in the meantime—oh, to have a particle of the faith that God had in humanity! Dear, trusting God, forever trying them beyond their feeble powers, ordering terrible tests, fatal trials by nonsense (the crazy bishop). And keeping Monsignor steadily warming up on the side lines, ready to rush in, primed for the day that would perhaps never dawn.

At one time, so the talk went, there had been reason to think that Monsignor was headed for a bishopric. Now it was too late; Monsignor's intercessors were all dead; the cupboard was bare; he knew it at heart, and it galled him to see another man, this *crazy* man, given the opportunity, and making such a mess of it.

Father Eudex searched for and found a little salt for Monsignor's wound. "The word's going around he'll be the next archbishop," he said.

"I won't believe it," Monsignor countered hoarsely. He glanced at the newspaper on the swing and renewed his horror. "If that fellow's right, Father, I'm"—his voice cracked at the idea—*"wrong!"*

Father Eudex waited until Monsignor had started down the steps to the car before he said, "It could be."

"I'll be back for lunch, Father. I'm taking her for a little spin."

Monsignor stopped in admiration a few feet from the car—her. He was as helpless before her beauty as a boy with a birthday bicycle. He could not leave her alone. He had her out every morning and afternoon and evening. He was indiscriminate about picking people up for a ride in her. He kept her on a special diet—only the best of gas and oil and grease, with daily rubdowns. He would run her only on the smoothest roads and at so many miles an hour. That was to have stopped at the first five hundred, but only now, nearing the thousand mark, was he able to bring himself to increase her speed, and it seemed to hurt him more than it did her.

Now he was walking around behind her to inspect the tires. Apparently O.K. He gave the left rear fender an amorous chuck and eased into the front seat. Then they drove off, the car and he, to see the world, to explore each other further on the honeymoon.

Father Eudex watched the car slide into the traffic, and waited, on edge. The corner cop, fulfilling Father Eudex's fears, blew his whistle and waved his arms up in all four directions, bringing traffic to a standstill. Monsignor pulled expertly out of line and drove down Clover Boulevard in a one-car parade; all others stalled respectfully. The cop, as Monsignor passed, tipped his cap, showing a bald head. Monsignor, in the circumstances, could not acknowledge him, though he knew the man well—a parishioner. He was occupied with keeping his countenance kindly, grim, and exalted, that the cop's faith remain whole, for it was evidently inconceivable to him that Monsignor should ever venture abroad unless to bear the Holy Viaticum, always racing with death.

Father Eudex, eyes baleful but following the progress of the big black car, saw a hand dart out of the driver's window in a wave. Monsignor would combine a lot of business with pleasure that morning, creating what he called "good will for the Church"—all morning in the driver's seat toasting passers-by with a wave that was better than a blessing. How he loved waving to people!

Father Eudex overcame his inclination to sit and stew about things by going down the steps to meet the mailman. He got the usual handful for the Monsignor—advertisements and amazing offers, the unfailing crop of chaff from dealers in church goods, organs, collection schemes, insurance, and sacramental wines. There were two envelopes addressed to Father Eudex, one a mimeographed plea from a missionary society which he might or might not acknowledge with a contribution, depending upon what he thought of the cause—if it was really lost enough to justify a levy on his poverty—and the other a check for a hundred dollars.

The check came in an eggshell envelope with no explanation except a tiny card, "Compliments of the Rival Tractor Company," but even that was needless. All over town clergymen had known for days that the checks were on the way again. Some, rejoicing, could hardly wait. Father Eudex, however, was one of those who could.

With the passing of hard times and the coming of the fruitful war years, the Rival Company, which was a great one for public relations, had found the best solution to the excess-profits problem to be giving. Ministers and even rabbis shared in the annual jackpot, but Rival employees were largely Catholic and it was the checks to the priests that paid off. Again, some thought it was a wonderful idea, and others thought that Rival, plagued by strikes and justly so, had put their alms to work.

There was another eggshell envelope, Father Eudex saw, among the letters for Monsignor, and knew his check would be for two hundred, the premium for pastors.

Father Eudex left Monsignor's mail on the porch table by his cigars. His own he stuck in his back pocket, wanting to forget it, and went down the steps into the yard. Walking back and forth on the shady side of the rectory where the lilies of the valley grew and reading his office, he gradually drifted into the back yard, lured by a noise. He came upon Whalen, the janitor, pounding pegs into the ground.

Father Eudex closed the breviary on a finger. "What's it all about, Joe?"

Joe Whalen snatched a piece of paper from his shirt and handed it to Father Eudex. "He gave it to me this morning."

He—it was the word for Monsignor among them. A docile pronoun only, and yet when it meant the Monsignor it said, and concealed, nameless things.

The paper was a plan for a garden drawn up by the Monsignor in his fine hand. It called for a huge fleur-de-lis bounded by smaller crosses—and these Maltese—a fountain, a sundial, and a cloister walk running from the rectory to the garage. Later there would be birdhouses and a ten-foot wall of thick gray stones, acting as a moat against the eyes of the world. The whole scheme struck Father Eudex as expensive and, in this country, Presbyterian.

When Monsignor drew the plan, however, he must have been in his medieval mood. A spouting whale jostled with Neptune in the choppy waters of the fountain. North was indicated in the legend by a winged cherub huffing and puffing.

Father Eudex held the plan up against the sun to see the watermark. The stationery was new to him, heavy, simulated parchment, with the Church of the Holy Redeemer and Monsignor's name embossed, three initials, W. F. X., William Francis Xavier. With all those initials the man could pass for a radio station, a chancery wit had observed, or if his last name had not been Sweeney, Father Eudex added now, for high Anglican.

Father Eudex returned the plan to Whalen, feeling sorry for him and to an extent guilty before him—if only because he was a priest like Monsignor (now turned architect) whose dream of a monastery garden included the overworked janitor under the head of "labor."

Father Eudex asked Whalen to bring another shovel. Together, almost without words, they worked all morning spading up crosses, leaving the big fleur-de-lis to the last. Father Eudex removed his coat first, then his collar, and finally was down to his undershirt.

Toward noon Monsignor rolled into the driveway.

He stayed in the car, getting red in the face, recovering from the pleasure of seeing so much accomplished as he slowly recognized his curate in Whalen's helper. In a still, appalled voice he called across the lawn, "Father," and waited as for a beast that might or might not have sense enough to come.

Father Eudex dropped his shovel and went over to the car, shirtless.

Monsignor waited a moment before he spoke, as though annoyed by the everlasting necessity, where this person was concerned, to explain. "Father," he said quietly at last, "I wouldn't do any more of that—if I were you. Rather, in any event, I wouldn't."

"All right, Monsignor."

"To say the least, it's not prudent. If necessary"—he paused as Whalen came over to dig a cross within earshot—"I'll explain later. It's time for lunch now."

The car, black, beautiful, fierce with chromium, was quiet as Monsignor dismounted, knowing her master. Monsignor went around to the rear, felt a tire, and probed a nasty cinder in the tread.

"Look at that," he said, removing the cinder.

Father Eudex thought he saw the car lift a hoof, gaze around, and thank Monsignor with her headlights.

Monsignor proceeded at a precise pace to the back door of the rectory. There he held the screen open momentarily, as if remembering something or reluctant to enter before himself—such was his humility—but then called to Whalen with an intimacy that could never exist between them.

"Better knock off now, Joe."

Whalen turned in on himself. "*Joe*—is it!"

Father Eudex removed his clothes from the grass. His hands were all blisters, but in them he found a little absolution. He apologized to Joe for having to take the afternoon off. "I can't make it, Joe. Something turned up."

"Sure, Father."

Father Eudex could hear Joe telling his wife about it that night—yeah, the young one got in wrong with the old one again. Yeah, the old one, he don't believe in it, work, for them.

Father Eudex paused in the kitchen to remember he knew not what. It was in his head, asking to be let in, but he did not place it until he heard Monsignor in the next room complaining about the salad to the housekeeper. It was the voice of dear, dead Aunt Hazel, coming from the summer he was ten. He translated the past into the present: I can't come out and play this afternoon, Joe, on account of my monsignor won't let me.

In the dining room Father Eudex sat down at the table and said grace. He helped himself to a chop, creamed new potatoes, pickled beets, jelly, and bread. He liked jelly. Monsignor passed the butter.

"That's supposed to be a tutti-frutti salad," Monsignor said, grimacing at his. "But she used green olives."

Father Eudex said nothing.

"I said she used green olives."

"I like green olives all right."

"*I* like green olives, but *not* in tutti-frutti salad."

Father Eudex replied by eating a green olive, but he knew it could not end there.

"Father," Monsignor said in a new tone. "How would you like to go away and study for a year?"

"Don't think I'd care for it, Monsignor. I'm not the type."

"You're no canonist, you mean?"

"That's one thing."

"Yes. Well, there are other things it might not hurt you to know. To be quite frank with you, Father, I think you need broadening."

"I guess so," Father Eudex said thickly.

"And still, with your tendencies . . . and with the universities honeycombed with Communists. No, that would never do. I think I meant seasoning, not broadening."

"Oh."

"No offense?"

"No offense."

Who would have thought a little thing like an olive could lead to all this, Father Eudex mused—who but himself, that is, for his association with Monsignor had shown him that anything could lead to everything. Monsignor was a master at making points. Nothing had changed since the day Father Eudex walked into the rectory saying he was the new assistant. Monsignor had evaded Father Eudex's hand in greeting, and a few days later, after he began to get the range, he delivered a lecture on the whole subject of handshaking. It was Middle West to shake hands, or South West or West in any case, and it was not done where he came from, and—why had he ever come from where he came from? Not to be reduced to shaking hands, you could bet! Handshaking was worse than foot washing and unlike that pious practice there was nothing to support it. And from handshaking Monsignor might go into a general discussion of Father Eudex's failings. He used the open forum method, but he was the only speaker and there was never time enough for questions from the audience. Monsignor seized his examples at random from life. He saw Father Eudex coming out of his bedroom in pajama bottoms only and so told him about the dressing gown, its purpose, something of its history. He advised Father Eudex to barber his armpits, for it was being done all over now. He let Father Eudex see his bottle of cologne, "Steeple," special for clergymen, and said he should not be afraid of it. He suggested that Father Eudex shave his face oftener, too. He loaned him his Rogers Peet catalogue, which had sketches of clerical blades togged out in the latest, and prayed that he would stop going around looking like a rabbinical student.

He found Father Eudex reading *The Catholic Worker* one day and had not trusted him since. Father Eudex's conception of the priesthood was evangelical in the worst sense, barbaric, gross, foreign to the mind of the Church, which was one of two terms he used as sticks to beat him with. The other was taste. The air of the rectory was often heavy with The Mind of the Church and Taste.

Another thing. Father Eudex could not conduct a civil conversation. Monsignor doubted that Father Eudex could even think to himself with anything like agreement. Certainly any discussion with Father Eudex ended inevitably in argument or sighing. Sighing! Why didn't people talk up if they had anything to say? No, they'd rather sigh! Father, don't ever, ever sigh at me again!

Finally, Monsignor did not like Father Eudex's table manners. This came to a head one night when Monsignor, seeing his curate's plate empty and all the silverware at his place unused except for a single knife, fork, and spoon, exploded altogether, saying it had been on his mind for weeks, and then descending into the vernacular he declared that Father Eudex did not know the forks—now perhaps he could understand that! Meals, unless Monsignor had guests or other things to struggle with, were always occasions of instruction for Father Eudex, and sometimes of chastisement.

And now he knew the worst—if Monsignor was thinking of recommending him for a year of study, in a Sulpician seminary probably, to learn the forks. So this was what it meant to be a priest. *Come, follow me. Going forth, teach ye all nations. Heal the sick, raise the dead, cleanse the lepers, cast out devils.* Teach the class of people we get here? Teach Mr. Memmers? Teach Communists? Teach Monsignors? And where were the poor? The lepers of old? The lepers were in their colonies with nuns to nurse them. The poor were in their holes and would not come out. Mr. Memmers was in his bank, without cheer. The Communists were in their universities, awaiting a sign. And he was at table with Monsignor, and it was enough for the disciple to be as his master, but the housekeeper had used green olives.

Monsignor inquired, "Did you get your check today?"

Father Eudex, looking up, considered. "I got *a* check," he said.

"From the Rival people, I mean?"

"Yes."

"Good. Well, I think you might apply it on the car you're wanting. A decent car. That's a worthy cause." Monsignor noticed that he was not taking it well. "Not that I mean to dictate what you shall do with your little windfall, Father. It's just that I don't like to see you mortifying yourself with a Model A—and disgracing the Church."

"Yes," Father Eudex said, suffering.

"Yes. I dare say you don't see the danger, just as you didn't a while ago when I found you making a spectacle of yourself with Whalen. You just don't see the danger because you just don't think. Not to dwell on it, but I seem to remember some overshoes."

The overshoes! Monsignor referred to them as to the Fall. Last winter

Father Eudex had given his overshoes to a freezing picket. It had got back to Monsignor and—good Lord, a man could have his sympathies, but he had no right clad in the cloth to endanger the prestige of the Church by siding in these wretched squabbles. Monsignor said he hated to think of all the evil done by people doing good! Had Father Eudex ever heard of the Albigensian heresy, or didn't the seminary teach that any more?

Father Eudex declined dessert. It was strawberry mousse.

"Delicious," Monsignor said. "I think I'll let her stay."

At that moment Father Eudex decided that he had nothing to lose. He placed his knife next to his fork on the plate, adjusted them this way and that until they seemed to work a combination in his mind, to spring a lock which in turn enabled him to speak out.

"Monsignor," he said. "I think I ought to tell you I don't intend to make use of that money. In fact—to show you how my mind works—I have even considered endorsing the check to the strikers' relief fund."

"So," Monsignor said calmly—years in the confessional had prepared him for anything.

"I'll admit I don't know whether I can in justice. And even if I could I don't know that I would. I don't know why . . . I guess hush money, no matter what you do with it, is lousy."

Monsignor regarded him with piercing baby blue eyes. "You'd find it pretty hard to prove, Father, that *any* money *in se* is . . . what you say it is. I would quarrel further with the definition of 'hush money.' It seems to me nothing if not rash that you would presume to impugn the motive of the Rival company in sending out these checks. You would seem to challenge the whole concept of good works—not that I am ignorant of the misuses to which money can be put." Monsignor, changing tack, tucked it all into a sigh. "Perhaps I'm just a simple soul, and it's enough for me to know personally some of the people in the Rival company and to know them good people. Many of them Catholic . . ." A throb had crept into Monsignor's voice. He shut it off.

"I don't mean anything that subtle, Monsignor," Father Eudex said. "I'm just telling you, as my pastor, what I'm going to do with the check. Or what I'm not going to do with it. I don't know what I'm going to do with it. Maybe send it back."

Monsignor rose from the table, slightly smiling. "Very well, Father. But there's always the poor."

Monsignor took leave of Father Eudex with a laugh. Father Eudex felt it was supposed to fool him into thinking that nothing he had said would be used against him. It showed, rather, that Monsignor was not winded, that he had broken wild curates before, plenty of them, and that he would ride again.

Father Eudex sought the shade of the porch. He tried to read his office, but was drowsy. He got up for a glass of water. The saints in Ireland used to stand up to their necks in cold water, but not for drowsiness. When he came back to the porch a woman was ringing the doorbell. She looked like a customer for rosary beads.

"Hello," he said.

"I'm Mrs. Klein, Father, and I was wondering if you could help me out."

Father Eudex straightened a porch chair for her. "Please sit down."

"It's a German name, Father, Klein was German descent," she said, and added with a silly grin, "It ain't what you think, Father."

"I beg your pardon."

"Klein. Some think it's a Jew name. But they stole it from Klein."

Father Eudex decided to come back to that later. "You were wondering if I could help you?"

"Yes, Father. It's personal."

"Is it matter for confession?"

"Oh no, Father." He had made her blush.

"Then go ahead."

Mrs. Klein peered into the honeysuckle vines on either side of the porch for alien ears.

"No one can hear you, Mrs. Klein."

"Father—I'm just a poor widow," she said, and continued as though Father Eudex had just slandered the man. "Klein was awful good to me, Father."

"I'm sure he was."

"So good . . . and he went and left me all he had." She had begun to cry a little.

Father Eudex nodded gently. She was after something, probably not money, always the best bet—either that or a drunk in the family—but this one was not Irish. Perhaps just sympathy.

"I come to get your advice, Father. Klein always said, 'If you got a problem, Freda, see the priest.' "

"Do you need money?"

"I got more than I can use from the bakery."

"You have a bakery?"

Mrs. Klein nodded down the street. "That's my bakery. It was Klein's. The Purity."

"I go by there all the time," Father Eudex said, abandoning himself to her. He must stop trying to shape the conversation and let her work it out.

"Will you give me your advice, Father?" He felt that she sensed his indifference and interpreted it as his way of rejecting her. She either had no idea how little sense she made or else supreme faith in him, as a priest, to see into her heart.

"Just what is it you're after, Mrs. Klein?"

"He left me all he had, Father, but it's just laying in the bank."

884   J. F. POWERS

"And you want me to tell you what to do with it?"

"Yes, Father."

Father Eudex thought this might be interesting, certainly a change. He went back in his mind to the seminary and the class in which they had considered the problem of inheritances. Do we have any unfulfilled obligations? Are we sure? . . . Are there any impedimenta? . . .

"Do you have any dependents, Mrs. Klein—any children?"

"One boy, Father. I got him running the bakery. I pay him good—too much, Father."

"Is 'too much' a living wage?"

"Yes, Father. He ain't got a family."

"A living wage is not too much," Father Eudex handed down, sailing into the encyclical style without knowing it.

Mrs. Klein was smiling over having done something good without knowing precisely what it was.

"How old is your son?"

"He's thirty-six, Father."

"Not married?"

"No, Father, but he's got him a girl." She giggled, and Father Eudex, embarrassed, retied his shoe.

"But you don't care to make a will and leave this money to your son in the usual way?"

"I guess I'll have to . . . if I die." Mrs. Klein was suddenly crushed and haunted, but whether by death or charity, Father Eudex did not know.

"You don't have to, Mrs. Klein. There are many worthy causes. And the worthiest is the cause of the poor. My advice to you, if I understand your problem, is to give what you have to someone who needs it."

Mrs. Klein just stared at him.

"You could even leave it to the archdiocese," he said, completing the sentence to himself: but I don't recommend it in your case . . . with your tendencies. You look like an Indian giver to me.

But Mrs. Klein had got enough. "Huh!" she said, rising. "Well! You *are* a funny one!"

And then Father Eudex realized that she had come to him for a broker's tip. It was in the eyes. The hat. The dress. The shoes. "If you'd like to speak to the pastor," he said, "come back in the evening."

"You're a nice young man," Mrs. Klein said, rather bitter now and bent on getting away from him. "But I got to say this—you ain't much of a priest. And Klein said if I got a problem, see the priest—huh! You ain't much of a priest! What time's your boss come in?"

"In the evening," Father Eudex said. "Come any time in the evening."

Mrs. Klein was already down the steps and making for the street.

"You might try Mr. Memmers at the First National," Father Eudex called, actually trying to help her, but she must have thought it was just some more of his nonsense and did not reply.

After Mrs. Klein had disappeared Father Eudex went to his room. In the hallway upstairs Monsignor's voice, coming from the depths of the clerical nap, halted him.

"Who was it?"

"A woman," Father Eudex said. "A woman seeking good counsel."

He waited a moment to be questioned, but Monsignor was not awake enough to see anything wrong with that, and there came only a sigh and a shifting of weight that told Father Eudex he was simply turning over in bed.

Father Eudex walked into the bathroom. He took the Rival check from his pocket. He tore it into little squares. He let them flutter into the toilet. He pulled the chain—hard.

He went to his room and stood looking out the window at nothing. He could hear the others already giving an account of their stewardship, but could not judge them. I bought baseball uniforms for the school. I bought the nuns a new washing machine. I purchased a Mass kit for a Chinese missionary. I bought a set of matched irons. Mine helped pay for keeping my mother in a rest home upstate. I gave mine to the poor.

And you, Father?

⬦

J. F. Powers was born in Jacksonville, Illinois, in 1917, went to a Franciscan high school, studied English at Northwestern, lived in Ireland, and has taught writing at Marquette, the University of Minnesota, and Smith College. He has received fellowship awards from both the Guggenheim and Rockefeller foundations, a grant from the National Academy of Arts and Letters, and has won the National Book Award. He has published two volumes of short stories, Prince of Darkness *(1947) and* The Presence of Grace *(1956), and one novel,* Morte D'Urban *(1963). Powers' novel and the best of his stories are about American Catholic priests and their problems; he writes so well about them—and almost everybody else who tries it does so poorly (except for George P. Elliott, who has written interestingly about monks)—that he has made the province almost entirely his own.*

In "The Forks" the Father and the Monsignor differ from one another in social class, and some of the conflict between them is founded in these differences. But unlike the other stories in this section, class as such is not itself either the main subject of the story or the basis on which the action turns. The real conflict between the Monsignor and Father Eudex is between worldly and commercial values on the one hand and idealistic and spiritual values on the other. But Powers associates the integrity of the Father with his simple "rural origins," and the worldliness of the Monsignor with his urban, urbane sophistication. Clothes are again used as a way of marking the differences: The Monsignor wants Father Eudex to "stop going around looking like a rabbinical student" and order dapper clerical clothes from Rogers Peet in New York; Father Eudex, on the other hand, will take his coat and collar right off to do physical labor helping the janitor. And again automobiles are used to mark the differences: the Monsignor practically violates his vow of chastity with love and lust for his long, black, sleek *"politician's"* car; Father Eudex keeps his vows of poverty to such an extent that all he wants or can afford is an old Model A. Differences of this sort between them are all pointedly made in the story, and there is no need to list them. What they all represent is that Father Eudex supposedly has no manners, no *"taste,"* does not know how to use *"the forks."* There is irony in this, of course: nothing could be more tasteless than Monsignor's advice that Father Eudex *"barber his armpits"* and use *"Steeple,"* a cologne made *"special for clergymen."* But beyond the irony is the basic difference between the two men: one honest and insightful but powerless; the other powerful but without integrity or insight. Father Eudex, simple and without knowledge of the forks as he is, actually has a finer conscience and finer consciousness than the Monsignor. The Monsignor has the conservative's stock cluster of attitudes that determines his reaction to any situation without difficulty. He is able *"to avoid the snares set in the path of the just man. . . . He would not be trapped as so many good shepherds before him had been trapped, poor souls—caught in fair-seeming dilemmas of justice that were best left alone, like the first apple."* Father Eudex becomes just such a poor soul, caught in just such a fair-seeming dilemma, when he insightfully and honestly confronts the question of what to do with his check from the Rival Tractor Company. The forks stand not only as an ironical symbol of the right way of doing things but also as a symbol of the prongs of this dilemma. The checks are the catalytic element in the story, bringing the situation to the point of action. The whole story may be read as a modern version of the parable of the talents, emphasizing the ambiguities and paradoxes of that parable in a commercial society. When the other priests who have received the company's checks are *"giving an account of their stewardship,"* what will Father Eudex say? He has faced squarely the fact that the check represents *"hush money,"* designed to influence the clergy in favor of a company that exploits its workers— a fact that the Monsignor blinks at, or winks at, or perhaps doesn't even know. Father Eudex sees clearly that it is wrong of the company to do this, and wrong of the priests, by accepting the money, to allow them to do it. And he sees that it is wrong to use such bad money, even to pass it on to a worthy cause. His action at the end is surprising, even shocking; but the whole story is so constructed as to prepare for it. What he does is not as an act of pique, not *"getting back at"* the Monsignor; nor is it *"holier than thou"* or *"touch me not."* Readers inclined to Freudian interpretation will point to the well-known association between feces and money and explain that Father Eudex is simply a prey to these associations, con-

sciously or unconsciously, when he flushes the dirty money down the toilet. But a broader interpretation of his act would take into consideration how his course has been determined by the action that just precedes it, his conversation with the woman who comes to the rectory "seeking good counsel," as he mockingly puts it. That she should come there convinced that the priests will know a good stock-market tip startles him. He realizes then how very deeply the worldliness and commercialism of our times have penetrated what should be the uninfected heart of society's virtue, the priesthood. What he does then, under these circumstances and in the grip of this realization, can be seen as the only pure act possible for him: he destroys, symbolically at least, what he sees as the root and source of evil worldliness. This action may seem futile and ineffectual and even wasteful, but that is not to say—even in these pragmatic times we live in now—that it is in any way meaningless.

◇—◇

In these four stories we have seen some of the ways in which competition for prestige works in that part of a middle America which believes itself to be "classless." Clearly, nobody does actually believe that everybody is "the same," and for those who not only recognize that other ways of doing or being are more prestigeful or "sophisticated," but also see that these ways are a matter of choice, a possible option—for them life is complex and full of doubts and frustrations and the possibility of error. The emphasis seems to have shifted from how to "get ahead" and how to "achieve success" to how to define success, how to recognize status and how to deal with the pressures of having to conform to systems of values and ways of life which are not only different but seem to be constantly changing and thus, in a sense, valueless. Whether it is the subtleties of academic intellectual one-upmanship, the "blood and bone" claims of inherited wealth, the easy skill with complex leisure and cultural pursuits, or merely a matter of a "sophisticated smile" and its implications, the differences must be measured against past as well as current and future expectations and aspirations. The result is often that defeat comes not from an inability to change from old ways to new ways but from the contradiction between the apparently unlimited possibilities open to the individual and the specific definitions and limitations of any particular way of life. Only an ascetic parish priest can refuse to participate in this chaotic race for bought-and-paid-for status by refusing to participate in the dilemma of how to spend money. For all the rest of us in this ordinary American "classless" middle class the fact of having some money, mobility and education brings with it the possibility of choosing an individual style of life and thus the realization that what we are is not a result of traditions or fate but all our own fault, the result of choices we have made.

✧—✧—✧

While we may long for a world of summer hammock reading in which a Trollope of our times, or a James or an Edith Wharton, could dish out an intricate but more or less complete world for our delectation, edification, and escape from the dullness of our own world, that such worlds no longer exist is no proof that fiction today does not have a lot to tell us about our own. It is more likely that lovers of facts have lost patience with fiction simply because it does tell us too much about the differentiations and confusions of our times; we are each so busy arranging our own little islands of personal balance in a precarious sea of constantly changing expert evaluations of the meaning, purpose, and "realities" of life that we cannot afford to give too close attention to alternative ways of life, other people's problems. Yet it is in the very nature of urbanized, industrialized, bureaucratized mass society to expose us to these problems and challenge our precious "facts" about "normal" life. The pervasive notion that it is up to each individual to do right and be better, that each one of us in America has all the opportunities he needs for a "happy" and "successful" life, means that we delegate responsibility for understanding what actually goes into any particular action or issue to the professionals and their sciences. Let psychology take care of the crazy, the social workers take care of the poor, the hospitals take care of the sick and the elderly—just leave me alone: I've got troubles of my own.

The writer of fiction has no such easy way out of his responsibilities because he is not dealing with "facts" but with human experience. He is, as he has always been, as all artists are, the conscience of his society. His accurate and skillful observations about the differentiations and confusions among us make us reevaluate our protective systems of theory and facts in the light of other people's experience of the way we live now.

The Eye of Fiction

IN SOME OVERVIEWS

·

IN SOME STRATAGEMS

Part Three

THE EYE OF FICTION

A PIECE OF FICTION *(a novel or a story) differs from an ordinary piece of prose writing in that it tells a story of something that happened to someone. Prose may do this too, but fiction must do it. If something doesn't happen to someone, then the work at hand is a sketch or an essay or something else. More importantly, what fiction has always provided the reader is a sort of "imagined" experience of this something that happened, a sort of pseudo-experience, somewhat between the reader's being told of something that happened and experiencing it himself. That is, reading of characters and events in a successful piece of fiction is received by the reader in a way that more closely resembles (or differs less from) experiencing such characters and events himself than does the simple reception of a piece of information, a fact, or even hearing a description of an actual person or event. Fiction's methods are thus necessarily entirely different from other methods of reporting the way things are, because the reality, the believability of the story, depends on "any resemblance to actual persons, places, and events" being "entirely coincidential." The one thing fiction is supposed not to do is report an actual event, describe an actual person. The illusion of the fictional reality is to some extent destroyed when we recognize characters and events as being too close to some character or event of "real" life, for we are then more aware of the additions and alterations made to actuality, and the "imagined" reality of fiction is more difficult for the writer to create, for the reader to experience.*

How, then, can fiction have so much to tell us about the way we live now? Why do we turn to the novels and stories of the past to find out the way people lived then? It is because, in order to be believable, fiction must present us with more than facts; it must convey all the nuances of feeling and interpretation, all the inarticulate reports of the senses that make up our experience of reality in everyday life. Fiction gives an experience of the times in which the story was written through the writer's eyes: through his perceptions, our perceptions are instructed. Even when a story is set in the past or the future, its relevance devolves from how the writer shapes or uses this material to make a comment on his own times. Each age reshapes the myths, re-creates them to express its own meanings and

891

its own experience. Unlike actual experience, in which the meanings and conclusions to be drawn from the event are drawn by oneself, the imagined experience of a fictional story comes all shaped and freighted with meaning and significance provided by the author. Reading a story is, therefore, never a cold learning of fact (even should the authorial voice present it as such) but a vivid learning of a specific dynamic, an internalization of something that happened during our reading which enriches our ability to see and feel in our own lives by extending our sensibilities to what the writer has presented as important to see and feel. Experiencing fiction does not so much take us away from actual reality as give us the opportunity to involve ourselves in an experience not specifically ours. Thus reading fiction is not an escape from reality but an addition to it.

Our ability to experience this reality depends on the writer's skill and accuracy with the written word to convey in the form of a meaningful and absorbing story his vision of how things are. For, of course, unlike the poetic, the dramatic, and the older tale-telling forms, modern fiction is uniquely committed to the sole medium of the written word. How does the written work of the writer's imagination translate itself into an experience of reality for the reader? Nobody knows, of course, exactly how this works, nor is it necessary or possible to know it with mechanical precision since each act of writing and each act of reading is unique to the time, place, and person involved. The methods are myriad, but perhaps they can be considered as three different types of processes—"distillation," "dramatization," and "distortion"—with the understanding that any one method in fiction is inseparable from any other method.

Distillation, by the dictionary a slow, drop-by-drop process of arriving at "the abstract or essence of anything," is as good a name as any for the way in which the writer transforms the reality of what he knows into the reality of the story. Fiction gives the author the license to abstract from the raw material of what he knows, feels, and believes (including his direct experience with people and things as well as his reading, his dreams, and fantasies—the whole encyclopedia of his mind) an essence that takes on the shape of reality in the story. He gives us a picture of the way things happen, describes the manners and mores of our times, in a language that has been formed in these times, through his particular vision, which must in part reflect his interaction with his times. This essence the writer distills is itself a volatile substance that, in the reading and after the reading, interacts with the reader's store of knowledge and takes on a multiplicity of meanings that are specific to the reader's own experience of his own times. This is one of the reasons it is more comfortable to read the fiction of other times: it does not challenge our concepts of the realities we live with.

Dramatization is the method by which the imagination is directly engaged. It is the method of making something happen in a story, of bringing alive the elements of character, plot, and setting, not only making them seem important, interesting, and believable but also putting them in motion, making them dynamic. It is this dynamic aspect that most differentiates fiction from other prose writing and that is responsible for the reader's sense of involvement—his loss of sense of actual self, and his sense of experiencing the imagined reality of the story. It is also what makes fiction so accurate a representation of social process: it conveys the sense of the thing happening, the particular way in which a particular event happens under particular circumstances. So that, although a story is a distillation, an essence abstracted from a variety of realities, it is nevertheless always presented and experienced as unique, specific, and individual. It shows character in action and at a crucial point. And it is this very method of detailed, dramatized depiction of the individual in action that enables the fiction writer to render the norms of his society in all their complexity and variations, to show in action the effects of the variety of variables that comprise what is "typical" in our times. The method of fictional dramatization creates a dynamic present in which what people say and do and think and dream and feel is inseparable, as it is in real life, from the way in which they interact with their times.

Distortion is an essential and inevitable technique of fiction: the reality presented in a story as the product of a distillation from a number of realities must be a distortion of any one of them; the selective exaggeration that is the essence of the dramatization of event and character and place, the presentation of crucial moments for dramatic effect, is a distortion of everyday reality; the writer of fiction must distort to reveal: it is part of his method. Distortion, like dramatization, is a method distinctive to fiction, differentiating it from the other sorts of prose writing that describe our times, the work of the journalist and the social scientist. The analogy is to the difference between the flat, white-light "accuracy" of a photograph and the painting of a fine artist, who gives dimension by emphasizing depths and shadows, who subtly distorts or even exaggerates features so as to point up that which, according to his vision and technique, he sees as significant, as the real nature of his subject. For the work to succeed as art, the distortions must have an inner consistency, must form an organic "harmonious" whole. When there is consistency as well from work to work in the bias of the author's distortions we recognize this as the author's distinctive "voice" and "world view"—as, for instance, the "world" and "voice" of Hemingway and Faulkner are original and distinct from one another. Their subject matter, their plots and characters, their language—indeed, all aspects of their work—reflect (through their choice) their unique vision of the times. However much, in the mode of many modern writers under the influence of James and Joyce, an author may want to feel that he stands so far behind and so far apart from his work that the reader is unaware of an authorial presence guiding his judgments about it, the nature of the writer's vision is nevertheless implicitly apparent in the content and tech-

nique of the story. Since everything in both the form and content of a work of fiction (as a created work of the imagination) exists as a result of the author's choice of it (his decision, conscious or unconscious, to include it) for the purpose of telling his story, then the story must reflect the author's moral judgments, for choice is the basis of expressions of value and ultimately of moral commitment. But every written presentation may be said to contain elements of choice. Although the scientist and the journalist base the legitimacy of their presentations of reality on their stand as simple "observers," who report "the facts as they are" in some systematic fashion that they believe precludes any distortion on the part of the writer, this stand is, of course, neither humanly possible nor humanistically desirable. What the objective method does, what "sticking to the facts" does, is provide the writer of nonfiction with a kind of freedom from the responsibility of choice. Since no distortion is recognized, no responsibility is assumed. And it is this very freedom that imposes a limitation on vision in any larger sense, by denying the participation of a distorting creator. Because distortion is inevitably the most distinctive part of each fiction writer's method in presenting the reality of a story, the author is held responsible for making "accurate" distortions: indeed his work will not be convincing, will not be successful in conveying an imagined reality to the reader unless his distortions are accurate as well as consistent. Thus the distortion of literary art is never really distortion, and freedom to distort is never really freedom. The fiction writer's responsibility for the choices implicit in his imagined, created work thus requires both accuracy and morality if his work is to be esthetically successful. For him, accuracy and morality are virtually the same thing, since the distortions in his work are the product of the truth of his vision, the evidence of his acuteness as an observer of our times.

Critics of modern fiction are always pointing to a great difference between the eye of fiction in our time and the eye of fiction in eighteenth- or nineteenth-century England and Europe. What Dickens or Dostoievsky "saw" or "imagined" or "reported" of the activities and dilemmas of their contemporaries is different from what our writers see, imagine, or report of today, not only because the society they live in is different but because their way of seeing it is different. The form of literary fiction is a reflection or expression or extension of the content, and the content must be an accurate reflection or expression or extension of the times in which it is created. Different ages, different forms: it is nearly as simple as that. We may prefer to read the simpler and more pleasant fiction of an earlier era, as we might prefer to live in a simpler and more pleasant time. But just as we must live in these times, our writers must write in these times. The times are not pleasant and they are not simple. Neither is our fiction. If it seems to many people today that the eye of modern American fiction is overly baleful, is turned within, looks through lenses that are cracked and darkened, then they must realize that fiction of this time and place is, as art always is, a product of the nature of that time and place, can only reflect it, perceive it, render it. Our times are complex and disturbing; so is our fiction. The fiction writer's commitment to the moral accuracy of his vision of his material—and this material can be provided only by the world he lives in—locks him in with the modes of feeling of his age. He cannot escape the necessity for accuracy of choice and vision—and vision determines technique as surely as form follows content. This is why and how fiction, through the unique vision of the individual author, not only does but must accurately depict and truthfully express the times in which it is created. It cannot do anything else.

The Eye of Fiction

IN SOME OVERVIEWS

There is much criticism of contemporary fiction, but most of it consists
of one or a combination of three complaints: that it is "negative" and/or
"inaccessible" and/or "interior." The "negative" and "inaccessible" charges
are considered later (pages 982 and 988, respectively), but here it is neces-
sary to insist that the charge that modern fiction is overpreoccupied with
the interior life of the individual and fails to depict the society in which we
live is either (depending on how the charge is made) wrong, or is actually
pointing to what is not a fault but a strength—and a strength not just of
modern fiction but of all fiction.

For fiction does emphasize, and quite correctly, the importance of the
action of the story to the individual—it is in the nature of fiction that it
do so. Fiction, unlike poetry or drama, is usually now seen from the point
of view of a single character, and the very meaning of the story may reside
in what "happens" to that character. Fiction, to an extent that is unique
among the literary arts, has the ability to observe and "report" what's going
on in the mind of a character, and it is natural and praiseworthy that mod-
ern writers exploit this opportunity. The interior life of another man is
inaccessible to most of us, especially in this anonymous mass society when
communication between people seems so minimal; and it is outrageous to
criticize modern fiction for providing us with what we most lack: insight
into the emotions of others.

Often the "interior" criticism against modern fiction is so phrased as to
make the point that it is only the big slick best sellers that deal with "im-
portant" matters like affairs of state and power and politics. But the stories
in the first two parts of this book show clearly that all our good writers are
very much concerned with the condition of the country-as-a-whole, and
especially (and most usefully) with the point where the normative cultural
forces come in contact with the individual. As to writing directly about
politicians and statesmen: most public figures are nowadays more "images"
than persons, and as characters in fiction they always emerge as nearly
recognizable amalgams of various public images, rather than as convincing
characters created by the author. Only journalists are familiar with the cor-
ridors of power; and as is notorious, they seldom tell us the truth. What

897

happens in a cabinet meeting during a national crisis is subject for memoir-
ists and historians and perhaps satirists. It is not material for the modern
writer of fiction because it is not as such the way we live now. In his "in-
terior" emphasis on the individual—even on, perhaps, himself—the modern
writer is far more likely to describe "ourselves" than he is if he writes of
high-level machinations in the auto industry or behind-the-scenes goings-on
at a Presidential nominating convention.

The stories that follow nevertheless show how the "eye" of fiction ranges
wide and deep over our society. The stories are grouped together here not
because they don't refer directly to such institution-categories as "family"
and "community"—for in fact some of them do—but because they refer
back to them collectively in a way that is causative and significant. They
describe aspects of the American temper and the American society in more
general terms, and their themes suggest specific underlying reasons for
some of the dislocations in the way we live now.

Grand Guy Grand

◇◇◇◇◇◇◇

OUT OF THE GRAY granite morass of Wall Street rises one building like a heron of fire, soaring up in blue-white astonishment—*Number 18 Wall*—a rocket of glass and blinding copper. It is the *Grand Investment Building,* perhaps the most contemporary business structure in our country, known in circles of high finance simply as *Grand's.*

Offices of *Grand's* are occupied by companies which deal in *mutual funds*—giant and fantastic corporations whose policies define the shape of nations.

August Guy Grand himself was a billionaire. He had 180 millions cash deposit in New York banks, and this ready capital was of course but a part of his gross holdings.

In the beginning, Grand's associates, wealthy men themselves, saw nothing extraordinary about him; a reticent man of simple tastes, they thought, a man who had inherited most of his money and had preserved it through large safe investments in steel, rubber, and oil. What his associates managed to see in Grand was usually a reflection of their own dullness: a club member, a dinner guest, a possibility, a threat—a man whose holdings represented a prospect and a danger. But this was to do injustice to Grand's private life, because his private life was atypical. For one thing, he was the last of the big spenders; and for another, he had a very unusual attitude towards *people*—he spent about ten million a year in, as he expressed it himself, *"making it hot for them."*

At fifty-three, Grand had a thick trunk and a large balding bullet-head; his face was quite pink, so that in certain half-lights he looked like a fat radish-man—though not displeasingly so, for he always sported well-cut clothes and, near the throat, a diamond the size of a nickel . . . a diamond now that caught the late afternoon sun in a soft spangle of burning color when Guy stepped through the soundless doors of *Grand's* and into the blue haze of the almost empty street, past the huge doorman appearing larger than life in gigantic livery, he who touched his cap with quick but easy reverence.

"Cab, Mr. Grand?"

"Thank you no, Jason," said Guy, "I have the car today." And with a pleasant smile for the man, he turned adroitly on his heel, north towards Worth Street.

Guy Grand's gait was brisk indeed—small sharp steps, rising on the toes. It was the gait of a man who appears to be snapping his fingers as he walks.

Half a block on he reached the car, though he seemed to have a momentary difficulty recognizing it; beneath the windshield wiper lay a big parking ticket, which Grand slowly withdrew, regarding it curiously.

"Looks like you've got a *ticket,* bub!" said a voice somewhere behind him.

Out of the corner of his eye Grand perceived the man, in a dark summer suit, leaning idly against the side of the building nearest the car: There was something terse and smug in the tone of his remark, a sort of nasal piousness.

"Yes, so it seems," mused Grand, without looking up, continuing to study the ticket in his hand. "How much will you eat it for?" he asked then, raising a piercing smile at the man.

"How's that, mister?" demanded the latter with a nasty frown, pushing himself forward a bit from the building.

Grand cleared his throat and slowly took out his wallet—a long slender wallet of such fine leather it would have been limp as silk, had it not been so chock-full of thousands.

"I asked what would you take to *eat* it? You know . . ." Wide-eyed, he made a great chewing motion with his mouth, holding the ticket up near it.

The man, glaring, took a tentative step forward.

"Say, I don't *get* you, mister!"

"Well," drawled Grand, chuckling down at his fat wallet, browsing about in it, "simple enough really . . ." And he took out a few thousand. "I have this ticket, as you know, and I was just wondering if you would care to *eat* it, for, say"—a quick glance to ascertain—"six thousand dollars?"

"What do you mean, *'eat it'?"* demanded the dark-suited man in a kind of a snarl. "Say, what're you anyway, bub, a *wise*-guy?"

" *'Wise*-guy' or *'grand* guy'—call me anything you like . . . as long as you don't call me *'late-for-chow!'* Eh? Ho-ho." Grand rounded it off with a jolly chortle, but was quick to add, unsmiling, "How 'bout it, pal—got a taste for the easy green?"

The man, who now appeared to be openly angry, took another step forward.

"Listen, mister . . ." he began in a threatening tone, half clenching his fists.

"I think I should warn you," said Grand quietly, raising one hand to his breast, "that I am armed."

"*Huh?*" The man seemed momentarily dumbfounded, staring down in dull rage at the six bills in Grand's hand; then he partially recovered, and cocking his head to one side, regarded Grand narrowly, in an attempt at shrewd skepticism, still heavily flavored with indignation.

"Just who do you think you *are*, Mister! Just what is your *game?*"

"Grand's the name, easy-green's the game," said Guy with a twinkle. "Play along?" He brusquely flicked the corners of the six crisp bills, and they crackled with a brittle, compelling sound.

"*Listen . . .*" muttered the man, tightlipped, flexing his fingers and exhaling several times in angry exasperation, ". . . are *you* trying . . . are you trying to tell ME that you'll give *six thousand dollars* . . . to . . . to EAT that"—he pointed stiffly at the ticket in Guy's hand—"to *eat* that TICKET?!?"

"That's about the size of it," said Grand; he glanced at his watch. "It's what you might call a 'limited offer'—expiring in, let's say, *one minute.*"

"Listen, mister," said the man between clenched teeth, "if this is a gag, *so help me . . .*" He shook his head to show how serious he was.

"No threats," Guy cautioned, "or I'll shoot you in the temple—well, what say? Forty-eight seconds remaining."

"Let's *see* that goddamn money!" exclaimed the man, quite beside himself now, grabbing at the bills.

Grand allowed him to examine them as he continued to regard his watch. "Thirty-nine seconds remaining," he announced solemnly. "Shall I start the *big count down?*"

Without waiting for the latter's reply, he stepped back and, cupping his hands like a megaphone, began dramatically intoning, "*Twenty-eight . . . twenty-seven . . . twenty-six . . .*" while the man made several wildly gesticulated and incoherent remarks before seizing the ticket, ripping off the quarter of it with his teeth and beginning to chew, eyes blazing.

"*Stout fellow!*" cried Grand warmly, breaking off the count down to step forward and give the chap a hearty clap on the shoulder and hand him the six thousand.

"You needn't actually eat the ticket," he explained. "I was just curious to see if you had your price." He gave a wink and a tolerant chuckle. "Most of us have, I suppose. Eh? Ho-ho."

And with a grand wave of his hand, he stepped inside his car and sped away, leaving the man in the dark summer suit standing on the sidewalk staring after him, fairly agog.

Grand's own idea of what he was doing—"making it hot for people"—had formed crudely, literally, and almost as an afterthought, when, early one summer morning in 1938, just about the time the Spanish Civil War was ending, he flew out to Chicago and, within an hour of arrival, purchased a property on one of the busiest corners of the Loop. He had the modern two-story structure torn down and the debris cleared off that day—that very morning, in fact—by a demolition crew of fifty men and machines; and then he directed the six carpenters, who had been on stand-by since early morning, when they had thrown up a plank barrier at the sidewalk, to construct the wooden forms for a concrete vat of the following proportions: fifteen feet square, five feet deep. This construction was done in an hour and a half, and it seemed that the work, except for pouring the concrete, was ended; in fact the carpenters had put on their street clothes and were ready to leave when, after a moment of reflection, Grand assembled them with a smart order to take down this present structure, and to rebuild it, but on a two-foot elevation—giving clearance beneath, as he explained to the foreman, to allow for the installation of a heating apparatus there.

"That'll make it hot for them," he said—but he wasn't speaking to the foreman then, nor apparently to anyone else.

It was mid-afternoon, and collecting from the flux of the swollen summer street were the spectators, who hung in bunches at the sturdy barrier, gatherings in constant change, impressed in turn by the way the great man from the East snapped his commands, expensively dressed as he was, shirt turned back at the cuff.

And when the work was going ahead correctly, Grand might give the crowd a moment of surveillance from where he stood in the center of the lot, finally addressing them, hands cupped to his mouth as if he had to shout—though, actually, they were only a few yards away.

"Tomorrow . . ." he would say, *". . . back . . . tomorrow! Now . . . getting . . . it . . . ready!"*

When an occasional wiseacre could get his attention and attempt some joke as to what was going on there beyond the barrier, Grand Guy Grand would smile wearily and shake a scolding finger at him.

"Now . . . getting . . . it . . . ready," he would shout slowly, or something else equally irrelevant to the wiseacre's jibe; but no one took offense, either because of not understanding or else because of the dignity and bearing of the man, and the big diamond he wore at his throat.

Another contractor, three workers, a truck of sand and gravel, and six sacks of quick-drying cement arrived at the working site at two o'clock, but were forced to wait until the new forms were complete. Then a sheet of metal was lowered into place and the concrete was poured into the forms. Under Grand's spirited command, it was all so speedily done that well before dusk the work was ended, including the installation of a great gas burner there, star-shaped with a thousand dark jets, like a giant upturned squid stretched beneath the structure. It was apparent now that when the board forms were removed, the whole would resemble a kind of white stone bath, set on four short columns, with a heating apparatus beneath, and small ramps leading up the vat on each of its sides.

Before dinner Guy Grand completed arrangements begun earlier in the day with the Chicago stockyards: these provided for the delivery of three hundred cubic feet of manure, a hundred gallons of urine, and fifty gallons of blood, to an address in the suburbs. Grand met them there and had the whole stinking mess transferred to a covered dump truck he had purchased that morning. These arrangements cost Grand a pretty penny, because the stockyards do not ordinarily conserve or sell urine, so that it had to be specially collected.

After securing the truck's cover, Grand climbed into the cab, drove back towards the stockyards and parked the truck there, where the stench of it would be less noticeable.

Then he took a taxi into town, to the near North Side and had a quiet dinner at the Drake.

At nine o'clock, while it was still light, he returned to the working site, where he was met by some of the crew, and saw to the removal of the board forms and the barrier. He inspected the vat, and the burner below— which he tested and found in good working order. Then he dismissed the crew and went back to his hotel.

He sat at his desk writing business letters until his thin gold wrist-clock sounded three A.M. Exactly then he put away his writing things, freshened himself up, and, just before leaving the room, paused near the door and collected a big leather brief case, a gas mask, a wooden paddle, a bucket of black paint, and an old, stiff paintbrush. He went downstairs and took a cab out to the place where he had parked the dump truck. Leaving the cab, he got into the truck and drove back to the working site. There he backed the truck carefully up one of the ramps and then emptied all that muck into the vat. The stench was nearly overpowering, and Grand, as soon as he had parked the truck and gotten out of it, was quick to don the gas mask he had brought.

Stepping up one of the ramps, he squatted on the parapet of the vat and opened the brief case, out of which he began taking, a handful at a time, and dropping into the vat, ten thousand one-hundred-dollar bills, slowly stirring them in with his wooden paddle.

And he was in this attitude, squatting at the edge of the vat, gas mask covering his face, stirring with his paddle and dumping bills into the muck, the work only half begun, when a passing police patrol car pulled up to investigate the activity and, above all, the stench. But before the officers could properly take account, Grand had closed the brief case, doffed his mask, given them five thousand dollars each, and demanded to be taken at once to their precinct captain. After a few hushed words between them, and a shrugging of shoulders, they agreed.

At the station, Grand spoke privately with the captain, showing him several business cards and explaining that it was all a harmless promotion stunt for a new product.

"Naturally my firm is eager to cooperate with the authorities," he said, and handed the captain twenty-five thousand.

And so it was finally agreed that Grand might return to the site and proceed, as long as whatever he was doing did not involve criminal violence within the precinct. Moreover, while the captain could make no definite promise about it, he was attentive enough to Grand's proposal of an additional fifty thousand on the following noon if the police would be kept away from the site for a few hours that morning.

"Think it over," said Grand pleasantly. "Better sleep on it, eh?"

Back at the site, Grand Guy donned his mask again, and dumped the remaining contents of the brief case into the vat. Then he stepped down, opened the can of paint, gave it a good stirring, and finally, using his left hand so that what resulted looked childish or illiterate, he scrawled across the vat FREE $ HERE in big black letters on the sides facing the street.

He climbed up for a final check on the work. Of the bills in the muck, the corners, edges, and denomination figures of about five hundred were visible. After a moment he stepped down and, half crouching beneath the vat, took off his mask and saw to his burners. He did a short terse count down and turned the valve full open; then he removed the handle so that it could not easily be interfered with. As he touched off the match, the thousand flames sprang up, all blue light, and broke back doubling on the metal plate, and on the wet concrete—a color of sand in summer moonlight: one of those chosen instants, lost to childhood, damp places in reflection, surface of cement under the earth, the beautifully cool buried places . . . the stench became unbearable; he stood and quickly donned his mask, turned away from the site and walked across the street where he paused at the corner and surveyed the whole. Already in the pale eastern light, the moronic scrawl, FREE $ HERE, loomed with convincing force, while below the thousand flames beat up, blue-white and strangely urgent for this hour of morning on a downtown corner of Chicago.

"Say . . ." mused Grand, half-aloud, *"That'll* make it hot for them all right!" And he leaped into the big dump truck and drove like the wind back to his hotel. At dawn he caught the plane for New York.

The commotion that occurred a few hours later on that busy corner of the Loop in downtown Chicago was the first and, in a sense perhaps, the most deliberately literal of such projects eventually to be linked with the name of "Grand Guy" Guy Grand, provoking the wrath of the public press against him, and finally earning him the label, "Eccentric" and again towards the end, "Crack-pot."

Evidently Grand liked playing the donkeyman. In any case, he had bought himself a large motion-picture house in Philadelphia. The house had been losing money badly for six months, so it was natural that the manager and his staff, who knew nothing of Grand's background, should be apprehensive over the probable shake-up.

The manager was a shrewd and capable man of many years' experience in cinema management, a man whose position represented for him the fruit of a life's work. He decided that his best move, under the circumstances, would be to go to Grand and cheerfully recommend salary cuts for all.

During their first conference, however, it was Grand, in his right as new owner, who held the initiative throughout.

By way of preliminary, and while the manager sat alertly on the edge of a big leather chair, Grand paced the floor of the comfortable office, his hands clasped at his back, and a slight frown on his face. Finally he stopped in the center of the room and addressed the manager:

"The *Chinese* have an expression, Mr. . . . *Mister Manager*. I believe it occurs in the book of the *I Chiang:* "Put your house in order," they say, *"that* is the first step.""

This brought a flush to the manager's face and caused him to shift in his chair.

"My dad," said Grand then, and with severe reverence, "pushed out here in . . . 1920. There were few frontiers open for him at that time. There are fewer still . . . open-for-us-today!"

He faced the manager and would have let him speak; in fact, by looking straight into his face, he invited him to do so, but the man could only nod in sage agreement.

"If there is one unexplored territory," Grand continued, waxing expansive now, "one virgin wood alive today in this man's land of ours—it is cinema management! My dad—'Dad Grand'—was a championship golfer. That *may* be why . . . now this is only a guess . . . but that *may* be why he always favored the maxim: 'If you want them to play your course —don't put rocks on the green!' "

Grand paused for a minute, staring down at the manager's sparkling shoes as he allowed his great brow to furrow and his lips to purse, frantically pensive. Then he shot a question:

"Do you know the story of the Majestic Theatre in Kansas City?"

The manager, a man with thirty years' experience in the field, who knew the story of every theatre in the country, did not know this one.

"In August, 1939, the management of the K.C. Majestic changed hands, *and* policy. Weston seats were installed—four inches wider than standard —and 'a.p.'s,' admission prices, were cut in half . . . and two people were to occupy each seat. The new manager, Jason Frank, who died of a brain hemorrhage later the same year, had advanced Wyler Publicity nine hundred dollars for the catch-phrase, 'Half the Price, and a Chance for Vice,' which received a wide private circulation."

Grand broke off his narrative to give the manager a searching look before continuing:

". . . *but* it didn't work, sir! It *did not* work . . . and I'll tell you why: it was a *crackpot* scheme. A crackpot scheme, and rocks on the green! It cost Frank his license, his health, and in this case perhaps his very life."

Grand paused for effect and crossed to the desk where he took up a sheaf of onionskin papers and threshed them about before the manager. Each sheet was black with figures.

"According to my figures," he said tersely, "this house will fold in nine months' time unless there is, at minimum, an eight percent climb in 'p.a.'s' —paid admission." Here he frowned darkly, let it pass, forced a smile, and then flapped his arms a time or two, as he resumed speaking, in a much lighter tone now:

"Of course there are a number of . . . of *possibilities* for us here . . . I have certain plans . . . oh granted they're tentative, under wrap, irons in the fire, if you like—but I *can* tell you *this:* I am retaining you and your staff. We are not ploughing the green under. Do you follow? Right. Now I have arranged for this increase in your salaries: ten percent. I won't say it is a *substantial* increase; I say simply: *ten percent* . . . which means, of course, that all . . . *all these figures*"—he waved the sheaf of papers in a gesture of hopelessness and then dropped them into the wastebasket—"will have to be *revised!* More time lost before we know where we stand! Yet that can't be helped. It *is* a move—and *I* say it is a move . . . in the right direction!"

He spoke to the manager for an hour, thinking aloud, getting the feel of things, keeping his hand in, and so on. Then he dismissed him for three months' paid vacation.

Grand's theatre was one of the city's largest and had first-run rights on the most publicized films. In the manager's absence, things proceeded normally for a while; until one night when the house was packed for the opening of the smart new musical, *Main Street, U.S.A.*

First there was an annoying half-hour delay while extra camp-stool seats were sold and set up in the aisles; then, when the house lights finally dimmed into blackness, and the audience settled back to enjoy the musical, Grand gave them something they weren't expecting: a cheap foreign film.

The moment the film began, people started leaving. In the darkness, however, with seats two-abreast choking the aisles, most of them were forced back. So the film rolled on; and while the minutes gathered into quarter-hours, and each quarter-hour cut cripplingly deep into the evening, Grand, locked in the projection room high above, stumbled from wall to wall, choking with laughter.

After forty-five minutes, the film was taken off and it was announced over the public-address system, and at a volume strength never before used, anywhere, that a mistake had been made, that this was *not* the new musical.

Shouts of *"And how!"* came from the crowd, and *"I'll say it's not!"* and *"You're telling me! God!"*

Then after another delay for rewinding, the cheap foreign film was put on again, upside down.

By ten thirty the house was seething towards angry panic, and Grand gave the order to refund the money of everyone who wished to pass by the box office. At eleven o'clock there was a line outside the theatre two blocks long.

From his office above, Grand kept delaying the cashier's work by phoning every few minutes to ask: "How's it going?" or "What's up?"

The next day there was a notice on the central bulletin board:

"Rocks on the green! All hands alert!"

It also announced another fat pay-hike.

Into certain films such as *Mrs. Miniver,* Grand made eccentric inserts.

In one scene in *Mrs. Miniver,* Walter Pidgeon was sitting at evening in his firelit study and writing in his journal. He had just that afternoon made the acquaintance of Mrs. Miniver and was no doubt thinking about her now as he paused reflectively and looked towards the open fire. In the original version of this film, he took a small penknife from the desk drawer and meditatively sharpened the pencil he had been writing with. During this scene the camera remained on his *face,* which was filled with quiet reflection and modest hopefulness, so that the intended emphasis of the scene was quite clear: his genteel and wistfully ambitious thoughts about Mrs. Miniver.

The insert Grand made into this film, was, like those he made into others, professionally done, and as such, was technically indiscernable. It was introduced just at the moment where Pidgeon opened the knife, and it was a three-second close shot of the fire-glint blade.

This simple insert misplaced the emphasis of the scene; the fire-glint blade seemed to portend dire evil, and occurring as it did early in the story, simply "spoiled" the film.

Grand would hang around the lobby after the show to overhear the remarks of those leaving, and often he would join in himself:

"What was that part about the *knife?*" he would demand querulously, stalking up and down the lobby, striking his fist into his open hand, ". . . he *had* that knife . . . I thought he was going to try and *kill* her! Christ, I don't *get* it!"

In some cases, Grand's theatre had to have two copies of the film on hand, because his alterations were so flagrant that he did not deem it wise to project the altered copy twice in succession. This was the case with a popular film called *The Best Years of Our Lives.* This film was mainly concerned, in its attempt at an odd kind of realism, with a young veteran of war, who was an amputee and had metal hooks instead of hands. It was a story told quite seriously and one which depended for much of its drama upon a straight-faced identification with the amputee's situation and attitude. Grand's insert occurred in the middle of the film's big scene. This original scene was a seven-second pan of the two principal characters, the amputee and his pretty home-town fiancée while they were sitting on the family porch swing one summer evening. The hero was courting her, in his quiet way—and this consisted of a brave smile, more or less in apology, it would seem, for having the metal hooks instead of hands—while the young girl's eyes shone with tolerance and understanding . . . a scene which was interrupted by Grand's insert: a cut to below the girl's waist where the hooks were seen to hover for an instant and then disappear, grappling urgently beneath her skirt. The duration of this cut was less than one-half second, but was unmistakably seen by anyone not on the brink of sleep.

It brought some of the audience bolt upright. Others the scene affected in a sort of double-take way, reacting to it as they did only minutes later. The rest, that is to say about one-third of the audience, failed to notice it at all; and the film rolled on. No one could believe his eyes; those who were positive they had seen something funny in the realism there, sat through the film again to make certain—though, of course, the altered version was never run twice in succession—but *all* who had seen were so obsessed by what they had seen, or what they imagined they had seen, that they could no longer follow the story line, though it was, from that point on, quite as it was intended, without incongruity or surprise.

Grand had a good deal of trouble about his alterations of certain films and was eventually sued by several of the big studios. You can bet it cost him a pretty to keep clear in the end.

Grand upset the equilibrium of a rather smart Madison Avenue advertising agency, Jonathan Reynolds, Ltd., by secretly buying it—*en passant,* so to speak—and putting in as president a pygmy.

At that time it was rare for a man of this skin-pigmentation or stature (much the less both) to hold down a top-power post in one of these swank agencies, and these two handicaps would have been difficult to overcome—though perhaps could have been overcome in due time had the chap shown a reasonable amount of savoir-faire and general ability, or the promise of developing it. In this case, however, Grand had apparently paid the man to behave in an eccentric manner—to scurry about the offices like a squirrel and to chatter raucously in his native tongue. It was more than a nuisance.

An account executive, for example, might be entertaining an extremely important client in his own office, a little tête-à-tête of the very first seriousness—perhaps with an emissary of one of the soap-flake kings—when the door would burst open and in would fly the president, scrambling across the room and under the desk, shrieking pure gibberish, and then out he'd go again, scuttling crabwise over the carpet, teeth and eyes blazing.

"What in God's name was that?" the client would ask, looking slowly about, his face pocked with a terrible frown.

"Why, that . . . that . . ." But the a.e. could not bring himself to tell, not after the first few times anyway. Evidently it was a matter of pride.

Later this a.e. might run into one of his friends from another agency, and the friend would greet him:

"Say, hear you've got a new number one over at J.R., Tommy—what's the chap like?"

"Well, as a matter of fact, Bert . . ."

"You don't mean the old boy's got you on the *mat* already, Tommy. Ha-ha. *That* what you're trying to say?"

"No, Bert, it's . . . well I don't know, Bert, I *just don't know.*"

It was a matter of pride, of course. As against it, salaries had been given a fairly stiff boost, *and* titles. If these dapper execs were to go to another agency now, it would be at a considerable loss of dollars and cents. Most of the old-timers—and the younger ones too, actually—had what it took to stick it out there at J.R.

Grand made quite a splash in the fall of '58 when he entered the "big-car" field with his sports line of Black Devil Rockets, a gigantic convertible. There were four models of the Rocket, each with a different fanciful name, though, except for the color of the upholstery, all four cars were identical. The big convertible was scaled in the proportions of an ordinary automobile, but was tremendous in size—was, in fact, *longer and wider than the largest Greyhound Bus in operation.*

"There's power to spare under this big baby's forty-foot hood!" was a sales claim that gained attention.

Fronting the glittering crystal dash were two "racing-cup" seats with a distance of ten feet between them, and the big "gang's-all-here" seat in back would accommodate twelve varsity crewmen abreast in roomy comfort.

"Buy Yourself One *Whale* of a Car, Buddy!" read the giant ads. "From Stem to Stern She's a Flat One Hundred Feet! Ladylike Lines on a He-Man Hunk of Car!"

Performance figures were generally side-stepped, but a number of three-color billboards and full-page ads were headed: *"Performance?* Ask the Fella Behind the Wheel!" and featured, in apparently authentic testimonial, one of the Indianapolis speed kings behind the wheel of the mammoth convertible. A larger than average man, he was incredibly dwarfed by the immense dimensions of the car. His tiny face, just visible at the top of the wheel, was split in a grin of insanity, like a toothpaste ad, a madman's laugh frozen at the nightmare peak of hilarity, and it was captioned:

"Getting the feel of this big baby has been one real thrill, believe you me!"

The four identical models were shown at a display room on Fifth Avenue, and though considered beyond the price range of most, were evidently sold. At any rate, on the last day of the exposition they were driven away, out and into the streets of midtown Manhattan during the five o'clock rush.

Despite their roominess, power, and road-holding potential, the big cars did prove impractical in the city, because their turning-arc—for the ordinary 90° change of direction—was greater than the distance between the street-angled buildings, so that by five thirty all four of the sleek Devil Rockets were wedged at angles across various intersections around Columbus Circle, each a barrier to thoroughfare in four directions, and causing quite a snarl indeed until cranes and derricks could be brought up from the East River to pry the big cars out.

New York authorities were quick to respond to the flood of protests and got out an injunction to prevent Black Devil Rocket Corp. from further production.

"Personally," said one high-ranking city official, in an off-the-record remark in defense of the court's ruling—which was, after all a flagrant infringement on the rights of free enterprise—". . . *personally* I frankly think the car is an ugly car and a . . . a *pretentious* car, and, as experience has shown us, it is an impractical car. I'll bet it's plenty expensive to run, too."

At last account though, Grand—himself fairly well in the background— was carrying on, pressing his fight to get the go-ahead and swing into full production with the big baby.

It was along towards the end though that Grand achieved, in terms of public outrage, his *succès d'estime,* as some chose to call it, when he put out to sea in his big ship, the S.S. *Magic Christian* . . . the ship sometimes later referred to as "The Terrible Trick Ship of Captain Klaus." Actually it was the old *Griffin,* a passenger liner which Grand bought and had reconditioned for about fifty million.

A vessel of 30,000 tons, the *Christian* had formerly carried some eleven-hundred-odd passengers. Grand converted it into a one-class ship, outfitted to accommodate four hundred passengers, in a style and comfort perhaps unknown theretofore outside princely domains of the East. Each cabin on the *Christian* was a palace in miniature; the appointments were so lavish and so exquisitely detailed that they might better be imagined than described. All the cabins were of course above deck and outside, each with a twenty-foot picture window and French doors to a private patio commanding a magnificent expanse of sea and sky. There were fine deep rugs throughout each suite and period-furnishings of first account, private bars, chaise longues, log-burning fireplaces, king-sized beds (canopy optional), an adjoining library-den (with a set of the *Britannica* and the best in smart fiction), tape recorders, powder rooms, small Roman bath and steam cabinet. Walls were generally in a quiet tone of suede with certain paneling of teak and rosewood.

Ship's dining room was styled after Maxim's in Paris whose staff had been engaged to prepare the meals and to serve them with inconspicuous grace against a background of soft music provided by the Juilliard String Quartette. The balance of ship's appointments were in harmonious key—

there was, for example, a veritable jewel box of a theatre, seating just four hundred, fashioned in replica of the one in the Monte Carlo Casino; and the versatile repertory group, Old Vic Players, were on stand-by for two shows a day.

Ship's doctor, aside from being an able physician, was also a top-flight mental specialist, so that Problem-Counseling was available to the passengers at all hours.

But perhaps the most carefully thought-out nicety of the *Christian* was its principal lounge, the Marine Room—a large room, deep below decks, its walls (that which was part of ship's hull) glassed so that the passengers sat looking out into the very heart of the sea. An ocean-floor effect was maintained by the regular release of deep-sea creatures from a waterline station near the bow, and through the use of powerful daylight kliegs there was afforded a breath-taking panorama—with giant octopi, huge rainbow-colored ray, serpents, great snowy angelfish, and fantastic schools of luminous tetra constantly gliding by or writhing in silent majestic combat a few feet from the relaxed passengers.

Though the *Magic Christian* received its share of prevoyage hullabaloo (*Life* magazine devoted an issue to photographs, enthusiastically captioned), its only form of paid advertisement was a simple announcement of its sailing date, which appeared in *The Times* and in the *National Geographic*. The fare was not mentioned (though *Life* had said it was "about five thousand") and the announcement was set in small heavy type, boxed with a very black border. "For the Gracious Few . . ." it opened, and went on to state in a brief, restrained apology, that *not everyone* could be accepted, that applications for passage on the *Christian* were necessarily carefully screened, and that those who were refused should not take offense. "Our criteria," it closed, "may *not* be yours."

Ship's quarters were not shown until the applicant had been accepted, and then were shown by appointment.

The ship was christened by the Queen of England.

All of this had a certain appeal and the applications poured in. More than a few people, in fact, were *demanding* passage on the *Christian's* first voyage. Those just back from holiday were suddenly planning to go abroad again; scores rushed home simply to qualify and make the trip. For many, the maiden voyage of the *Magic Christian* became a must.

Meanwhile Guy Grand, well in the background, was personally screening the applications according to some obscure criteria of his own, and apparently he had himself a few laughs in this connection. In the case of one application, for example, from a venerable scioness of Roman society, he simply scrawled moronically across it in blunt pencil: "Are *you* kidding?!? No wops!" The woman was said to have had a nervous breakdown and did later file for a million on defamation. It cost Grand a pretty to clear it.

On the other hand, he accepted—or rather, engaged—as passengers, a group from a fairly sordid freak show, most of whom could not be left untended, along with a few gypsies, Broadway types, and the like, of offensive appearance and doubtful character. These, however, were to be kept below decks for the first few days out, and, even so, numbered only about forty in all, so that a good nine-tenths of the passenger list, those on deck when the *Christian* set sail in such tasteful fanfare that Easter morn, were top-drawer gentry and no mistake.

Unique among features of the *Christian* was its video communication system from the bridge to other parts of the ship. Above the fireplace in each cabin was a small TV screen and this provided direct visual communication with the Captain at the wheel and with whatever other activity was going on there, giving as it did a view of almost the entire bridge. These sets could be switched *on* or *off*, but the first day they were left *on* before the passengers arrived, in order to spare anyone the embarrassment of not knowing what the new gimmick was. So that when passengers entered their cabins now they saw at once, there on the screen above the fireplace: the Captain at the wheel. Captain Klaus. And for this person, Guy Grand had engaged a professional actor, a distinguished silver-haired man whose every gesture inspired the deepest confidence. He wore a double row of service ribbons on his dark breast and deported himself in a manner both authoritative and pleasingly genial—as the passengers saw when he turned to face the screen, and this he did just as soon as they were all settled and under way.

He was filling his pipe when he turned to camera, but he paused from this to smile and touch his cap in easy salute.

"Cap'n Klaus," he said, introducing himself with warm informality, though certainly at no sacrifice to his considerable bearing. "Glad to have you aboard."

He casually picked up a pointer stick and indicated a chart on the nearby wall.

"Here's our course," he said, "nor' by nor'east, forty-seven degrees."

Then he went on to explain the mechanics and layout of the bridge, the weather and tide conditions at present, their prospects, and so on, using just enough technical jargon throughout all this to show that he knew what he was about. He said that the automatic-pilot would be used from time to time, but that he personally preferred handling the wheel himself, adding good-humoredly that in his opinion "a ship favored men to machines."

"It may be an old-fashioned notion," he said, with a wise twinkle, ". . . but to me, a ship is a woman."

At last he gave a final welcome-salute, saying again: "Glad to have you aboard," and turned back to his great wheel.

This contact with the bridge and the fatherly Captain seemed to give the passengers an added sense of participation and security; and, indeed, things couldn't have gone more smoothly for the first few hours.

It was in the very early morning that something untoward occurred, at about three A.M.—and of course almost everyone was asleep. They had watched their screens for a while: the Captain in the cozy bridge house, standing alone, pipe aglowing, his strong eyes sweeping the black water ahead—then they had switched off their sets. There were a few people though who were still up and who had their sets on; and, of these few, there were perhaps three who happened to be watching the screen at a certain moment—when in the corner of the bridge house, near the door, there was a shadow, an odd movement . . . then suddenly the appearance of a sinister-looking person, who crept up behind the Captain, hit him on the head, and seized the wheel as the screen blacked out.

The people who had seen this were disturbed and, in fact, were soon rushing about, rousing others, wanting to go to the bridge and so on. And they did actually get up a party and went to the bridge—only to be met at the top of the ladder by the Captain himself, unruffled, glossing it over, blandly assuring them that nothing was wrong, nothing at all, just a minor occurrence. And, of course, back in the cabins, there he was on the screen again, Captain Klaus, steady at the helm.

Those three who had seen the outrage, being in such a hopeless minority, were thought to have been drunk or in some way out of their minds, and were gently referred to ship's doctor, the mental specialist, so the incident passed without too much notice.

And things went smoothly once more, until the next evening—when, in the exquisite gaming rooms just off the Marine Lounge, one of the roulette croupiers was seen, by several people, to be cheating . . . darting his eyes about in a furtive manner and then interfering with the bets, snatching them up and stuffing them in his pocket, that sort of thing.

It was such an unheard-of outrage that one old duke fainted dead away. The croupier was hustled out of the gaming room by Captain Klaus himself, who deplored the incident profusely and declared that the next dozen spins were on the house, losing bets to remain untouched for that time—gracious recompense, in the eyes of a sporting crowd, and applauded as such; still, the incident was not one easily forgotten.

Another curious thing occurred when some of the ladies went, individually, to visit the ship's doctor. For the most part they had simply dropped around to pick up a few aspirin, sea-sickness pills—or merely to have a reassuring chat with the amiable physician. Several of these ladies, however, were informed that they looked "rather queer" and that an examination might be in order.

"Better safe than sorry," the doctor said, and then, during the examination, he invariably seemed to discover what he termed "a latent abrasion" —on the waist, side, hip, or shoulder of the woman—and though the abrasion could not be seen, the doctor deemed it required a compress.

"Nothing serious," he explained, "still it's always wise to take precautions." And so saying he would apply a *huge compress* to the area, a sort of gigantic Band-Aid about a foot wide and several inches thick, with big adhesive flaps that went halfway around the body. The tremendous bulk of these compresses was a nuisance, causing as they did, great deforming bulges beneath the women's smart frocks. They were almost impossible to remove. One woman was seen running about with one on her head, like a big white hat.

First lifeboat drill was scheduled for the following morning. Shortly before it, Captain Klaus came on the screen and smilingly apologized for the inconvenience and gave a leisurely and pleasantly informative talk about the drill and its necessity.

"Better safe than sorry," he said in a genial close to his little talk.

When the drill signal sounded, they all got into life jackets—which were the latest thing and quite unlike standard passengership equipment—and then, grumbling goodnaturedly, they started for their boat stations; but an extraordinary thing happened: two minutes after they had put them on, the life jackets began inflating in a colossal way. Apparently the very act of donning the jacket set off some device which inflated it. The extraordinary thing was that each one blew up so big that it simply obscured the person wearing it, ballooning out about them, above their heads, below their feet, and to a diameter of perhaps twelve feet—so that if they were in an open space, such as their cabins, the lounge, or on deck, they simply rolled or lolled about on the floor, quite hidden from view, whereas if they were in a corridor, they were hopelessly stuck.

In any event, almost no one escaped the effects of the faulty life jacket; so it was—after they deflated—with a good deal of annoyance that they came back to the cabins, quite ready to hear Captain Klaus' explanation of what had gone amiss.

Unfortunately though, the foghorn, which had been put to practice during the drill, was now evidently jammed. At any rate, it continued steadily during the Captain's afterdrill talk and completely shut out his voice, so that it was like looking at someone talk behind several layers of glass. The Captain himself didn't seem to realize that he wasn't coming through, and he went on talking for quite a while, punctuating his remarks with various little facial gestures to indicate a whole gamut of fairly intense feelings about whatever it was he was saying.

The business with the foghorn was more serious than at first imagined; it continued, blasting without let-up, for the rest of the voyage.

Quite incidental to what was happening during the drill, fifty crew members took advantage of the occasion to go around to the cabins, lounges, and dining rooms, and to substitute a thin length of balsa wood for one leg of every chair, table, and dresser on ship.

When the Captain finished his lengthy and voiceless discourse, he smiled, gave an easy salute and left the bridge house. It was about this time that all the furniture began to collapse—in half an hour's time there wasn't one standing stick of it aboard the *Christian*.

Strange and unnatural persons began to appear—in the drawing rooms, salons, at the pool. During the afternoon tea dance, a gigantic *bearded-woman,* stark naked, rushed wildly about over the floor, interfering with the couples, and had to be forcibly removed by ship's doctor.

The plumbing went bad, too; and finally one of the *Christian's* big stacks toppled—in such a way as to give directly on to ship's dining room, sending oily smoke billowing through. And, in fact, from about this point on, the voyage was a veritable nightmare.

Large curious posters were to be seen in various parts of the ship:

SUPPORT MENTAL HEALTH

LET'S KEEP THE CLAP OUT
OF CHAPPAQUIDDICK

as well as rude slogans, vaguely political, scrawled in huge misshapen letters across walls and decks alike:

DEATH TO RICH!
BLOW UP U.S.!

Due to the strain of untoward events, more than one passenger sought solace and reassurance from the problem-counselor, the ship's distinguished doctor.

"Doctor, what *in the name of God* is going on here!" the frenzied passenger would demand.

The doctor would answer with a quizzical smile, arching his brows, only mildly censorious. "Fair-weather sailor?" he would gently chide, ". . . hmm? Cross and irritable the moment things aren't going exactly to suit you? Now just what seems to be the trouble?"

" *'Trouble'!?!"* exclaimed the outraged passenger. "Good Lord, Doctor, surely you don't think my complaint is an . . . an unreasonable one?"

The doctor would turn his gaze out to sea, thin fingers pressed beneath his chin in a delicate pyramid of contemplation, wistfully abstract for a moment before turning back to address the patient frankly.

"Deep-rooted and unreasonable fears," he would begin in a grand, rich voice, "are most often behind our anxieties . . ." and he would continue in this vein until the passenger fairly exploded with impatience.

"Great Scott, Doctor! I didn't come here for a lecture on *psychology*—I came to find out what *in the name of Heaven* is going on *aboard this ship!"*

In the face of these outbursts, however, the doctor almost invariably retained his calm, regarding the patient coolly, searchingly, making a few careful notes on his pad.

"Now, you say that 'the life jacket *over inflated,"* and that you were 'stuck in the corridor'—that was your expression, I believe, *'stuck in the corridor'*—and at that moment you felt a certain *malaise,* so to speak. Now, let me ask you *this . . ."* Or again, on other occasions, he might behave eccentrically, his head craned far to one side, regarding the patient out of the corners of his eyes, a sly, mad smile on his lips which moved in an inaudible whisper, almost a hiss.

Finally, the patient, at the end of his tether, would leap to his feet.

"Well, in the name of God, Doctor, the least you can do is let me have some *tranquillizers!"*

But the doctor, as it turned out, was not one given to prescribing drugs promiscuously.

"Escape into drugs?" he would ask, wagging his head slowly. "Mask our fears in an artificial fog?" And there was always a trace of sadness in his smile, as he continued, "No, I'm afraid the trouble is *in ourselves,* you see." Then he would settle back expansively and speak with benign countenance. "Running away from the problems is scarcely the solution to them. I *believe* you'll thank me in years to come." And at last he would lean forward in quiet confidence. "Do you mind if I ask you a few questions about your . . . your *early childhood?"*

When Captain Klaus next appeared on the screen, he looked as though he had been sleeping in two feet of water. Completely disheveled, his ribbons dangling in unsightly strands, his open coat flapping, his unknotted tie strung loosely around his collar, he seemed somewhat drunk as well. With a rude wave of his hand he dismissed bridge personnel and lurched toward the video screen, actually crashing into it, and remaining so close that his image was all distorted.

"We'll get the old tub through!" he was shouting at deafening volume, and at that moment he was attacked from behind by a ruffian type who was carrying a huge hypodermic and appeared to overpower the Captain and inject something into the top of his head, then to seize the wheel, wrenching it violently, before the screen went black.

Also, it was learned about this time that because of fantastic miscalculation on the part of the ship's-stores officer, the only food left aboard now was potatoes.

Thus did the *Christian* roar over the sea, through fair weather and foul.

Guy Grand was aboard of course, as a passenger, complaining bitterly, and in fact kept leading assault parties in an effort to find out, as he put it, "What the devil's going on on the bridge!"

But they were always driven back by a number of odd-looking men with guns and knives near the ladder.

"Who the deuce are those chaps?" Grand would demand as he and the others beat a hasty retreat along the deck. "I don't like the looks of this!"

Occasionally the communications screen in each of the cabins would light up to reveal momentarily what was taking place on the bridge, and it was fairly incredible. The bridge house itself now was a swaying rubble heap and the Captain was seen intermittently, struggling with various assailants, and finally with what actually appeared to be a gorilla—the beast at last overpowering him and flinging him bodily out of the bridge house and, or so it seemed, into the sea itself, before seizing the wheel, which he seemed then to be trying to tear from its hub.

It was about this time that the ship, which, as it developed, had turned completely around in the middle of the ocean, came back into New York harbor under full steam, and with horns and whistles screaming, ploughed headlong into the big Forty-Seventh Street pier.

Fortunately no one was injured on the cruise; but, even so, it went far from easy with Grand—he had already sunk plenty into the project, and just how much it cost him to keep clear in the end, is practically anyone's guess.

The S.S. *Magic Christian* was Grand's last major project—at least it was the last to be brought into open account. After that he began to taper off. However, he did like "keeping in touch," as he expressed it, and, for one thing, he bought himself a grocery store in New York City. Quite small, it was more or less indistinguishable from the several others in the neighborhood, and Grand put up a little sign in the window.

NEW OWNER—NEW POLICY

BIG GET-ACQUAINTED SALE

Grand was behind the counter himself, wearing a sort of white smock, when the store opened that evening.

His first customer was a man who lived next door to the store. He bought a carton of Grape-Ade.

"That will be three cents," said Grand.

"How much?" asked the man, with a frown.

"Three cents."

"Three *cents?* For six Grape-Ade? Are you kidding?"

"It's our two-for-one Get-Acquainted on Grape-Ade," said Grand. "It's new policy."

"Boy, *I'll* say it's new," said the man. "And how! Three *cents?* Okay by me, brother!" He slapped three cents on the counter. "There it is!" he said and still seemed amazed when Grand pushed the carton towards him.

"Call again," said Grand.

"That's some policy all right," said the man, looking back over his shoulder as he started for the door. At the door, however, he paused.

"Listen," he said, "do you sell it . . . uh, you know, by the *case?*"

"Well, yes," said Grand, "you would get some further reduction if you bought it by the case—not too much, of course; we're working on a fairly small profit-margin during the sale, you see and—"

"Oh, I'll pay the two-for one all right. Christ! I just wanted to know if I could *get* a case at that price."

"Certainly, would you like a case?"

"Well, as a matter of fact, I could *use* more than one case . . ."

"How many cases could you use?"

"Well, uh . . . how many . . . how many have you *got?*"

"Could you use a thousand?"

"A *thousand?!?* A thousand cases of Grape-Ade?"

"Yes, I could give you . . . say, ten percent off on a thousand . . . and at twenty-four bottles to the case, twelve cents a case . . . would be one hundred and twenty dollars, minus ten percent, would be one hundred and eight . . . call it one-naught-five, shall we?"

"No, no. I couldn't use a thousand cases. Jesus! I meant, say, *ten* cases."

"That would be a dollar twenty."

"Right!" said the man. He slapped down a dollar twenty on the counter. "Boy, that's some policy you've got there!" he said.

"It's our Get-Acquainted policy," said Grand.

"It's some policy all right," said the man.

"Have you got any other . . . *specials* on? You know, 'two-for-one,' that sort of thing?"

"Well, most of our items have been reduced for the Get-Acquainted."

The man hadn't noticed it before, but price tags were in evidence, and all prices had been sharply cut: milk, two cents a quart—butter, ten cents a pound—eggs, eleven cents a dozen—and so on.

The man looked wildly about him.

"How about cigarettes?"

"No, we decided we wouldn't carry cigarettes; since they've been linked, rather authoritatively, to cancer of the lung, we thought it wouldn't be exactly in the best of taste to sell them—being a *neighborhood* grocery, I mean to say."

"Uh-huh, well—listen, I'm just going home for a minute now to get a sack, or a . . . trunk, or maybe a truck . . . I'll be right back . . ."

Somehow the word spread through the neighborhood and in two hours the store was clean as a whistle.

The next day, a sign was on the empty store:

MOVED TO NEW LOCATION

And that evening, in another part of town, the same thing occurred—followed again by a quick change of location. The people who had experienced the phenomenon began to spend a good deal of their time each evening looking for the new location. And occasionally now, two such people meet—one who was at the big Get-Acquainted on West 4th Street, for example, and the other at the one on 139th—and so, presumably, they surmise not only that it wasn't a dream, but that it's still going on.

And some say it does, in fact, still go on—they say it accounts for the strange searching haste which can be seen in the faces, and especially the eyes, of people in the cities, every evening, just about the time now it starts really getting dark.

❖

Terry Southern was born in Texas in 1928, educated at the University of Chicago and Northwestern, spent many years in Paris and Switzerland, then in New York and Connecticut, and now lives in Los Angeles, where he writes for the movies. His first novel was Flash and Filigree *(1958); his second,* The Magic Christian *(1960), from which the excerpts comprising "Grand Guy Grand" have been taken. His short stories and humor pieces have been collected in* Red Dirt Marijuana *(1967). And he is also co-author of two extraordinary works. With Mason Hoffenberg he wrote* Candy *as a dirty book for The Olympia Press in Paris; when it was published in America in 1964 it was widely read and admired as a comic novel parodying pornography. With Stanley Kubrick he wrote* Dr. Strangelove, *a satirical film of great power based on the melodrama* Red Alert, *by Peter George, who also collaborated on the screenplay. The extent to which Southern is or isn't responsible for these works is obscure, but they both have his characteristic style, a style that's hard to analyze, especially as many elements of it have become common. One of the trademarks is to throw words into emphasis by using italics in unexpected but effective places—usually in dialogue but not always. This is especially effective in his stories about hipsters and Negroes: he is one of the few people who seem able to write and accent Beat or hip dialect convincingly. Another aspect of the Southern style is the put-on: the assumption by one person of an eager or stuffy or anxious manner to fake the other into some sort of compensatory attitude, upon which the trap may or may not be pulled. Southern's seemingly very original style was so instantly co-opted by media of all sorts that one can't tell what was his and what was our times' to begin with. Humor in America, like everything else, now changes so swiftly—from the sick jokes, to the absurdity of elephant and space jokes, to whatever sort of backlash the vicious anti-Polish jokes expressed or repressed, to whatever is current now—and is so involved with other matters—the "absurd" in theater and other arts, with "black humor," with the "camp" sensibility—that it is of course impossible to make anything resembling a sensible comment on it. Except, perhaps, one might say: the style of Terry Southern has a central place in it somewhere.*

"Grand Guy Grand" makes a savage and scathing comment on the contemporary American character in the form of what seems to be just a series of gags, a sequence of ever more elaborate practical jokes. It is said that the confidence man relies on the greed of his victims and without it cannot pull his tricks, and the same is true of Guy's tricks: his victims are his collaborators. The common underlying purpose behind most of what he does is seen most clearly in "the first and, in a sense perhaps, the most deliberately literal of such projects": in downtown Chicago he slowly stirs ten thousand $100 bills into a huge vat of urine, manure, and blood from the stockyards, heated "to make it hot" for those who try to get the free money. By "making it hot" for people Guy means putting their avarice in direct conflict with some other quality that they prize. There is, for instance, the smug "nasal piousness" of the man who is made to realize he would eat the parking ticket, who is made to see that he has "his price." The advertising men prize their professionalism, but when Guy buys the agency and installs the mad pygmy as president, he raises salaries and titles at the same time. "If these dapper execs were to go to another agency now, it would be at a considerable loss of dollars and cents." Of course dollars win over pride, and they stay, but Southern's wording is mocking: they "had what it took to stick it out there." Much of the idea behind his pranks is to humiliate the smug, the hypocritical, the pompous. The purported luxury and exclusiveness of the S.S. Magic Christian *so attract "the Gracious Few" that they struggle to get on board: they collaborate wonderfully in Guy's plans to make it hot for them. Pride of all sorts, conviction and belief of all sorts, dignity of any sort—all is shown to be hypocrisy, all is shown to crumble before the power of money. Everyone is willingly ridiculed, debased, corrupted, soiled, in the scramble for Guy's dollars; everyone rushes to sell out. And of course Guy's dollars are symbolic of our money economy's success in buying out talent and integrity in all areas of American life. It is a savagely outraged book, Swiftian in the contempt it expresses for modern man's greedy gullibility. In the final sequence, in which Guy's pranks are raised to a sort of legendary level, even common sense is shown to be powerless against the fantastic bargains of the grocery's Get-Acquainted Sale—the ultimate insane projection of the advertising bargains with which Americans are always duping one another. People are said still to search now from neighborhood to neighborhood, surmising "not only that it wasn't a dream, but that it's still going on." Then Southern concludes his book: "And some say it does, in fact, still go on—they say it accounts for the strange searching haste which can be seen in the faces, and especially the eyes, of people in the cities. . . ."*

VLADIMIR NABOKOV

Traveling with Lolita

◇◇◇◇◇◇◇◇

IT WAS THEN that began our extensive travels all over the States. To any other type of tourist accommodation I soon grew to prefer the Functional Motel—clean, neat, safe nooks, ideal places for sleep, argument, reconciliation, insatiable illicit love. At first, in my dread of arousing suspicion, I would eagerly pay for both sections of one double unit, each containing a double bed. I wondered what type of foursome this arrangement was ever intended for, since only a pharisaic parody of privacy could be attained by means of the incomplete partition dividing the cabin or room into two communicating love nests. By and by, the very possibilities that such honest promiscuity suggested (two young couples merrily swapping mates or a child shamming sleep to earwitness primal sonorities) made me bolder, and every now and then I would take a bed-and-cot or twin-bed cabin, a prison cell of paradise, with yellow window shades pulled down to create a morning illusion of Venice and sunshine when actually it was Pennsylvania and rain.

We came to know—*nous connûmes,* to use a Flaubertian intonation— the stone cottages under enormous Chateaubriandesque trees, the brick unit, the adobe unit, the stucco court, on what the Tour Book of the Automobile Association describes as "shaded" or "spacious" or "landscaped" grounds. The log kind, finished in knotty pine, reminded Lo, by its golden-brown glaze, of fried-chicken bones. We held in contempt the plain whitewashed clapboard Kabins, with their faint sewerish smell or some other gloomy self-conscious stench and nothing to boast of (except "good beds"), and an unsmiling landlady always prepared to have her gift (". . . well, I could give you . . .") turned down.

Nous connûmes (this is royal fun) the would-be enticements of their repetitious names—all those Sunset Motels, U-Beam Cottages, Hillcrest Courts, Pine View Courts, Mountain View Courts, Skyline Courts, Park Plaza Courts, Green Acres, Mac's Courts. There was sometimes a special line in the write-up, such as "Children welcome, pets allowed" *(You are* welcome, *you* are allowed). The baths were mostly tiled showers, with an endless variety of spouting mechanisms, but with one definitely non-Laodicean characteristic in common, a propensity, while in use, to turn instantly beastly hot or blindingly cold upon you, depending on whether your neighbor turned on his cold or his hot to deprive you of a necessary complement in the shower you had so carefully blended. Some motels had instructions pasted above the toilet (on whose tank the towels were unhygienically heaped) asking guests not to throw into its bowl garbage, beer cans, cartons, stillborn babies; others had special notices under glass, such as Things to Do (Riding: *You will often see riders coming down Main Street on their way back from a romantic moonlight ride.* "Often at 3 A.M.," sneered unromantic Lo).

Nous connûmes the various types of motor court operators, the reformed criminal, the retired teacher and the business flop, among the males; and the motherly, pseudo-ladylike and madamic variants among the females. And sometimes trains would cry in the monstrously hot and humid night with heartrending and ominous plangency, mingling power and hysteria in one desperate scream.

We avoided Tourist Homes, country cousins of Funeral ones, old-fashioned, genteel and showerless, with elaborate dressing tables in depressingly white-and-pink little bedrooms, and photographs of the landlady's children in all their instars. But I did surrender, now and then, to Lo's predilection for "real" hotels. She would pick out in the book, while I petted her in the parked car in the silence of a dusk-mellowed, mysterious side-road, some highly recommended lake lodge which offered all sorts of things magnified by the flashlight she moved over them, such as congenial company, between-meals snacks, outdoor barbecues—but which in my mind conjured up odious visions of stinking high school boys in sweatshirts and an ember-red cheek pressing against hers, while poor Dr. Humbert, embracing nothing but two masculine knees, would cold-humor his piles on the damp turf. Most tempting to her, too, were those "Colonial" Inns, which apart from "gracious atmosphere" and picture windows, promised "unlimited quantities of M-m-m food." Treasured recollections of my father's palatial hotel sometimes led me to seek for its like in the strange country we traveled through. I was soon discouraged; but Lo kept following the scent of rich food ads, while I derived a not exclusively economic kick from such roadside signs as TIMBER HOTEL, *Children under 14 Free.* On the other hand, I shudder when recalling that *soi-disant* "high-class" resort in a Midwestern state, which advertised "raid-the-icebox" midnight snacks and, intrigued by my accent, wanted to know my dead wife's and dead mother's maiden names. A two-days' stay there cost me a hundred and twenty-four dollars! . . .

Immediately upon arrival at one of the plainer motor courts which became our habitual haunts, she would set the electric fan a-whirr, or induce me to drop a quarter into the radio, or she would read all the signs and inquire with a whine why she could not go riding up some advertised trail or swimming in that local pool of warm mineral water. Most often, in the slouching, bored way she cultivated, Lo would fall prostrate and abominably desirable into a red springchair or a green chaise longue, or a steamer chair of striped canvas with footrest and canopy, or a sling chair, or any other lawn chair under a garden umbrella on the patio, and it would take hours of blandishments, threats and promises to make her lend me for a few seconds her brown limbs in the seclusion of the five-dollar room before undertaking anything she might prefer to my poor joy.

A combination of naïveté and deception, of charm and vulgarity, of blue sulks and rosy mirth, Lolita, when she chose, could be a most exasperating brat. I was not really quite prepared for her fits of disorganized boredom, intense and vehement griping, her sprawling, droopy, dopey-eyed style, and what is called goofing off—a kind of diffused clowning which she thought was tough in a boyish hoodlum way. Mentally, I found her to be a disgustingly conventional little girl. Sweet hot jazz, square dancing, gooey fudge sundaes, musicals, movie magazines and so forth—these were the obvious items in her list of beloved things. The Lord knows how many nickels I fed to the gorgeous music boxes that came with every meal we had! I still hear the nasal voices of those invisibles serenading her, people with names like Sammy and Jo and Eddy and Tony and Peggy and Guy and Patty and Rex, and sentimental song hits, all of them as similar to my ears as her various candies were to my palate. She believed, with a kind of celestial trust, any advertisement or advice that appeared in *Movie Love* or *Screen Land*—Starasil Starves Pimples, or "You better watch out if you're wearing your shirttails outside your jeans, gals, because Jill says you shouldn't." If a roadside sign said: VISIT OUR GIFT SHOP—we *had* to visit it, *had* to buy its Indian curios, dolls, copper jewelry, cactus candy. The words "novelties and souvenirs" simply entranced her by their trochaic lilt. If some café sign proclaimed Icecold Drinks, she was automatically stirred, although all drinks everywhere were ice-cold. She it was to whom ads were dedicated: the ideal consumer, the subject and object of every foul poster. And she attempted—unsuccessfully—to patronize only those restaurants where the holy spirit of Huncan Dines had descended upon the cute paper napkins and cottage-cheese-crested salads. . . .

Every morning during our yearlong travels I had to devise some expectation, some special point in space and time for her to look forward to, for her to survive till bedtime. Otherwise, deprived of a shaping and sustaining purpose, the skeleton of her day sagged and collapsed. The object in view might be anything—a lighthouse in Virginia, a natural cave in Arkansas converted to a café, a collection of guns and violins somewhere in Oklahoma, a replica of the Grotto of Lourdes in Louisiana, shabby photographs of the bonanza mining period in the local museum of a Rocky Mountain resort, anything whatsoever—but it had to be there, in front of us, like a fixed star, although as likely as not Lo would feign gagging as soon as we got to it.

By putting the geography of the United States into motion, I did my best for hours on end to give her the impression of "going places," of rolling on to some definite destination, to some unusual delight. I have never seen such smooth amiable roads as those that now radiated before us, across the crazy quilt of forty-eight states. Voraciously we consumed those long highways, in rapt silence we glided over their glossy black dance floors. Not only had Lo no eye for scenery but she furiously resented my calling her attention to this or that enchanting detail of landscape; which I myself learned to discern only after being exposed for quite a time to the delicate beauty ever present in the margin of our undeserving journey. By a paradox of pictorial thought, the average lowland North-American countryside had at first seemed to me something I accepted with a shock of amused recognition because of those painted oilcloths which were imported from America in the old days to be hung above washstands in Central-European nurseries, and which fascinated a drowsy child at bed time with the rustic green views they depicted—opaque curly trees, a barn, cattle, a brook, the dull white of vague orchards in bloom, and perhaps a stone fence or hills of greenish gouache. But gradually the models of those elementary rusticities became stranger and stranger to the eye, the nearer I came to know them. Beyond the tilled plain, beyond the toy roofs, there would be a slow suffusion of inutile loveliness, a low sun in a platinum haze with a warm, peeled-peach tinge pervading the upper edge of a two-dimensional, dove-gray cloud fusing with the distant amorous mist. There might be a line of spaced trees silhouetted against the horizon, and hot still noons above a wilderness of clover, and Claude Lorrain clouds inscribed remotely into misty azure with only their cumulus part conspicious against the neutral swoon of the background. Or again, it might be a stern El Greco horizon, pregnant with inky rain, and a passing glimpse of some mummy-necked farmer, and all around alternating strips of quick-silverish water and harsh green corn, the whole arrangement opening like a fan, somewhere in Kansas.

Now and then, in the vastness of those plains, huge trees would advance toward us to cluster self-consciously by the roadside and provide a bit of humanitarian shade above a picnic table, with sun flecks, flattened paper cups, samaras and discarded ice-cream sticks littering the brown ground. A great user of roadside facilities, my unfastidious Lo would be charmed by toilet signs—Guys-Gals, John-Jane, Jack-Jill and even Buck's-Doe's; while lost in an artist's dream, I would stare at the honest brightness of the gasoline paraphernalia against the splendid green of oaks, or at a distant hill scrambling out—scarred but still untamed—from the wilderness of agriculture that was trying to swallow it.

At night, tall trucks studded with colored lights, like dreadful giant

Christmas trees, loomed in the darkness and thundered by the belated little sedan. And again next day a thinly populated sky, losing its blue to the heat, would melt overhead, and Lo would clamor for a drink, and her cheeks would hollow vigorously over the straw, and the car inside would be a furnace when we got in again, and the road shimmered ahead, with a remote car changing its shape mirage-like in the surface glare, and seeming to hang for a moment, old-fashionedly square and high, in the hot haze. And as we pushed westward, patches of what the garage-man called "sage brush" appeared, and then the mysterious outlines of table-like hills, and the red bluffs ink-blotted with junipers, and then a mountain range, dun grading into blue, and blue into dream, and the desert would meet us with a steady gale, dust, gray thorn bushes, and hideous bits of tissue paper mimicking pale flowers among the prickles of wind-tortured withered stalks all along the highway; in the middle of which there sometimes stood simple cows, immobilized in a position (tail left, white eyelashes right) cutting across all human rules of traffic.

My lawyer has suggested I give a clear, frank account of the itinerary we followed, and I suppose I have reached here a point where I cannot avoid that chore. Roughly, during that mad year (August 1947 to August 1948), our route began with a series of wiggles and whorls in New England, then meandered south, up and down, east and west; dipped deep into *ce qu'on appelle* Dixieland, avoided Florida . . . , veered west, zigzagged through corn belts and cotton belts (this is not too clear I am afraid . . . but I did not keep any notes, and have at my disposal only an atrociously crippled tour book in three volumes, almost a symbol of my torn and tattered past, in which to check these recollections); crossed and recrossed the Rockies, straggled through southern deserts where we wintered; reached the Pacific, turned north through the pale lilac fluff of flowering shrubs along forest roads; almost reached the Canadian border; and proceeded east, across good lands and bad lands, back to agriculture on a grand scale, avoiding, despite little Lo's strident remonstrations, little Lo's birthplace, in a corn, coal and hog producing area; and finally returned to the fold of the East, petering out in the college town of Beardsley.

Now, in perusing what follows, the reader should bear in mind not only the general circuit as adumbrated above, with its many sidetrips and tourist traps, secondary circles and skittish deviations, but also the fact that far from being an indolent *partie de plaisir*, our tour was a hard, twisted, teleological growth, whose sole *raison d'être* (these French clichés are symptomatic) was to keep my companion in passable humor from kiss to kiss.

Thumbing through that battered tour book, I dimly evoke that Magnolia Garden in a southern state which cost me four bucks and which, according to the ad in the book, you must visit for three reasons: because John

Galsworthy (a stone-dead writer of sorts) acclaimed it as the world's fairest garden; because in 1900 Baedeker's Guide had marked it with a star; and finally, because . . . O, Reader, My Reader, guess! . . . because children (and by Jingo was not my Lolita a child!) will "walk starry-eyed and reverently through this foretaste of Heaven, drinking in beauty that can influence a life." "Not mine," said grim Lo, and settled down on a bench with the fillings of two Sunday papers in her lovely lap.

We passed and re-passed through the whole gamut of American roadside restaurants, from the lowly Eat with its deer head (dark trace of long tear at inner canthus), "humorous" picture post cards of the posterior "Kurort" type, impaled guest checks, life savers, sunglasses, adman visions of celestial sundaes, one half of a chocolate cake under glass, and several horribly experienced flies zigzagging over the sticky sugar-pour on the ignoble counter; and all the way to the expensive place with the subdued lights, preposterously poor table linen, inept waiters (ex-convicts or college boys), the roan back of a screen actress, the sable eyebrows of her male of the moment, and an orchestra of zoot-suiters with trumpets.

We inspected the world's largest stalagmite in a cave where three southeastern states have a family reunion; admission by age; adults one dollar, pubescents sixty cents. A granite obelisk commemorating the Battle of Blue Licks, with old bones and Indian pottery in the museum nearby, Lo a dime, very reasonable. The present log cabin boldly simulating the past log cabin where Lincoln was born. A boulder, with a plaque, in memory of the author of "Trees" (by now we are in Poplar Cove, N.C., reached by what my kind, tolerant, usually so restrained tour book angrily calls "a very narrow road, poorly maintained," to which, though no Kilmerite, I subscribe). From a hired motorboat operated by an elderly, but still repulsively handsome White Russian, a baron they said (Lo's palms were damp, the little fool), who had known in California good old Maximovich and Valeria, we could distinguish the inaccessible "millionaires' colony" on an island, somewhere off the Georgia coast. We inspected further: a collection of European hotel picture post cards in a museum devoted to hobbies at a Mississippi resort, where with a hot wave of pride I discovered a colored photo of my father's Mirana, its striped awnings, its flag flying above the retouched palm trees. "So what?" said Lo, squinting at the bronzed owner of an expensive car who had followed us into the Hobby House. Relics of the cotton era. A forest in Arkansas and, on her brown shoulder, a raised purple-pink swelling (the work of some gnat) which I eased of its beautiful transparent poison between my long thumbnails and then sucked till I was gorged on her spicy blood. Bourbon street (in a town named New Orleans) whose sidewalks, said the tour book, "may [I liked the 'may'] feature entertainment by pickaninnies who will [I liked the 'will' even better] tap-dance for pennies" (what fun), while "its numerous small and intimate night clubs are thronged with visitors" (naughty). Collections of frontier lore. Antebellum homes with iron-trellis balconies and hand-worked stairs, the kind down which movie ladies with sun-kissed shoulders run in rich Technicolor, holding up the fronts of their flounced skirts with both little hands in that special way, and the devoted Negress shaking her head on the upper landing. The Menninger Foundation, a psychiatric clinic, just for the heck of it. A patch of beautifully eroded clay; and yucca blossoms, so pure, so waxy, but lousy with creeping white flies. Independence, Missouri, the starting point of the Old Oregon Trail; and Abilene, Kansas, the home of the Wild Bill Something Rodeo. Distant mountains. Near mountains. More mountains; bluish beauties never attainable, or ever turning into inhabited hill after hill; south-eastern ranges, altitudinal failures as alps go; heart and sky-piercing snow-veined gray colossi of stone, relentless peaks appearing from nowhere at a turn of the highway; timbered enormities, with a system of neatly overlapping dark firs, interrupted in places by pale puffs of aspen; pink and lilac formations, Pharaonic, phallic, "too prehistoric for words" (blasé Lo); buttes of black lava; early spring mountains with young-elephant lanugo along their spines; end-of-the-summer mountains, all hunched up, their heavy Egyptian limbs folded under folds of tawny moth-eaten plush; oatmeal hills, flecked with green round oaks; a last rufous mountain with a rich rug of lucerne at its foot.

Moreover, we inspected: Little Iceberg Lake, somewhere in Colorado, and the snow banks, and the cushionets of tiny alpine flowers, and more snow, down which Lo in red-peaked cap tried to slide, and squealed, and was snowballed by some youngsters, and retaliated in kind *comme on dit.* Skeletons of burned aspens, patches of spired blue flowers. The various items of a scenic drive. Hundreds of scenic drives, thousands of Bear Creeks, Soda Springs, Painted Canyons. Texas, a drought-struck plain. Crystal Chamber in the longest cave in the world, children under 12 free, Lo a young captive. A collection of a local lady's homemade sculptures, closed on a miserable Monday morning, dust, wind, witherland. Conception Park, in a town on the Mexican border which I dared not cross. There and elsewhere, hundreds of gray hummingbirds in the dusk, probing the throats of dim flowers. Shakespeare, a ghost town in New Mexico, where bad man Russian Bill was colorfully hanged seventy years ago. Fish hatcheries. Cliff dwellings. The mummy of a child (Florentine Bea's Indian contemporary). Our twentieth Hell's Canyon. Our fiftieth Gateway to something or other *fide* that tour book, the cover of which had been lost by that time. A tick in my groin. Always the same three old men, in hats and suspenders, idling away the summer afternoon under the trees near the public fountain. A hazy blue view beyond railings on a mountain pass, and the backs of a family enjoying it (with Lo, in a hot, happy, wild, intense, hopeful, hopeless whisper—"Look, the McCrystals, please, let's talk to them, please"—let's talk to them, reader!—"please! I'll do anything you want, oh, please . . ."). Indian ceremonial dances, strictly commercial.

ART: American Refrigerator Transit Company. Obvious Arizona, pueblo dwellings, aboriginal pictographs, a dinosaur track in a desert canyon, printed there thirty million years ago, when I was a child. A lanky, six-foot, pale boy with an active Adam's apple, ogling Lo and her orange-brown bare midriff, which I kissed five minutes later, Jack. Winter in the desert, spring in the foothills, almonds in bloom. Reno, a dreary town in Nevada, with a nightlife said to be "cosmopolitan and mature." A winery in California, with a church built in the shape of a wine barrel. Death Valley. Scotty's Castle. Works of Art collected by one Rogers over a period of years. The ugly villas of handsome actresses. R. L. Stevenson's footprint on an extinct volcano. Mission Dolores: good title for book. Surf-carved sandstone festoons. A man having a lavish epileptic fit on the ground in Russian Gulch State Park. Blue, blue Crater Lake. A fish hatchery in Idaho and the State Penitentiary. Somber Yellowstone Park and its colored hot springs, baby geysers, rainbows of bubbling mud—symbols of my passion. A herd of antelopes in a wildlife refuge. Our hundredth cavern, adults one dollar, Lolita fifty cents. A chateau built by a French marquess in N.D. The Corn Palace in S.D.; and the huge heads of presidents carved in towering granite. The Bearded Woman read our jingle and now she is no longer single. A zoo in Indiana where a large troop of monkeys lived on concrete replica of Christopher Columbus' flagship. Billions of dead, or halfdead, fish-smelling May flies in every window of every eating place all along a dreary sandy shore. Fat gulls on big stones as seen from the ferry *City of Cheboygan,* whose brown woolly smoke arched and dipped over the green shadow it cast on the aquamarine lake. A motel whose ventilator pipe passed under the city sewer. Lincoln's home, largely spurious, with parlor books and period furniture that most visitors reverently accepted as personal belongings.

We had rows, minor and major. The biggest ones we had took place: at Lacework Cabins, Virginia; on Park Avenue, Little Rock, near a school; on Milner Pass, 10,759 feet high, in Colorado; at the corner of Seventh Street and Central Avenue in Phoenix, Arizona; on Third Street, Los Angeles, because the tickets to some studio or other were sold out; at a motel called Poplar Shade in Utah, where six pubescent trees were scarcely taller than my Lolita, and where she asked, *à propos de rien,* how long did I think we were going to live in stuffy cabins, doing filthy things together and never behaving like ordinary people? On N. Broadway, Burns, Oregon, corner of W. Washington, facing Safeway, a grocery. In some little town in the Sun Valley of Idaho, before a brick hotel, pale and flushed bricks nicely mixed, with opposite, a poplar playing its liquid shadows all over the local Honor Roll. In a sage brush wilderness, between Pinedale and Farson. Somewhere in Nebraska, on Main Street, near the First National Bank, established 1889, with a view of a railway crossing in the vista of the street, and beyond that the white organ pipes of a multiple silo. And on

McEwen St., corner of Wheaton Ave., in a Michigan town bearing his first name.

We came to know the curious roadside species, Hitchhiking Man, *Homo pollex* of science, with all its many sub-species and forms: the modest soldier, spic and span, quietly waiting, quietly conscious of khaki's viatic appeal; the schoolboy wishing to go two blocks; the killer wishing to go two thousand miles; the mysterious, nervous, elderly gent, with brand-new suitcase and clipped mustache; a trio of optimistic Mexicans; the college student displaying the grime of vacational outdoor work as proudly as the name of the famous college arching across the front of his sweatshirt; the desperate lady whose battery has just died on her; the clean-cut, glossy-haired, shifty-eyed, white-faced young beasts in loud shirts and coats, vigorously, almost priapically thrusting out tense thumbs to tempt lone women or sadsack salesmen with fancy cravings.

"Let's take him," Lo would often plead, rubbing her knees together in a way she had, as some particularly disgusting *pollex,* some man of my age and shoulder breadth, and the face *à claques* of an unemployed actor, walked backwards, practically in the path of our car.

Oh, I had to keep a very sharp eye on Lo, little limp Lo! Owing perhaps to constant amorous exercise, she radiated, despite her very childish appearance, some special languorous glow which threw garage fellows, hotel pages, vacationists, goons in luxurious cars, maroon morons near blued pools, into fits of concupiscence which might have tickled my pride, had it not incensed my jealousy. For little Lo was aware of that glow of hers, and I would often catch her *coulant un regard* in the direction of some amiable male, some grease monkey, with a sinewy golden-brown forearm and watch-braceleted wrist, and hardly had I turned my back to go and buy this very Lo a lollipop, than I would hear her and the fair mechanic burst into a perfect love song of wisecracks.

When, during our longer stops, I would relax after a particularly violent morning in bed, and out of the goodness of my lulled heart allow her—indulgent Hum!—to visit the rose garden or children's library across the street with a motor court neighbor's plain little Mary and Mary's eight-year-old brother, Lo would come back an hour late, with barefoot Mary trailing far behind, and the little boy metamorphosed into two gangling, golden-haired high school uglies, all muscles and gonorrhea. The reader may well imagine what I answered my pet when—rather uncertainly, I admit—she would ask me if she could go with Carl and Al here to the roller-skating rink.

I remember the first time, a dusty windy afternoon, I did let her go to one such rink. Cruelly she said it would be no fun if I accompanied her, since that time of day was reserved for teenagers. We wrangled out a compromise: I remained in the car, among other (empty) cars with their noses to the canvas-topped open-air rink, where some fifty young people, many in pairs, were endlessly rolling round and round to mechanical music, and the wind silvered the trees. Dolly wore blue jeans and white high shoes, as most of the other girls did. I kept counting the revolutions of the rolling crowd—and suddenly she was missing. When she rolled past again, she was together with three hoodlums whom I had heard analyze a moment before the girl skaters from the outside—and jeer at a lovely leggy young thing who had arrived clad in red shorts instead of those jeans or slacks. . . .

There were other unpleasant incidents. There was the movie theatre once, for example. Lo at the time still had for the cinema a veritable passion (it was to decline into tepid condescension during her second high school year). We took in, voluptuously and indiscriminately, oh, I don't know, one hundred and fifty or two hundred programs during that one year, and during some of the denser periods of movie-going we saw many of the news-reels up to a half-a-dozen times since the same weekly one went with different main pictures and pursued us from town to town. Her favorite kinds were, in this order: musicals, underworlders, westerners. In the first, real singers and dancers had unreal stage careers in an essentially grief-proof sphere of existence wherefrom death and truth were banned, and where, at the end, white-haired, dewy-eyed, technically deathless, the initially reluctant father of a show-crazy girl always finished by applauding her apotheosis on fabulous Broadway. The underworld was a world apart: there, heroic newspapermen were tortured, telephone bills ran to billions, and, in a robust atmosphere of incompetent marksmanship, villains were chased through sewers and storehouses by pathologically fearless cops (I was to give them less exercise). Finally there was the mahogany landscape, the florid-faced, blue-eyed roughriders, the prim pretty schoolteacher arriving in Roaring Gulch, the rearing horse, the spectacular stampede, the pistol thrust through the shivered windowpane, the stupendous fist fight, the crashing mountain of dusty old-fashioned furniture, the table used as a weapon, the timely somersault, the pinned hand still groping for the dropped bowie knife, the grunt, the sweet crash of fist against chin, the kick in the belly, the flying tackle; and immediately after a plethora of pain that would have hospitalized a Hercules (I should know by now), nothing to show but the rather becoming bruise on the bronzed cheek of the warmed-up hero embracing his gorgeous frontier bride. I remember one matinee in a small airless theatre crammed with children and reeking with the hot breath of popcorn. The moon was yellow above the neckerchiefed crooner, and his finger was on his strumstring, and his foot was on a pine log, and I had innocently encircled Lo's shoulder and approached my jawbone to her temple, when two harpies behind us started muttering the queerest things— I do not know if I understood aright, but what I thought I did, made me withdraw my gentle hand, and of course the rest of the show was fog to me.

Another jolt I remember is connected with a little burg we were traversing at night, during our return journey. Some twenty miles earlier I had happened to tell her that day the school she would attend at Beardsley was a rather high-class, non-coeducational one, with no modern nonsense, whereupon Lo treated me to one of those furious harangues of hers where entreaty and insult, self-assertion and double talk, vicious vulgarity and childish despair, were interwoven in an exasperating semblance of logic which prompted a semblance of explanation from me. Enmeshed in her wild words (swell chance . . . I'd be a sap if I took your opinion seriously . . . Stinker . . . You can't boss me . . . I despise you . . . and so forth), I drove through the slumbering town at a fifty-mile-per-hour pace in continuance of my smooth highway swoosh, and a twosome of patrolmen put their spotlight on the car, and told me to pull over. I shushed Lo who was automatically raving on. The men peered at her and me with malevolent curiosity. Suddenly all dimples, she beamed sweetly at them as she never did at my orchideous masculinity; for, in a sense, my Lo was even more scared of the law than I—and when the kind officers pardoned us and servilely we crawled on, her eyelids closed and fluttered as she mimicked limp prostration.

At this point I have a curious confession to make. You will laugh—but really and truly I somehow never managed to find out quite exactly what the legal situation was. I do not know it yet. Oh, I have learned a few odds and ends. Alabama prohibits a guardian from changing the ward's residence without an order of the court; Minnesota, to whom I take off my hat, provides that when a relative assumes permanent care and custody of any child under fourteen, the authority of a court does not come into play. Query: is the stepfather of a gaspingly adorable pubescent pet a stepfather of only one month's standing, a neurotic widower of mature years and small but independent means, with the parapets of Europe, a divorce and a few madhouses behind him, is he to be considered a relative, and thus a natural guardian? And if not, must I, and could I reasonably dare notify some Welfare Board and file a petition (how do you file a petition?), and have a court's agent investigate meek, fishy me and dangerous Dolores Haze? The many books on marriage, rape, adoption and so on, that I guiltily consulted at the public libraries of big and small towns, told me nothing beyond darkly insinuating that the state is the super-guardian of minor children. Pilvin and Zapel, if I remember their names right, in an impressive volume on the legal side of marriage, completely ignored stepfathers with motherless girls on their hands and knees. My best friend, a social service monograph (Chicago, 1936), which was dug out for me at great pains from a dusty storage recess by an innocent old spinster, said "There is no principle that every minor must have a guardian; the court is passive and enters the fray only when the child's situation becomes conspicuously perilous." A guardian, I concluded, was appointed only when he expressed his solemn and formal desire; but months might elapse before he was given notice to appear at a hearing and grow his pair of gray wings, and in the meantime the fair daemon child was legally left to her own devices which, after all, was the case of Dolores Haze. Then came the hearing. A few questions from the bench, a few reassuring answers from the attorney, a smile, a nod, a light drizzle outside, and the appointment was made. And still I dared not. Keep away, be a mouse, curl up in your hole. Courts became extravagantly active only when there was some monetary question involved: two greedy guardians, robbed orphan, a third, still greedier, party. But here all was in perfect order, an inventory had been made, and her mother's small property was waiting untouched for Dolores Haze to grow up. The best policy seemed to be to refrain from any application. Or would some busybody, some Humane Society, butt in if I kept too quiet? . . .

I decided that at Beardsley (the site of Beardsley College for Women) I would have access to works of reference that I had not yet been able to study, such as Woerner's Treatise "On the American Law of Guardianship" and certain United States Children's Bureau Publications. I also decided that anything was better for Lo than the demoralizing idleness in which she lived. I could persuade her to do so many things—their list might stupefy a professional educator; but no matter how I pleaded or stormed, I could never make her read any other book than the so-called comic books or stories in magazines for American females. Any literature a peg higher smacked to her of school, and though theoretically willing to enjoy A Girl of the Limberlost or the Arabian Nights, or Little Women, she was quite sure she would not fritter away her "vacation" on such highbrow reading matter.

I now think it was a great mistake to move east again and have her go to that private school in Beardsley, instead of somehow scrambling across the Mexican border while the scrambling was good so as to lie low for a couple of years in subtropical bliss until I could safely marry my little Creole: for I must confess that depending on the condition of my glands and ganglia, I could switch in the course of the same day from one pole of insanity to the other—from the thought that around 1950 I would have to get rid somehow of a difficult adolescent whose magic nymphage had evaporated—to the thought that with patience and luck I might have her produce eventually a nymphet with my blood in her exquisite veins, a Lolita the Second, who would be eight or nine around 1960, when I would still be dans la force de l'âge; indeed, the telescopy of my mind, or un-mind, was strong enough to distinguish in the remoteness of time a vieillard encore vert—or was it green rot?—bizarre, tender, salivating Dr. Humbert, practicing on supremely lovely Lolita the Third the art of being a granddad.

In the days of that wild journey of ours, I doubted not that as father to Lolita the First I was a ridiculous failure. I did my best; I read and reread a book with the unintentionally biblical title Know Your Own Daughter, which I got at the same store where I bought Lo for her thirteenth birthday a de luxe volume with commercially "beautiful" illustrations, of Andersen's *The Little Mermaid*. But even at our very best moments, when we sat reading on a rainy day (Lo's glance skipping from the window to her wrist watch and back again), or had a quiet hearty meal in a crowded diner, or played a childish game of cards, or went shopping, or silently stared, with other motorists and their children, at some smashed, blood-bespattered car with a young woman's shoe in the ditch (Lo, as we drove on: "That was the exact type of moccasin I was trying to describe to that jerk in the store"); on all those random occasions, I seemed to myself as implausible a father as she seemed to be a daughter. Was, perhaps, guilty locomotion instrumental in vitiating our powers of impersonation? Would improvement be forthcoming with a fixed domicile and a routine schoolgirl's day?

In my choice of Beardsley I was guided not only by the fact of there being a comparatively sedate school for girls located there, but also by the presence of the women's college. In my desire to get myself *casé*, to attach myself somehow to some patterned surface which my stripes would blend with, I thought of a man I knew in the department of French at Beardsley College; he was good enough to use my textbook in his classes and had attempted to get me over once to deliver a lecture. I had no intention of doing so, since, as I have once remarked in the course of these confessions, there are few physiques I loathe more than the heavy low-slung pelvis, thick calves and deplorable complexion of the average coed (in whom I see, maybe, the coffin of coarse female flesh within which my nymphets are buried alive); but I did crave for a label, a background, and a simulacrum. . . .

Finally, there was the money question. My income was cracking under the strain of our joy-ride. True, I clung to the cheaper motor courts; but every now and then, there would be a loud hotel de luxe, or a pretentious dude ranch, to mutilate our budget; staggering sums, moreover, were expended on sightseeing and Lo's clothes, and the old Haze bus, although a still vigorous and very devoted machine, necessitated numerous minor and major repairs. In one of our strip maps that has happened to survive among the papers which the authorities have so kindly allowed me to use for the purpose of writing my statement, I find some jottings that help me compute the following. During that extravagant year 1947–1948, August to August, lodgings and food cost us around 5,500 dollars; gas, oil and repairs, 1,234, and various extras almost as much; so that during about 150 days of actual motion (we covered about 27,000 miles!) plus some 200 days of interpolated standstills, this modest *rentier* spent around 8,000 dollars, or better say 10,000 because, unpractical as I am, I have surely forgotten a number of items.

And so we rolled East. I more devastated than braced with the satisfaction of my passion, and she glowing with health, her bi-iliac garland still as brief as a lad's although she had added two inches to her stature and eight pounds to her weight. We had been everywhere. We had really seen nothing. And I catch myself thinking today that our long journey had only defiled with a sinuous trail of slime the lovely, trustful, dreamy, enormous country that by then, in retrospect, was no more to us than a collection of dog-eared maps, ruined tour books, old tires, and her sobs in the night—every night, every night—the moment I feigned sleep.

◇

Vladimir Nabokov was born in St. Petersburg, Russia, in 1899, left Russia in 1919, took his degree at Trinity College, Cambridge University in England, lived in many parts of Western Europe until 1940, when he came to the United States, taught at Stanford, Wellesley, and Cornell, became an American citizen in 1945, and in recent years has been living in Switzerland. He has twice been awarded Guggenheim fellowships and has also had an award from the National Academy of Arts and Letters. We will not attempt his bibliography, for Nabokov began writing novels in Russian in 1924, there are many of them, and he has been reissuing them in his own English translation or in translations supervised by him. His fiction with an American setting seems limited to three books so far: Lolita, *which was written between 1949 and 1954, published by the Olympia Press in Paris in 1955 and by G. P. Putnam's Sons in New York in 1958;* Pnin (1957), *an amusing and poignant account of the adventures of a Russian emigré professor on an American college campus; and* Pale Fire (1963), *a thousand-line poem annotated by a madman, in which the American setting, although relevant, is not used to the extent it is in* Pnin *and* Lolita. *It may be objected that it is not playing the game fairly to include Nabokov's work in an anthology designed to prove the excellence of contemporary American fiction, on the ground that he is a high-powered European ringer. To this contention we answer with the fact, mentioned above, that he is an American citizen; with his own statement, quoted below, that he is "trying to be an American writer"; and with the countercontention that to deny ourselves Nabokov as an American writer would be equivalent to excluding Joseph Conrad from the ranks of English novelists.*

As everyone must know, even if he had not deduced it from the excerpt reprinted above, Lolita *purports to be the memoir of one Humbert Humbert, a middle-aged European man who is attracted only by "nymphets," who manages, first by marrying the widowed Charlotte Haze and then by quick action after her timely death, to abscond with her twelve-year-old daughter, Dolores. The sections excerpted above for the accuracy and beauty with which they describe the American roadside scene, as experi-*

enced by Humbert and Dolores on their first transcontinental ramble, should be thought of only as an introduction, not as a sample, to anyone who has not read the whole of this marvelous novel. In a note appended to the American edition of Lolita, Nabokov has some interesting things to say about the reaction of readers: "An otherwise intelligent reader who flipped through the first part described Lolita as 'Old Europe debauching young America,' while another flipper saw it: 'Young America debauching old Europe.'" Nabokov continues:

"Another charge which some readers have made is that Lolita is anti-American. This is something that pains me considerably more than the idiotic accusation of immorality. Considerations of depth and perspective (a suburban lawn, a mountain meadow) led me to build a number of North American sets. I needed a certain exhilarating milieu. Nothing is more exhilarating than philistine vulgarity. But in regard to philistine vulgarity there is no intrinsic difference between Palearctic manners and Nearctic manners. Any proletarian from Chicago can be as bourgeois (in the Flaubertian sense) as a duke. I chose American motels instead of Swiss hotels or English inns only because I am trying to be an American writer and claim only the same rights that other American writers enjoy. On the other hand, my creature Humbert is a foreigner and an anarchist, and there are many things, besides nymphets, in which I disagree with him. And all my Russian readers know that my old worlds—Russian, British, German, French—are just as fantastic and personal as my new one is. . . .

"After Olympia Press, in Paris, published the book, an American critic suggested that Lolita was the record of my love affair with the romantic novel. The substitution 'English language' for 'romantic novel' would make this elegant formula more correct. But here I feel my voice rising to a much too strident pitch. None of my American friends have read my Russian books and thus every appraisal on the strength of my English ones is bound to be out of focus. My private tragedy, which cannot, and indeed should not, be anybody's concern, is that I had to abandon my natural idiom, my untrammeled, rich, and infinitely docile Russian tongue for a second-rate brand of English, devoid of any of those apparatuses—the baffling mirror, the black velvet backdrop, the implied associations and traditions—which the native illusionist, frac-tails flying, can magically use to transcend the heritage in his own way."

It is not characteristic of Nabokov to denigrate his work; even if one thought he were more serious, it would be necessary to disagree with his assessment as "a second-rate brand of English" the wonderfully fluid and rich prose used in Lolita to describe American countryside, to show how it has been despoiled by the motels, signs, junkyards, gas stations, and other uglinesses cast up or off by our careless commercial culture. The roadside view of our "lovely, trustful, dreamy, enormous country" has been defiled and corrupted by this commercialism in a way that seems analogous to the "sinuous trail of slime" left by poor Dolores and Humbert.

WARREN MILLER

Chaos, Disorder and the Late Show

◇◇◇◇◇◇◇

I AM A CERTIFIED PUBLIC ACCOUNTANT and a rational man. More exactly, and putting things in their proper order, I am a rational man first and an accountant second. I insist on order; I like the symbols of order—a blunt, hardy plus sign or a forthright minus delights me. I make lists, I am always punctual, I wear a hat. Maltz believes this has caused my hairline to recede. Maltz is one of my associates at the office. He married too young and he regrets it.

In fact, there is no scientific foundation for his view that wearing a hat causes the hairline to recede. Such things are largely a matter of heredity, although my father has a luxuriant head of hair. But what of my grandfathers? I have no doubt that one of them accounts for my high forehead. Talent, I believe I have read somewhere, often skips a generation or jumps from uncle to nephew. Studies have been made. Naturally there are exceptions. But it provides one with the beginning of an explanation. The notion of having been an adopted child is a fancy I have never indulged. I have never doubted that my parents are my true parents. But I sometimes suspect they think I am not their true son.

Let me say just this about my father: He is a high-school history teacher, and every summer for twenty-five years he has had a three-month vacation. Not once has he ever put this time to any real use. He could have been a counselor at a camp, taught the summer session, clerked at a department store or . . . any number of things. I recall that he spent one entire summer lying on the sofa, reading. Some years he goes to the beach. Once he went to Mexico. His income is, to be sure, adequate, But I am certain that one major illness would wipe out his savings. I have tried to speak to him about preplanning; he listens, but he does not seem to hear.

My mother—I think this one example will suffice—my mother believes that Leslie Howard, who was a Hollywood actor killed in the war, is still alive. My father merely smiles when she speaks of Leslie Howard—I believe he actually enjoys it—but I have brought home almanacs and circled references in *Harper's* and other magazines attesting to the fact that Leslie Howard is, in fact and in truth, dead. Definitive proof.

Not that I care; not that I care very deeply. It is a harmless-enough delusion; but it is sloppy. I believe that the world tends naturally to chaos and that we all have to make our daily—even hourly—contribution toward order. My parents, in my opinion, are unwilling to shoulder their share of this responsibility.

I have, once or twice, discussed the matter with Maltz, whose wife has proved to be unreliable in some ways and who has a sympathy in matters of this kind. Maltz agrees that my father is mistaken in his indulgent attitude; on the other hand, he believes it would, perhaps, be better psychologically if I ignored my mother's pitiful little delusion—as he called it.

But it is like a pebble in my shoe or loose hair under my shirt collar. Chaos and disorder in the world, in the natural scheme of things, is bad enough; one does not want to have to put up with it at home too. The subways are dirty and unreliable; the crosstown buses are not properly spaced; clerks in stores never know where their stock is.

The extent of the breakdown is incredible. Every year at this time I rent an empty store on upper Broadway and help people with their income-tax returns. These people keep no records! They have no receipts! They lose their canceled checks! They guess! The year just past is, to them, a fast-fading and already incomplete collection of snapshots. It was full of medical and business expenses and deductions for entertaining, yet they remember nothing. Believe me, the chaos of subways and crosstown buses and our traffic problems is as nothing compared to the disorder in the heads of *people*. Every year I am struck with this anew.

This extra-time work continues for three months and becomes more intense as deadline time draws near. It is amazing how many people wait until the last possible moment. Often I am there until nearly midnight.

At the beginning of March I hire Maltz and pay him by the head. He is not as fast as I would like, but he is reliable and, because of his wife and her extravagances, he needs the money. "It would embarrass me," he says, "if I had to tell you how much she spends every week on magazines alone."

Poor guy.

I live with my parents. The store I rent is near their apartment, a matter of three blocks, walking distance. It is a neighborhood of small shops and large supermarkets which once were movie houses; their marquees now advertise turkeys and hams. Maltz occasionally will walk me to my door.

That night, the night of the incident, it was snowing. It had been snowing all day. No one had cleaned his sidewalk, and it made walking treacherous. I almost slipped twice.

"Isn't there a city ordinance about people cleaning their sidewalks? Isn't it mandatory?" I asked.

Maltz said, "There is such an ordinance, Norman, but it is more honored in the breach than in the practice."

The sadness of his marriage has given Maltz a kind of wisdom. The next time he slipped I took his arm, and I thought, Here is a man who might one day be my friend. The loneliness of the mismated is a terrible thing to see. It touches me. I believe I understand it. At the door of my building I said good night and I watched for a moment as Maltz proceeded reluctantly toward home.

The elevator was out of order again. When a breakdown occurs, tenants must use the freight elevator at the rear of the lobby. I had to ring for it three times and wait more than five minutes; then I had to ride up with two open garbage cans. It was not very pleasant. The elevator man said, "How's business, Mr. Whitehead?"

"Very good, thank you, Oscar," I said.

"I'll be in to see you real soon, Mr. Whitehead."

I nodded. I knew he'd wait, as he did last year, until the last possible moment. I tried to shrug it off. It's no good trying to carry the next man's share on your own shoulders, I told myself. Forget it, I thought.

Because I had come up in the freight elevator, I therefore entered our apartment by way of the kitchen. I took off my rubbers and carried them in with me, my briefcase in the other hand. As a result the door slammed shut, since I had no free hand to close it slowly.

"Is it you?" my mother called.

She was at the kitchen table having her midnight cup of tea; she said it calmed her and made sleeping easier to have tea before bed. I have tried to explain to her that tea has a higher percentage of caffeine than coffee, but she continues to drink it.

She was smiling.

"What is it?" I said.

"Mr. Know-it-all, come here and I would like to show you something."

She had a newspaper on the table. I did not move. "What is it?" I asked.

"Come here and I will show you, Norman," she said, still smiling.

At this point my father shouted something unintelligible from their bedroom.

"What did you say, dear? What?"

"Bette Davis on the late show. *Dark Victory!*"

My mother put her hand to her heart. "I remember the day I saw it," she said. "At the Rivoli, with Millie Brandon." She sat there, staring at nothing; she had forgotten all about me.

"What was it you wanted, Mother?" I said.

"Twenty-five cents if you got there before noon, would you believe it," she said.

I looked at the newspaper. I was astonished to see that she had brought such a newspaper into the house. There it was, beside her teacup, one of those weekly papers that always has headlines such as: MOTHER POISONS HER FIVE BABIES or TAB HUNTER SAYS "I AM LONELY." The inside pages, I have been told, are devoted to racing news.

"Mr. Know-it-all," she said and began to smile again.

"What are you doing with *that* paper, Mother?"

"Millie called me this afternoon and I ran out and bought it. Look!" she cried, and with an all-too-typical dramatic flourish she unfolded it and showed me the front page. The headline read: LESLIE HOWARD STILL ALIVE.

"So much for your almanacs and your definitive proof," she said. "Now what have you got to say, my dear?"

"Two minutes, dear," my father called in to her. "Commercial on now."

"Coming," she called back.

"Mother," I said, "you know very well what kind of paper this is."

"Why should they pick this subject?" she said, tapping the headline with her fingernail. "Why should they pick this particular subject right out of the blue? I would like to ask you that."

"Did you read the article itself, Mother? Is there one iota of hard fact in it?"

"There are facts, and there are facts, my dear boy."

I was very patient with her. "Mother," I said, "he is dead. It is well known that he is dead. He went down at sea in a transport plane. . . ."

"First of all, Mr. Smart One, it was not a transport. It was a Spitfire. He always flew Spitfires. He and David Niven."

"Well, then, Mother, just tell me this," I said. "If he's alive, where is he? Where is he?"

"It's starting, dear," my father called.

"The loveliest man who ever walked this earth," she said.

"I have never had the pleasure of seeing him, Mother."

"Steel-rimmed glasses. A pipe. Tweed jackets."

"Well, where is he, Mother?"

"So gentle. Gentle, yet dashing. If everybody was like Leslie Howard, wouldn't this be one beautiful world. Oh, what a beautiful world it would be!"

"Under no circumstances would I trust that particular newspaper," I said.

"This newspaper, my dear boy, is like every other newspaper. It is sometimes right."

I put my rubbers under the sink.

"The year you were born I saw him in *Intermezzo,* Ingrid Bergman's first American movie. Produced by Selznick, who was then still married, I believe, to Louis B. Mayer's daughter Irene." She sipped her tea and looked at the headline. She said, "These days they don't even name boys Leslie anymore. *Girls* are now named Leslie. Before the war people had such lovely names. Leslie, Cary, Myrna, Fay, Claudette. What has happened?"

She looked at me as if it were all my fault. "I don't know what's happened, Mother," I said, perhaps a little testily.

"It's your world, my dear; therefore you should know," she said. "Nowadays they even name them after the days of the week."

"I have named no one after any day of the week, Mother," I said, but she was not listening.

"You could always find a parking place. People were polite. Self-service was unheard of. Frozen food was something to be avoided at all costs."

"I can put no confidence at all in that particular newspaper," I said. "Absolutely none."

"Then I am sorry for you and I pity you," she said in a manner that I thought entirely uncalled for.

"Why? Why should you be sorry for me and pity me?" I asked.

I waited for her to answer, but she went back to sipping her tea and reading the headline.

"I have a good job," I said, "and I am doing the work I like."

"Nevertheless, Norman, I feel sorry for you."

I had not even taken off my overcoat, and I was forced to put up with an attack of this nature! I was struck by the unfairness of it. I said, "You *know* what a silly newspaper that is, Mother. What is the matter with you? You know he is dead. I know you know it. Everybody knows that he is dead."

She banged down her cup. "He is not!" she said. "He is not dead! He is not!"

"What's going on in there?" my father called.

"He is alive!"

"Then where is he?" I demanded, and I raised my voice, too; I admit that I raised my voice. "Where is he?"

"Oh," she said as if she were completely disgusted with me. "Oh, Mr. Born Too Late, I'll tell you where he is," she said, getting up from her chair, the newspaper in her hand. And she began to hit me on the head with it. She hit me on the head with it. Every time she mentioned a name she hit me. "I'll tell you where he is, I'll tell you where he is. He is with Carole Lombard and Glenn Miller and Will Rogers and Franklin . . ."

I ran out of the room. Why argue? She has a harmless delusion. From now on I will try to ignore her when she gets on this particular subject. Maltz may be right about this. I hung up my coat. Fortunately it is only when I stand at my closet door that I can hear the sound of their television set, which often goes on until three in the morning. Once I shut that door, however, my room is perfectly silent.

◇

Warren Miller called his second novel The Way We Live Now, *a title that Anthony Trollope had used a hundred years before and that we now use for the first part of this book. There is something about the phrase "the way we live now" that implies that it isn't the way we ought to live; it reflects something of the disapproval writers have always felt for the society in which they live. Trollope's novel describes the unhappiness caused by marriages arranged to exchange money for titles in mid-nineteenth-century London; Miller's novel describes the unhappiness of the young divorced adrift in mid-twentieth-century New York. The marriage customs described could scarcely be more different—and there seems even more than a century's difference in tone and method between Trollope and Miller—yet the two books both brilliantly do what fiction does best: they describe how things are and how things work in a given time and place, demonstrating cultural patterns dynamically in action, and then indicating the true meaning of them, their consequences to the individual. Miller's work is always splendidly in this tradition, always emphasizing the particularity of the point of view as he develops his social satire, always speaking as well as seeing through a highly individualized narrator. Miller died in 1966, when he was forty-five, so we won't have the Trollope-wide shelf of novels we might have had from him to illuminate our times as Trollope's did his—for while he lived Miller was prolific too, publishing often under pseudonyms—and also political, one of the few contemporary writers who successfully mix fiction and politics. He wrote a nonfiction book about Cuba under Castro,* Ninety Miles from Home *(1961), and many short stories and articles that have not yet been collected. And he published six novels:* The Sleep of Reason, *a roman à clef about the McCarthy hearings, published in England in 1956 but in America not until 1960;* The Way We Live Now *(1958);* The Cool World *(1959), a popular and revealing book about gang wars in New York City;* Flush Times *(1962), about Cuba before and during the revolution;* Looking for the General *(1964), a chronicle of the lunatic fringe in America; and* The Siege of Harlem *(1964), in which Harlem is imagined to have declared itself a separate country. All his work tells us much about our times, but times—as we have constantly noted—change rapidly now. Miller's work was always very topical, and although the loss of such a fine, serious, and prolific writer is already deeply felt, it is certain to be even more so as we find ourselves without his comment on the decades to come.*

In "Chaos, Disorder and the Late Show" Miller uses the limitations of the special language and point of view of the self-styled "rational man" to give us a humorous, lightly sketched but entirely believable portrait of the conflict between rational man and the irrational forces of faith, fantasy, pleasure, and indulgence reduced to its lowest common denominators—the CPA and TV. Although he tries to exorcise it "psychologically," his mother's "pitiful little delusion" about the immortality of Leslie Howard irritates Norman because it is "sloppy"; chaos and disorder frame his world, attack him at every turn, whereas the Late Show sustains those who can believe in movie stars as gods and heroes. While the tone of the story is light, the sense of the restrictions, fears, and final "silence" of the rational man are suffocating, as Miller meant them to be. The "incident" in the story turns on the question of faith in the immortality of an ideal, of the continued existence "somewhere" of the "gentle, yet dashing" Leslie Howard, but the nature of each of the conflicting belief systems of these "mismated" generations is indicated by evocative detail. This apparently meandering little tale follows an exacting progression in the development of the characteristics of rational man. He believes in "putting things in their proper order," which involves him in mathematics and the "scientific foundation" of the facts available—"studies have been made"—as "the beginning of an explanation" for anything, from hairlines to heredity. "Real use" of time does not include his father's way of reading for pleasure, traveling, or going to the beach; "real use" of time means "preplanning" for illness and disaster. "Definitive proof" is the responsibility of man because "the world tends naturally to chaos" and "breakdown" and "the disorder in the heads of people" (other people) is the worst of all. Even walking home in the snow is "treacherous." It is rational man who is shown to be foolish, troubled, frightened, and alone, helpless against the chaos and disorder he sees everywhere because he cannot take anything on faith, nor can he tolerate the idea that anyone else can. Finally, Norman and his mother and father and Maltz are far from being extraordinary, heroic, or extreme people; the familiarity of their actions and reactions functions as a reminder of the way in which rationality has become part of the way we see the world we live in, and as a reminder that only faith in the unprovable can stand up to the poverty of spirit of the rational man in all of us.

HUGHES RUDD

Nightwatch
at Vernal Equinox

◇◇◇◇◇◇◇

"YOU CAN DO ENNYTHANG, but keep offa mah blue suede shoes!" shouts the man in the jukebox. "You can burn down mah house, you can steal mah cah, you can drink mah lickah fum a ole fruit jah!"

It is a song: he shouts it from a tight, excited throat against the frantic drumming of the rural guitars. The hidden record spinning in the bloated, winking jukebox blasts the walls of the bus station café, walls and ceiling shiny with old white enamel and the congealed grease given off by a million hamburgers; the sound bursts along the counters and booms and rattles in the glass cases of dead pie slices, crusted cake segments and soggy, oily sweet rolls.

The listless waitresses stand in the jukebox roar, their thin arms folded across their flat chests, their pimpled faces sad, stern, empty, their bodies draped in nylon uniforms. The counter top is formica, the ketchup and mustard bottles are polyethylene, the jukebox a geological age of laminated, scrolled and twisted plastics. The menus are slick in envelopes of heavy cellophane, the counter bears islands of stiffened Pliofilm turrets, scratched and blurred, squatting guard over more pie slices and cake hunks. Along the floor, lapping around the pedestals of the counter stools and the heavy base of the jukebox, running back into the darkness at the rear of the café, where the toilets are, is the dark green linoleum, filmy, curling, scaly around the pedestals.

"I'm waiting for a climax," says a man seated at the counter. He is fortyish, burly, heavy-shouldered with thick black hair brushed back from his forehead. His hands cradle a mug of coffee, and on the backs of his hands the hair is black and curling and thick. He wears a brown suit, brown shoes, and a muffler in place of a necktie. The muffler is of Paisley

---

silk, the sort of muffler one saw twenty years ago, smooth from his chin to the buttoned V of his suit coat. On his dark, heavy, closely shaved jowls the man wears rouge, and on his mouth lipstick glares against his dark skin.

"I'm waiting for a climax," he says, not saying it to anyone in particular, staring straight ahead between two waitresses. They do not look at him: one slowly lifts an arm and carefully, as though avoiding pain, picks her teeth with a toothpick. The waitresses on the night watch don't listen to anything other than orders for hamburgers, pie, cake or coffee. They do not hear the word "climax," do not wonder at the man's meaning, do not suspect him of speaking of sex, since they have another word for that part of sex but never use it, since they have never experienced it and cannot, except to please their men and repeat by rote some faintly recalled dirty jokes, even believe in it.

And they are right. The man is not talking about that: he is just waiting, waiting, as he has waited in the midwestern town's bus station café for how many nights, waiting for the buses pounding down the bricks of U.S. Highway 81, pounding out of the night, through the sleeping countryside and into the dozing, fitful city, a barren city of grain elevators, department stores, the hot iron and grit and slam of railroad yards, and the people, midwestern people.

But these are not the midwestern people here in the café of the bus station or its café. The night people are unknown to the owners of the home, packed in the red and brown brick buildings near the center of town, ranked in the white frame houses farther out, and arranged in the ranch-style ramblers, farther out still. The farther you live from the center of town the less likely it is that you have ever seen the interior of the bus station or its café. The night people are unknown to the owners of the ranch-style ramblers, who have their own problems and disasters: obesity, fallen wombs, perforated stomach linings, sleeplessness in the nights and drowsiness in the afternoons, breast lumps, monstrous uterine cauliflowers and the occasional child who is not quite right in the head, the matching automatic washers and dryers in the new pastel shades, the walk-in deep freezers, the problems of space, of where to store things.

In one of the ramblers lives a young woman with husband and children. In college she did many things: she read some of Franz Kafka, for instance, but mistook him for a science fiction writer. She is fascinated by grotesques but has never, to her knowledge, known any. Although the state has gone Republican in every election since it was admitted to the union she always votes Democratic and is a Democratic worker, giving teas for lady Democrats, organizing discussion groups, attending night classes in the humanities at the city's university, interested in high fidelity phonograph records, a subscriber to *The Reporter* magazine, a giver of patio barbecue dinners in the California manner, a singer of American folk songs with her husband and children, a writer of protest letters to the city's newspaper, a subscriber to symphony concerts, a follower of much of John Dewey's philosophy, a smiling believer in the newer versions of psychoanalysis, an indignant racist in reverse, intellectually anti-Communist, a foe of private power projects on the public domain, and not too certain of her attitude toward the distant and historic Moral Rearmament movement. Her husband keeps an atomizer full of vermouth with which he makes his celebrated martinis, earns twelve thousand dollars a year and is extremely interested in the Great Books program. The city is not really their kind of city, but there are the children and their little friends to be thought of, and the children have a subscription to the *National Geographic* and own all of the Little Golden Books.

So the night people in the bus station are far, far from the rambler folk. Some of the students at the university are aware of this distance, and they come to the bus station café after a night of drinking cheap whiskey or alcohol and grape juice. They want to see life as it is really lived, stripped of all illusion. They feel, after a course in the university's humanities sequence (modeled on that of the University of Chicago), that something is wrong: for a time they are uncomfortable with their illusions and those of the parents who are supporting them, and they come to the bus station café to see life without illusions, to lose, if possible, their own. The town is not large; the bus station café must serve as their Montparnasse, their North Beach, their Greenwich Village, their underground. It never works the other way: the night people do not go out into the suburbs to peer through picture windows into lighted living rooms, to finger the chill metal of cars in the nighttime driveways. Very probably they would be arrested if they did, but there's more to it than that: they don't want to go to the suburbs. It is this fact, more than any other thing they know about the night people, which disturbs and attracts the students. Is this what happens in an illusionless world? Peculiar!

Because the students are in transition, spies and yet not really spies, thieves of experience and yet not really thieves. They have not yet suffered that corrosion which will eat away their passion for intangibles and clear them out, making room for objects, for things, machinery, appliances, insurance policies, memberships, the older identity. At present all they want of that identity is new clothes, a motor car and spending money, as it is called, and these are not the same as the other appliances and machinery. These are for sex, they say: without them there can be no sex, since their girls have not yet been cleared out either and so will not go to a motel or a hotel to do the things they will do in parked motor cars. Conversely, the waitresses in the bus station café will not do the things in a motor car they will do in a motel or a hotel, but most of the students are not aware of that, and in any case the waitresses would not suffice. As part-time spies and thieves the students find the waitresses a little too obvious, not mysterious, as are the girls in the parked motor cars. Occasionally a student couples with a waitress or a prostitute, but the experience is never entirely satisfactory. It is too straightforward, too well illuminated, not like the movies at all: the wrestling in the parked car with its invisible culmination is more like the movies, since the radio plays its background music and the darkness is glamorous and kind to errors.

But the experience in the parked cars does not strike the students with the blow of reality, since reality must be unpleasant: otherwise, they believe, it is fraudulent, middle-class. The experiences in the parked cars exist in darkness, unreal, without sociological coordinates. Here, in the bus station café, is reality, think the students, since reality is, after all, life stripped of all illusion. That nakedness makes reality a little dangerous, of course: the students are rather nervous in the café, they talk among themselves in low voices, watching the café customers furtively, nudging each other when the man in rouge and lipstick says he is waiting for a climax. But the students are ignored. To the waitresses and the customers there is nothing odd or vulnerable about the students whatever. They are recognized as fellows from the college out south, no more, and the students come to the café to sit and watch and listen, drinking the bitter coffee to clear their heads of alcohol, perhaps wasting their substances, perhaps not. It is too early to tell.

The students are not concerned with substance yet, unless their substance is to be their sex and the totems of their sex: the spending money and the motor cars now, the washer-dryer later in pastel pink, the battery-operated martini mixing rods which still lie somewhere in their futures. The professors at the university do not alarm the students much about the future: it is somebody else's future the professors are talking about, and the students are not very interested in somebody else's future. There has been too much of that sort of interest already, they tell each other in the dormitories and the beer joints, and that sort of interest has no real use whatever, so the professors drone away without alarming the students, and the students don't alarm the professors. Of course there is always one professor who is alarmed, and each semester he manages to alarm one or two students, but no more than that. He tells the students they enter as cabbage heads and they will leave as cabbage heads, but the students smile at the professor's accent, which is French. Except for one or two students who don't smile at all, but frown, and chew on pencil ends, and shift uneasily on the varnished wooden chairs in quiet, new alarm. Sometimes they raise their hands to argue, or stop the professor in the hall, and rarely, very rarely, they are so upset and gutted with alarm they go out and get drunk, or insult their parents, or join the ministry. One time, several years ago, the professor moved one girl to hopeless prostitution with his lectures on *The Brothers Karamazov,* and the girl was seen no more on campus. The professor remembers her: he thinks about her often, rather proudly, and sometimes tells new instructors about her, but never the dean.

Things like that are pretty unusual, though, and the professor who is alarmed knows they are unusual, and contents himself with less, out of necessity. Once, when he had worked himself into a state of terrible ecstasy and thunder over *War and Peace* on the final lecture of the course, he found the only response to be a question from a boy who wanted to know if they'd be required to know all that for the final examination, and this so enraged the professor that he shouted, yes, they would be required to know it, along with the number of rounds fired at the Battle of Borodino, the number of legs amputated and the number of meters of gauze used in dressing the wounds of the survivors. But he had gone too far of course: the students smiled, and there were no final examination questions about the Battle of Borodino at all.

Now, on this particular night, when the man at the bus station counter said he was waiting for a climax, at a few minutes past midnight, one of the rambler folk was dying in his ranch-style bungalow out south, three blocks from the rambler where the girl who had read Kafka lay sleepless in her half of the twin beds, thinking of Mrs. Roosevelt, Frank Lloyd Wright and her martini-famous husband, who was in Chicago attending a convention of air-conditioning engineers.

It was a dreadful night for dying, one of the first full nights of the midwestern spring. The smell of grass and damp earth came through the bedroom windows, and the birds despite the late hour made noises in the budding trees. Still, a rambler owner lay dying in his bedroom, attended by his wife and physician. His son, fourteen years old, sat on the living room couch in pajamas and bathrobe, leafing through a copy of *Motor Age*.

The dying man's wife stood by the bedside in negligee, wrung by sorrow and incomprehension, and faintly troubled by the thought of what might happen to the mattress. She could not prevent the thought: once, long ago, when she and the dying man had first been married, when she was a young housewife, crisp and fresh and sweet-tasting, a door-to-door photographer had died in the apartment next door, just as he was bending over his camera to snap the portrait of the neighbors' children. He had straightened up, gasped, and fallen backward as solidly and terrifically as a collapsing building, and before the police ambulance removed him his sphincter had relaxed and soiled the rug. The wife could not keep this out of her mind, as she sobbed and called the dying man's name.

The dying man was of some importance in the town, a builder of ranch-style ramblers, a planner of residential districts, a respected customer of banks, an outstanding member of the Toastmasters Club, a past state commander of the American Legion, a citizen in every respect. His life had run on ballasted rails, not at all like that of the long-dead door-to-door photographer, who had followed one of those uncertain and insecure callings in which, more often than not, death comes on someone else's property. And that is an awful thing, not to die in your own place, to be, to the last, dependent on harassed, impatient strangers. Your uniqueness cannot survive that.

And so the individuality, the uniqueness of the planner of subdivisions, was being preserved: the borrower of millions of dollars, the earner of hundreds of thousands, the husband, the father, the veteran, was dying at home, decaying in the bedroom of the big ranch-style rambler into a small monument, providing a reference point in the city and the family. He had not been at home, in his bed, this early for many years. He had been, as he said, active in so many organizations, and of course business did not end with the five o'clock whistle, he often said. But he had been a good family man, everyone said. Each Friday night, if he was in the city, he took his wife and son out to dinner. He had done this for many years.

It was always the same. They would be seated in the restaurant, always a quiet, wholesome place where the lighting was too bright and everything looked clean, and they would each be given a menu by the waitress, who always knew them. They would look at the items printed on the menu and the builder would talk to his wife and son:

"All right, now. See anything you like? How about the roast loin of pork with sweet potatoes and marshmallow sauce and chef's tossed green salad? You get a choice of beverage with that. Hot coffee, tea, or milk. Or the breaded veal cutlets with cream sauce, scalloped potatoes and salad Waldorf? Hm? See anything you like? They have iced tea with lemon. Fifteen cents. Hm? Or how about a nice steak? They have the club house with french fried long branch potatoes and a tossed green salad. Two seventy-five. You have a choice of delicious ice-cold tomato juice or a cup of today's soup with that. Chicken and rice with noodles, cup ten cents, bowl twenty-five. Hm? Get whatever you want, now."

He was a good man, perhaps, but it had been difficult to measure him. He had been the husband, the businessman, the father. It had been difficult to measure him.

And now he was dying, with many projects unfinished, many things left undone on this full night of spring. His voice mechanism had failed when the heart within him gave that terrible, awesome lurch and gurgle, and he lay on the bed in his underwear, looking up at the doctor and at his wife, unable to speak, smelling the damp earth smell on the air which moved softly through the bedroom windows, since it would not be necessary to turn on the air-conditioning units and seal up the house for a month or more. The heat was at least a month away. Of course, the air-conditioning units were expensive to install and to operate, but they made possible sleep in summer, and they made housekeeping much easier, too: the dust couldn't get in. The time was coming when every new house would include an air-conditioning unit as matter of factly as garbage disposal units were now included, there was no doubt about it. The ramblers would be air-conditioned. When you could offer an air-conditioned home for eleven or twelve five, why, that would be something, all right. Or even thirteen five.

Lying in his bedroom near the center of the enormous, rolling, soft, jagged and blank continent, the builder thought thus of fortifying against that intense, sinister heat which lies on the plains in summer, whether to help others to withstand nature or simply to make money for himself it was difficult to say, since it was much too complicated for such simple measurement: proud of the ranch-style homes, the subdivisions on serpentined streets planted with fully-grown trees from nurseries, hard and committed forever against the experimental in architecture, the "organic" as the great experimenter called it. And a thousand miles to the west the experimenter himself lay in his great camp of stone, wood and canvas in the desert, in the fitful sleep of the very old; and the desert camp was the generator, the source of all the split-level ramblers, as the dying man was of the youth who read *Motor Age* in the living room. A beautiful Bedouin encampment of stone, wood and canvas from which the assault was mounted each morning in the desert, the trumpet and campaign of architecture-made man, warring with the builder's man-made architecture, houses against homes.

The girl who had once read Kafka couldn't sleep. She lay on her half of the twin beds in a pink nylon nightgown, her body fresh and warm and soft, her mind urgent with indecision. The legends of gods and of Christ had been invented to make man feel guilty, and yet it began to look as though psychoanalysis was not a satisfactory substitute. There was always another guilt lying beneath the one the analyst pulled off. She was not aware of any particularly strong feelings of guilt in herself, nor had she ever visited an analyst, but the subject was interesting, and important. Many of her friends had suffered *post partem* breakdowns or crackups, because they had failed to keep their minds occupied. They had stagnated into housewives, and when the pressures came that was not enough, she knew. They should have kept themselves interested in important things. Her husband always agreed with her. The town really was not their kind of place at all, in spite of the fact that the nation's most famous psychiatric clinic was only sixty miles away. The *post partem* cases whose parents could afford it were sent there, where they made costume jewelry from sterling silver wire, as they regained their equilibrium in the occasional company of disturbed movie stars. The clinic was an annex of the good life and the staff was remarkably successful in returning rehabilitated housewives to the subdivisions, the returnees were encouraged to talk freely of their experiences to those of their friends who had not yet been to the clinic. It was even suggested smilingly that the use of such expressions as "When I was in the bughouse" or "While the headshrinkers had me" would help remove the embarrassment the friends were sure to feel in the returnees' presence. There was nothing to be ashamed of: the staff emphasized that quite strongly.

And of course there was not, the girl who had once read Kafka told herself. The fact that the clinic's staff would even feel it necessary to point that out showed you how this part of the country really wasn't what you'd like it to be.

Impatiently, she rose from her airfoam mattress and walked to the open window. She stood looking out into the darkness, a gentle breeze pressing the pink nylon against her body. The smell of the night made her sad, nostalgic for some time or place she couldn't name; she thought of sea-coasts and forests, of wild birds migrating, of surf bursting on rocks she'd never seen. She smelled the hot pine gum of faraway woods, the dust of deserts and southwestern towns, the perfume of bakeries at midnight in strange cities. Life, it seemed to her, was being lived elsewhere, not here in her city. She felt that her ideas and interests were false, second-hand: she was only a spectator, and terribly removed from the spectacle. She sighed, she ran her fingers through her hair and thought, I'll go out for a drive. I can't sleep, I'll go out for a drive, and guiltily, she dressed.

It was a night when sailors walk the streets and giggle, calling to the girls, sailors combing their hair with combs they take from blouse pockets bulged with cigarette packs, saying, "Hey! Where ya goin'?" whipping the combs through their hair and then restoring them to tiny pockets in the blouses.

I'll get old and nothing will ever happen to me, thought the girl who had once read Kafka, driving slowly down the main street, watching the sailors, the delivery boys, the soldiers, the salesmen and the girls. It's Saturday night for everybody but me, she thought, listening to the music on the car radio. Cats moved toward black alleys, as certain and contemptuous as Arabs, and the store windows spilled blue-white light onto the gritty side-walks to throw crumpled candy wrappers into crisp relief. Objects filled the windows: synthetic silk stockings displayed on clear plastic legs kicked and died in the cold fluorescence; cellulose fibers from the giant molecules were fluffed to look like fur, and one window was crammed with hideously tortured handbags of simulated Mexican leather, burned and scarred with imitation Mexican designs, as shiny as varnish, as slick as grease. Above the popcorn stand an electric bug killer snapped and popped, electrocuting moths and June bugs: ten thousand corpses lay around the popcorn vendor's feet as he ladled hot coconut oil over the swollen kernels.

The girl in the car drove on toward the bus station café and passed it and crossed the Santa Fe tracks and turned onto the bridge, crossing the river and picking up speed, hoping to catch up with something. On the horizon lightning glared, swelling and fading, far away and silent, playing in the terrible beginning thunderheads of summer's coming, at thirty thousand feet.

And oh, dear reader, how pleasant it would be if the girl who couldn't sleep had perhaps picked up a sailor, or dropped by the bus station café for coffee and saved the lipsticked man who was waiting for a climax, or had met the students and they had all resolved one another, leading to divorce, to scandal and farewell to the rambler and the vermouth atomizer! Would that be pleasant? Or perhaps the girl should've found that life was busy in the city along with death, and discovered a June bug's oily corpse in a bag of hot popcorn, and thought of her children, those devoted readers of the Golden Books, and returned to her airfoam bed a wiser woman with a husband all unknowing at his convention in Chicago, her connubial obligations all intact, ready now to wait, no matter where she was in summer, for compassion to come and fill her up. Would that be pleasant?

Well, that's not the way that summer was, a long five years ago, dear reader: the great old man is dead, and the man who built the ramblers is dead, and his son sells used motor cars in Los Angeles, and there are new students in the bus station café each night, and very often the girl who had read Kafka cannot sleep. She can't understand that sleeplessness, not really: her husband now makes seventeen thousand dollars a year because the rambler builder had been right, almost every home is air-conditioned now, and air-conditioning engineers are doing very well, and the children are doing very well in school (they now get all the Landmark Series instead of the Golden Books), and she has avoided, so far, the great psychiatric clinic sixty miles away, although it seems a little closer, more accessible and less expensive, each time that summer comes.

❖

Hughes Rudd was born in Waco, Texas, in 1921, was educated at the University of Missouri before World War II, in which he flew a Piper Cub as an artillery observer and was wounded and decorated; after the war he worked as a newspaper reporter in the Midwest, attended the University of Minnesota, and then in the early 1950s went to Stanford on a fellowship to the writing program. In recent years he has been correspondent and bureau chief in Atlanta, Chicago, Moscow, and now Bonn for the Columbia Broadcasting System. He has published one book, My Escape from the C.I.A. (and Other Improbable Events) *(1966), a collection of short stories, memoirs that read like stories, a sequence of excellent combat stories, a novel section, and an extraordinarily evocative account of the death of William Faulkner. In Rudd's work, more so even than in most modern writers, the hopelessly tragic and the hopelessly comic seem to exist side by side—sometimes, but not always, conjoined in the grotesque.*

In "Nightwatch at Vernal Equinox" the journalist's eye and the fiction writer's art are both at work to give us a marvelously precise and specific view of a kind of symbolic centerpoint on our continent, a microcosm of an America that seems to have no story, no "organic" necessity. The "story"—if it can be called that—shows that there are no "pleasant" fictional resolutions to anyone's nightwatch at vernal equinox, to anyone's vague doubts that where they are is "not their kind of place at all." America is as visible in the rouged man waiting for his "climax" in the bus station café as it is in Frank Lloyd Wright's "desert camp." Rudd implies that all of these are related to each other: that the desert camp is "the source of all the split-level ramblers," just as the suburbia is the beginning and the end for the students who "come to the bus station café to see life without illusions, to lose, if possible, their own." Yet there are insurmountable distances within the town that make these people unknown, invisible, to one another. Each way of life has "problems and disasters" ranging from the tragic to the ridiculous—and one is seen to be a part of the other. In the bus station café the waitresses and the students and the man at the counter all belong to separate worlds, all of which are different from the worlds of "the midwestern people." For the people, the good folks, are at home asleep, anyway at home, "packed in the red and brown brick buildings near the center of town, ranked in the white frame houses farther out, and arranged in the ranch-style ramblers, farther out still." Those three verbs clearly evoke the very different lives of the service workers "packed" in the center, the clerks and mechanics "ranked" farther out, and the managers and executives "arranged" in the suburbs. The story is built on the comparison of lists of belongings and attitudes of different groups, as if it were not a story. Much is made of the fact that nothing happens. A central point of the story of course is that nothing can happen—except that our great commercial society will continue to isolate itself from "the smell of grass and damp earth" with its air conditioners, which make everybody richer and cleaner, that kids will go through their educational cycles of standardized books and bus station café "reality," and that anyone who cannot sleep, like the girl who once read Kafka, is a little closer to that other "annex of the good life," the psychiatric clinic where they are "remarkably successful in returning rehabilitated housewives to the subdivisions." But even that isn't supposed to mean anything. The view is of the stifling meaninglessness of the interconnections in this microcosm of America. Yet these interconnections are seen as both layered, recurring, inevitable results of the way individual life goes on and dies out in its miniscule patterns and as the invisible, meaningless, superficial juxtaposition of a people whose search for ultimate meaning is defined by "hoping to catch up with something."

JOHN CHEEVER

The Death of Justina

❖❖❖❖❖❖❖

SO HELP ME GOD it gets more and more preposterous, it corresponds less and less to what I remember and what I expect as if the force of life were centrifugal and threw one further and further away from one's purest memories and ambitions; and I can barely recall the old house where I was raised, where in midwinter Parma violets bloomed in a cold frame near the kitchen door, and down the long corridor, past the seven views of Rome— up two steps and down three—one entered the library where all the books were in order, the lamps were bright, where there was a fire and a dozen bottles of good bourbon locked in a cabinet with a veneer like tortoise shell whose silver key my father wore on his watch chain. Fiction is art and art is the triumph over chaos (no less) and we can accomplish this only by the most vigilant exercise of choice, but in a world that changes more swiftly than we can perceive there is always the danger that our powers of selection will be mistaken and that the vision we serve will come to nothing. We admire decency and we despise death but even the mountains seem to shift in the space of a night and perhaps the exhibitionist at the corner of Chestnut and Elm streets is more significant than the lovely woman with a bar of sunlight in her hair, putting a fresh piece of cuttlebone in the nightingale's cage. Just let me give you one example of chaos and if you disbelieve me look honestly into your own past and see if you can't find a comparable experience. . . .

On Saturday the doctor told me to stop smoking and drinking and I did. I won't go into the commonplace symptoms of withdrawal but I would like to point out that, standing at my window in the evening, watching the brilliant afterlight and the spread of darkness, I felt, through the lack of these humble stimulants, the force of some primitive memory in which the coming of night with its stars and its moon was apocalyptic. I thought suddenly of the neglected graves of my three brothers on the mountainside and that death is a loneliness much crueler than any loneliness hinted at in life. The soul (I thought) does not leave the body but lingers with it through every degrading stage of decomposition and neglect, through heat, through cold, through the long winter nights when no one comes with a wreath or a plant and no one says a prayer. This unpleasant premonition was followed by anxiety. We were going out for dinner and I thought that the oil burner would explode in our absence and burn the house. The cook would get drunk and attack my daughter with a carving knife or my wife and I would be killed in a collision on the main highway, leaving our children bewildered orphans with nothing in life to look forward to but sadness. I was able to observe, along with these foolish and terrifying anxieties, a definite impairment of my discretionary poles. I felt as if I were being lowered by ropes into the atmosphere of my childhood. I told my wife—when she passed through the living room—that I had stopped smoking and drinking but she didn't seem to care and who would reward me for my privations? Who cared about the bitter taste in my mouth and that my head seemed to be leaving my shoulders? It seemed to me that men had honored one another with medals, statuary, and cups for much less and that abstinence is a social matter. When I abstain from sin it is more often a fear of scandal than a private resolve to improve on the purity of my heart, but here was a call for abstinence without the worldly enforcement of society, and death is not the threat that scandal is. When it was time for us to go out I was so lightheaded that I had to ask my wife to drive the car. On Sunday I sneaked seven cigarettes in various hiding places and drank two Martinis in the downstairs coat closet. At breakfast on Monday my English muffin stared up at me from the plate. I mean I *saw* a face there in the rough, toasted surface. The moment of recognition was fleeting, but it was deep, and I wondered who it had been. Was it a friend, an aunt, a sailor, a ski instructor, a bartender, or a conductor on a train? The smile faded off the muffin but it had been there for a second—the sense of a person, a life, a pure force of gentleness and censure—and I am convinced that the muffin had contained the presence of some spirit. As you can see, I was nervous.

On Monday my wife's old cousin, Justina, came to visit her. Justina was a lively guest although she must have been crowding eighty. On Tuesday my wife gave her a lunch party. The last guest left at three and a few minutes later Cousin Justina, sitting on the living-room sofa with a glass of good brandy, breathed her last. My wife called me at the office and I said that I would be right out. I was clearing my desk when my boss, Mac-Pherson, came in.

"Spare me a minute," he asked. "I've been bird dogging all over the place, trying to track you down. Pierce had to leave early and I want you to write the last Elixircol commercial."

"Oh, I can't, Mac," I said. "My wife just called. Cousin Justina is dead."

"You write that commercial," he said. His smile was satanic. "Pierce had to leave early because his grandmother fell off a stepladder."

Now I don't like fictional accounts of office life. It seems to me that if you're going to write fiction you should write about mountain climbing and tempests at sea, and I will go over my predicament with MacPherson briefly, aggravated as it was by his refusal to respect and honor the death of dear old Justina. It was like MacPherson. It was a good example of the way I've been treated. He is, I might say, a tall, splendidly groomed man of about sixty who changes his shirt three times a day, romances his secretary every afternoon between two and two-thirty and makes the habit of continuously chewing gum seem hygienic and elegant. I write his speeches for him and it has not been a happy arrangement for me. If the speeches are successful MacPherson takes all the credit. I can see that his presence, his tailor and his fine voice are all a part of the performance but it makes me angry never to be given credit for what was said. On the other hand if the speeches are unsuccessful—if his presence and his voice can't carry the hour—his threatening and sarcastic manner is surgical and I am obliged to contain myself in the role of a man who can do no good in spite of the piles of congratulatory mail that my eloquence sometimes brings in. I must pretend—I must, like an actor, study and improve on my pretension—to have nothing to do with his triumphs, and I must bow my head gracefully in shame when we have both failed. I am forced to appear grateful for injuries, to lie, to smile falsely and to play out a role as inane and as unrelated to the facts as a minor prince in an operetta, but if I speak the truth it will be my wife and my children who will pay in hardships for my outspokenness. Now he refused to respect or even to admit the solemn fact of a death in our family and if I couldn't rebel it seemed as if I could at least hint at it.

The commercial he wanted me to write was for a tonic called Elixircol and was to be spoken on television by an actress who was neither young nor beautiful but who had an appearance of ready abandon and who was anyhow the mistress of one of the sponsor's uncles. *Are you growing old?* I wrote. *Are you falling out of love with your image in the looking glass? Does your face in the morning seem rucked and seamed with alcoholic and sexual excesses and does the rest of you appear to be a grayish-pink lump, covered all over with brindle hair? Walking in the autumn woods do you feel that a subtle distance has come between you and the smell of wood smoke? Have you drafted your obituary? Are you easily winded? Do you wear a girdle? Is your sense of smell fading, is your interest in gardening waning, is your fear of heights increasing, and are your sexual drives as ravening and intense as ever and does your wife look more and more to you like a stranger with sunken cheeks who has wandered into your bedroom by mistake? If this or any of this is true you need Elixircol, the true juice of youth. The small economy size (business with the bottle) costs seventy-five dollars and the giant family bottle comes at two hundred and fifty. It's a lot of scratch, God knows, but these are inflationary times and who can put a price on youth? If you don't have the cash borrow it from your neighborhood loan shark or hold up the local bank. The odds are three to one that with a ten-cent water pistol and a slip of paper you can shake ten thousand out of any fainthearted teller. Everybody's doing it. (Music up and out.)* I sent this in to MacPherson via Ralphie, the messenger boy, and took the 4:16 home, traveling through a landscape of utter desolation.

Now my journey is a digression and has no real connection to Justina's death but what followed could only have happened in my country and in my time and since I was an American traveling across an American landscape the trip may be part of the sum. There are some Americans who, although their fathers emigrated from the Old World three centuries ago, never seem to have quite completed the voyage and I am one of these. I stand, figuratively, with one wet foot on Plymouth Rock, looking with some delicacy, not into a formidable and challenging wilderness but onto a half-finished civilization embracing glass towers, oil derricks, suburban continents and abandoned movie houses and wondering why, in this most prosperous, equitable, and accomplished world—where even the cleaning women practice the Chopin preludes in their spare time—everyone should seem to be so disappointed.

At Proxmire Manor I was the only passenger to get off the random, meandering and profitless local that carried its shabby lights off into the dusk like some game-legged watchman or beadle making his appointed rounds. I went around to the front of the station to wait for my wife and to enjoy the traveler's fine sense of crisis. Above me on the hill were my home and the homes of my friends, all lighted and smelling of fragrant wood smoke like the temples in a sacred grove, dedicated to monogamy, feckless childhood, and domestic bliss but so like a dream that I felt the lack of viscera with much more than poignance—the absence of that inner dynamism we respond to in some European landscapes. In short, I was disappointed. It was my country, my beloved country, and there have been mornings when I could have kissed the earth that covers its many provinces and states. There was a hint of bliss; romantic and domestic bliss. I seemed to hear the jinglebells of the sleigh that would carry me to grandmother's house although in fact grandmother spent the last years of her life working as a hostess on an ocean liner and was lost in the tragic sinking of the S.S. *Lorelei* and I was responding to a memory that I had not experienced. But the hill of light rose like an answer to some primitive dream of homecoming. On one of the highest lawns I saw the remains of a snowman who still smoked a pipe and wore a scarf and a cap but whose form was wasting away and whose anthracite eyes stared out at the view with terrifying bitterness. I sensed some disappointing greenness of spirit in the scene although I knew in my bones, no less, how like yesterday it was that my father left the Old World to found a new; and I thought of the forces that had brought stamina to the image: the cruel towns of Calabria with their cruel princes, the badlands northwest of Dublin, ghettos, despots, whorehouses, bread lines, the graves of children, intolerable hunger, corruption, persecution, and despair had generated these faint and mellow lights and wasn't it all a part of the great migration that is the life of man?

My wife's cheeks were wet with tears when I kissed her. She was distressed, of course, and really quite sad. She had been attached to Justina. She drove me home, where Justina was still sitting on the sofa. I would like to spare you the unpleasant details but I will say that both her mouth and her eyes were wide open. I went into the pantry to telephone Dr. Hunter. His line was busy. I poured myself a drink—the first since Sunday—and lighted a cigarette. When I called the doctor again he answered and I told him what had happened. "Well, I'm awfully sorry to hear about it, Moses," he said. "I can't get over until after six and there isn't much that I can do. This sort of thing has come up before and I'll tell you all I know. You see, you live in Zone B—two-acre lots, no commercial enterprises and so forth. A couple of years ago some stranger bought the old Plewett Mansion and it turned out that he was planning to operate it as a funeral home. We didn't have any zoning provision at the time that would protect us and one was rushed through the village council at midnight and they overdid it. It seems that you not only can't have a funeral home in Zone B—you can't bury anything there and you can't die there. Of course it's absurd, but we all make mistakes, don't we? Now there are two things you can do. I've had to deal with this before. You can take the old lady and put her into the car and drive her over to Chestnut Street, where Zone C begins. The boundary is just beyond the traffic light by the high school. As soon as you get her over to Zone C, it's all right. You can just say she died in the car. You can do that or if this seems distasteful you can call the mayor and ask him to make an exception to the zoning laws. But I can't write you out a death certificate until you get her out of that neighborhood and of course no undertaker will touch her until you get a death certificate."

"I don't understand," I said, and I didn't, but then the possibility that there was some truth in what he had just told me broke against me or over me like a wave, exciting mostly indignation. "I've never heard such a lot of damned foolishness in my life," I said. "Do you mean to tell me that I can't die in one neighborhood and that I can't fall in love in another and that I can't eat . . ."

"Listen. Calm down, Moses. I'm not telling you anything but the facts and I have a lot of patients waiting. I don't have the time to listen to you fulminate. If you want to move her, call me as soon as you get her over to the traffic light. Otherwise, I'd advise you to get in touch with the mayor or someone on the village council." He cut the connection. I was outraged but this did not change the fact that Justina was still sitting on the sofa. I poured a fresh drink and lit another cigarette.

Justina seemed to be waiting for me and to be changing from an inert into a demanding figure. I tried to imagine carrying her out to the station wagon but I couldn't complete the task in my imagination and I was sure that I couldn't complete it in fact. I then called the mayor but this position in our village is mostly honorary and as I might have known he was in his New York law office and was not expected home until seven. I could cover her, I thought, that would be a decent thing to do, and I went up the back stairs to the linen closet and got a sheet. It was getting dark when I came back into the living room but this was no merciful twilight. Dusk seemed to be playing directly into her hands and she gained power and stature with the dark. I covered her with a sheet and turned on a lamp at the other end of the room but the rectitude of the place with its old furniture, flowers, paintings, etc., was demolished by her monumental shape. The next thing to worry about was the children, who would be home in a few minutes. Their knowledge of death, excepting their dreams and intuitions of which I know nothing, is zero and the bold figure in the parlor was bound to be traumatic. When I heard them coming up the walk I went out and told them what had happened and sent them up to their rooms. At seven I drove over to the mayor's.

He had not come home but he was expected at any minute and I talked with his wife. She gave me a drink. By this time I was chain-smoking. When the mayor came in we went into a little office or library, where he took up a position behind a desk, putting me in the low chair of a supplicant. "Of course I sympathize with you, Moses," he said, "it's an awful thing to have happened, but the trouble is that we can't give you a zoning exception without a majority vote of the village council and all the members of the council happen to be out of town. Pete's in California and Jack's in Paris and Larry won't be back from Stowe until the end of the week."

I was sarcastic. "Then I suppose Cousin Justina will have to gracefully decompose in my parlor until Jack comes back from Paris."

"Oh no," he said, "oh *no*. Jack won't be back from Paris for another month but I think you might wait until Larry comes from Stowe. Then we'd have a majority, assuming of course that they would agree to your appeal."

"For Christ's sake," I snarled.

"Yes, yes," he said, "it is difficult, but after all you must realize that this is the world you live in and the importance of zoning can't be overestimated. Why, if a single member of the council could give out zoning exceptions, I could give you permission right now to open a saloon in your garage, put up neon lights, hire an orchestra and destroy the neighborhood and all the human and commercial values we've worked so hard to protect."

"I don't want to open a saloon in my garage," I howled. "I don't want to hire an orchestra. I just want to bury Justina."

"I know, Moses, I know," he said. "I understand that. But it's just that it happened in the wrong zone and if I make an exception for you I'll have to make an exception for everyone and this kind of morbidity, when it gets out of hand, can be very depressing. People don't like to live in a neighborhood where this sort of thing goes on all the time."

"Listen to me," I said. "You give me an exception and you give it to me now or I'm going home and dig a hole in my garden and bury Justina myself."

"But you can't do that, Moses. You can't bury anything in Zone B. You can't even bury a cat."

"You're mistaken," I said. "I can and I will. I can't function as a doctor and I can't function as an undertaker, but I can dig a hole in the ground and if you don't give me my exception, that's what I'm going to do."

"Come back, Moses, come back," he said. "Please come back. Look, I'll give you an exception if you'll promise not to tell anyone. It's breaking the law, it's a forgery but I'll do it if you promise to keep it a secret."

I promised to keep it a secret, he gave me the documents and I used his telephone to make the arrangements. Justina was removed a few minutes after I got home but that night I had the strangest dream. I dreamed that I was in a crowded supermarket. It must have been night because the windows were dark. The ceiling was paved with fluorescent light—brilliant, cheerful but, considering our prehistoric memories, a harsh link in the chain of light that binds us to the past. Music was playing and there must have been at least a thousand shoppers pushing their wagons among the long corridors of comestibles and victuals. Now is there—or isn't there—something about the posture we assume when we push a wagon that unsexes us? Can it be done with gallantry? I bring this up because the multitude of shoppers seemed that evening, as they pushed their wagons, penitential and unsexed. There were all kinds, this being my beloved country. There were Italians, Finns, Jews, Negroes, Shropshiremen, Cubans—anyone who had heeded the voice of liberty—and they were dressed with that sumptuary abandon that European caricaturists record with such bitter disgust. Yes, there were grandmothers in shorts, big-butted women in knitted pants and men wearing such an assortment of clothing that it looked as if they had dressed hurriedly in a burning building. But this, as I say, is my own country and in my opinion the caricaturist who vilifies the old lady in shorts vilifies himself. I am a native and I was wearing buckskin jump boots, chino pants cut so tight that my sexual organs were discernible and a rayon-acetate pajama top printed with representations of the *Pinta,* the *Niña* and the *Santa María* in full sail. The scene was strange—the strangeness of a dream where we see familiar objects in an unfamiliar light—but as I looked more closely I saw that there were some irregularities. Nothing was labeled. Nothing was identified or known. The cans and boxes were all bare. The frozen-food bins were full of brown parcels but they were such odd shapes that you couldn't tell if they contained a frozen turkey or a Chinese dinner. All the goods at the vegetable and the bakery counters were concealed in brown bags and even the books for sale had no titles. In spite of the fact that the contents of nothing was known, my companions of the dream—my thousands of bizarrely dressed compatriots —were deliberating gravely over these mysterious containers as if the choices they made were critical. Like any dreamer, I was omniscient, I was with them and I was withdrawn, and stepping above the scene for a minute I noticed the men at the check-out counters. They were brutes. Now sometimes in a crowd, in a bar or a street, you will see a face so full-blown in its obdurate resistance to the appeals of love, reason and decency, so lewd, so brutish and unregenerate, that you turn away. Men like these were stationed at the only way out and as the shoppers approached them they tore their packages open—I still couldn't see what they contained—but in every case the customer, at the sight of what he had chosen, showed all the symptoms of the deepest guilt; that force that brings us to our knees. Once their choice had been opened to their shame they were pushed—in some cases kicked—toward the door and beyond the door I saw dark water and heard a terrible noise of moaning and crying in the air. They waited at the door in groups to be taken away in some conveyance that I couldn't see. As I watched, thousands and thousands pushed their wagons through the market, made their careful and mysterious choices and were reviled and taken away. What could be the meaning of this?

We buried Justina in the rain the next afternoon. The dead are not, God knows, a minority, but in Proxmire Manor their unexalted kingdom is on the outskirts, rather like a dump, where they are transported furtively as knaves and scoundrels and where they lie in an atmosphere of perfect neglect. Justina's life had been exemplary, but by ending it she seemed to have disgraced us all. The priest was a friend and a cheerful sight, but the undertaker and his helpers, hiding behind their limousines, were not; and aren't they at the root of most of our troubles, with their claim that death is a violet-flavored kiss? How can a people who do not mean to understand death hope to understand love, and who will sound the alarm?

I went from the cemetery back to my office. The commercial was on my desk and MacPherson had written across it in grease pencil: *Very funny, you broken-down bore. Do again.* I was tired but unrepentant and didn't seem able to force myself into a practical posture of usefulness and obedience. I did another commercial. *Don't lose your loved ones,* I wrote, *because of excessive radioactivity. Don't be a wallflower at the dance because of strontium 90 in your bones. Don't be a victim of fallout. When the tart on Thirty-sixth Street gives you the big eye does your body stride off in one direction and your imagination in another? Does your mind follow her up the stairs and taste her wares in revolting detail while your flesh goes off to Brooks Brothers or the foreign exchange desk of the Chase Manhattan Bank? Haven't you noticed the size of the ferns, the lushness of the grass, the bitterness of the string beans and the brilliant markings on the new breeds of butterflies? You have been inhaling lethal atomic waste for the last twenty-five years and only Elixircol can save you.* I gave this to Ralphie and waited perhaps ten minutes when it was returned, marked again with grease pencil. *Do,* he wrote, *or you'll be dead.* I felt very tired. I put another piece of paper into the machine and wrote: *The Lord is my shepherd; therefore can I lack nothing. He shall feed me in a green pasture and lead me forth beside the waters of comfort. He shall convert my soul and bring me forth in the paths of righteousness for his Name's sake. Yea, though I walk through the valley of the shadow of death I will fear no evil for thou art with me; thy rod and thy staff comfort me. Thou shalt prepare a table before me in the presence of them that trouble me; thou hast anointed my head with oil and my cup shall be full. Surely thy loving-kindness and mercy shall follow me all the days of my life and I will dwell in the house of the Lord for ever.* I gave this to Ralphie and went home.

⋄

In "The Death of Justina" John Cheever contrasts the incomprehensible chaos of modern life, which distorts the nature of things, with the orderliness of older ways, which attempted to make sense of things by recognizing them for what they are. This comparison is made throughout the story in various ways, but the main consideration is how our society attempts the final inconceivable absurdity: denial of death. Moses' funny commercials for Elixircol, "the juice of youth," are really just exaggerations (by being put in the form of direct statements) of what MacPherson wants him merely to imply—that Elixircol can keep you young, reverse aging, deny death—which is the hidden message in most of the marketing methods of our commercial society. Owing to a hastily written provision, the zoning code in Moses' village says no one may die in Zone B. As the doctor tells Moses: "Of course it's absurd, but we all make mistakes, don't we?" Denial of the right to die is bureaucratic encroachment on individual rights carried to an ultimate extreme. In Moses' wonderfully ludicrous and terrifying dream, modern American life is likened to a supermarket, a good choice of analogy for a consumer society in which one is defined and identified by his choice. But in this supermarket none of the containers is labeled, and all choices are meaningless because nothing is recognizable as what it is. The people "were all kinds, this being my beloved country," of all races and origins; but now they are all "penitential and unsexed," pushing their shopping carts, all dressed alike in their bizarre American leisure wear, variegated but essentially undifferentiated and anonymous. They "were deliberating gravely" over these meaningless choices, but when they reach the check-out counter (death, of course) and are confronted with what they have chosen, the poor souls experience deep guilt and shame: the inevitable consequence of having had to choose in a world where nothing is recognizable as what it is. Then they are thrown into "some conveyance" and carted away. At the cemetery—it is "on the outskirts, rather like a dump" to which the dead "are transported furtively"— Moses sees the undertakers "hiding behind their limousines." He asks first: "Aren't they at the root of most of our troubles, with their claim that death is a violet-flavored kiss?" Then he asks the question that states the theme of the story: "How can a people who do not mean to understand death hope to understand love, and who will sound the alarm?" The second commercial Moses does for Elixircol emphasizes the freakish mutations and lush, sick brilliance of modern life under the bomb. MacPherson returns it with the note, "Do, or you'll be dead"—and by "dead" he means out-of-a-job. Moses then, in an attempt to find something that will make some sensible and meaningful reference to death, goes back to an older ritual statement of faith; as the final, ultimate Elixircol commercial, he types out the Twenty-third Psalm.

The extraordinary thing about "The Death of Justina" is that all this is done within an additional frame of meaning established by the statement in the opening paragraph. This paragraph is an example of Cheever's writing at its finest and shows how the author not only triumphs over but actually exploits for his own purposes what many critics and some writers have seen as an insuperable problem for contemporary American writers dealing with contemporary American life: the difficulty of rendering in fiction such a period of social disorganization and change. But it is ridiculous to try to paraphrase the paragraph, for Cheever says explicitly:

"Fiction is art and art is the triumph over chaos (no less) and we can accomplish this only by the most vigilant exercise of choice, but in a world that changes more swiftly than we can perceive there is always the danger that our powers of selection will be mistaken and that the vision we serve will come to nothing."

It should be explained that "The Death of Justina" appears in Cheever's unusual book, Some People, Places, and Things That Will Not Appear in My Next Novel, *and that collected under this outlandish title are eight short stories and a wonderful section at the end called "A Miscellany of Characters That Will Not Appear." "The Death of Justina" and two other stories were published in* Esquire *and all the rest of the book was published in*

The New Yorker, *but the book is much more than a collection of magazine pieces: it serves as something of an informal treatise on the joys and sorrows of writing fiction about America today. In a note at the beginning Cheever is quoted as saying: "In order to become readable again, to say nothing of recouping some of its lost importance, fiction can no longer operate as a sixth-rate boarding house." So these are the characters and situations he throws out of his next novel, and they are a marvelous group. Each of the stories begins with an expression of discontent about the material—the people or situations—that is about to be made into a story. Often these are marvelously phrased, like the opening paragraph of "The Death of Justina," or the first paragraph of "The Brigadier and the Golf Widow," which begins his most recent collection of short stories and seemingly concludes his restatements of this complaint:*

"I would not like to be one of those writers who begin each morning by exclaiming, 'O Gogol, O Chekhov, O Thackeray and Dickens, what would you have made of a bomb shelter ornamented with four plaster-of-Paris ducks, a birdbath, and three composition gnomes with long beards and red mobcaps?' As I say, I wouldn't want to begin a day like this, but I often wonder what the dead would have done. But the shelter is as much a part of my landscape as the beech and horse-chestnut trees that grow on the ridge. I can see it from this window where I write. . . ."

Of course Cheever then does go on to tell a brilliant story of a brigadier and a golf widow and a key to a fallout shelter, just as he goes on to make an interesting story out of all the unattractive and unlikely material in the other book. It is in each case the same creating of art by triumphing over chaos, refashioning the ugly and temporal into something beautiful and enduring, that we remarked on in discussing the Grecian-urn parallei in the last paragraph of "The Country Husband" (page 487). Cheever has a magician's way with his material, and his disclaimers have the effect of the magician's opening con, improving his trick. He plays to the hilt the role of the artist as sorcerer/artificer/artisan: "See," he says, "I'm going to take this ordinary lump of clay. . . . Sordid and familiar, isn't it? . . . Now see what I make out of it!"

In "A Miscellany of Characters That Will Not Appear" he presents a half-dozen beautifully realized vignettes of weak, distasteful characters, and then in the last sketch amusingly summarizes the career of a writer named Royden Blake, a marvelously malicious mixture of O'Hara and Hemingway. At the end, Royden is dying, but he's still working and from his deathbed describes his new novel. It has to do with three strangers who meet in the station café at a mountain stop of the Transalpini: a tall, bald-headed man in a sable-lined coat, a beautiful American woman whose son has been killed in a mountain-climbing accident, and a white-haired Italian woman addressed as "Your Majesty" by the waiter. Royden goes on:

"Avalanche warnings had been posted earlier in the day. . . ." Then, says Cheever:

"Then he put his head back on the pillow and died—indeed, these were his dying words, and the dying words, it seemed to me, of generations of storytellers, for how could this snowy and trumped-up pass, with its trio of travelers, hope to celebrate a world that lies spread out around us like a bewildering and stupendous dream?"

We have used the last words of this quotation as the epigraph of this book; "to celebrate a world that lies spread out around us like a bewildering and stupendous dream" seems to us the best possible statement of what are the difficulties, what ought to be the purpose, and what in fact has been the achievement of contemporary fiction.

◇–◇

The stories in this section have all shown—directly in some cases, very indirectly in others—that it is commercialism of one sort or another, made manifest in a great variety of ways, that may be at the root of what's wrong with how we live now. Commercialism has always been the basis of the American society—the force behind the giant forces that are working such indiscriminate change in our institutions and way of life. Southern shows it as endemic in the modern American character—everyone so anxious for money as to collaborate eagerly in a rich jokester's projects to "make things hot" for those who want it. Nabokov describes a once-lovely country, now ravaged by the ugliness of sleazy commercial establishments from coast to coast, with youth corrupted easily and early by our money culture's constant selling of sex and youth as the only virtues. Warren Miller shows us the calculating rationality of the CPA mind that despises a high school history teacher for spending a summer lying on a couch reading when he could be making money moonlighting as a clerk in a department store. Hughes Rudd shows the emptiness and segmentation of a representative community, from the bus station café at the center to the farthest regimented suburb, where a great architectural idea has been commercialized into standardized rows of ranch houses, all air-conditioned against the spring air. And John Cheever shows us the ultimate insanity of our commercially minded culture, mass-marketing products like Elixircol as "the juice of youth" and trying to sell us the idea that death is "a violet-flavored kiss."

But commercialism is not the only theme expressed in these stories, and they do not all have the same central idea; that it can be made to seem so is only further demonstration that serious fiction always takes account of basic issues and thus it is almost always possible to see some central force at work in any complex story about the way we live now. The eye of fiction is inseparable from the society that it reflects, distorts, remolds, and finally gives us back again as if the story were a completely independent world of its own. But in this process of translating from one reality to another the writer himself is not a simple instrument but a man whose intense belief in the necessity of what he is doing sustains him through the incredible difficulties of creating a world that is both believable as something that could have happened and is a comment on it.

In the next section we see some of the stratagems of method which express different aspects of the fiction writer's role as mediator between believable reality and a compelling vision of truth that transforms reality.

The Eye of Fiction

IN SOME STRATAGEMS

There is nothing limiting about fiction as a medium, as some writers and readers seem to believe today. The work of Henry James and James Joyce are not extremes of what the novel form is capable of, but only examples. The short story can range from something approaching the freedom of the novel to something that approaches the compression of poetry. Fiction can still reveal through realistic depiction of how we live, in entertaining stories replete with "story values" of character and plot. Or fiction can occur in forms that may seem not to be fiction at all, but resemble no other form more closely. We conclude this anthology with three short examples of this sort of fiction that doesn't seem like fiction, not in the least because we feel this is a direction in which modern fiction is going, or should go, or must go—but simply to show where it may go when subject and vision require. The limitations of an anthology prevent us from even suggesting the huge wide fields of possibility for the novel that are being exploited now by our writers. But here we can show three splendid examples of how fiction is capable of compressing and expressing the largest conceptions even toward the smaller end of the infinite scale of forms available.

And, neatly enough, each of the three stories that follow can be interpreted as presenting an analogy, three metaphors of the role of the writer: the writer as savior/immortalizer; the writer as survivor/nay-sayer; and the writer as creator/maker.

JOHN UPDIKE

Lifeguard

❖❖❖❖❖

BEYOND DOUBT, I am a splendid fellow. In the autumn, winter, and spring, I execute the duties of a student of divinity; in the summer I disguise myself in my skin and become a lifeguard. My slightly narrow and gingerly hirsute but not necessarily unmanly chest becomes brown. My smooth back turns the color of caramel, which, in conjunction with the whipped cream of my white pith helmet, gives me, some of my teenage satellites assure me, a delightfully edible appearance. My legs, which I myself can study, cocked as they are before me while I repose on my elevated wooden throne, are dyed a lustreless maple walnut that accentuates their articulate strength. Correspondingly, the hairs of my body are bleached blond, so that my legs have the pointed elegance of, within the flower, umber anthers dusted with pollen.

For nine months of the year, I pace my pale hands and burning eyes through immense pages of Biblical text barnacled with fudging commentary; through multivolumed apologetics couched in a falsely friendly Victorian voice and bound in subtly abrasive boards of finely ridged, pre-faded red; through handbooks of liturgy and histories of dogma; through the bewildering duplicities of Tillich's divine politicking; through the suave table talk of Father D'Arcy, Etienne Gilson, Jacques Maritain, and other such moderns mistakenly put at their ease by the exquisite antique furniture and overstuffed larder of the hospitable St. Thomas; through the terrifying attempts of Kierkegaard, Berdyaev, and Barth to scourge God into being. I sway appalled on the ladder of minus signs by which theologians would surmount the vo'd. I tiptoe like a burglar into the house of naturalism to steal the silver. An acrobat, I swing from wisp to wisp. Newman's iridescent cobwebs crush in my hands. Pascal's blackboard mathematics are erased by a passing shoulder. The cave drawings, astoundingly vital by candlelight, of those aboriginal magicians, Paul and Augustine, in daylight fade into mere anthropology. The diverting productions of literary flirts like Chesterton, Eliot, Auden, and Greene—whether they regard Christianity as a pastel forest designed for a fairyland romp or a deliciously miasmic pit from which chiaroscuro can be mined with mechanical buckets—in the end all infallibly strike, despite the comic variety of gongs and mallets, the note of the rich young man who on the coast of Judaea refused in dismay to sell all that he had.

Then, for the remaining quarter of the solar revolution, I rest my eyes on a sheet of brilliant sand printed with the runes of naked human bodies. That there is no discrepancy between my studies, that the texts of the flesh complement those of the mind, is the easy burden of my sermon.

On the back rest of my lifeguard's chair is painted a cross—true, a red cross, signifying bandages, splints, spirits of ammonia, and sunburn unguents. Nevertheless, it comforts me. Each morning, as I mount into my chair, my athletic and youthfully fuzzy toes expertly gripping the slats that make a ladder, it is as if I am climbing into an immense, rigid, loosely fitting vestment.

Again, in each of my roles I sit attentively perched on the edge of an immensity. That the sea, with its multiform and mysterious hosts, its savage and senseless rages, no longer comfortably serves as a divine metaphor indicates how severely humanism has corrupted the apples of our creed. We seek God now in flowers and good deeds, and the immensities of blue that surround the little scabs of land upon which we draw our lives to their unsatisfactory conclusions are suffused by science with vacuous horror. I myself can hardly bear the thought of stars, or begin to count the mortalities of coral. But from my chair the sea, slightly distended by my higher perspective, seems a misty old gentleman stretched at his ease in an immense armchair which has for arms the arms of this bay and for an antimacassar the freshly laundered sky. Sailboats float on his surface like idle and unrelated but benevolent thoughts. The soughing of the surf is the rhythmic lifting of his ripple-stitched vest as he breathes. Consider. We enter the sea with a shock; our skin and blood shout in protest. But, that instant, that leap, past, what do we find? Ecstasy and buoyance. Swimming offers a parable. We struggle and thrash, and drown; we succumb, even in despair, and float, and are saved.

With what timidity, with what a tense of trespass, do I set forward even this obliquely a thought so official! Forgive me. I am not yet ordained; I am too disordered to deal with the main text. My competence is marginal, and I will confine myself to the gloss of flesh with which this particular margin, this one beach, is annotated each day.

Here the cinema of life is run backwards. The old are the first to arrive. They are idle, and have lost the gift of sleep. Each of our bodies is a clock that loses time. Young as I am, I can hear in myself the protein acids ticking; I wake at odd hours and in the shuddering darkness and silence feel my death rushing toward me like an express train. The older we get, and the fewer the mornings left to us, the more deeply dawn stabs us awake.

The old ladies wear wide straw hats and, in their hats' shadows, smiles as wide, which they bestow upon each other, upon salty shells they discover in the morning-smooth sand, and even upon me, downy-eyed from my night of dissipation. The gentlemen are often incongruous; withered white legs support brazen barrel chests, absurdly potent, bustling with white froth. How these old roosters preen on their "condition"! With what fatuous expertness they swim in the icy water—always, however, prudently parallel to the shore, at a depth no greater than their height.

Then come the middle-aged, burdened with children and aluminum chairs. The men are scarred with the marks of their vocation—the red forearms of the gasoline-station attendant, the pale X on the back of the overall-wearing mason or carpenter, the clammer's nicked ankles. The hair on their bodies has as many patterns as matted grass. The women are wrinkled but fertile, like the Iraq rivers that cradled the seeds of our civilization. Their children are odious. From their gaunt faces leer all the vices, the greeds, the grating urgencies of the adult, unsoftened by maturity's reticence and fatigue. Except that here and there, a girl, the eldest daughter, wearing a knit suit striped horizontally with green, purple, and brown, walks slowly, carefully, puzzled by the dawn enveloping her thick smooth body, her waist not yet nipped but her throat elongated.

Finally come the young. The young matrons bring fat and fussing infants who gobble the sand like sugar, who toddle blissfully into the surf and bring me bolt upright on my throne. My whistle tweets. The mothers rouse. Many of these women are pregnant again, and sluggishly lie in their loose suits like cows tranced in a meadow. They gossip politics, and smoke incessantly, and lift their troubled eyes in wonder as a trio of flat-stomached nymphs parades past. These maidens take all our eyes. The vivacious redhead, freckled and white-footed, pushing against her boy and begging to be ducked; the solemn brunette, transporting the vase of herself with held breath; the dimpled blond in the bib and diapers of her Bikini, the lambent fuzz of her midriff shimmering like a cat's belly. Lust stuns me like the sun.

You are offended that a divinity student lusts? What prigs the unchurched are. Are not our assaults on the supernatural lascivious, a kind of indecency? If only you knew what de Sadian degradations, what frightful psychological spelunking, our gentle transcendentalist professors set us to, as preparation for our work, which is to shine in the darkness.

I feel that my lust makes me glow; I grow cold in my chair, like a torch of ice, as I study beauty. I have studied much of it, wearing all styles of bathing suit and facial expression, and have come to this conclusion: a woman's beauty lies, not in any exaggeration of the specialized zones, nor in any general harmony that could be worked out by means of the *sectio aurea* or a similar aesthetic superstition; but in the arabesque of the spine.

The curve by which the back modulates into the buttocks. It is here that grace sits and rides a woman's body.

I watch from my white throne and pity women, deplore the demented judgment that drives them toward the braggart muscularity of the mesomorph and the prosperous complacence of the endomorph when it is we ectomorphs who pack in our scrawny sinews and exacerbated nerves the most intense gift, the most generous shelter, of love. To desire a woman is to desire to save her. Anyone who had endured intercourse that was neither predatory nor hurried knows how through it we descend, with a partner, into the grotesque and delicate shadows that until then have remained locked in the most guarded recess of our soul; into this harbor we bring her. A vague and twisted terrain becomes inhabited; each shadow, touched by the exploration, blooms into a flower of act. As if we are an island upon which a woman, tossed by her laboring vanity and blind self-seeking, is blown, and there finds security, until, an instant before the anticlimax, Nature with a smile thumps down her trump and the island sinks beneath the sea.

There is great truth in those motion pictures which are slandered as true neither to the Bible nor to life. They are—written though they are by demons and drunks—true to both. We are all Solomons lusting for Sheba's salvation. The God-filled man is filled with a wilderness that cries to be populated. The stony chambers need jewels, furs, tints of cloth and flesh, even though, as in Samson's case, the temple comes tumbling. Women are an alien race of pagans set down among us. Every seduction is a conversion.

Who has loved and not experienced that sense of rescue? It is not true that our biological impulses are tricked out with ribands of chivalry; rather, our chivalric impulses go clanking in encumbering biological armor. Eunuchs love. Children love. I would love.

My chief exercise, as I sit above the crowds, is to lift the whole mass into immortality. It is not a light task; the throng is so huge, and its members so individually unworthy. No *memento mori* is so clinching as a photograph of a vanished crowd. Cheering Roosevelt, celebrating the Armistice, there it is, wearing its ten thousand straw hats and stiff collars, a fearless and wooden-faced bustle of life: it is gone. A crowd dies in the street like a derelict; it leaves no heir, no trace, no name. My own persistence beyond the last rim of time is easy to imagine; indeed, the effort of imagination lies the other way—to conceive of my ceasing. But when I study the vast tangle of humanity that blackens the beach as far as the sand stretches, absurdities crowd in on me. Is it as maiden, matron, or crone that the females will be eternalized? What will they do without children to watch and gossip to exchange? What of the thousand deaths of memory and bodily change we endure—can each be redeemed at a final Adjustments Counter? The sheer numbers involved make the mind scream. The race is no longer a tiny clan of simian aristocrats lording it over an ocean of grass; mankind is a plague racing like fire across the exhausted continents. This immense clot gathered on the beach, a fraction of a fraction— can we not say that this breeding swarm is its own immortality and end the suspense? The beehive in a sense survives; and is each of us not proved to be a hive, a galaxy of cells each of whom is doubtless praying, from its pew in our thumbnail or esophagus, for personal resurrection? Indeed, to the cells themselves cancer may seem a revival of faith. No, in relation to other people oblivion is sensible and sanitary.

This sea of others exasperates and fatigues me most on Sunday mornings. I don't know why people no longer go to church—whether they have lost the ability to sing or the willingness to listen. From eight-thirty onward they crowd in from the parking lots, ants each carrying its crumb of baggage, until by noon, when the remote churches are releasing their gallant and gaily dressed minority, the sea itself is jammed with hollow heads and thrashing arms like a great bobbing backwash of rubbish. A transistor radio somewhere in the sand releases in a thin, apologetic gust the closing peal of a transcribed service. And right here, here at the very height of torpor and confusion, I slump, my eyes slit, and the blurred forms of Protestantism's errant herd seem gathered by the water's edge in impassioned poses of devotion. I seem to be lying dreaming in the infinite rock of space before Creation, and the actual scene I see is a vision of impossibility: a Paradise. For had we existed before the gesture that split the firmament, could we have conceived of our most obvious possession, our most platitudinous blessing, the moment, the single ever-present moment that we perpetually bring to our lips brimful?

So: be joyful. Be Joyful in my commandment. It is the message I read in your jiggle. Stretch your skins like pegged hides curing in the miracle of the sun's moment. Exult in your legs' scissoring, your waist's swivel. Romp; eat the froth; be children. I am here above you; I have given my youth that you may do this. I wait. The tides of time have treacherous undercurrents. You are borne continually toward the horizon. I have prepared myself; my muscles are instilled with everything that must be done. Someday my alertness will bear fruit; from near the horizon there will arise, delicious, translucent, like a green bell above the water, the call for help, the call, a call, it saddens me to confess, that I have yet to hear.

◈

Of all the myriad meanings and implications of "Lifeguard" we will consider only one: that the lifeguard's peculiar role and situation has analogies to the peculiar situation and role of the author of fiction. In his lifeguard,

Updike has created a complacent, "splendid" figure of a monologist, and this characterization gives license for a fancy series of conceits, a good deal of ornate language, and a lot of general showing-off. Lifeguards are show-offs, as everyone knows; but it is the writer who is showing off here and has deliberately created the point-of-view character so that he can do so. The job of the author and the lifeguard is like that of the savior: to thwart death. The lifeguard says, "My chief exercise, as I sit above the crowds, is to lift the whole mass into immortality," and that is clearly the Sisyphean labor that every serious writer sets himself. "It is not a light task; the throng is so huge, and its members so individually unworthy," the lifeguard says, echoing the plaints of modern writers that the complexity of modern life and the unheroic nature of modern man make their material difficult to transform into fiction, the chaos too vast to be ordered. The lifeguard speaks of a photograph of a vanished crowd as a clinching memento mori: *what the lifeguard/author must do is save all these people in his own crowded times from death, immortalizing them by his work. He sits on his tower above them, observing them; he is of them, lusts for them, but is not himself with them. An accurate observer and assessor and interpreter of them, he holds the truth and would use it for their salvation. They look up to him in admiration, and from time to time he has the opportunity to warn them; in this too he reflects the position of the writer in our times. But although his purpose as lifeguard and student of God's Truth is based on past training for future events, his daily preoccupation (and his work as a writer) is with the present moment when on his tower he becomes part of the scene which he evokes and controls. His purpose is not literally to save (either souls or bodies) but to communicate the joy and beauty of the possibilities of immortality in what he sees of life around him—to hold time still for us so that we experience the moment.*

JOHN BARTH

Night-Sea Journey

◇◇◇◇◇◇◇

"ONE WAY OR ANOTHER, no matter which theory of our journey is correct, it's myself I address; to whom I rehearse as to a stranger our history and condition, and will disclose my secret hope though I sink for it.

"Is the journey my invention? Do the night, the sea, exist at all, I ask myself, apart from my experience of them? Do I myself exist, or is this a dream? Sometimes I wonder. And if I am, who am I? The Heritage I supposedly transport? But how can I be both vessel and contents? Such are the questions that beset my intervals of rest.

"My trouble is, I lack conviction. Many accounts of our situation seem plausible to me—where and what we are, why we swim and whither. But implausible ones as well, perhaps especially those, I must admit as possibly correct. Even likely. If at times, in certain humors—stroking in unison, say, with my neighbors and chanting with them 'Onwards! Upwards!'—I have supposed that we have after all a common Maker, Whose nature and motives we may not know, but Who engendered us in some mysterious wise and launched us forth toward some end known but to Him—if (for a moodslength only) I have been able to entertain such notions, very popular in certain quarters, it is because our night-sea journey partakes of their absurdity. One might even say: I can believe them *because* they are absurd.

"Has that been said before?

"Another paradox: it appears to be these recesses from swimming that sustain me in the swim. Two measures onward and upward, flailing with the rest, then I float exhausted and dispirited, brood upon the night, the sea, the journey, while the flood bears me a measure back and down: slow progress, but I live, I live, and make my way, aye, past many a drowned comrade in the end, stronger, worthier than I, victims of their unremitting *joie de nager*. I have seen the best swimmers of my generation go under. Numberless the number of the dead! Thousands drown as I think this thought, millions as I rest before returning to the swim. And scores,

974

hundreds of millions have expired since we surged forth, brave in our innocence, upon our dreadful way. 'Love! Love!' we sang then, a quarter-billion strong, and churned the warm sea white with joy of swimming! Now all are gone down—the buoyant, the sodden, leaders and followers, all gone under, while wretched I swim on. Yet these same reflective intervals that keep me afloat have led me into wonder, doubt, despair—strange emotions for a swimmer!—have led me, even, to suspect . . . that our night-sea journey is without meaning.

"Indeed, if I have yet to join the hosts of the suicides, it is because (fatigue apart) I find it no meaningfuller to drown myself than to go on swimming.

"I know that there are those who seem actually to enjoy the night-sea; who claim to love swimming for its own sake, or sincerely believe that 'reaching the Shore,' 'transmitting the Heritage' (*Whose* Heritage, I'd like to know? And to whom?) is worth the staggering cost. I do not. Swimming itself I find at best not actively unpleasant, more often tiresome, not infrequently a torment. Arguments from function and design don't impress me: granted that we can and do swim, that in a manner of speaking our long tails and streamlined heads are 'meant for' swimming; it by no means follows—for me, at least—that we *should* swim, or otherwise endeavor to 'fulfill our destiny.' Which is to say, Someone Else's destiny, since ours, so far as I can see, is merely to perish, one way or another, soon or late. The heartless zeal of our (departed) leaders, like the blind ambition and good cheer of my own youth, appalls me now; for the death of my comrades I am inconsolable. If the night-sea journey has any justification, it is not for us swimmers ever to discover it.

"Oh, to be sure, 'Love!' one heard on every side: 'Love it is that drives and sustains us!' I translate: We don't know *what* drives and sustains us, only that we are most miserably driven and, imperfectly, sustained. *Love* is how we call our ignorance of what whips us. 'To reach the Shore,' then: but what if the Shore exists only in the fancies of us swimmers, who dream it to account for the dreadful fact that we swim, have always and only swum, and continue swimming without respite (myself excepted) until we die? Supposing even that there *were* a Shore—that, as a cynical companion of mine once imagined, we rise from the drowned to discover that all those vulgar superstitions and exalted metaphors are literal truths: the giant Maker of us all, the Shores of Light beyond our night-sea journey!—whatever would a swimmer do there? The fact is, when we imagine the Shore, what comes to mind is just the opposite of our present condition: no more night, no more sea, no more journeying. In short, the blissful estate of the drowned.

" 'Ours not to stop and think; ours but to swim and sink. . . .' Because a moment's thought reveals the pointlessness of swimming. 'No matter,' I've heard some say, even as they gulped their last: 'The night-sea journey may be absurd, but here we swim, will-we nill-we, against the flood, onward and upward, toward a Shore that may not exist and couldn't be reached even if it did.' The thoughtful swimmer's choices, then, they say, are two: give over thrashing and go under for good, or embrace the absurdity: affirm in and for itself the night-sea journey; swim on with neither motive nor destination, for the sake of swimming, and compassionate moreover with your fellow swimmer, we being all at sea and equally in the dark. I find neither course acceptable. If not even the hypothetical Shore can justify a sea full of drowned comrades, to speak of the swim-in-itself as somehow doing so strikes me as obscene. I continue to swim—but only because blind habit, blind instinct, and blind fear of drowning are still more strong than the horror of our journey. And if on occasion I have assisted a fellow thrasher, joined in the cheers and songs, even passed along to others strokes of genius from the drownèd great, it's that I shrink by temperament from making myself conspicuous. To paddle off in one's own direction, assert one's independent right-of-way, overrun one's fellows without compunction in pursuit of selfish ends, or dedicate oneself entirely to pleasures and diversions without regard for conscience—I can't finally condemn those who journey in this wise; in half my moods I envy them and despise the weak vitality that keeps me from following their example. But in reasonabler moments I remind myself that it's their very freedom and self-responsibility I reject, as more dramatically absurd, in our senseless circumstances, than tailing along in conventional fashion. Suicides, rebels, affirmers of the paradox—nay-sayers and yea-sayers alike to our fatal journey—I finally shake my head at them. And I splash sighing past their corpses, one by one, as past a hundred sorts of others: friends, enemies, brothers, fools, sages, brutes—and nobodies, million upon million. I envy them all.

"A poor irony: that I, who find abhorrent and tautological the doctrine of survival of the fittest (*fitness* meaning, in my experience, nothing more than survival ability, a talent whose only demonstration is the fact of survival, but whose chief ingredients seem to be strength, guile, and callousness), may be the sole remaining swimmer! But the doctrine is false as well as repellent: Chance drowns the worthy with the unworthy, bears up the unfit with the fit by whatever definition, and makes the night-sea journey essentially *haphazard* as well as murderous and unjustified.

" 'You only swim once.' Why bother, then?

" 'Except ye drown, ye shall not reach the Shore of Life.' Poppycock.

"One of my late companions—that same cynic with the curious fancy, among the first to drown—entertained us with odd conjectures while we waited to begin our journey. A favorite theory of his was that the Father does exist, and did indeed make us and the sea we swim—but not a-purpose or even consciously; He made us as it were despite Himself, as we make waves with every tail thrash, and may be unaware of our existence. Another was that He knows we're here but doesn't care what happens to us, inasmuch as He creates (voluntarily or not) other seas and swimmers at more or less regular intervals. In bitterer moments, such as just before he drowned, my friend even supposed that our Maker wished us unmade; there was indeed a Shore, he'd argue, which could save at least some of us from drowning and toward which it was our function to struggle—but for reasons unknowable to us He wanted desperately to prevent our reaching that happy place and fulfilling our destiny. Our 'Father,' in short, was our adversary and would-be killer! No less outrageous, and offensive to traditional opinion, were the fellow's speculations on the nature of our Maker: That He might well be no swimmer Himself at all, but some sort of monstrosity, perhaps even tailless; that He might be stupid, malicious, insensible, perverse, or asleep and dreaming; that the end for which He created and launched us forth, and which we flagellate ourselves to fathom, was perhaps immoral, even obscene. *Et cetera, et cetera:* there was no end to the chap's conjectures, or the impoliteness of his fancy; I have reason to suspect that his early demise, whether planned by 'our Maker' or not, was expedited by certain fellow swimmers indignant at his blasphemies.

"In other moods, however (he was as given to moods as I), his theorizing would become half-serious, so it seemed to me, especially upon the subjects of Fate and Immortality, to which our youthful conversations often turned. Then his harangues, if no less fantastical, grew solemn and obscure, and if he was still baiting us, his passion undid the joke. His objection to popular opinions of the hereafter, he would declare, was their claim to general validity. Why need believers hold that *all* the drownèd rise to be judged at journey's end, and nonbelievers that drowning is final without exception? In *his* opinion (so he'd vow at least), nearly everyone's fate was permanent death; indeed he took a sour pleasure in supposing that every 'Maker' made thousands of separate seas in His creative lifetime, each populated like ours with millions of swimmers, and that in almost every instance both sea and swimmers were utterly annihilated, whether accidentally or by malevolent design. (Nothing if not pluralistical, he imagined there might be millions and billions of 'Fathers,' perhaps in some 'night-sea' of their own!) However—and here he turned infidels against him with the faithful—he professed to believe that in possibly a single night-sea per thousand, say, one of its quarter-billion swimmers (that is, one swimmer in two-hundred-fifty billions) achieved a qualified immortality. In some cases the rate might be slightly higher; in others it was vastly lower, for just as there are swimmers of every degree of proficiency, including some who drown before the journey starts, unable to swim at all, and others created drownèd, as it were, so he imagined what can only be termed impotent Creators, Makers unable to Make, as well as uncommonly fertile ones and all grades between. And it pleased him to deny any necessary relation between a Maker's productivity and His other virtues—including, even, the quality of His creatures.

"I could go on (*he* surely did) with his elaboration of these mad notions

—such as that swimmers in other night-seas needn't be of our kind; that Makers themselves might belong to different *species,* so to speak; that our particular Maker mightn't Himself be immortal, or that we might be not only His emissaries but His 'immortality,' continuing His life and our own, transmogrified, beyond our individual deaths. Even this modified immortality (meaningless to me) he conceived as relative and contingent, subject to accidental or deliberate termination: his pet hypothesis was that Makers and swimmers *each generate the other*—against all odds, their number being so great—and that any given 'immortality chain' could terminate after any number of cycles, so that what was 'immortal' (still speaking relatively) was only the cyclic process of incarnation, which itself might have a beginning and an end. Alternatively he liked to imagine cycles within cycles, either finite or infinite: for example, the 'night-sea,' as it were, in which Makers 'swam' and created night-seas and swimmers like ourselves, might be the creation of a larger Maker, Himself one of many, Who in turn, etc. Time itself he regarded as relative to our experience, like magnitude: who knew but what, with each thrash of our tails, minuscule seas and swimmers, whole eternities, came to pass—as ours, perhaps, and our Maker's Maker's, was elapsing between the strokes of some super-tail, in a slower order of time?

"Naturally I hooted with the others at this nonsense. We were young then, and had only the dimmest notion of what lay ahead; in our ignorance we imagined night-sea journeying to be a positively heroic enterprise. Its meaning and value we never questioned; to be sure, some must go down by the way, a pity no doubt, but to win a race requires that others lose, and like all my fellows I took for granted that I would be the winner. We milled and swarmed, impatient to be off, never mind where or why, only to try our youth against the realities of night and sea; if we indulged the skeptic at all it was as a droll, half-contemptible mascot. When he died in the initial slaughter, no one cared.

"And even now I don't subscribe to all his views—but I no longer scoff. The horror of our history has purged me of opinions, as of vanity, confidence, spirit, charity, hope, vitality, everything—except dull dread and a kind of melancholy, stunned persistence. What leads me to recall his fancies is my growing suspicion that I, of all swimmers, may be the sole survivor of this fell journey, tale bearer of a generation. This suspicion, together with the recent sea change, suggests to me now that nothing is impossible, not even my late companion's wildest visions, and brings me to a certain desperate resolve, the point of my chronicling.

"Very likely I have lost my senses. The carnage at our setting out; our decimation by whirlpool, poisoned cataract, and sea convulsion; the panic stampedes, mutinies, slaughters, mass suicides; the mounting evidence that none will survive the journey—add to these anguish and fatigue; it were a miracle if sanity stayed afloat. Thus I admit, with the other possibilities, that the present sweetening and calming of the sea, and what seems to be a kind of vasty presence, song, or summons from the near upstream, may be hallucinations of disordered sensibility. . . .

"Perhaps, even, I am drowned already. Surely I was never meant for the rough-and-tumble of the swim; not impossibly I perished at the outset and have only imaged the night-sea journey from some final deep. In any case I'm no longer young, and we spent old swimmers, disabused of every illusion, are most vulnerable to dreams.

"Sometimes I think I am my drownèd friend.

"Out with it: I've begun to believe, not only that *She* exists, but that She lies not far ahead, and stills the sea, and draws me Herward! Aghast, I recollect his maddest notion: that our destination (which existed, mind, in but one night-sea out of hundreds and thousands) was no Shore, as commonly conceived, but a mysterious being, indescribable except by paradox and vaguest figure: wholly different from us swimmers, yet our complement; the death of us, yet our salvation and resurrection; simultaneously our journey's end, midpoint, and commencement; not membered and thrashing like us, but a motionless or hugely gliding sphere of unimaginable dimension; self-contained, yet dependent absolutely, in some wise, upon the chance (always monstrously improbable) that one of us will survive the night-sea journey and reach . . . Her! *Her,* he called it, or *She,* which is to say, Other-than-a-he. I shake my head; the thing is too preposterous; it is myself I talk to, to keep my reason in this awful darkness. There is no She! There is no You! I rave to myself; it's Death alone that hears and summons. To the drowned, all seas are calm. . . .

"Listen: my friend maintained that in every order of creation there are two sorts of creators, contrary yet complementary, one of which gives rise to seas and swimmers, the other to the Night-which-contains-the-sea and to What-waits-at-the-journey's-end: the former, in short, to destiny, the latter to destination (and both profligately, involuntarily, perhaps indifferently or unwittingly). The 'purpose' of the night-sea journey—but not necessarily of the journeyer or of either Maker!—my friend could describe only in abstractions: *consummation, transfiguration, union of contraries, transcension of categories.* When we laughed he would shrug and admit that he understood the business no better than we, and thought it ridiculous, dreary, possibly obscene. 'But one of you,' he'd add with his wry smile, 'may be the Hero destined to complete the night-sea journey and be one with Her. Chances are, of course, you won't make it.' He himself, he declared, was not even going to try; the whole idea repelled him; if we chose to dismiss it as an ugly fiction, so much the better for us; thrash, splash, and be merry, we were soon enough drowned. But there it was, he could not say how he knew or why he bothered to tell us, any more than he could say what would happen after She and the Hero, Shore and Swimmer, 'merged identities' to become something both and neither. He quite agreed with me that if the issue of that magical union had no memory of the night-sea journey, for example, it enjoyed a poor sort of immortality; even poorer if, as he rather imagined, a swimmer-hero plus a She equalled or became merely another Maker of future night-seas and the rest, at such incredible expense of life. This being the case—he was persuaded it was—the merciful thing to do was refuse to participate; the genuine heroes, in his opinion, were the suicides, and the hero of heroes would be the swimmer who, in the very presence of the Other, refused Her proffered 'immortality' and thus put an end to at least one cycle of catastrophes.

"How we mocked him! Our moment came, we hurtled forth, pretending to glory in the adventure, thrashing, singing, cursing, strangling, rationalizing, rescuing, killing, inventing rules and stories and relationships, giving up, struggling on, but dying all, and still in darkness, until only a battered remnant was left to croak 'Onward, upward,' like a bitter echo. Then they too fell silent—victims, I can only presume, of the last frightful wave—and the moment came when I also, utterly desolate and spent, thrashed my last and gave myself over to the current, to sink or float as might be, but swim no more. Whereupon, marvelous to tell, in an instant the sea grew still! Then warmly, gently, the great tide turned, began to bear me, as it does now, onwards and upwards will-I nill-I, like a flood of joy—and I recalled with dismay my dead friend's teaching.

"I am not deceived. This new emotion is Her doing; the desire that possesses me is Her bewitchment. Lucidity passes from me; in a moment I'll cry 'Love!', bury myself in Her side, and be 'transfigured.' Which is to say, I die already; this fellow transported by passion is not I; *I am he who abjures and rejects the night-sea journey! I.* . . .

"I am all love. 'Come!' She whispers, and I have no will.

"You who I may be about to become, whatever You are; with the last twitch of my real self I beg You to listen. It is *not* love that sustains me! No; though Her magic makes me burn to sing the contrary, and though I drown even now for the blasphemy, I will say the truth. What has fetched me across this dreadful sea is a single hope, gift of my poor dead comrade: that You may be stronger-willed than I, and that by sheer force of concentration I may transmit to You, along with Your official Heritage, a private legacy of awful recollection and negative resolve. Mad as it may be, my dream is that some unimaginable embodiment of myself (or myself plus Her if that's how it must be) will come to find itself expressing, in however garbled or radical a translation, some reflection of these reflections. If against all odds this comes to pass, may You to whom, through whom I speak, do what I cannot: terminate this aimless, brutal business! Stop Your hearing against Her song! Hate love!

"Still alive, afloat, afire. Farewell then my penultimate hope: that one may be sunk for direst blasphemy on the very shore of the Shore. Can it be (my old friend would smile) that only utterest nay-sayers survive the night? But even that were Sense, and there is no sense, only senseless love, senseless death. Whoever echoes these reflections: be more courageous than their author! An end to night-sea journeys! Make no more! And forswear me when I shall forswear myself, deny myself, plunge into Her who summons, singing . . .

" 'Love! Love! Love!' "

❖

John Barth's "Night-Sea Journey" shows how material that in conception seems part philosophical tract and part satirical fantasy can be successfully cast in a fiction form. What we have been saying about fiction's preoccupation with the individual and specific (with implications that are general) is almost comically demonstrated in this case—for among the quarter-billion human sperm making this journey, the author has chosen to tell the story from the point of view of a single one. (How we would like to say that it states the problem of an individual in a mass society!) And, too, "something happens" to the character in question. At the beginning, the author deliberately keeps the reader in the dark about just what this night-sea journey is, permitting him to develop his commentary on the preposterousness of human life without resistance. The reader is able to gather the situation only through clues offered, and these are presented mostly as the outrageous speculations of the dead "cynical companion" who entertained the other swimmers with his "odd conjectures." The reader who draws his conclusions from these absurd and fantastic speculations is thus forced to admit their validity as a description of human life. Throughout, but especially in the beginning, the sperm's journey through the dark to life (through a guessed-at union, with the egg) is equated with the human journey through life to death (and a guessed-at union, with God). Many arguments and observations are made, but the telling combination is this: that if no further purpose is realized by this journey, then it is senseless and meaningless; if the only purpose realized is the perpetuation of such journeys (both the one to life and the one through life), then not only is it doubly purposeless, but it is "at such incredible expense of life" that "the merciful thing to do was refuse to participate." It is love, of course, that perpetuates life so cruelly, and the final message, before the sperm succumbs, is "Hate love!" Barth has great fun in the story, punning and parodying and paradoxing, mocking all sorts of ideas and styles, and fancifully suggesting that in some strange way this "private legacy of awful resolution and negative resolve" may have been transmitted "by sheer force of concentration." As the other swimmers expire, our hero-sperm has his "growing suspicion that I, of all swimmers, may be the sole survivor of this

fell journey, tale bearer of a generation." Thus the story plays off the ven-
erated literary tradition of the lone survivor returned to tell the tale—it is
used in Moby Dick *and* Rime of the Ancient Mariner, *for instance, and*
in this anthology Wilner jokes with it in his opening to "Dovisch in the
Wilderness." It suggests another metaphor for the writer's role, that of
survivor: the one who has seen and experienced what other men have not
and who has come back to tell the truth about the world. The epithet "tale
bearer of a generation" works as a funny pun in this story, but it is also
a good phrase for the author's role as survivor/nay-sayer. "Can it be," the
hero-sperm wonders in the last few lines of his monologue, ". . . that only
utterest nay-sayers survive the night?" (Those who utter most are writers.)
One is reminded, by both image and meaning, of Yeats' "The Second
Coming":

> *Mere anarchy is loosed upon the world,*
> *The blood-dimmed tide is loosed, and everywhere*
> *The ceremony of innocence is drowned;*
> *The best lack all conviction. . . .*

The suggestion is that salvation, if it occurs, is to be only through refusal.
The story asserts (or admits) the power of love but denies its goodness. The
negativism of the story is intense; it is not so much alleviated by the wit
as emphasized by it. Barth's description of the ludicrous circumstances of
the human condition, from inception to expiration, is in terms of all time
and all place: there is nothing that implies that this conception will take
place in twentieth-century America. Yet it is clearly a modern story: the
black-humored manner and the witty cold intellectualism embody the deep-
est pessimism in a way that is characteristic of our times.

Much criticism of contemporary fiction has been made on this ground,
that it is excessively negative. Three answers to the charge suggest them-
selves: first that all great fiction has always been negative; second, that con-
temporary fiction isn't really negative; and third, that contemporary fiction
has a right to be negative. The reason these answers don't cancel one an-
other out is that the whole discussion depends on what is meant by negative.
Certainly a case could be made that all great literature from Homer to
Hemingway has been deeply pessimistic. Melville's much-quoted letter to
Hawthorne specified that the author's role is precisely to say "No, in thun-
der." We accept and understand and even approve this dark vision in
Melville and Hawthorne and Thoreau, but it seems simply antagonistic
or faddishly bleak in Bellow or Mailer or Malamud. Whatever arguments
are used about negativism in modern writing must be seen to apply as well
to great writing from the past. For a case can be made equally that under-
neath an apparent negativism every great writer is at heart the most moral
and positive of men. The contemporary novelist portrays the evil and
banality he sees around him, he doesn't create it. And to all but the most

unsophisticated readers it must be apparent that he doesn't approve of it. The scenes of sex and violence in modern writing that so appall some readers are meant to appall them. Much of the dark vision of contemporary writers is often an expression of a greater sorrow or anger than is felt by most of us over the discrepancy between the potential they imagine for modern man and the actuality of how we live. It is a time when faiths of all sorts have failed—faith in religion, faith in science, faith in man, faith in society. No one really much believes in anything anymore. Those who leap to deny this would be the first to confirm it by saying: "That's the trouble with people today, they don't believe in anything anymore." So if the contemporary writer seems especially negative about contemporary society, hasn't he special reasons? Isn't he simply being accurate and insightful about how we live now? There is much that is wrong with our society, and it is the obligation of the writer to point it out. Where it is most wrong is precisely in the area where fiction focuses most intensely—where the individual and the culture come into contact and conflict. The negativism in contemporary fiction is actually a relevant and accurate negativism—accurate and relevant as both depiction and expression. Literature has never ultimately been wrong about its characterization of the times in which it was created before, and to think that our contemporary writers are now wrong about the times in which we live, and to reject their work as excessively negative, is dangerous and damaging wishful thinking.

RICHARD WILBUR

A Game of Catch

◇◇◇◇◇◇◇

MONK AND GLENNIE were playing catch on the side lawn of the fire-house when Scho caught sight of them. They were good at it, for seventh-graders, as anyone could see right away. Monk, wearing a catcher's mitt, would lean easily sidewise and back, with one leg lifted and his throwing hand almost down to the grass, and then lob the white ball straight up into the sunlight. Glennie would shield his eyes with his left hand and, just as the ball fell past him, snag it with a little dart of his glove. Then he would burn the ball straight toward Monk, and it would spank into the round mitt and sit, like a still-life apple on a plate, until Monk flipped it over into his right hand and, with a negligent flick of his hanging arm, gave Glennie a fast grounder.

They were going on and on like that, in a kind of slow, mannered, luxurious dance in the sun, their faces perfectly blank and entranced, when Glennie noticed Scho dawdling along the other side of the street and called hello to him. Scho crossed over and stood at the front edge of the lawn, near an apple tree, watching.

"Got your glove?" asked Glennie after a time. Scho obviously hadn't.

"You could give me some easy grounders," said Scho. "But don't burn 'em."

"All right," Glennie said. He moved off a little, so the three of them formed a triangle, and they passed the ball around for about five minutes, Monk tossing easy grounders to Scho, Scho throwing to Glennie, and Glennie burning them in to Monk. After a while, Monk began to throw them back to Glennie once or twice before he let Scho have his grounder, and finally Monk gave Scho a fast, bumpy grounder that hopped over his shoulder and went in to the brake on the other side of the street.

"Not so hard," called Scho as he ran across to get it.

"You should've had it," Monk shouted.

It took Scho a little while to find the ball among the ferns and dead leaves, and when he saw it, he grabbed it up and threw it toward Glennie. It struck the trunk of the apple tree, bounced back at an angle, and rolled steadily and stupidly onto the cement apron in front of the firehouse, where one of the trucks was parked. Scho ran hard and stopped it just before it rolled under the truck, and this time he carried it back to his former position on the lawn and threw it carefully to Glennie.

"I got an idea," said Glennie. "Why don't Monk and I catch for five minutes more, and then you can borrow one of our gloves?"

"That's all right with me," said Monk. He socked his fist into his mitt, and Glennie burned one in.

"All right," Scho said, and went over and sat under the tree. There in the shade he watched them resume their skillful play. They threw lazily fast or lazily slow—high, low, or wide—and always handsomely, their expressions serene, changeless, and forgetful. When Monk missed a low backhand catch, he walked indolently after the ball and, hardly even looking, flung it sidearm for an imaginary put-out. After a good while of this, Scho said, "Isn't it five minutes yet?"

"One minute to go," said Monk, with a fraction of a grin.

Scho stood up and watched the ball slap back and forth for several minutes more, and then he turned and pulled himself up into the crotch of the tree.

"Where you going?" Monk asked.

"Just up the tree," Scho said.

"I guess he doesn't want to catch," said Monk.

Scho went up and up through the fat light-gray branches until they grew slender and bright and gave under him. He found a place where several supple branches were knit to make a dangerous chair, and sat there with his head coming out of the leaves into the sunlight. He could see the two other boys down below, the ball going back and forth between them as if they were bowling on the grass, and Glennie's crew-cut head looking like a sea urchin.

"I found a wonderful seat up here," Scho said loudly. "If I don't fall out." Monk and Glennie didn't look up or comment and so he began jouncing gently in his chair of branches and singing "Yo-ho, heave ho" in an exaggerated way.

"Do you know what, Monk?" he announced in a few moments. "I can make you two guys do anything I want. Catch that ball, Monk! Now you catch it, Glennie!"

"I was going to catch it anyway," Monk suddenly said. "You're not making anybody do anything when they're already going to do it anyway."

"I made you say what you just said," Scho replied joyfully.

"No, you didn't," said Monk, still throwing and catching but now less serenely absorbed in the game.

"That's what I wanted you to say," Scho said.

The ball bounded off the rim of Monk's mitt and plowed into a gladiolus bed beside the firehouse, and Monk ran to get it while Scho jounced in his treetop and sang, "I wanted you to miss that. Anything you do is what I wanted you to do."

"Let's quit for a minute," Glennie suggested.

"We might as well, until the peanut gallery shuts up," Monk said.

They went over and sat crosslegged in the shade of the tree. Scho looked down between his legs and saw them on the dim, spotty ground, saying nothing to one another. Glennie soon began abstractedly spinning his glove between his palms; Monk pulled his nose and stared out across the lawn.

"I want you to mess around with your nose, Monk," said Scho, giggling. Monk withdrew his hand from his face.

"Do that with your glove, Glennie," Scho persisted. "Monk, I want you to pull up hunks of grass and chew on it."

Glennie looked up and saw a self-delighted, intense face staring down at him through the leaves. "Stop being a dope and come down and we'll catch for a few minutes," he said.

Scho hesitated, and then said, in a tentatively mocking voice, "That's what I wanted you to say."

"All right, then, nuts to you," said Glennie.

"Why don't you keep quiet and stop bothering people?" Monk asked.

"I made you say that," Scho replied, softly.

"Shut up," Monk said.

"I made you say that, and I want you to be standing there looking sore. And I want you to climb up the tree. I'm making you do it!"

Monk was scrambling up through the branches, awkward in his haste, and getting snagged on twigs. His face was furious and foolish, and he kept telling Scho to shut up, shut up, shut up, while the other's exuberant and panicky voice poured down upon his head.

"Now you shut up or you'll be sorry," Monk said, breathing hard as he reached up and threatened to shake the cradle of slight branches in which Scho was sitting.

"I *want*——" Scho screamed as he fell. Two lower branches broke his rustling, crackling fall, but he landed on his back with a deep thud and lay still, with a strangled look on his face and his eyes clenched. Glennie knelt down and asked breathlessly, "Are you O.K., Scho? Are you O.K.?" while Monk swung down through the leaves crying that honestly he hadn't even touched him, the crazy guy just let go. Scho doubled up and turned over on his right side, and now both the other boys knelt beside him, pawing at his shoulder and begging to know how he was.

Then Scho rolled away from them and sat partly up, still struggling to get his wind but forcing a species of smile onto his face.

"I'm sorry, Scho," Monk said. "I didn't mean to make you fall."

Scho's voice came out weak and gravelly, in gasps. "I meant—you to do it. You—had to. You can't do—anything—unless I want—you to."

Glennie and Monk looked helplessly at him as he sat there, breathing a bit more easily and smiling fixedly, with tears in his eyes. Then they picked up their gloves and the ball, walked over to the street, and went slowly away down the sidewalk, Monk punching his fist into the mitt, Glennie juggling the ball between glove and hand.

From under the apple tree, Scho, still bent over a little for lack of breath, croaked after them in triumph and misery, "I want you to do whatever you're going to do for the whole rest of your life!"

⬦

Richard Wilbur was born in 1921 in New York City, has his B.A. from Amherst and his M.A. from Harvard, and has taught at Harvard and Wellesley and now is at Wesleyan. He has published four volumes of poetry: The Beautiful Changes *(1947),* Ceremony and Other Poems *(1950),* Things of This World *(1957), and* Advice to a Prophet *(1961). His work has won him many awards: two Guggenheim fellowships, a Ford Foundation fellowship, the Prix de Rome fellowship of the American Academy of Arts and Letters, the Pulitzer Prize for poetry, the National Book Award for poetry, and others. He very rarely writes fiction: when "A Game of Catch" was published in 1953, he said it was the first story he had written in ten years, and he doesn't seem to have done many more since.*

"A Game of Catch" is a sort of prose lyric, capturing or creating virtually entirely an evocative moment, rendering it timeless, eternal. There are pictures of boys throwing and catching balls on Grecian vases: no doubt they did it easily, lazily, as "a kind of slow, mannered, luxurious dance in the sun." Here a poet has depicted the scene again, in a sketch-story that can be read as a third analogy of the literary artist's role in relation to his times—this time as creator/maker. Scho "shows" how the artist is excluded from efficient modern society, represented by the skillful baseball players, Monk and Glennie: the artist is the stranger, the longer-after-life, the outsider. Up in his tree, like Updike's lifeguard up on his tower, he observes; and through observing action, it seems to him that he creates it. He feels that he has power over the others, can make them do what he wants. The argument "I made you do that" is infuriating because it is unarguable: it has already happened and is not subject to any sort of rational disproof. Like repeating everything a person says, it is the kind of thing children delight in, and so do authors: it gives them power over what has been said, by making it their own. The others are angered by Scho: to make him stop they first try bribing him by offering him a place in the game; when he refuses, they harm him, then worry that they've harmed him. Left alone at the end, he persists "in triumph and misery" in describing his vision, his version of how things are. Scho has the artist's

illusion that he himself is creating reality, is the maker of experience. And Wilbur shows in this story that, in a way, that is exactly what the artist does: for after all, he created Glennie and Monk and Scho, and now he has been able to make them do exactly what he wants them to—forever.

◇—◇

It may seem wrong-headed to end a one-thousand-page anthology of fiction with a four-page sketch by a poet, but doing so enables us to make three points. The first is to emphasize what we said in the introduction to this section: that modern fiction is a far-ranging form, embracing works of all sorts, shapes, and sizes.

And secondly, it gives us a chance to repeat the apology, offered in advance in our introductory note, about the obtrusiveness or overanxiousness of our interpretations and analyses of the stories. "A Game of Catch" has such a lovely, delicate, lyrical tone, is so perfectly wrought, so every-word-in-place that to an even greater extent than the other stories in this volume it seems entitled to remain sacrosanct from analysis and paraphrase. Such a story—and perhaps all stories—should be appreciated simply for the realization of moment and scene evoked. But appreciation often comes only after understanding, and in our anxiousness that contemporary fiction be better appreciated we have undoubtedly explained the obvious in many cases, possibly misinterpreted in others, and continually violated the basic premise of appreciation: that literary art cannot be paraphrased; that a story says what it says only in the way that it says it, not in any other way. This represents the well-known fusion of form and content, in which Art is said to reside.

The trouble has been that many readers have gotten the idea that much contemporary fiction is hard-to-read and impossible-to-understand, in the same way that much contemporary poetry or contemporary art or music seems incomprehensible. This is simply not true. Experimental and impressionistic avant-garde fiction is now not much written in America, except by beginners who use obscurity to conceal ineptness and as an excuse for not being able to get their work published. At any rate, most readers seldom encounter it. But they still complain that modern short stories seem to them to lack endings; modern novels don't seem to them to have the big narrative sweep, the "story values" of big characters and action-filled plots of older-fashioned fiction. It is true perhaps that modern fiction may demand a bit more from modern readers, but that is because of its subtlety, its complexity, its excellence. We believe that the stories in this book show that a lot does in fact "happen" to characters in modern fiction, and what happens is for the most part a great deal more real and more sig-

nificant than much of the often very simple-minded, superficially exciting but actually fairly meaningless event that occurs in many of the favorite novels of the past. The issues, themes, and situations of modern fiction aren't always subject to arbitrary endings in the form of such events as getting married or becoming rich or being vindicated—perhaps because in modern life such events are never very final. Most complaints about the inaccessibility of contemporary fiction come from judging the whole by a few examples or from careless reading. For good fiction—modern or otherwise—cannot be read carelessly. It is not like watching television. No one would want to deny that the reading of fiction should provide entertainment, but long ago it was established that good fiction provides more than entertainment and escape. There is obviously no pleasure at all, much less entertainment, in reading fiction if one doesn't understand it—doesn't understand either what happens in the story or what the meaning is of what happens. But contemporary fiction is not in itself difficult. There is no need for it to go un-understood and hence unappreciated—unless we have turned into a nation of mindless viewers, stunned by the meaninglessness of television. Fiction is like any other art: if merely glanced at, it goes uncomprehended and unappreciated and provides no pleasure. But like any other art, when fiction is considered appreciatively, its meanings and values and excellences become apparent and provide entertainment and pleasure—and something more.

The third reason for ending our book with a story by a poet who seldom writes fiction is that it suggests the point documented in the Appendix that follows. The very great achievement of contemporary fiction is not the work of just a few giant figures, as has been the case in other literary eras. It is the accomplishment of many writers, perhaps a dozen great ones, hundreds that are merely excellent.

◇◇◇

In Defense of Contemporary Fiction

Appendix

IN DEFENSE OF CONTEMPORARY FICTION

Anyone *who has read the fiction in this book will see no need for a defense of fiction in our times. If the reader is curious about why there is such a disparity between the very great achievement of modern fiction and its rather dismal reputation, he will find us trying to provide some answers and reasons here. But he should be warned that compared to what has gone before, there is no pleasure in what follows.*

What we want to do here is make some additional arguments in the case for modern American fiction and try to avoid repeating what we have said elsewhere. As we pointed out in our Introductory Note, we believe that the fiction in this book is itself the best demonstration of the excellence of modern fiction. As we point out in the Final Note, which follows, we believe that modern fiction as a whole demonstrates this even better than the fiction chosen here. In the introduction to Part III, "The Eye of Fiction" (pp. 891ff.), we gave what statement we could to our conviction that fiction has a particular and powerful way of expressing and depicting the times in which we live. The standard complaints about modern fiction—that it is "interior" and/or "negative" and/or "inaccessible"—we have discussed separately earlier (pp. 897ff., 982ff., and 988ff., respectively). The argument that our times are too chaotic or bizarre to be successfully rendered in fiction is considered in the two discussions of John Cheever's work (pp. 487 and 961). Other bits and pieces of what might have been a coherent defense of fiction in our time are scattered throughout the book, introduced at what seemed to us relevant places.

The remnants of the argument follow. First we consider the currently widespread idea that nonfiction rather than fiction may be the characteristic literary form of our era. Then we consider possible reasons for the decline in the popularity of fiction—not in terms of the fiction itself but in terms of the ways fiction is "approached" today—the approaches of the literary critic and the cultural critic. Then we try to show that contrary to general opinion America today has more good fiction writers than any time or any place ever had; we do this mainly by listing several hundred of their names. Then we make a brief mention of how publishing practices in America may contribute to the difficulty our readers and writers have in getting together.

All this is done somewhat argumentatively and contentiously, in a tone and frame of mind we have tried to keep out of the rest of the book, because most of it refers to the professional mood and rationalizations of the special worlds of magazine and book publishing and education that are themselves irrelevant to the singular relationship this book was designed to celebrate—that of the serious contemporary reader to the serious contemporary piece of fiction. We feel strongly that anyone who read this Appendix instead of *the fiction in the book itself would have virtually no comprehension of what the book is trying to prove.*

As mentioned previously, the idea is very current and widespread that nonfiction rather than fiction is the characteristic form of literary expression of our time, the form that tells us most about ourselves and the way we live now. The view that fiction is in some sort of "decline" is stated virtually every day and five times on Sunday by those who review books for The New York Times. *The National Book Council reports that the ratio of nonfiction books to fiction books published each year has dropped from about 4.5 to 1 in 1936 to 9 to 1 in 1966. One of the biggest successes of recent publishing seasons was Truman Capote's factual account of a Kansas murder,* In Cold Blood; *and this book was so detailed and so suspenseful and so well written that when the author started the silly business of calling it a "nonfiction novel," many who reviewed the book took the opportunity to launch into another round of laments about the fatigue of contemporary fiction and make proclamations about the vitality of the "new" nonfiction.*

The worst of it is that the conviction that fiction is finished, repeated so often and in so many ways, not only convinces, it causes. *The magazines that once featured fiction either have gone out of business or now publish more articles than short stories on a 10-to-1 basis, and most of the new magazines that start up never publish fiction at all. A magazine editor hearing over and over again that fiction has lost its vitality may decide to drop it entirely. Novelists who find short stories difficult to write are already too fond of the excuse that there's no good short fiction being written because "the market's gone." Book publishers, who always prefer riding trends to bucking them, regretfully turn down novels and enterprisingly think up nonfiction book ideas of their own and give authors big advances to write them—and it may be that they give the big advance and the idea to a* fiction *writer. Good-bye novelist. Enterprising magazines* (Holiday, Esquire, *etc.) are always commissioning our best novelists to do articles (on politics or travel or on one another), and the between-novel energy that used to go into craft-sharpening short stories in the good old days that everyone now misses so (when Scribner's would publish a book of short* stories by Hemingway or Fitzgerald or Wolfe alternately with their novels), all goes now into nonfiction that blunts the fiction technique. The short story is now, as a result, thought of as form only for beginners. The reader-ship for a new novelist is scarcely larger than that for a new poet. What is described as already true—that fiction is in some sort of decline—may actually become true as a result of the conviction.

But any "decline" in fiction which may now exist is a decline in popularity rather than a decline in quality. Critics of contemporary fiction, when they aren't simply confusing the two, tend to try to put them into a cause-and-effect relationship. Sometimes the argument is that if contemporary fiction isn't much read, that must be because it isn't much good. Sometimes the causal factor is reversed: fiction is losing its vitality because it lacks a regular responsive readership. The decrease in the amount of fiction run in national commercial magazines is sometimes seen as the result, some-times the cause, of the "fact" that the short story is a dying form in America today. And, if the short story is a dying form, it is a simple further misstep to the conclusion that the nonfiction article that has replaced it in our magazines must be "the characteristic literary form of our era"—a view actually put forward by Norman Podhoretz and John Fischer in Commentary and Harper's a number of years ago, and much repeated by others since.

But the fact is that most magazine articles are cliché structured from opening anecdote through supporting statistics to hope-for-the-future ending. Most of them are written to order by professional journalists from ideas thought up in editorial committee—thus not only from the ideas of others but from those whose job depends on conceiving ideas that will increase either the magazine's circulation or its advertising linage. Virtually always, a fiction writer writes better than a nonfiction writer, has at his command more language and style as well as profoundly more insight and conviction and integrity to bring alive his vision of the way things are now. He is more economical, his eye and ear are better, his observations more accurate and acute. He is infinitely more original. The best magazine articles, in fact, are those that are done by fiction writers, or by those who use fiction-like techniques. When a fiction writer like Mailer or Baldwin or Capote does a personal essay or a job of reportage, it is demonstrably far better written and intrinsically far more interesting than the work of journalists and critics who do nonfiction routinely. Those who attack con-temporary fiction point to the excellence of such nonfiction by fiction writers to prove that the magazine article is the characteristic literary form now, but in fact it proves just the opposite. What it proves is not that fiction is on the decline but rather that modern fiction is so vital and its practi-tioners so skillful that when they apply their techniques and insights to nonfiction they are conspicuously successful. Everyone misses the irony that it is fiction methods—direct dialogue, scene setting, use of a participant *point-of-view narrator, and so forth—that are being used to make these fact pieces seem more "real" and "true."*

No one wants to belabor the meager thing that is the average magazine article, but neither does one like to see it puffed up in importance so as to justify not running fiction in magazines. Book publishers similarly over-praise nonfiction books to justify not publishing novels and collections of stories, but most of them know that the real reason they don't publish much fiction is because it doesn't sell. A good deal of the disparagement of modern fiction occurs as a result of the rationalizations and justifications of magazine editors and book editors for not publishing more of it. That their convictions rest on the hard economic facts of modern publishing as a big business with all the problems of mass distribution and competitive shelf space associated with marketing laundry soap or shaving cream is immaterial here, since we are supposing that even if editors and publishers aren't capable of dealing with the economics of their business in order to follow their convictions, they still ought to be able to separate the two in their minds. At any rate, there has come to be a kind of cumulative, accelerating, snow-balling, band-wagon quality to this misconception that modern fiction is "in decline." And unfortunately, it is a misconception that threatens to lead to a situation in which a whole generation of fine fiction writers will have virtually no readership in their own time.

We have said that any decline in fiction which exists today is a decline in popularity, not a decline in quality. But what has caused the decline in popularity, if the quality is good? There are many factors, some having to do with the nature of modern life, some with the nature of modern readers, some with the nature of modern fiction. It seems to us that far more of the fault can be found with modern readers than with modern writers.

It is often said that television has stolen fiction's audience, and if the average American family's set is on for eight hours a day (as we are told it is), that might have something to do with it; but so just as much might the boom in boating or bowling, for the sort of fiction reader who now goes to TV for his weekly quota of entertainment and escape never was much of a reader of literature anyway. Those who talk about a decline in fiction reading usually fail to make the distinction between the old "popular" "slick" magazine fiction (which is now indeed pretty much gone, and probably over to TV, both the reader of it and the writer of it) and the "serious" "literary" fiction (which perhaps never was read by many but is now read by proportionately even fewer). What has happened is that as a supposedly literate, college-educated population has grown in the United States, literary fiction has failed to keep its share of readers. Again, it should be clear that the serious reader of serious fiction has been lost not to TV but to nonfiction, especially to nonfiction books. One is constantly encountering well-informed, well-educated men and women who feel no reluctance admitting that they haven't read (or finished) a modern novel in years. In fact, it might be safe to say that the most serious and literate segment of modern American readers, those who read most and most intelligently, virtually never read fiction—unless it be an occasional mystery novel for entertainment and escape.

As the stories in this anthology have shown, our times are unsettled and complex, and our people are troubled and anxious. It is natural that the most educated and concerned Americans would turn to books that directly describe themselves and their society, books that will expose to them the lives of others, whether it be their neighbors or their leaders; books in recent history, in popular psychology, in the social sciences; books like The Exurbanites, The Lonely Crowd, The American Way of Death, Games People Play, The Affluent Society, *and so on; books that are presented as offering them some new understanding of how they and others live now. They want* facts—*or at least they think that is what they want. What is really wanted is not so much facts, or at any rate not just more facts, but rather the truth, or at any rate more truth. It is inevitable that in the search for facts they will turn first to nonfiction. And virtually no one seeks for the truth about ourselves and our times where it is most certainly and most logically to be found—in our literary art, our contemporary fiction.*

The way Americans now read has a good deal to do with the problem. Any sort of speed reading, quick scanning of pages solely for content, finds little of value in literature, where the meaning resides as much in the form as the content. The majority of book readers are too hurried, too pragmatic, too impatient to submit to the experience of an imagined reality required by fiction. And then too often they turn to the experts, the specialists, the professionals, to be told what their literature says. Unfortunately, professional criticism today seems to consist in one or both of two "approaches" to literature—that of the cultural critic and that of the literary critic— both of whom tend, in entirely different ways, to obscure from the general reader how much our best fiction could tell us about ourselves and our times.

The cultural critic's approach—similar to what is sometimes called "the sociology of literature"—when it is directed to contemporary writing, finds at least as much significance in the analysis of popular "slick" writing as it does in the study of serious "literary" fiction, in which the underlying ideas and assumptions are usually much less apparent. There is undoubtedly much to learn about our times from a study of our popular culture: from comic books, popular songs, films, TV series dramas and domestic comedies, advertising campaigns, and so forth. Critical reading of the "true confessions" magazines, of the more sensational men's magazines, and of the slick romantic magazines for women reveals a great deal about the falsity and fantasy implicit in the fiction and hence in the society: it exposes the nation's daydreams, so to speak. And such stories also depict, often quite accurately, the superficial manners and mores of our time—revealing a good deal about the norms of the society. In a mass society the mass culture disseminated through mass media has certainly got to be significant, and none of the serious study given it is in any way wasted.

But in such critical readings and in every analysis of popular culture, the truth lies in the analysis rather than in the material. Bad art inadvertently reveals more to such reading than real art purposefully will. By this approach, one attempts to understand the author's purpose in order to mock him, not to learn from him. So pervasive is this kind of approach to culture today that cults grow up for that which is worst. The so-called "camp" sensibility most admires the most false and the most vulgar. Sometimes it seems that there are more serious readers for the books and the magazine features that analyze and interpret our popular culture than there are for the literature that is our real culture, which truly (not falsely) depicts and expresses our times. Popular literature (like the advertising that usually supports it) is deliberately designed accurately to reflect readers' (consumers') expectations and hopes (secret or otherwise), and in that sense is not "false." But what is revealed is how widespread are certain misconceptions, how pervasive are certain daydreams and delusions and vulgarities. As an expression of the reader-audience-consumer rather than of the writer's own vision, popular literature truly reflects the false values of our culture. But always we are depending on the acuteness and insight and accuracy of the interpreter rather than on the vision and perception and accuracy of the creator for the truth of what this kind of fiction reveals about our times. And because this "approach" gets most from what is bad, it tends to separate us further from what is good.

The literary critic's approach has the opposite effect: the emphasis is so completely on finding the esthetic excellence of the work that everything else in the work is overlooked. The way students are now taught to read literature in our colleges and universities obscures from them what literature can tell us about ourselves and the way we live. In their famous first "Letter to the Teacher" (1938) in Understanding Poetry, *Cleanth Brooks and Robert Penn Warren stressed that "though one may consider a poem as an instance of historical or ethical documentation, the poem in itself, if literature is to be studied as literature, remains the final object of study," and that "a poem should always be treated as an organic system of relationships." As everyone knows, this textbook had a tremendous influence: it introduced to the undergraduate teaching of all literature (not just poetry) the meticulous critical methods of the so-called New Criticism, methods based in the ultimate of esthetic theory, that Art should be considered as Art and not as anything else. The art object (the poem or story) should be judged neither as* expression *of the artist nor as* communication *to the reader but as an independent* object—*and its worth calculated through an internal analysis of its "organic" system of relationships. The introduction of these principles into the classroom was a great corrective to much foolishness in the way literature had been taught; but what began as a system of critical technique has now become the pervasive manner of teaching and studying literature, and the exercise of the technique has become an art in itself.*

The question of evaluation is clearly what has been allowed to fog the issue here, for while literature should be judged as literature, it can be read in many ways. A critic evaluating a literary work of art is surely correct to consider the work as art and not as anything else. But not all undergraduates are training to be critics. When a student is taught to read literature as literature and not as anything else, then whatever else literature might have been to him is denied him. Contemporary literature may offer inspired insights into our times and troubles, but these insights are considered irrelevant. And so they may be—to a literary critic. What is unfortunate in this otherwise salutary revolution in teaching is the side effect: students are taught to read literature "correctly"—that is, as literature—but more or less exclusively so; and few professors seem able to go on and show them that there is another great kind of value in reading literature "incorrectly"— that is, as some kind of "historical or ethical documentation." A short story is not to be considered simply as a piece of sociology, but neither should it be the precious, exclusive province of the literary cognoscenti and critics. The importance of "understanding" fiction (as well as poetry) has had the effect of making the nonspecialized reader obsolete. While increasing the understanding of the literary specialist, it has alienated the general student from all except a few more or less underground "bibles"—The Catcher in the Rye, Catch-22, Lord of the Flies, *the Tolkien series, and so forth— that to successive student generations become secret talismans of belonging. Right from his freshman English class it is obscured from the student that literature, even when read "incorrectly" as something it isn't even supposed to be, has as much of the truth to reveal about a civilization (our own, for instance) as have his textbooks in social science and history, which set out to describe that culture directly.*

Like virtually everything else in America, reading fiction with intent to understand thus seems to have fallen into the grips of the experts, the specialists, the professionals. And like most experts, these two sorts of professional readers—the cultural critics and the literary critics—are interested more in finding further proof of what they already know or believe they know, than in learning from what they read. If the danger of the cultural critic's approach to literature is that he reads only to find further proof of some theory he holds about society, the danger of the literary critic's approach is that he reads only what he (and almost everyone else) knows is good in search of further proof of its excellence. The cultural critic finds most proof of what he already knows about society in bad art. The literary critic finds it easiest to prove again the excellence of classics of the past, and we have new interpretations of Donne sonnets rather than helpful exegeses of contemporary works that might yield to the analytical critical methods—works like Barth's Giles Goat-Boy *or Salinger's* Seymour: An Introduction. *To these two kinds of professional readers can now be counterposed only those few general readers who keep turning to new fiction in search of entertainment and escape, only to be disappointed by the seriousness (even of the humorists) they find there. Surely there must be a way of reading modern literature that rests between the professional and the mindless. Our fiction writers very much need and surely deserve the attention of serious amateur readers: readers willing to undergo the particular experience of the particular reality of a particular work of fiction, readers approaching the novel or story with not only the intent to understand it, but the willingness to learn from the author. Today we think so little of our fiction writers that it seems naïve to say that we might actually* learn *something from reading their novels. The sort of readership that we call for can be available only when there is some initial trust or confidence in the excellence of the work. It cannot exist when the general opinion has it that our modern fiction is "in decline" and that we are without writers of stature.*

Those who assert that contemporary fiction is "in decline" constantly raise the question: "Where are the Faulkners, Fitzgeralds, and Hemingways of the future?" It is in many ways an idiot question, highly loaded; for there are of course never equivalents, one era to another, for the original vision of any great writer. The question can perhaps be more sensibly phrased something like this: "Granted there are many, many fiction writers in America now, perhaps more than ever, and some of them are undoubtedly very talented; but where are the giants, the towering figures that dominate a literary era and inspire it?" Then the question is answerable, and in an either/or way. Either we can admit that there are no giants, that the achievement of modern American fiction is a collective achievement of dozens, perhaps hundreds, of excellent writers, no one of them or no several of them standing significantly above a secondary rank of them— which is hardly a damaging admission. Or we can revert to the seemingly unavoidable cliché and say that it may be a question of not being able to see the forest for the trees. A period that has Saul Bellow and Vladimir Nabokov, and also John Barth, John Cheever, and Norman Mailer all regularly writing—such a period will certainly seem flourishing to the literary historians of the future. Perhaps our trouble is that there are too many other writers who may be just as good or better—Bernard Malamud, Truman Capote, J. D. Salinger, William Styron, Nelson Algren, Philip Roth, John Updike, Evan S. Connell, Jr., J. P. Donleavy, and so on. And between these larger trees are others, nearly the same size, or perhaps even bigger, for (to take the metaphor further in an attempt to justify using the

*cliché in the first place) writers, like trees in a forest, come in different
species, and/but their growth is individual and dependent on many factors.
It may not be possible to judge either their potential growth or actual
strength by the height at which they may be standing now. For who is to
say that all the writers mentioned above are "better" or "stronger" or
"greater" writers than William Humphrey, Joseph Heller, Thomas Berger,
Mary McCarthy, Thomas Pynchon, Vance Bourjaily, Ralph Ellison, Wright
Morris, Kay Boyle, and so on and on and on. Making comparisons between such disparate types of talent is ridiculous in itself, of course; but
the ridiculousness of doing it indicates how deep and widespread excellence
is in the ranks of our contemporary writers.*

*The writers on the list that follow all vary greatly in both kind and de-
gree of both excellence and achievement. Some of them have already written
a great amount of excellent work and have deserved, earned reputations
far greater than many, or perhaps even most, of the writers whose work is
included in this book. Some of them have so far done very little. Some
belong to the generation of writers famous before World War II who happen still to be alive; they may not have written anything, or anything interesting, in years, but sometimes such writers can find a new burst of energy
and inspiration for a final book as good as any they have ever done. Some
have written first novels of great promise but since then only routine stuff;
sometimes such writers can work themselves back to where they started.
Some of them have never written anything that wasn't brilliant and complex, but have now got themselves into such a complicated corner of vision
and technique that they are unable to write more at all; sometimes such
writers will suddenly find themselves turned on again. Some of them write
serious but dull books, steadily and regularly; sometimes such writers
improve simply by practice, and their work is ultimately impressive simply
because so much was so conscientiously done. Of all of them it is possible to
say at the very least this: that it is not inconceivable that they will produce
something good.*

*But if all this sounds unknowingly and unduly hopeful, let us insist that
it is not really necessary to be so hopeful. The list contains the names of
some three hundred writers; the greater part of them could be discounted,
and there would still be more good writers than we regularly read from
other times. One of the reasons that writing from the past seems so very
good to us is that it has been sifted and screened and resifted and rescreened
so that only the very best is regularly read now. Writing by the authors
listed below, sifted and screened by the future, will surely seem the equal
of any other period. The list is not presented as comprehensive; although
we have done our best, there are undoubtedly many good writers we have
never heard of. And, quite seriously, the list is not meant to be controversial. It is inevitable that such a list, if it is read at all, will be scanned only
in search of names we have forgotten or deliberately omitted—fortunately*

no one can ever know which. Our only hope is that those who do this will at the same time realize the point the list is intended to make: that far from suffering a dearth of good or promising writers, America now probably has more of them than any other land in any other time.

Junius Adams
Nelson Algren
Juan Alonso
L. J. Amster
Roger Angell
Louis Auchincloss
Elliott Baker
Anthony Bailey
James Baldwin
Richard Bankowsky
B. L. Barrett
John Barth
Donald Barthelme
Jonathon Baumbach
Ann Bayer
Peter S. Beagle
Stephen Becker
Charles G. Bell
Saul Bellow
Thomas Berger
Gina Berriault
John Berry
Wendell Berry
Jesse Bier
Sallie Bingham
Burt Blechman
Ralph Blum
Roy Bongartz
Ann Borowick
Keith Botsford
Vance Bourjaily
Robert O. Bowen
Jane Bowles
Paul Bowles
Kay Boyle
William Brammer
Paul Brodeur
Harold Brodkey
Chandler Brossard

Brock Brower
Anatole Broyard
James Buechler
Frederick Buechner
Jackson Burgess
William Burroughs
Erskine Caldwell
Hortense Calisher
Truman Capote
Don Carpenter
R. V. Cassill
Fred Chapell
Jerome Charyn
John Cheever
Alfred Chester
Walter Van T. Clark
Walter Clemmons
Robert Coates
Leonard Cohen
Burt Cole
Tom Cole
Evan S. Connell, Jr.
Frank Conroy
Clarence L. Cooper
Robert Coover
John W. Corrington
James Gould Cozzens
Robert Creeley
Montgomery Culver
Daniel Curley
Edward Dahlberg
Christopher Davis
Wesley Ford Davis
Robert DeMaria
Benjamin de Mott
Peter De Vries
Joan Didion
J. P. Donleavy
H. E. F. Donohue

Sonya Dorman
John Dos Passos
Ellen Douglas
Rosalind Drexler
William Eastlake
Stanley Elkin
George P. Elliott
Ralph Ellison
Seymour Epstein
James T. Farrell
Irvin Faust
Peter S. Feibleman
Leslie Fiedler
Jesse Hill Ford
William Price Fox
Bruce Jay Friedman
Sanford Friedman
Daniel Fuchs
Blair Fuller
William Gaddis
Ernest J. Gaines
George Garrett
William Gass
Merrill Joan Gerber
Herbert Gold
Ivan Gold
William Goldman
Mitchell Goodman
Paul Goodman
Caroline Gordon
Robert Gover
William Goyen
Shirley Ann Grau
Joanne Greenberg
Philip L. Greene
Alfred Grossman
A. B. Guthrie, Jr.
Charles Haldeman
Hope Hale

James B. Hall
James Baker Hall
Lawrence S. Hall
Oakley Hall
Mac Hammond
Elizabeth Hardwick
Donald Harington
Curtis Harnack
Alan Harrington
Macdonald Harris
Mark Harris
John Hawkes
Shirley Hazzard
Arthur Heiserman
Joseph Heller
Robert Henderson
James Leo Herlihy
John Hersey
Pati Hill
Chester Himes
Edward Hoagland
William Hoffman
John Clellon Holmes
Paul Horgan
Maureen Howard
H. L. Humes
William Humphrey
James Jones
Jean Ross Justice
M. R. Kadish
Edmund Keeley
William Melvin Kelly
Mark Kennedy
Calvin Kentfield
Jack Kerouac
Ken Kesey
Richard Kim
John Knowles
Victor Kolpacoff
Edith Konecky
Jonathon Kozol
Jeremy Larner
Albert Lebowitz
Harper Lee

John Leggett
Meyer Liben
Leo Litwak
Jack Ludwig
Alison Lurie
Andrew Lytle
Mary McCarthy
Edward McClannahan
Carson McCullers
Joseph McElroy
Georgia McKinley
John McPhee
Robie Macauley
Ben Maddow
Norman Mailer
Bernard Malamud
George Mandel
Wallace Markfield
John P. Marquand
Paule Marshall
Harry Mathews
Peter Matthiesson
William Maxwell
Tom Mayer
Julian Mazor
James Merrill
Shirley Mezvinski
Arthur Miller
Henry Miller
Mark Mirsky
Marion Montgomery
Wright Morris
William Murray
Vladimir Nabokov
Howard Nemerov
Jay Neugeboren
Charles Newman
John Nichols
Hugh Nissenson
Joyce Carol Oates
John O'Hara
Tillie Olsen
Neal Oxenhandler
Cynthia Ozick

Nancy H. Packer
Grace Paley
Joseph Papaleo
William Peden
Walker Percy
Harry Mark Petrarkis
Katherine Anne Porter
Charles Portis
Nancy Potter
Reynolds Price
James Purdy
Thomas Pynchon
Burton Raffel
Vera Randall
John Rechy
Leonard W. Robinson
Thomas Rogers
Gil Rogin
Frank Rooney
Norma Stahl Rosen
Henry Roth
Philip Roth
Earl Rovit
Hughes Rudd
Michael Rumaker
Martin Russ
J. D. Salinger
James Salter
William Saroyan
May Sarton
Stephen Schneck
Mark Schorer
Budd Schulberg
Richard Scowcroft
Allan Seager
Lore Segal
Hubert Selby
Thalia Selz
Irwin Shaw
Wilfred Sheed
Charles Simmons
Herbert Simmons
Isaac Bashevis Singer
Leo Skir

Barbara P. Solomon	Mack Thomas	Thornton Wilder
Susan Sontag	Lionel Trilling	Joan Williams
Peter Sourian	Alexander Trocchi	John Williams
Terry Southern	Nicolo Tucci	John A. Williams
John Speicher	John Updike	Tennessee Williams
Jean Stafford	Gore Vidal	Thomas Williams
Max Steele	Kurt Vonnegut, Jr.	Calder Willingham
Wallace Stegner	David Wagoner	Herbert Wilner
John Steinbeck	Janice Warnke	Donald Windham
George Steiner	Robert Penn Warren	Janet Lewis Winters
Richard G. Stern	Eudora Welty	Bernard Wolfe
Edward Stewart	Glenway Wescott	Malcolm Wood
Robert Stone	Alan Wheelis	Douglas Woolf
William Styron	Thomas Whitbread	Charles Wright
Harvey Swados	Robin White	Richard Yates
Barry Targan	Wallace White	Marguerite Young
Peter Taylor	Joseph Whitehill	John Yount

There may be a great many writers on this list who are unknown to most readers—and yet all have written and may again write a piece of fiction that deserves serious attention. And there are many other good writers who are not on this list. It is the business of the agents and publishers and editors and critics of fiction to keep up with such writers as well as to discover new ones. But what of the reader who is not privy to the counsel of dozens of professional readers and agents and reviewers and teachers—how is he to know which of approximately 3000 works of fiction published each year he should definitely read? He can join a book club and be sent books chosen by a committee of authorities; he can peruse the reviewing media and make his choices on that basis; he can buy the books he "hears" most about, and he can simply rely on the roulette principle that the title (or cover!) his hand leads him to on the paperback stand will be one of the serious novels published in that form. But all of these methods of choice tend to lead to the same books, those chosen by a combination of publishing enthusiasm and know-how that are picked up by the book clubs, given the most reviewing attention, most talked about on radio and television, and most likely to be given prominent shelf space in the bookstores and on the paperback racks. This means that there is to some extent a star system, like the brand-name system in mass marketing, in American fiction publishing.

The best-known writers are given the biggest advances and hence the biggest advertising and promotion budgets—and hence become even better known. We are constantly being told how the paperback revolution has made fiction available in every drugstore and stationery store across the country. True enough, but too often in each and every drugstore it is the same titles—*Jacqueline Susann's* Valley of the Dolls *and James Michener's* The Source, *along with others, more or less the same each month—in each of the thousands of outlets. There is mass distribution for few, negligible distribution for many. The system provides a flashing acceptance for a few, virtually complete neglect for most. In Norman Mailer's overheated words: "America is a cruel soil for talent. It stunts it, blights it, uproots it, or overheats it with cheap fertilizer."*

So there is a double irony in all this. Amid the laments of "Our fiction is in decline" and "We have no major writers today," a situation exists in which writers—major or minor—have never had it so good, in America or anywhere else ever. Few writers starve. There is for them a seeming infinity of grants, awards, writer-in-residencies, fellowships, prizes—financial support on all sides, especially from the colleges and universities year in and year out, but also from publishers and foundations and government and patrons of all sorts. Writers are as cool as anyone else when the money nerve is touched, and no doubt more of the same would be more and more welcome. Poverty should not have to be one of the vows of creativity. Yet there is a sense in this attitude toward writers as permanent fixtures on a college campus, of the co-optation, the take-over of the writer as heroic purveyor of dreams and truth, not simply to support him in his lonely and difficult work but to possess the goose that lays the golden egg, to have a lien on the potential superhero, the man who will write (as Christ must come again) The Great American Novel. Romantic and possessive, in true American style, this new mass supercult of The Writer Who Knows All, and Tells, still falls short of the dream of all writers, good, medium, and great, which is to have people read their stuff seriously, as if the value of the work were in the work itself. It seems to many of them, and to us, preposterous that they should have fallen on such good times and still be without what their very great achievements should in all common sense provide in great abundance: readers.

A Final Note

*Anyone who edits an anthology feels that he has to say something to jus-
tify his choices, to hedge against the complaints of those who have favorite
stories or authors that are left out. Our disclaimer is simply that in an
anthology like this, which must by its nature be balanced and has no room
for two overlapping stories that make similar points about how we live,
we not only have had to pick and choose, but have had to fit it all together,
which sometimes meant not using good stories for all sorts of wrong but
necessary reasons. So while our method was first to choose stories we
thought were good and had a lot to tell us about life now, and then only
afterward to fit them into sections that developed out of the selected fiction
itself, once these sections were established we had to forgo using equally
good stories in the same area. The thing that is at once discouraging about
our efforts and so very encouraging about the state of fiction today is that
we finally had the feeling, when finished, that we could have made a book
of equal quality—or even several books of nearly equal quality—using
entirely different stories, novel excerpts, and novellas. To some extent this
might have meant using different stories by the same writers—in the same
areas or elsewhere—for there are many writers whose work as a whole
gives a perhaps even better picture of how we live than does this book as
a whole. But what an entirely different book would more likely have meant
is an entirely different system of organization—taking its form from the
selections made—because the "institutional" categories used here (family,
community, work, etc.), while straightforward enough, have no value in
and of themselves for categorizing fiction. More imaginative orderings might
have been done according to theme or problems or questions about our
times. The twin purposes of the book—to prove that modern American
fiction is excellent and to prove that it has much to tell us about ourselves
and our times—were sometimes in conflict, although not as often as one
might have supposed. And it might as well be admitted somewhere that
the selections represent a somewhat establishmentarian choice: little of
the avant-garde—outlawed, experimental, unrecognized, and unknown—is
included here.*

At any rate, what we finally want to say about our choices is this: that although we are convinced that what we have included in the book is good, we are by no means convinced it is the best of modern American fiction. It has not seemed to us our job to say who the best writers are. We have not misrepresented modern American fiction by skimming off only the best and serving it up as representative. It is representative, so far as we can see. The culling and sifting processes by which the classics of our time will be established will be done by the literary critics of the future. Those books that are thought to reveal most about the essence and life of mid-twentieth-century America (chances are they will be the same books as the classics) will be chosen by the cultural historians of the future. Again: we do not believe, and certainly do not want others to believe, that we have chosen "the best" in American fiction of the last ten or fifteen years. We do believe that the stories in this book and the writers represented are in fact excellent—but this is far from being the only good writing; these are certainly not all the good writers.

But these limitations of our methods are immaterial to the purpose of this anthology—to collect good contemporary stories and present them within a systematic context that celebrates both their excellence and their relevance to the way we live now, thus, we hope, convincing the serious reader that he must pay serious attention to the serious fiction of his times.